PENGUIN BOOKS

THE PENGUIN BOOK OF WESTERN FAIRY TALES

Jack Zipes is a professor of German at the University of Minnesota. A specialist in folklore, fairy tales, and children's literature, he is the author of several books on fairy tales, including *Breaking the Magic Spell*, *Fairy Tales and the Art of Subversion*, and *Don't Bet on a Prince*, and the editor and translator of *The Complete Tales of the Brothers Grimm*, *Fairy Tales and Fables from Weimar Days*, and *Beauties, Beasts, and Enchantment: Classic French Fairy Tales*. In 1992, he was presented with the Distinguished Scholar Award by the International Association for the Fantastic in the Arts.

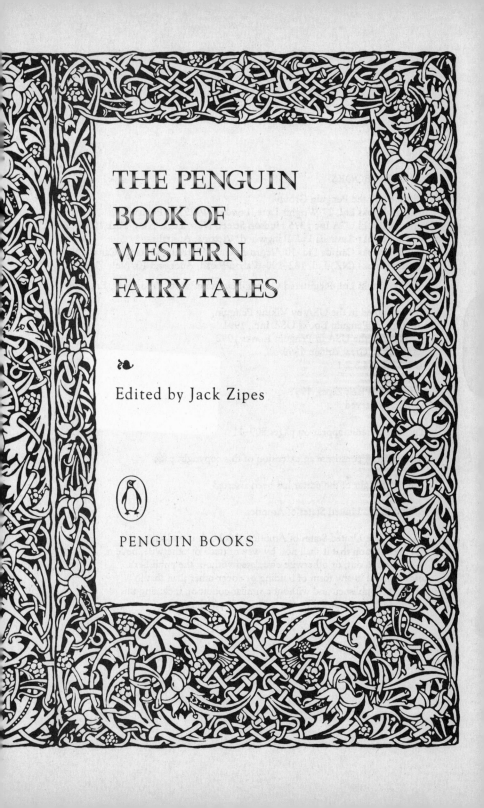

THE PENGUIN
BOOK OF
WESTERN
FAIRY TALES

Edited by Jack Zipes

PENGUIN BOOKS

PENGUIN BOOKS

Published by the Penguin Group
Penguin Books Ltd, 27 Wrights Lane, London W8 5TZ, England
Penguin Books USA Inc., 375 Hudson Street, New York, New York 10014, USA
Penguin Books Australia Ltd, Ringwood, Victoria, Australia
Penguin Books Canada Ltd, 10 Alcorn Avenue, Toronto, Ontario, Canada M4V 3B2
Penguin Books (NZ) Ltd, 182–190 Wairau Road, Auckland 10, New Zealand

Penguin Books Ltd, Registered Offices: Harmondsworth, Middlesex, England

First published in the USA by Viking Penguin,
a division of Penguin Books USA Inc., 1991
Published in the USA in Penguin Books 1992
Published in Great Britain 1993
10 9 8 7 6 5 4 3 2 1

Illustration credits appear on pages 809–11

Pages 812–14 constitute an extension of this copyright page

The moral right of the editor has been asserted

Printed in the United States of America

For Carol and Hanna
Who have kept the magical hope
of the tales alive

—§§—

CONTENTS

INTRODUCTION

t has generally been assumed that fairy tales were first created for children and are largely the domain of children. But nothing could be further from the truth.

From the very beginning, thousands of years ago, when tales were told to create communal bonds in face of the inexplicable forces of nature, to the present, when fairy tales are written and told to provide hope in a world seemingly on the brink of catastrophe, mature men and women have been the creators and cultivators of the fairy tale tradition. When introduced to fairy tales, children welcome them mainly because they nurture their great desire for change and independence. On the whole, the literary fairy tale has become an established genre within a process of Western civilization that cuts across all ages. Even though numerous critics and shamans have mystified and misinterpreted the fairy tale because of their spiritual quest for universal archetypes or their need to save the world through therapy, both the oral and the literary forms of the fairy tale are grounded in history: they emanate from specific struggles to humanize bestial and barbaric forces, which have terrorized our minds and communities in concrete ways, threatening to destroy free will and human compassion. The fairy tale sets out to conquer this concrete terror through metaphors.

Though it is difficult to determine when the first *literary* fairy tale was conceived, and also extremely difficult to define exactly what a fairy tale is, we do know that oral folk tales, which contain wondrous and marvelous elements, have existed for thousands of years and were told largely by adults for adults. Motifs from these tales, which were memorized and passed on by word of mouth, made their way into the Bible and the Greek classics such as *The Iliad* and *The Odyssey*. The early oral tales that served as the basis for the development of the literary fairy tales were closely tied to the rituals, customs, and beliefs of tribes, communities, and trades. They fostered a sense of belonging and the hope that miracles involving some kind of magical transformation were possible to bring about a better world. They instructed, amused, warned, initiated, and enlightened. They opened windows to imaginative worlds inside that needed concrete expression outside, in reality. They were to be shared and exchanged, used and modified according to the needs of the tellers and the listeners.

Tales are marks that leave traces of the human struggle for immortality. Tales are human marks invested with desire. They are formed like musical compositions, except that the notes constitute words and are chosen to enunciate the speaker/writer's position in the world, including his or her dreams, needs, wishes, and experiences. The speaker/writer posits the self against language to establish identity and to test the self with and against language, and each word marks a way toward a future different from what may have been decreed, certainly different from what is being experienced in the present: the words that are selected in the process of creating a tale allow the speaker/writer freedom to play with options that no one has ever glimpsed. The marks are magical.

The fairy tale celebrates the marks as magical: marks as letters, words, sentences, signs. More than any other literary genre, the fairy tale has persisted in emphasizing transformation of the marks with spells, enchantments, disenchantments, resurrections, re-creations. During its inception, the fairy tale distinguished itself as a genre both by appropriating the oral folk tale and by expanding it, for it became gradually necessary in the modern world to adapt the oral tale to standards of literacy and make it acceptable for diffusion in the public sphere. The fairy tale is only one type of appropriation of a particular oral storytelling tradition: the wonder folk tale, often called the *Zaubermärchen* or the *conte merveilleux*. As more and more wonder tales were written down in the fifteenth, sixteenth, and seventeenth centuries, they constituted the genre of the literary fairy tale, which began establishing its own conventions, motifs, *topoi*, characters, and plots, based to a large extent on those developed in the oral tradition but altered to address a reading public formed by the aristocracy and the middle classes. Though the peasants were excluded in the formation of this literary tradition, it was their material, tone, style, and beliefs that were incorporated into the new genre.

What exactly is the oral wonder tale?

Vladimir Propp, in his now famous study, *The Morphology of the Folk Tale,* outlined thirty-one basic functions that constitute the formation of a paradigm, an archetypal story form that still is common in Europe. By functions, Propp meant the fundamental and constant components of a tale that are the acts of a character, necessary for driving the action forward. To summarize the functions, with a different emphasis:

1. The protagonist is confronted with an interdiction or prohibition, which he or she violates in some way.

2. Departing or banished, the protagonist has either been given or assumes a task related to the interdiction or prohibition. The task is *assigned,* and it is a *sign.* That is, the protagonist's character will be marked by the task that is his or her sign.

3. There is an encounter with: (*a*) a villain; (*b*) a mysterious individual or creature, who gives the protagonist gifts; (*c*) three different animals or creatures, who are helped by the protagonist and promise to repay him or her; or (*d*) three animals or creatures who offer gifts to help the protagonist, who is in trouble. The gifts are often magical agents, which bring about miraculous change.

4. The endowed protagonist is tested and moves on to battle and conquer the villain or inimical forces.

5. There is a peripety or sudden fall in the protagonist's fortunes, which is generally only a temporary setback. A wonder or miracle is needed to reverse the wheel of fortune.

6. The protagonist makes use of endowed gifts (and this includes the magical agents and cunning) to achieve his or her goal. The result is: (*a*) three battles with the villain; (*b*) three impossible tasks that are nevertheless made possible; or (*c*) the breaking of a magic spell.

7. The villain is punished or the inimical forces are vanquished.

8. The success of the protagonist usually leads to: (*a*) marriage; (*b*) the acquisition of money; (*c*) survival and wisdom; or (*d*) any combination of the first three.

Rarely do wonder tales end unhappily. They triumph over death. The tale begins with "Once upon a time" or "Once there was" and never really ends when it ends. The ending is actually the beginning. The once upon a time is not a past designation but futuristic: the timelessness of the tale and its lack of geographical specificity endow it with utopian connotations— "utopia" in its original meaning designated "no place," a place that no one had ever envisaged. We form and keep the utopian kernel of the tale safe in our imaginations with hope.

The significance of the paradigmatic functions of the wonder tale is that they facilitate recall for teller and listeners. They enable us to store, remember, and reproduce the utopian spirit of the tale and to change it to fit our experiences and desires, owing to the easily identifiable characters who are associated with particular assignments and settings. For instance, we have the simpleton, who turns out to be remarkably cunning; the third and youngest son, who is oppressed by his brothers and/or father; the beautiful but maltreated youngest daughter; the discharged soldier, who has been exploited by his superiors; the shrew who needs taming; the evil witch; the kind elves; the cannibalistic ogre; the clumsy, stupid giant; terrifying beasts like dragons, lions, wild boars; kind animals like ants, birds, deer, bees, ducks, fish; the clever tailor; the evil and jealous stepmother; the clever peasant; the power-hungry and unjust king; treacherous nixies; the beast bridegroom. There are haunted castles; enchanted forests; mysterious huts in woods; glass mountains; dark, dangerous caves; underground kingdoms. There are seven-league boots, which enable the protagonist to move faster than jet planes; capes that make a person invisible; magic wands, which can perform extraordinary feats of transformation; animals that produce gold; tables that provide all the delicious and sumptuous food you can eat; musical instruments with enormous captivating powers; swords and clubs capable of conquering anyone or anything; lakes, ponds, and seas that are difficult to cross and serve as the home for supernatural creatures.

The characters, settings, and motifs are combined and varied according to specific functions to induce *wonder*. It is this sense of wonder that distinguished the wonder tales from such other oral tales as the legend, the fable, the anecdote, and the myth; it is clearly the sense of wonder that distinguishes the *literary* fairy tale from the moral story, novella, sentimental tale, and other modern short literary genres. Wonder causes astonishment, and as manifested in a marvelous object or phenomenon, it is often regarded as a supernatural occurrence and can be an omen or a portent. It gives rise to admiration, fear, awe, and reverence. The *Oxford Universal Dictionary* states that wonder is "the emotion excited by the perception of something novel and unexpected, or inexplicable; astonishment mingled with perplexity or bewildered curiosity." In the oral wonder tale, we are to wonder about the workings of the universe, where anything can happen at any time, and these happy or fortuitous events are never to be explained. Nor do the characters demand an explanation—they are opportunistic, are encouraged to be so, and if they do not take advantage of the opportunity that will benefit them in their relations with others, they are either dumb or mean-spirited. The tales seek to awaken our regard for the miraculous condition of life and to evoke in a religious sense profound feelings of awe and respect for life as a miraculous process, which can be altered and changed to compensate for the lack of power, wealth, and pleasure that is most people's lot. Lack, deprivation, prohibition, and interdiction motivate people to look for signs of fulfillment and emancipation.

In the wonder tales, those who are naive and simple are able to succeed because they are untainted and can recognize the wondrous signs. They have retained their belief in the miraculous condition of nature, revere nature in all its aspects. They have not been spoiled by conventionalism, power, or rationalism. In contrast to the humble characters, the villains are those who use words intentionally to exploit, control, transfix, incarcerate, and destroy for their benefit. They have no respect or consideration for nature and other human beings, and they actually seek to abuse magic by preventing change and causing everything to be transfixed according to their interests. Enchantment equals petrification. Breaking the spell equals emancipation. The wondrous protagonist wants to keep the process of natural change flowing and indicates possibilities for overcoming the obstacles that prevent other characters or creatures from living in a peaceful and pleasurable way.

The focus on wonder in the oral folk tale does not mean that all wonder tales and, later, the literary fairy tales served and serve an emancipatory purpose. The nature and meaning of folk tales have depended on the stage of development of a tribe, community, or society. Oral tales have served to stabilize, conserve, or challenge the common beliefs, laws, values, and norms of a group. The ideology expressed in wonder tales always stemmed from the position that the narrator assumed with regard to the developments in his or her community, and the narrative plot and changes made in a tale depended on the sense of wonder or awe that the narrator wanted to evoke. In other words, the sense of wonder in the tale and the intended emotion sought by the narrator are ideological.

Since these wonder tales have been with us for thousands of years and have undergone so many different changes in the oral tradition, it is difficult to determine the ideological intention of the narrator, and when we disregard the narrator's intention, it is often difficult to reconstruct (and/or deconstruct) the ideological meaning of a tale. In the last analysis, even if we cannot establish whether a wonder tale is ideologically conservative, sexist, progressive, emancipatory, etc., it is the celebration of wonder that constitutes its major appeal. No matter what the plot may be, this type of tale calls forth our capacity as readers and potential transmitters of its signs and meanings to wonder. We do not want to know the exact resolution, the "happily ever after," of a tale—that is, what it is actually like. We do not want to name God, gods, goddesses, or fairies, who will forever remain mysterious and omnipotent. We do not want to form graven images. We do not want utopia designated for us. We want to remain curious, startled, provoked, mystified, and uplifted. We want to glare, gaze, gawk, behold, and stare. We want to be given opportunities to change, and ultimately we want to be told that we can become kings and queens, or lords of our own destinies. We remember wonder tales and fairy tales to keep our sense of wonderment alive and to nurture our hope that we can seize possibilities and opportunities to transform ourselves and our worlds.

Ultimately, the definition of both the wonder tale and the fairy tale, which derives from it, depends on the manner in which a narrator/author arranges *known* functions of a tale aesthetically and ideologically to induce wonder and then transmits the tale as a whole according to customary usage of a society in a given historical period. The first stage for the literary fairy tale involved a kind of class and perhaps even gender appropriation. The voices of the nonliterate tellers were submerged, and since women in most cases were not allowed to be scribes, the tales were scripted according to male dictates or fantasies, even though they may have been told by women. Put crudely, it could be said that the literary appropriation of the oral wonder tales served the hegemonic interests of males within the upper classes of particular communities and societies, and to a great extent this is true. However, such a statement must be qualified, for the writing down of the tales also preserved a great deal of the value system of those deprived of power. And the more the literary fairy tale was cultivated and developed, the more it became individualized and varied by intellectuals and artists, who often sympathized with those society marginalized or were marginalized themselves. The literary fairy tale allowed for new possibilities of subversion in the written word and in print, and therefore it was always looked upon with misgivings by the governing authorities in the civilization process.

During early Christianity, there were not many signs that the oral folk tales would develop and flourish as a major literary genre in the West, and there were obvious reasons for this lack: most people were nonliterate and shared strong oral cultural traditions; the tales had not been changed sufficiently to serve the tastes and interests of the ruling classes; Latin was the dominant intellectual and literary language until the late Middle Ages, when the vernacular languages gradually formed general standards of grammar and orthography for communication; the technology of printing did not make much progress until the fifteenth century, so that the distribution of literary works was limited. Consequently it is not surprising that the first appearance of a major literary fairy tale, Apuleius's "Cupid and Psyche," was in Latin and came in the second century. Moreover, it was included in a book, *The Golden Ass*, that dealt with metamorphoses, perhaps the key theme of the fairy tale up to the present. However, whereas many oral wonder tales had been concerned with the humanization of natural forces, the literary fairy tale, beginning with "Cupid and Psyche," shifted the emphasis more toward the civilization of the protagonist, who must learn to respect particular codes and laws to become accepted in society and/or united to reproduce and continue the progress of the world toward perfect happiness.

At first this new literary fairy tale could not stand by itself—that is, it did not have a receptive audience and had to be included within a frame story or in a collection of instructive and amusing stories and anecdotes. Therefore, up to the fifteenth century, the only other evidence we have of complete fairy tales are within such manuscripts as the *Gesta Romanorum* (c. 1300) or in sermons delivered by priests. Tales like "Of Feminine Subtlety" were generally used to provide instruction for the education of young Christian boys and had a strong moralistic strain. In addition, like "Cupid and Psyche," the early Latin fairy tales were largely addressed to the male sex and focused on their acquisition of the moral values and ethics that would serve them in their positions of power in society.

It was not until the publication of Giovanni Straparola's *Le piacevoli notti* (*The Delectable Nights*) in 1550–53 that fairy tales were first published in the vernacular and for a mixed audience of (upper-class) men and women. Straparola brings together a group of aristocrats who flee Milan for political reasons and decide to tell tales to amuse one another during their exile. The frame narrative is set up to include erotic anecdotes, fables, and fairy tales like "The Pig Prince," and it is modeled after Boccaccio's *Decameron*. But since Boccaccio did not include fairy tales in his collection, Straparola can be considered the first writer in Europe to have published fairy tales in the vernacular for an educated audience. His tales did not achieve the popularity of Boccaccio's collection, yet they were reprinted several times in Italian during the next few centuries, and by the nineteenth century they were translated into French, German, and English.

There is no direct evidence whether Straparola influenced Giambattista Basile, whose *Lo Cunto de li Cunti* (*The Story of Stories*), also known as *The Pentameron*, was published posthumously in 1634. Basile, who wrote in Neapolitan dialect, was the first to use an old folktale motif about laughter to frame an entire collection. His book of fifty fairy tales begins with a story about a princess named Zoza, who cannot laugh, no matter what her father, the king of Vallepelosa, does to try to assuage her melancholy. Finally, the king orders a fountain of oil erected before the palace gate so that people will skip and jump to avoid being soiled. The king hopes that their antics will overcome his daughter's melancholy. Indeed, the princess does laugh, but at the wrong person, an old witch of a woman, who places a curse on her and declares that if Zoza is ever to marry, she must wed Taddeo, a bewitched sleeping prince, whom only she can wake and save with her tears. With the help and advice of three fairies, Zoza succeeds in weeping a sufficient amount of tears, but she then falls asleep before she can achieve the rescue of Taddeo. In the meantime, a malicious slave steals Zoza's vessel of tears and claims the honor of liberating Taddeo, who marries her. Yet this does not deter Zoza, who rents a fine house opposite Taddeo's palace and manages through her beauty to attract his attention. The slave, who is pregnant, learns about this and threatens to kill her unborn child if Taddeo does not obey her every whim. Zoza responds by enticing the slave with three gifts she had received from the fairies. The third of these is a doll that causes the slave to be addicted to fairy tales, and she forces Taddeo to gather storytellers, who will amuse her during the final ten days of her pregnancy. So Taddeo gathers a group of ten motley women, who tell five fairy tales a day until Zoza concludes the sessions with her own tale, which exposes the slave's theft and brings the frame story to its conclusion. As a result, Taddeo has the pregnant slave put to death and takes Zoza for his new wife.

Basile was familiar with the customs and behavior of the Neapolitans and had also traveled widely in Italy and served at different courts. Therefore, he was able to include in his fairy tales a wealth of folklore, anecdotes, and events that celebrate miraculous changes and communion. A good example is "The Merchant's Two Sons," which has many different folk and literary versions. As in the frame narrative, the humane ties between people based on compassion and love can be solidified only if the protagonists recognize what and where evil is. The fairy tale involves arousing the protagonists and sharpening their perception of what is occurring so that they can make or bring about changes and master their own destinies. Thus the narrative structure is conceived so that the listener will learn to distinguish between destructive and beneficial forces, for the art of seeing and intuiting is nurtured by the fairy tale.

It is not by chance that in Europe the literary fairy tale flourished in Italy first. During the fifteenth and sixteenth centuries, the Italian cities and duchies had prospered by developing great commercial centers, and the literacy rate had grown immensely. Cultural activity at the courts and in the city-states was high, and there was a great deal of foreign influence on storytelling, as well as strong native oral traditions among the people. Although it cannot be fully documented, it is highly likely that the Italian literary fairy tales were gradually spread in print and by word of mouth throughout Europe. Interestingly, England, also a powerful maritime country, was the other nation that began cultivating a literary fairy tale tradition. There are fairy tale elements in Chaucer's *The Canterbury Tales* (c. 1386–1400), in Spenser's *The Faerie Queen* (1590–96), and, of course, in many of Shakespeare's plays, such as *King Lear, A Midsummer Night's Dream, The Taming of the Shrew,* and *The Tempest,* all written between 1590 and 1611. However, owing to the Puritan hostility toward amusement during the seventeenth century, the fairy tale as a genre was not able to flourish in England. France offered more propitious conditions, and the genre bloomed in full force there toward the end of the ancien régime, from 1690 to 1714.

Many factors account for the rise and spread of the fairy tale in France at this time. First of all, France had become the most powerful country in

Europe, and French, considered the most cultivated of languages, was used at most courts throughout Europe. Second, the evolution of printing favored experimentation with different kinds of literature. Third, there was great cultural creativity and innovation in France. Finally, about the middle of the seventeenth century, the fairy tale gradually became more accepted at literary salons and at the court, particularly in theatrical form. Fairy tale recitations and games were devised, generally by women in their salons, and these led to the publication of the tales during the 1690s. Perhaps the most prodigious (and most prolific) of the French fairy tale writers was Marie-Catherine D'Aulnoy, whose first tale, "The Island of Happiness," was embedded in her novel *L'Histoire d'Hippolyte* (1690). It was not until she had established a popular literary salon, in which fairy tales were regularly presented, that she herself published four volumes of fairy tales, between 1696 and 1698. Though Charles Perrault is generally considered to be the most significant French writer of fairy tales of this period, Mme D'Aulnoy was undoubtedly more typical and more a catalyst for other writers. Her long and rambling narratives focus on the question of *tendresse*—true and natural feelings between a man and a woman, whose nobility will depend on their manners and the ways they uphold standards of civility in defending their love. "Green Serpent" exemplifies Mme D'Aulnoy's concerns and reflects the influence of Apuleius's "Cupid and Psyche" and her familiarity with the Italian tradition of fairy tales, not to mention French folklore. In turn, her fairy tales set the stage for the works of Mlle L'Héritier, whose "Ricdin-Ricdon" (1696) is a remarkable courtly interpretation of "Rumpelstiltskin," and Mlle de La Force, whose "Parslinette" (1697) is a fascinating version of "Rapunzel." Of course, the writer whose name has become practically synonymous with the term *conte de fée* is Charles Perrault, who wrote two verse tales, "The Foolish Wishes" (1693) and "Donkey Skin" (1694), and then published the famous prose renditions of "Cinderella," "Little Red Riding Hood," "Sleeping Beauty," "Blue Beard," "Tom Thumb," "Riquet with the Tuft," and "The Fairies" in *Histoires ou contes du temps passé* (1697). Perrault frequented the literary salons in Paris, and he purposely sought to establish the literary fairy tale as an innovative genre which exemplified a modern sensibility that was coming into its own and was to be equated with the greatness of French *civilité*. Not all the French writers of this period intended to celebrate the spendor of the ancien régime, but they all were concerned with questions of manners, norms, and mores in their tales and sought to illustrate correct behavior and what constituted noble feelings. Almost all the writers lived in Paris, where their tales were published. Therefore, the "mode" of writing fairy tales was concentrated within a feudal sphere and led to what could be called the institutionalization of the genre, for after this point—that is, after the appearance of *The Thousand and One Nights* (1704–17) in twelve volumes, translated and adapted into French by Antoine Galland—the literary fairy tale became an acceptable social symbolic form through which conventionalized motifs, characters, and plots were selected, composed, arranged, and rearranged to comment on the civilizing process and to keep alive the possibility of miraculous change and a sense of wonderment.

The very name of the genre itself—fairy tale—originated during this time, for the French writers coined the term *conte de fée* during the seventeenth century, and it has stuck to the genre in Europe and North America ever since. This "imprint" is important, because it reveals something crucial about the fairy tale that has remained part of its nature to the present. The early writers of fairy tales placed the power of metamorphosis in the hands of women—the redoubtable fairies. In addition, this miraculous power was not associated with a particular religion or mythology, through which the world was to be explained. It was a secular mysterious power of compassion that could not be explained, and it derived from the creative imagination of the writer. Anyone could call upon the fairies for help, and it is clear that the gifted French women writers of the seventeenth century preferred to address themselves to a fairy and to have a fairy resolve the conflicts in their tales rather than the Church, with its male-dominated hierarchy. After all, it was the Church that had eliminated hundreds of thousands of so-called female witches during the previous two centuries in an effort to curb heretical and nonconformist beliefs. However, those "pagan" notions survived in the tradition of the oral wonder tale and surfaced in published form in France when it became safer to introduce in a symbolical code supernatural powers and creatures other than those officially sanctioned by the Christian code. In short, there was something subversive about the institutionalization of the fairy tale in France during the 1690s, for it enabled writers to create a dialogue about norms, manners, and power that evaded court censorship and freed the fantasy of the writers and readers, while at the same time paying tribute to the French code of *civilité* and the majesty of the aristocracy. Once certain discursive paradigms and conventions were established, a writer could demonstrate his or her "genius" by rearranging, expanding, deepening, and playing with the known functions of a genre that, by 1715, had already formed a type of canon, which consisted not only of the great classical tales—"Cinderella," "Sleeping Beauty," "Rapunzel," "Rumpelstiltskin," "Puss in Boots," "Little Red Riding Hood," "Beauty and the Beast," "Bluebeard," "The Golden Dwarf," "The Blue Bird," and "The White Cat"—but also the mammoth collection *The Arabian Nights.*

Galland's project of translating the Arabic tales from original manuscripts, which stemmed from the fourteenth century and were based on an oral tradition, was important for various reasons: his translation was not literal, and he introduced many changes influenced by French culture into his adaptations; eight of the tales, among them "Prince Ahmed and the Fairy Pari-Banou," were obtained from a Maconite scholar named Youhenna Diab, living at that time in Paris, and were in part Galland's literary re-creations; the exotic setting and nature of these Oriental tales attracted not only French but numerous European readers, so that Galland's work stimulated the translation of other Arabic writings, such as *The Adventures of Abdalah, Son of Anif* (1712–14), by the abbot Jean-Paul Bignon, as well as hundreds of translations from the French into English, Italian, German, Spanish, etc.

The infusion of the Oriental tales into the French literary tradition enriched and broadened the paradigmatic options for Western writers during the course of the eighteenth century, and it became a favorite device (and still is) to deploy the action of a tale to the Orient while discussing sensitive issues of norms and power close to home. Aside from the impact of the Arabic and Persian tales on Western writers through translations, another development was crucial for the institutionalization of the fairy tale in the eighteenth century. Soon after the publication of the tales by D'Aulnoy, Perrault, L'Héritier, Galland, and others, they were reprinted in a series of chapbooks called the *Bibliothéque Bleue,* and these inexpensive volumes were distributed by peddlers called *colporteurs* to the lower classes throughout France and Central Europe. The fairy tales were often abridged; the language was simplified; and there were multiple versions, which were read to children and nonliterates. Many tales were appropriated by oral storytellers, so that the literary tradition became a source for an oral tradition. The increased popularity of the literary fairy tale as chapbook led to the cultivation of the literary fairy tale for children. Already during the 1690s, Fénelon, the important theologian and archbishop of Cambrai, who was in charge of the dauphin's education, had written several didactic fairy tales as an experiment to make the prince's lessons more enjoyable. However, they were not published, as they were considered insufficiently proper and useful for the grooming of children from the upper classes. They were first printed in 1730, after Fénelon's death, and thereafter it became more acceptable to write and publish fairy tales for children just so long as they indoctrinated gender-specific roles and class codes. The most notable example here, aside from Fénelon's tales, is the voluminous work of Mme Leprince de Beaumont, whose *Magasin des Enfants* (1743) included "Beauty and the Beast," "Prince Chéri," and other overtly moralistic tales for children. Mme de Beaumont used a frame story in which a governess engages several young girls between six and ten in discussions about morals, manners, ethics, and gender roles, which lead her to tell didactic stories to illustrate her points. The method was based on her work as a governess in England, and the frame was adaptable to institutionalizing a type of storytelling in homes of the upper classes. It was only as part of the civilizing process that storytelling developed within the aristocratic and bour-

geois homes, in the seventeenth and eighteenth centuries through governesses
and nannies, and later in the eighteenth and the nineteenth centuries through
mothers, who told bedtime stories.

As the literary fairy tale spread in France to every age group and every
social class, it began to serve different functions, depending on the writer's
interests. It represented the glory and ideology of the French aristocracy. It
provided a symbolic critique, with utopian connotations, of the aristocratic
hierarchy, largely within the aristocracy itself and from the female viewpoint.
It introduced the norms and values of the bourgeois civilizing process as more
reasonable and egalitarian than the feudal code. As a *divertissement* for the
aristocracy and bourgeoisie, the fairy tale diverted the attention of listeners/
readers from the serious sociopolitical problems of the times, compensating
for the deprivations that the upper classes perceived themselves to be suffering.
There was also an element of self-parody, revealing the ridiculous notions in
previous fairy tales and representing another aspect of court society to itself;
such parodies can be seen in Jacques Cazotte's "A Thousand and One Follies"
(1746), Jean-Jacques Rousseau's "The Queen Fantasque" (1758), and Voltaire's "The White Bull" (1774). Finally, fairy tales with clear didactic and
moral lessons were approved as reading matter to serve as a subtle, more
pleasurable means of initiating children into the class rituals and customs that
reinforced the status quo.

The climax of the French institutionalization of the fairy tale was the
publication, between 1785 and 1789, of Charles Mayer's forty-one-volume
Cabinet des Fées, which collected most of the important French tales written
during the previous hundred years. Thereafter, most writers, whether they
wrote for adults or children, consciously held a dialogue with a fairy tale
discourse that had become firmly established in the Western intellectual tradition. For instance, the French fairy tale, which, we must remember, now
included *The Arabian Nights,* had a profound influence on the German clas-
sicists and the Romantics, and the development in Germany provided the
continuity for the institution of the genre in the West as a whole. Like the
French authors, German middle-class writers like Johann Karl August Musäus,
in his collection *Volksmärchen der Deutschen* (1782–86), which included "Libussa," began employing the fairy tale to celebrate German customs. Musäus
combined elements of German folklore and the French fairy tale in a language
clearly addressed to educated Germans. At the same time, Christoph Martin
Wieland translated and adapted numerous tales from the *Cabinet des Fées* in
Dschinnistan (1786–89). "The Philosophers' Stone" is his own creation but
reveals how he, too, consciously used the fairy tale to portray the decadence
of German feudal society and introduced Oriental motifs to enhance the tale's
exoticism and to conceal his critique of his own society. Numerous French
fairy tales also became known in Germany by the turn of the century through

the popular *Blaue Bibliothek* series and other translations. In fact, some, like "Sleeping Beauty," "Cinderella," and "Little Red Riding Hood," even worked their way into the brothers Grimm collection of the *Kinder- und Hausmärchen* (*Children's and Household Tales*, 1812–15), which were considered to be genuinely German. Romantic writers such as Wilhelm Heinrich Wackenroder, Ludwig Tieck, Novalis, Joseph von Eichendorff, Clemens Brentano, Adalbert von Chamisso, Friedrich de La Motte-Fouqué, and E.T.A. Hoffmann wrote extraordinary tales that revealed a major shift in the function of the genre: the fairy tale no longer represented the dominant aristocratic ideology. Rather it was written as a critique of the worst aspects of the Enlightenment and absolutism. This viewpoint was clearly expressed in Johann Wolfgang Goethe's classical narrative simply entitled "The Fairy Tale" (1795), as though it were the fairy tale to end all fairy tales. Goethe optimistically envisioned a successful rebirth of a rejuvenated monarchy, which enjoyed the support of all social classes, in his answer to the chaos and destruction of the French Revolution. In contrast, the Romantics were generally more skeptical about the prospects for individual autonomy, the reform of decadent institutions, and a democratic public sphere in a Germany divided by the selfish interests of petty tyrants and the Napoleonic Wars. Very few of the German Romantic tales end on a happy note. The protagonists either go insane or die. The evil forces assume a social hue, for the witches and villains no longer are allegorical representations of evil in the Christian tradition but are symbolically associated with the philistine bourgeois society or the decadent aristocracy. Nor was the purpose of the Romantic fairy tale to amuse in the traditional sense of *divertissement*. Instead, it sought to engage the reader in a serious discourse about art, philosophy, education, and love. It is not by chance that the German term for the literary fairy tale is *Kunstmärchen* (art tale), for in the Romantic narratives, the utopian impulse for a better future was often carried on by an artist or a creative protagonist, and his fate indicated to what extent the civilizing process in Germany inhibited or nurtured the creative and independent development of the citizens.

While the function of the fairy tale for adults underwent a major shift—and this was clear in other countries as well—that made it an appropriate means to maintain a dialogue about social and political issues within the bourgeois public sphere, the fairy tale for children remained suspect until the 1820s. Although various collections were published for children in the latter part of the eighteenth century and at the turn of the century, along with individual chapbooks containing "Cinderella," "Jack the Giant Killer," "Beauty and the Beast," "Little Red Riding Hood," and "Sleeping Beauty," they were not regarded as the prime reading material for children. Nor were they considered to be "healthy" for the development of children's minds. For the most part, church leaders and educators favored other genres of stories, realistic, sentimental, didactic, which were intended to demonstrate what good manners and morals were. Even the brothers Grimm, in particular Wilhelm, began in 1819 to revise their collected tales, targeting them more for children than they had done in the beginning and cleansing their narratives of erotic, cruel, or bawdy passages. However, the fantastic and wondrous elements were retained, so that the stories were not at first fully accepted by the bourgeois reading public, which only began changing its attitude toward the fairy tale for children during the course of the 1820s and 1830s throughout Europe. It was signaled in Germany by the publication of Wilhelm Hauff's *Märchen Almanach* (1826) and in England by Edward Taylor's translation of the Grimms' *Kinder- und Hausmärchen,* under the title *German Popular Stories* (1823), with illustrations by the famous George Cruikshank. The more tolerant acceptance of the literary fairy tale for children may be attributed to the realization on the part of educators and parents, probably owing to their own reading experiences, that fantasy literature and amusement would not necessarily destroy or pervert children's minds. Whether children were of the middle classes and attended school, or were of the lower classes and worked on the farm or in a factory, they needed a recreation period—the time and space to re-create themselves without having morals and ethics imposed on them, without having the feeling that their reading or listening had to involve indoctrination.

Significantly, it was from 1830 to 1900, during the rise of the middle classes, that the fairy tale came into its own for children. It was exactly during this time—from 1835 onward, to be precise—that Hans Christian Andersen, greatly influenced by the German Romantic writers and the Grimms, began publishing his tales, which became extremely popular throughout Europe and America. Andersen combined humor, Christian sentiments, and fantastic plots to form tales that at once amused and instructed both young and older readers. More than any writer of the nineteenth century, he fully developed what Perrault had begun: writing tales, such as "The Red Shoes," that could be readily grasped by children and adults alike but with a different understanding. Some of his narratives, like "The Shadow," were clearly intended for adults alone, and it is a good example of his use of the *doppelgänger* motif, developed by E.T.A. Hoffmann, and his exploration of paranoia within the fairy tale genre to express his individual and very peculiar fears of the diminished possibilities for autonomy in European society and the growing alienation of people from themselves.

In fact, the flowering of the fairy tale in Europe and America during the latter half of the nineteenth century has a great deal to do with alienation. As daily life became more structured, work more rationalized, and institutions more bureaucratic, there was little space left for daydreaming and the imagination. It was the fairy tale that provided room for amusement, nonsense, and recreation. This does not mean that it abandoned its more traditional role in the civilizing process as agent of socialization. For instance, up until the 1850s, the majority of fairy tale writers for children, including Catherine Sinclair, George Cruikshank, and Alfred Crowquill in England, Collodi in Italy, Comtesse Sophie de Ségur in France, and Ludwig Bechstein in Germany, emphasized lessons to be learned, in keeping with the principles of the Protestant ethic—industriousness, honesty, cleanliness, diligence, virtuousness—and male supremacy. However, just as the "conventional" fairy tale for adults had become subverted at the end of the eighteenth century, there was a major movement to write parodies of fairy tales, which were intended for both children and adults. In other words, the classical tales were turned upside down and inside out to question the value system upheld by the dominant socialization process and to keep wonder, curiosity, and creativity alive. By the 1860s, it was clear that numerous writers were using the fairy tale to subvert the formal structure of the canonized tales as well as the governing forces in their societies that restricted free expression of ideas. Such different authors as William Makepeace Thackeray ("Bluebeard's Ghost," 1843), Nathaniel Hawthorne ("Feathertop," 1846), Theodor Storm ("Hinzelmeier," 1857), Gottfried Keller ("Spiegel the Cat," 1856), George MacDonald ("The Day Boy and the Night Girl," 1879), Mary De Morgan ("The Three Clever Kings," 1888), Oscar Wilde ("The Fisherman and His Soul," 1891), and Hugo von Hofmannsthal ("The Tale of the 672nd Night," 1895) were concerned with exploring the potential of the fairy tale to reform both the prescribed way it had become cultivated and the stereotypes and prejudices in regard to gender and social roles that it propagated. The best example of the type of subversion attempted during the latter part of the nineteenth century is Lewis Carroll's *Alice in Wonderland* (1865), which has had a major influence on the fairy tale genre to this day.

Although many of the fairy tales were ironical or ended on a tragic note, they still subscribed to the utopian notion of the transformation of humans—that is, the redemption of the humane qualities and the overcoming of bestial drives. In America, for instance, Frank Stockton, who could be considered the "pioneer" writer of the fairy tale in America, and Howard Pyle, one of the finest writer-illustrators of fairy tales, touch upon the theme of redemption in their tales "The Griffin and the Minor Canon" (1885) and "Where to Lay the Blame" (1895). But the most notable American fairy tale of the nineteenth century was L. Frank Baum's *The Wizard of Oz* (1900), which depicts Dorothy's great desire and need to break out of Kansas and determine her own destiny, a theme that Baum also explored in "The Queen of Quok" (*American Fairy Tales*, 1901).

By the beginning of the twentieth century, the fairy tale had become fully institutionalized in Europe and America, and its functions had shifted and expanded. The institutionalization of a genre means that a specific process of production, distribution, and reception has become regularized within the public sphere of a society and plays a role in forming and maintaining the cultural heritage of that society. Without such institutionalization in advanced industrialized and technological countries, the genre would perish, and thus the genre itself becomes a kind of self-perpetuating institute involved in the socialization and acculturation of readers. Thus it is the interaction of writer/publisher/audience within a given society that makes for the definition of the genre in any given epoch. The aesthetics of each fairy tale will depend on how and why an individual writer wants to intervene in the discourse of the genre as institution.

By the beginning of the twentieth century, the fairy tale as institution had expanded to include drama, poetry, ballet, music, and opera. In fact, one could perhaps assert that the pageants at the various European courts in the sixteenth and seventeenth centuries, especially the court of Louis XIV, had influenced and helped further the development of the literary fairy tale. Certainly, after Mozart's *The Magic Flute* (1791), fairy tale themes became abundant in the musical world of Europe in the nineteenth century, as can be seen in E.T.A. Hoffmann's own *Undine* (1814), Robert Schumann's *Kreisleriana* (1835–40), Léo Delibes's *Coppélia* (1870), Tchaikovsky's *Sleeping Beauty* (1889) and *The Nutcracker* (1892), Engelbert Humperdinck's *Hänsel and Gretel* (1893), and Jacques Offenbach's *The Tales of Hoffmann* (1881). Again, the manner in which the fairy tale incorporated other art forms reveals the vital role adults have played in maintaining the genre. Never has the fairy tale lost its appeal to adults, and the fairy tale for adults or mixed audiences underwent highly significant changes in the twentieth century.

During the first half of the century, the major shift in the function of the literary tale involved greater and more explicit politicization. In France, Apollinaire, who wrote "Cinderella Continued" (1919), joined with a group of experimental writers to publish their fairy tales in *La Baïonette* as commentary on the ravages of World War I. Hermann Hesse, who had written "The Forest Dweller" (1917–18) to criticize the conformity of his times, published "Strange News from Another Planet" in 1919 to put forward his pacifist views, and Thomas Mann made a major contribution to the fairy tale novel with *The Magic Mountain* (1924), which is filled with political debates about nationalism and democracy. Moreover, there was a wave of innovative and expressionistic fairy tales in Germany written by Edwin Hoernle, Hermynia zur Mühlen, Mynona, Franz Hessel, Kurt Schwitters, Oskar Maria Graf, Bertolt Brecht, Alfred Döblin, and others, which were politically tendentious. In England, the experimentation was not as great. Nevertheless, a volume entitled *The Fairies Return, Or, New Tales for Old* appeared in 1934, and it contained tales with unusual social commentaries by A. E. Coppard,

Lord Dunsany, Eric Linklater, Helen Simpson, E. O. Somerville, Christina Stead, and G. B. Stern. Of course, after the Nazi rise to power and during the Spanish Civil War, the fairy tale became more and more the means to convey political sentiments. In Germany, the fairy tale was interpreted and produced according to Nazi ideology, and there are numerous examples of *völkisch* and Fascist fairy tale products. In turn, they brought out a response of writers opposed to Nazism, such as the American H. I. Phillips in "Little Red Riding Hood as a Dictator Would Tell It" (1940). Germany offers an extreme case of how the fairy tale became politicized or used for political purposes. But this extreme case does illustrate a general trend in the political intonation of fairy tales, which continued into the 1940s and 1950s. For example, J.R.R. Tolkien's *The Hobbit* (1937) was written with World War I in mind and with the intention of warning against a second world war. James Thurber's "The Girl and the Wolf" (1939) focused on power and violation. Georg Kaiser's "The Fairy Tale of the King" (1943) reflected upon dictatorship. Erich Kästner's "The Fairy Tale About Reason" (1948) projected the possibility of world peace. Ingeborg Bachmann's "The Smile of the Sphinx" (1949) recalled the terror of the Holocaust.

Following World War II, the fairy tale set out once again to combat terror, but this time the terror concerned not the inhibitions of the civilizing process, rationalization and alienation, but the demented and perverse forms of civilization that had in part caused atrocities and threatened to bring the world to the brink of catastrophe. Confronted with such a prospect at the onset of the Cold War, with other wars to follow, writers like Henri Pourrat and Italo Calvino sought to preserve spiritual and communal values of the oral wonder tales in revised versions, while numerous other writers drastically altered the fairy tale to question whether the utopian impulse could be kept alive and whether our sense of wonderment could be maintained. If so, then the fairy tale had to deal with perversity and what Hannah Arendt called the "banality of evil." Writers like Philip K. Dick ("The King of the Elves," 1953), Naomi Mitchison ("Five Men and a Swan," 1957), Sylvia Townsend Warner ("Bluebeard's Daughter," 1960), Christoph Meckel ("The Crow," 1962), Stanislaw Lem ("Prince Ferrix and the Princess Crystal," 1967), and Robert Coover ("The Dead Queen," 1973) provoke readers not by playing with their expectations but by disturbing expectations. To a certain extent, they know that most of their readers have been "Disneyized"—that is, subjected to the saccharine sexist and illusionary stereotypes of the Disney culture industry—and therefore they have felt free to explode the illusion that happy ends are possible in real worlds that are held together by the deceit of advertising and government. Especially since the 1970s, the fairy tale for adults has become more aggressive, aesthetically more complex and sophisticated, and more insistent on *not* distracting readers but helping them focus on key social problems and issues in their respective societies. This standpoint is especially apparent in the works of Janosch, Günter Kunert, Michael Ende, Michel Tournier, Donald Barthelme, Michael de Larrabeiti, and Peter Redgrove. Perhaps the major social critique carried by the fairy tale can be seen in the restructuring and reformation by feminists of the fairy tale genre itself. The result has been a remarkable production of nonsexist fairy tales for children and adults as well theoretical works that have explored the implications of gender roles in fairy tales. Not only have individual authors such as Anne Sexton, Angela Carter, Jane Yolen, Tanith Lee, Rosemarie Künzler, Jay Williams, and Robin McKinley created highly innovative tales that reverse and question traditional sex roles, but there have been collective enterprises in Italy, England, Ireland, and the United States that have reacted critically to the standard canon representing catatonic females flat on their backs waiting to be brought to life by charming princes.

Of course, there are numerous fairy tale works for adults that are blissfully serene and depict intact worlds that need no changing. Or there are placid revisions and patchwork reproductions of classical fairy tales meant to provide amusement and/or *divertissement*. For instance, there has been a great commercialization of the fairy tale since the 1950s. In all forms and shapes, the classical fairy tales continue to be money-makers and thrive on basic sexist messages and conservative notions of social behavior. While the production of classical fairy tale books continues to be a profitable enterprise—and publishers are often indiscriminate as long as the fairy tales are like money in the bank and produce a healthy interest—even more money is generated through fairy tale films, plays, telecasts, and videos. *Faerie Tale Theatre*, a television and video product created by Shelley Duvall, is a case in point.

The theatrical and cinematic use of the fairy tale is extremely significant since Western society has become more oriented toward viewing fairy tale films, plays, and pictures rather than reading them. Here, two fairy tale productions might serve to illustrate a shift in function that is still in process. The 1987 Broadway musical *Into the Woods*, an amusing and trite collage, is typical of one aspect of the shift. It plays eclectically with all sorts of fairy tale motifs and characters in a conventional Broadway musical manner, only to arrive at a stale happy end to "divert" audiences from thinking creatively about their lives. If it is true that the fairy tale in the seventeenth century was bound by the rules and regulations of court society and that it largely served to represent court society to itself and to glorify the aristocracy, and if it is true that social and political development in the nineteenth century set art free so that the fairy tale as a genre became autonomous on the free market and in the public sphere, then it appears that there is a return, at least in the theater, television, and cinema, to the representative function of the fairy tale. Of course, this time the society that is being represented to itself as glorious is the capitalist consumer society. In addition, the fairy tale implicitly and explicitly reflects the state's endeavors to reconcile divergent forces, to pacify malcontents, to show how there are basically good elements within the bourgeois elite groups vying for control of American society. These agents (often understood as heroes) are portrayed as seeking the happiness of *all* groups, especially the disenfranchised, who create the drama in real life and in the fairy tale productions.

The 1987–89 television series *Beauty and the Beast* is a good example of how the fairy tale as representation (and legitimation) of elite bourgeois interests functions. No matter which thirty-minute episode a viewer watched, the basic plot of this television adaptation of the classic tale followed the same lines: the young woman, Catherine, who is from the upper classes, devotes her talents to serving as a legal defender of the oppressed; and the Beast, Vincent, represents the homeless and the outcasts in America, forced to live underground. These two continually unite, because of some elective affinity, to oppose crime and corruption and clear the way for the moral forces to triumph in America. Though the different episodes do expose the crimes of the upper as well as the lower classes, the basic message is that there can be a reconciliation between beauty and beast, and we can live in a welfare state without friction.

Despite the tendency of the film and television industry to use the fairy tale to induce a sense of happy end and ideological consent and to mute its subversive potential for the benefit of those social groups controlling power in the public sphere, the fairy tale as institution cannot be defined one-dimensionally or totally administered by its most visible producers in the mass media and publishing. The readers, viewers, and writers of fairy tales constitute its broadest meaning, perhaps not in the old communal way but in an individualized way that allows for free expression and subversion of norms that are hypocritically upheld and serve to oppress people. A good case in point is Salman Rushdie's inventive fairy tale novel *Haroun and the Sea of Stories* (1990), which concerns a young boy's quest to save his father's storytelling gifts, which are ultimately employed to undermine oppression in the country of Alifbay, so ruinously sad that it had forgotten its name. Rushdie's fairy tale allows him to diagnose the sickness of the country by symbolically naming names. Himself suffering oppression, he has written a fairy tale in which he urges readers to question authoritarianism and to become inventive, daring, and cunning. He wants to leave his mark in society during troubled times, providing hope for solutions without supplying the definitive answers.

This is the ultimate paradox of the literary fairy tale: it marks reality without leaving a trace of how it creates the wondrous effects. There is no doubt that the fairy tale has become totally institutionalized in Western society, part of the public sphere, with its own specific code and forms through which we communicate about social and psychic phenomena. We initiate children and expect them to learn the fairy tale code as part of our responsibility in the civilizing process. This code has its key words and keynotes, but it is not static. As in the oral tradition, its original impulse of hope for better lives has not vanished in the literary tradition, although many of the signs have been manipulated in the name of male authoritarian forces. As long as the fairy tale continues to awaken our wonderment and enable us to project worlds counter to our present society, it will serve a meaningful social and aesthetic function, not just for compensation but for revelation: for the worlds portrayed by the best of our fairy tales are like magic spells of enchantment that actually free us. Instead of petrifying our minds, fairy tales arouse our imagination and compel us to realize how we can fight terror and cunningly insert ourselves into our daily struggles and turn the course of the world's events in our favor.

A NOTE ON THE
TEXTS AND ACKNOWLEDGMENTS

In selecting the texts for this anthology, I intended to provide as comprehensive a view as possible of the major literary fairy tales written for adults in Western culture from the second century to the present. Occasionally I have included tales that were written for readers both young and old, especially if the author made a vital contribution to the development of the fairy tale genre. Unfortunately, the mammoth size of the project and the unavailability of certain tales prevented my inclusion of all the texts I would have liked to publish. Nevertheless, I believe that the anthology is representative of all the types of *literary* fairy tales that were conceived during the major literary movements in Europe and North America up to the contemporary period. My focus has been on the work of gifted and famous authors, to show how the genre has attracted some of the most creative minds to experiment with the magic ingredients of the fairy tale. Moreover, since creativity is not a property of famous authors alone, I have chosen some texts by "unknown" writers whose tales have been unduly neglected and yet provide illuminating examples of how the genre was and can be developed in unique and fascinating ways.

If the majority of the tales have been taken from the work of Italian, French, German, British, and American authors, it is not because other Western countries have not cultivated their own significant literary fairy tale traditions. It is because the selected tales constitute what has become a *known* and fertile tradition in the West, particularly in English-speaking countries. To a certain degree, these tales have selected themselves for this anthology, and it is the first time that they have ever been brought together in such a manner that their affinities and their uniqueness can be appreciated. Ironically, as well known as many of the fairy tales are, most readers are probably unaware of how extensive and prevalent the fairy tale tradition for adults has been in the West, because the major texts have never been reproduced in one volume.

Most of the tales in the anthology are translations, and they have been arranged chronologically so that the reader can gain a historical overview of the genre's development. Wherever an existing translation was of high quality, I have included it; otherwise, I have done all the translating. In some instances, I have made changes in translations that were either antiquated (as was the case with Straparola's "The Pig Prince") or stylistically clumsy (as was the case with Gottfried Keller's "Spiegel the Cat"). For the most part, I have tried to introduce major texts, which are key to understanding the history of the fairy tale, yet have been unavailable to English-speaking readers. Therefore, I have provided original translations of tales by Mme de La Force, Mlle L'Héritier, Antoine Galland, Jean-Jacques Rousseau, Johann Karl August Musäus, Christoph Martin Wieland, and others. In preparing my translations, I have endeavored to respect the individual style of the author without succumbing to historical quaintness. I hope that the translations in their modern idiom capture their original indelible qualities and remain alive and stimulating for contemporary readers.

I should like to thank the John Simon Guggenheim Foundation, which provided me with a grant in 1989–90 that enabled me to complete this anthology as well as a study on the origins of the literary fairy tale. In addition, I have benefited from the support and advice of Michael Millman at Viking and the fine work of Beena Kamlani and copyeditor Marjorie Horvitz.

Jack Zipes
Minneapolis, 1991

THE PENGUIN
BOOK OF
WESTERN
FAIRY TALES

‹ *Cupid and Psyche* ›

APULEIUS

nce upon a time there lived a king and queen who had three very beautiful daughters. They were so beautiful, in fact, that it was only just possible to find words of praise for the elder two, and to express the breath-taking loveliness of the youngest, the like of which had never been seen before, was beyond all power of human speech. Every day thousands of her father's subjects came to gaze at her, foreigners too, and were so dumbfounded by the sight that they paid her the homage due to the Goddess Venus alone. They pressed their right thumbs and forefingers together, reverently raised them to their lips and blew kisses towards her. The news of her matchless beauty spread through neighbouring cities and countries. Some reported: "Immortal Venus, born from the deep blue sea and risen to Heaven from its foam, has descended on earth and is now incarnate as a mortal at whom everyone is allowed to gaze." Others: "No, this time the earth, not the sea, has been impregnated by a heavenly emanation and has borne a new Goddess of Love, all the more beautiful because she is still a virgin." The princess's fame was carried farther and farther to distant provinces and still more distant ones and people made long pilgrimages over land and sea to witness the greatest wonder of their age. As a result, nobody took the trouble to visit Venus's shrines at Cyprian Paphos or Carian Cnidos or even in the isle of Cythera, where her lovely foot first touched dry land; her

festivals were neglected, her rites discontinued, the cushions on which her statues had been propped at her sacred temple feasts were kicked about the floor, the statues themselves were left without their usual garlands, her altars were unswept and cluttered with the foul remains of months-old burned sacrifices, her temples were allowed to fall into ruins.

When the young princess went out on her morning walks through the streets, victims were offered in her honour, sacred feasts spread for her, flowers scattered in her path, and rose garlands presented to her by an adoring crowd of suppliants who addressed her by all the titles that really belonged to the great Goddess of Love herself. This extraordinary transfer of divine honours to a mortal naturally angered the true Venus. Unable to suppress her feelings, she shook her head menacingly and said to herself: "Really now, whoever would have thought that I'd be treated like this? I, all the world's lovely Venus whom the philosophers call "the Universal Mother" and the original source of all five elements! So I'm expected to share my sovereignty, am I, with a mortal who goes about pretending to be myself? And to watch my bright name, which is registered in Heaven, being dragged through the dirty mud of Earth! Oh, yes, and I must be content, of course, with the reflected glory of worship paid to this girl, grateful for a share in the expiatory sacrifices offered to her instead of me? It meant nothing, I suppose when the shepherd Paris, whose just and honest verdict Jupiter himself confirmed, awarded me the apple of beauty over the heads of my two goddess rivals? No, it's quite absurd. I can't let this silly creature, whoever she may be, usurp my glory any longer. I'll very soon make her sick and sorry about her good looks: they are dead against the rules."

She at once called her winged son, Eros, alias Cupid, that very wicked boy, with neither manners nor respect for the decencies, who spends his time running from building to building all night long with his torch and his arrows, breaking up respectable homes. Somehow he never gets punished for all the harm he does, though he never seems to do anything good in compensation. Venus knew that he was naturally bent on mischief, but she tempted him to still worse behaviour by bringing him to the city where the princess lived— her name, by the way, was Psyche—and telling him the whole story of the new cult that had grown up around her. Groaning with indignation she said: "I implore you, darling, as you love your mother, to use your dear little arrows and that sweet torch of yours against this impudent girl. If you have any respect for me, you'll give me my revenge, revenge in full. You'll see that the princess falls desperately in love with some perfect outcast of a man— someone who has lost rank, fortune, everything, someone who goes about in terror of his life and in such complete degradation that nobody viler can be found in the whole world."

She kissed him long and tenderly and then went to the near by sea shore, where she ran along the tops of the waves as they danced foaming towards her. At the touch of her rosy feet the whole sea suddenly calmed, and she had no sooner willed the powers of the deep to appear, than up they bobbed as though she had shouted their names. The Nereids were there, singing a part song; and Neptune, sometimes called Portumnus, with his blueish beard; his wife Salacia, the naughty goddess of the deep sea, with a lapful of aphrodisiac fish; and little Palaemon, their charioteer, riding on a dolphin. After these came troops of Tritons swimming about in all directions, one blowing softly on his conch-shell, another protecting Venus from sunburn with a silk parasol, a third holding a mirror for her to admire herself in, and a whole team of them, yoked two and two, harnessed to her car. When Venus goes for an ocean cruise she's attended by quite an army of retainers.

Meanwhile Psyche got no satisfaction at all from the honours paid her. Everyone stared at her, everyone praised her, but no commoner, no prince, no king even, dared to make love to her. All wondered at her beauty, but only as they might have wondered at an exquisite statue. Both her less beautiful elder sisters, whose reputation was not so great, had been courted by kings and successfully married to them, but Psyche remained single. She stayed at home feeling very miserable and rather ill, and began to hate the beauty which everyone else adored.

Her poor father feared that the gods might be angry with him for allowing his subjects to make so much of her, so he went to the ancient oracle of Apollo at Miletus and, after the usual prayers and sacrifices, asked where he was to find a husband for his daughter whom nobody wanted to marry. Apollo, though an Ionian Greek and the true founder of Miletus, chose to deliver the following oracle in Latin verse:

> On some high mountain's craggy summit place
> The virgin, decked for deadly nuptial rites,
> Nor hope a son-in-law of mortal birth
> But a dire mischief, viperous and fierce,
> Who flies through aether and with fire and sword
> Tires and debilitates all things that are,
> Terrific to the powers that reign on high,
> Great Jupiter himself fears this winged pest
> And streams and Stygian shades his power abhor.

The king, who until now had been a happy man, came slowly back from the oracle feeling thoroughly depressed and told his queen what an unfavourable answer he had got. They spent several miserable days brooding over their daughter's fate and weeping all the while. But time passed, and the cruel oracle had to be obeyed.

The hour came when a procession formed up for Psyche's dreadful wedding. The torches chosen were ones that burned low with a sooty, spluttering flame; instead of the happy wedding-march the flutes played a querulous Lydian lament; the marriage-chant ended with funereal howls, and the poor bride wiped the tears from her eyes with the corner of her flame-coloured veil. Everyone turned out, groaning sympathetically at the calamity that had overtaken the royal house, and a day of public mourning was at once proclaimed. But there was no help for it: Apollo's oracle had to be obeyed. So when the preliminaries of this hateful ceremony had been completed in deep grief, the bridal procession moved off, followed by the entire city, and at the head of it walked Psyche with the air of a woman going to her grave, not her bridal bed.

Her parents, overcome with grief and horror, tried to delay things by holding up the procession, but Psyche herself opposed them. "Poor Father, poor Mother, why torment yourselves by prolonging your grief unnecessarily? You are old enough to know better. Why increase my distress by crying and shrieking yourselves hoarse? Why spoil the two faces that I love best in the world by crying your eyes sore and pulling out your beautiful white hair? Why beat your dear breasts until my own heart aches again? Now, too late, you at last see the reward that my beauty has earned you; the curse of divine jealousy for the extravagant honours paid me. When the people all over the world celebrated me as the New Venus and offered me sacrifices, then was the time for you to grieve and weep as though I were already dead; I see now, I see it as clearly as daylight, that the one cause of all my misery is this blasphemous use of the Goddess's name. So lead me up to the rock of the oracle. I am looking forward to my lucky bridal night and my marvellous husband. Why should I hesitate? Why should I shrink from him, even if he has been born for the destruction of the whole world?"

She walked resolutely forward. The crowds followed her up to the rock at the top of the hill, where they left her. They returned to their homes in deep dejection, extinguishing the wedding-torches with their tears, and throwing them away. Her broken-hearted parents shut themselves up in their palace behind closed doors and heavily curtained windows.

Psyche was left alone weeping and trembling at the very top of the hill, until a friendly west wind suddenly sprang up. It played around her, gradually swelling out her skirt and veil and cloak until it lifted her off the ground and carried her slowly down into a valley at the foot of the hill, where she found herself gently laid on a bed of the softest turf, starred with flowers.

It was such a cool, comfortable place to lie that she began to feel rather more composed. She stopped crying and fell asleep, and when she awoke, feeling thoroughly refreshed, it was still daylight. She rose and walked calmly towards the tall trees of a near-by wood, through which a clear stream was flowing. This stream led her to the heart of the wood where she came upon a royal palace, too wonderfully built to be the work of anyone but a god; in fact, as soon as she came in at the gates she knew that some god must be in residence there.

The ceiling, exquisitely carved in citrus wood and ivory, was supported by golden columns; the walls were sheeted with silver on which figures of all the beasts in the world were embossed and seemed to be running towards Psyche as she came in. They were clearly the work of some demi-god, if not a full god, and the pavement was a mosaic of all kinds of precious stones arranged to form pictures. How lucky, how very lucky anyone would be to have the chance of walking on a jeweled floor like that! And the other parts of the palace, which was a very large one, were just as beautiful, and just as fabulously costly. The walls were faced with massive gold blocks which glittered so brightly with their own radiance that the house had a daylight of its own even when the sun refused to shine: every room and portico and doorway streamed with light, and the furniture matched the rooms. Indeed, it seemed the sort of palace that Jupiter himself might have built as his earthly residence. Psyche was entranced. She went timorously up the steps, and after a time dared to cross the threshold. The beauty of the hall lured her on; and every new sight added to her wonder and admiration. When well inside the palace she came on splendid treasure chambers stuffed with unbelievable riches; every wonderful thing that anyone could possibly imagine was there. But what amazed her even more than the stupendous wealth of this world treasury, was that no single chain, bar, lock or armed guard protected it.

As she stood gazing in rapt delight, a voice suddenly spoke from nowhere: "Do these treasures astonish your Royal Highness? They are all yours. Why not go to your bedroom now, and rest your tired body. When you feel inclined for your bath, we will be there to help you—this is one of your maids speaking—and afterwards you will find your wedding banquet ready for you."

Psyche was grateful to the unknown Providence that was taking such good care of her and did as the disembodied voice suggested. First she found her bedroom and dozed off again for awhile, then she went to the bath, where invisible hands undressed her, washed her, anointed her and dressed her again in her bridal costume. As she wandered out of the bathroom she noticed a semi-circular table with a comfortable chair in front of it; it was laid for a banquet, though there was nothing yet on it to eat or drink. She sat down expectantly—and at once nectarous wines and appetizing dishes appeared by magic, floating up to her of their own accord. She saw nobody at all; the waiters were mere voices, and when someone came in and sang and someone else accompanied him on the lyre, she saw neither of them, nor the lyre either. Then a whole invisible choir burst into song. When this delightful banquet was over, Psyche thought it must be about time to go to bed, so she went to her bedroom again and undressed and lay awake for a long time.

Towards midnight she heard a gentle whispering near her, and began to feel lonely and scared. Anything might happen in a vast uninhabited place like this, and she had fears for her chastity. But no, it was the whisper of her unknown husband.

Now he was climbing into bed with her. Now he was taking her into his arms and making her his wife.

He left her hastily just before daybreak, and almost at once she heard the voices of her maids reassuring her that though she had lost her virginity, her chastity was safe. So she went to sleep again.

The next day she made herself more at home in her palace, and on the following night her invisible husband paid her another visit. The third day and night were spent in the same way until, as one might expect, the novelty of having invisible servants wore off and she settled down to what was a very enjoyable routine; at any rate she could not feel lonely with so many voices about her.

Meanwhile the old king and queen were doing exactly what she had asked them not to do—wasting their time in unnecessary grief and tears; and the news of Psyche's sad fate spread from country to country until both her elder sisters heard all the details. They left their palaces and hurried back in deep grief to their native city to console their parents.

On the night of their arrival Psyche's husband, whom she still knew only by touch and hearing, warned her: "Lovely Psyche, darling wife, the Fates are cruel: you are in deadly danger. Guard against it vigilantly. Your elder sisters are alarmed at the report of your death. They will soon be visiting the rock from which the West Wind blew you down into this valley, to see whether they can find any trace of you there. If you happen to hear them mourning for you up there, pay no attention at all. You must not answer them, nor even look up to them; for that would cause me great unhappiness and bring utter ruin on yourself."

Psyche promised to do as her husband asked; but when the darkness had vanished, and so had he, the poor girl spent the whole day in tears, complaining over and over again that not only was she a prisoner in this wonderful palace without a single human being to chat with, but her husband had now forbidden her to relieve the minds of her poor sisters, or even to look up at them without speaking. That night she went to bed without supper or bath or anything else to comfort her, and soaked her pillow with tears. Her husband came in earlier than usual, drew her to him, still weeping, and expostulated gently with her, "O Psyche, what did you promise me? What may I expect you to do next? You have cried all day and all evening and even now when I hold you close to me, you go on crying. Very well, then, do as you like, follow your own disastrous fancies; but I warn you solemnly that when you begin to wish you had listened to me, the harm will have been done."

She pleaded earnestly with him, swearing she would die unless she were allowed to see her sisters and comfort them and have a short talk with them. In the end she forced him to consent. He even said that she might give them as much jewellery as she pleased; but he warned her with terrifying insistence that her sisters were evil-minded women and would try to make her discover what he looked like. If she listened to them, her sacrilegious curiosity would mean the end of all her present happiness, and she would never lie in his arms again.

She thanked him for his kindness and was quite herself again. "No, no," she protested, "I'd rather die a hundred times over than lose you. I have no idea who you are, but I love you. I love you desperately, I love you as I love my own soul; I wouldn't exchange your kisses for the kisses of the God Cupid himself. So please, please grant me one more favour! Tell your servant, the West Wind, to carry my sisters down here in the same delightful way that he carried me." She kissed him coaxingly, whispered-love words in his ear, wound her arms and legs more closely around him and called him: "My honey, my own husband, soul of my soul!" Overcome by the power of her love he was forced to yield, however reluctantly, and promised to give her what she asked. But he vanished again before daybreak.

Meanwhile Psyche's sisters enquired their way to the rock where she had been abandoned. Hurrying there they wept and beat their breasts until the cliffs re-echoed. "Psyche! Psyche!" they screamed. The shrill cry reached the valley far below and Psyche ran out of her palace in feverish excitement, crying: "Sisters, dear sisters, why are you mourning for me? There's no need for that at all. Here am I, Psyche herself! Please, please stop that terrible noise and dry your tears. In a moment you'll be able to embrace me."

Then she whistled up the West Wind, and gave him her husband's orders. He at once obliged with one of his gentle puffs, and wafted them safely down to her. The three sisters embraced and kissed rapturously. Soon they were shedding tears of joy, not of sorrow. "Come in now," said Psyche, "come in with me to see my new home. It will make you both very happy." She showed them her treasure chambers and they heard the voices of the big retinue of invisible slaves. She ordered a wonderful bath for them and feasted them splendidly at her magical table. But this revelation of Psyche's goddess-like prosperity made them both miserably jealous—particularly the younger one, who was always very inquisitive. She was dying to know who owned all this fabulous wealth; so she pressed Psyche to tell her what sort of a man her husband was, and how he treated her.

Psyche was loyal to her promise and gave away nothing: but she made up a story for the occasion. She said lightly that, oh, her husband was a very handsome young man, with a little downy beard, and spent all his time hunting in the neighbouring hills and valleys. But when her sisters began to cross-examine her she grew afraid. Suppose she contradicted herself or made a slip or broke her promise? She loaded them both with jewelled pins and rings, festooned them with precious necklaces, then summoned the West Wind and asked him to fetch them away at once. He carried them up to the rock, and on their way back to the city the poison of envy began working again in their hearts.

The elder said: "How blindly and cruelly and unjustly Fortune has treated us! Do *you* think it fair that we three sisters should be given such different destinies? You and I are the two eldest, yet we get exiled from our home and friends and married off to foreigners who treat us like slaves; while Psyche, the result of Mother's last feeble effort at child-bearing, is given the most marvellous palace in existence and a god for a husband, and doesn't even know how to make proper use of her tremendous wealth. Did you ever see such masses of amazing jewels, such cupboardsful of embroidered dresses? Why, the very floors were made of gems set in solid gold! If her husband is really as good-looking as she says, she is quite the luckiest woman in the whole world. The chances are that if he remains as fond of her as he is at present he will make her a goddess. And my goodness, wasn't she behaving as if she were one already, with her proud looks and condescending airs? She's only flesh and blood after all, yet she orders the winds about and has a palaceful of invisible attendants. How I hate her! My husband's older than Father, balder than a pumpkin and as puny as a little boy; and he locks up everything in the house with bolts and chains."

"My husband," said the younger sister, "is even worse than yours. He's doubled up with sciatica, which prevents him from sleeping with me more than once in a blue moon, and his fingers are so crooked and knobby with gout that I have to spend half my time massaging them. You remember what beautiful white hands I used to have? Well, look what a state they are in now from messing about with his stinking fomentations and disgusting salves and filthy plasters! I'm treated more like a surgeon's assistant than a queen. You're altogether too patient, my dear; in fact, if you will excuse my saying so, you're positively servile, the way you accept this monstrous state of affairs. Personally, I simply can't stand seeing my youngest sister living in such un-deserved style. I'm glad you noticed how haughtily she treated us, how she bragged of her wealth and how stingy with her presents she was. Then, the moment she got bored with our visit, she whistled up the wind and had us blown off the premises. But I'll be ashamed to call myself a woman, if I don't see that she gets toppled down from her pinnacle before long and flung into the gutter. And if you feel as bitter as you ought to feel at the way she's insulted us both, what about joining forces and working out some plan for humbling her?"

"I'm with you," said the elder sister. "And in the first place I suggest that we show nobody, not even Father and Mother, these presents of hers, and let nobody know that she's still alive. It's bad enough to have seen her revelling in her good luck, without having to bring the news home to be spread all over the place; and there's no pleasure in being rich unless people hear about it. Psyche must be made to realize that we're not her servants but her elder sisters."

"Good," said the younger one. "We'll go back to our shabby homes and our shabby old husbands without telling Father and Mother anything. But when either of us thinks of a good plan for humbling Psyche's pride, let's come here again and boldly put it into operation."

The two bad sisters shook hands on this. They hid the valuable presents that Psyche had given them and, as they neared their father's palace, each began scratching her face and tearing out her hair in pretended grief at having found no trace of their sister; which made the king and queen sadder than ever. Then they separated: each went back full of malicious rage to her own adopted country, thinking of ways for ruining her innocent sister, even if it meant killing her.

Meanwhile, Psyche's unseen husband gave her another warning. He asked her one night: "Do you realize that a dangerous storm is brewing in the far distance? It will soon be on you and unless you take the most careful precautions, it will sweep you away. These treacherous bitch-wolves are scheming for our destruction: they will urge you to look at my face, though as I have often told you, once you see it, you lose me for ever. So if these hateful vampires come to visit you again—and I know very well that they will—you must refuse to speak to them. Or, if this is too difficult for a girl as open-hearted and simple as yourself, you must at least take care not to answer any questions about me. Pretend that you have not heard them. This is most important, because we have a family on the way: though you are still only a child, you will soon have a child of your own which shall be born divine if you keep our secret, but mortal if you divulge it."

Psyche was exultant when she heard that she might have a god for a baby. She began excitedly counting the months and days that must pass before it was born. But she knew very few of the facts of life and could not make out why the mere breach of her maidenhead was having so odd an effect on her figure.

The wicked sisters were now hurrying to Psyche's palace again, with the ruthless hate of Furies, and once more she was warned: "Today is the fatal day. Your enemies are near. They have struck camp, marshalled their forces and sounded the 'Charge.' They are enemies of your own sex and blood. They are your elder sisters, rushing at you with drawn swords aimed at your throat. O darling Psyche, what dangers surround us! Have pity on yourself and on me and on our unborn child! Keep my secret safe and so guard us all from the destruction that threatens us. Refuse to see those wicked women. They have forfeited the right to be called your sisters because of the deadly hate they bear you. Forbid them to come here, refuse to listen to them when, like Sirens leaning over the cliff, they make the rocks echo with their unlucky voices. Preserve absolute silence."

Psyche, her voice broken with sobs, said: "Surely you can trust me? The last time my sisters came to visit me I gave you convincing proof of my loyalty and my power of keeping a secret; it will be the same again tomorrow. Only tell the West Wind to do his duty as before, and allow me to have a sight, at least, of my sisters; as a very poor consolation for never seeing you, my darling. These fragrant curls dangling all round your head; these cheeks as tender and smooth as my own; this breast which gives out such extraordinary heat; oh, how I look forward to finding out what you are really like by studying my baby's face! So please, be sweet and humour my craving—it will be bad for the baby if you refuse—and make your Psyche happy. You and I love each other so much. I promise that if you let me see them I won't be so frightened of the dark or so anxious to look at you when I have you safe in my arms, light of my life!" Her voice and sweet caresses broke down his resistance. He wiped her eyes dry with his hair, granted what she asked, and as usual disappeared again before the day broke.

The wicked sisters landed together at the nearest port and, not even troubling to visit their parents, hurried straight to the rock above the valley and with extraordinary daring leaped down from it without waiting for the breeze to belly out their robes. However, the West Wind was bound to obey standing orders, reluctant though he might be: he caught them in his robe as they fell and brought them safely to the ground.

They rushed into the palace crying: "Sister, dear sister, where are you?" and embraced their victim with what she took for deep affection. Then, with cheerful laughter masking their treachery, they cried: "Why, Psyche, you're not nearly so slim as you used to be. You'll be a mother before very long. We're dying to see what sort of a baby it's going to be, and Father and Mother will be absolutely delighted with the news. Oh, how we shall love to nurse your golden baby for you. If it takes after its parents, as it ought to, it will be a perfect little Cupid."

They gradually wormed themselves into her confidence. Seeing that they were tired, she invited them to sit down and rest while water was heated for them; and when they had taken their baths, she gave them the most delicious supper they had ever tasted, course after course of tasty dishes, from spiced sausages to marzipan, while an unseen harpist played for them at her orders, and an unseen flautist, and a choir sang the most ravishing songs. But even such heavenly music as that failed to soften the hard hearts of the sisters.

They insidiously brought the conversation round to her husband, asking her who he was, and from where his family came.

Psyche was very simple-minded and, forgetting what story she had told them before, invented a new one. She said that he was a middle-aged merchant from the next province, very rich, with slightly grizzled hair. Then breaking the conversation off short, she loaded them with valuable presents and sent them away in their windy carriage.

As they rode home the younger sister said: "Now, what do you make of the monstrous lies she tells us? First the silly creature says that her husband is a very young man with a downy beard, and then she says that he's middle-aged with grizzled hair! Quick work, eh? You may depend upon it that the beast is either hiding something from us, or else she doesn't know herself what her husband looks like."

"Whatever the truth may be," said the elder sister, "we must ruin her as soon as possible. But if she really has never seen her husband, then he must be a god, and her baby will be a god too."

"If anything like that happens, which Heaven forbid," said the younger, "I'll hang myself at once—I couldn't bear Psyche to mother an immortal. I think we have a clue now to the best way of tricking her. Meanwhile, what about calling on Father and Mother?"

They went to the palace, where they gave their parents an off-hand greeting. The violence of their passions kept them awake all night. As soon as it was morning they hurried to the rock and floated down into the valley as usual with the help of the West Wind. Rubbing their eyelids hard until they managed to squeeze out a few tears, they went to Psyche and said: "Oh, sister, ignorance is indeed bliss! There you sit calmly and happily without the least suspicion of the terrible misfortune that has befallen you, while we are in absolute anguish about it. You see, we watch over your interests like true sisters, and since we three have always shared the same sorrows and joys it would be wrong for us to hide your danger from you. It is this, that the husband who comes secretly gliding into your bed at night is an enormous snake, with widely gaping jaws, a body that could coil around you a dozen times and a neck swollen with deadly poison. Remember what Apollo's oracle said: that you were destined to marry a savage wild beast. Several of the farmers who go hunting in the woods around this place have met him coming home at nightfall from his feeding ground, and ever so many of the people in the nearest village have seen him swimming across the ford there. They all say that he won't pamper you much longer, but that when your nine months are nearly up he will eat you alive; apparently his favourite food is a woman far gone in pregnancy. So you had better make up your mind whether you will come away and live with us—we would do anything in the world to save you—or whether you prefer to stay here with this fiendish reptile until you finish up in his guts. Perhaps you're fascinated by living here alone with your voices all day, and at night having secret and disgusting relations with a poisonous snake; if so, you are welcome to the life, but at all events we have done our duty as affectionate sisters by warning you how it must end."

Poor silly Psyche was aghast at the dreadful news. She lost all control of herself, trembled, turned deathly pale, and forgetting all the warnings her husband had given her, and all her own promises, plunged headlong into the abyss of misfortune. She gasped out brokenly: "Dearest sisters, thank you for being so kind. You're quite right to warn me, and I believe that the people who told you were not making it up. The fact is, I have never seen my husband's face and haven't the least idea who he is or where he comes from. I only hear him speaking to me at night in whispers, and find it very hard to be married to someone who hates the light of day as much as he does. So I have every reason to suppose, as you do, that he must be some sort of monster. Besides, he is always giving me frightful warnings about what will happen if I try to see what he looks like. So please, if you can advise me what to do in this dreadful situation, tell me at once, like the dear sisters you are: otherwise, all the trouble you have been kind enough to take will be wasted."

The wicked women saw that Psyche's defences were down, and her heart laid open to their attacks. They pressed their advantage savagely. The younger said: "Blood is thicker than water; the thought of your danger makes us forget our own. We two have talked the matter over countless times since yesterday and have come to the conclusion that you have only one chance of saving yourself. It is this. Get hold of a very sharp carving knife, make it sharper still by stropping it on your palm, then hide it somewhere on your side of the bed. Also, get hold of a lamp, have it filled full of oil, trim the wick carefully, light it and hide it behind the bedroom tapestry. Do all this with the greatest secrecy and when the monster visits you as usual, wait until he is stretched out at full length, and you know by his deep breathing that he's fast asleep. Then slip out of bed with the knife in your hand and tiptoe barefooted to the place where you have hidden the lamp. Finally, with its light to assist you, perform your noble deed, plunge the knife down with all your strength at the nape of the creature's poisonous neck, and cut off his head. We promise to stand close by and keep careful watch. The moment you have saved yourself by killing it, we shall come running in and help you to get away at once with all your treasure. After that, we'll marry you to a decent human being."

When they saw that Psyche was now determined to follow their suggestion, they went quietly off, terrified to be anywhere near her when the catastrophe came; they were helped up to the rock by the West Wind, ran back to their ships as fast as they could, and sailed off at once.

Psyche was left alone, except in so far as a woman who had decided to kill her husband is haunted by the Furies. Her mind was as restless as a stormy sea. When she first began making preparations for her crime, her resolve was firm; but presently she wavered and started worrying about what would happen if she succeeded and what would happen if she failed. She hurried, then she dawdled, not feeling quite sure whether after all she was doing the right thing, then got furiously angry again. The strange part of the story is that though she loathed the idea of sleeping with a poisonous snake, she was still in love with her husband. However, as the evening drew on, she finally made up her mind and hurriedly got the lamp and carving knife ready.

Night fell, and her husband came to bed, and as soon as they had finished kissing and embracing each other, he fell fast asleep. Psyche was not naturally either very strong or very brave, but the cruel power of fate made a virago of her. Holding the carving knife in a murderous grip, she uncovered the lamp and let its light shine on the bed.

At once the secret was revealed. There lay the gentlest and sweetest of all wild creatures, Cupid himself, the beautiful Love-god, and at sight of him the flame of the lamp spurted joyfully up and the knife turned its edge for shame.

Psyche was terrified. She lost all control of her senses, and pale as death, fell trembling to her knees, where she desperately tried to hide the knife by plunging it in her own heart. She would have succeeded, too, had the knife not shrunk from the crime and twisted itself out of her hand. Faint and unnerved though she was, she began to feel better as she stared at Cupid's divine beauty: his golden hair, washed in nectar and still scented with it, thick curls straying over white neck and flushed cheeks and falling prettily entangled on either side of his head—hair so bright that the flame of the lamp winked in the radiant light reflected from it. At his shoulders grew soft wings of the purest white, and though they were at rest, the tender down fringing the feathers quivered naughtily all the time. The rest of his body was so smooth and beautiful that Venus could never have been ashamed to acknowledge him as her son. At the foot of the bed lay this great god's bow, quiver and arrows.

Psyche's curiosity could be satisfied only by a close examination of her husband's sacred weapons. She pulled an arrow out of the quiver and touched the point with the tip of her thumb to try its sharpness; but her hand was trembling and she pressed too hard. The skin was pierced and out came a drop or two of blood. So Psyche accidentally fell in love with Love. Burning with greater passion for Cupid even than before, she flung herself panting upon him, desperate with desire, and smothered him with kisses; her one fear now being that he would wake too soon.

While she clung to him, utterly bewildered with delight, the lamp, which she was still holding, whether from treachery or from envy, or because it longed as it were to touch and kiss such a marvellously beautiful body, spurted a drop of scalding oil on the God's right shoulder. What a bold and impudent lamp, what a worthless vessel at the altar of Love—for the first lamp was surely invented by some lover who wished to prolong all night the passionate delights of his eye—so to scorch the God of all fire! Cupid sprang up in pain, and taking in the whole disgraceful scene at a glance, spread his wings and flew off without a word; but not before the poor girl had seized his right leg with both hands and clung to it. She looked very queer, carried up like that through the cloudy sky; but soon her strength failed her and she tumbled down to earth again.

Cupid did not desert her immediately, but alighted on the top of a cypress near by, where he stood reproaching her. "Oh, silly, foolish Psyche, it was for your sake that I disobeyed the orders of my mother Venus! She told me to inflame you with passion for some utterly worthless man, but I preferred to fly down from Heaven and become your lover myself. I know only too well that I acted thoughtlessly, and now look at the result! Cupid, the famous archer, wounds himself with one of his own arrows and marries a girl who mistakes him for a monster; she tries to chop off his head and darken the eyes that have beamed such love upon her. This was the danger of which I warned you again and again, gently begging you to be on your guard. As for those sisters of yours who turned you against me and gave you such damnable advice, I'll very soon be avenged on them. But your punishment will simply be that I'll fly away from you." He soared up into the air and was gone.

Psyche lay motionless on the ground, following him with her eyes and moaning bitterly. When the steady beat of his wings had carried him clean out of her sight, she climbed up the bank of a river that flowed close by and flung herself into the water. But the kindly river, out of respect for the god whose warm power is felt as much by water-creatures as by beasts and birds, washed her ashore with a gentle wave and laid her high and dry on the flowery turf.

Pan, the goat-legged country god, happened to be sitting near by, caressing the mountain nymph Echo and teaching her to repeat all sorts of pretty songs. A flock of she-goats roamed around, browsing greedily on the grass. Pan was already aware of Psyche's misfortune, so he gently beckoned to the desolate girl and did what he could to comfort her. "Pretty dear," he said soothingly. "Though I'm only an old, old shepherd and very much of a countryman, I have picked up a good deal of experience in my time. So if I am right in my conjecture—or my divination, as sensible people would call it—your unsteady walk, your pallor, your constant sighs, and your sad eyes show that you're desperately in love. Listen: make no further attempt at suicide by leaping from a precipice, or doing anything else violent. Stop crying, try to be cheerful, and open your heart to Cupid, the greatest of us gods; he's a thoroughly spoilt young fellow, whom you must humour by praying to him only in the gentlest, sweetest language."

It is very lucky to be addressed by Pan, but Psyche made no reply. She merely curtseyed dutifully and went on. She trudged along the road by the river for awhile, until for some reason or other she decided to follow a lane that led off it. Towards evening it brought her to a city, of which she soon found out that her eldest sister was the queen. She announced her arrival at the palace and was at once admitted.

After an exchange of embraces, the queen asked Psyche why she had come. Psyche answered: "You remember your advice about that carving knife and the monstrous snake who pretended to be my husband and was going to swallow me? Well, I took it, but no sooner had I shone my lamp on the bed than I saw a marvellous sight: Venus's divine son, Cupid himself, lying there in tranquil sleep. The joy and relief were too great for me. I quite lost my head and didn't know how to satisfy my longing for him; but then, by a dreadful accident, a drop of burning oil from the lamp spurted on his shoulder. The pain woke him at once. When he saw me holding the lamp and the knife, he shouted: 'Wicked woman, out of this bed at once! I divorce you here and now. I am going to marry your eldest sister instead.' Then he called for the West Wind, who blew me out of the palace and landed me here."

Psyche had hardly finished her story before her sister, madly jealous of her for having been in bed with a god and burning with desire to have the same experience, rushed off to her husband with a story that her parents were dead, and that she must sail home at once. Off she went, and when at last she reached the rock, though another wind altogether was blowing, she shouted confidently: "Here I come, Cupid, a woman worthy of your love. West Wind, convey your mistress to the Palace at once!" Then she took a headlong leap; but she never reached the valley, either dead or alive, because the rocks cut her to pieces as she fell and scattered her flesh and guts all over the mountainside. So she got what she deserved, and the birds and beasts feasted on her remains.

Psyche wandered on and on until she came to another city, where the other sister was queen, and told her the same story. The wicked woman, wishing to supplant Psyche in Cupid's love, set sail at once, hurried to the rock, leaped off it, and died in exactly the same way.

Psyche continued on her travels through country after country, searching for Cupid; but he was in Heaven, lying in bed in his mother's royal suite, groaning for pain. Meanwhile a white gull, of the sort that skims the surface of the sea flapping the waves with its wings, dived down into the water; there it met Venus, who was enjoying a dip, and brought her the news that her son Cupid was confined to bed by a severe and painful burn, from which it was doubtful whether he would recover. It told her, too, that every sort of scandal about the Venus family was going around. People were saying that her son had flown down to some mountain or other for an indecent affair with a girl, and that she herself had abandoned her divine tasks and gone off for a seaside holiday. "The result is," screamed the gull, "that Pleasure, Grace, and Wit have disappeared from the earth and everything there has become ugly, dull, and slovenly. Nobody bothers any longer about his wife, his friends or his children; and the whole system of human love is in such complete disorder that it is now considered disgusting for anyone to show even natural affection."

This talkative, meddlesome bird succeeded in setting Venus against her son. She grew very angry and cried: "So my promising lad has already taken a mistress, has he? Here, gull—you seem to be the only creature left with any true affection for me—tell me, do you know the name of the creature who has seduced my poor simple boy? Is she one of the Nymphs, or one of the Hours, or one of the Muses, or one of my own train of Graces?"

The gull was very ready to spread the scandal it had picked up. "I cannot say for certain, Your Majesty, but unless my memory is playing me tricks, I think the story is that your son has fallen desperately in love with a human named Psyche."

Venus was absolutely furious. "What! With her, of all women? With Psyche, the usurper of my beauty, the rival of my glory? This is worse and worse. It was through me that he got to know the girl. Does the impudent young wretch take me for a procuress?"

She rose from the sea at once and hurried aloft to her golden room, where she found Cupid lying ill in bed, as the gull had told her. As she entered she bawled out at the top of her voice: "Now *is* this decent behaviour? A fine credit you are to your divine family and a fine reputation you're building up for yourself. You trample your mother's orders underfoot as though she had no authority over you whatsoever, and instead of tormenting her enemy with a dishonourable passion, as you were ordered to do, you have the impudence to sleep with the girl yourself. At your age, you lecherous little beast! I suppose you thought that I'd be delighted to have her for a daughter-in-law, eh? And I suppose, you also thought, you scamp, you debauched detestable brat, that you're my heir and that I'm past the age of child-bearing! Please understand that I'm quite capable of having another son, if I please, and a far better one than you, and quite prepared to disinherit you in his favour. However, to make you feel the disgrace still more keenly, I think I'll legally adopt the son of one of my slaves and hand over to him your wings, torch, bow, and arrows, which you have been using in ways for which I never intended them. And I have every right to do that, because not one of them was supplied by your father, Vulcan. The fact is, that you have been mischievous from your earliest years and always delighted in hurting people. You have often had the bad manners to shoot at your elders, and as for me, your mother, you shame me before the whole world day after day, you matricidal wretch, by sticking me full of your horrible little arrows. You sneer at me and call me 'the widow,' I suppose because your father and I are no longer on speaking terms, and show not the slightest respect for your brave, invincible stepfather, Mars; in fact, you do your best to annoy me by setting him after other women and making me madly jealous. But you'll soon be sorry that you played all those tricks; I warn you that this marriage of yours is going to leave a sour, bitter taste in your mouth."

He did not answer, so she complained to herself in an undertone: "This is all very well, but everyone is laughing at me and I haven't the faintest idea what to do or where to go. How in the world am I to catch and cage the nasty little lizard? I suppose I'd better go for help to old Sobriety, to whom I've always been so dreadfully rude for the sake of this spoilt son of mine. Must I really have anything to do with that dowdy, countrified old bore, my natural foe? The idea makes me shudder, yet revenge is sweet from whatever quarter it comes. Yes, I fear that she's the only person who can do anything for me. She'll give the little beast the thrashing of his life; confiscate his quiver, blunt his arrows, tear the string off his bow, and quench his torch. Worse than that, she'll shave off his golden hair, which I used to curl so carefully with my own hands, and clip those lovely wings of his, which I once whitened with the dazzling milk of my own breast. When that's been done, perhaps I'll feel a little better."

She rushed off again and at once ran into her step-mother, Juno, and her aunt Ceres, who noticed how angry she looked and asked her why she was spoiling the beauty of her bright eyes with so sullen a frown. "Thank goodness I met you," she answered. "I needed you to calm me down. There is something you can do for me, if you'll be kind enough. Please make careful enquiries for the whereabouts of a runaway creature called Psyche—I'm sure you must have heard all about her and the family scandal she's caused by her affair with . . . with you know whom!"

Of course, they knew all about it, and tried to soothe her fury. "Darling," Juno said, "you mustn't take this too much to heart. Why try to thwart his pleasures and kill the girl with whom he's fallen in love? What terrible sin has he committed? It is no crime, surely, to sleep with a pretty girl?"

And Ceres said: "Darling, you imagine that he's still only a boy because he carries his years so gracefully, but you simply must realize that he's a young man now. Have you forgotten his age? And, really, Juno and I think it very strange that, as a mother and a woman of the world, you persist in poking your nose into what is really his own business, and that when you catch him out in a love affair you blame the poor darling for those very talents and inclinations that he inherits directly from yourself. What god or man will have any patience with you, you go about all the time waking sexual desire in people but at the same time try to repress similar feelings in your own son? Is it really your intention to close down the sole existing factory of woman's universal weakness?"

The goddesses were not quite honest in their defence of Cupid: they were afraid of his arrows and thought it wiser to speak well of him even when he was not about. Venus, seeing that they refused to take a serious view of her wrongs, indignantly turned her back on them and hurried off again to the sea.

Meanwhile, Psyche was restlessly wandering about day and night in search of her husband. However angry he might be, she hoped to make him relent either by coaxing him in their own private love-language or by going down on her knees in abject repentance. One day she noticed a temple on the top of a steep hill. She said to herself: "I wonder if my husband is there?" So she walked quietly towards the hill, her heart full of love and hope, and reached the temple with some difficulty, after climbing ridge after ridge. But when she arrived at the sacred couch she found it heaped with votive gifts of wheat-sheaves, wheat-chaplets and ears of barley, also sickles and other harvest implements; but all scattered about untidily, as though flung down at the close of a hot summer day by careless reapers.

She began to sort all these things carefully, and arrange them in their proper places, feeling that she must behave respectfully towards every deity whose temple she happened to visit and implore the help of the whole Heavenly family one by one. The temple belonged to the generous Goddess Ceres, who saw her busily at work and called out from afar: "Oh, you poor Psyche! Venus is furious and searching everywhere for you. She wants to be cruelly revenged on you. I am surprised that you can spare the time to look after my affairs for me, or think of anything at all but your own safety."

Psyche's hair streamed across the temple floor as she prostrated herself at the Goddess's feet, which she wetted with her tears. She implored her protection: "I beseech you, Goddess, by the corn-stalks in your hand, by the happy ceremony of harvest-home, by the secret contents of the wicker baskets carried in your procession, by the winged dragons of your chariot, by the furrows of Sicily from which a cruel god once ravished your daughter Proserpine, by the wheels of his chariot, by the earth that closed upon her, by her dark descent and gloomy wedding, by her happy torch-lit return to earth, and by the other mysteries which Eleusis, your Attic sanctuary, silently conceals—help me, oh please help your unhappy suppliant Psyche. Allow me, just for a few days, to hide myself under that stack of wheat-sheaves, until the great Goddess's rage has had time to cool down; or if not for so long as that, at least let me have a short rest, because, honestly, I am very, very tired, and haven't stopped travelling for a moment since I set out."

Ceres answered: "Your tears and prayers go straight to my heart, and I would dearly love to help you; but the truth is that I can't afford to offend my niece. She has been one of my best friends for ages and ages and really has a very good heart when you get to know her. You'd better leave this temple at once and think yourself lucky that I don't have you placed under arrest."

Psyche went away, twice as sad as she had come: she had never expected such a rebuff. But soon she saw below her in the valley another beautiful temple in the middle of a dark sacred grove. She feared to miss any chance, even a remote one, of putting things right for herself, so she went down to implore the protection of the deity of the place, whoever it might be. She saw various splendid offerings hanging from branches of the grove and from the temple door-posts; among them were rich garments embroidered with gold letters that spelt out the name of the goddess to whom all were dedicated, namely Juno, and recorded the particular favours which she had granted their donors.

Psyche fell on her knees, wiped away her tears, and embracing the temple altar, still warm from a recent sacrifice, began to pray. "Sister and wife of great Jupiter, I cannot tell where you may be at the moment. You may be residing in one of your ancient temples on Samos—the Samians boast that you were born in their island and spent your whole impassioned childhood there. Or you may be visiting your happy city of Carthage on its high hill, where you are adored as a virgin travelling across Heaven in a lion-drawn chariot. Or you may be watching over the famous walls of Argos, past which the river Inachus flows, where you are adored as the Queen of Heaven, the Thunderer's bride. Wherever you are, you whom the whole East venerates as Zygia the Goddess of Marriage, and the whole West as Lucina, Goddess of Childbirth, I appeal to you now as Juno the Protectress: I beg you to watch over me in my overwhelming misfortune, and rescue me from the dangers that threaten me. You see, Goddess, I am very, very tired, and very, very frightened and I know that you're always ready to help women who are about to have babies, if they get into any sort of trouble."

Juno appeared in all her august glory and said: "My dear, I should be only too pleased to help you, but unfortunately divine etiquette forbids. I can't possibly go against the wishes of Venus, who married my son Vulcan, you know, and whom I have always loved as though she were my own child. Besides, I am forbidden by law—one of the Fabian laws—to harbour any fugitive slave-girl without her owner's consent."

Psyche was distressed by this second shipwreck of her hopes, and felt quite unable to go on looking for her winged husband. She gave up all hope of safety and said to herself: "Where in the world, or out of it, can I turn for help, now that even these powerful goddesses will do nothing for me but express their sympathy? My feet are so tangled in the snares of fate that it seems useless to ask them to take me anywhere else. Where is there a building in which I can hide myself from the watchful eyes of great Venus, even with all doors and windows locked? The fact is, my dear Psyche, that you must borrow a little male courage, you must boldly renounce all idle hopes of escape and make a voluntary surrender to your sovereign mistress. It may be too late, but you must at least try to calm her rage by submissive behaviour. Besides, after this long, useless search, you have quite a good chance of finding your husband at your mother-in-law's house."

Psyche's decision to do her duty was risky and even suicidal, but she prepared herself for it by considering what sort of appeal she ought to make to her Mistress.

Venus meanwhile had declined to use any human agencies in her search for Psyche and returned to Heaven, where she ordered her chariot to be got ready. It was of burnished gold, with coach-work of such exquisite filigree that its intrinsic value was negligible compared with its value as a work of art. It had been her husband Vulcan's wedding present to her. Four white doves from the flock in constant attendance on her flew happily forward and offered their rainbow-coloured necks to the jewelled harness and, when Venus mounted, drew the chariot along at a spanking rate. Behind flew a crowd of naughty sparrows and other little birds that sang very sweetly in announcement of the Goddess's arrival.

Now the clouds vanished, the sky opened and the high upper air received her joyfully. Her singing retinue were not in the least afraid of swooping eagles or greedy hawks, and she drove straight to the royal citadel of Jupiter, where she demanded the immediate services of Mercury, the town-crier of Heaven, in a matter of great urgency. When Jupiter nodded his sapphire brow in assent, Venus was delighted; she retired from his presence and gave Mercury, who was now accompanying her, careful instructions: "Brother from Arcady, you know I have never in my life undertaken any business at all without your assistance, and you know how long I have been without news of my runaway slave girl. So you simply must make a public announcement offering a reward to the person who finds her, and insist on my orders being obeyed at once. Her person must be accurately described so that nobody will be able to plead ignorance as an excuse for harbouring her. Here is her dossier; Psyche is the name, and all particulars are included."

She handed him a little book and immediately went home. Mercury did as he was told. He went from country to country, crying out: "Oyez, oyez! If any person can apprehend and seize the person of a runaway princess, one of the Lady Venus's slave-girls, by name PSYCHE, or give any information that will lead to her discovery, let such a person go to Mercury, Town-crier of Heaven, in his temple just outside the precincts of Our Lady of the Myrtles, Aventine Hill, Rome. The reward offered is as follows: seven sweet kisses from the mouth of the said Venus herself, and one exquisitely delicious thrust of her honeyed tongue between his pursed lips."

A jealous competitive spirit naturally fired all mankind when they heard this reward announced, and it was this that put an immediate end to Psyche's hesitation. She was already near her mistress's gate when she was met by one of the household, named Old Habit, who screamed out at once at the top of her voice: "You wicked slut, you! So you've discovered at last that you have a mistress, eh? But don't pretend, you brazen-faced thing, that you haven't heard of the huge trouble that you've caused us in our search for you. Well, I'm glad you've fallen into my hands, not some other slave's, because you're safe here—safe in the jaws of Hell, and there won't be any delay in your punishment either, you obstinate, impertinent baggage!" She twisted her fingers in Psyche's hair and dragged her into Venus's presence, though she came along willingly enough.

Venus burst into the hysterical laugh of a woman who is desperately angry. She shook her head menacingly and scratched her ear—the right ear, behind which the Throne of Vengeance is said to be situated. "Ah," she cried, "so you condescend to pay your respects to your mother-in-law, is that it? Or perhaps you have come to visit your husband's sick-bed, hearing that he's still dangerously ill from the burn you gave him? But make yourself at home. I promise you the sort of welcome that a good mother-in-law is bound to give her son's wife." She clapped her hands for her slaves, Anxiety and Grief, and when they ran up, gave Psyche over to them for punishment. They led her off, flogged her cruelly and tortured her in other ways besides, after which they brought her back to Venus's presence.

Once more Venus yelled with laughter: "Just look at her!" she cried. "Look at the whore! That big belly of hers makes me feel quite sorry for her. By Heaven, it wrings my grandmotherly heart! Grandmother, indeed! How wonderful to be made a grandmother at my time of life! And to think that the son of this disgusting slave will be called Venus's own grandchild! No, but of course that is nonsense. A marriage between a god and a mortal, celebrated in the depth of the country without witnesses and lacking even the consent of the bride's father, can't possibly be recognized at Law; your child will be a bastard, my girl, even if I permit you to bring it into the world."

With this, she flew at poor Psyche, tore her clothes to shreds, pulled out handfuls of her hair, then grabbed her by the shoulders and shook her until she nearly shook her head off, giving her a terrible time. Next she called for quantities of wheat, barley, millet, lentils, beans and the seeds of poppy and vetch, and mixed them all together into a huge heap. "You look such a dreadful sight, slave," she said, "that the only way that you are ever likely to get a lover is by hard work. So now I'll test you myself, to find out whether you're industrious. Do you see this pile of seeds all mixed together? Sort out the different kinds, stack them in separate little heaps, and prove that you're quick-fingered by getting every grain in its right place before nightfall." Without another word, she flew off to attend some wedding breakfast or other.

Psyche made no attempt to set about her stupendous task, but sat gazing dumbly at it, until a very small ant, one of the country sort, happened to pass and realized what was going on. Pity for Psyche as wife of the mighty God of Love set the little thing shrieking wild curses at the cruel mother-in-law and scurrying about to round up every ant in the district. "Take pity on her, sisters, take pity on this pretty girl, you busy children of the generous Earth. She's the wife of Love himself and her life is in great danger. Quick, quick, to the rescue!"

They came rushing up as fast as their six legs would carry them, wave upon wave of ants, and began working furiously to sort the pile out, grain by grain. Soon they had arranged it all tidily in separate heaps, and run off again at once.

Venus returned that evening, a little drunk, smelling strongly of aphrodisiac ointments, and simply swathed in rose-wreaths. When she saw with what prodigious speed Psyche had finished the task, she said: "You didn't do a hand's stroke yourself, you wicked thing. This is the work of someone whom you have bewitched, poor fellow! But you'll be 'poor fellow' too, before I have done." She threw her part of a coarse loaf and went to bed.

Meanwhile she had confined Cupid to his bedroom, partly to prevent him from playing his usual naughty tricks and so making his injury worse; partly to keep him away from his sweetheart. So the lovers spent a miserable night, unable to visit each other, although under the same roof.

As soon as the Goddess of Dawn had set her team moving across the sky, Venus called Psyche and said: "Do you see the grove fringing the bank of that stream over there, with fruit bushes hanging low over the water? Shining golden sheep are wandering about in it, without a shepherd to look after them. I want you to fetch me a hank of their precious wool, and I don't care how you get it."

Psyche rose willingly enough, but with no intention of obeying Venus's orders: she had made up her mind to throw herself in the stream and so end her sorrows. But a green reed, of the sort used in Pan's pipes, was blown upon by some divine breeze and whispered to her: "Wait, Psyche, wait! I know what dreadful sorrows you have suffered, but you must not pollute these sacred waters by a suicide. And, another thing, you must not go into the grove, to risk your life among those dangerous sheep; not yet. The heat of the sun so infuriates the beasts that they kill any human being who ventures among them. Either they gore them with their sharp horns, or butt them to death with their stony foreheads or bite them with their poisonous teeth. Wait, Psyche, wait until the afternoon wears to a close, and the serene whispers of these waters lull them asleep. Hide meanwhile under that tall plane-tree who drinks the same water as I do, and as soon as the sheep calm down, go into the grove and gather the wisps of golden wool that you'll find sticking on every briar there."

It was a simple, kindly reed and Psyche took its advice, which proved to be sound: that evening she was able to return to Venus with a whole lapful of the delicate golden wool. Yet even her performance of this second dangerous task did not satisfy the Goddess, who frowned and told her with a cruel smile: "Someone has been helping you again, that's quite clear. But now I'll put your courage and prudence to a still severer test. Do you see the summit of that high mountain over there? You'll find that a dark-coloured stream cascades down its precipitous sides into a gorge below and then floods the Stygian marshes and feeds the hoarse River of Wailing. Here is a little jar. Go off at once and bring it back to me brimful of ice-cold water fetched from the very middle of the stream at the point where it bursts out of the rock."

She gave Psyche a jar of polished crystal and packed her off with renewed threats of what would happen if she came back empty-handed.

Psyche started at once for the top of the mountain, which was called Aroanius, thinking that there at least she would find a means of ending her wretched life. As she came near, she saw what a stupendously dangerous and difficult task had been set her. The dreadful waters of the Styx burst out from half-way up an enormously tall, steep, slippery precipice; cascaded down into a narrow conduit which they had hollowed for themselves in the course of centuries, and flowed unseen into the gorge below. On both sides of their outlet she saw fierce dragons crawling, never asleep, always on guard with unwinking eyes, and stretching their long necks over the sacred water. And the waters sang as they rolled along, varying the words every now and then: "Be off! Be off!" and "What do you wish, wish, wish? Look! Look!" and "What are you at, are you at? Care, take care!". "Off with you, off with you, off with you! Death! Death!"

Psyche stood still as stone, her mind far away: the utter impossibility of escaping alive from the trap that Venus had set for her was so overwhelming that she could no longer even relieve herself by tears—that last comfort of women when things go wrong with them. But the kind, sharp eyes of Providence notice when innocent souls are in trouble. At her suggestion Jupiter's royal bird, the rapacious eagle, suddenly sailed down to her from Heaven. He gratefully remembered the ancient debt that he owed to Cupid for having helped him to carry Ganymede, the beautiful Phrygian prince, up to Heaven to become Jupiter's cup-bearer; and since Psyche was Cupid's wife he screamed down at her: "Silly, simple, inexperienced Psyche, how can you ever hope to steal one drop of this frightfully sacred stream? Surely you have heard that Jupiter himself fears the waters of Styx, and that just as you swear by the Blessed Gods, so they swear by the Sovereign Styx. But let me take that little jar." He quickly snatched it from her grasp and soared off on his strong wings, steering a zigzag course between the two rows of furious fangs and vibrating three-forked tongues, until he reached the required spot. The stream was reluctant to give up its water and warned him to escape while he still could, but he explained that the Goddess Venus wanted the water and that she had commissioned him to fetch it; a story which carried some weight with the stream. He filled the jar with the water and brought it safely back to the delighted Psyche.

She returned with it to Venus but could not appease her fury even with this latest success. Venus was resolved to set a still more outrageous test, and said with a sweet smile that seemed to spell her complete ruin: "You must be a witch, a very clever, very wicked witch, else you could never have carried out my orders so exactly. But I have still one more task for you to perform, my dear girl. Please take this box and go down to the Underworld to the death-palace of Pluto. Hand it to Queen Proserpine and say: 'The Lady Venus's compliments, and will you please send this box back to her with a little of your beauty in it, not very much but enough to last for at least one short day. She has had to make such a drain on her own store as a result of sitting up at night with her sick son, that she has none left.' Then come back with the box at once, because I must use her make-up before I appear at the Olympic Theatre tonight."

This seemed the end of everything, since her orders were to go down to the Underworld of Tartarus. Psyche saw that she was openly and undisguisedly being sent to her death. She went at once to a high tower, deciding that her straightest and easiest way to the Underworld was to throw herself down from it. But the tower suddenly broke into human speech: "Poor child," it said, "do you really mean to commit suicide by jumping down from me? How rash of you to lose hope just before the end of your trials. Don't you realize that as soon as the breath is out of your body you will indeed go right down to the depths of Tartarus, but that once you take that way there's no hope of return? Listen to me. The famous Greek city of Lacedaemon is not far from here. Go there at once and ask to be directed to Taenarus, which is rather an out-of-the-way place to find. It's on a peninsula to the south. Once you get there you'll find one of the ventilation holes of the Underworld. Put your head through it and you'll see a road running downhill, but there'll be no traffic on it. Climb through at once, and the road will lead you straight to Pluto's palace. But don't forget to take with you two pieces of barley bread soaked in honey water, one in each hand, and two coins in your mouth.

"When you have gone a good way along the road you'll meet a lame ass loaded with wood, and its lame driver will ask you to hand him some pieces of rope for tying up part of the load which the ass has dropped. Pass him by in silence. Then hurry forward until you reach the river of the dead, where Charon will at once ask you for his fee and ferry you across in his patched boat among crowds of ghosts. It seems that the God Avarice lives thereabouts, because neither Charon nor his great father Pluto does anything for nothing. (A poor man on the point of death is expected to have his passage-fee ready; but if he can't get hold of a coin, he isn't allowed to achieve true death, but must wander about disconsolately forever on this side of Styx.) Anyhow, give the dirty ruffian one of your coins, but let him take it from your mouth, not from your hand. While you are being ferried across the sluggish stream, the corpse of an old man will float by; he will raise a putrid hand and beg you to haul him into the boat. But you must be careful not to yield to any feeling of pity for him; that is forbidden. Once ashore, you will meet three women some distance away from the bank. They will be weaving cloth and will ask you to help them. To touch the cloth is also forbidden. All these apparitions, and others like them, are snares set for you by Venus; her object is to make you let go one of the sops you are carrying, and you must understand that the loss of even one of them would be fatal—it would prevent your return to this world. They are for you to give to Cerberus, the huge, fierce, formidable hound with three heads on three necks, all barking in unison, who terrifies the dead; though of course the dead have no need to be frightened by him because they are only shadows and he can't injure shadows.

"Cerberus keeps perpetual guard at the threshold of Proserpine's dark palace, the desolate place where she lives with her husband, Pluto. Throw him one of your sops and you'll find it easy to get past him into the presence of Proserpine herself. She'll give you a warm welcome, offer you a cushioned chair, and have you brought a magnificent meal. But sit on the ground, ask for a piece of common bread and eat nothing else. Then deliver your message, and she'll give you what you came for.

"As you go out, throw the cruel dog the remaining sop as a bribe to let you pass; then pay the greedy ferryman the remaining coin for your return fare across the river, and when you're safely on the other bank follow the road back until you see once again the familiar constellations of Heaven. One last, important warning; be careful not to open or even look at the box you carry back; that hidden receptacle of divine beauty is not for you to explore."

It was a kind and divinely inspired tower and Psyche took its advice. She went at once to Taenarus where, armed with the coins and the two sops she ran down the road to the Underworld. She passed in silence by the lame man with the lame ass, paid Charon the first coin, stopped her ears to the entreaties of the floating corpse, refused to be taken in by the appeal of the spinning women, pacified the dreadful dog with the first sop and entered Proserpine's palace. There she refused the comfortable chair and the tempting meal, sat humbly at Proserpine's feet, content with a crust of common bread, and finally delivered her message. Proserpine secretively filled the box, shut it and returned it to her; then Psyche stopped the dog's barking with the second sop, paid Charon with the second coin and returned from the Underworld, feeling in far better health and spirits than while on her way down there. When she saw the daylight again she offered up a prayer of praise for its loveliness. Though she was in a hurry to complete her errand she foolishly allowed her curiosity to get the better of her. She said to herself: "I should be a fool to carry this little boxful of divine beauty without borrowing a tiny touch of it for my own use: I must do everything possible to please my beautiful lover."

She opened the box, but it contained no beauty nor anything else, so far as she saw: but out crept a truly Stygian sleep which seized her, and wrapped her in a dense cloud of drowsiness. She fell prostrate and lay there like a corpse, the open box beside her.

Cupid, now recovered from his injury and unable to bear Psyche's absence a moment longer, flew out through the narrow window of the bedroom where his mother had been holding him a prisoner. His wings, invigorated by their long rest, carried him faster than ever before. He hurried to Psyche, carefully brushed away the cloud of sleep from her body, and shut it up again in its box, then roused her with a harmless prick of an arrow. "Poor girl," he said, "your curiosity has once more nearly ruined you. Hurry now and complete the task which my mother set you; and I'll see to everything else." He flew off, and she sprang up at once to deliver Proserpine's present to Venus.

But Cupid, who had fallen more deeply in love with Psyche than ever and was alarmed by his mother's sudden conversion to respectability, returned to his naughty tricks. He flew at great speed to the very highest heaven and flung himself as a suppliant at Jupiter's feet, where he pleaded his case. Jupiter pinched his handsome cheeks and kissed his hand. Then he said: "My masterful child, you never pay me the respect which has been decreed me by the Council of Gods, and you're always shooting your arrows into my divine heart—the very seat of the laws that govern the four elements and all the constellations of the sky. Often you defile it with mortal love affairs, contrary to the Laws of Heaven, the Julian edict against adultery, and public peace, injuring my reputation and authority by involving me in sordid love intrigues and transmogrifying my serene appearance into that of serpent, fire, wild beast, bird or farmyard bull. Nevertheless, I can't forget how often I've nursed you on my knees and how soft-hearted I can be, so I'll do whatever you ask. But please realize that you must protect yourself against a Certain Person who might envy you your beautiful wife, and at the same time reward him for what he's going to do for you; so I advise you to introduce me to whatever other girl of really outstanding beauty happens to be about on the earth today."

Then he ordered Mercury to call a Council of all Heavens, with a penalty of ten thousand drachmae for non-appearance. Everyone was afraid to be fined such a sum, so the Celestial Theatre filled up at once, and Almighty Jupiter from his sublime throne read the following address:

> Right honourable gods and goddesses whose names are registered in the White Roll of the Muses, you all know the young fellow over there whom I have brought up from boyhood and whose passionate nature must, in my opinion, be curbed in some way or other. It is enough to remind you of the daily complaints that come in of his provoking someone or other to adultery or a similar crime. Well, I have decided that we must stop the young rascal from doing anything of the sort again by fastening the fetters of marriage securely upon him. He has found and seduced a pretty girl called Psyche, and my sentence is that he must have her, hold her, possess her and cherish her from this time forth and for evermore.

Then he turned to Venus: "My dear, you have no occasion to be sad, or ashamed that your rank and station in Heaven has been disgraced by your son's match; for I'll see that the marriage is one between social equals, perfectly legitimate and in complete accordance with civil law." He ordered Mercury to fetch Psyche at once and escort her into his presence. When she arrived he took a cup of nectar and handed it to her. "Drink, Psyche, and become an immortal," he said. "Cupid will now never fly away from your arms, but must remain your lawful husband for ever."

Presently a great wedding breakfast was prepared. Cupid reclined in the place of honour with Psyche's head resting on his breast; Jupiter was placed next, with Juno in the same comfortable position, and then all the other gods and goddesses in order of seniority. Jupiter was served with nectar and ambrosia by apple-cheeked Ganymede, his personal cup-bearer; Bacchus attended to everyone else. Vulcan was the chef; the Hours decorated the palace with red roses and other bridal flowers; the Graces sprinkled balsam water; the Muses chanted the marriage-hymn to the accompaniment of flute and pipe-music from the godlings Satyrus and Peniscus. Finally Apollo sang to his own lyre and the music was so sweet that Venus came forward and performed a lively step-dance in time to it. Psyche was properly married to Cupid and in due time she bore him her child, a daughter whose name was Pleasure.

—§—

Translated by Robert Graves

Of Feminine Subtlety ›
Gesta Romanorum

King Darius was a circumspect prince and had three sons, whom he loved very much. On his deathbed, he bequeathed the kingdom to his firstborn; all his personal acquisitions to his second; and a golden ring, a necklace, and a piece of valuable cloth to his third. The ring had the power to render beloved anyone who wore it on his finger, and could also obtain for him whatever he sought. The necklace enabled the person who wore it upon his breast to accomplish his heart's desire. And the cloth had the virtue of instantaneously transporting whoever sat upon it to wherever he wanted to go. The king conferred these three gifts upon the younger son for the purpose of aiding his studies, but his mother was to retain them until he reached maturity.

Soon after making the bequests, the old monarch gave up the ghost and was magnificently buried. The two elder sons then took possession of their legacies, while the mother brought the youngest the ring and cautioned him to beware of the artifices of women, otherwise he would lose the ring. Jonathan (for that was his name) took the ring and applied himself zealously to his studies, in which he made himself proficient. But one day, while he was walking through the streets, he noticed a very beautiful woman, who struck him so much that he took her to him. However, he continued to use the ring and found favor with everyone, which enabled him to obtain whatever he desired.

Now the lady was very much surprised that he lived so splendidly even though he had no possessions. And once, when he was particularly exhilarated, she embraced him tenderly and maintained that there was not a creature under the sun whom she loved so much as she did him. Therefore, she suggested, he ought to tell her how he managed to support his magnificent way of life. He explained the virtues of the ring, and she pleaded with him to be careful with such a valuable treasure.

"Since you may lose it in your daily contact with men," she added, "I beg you to place it in my custody."

Overcome by her entreaties, he gave up the ring. But when he was in need of something, she said that it had been stolen. He lamented bitterly, but now he had no means at all of subsistence. So he hastened to his mother and explained to her how he had lost his ring.

"My son," said she, "I warned you what might happen, but you did not pay any attention to my advice. Here is the necklace, but guard it more carefully. If you lose it, you will always be lacking a thing of the greatest honor and value."

Jonathan took the necklace and returned to his studies. At the gate of the city, his concubine met him and welcomed him with the appearance of great joy. He remained with her and wore on his breast the necklace that enabled him to accomplish his heart's desire. Once again he began to live in splendor, so that the lady was astonished, since she knew that he had neither gold nor silver. Consequently she guessed that he was carrying another talisman and cunningly drew from him the history of the miraculous necklace.

"Why do you always take it with you?" she asked. "You can accomplish more that your heart desires in one moment than can be made use of in a year. Let me keep it."

"No," he replied. "You'll lose the necklace just as you lost the ring. And thus I'll be damaged in the worst possible way."

"Oh, my lord," she replied. "After having the ring in my custody, I've learned my lesson and know how to guard the necklace. I assure you, no one will be able to get it from me."

The foolish youth trusted her words and gave her the necklace.

Now when he had spent all that he had owned, he sought his talisman, and just as before, she solemnly protested that it had been stolen. Jonathan was extremely distressed by this news.

"Am I going mad?" he cried. "After the loss of my ring, I've now had to lose the necklace!"

He immediately hastened to his mother and told her the entire story. Disturbed by his account, she said, "Oh, my dear child, how can you place your trust in a woman who has deceived you twice? People will think you a fool. Try to be wise, for I have nothing more for you than the valuable cloth which your father left you. If you lose that, there will be no sense at all in your returning to me."

Jonathan took the cloth and again went back to his studies. The concubine seemed quite joyful, and as he spread out the cloth, he said, "My dear girl, my father bequeathed me this beautiful cloth. Sit down upon it by my side."

She complied, and Jonathan secretly wished that they were in a desert place out of reach of man. The talisman took effect. They were carried into a forest on the uttermost border of the world, where there was not a trace of humanity. The lady wept bitterly, but Jonathan paid no attention to her tears. He solemnly vowed to Heaven that he would leave her a prey to the wild beasts unless she restored his ring and necklace, and this she promised to do. Soon thereafter, the foolish Jonathan yielded to her request and revealed to her the secret behind the cloth's power. Meanwhile he became weary and placed his head in her lap. As he slept, she managed to draw away that part of the cloth upon which he reposed, and once she was sitting upon it alone, she wished herself where she had been in the morning. The cloth immediately carried out her wish and left Jonathan slumbering in the forest.

When he awoke and found that his cloth and his concubine had departed, he burst into an agony of tears. He had no idea of where to turn. Nevertheless, he arose and fortified himself with the sign of the cross. Then he began walking along a path until he reached a deep river, over which he had to pass. But he found the water so bitter and hot that it separated the flesh from his bones. Full of grief, he carried away with him a small quantity of that water. Proceeding a little farther, he felt hungry. A tree upon which hung the most tempting fruit invited him to partake, whereupon he did so and immediately became a leper. Now he also gathered some of that fruit and carried it away with him. After traveling for some time, he reached another stream, which had the power to restore the flesh to his feet. Some of that water he took with him. He also ate the fruit from another tree, which cleaned him of his leprosy. Therefore, he also took some of that fruit with him.

Walking in this manner day after day, he finally came to a castle, where he encountered two men, who inquired what he was.

"I am a physician," he responded.

"This is lucky," one of the men said. "The king of this country is a leper, and if you can cure him of his leprosy, you will be rewarded handsomely."

He promised to try his skill, and they led him to the king. The result was fortunate. Jonathan supplied him with the fruit of the second tree, and the leprosy disappeared. And when the flesh next was washed in the water, it was completely restored.

After being rewarded most generously, Jonathan boarded a vessel that was bound for his native city. Disembarking, he circulated a report that a great physician had arrived. Now the lady who had cheated him of the talismans was sick to death, and she immediately sent for him. Jonathan was so well disguised that she could not recognize him, but he remembered her very well. As soon as he came to her, he declared that the medicine would not be able to help her unless she first confessed her sins. And if she had defrauded anyone, the goods had to be restored. Since she was on the very verge of death, the lady admitted in a low voice that she had cheated Jonathan of his ring, necklace, and cloth and had left him in a desert place to be devoured by wild beasts. After she had said all this, the disguised physician asked, "Tell me, lady, where are these talismans?"

"In that chest," she answered, and gave him the keys that enabled him to obtain possession of his treasures.

Then Jonathan gave her some of the fruit which produced leprosy, and after she ate it, he gave her some of the water which separated the flesh from the bones. As a result, she was tortured with agony.

Meanwhile Jonathan hastened to his mother, and the whole kingdom rejoiced at his return. Then he recounted how God had saved him from various dangers, and after living many years, he ended his days in peace.

§

Translated by Charles Swan

‹ *The Pig Prince* ›
GIOVANNI FRANCESCO STRAPAROLA

 aleotto, king of Anglia, was a man with many blessings. He was very wealthy, and his wife, Ersilia, daughter of Matthias, king of Hungary, was a princess whose beauty and virtues outshone those of all other ladies of the time. Moreover, Galeotto was a wise king, who ruled his land in such a way that no one ever raised a complaint against him. However, though he and Ersilia had been married for several years, they had no children, and they were both most sad about this situation.

One day, while Ersilia was walking in her garden, she suddenly felt tired, and noticing a spot nearby covered with fresh green grass, she went over to it and sat down. Overcome by weariness and soothed by the sweet singing of the birds in the green bushes, she fell asleep. While she slept, three fairies happened to pass by, and all three held mankind somewhat in scorn. So when they beheld the sleeping queen they stopped and, gazing at her beauty, conferred together how they might protect her with some spell.

Once they reached an agreement, the first fairy cried out, "I wish that no man shall be able to harm her, and that the next time she lies with her husband she will become pregnant, and that she shall bear a son who will be the most handsome child in the world."

Then the second fairy declared, "I wish that no one shall ever have the power to offend her, and that the prince, her son, will be endowed with every virtue under the sun."

And the third fairy said, "I wish that she will be the wisest among women but that the son she conceives will be born in the skin of a pig, with a pig's ways and manners, and he will be obliged to live like this until he has wed three times."

As soon as the three fairies had flown away, Ersilia awoke, stood up, and returned directly to the palace, taking with her the flowers that she had plucked. It was only a few days later that she felt she had become pregnant. When the time of her delivery arrived, she gave birth to a son with body and limbs like those of a pig. The king and queen lamented this prodigy a great deal, and the king, bearing in mind how good and wise his wife was, felt moved more than once to put this offspring of hers to death and cast it into the sea so that she might be spared the shame of having given birth to him. But when he debated in his mind and considered that this son, whatever he might be, was of his own begetting, he discarded the cruel plans he had been deliberating, and seized with pity and grief, he decided that the son should be brought up and nurtured like a rational being and not a brute beast.

Therefore, the child was nursed with the greatest of care and would often be brought to the queen. Then he would put his little snout and his little paws in his mother's lap, and moved by natural affection, she would caress him by stroking his bristly back with her hand and embrace and kiss him as though he were human. In turn, he would wag his tail and give other signs to show that he was conscious of his mother's affection.

When he grew older, the piglet began to talk like a human being and to wander around the city, but if ever he came near any mud or dirt, he would wallow in it as pigs are accustomed to do and return home covered with filth. Then, when he would approach the king and queen, he would rub his sides against their fair garments, defiling them with all kinds of dirt. Nevertheless, they endured it all because he was their son.

One day he came home covered with mud and filth, as was his wont, and he lay down on his mother's rich robe and said in a grunting tone, "Mother, I want to get married."

When the queen heard this, she replied, "Don't talk so foolishly. What maid would ever take you for a husband? Furthermore, do you think that any noble or knight would ever give his daughter to someone so dirty and stinking as you?"

But he kept on grunting that he must have a wife of one sort or another. Not knowing how to manage him in this instance, the queen consulted the king about this problem and said to him, "Our son wishes to marry, but where shall we find anyone who will take him as a husband?"

In the meantime the pig came to his mother every day with the same demand. And one day he said, "I must have a wife, and I'll never leave you in peace until you obtain a maiden for me, and I've seen one today who pleases me a great deal."

It happened that this maiden was the daughter of a poor woman who had three daughters, each of whom was very lovely. When the queen heard this, she summoned the woman and her eldest daughter and said, "Good mother, you are poor and burdened with children. If you agree to what I am about to say to you, you will be rich. I have a son who is, as you see, in the form of a pig, and I would like to marry him to your eldest daughter. You mustn't regard him but think of the king and of me, and remember that your daughter will inherit this whole kingdom when the king and I die."

When the young girl heard the words of the queen, she was very disturbed and blushed red for shame. Then she said that on no account would she listen to the queen's proposition. However, her mother pleaded with her so forcefully that she at last yielded. So when the pig came home that day, all covered with dirt as usual, his mother said to him, "My son, we've found for you the wife you desire." And she commanded the bride to be brought into the chamber, and by this time she had been dressed in magnificent regal attire and was presented to the pig prince.

When he saw her, so lovely and desirable, he was filled with joy, and despite the fact that he was all stinking and dirty, he jumped around her and endeavored to show his affection by pawing and nuzzling her. But she found that he was soiling her beautiful dress and thrust him aside, whereupon the pig said to her, "Why are you pushing me like that? Haven't I had these garments made for you yourself?"

Then she answered disdainfully, "No, neither you nor any other of the whole kingdom of hogs has done this thing."

And when the time for going to bed arrived, the young girl said to herself, "What am I to do with this foul beast? There's only one solution: tonight, while he's sound asleep, I'll kill him."

Now the pig prince, who was not far off, heard these words but said nothing, and when the two retired to their chamber, he got into bed next to her. Stinking and dirty as he was, he defiled the sumptuous bed with his filthy paws and snout. Soon after, his wife fell asleep, and then he struck her with his sharp hooves, driving them into her breast so that he killed her.

The next morning the queen went to visit her daughter-in-law, and to her great grief, she found that the pig had killed her. When he came back from wandering about the city, he said in reply to the queen's bitter reproaches that he had only dealt with his wife as she had intended to deal with him. Then he retired in a bad mood.

Not many days passed before the pig prince began to beseech the queen to allow him to marry one of the other sisters, but at first the queen would not listen to his request. However, he persisted, threatening to ruin everything in the palace if he could not wed the maiden. Hearing this, the queen went to the king and told him everything, and he answered that perhaps it would be wiser to kill their ill-fated offspring before he did some fatal mischief in the city. Yet the queen felt all the tenderness of a mother toward him and loved him very dearly in spite of his brutal nature, and she could not endure the thought of his being put to death. So once again she summoned the poor woman to the palace, along with her second daughter, and she had a long talk with her, begging her to give the daughter in marriage. At last the girl consented to take the pig for a husband, but her fate was no happier than her sister's, for the bridegroom killed her as he had killed his other bride, and then fled headlong from the palace.

When he came back, dirty as usual and stinking so dreadfully that no one could approach him, the king and queen reprimanded him gravely for the outrage he had committed. But again he cried out boldly that if he had not killed her, she would have killed him. Then, as he had done before, the pig began in very short order to plead with his mother to let him wed the youngest sister, who was more beautiful than either of the others. When his request was steadfastly refused, he became more insistent than ever, and in the end, using violent and bloodthirsty language, he began to threaten the queen's life if he was refused the girl for his wife. When she heard this shameful and unnatural speech, the queen was almost brokenhearted and felt she might go out of her mind. But putting all other considerations aside, she summoned the poor woman and her third daughter, whose name was Meldina, and she said to the girl, "Meldina, my child, I would be greatly pleased if you would take the pig prince for your husband. Pay no regard to him, but to his father and to me. Then, if you're prudent and tolerate him, you may become the happiest woman in the world."

In response, Meldina said with a grateful smile that she was quite content to do as the queen requested and thanked her humbly for deigning to choose her as a daughter-in-law, for since she herself had nothing in the world, it was indeed her good fortune that she, a poor girl, should become the daughter-in-law of a powerful sovereign. When the queen heard this modest and amiable reply, she could not keep back the tears for the happiness she felt, but she also feared that the same fate might be in store for Meldina as that which her sisters had suffered.

After the new bride was dressed in rich attire and decked with jewels, she awaited the bridegroom, and the pig prince came in filthier and muddier than ever. However, she spread out her rich gown and asked him to lie down by her side. Thereupon the queen told her to thrust him away, but she would not consent and said, "There are three wise sayings, gracious lady, which I remember very well. The first is that it is folly to waste time in searching for that which cannot be found. The second is that we should believe nothing we may hear except that which bears the marks of sense and reason. The third is that when you have once obtained possession of some rare and precious treasure, prize it well and keep a firm hold upon it."

When the maiden had finished speaking, the pig prince, who had been wide awake and had heard all that she said, got up and kissed her on the face and neck and bosom and shoulders with his tongue. And she did not shy away from returning his caresses, so that he felt a warm love for her. As soon as the time arrived for retiring for the night, the bride went to bed and awaited her unseemly spouse, and when he came, she raised the cover and asked him to lie near her and put his head on the pillow. Covering him carefully with the nightclothes, she drew the curtains so that he would not feel cold.

When morning came, the pig got up and went out to pasture, as was his custom, and very soon after, the queen went to the bride's chamber, expecting to find that she had met with the same fate as her sisters. But when she saw her lying in the bed, all defiled as it was, and looking pleased and contented, she thanked God that her son had at last found a suitable spouse.

One day soon after this, when the pig prince was conversing pleasantly with his wife, he said to her, "Meldina, my beloved wife, if I could be completely certain that you could keep a secret, I'd tell you one of mine, something I have kept hidden for many years. Since I feel you are very prudent and wise and that you love me truly, I'd like to share this secret with you."

"You may safely tell it to me, if you want," said Meldina, "for I promise never to reveal it to anyone without your consent."

Since he was sure of his wife's discretion and fidelity, he immediately shook off the dirty and stinking skin of the pig from his body, and he stood revealed as a handsome and well-shaped young man, and all that night he rested closely folded in the arms of his beloved wife. However, he ordered her solemnly to keep silent about this miracle she had seen, for the time had not come for his complete delivery from this misery. Therefore, when he left the bed, he donned the dirty pig's hide once more.

Of course, Meldina was overjoyed that, instead of a pig, she had gained a handsome and gallant young prince for a husband. And not long after this it turned out that she was pregnant. In due time she gave birth to a fair and shapely boy, and the king and queen were beside themselves with joy, especially when they found that the newborn child had the form of a human being and not that of a beast.

But the burden of the strange secret which her husband had confided to her weighed heavily on Meldina, and one day she went to her mother-in-law and said, "Gracious queen, when I first married your son, I believed I was married to a beast, but now I find that you have given me the handsomest, the worthiest, and the most gallant young man ever born into the world to

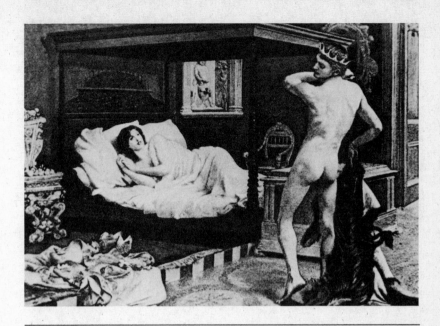

be my husband. I want you to know that when he comes to my chamber to lie by my side, he casts off his dirty hide and leaves it on the ground, and is changed into a graceful, comely youth. It is impossible for anyone to believe this miracle if you don't see it with your own eyes."

When the queen heard these words, she thought that her daughter-in-law must be jesting with her, but Meldina insisted that what she said was true. So the queen inquired how she could witness the miracle with her own eyes to determine whether it was true, and Meldina replied, "Come to my chamber tonight when we fall asleep. The door will be open, and you'll find that what I tell you is the truth."

That same night, when the appointed time had arrived and everyone had gone to bed, the queen had torches kindled and went to her son's chamber, accompanied by the king. Upon entering, she saw the pig's skin lying on the floor in a corner of the room, and when she went to the bedside, she found a handsome young man with his arms wrapped around Meldina. To say the least, the queen and king were extremely delighted, and the king ordered the pig's hide to be torn to shreds before anyone was allowed to leave the room. Their joy was in fact so great that they almost died from it.

King Galeotto, knowing that he had such a fine son, and a grandchild as well, put aside his diadem and his royal robes and had his son crowned king in his place, with exceeding pomp. Thereafter, his son was known as

King Pig, and to the supreme satisfaction of all the people in the realm, the young king began his reign, and he lived long and happily with Meldina, his beloved wife.

Translated by W. G. Waters

‹ *The Merchant's Two Sons* ›
Giambattista Basile

here was once a very rich merchant called Antoniello, who had two sons, Cienzo and Meo, so much alike that you could not tell one from the other. Now it happened that Cienzo, the elder, having challenged the king of Naples's son to a battle of stones at the Arenaccia, broke the prince's head.

Antoniello, in a fury at this incident, said to his son: "Bravo, now you've done a fine thing! Publish it abroad, boast of it, you windbag, or I will rip you up. Put it on a perch where all can see it, for you have broken something worth six *grani!* You have broken the head of the king's son! Didn't you have the cane to measure your distance, you goat's son? Now what will happen to you? You've cooked your goose so well that I wouldn't wager three *calli* on you. Even if you could creep back into what you came out of, I couldn't save you from the long arm of the king, for you know that it reaches everywhere. He will do something terrible!"

His father talked and talked, and at last Cienzo replied: "My good sir, I have always heard that it is better to have the court than the doctor in the house. Wouldn't it have been worse if he had broken *my* head? We are only boys. I was challenged and we fought; it is a first offense. The king is a reasonable man; and after all, what can he do to me? Let him who will not give me the mother give me the daughter; let him who will not send me cooked meat send me raw meat. There is the whole world open to us, and let him who fears become a constable."

"What can he do to you?" replied Antoniello. "He can send you for a change of air, send you packing out of this world. He can make you a schoolmaster where you will have a birch twenty-four feet long to thrash the fishes with till they learn to speak. He can send you off to marry the widow in a well-starched collar three feet wide, but instead of touching the lady's hand, you will feel the hangman's foot. So don't stay here at the risk of your life between the cloth and the tailor's scissors, but be off this very moment and let nothing fresh or old be heard of your doings if you don't want to get caught by the foot. The bird in the field fares better than the bird in the cage. Here is some money for you; take one of the two enchanted horses that I have in the stable and a dog which is also enchanted, and delay no longer. It is better to take to your heels than to feel the heels of another; better to put your legs to your shoulders than to find two legs round your neck; better to run a thousand feet than wait here for three feet of rope. Take yourself off with your knapsack at once, for not even the lawyers Baldo and Bartolo can help you!"

Cienzo asked his father's blessing, mounted his horse, and, carrying his dog under his arm, rode out of the city. But when he had passed through the Capuan gate, he turned to look back and began to say: "Ah! my beautiful Naples, behold, I am leaving you, and who knows if it will be my lot ever to see you again: you whose bricks are of sugar, whose walls are of sweet pastry; where the stones are manna, the rafters are sugarcanes and the doors and windows are wafer cakes! Oh, woe is me! Now that I am leaving you, my beautiful Pennino, I feel as if setting forth with the pennant. My spirit sinks as I leave you, Piazza Larga, and I feel I lose my very soul as I say farewell to you, Piazza dell' Olmo. Parting from you, Lancieri, is to be pierced by a Catalan lance. Tearing myself from you, Forcella, my spirit is torn from the pit of my soul! Where shall I find another Porto, thou beautiful port of the world's whole wealth? Where another Gelsi, where the silkworms of love continually weave cocoons of pleasure? Where another Pertuso, resort of all virtuous men? Where another Loggia, where plenty is lodged and pleasure is refined? Ah, Lavinaro, I cannot tear myself from you without a lava of tears streaming from my eyes, nor from you, Mercato, without a load of grief as merchandise! Beautiful Piaggia, I cannot leave you without a thousand wounds tormenting my heart! Farewell, parsnips and beetroots, farewell, fritters and cakes; farewell, cauliflowers and pickled tuna fish; farewell, tripe and liver; farewell, minced meat and grated cheese! Farewell, flower of cities, glory of Italy, painted egg of Europe, mirror of the world! Farewell, Naples, the *non plus ultra*, where virtue has set her limits and grace her boundaries! I leave you and shall be deprived of your cabbage soups; driven out of this dear village, oh, my broccoli, I must leave you behind!" So saying, and making a winter of weeping in a summer of sighs, he journeyed forward till at the end of the first day, on nearing Cascano, he reached a wood which enjoyed both silence and shade while the Sun held its mule without the confines. There he found a tumbledown old house at the foot of a tower. He knocked at the door of the tower, but the master was afraid of robbers, for it was already night, and refused to open. So poor Cienzo was obliged to stay in the old ruin, and having tethered his horse in the middle of a field, threw himself down to sleep on a little straw which he found inside, with his dog beside him.

He had no sooner closed his eyes and was falling asleep than he was roused by the barking of the dog and heard the clattering of old shoes in the house. Cienzo, who was bold and venturesome, put his hand to his sword and struck out fiercely in the dark. But finding that with his wild aim he hit no one, he lay down again on the straw. After a while he felt his feet being gently pulled and, reaching for his sword, got up again, calling out: "Ho, there! Now you've really annoyed me. There's no sense in playing these tricks. If you have any pluck, show yourself and let's have it out together, for you will find you have met your match."

In answer to this came a side-splitting laugh, and then a deep voice said: "Come down here and I will let you know who I am." Cienzo, without losing courage, replied: "Wait a bit, I am coming." He groped about and found a ladder leading into a cellar, and when he had gone down he saw there a lighted lamp and what appeared to be three goblins, who were making a pitiful lamentation, calling out: "Oh, my beautiful treasure, must I lose you?"

Cienzo thought he had better join in the hullabaloo for the sake of good-fellowship. He did so for some time, and the moon had already cleaved the bar of heaven with the ax of her rays when the three who had been chanting the dirge said to him: "Now go and take this treasure, which is destined for you alone; but take care to guard it well." Then they suddenly disappeared just as if they were the fellow you never see!

Cienzo, seeing sunlight through a hole, wanted to climb up again out of the cellar; but he could not find the ladder. So he began to shout, and shouted so loudly that the master of the tower, who had come within those ruined walls to perform an act of nature, heard him and asked what he was doing there, and when Cienzo told him what had happened he went to fetch a ladder and came down into the cellar. As soon as he reached the bottom he saw before him a great treasure of which he at once took possession, but not without offering Cienzo his proper share; Cienzo refused it, however, and taking his dog in his arms, he got on his horse and set out again on his journey.

After a few hours he came to a lonely, desolate forest, so gloomy that it made one shudder with fright. Here on the bank of a river, which to please the shadows it loved wound snakelike through the meadows, leaping over stones, he found a fairy surrounded by a band of robbers, who were trying to deprive her of her honor. Cienzo, as soon as he saw the evil intentions of these miscreants, drew his sword and made a shambles of the band. The fairy overwhelmed him with compliments and thanks for what he had done in her defense, and invited him to a palace nearby, where she would reward him for his services. But Cienzo replied: "Oh, that was nothing at all. A thousand thanks, but I am in great haste now on important business; I must accept your favors at some other time." And he went on his way.

When he had traveled another long stretch, he found himself before a king's palace, all hung with mourning drapery which made one's heart grow dark to see it. Cienzo inquired the meaning of this mourning and was told that there had appeared in the country a seven-headed dragon, the most terrible that had ever been seen in the world. It had the crest of a cock, the head of a cat, eyes of fire, the jaws of a race-hound, the wings of a bat, the claws of a bear and the tail of a serpent. "Now this dragon," they told him, "swallows a Christian every day, and so it has gone on up till today, when now the lot has fallen upon the king's daughter, Menechella. This is the reason of the distress and mourning in the royal palace, for the fairest lady of the land is to be swallowed and devoured by this horrible beast."

When Cienzo had received this information, he stood aside and saw Menechella approaching in a mourning procession accompanied by the court ladies and all the women of the country, wringing their hands, tearing out their hair by handfuls, and bewailing the lot of the unfortunate princess, crying out: "Who could have thought that this maiden would give up the joys of life inside the body of this evil brute! Who would have thought that this lovely goldfinch should be caged in the belly of a dragon! Who would have thought that this beautiful silkworm would have left the seed of its vital stamen in a black cocoon!" While they were thus lamenting, lo! out came the dragon from the depths of a great cavern—oh, Mother mine, how hideous it was! The sun for terror hid behind the clouds, the sky darkened, and the hearts of all the folk became mummified; so great was their trembling that it would have been impossible to pierce them with a pig's bristle.

Cienzo, at this sight, rushed forward and—whiz!—with a blow of his sword down fell one of the heads. But the dragon rubbed his neck on a plant which was growing close by, and immediately the head reattached itself: just as a lizard joins itself on at the tail. Cienzo thought to himself: "Without perseverance there will be no offspring," and clenching his teeth gave such a tremendous blow that he cut off all the seven heads at once, and they leapt from the dragon's neck like peas out of a frying pan. Then he tore out all the tongues and put them in his pocket and hurled the heads a mile away from the body lest they might be reunited with it; he also gathered a handful of the plant with which the dragon had joined his head on again to his neck. When all this was done, he sent Menechella back to her father's house and went off to rest himself at an inn.

. No words can describe the king's joy on seeing his daughter again. When he heard in what manner she had been freed, he ordered a proclamation to be made that whosoever had killed the dragon should come and claim the princess for his wife.

Now a rascally peasant, when he saw the proclamation, collected all the dragon's heads, took them to the king, and said: "It was the deed of the man you see before you that saved Menechella; these are the hands that freed the country from destruction. Behold the dragon's heads, which are proof of my valor! Therefore, your promise must be duly fulfilled." The king took the crown from his own head and put it on the rustic's pate, which now looked like the head of a bandit on the top of a pole.

The news of these doings soon spread abroad and reached the ears of Cienzo, who said to himself: "I really am a great fool! I held Fortune by the hair of her head and have let her slip through my hands. One man offers half a fortune and I make no more of it than a German would of a glass of cold water. A fairy offers me her favors in her palace and it means to me no more than music does to an ass. Now I have the chance of a crown and stand here like a tipsy woman with her spindle, letting a hairy-footed swindler get before me and cheat me out of my ace of trumps."

With these reflections, he took a pen from the inkstand, spread out a sheet of paper, and began to write as follows: "To the most beautiful jewel of all women, Menechella the daughter of Perdisenno: Having, by the grace of Sol in Leo, saved your life, I learn that another claims my deeds and the service I did you as his own. But you, who were present at the fray, can assure the king of the truth and will not allow the vacant place for which I have labored to be taken by another. Thus shall your queenly graciousness have its due effect and the strong hand of Scannarebecco its well-deserved reward. In conclusion I kiss your dainty hands. —Dated, Inn of the Orinale, today, Sunday."

Cienzo, having written this letter and sealed it with a wafer, put it in his dog's mouth and said to him: "Now go, run fast and carry it to the king's daughter; give it only into the hands of the silver-faced maiden." The dog arrived at the palace almost as quickly as if he had flown, went up the stairs, and found the king still paying compliments to the bridegroom. And he, seeing the dog come in with the letter in his mouth, ordered that it should be taken from him. But the dog would not allow anyone to touch it, but jumped into Menechella's lap and put the letter in her hand. Menechella rose from her seat, made a curtsy to the king, and handed him the letter to read.

When the king had read the letter, he at once ordered that the dog should be followed to see what house it would go to, and that the dog's master should be immediately brought before him. Two of the courtiers followed the dog, came to the inn, where they found Cienzo, and when they had delivered their message, brought him back to the palace.

When Cienzo arrived in the royal presence, the king asked him how he dared boast of having killed the dragon, when the seven heads had been brought by the man now sitting beside him with the crown on his head. To which Cienzo replied: "That fellow deserves a cardboard miter instead of a crown, for his impudence in telling you such false tales. And so that I may prove that it was I who did the deed, and not this bearded goat, order the dragon's heads to be brought here. Not one of them can bear witness, for not one has a tongue. All the tongues I have brought with me to judgment, so that they may bear witness."

He showed them the tongues, and the rustic was utterly dismayed and could not think what had happened. Then Menechella called out: "This is the man! Oh, you wretched dog, what a trick you have played me!" The king immediately took the crown away from the thickheaded rustic and put it on Cienzo's head. He would have sent the man to the galleys, but Cienzo, repaying wickedness with kindness, begged and obtained his pardon. Then the tables were spread and there was a great feast, after which the bride and bridegroom retired to a beautiful bed all fragrant with fresh linen, where Cienzo, having carried off the trophies of his victory over the dragon, triumphantly entered the citadel of love.

When morning came and the Sun, brandishing light's two-handed sword amidst the stars, called out: "Back, you rabble!" Cienzo, who was dressing in front of the window, saw a beautiful girl at the opposite window. "Who is the lovely girl who lives in the opposite house?" asked Cienzo, turning to Menechella. "What do you want with that rubbish?" replied his wife. "Why are you staring at her? Has some foolish idea come into your head? Are you surfeited with good things? Isn't the meat you have at home good enough for you?"

Cienzo hung his head like a cat caught thieving and said not a word, but pretending to go out of the room for something, he left the palace and went to the house of the beautiful girl. She really was a dainty morsel: like a soft cream cheese or a sugar cake! She never turned the pupils of her eyes without branding some heart with their message of love; she never opened the caldron of her lips without scalding some heart; she never moved her foot without giving the final blow to the shoulder of some poor wretch who hung suspended by the cord of hope. But besides all these bewitching charms she had the power whenever she wished of enchanting, binding, fastening, knotting, enchaining, and entangling men with her hair. This she did to Cienzo, who, as soon as he set foot in the house, was caught and tethered like a young colt.

While all these things were happening, Meo, the younger brother, not having had any news of Cienzo, began to think he would go in search of him. He obtained permission of his father and also received an enchanted horse and an enchanted dog. He started on his journey and arrived one evening at the tower where Cienzo had been. The master, mistaking him for his brother, was most kind to him and wanted to give him a handsome present of money, which Meo would not accept; but all these attentions made him

think that his brother must have been there, which gave him hope of finding him. As soon as the Moon, the enemy of poets, had turned her back on the Sun, he started again on his way and came to the palace of the fairy, who also took him for Cienzo and received him joyfully, saying, "Welcome, my friend who saved my life!" Meo thanked her for her kindness, but said: "Forgive me for not staying now, for I am in great haste. Farewell till we meet again on my return." Delighted at always finding traces of his brother, he continued his journey and arrived at the king's palace the very day that his brother had been captured by the witch's hair. He entered the palace and was received by the servants with great honor and was most affectionately embraced by the bride, who said: "Welcome, my husband. Day has passed and evening comes, and if every bird goes out to seek food, yet the owl

returns. Why are you so late, my Cienzo? How can you stay away so long from your Menechella? You took me out of the dragon's jaws, but you thrust me back into a dark gullet of suspicion when your eyes are not mirrored in mine!" Meo, who was crafty, guessed at once that this must be his brother's wife; he embraced her and excused himself for being late, and they sat down to dinner together.

When the Moon, like a brood hen, called the stars to peck up the dewdrops, the two retired to bed. But Meo, who respected his brother's honor, divided the sheets to avoid touching Menechella, taking one for himself and leaving the other for her. Menechella, at this strange proceeding, with scowling looks and the face of a stepmother, said: "Goodness me! What's all this about? What are we playing at? What sort of a joke is this? Are we two quarreling peasants that we have to have boundaries marked out? Are we enemy armies that a trench must be dug between us? Are we wild horses that you put up a palisade?" Meo, who could count up to thirteen, replied: "Do not be angry with me, beloved, but with the doctor who has ordered me to diet, wishing to purge me; besides, I've come back worn out with the fatigue of a whole day's hunting." Menechella, who knew not how to trouble water, swallowed this story and went to sleep.

But when Night, exiled by the Sun, was helped by the hours of twilight to pack her bundles, Meo began to dress himself before the window, as his brother had done. He saw the same beautiful girl who had captivated Cienzo, and since he also found her pleasing, he said to Menechella: "Who is that coquette at the window?" And she in a great rage answered: "Now it is beginning again! Yesterday, too, you made a song about the ugly wretch. I fear the tongue goes where the tooth hurts. You ought to show me more respect, for I am a king's daughter and all dung has its own odor. There was some reason for your playing the imperial eagle this night, shoulder to shoulder! Not without a purpose have you retired with your capital! I understand you: dieting in my bed means banqueting elsewhere. If I find this out, for certain I shall do something violent and chips will be sent flying through the air." Meo, who had eaten bread out of more than one oven, calmed her with fair words. He assured her on his oath that he would not change her for the most beautiful courtesan in the world and that she was the apple of his eye. Menechella, quite consoled, went to her dressing room for her waiting maids to pass the glass over her forehead, dress her hair, tint her eyelashes, color her cheeks, and adorn her in every way so that she might appear more beautiful to the man she thought was her husband.

In the meanwhile, Meo, suspecting, from what Menechella had said, that Cienzo must be in the beautiful girl's house, took his dog, left the palace, and went into the opposite house. No sooner had he arrived than the beautiful witch said: "Hair of my head, bind this man!" But Meo promptly called: "Eat up this woman, my dog!" Whereupon the dog flew at her and swallowed her down like the yolk of an egg. Meo then went right into the house and found his brother under a spell; but he took two of the dog's hairs and put them on Cienzo, who then woke as if from a deep sleep.

Meo began to tell Cienzo all that had happened on his journey, and lastly at the palace, and how he had slept with Menechella because she mistook him for his brother, and would have gone on to speak of the divided sheets, when Cienzo, moved by the devil, seized an old sword and cut off his brother's head as if it had been a cucumber. The king's daughter, hearing this disturbance, rushed in and saw that Cienzo had killed a man exactly like himself. When she asked his motive, Cienzo replied: "Ask yourself: you have slept with my brother thinking it was I; that is why I killed him." "Alas, how many are wrongfully slain!" exclaimed Menechella. "This is a fine thing you have done! You do not deserve such a good brother. Now you shall know what happened: when he found himself in the same bed with me, he, with the greatest modesty, divided our sheets, saying: 'You keep to your side and I will keep to mine.' "

Cienzo repented bitterly of his terrible mistake, which had been born of a hasty judgment and had become father to a foolish deed, and he tore the skin from his face. But recollecting the plant he had seen the dragon use, he rubbed it on his brother's neck, and immediately the head was joined on again and his brother stood up alive and well. He embraced him with joy and begged forgiveness for having given way to anger. Then they all went back to the king's palace. Antoniello was sent for and came with all his family. He became a very dear friend to the king, and in what had happened to his son, saw the truth of the saying:

'*Tis the crooked ship goes straight to port.*

Translated by N. M. Penzer

‹ *Ricdin-Ricdon* ›
MARIE-JEANNE L'HÉRITIER

nce there was a king who reigned over one of the most beautiful kingdoms of Europe, whose name, however, historians can no longer trace. The king was known for his sense of justice, rectitude, and paternal love for his subjects, and thus he had acquired the glorious name of King Prud'homme, which during those times signified a king full of integrity and honor. This king was married to a lady who had many virtues as well. Since she was especially lively and active and constantly occupied herself with some pleasant work, the people called her Queen Laborieuse. The king and queen had an only son, whose inclinations were still as virtuous as at birth, but since this prince had inherited the vivacity of the queen his mother and was not obliged to work during his youth, he expended his energies in pleasure. He took a great liking to the theater and balls, tournaments and hunting parties. In short, he was extremely eager to do anything that would furnish him diversion of whatever kind, and thus he came to be known by the name of Amour joie.

The king and queen regarded their son's manner of amusing himself as innocent and did not oppose his penchant for pleasure. Indeed, they felt that the eagerness he displayed for amusements would be but a passing phase of his youth. Aside from this, the prince was quite likable, and it was clear from all his actions that he had a fiery spirit.

What surprised most people, however, was that such a vivacious prince had not yet fallen in love and did not regard affairs of the heart as significant. The only desire of his heart was to participate at the gallant festivals and in the hunts, which he found stimulating because they tended to be unique and various. At times, while pursuing a stag, he would become separated from the rest of his hunting party, and sometimes he would become so famished before he could find his people again that he would enter the home of the first country gentleman or the first peasant whom he encountered on his way. Since he ordinarily did not reveal who he was, he enjoyed many a bizarre adventure. Later, at the court, he would relate them to his father with extreme delight.

One day, when he had again been separated from his entourage, he came across a village that at first appeared deserted. Suddenly he saw a dazzling maiden emerge from a garden. An old woman with an unpleasant face was dragging her violently toward a rustic cottage on the other side of the road. The maiden had a distaff packed with linseed at her side and harbored in the folds of her dress a bunch of flowers, which she had gathered in the garden. The old woman tore the flowers from her, threw them down in the middle of the road, and gave the lovely girl some harsh blows. Then she took her by the arm again and said in a furious tone, "Let's go, let's go, you miserable creature! Back to the house! I'll teach you what it means to be so impudent and disobedient!"

The prince, who had stopped to watch this spectacle, approached the old woman just as she was about to enter the cottage, and he asked her in a gentle voice, "Why are you abusing this young girl, my good woman? What has she done to make you so angry?"

The peasant woman, who was in a fit of fury and did not like anyone to mix into her affairs, was about to respond insolently to the prince. But when she glanced at his garments and judged by their splendor that they clothed a person of distinction, she controlled her fury and contented herself by answering in a bitter voice. "My lord, I'm quarreling with my daughter because she always does the opposite of what I tell her. I don't want her to spin anymore, and yet she spins from morning until night and is so diligent that nobody can match her work. It is only because she spins too much that I scold her."

"What!" said the prince. "Is that a reason to complain about this poor child? Ah, truly, my good woman, if you dislike girls because they enjoy spinning too much, you should give your daughter to my mother, the queen, who finds this occupation most pleasant and loves girls who know how to spin. The queen will make your daughter rich."

"Alas, my lord," responded the old woman, "if this conceited snip here, with her pretty skills, seems suitable for your good queen, you can have

her right away, for she has long been a burden to me and I'd like to get rid
of her."

Just then a number of the prince's hunting party rejoined him, and he
told one of his valets to place the beautiful maiden on the rump of the horse
behind him. The girl's face was still covered with tears because of the old
woman's threats and treatment, but her crying did not detract at all from her
charms. The prince tried to console her, assuring her that with the skills she
possessed she could not fail to find a great deal of favor in the eyes of the
queen. However, the poor girl was so bewildered by the numerous men surrounding her that she did not even hear half of what the prince said to her.
Her mother watched her departure without evincing the slightest interest in
her daughter's destiny, while the few villagers who had appeared could not
open their eyes wide enough as they watched her in the midst of all those
great lords garnished with gold. These, the prince's officers, were leading her
to the queen, and thus she was the envy of all the peasant girls who saw her
as she passed.

Along the way the prince learned that the beauty's name was Rosanie,
and as soon as they arrived at the palace, he presented her to the queen as
the most skillful and diligent spinner in the entire kingdom. The queen gave
her a kind welcome, regarded her attentively, and praised her modest and
touching charms, which mortified certain ladies of the court who prided
themselves on their perfect beauty. The queen provided lodgings for Rosanie
in the palace, where there was a suite of rooms completely filled with large
masses of the best filasse in the world. There was hemp from Syria and Brittany
and flax from isle of Ithaca, from Picardy and Flanders. In fact, there was
even that famous incombustible flax out of which one can make a marvelous
cloth that the most scorching fire cannot damage. Rosanie was told, as if it
were good news, that she had only to choose among the flax and hemp, and
she could set to work whenever she wished. Then someone added that, since
she was stronger and more skillful than anyone else, the queen wanted to
keep her a long time and do much good for her, having destined her to spin
all the fibers in the apartment.

When the poor girl was alone, she fell into the utmost despair, for in
truth she had such an insurmountable aversion to the métier of spinning that
she regarded just a few hours of this work as an atrocious punishment. It was
true that when she was energetic enough to occupy herself with spinning,
she performed the work with infinite skill. Her yarn was perfectly even and
fine, but she spun so terribly slowly that even if she could ultimately have
gathered her strength and retained her assiduity from morning until night,
she hardly would have been able to spin more than half a spindle of yarn
each day.

Given her disposition, one can judge the pain she felt in respect to the queen's attitude. Rosanie did not know how she would be able to get herself out of this predicament, created by her malicious mother. Still, she was glad to be out of the hands of the old woman, who had only harsh feelings toward her. The gracious and kind welcome by the queen had captured her imagination. The court, which she had viewed as in a flash of lightning, seemed to her already a most pleasant place. She was charmed by all the objects her eyes encountered. Yet knowing she could sustain herself at court only by showing what a nimble spinner she was, she was well aware that she did not have the talent for this. Preoccupied by these cruel thoughts, she did not sleep a wink that first night. Nor did the prince sleep. The naive grace and charms of Rosanie had made so striking an impression on his heart that he spent the entire night envisaging only her.

As soon as it became day, the queen sent a message to Rosanie, ordering her to come and talk with her. Everyone was in full dress in the queen's chambers that morning, and when Rosanie arrived, a group of ladies avidly cast glances at her face. The king, who had not seen her until then, happened to be there and regarded the young beauty avidly, bestowing praise on her. The prince was also in his mother's chambers, and though he thought the girl even more beautiful than his father did, he said nothing. Despite the simplicity of her violet corset and the rustic manner of her coiffure, Rosanie truly captivated the eyes of all who regarded her, for she had a fine and well-shaped figure and a free and easy manner. Indeed, though she lacked of education, she did not have the awkward air of a village maiden. Her hair was the most beautiful ash blond, and her face was ornamented by glistening blue eyes, which were as soft as they were alert. Her nose was perfectly proportioned, and she had a small mouth, pleasantly shaped. Moreover, she had splendid teeth, as is necessary for one to be perfectly beautiful, and her complexion was dazzling white and enriched by a tinge of red that made her glow. Her remarkable features and complexion did not blind one to the lively charms of her face and her personality and whatever else contributes to the soul of beauty.

Though she had not slept that night, she did not seem at all downcast. The confusion she experienced on being exposed to the view of numerous people at court made her blush, so that her attractive features were only heightened. It was clear to see that since she was a spinner and had been obligated to stay within four walls, her complexion had been protected from the ravages of the sun. Those ladies who considered themselves beautiful felt extremely spiteful toward Rosanie, and they tried to find fault with her face and figure, while the astonished young men conceived a thousand ridiculous plans to win her. In sum, no matter how one viewed her, she drew the attention of the entire court.

Before the king departed, he advised the queen to give another dress to the beautiful spinner, since hers was too different from that of all the other young women at the palace. The queen had already devoted some thought to this, and in fact, a few hours later, a servant brought Rosanie a dress and headdress that perfectly conformed to the prevailing mode at the court of King Prud'homme. The queen's chambermaids dressed her and combed her hair with a great deal of care. Afterward they showed her exactly how she was to go about grooming herself and fixing her clothes thenceforward. The garments fitted her splendidly, and she appeared in perfect array at the chapel, where the prince found her more beautiful than ever and heaped praise on her for all to hear. All those at court who had not seen her in the queen's chambers regarded her with eager curiosity, and since the king had called her the beautiful spinner, this flattering designation stuck with her. In less than twenty-four hours she had become the cynosure of fashion at the court and in the city, so that there was not a single conversation in which the beautiful spinner did not enter for some reason.

Nevertheless, though there were a hundred beautiful young women at the court jealous of her good fortune and tired of hearing everyone talk so much about her, the young maiden in question was experiencing some sad moments. During the course of the first day she had spent at the palace, she had found a way to excuse herself from spinning by saying she had cramps in her fingers. The anxiety she felt about the constraining work for which she was destined was offset by the delight she had in being so richly dressed and in hearing her beauty praised a thousand times.

The queen's ladies-in-waiting, most of whom were no longer young and could no longer boast about their beauty, took a great liking to Rosanie. And she responded to their affection with extreme complaisance. They promenaded with her all over the palace and in different places of the city, and these walks were a great distraction for this new member of the court, whose eyes were not accustomed to seeing so many magnificent things. Yet when she returned in the evening to that fateful apartment filled with flax, she was repelled by the odious sight and sank once again into a state of despair. Still, she was able to regain some of her tranquillity and to sleep much better than she had the first night. The next day, after she had arisen, she thought about putting on the beautiful clothes that the queen had given her. But she did not remember how to get dressed properly, in the way that the queen's chambermaids had taught her. She tried twenty different times to make herself appear tolerably well dressed but could not succeed. Finally, after many fruitless attempts, she decided that her headdress and garments would have to remain odd and awkward on her. Greatly depressed by her lack of success, she sought to compensate for it in some other way. So she loaded her distaff and began to spin, but her hand was just as slow as ever. Despite all her efforts, she only succeeded in spinning a quarter of a spindle of yarn from ten o'clock, the time when she had finished dressing, until twelve-thirty, when a messenger arrived from the queen, saying that her majesty wanted to see her work.

Rosanie received the message and burst into tears. Then she applied herself to thinking up a new excuse to help her out of this predicament. Appearing downcast before the queen, she told her that she had been overwhelmed by a violent attack of rheumatism that affected her arm and prevented her from working in her usual assiduous manner. She added that she had tried with all her might to overcome this malady and had attempted twenty different times to use the distaff and the spindle, but all in vain. Despite her perseverance, she had only been able to spin a small amount of yarn, which she showed the queen. Now Queen Laborieuse found her work remarkably beautiful, and it confirmed her opinion of Rosanie's dexterity. Since the queen was a good woman, she told Rosanie not to force herself to work and recommended the ministrations of her chief doctor. Rosanie, fearful that the doctor might discover that nothing was wrong with her, told the queen that she did not need any remedy for this malaise. Whenever she had been incapacitated by such an attack before, she had needed only to rest for it to pass. The queen was satisfied with this explanation, but after Rosanie withdrew, the queen's attendants, jealous of the great favors the queen had shown the newcomer at court, remarked very loudly that the cramps and the rheumatism assuredly resulted from the queen's orders. Most likely, this beauty, whom everyone believed so skillful and diligent, was nothing but a clumsy, dawdling worker.

Poor Rosanie, who had heard these remarks, was greatly affected by them. To complete her disgrace, the queen's daughters and other ladies-in-waiting, having noticed how poorly she had dressed herself and positioned her headdress, burst out into peals of laughter and made a thousand jokes about the violet bodice and short skirt that she had worn on her arrival. Indeed, they maintained that it had been a great mistake to take those things away from her, since they suited her better than the garments of a young lady of the court.

Rosanie could not withstand such provocations. So she left the palace and went toward the gardens. Once there, she kept walking until she found herself in a very dense wood. She felt exhausted and sat down at the edge of a rippling stream that wound its way through the trees. She began to mope and ponder her bad fortune and what role it had played in bringing about the sad state she was in. For a moment, she almost decided to return to her mother, but when she thought about that woman's harsh treatment of her ever since the loss of her father, she reproached herself for having the slightest idea of returning. Young and curious about the world as she was, she felt an aversion to the village and its ways, and her stay in court, however brief, had certainly not diminished this feeling. On the other hand, she saw clearly that the queen, indignant, would expel her from the palace in shame and perhaps even punish her if she realized that Rosanie had deceived her about her skill in spinning. Knowing that the truth was about to manifest itself, she was defeated and worn out. She could no longer feign cramps or rheumatism with success. Nor did she want to allow those people who envied her to make her a laughingstock.

Thus cruelly reflecting, she abandoned herself completely to her despair; there was nothing left for her to do but die. With this idea in mind, and forgetting her weariness, she stood up to walk to a high open pavilion at the other end of the wood, which the ladies had shown her the day before during their promenade. She intended to climb to the top and throw herself to the ground. Nevertheless, her natural love for life, thoughts about her tender youth, and, above all, her secret vanity regarding her own beauty, all made her weep in anticipation of her death, and she sought to walk very slowly toward the fatal spot where she had condemned herself to die.

As she was about to cross a path that led to the pavilion, a large, dark, and well-dressed man suddenly emerged. He was somber in appearance but had a jovial and gracious air about him as he spoke.

"Where are you going, my pretty child?" he inquired. "It seems to me that I see tears streaming from your eyes. Tell me what's bothering you. It would have to be something extraordinary for me not to be able to help you."

"Alas!" responded Rosanie. "There's nothing anyone can do against the troubles that have overwhelmed me. Therefore, it's useless for me to reveal anything to you."

"Perhaps," replied the stranger, "help is not so impossible as you think in your despair. At the very least, you can relieve yourself by talking about your troubles. Tell me all about them. There's nobody better you can confide in."

"Since you insist," answered Rosanie, "I'll tell you my entire history.

"I had the misfortune of being born in obscure circumstances. My father was a peasant, a good man of integrity and intelligence, and he developed a fine reputation among the inhabitants of our village and the villages nearby, so that they asked him to arbitrate all their differences. Since he was very reserved and disliked idle talk, he was called Disantpeu. Having once been in the army, where his captain had esteemed him highly, he did not have those repulsive rustic manners and speech of people who never leave their village. My father had a tender love for me, and from my earliest childhood he took care to teach me all that he knew. If I have a great love for virtue and am somewhat intelligent, I owe it all to him, for my mother is a frightfully coarse woman. Moreover, she never took any pains to teach me what she knew. In fact, she was always hard with me and disliked me. All her tenderness was reserved for my brother.

"Despite my village background and my limited education, I have the feelings and inclinations of someone much above my station. Of course, the fact that I am of low birth causes me great despair. The only consolation I have resides in my fair features. They allow me to hope that I may have a happy future. When I was only twelve years old, I would go often to a spring or brook, into which I would gaze, telling myself that I would never remain beneath a thatched roof. Given such ideas, I scorned the compliments the young boys of the village paid me. However, I had barely turned fourteen when my father received some of the best proposals for my hand that a person of my rank could hope for. When he told me about them, I dissolved in tears and told him forcefully that I would prefer to die than enter into any marriage of that kind. Thanks to his love for me, he did not force me to accept any of the proposals. My mother kept complaining that he was spoiling me by blindly complying with my will. Yet despite her words, he did not change his kind nature. On the contrary, he often reproached my mother for not loving me and asserted that only her son was dear to her. Alas! It did not take long for her to prove the truth of my father's words. He went on a journey and did not inform us why or where he was going. Though he assured us that he would return soon, he must have died during this unfortunate journey, for a great deal of time has passed, and he has not come back.

"My mother began regarding herself as my absolute mistress, and she treated me as harshly as was possible. Finally, two days ago, after scolding me cruelly for spinning insufficiently, she started dragging me toward our cottage, and at just that time the king's son happened to pass by and ask why she was abusing me. She answered him mockingly and told him that it was because I spun too much. The prince thought she was serious, and since our queen is favorably disposed toward all kinds of work and especially takes great delight in spinning, the prince immediately asked my mother whether she would give me to the queen. My mother was overjoyed to get rid of me and placed me in the hands of the prince's men right on the spot.

"They presented me to the queen as the best and most diligent spinner in the entire kingdom, though I am truly the last person in the world to possess such qualities as those. Nevertheless, the queen believed that I had them and gave me such a terrible amount of work to do that just the sight of it sends shivers up my spine. I think that she has gathered together all the best flax in the world in order to overwhelm me. Given how much I hate spinning and how slowly I accomplish it, I don't know where to begin or how I can finish such boring and enervating work. On the other hand, I have no other choice if I want to stay at court. Alas! How happy I was at first when I found myself at the palace and heard my beauty praised. I recalled the dreams of vanity from my youth and flattered myself that some nobleman at the court or, at least, one of the royal officers would be sufficiently taken by me to want to marry me and share his fortune with me. I even for a few moments believed—oh, what presumption!—that the prince would regard me with passion. And now what is left of all that? How depressing to feel that I lack the skill even to dress myself properly, thus distorting the gifts nature has bestowed upon me. Nor do I have the skill to spin quickly. Because of all this I'll be expelled in shame by the queen and become the laughingstock of all the envious young women, who previously trembled because of my beauty and the favors I received.

"So, monsieur," Rosanie concluded, "although you don't know me, you can clearly see that there is no remedy for my troubles. I hope to end my torments through some fatal means, which I shan't reveal."

The stranger responded: "What if, instead of these fatal means, someone were to give you some sweet and pleasant way to settle these troubles; wouldn't you feel obligated to this person and wouldn't you do this person a favor in return?"

"I'd do anything I could reasonably do," Rosanie answered with alacrity. "With the exception of my honor, there is nothing that I wouldn't sacrifice to show my gratitude."

"Since you feel the way you do," the stranger replied, "I myself should like to serve you, and with pleasure. But before I undertake this, let us agree upon the exact conditions. Now look at the wand that I hold in my hand, and take it in your own hand."

Rosanie took the wand he proffered and regarded it. It was quite small and made of an unfamiliar gray-brown wood, very bright. It was adorned by a changing stone that was neither ruby nor carnelian nor any other stone known to her. In short, it was impossible to tell what the stone was or the wood. After Rosanie inspected the wand for some time, she returned it to the stranger, who said to her, "Look at this wand very carefully. It has remarkable powers. As soon as you touch it to flax and hemp, the wand will spin as much as you want each day and of the finest quality. It has another feature: touch wool, silk, or canvas, and it instantly produces tapestries more beautiful than any in the world and works of petit point that excel those made by the best of manufacturers. I'll lend you this marvelous wand for three months, provided that you agree with the terms I am about to offer you. If, three months from today, three months to this very day, I return to retrieve my wand and you say to me, 'Take it, Ricdin-don. Here is your wand,' I'll take back my wand without your being obligated to me in any way whatsoever. But if, on the appointed day, you cannot recall my name, and you simply say, 'Here, take back your wand,' I shall be master of your destiny and lead you wherever I please, and you will be obliged to follow me."

Rosanie took a few moments to respond. It seemed to her that it would be easy to retain the name Ricdin-don and that it would not be risky to accept the propitious help of the marvelous wand. She was already imagining her secret delight in watching the astonished faces of her vain opponents when she produced the beautiful yarn spun by the wand. However, she was troubled about one thing: she imagined that the artlessness with which she dressed herself and groomed her hair had detracted greatly from the advantages provided by her beauty. It would be a torment to stay in the palace dressed and groomed so unbecomingly. All these thoughts prevented her from responding to the stranger immediately, but finally she said to him, "Monsieur Ricdin-don, I shall accept your proposal if you will include one more condition. Along with the virtue of producing beautiful yarn and tapestries, I would like your wand to be able to transform my coiffure and dress so that they will please everyone. If you can enrich the properties of your wand, already so useful, with a virtue as necessary to beautiful women as food, you can consider our agreement settled."

"Ah!" exclaimed Ricdin-don. "Nothing is easier than to grant what you demand. My comrades and I never refuse the fair sex the virtue of looking just as they would like. That goes without saying among us. It is why you see girls of twelve already capable of grooming themselves with remarkable skill and adjusting a beauty patch on themselves just as judiciously as a woman of fifty. Therefore, I declare that as soon as my wand touches your coiffure and garments, they will have a first-rate appearance and flutter so gracefully that they will entrance all the handsome young men."

"Then I accept your proposition," Rosanie said.

"But you must swear an oath," Ricdin-don responded.

"Well then, I swear," she answered. "You have my solemn word."

"That will do," said Ricdin-don, "and now that I have your promise in such good form, I am your servant until we see each other again."

Upon saying these words, he bestowed the wand on her and departed. The first thing Rosanie did was to touch the wand to her coiffure and clothes. Then she looked at herself in the nearest stream and found herself so beautiful and so well dressed that she was immensely gratified that she had concluded the agreement and remembered every detail. Her eyes caressed the obliging wand, and she told herself delightedly that she had just acquired a very useful article at very little cost.

Immersed in diverse thoughts, she walked through the wood and the park and returned to the palace. No sooner did she reach the entrance than she encountered the prince. He had not seen her that day, but certain malicious jesters, who overran the court, had not failed to tell him about the clumsy manner in which the beautiful spinner had dressed and groomed herself. The prince had listened to everything without a smile. Indeed, he did not dare show them how much he was convinced that Rosanie was always charming no matter what garments she wore, for he feared they would discover his feelings for the beautiful maiden.

Seeing her now, he was as enchanted by her attractions as always, and upon examining her perfect appearance, he turned toward one of those cold jesters, who had exhausted him some hours ago with an insipid story about Rosanie that the man had believed to be very funny. The prince made a hundred remarks, both subtle and pointed, about the slanderous story. Then he greeted Rosanie with such chivalry that it seemed as if she were one of the most distinguished people at court. He asked her graciously if she had seen the waterworks, and when she responded no, he told her that he would have them played for her next day. Then Rosanie made a low curtsy and withdrew to her apartment, still rejoicing in the marvelous wand, though in her ecstasy she forgot the name of the man who had given it to her. That night her joy prevented her from sleeping, just as her sorrow had the first night she spent in the palace. And during all those hours that she should have been sleeping, her mind was occupied only by ideas so pleasant they made her more content than the most gratifying dreams could have done.

In the morning, her wand was at her service instantly, as was Coquette, the most skillful of the chambermaids and her favorite. Then she hastened to test the wand's powers on a small batch of the queen's flax, which, through the virtue of this enchanted stick of wood, immediately became a pound of yarn resembling the most beautiful yarn of Flanders. Overjoyed by the prowess of the wand, Rosanie took some yarn to the queen that evening, to demonstrate that she was the most diligent worker in the world. Later she watched the waterworks that had been ordered by the prince, and they were better that day than they had been for a long time. When the day was over, she waited for the queen at the passage where she normally began her walk. The queen appeared, and Rosanie told her that the cramps and rheumatism were gone and she had spent the day working. Therefore, she had taken the liberty to come and show her what she had accomplished. The queen took the yarn and regarded it with eagerness. However, the sun had set and the halls had not been illuminated, so the queen ordered that the torches be lit at once. Once she could see, she was enchanted by the beauty of Rosanie's yarn and enjoyed herself so, examining and praising it, that she forgot all about her nightly hour-long promenade. Finally, she remarked that she did not want any of her ladies at court to say anything against the beautiful spinner anymore. To Rosanie she said many gracious things and ordered her to come to her morning audience next day.

That night Rosanie slept very well, and the next morning she did not fail to be in the queen's chamber on time, and she brought with her the other part of the pound of yarn that she had spun. "Madam," she said to the queen, as she presented the yarn, "since I saw that my little work had the good fortune of pleasing you and could perhaps contribute to diverting you, I spent the night making something new for you so you can see how zealous I am."

"Ah, poor child!" exclaimed the queen, turning toward her lady of honor. "She is just as affectionate as she is skillful and diligent. But, my child"— she turned back to address Rosanie—"I don't want you to make a habit of spending the night like this. It will ruin your health, which seems so solid and excellent."

"Madam," Rosanie answered, "it will be an honor for me to work for you, however much, and I shan't harm myself. I have the good health and strength of a girl of seventeen, and at that age there is nothing that can trouble me. I only beg you to be so kind as to permit me to entertain you for a few hours each day. If you grant this, it will not cost me anything to spend the night working."

The queen assured Rosanie that if she did not stay awake the entire night, she would grant Rosanie some time to entertain her each day. After receiving the queen's guarantee, Rosanie answered, "Until I had shown you what I can do with the distaff and the spindle, I didn't dare tell you that I can weave tapestry just as well as I can spin yarn. Now that you have seen a sample of my spinning, I feel free to tell you that if you would like to give me some wool, silk, and canvas, I'll weave all kinds of tapestries and do some petit point for you, as you wish."

"Truly," the queen exclaimed, "this little girl has prodigious talents! Go, my child," she continued, "go and gather strawberries in the garden with my ladies. Later I'll give you all that you will need to make tapestries, and you can work on it tomorrow."

"Before I go, madam, I have another favor to ask of you. Would you be so kind as to give orders that I am to be left alone and undisturbed while I am at work in the apartment that you have given me? I cannot tolerate anyone watching me while I work, for it upsets my concentration."

"Consider your request granted," the queen responded. "You will be completely free and have your peace and quiet."

When the conversation concluded, Rosanie withdrew and spent the rest of the day amusing herself, and that night she slept quite well. Even though she had forgotten the name of the man who had given her the wand, she did not think about this much. And when she did ponder it, she was not unduly worried, for she was sure she would remember the name once she took the trouble to recall it. Besides, she had been given three months, and she wanted to profit from this time and use the wand in peace. Indeed, these three months appeared to her just as long as half a century might appear to someone else.

Meanwhile the prince thought only about his love for her. The pleasure he had previously taken from his amusements was no longer so sweet. To go hunting or to the theater seemed insipid, and he was bored by everything at the court unless Rosanie was present. She was the object of all his wishes: to see her, talk to her about his tender feelings, and prove his love for her by some great feat that would move her heart. He did not dare to express these wishes as much as he was inclined to do, for fear that the people at court would notice his fervor. But despite the precautions he took, the old courtiers had largely discerned his true feelings, and this discovery contributed toward their showing Rosanie a great deal of attention and consideration. As far as the young men were concerned, they did not have the slightest idea that the prince was attracted to this young beauty, and they mainly thought of her as the object of a pleasant conquest.

The queen had ordered one of her ladies, named Vigilentine, to accompany Rosanie everywhere she went and to serve as her mother. Vigilentine was delighted by this assignment. She found Rosanie totally charming, and it gave her great pleasure to impart all she knew about polite manners and to exhort the girl to conduct herself well in all the courtly proceedings. Since this woman had a good deal of intelligence and practical experience, she was able in a very short time to facilitate Rosanie's cultivation.

Now in the capital city of King Prud'homme's realm, there was a public garden in which the beautiful ladies from the court and the city exhibited their attractions with great pomp. All the gallant young men displayed themselves to their best there too, and the coy young women suspended their ordinary judgments. The air was so hot and inflamed that not even the four winds could cool it. One ran the risk of becoming more intoxicated by all the flowery talk than by the flowers themselves. Vigilentine did not take Rosanie to this tempestuous place until she had instructed her on how to avoid all the dangers. Aside from Rosanie's good taste and gallant clothes, all accomplished with the help of the wand, Vigilentine's lessons taught her to assume a modest appearance, enhancing her natural charms and radiant air so that she appeared to be a remarkable person, suited to inspire just as much respect as love. She was regarded with jealous eyes by four or five beautiful women, who were à la mode and had come from the provinces to the capital with plans to find their fortune through tying the nuptial knot with some well-endowed young man. Relying on their attractive features, they imagined that they had merely to appear in this large city, where the most cultivated, wealthy, and distinguished men of high rank lived, and these men would come running to offer them their hearts and hands in marriage. However, they had been erroneously informed that the men were moved more by two beautiful eyes than by the luster of gold. In vain they made a thousand efforts to advertise their charms with great fanfare. Hardly anyone thought of them in terms of a solid matrimonial bond, and in spite of all the care they took, the only thing left for them was the frivolous glory of being courted by foreigners obsessed with these giddy creatures, who were secretly bid on by financiers. The only thing in their favor was that the public rendered justice to their virtue, being persuaded that they truly knew how to guard against the many different traps that had been set for them.

Ordinarily, these beautiful women would have been divided among one another, but they united their forces against Rosanie. The flattery that she received from all sides, the acclamations she inspired when she appeared in public, made those other young ladies extremely bitter. They could not tolerate some rustic villager's having come and taken over the empire of beauty that each one of them claimed as her own. At least they now desired to share it among themselves. Since each of them had a following, their different supporters went to great lengths to decry Rosanie's charms in all their conversations. One found her nose too long; the other thought her mouth too large. Someone else said her eyes were lusterless and her complexion was too dark. They spread their stories with such cleverness that those who had never seen Rosanie, or who had only caught a glimpse of her, were deceived by the false pictures. As a result, they began saying to each other that the queen's beautiful spinner, who was the talk of the entire city, was not such a marvelous beauty after all. On the contrary, she had many faults, and one should be cautious about expressing admiration for her.

Yet despite all the trouble her opponents took to spread these notions, they evaporated as soon as Rosanie appeared. Those people who had already seen her once regarded her now with more attention and found her more beautiful than before. Those who had only heard rumors about her recognized, once they saw her, that there had been a great deal of malice or bad taste in the pictures that had been painted. Vigilentine took Rosanie to the theater, and the crowd that filled this vast edifice overwhelmed her with such loud applause that she was embarrassed about it and even upset. To be sure, she was not angry that the people admired her, for she was no different than most beautiful women, desirous as they are of praise. However, Vigilentine had told her that nothing was more fatal for a young woman than to be noticed too much, and since people regarded her too much, Vigilentine decided that it would be best not to go on public walks or to the theater all that often. This saddened Rosanie, because she enjoyed those places where there were so many stimulating things to see.

However, she soon had something to console her for this minor disappointment, and it was due to the fortunate success of her wand. Even though she spent the day largely amusing herself and taking walks, she always found time to have the obliging wand do the tasks of a worker skilled beyond others. Thus she continued to show the most beautiful yarn in the world to the queen, and when eight or ten days passed after she had been given wool, silk, and canvas, she produced tapestry that was more beautiful and better made than that of Arachne. The queen, whose passion for such work was sometimes a bit extreme, was ecstatic when she saw Rosanie's tapestry. She bestowed on her great praise and numerous caresses, and from that day, the beautiful girl was overwhelmed by gestures and signs of favor. It seemed that one even forgot that she came of a lowborn family, for she was placed with the maids of honor at all the courtly celebrations and was indeed considered to be among the most distinguished of them. These young ladies were very much irritated by this, except for one, whose name was Sirene. This young woman had a pleasant face and a generous soul. She paid tribute to Rosanie's beauty and skills, and instead of scorning her low birth, she said that one should give her more credit than one would a person born into an illustrious family, who is not obliged to cultivate noble sentiments and conduct. It was because this just young lady had such a beautiful voice and sang so pleasantly that she had acquired her name. Moreover, the people at court deemed her temperament just as sweet as her voice. Rosanie, who sensed Sirene's favorable disposition toward her, developed true feelings of friendship in return. Sirene was always gracious and obliging and acted this way out of inclination and joy, while her companions did so only out of politics and with vexation. Not only were they ashamed that they were obliged to behave courteously to Rosanie, but as I have already said, they were annoyed by the distinguished honors and lavish praise she received.

The prince was delighted by the consideration the people at court were giving to his beloved. Yet he was at the same time dismayed by the difficulty he encountered in revealing his tender feelings to her. He had succeeded in managing to see her often and could not complain about this. However, he was not able to get her to himself and converse with her for a single moment. Nor was he among those who were permitted to enter her apartment, and whenever she left it, Vigilentine was at her side. Furthermore, he had organized some balls in vain. Ordinarily, one can find a way to speak to the woman one loves at a ball, but Rosanie did not know how to dance. Although she had been given a dancing master soon after she arrived at the palace, she had barely had enough lessons to achieve a good curtsy. At balls, therefore, she was obliged to be a spectator among a group of others, affording him no suitable occasion to disclose his feelings toward her.

To be sure, the prince had sought to make her understand his sentiments through a thousand gallant acts and diverse hints whenever he spoke, and to be sure, he had overheard a hundred small things she had said, such that she would have killed herself had she realized he heard them. But it was not enough for a love as passionate as his to be known by that which he had aroused in her. He wanted to ascertain for sure whether he had made some favorable impressions on her heart. He saw with great resentment that many of the men of the court and city had already dared to declare their feelings in front of Rosanie and right under the eyes of Vigilentine. He even knew that an ambassador, forgetting the dignity of his position, had been so bold as to want to tempt her virtue by offering her a prodigious sum of money to be his mistress. Of course, this was extremely disturbing for the beautiful maiden, who had always cultivated nothing but noble and elevated feelings.

Aside from this, she was very much a child in her inclinations and pleasures. She had a boundless love for ribbons, dogs, and birds. Whenever the ladies had a serious conversation, she would become impatient in a very short time, and she amused herself best with girls her own age. If she loved a play at the theater, it was not so much for the play itself but because she enjoyed seeing such a large group of bustling people gathered together in one spot. The poor girl understood very little of the satirical lines in a comedy, and even less of the political allusions and the tender poetry of a tragedy. And if it were not for the pleasure of seeing and being seen, she would have preferred to amuse herself by playing blindman's buff or bagatelle rather than attend the theater to see such plays as *Cinna, Iphigenia,* or *The Misanthrope.*

Despite these childish inclinations, however, as well as her natural tenderness and affection, she did not succumb to the ardent prince. Her penchant for virtue set her in opposition to her own feelings for so amiable a lover. She continually told herself that his elevated rank compelled her to close her eyes toward his love and accomplishments, since this rank was an invincible obstacle to their ever being united in a sacred bond.

The beautiful Rosanie continued to use the wand in glorious spinning and weaving, as well as adorning her own graceful and fine appearance to the admiration of all. She succeeded in learning to dance very well, even without the benefit of magic. Indeed, she had no other advantage here than a good dancing master. On the other hand, despite the same benefits, her progress in reading and writing was weak. She found forming letters and tracing their characters boring and lacked the strength to apply herself to something that did not divert her.

The prince still burned with impatience to reveal his feelings to Rosanie, if only for a few moments. The way he was forced to restrain himself put him into a bad mood. Now among the more assiduous young men at court there was a very bright chevalier by the name of Bonavis, who had been endowed with many fine qualities. To him the prince confided his longings, and Bonavis, who was ingenious, quickly found a means to help him. He accompanied his lord wherever he went, and thus, when the prince encountered Rosanie, Bonavis cleverly managed to occupy Vigilentine in conversation about a matter that seemed of great importance to her. The prince, free to talk to Rosanie about his love, drew such moving and tender pictures that she was quite touched. But such was the sensitivity of this beautiful young woman that she told him he must extinguish his ardor since, despite all his accomplishments, she would never stoop so low as to become his mistress, and clearly she had not been born high enough to become his wife. The prince responded that it was no longer a novelty for kings to marry a villager: nobody would see anything strange in a bond of love and merit. Though Rosanie did not understand the figurative manner of speaking customary in the theater, she grasped these words perfectly well because they emanated from the mouth of a lover whom she cherished. The prince assured her that he loved her more ardently than anyone had ever loved before. He solemnly declared that he would rather renounce his claim to the throne than give her up. He swore oath upon oath that no matter what might happen, he would never marry anyone but her, and he would make to her the same solemn vows he would make to the highest princess on earth. In short, he spoke in such a passionate and natural manner that Rosanie let herself be convinced that his love was sincere and pure, and she gave him permission to talk to her about it from time to time, provided that he kept his promise regarding respect and loyalty.

The amorous prince swore to her again that he would never think about pleasing anyone except her, that he had feelings only for her, and he swore all this with the most binding of oaths.

After that day when the hearts of the two lovers had reached an understanding, their eyes were in perfect agreement, too, and often gave tender signs of their secret feelings. Bonavis knew how to arrange for diverse conversations to take place, but he was not always able to succeed with such skill in covering up the prince's attachment to Rosanie. Therefore, the king and queen were forewarned. Still, the king regarded his son's inclination as a passing fancy. As for the queen, she had so much confidence in Rosanie's virtue that she did not harbor the slightest fear their attachment would be fatal. The prince made every effort to conceal his love from the eyes of the court, but love is one of those turbulent passions that one can conceal only under the veil of discretion, and even then, only rarely.

As soon as Rosanie's opponents had been informed about her illustrious conquest, their jealousy and hate doubled. Among those young women who let themselves be swayed by such unjust feelings, none was more tyrannized than one of the queen's handmaidens, who had been secretly in love with the prince for a long time. This Penséemorne was somewhat of a beauty and greatly ambitious, had a violent penchant for love, and a dark soul. Furthermore, she was as vindictive as she was crafty. As long as she saw that the prince was indifferent toward all the beautiful women at court, she consoled herself about not being able to touch a heart that no one else at court could move, and she flattered herself that if he were ever to leave himself open to love, he would lean toward her. She counted a great deal on the strength of her charms. In fact, she had made so many advances to the prince that she could not believe they had been lost on him. However, when she saw that the prince, the sole object of her desires, not only responded to her tender advances with ingratitude but had also given himself to a rival whom she already hated more than death, all her love turned to fury, and she concerned herself exclusively with plans for a savage revenge. She sought out a pernicious sorceress, who had already failed in utilizing the secrets of her art to make the prince fall in love with the queen's handmaid.

"In spite of your good intentions," Penséemorne told her, "you have not been able to further the cause of my love. But I know that you will be able to bend your great art to the cause of vengeance. I want that ingrate of a prince to perish, for he has scorned me, and at the same time I want my unworthy rival to perish in a truly terrible way, for he has preferred her over me."

The sorceress assured her that she would adopt these vengeful feelings as though they were her own and promised to serve Penséemorne as best she could.

Now that the prince's tender feelings had been more satisfied than ever before, he began to pursue his customary pleasures once again. He went hunting deep in the forest, and not for the first time he became separated from his party while pursuing an animal with too much zeal. After killing it, he found himself in front of a magnificent palace. He was amazed to see so splendid an edifice in so desolate a spot. But his astonishment only increased when he saw a dazzlingly beautiful lady, magnificently attired, come out of the palace. She was followed by a retinue of ladies, who seemed to attend her with great respect. This beautiful lady approached him graciously and said, "Prince, if you love glory, and if you have sympathy for the troubles of the misfortunate, enter into this palace with me and do not refuse to listen to me."

In silence, the prince made a low bow and offered his hand to her. They entered the palace and proceeded to an apartment where gold and precious stones glistened in emulation of one another. The prince demonstrated his impatience to hear the lady's story and to learn whether there was some service he could render her. She asked him to sit down, then spoke as follows:

"You see before you, my lord, an unhappy princess, the closest relative and heir of a king who during his lifetime was master of a prosperous kingdom, which a cruel tyrant overcame fifteen years ago. If you think carefully about the picture I am painting, you will undoubtedly recognize the realm of Fiction, which the barbarian Songecreux seized after having defeated and killed King Planjoli in that amiable king's last battle. The queen Riante-image, wife of King Planjoli, was taken prisoner. She was pregnant at the time, and the tyrant had her child killed after she gave birth. The poor queen he has kept in captivity ever since. I was still in my cradle when King Planjoli was dethroned, and owing to his death and that of his child, I found myself heir to the realm of Fiction. Fortunately, my mother, a highborn princess, found a way to remove me from the tyrant's power, and a wise sorcerer, master of this palace, offered us as a retreat a solitary château that often served as an asylum for illustrious people in distress. My mother raised me in that château with all possible care, but a year ago I had the misfortune of losing my mother, and the sorcerer became my only support. He led me to this superb palace, where I am served with a splendor worthy of my rank. A short time ago he divined that the time had arrived for me to regain possession of my kingdom and to punish the usurper. But first I must find a protector of royal blood, who will use his valor and arms for me and protect my interests under conditions that the sage magician will propose. Seeing you, my lord," the unknown princess added, lowering her eyes, "I could tell at once that you had something great to offer us. So I shall ask my wise adviser to make you a proposal. Now I am going to withdraw, while he discusses everything with you. I shall be happy indeed if the eloquent speech of this generous old man will dispose you kindly to my affair."

The old man who appeared upon the princess's retiring had a fine appearance despite the gauntness and emaciation that were due to his extreme age.

"Prince," he said, after greeting him respectfully, "the qualities with which you have been endowed have caused me to take an interest in you, and I would gladly employ the powers at my command for your happiness and glory. Please, then, deign to let yourself be guided by me. The beautiful princess whom you have just seen regards you with the tenderest of feelings. She is heiress to a great kingdom, and with the advice and help of Labouréelamboy—which is how I am called—you may unite her crown with that other for which heaven has destined you. It is entirely up to you." He pulled a ring from his finger. "Here you have a ring that has the power of bringing inevitable victory to him who wears it. If you have any enemies, they will succumb to your power as soon as you have this ring. Nothing can withstand it. If you will swear eternal love to our princess, I shall give you this rare ring as a gift. The princess has a loyal following in the realm of Fiction, dedicated to oppose the tyrant Songecreux. Place yourself at its head and you will conquer him, then have a hundred new triumphs after his defeat. You will become master of the dominions of many kings and one of the greatest conquerors who has ever dwelled on earth."

The prince had listened astonished to this speech, and as soon as he saw that the sorcerer was waiting for a response, he said to him without hesitating, "I cannot offer my love to any woman. My heart and my loyalty are already committed to a lady whom I shall love until I breathe my very last. Despite this, I am prepared to offer my compassion and goodwill to the beautiful princess whom I have just seen, and I am willing to fight against her enemies. However, I do not want to accept your ring. I love glory, and a victory in a battle of arms is to me the most exciting thing in the world. I shall seek victory with all possible zeal, but I want to triumph only through my own courage and the strength of my arm. Therefore, I shall refrain from accepting the help of a supernatural power."

"You are very fastidious, my lord," replied Labouréelamboy. "I know a great many princes and generals who would go to a great deal of trouble to obtain that which you are rejecting. But even if you disdain the help of my art, do not scorn my advice, which comes from experience. I have lived a long time and have acquired a certain right to give advice to people your age. So please bear with me when I tell you that the scruples you have because of the oath you have given to another woman should not prevent you from offering your heart to the heiress of the realm of Fiction. The princess has a powerful following in her dominions. You have only to put yourself at the head of this party, and it is certain that you will triumph over the tyrant without the help of the ring that you have rejected. After his fall, you will marry the princess and acquire a kingdom that you will one day join to your destined realm. Moreover, you will be performing a generous act to benefit an amiable princess, who has the most passionate and tender feelings for you."

The prince again responded that his heart and fidelity were no longer his to dispose of. Now the princess suddenly returned, her face bathed in tears, and she threw herself on her knees and said to him, "O my lord, if my weak attractions are not able to move you, then at least have compassion for my misfortunes. I shall die if you continue to disdain the ardent proof of my feelings for you."

The prince was confused and embarrassed. He had fallen to his knees when the princess had. But after he lifted her up, he stood silent and anxious while regarding her. Her face radiated charm but nonetheless bore an expression of pain. He secretly accused himself of being a barbarian for responding so coldly to the wishes of such an appealing woman. On the other hand, the tender love and sacred oaths that committed him to Rosanie prevented his feeling the least spark of fire for the princess. Maintaining his fidelity, he believed that at the same time he could satisfy the princess with his generosity and politesse.

"Beauty such as yours, madam," he said, "deserves undivided love and a completely devoted heart. I no longer have power over my heart. The strongest ties have committed me to a lady worthy of all my tender feelings. Still, if I cannot give you my heart, madam, I shall consecrate my profound respect for you and dedicate all the efforts of my arm to your cause. Let us depart. I shall be delighted to support the zeal of your loyal subjects, and I shall spill my blood with joy to vanquish the usurper of your crown."

"You ingrate!" the princess exclaimed in rage. "I don't want your help if you refuse to give me your heart. It is your heart alone that I desire. Alas! My wrath . . ."

As she uttered these words, a dazzling young child appeared, carrying a golden scepter in his hand. He touched the princess and the sorcerer with it, and they immediately began to flee, uttering terrible shrieks. The walls of the room he touched also, and the palace disappeared. The prince found himself in the middle of the forest, the bright child in front of him.

"Prince," he said, "I have just dissipated the fatal illusion that clouded your mind in order to reward the fidelity which you demonstrated by honoring your oath. If heaven severely punishes liars, then it is only just that people of good faith are equally rewarded. Indeed, you deserve divine grace for the way you proved yourself toward Rosanie. I want you to know that the creature that was just before you in the guise of a beautiful princess was a demon occupying a ghostly body through the magic spell of a perfidious sorceress. This dark spirit disguised as a princess sought to deceive you by saying she was the heiress to the kingdom of Fiction. In fact, all the relatives of King Planjoli are old, and he left behind but a single child, whose identity will become known one day. The old man who appeared to you was a demon too. If your heart had been seduced by the beauty of the princess, or by the flattering promises of the old man, and if you had violated the oath that you had sworn to the lady of your heart, these cruel demons would have taken immediate possession of you, and you would have remained in their power for centuries. But since you have graciously triumphed over them, Heaven wants to liberate you once and for all from their traps. So take this, sincere lover," the charming child continued. "Here is a ring, which is completely different from the one the seductive spirit wanted to give you. His was the ring of falsehood, while this is the ring of truth. Wear it always, and it will prevent the dangerous illusions of hell from ever obtaining power over you; unbeknownst to them, you will see sorcerers and demons performing their dark deeds."

Gesturing graciously, the child put the ring on the prince's finger and then disappeared. The prince throughout had been so thunderstruck and speechless that he was only able to demonstrate his feelings to this child, who had seemed to be divine, by signs of respect and gratitude. Now the prince managed to gather himself together, and he gave fervent thanks to Heaven for helping him avoid the terrible dangers that had threatened him that day. Sounding his horn, he eventually found his retinue. Once he had returned to the palace, Rosanie's presence and the tender innocence that he discerned in her beautiful eyes made him forget the troubling incidents of the hunt.

Penséemorne and her confidante the sorceress were distressed that their vengeful stratagem had failed. They had counted on the palace in the solitary forest and had watched in mortal agony as the prince slipped through their net. Penséemorne resolved to revenge herself in the most pernicious way that human cunning and wickedness could inspire. Since she had spies all around Rosanie and those who took an interest in her, she knew that the ambassador who had made her an insulting offer was still so much in love with her that he was willing to sacrifice his fortune to attain her.

In short, once the ambassador became convinced that it was impossible to possess Rosanie except through marriage, he decided to wed her. Asking her pardon for his offensive behavior toward her, he offered her his hand and assured her that the minor annoyance of spending her life in a foreign country would be completely eased by the luster of her rank and by her husband's boundless and eternal complaisance. Rosanie replied that though she was very gratified that he wanted to marry her, she must decline the honor because she could never think of separating herself from the queen, her mistress, to whom she was passionately attached and from whom she had received such kind treatment. The ambassador, a violent man, nevertheless concealed his rage and contented himself by resolving that he would fulfill his love, no matter the cost.

When Penséemorne learned that Rosanie had rejected a marriage that was very advantageous for a person of her rank, she burst into an indescribable fury and exclaimed, "How could this audacious peasant think that so young, handsome, and wealthy a lord as the ambassador is not good enough for her! I see that she wants to sit on the throne and will settle for nothing less than lovers who wear crowns on their heads. Ah, believe me, I shall knock this insolent, proud creature from her high horse!"

She consulted with the ambassador's confidant, who was her ally, and he came up with the idea of abducting Rosanie. The ambassador, madly in love and extremely spiteful, gave his immediate approval to this daring plan, saying, "I shall be delighted to take this beautiful booty with me when I leave King Prud'homme's realm."

He chose a time when the king and the prince had taken a trip to a country villa; the queen could not accompany them because of some indisposition. The palace was thus rather emptier than usual.

One evening, Rosanie had been taking the air in the public park and was returning with Vigilentine to the castle through the kitchen courtyards, when four masked men seized the girl brusquely and dragged her through a hidden door. She found herself on a deserted street, and they forced her, resisting, into a carriage, which departed with such great speed that it seemed to be flying. After some time, the carriage, escorted by a band of cavaliers, stopped at a relay station for fresh horses. There the audacious ambassador climbed into the carriage, whereupon the sad and despondent Rosanie augmented her cries and tears.

"Don't torture yourself," he told her. "I have no intention of harming you. I only want to conduct you to my country, where I shall marry you and assure you of a fortunate destiny."

"Ah, my lord!" Rosanie cried out, her voice tearful. "No matter your intentions, they are no longer valid once you employ force to achieve them. In the name of all that you cherish, please return me to the queen, my mistress. I shall be so obligated that my sympathy for your desires will induce me to leave my queen and spend my time with you. But if I don't return, what will this great queen think of me? Alas! She will believe that I failed to ask her advice regarding my destiny. In the name of God, my lord, permit me to go and eliminate her suspicions."

"No, no, you ingrate," responded the ambassador. "I won't let go of you. I see your trickery. Once you are away from me, you will mock my love again. After so much trouble to get my heart's desire, I shall be on my guard and won't let you get away."

"Wicked creature!" Rosanie replied. "Since you have little regard for my prayers, I shall not demean myself any more by begging you. But I hope that heaven will help me from your unworthy hands, nor let your crime go unpunished."

The carriage, meanwhile, sped on. But since the coachman was concerned with driving as fast as he could, he lost the way. Once he realized he was no longer following the route his master had ordered him to take, he sought to regain it, and in so doing turned the carriage with a great deal of force. It broke apart, and Rosanie was thrown into the middle of the road near a dense wood. She was neither injured nor terrified, and regarded the accident as a fortuitous sign. The ambassador was swearing furiously at the squire, the coachman, and the entire entourage, who tried to pull the carriage upright and set it back on the road. Their predicament gave Rosanie more courage, and she uttered cries with all her might to attract the attention of some peasants. She would have liked to flee, but that was impossible: the ambassador had ordered his servants to hold her by the arms. Afraid that her cries had been in vain, and wavering between hope and fear, she looked up at the moon, which was very radiant that night, and hoped for someone to appear. It was not long before she saw three men emerge from the wood.

"My lords!" she cried out as soon as she saw them. "Please help an unfortunate girl who is being abducted against her will!"

The three strangers drew their swords immediately and went to do combat with the ambassador and his men, who hadn't time to get back on their horses. Every blow delivered by the three strangers was mortal. One stranger especially distinguished himself through his incomparable skills and valor. It was he who killed the confidant and two others. The ambassador, enraged, began to fight like a furious lion. The brave stranger took him on, and though he was wounded on the left shoulder, he delivered so terrible a blow that the ambassador fell down at his feet, dead. The rest of the ambassador's men took flight. Then the valiant stranger approached Rosanie, who was trembling with horror at seeing so much blood shed in her behalf.

"You are free, beautiful maiden," he cried. "Your kidnappers have vanished."

At the sound of this voice, Rosanie became ecstatic and felt more joy than she had ever known. Indeed, it was her dear prince who had liberated her. You cannot imagine all the tender things that the two lovers had to say to each other. The prince was ecstatic that he had been given the opportunity to save the woman he loved. And Rosanie could not stop praising her illustrious defender. The two men with the prince were the loyal Bonavis and another gentleman of the royal house who was the prince's confidant; thus Rosanie was not constrained by their presence.

They bandaged the prince's wound, which fortunately was only minor. When the brave and sensitive prince recognized the ambassador, he at first agonized over having killed a man whose distinguished position gave him sacred rights. But he thought of this unworthy minister's forfeiting his privileges by his odious behavior and rejoiced that he had been chosen by heaven to punish the man for flagrantly violating the rights his people had vouchsafed him, and doing so in the domain of a king who had treated him with great generosity and consideration.

The prince, though inconvenienced by his wound, escorted the charming Rosanie to the king's country seat, at the other end of the forest. As they walked, she told him the story of her abduction, and he in his turn related to the beautiful maiden how he had been overcome by sorrow at their separation and, realizing that he would be unable to sleep, had resolved to spend a good part of the night in the forest with his two companions. No sooner had the prince placed Rosanie in the hands of two ladies at the château than he was told that one of the queen's chevaliers had just arrived and wished to speak to him. This nobleman informed him that someone had kidnapped Rosanie from the palace, practically under the queen's very eyes, and she, enraged by such insolence, wanted to alert the prince and the king so that they could take measures to apprehend and punish the kidnapper; she had already given her people similar orders. The prince sent the nobleman right back to his mother with the report about the fortunate coincidence that led to his saving Rosanie and punishing her abductor.

The next day, the king returned to the capital and brought the beautiful spinner to the queen. The pleasant maiden was received with such signs of kindness and benevolence that the envious Penséemorne was practically dying with rage. Not only had Rosanie had the good fortune to escape the abduction; she had been saved through the prince's valor! Despite the several obvious signs that heaven was opposed to her vengeance, Penséemorne did not stop seeking to satisfy it, and once again she sought success.

Rosanie, despite her joy in being rescued from her kidnapper by a dear lover, showered with glory, was disturbed by a secret anxiety that she could barely conceal. Sirene, who increasingly demonstrated a tender friendship for her, perceived Rosanie's agitation and wanted to know the cause. Rosanie hesitated to confide in her, nor was she wrong in this. The fact was that she sensed that the date set by the man with the wand was imminent; he would come soon to seek his precious stick of wood. Her mind had still not recalled the man's bizarre name, though she had endeavored a thousand times to recollect it. She knew that if she could not remember his name, she was bound by her inviolable oath to follow him wherever he wanted to lead her, and her recent abduction made her dread more than ever the mortal anguish of being eternally separated from the prince.

Though Rosanie still had difficulty in forming the letters of the alphabet, she wanted to see whether they might help her recall the name she passionately sought. She applied herself as best she could, until she wrote down *Racdon*, then *Ricordon*, and finally *Ringaudon*. A few times she was on the verge of joy, thinking she was about to find the name. But then she would fall into despair, convinced that the names her memory called forth were nowhere near the right and proper name. Tired of prodding her memory with so little success, she abandoned the writing and was plunged once more into sadness.

Meanwhile Penséemorne intended to give her reason for even greater anguish. Not only had the prince escaped her vengeance, he had also enabled Rosanie to escape it, and the cruel Penséemorne wanted to gratify her fury by having the young hero killed. Since this wicked young lady was beautiful, highborn, and extremely wealthy, she had many suitors. But most of them were without titles, money, or manners, their characters just as wanting as their fortunes. Among these shabby lovers Penséemorne chose three, and she spoke to each of them in private, saying, "If you perform this task that I ask of you, I shall marry you, and you will become my lord and command my fortune. Since the prince has insulted me, my anger can only be appeased by his death. You must follow him closely and take his life when he is separated during a hunt. Two of my friends will accompany you to provide you with support. I shall give each of you a magic sword made by a wise sorceress, a sword that will enable you to wound your opponent and never be wounded yourself. And she will use her magic powers to prevent anyone from discovering that it was you who killed the prince."

Not one of these villains refused Penséemorne's horrible proposition. She gave them the swords over which the sorceress had mumbled a magic spell, and then all three prepared to carry out the abominable assassination that Penséemorne had demanded. Ever since the prince had escaped the traps she had set for him in the enchanted palace, Penséemorne no longer counted with certainty on the power of magic. She was convinced that she needed the combination of supernatural powers and three heavily armed men to take the life of an individual whom they would attack at their advantage.

The king meanwhile repaired to his country residence without the queen and the prince, and the young lover, now fully recovered from his wound, was so disturbed by Rosanie's gloomy mood that he decided to go hunting to distract himself. Preoccupied by his cares, the prince became separated from his party and was so steeped in his thoughts that nightfall surprised him before he could rejoin his retinue. As he passed through a desolate spot near a derelict castle, he was surprised to see a great number of lights inside. He approached the windows, which were gaping open, and peered through the trees that surrounded them, and he saw in the glimmer of a bright violet light many people with repulsive faces and bizarre garments. They surrounded a gaunt, dark man with a ferocious and terrifying face. He appeared to be in a cheerful mood, for he sauntered and jumped around with inconceivable agility. The prince shuddered on viewing these atrocious creatures and was convinced they were from hell. But he remembered that he was wearing the ring of truth and was not afraid of their odious power. Among the group gathered around the terrifying man was a woman, who was pleading with him.

"No," he said. "My power does not extend to him. A celestial spirit, my sworn enemy, is protecting him against me and clearly demonstrated to me a short while ago that I cannot have much luck under the name of Labouréelamboy. My other name is much more advantageous. I've already acquired a great number of beautiful young women under this name, and I hope that tomorrow, at this very hour, I'll have acquired one who is worth more than all the others."

After saying these words, the dreadful man began to leap about and sing, his voice terrible:

> *If a young and tender female,*
> *Loving only childish pleasures,*
> *Had fixed it in her mind*
> *That my name is Ricdin-don,*
> *She would not fall in my trap.*
> *But the beauty will be mine,*
> *For my name has slipped her mind.*

Once the demon, for that is what he was, had finished his ditty, he turned once more to the woman.

"Since men are educated and more cultivated than women, we ordinarily have more trouble in duping them, unless we make use of the more gullible sex to get men to fall into our traps. On the other hand, men often cause women to fall into our snares. I myself have acquired more young girls by exploiting their desire to appear beautiful than have twenty of my comrades who have tried one hundred other means to capture them. And this powerful passion that makes them want so desperately to acquire beauty and elegance stems from their boundless desire to captivate men. Thus it is very often men who cause women to become our spoils. For example, I am certain that your good friend is not going to escape us. Aren't I right? Isn't it her passion to please a man that will make her our booty? But who would have believed that this young prince who has charmed her could have rendered ineffectual all the devices we have used against him? Nothing has been able to induce him to betray the oath of fidelity that he swore to his mistress, and he has never been tempted by anything of value and glory derived from magic. On the contrary, his two virtuous deeds have secured him a defender, who makes all the powers of hell useless against him. Thus you implore my help in vain. Neither you nor I can harm him. Everything regarding him will take its natural course."

The prince, listening to these words, recognized the person he was hearing as the demon who had spoken to him in the guise of an old man, and he was just as certain that the woman was the sorceress who was planning something wicked against him, as the celestial child had warned him. He was tempted to act immediately and punish this wicked woman and all the villains gathered there. But he abandoned this idea: these miserable creatures were not worth his vengeance. He resolved to get far away from this odious group and try to rejoin his men, or at least to find his way out of the forest.

He had not walked very long when he was abruptly attacked by three men who jumped out of a thicket. The prince defended himself with heroic valor, backed against a tree so that he could not be attacked from the rear. He fought with so much courage and skill that after he had killed one of his adversaries and knocked another to the ground, he saw the third take flight. With no thought for pursuing this man, he continued on his way, for he was very tired and had received a wound on his arm, causing him to lose much blood and feel quite weak. Fortunately, he eventually encountered some of his men, and in spite of his wound, he mounted a horse and raced to the palace. The queen was visibly upset when she saw her son's wound, even though the doctors she had summoned assured her that it was not a serious one. Rosanie, too, was distressed by his condition.

Nobody could guess who was behind this abominable assassination attempt against a prince so gentle and obliging. Even he, though, aware of Penséemorne's feelings for him and the depth of her frustration, could not imagine her capable of such wickedness.

Now while the prince had been the uneasy spectator at a witches' sabbath and the object of a wicked lover's fury, his father had been having a very pleasant time. In fact, he had learned some secrets that gave him immense joy. That same day, the king received a messenger, who demanded an audience for a charming and beautiful lady with a dazzling air about her. She was accompanied by an old man with a goodly countenance, who appeared to be someone of quality, and another man, a villager, it seemed, with a prudent and honest aspect that predisposed people in his favor.

"My lord," the lady said to the king, "you see before you a queen who has come to pay you the homage that she owes you and your wife for your services."

"I don't believe, madam," the king responded, "that either the queen or I have had the pleasure of rendering you a single service."

"It is true," replied the lady, "that I have not personally received the favors for which I have come to thank you. But they have been bestowed upon someone who is more dear to me than myself, for I am speaking about my daughter, the princess Rosanie."

"What, madam!" cried the king. "The beautiful Rosanie is your daughter! That is difficult to believe. Though that charming creature is still almost a child, you are too beautiful and youthful to be her mother."

"My lord," replied the lady, "I know how to deal with sweet words such as you have spoken, the gallant and gracious lies that men of elevated rank have translated into politesse. But, my lord, if you deign to listen to me, I shall tell you some serious truths, which I believe will surprise you greatly."

"It will be my pleasure to listen to you," replied the king.

So she began: "You see in me, my lord, Queen Riante-image, widow of King Planjoli, whose sad fate is well known to everyone. When the cruel Songecreux defeated and killed my husband, he seized his throne, locked me up in an obscure prison, and thought only about strengthening his hold on our realm. Since he knew that I was pregnant, he decided to have my child killed if I gave birth to a boy. But if it was a girl, he wanted to look after her life with great care so that his young son could marry her one day. When I learned about the tyrant's sinister plans, I shuddered at the thought of either fate for my unborn child. I resolved that no matter what the sex of the child that heaven was sending me, I would try to remove my babe from the tyrant's power, even if it were to cost me my life.

"The loyal chevalier whom you see before you," the queen continued, pointing to the old man, "had always been devoted to me. So wise and prudent was he always in all his actions that people gave him the name Longuevue. Well, this chevalier, who escaped the cruelty of the tyrant through a disguise, won over some of my guards and found a way to come and speak to me in my prison. Delighted to see him, I took the appropriate steps to give him my child as soon as it was born. The tyrant had ordered that I was to be treated with a great deal of care because of my pregnancy. Therefore, the governor of the fortress in which I was imprisoned made sure that I had all the necessary comforts so that I would remain in good health. When I knew I was close to giving birth, I expressed a desire to eat a pie made of wild boar. The governor acceded, and one of my clever ladies arranged that the loyal Longuevue, disguised as a peasant, was charged with making this pie. Longuevue gave it to my guards, who carried it to me. We opened it, my chambermaid and I, and found a dead baby, but recently born. All this was according to the plan I had conceived with Longuevue. The prudent chevalier had also given me the means to conserve the body of this innocent child until the time that I would need to show it. Soon thereafter I happily gave birth to a daughter, who had a birthmark above her elbow in the shape of a rose. Consequently I gave her the name Rosanie. My chambermaid hid the princess and placed the dead baby next to me. Then she began to shed tears, cry for help, and tell everyone that I had just given birth to a dead baby boy.

"There were many who hated Songecreux and his tyranny, and these people spread the news that I had given birth to a boy, whom he had killed. The guards had put the dead child into a coffin, but my chambermaid replaced him with my live daughter and disposed of the dead infant without arousing the slightest suspicion. Finally, they carried away the coffin, and even though we had given my daughter a great deal of nourishment, I trembled with fear that her cries might betray our secret. But fortune was on our side, and she did not cry. Longuevue, who had gained the trust of the governor, was charged with the burial, which took place without a ceremony. As soon as he could, Longuevue took Rosanie from the coffin, and thanks to heaven's protection, he found her in the best of health. From then on he took very good care of the child and did not rest until he had left the country that suffered under the barbarian Songecreux's tyrannical rule. What happened after this, my lord, I shall let the noble Longuevue tell you."

The queen turned to Longuevue, who addressed the king as follows:

"I left the realm of Fiction without encountering any trouble, my lord, and along with the little princess, I took with me a wet nurse, whom I passed off as her mother. Even though I had taken great care in choosing this woman, I concealed from her the true birth and the destiny of the child whom she was nursing. I arrived in your dominions, my lord, and I crossed a good part of your country without meeting a person to whom I felt I could entrust the precious creature who was in my charge. I would have been delighted to place her in good hands, for it was imperative for me to return to the realm of Fiction to protect the interests of the queen and princess.

"Finally, one day, in order to give the nurse and the princess some rest, I stopped under some trees on the edge of a large road that served two or three villages. While the nurse was sitting, I walked along the trees, and I was already some distance from the nurse when I heard two peasants walking behind me, and one said to the other, 'Well, then, obstinate Disantpeu, are you going to stay in that mood which has caused such an uproar?'

" 'What do you want me to say?' replied the second peasant. 'I'm satisfied with pitying the bad luck of my neighbor without blaming him for it, nor am I too curious to find out what has caused it. So you see, I don't know a thing about it and can't answer your questions.'

" 'Come on!' the first peasant said. 'None of the other people from your village have such a closed mouth. I know very well what I want to know without your telling me. And since you don't want to tell me anything, I'm going to hurry and arrive in your village before you. That will give me some time to talk with the townsfolk. I can't stay there too long, and anyway, since you are burdened by your child, you cannot go as fast as I can.'

"When the peasant with the child was alone, I approached him and began asking questions. The child he carried was his daughter, about a month old. His wife had been unable to nurse her, and he had taken the child to a wet nurse in a village some distance from their own. Now his wife's breasts had healed, and he was bringing back their daughter for her to nurse herself. I listened to his story with a great deal of attention, and the man's appearance pleased me. I believe, my lord, that you will find that I was right, for that good peasant is the same old man whom you see behind the queen, my mistress. I learned that he had been given the name Disantpeu because of his penchant for silence. All of this predisposed me in his favor, and I resolved to hire him to be Princess Rosanie's guardian, without revealing to him the secret of her birth. Of course, I made considerable promises to him and gave him gold and precious stones, as well as an immensely valuable bracelet from the queen as a means to recognize the princess one day. I demanded that he never tell anyone about this incident, not even his wife, and he took an oath accordingly, and here is what we did so that the secret would remain ours alone: "Since the child of Disantpeu was exactly Rosanie's age, he would take the princess to his wife as though she were their daughter, brought back from the village where she had been nursed. We were certain that he would be able to fool the mother, who had only seen her child when she gave birth. I myself carried Disantpeu's daughter to Rosanie's nurse, and I took the princess from her arms and placed her in the hands of the good peasant. We agreed, Disantpeu and I, that I would take the nurse to a comfortable home in a village that he named about six miles distant, and I assured him that I would take care of his daughter as if she were my own. After these guarantees, he gave me his daughter, and I, in turn, presented her to Rosanie's nurse. This good woman was shocked by my exchange of babies, and I told her that I had my reasons for doing it. I led her to the very next village and found lodgings for her. Then I made for the peasant's village to inquire about his character, which was indeed vouched for. Returning to the nurse, I escorted her and the baby to the village named by Disantpeu, and after arranging for comfortable quarters there, I returned to the realm of Fiction.

"Queen Riante-image was still imprisoned there, and the barbarian Songecreux continued to exercise his tyranny. Various people who hated Songecreux had come together to form a party, but it was not yet powerful enough to declare itself openly against the tyrant. Although some loyal followers of the late king and I spent all our energy in strengthening this movement, we were not able to succeed, and many years rolled by before we were in a position to act. Songecreux by his tyranny had captured the minds of the people, who were discouraged not to have a leader to succeed their late king. I did not dare reveal Rosanie's existence for fear that someone might betray the secret and the tyrant would find a way to take her life. I received news about her often enough, and I managed to convey everything to the queen, though with difficulty. But this news was the only consolation the queen had in her sad captivity.

"Some time after I had returned to the realm of Fiction, the nurse informed me that Disantpeu's daughter had died. As I was making arrangements to bring the nurse home to the Realm of Fiction, she, too, died in the village where I had left her, without ever knowing the truth of Rosanie's birth. Her death was an even greater guarantee that the secret would remain safe, and it remained enshrouded in profound silence for a long time. There came a time when the family of Songecreux, which had become extremely numerous, had committed so many atrocious acts that the hatred many people bore the tyrant reawakened. The opposition party had meantime become much stronger, and its members finally saw themselves in a position to take action.

"Their first act was to attack the principal fortresses of Songecreux, and they began a campaign under the command of General Belles-idées, who had led many victorious armies during the regime of the late king. At first this general made considerable progress and defeated Songecreux's troops in two battles. But the tyrant did not surrender. Instead, he requested help from different kingdoms of Europe and auxiliary troops from the Arab countries. The Arabs so distinguished themselves, defeating and wounding General Belles-idées, that it was believed they would destroy the loyal subjects of King Planjoli and Queen Riante-image down to the last person. They promised that if they were allowed to plunder the realm of Fiction in keeping with *A Thousand and One Nights*, they would guarantee Songecreux an eternal victory. Fortunately, a general named Bongout, from the country of Politesse, arrived with his troops to fortify General Belles-idées' army, and our cause was joined again. Despite the endless squadrons of Arabs and their fantastic formations, they were forced to yield to Belles-idées and Bongout.

"I felt it was now time to confide to the commanders of our party that their king had left an heir, Rosanie. Since there still might be traitors among our troops, we did not think it appropriate to divulge this secret for fear that the princess might somehow be sacrificed. Meanwhile we sent a messenger for Disantpeu, so that he could verify what I had told the leaders of the former king's party. It would have been a joy to hear the testimony from the queen herself, but the tyrant had changed the administration of the fortress where she was held prisoner, and news about her had been impossible to obtain.

Disantpeu, alas, was taken prisoner by Songecreux's soldiers as soon as he had crossed the border into the realm of Fiction. We continued our progress on the battlefield, but, despite the prudence and intrepidity of our commanders and the bravery of our soldiers, we did not immediately overcome the strong resistance that faced us. It took us ten days to crush the tyrant's forces. We found Disantpeu, and then we had the immense joy of rescuing the queen. She was ecstatic when she learned from Disantpeu that Princess Rosanie's soul was just as beautiful as her face. Since the tyrant Songecreux had fled the realm of Fiction, we declared to the people of the kingdom that they would regain their true monarch, in the person of a girl child whom the former king had left behind. The memory of King Planjoli had been extremely dear to the citizens of the realm of Fiction, and they expressed delight at living under a princess who descended from his bloodline.

"Queen Riante-image felt that the moment when she would see her daughter could not come soon enough. We left the government in the hands of Belles-idées and Bongout, and, with the queen mother and a huge retinue, made the long journey to your dominions. Disantpeu led us to his village, where the queen believed that she would find Rosanie and surprise her. But we learned there, my lord, that your wife, Queen Laborieuse, had invited the girl to your court, where she was called the beautiful spinner and had received a thousand signs of kindness from this great queen and yourself. At the same time we learned that you were at your country seat, so the queen, my mistress, hastened here to thank you for all you have done for Rosanie."

"Yes, my lord." Queen Riante-image resumed talking. "This is why I have come. I had thought that I would be able to thank you and your wife at the same time, for I believed that she was in this château with you. And I counted on finding my daughter with the queen as well."

"No, madam," the king responded. "Princess Rosanie is not here, but it will not take long for you to see this charming princess. She is staying with the queen in my capital city, and I shall accompany you there tomorrow. But, madam," he added, "I don't know how we shall be able to apologize sufficiently for all the mistakes we made, not knowing how highborn your daughter was."

The king gave orders to prepare the carriages and equipment, and after treating the queen and her retinue in regal fashion, they set out the next day for the capital.

Rosanie, meanwhile, was undergoing mortal agony. Greatly distressed as she was by the wound sustained by her dear lover, his injury was not her major concern. For she saw the inexorable approach of the dreadful instant when the master of the magic wand would demand his fatal stick. She had still not recalled the name of this stranger, and knew that the inviolable commitment of her oath would oblige her to follow him wherever he wished to lead her. Streams of tears bathed her cheeks when she thought of being forever parted from the queen who had showered her with so much kindness and for whom she felt such a sincere attachment. She would miss, too, the pleasant Sirene and regret the loss of Vigilentine's care, but her pain was most agonizing when she thought that she would be eternally condemned never to see the prince again. It is impossible to express all that she suffered when she thought about such a cruel separation, and she could not stop weeping for nights at a time.

One morning, still preoccupied by such gloomy thoughts, she received a queen's messenger, who told her that the queen wanted to see her in the prince's chamber. At her entrance, the queen cried out, "I have some strange news for you, my dear Rosanie! Alas, there's a monster among my ladies of honor!" And the queen proceeded to inform her about what she had recently learned. One of the prince's attackers had dragged himself, wounded, to the next village, where the doctor told him that he was going to die. This miserable man began excoriating Penséemorne and recounted all the circumstances that had led up to the odious and criminal attack. Then he died, heaping curses on his guilty mistress. Apparently, someone alerted this unworthy girl to the villain's confession, for, it had been learned, Penséemorne left the palace in a fury, flew to the wicked sorceress, and strangled her, then she strangled herself.

Rosanie trembled a thousand times as she listened to this story. When the queen had finished, she said that she was going to the temple and wanted Rosanie to distract her son so that he would feel less pain from his wound. She also requested that Sirene go and sing to him. This pleasant girl sang with great charm, but neither the prince nor Rosanie heard her. They were so preoccupied that they were insensitive to the sweetness of music. Aware of their distraction, Sirene stopped singing, got up, and went to the window to look at the swans that glided on the river and swam over to take bread crumbs from the hands of palace officers. As soon as the prince believed that only Rosanie could hear his words, he said to her, "Beautiful Rosanie, why have you become so terribly sad? You seemed to have plunged yourself into gloom. Can't my ardent feelings with all their tenderness provide you with some joy? That is, unless you've become totally insensitive to my love."

"My lord," Rosanie replied, "do you believe that I can see you in such pain and think about all the dangers you've been exposed to without feeling extreme sorrow?"

"But the dangers have passed," responded the prince, "and even I don't have the slightest fear that there will be any more trouble. And since I don't want to hide anything from you, charming Rosanie, I want you to learn how I was so fortunate as to have escaped these dangers."

He told her about his adventure in the enchanted palace of the forest, about the traps that had been set for him by that princess, who had pretended to be so unfortunate, and about the ring of truth that had been given to him by the unknown marvelous child. Next he told the story of his adventure at the ruined palace and all the diabolic ranting he had heard. Finally, he came to the point of his story where he recalled the ditty sung by the demon, and he repeated it to Rosanie word for word:

> If a young and tender female,
> Loving only childish pleasures,
> Had fixed it in her mind
> That my name is Ricdin-don,
> She would not fall in my trap.
> But the beauty will be mine,
> For my name has slipped her mind.

Rosanie had uttered such a loud cry that he was at first frightened. But the prince was reassured when he heard Rosanie exclaim with joy, "Heaven be praised for its infinite kindness to me!"

The prince asked her to explain the meaning of her words, but he realized that she did not want to disclose anything in the presence of Sirene, who had approached when she heard Rosanie's cry. When Sirene returned to the window, Rosanie told the prince all about the wand. She had been shocked on learning that this man was a demon. The prince could not but criticize her a little for having come to an agreement so easily with a stranger. But since one is always ready to excuse anything done by a beloved person, he blamed the imprudent act on her extreme youth and lack of experience. She, of course, was delighted beyond belief; her lover's memory had helped her escape the greatest danger of her life. The prince even wrote the name Ricdin-don on a slate right then and there and gave it to Rosanie, who could not find words enough to express her gratitude.

"My lord!" she said to him. "Your abundant valor had already saved me from the hands of a cruel kidnapper. But today your excellent memory has pulled me out of the grasp of an enemy much more formidable."

Toward noon, a venerable old man, dressed simply but properly, entered the prince's room. As soon as Rosanie saw him, she ran to him with open arms, crying out, "Oh, my dear father! What joy to be able to embrace you after thinking you were dead! My lord," she continued addressing the prince, "please pardon the ecstasy of a girl who has just seen once more the best father in the world and the one most worthy to be cherished. In spite of the obscurity of his rank, I am not shamed to admit that I was born from him. The honesty and the elevated feelings with which nature endowed him make up for the lowliness of his birth. I should also like to ask him, my lord, about my mother, whom I have not forgotten, despite her rough treatment of me."

"Madam," responded the old man, "you are not my daughter. You have too many wonderful qualities to have come from a man like me. You are the daughter of a great king, who is dead. However, the queen, your mother, has just arrived in this palace and is presently with Queen Laborieuse. She will come here to embrace you and verify all that I have just told you."

Rosanie was at first speechless at his words. But finally she regained control of herself and cried out, "Alas! What is going on, Father? Do you want to deceive the prince to whom I have just boasted about your honest character with such great pleasure?"

"I am not deceiving anyone, madam," replied the old man. "The queen, your mother, who has just entered this room, will testify to this."

Indeed, just then, Queen Riante-image, King Prud'homme, Queen Laborieuse, and Lord Longuevue entered the prince's chamber, along with many other illustrious people, who were transported by delight. Queen Riante-image was speechless to find Rosanie so beautiful, and she hugged her tenderly in her arms. The charming girl kissed her mother's hands, soaking them with tears of joy.

After the first ecstasy of the reunion, the king and Longuevue told Rosanie about her exalted birth and her destiny. She was much less impressed by the throne and the glory of reigning than by the great pleasure she would take in offering a scepter to a lover who had planned to offer a crown to a mere villager. As for the prince, he felt such a range of sweet and glorious emotions that he could hardly bear it. He complimented himself for having distinguished Rosanie's merits and charms beneath the thick veils of her humble upbringing. He was delighted to have become the object of this beautiful maiden's love, ecstatic to have performed two considerable services for her, and in the flattering hope that he would be united with her soon, he only envisaged the joy of being with her as she had been without the luster of the throne that fortune had just given her.

Longuevue, accompanied by Disantpeu, now approached Rosanie and said, "Please grant us permission, madam, to show your mother, the queen, the mark that you have on your arm and that inspired the name that you bear."

"Oh!" cried out Riante-image. "I don't need any proof to recognize my own blood! If I had not had the testimony of such honest men as you both are, I still would have recognized her because she resembles my former husband so much, and this resemblance is sufficient enough to convince me that she is my daughter."

In spite of the queen's protestations, the chambermaid who had saved Rosanie's life when she was born approached that charming princess, and after rolling up the sleeve of her dress, she showed the company an arm that was whiter than alabaster. Everyone surrounded the new princess, and they saw the figure of a little rose perfectly represented on her arm above her elbow.

The two queens began once more to hug her. Then Disantpeu presented Queen Riante-image with the bracelet of diamonds and other precious stones that Longuevue had given him so many years before. The queen mother handed them to her daughter, who received them with respect.

"Now you see, madam," Disantpeu said with a laugh to Rosanie, "that I was completely right to refuse all those good matches that were proposed to you at the village. I knew that even if you had never been recognized, the least valuable of these precious stones that I was keeping for you would have made you richer than all the possessions of those suitors put together."

Rosanie said a thousand grateful things to her good protector, assured him that she would show her appreciation in many different ways, and added that since his wife had been her nurse, she, too, would receive a great deal of wealth, as would their son. The young princess did not forget to speak of her gratitude to Longuevue and the loyal chambermaid. She gave one hundred caresses to Sirene, who from that moment on was regarded as the new queen's favorite. King Prud'homme did not wait long before he requested Rosanie's hand in marriage for his son from Queen Riante-image. Of course, she consented right away, and the day of the wedding was set so as to satisfy the two lovers and the two mothers.

That evening they dined in splendor, and after the meal, they all withdrew to their rooms to rest. Rosanie had not been in her chamber very long when a messenger came to tell her that a man dressed in black, with a very somber face, wanted to speak with her. She gave the order to let him enter, and at once recognized him as the man who had given her the wand. Even though she knew his name, the sight of him made her shudder, for she knew how dangerous he was. Without saying a single word, she stood up, fetched the wand, and handed it to him. "Take it, Ricdin-don," she said. "Here is your wand."

The evil spirit, who had not expected to hear this, disappeared while uttering terrible howls. And thus he was duped, something that happens to him when he tries to ensnare the innocent, who do not realize that he is after their soul.

Rosanie spent many long years with the prince in a perfect union of extreme happiness. They arranged a marriage between Bonavis and Sirene, who remained their favorites. They heaped gifts upon all those who rendered them service. Longuevue, Disantpeu, the queen's chambermaid, and Vigilentine were very content with the tokens of gratitude they received.

The admirable royal couple were loved by most of their subjects, and the most noble of them were delighted to see the descendants of King Planjoli and Queen Riante-image reign over them. However, since it is difficult to please all people equally, the party of Songecreux rouses itself from time to time and becomes powerful enough to cause disruptions that affect the capital city itself. It is even said that in spite of the gracious manners of the legitimate sovereigns of the country and the care taken by the generals Belles-idées and Bongout, the followers of Songecreux will never be entirely destroyed.

Translated by Jack Zipes

‹ *Riquet with the Tuft* ›
CHARLES PERRAULT

Once upon a time there was a queen who gave birth to a son so ugly and misshapen that for a long time everyone doubted if he was in fact human. A fairy who was present at his birth assured everyone, however, that he could not fail to be pleasant because he would have a great deal of intelligence. She added that he would have the ability to impart the same amount of intelligence to that person he came to love by virtue of this gift she was giving him. All this somewhat consoled the poor queen, who was very much distressed at having brought such a hideous little monkey into the world. Sure enough, as soon as the child was able to talk, he said a thousand pretty things. Furthermore, there was an indescribable air of thoughtfulness in all his actions that charmed everyone. I have forgotten to say that he was born with a little tuft of hair on his head, and this was the reason why he was called Riquet with the Tuft (Riquet being the family name).

At the end of seven or eight years, the queen of a neighboring kingdom gave birth to two daughters. The first of them was more beautiful than daylight, and the queen was so delighted that people feared her great joy might cause her some harm. The same fairy who had attended the birth of little Riquet with the Tuft was also present on this occasion, and to moderate the queen's joy, she declared that this little princess would be as stupid as she was beautiful.

The queen was deeply mortified by this, but a few minutes later her chagrin became even greater still, for she gave birth to a second child, who turned out to be extremely ugly.

"Don't be too upset, madam," the fairy said to her. "Your daughter will be compensated in another way. She'll have so much intelligence that her lack of beauty will hardly be noticed."

"May Heaven grant it," replied the queen. "But isn't there some way to give a little intelligence to my older daughter, who is so beautiful?"

"I can't do anything for her, madam, in the way of wit," said the fairy, "but I can do a great deal in matters of beauty. Since there's nothing I would not do to please you, I shall endow her with the ability to render any person who pleases her with a beautiful or handsome appearance."

As these two princesses grew up, their qualities increased in the same proportion. Throughout the realm everyone talked about the beauty of the older daughter and the intelligence of the younger. It is also true that their defects greatly increased as they grew older. The young daughter became uglier, and the older, more stupid every day. She either gave no answer when addressed, or she said something foolish. At the same time she was so awkward that she could not place four pieces of china on a mantel without breaking one of them, nor drink a glass of water without spilling half of it on her clothes. Despite the great advantage of beauty in the older sister, the younger sister always outshone the elder whenever they were in society. At first everyone gathered around the more beautiful girl to admire her, but soon left her for the more intelligent sister, to listen to the thousand pleasant things she said. In less than a quarter of an hour, not a soul would be standing near the elder sister, while everyone would be surrounding the younger. Though very stupid, the elder sister noticed this and would have willingly given up all her beauty for half the intelligence of her sister.

The queen, discreet though she was, could not help reproaching the elder daughter whenever she did stupid things, and that made the poor princess ready to die of grief. One day, when she was withdrawn into the woods to bemoan her misfortune, she saw a little man coming toward her. He was extremely ugly and unpleasant, but was dressed in magnificent attire. It was young Riquet with the Tuft. He had fallen in love with her from seeing her portraits, which had been sent all around the world, and he had left his father's kingdom to have the pleasure of seeing and speaking to her. Delighted to meet her thus alone, he approached her with all the respect and politeness imaginable. After paying the usual compliments, he remarked that she was very melancholy.

"I cannot comprehend, madam," he said, "how a person so beautiful as you are can be so sad as you appear. Though I may boast of having seen an infinite number of lovely women, I can assure you that I've never beheld one whose beauty could begin to compare with yours."

"It's very kind of you to say so, sir," replied the princess, and there she stopped.

"Beauty is such a great advantage," continued Riquet, "that it ought to surpass all other things. If one possesses it, I don't see anything that could cause one much distress."

"I'd rather be as ugly as you and have intelligence," said the princess, "than be as beautiful and stupid as I am."

"There's no greater proof of intelligence, madam, than the belief that we do not have any. It's the nature of the gift that the more we have, the more we believe we are deficient in it."

"I don't know whether that's the case," the princess said, "but I know full well that I am very stupid, and that's the cause of the grief which is killing me."

"If that's all that's troubling you, madam, I can easily put an end to your distress."

"And how do you intend to manage that?" the princess asked.

"I have the power, madam, to give as much intelligence as anyone can possess to the person I love," Riquet with the Tuft replied. "And as you are that person, madam, it will depend entirely on whether or not you want to have so much intelligence, for you may have it, provided that you consent to marry me."

The princess was thunderstruck and did not say a word.

"I see that this proposal torments you, and I'm not surprised," said Riquet with the Tuft. "But I'll give you a full year to make up your mind."

The princess had so little intelligence, and at the same time had such a strong desire to possess a great deal, that she imagined the year would never come to an end. So she immediately accepted his offer. No sooner did she promise that she would marry Riquet with the Tuft twelve months from that day than she felt a complete change come over her. She found she possessed an incredible facility to say anything she wished and to say it in a polished yet easy and natural manner. She commenced right away, maintaining an elegant conversation with the prince. Indeed, she was so brilliant that he believed that he had given her more wit than he had kept for himself.

When she returned to the palace, the whole court was at a loss to account for such a sudden and extraordinary change. Whereas she had formerly said any number of foolish things, she now made sensible and exceedingly clever observations. The entire court rejoiced beyond belief. Only the younger sister was not quite pleased, for she no longer held the advantage of intelligence over her elder sister. Now she merely appeared as an ugly woman by her side, and the king let himself be guided by the elder daughter's advice. Sometimes he even held the meetings of his council in her apartment.

The news of this change spread abroad, and all the young princes of the neighboring kingdoms exerted themselves to the utmost to gain her affection.

Nearly all of them asked her hand in marriage, but since she found none of
them sufficiently intelligent, she listened to them without promising herself
to anyone in particular. At last a prince arrived who was so witty and handsome
that she could not help feeling attracted to him. Her father noticed this and
told her that she was at perfect liberty to choose a husband for herself and
that she only had to make her decision known. Now, the more intelligence
one possesses, the greater the difficulty one has in making up one's mind
about such a weighty matter. So she thanked her father and requested some
time to think it over.

By chance she took a walk in the same woods, where she had met Riquet
with the Tuft to ponder with greater freedom what she should do. While she
was walking, deep in thought, she heard a dull rumble beneath her feet, as
though many people were running busily back and forth. Listening more
attentively, she heard voices say, "Bring me that cooking pot." "Give me
that kettle." "Put some wood on the fire." At that same moment the ground
opened, and she saw below what appeared to be a large kitchen full of cooks,
scullions, and all sorts of servants necessary for the preparation of a magnificent
banquet. A group of approximately twenty to thirty cooks came forth, and
they took places at a very long table set in a path of the woods. Each had a
larding pin in hand and a cap on his head, and they set to work, keeping
time to a melodious song. Astonished at this sight, the princess inquired who
had hired them.

"Riquet with the Tuft, madam," the leader of the group replied. "His
marriage is to take place tomorrow."

The princess was even more surprised than she was before, and suddenly
she recalled that it was exactly a year ago that she had promised to marry
Prince Riquet with the Tuft. How she was taken aback! The reason why she
had not remembered her promise was that when she had made it, she had

still been a fool, and after receiving her new mind, she had forgotten all her follies. Now, no sooner had she advanced another thirty steps on her walk when she encountered Riquet with the Tuft, who appeared gallant and magnificent, like a prince about to be married.

"As you can see, madam," he said, "I've kept my word to the minute, and I have no doubt but that you've come here to keep yours. By giving me your hand, you'll make me the happiest of men."

"I'll be frank with you," the princess replied. "I've yet to make up my mind on that matter, and I don't believe I'll ever be able to do so to your satisfaction."

"You astonish me, madam."

"I can believe it," the princess responded, "and assuredly, if I had to deal with a stupid person—a man without intelligence—I'd feel greatly embarrassed. 'A princess is bound by her word,' he'd say to me, 'and you must marry me as you promised to do so.' But since the man with whom I'm speaking is the most intelligent man in the world, I'm certain he'll listen to reason. As you know, when I was no better than a fool, I could not decide whether I should marry you. Now that I have the intelligence that you've given me and that renders me much more difficult to please than before, how can you expect me to make a decision today that I couldn't make then? If you seriously thought of marrying me, you made a big mistake in taking away my stupidity and enabling me to see clearer."

"If a man without intelligence would be justified in reproaching you for your breach of promise," Riquet with the Tuft replied, "why do you expect, madam, that I should not be allowed to do the same? This matter affects the entire happiness of my life. Is it reasonable that intelligent people should be placed at a greater disadvantage than those who have none? Can you presume this, you who have so much intelligence and have so earnestly desired to possess it? But let us come to the point, if you please. With the exception of my ugliness, is there anything about me that displeases you? Are you dissatisfied with my birth, my intelligence, my temperament, or my manners?"

"Not in the least," replied the princess. "I admire you for everything you've just mentioned."

"If so," Riquet with the Tuft responded, "I'll gain my happiness, for you have the power to make me the most pleasing of men."

"How can that be done?"

"It can if you love me sufficiently to wish that it should be. And to remove your doubts, you should know that the same fairy who endowed me at birth with the power to give intelligence to the person I chose also gave you the power to render handsome any man who pleases you."

"If that's so," the princess said, "I wish with all my heart that you may become the most charming and handsome prince in the world."

No sooner had the princess pronounced these words than Riquet with the Tuft appeared to her eyes as the most handsome, strapping, and charming man she had ever seen. There are some who assert that it was not the fairy's spell but love alone that caused this transformation. They say that the princess, having reflected on her lover's perseverance, prudence, and all the good qualities of his heart and mind, no longer saw the deformity of his body nor the ugliness of his features. His hunch appeared to her as nothing more than the effect of a man shrugging his shoulders. Likewise, his horrible limp appeared to be nothing more than a slight sway that charmed her. They also say that his eyes, which squinted, seemed to her only more brilliant for the proof they gave of the intensity of his love. Finally, his great red nose had something martial and heroic about it. However this may be, the princess promised to marry him on the spot, provided that he obtained the consent of the king, her father.

On learning of his daughter's high regard for Riquet with the Tuft, whom he also knew to be a very intelligent and wise prince, the king accepted him with pleasure as a son-in-law. The wedding took place the next morning, just as Riquet with the Tuft had planned it.

Moral

That which you see written down here
Is not so fantastic because it's quite true:
We find what we love is wondrously fair,
In what we love we find intelligence, too.

Another Moral

Nature very often places
Beauty in an object that amazes,
Such that art can ne'er achieve.
Yet even beauty can't move the heart
As much as that charm hard to chart,
A charm which only love can perceive.

Translated by Jack Zipes

nce upon a time there was a great queen who, having given birth to twin daughters, invited twelve fairies who lived nearby to come and bestow gifts upon them, as was the custom in those days. Indeed, it was a very useful custom, for the power of the fairies generally compensated for the deficiencies of nature. Sometimes, however, they also spoiled what nature had done its best to make perfect, as we shall soon see.

When the fairies had all gathered in the banquet hall, they were about to sit at the table and enjoy a magnificent meal. Suddenly the fairy Magotine entered. She was the sister of Carabossa and no less malicious. Shuddering when she saw her, the queen feared some disaster, since she had not invited her to the celebration. However, she carefully concealed her anxiety, personally went looking for an armchair for the fairy, and found one covered with green velvet and embroidered with sapphires. Since Magotine was the eldest of the fairies, all the rest made way for her to pass and whispered to one another, "Let us quickly endow the infant princesses, sisters, so that we may get the start on Magotine."

When the armchair was set up for her, she rudely declined it, saying that she was big enough to eat standing. She was mistaken in this, though, because the table was rather high and she was not tall enough to see over it. This annoyance increased her foul mood even more.

"Madam," the queen said, "I beg you to take your seat at the table."

"If you had wished me to do so," the fairy replied, "you would have sent an invitation to me as you did to the others, but you only want beauties with fine figures and fine dresses, like my sisters here. As for me, I'm too ugly and old. Yet despite it all, I have just as much power as they. Yea, without boasting about it, I may even have more."

All the fairies urged her strongly to sit at the table, and at length she consented. A golden basket was placed before them, containing twelve bouquets composed of jewels. The fairies who had arrived first each took a bouquet, leaving none for Magotine. As she began to mutter between her teeth, the queen ran to her room and brought her a casket of perfumed Spanish morocco covered with rubies and filled with diamonds, and asked her to accept it. But Magotine shook her head and said, "Keep your jewels, madam. I have more than enough to spare. I came only to see if you had thought of me, and it's clear you've neglected me shamefully."

Thereupon she struck the table with her wand, and all the delicacies heaped on it were turned into fricasseed serpents. This sight horrified the fairies so much that they flung down their napkins and fled the table. While they talked with one another about the nasty trick Magotine had played on them, that cruel fairy approached the cradle in which the princesses, the loveliest children in the world, were lying wrapped in golden swaddling. "I endow you with perfect ugliness," she quickly said to one of them, and she was about to utter a malediction on the other when the fairies, greatly disturbed, ran and stopped her. Then the mischievous Magotine broke one of the windowpanes, dashed through it like a flash of lightning, and vanished from sight.

All the good gifts that the benevolent fairies proceeded to bestow on the princess did not alleviate the misery of the queen, who found herself the mother of the ugliest being in the universe. Taking the infant in her arms, she had the misfortune of watching it grow more hideous by the moment. She struggled in vain to suppress her tears in the presence of their fairy ladyships, whose compassion is impossible to imagine. "What shall we do, sisters?" they said to one another. "How can we ever console the queen?" They held a grand council about the matter, and at the end they told the queen not to give in to her grief, since a time would come when her daughter would be very happy.

"But," the queen interrupted, "will she become beautiful again?"

"We can't give you any further information," the fairies replied. "Be satisfied, madam, with the assurance that your daughter will be happy."

She thanked them very much and did not forget to give them many presents. Although the fairies were quite rich, they always liked people to give them something. Throughout the world this custom has been passed down from that day to our own, and time has not altered it in the least.

The queen named her elder daughter Laidronette and the younger Bellotte. These names suited them perfectly, for Laidronette, despite her boundless intelligence, became too frightful to behold, whereas her sister's beauty increased hourly, until she looked thoroughly charming.

After Laidronette had turned twelve, she went to the king and queen and threw herself at their feet. "Please, I implore you, allow me to shut myself up in a lonely castle so that I will no longer torment you with my ugliness." Despite her hideous appearance, they could not help being fond of her, and not without some pain did they consent to let her depart. However, since Bellotte remained with them, they had ample consolation.

Laidronette begged the queen not to send anyone except her nurse and a few officers to wait on her. "You needn't worry, madam, about my being abducted. I can assure you that, looking as I do, I shall avoid even the light of day."

After the king and queen had granted her wishes, she was conducted to the castle she had chosen. It had been built many centuries before, and the sea crashed beneath its windows and served it as a moat. In the vicinity was a large forest in which one could stroll, and in several fields leading to the forest, the princess played various instruments and sang divinely.

Two years she spent in this pleasant solitude, even writing several volumes recording her thoughts, but the desire to see her father and mother again induced her to take a coach and revisit the court. She arrived just as they were to celebrate the marriage of Bellotte. Everyone had been rejoicing, but the moment they saw Laidronette, their joy turned to distress. She was neither embraced nor hugged by any of her relatives. Indeed, the only thing they said to her was that she had grown a good deal uglier, and they advised her not to appear at the ball. "However, if you wish to see it, we shall find some hole for you to peep through."

She replied that she had come there neither to dance nor to hear the music, that she had been in the desolate castle so long that she had felt a longing to pay her respects to the king and the queen. Painfully aware that they could not endure the sight of her, she told them that she would therefore return to her wilderness, where the trees, flowers, and springs she wandered among did not reproach her for her ugliness. When the king and queen saw how hurt she was, they told her reluctantly that she could stay with them two or three days. Good-natured as always, though, she replied, "It would be harder for me to leave you if I were to spend so much time in your good company." Since they were all too eager for her to depart, they did not press her to stay but coldly remarked that she was quite right.

For coming to her wedding the princess Bellotte gave her a gift of an old ribbon that she had worn all winter in a bow on her muff, and Bellotte's fiancé gave her some magenta taffeta to make a petticoat. If she had expressed what she thought, she would have surely thrown the ribbon and the rag of taffeta in her generous donors' faces, but she had such good sense, prudence, and judgment that she revealed none of her bitterness. With her faithful nurse, she left the court to return to her castle, her heart so filled with grief that she did not say a word during the entire journey.

One day, as she was walking on one of the gloomiest paths in the forest, she saw a large green serpent at the foot of a tree. As it reared its head, it said to her, "Laidronette, you aren't the only unhappy creature. Look at my horrible form. And yet at birth I was even handsomer than you."

Terrified, the princess heard not one half of this. She fled from the spot and for many days thereafter did not dare to leave the castle, so afraid was she of another such encounter.

Eventually she tired of sitting alone in her room, however, and one evening she went for a walk along the beach. She was strolling slowly, pondering her sad fate, when she noticed a small gilt barque painted with a thousand different emblems gliding toward her. Its sail was made of gold brocade, its mast of cedar, its oars of eagle wood, and it appeared to be drifting at random. When it landed on the shore, the curious princess stepped on board to inspect all its beautiful decorations. She found its deck laid with crimson velvet trimmed in gold, and all the nails were diamonds.

Suddenly the barque drifted out to sea again, and the princess, alarmed at her impending danger, grabbed the oars and endeavored in vain to row back to the beach. The wind rose and the waves became high. She lost sight of land and, seeing nothing around her but sea and sky, resigned herself to her fate, fully convinced not only that it was unlikely to be a happy one, but also that this was another one of the fairy Magotine's mean tricks. "If I must die, why do I have such a secret dread of death?" she asked. "Alas, have I ever enjoyed any of life's pleasures so much that I should now feel regret at dying? My ugliness disgusts even my family. My sister is a great queen, and I'm consigned to exile in the depths of a wilderness where the only companion I've found is a talking serpent. Wouldn't it be better for me to perish than to drag out such a miserable existence?" Having thus reflected, she dried her tears and courageously peered out to discover whence death would come, inviting its speedy approach. Just then she saw a serpent riding the billows toward the vessel, and as it approached her, it said: "If you're willing to be helped by a poor green serpent like me, I have the power to save your life."

"Death is less frightful to me than you are," the princess exclaimed, "and if you want to do me a kind favor, never let me set eyes on you again."

The green serpent gave a long hiss (the manner in which serpents sigh), and without saying a word it immediately dove under the waves.

"What a horrible monster!" the princess said to herself. "He has green wings, a body of a thousand colors, ivory claws, fiery eyes, and a bristling mane of long hair on his head. Oh, I'd much rather die than owe my life to him! But what motive does he have in following me? How did he obtain the power of speech that enables him to talk like a rational creature?"

As she was entertaining these thoughts, a voice answered her: "You had better learn, Laidronette, that the green serpent is not to be despised. I don't mean to be harsh, but I assure you that he's less hideous in the eyes of his species than you are in the eyes of yours. However, I desire not to anger you but to lighten your sorrows, provided you consent."

The princess was dumbfounded by this voice, and the words it uttered seemed so unjust to her that she could not suppress her tears. Suddenly, though, a thought occurred to her. "What am I doing? I don't want to cry about my death just because I'm reproached for my ugliness," she exclaimed. "Alas, shouldn't I perish as though I were the grandest beauty in the world? My demise would be more of a consolation to me."

Completely at the mercy of the winds, the vessel drifted on until it struck a rock and immediately shattered into pieces. The poor princess realized that mere philosophizing would not save her in such a catastrophe, and she grabbed onto some pieces of the wreck, so she thought, for she felt herself buoyed in the water and fortunately reached the shore, coming to rest at the foot of a towering boulder. Alas, she was horrified to discover that her arms were wrapped tightly around the neck of the green serpent! When he realized how appalled she was, he retreated from her and said, "You'd fear me less if you knew me better, but it is my hard fate to terrify all those who see me."

With that he plunged into the surf, and Laidronette was left alone by the enormous rock. No matter where she glanced, she could see nothing that might alleviate her despair. Night was approaching. She was without food and knew not where to go. "I thought I was destined to perish in the ocean," she said sadly, "but now I'm sure that I'm to end my days here. Some sea monster will come and devour me, or I'll die of hunger." Rising, she climbed to the top of the crag and sat down. As long as it was light, she gazed at the ocean, and when it became dark, she took off her taffeta petticoat, covered her head with it, and waited anxiously for whatever was to happen next. Eventually she was overcome by sleep, and she seemed to hear the music of some instruments. She was convinced that she was dreaming, but a moment later she heard someone sing the following verse, which seemed to have been composed expressly for her:

> Let Cupid make you now his own.
> Here he rules with gentle tone.
> Love with pleasure will be sown.
> On this isle no grief is known.

The attention she paid to these words caused her to wake up. "What good or bad luck shall I have now?" she exclaimed. "Might happiness still be in store for someone so wretched?" She opened her eyes timidly, fearing that she would be surrounded by monsters, but she was astonished to find that in place of the rugged, looming rock was a room with walls and ceiling made entirely of gold. She was lying in a magnificent bed that matched perfectly the rest of this palace, which was the most splendid in the universe. She began asking herself a hundred questions about all of this, unable to believe she was wide awake. Finally, she got up and ran to open a glass door

that led onto a spacious balcony, from which she could see all the beautiful things that nature, with some help from art, had managed to create on earth: gardens filled with flowers, fountains, statues, and the rarest trees; distant woods, palaces with walls ornamented with jewels, and roofs composed of pearls so wonderfully constructed that each was an architectural masterpiece. A calm, smiling sea strewn with thousands of vessels, whose sails, pendants, and streamers fluttered in the breeze, completed the charming view.

"Gods! You just gods!" the princess exclaimed. "What am I seeing?

Where am I? What an astounding change! What has become of the terrible rock that seemed to threaten the skies with its lofty pinnacles? Am I the same person who was shipwrecked last night and saved by a serpent?" Bewildered, she continued talking to herself, first pacing, then stopping. Finally, she heard a noise in her room.

Reentering it, she saw a hundred pagods advancing toward her. They were dressed and made up in a hundred different ways. The tallest were a foot high, and the shortest no more than four inches—some were beautiful, graceful, pleasant, others hideous, dreadfully ugly. Their bodies were made of diamonds, emeralds, rubies, pearls, crystal, amber, coral, porcelain, gold, silver, brass, bronze, iron, wood, and clay. Some were without arms, others without feet, others had mouths extending to their ears, eyes askew, noses broken. In short, nowhere in the world could a greater variety of people be found than among these pagods.

Those pagods who presented themselves to the princess were the deputies of the kingdom. After a speech containing some very judicious ideas, they informed her that they had traveled about the world for some time past, but in order to obtain their sovereign's permission to do so, they had to take an oath not to speak during their absence. Indeed, some were so scrupulous that they would not even shake their heads or move their hands or feet, but the majority of them could not help it. This was how they had traveled about the universe, and when they returned, they amused the king by telling him everything that had occurred, even the most secret transactions and adventures in all the courts they had visited. "This is a pleasure, madam," one of the deputies added, "which we shall have the honor of occasionally affording you, for we have been commanded to do all we can to entertain you. Instead of bringing you presents, we now come to amuse you with our songs and dances."

They began immediately to sing the following verses while simultaneously dancing to the music of tambourines and castanets:

> Sweet are pleasures after pains.
> Lovers, do not break your chains.
> Trials though you may endure,
> Happiness they will ensure.
> Sweet are pleasures after pains,
> Joy from sorrow luster gains.

When they stopped dancing and singing, their spokesman said to the princess, "Here, madam, are a hundred pagodines, who have the honor of being selected to wait on you. Any wish you may have in the world will be fulfilled, provided you consent to remain among us."

The pagodines appeared in their turn. They carried baskets cut to their own size and filled with a hundred different articles, so pretty, so useful, so well made, and so costly that Laidronette never tired of admiring and praising them, uttering exclamations of wonder and delight at all the marvels they showed her. The most prominent pagodine, a tiny figure made of diamonds, advised her to enter the grotto of the baths, since the heat of the day was increasing. The princess proceeded in the direction indicated between two ranks of bodyguards, whose appearance was enough to make one die with laughter.

She found two baths of crystal in a grotto ornamented with gold and filled with scented water so delicious and uncommon that she marveled at it. Shading the baths was a pavilion of green and gold brocade. When the princess inquired why there were two, they answered that one was for her and the other for the king of the pagods.

"But where is he, then?" the princess asked.

"Madam," they replied, "he is presently with the army, waging war against his enemies. You'll see him as soon as he returns."

The princess then inquired if he was married. They answered no. "He is so charming that no one has yet been found who would be worthy of him." She indulged her curiosity no further, but disrobed and entered the bath. All the pagods and pagodines began to sing and play on various instruments. Some had theorbos made out of nutshells; others, bass viols made out of almond shells, for it was, of course, necessary that the instruments fit the size of the performers. But all the parts were arranged in such perfect accord that nothing could surpass the delight their concert gave her.

When the princess emerged from her bath, they gave her a magnificent dressing gown. A pair of pagods playing a flute and an oboe marched before her, and a train of pagodines singing songs in her praise trailed behind. In this state did she enter a room where her toilet was laid out. Immediately the pagodines-in-waiting, and those of the bedchamber, bustled about, dressed her hair, put on her robes, and praised her. There was no longer talk of her ugliness, of taffeta petticoats or greasy ribbons.

The princess was truly taken aback. "To whom can I be indebted for such extraordinary happiness?" she asked herself. "I was on the brink of destruction, I was waiting for death to come and had lost hope, and yet I suddenly find myself in the most magnificent place in the world, where I've been welcomed with the greatest joy!"

Since the princess was endowed with a great deal of good sense and breeding, she conducted herself so well that all the wee creatures who approached her were enchanted by her behavior. Every morning when she arose, she was given new dresses, new lace, new jewels. Though it was a pity she was so ugly, she who could not abide her looks began to think they were more appealing because of the great pains they took in dressing her. She rarely spent an hour without some pagods coming to visit and recounting to her the most curious and private events of the world: peace treaties, offensive and defensive alliances, lovers' quarrels and betrayals, unfaithful mistresses, distractions, reconciliations, disappointed heirs, matches broken off, old widows remarrying foolishly, treasures discovered, bankruptcies declared, fortunes made in a minute, favorites disgraced, office seekers, jealous husbands, coquettish wives, naughty children, ruined cities. In short, they told the princess everything under the sun to entertain her. She occasionally saw some pagods who were so corpulent and had such puffed-out cheeks that they were wonderful to behold. When she asked them why they were so fat, they answered, "Since we're not permitted to laugh or speak during our travels and are constantly witnessing all sorts of absurdities and the most intolerable follies, our inclination to laugh is so great that we swell up when we suppress it and cause what may properly be called risible dropsy. Then we cure ourselves as soon as we get home." The princess admired the good sense of the pagodine people, for we, too, might burst with laughter if we laughed at all the silly things we see every day.

Scarcely an evening passed without a performance of one of the best plays by Corneille or Molière. Balls were held frequently, and the smallest pagods danced on a tightrope in order to be better seen. What's more, the banquets in honor of the princess might have served for feasts on the most solemn occasions. They also brought her books of every description—serious, amusing, historical. And so the days passed like minutes, although to tell the truth, all these sprightly pagods seemed insufferably little to the princess. For instance, whenever she went out walking, she had to put some thirty or so into her pockets in order for them to keep up. It was the most amusing thing in the world to hear the chattering of their little voices, shriller than those of puppets in a show at the fair.

One night, when the princess was unable to fall asleep, she said to herself, "What's to become of me? Am I to remain here forever? My days are more pleasant than I could have dared to hope, yet my heart tells me something's missing. I don't know what it is, but I'm beginning to feel that this unvarying routine of amusements is rather insipid."

"Ah, Princess," a voice said, as if answering her thoughts, "isn't it your own fault? If you'd consent to love, you'd soon discover that you can abide with a lover for an eternity without wishing to leave. I speak not only of a palace but even of the most desolate spot."

"What pagodine addresses me?" the princess inquired. "What pernicious advice are you giving me? Why are you trying to disturb my peace of mind?"

"It is not a pagodine who forewarns you of what will sooner or later come to pass," the voice replied. "It's the unhappy ruler of this realm, who adores you, madam, and who can't tell you this without trembling."

"A king who adores me?" the princess replied. "Does this king have eyes, or is he blind? Doesn't he know that I'm the ugliest person in the world?"

"I've seen you, madam," the invisible being answered, "and have found you're not what you represent yourself to be. Whether it's for your person, merit, or misfortunes, I repeat: I adore you. But my feelings of respect and timidity oblige me to conceal myself."

"I'm indebted to you for that," the princess responded. "Alas, what would befall me if I were to love anyone?"

"You'd make a man who can't live without you into the happiest of beings," the voice said. "But he won't venture to appear before you without your permission."

"No, no," the princess said. "I wish to avoid seeing anything that might arouse my interest too strongly."

The voice fell silent, and the princess continued to ponder this incident for the rest of the night. No matter how strongly she vowed not to say the least word to anyone about it, she could not resist asking the pagods if their king had returned. They answered in the negative. Since this reply did not correspond in the least with what she had heard, she was quite disturbed. She continued making inquiries. Was their king young and handsome? They told her he was young, handsome, and very charming. She asked if they frequently received news about him.

They replied, "Every day."

"But," she added, "does he know that I reside in his palace?"

"Yes, madam," her attendants answered. "He knows everything that occurs here concerning you. He takes great interest in it, and every hour a courier is sent off to him with an account about you."

Lapsing into silence, she became far more thoughtful than she had ever been before.

Whenever she was alone, the voice spoke to her. Sometimes she was alarmed by it, but at others she was pleased, for nothing could be more polite than its manner of address. "Although I've decided never to love," the princess said, "and have every reason to protect my heart against an attachment that could only be fatal to it, I nevertheless confess to you that I yearn to see a king who has such strange tastes. If it's true that you love me, you're perhaps the only being in the world guilty of such weakness for a person so ugly."

"Think whatever you please, adorable princess," the voice replied. "I find that you have sufficient qualities to merit my affection. Nor do I conceal myself because I have strange tastes. Indeed, I have such sad reasons that if you knew them, you wouldn't be able to refrain from pitying me."

The princess urged him to explain himself, but the voice stopped speaking, and she heard only long, heavy sighs.

All these conversations made her very uneasy. Although her lover was unknown and invisible to her, he paid her a thousand attentions. Moreover, the beautiful place she inhabited led her to desire companions more suitable than the pagods. That had been the reason why she had begun feeling bored, and only the voice of her invisible admirer had the power to please her.

One very dark night she awoke to find somebody seated beside her. She thought it was the pagodine of pearls, who had more wit than the others and sometimes came to keep her company. The princess extended her arm to her, but the person seized her hand and pressed it to a pair of lips. Shedding a few tears on it, the unseen person was evidently too moved to speak. She was convinced it was the invisible monarch.

"What do you want of me?" she sighed. "How can I love you without knowing or seeing you?"

"Ah, madam," he replied, "why do you make conditions that thwart my desire to please you? I simply cannot reveal myself. The same wicked Magotine who's treated you so badly has condemned me to suffer for seven years. Five have already elapsed. There are two remaining, and you could relieve the bitterness of my punishment by allowing me to become your husband. You may think that I'm a rash fool, that I'm asking an absolute impossibility. But if you knew, madam, the depth of my feelings and the extent of my misfortunes, you wouldn't refuse this favor I ask of you."

As I have already mentioned, Laidronette had begun feeling bored, and she found that the invisible king certainly had all the intelligence she could wish for. So she was swayed by love, which she disguised to herself as pity, and replied that she needed a few days to consider his proposal.

The celebrations and concerts recommenced with increased splendor, and no songs were heard but those about marriage. Presents were continually brought to her that surpassed all that had ever been seen. The enamored voice assiduously wooed her as soon as it turned dark, and the princess retired at a earlier hour in order to have more time to listen to it. Finally, she consented to marry the invisible king and promised him that she would not attempt to look upon him until the full term of his penance had expired. "It's extremely important," the king said, "both for you and for me. Should you be imprudent and succumb to your curiosity, I'll have to begin serving my sentence all over again, and you'll have to share in my suffering. But if you can resist the evil advice that you will soon receive, you'll have the satisfaction of finding in me all that your heart desires. At the same time you'll regain the marvelous beauty that the malicious Magotine took from you."

Delighted by this new prospect, the princess vowed a thousand times that she would never indulge her curiosity without his permission. So the wedding took place without any pomp and fanfare, but the modesty of the ceremony affected their hearts not a whit.

Since all the pagods were eager to entertain their new queen, one of them brought her the history of Psyche, written in a charming style by one of the most popular authors of the day. She found many passages in it that paralleled her own adventures, and they aroused in her a strong desire to see her father, mother, sister, and brother-in-law. Nothing the king could say to her sufficed to quell this whim.

"The book you're reading reveals the terrible ordeals Psyche experienced. For mercy's sake, try to learn from her experiences and avoid them."

After she promised to be more than cautious, a ship manned by pagods and loaded with presents was sent with letters from Queen Laidronette to her mother, imploring her to come and pay a visit to her daughter in her own realm. (The pagods assigned this mission were permitted, on this one occasion, to speak in a foreign land.)

And in fact, the princess's disappearance had affected her relatives. They believed she had perished, and consequently her letters filled them with gladness. The queen, who was dying to see Laidronette again, did not lose a moment in departing with her other daughter and her son-in-law. The pagods, the only ones who knew the way to their kingdom, safely conducted the entire royal family, and when Laidronette saw them, she thought she would die from joy. Over and over she read the story of Psyche, to be completely on her guard regarding any questions that they might put to her and to make sure she would have the right answers. But the pains she took were all in vain—she made a hundred mistakes. Sometimes the king was with the army; sometimes he was ill and in no mood to see anyone; sometimes he was on a pilgrimage and at others hunting or fishing. In the end it seemed that the barbarous Magotine had unsettled her wits and doomed her to say nothing but nonsense.

Discussing the matter together, her mother and sister concluded that she was deceiving them and perhaps herself as well. With misguided zeal they told her what they thought and in the process skillfully plagued her mind with a thousand doubts and fears. After refusing for a long time to acknowledge the justice of their suspicions, she confessed at last that she had never seen her husband, but his conversation was so charming that just listening to him was enough to make her happy. "What's more," she told them, "he has only two more years to spend in this state of penance, and at the end of that time I shall not only be able to see him but become myself as beautiful as the orb of day."

"Oh, unfortunate creature!" the queen exclaimed. "What a devious trap they've set for you! How could you have been so naive as to listen to such tales? Your husband is a monster, and that's all there is to it, for all the pagods he rules are downright monkeys."

"I believe differently," Laidronette replied. "I think he's the god of love himself."

"What a delusion!" Princess Bellotte cried. "They told Psyche that she had married a monster, and she discovered that it was Cupid. You're positive that Cupid is your husband, and yet it's certain he's a monster. At the very least, put your mind to rest. Clear up the matter. It's easy enough to do."

This was what Bellotte had to say, and her husband was even more emphatic. The poor princess was so confused and disturbed that after having sent her family home loaded with presents that sufficiently repaid the magenta taffeta and the muff ribbon, she decided to catch a glimpse of her husband, come what may. Oh, fatal curiosity, which never improves in us despite a thousand dreadful examples, how dearly you are about to make this unfortunate princess pay! Thinking it a great pity not to imitate her predecessor, Psyche, she shone a lamp on their bed and gazed upon the invisible king so dear to her heart. When she saw, however, the horrid green serpent with his long, bristling mane instead of a tender Cupid, young, white, and fair, she let out the most frightful shrieks. He awoke in a fit of rage and despair.

"Cruel woman," he cried, "is this the reward for all the love I've given you?"

The princess did not hear a word. She had fainted from fright. Within seconds the serpent was far away. Upon hearing the uproar caused by this tragic scene, some pagods ran to their post, carried the princess to her couch, and did all they could to revive her. No one can possibly fathom Laidronette's depths of despair upon her regaining consciousness. How she reproached herself for the misfortune she had brought upon her husband! She loved him tenderly, but she abhorred his form and would have given half her life if she could have taken back what she had done.

These sad reflections were interrupted by several pagods, who entered her room with fear written on their faces. They came to warn her that several ships of puppets, with Magotine at their head, had entered the harbor without encountering any resistance. Puppets and pagods had been enemies for ages and had competed with each other in a thousand ways, for the puppets had always enjoyed the privilege of talking wherever they went—a privilege denied the pagods. Magotine was the queen of the puppets, and her hatred for the poor green serpent and the unfortunate Laidronette had prompted her to assemble her forces in order to torment the two of them just when their suffering was most acute.

This goal she easily accomplished because the princess was in such despair that although the pagods urged her to give the necessary orders, she refused, insisting that she knew nothing of the art of war. Nevertheless, she ordered them to convene all those pagods who had been in besieged cities or on the councils of the greatest commanders and told them to take the proper steps. Then she shut herself up in her room and regarded everything happening around her with utter indifference.

Magotine's general was that celebrated puppet Punch, and he knew his business well. He had a large body of wasps, mayflies, and butterflies in reserve, and they performed wonders against some lightly armed frogs and lizards. The latter had been in the pay of the pagods for many years and were, if truth be told, much more frightening in name than in action.

Magotine amused herself for some time by watching the combat. The pagods and pagodines outdid themselves in their efforts, but the fairy dissolved all their superb edifices with a stroke of her wand. The charming gardens, woods, meadows, fountains, were soon in ruins, and Queen Laidronette could not escape the sad fate of becoming the slave of the most malignant fairy that ever was or will be. Four or five hundred puppets forced her to go before Magotine.

"Madam," Punch said to the fairy, "here is the queen of the pagods, whom I have taken the liberty of bringing to you."

"I've known her a long time," Magotine said. "She was the cause of my being insulted on the day she was born, and I'll never forget it."

"Alas, madam," the queen said, "I believed you were sufficiently avenged. The gift of ugliness that you bestowed on me to such a supreme degree would have satisfied anyone less vindictive than you."

"Look how she argues," the fairy said. "Here is a learned doctor of a new sort. Your first job will be teaching philosophy to my ants. I want you to get ready to give them a lesson every day."

"How can I do it, madam?" the distressed queen replied. "I know nothing about philosophy, and even if I were well versed in it, your ants are probably not capable of understanding it."

"Well now, listen to this logician," exclaimed Magotine. "Very well, Queen. You won't teach them philosophy, but despite yourself you'll set for the entire world an example of patience that will be difficult to imitate."

Immediately thereafter, Laidronette was given a pair of iron shoes so small that she could fit only half her foot into each one. Compelled nevertheless to put them on, the poor queen could only weep in agony.

"Here's a spindle of spiderwebs," Magotine said. "I expect you to spin it as fine as your hair, and you have but two hours to do it."

"I've never spun, madam," the queen said. "But I'll try to obey you even though what you desire strikes me to be impossible."

She was immediately led deep into a dark grotto, and after they gave her some brown bread and a pitcher of water, they closed the entrance with a large rock. In trying to spin the filthy spiderwebs, she dropped her spindle a hundred times because it was much too heavy. Even though she patiently picked it up each time and began her work over again, it was always in vain. "Now I know exactly how bad my predicament is. I'm wholly at the mercy of the implacable Magotine, who's not satisfied with having deprived me of all my beauty but wants some pretext for killing me." She began to weep as she recalled the happiness she had enjoyed in the kingdom of Pagodia. Then she threw down her spindle and exclaimed, "Let Magotine come when she will! I can't do the impossible."

"Ah, Queen," a voice answered her. "Your indiscreet curiosity has caused you these tears, but it's difficult to watch those we love suffer. I have a friend whom I've never mentioned to you before. She's called the Fairy Protectrice, and I trust she'll be of great service to you."

All at once she heard three taps, and without seeing anyone, she found her web spun and wound into a skein. At the end of the two hours Magotine, who wanted to taunt her, had the rock rolled from the grotto mouth and entered it, followed by a large escort of puppets.

"Come, come, let us see the work of this idle hussy who doesn't know how to sew or spin."

"Madam," the queen said, "it's quite true I didn't know how, but I was obliged to learn."

When Magotine saw the extraordinary result, she took the skein of spiderweb and said, "Truly, you're too skillful. It would be a great pity not to keep you employed. Here, Queen, make me some nets with this thread strong enough to catch salmon."

"For mercy's sake!" the queen replied. "You see that it's barely strong enough to hold flies."

"You're a great casuist, my pretty friend," Magotine said, "but it won't help you a bit." She left the grotto, had the stone replaced at the entrance, and assured Laidronette that if the nets were not finished in two hours, she was a lost creature.

"Oh, Fairy Protectrice!" the queen exclaimed. "If it's true that my sorrows can move you to pity, please don't deny me your assistance."

Even as she spoke, the nets were made, to Laidronette's astonishment. With all her heart she thanked the friendly fairy who had granted her this favor, and it gave her pleasure to think that it must have been her husband who had provided her with such a friend. "Alas, green serpent," she said, "you're much too generous to continue loving me after the harm I've done you."

No reply was forthcoming, for at that moment, Magotine entered. She was nonplussed to find the nets finished. Indeed, they were so well made that the work could not have been done by common hands. "What?" she cried. "Do you have the audacity to maintain that it was you who wove these nets?"

"I have no friend in your court, madam," the queen said. "And even if I did, I'm so carefully guarded that it would be difficult for anyone to speak to me without your permission."

"Since you're so clever and skillful, you'll be of great use to me in my kingdom."

She immediately ordered her fleet to make ready the sails and all the puppets to prepare themselves to board. The queen she had heavily chained down, fearing that in some fit of despair she might fling herself overboard.

One night, when the unhappy princess was deploring her sad fate, she perceived by the light of the stars that the green serpent was silently approaching the ship.

"I'm always afraid of alarming you," he said, "and despite the reasons I have for not sparing you, you're extremely dear to me."

"Can you pardon my indiscreet curiosity?" she replied. "Would you be offended if I said:

> *Is it you? Is it you? Are you again near?*
> *My own royal serpent, so faithful and dear!*
> *May I hope to see my fond husband again?*
> *Oh, how I've suffered since we were parted then!*

The serpent replied as follows:

> *To hearts that love truly, to part causes pain,*
> *With hope even to whisper of meeting again.*
> *In Pluto's dark regions what torture above*
> *Our absence forever from those whom we love?*

Magotine was not one of those fairies who fall asleep, for the desire to do mischief kept her continually awake. Thus she did not fail to overhear the conversation between the serpent king and his wife. Flying like a Fury to interrupt it, she said, "Aha, you amuse yourselves with rhymes, do you? And you complain about your fate in bombastic tones? Truly, I'm delighted to hear it. Proserpine, who is my best friend, has promised to pay me if I lend her a poet. Not that there is a dearth of poets below, but she simply wants more. Green serpent, I command you to go finish your penance in the dark manor of the underworld. Give my regards to the gentle Proserpine!"

Uttering long hisses, the unfortunate serpent departed, leaving the queen in the depths of sorrow. "What crime have we committed against you, Magotine?" she exclaimed heatedly. "No sooner was I born than your infernal curse robbed me of my beauty and made me horrible. How can you accuse me of any crime when I wasn't even capable of using my mind at that time? I'm convinced that the unhappy king whom you've just sent to the infernal regions is as innocent as I was. But finish your work. Let me die this instant. It's the only favor I ask of you."

"You'd be too happy if I granted your request," Magotine said. "You must first draw water for me from the bottomless spring."

As soon as the ships had reached the kingdom of puppets, the cruel

Magotine took a millstone and tied it around the queen's neck, ordering her to climb to the top of a mountain that soared high above the clouds. Upon arriving there, she was to gather enough four-leaf clovers to fill a basket, descend into the depths of the next valley to draw the water of discretion in a pitcher with a hole in the bottom, and bring her enough to fill her large glass. The queen responded that it was impossible to obey: the millstone was more than ten times her own weight, and the pitcher with a hole in it could never hold the water she wished to drink. "Nay, I cannot be induced to attempt anything so impossible."

"If you don't," Magotine said, "rest assured that your green serpent will suffer for it."

This threat so frightened the queen that she tried to walk despite her handicap. But alas, the effort would have been for naught if the Fairy Protectrice, whom she invoked, had not come to her aid.

"Now you can see the just punishment for your fatal curiosity," the fairy said. "Blame no one but yourself for the condition to which Magotine has reduced you."

After saying this, she transported the queen to the top of the mountain. Terrible monsters that guarded the spot made supernatural efforts to defend it, but one tap of the Fairy Protectrice's wand made them gentler than lambs. Then she proceeded to fill the basket for her with four-leaf clovers.

Protectrice did not wait for the grateful queen to thank her, for to complete the mission, everything depended on her. She gave the queen a chariot drawn by two white canaries who spoke and whistled in a marvelous way. She told her to descend the mountain and fling her iron shoes at two giants armed with clubs who guarded the fountain. Once they were knocked unconscious, she had only to give her pitcher to the canaries, who would easily find the means to fill it with the water of discretion. "As soon as you have the water, wash your face with it, and you will become the most beautiful person in the world." She also advised her not to remain at the fountain, or to climb back up the hill, but to stop at a pleasant small grove she would find on her way. She could remain there for three years, since Magotine would merely suppose that she was either still trying to fill her pitcher with water or had fallen victim to one of the dangers during her journey.

Embracing the knees of the Fairy Protectrice, the queen thanked her a hundred times for the special favors she had granted her. "But, madam," the queen added, "neither the success I may achieve nor the beauty you promise me will give me the least pleasure until my serpent is transformed."

"That won't occur until you've spent three years in the mountain grove," the fairy said, "and until you've returned to Magotine with the four-leaf clovers and the water in the leaky pitcher."

The queen promised the Fairy Protectrice that she would scrupulously follow her instructions. "But, madam," she added, "must I spend three years without hearing any news of the serpent king?"

"You deserve never to hear anymore about him for as long as you live," the fairy responded. "Indeed, can anything be more terrible than having made him begin his penance all over again?"

The queen made no reply, but her silence and the tears flowing down her cheeks amply showed how much she was suffering. She got into her little chariot, and the canaries did as commanded. They conducted her to the bottom of the valley, where the giants guarded the fountain of discretion. She quickly took off her iron shoes and threw them at their heads. The moment the shoes hit them, they fell down lifeless like colossal statues. The canaries took the leaky pitcher and mended it with such marvelous skill that there was no sign of its having ever been broken.

The name given to the water made her eager to drink some. "It will make me more prudent than I've been," she said. "Alas, if I had possessed those qualities, I'd still be in the kingdom of Pagodia." After she had drunk a long draft of the water, she washed her face with some of it and became so very beautiful that she might have been mistaken for a goddess rather than a mortal.

The Fairy Protectrice immediately appeared and said, "You've just done something that pleases me very much. You knew that this water could embellish your mind as well as your person. I wanted to see which of the two you would prefer the most, and it was your mind. I praise you for it, and this act will shorten the term of your punishment by four years."

"Please don't reduce my sufferings," the queen replied. "I deserve them all. But comfort the green serpent, who doesn't deserve to suffer at all."

"I'll do everything in my power," the fairy said, embracing her. "But since you're now so beautiful, I want you to drop the name of Laidronette, which no longer suits you. You must be called Queen Discrète."

As she vanished, the queen found she had left a pair of dainty shoes that were so pretty and finely embroidered that she thought it almost a pity to wear them. Soon thereafter she got back into her little chariot with her pitcherful of water, and the canaries flew directly to the grove of the mountain.

Never was a spot as pleasant as this. Myrtle and orange trees intertwined their branches to form long arbors and bowers that the sun could not penetrate. A thousand brooks running from gently flowing springs brought a refreshing coolness to this beautiful abode. But most curious of all were the animals there, which gave the canaries the warmest welcome in the world.

"We thought you had deserted us," they said.

"The term of our penance is not over yet," the canaries replied. "But here is a queen whom the Fairy Protectrice has ordered us to bring you. Try to do all you can to amuse her."

She was immediately surrounded by all sorts of animals, who paid her their best compliments. "You shall be our queen," they said to her. "You shall have all our attention and respect."

"Where am I?" she exclaimed. "What supernatural power has enabled you to speak to me?"

One of the canaries whispered in her ear. "You should know, madam, that several fairies were distressed to see, on their travels, various persons fall into bad habits. At first they imagined that they needed merely to advise them to correct themselves, but their warnings were paid no heed. Eventually the fairies became quite upset and imposed punishments on them. Those who talked too much were changed into parrots, magpies, and hens. Lovers and their mistresses were transformed into pigeons, canaries, and lapdogs. Those who ridiculed their friends became monkeys. Gourmands were made into pigs and hotheads into lions. In short, the number of persons they punished was so great that this grove has become filled with them. Thus you'll find people with all sorts of qualities and dispositions here."

"From what you've just told me, my dear canary," the queen said, "I've reason to believe that you're here only because you loved too well."

"It's quite true, madam," the canary replied. "I'm the son of a Spanish grandee. Love in our country has such absolute power over our hearts that one cannot resist it without being charged with the crime of rebellion. An English ambassador arrived at the court. He had a daughter who was extremely beautiful but insufferably haughty and sardonic. In spite of all this, I was attracted to her. My love, though, was greeted with so much disdain that I lost all patience. One day, when she had exasperated me, a venerable old woman approached and reproached me for my weakness. Yet everything she said only made me more obstinate. When she perceived this, she became angry. 'I condemn you,' she said, 'to be a canary for three years and your mistress to be a wasp.' Instantly I felt an indescribable change come over me. Despite my affliction, I could not restrain myself from flying into the ambassador's garden to determine the fate of his daughter. No sooner had I arrived than I saw her approach in the form of a large wasp buzzing four times louder than all the others. I hovered around her with the devotion of a lover that nothing can destroy, but she tried several times to sting me. 'If you want to kill me, beautiful wasp,' I said, 'it's unnecessary to use your sting. You only have to command me to die, and I'll obey you.' The wasp did not reply but landed on some flowers that had to endure her bad temper.

"Overwhelmed by her contempt and the condition to which I was reduced, I flew away without caring where my wings would take me. I eventually arrived at one of the most beautiful cities in the universe, which they call Paris. Wearily, I flung myself on a tuft of large trees enclosed within some garden walls, and before I knew who had caught me, I found myself behind

the door of a cage painted green and ornamented with gold. The apartment
and its furniture were so magnificent that I was astounded. Soon a young lady
arrived. She caressed me and spoke to me so sweetly that I was charmed by
her. I did not live there long before learning whom her sweetheart was. I
witnessed this braggart's visits to her, and he was always in a rage because
nothing could satisfy him. He was always accusing her unjustly, and one time
he beat her until he left her for dead in the arms of her women. I was quite
upset at seeing her suffer this unworthy treatment, and what distressed me
even more was that the blows he dealt the lovely lady served only to increase
her affection.

"Night and day I wished that the fairies who had transformed me into
a canary would come and set to rights such ill-suited lovers. My wish was
eventually fulfilled. The fairies suddenly appeared in the apartment just as
the furious gentleman was beginning to make his usual commotion. They
reprimanded him severely and condemned him to become a wolf. The patient
being who had allowed him to beat her they turned into a sheep and sent to
the grove of the mountain. As for myself, I easily found a way to escape.
Since I wanted to see the various courts of Europe, I flew to Italy and fell
into the hands of a man who had frequent business in the city. Since he was
very jealous of his wife and did not want her to see anyone during his absence,
he took care to lock her up from morning until night, and I was given the
honor of amusing this lovely captive. However, she had other things to do
than to attend to me. A certain neighbor who had loved her for a long time
came to the top of the chimney in the evening and slid down it into the
room, looking blacker than a devil. The keys that the jealous husband kept
with him served only to keep his mind at ease. I constantly feared that some
terrible catastrophe would happen, when one day the fairies entered through
the keyhole and surprised the two lovers. 'Go and do penance!' the fairies
said, touching them with their wands. 'Let the chimney sweeper become a
squirrel and the lady an ape, for she is a cunning one. And your husband,
who is so fond of keeping the keys of his house, shall become a mastiff for
ten years.'

"It would take me too long to tell you all the various adventures I had,"
the canary said. "Sometimes I was obliged to visit the grove of the mountain,
and I rarely returned there without finding new animals, for the fairies were
always traveling and were continually upset by the countless faults of the
people they encountered. But during your residence here you'll have plenty
of time to entertain yourself by listening to the accounts of all the inhabitants'
adventures."

Several of them immediately offered to relate their stories whenever she
desired. She thanked them politely, but since she felt more inclined to med-
itate than to talk, she looked for a spot where she could be alone. As soon

as she found one, a little palace arose on it, and the most sumptuous banquet in the world was prepared for her. It consisted only of fruits, but they were of the rarest kind. They were brought to her by birds, and during her stay in the grove there was nothing she lacked.

Occasionally she was pleased by the most unique entertainments: lions danced with lambs; bears whispered tender things to doves; serpents relaxed with linnets; a butterfly courted a panther. In short, no amour was categorized according to species, for it mattered not that one was a tiger or another a sheep, but simply that they were people whom the fairies had chosen to punish for their faults.

They all loved Queen Discrète to the point of adoration, and everyone asked her to arbitrate their disputes. Her power was absolute in this tiny republic, and if she had not continually reproached herself for causing the green serpent's misfortunes, she might have accepted her own misfortune with some degree of patience. However, when she thought of the condition to which he was reduced, she could not forgive herself for her indiscreet curiosity.

Finally, the time came for her to leave the grove of the mountain, and she notified her escorts, the faithful canaries, who wished her a happy return. She left secretly during the night to avoid the farewells and lamentations, which would have cost her some tears, for she was touched by the friendship and respect that all these rational animals had shown her.

She did not forget the pitcher of discretion, the basket of four-leaf clovers, or the iron shoes. Just when Magotine believed her to be dead, she suddenly appeared before her, the millstone around her neck, the iron shoes on her feet, and the pitcher in her hand. Upon seeing her, the fairy uttered a loud cry. "Where have you come from?"

"Madam," the queen said, "I've spent three years drawing water into the broken pitcher, and I finally found the way to make it hold water."

Magotine burst into laughter, thinking of the exhaustion the poor queen must have experienced. But when she examined her more closely, she exclaimed, "What's this I see? Laidronette has become quite lovely! How did you get so beautiful?"

The queen informed her that she had washed herself with the water of discretion and that this miracle had been the result. At this news, Magotine dashed the pitcher to the ground. "Oh, you powers that defy me," she exclaimed, "I'll be revenged. Get your iron shoes ready," she said to the queen. "You must go to the underworld for me and demand the essence of long life from Proserpine. I'm always afraid of falling ill and perhaps dying. Once I have that antidote in my possession, I won't have any more cause for alarm. Take care, therefore, that you don't uncork the bottle or taste the liquor she gives you, or you'll reduce my portion."

The poor queen had never been so taken aback as she was by this order.

"Which way is it to the underworld?" she asked. "Can those who go there return? Alas, madam, won't you ever tire of persecuting me? Under what unfortunate star was I born? My sister is so much happier than I. Ah, the stars above are certainly unfair."

As she began to weep, Magotine exulted at her tears. She laughed loudly and cried, "Go! Go! Don't put off your departure a moment, for your journey promises to benefit me a great deal." Magotine gave her some old nuts and black bread in a bag, and with this handsome provision the poor queen started on her journey. She was determined, however, to dash her brains out against the first rock she saw, to put an end to her sorrows.

She wandered at random for some time, turning this way and that, thinking it most extraordinary to be sent like this to the underworld. When she became tired, she lay down at the foot of a tree and began to think of the poor serpent, forgetting all about her journey. Just then appeared the Fairy Protectrice, who said to her, "Don't you know, beautiful queen, that if you want to rescue your husband from the dark domain where he is being kept under Magotine's orders, you must seek the home of Proserpine?"

"I'd go much farther, if it were possible, madam," she replied, "but I don't know how to descend into that dark abode."

"Wait," said the Fairy Protectrice. "Here's a green branch. Strike the earth with it and repeat these lines clearly." The queen embraced the knees of her generous friend and then said after her:

> _You who can wrest from mighty Jove the thunder!_
> 　_Love, listen to my prayer!_
> 　_Come, save me from despair,_
> _And calm the pangs that rend my heart asunder!_
> _As I enter the realm of Tartarus, be my guide:_
> _Even in those dreary regions you hold sway._
> _It was for Proserpine, your subject, that Pluto sighed:_
> _So open the path to their throne and point the way._
> _A faithful husband from my arms they tear!_
> _My fate is harder than my heart can bear._
> 　_More than mortal is its pain,_
> 　_Yet for death it sighs in vain!_

No sooner had she finished this prayer than a young child more beautiful than anything we shall ever see appeared in the midst of a gold and azure cloud. He flew down to her feet, with a crown of flowers encircling his brow. The queen knew by his bow and arrows that it was Love. He addressed her in the following way:

I have heard your tender sighs
And for you have left the skies.
Love will chase your tears away
And try his best in every way.
Shortly shall your eyes be blest
With his sight you love the best.
Then the penance will be done,
And your foe will be overcome.

The queen was dazzled by the splendor that surrounded Love and delighted by his promises. Therefore, she exclaimed:

Earth, my voice obey!
Cupid's power is like my own.
Open for him and point the way
To Pluto's dark and gloomy throne!

The earth obeyed and opened her bosom. The queen went through a dark passage, in which she needed a guide as radiant as her protector, and finally reached the underworld. She dreaded meeting her husband there in the form of a serpent, but Love, who sometimes employs himself by doing good deeds for the unfortunate, had foreseen all that was to be foreseen: he had already arranged that the green serpent become what he was before his punishment. Powerful as Magotine was, alas, there was nothing she could do against Love.

The first object the queen's eyes encountered was her husband. She had never seen him in such a charming form, and he had never seen her as beautiful as she had become. Nevertheless, a presentiment, and perhaps Love, who made up the third in the party, caused each of them to guess who the other was. With extreme tenderness, the queen said to him:

I come to share your prison and your pain.
Though doomed no more the light of heaven to see,
Here let but love unite our hearts again.
No terrors these sad shades will have for me!

Carried away by his passion, the king replied to his wife in a way that demonstrated his ardor and pleasure. But Love, who is not fond of losing time, urged them to approach Proserpine. The queen offered Magotine's regards and asked her for the essence of long life. Proserpine immediately gave the queen a vial that was very badly corked in order to induce her to open it. Love, who is no novice, warned the queen against indulging a curiosity that would again be fatal to her. Quickly the king and queen left those dreary regions and returned to the light of day, with Love accompanying them. He led them back to Magotine and hid himself in their hearts so that she would not see him. His presence, however, inspired the fairy with such humane sentiments that she received these illustrious unfortunates graciously, although she knew not why. With a supernatural effort of generosity, she restored the kingdom of Pagodia to them, and they returned there immediately and spent the rest of their days in as much happiness as they had previously endured trouble and sorrow.

> Too oft is curiosity
>   The cause of fatal woe.
> A secret that may harmful be
>   Why should we seek to know?
> It is a weakness of womankind,
>   For witness the first created,
> From whom Pandora was designed
>   And Psyche imitated.
> Each one, despite a warning, on the same
>   Forbidden quest intent,
> Did bring about her misery and became
>   Its fatal instrument.
> Psyche's example failed to save
>   Poor Laidronette from erring.
> Like warning she was led to brave,
>   Like punishment incurring.
> Alas, for human common sense,
>   No tale, no caution, schools!
> The proverb says, Experience
>   Can make men wise, and even lazy fools.
> But when we're told, yet fail to listen
>   To the lessons of the past,
> I fear the proverb lies quite often,
>   Despite the shadows forward cast.

Translated by Jack Zipes

<h1 style="text-align:center">‹ Parslinette ›</h1>

CHARLOTTE-ROSE DE LA FORCE

After a long period of courtship, two young lovers were married, and nothing could equal their ardor. They lived content and happy, and to complete their felicity, the young wife became pregnant. They had strongly desired a child, and their wish was now fulfilled.

Within the vicinity of their house there lived a fairy, who was fond of cultivating a beautiful garden that had an abundance of all kinds of fruits, plants, and flowers. At the time of this story, parsley was very rare in that country, and the fairy had it brought from the Indies. Indeed, one could not find any parsley in that country except in her garden.

Now the expectant wife had a great desire to eat some parsley, and since she knew that it would be difficult to satisfy her wants because nobody was allowed in the fairy's garden, she became so sad and wretched that her husband's eyes could barely recognize her. He kept urging her to tell him what had brought about such a huge change not only in her spirits but in her body, and after resisting for some time, his wife finally confessed that she had a great desire to eat some parsley. Her husband sighed and was troubled by this desire, which would indeed be difficult to satisfy. Nevertheless, since nothing appears difficult if one is in love, he walked along the walls of the garden day and night to try to find a way to climb over. But it was impossible because they were so high.

Finally, one evening, he saw that one of the doors to the garden was open. He crept through quietly, and, happily, he grabbed a fistful of parsley as fast as he could. Then he left as he had entered and carried the loot to his wife, who ate the parsley with avidity. Two days later she felt a desire, even greater than before, to eat some more.

To be sure, the parsley must have been extremely delectable.

The poor husband returned to the garden many times afterward, but in vain. Eventually, however, his perseverance was rewarded, for he found the door to the garden open again. He entered and was extremely surprised to find the fairy herself, who snarled at him because he had been so audacious as to set foot in a place where admission was not simply granted to anyone who thought he could enter. The bewildered young man fell to his knees, begged her pardon, and told her that his wife would die if she could not eat a little parsley, for she was pregnant, and her desire was thus understandable and indeed forgivable.

"Well then," said the fairy, "I'll give you as much parsley as you like if you will give me your child when your wife gives birth."

After short deliberation, the husband promised, and he took as much parsley as he liked.

When the time arrived, the fairy went to be near the mother, who gave birth to a daughter, whom the fairy called Parslinette. She wrapped her in sheets of gold and sprinkled her face with some precious water that she had in a crystal vase, which immediately made her the most beautiful creature in the world. After performing these ceremonies to ensure the child's beauty, the fairy took little Parslinette to her home and raised her with the utmost care imaginable. Before Parslinette reached the age of twelve, she was a marvel to behold, and since the fairy was fully aware of what fate had in store for the child, she decided to shield her from her destiny.

In order to accomplish her goal, she used her magic to build a silver tower in the middle of a forest. This mysterious tower did not have a door by which one could enter it. There were large and beautiful apartments, so bright it seemed as if the sun penetrated them, but they actually received light through the fire of carbuncles that glistened in all the chambers. The fairy had splendidly provided everything necessary for life, and all the rarest things were gathered together in this place. Parslinette had only to open the drawers of her dressers, and she would find the most beautiful jewels. Her wardrobe was just as magnificent as that of the queens of Asia, and she always anticipated the latest fashion. Alone in this beautiful residence, she had nothing to desire other than some company. Except for that, all her desires were anticipated and fulfilled.

Needless to say, all the meals were as delicious as one could imagine, and I assure you that even though she did not know anyone except the fairy, she was not bored in her solitude. She read, painted, played musical instruments, and entertained herself with all the things that a girl knows how to do when she has been perfectly educated.

The fairy ordered her to sleep at the top of the tower, where there was but a single window, and after helping Parslinette get settled in this charming seclusion, she departed via this window and returned to her own home. Parslinette continued to amuse herself with a hundred different things, and even when she was merely searching around in her caskets, she felt fully occupied. Indeed, how many people would not like to feel as contented as she was!

The view from the window of the tower was the most beautiful in the world, for one could see the ocean at one side and at the other the vast forest, two sights that were rare and fascinating. Since Parslinette had a divine voice, she loved to sing aloud. This was one of the ways she entertained herself, especially during the hours when she awaited the arrival of the fairy, who came to see her often, calling from the bottom of the tower, "Parslinette, let your hair down so I can climb up."

One of Parslinette's most beautiful attributes was her hair, which was thirty yards long and did not incommode her at all. It was as blond as gold and braided with ribbons of all colors. And when she heard the fairy's voice, she would undo her hair and let it fall, and the fairy would climb up.

One day Parslinette was alone at her window, and she began to sing in her extraordinary way. Just at this very moment, a young prince happened to be hunting in the forest. He had lost the rest of his company in pursuit of a stag. Upon hearing such a pleasurable voice in this wilderness, he approached the tower and saw the young Parslinette. Her beauty moved him. Her voice captivated him. He went around that fateful tower twenty times, and when he could not find an entrance, he thought he would die of agony, for he had fallen in love. But since he was daring, he kept looking for a way to scale the tower.

As for Parslinette, she had become speechless. She gazed at this comely man for a long time, but all at once she withdrew from the window, for she remembered that she had heard there were men who could kill with their eyes, and this man's looks were very dangerous.

When she disappeared from his sight, the prince became despondent. He made inquiries in the nearest village, where he was told that a fairy had built that tower and locked up a young girl within. So he prowled around the tower every day, until finally he saw the fairy arrive and heard her say: "Parslinette, let your hair down so I can climb up." Immediately the beautiful girl began to undo her long plaits of hair, and soon after, the prince saw how

the fairy mounted by taking hold of the hair. To be sure, he was very surprised
by this unusual manner of making a visit.

The next day, he waited impatiently until nightfall. Then, sure that the
hour for the fairy to enter the tower had passed, he stood under Parslinette's
window and disguised his voice admirably to make it sound like the fairy's,
and he said, "Parslinette, let your hair down so I can climb up."

Poor Parslinette, deceived by the sound of this voice, ran to the window
and undid her beautiful hair. The prince climbed up, and when he was at
the top and looked at her through the window and saw how exquisite she
was up close, he thought he would fall back down to the bottom. Nevertheless,
he recovered his natural boldness and jumped into the chamber. Then he
bowed down before Parslinette and embraced her knees with ardor, to persuade
her of his love. But she was afraid. She cried, and the next moment she
trembled, and there was nothing that could calm her, for she found her heart
full of all the love she could possibly feel for this prince. Meanwhile he was
saying all the most beautiful things in the world to her, and she responded
with a confusion that gave the prince hope. Finally, he became bolder and
proposed to marry her right then and there, and she consented, though she
hardly knew what she was doing. Even so, she was able to complete the
ceremony.

Now the prince was happy, and Parslinette grew accustomed to loving
him. They saw each other every day, and in a short time she became pregnant.
Since she had no idea what her condition signified, she was upset. Although
the prince knew, he did not want to explain it to her for fear of frightening
her. But the fairy had come to see her, and no sooner did she look at her
than she understood the situation.

"Ah, how unfortunate for you!" she said. "You've made a great mistake,
and you're going to be punished for it. Fate has had its way, and all the
precautions I took were in vain."

After saying this, she asked Parslinette in an imperious tone to confess
all that had happened. And Parslinette complied, her eyes filled with tears.
The fairy did not appear to be moved by Parslinette's touching story of love,
and taking her by her hair, she cut off the precious braids. Then she made
Parslinette climb down the tower by means of the braids, and she followed
her to the bottom. There she covered Parslinette in a cloud that carried both
of them to the seaside and deposited them at a spot that was isolated but
pleasant enough. There were meadows, woods, a brook with fresh water, and
a small cabin made of foliage that was perpetually green. Inside there was a
bed made of shrubs, and beside it a basket filled with unusual biscuits that
were continually replenished. Such was the place to which the fairy had
conducted Parslinette, and there she left her after reproaching her severely.
These reproaches seemed to Parslinette a hundred times more cruel than her
own woes.

It was in this place that she gave birth to a little prince and a little princess, and it was in this place that she nursed them and had all the time in the world to cry about her misfortune.

But the fairy did not find this vengeance sufficient. She wanted to punish the prince as well. As soon as she left the wretched Parslinette, she returned to the top of the tower and began singing as Parslinette had done. The prince, fooled by this voice, asked Parslinette to lower her hair so that he could climb up in the accustomed way. The perfidious fairy, who had expressly cut Parslinette's hair for this purpose, let it down for him. When the poor prince appeared at the window, he was surprised and more than a little distressed not to find his mistress, and he searched for her with his eyes.

"You reckless fool!" the fairy said to him. "Your crime is immense. Your punishment will be terrible!"

But the prince shrugged off these menacing threats and responded, "Where is Parslinette?"

"She is no longer here for you!" the fairy replied.

And invoking her power, she caused the prince to throw himself from the top of the tower. Although his body should have broken into a thousand pieces when it reached the ground, the only agony he suffered was the loss of his sight.

The prince was horrified when he realized that he could no longer see. He remained for a time at the foot of the tower, groaning and repeating Parslinette's name a hundred times. Then he began groping about and tried to proceed as best he could. Slowly he gained confidence and could make his way in the dark world he now inhabited. For a long time he did not encounter anyone who could help and guide him. He nourished himself by eating herbs and roots that he found when he became hungry.

At the end of some years, he found himself one day more troubled by his lost love than usual. He lay under a tree and was consumed by sad reflection, a cruel preoccupation for someone who deserved a better fate. But suddenly he was wakened from his reverie by a beguiling voice. The first sounds pierced his heart, producing sweet feelings as of old.

"O gods!" he cried out. "It is Parslinette's voice!"

He was not mistaken. Without knowing it, he had reached her solitary spot. She was seated at the door of her cabin and singing a song about her unfortunate love. Her two children, more beautiful than the day was bright, were playing a little distance from her. They came upon the tree under which the prince was lying. No sooner did they see him than one and then the other ran and hugged him a thousand times.

"It's my father!" they said at one and the same time, and called their mother. In fact, they made such a cry that she came running, for she could not imagine what the matter could be. Until that moment, nothing had ever happened in that solitary place.

Imagine her surprise and joy when she recognized her dear husband! It is impossible to describe it. She uttered a piercing cry above him and quite naturally burst forth into tears. But what a miracle! No sooner had her precious tears fallen on the prince's eyes than he regained his full vision. Now he could see just as clearly as he had seen before, and all this was due to the tenderness of the impassioned Parslinette, who now took him into her arms. He responded with endless hugs, more than he had ever given her before.

It was touching indeed to see the handsome prince, the charming princess, and the lovely children express such ecstatic joy and tenderness. The rest of the day continued just as pleasant, and when night came, the little family finally realized it was time to eat. The prince took a biscuit, but it turned to stone. This miracle caused him to groan with terror. The poor children cried, and the distraught mother wanted at least to give them some water, but it changed into crystals. What a night! They believed this terrible time would last forever.

When the sun appeared, they arose and decided to gather herbs. But to their astonishment, the herbs turned to toads and venomous snakes. The most innocent birds became dragons, and vixens flew around them, glaring in a terrifying way.

"I can't go on like this!" the prince cried. "My dear Parslinette, I did not want to find you, only to lose you in such a terrible way."

"Let us die together, my dear prince," she responded, embracing him tenderly, "and let us make our enemies envious by the sweetness of our death."

The poor little children were in their arms, all of them so faint that they were on the brink of death. Who would not have been touched by the sight of this poor dying family? They needed a miracle.

Fortunately, the fairy was finally moved, and recalling at this moment all the tenderness she had once felt for the amiable Parslinette, she flew to the spot where they were, appearing in a glittering golden chariot covered with gems. She summoned the now fortunate lovers, each of them at one side of her, and after placing their delightful children on magnificent pillows at their feet, she transported them to the palace of the prince's father, the king. There was no end of rejoicing. The handsome prince, whom his parents had long believed lost, was received like a god, and he found himself quite content to be settled after the torments of his stormy life. Nothing in the world could be compared to the happiness in which he lived with his perfect wife.

> Oh, tender couples learn to view
> How advantageous it is always to be true.
> The pains, the work, the most burdensome worry,
> All this will eventually turn out quite sweet,

When the ardor is shared in a love complete.
Together there's nothing a couple can't do,
And fortune and fate will be overcome too.

Translated by Jack Zipes

‹ Prince Ahmed ›
and the Fairy Pari-Banou
ANTOINE GALLAND

here was once a sultan of the Indies, who reigned peacefully for a long time and reached a good old age. He had three virtuous sons, worthy of his dignity, and one niece, the chief ornament of his court. The eldest son was called Houssain, the second, Ali, the youngest, Ahmed. His niece was Nouronnihar, and she was the daughter of the sultan's favorite brother, whom he had endowed with great wealth on the occasion of his marriage. However, this brother had died young, and the sultan took charge of his niece's education and had her brought up in the palace with the three princes. Aside from her perfect beauty and fine figure, she was also highly intelligent and known for being irreproachably virtuous. When she reached the proper age, the sultan began considering an alliance for her with a neighboring prince, especially when he discovered that all three of his sons were passionately in love with her. Indeed, this discovery distressed him very much—not because his own plans for his niece would be dashed, but because he realized how difficult it would be to get the two younger sons to cede to the eldest.

He spoke to each of them alone and demonstrated the impossibility of one princess becoming the wife of three brothers, and the troubles they would create if they continued in their passionate inclinations. He did all he could to persuade them either to abide by a declaration of the princess in favor of one of them or to renounce their claims to her hand, marry some other woman of their choice, and let her marry a stranger. But since he found them equally obstinate, he sent for them again and said, "My sons, since I have not succeeded in convincing you of what I think would be for your own good and peace of mind, and since I am not inclined to use my authority to give the princess, your cousin, to one of you in preference over another, I have thought of an expedient which will please you all and preserve harmony among you, if you will but hear me and follow my advice: I propose that you are to travel separately to different countries so you will not meet one another. As you know, I'm intrigued by rare objects, and I promise my niece in marriage to whoever brings me the most extraordinary discovery. You yourselves will judge which one among you deserves the princess. I'll give each of you a sum suitable to your age for expenses, but you are not to use the money to buy equipment for a retinue, since this would reveal your royal status. The money should provide you with the opportunity to observe things that deserve attention in foreign lands so that you make the best of your voyage."

Since the three princes had always respected the wishes of the sultan, and since each one flattered himself that fortune would decide in his favor and enable him to gain the hand of Princess Nouronnihar, they indicated that they would obey him. Without delay, the sultan gave them the money and issued orders for travel preparations. Then the princes took leave of their father so that they could rest up for their journey. Early the next morning, they all left through the city gate, each well equipped and dressed like a merchant, and attended by a trusted officer disguised as a slave. They undertook the first day's travel together, until they reached a crossroads, where their paths would diverge in three different directions. While eating supper at an inn there, they agreed to meet a year later at this very same place. The first to arrive was to wait for the others, and the first two were to wait for the last, so that all three of them might return together to the sultan, just as they had left him. At dawn the next morning, after they had embraced and wished each other good luck, they mounted their horses, and each took a different road.

Prince Houssain, the eldest brother, who had heard of the grandeur, power, riches, and splendor of the kingdom of Bisnagar, headed toward the coast of the Indian Ocean. After traveling three months with different caravans, sometimes over deserts and barren mountains, and sometimes through very populous countries, the best cultivated and the most fertile on the face of the earth, he arrived at the capital city of Bisnagar, which was also the king's residence. Houssain took lodgings at a khan for foreign merchants and soon learned that there were four principal quarters of the city, where all kinds of merchants kept their shops. In the center of the city stood the king's vast palace, surrounded by three courts, whose gates were two miles distant from one another.

The prince could not help but admire everything that he saw in the quarter in which he was staying. It was immense, with numerous intersecting streets that were protected from the sun by canopies, and yet they were still very bright. The shops were all the same size and shape, and merchants with the same kinds of articles to sell gathered on the same street, which also housed the artisans. The majority of the shops were filled with merchandise, such as the finest cloth from different parts of India, bright-colored cloth painted with people, landscapes, trees, and flowers, silk and brocade from Persia and China, porcelain from China and Japan, rugs of all different sizes. All of this was so extraordinary that the prince did not know whether he should believe his eyes. Moreover, when he reached the shops of the gold-smiths and jewelers—the two professions were practiced by the same merchants—he became ecstatic upon seeing prodigious quantities of wrought gold and silver, and he was dazzled by the luster of the pearls, diamonds, rubies, emeralds, sapphires, and other precious stones that were being offered for sale. If he was astonished by such an enormous amount of wealth gathered on one single spot, he was even more stunned when he walked around and calculated the richness of the kingdom in general. Excluding the Brahmins and the guardians of the idols, who practiced a life that dismissed the vanity of the world, he could only see, no matter where he looked, men and women wearing necklaces, bracelets, and ornaments on their feet or legs, and the pearls and precious stones appeared to glisten even more because the people were very dark, so that their skin brought out the brightness of the gems. In addition, Prince Houssain noticed that there were an unusual number of vendors selling roses. It was apparent that the Indians loved this flower, since there was not one person who did not carry a bouquet of roses in the hand or wear a garland on the head, hardly a merchant who did not have many vases filled with roses in his shop. The entire quarter smelled totally of roses.

After having walked street by street through the quarter, the prince, overcome by impressions of so much wealth, needed a rest. A merchant, seeing how tired he was, politely invited him to sit down inside his shop. Houssain consented, and no sooner was he seated than he saw a vendor pass by with a carpet on his arm, which he was offering to sell for thirty purses of gold. The prince called to the vendor and examined the carpet. He told the vendor that he could not understand how such a small carpet, some six feet square, which was not particularly unusual in appearance or high in quality, could be set at so high a price.

The vendor, who assumed that Prince Houssain was a merchant, replied, "My lord, if this price appears excessive to you, your astonishment will be even greater when I tell you that I was ordered to raise the price to forty purses if I could find a person who could pay this sum."

"There must be something extraordinary about it," replied Prince Houssain, "which I don't know."

"You have guessed right, sir," replied the vendor. "Know that whoever sits on this carpet and makes a wish will instantly be transported wherever he desires."

The prince recalled the principal purpose of his voyage, and considering that he was supposed to bring his father some rare object that nobody had ever seen before, he judged that there was nothing that could satisfy the sultan more than this carpet.

"If the carpet does indeed possess this virtue," the prince said, "I shall not think forty purses too much to pay for it. In addition, I shall pay you a bonus with which I'm sure you will be content."

"Sir," replied the vendor, "I have told you the truth, and it will be easy to convince you now that you are willing to conclude the bargain at forty purses. Since I assume that you do not have the money here, and since it will be necessary for me to accompany you to fetch the purses, I shall ask permission of the master of this shop, and we shall go into the back room, where I shall spread the carpet. When we have both sat down, you will make the wish to be transported back to your lodgings. If we are not flown there immediately, there will be no bargain, and you won't be held to anything. As for the present, since it is generally the owner of this carpet who is supposed to compensate me for my work, it is extremely gracious of you to offer me a bonus, and I shall be in your debt."

The prince agreed to the proposal, and after obtaining the merchant's permission, they went into the back room, where they both sat down on the carpet. As soon as the prince made his wish to be transported back to his room at the khan, he instantaneously found himself and the vendor there. After this convincing proof of the carpet's virtue, he counted out forty purses of gold to the vendor and made him happy by giving him twenty additional pieces for himself.

In this manner Prince Houssain became the owner of the carpet and was overjoyed to have found at Bisnagar such a rare item, which would surely enable him to win Nouronnihar. Indeed, he considered it impossible that his younger brothers would find anything that would compare with what he had been so fortunate to obtain. Now he did not have to make his stay at Bisnagar very long, and he could be at the place of rendezvous that very day simply by sitting on the carpet. However, he would have been obliged to wait a long time there for his brothers. Therefore, curious to see the king of Bisnagar and his court and to discover more about the power, the laws, the customs, and the condition of the realm, he decided to spend several months satisfying his curiosity.

The custom of the king of Bisnagar was to hold an audience once a week for foreign merchants, and since the prince did not want to reveal who he was, it was in the disguise of a merchant that he saw the king many times.

Given the fact that the prince was handsome, immensely intelligent, and fully cultivated, he distinguished himself among the merchants who appeared before the king, and thus the king most often addressed himself to him when he wanted information about the sultan of the Indies, his power, his wealth, and the government of his empire.

During the other days of the week, the prince tried to see all that was most remarkable in the city and the surrounding area. Among the marvelous things he encountered was a temple made completely out of bronze. It was ten feet wide and fifteen high. The most beautiful thing in the temple was a man-sized idol made totally out of gold. The eyes were rubies, so skillfully set in place that they seemed to follow anyone who looked at them. The prince saw another remarkable idol in a village where a field of some ten acres was strewn with roses and other flowers pleasing to the eye. The entire space was surrounded by a wall that had been constructed to keep out the animals. In the middle of the field was a terrace, about the height of a man and made out of different stones joined in such a way that it appeared as if it were made out of a single stone. A domed temple was set in the middle of the terrace and was fifty feet in height, with a length of thirty feet and a width of twenty. And the red marble with which it was built was extremely polished. The arch of the dome was ornamented with three rows of paintings, colorful and tasteful, and the entire temple was generally filled with so many bas-reliefs and idols that there was no more space from top to bottom for anything more.

From evening to morning, there were superstitious ceremonies in this temple, which were followed by games, musical concerts, dances, songs, and feasts. The priests of the temples and the inhabitants of this place subsisted only on the offerings made by pilgrims who came from far and wide to fulfill their vows.

Prince Houssain was a spectator at a solemn festival that was celebrated every year at the court of Bisnagar. The governors of the provinces, the commanders of the fortresses, the judges of the cities, and the most famous of the Brahmins were all obligated to attend. One of them had traveled four months to get there. The gathering, composed of a countless mass of Indians, took place on a vast plain, where they produced an amazing spectacle, whatever one could see of it. In the middle of this plain there was a huge space closed on one side by a superb structure in the form of a scaffold nine stories high, supported by four columns and designated for the king, his court, and the foreigners whom he honored at his weekly audience. It was ornamented inside and furnished in magnificent style, and the outside had paintings of landscapes, animals, birds, insects, and even fleas and gnats, all rendered naturalistically. Other scaffolds, about four or five stories high and all painted more or less in the same way, formed the three other sides. And the unique thing about these scaffolds was that they could be turned and their decorations changed from time to time.

On each side of this place, at some distance from one another, there were a thousand elephants with sumptuous harnesses, each carrying a square tower made of gilded wood, and musicians and comedians occupied each tower. The trunks of the elephants, their ears, and the rest of their bodies were painted with vermilion and other colors in grotesque patterns.

Throughout the entire spectacle, aside from admiring the industriousness, skill, and inventive genius of the Indians, Prince Houssain was particularly taken by one of the elephants, the largest and most powerful of all, his four feet balanced on a post, his trunk swinging in the air in time to the music. Another elephant, just as powerful, stood at one end of a huge wooden log set up like a seesaw, and at the other end was an enormous rock to balance him, and as the Indians used their force to send him up and down, he kept time to the music with his swinging trunk and body.

Prince Houssain lingered long at the court and in the kingdom of Bisnagar, up to the last day of the year, when he was supposed to join his brothers at the place agreed upon for their meeting. And though he was fully satisfied with everything he saw, he had been continually preoccupied with the object of his love. Ever since he had acquired the magic carpet, the intensity of his feelings for the beauty and charms of Princess Nouronnihar increased day by day, and he felt certain that he would be much more tranquil as soon as he was close to her. After having paid for his lodgings at the khan, he told the concierge when he could come and fetch the key. Then the prince returned to his rooms, left the key on a table, spread the carpet on the floor, and sat down on it with the officer who had accompanied him. Finally, he collected his thoughts, and after having made the wish to be at the meeting place with his brothers, he perceived that he had arrived.

Prince Ali, the second brother, who had planned to travel to Persia in accordance with his father's wishes, joined a caravan after he had separated from his brothers and, in four months, arrived at Shiraz, the capital of that empire. Since he had made the acquaintance along the way with a number of merchants and pretended himself to be a seller of jewelry, he took lodgings with them in the same khan.

The next morning, while the merchants unpacked their wares, the prince, who was carrying with him just those things that were necessary for his own comfort, got dressed and was conducted to the market where they sold gems, silver and gold objects, brocade, silk, fine cloth, and other rare and precious items. This place, which was spacious and built solidly, was covered by a canopy, and the canopy was supported by huge pillars. The shops were set up around these pillars and along a wall, inside and outside, and the spot was known in Shiraz as the jewelers market. Prince Ali walked up and down the market on all sides, and he admired the riches and the prodigious quantity of valuable merchandise spread out before his eyes. As he regarded the vendors who passed back and forth with samples of several sorts of goods, he was surprised to see one who held in his hand an ivory tube about a foot long and an inch thick, which he was selling for thirty purses of gold. At first he thought the vendor was a bit crazy, and he approached a merchant standing in front of his shop and said, "Please tell me, my lord, that man over there who's selling the small ivory tube—is he in his right mind?"

"My lord," responded the merchant, "unless he's lost his mind since I saw him yesterday, I can assure you that he is our shrewdest vendor and the one who is most employed, since everyone has confidence in him, especially when it concerns something valuable. As for the tube that he's selling for thirty purses of gold, it must be worth it, and there must be something special about it that we can't see. He's going to pass by here again in a moment. We'll call him, and you can ask him yourself. Meanwhile sit down on my sofa and rest."

Prince Ali did not refuse the merchant's gracious offer, and a short time after he was seated, the vendor passed by. The merchant called his name and, when he approached, asked him in front of Prince Ali, "This gentleman seated here would like to know whether you're in your right mind, asking thirty purses of gold for an ivory tube that does not seem to be very valuable. I would be astonished myself at the price if I didn't know that you are a shrewd man."

Addressing Prince Ali, the vendor replied, "Sir, you are not the only person who thinks I'm a madman on account of this tube. But when I have told you about its power, you shall judge for yourself whether I'm mad or not. And I hope that you will make a bid like those to whom I've already shown the tube and who had just as bad an opinion of me as you. First of all, my lord"—and he handed the tube to the prince—"notice that it is covered by glass at each end. One looks through one end and wishes to behold something, and one sees it immediately."

"I am ready to make amends to your honor," Prince Ali replied, "if you are telling the truth." He was still holding the tube in his hands and examining the two lenses. "Show me how to use the tube," Ali continued, "so that I may know whether it works."

And the vendor showed him. Holding up the tube, he wished to see his father, and immediately he saw him, in perfect health, sitting on his throne in the middle of his council. Next, since there was nothing in the world so dear to him, after the sultan, as the princess Nouronnihar, he wished to see her, and he instantly beheld her laughing and in a gay mood, with her women about her. Prince Ali needed no other proof to persuade him that this tube was the most valuable article not only in the city of Shiraz but in the entire world. So he decided to negotiate with the vendor to buy it, for he would never find another such rare object to bring back from his voyage, either at Shiraz, even if he were to live there ten years, or elsewhere.

"I want to retract the derisive remarks I made about your sanity," Prince Ali said to the vendor. "But I believe that you will be fully satisfied with the remuneration that I am prepared to offer you for the tube. Since I'd be angry if someone other than myself bought the tube, tell me the minimum price that the owner has fixed so that I can purchase it. Then you won't have to run about anymore and tire yourself out. You have only to return with me to my lodgings, and I shall pay the sum you ask."

The vendor assured him on his word of honor that he had been given orders not to let the tube go for less than forty purses. Prince Ali believed him and took the vendor to the khan where he was staying. Giving him the gold, he became the owner of the tube. Prince Ali was delighted by his purchase, and he was convinced that, since his brothers would not be able to find anything as remarkable and rare as his tube, the princess Nouronnihar would be the reward of his exhausting travels. Now he thought about visiting the court of Persia without making his identity known and seeing whatever was unusual in Shiraz and the surrounding area, until the caravan with which he had come was ready to depart.

He satisfied his curiosity, and when the caravan was leaving, he rejoined the party of merchants. Once on their way, they had no accidents, troubles, or interruptions, and though the days were long and the journey was strenuous, they arrived happily at the appointed place. There he found Prince Houssain, and both waited for their younger brother.

Prince Ahmed had taken the road to Samarcand, and like his brothers, he went to the market the day after his arrival. After walking for a short time, he heard a vendor offering an artificial apple for sale at thirty-five purses. Prince Ahmed stopped the vendor and said to him, "Let me see that apple, and tell me what power or extraordinary virtue it has that you are selling it at such a high price."

"My lord," replied the vendor, placing it in his hand, "if you look at the mere outside of this apple, it is not very remarkable. But if you consider its power, its virtues, and the way one can use it to help people, you will say it is priceless and that he who possesses it is the owner of a great treasure. In truth, it cures anyone who becomes sick, no matter what the disease, whether it be a fever, a purpura, pleurisy, a plague, or any other kind of malady, and even if the sick person is dying, it will bring about an immediate recovery and restore him to perfect health. And it is extremely easy to provide the cure, for the only thing the sufferer has to do is to smell it."

"If you are to be believed," Prince Ahmed replied, "the virtues of this apple are wonderful, and it is indeed priceless. But how am I to know, an honest man like me, interested in purchasing the apple, whether you aren't pretending and exaggerating the high praises that you bestow on it?"

"Sire," replied the vendor, "the truth is known and can be verified by the whole city of Samarcand. You don't have to go very far. Ask all these merchants you see here, and listen to what they have to say. You'll find several of them who'll tell you that they would not be alive this very day if they had not made use of this excellent remedy. But let me tell you first how this apple was invented and why it has such virtues. Indeed, it is the fruit of long research undertaken by the most famous philosopher of this city. He dedicated his entire life to the study of plants and minerals and finally succeeded in inventing this apple that you see before you. In fact, he used it to bring about such surprising cures in this city that people will never forget him. However, his own death came so suddenly that he did not have the time to cure himself. This was not too long ago. Since he left his widow with very little money and since she must look after a number of children who are still quite young, she finally decided to sell the apple to make her family and herself more comfortable."

While the vendor was explaining the virtues of the artificial apple to Prince Ahmed, many people gathered around them and confirmed his account. One of the men said that he had a friend who was dangerously ill and on the point of death; he would offer an opportunity to show what the apple could do. Thereupon Prince Ahmed told the vendor that he would give him forty purses of gold for the apple if the sick person was cured by smelling it.

Since the vendor had been told to sell the apple at that price, he said to Prince Ahmed, "Come, sir. Let us go and conduct this test, and the apple will be yours. As I've told you, I'm confident that it will bring back this sick person from the gates of death, as it has always done in the past."

The test was a success, and after the prince paid the vendor forty purses, he received the apple. Then he waited eagerly for the first caravan to return to India and spent his time by seeing all that deserved his attention in and around Samarcand, such as the valley of Sogde, named after a river with the same name. The Arabs consider this valley one of the four paradises of the world because of the beauty of its countryside and of the gardens surrounding the palace, the richness of all kinds of fruit, and the delights it provides during the bountiful season.

Finally, Ahmed joined a caravan headed for India, and despite all the inconveniences of such a long journey, he arrived in perfect health at the inn where his brothers were waiting for him.

Prince Ali, who had arrived some time before his brother Ahmed, had asked Prince Houssain, who had been the first one there, how long he had been waiting there. When he learned that Houssain had been there almost three months, he replied, "You must not have gone very far."

"I'm not going to tell you anything right now about the place that I came from," answered Prince Houssain. "But I can assure you that it took me three months to get there."

"If that's the case," said Prince Ali, "then you didn't spend much time there."

"My brother," said Houssain, "you are wrong. I spent about four or five months there, and I could have stayed longer if I had wanted to."

"Unless you returned by flying," responded Ali, "I don't understand how you've been waiting here for three months, as you want me to believe."

"I'm telling you the truth," Prince Houssain added, "and I'll solve this riddle for you only when our brother, Prince Ahmed, arrives, and at the same time I'll tell you about the rare object I found during my journey. And you? What have you brought back? It must be something small, for I've noticed that you are carrying little more than you had at the beginning of your trip."

"And you, my brother?" replied Prince Ali. "Aside from a carpet on your sofa that you obviously purchased but does not look remarkable at all, I could say the same thing about you. But since it seems that you want to make a mystery out of the rare object that you've brought back with you, I'm sure that you will understand when I do the same with my acquisition."

In response, Prince Houssain declared, "I believe that the rare object that I have brought back with me is worth so much more than any other thing that exists in the world that it would be no trouble for me to show it to you and convince you that I am right. But it is appropriate for us to wait for Prince Ahmed to arrive. Then we can share our experiences in a spirit of benevolence while talking about how fortune has been kind to us."

Prince Ali did not want to continue the conversation or contest his brother's opinion about the worth of his rare object. He contented himself with the conviction that his tube was better than anything else could possibly be and agreed with his brother to wait until Prince Ahmed arrived before showing their rare objects.

Ahmed finally joined his brothers, and they all embraced tenderly. Then Prince Houssain, as the eldest, began to speak. "My brothers, we shall have plenty of time to converse about the unusual things we each experienced during our travels. Therefore, let us talk about what is most important to know. And since I am certain that you, like me, recall the principal reason for our journeys, let us not hide the rare objects that we have brought back. It is only fair that we judge these things in advance, and then we shall see which one our father will prefer. Since I have made this proposal and should set an example, I would like to tell you that the rare object that I have brought back from my journey to the kingdom of Bisnagar is the carpet on which I am sitting. As you can see, it seems a common, ordinary rug, but when I tell you about its power, I'm sure you will be more astonished than you've ever been before. In short, if you sit on this carpet, as I do now, and desire to be transported to a certain place, no matter how far, you will be there almost as you make the wish. I tested it before paying the forty purses of gold that it cost, and I don't regret what I paid for it. When I had fully satisfied my curiosity at the court of Bisnagar and wanted to return, I simply made use of this marvelous carpet to transport me here, along with my servant, who can tell you how long it took for us to come here. I shall be glad to let each one of you try the rug whenever you think it suitable. Now I'll wait to see if what you have brought can possibly compare with my carpet."

After Prince Houssain had finished praising his carpet, Prince Ali began speaking. "My brother," he said, "I must admit that your carpet is one of the most marvelous things imaginable if it has the power that you've just described, and I have no reason to doubt this. But you will admit that there are perhaps other things that are—I won't say more—at least as marvelous, in a different way. And in order to get you to agree," he continued, "let me show you this ivory tube, which, like your carpet, does not seem to deserve much attention as a rare object. However, I paid the exact price for this tube that you paid for your carpet, and I am just as content with my purchase as you. Since you are all fair men, I am sure that once you know its virtue and have tested it, you will agree that I haven't made a mistake. Just look through one end and make a wish, and you can see anything you want to see. I don't want you to take my word for this," Prince Ali added. "Here is the tube. See if I am telling the truth."

Prince Houssain took the ivory tube from Ali's hand, and when he put one end to his eye, as his brother had indicated, he decided to see how Princess Nouronnihar was faring. Ali and Ahmed were watching him and were extremely surprised to see his face suddenly become greatly distressed. Prince Houssain did not give them time to ask what the matter was, but cried out, "Alas! Brothers, we've undertook our difficult voyages to win the hand of the charming Princess Nouronnihar in vain! In a few moments that lovely princess will no longer be alive! I've just seen her in bed surrounded by her women and eunuchs, all of them in tears, awaiting her death. Take the tube and look for yourselves at the miserable state she is in, and let your tears flow with mine!"

Prince Ali took the ivory tube out of Houssain's hand, and after he had seen the same thing, he handed the tube to Ahmed, his grief apparent. Then Ahmed took it to behold the distressing sight that so concerned them all. When he saw that Nouronnihar's end was near, he turned to his brothers and said, "There is no doubt but that Princess Nouronnihar, whom we each love, is truly at death's door. But provided that we hurry and don't lose any time, we may still save her life."

Then the prince took the artificial apple out of a pocket and showed it to his brothers.

"This apple which you see," he said, "cost the same amount as the carpet and the ivory tube. The present occasion is a perfect opportunity to show you its marvelous power and to explain why I have no regrets that I paid forty purses of gold for it. But I don't want to hold you in suspense: its miraculous power will enable a sick person to regain life just by smelling the apple, no matter what the malady is. I have already tested it and can show you how it can work wonders with the Princess Nouronnihar herself, but we must hurry if we are to save her."

"If that be all," replied Prince Houssain, "we cannot hurry any faster than my carpet, which can convey us immediately to her chamber. Let's not lose any time! Come over here and sit down. It is large enough to hold the three of us. But let us first tell our servants to leave at once and meet us at the palace."

The order given, Ali and Ahmed sat next to Houssain, and since all had the same goal, they all made the same wish and were transported instantaneously to Princess Nouronnihar's chamber. The sudden appearance of the three princes alarmed the women and eunuchs gathered around the princess. They could not grasp what magic had brought the three men into the chamber, and since the eunuchs did not at first recognize them, they were ready to pounce on the princes as if they were people who had wandered into a part of the palace where they were not allowed to enter. But they soon perceived their error.

No sooner did Prince Ahmed realize that he was in Nouronnihar's chamber than he stepped off the carpet, went to her bedside, and put the apple to her nostrils. Moments later, the princess opened her eyes and turned her head from side to side, looking at the people gathered around her. She sat up then and asked to be dressed, just as if she had awakened out of a sound sleep. Soon thereafter her chambermaids informed her that it was due to her three cousins, and particularly to Prince Ahmed, that she had made the sudden recovery from her sickness. She immediately expressed her joy at seeing them and thanked them all, Prince Ahmed in particular. Since she wished to dress, the princes contented themselves with telling her how great a pleasure it was to have arrived in time to rescue her, and how ardently they wished her a long life.

The three brothers went to prostrate themselves at their father's feet and pay him their respects. The sultan had already been informed by the princess's chief eunuch of their unexpected arrival and of the princess's cure, and for both these joys he embraced them with deep emotion. After the usual compliments, each of the brothers presented the rare object that he had brought: Prince Houssain his carpet; Prince Ali his ivory tube; and Prince Ahmed his apple. Then each, according to his age, put his present into the sultan's hands and praised its virtues, and all three begged him to pronounce their fate, declaring which of them would receive the Princess Nouronnihar, as promised.

The sultan of the Indies had listened benevolently to all that the princes had to say in favor of their rare objects, but now he remained silent, meditating how best to respond. At last he broke the silence and uttered these words of wisdom: "My sons, I would choose one of you if I could do so with justice.

But think yourselves whether this is possible. It is true, Ahmed, that the princess was cured by your artificial apple. But let me ask you whether you could have managed to cure her if you had not discovered through Ali's ivory tube that she was in danger and if Houssain's carpet had not brought you to her so soon. Your tube, Ali, revealed to you and your brothers the illness of your cousin, but you must acknowledge that the discovery of her illness would have been useless without the apple and the carpet. As for you, Houssain, the princess would be an ingrate if she did not recognize that your carpet was essential in bringing about her cure. But you must also grant that it would not have been of much use if you had not known about her illness through Ali's tube, or if Ahmed had not employed his apple. Therefore, since the carpet, the ivory tube, and the artificial apple have proved that they have no advantage over each other but rather played an equal role in helping cure the princess, I cannot grant her to any one of you. The only fruit you have reaped from your travels is the glory of having equally contributed to the restoration of her health.

"Since this is the case," he added, "I must resort to other means to determine the choice I ought to make. Indeed, there is still enough time between now and nightfall. So I shall do it right away. I want each of you to fetch a bow and arrow. Then proceed to the field where the horses are exercised. I'll join you there and will give the princess Nouronnihar to whoever shoots the farthest.

"Now I have not forgotten that I ought to thank you for the gifts you have brought me. I have some very rare objects in my treasury, but none comes close to the uniqueness of the carpet, the ivory tube, and the artificial apple, all of which will augment and enrich my collection. I shall prize these three articles the most and shall look after them very carefully. Indeed, I intend to make use of their powers."

The three princes could not object to the sultan's decision, and after they were dismissed, each fetched a bow and arrow. They then proceeded to the designated field, followed by a large crowd of people. As soon as the sultan arrived, Prince Houssain took his bow and arrow and, as the eldest, shot first. Prince Ali shot next and far beyond him, and Prince Ahmed last of all, but it so happened that nobody saw where his arrow fell. They ran. They looked. But despite a far-flung search made by him and all the spectators, the arrow could not be found. It was evident that he had shot the farthest and thus deserved the princess. Yet since it was necessary to retrieve the arrow to determine the winner, the sultan decided in favor of Prince Ali and, in spite of Ahmed's objections, ordered preparations to be made for the wedding between Ali and Nouronnihar, which was celebrated a few days after with great splendor.

Prince Houssain refused to honor the feast with his presence. So passionate and deep were his feelings for Princess Nouronnihar, he did not have sufficient forbearance to witness her marriage to Prince Ali, who, he said, did not deserve her since he did not love her as completely as he himself. His grief was so great that he left the court and renounced all right of succession to the throne in order to turn dervish. He put himself under the discipline of a famous sheikh, who had gained a great reputation for his exemplary life and had established a dwelling place for himself and numerous disciples in a pleasant, secluded place.

It was for the same reasons that Prince Ahmed did not attend the wedding. Unlike his brother Houssain, however, he did not renounce the world. Since he did not understand how his arrow had become invisible, he left his retinue and decided to search for it. Indeed, he was determined to look in such a way that he would not be able to reproach himself later. So he returned to the spot where the three princes had gathered for the contest. From there he marched straight ahead, looking right and left. He walked extremely far but without success, so that eventually he began to think that his efforts were in vain. Yet he felt compelled to proceed, until he came to some high rocks, which completely prevented further progress. Extremely steep, they were situated in a barren spot about four miles from where he had begun his search.

As he approached the rocks, he perceived an arrow, which, astonishingly, was the same one he had shot. "That's mine," he said to himself, "but neither I, nor any living man, could shoot an arrow so far. There's something mysterious about this extraordinary phenomenon, and perhaps it will turn out to be to my advantage. It could be that fortune wants to make amends for depriving me of what I thought would be the greatest happiness of my life. Perhaps it has reserved a greater blessing as consolation."

With this in mind, the prince entered one of the craggy recesses of the rocks. Looking around him, he caught sight of an iron door, apparently locked. But he pushed against it, and the door opened, disclosing a staircase, which he descended, the arrow in his hand. At first he thought he was moving into darkness, but soon he was surrounded by light and beheld a magnificent palace, a remarkable edifice, which he did not have time to admire, for at that moment he beheld a majestic lady, whose beauty was heightened by the richness of the jewels that adorned her. She was attended by an entourage of ladies, all magnificently appareled.

As soon as Ahmed perceived the lady, he hastened to pay his respects, but she addressed him first and said, "Approach, Prince Ahmed, you are welcome."

The prince was astounded when he heard his name uttered in a realm he had never heard of, even though it bordered on his father's kingdom. Nor did he understand how he could be known by a lady whom he did not know. Finally, he threw himself at her feet and said, "Madam, I hope that my curiosity has not made me an intruder in your realm, and I want to thank you a thousand times for welcoming me. But without wanting to be impolite, may I ask how it's been possible that I've never made your acquaintance until today, even though we are close neighbors?"

"Prince," she said to him, "let us enter into this salon, and I shall answer your questions in a more comfortable atmosphere."

And the lady led Prince Ahmed into a marvelous salon. Its arch was embellished by gold and azure. The immense richness of the furnishings was such that he could only express his admiration by saying that he had never seen anything like it in his life.

"Nevertheless," she commented, "I can assure you that this room is the least beautiful one in my palace, and you will agree with me when you have seen the rest of the apartments." Then she sat down on a sofa, requesting that the prince sit down by her side. "Prince, you are surprised, you said, that I know you without your knowing me. But your surprise will cease when I tell you who I am. Undoubtedly you are aware, as your religion has instructed you, that the world is inhabited by jinns as well as people. Well, I am Pari-Banou, daughter of one of the most powerful and distinguished of these jinns. So you can understand that I know you, your father the sultan, your brothers, and the princess Nouronnihar. In fact, I know all about your love for the princess and your travels. The artificial apple that you bought at Samarcand, the carpet that Prince Houssain purchased at Bisnagar, and the tube that Prince Ali brought from Shiraz were all devised by me. That should suffice to make you understand that I know everything that concerns you. I want only to add that you seemed to me to be worthy of a happier fate than to marry Princess Nouronnihar, and that is why I caused your arrow to fly out of sight. It is in your power to take advantage of this favorable opportunity and achieve great happiness."

Since the fairy Pari-Banou uttered these last words with a different tone and at the same time looked tenderly at the prince, her eyes lowered and a modest blush on her cheeks, it was not difficult for him to comprehend what happiness she meant. Indeed, he realized that Princess Nouronnihar could no longer be his, and that the fairy Pari-Banou surpassed her infinitely in beauty, charms, and intelligence, and even in wealth, as indicated by the magnificence of the palace in which he found himself. And blessing the moment when he determined to go and look for the arrow a second time, he yielded to the new inclinations that inflamed his heart. "Madam," he replied, "if I were to have the good fortune of becoming your slave and the admirer of your ravishing charms, I should think myself the most fortunate of mortals. Pardon the boldness that has inspired me to request this honor, and please admit into your court a prince who will be totally devoted to you."

"Prince," answered the fairy, "since I have been mistress of my own life for a long time, with the consent of my parents, it is not as a slave that I want to admit you into my court but as the lord of all that belongs to me and can belong to me, conjointly upon your pledging your faith to me and agreeing to marry me. I hope that you do not find it offensive that I have made this proposal before you could have anticipated it. I have already told you that I am my own mistress. I should like to add that we have customs in the realm of fairies that are not common among ordinary women, who would find it dishonorable to make such a proposal. We, however, make such offers, and we expect an obligation in return."

Prince Ahmed, filled with gratitude, believed that the best way to respond to the fairy's speech was to approach her and kiss the bottom of her gown. Yet she did not give him the time to do this. Instead, she extended her hand, which he kissed, and, holding on to his, said, "Prince Ahmed, are you going to pledge yourself to me as I have pledged myself to you?"

"Ah, madam!" replied the prince, radiant with joy. "There's nothing in the world that could bring me greater pleasure than this! Yes, my empress, my queen, I shall pledge myself to you with all my heart and without reservation."

"If that is the case," responded the fairy, "you are my husband, and I am your wife. Our fairy marriages are contracted with no other ceremony but mutual consent. They are more constant and more indissoluble than those among humans in spite of all their ceremonies. Now, while my servants prepare our wedding feast for this evening, you shall be given a light meal, since you have had nothing to eat today. Then I shall show you the apartments of my palace, and you will be able to judge for yourself whether I told the truth when I said that this salon is the least beautiful in my palace."

Some of the fairy's ladies-in-waiting, who had entered the salon with her and had understood her intentions, left the room and soon returned with food and wine. After Prince Ahmed had eaten and drunk as much as he desired, the fairy Pari-Banou led him through the apartments of the palace, where he saw diamonds, rubies, emeralds, and all sorts of fine jewels mixed with agate, jasper, porphyry, and precious marble, along with the richest furniture, arranged in the most elegant manner. Everything was laid out with such astonishing profusion that the prince had to admit that there was nothing quite like it on the face of the earth.

"Prince," the fairy said to him, "if you so admire my palace, which truly has grand and beautiful features, what would you say about the palaces of the chiefs of our jinns, which are much more beautiful, spacious, and magnificent? I could also let you admire the beauty of my garden, but that will be for another time. Night is approaching, and it's time for our evening meal."

The fairy led Prince Ahmed to the only room in the palace that he had not seen, and it was just as splendid as all the other rooms. An infinite number of candles, scented with amber, were arranged so symmetrically that it was a pleasure to regard them. There was a large buffet table, covered with plates of gold that were made more precious by their artful design. Choirs of women, all ravishingly beautiful and richly dressed, began a vocal concert accompanied by all sorts of instruments, and they produced the most harmonious music that the prince had ever heard. Pari-Banou and Ahmed sat down at the table, and the fairy took great care to serve the prince delicious dishes, which she first named and then invited him to taste. The prince had never heard of these foods, and when he tasted them he found them so exquisite that he heaped praises on them and told her that they surpassed anything that he had ever eaten among humans. He said the same thing about the wine that came right before the dessert, which consisted of fruit, cakes, and other delights.

Finally, after dessert, the fairy Pari-Banou and Prince Ahmed got up from the table, which was immediately taken away, and sat down on a sofa that had soft needlework cushions of different colors made with great finesse. Numerous jinns and fairies entered the hall and began an astounding dance, which continued until the fairy and the prince arose. Then the jinns and the fairies left the hall, still dancing, and led the newly married couple up to the door of their chamber, where the nuptial bed had been prepared. When all arrived at the door, the company formed a row to let the bridal pair enter. Then the escort withdrew and allowed the couple time to be alone together.

The marriage celebration continued the next day, or, rather, the days that followed the marriage were a continual celebration that Pari-Banou, for whom everything was easy, knew how to diversify. She introduced new dishes at the feasts, new concerts, new dances, new plays, and new amusements, all so extraordinary that Prince Ahmed could never have imagined anything the like, even had he lived to be a thousand years old. The fairy's intention was not only to give the prince convincing proof of her love but to let him know that his father's court could offer him nothing more than he had here and that there was no place in the world where he could find the happiness he enjoyed with her. By these means she hoped that Ahmed would become completely attached to her and that they would never separate. Indeed, she succeeded perfectly in her plans: the love of Prince Ahmed did not diminish at all after he possessed her. In fact, it was no longer in his power to stop loving her, even if she herself would have stopped loving him.

At the end of six months, Prince Ahmed, who had always loved and honored his father, felt a great desire to find out how he was, and he could only satisfy this desire by visiting the sultan's court. Pari-Banou was alarmed that this might only be an excuse to leave her.

"What could I have done to have displeased you and make you ask for permission to leave me?" the fairy asked. "Is it possible that you have forgotten your pledge to me and that you no longer love me, the woman who loves you so passionately? You should be convinced of this by the signs of affection that I continually show you."

"My queen," replied the prince, "I am convinced that you love me, and I would be unworthy of your love if I did not reciprocate it. If you are offended by my request, I beg you to pardon me. There is nothing I would not be willing to do to make amends. I made this request not with any intention of displeasing you but out of respect for my father, who has undoubtedly been distressed by my long absence and must assume that I am dead. But since you do not approve of my going to comfort him, I shall deny myself the pleasure, because there is nothing I would not give up to please you."

Prince Ahmed was not pretending, for he loved her with all his heart. He stopped requesting permission to leave, and the fairy showed him how satisfied she was that he had submitted to her wishes. However, he managed to allude to the fine qualities of the sultan of the Indies from time to time and especially to the signs of affection that he, as son, was obliged to show his father. In doing this, he hoped that the fairy would finally consent to his visiting the sultan.

In fact, Prince Ahmed had judged the situation correctly. While celebrating wholeheartedly the marriage of Prince Ali and Princess Nouronnihar, the sultan had been deeply disturbed by the absence of his two sons. He was soon informed about Prince Houssain's resolve to forsake the world and about the place to which he had retreated. As a good father, he would have preferred his sons to have remained at court, close to him, especially since they had proved themselves worthy of his affection. Yet he could not disapprove of Houssain's desire to achieve the state of perfection, and thus he could stand his absence with patience. With regard to Ahmed, however, he made the most diligent search to obtain news about him and sent messengers to all the provinces of his dominions, with orders to the governors to detain Ahmed and compel him to return to the court. Despite all the pains he took, he had no success, and his distress increased instead of diminishing. Indeed, he often talked with his grand vizier about his sorrow.

"Vizier," he said, "you know that Ahmed is the one whom I always loved the most among my sons, and you are fully aware of the many efforts I have made to try to find him without success. The pain I feel is so excruciating that I shall succumb to it in the end unless you sympathize with me. If you have the least bit of consideration for my life, I implore you to help me with your advice."

The grand vizier, who was loyally attached to the sultan, just as he was zealous in his duties to the state, bethought himself of a way of providing solace for the sultan. He recalled having heard about a sorceress who could do marvelous things, and suggested to the sultan that she be brought to the court for consultation. The sultan consented, and after sending someone to search for her, the vizier himself brought her before the sultan, who addressed her as follows: "The sorrow which I have felt ever since the marriage of Prince Ali and Princess Nouronnihar occasioned the absence of Prince Ahmed is so well known and public that I am sure you know about it. Is it possible that through your art you can tell me what has become of him? Does he still live? Where is he? What is he doing? Can I hope to see him again?"

"Sire," she replied, "despite the skill I may have in my profession, I'm unable to satisfy your majesty's request on the spot. But if you'll give me till tomorrow, I shall respond to you then."

The sultan granted her request and promised to reward her generously if her response satisfied him.

The sorceress returned the next day, and the grand vizier presented her to the sultan a second time.

"Sire," she said, "despite all my efforts to use my art to discover what you want to know, I haven't been able to learn anything except that Prince Ahmed is alive. That is very certain, and you can rest assured about it. However, I cannot discover where he is."

The sultan had to content himself with this answer, which relieved somewhat his anxiety about the prince.

Meanwhile Prince Ahmed kept his promise to the fairy Pari-Banou, though his frequent references to his father made her aware that he still wanted to see the sultan. The prince's disinclination to displease her by again requesting permission to visit his father convinced her of his love for her. Indeed, he continued to show his affection in different ways. Gradually, her own feelings that it was unjust to make a son renounce his natural inclinations toward a father induced her to grant him what he ardently desired. "Prince," she said to him one day, "when you told me you wished to visit your father, I feared that it was a sign of your inconstancy and desire to abandon me. Only for that did I refuse to grant you permission. But now your actions and words have convinced me that your love is constant and strong, and I shall give you leave to depart. However, there is one condition: you must swear that your absence will not be long and you'll return as soon as possible. I know from the sincerity of your love that this will not be difficult for you."

"My queen," Prince Ahmed said, "I cherish your graciousness. But my words are insufficient thanks. I implore you to forgive my inadequacy. Believe me, I think the way you do and even more so. The pledge you demand from me will not cause me to suffer, and I'll give it to you all the more freely because it is impossible for me to live without you. Once I depart, you'll become aware of my eagerness to return to you, not for fear of breaking my pledge but because I'll be following my desire to live with you for my whole life."

"Prince," she said, "you may leave whenever you wish. But before you depart, don't think ill of me if I give you some advice about how you should conduct yourself during your journey. First of all, I don't think it would be appropriate if you speak to your father about our marriage, or about my powers and the place where you have now made your home. Please content yourself simply with informing him that you are happy and have everything you need, and that the only reason you have returned is to put to rest his fears with regard to your fate."

On the day that he was to set out, she summoned twenty horsemen, well mounted and equipped, to attend him. When everything was ready, Prince Ahmed took his leave of the fairy, embraced her, and assured her that he would return soon. He was brought a richly harnessed charger, as splendid and valuable as any in the sultan's stables. He mounted it with extraordinary grace, and after bidding the fairy a last adieu, he set forth on his journey.

Since the capital was not very far, Prince Ahmed arrived there very soon. The people received him with great acclamation and followed him to the palace. There the sultan embraced him with joy, complaining with fatherly tenderness about the distress the long absence had caused him.

"Your absence," he added, "was all the more painful because I had reason to fear that you might be driven to commit some desperate act after destiny had decided in favor of your brother Prince Ali."

"Sire," replied Prince Ahmed, "I shall let Your Majesty consider whether, after having lost Princess Nouronnihar, who had been the sole object of my desires, I could bring myself to witness the happiness of Prince Ali. If I had been capable of an indignity of this kind, what would the people at the court and in the city have thought about my love for her? What would your majesty yourself have thought? Love is a feeling that one cannot abandon when one wishes. It dominates you, it commands you, it does not give a true lover any time to use his reason. Your Majesty knows that when I shot my arrow, something extraordinary happened. And you know it was impossible to find it, either on the exercise field or on the plains. This symbolized my loss of a valuable object. Defeated by the caprice of fate, I did not lose any time in complaining uselessly. Instead, I wanted to calm my mind, disturbed by this incomprehensible event. Therefore, I left my attendants without their noticing and returned alone to look for the arrow. I looked high and low in the field where Houssain's and Ali's arrows had been found and where I imagined mine must have fallen, but in vain. However, I did not give up. I continued searching on a straight line in the same direction. I walked for more than a mile, looking right and left, and I even went out of the way to pick up the slightest thing that resembled an arrow. When I realized that it would have been impossible for an arrow to have gone so far, I asked myself whether I was crazy enough to believe that I had the strength to shoot an arrow so much farther than any of our old and famous archers ever did. I was about to abandon my search and return home, when I found myself drawn forward against my will. After going four miles, to the end of the field where it is bordered by rocks, I noticed an arrow. I ran, picked it up, and recognized it as the same one I had shot. Far from blaming Your Majesty for deciding in favor of my brother Ali, I was sure that there was some mystery behind what had happened, and in fact I did not have to go far to clear it up. But as to revealing this mystery, I beg that you will not be offended if I remain silent. I just hope that you will be satisfied to know from my own mouth that I am happy and content with my fate. The only thing that has troubled my happiness was the uneasiness I might have caused you because you didn't know what had become of me. I believed it was my duty to come here. Now you know why I've come. The only favor I ask is your permission to come occasionally to pay my respects and see how you fare."

"Son," the sultan answered, "I cannot refuse your request. However, I would have preferred it had you decided to live at my court. At least let me know how I can contact you when you cannot come yourself to tell me how you are, or where I can reach you if your presence is necessary."

"Sire," Prince Ahmed replied, "please allow me to be silent in regard to this one matter. I shall return as frequently as possible in accordance with my duties and shall be here whenever necessary."

"I don't wish to pry into your secrets," the sultan said. "I can only tell you that your presence has made me happier than I have been for a long time. You shall be welcome whenever you can come and visit me."

Prince Ahmed stayed only three days at his father's court, and early on the fourth he returned to the fairy Pari-Banou, who received him with great joy, since she had not expected him so soon. His diligence made her reproach herself once again for having suspected he might be disloyal and capable of breaking his solemn promise. She did not hide anything from the prince, and after revealing her weakness, she apologized to him. Thereafter the union of the two lovers was so perfect that they were always of the same mind.

A month after the prince's return, the fairy Pari-Banou became aware that after telling her all about his journey and his conversations with his father, the prince had stopped speaking about the sultan, as if he were no longer on this earth. She concluded that this was done out of consideration for her, and one day she took the opportunity to say, "Prince, have you forgotten all about your father? Don't you recall the promise that you made to him to see him from time to time? I haven't forgotten what you told me after your return, and I would like to remind you about it so that you won't wait very long to keep your promise."

"Madam," replied the prince in the same light tone as the fairy's, "since I don't feel guilty about forgetting my father, I would prefer to suffer your reproach, even though I don't deserve it, than to expose myself to a rejection if I were to try to obtain something from you that would cause you pain."

"Prince," she stated, "I no longer want you to take my feelings into consideration, nor should anything like this happen again. I don't think you should stay away from your father longer than a month. Go to him tomorrow, and after that, visit him each month without discussion by either of us. I readily consent to such an arrangement."

The next morning Prince Ahmed set out, attended as before but much more magnificently mounted, equipped, and dressed, and he was received by the sultan with the same joy and contentment. For several months he paid him visits and always with a more splendid equipage.

The sultan's councillors, who judged by his appearance that Prince Ahmed must be very powerful, abused their privileges and sought to make the sultan suspicious. They told him that he would be wise to find out where his son's retreat was, and where he obtained his funds to make such great expenditures, especially since the sultan had not granted him an allowance. The prince seemed to come to court only to let everyone see that he did not have need of the sultan's generosity to live as a prince. The councillors even claimed that his son might want to dethrone him.

The sultan found such an idea inconceivable. "You're mocking me," he said. "My son loves me, and I am certain of his loyalty. Nor can I remember ever having given him the slightest reason to be displeased with me."

One of his councillors responded, "Sire, though Your Majesty, who is generally most sound in his judgments, could not have done any better in resolving the matter among the three princes in regard to the marriage of Princess Nouronnihar, who knows whether Prince Ahmed has accepted his lot with the same resignation as Prince Houssain? Isn't it possible that he has imagined that he alone deserved her and that Your Majesty, instead of showing him preference over his siblings, has done him an injustice by allowing fate to decide the outcome?

"Your Majesty could say," added the malicious councillor, "that Prince Ahmed has not shown a sign of being malcontent, that our fears are foolish, that we are alarming ourselves too hastily, that we are wrong to arouse suspicions of this nature against a prince of royal blood. But, sire, perhaps these suspicions are well founded. Your Majesty knows well that in an affair as delicate and as important as this, one must side with the party that is the most certain. Your Majesty must realize that the prince may be deceiving you, and the danger is all the greater since it is obvious that the prince does not live all that far from the capital. Had Your Majesty paid as much attention as we have, you would have observed that every time he arrives, he and his men are fresh, their garments and the saddle cloths of the horses, along with their ornaments, have the same radiance as if they had just been finished and delivered from the hands of the craftsman. The horses themselves seem as if they had just come from a short promenade. The signs that Prince Ahmed lives nearby are so evident that we believe it would have been to neglect our duty if we had not humbly brought everything to your attention, for your own good and for the welfare of your realm."

To the councillor's long speech, the sultan replied, "No matter what you say, I don't believe that my son is as wicked as you would like me to believe. Nevertheless, I'm obliged to you for your advice, and I know that your intentions have been good."

The sultan of the Indies did not let his councillors know that their words had made a great impression on his mind. However, he did not permit himself to get alarmed by it, and he decided to have Prince Ahmed's steps watched. At the prince's next visit, the sultan had the sorceress come to him through a secret door in the palace, and she was led into his private room, where he said to her, "You told me the truth when you informed me that my son Ahmed wasn't dead, and I am much obliged to you. Now I want you to do another favor for me. Ever since I've found him again, I have not been able to ascertain where he lives, and I haven't wanted to embarrass him by prying into his secret. But I believe that you are clever enough to put an end to my curiosity without the knowledge of him or anyone at my court. The prince is accustomed to leaving the court without informing me or anyone else. Don't lose any time. Go right now and watch him; stay on his trail so that you find out where his retreat is, and bring me what I want to know."

Leaving the palace, the sorceress went to the spot where, according to the sultan's account, Prince Ahmed had found his arrow, and she hid herself behind the rocks. The next morning Prince Ahmed set out at daybreak, without bidding adieu to anyone at court. From her place of concealment, the sorceress observed him and his attendants until she suddenly lost sight of them in the rocks. The steepness of the rocks formed an insurmountable barrier to men, whether on horseback or on foot, and the sorceress surmised that the prince and his retinue had suddenly withdrawn into a cave or some subterraneous place where the jinns and fairies make their abode. Coming out of her hiding place, she explored the spot where she had lost sight of them. She proceeded until the path broke off into different directions. Looking all around her, she went back and forth many times. Despite her careful search, she did not discover a single opening into a cave; nor did she see the iron door that had not escaped Prince Ahmed's eyes, for in fact this door was visible only to certain men, who were welcome in the presence of the fairy Pari-Banou. Realizing that all her endeavors were in vain, the sorceress had to content herself with what she had just discovered, and she returned to the sultan. After recounting what she had done, she added, "As Your Majesty can understand from what I've just said, it will not be difficult for me to provide you with the information that you desire regarding Prince Ahmed's behavior. I shall not tell you at present what I think. I would prefer to tell you everything when I am more certain. In order to succeed, I only ask for more time and your permission to do what I want without my informing you of the means by which I shall accomplish my task."

The sultan replied, "You are in command of the situation. Go and do what you judge is appropriate. I shall await the results patiently."

To encourage her, he gave the sorceress a very valuable diamond and said that it was only part of the ample reward she would receive when she had completed her important task.

A day or two before Ahmed's next regular monthly trip, the sorceress went to the foot of the rock where she had lost sight of him and his attendants, and she waited there to carry out the plan she had conceived.

The next morning, when Prince Ahmed went out as usual through the iron gate with his attendants to begin his journey to the capital, he saw an unknown woman lying with her head on a rock and moaning as if she were in great pain. He took pity on her, turned his horse, and asked what he could do to assuage her pain. The cunning sorceress looked at the prince in a way that would increase his pity for her. Then she responded brokenly, as if she could hardly breathe, and said that she had left her home to go to the city, and along the way had been attacked by a violent fever. It had left her without strength, so that she had been forced to stop and rest where he had found her, far from any village and consequently without hope of being saved.

"Good woman," replied Prince Ahmed, "you are not as far from help as you believe. I shall take you to a place where you will be cared for and cured as rapidly as possible. Rise and let one of my men take you behind him."

The sorceress did not refuse the kind offer. She feigned attempts to rise, pretending that the severity of her illness prevented her. Two of the prince's attendants dismounted, helped her up, and placed her behind one of their companions. Then they mounted their horses and followed the prince, who turned back to the iron gate, which was opened by one of his retinue. Coming into the exterior court of the fairy's palace without dismounting, he sent one of the servants to tell Pari-Banou that he wanted to speak with her. When the fairy appeared, concerned that the prince had returned, Ahmed did not give her any time to ask the cause. "My princess," he said, pointing to the sorceress, whom two of his men were supporting on the ground, "I'd like you to have pity on this good woman, as I have. Right after I departed, I found her lying in her present deplorable condition, and I've promised to help her. I'd like to put her in your care and am convinced that you will not abandon her, not only because of my request but because of your own inclinations."

The fairy, who had her eyes fixed on the deceitful sorceress as the prince spoke, ordered two of her ladies to take her into an apartment of the palace and to care for her as they would their mistress. Next the fairy went up to Prince Ahmed and whispered into his ear, "Prince, I praise you for your compassion, which is worthy of you and your birth, and it will please me to carry out your good intentions. But permit me to tell you that I fear they will be poorly rewarded. It seems to me that this woman is not as sick as she pretends to be. I am quite certain that she has been sent here expressly to cause you trouble. But do not fear. No matter what she may be plotting against you, I'll save you from all the snares. Go and continue your journey."

The fairy's words did not alarm Prince Ahmed, and he replied, "My princess, since I don't recall that I've ever harmed anyone, and since I don't intend to, I don't believe that anyone would have a reason to harm me. No matter what, I won't stop helping people and doing good whenever I have the occasion."

So Prince Ahmed took leave of the fairy and set forth again for his father's capital, where he was greeted as usual by the sultan, who tried to hide the suspicions his councillors had planted in him.

In the meantime, the fairy's two ladies had conducted the sorceress into an elegant and richly furnished apartment. They sat her down on a sofa, supported by a cushion of gold brocade, while they prepared a bed for her. This bed had a satin mattress embroidered in silk, sheets of finest linen, and a cover and canopy of gold. When they were done, they helped her lie down in the bed, for the sorceress still pretended that the fever debilitated her. One of the ladies left the room and returned with an extraordinarily fine china cup full of a certain liquor. She offered it to the sorceress while the other lady helped her sit up.

"Drink this," said the lady with the cup. "It is water from the fountain of lions and a powerful remedy for any kind of fever that exists. You will feel its effect in less than an hour."

The sorceress pretended to an insurmountable repugnance against this potion. Finally, she took the cup and drank, shaking her head as if in a fit. When she lay down again, the two ladies covered her with care.

"Rest well," said the one who had brought the potion, "and sleep if you desire. We are going to leave you alone, and we hope to find you perfectly cured when we return in about an hour."

The sorceress, who had come only to discover the retreat of Prince Ahmed, would of course have liked to say that she had been cured on the spot, so that she could return to the sultan and inform him about her mission. But since they had told her that the potion did not take effect right away, she was obliged to wait for the return of the two ladies.

The women came back in an hour's time and found the sorceress on the sofa, dressed and sitting up. In fact, she stood and cried out, "Oh, what a remarkable potion! It took effect much sooner than you told me it would, and I've been waiting for you impatiently for some time, to ask you to lead me to your charitable mistress so I can thank her for her kindness. I'm eternally obliged to her, and since I'm now cured, as if by a miracle, I should like to continue my journey."

Telling the sorceress how glad they were that she had been cured so soon, the two women led her through several apartments, even more superb than the one she had inhabited, into a large hall, the most magnificently furnished of the entire palace.

Pari-Banou was seated in this hall upon a massive gold throne ornamented with diamonds, rubies, and pearls of an enormous size, and on her right and left she was attended by a great number of fairies, all beautifully charming and richly dressed. The sorceress was not only dazzled but so thunderstruck that after she had prostrated herself before the throne, she could not open her lips to thank the fairy as she had wanted to do. However, Pari-Banou saved her the trouble and said, "Good woman, I am glad that I had the opportunity to help you, and that you are able to continue your journey. I shall not detain you, but perhaps you would like to see my palace. Follow my ladies, and they will show it to you."

The old woman prostrated herself a second time, with her head on the carpet that covered the foot of the throne, and she took her leave without having the strength or the courage to say a single word. Accompanied by two fairies, she was shown, to her astonishment and continual exclamations, the same apartments, one by one, the same wealth, and the same magnificence that the fairy Pari-Banou had shown Prince Ahmed the first time he had been with her, as we know. But what awed the sorceress most was that after she had toured the entire palace, the two fairies told her that she had seen but a small example of the grandeur and the power of their mistress and that in the vast expanse of her realm she had countless palaces, each with a different architecture, which were no less superb and magnificent than the present one. The fairies conducted her to the iron gate through which Prince Ahmed had brought her, and after she said farewell to them and thanked them for their trouble, they opened it and wished her a pleasant journey.

After the sorceress had gone a little way, she turned to look at the door so that she might recognize it again, but it was all in vain, for it was invisible to all women, as we have seen. Except for this one circumstance, she was quite satisfied with her success. After she had arrived in the capital, she took the back alleys and entered the palace via the secret door. Informed that she was in the palace, the sultan had her come to him. Her visage was somber, and, assuming that she had not succeeded, he said to her, "Looking at you, I judge that your journey has been in vain and that you do not bring me the information I'd been expecting."

"Sire," responded the sorceress, "if your majesty will permit me, it is not by my visage that you should judge whether I've carried out the orders with which you've honored me. Judge me instead by the sincere report I shall give of everything that I've done and has happened to me, not forgetting anything so that I can render myself worthy of your approbation. What you see as somber in my countenance comes from another cause than that of not having succeeded in what I hope will make your majesty content. I shall not tell you this cause. The story that I have to tell you will explain everything, if you will bear with me."

So then the sorceress told the sultan of the Indies about how she had pretended to be sick and how the prince, upon leaving the cave, was touched with compassion and led her into the subterranean spot, where he himself presented and entrusted her to the most beautiful fairy in the universe and asked her aid in bringing the sorceress back to sound health. She explained to him how, kindly, the fairy immediately ordered two of her women to accompany her, take charge of her, and not to leave her until she had regained her health. All this made her realize that the fairy would not have condescended had she not been married to Prince Ahmed. The sorceress did not fail to describe her surprise at the fairy's palace, which she believed to be the most superb in the world. With regard to the majesty of the fairy, the sorceress described how she sat on a glistening throne of precious stones whose wealth surpassed anything in the sultan's kingdom. Finally, she told him about the other immensely rich things that she saw in the palace, asserting that their value was beyond estimation. When the sorceress came to the end of her report, she said, "What does Your Majesty think of the fairy's incredible wealth? Perhaps you'll say that you admire her and rejoice at the good fortune of your son, who shares everything in common with her. For my part, sire, pardon me if I take the liberty of telling you what I think about the matter. I shudder when I consider the bad things that might happen to you, and that is the reason I was not able to conceal the somber visage that you perceived. I would want to believe that your son, Prince Ahmed, is not himself capable, due to his natural goodness, of plotting anything against Your Majesty. But who can say whether the fairy might not use her charms and caresses to arouse your son perniciously against his father so that he may want to dethrone you and seize the crown of the Indies? It is up to Your Majesty to pay careful attention to an affair of such great importance."

The sultan refused to let himself be swayed by the sorceress's words, and said, "I thank you for your troubles and your well-intended advice. I recognize how important the affair is, and it appears to me that I cannot deliberate about it without taking counsel."

Since the sultan had been consulting with his courtiers when he had been informed of the sorceress's arrival, he ordered her now to follow him into the council chamber. First informing his councillors of all that he had learned and of the possibility of the fairy's malign influence over his son, he asked them what they would do to prevent such an occurrence.

One of his councillors spoke for all the rest and said, "Sire, since Your Majesty knows who it is that might commit this crime and since he is in Your Majesty's power, you should not hesitate. I don't say that you should take his life, for that would cause an uproar, but the least you should do is put him in a secure prison for the rest of his life."

The other councillors unanimously praised this advice. Then the sorceress, who found it too extreme, asked permission to speak and said, "Sire, I believe that your councillors' zeal for Your Majesty's interests has made them too insistent on arresting your son. Let me ask them to consider the fact that you must arrest his retinue along with your son. But they are all jinns. Won't they use their powers to make themselves invisible and return to the fairy, whom they will inform of her husband's imprisonment? And do you suppose that she will let this insult go unavenged? But if by some other, less striking means, the sultan would be able to protect himself from whatever evil designs Prince Ahmed may have, without his majesty's glory being compromised or without his being suspected of an evil intention, wouldn't it be more appropriate to put such a plan into practice? I believe, Your Majesty, that you could turn the prince's alliance to your advantage, especially since jinns and fairies can do things beyond the comprehension of mortals. All you have to do is impose some hard task on him, which will benefit you if he performs it and, if he fails, will give you an honorable pretext for making accusations against him. For instance, every time Your Majesty wants to undertake an expedition, you are obliged to spend a prodigious sum of money, not only for tents for yourself and your army but also for camels, mules, and other beasts of burden to carry all this equipment. Couldn't you request the prince, considering the great credit he has with the fairy, to procure a tent for you that can be carried in a man's hand and yet be large enough to shelter your entire army? This will be all to your advantage. If the prince brings the tent, there are many other requests of this kind that you can make, but in the end he'll have to succumb because of the difficulties or because it will be impossible to do, no matter how inventive may be the fairy whose enchantment has taken him away from you. As a result, he will feel too ashamed to appear at your court, and he will be constrained to spend his days with the fairy, cut off from contact with the rest of the world. Then Your Majesty will not have to fear his plots, and nobody will be able to reproach you for taking an odious action such as confining a son of your own blood in a prison for the rest of his life."

When the sorceress had finished speaking, the sultan asked his councillors if they had anything better to propose. They all kept silent, and he decided to follow her advice, since it seemed the most reasonable and, moreover, corresponded to the gentleness with which he had always governed his realm. So the next day, when the prince came to his father, the sultan said to him, "My son, when you returned and relieved the long sadness your absence had provoked in me, you made a mystery out of the abode which you have made into your retreat. And satisfied just to see you again and to learn that you were happy with your lot, I did not want to pry into your secret, especially when I understood that you did not want me to. I don't know what reason you had for doing such a foolish thing to your father, who has always, just as he is doing now, given you proof of how much he wants you to be happy. I know what this happiness is, and I wish to rejoice in it with you. So I want you to know that I approve of your marriage to a fairy, who, I have learned, is worthy of your love and is just as rich as she is powerful. Influential as I am, it still would have been impossible for me to arrange such a marriage for you. I ask only that you continue to live with me on good terms, as you have always done, but also request that you make use of your influence with your wife to do a great service for me. You know how expensive it is, not to mention how difficult, every time I go on an expedition, to provide mules, camels, and other beasts of burden to carry my tents and the tents of my generals, officers, and soldiers. Well, I am convinced that you could easily procure from your wife—especially if you tell her that it would be for me— a tent that might be carried in a man's hand and that would protect my entire army. Just because this thing is difficult should not deter you. Everyone knows that fairies are powerful and can do extraordinary things."

Prince Ahmed would not have expected his father to make such a request, which was not only difficult but probably impossible. Though he was fully aware that the power of jinns and fairies was great, he doubted that his wife could furnish a tent such as his father had asked for. Furthermore, up till then he had not demanded a single thing from Pari-Banou, for he had been content with the constant signs of affection she had shown him, and his only desire was to keep himself in her good graces. Therefore, he did not know what to say to his father.

"Sire," he replied, "if I made a mystery out of what happened to me after I had found my arrow, it was because it seemed unnecessary to inform you. I don't know how you found out about it. And I don't deny that what you discovered is true. I am the husband of a fairy, whom I love, and I'm convinced that she loves me as well. But with regard to the influence Your Majesty believes I have on her, I can't say anything. It is not only that I haven't put her to the test, but also that I've never had such a thought, and I would very much prefer that Your Majesty dispense with such an enterprise and let me enjoy the happiness of loving and being loved. But what a father requests is a command for a son, who should consider it a duty to obey his father in all things. Despite myself and with a certain repugnance, I'll make this request that my father desires, but I cannot promise that it will be granted. And if I stop visiting your court and rendering my homage, it will be a sign that I have not succeeded in obtaining your wish. Therefore, I'd like to request your pardon in advance and ask you to remember that it will be yourself who will have brought about such an extreme situation."

The sultan responded: "My son, I would be very angry if my request led to my not seeing you at my court anymore. I see clearly that you don't know the power that a husband can exercise on a wife. Your wife will show that she only loves you feebly if, with the power that she has as a fairy, she refuses you something of such small consequence that I have asked you to request out of love for me. Forget your timidity. It merely comes from the fact that you don't believe yourself to be loved as much as you love her. Go and just ask, and you'll see that the fairy loves you more than you believe, and remember that for want of not requesting anything, you will deprive yourself of great benefits. Just think that because you love her, you would never refuse anything she requested and that she would probably do the same."

The sultan did not convince Prince Ahmed, who would have preferred his father's requesting something other than his exposing himself to the displeasure of his beloved Pari-Banou. And because he felt so vexed, he left the court two days early. When he returned to the fairy, she noticed that he was not as cheerful as he always had been, and she asked him why he was melancholy. Instead of responding, he asked her how her health had been, and it was quite clear to her that he was avoiding her question.

"I'll respond to your question when you respond to mine," she said.

The prince kept denying that anything was wrong, but the more he denied, the more the fairy persisted.

"You must tell me what's bothering you," she said, "so that I can take care of it, no matter what it is. It would have to be something extraordinary if it were beyond my power, unless it were the death of your father, the sultan. In that case, aside from what I could try, time would certainly bring you consolation."

Prince Ahmed could no longer resist the fairy's insistent questions, and finally he said to her, "Madam, may God give my father a long life and keep him well till the end of his days! I left him full of life and in good health. So it's not that which has caused the chagrin that you've noticed. It's the sultan himself who is the cause. And that distresses me all the more, for he's put me in the terrible situation of intruding upon you. First of all, madam, you know with what care I've concealed the happiness I've had in loving you, in earning your good graces and your love, and in receiving your trust as I've given you mine. Yet he's discovered my secret, and I don't know how he's managed it."

Here the fairy Pari-Banou interrupted the prince. "I know. Remember what I predicted about the sick woman whom you brought here with such compassion? She's the one who revealed to the sultan everything that you kept from him. I had told you that she was no more sick than either you or I, and she revealed the truth to me. You see, after the two ladies whom I had placed in charge of her had given her some special water to cure her, she just pretended that the water had healed her, and when she came to me to take her leave, she wanted to bring her report to the sultan as soon as possible. She was in such a hurry that she would have left the palace without touring it if I had not commanded my two ladies to show it to her and had not made her realize that it would be worth her while. But continue your story, and let us see what your father has compelled you to do to trouble me, something, I assure you, you could never do."

"Madam," the prince continued, "you've noticed that until now I've been satisfied just to be loved by you, and I've never asked a favor of you. After marrying so lovable a wife as you, what more could I desire? Moreover, I am fully aware of your power, but I have made a point of never seeking any proof of it. Therefore, I would like you to realize that it is not me but the sultan, my father, who, it seems to me, has made an indiscreet request for a tent that one could hold in one's hand and that would protect him from injury when he goes on a campaign, as well as protecting his entire court and army. Again, it is not me but my father who has asked for this favor."

"Prince," replied the fairy, smiling, "I'm angry that such a small thing has caused you so much trouble and torment. I see clearly that two things have contributed to your anguish: one of them is the law that you've imposed on yourself to be content to love me and be loved by me and to abstain from making the least request that will put my power to a test; the other, I'm convinced, no matter what you might say, is that you have imagined that what the sultan has demanded is beyond my power. As far as the first is concerned, I praise you for it and love you even more because of it, if that's possible. As for the second, it will not be difficult to demonstrate to you that what your father has requested is a trifle, and given the opportunity, I could do something more difficult and more important for him. Therefore, rest assured that I do not feel put upon by you. On the contrary, I shall always take great pleasure in performing whatever you desire."

Pari-Banou then sent for her treasurer, and when she arrived, the fairy said, "Nourighan, bring me the largest tent in my treasury."

Nourighan soon returned with a small case concealed in the palm of her hand and presented it to her mistress, who gave it to the prince to look at. When Prince Ahmed saw the small case, which the fairy called the largest tent in her treasury, he believed that she wanted to make fun of him, and his face showed how surprised he was. Pari-Banou saw his expression and burst out laughing. "What is it, Prince?" she exclaimed, "Do you think that I'm jesting with you? You'll soon see that I'm not mocking you. Nourighan," she said to her treasurer, taking the tent out of Prince Ahmed's hands, "go and set it up so that the prince may judge whether his father will think it large enough."

The treasurer immediately left the palace, carried the tent a great distance away, and then set it up. When everything was done, the prince found it large enough to shelter two armies as large as that of his father.

"Well then, my princess," he said to Pari-Banou, "I beg your pardon a thousand times for my incredulity. After what I've seen, I don't think there's a thing you can't do once you set your mind to it."

"You've seen," said the fairy, "that the tent is larger than your father needs. But notice that it has one special property: it becomes larger or smaller according to the size of the army it is to cover."

The treasurer took down the tent, reduced it to its original size, and returned it to the prince's hands. The next day he mounted his horse and went, accompanied as usual by his attendants, to see the sultan.

His father was greatly surprised by the prince's gift. He took the tent and admired its small size, but when he had it set up on a great plain and saw that the tent was large enough to cover his whole army and two other armies as well, his amazement was so great that he could not control himself. Since the sultan indicated that the grand dimensions might be an inconvenience for him, the prince apprised him that the size of the tent would always be in accord with the proportions of his army. The sultan expressed his gratitude to the prince for such a noble present and asked him to thank the fairy for him. To show his son how valuable he found it, he ordered it to be carefully stored in his treasury. But in his secret bosom, he felt more jealous of his son than before, and this jealousy was greater than what his councillors and the sorceress had inspired, especially when he considered that thanks to the fairy, his son could perform things that were infinitely beyond his own power, despite his grandeur and his wealth. More intent than ever on bringing about his son's destruction, he went again to consult the sorceress, who advised him to ask the prince to bring him some of the water from the fountain of the lions.

In the evening, when the sultan was surrounded as usual by his entire court and the prince was present, the sultan addressed him in these words: "My son, I have already expressed my gratitude to you for the tent that you procured for me, which I consider the most valuable item in my treasury. But out of love for me, you must do one thing more, which will please me just as much. I have been told that your wife, the fairy, makes use of a certain water from the fountain of the lions, which cures all kinds of the most dangerous diseases. Since I am completely convinced that my health is very dear to you, I am positive that you will not mind asking for a flask of that water and will bring it to me so that I may use it whenever I need it. Do this important service for me, as a good son should do toward a tender father."

Prince Ahmed, who had believed that his father should have been satisfied with such a unique and useful tent as that which he had just brought and that he should not impose any new task on him, which might risk the fairy's displeasure, was thunderstruck by this new request, despite the fact that his wife had assured him that she would do everything for him that was within her power. After a long silence he said, "Sire, you may be certain that there is nothing I wouldn't undertake to procure something that might prolong your life, but I wish it would not have to be done through my wife. For this reason, I dare not promise that I can bring you the water. All I can do is to assure you that I shall request it from her, but I shall do this with great reluctance, just as I did when I asked for the tent."

The next morning Prince Ahmed returned to Pari-Banou and told her candidly and truthfully what had happened at his father's court, from the giving of the tent, which he reported that his father had received with utmost gratitude, to the new request he had imposed on him. Then he added, "My princess, I'm only telling you this as a frank account of what happened between me and my father. As for the rest, it is up to you as to whether you will satisfy or reject his new request. I only want what you want."

"No, no," replied the fairy. "It is perfectly all right with me that the sultan knows how important you are to me. I want to make him content, and whatever advice the sorceress may give him (for I see that he listens to her counsel), he shall find no fault with you or me. There is a great deal of malice in this request, and you will understand this by what I am going to tell you. The fountain of lions is situated in the middle of a court of a great castle. Its entrance is guarded by four extremely powerful lions, two of which sleep alternately with the other two. But do not let that frighten you. I shall supply you with the means to go by them without danger."

The fairy was working with her needle, and since she had several spools of thread at her side, she took one and gave it to Prince Ahmed.

"First of all, take this spool of thread," she said, "and I'll soon tell you how to use it. Second, you must have two horses. One you must ride yourself, and the other you must lead, and it must be loaded with a sheep cut into four quarters, which must be killed today. Third, you must have a flask for carrying the water. Set out early tomorrow morning, and when you have gone through the iron gate, throw the spool of thread in front of you, and it will roll until it reaches the gates of the castle. Follow it, and when it stops, you will see four lions, since the gates will be open. The two that are awake will wake the other two by their roaring. Don't be alarmed. Just throw each of them a quarter of the sheep. Once that is done, clap spurs to your horse right away and ride to the fountain. Fill your flask without dismounting, and return the way you came. The lions will be so busy eating that they will let you pass unmolested."

Prince Ahmed set out the next morning at the time designated by the fairy and followed her instructions exactly as she had ordered. He distributed the quarters of the sheep among the four lions, and after bravely passing right through their middle, he arrived at the fountain, filled his flask, and returned sound and safe, just as he had entered. When he had gone some distance, he turned around and noticed that two of the lions were running after him. Fearlessly, he drew his saber and prepared to defend himself. But then he saw one of the lions stop and signal with his head and tail that he had only come to march in front of him, while the other brought up the rear. So the prince put his saber back in its sheath and continued on his way until he reached the capital of the Indies, where he entered and was escorted by the lions, who did not leave him until he came to the sultan's door. At that point the lions went back the way they had come but not without alarming the populace, who fled or hid themselves to avoid them. Nevertheless, the lions walked gently and showed no signs of ferocity.

Many officers came to attend the prince when he dismounted, and they conducted him to the sultan, who was talking at the time with his councillors. Ahmed approached the throne, laid the bottle at the sultan's feet, kissed the rich carpet that covered the footstool, and, as he arose, said, "Sire, I have brought you that salutary water that you desired to place among the precious and unique things that enrich and adorn your treasury. But at the same time, I want to wish you such good health that you will never need to make use of it."

After the prince had concluded his compliment, the sultan placed him on his right hand and said, "Son, I am very much obliged to you for this valuable present, especially since you exposed yourself to great danger on my account." (He had been informed about the peril by the sorceress, who knew about the fountain and the lions and how dangerous it was to seek the water.) "Favor me by explaining how you managed or by what incredible power you obtained the water."

"Sire," replied Prince Ahmed, "I do not deserve your compliments. It was due to the fairy, my wife, that I had the glory of fetching the water. I just followed her good advice."

So he informed his father what his wife's good advice was, as he recounted the journey that he had undertaken and how he had conducted himself. When he had finished, the sultan, who expressed great joy while listening but in secret was even more jealous than before, arose and retired into the interior of his palace, where he sent for the sorceress.

Upon her arrival the sorceress spared the sultan the pain of talking about

Prince Ahmed and the success of his journey, which had reached her ears since it had caused such a clamor in the kingdom. She had already prepared a sure means to thwart the prince, and she related it to the sultan. So the next day, in front of the entire court, the sultan presented it to the prince in these terms: "My prince, I have only one more thing to ask of you, after which I won't ever demand a sign of your obedience or the help of your fairy wife. My request is that you bring me a man who is no more than a foot and a half high, whose beard is thirty feet long, who carries a bar of iron weighing five hundred pounds on his shoulder, which he uses as a quarter staff, and who can speak."

Prince Ahmed could not imagine any such man in the entire world, and he expressed reluctance to fulfill this request. But the sultan insisted, saying that the fairy could do things even more incredible than this.

The next day the prince returned to the underground realm of Pari-Banou and relayed his father's new demand, stating that he regarded the request as even more impossible to fulfill than the first two. "I can't imagine that there is or can be such a man in the whole world. There is no doubt but my father wants to see if I am naive enough to go looking, or if there is such a one, he intends that his plan will bring about my ruin. How could I possibly capture a man so small, who is armed as he described? What weapons could help me make him submit to me? If there is any way I may do it in an honorable way, I beg you to tell me."

"Do not alarm yourself, my prince," replied the fairy. "You ran a risk when you went to fetch the water of the fountain of lions, but there is no danger involved with regard to this man. He is my brother Schaibar. Though we both had the same father, he does not resemble me. Indeed, he has such a violent nature that his resentment flares up at the slightest offense. On the other hand, he is the most generous person in the world and is always ready to help people. He is built exactly as your father described him. He has no weapon other than the iron bar weighing five hundred pounds, which he always carries with him and uses to gain respect from others. I shall send for him, and you'll judge for yourself whether I'm telling the truth. But prepare yourself, and don't be frightened by this extraordinary creature when he appears before you."

"Well then," Prince Ahmed replied. "If Schaibar is your brother, I shall not be frightened, no matter how ugly or deformed he is. On the contrary, I shall love and honor him as your nearest kin."

The fairy ordered a gold chafing dish to be lit under the porch of her palace and also had a golden box brought to her. Then she took some incense from the box and threw it into the fire, causing a thick cloud of smoke to rise. Some moments after this ceremony, the fairy said to Ahmed, "Prince, here comes my brother. Do you see him?"

The prince immediately perceived Schaibar, who was no taller than a foot and a half and walked gravely with the iron bar of five hundred pounds on his shoulder. He also had a thick beard, thirty feet long, thrust in front of him, and it was matched by a bushy mustache that went from ear to ear and practically covered his face. His beastly eyes were plunged deep in his enormous head, which was covered by a pointed hat. To top it all off, he was hunchbacked.

If the prince had not been forewarned that Schaibar was Pari-Banou's brother, he would have been frightened to death by the dwarf's appearance. As it was, he stood firmly with the fairy and welcomed him without a sign of weakness. As the little man moved toward him, he looked at Ahmed with an eye that could have chilled the soul in his body, and when he was by his sister's side, he asked her who he was.

"My brother," she replied, "this is my husband. His name is Ahmed. He is the son of the sultan of the Indies. The reason I did not invite you to my wedding was because I did not want to deter you from a distant expedition in which you were engaged. I was pleased to learn you returned victorious from this venture, and I have now taken the liberty to call for you on my husband's behalf."

At these words, Schaibar glanced at Prince Ahmed more favorably, but this did not diminish either his fierceness or his savage look.

"Sister," he said, "is there something I can do for you? You have only to say it. It's enough for me that he is your husband."

"His father, the sultan," replied Pari-Banou, "is curious to see you, and I should like Ahmed to guide you to the sultan's court."

"Let him only lead the way, and I'll follow him," Schaibar answered.

"Brother," Pari-Banou replied, "it's too late to begin the journey today. I suggest that you start out tomorrow morning. In the meantime, we can speak about what has happened between the sultan of the Indies and Prince Ahmed since our marriage. I can do this tonight."

The next morning, informed about everything that he should know,

Schaibar set out with Prince Ahmed to visit the sultan. The people of the
capital took fright and hid themselves in their shops and houses as soon as
they saw the hideous Schaibar. Those who did not lock their doors took to
their heels and spread their fear to all the people they met, who did not stay
to look behind them. Consequently Schaibar and Prince Ahmed found the
streets and squares deserted. Even the palace guards ran away instead of
preventing Schaibar from entering. Thus the prince and the dwarf advanced
without hindrance to the council hall, where the sultan was seated on his
throne, surrounded by his grand vizier and his councillors, and holding audience. Schaibar haughtily approached the throne, and without waiting for
Prince Ahmed to present him, he addressed the sultan: "I've heard that you
sent for me. Well, what is it that you want?"

Instead of answering, the sultan raised his hands before his eyes. Enraged
by this uncivil and offensive reception after he had taken the trouble to come,
Schaibar lifted up his bar of iron and exclaimed, "Well, if you won't speak!"
And before Prince Ahmed could ask him to pardon his father, he let the bar
fall on the sultan's head, knocking him lifeless to the ground. The only thing
Ahmed could do was to save the grand vizier by praising the good advice he
had always given the sultan.

"Well, who are the ones who gave the sultan bad advice?" Schaibar
asked, and then proceeded to destroy the councillors right and left, who were
the enemies of Prince Ahmed. With each blow came a death, and the only
ones who managed to escape were those whom the terrible Schaibar did not
seize strongly enough to prevent their fleeing.

After completing this dreadful execution, Schaibar left the hall and went
into the middle of the court, with the bar of iron on his shoulder. Looking
at the grand vizier, who accompanied Ahmed, he cried out, "I know there
is a certain sorceress, an enemy of the prince, who stirred up the sultan to
demand my presence here. Let her be brought before me."

The grand vizier sent for her at once, and as soon as she arrived, Schaibar
also crushed her with his bar of iron and declared: "This is your reward for
giving wicked advice and pretending to be sick!"

"Nor is this enough," Schaibar declared. "Prince Ahmed, my brother-
in-law, must instantly be recognized as sultan of the Indies, otherwise I'll
destroy the entire city."

All those present agreed and let the air resound with cries of "Long live
Sultan Ahmed!" In a short time the whole city echoed with the same cries
and proclamations. Next Schaibar had the prince dressed in the robes of the
sultan and had him installed immediately on the throne. After paying him
homage and taking an oath of fidelity and allegiance, he went searching for
his sister Pari-Banou and, conducting her to the city in great pomp, had her
acknowledged as the sultana of the Indies.

With regard to Prince Ali and Princess Nouronnihar, Sultan Ahmed recognized that they had played no part in the conspiracy against him, and since he had been avenged, he granted them a very large province as their own dominion, where they spent the rest of their lives. Afterward he sent an officer to Houssain to inform him about the change of leadership and to offer him any province he might choose. But Prince Houssain was so happy in his solitude that he told the officer to thank his brother, the sultan, for the kind offer and to assure him of his allegiance. The only favor he requested was to be granted permission to live in the place that he had chosen for his retreat and solace.

Translated by Jack Zipes

The Queen Fantasque

Jean-Jacques Rousseau

nce upon a time there was a king who loved his people—"

"That's the way a fairy tale begins," the druid interrupted.

"Well, that's what it is," Jalamir responded.

So once upon a time, then, there was a king who loved his people, and consequently they adored him. Though he had made a great effort to find ministers who were just as concerned with the welfare of the people as he was, he eventually realized how foolish such an undertaking was and assumed the task of concealing as best he could the malicious activities of his ministers. Since he was obsessed by the bizarre goal of making his subjects happy, he concentrated all his energies on fulfilling this aim, and his comportment was considered totally ridiculous by the nobles of his kingdom. Blessed by the people, he was regarded as a fool at court. In short, he was a worthy individual. His name, incidentally, was Phoenix.

If this king was extraordinary, his wife was no less remarkable. Vivacious, absentminded, whimsical, she was a woman with crazy ideas, a wise heart, and a good nature, but she was also capriciously harmful. Such was the queen, and Fantasque was her name. Indeed, it was a famous name, passed on to her by her ancestors through the maternal line, and she bore it with honor and dignity. This woman, so illustrious and so intelligent, both enchanted and tortured her husband, so deeply did she love him.

Despite their love, many years went by without their being able to produce any fruit from their union. The king was distressed by this, while the queen had become so impatient that her good husband was not the only one to feel her frustration. She blamed everyone for her failure to have children. There was not a person at court whom she did not ask heedlessly about the secret of conceiving and whom she did not hold responsible for her poor success.

Of course, the queen did not forget the doctors. Indeed, she treated them in an unusually high-handed way. They ordered all sorts of drugs for her, which she had carefully prepared, only to throw them in their faces instead of taking them. Then the dervishes had their turn. She was supposed to appeal to Nouvena, to make vows and especially to give donations. But pity the poor priests at the temples to which her majesty made her pilgrimages! She ravaged everything, and under the pretext of wanting to breathe some fecund air, she would turn the monks' cells inside out. She also wore their relics and at various times dressed up ridiculously in their various garments. Sometimes it was a white girdle; at other times a leather belt, a hood, a scapular. There was not a single kind of monastic dress that her devotion did not lead her to try. And since she had a sprightly air about her, which rendered her charming in all her costumes, she never failed to have her portrait painted before she left.

Finally, owing to the exemplary way that she had performed her devotions and the wise way she had taken her medicine, heaven and earth granted the queen's wishes. She became pregnant just when everyone had begun to despair. I shall let you guess how joyful the king and his people were. As for the queen herself, she expressed her feelings as she normally did—with extravagance. In her ecstasy, she broke and smashed everything in sight. She embraced everyone she encountered, no matter who it was—men, women, courtesans, valets. Anyone she found in her way risked suffocation. As she put it, she knew of nothing so ravishing as having a child whom she could whip whenever she was in a bad mood.

Since her pregnancy had been totally unexpected, everyone considered it an extraordinary event. The doctors attributed it to their drugs; the monks, to their relics; the people, to their prayers; and the king, to his love. All were interested in the unborn child as if it were their own, and everyone wished sincerely that the child would be a prince: the people, the nobles, and the king were all in agreement on this one point. The queen considered it extremely bad-mannered that they ventured to prescribe to her what kind of child she should give birth to, and she declared that she intended to have a girl, adding that it seemed to her utterly presumptuous that anyone would dare contest her right to dispose of a treasure that incontestably belonged to her alone.

Phoenix tried in vain to make her listen to reason. But she told him unequivocally that it was no longer his business, and she locked herself in her room to sulk. This was one of her favorite occupations, which she regularly undertook at least six months out of the year. Of course, the six months were not consecutive. These sulky outbursts and withdrawals would have provided a respite for her husband had they not occurred at just the right intervals to distress him.

The king was quite aware of the fact that the whims of the mother do not determine the sex of a child. But he was upset that she had made her point in front of everyone at court. He would have sacrificed everything to obtain the universal approval that would justify his love for her, and the attempt he made on that occasion was not the only folly that undercut his ridiculous hope of making his wife listen to reason.

Not knowing any longer to which saint he should turn, he resorted to calling upon the fairy Discreet, the protectress of his kingdom. The fairy advised him to be sweet to his wife, that is, to apologize.

"The only goal of all female fantasies," the fairy said to him, "is to upset male conceit a little and accustom men to obeying women as suits them. The best means you have of curing the extravagances of your wife is to go along with them. From the time you stop opposing her whims, you can rest assured that she will stop having them, for she is only waiting to become good after having made you completely crazy. So do everything graciously, and try to give in on this occasion so that you can prevail at another time."

The king valued the fairy's advice, so he joined the queen's circle of friends, took her aside, and said quietly that he was sorry to have argued with her in this affair and would try to make up for his impolite behavior by improving his comportment in the future.

Fantasque, who feared that Phoenix merely wanted to cover up the ridiculous affair, hastened to respond that she felt his excuse was even more arrogant than his arguments, but since the wrongs of a husband did not authorize a wife to make mistakes, she would yield as she had always done. "My prince and my husband," she added in a loud voice, "has ordered me to give birth to a boy, and I know my duty very well and shall not fail to obey. I'm quite aware that when his majesty honors me with signs of his tenderness, he does this not so much because of his love for me but because he loves his people, whose interests occupy his mind night and day. And since I should accede to such noble impartiality, I'm going to ask at court for a memorandum instructing me about the number and sex of the children suitable for the royal family. This will be an important memorandum, pertinent to the welfare of the state, and every queen will have to learn how to regulate her conduct at night in accordance with it."

This eloquent statement was heard with great attention by the entire company, and I'll let you guess how many peals of laughter were awkwardly suppressed.

."Ah," thought the king sadly, shrugging his shoulders, "I see clearly that if one has a crazy wife, one cannot avoid being a fool."

The fairy Discreet, whose name and sex sometimes made for a pleasant contrast in her character, found this quarrel so amusing that she resolved to enjoy it to the very end. In public she said to the king that she had consulted the stars that presided over the birth of princes, and she could tell him that his child would be a boy. But privately she assured the queen that she would have a girl.

Thanks to this information, Fantasque became suddenly just as reasonable as she had been capricious before. It was with an infinite complaisance that she took all possible measures to make the king and the entire court feel sorry. She hastened to have the loveliest baby clothes made, so suitable for a boy, she claimed, that they would be ridiculous for a girl. This plan caused many fashions to change, and cost her nothing. She had a beautiful gold chain with glistening gems prepared and insisted that the king appoint the young prince's tutor in advance. As soon as she was sure that she was going to have a girl, she talked only about her son, and she took senseless precautions that made everyone forget about the important ones that should have been taken. She burst out laughing when she pictured the astonished and foolish faces of the nobles and magistrates, who were supposed to adorn her confinement bed with their presence. "It seems to me," she said to the fairy, "that I can see our venerable chancellor on one side, lifting his large glasses to verify the sex of the child, and, on the other, his sacred majesty, lowering his eyes and stammering, 'I believe . . . but the fairy told me . . . Gentlemen, it isn't my fault.' And other instructive sayings just as witty that will be collected by the scholars of the court and soon spread to the distant Indies."

She took malicious pleasure in imagining how this marvelous event would throw the entire gathering into dismay and disarray. She pictured the disputes, the agitation of all the ladies at court in order to claim, adjust, and conciliate the rights of their own charges. And the entire court would be set in an uproar because of a child's bonnet.

It was also during this time that Fantasque invented the custom of having the judges lecture the newborn prince. Phoenix sought to convince her that this would be degrading for the judiciary and serve no purpose. Moreover, it would turn the ceremonies of the court into an extravagant comedy, while exposing the child to a good deal of grotesque pomp before he could understand or respond.

"All the better," the queen replied spiritedly. "Won't it be smarter to let your son hear all the dumb things they have to say before he can understand them? Would you like them to save all their cant for later, when he has reached the age of reason and they can drive him crazy? For God's sake, let them harangue him at their convenience while we can be certain that he will understand nothing and be bored by it all. You of all people ought to know that a child would be lucky to get a good deal like this."

The queen had her way. By order of his majesty, the presidents of the senate and the academies had to begin composing, studying, erasing, and leafing through their Demosthenes in order to learn how to speak to an embryo.

Finally, the crucial moment arrived. The queen felt the first pains with unparalleled ecstasy and joy. She complained with such good grace and cried with such a pleasant air that one would have thought that giving birth was her greatest pleasure. The palace was in an uproar. Some of the servants ran to look for the king, while others went to fetch the princes, the ministers, and the senate. However, the majority of the servants, those who hurried the most, ran about for the sake of running about, and rolling their cask like Diogenes, they assumed a busy air for each step they took. In their hurry to gather together as many people as were necessary, the last person they thought about was the doctor, and the king, who was beside himself, inadvertently asked for a midwife. This mistake caused the ladies at court to laugh a great deal, and their laughter, along with the queen's good humor, made the birth the most cheerful one the world has ever known.

Although Fantasque had done her best to guard the fairy's secret, it was leaked to the women of the palace, and they kept it so carefully that the rumor took more than three days to spread throughout the entire city, so that there was a long time when the king was the only one who did not know anything about it. Therefore, everyone waited with suspense for the outcome. Since public concern furnished a pretext for all the curious to amuse themselves at the expense of the royal family, they arranged a celebration party in order to watch the faces of their majesties and to see how the fairy would extricate herself from the affair and keep her credibility after having made two contradictory promises.

"Now you must agree, monseigneur," said Jalamir, interrupting himself, "that it is up to me to hold you in suspense, in keeping with the rules of proper narrative style. For you certainly must feel that the moment has now arrived for the digressions, the portraits, and numerous other pretty things that every witty author always employs at the most interesting point of the plot to amuse his readers!"

"By God," said the druid, "do you think that there are fools who pay attention to those clever devices? You should know that most readers are smart enough to skip over all that, and in spite of the author, the readers can quickly leaf through the pretty pages. And you, who are acting as the logician here, do you think that your words are worth more than the witty remarks of others, and that to avoid the imputation of being foolish, you just have to say that only you know what it takes to keep me in suspense? Truly, by saying all this, you're proving how foolish you are. Unfortunately, there's no book at hand, and I can't resort to turning the pages."

"Console yourself," Jalamir told him softly. "Others will turn the pages for you if anyone ever writes this story down. No matter. Just believe that the entire court gathered in the queen's chamber, that it was the most beautiful occasion I have ever had to depict, that the most illustrious people were there, and that this is the only time you will ever have to get to know them."

"What in heaven do you mean?" the druid responded pleasantly. "I would recognize them quite well by their actions. So make them act if your story needs them, and don't say a word about them if they're of no use to you. I don't want anything but the facts."

"Since there is no way," said Jalamir, "to liven up my story by a little metaphysics, I'm going to resume telling my tale in a plain and simple fashion, but telling a tale for the sake of telling is boring. You don't know how many pretty things you're going to miss! Now please help me find my place, for I've lost track and don't know where I was in the story."

"You were with that queen," the druid said impatiently. "Remember, you had gone to a great deal of trouble to have her give birth, and you have kept me with her for an hour in labor."

"Oh, oh!" Jalamir responded. "Do you think that royal children are laid like the eggs of a thrush? You'll see whether it's not worth the trouble to elaborate."

Well, after much crying and laughing, the queen put an end to the curiosity of the court and the intrigue of the fairy by giving birth to a daughter and a son, more beautiful than the moon and the sun, and they resembled each other so much that it was very difficult to tell them apart, especially during their infancy, when it was such a pleasure to dress them the same way.

When the desired moment finally arrived, the king dropped all the formalities of his majesty to be natural and performed extravagant acts that he had previously prohibited his wife from doing. The pleasure of having children made him so childish that he ran to his balcony and cried at the top of his lungs: "*My friends! Rejoice, everyone! I've just had a son, and you now have a king who is a father and a queen who is a mother!*"

Since it was the first time that the queen had ever been at such an event, she did not understand the work that she had accomplished, and the fairy was happy to announce that she had given birth to a girl, as she had desired. The queen had the baby brought to her, and the spectators were surprised by the truly tender way that she embraced the child, but she did this with tears in her eyes and with an air of sadness that did not tally well with her mood just before.

I've already said that she was sincerely in love with her husband. Well, she had been touched by the compassion she had read in his looks when she had undergone some pain. To be sure, it was a strange time to do this, but she began to reflect on how cruel it was to torment such a good husband, and she could only think about how sorry the king would be when he was presented with a daughter and not a son. But Discreet, thanks to the good nature of her sex and her gifts as a fairy, had easily learned to read people's hearts, and she was able to grasp the feelings of the queen. Since there was no reason to conceal the truth from Fantasque, she had the young prince brought to her as well. Once the queen got over her surprise, she found the solution so pleasing that she burst into exuberant laughter, which was dangerous because of her condition. Indeed, she fainted, and they had a great deal of difficulty in reviving her. If the fairy had not been there to save her life, the most acute pangs of sorrow would have replaced the happiness in the king's heart and on the faces of the people at the court.

But this was the strangest thing about the entire adventure: the queen's sincere regret for the way she had tormented her husband made her much more affectionate toward the young prince than toward his sister. On the other hand, the king, who adored the queen, showed the very partiality toward the daughter that his wife had expected to have. Thus the indirect caresses that the husband and wife gave to each other soon indicated a definite preference, and the queen could not do without her son, nor the king without his daughter.

This double event gave great pleasure to everyone and at least reassured the people that they would not have to worry for a time about a successor to the throne. The people who always think they know better, who had made fun of the fairy's promises, found themselves mocked in their turn. But they did not acknowledge defeat, saying that they did not disallow lying even in a fairy, nor did they deny her the ability to counteract her own predictions. Other people at court, basing their views on the partiality that the royal couple had begun to show toward their children, became so impudent as to maintain that by giving a son to the queen and a daughter to the king, the event had completely belied the prophecy.

In the meantime, while everyone prepared to celebrate the baptism of the two newborns with pomp, and human pride polished itself to shine humbly at the altars of the gods—

"Wait a moment," interrupted the druid. "You're confusing me terribly. I'd like to know where all this is taking place. First, in order to make the queen pregnant, you promenaded her among the relics and the monks. After that you transported her to the Indies. Now you've just mentioned baptism and the altars of the gods. By the great Thamiris, given the ceremony you're preparing, I no longer know whether we are going to worship Jupiter, the holy Virgin, or Mohammed. To me, a druid, it's not all that important whether the two infants are baptized or circumcised. But you must be consistent in your story and not mislead me into taking a bishop for a mufti and the missal for the Koran."

"Why are you trying to make such a big deal out of this?" Jalamir responded. "People just as sophisticated as you have been wrong there too. God protects everyone from the evil of prelates who have harems and cannot distinguish the Latin of the breviary from the Arabic. God brings peace to all the honest hypocrites who follow the intolerance of the prophet of Mecca, always ready to massacre the human species for the greater glory of the creator. But you must remember that we are in a country of fairies, where nobody is sent to hell for the good of his soul, where one does not venture to look at the foreskin of people to damn or to absolve them, and where the cowl and the turban equally cover sacred heads in order to serve as signs to the eyes of both the wise and the fools. I realize that according to the laws of geography that regulate all the religions of the world the two newborns should be Muslims, but only males are circumcised, and I need both my twins to be treated in the same way. So you should rejoice that I'm having them baptized."

"Do it, do it," said the druid. "By my faith as a religious man, I've never in my life heard a better motivation for choosing a religion for children as yours!"

The queen, who took pleasure in upsetting all etiquette, wanted to get up at the end of six days and go out on the seventh, under the pretext that she felt well. The truth is that she was nursing her children, and so odious was this example that all the women strongly warned her of the consequences. But Fantasque felt it would be a shame to waste all that milk and argued that the pleasures of life should be gathered before death arrives, and when she died, her breasts would be withered whether she nursed or not. Furthermore, she added, in the tone of a duenna, the prettiest bosom in the eyes of a husband is that of a mother who nurses her children. When Fantasque mentioned husbands taking part in household affairs that men so seldom see, the women burst out laughing, and the queen, though too pretty to be regarded with impunity, appeared to them from that time on to be almost as ridiculous as her husband, whom they derisively called the bourgeois of Vaugirard.

"I see where you're coming from," the druid interjected. "You want me gradually to assume the role of Shah Bahan and ask whether there is also a

Vaugirard in the Indies, like a Madrid in the woods of Boulogne, an opera in Paris, and a philosopher at court. But continue your rhapsody, and don't set any more of these traps for me. Since I've never been married or a sultan, I do not wish to be made a fool."

Finally, Jalamir said without replying to the druid, when everything was ready, the day was reserved for opening the doors of heaven to the two newborns. It was a bright morning when the fairy went to the palace and declared to the royal couple that she was going to make a present to each of their children, to indicate the dignity of their birth and as tokens of her power.

"Before the magic water replaces my protection," she said, "I want to enrich them with my gifts and to give them names more effective than those designated by the Directory, to express the perfection that I've taken care to give them. But since you must be better acquainted than I am with the qualities that would suit the welfare of your family and your people, choose them yourself, performing this single act of good will for your children, what twenty years of education rarely accomplish during one's youth and what reason no longer does when one reaches an advanced age."

A tremendous altercation ensued between the king and queen. She claimed to be the only one who could regulate the character of the whole family the way she pictured it. And the good king, considering the choice of great importance, did not want to abandon the responsibility to the capriciousness of a woman whose follies he adored without sharing them. Fantasque preferred to have pretty children, and provided that they would shine at six years of age, she would not care if they did foolish things at thirty.

The fairy tried in vain to bring about an agreement between husband and wife. Soon the character of the newborns became merely the pretext for the dispute, and it was a question no longer of being right but of who would make the other submit. Finally, Discreet thought of a way to reconcile the two without either one of them having to concede: each was to mold the child of the same sex in the manner preferred. The king approved this expedient, since it provided the essentials for the heir presumptive to the crown and protected him from the bizarre wishes of the queen. And seeing the two children on the knees of their governess, he quickly took the prince and separated him from his sister, not without casting a look of commiseration at his daughter. Fantasque, who had no reason to object, ran like a madwoman to the young princess and embraced her. "You will exceed me in all attributes," she said. "But in order that the king's whims turn out to benefit one of his children despite himself, my wish is that the child I hold receive the exact opposite of that which he asks for the other. Now choose," she demanded of the king triumphantly. "And since you find it so charming to direct everything, decide the destiny of your entire family with a single word."

The fairy and the king tried in vain to dissuade her from this resolution, which placed the king in a rare predicament. But she refused to give in, and said that she was very pleased with the opportunity to endow her daughter with all the qualities that the king would not be able to give his son.

"Ah!" said the king, incensed at such spite. "You've always felt nothing but aversion for your daughter, and on the most important occasion of her life, you're proving just how you feel. But," he added, beside himself with anger, "in order to make her perfect in spite of you, I'm going to request that this child here resemble you."

"All the better for you and for him," the queen responded sharply, "but I'll be revenged, and your daughter will resemble you."

No sooner had they uttered these impetuous words than the king, despairing of his thoughtless act, wanted to retract them. But it was too late, and the children were endowed forever with the traits that were requested. The boy was called Prince Caprice, and the girl was given the bizarre name Princess Reason, which she rendered so illustrious that no woman has dared to bear it since.

There you have it. The future successor to the throne was adorned with all the perfections of a pretty woman, and the princess his sister was destined one day to possess all the virtues of an honest man and the qualities of a good king, a division that did not appear to be the best of arrangements but was irrevocable. The joke was that the mutual love of the royal couple had acted in this instance with all its usual due force, which had failed them often in crucial situations: the child who resembled each of them was found by each to have received the poorer part of the bargain, and instead of being content, the parents could only complain.

The king took his daughter into his arms and hugged her tenderly. "Alas," he said, "you'll have your mother's beauty, but you won't have the talent to make an asset of it. You'll be too reasonable to make people's heads turn."

Fantasque, more circumspect about her own virtues, did not say anything about the wisdom of the future king, but it was easy to see by the sad manner with which she caressed her son that, deep down in her heart, she did not think too highly of his part of the bargain.

The king looked at her, somewhat bemused, and reproached her gently for what had happened. "I feel that I've made some mistakes, but they are the results of your work. Our children could have become more distinguished than we are, and you're the reason why they will only resemble us."

"At least," she retorted, "I'm sure that they will love each other as much as it is possible to do."

Touched by the tenderness of this reply, Phoenix consoled himself with the thought that he had often had the opportunity to remark that natural goodness and a sensitive heart were sufficient to repair everything.

"I can guess the rest of the story quite well," said the druid, "and might as well finish the tale for you. Your Prince Caprice makes everyone's head turn and is so very much like his mother that he is bound to become her tormentor. He turns the kingdom upside down in desiring to reform it. To make his subjects happy, he brings them to the point of despair, always blaming others for his own mistakes. Unfair because he is imprudent, he commits new mistakes whenever he regrets his old ones. Since wisdom never guides him, the good that he wants to do augments the bad that he will have done. In short, even though he is basically good, sensitive, and generous, his virtues betray him, and only his thoughtlessness, concentrated in all its power, makes him more loathed than conscious maliciousness could. On the other hand, your Princess Reason, the new heroine of the land of fairies, becomes a prodigy of wisdom and prudence, and without having worshipers, she makes herself so loved by the people that everyone desires to be governed by her. Her goodness, beneficial to everyone and to herself, is only disadvantageous for her brother, whose eccentricities are constantly compared to her virtues. Indeed, the public bias is such that all the faults she lacks are attributed to him even when he does not have them. Soon the question arises whether the order of the succession to the throne should not be inverted, whether the fool should not be subjugated to the female heir, and chance to reason. The doctors emphatically explain the consequences of such an example and prove that it is better for the people to obey blindly madmen that chance may give them for lords than to choose reasonable leaders for themselves; that although one forbids a madman to govern his own estates, it is better to let him have supreme disposition over our welfare and our lives; that the most insane of men is still preferable to the wisest of women; and that even if the male or firstborn were a monkey or a wolf, it is necessary and politically preferable that a heroine or an angel born after him obey his will. The seditious will offer objections and answers, in which God will make your wit shine, as we shall see, for I know you. You take great pleasure in venting your anger by demeaning all that has been done, and your bitter candor appears to delight in the reproaches you supply."

"For God's sake, Father Druid, how you exaggerate!" Jalamir said, greatly surprised. "What a torrent of words! How did you ever learn to be so eloquent? I'm sure you've never preached this well in your sacred woods, even though you don't tell the truth. If I were to let you continue, you would soon turn a fairy tale into a political treatise, and one would some day find Bluebeard or Donkey-Skin as royal officials advising princes, rather than Machiavelli. But don't go to so much trouble to guess the ending of my tale. I'll show you that I have plenty of denouements if I need them, and I'll provide one for you now, perhaps not as clever as yours but just as predictable and certainly more unexpected."

You know of course that, as I've already remarked, the twins resembled each other very closely and were dressed identically. Thus the king believed that he had taken his son when he had really taken his daughter into his arms at the crucial moment, and the queen, fooled by her husband's choice, had also mistaken her son for her daughter. The fairy was able to benefit from this mistake by endowing the two children as would suit them best. So Caprice became the name of the princess, and Reason the name of her brother, the prince, and despite the bizarre behavior of the queen, everything found its natural order.

After the king died, Reason succeeded to the throne and neither waged war against foreigners nor violated his subjects, and he received more benedictions than praise. All the projects that his father had conceived during the preceding reign were completed during his, and in passing from the rule of the father to that of the son, the people were doubly happy, for they felt as though they had not changed rulers. The princess Caprice, after causing numerous lovers to lose either their lives or their minds, was finally married to a neighboring king, whom she preferred because he wore the longest mustache and hopped the best on one foot. As for Fantasque, she died of indigestion caused by a partridge leg in a ragout that she had wanted to eat before going to bed, where the king had shivered to death while waiting for her, for she had enticed him with her charms that night to come and sleep with her.

Translated by Jack Zipes

‹ *The White Bull* ›
Voltaire

I
HOW THE PRINCESS AMASIDIA
MEETS A BULL

he princess Amasidia, daughter of Amasis, king of Tanis in Egypt, took a walk upon the highway of Peluaium with the ladies of her train. She was sunk in deep melancholy. Tears gushed from her beautiful eyes. The cause of her grief was known, as well as the fears she entertained lest that grief should displease the king, her father. The old man Mambres, ancient magician and eunuch of the Pharaohs, was beside her and seldom left her. He was present at her birth. He had educated her and taught her all that a fair princess was allowed to know of the sciences of Egypt. The mind of Amasidia equaled her beauty. Her sensibility and tenderness rivaled the charms of her person, and it was this sensibility which cost her so many tears.

The princess was twenty-four years old; the magician Mambres about thirteen hundred. It was he, as everyone knows, who had that famous dispute with Moses, in which the victory was so long doubtful between these two profound philosophers. If Mambres yielded, it was owing to the visible protection of the celestial powers, who favored his rival. It required gods to overcome Mambres.

Amasis made him superintendent of his daughter's household, and he acquitted himself in this office with his usual prudence. His compassion was excited by the sighs of the beautiful Amasidia.

"O my lover!" said she to herself, "my young, my dear lover! O greatest of conquerors, most accomplished, most beautiful of men! Almost seven years hast thou disappeared from the world. What god hath snatched thee from thy tender Amasidia? Thou art not dead. The wise Egyptian prophets confess this. But thou art dead to me. I am alone in the world. To me it is a desert. By what extraordinary prodigy hast thou abandoned thy throne and thy mistress?—thy throne, which was the first in the world. However, that is a matter of small consequence; but to abandon me, who adores thee! O my dear Ne—"

She was going on.

"Tremble to pronounce that fatal name," said Mambres, the ancient eunuch and magician of the pharaohs. "You would perhaps be discovered by some of the ladies of your court. They are all very much devoted to you, and all fair ladies certainly make it a merit to serve the noble passions of fair princesses. But there may be one among them indiscreet, and even treacherous. You know that your father, although he loves you, has sworn to put you to death should you pronounce the terrible name always ready to escape your lips. This law is severe, but you have not been educated in Egyptian wisdom to be ignorant of the government of the tongue. Remember that Hippocrates, one of our greatest gods, has always his finger upon his mouth."

The beautiful Amasidia wept, and was silent.

As she pensively advanced toward the banks of the Nile, she perceived at a distance, under a thicket watered by the river, an old woman in a tattered gray garment, seated on a hillock. This old woman had beside her a she-ass, a dog, and a he-goat. Opposite to her was a serpent, which was not like the common serpents, for its eyes were mild, its physiognomy noble and engaging, while its skin shone with the liveliest and brightest colors. A huge fish, half immersed in the river, was not the least astonishing figure in the group, and on a neighboring tree were perched a raven and a pigeon. All these creatures seemed to carry on a very animated conversation.

"Alas!" said the princess, in a low tone. "These animals undoubtedly speak of their loves, and it is not so much as allowed me to mention the name of mine."

The old woman held in her hand a slender steel chain a hundred fathoms long, to which was fastened a bull, who fed in the meadow. This bull was white, perfectly well made, plump and at the same time agile, which is a thing seldom to be found. He was indeed the most beautiful specimen that was ever seen of his kind. Neither the bull of Pasiphaë, nor that in whose shape Jupiter appeared when he carried off Europa, could be compared to this

noble animal. The charming young heifer into which Isis was changed would have scarce been worthy of his company.

As soon as the bull saw the princess he ran toward her with the swiftness of a young Arabian horse that pricks up his ears and flies over the plains and rivers of the ancient Saana to approach the lovely consort whose image reigns in his heart. The old woman used her utmost efforts to restrain the bull. The serpent wanted to terrify him by its hissing. The dog followed him and bit his beautiful limbs. The she-ass crossed his way and kicked him to make him return. The great fish remounted the Nile and, darting himself out of the water, threatened to devour him. The he-goat remained immovable, apparently struck with fear. The raven fluttered round his head as if it wanted to tear out his eyes. The pigeon alone accompanied him from curiosity and applauded him by a sweet murmur.

So extraordinary a sight threw Mambres into serious reflections. In the meanwhile the white bull, dragging after him his chain and the old woman, had already reached the princess, who was struck with astonishment and fear. He threw himself at her feet. He kissed them. He shed tears. He looked upon her with eyes in which there was a strange mixture of grief and joy. He dared not to low, lest he should terrify the beautiful Amasidia. He could not speak. A weak use of the voice, granted by heaven to certain animals, was denied him; but all his actions were eloquent. The princess was delighted with him. She perceived that a trifling amusement could suspend for some moments even the most poignant grief.

"Here," said she, "is a most amiable animal. I could wish much to have him in my stable."

At these words the bull bent himself on his knees and kissed the ground.

"He understands me," cried the princess. "He shows me that he wants to be mine. Ah, heavenly magician! ah, divine eunuch! Give me this consolation. Purchase this beautiful bovine. Settle the price with the old woman, to whom he no doubt belongs. This animal must be mine. Do not refuse me this innocent comfort."

All the ladies joined their requests to the entreaties of the princess. Mambres yielded to them and immediately went to speak to the old woman.

II
HOW THE WISE MAMBRES, FORMERLY
MAGICIAN OF PHARAOH,
KNEW AGAIN THE OLD WOMAN, AND
WAS KNOWN BY HER

"Madam," said Mambres to her, "you know that ladies, and particularly princesses, have need of amusement. The daughter of the king is distractedly fond of your bull. I beg that you will sell him to us. You shall be paid in ready money."

"Sir," answered the old woman, "this precious animal does not belong to me. I am charged, together with all the beasts which you see, to keep him with care, to watch all his motions, and to give an exact account of them. God forbid that I should ever have any inclination to sell this invaluable animal."

Mambres, upon this discourse, began to have a confused remembrance of something which he could not yet properly distinguish. He eyed the old woman in the gray cloak with greater attention.

"Respectable lady," said he to her, "I either mistake, or I have seen you formerly."

"I make no mistake, sir," replied the old woman. "I have seen you seven hundred years ago, in a journey which I made from Syria into Egypt some months after the destruction of Troy, when Hiram the Second reigned at Tyre, and Nephel Keres in ancient Egypt."

"Ah, madam!" cried the old man. "You are the remarkable witch of Endor."

"And you, sir," said the sorceress, embracing him, "are the great Mambres of Egypt."

"Oh, unforeseen meeting! memorable day! eternal decrees!" said Mambres. "It certainly is not without permission of the universal providence that we meet again in this meadow, upon the banks of the Nile, near the noble city of Tanis. What, is it indeed you," continued Mambres, "who are so famous upon the banks of your little Jordan, and the first person in the world for raising apparitions?"

"What, is it you, sir," replied Miss Endor, "who are so famous for changing rods into serpents, the day into darkness, and rivers into blood?"

"Yes, madam, but my great age has in part deprived me of my knowledge and power. I am ignorant whence you have this beautiful bull, and who these animals are that, together with you, watch round him."

The old woman, recollecting herself, raised her eyes to heaven, and then replied:

"My dear Mambres, we are of the same profession, but it is expressly forbidden me to tell you who this bull is. I can satisfy you with regard to the other animals. You will easily know them by the marks which characterize them. The serpent is that which persuaded Eve to eat an apple and to make her husband partake of it. The ass, that which spoke to your contemporary Balaam in a remarkable discourse. The fish, which always carries its head above water, is that which swallowed Jonah a few years ago. The dog is he who followed Raphael and the young Tobit in their journey to Ragusa in Media, in the time of the great Salamanzar. This goat is he who expiates all the sins of your nation. The raven and the pigeon, those which were in the ark of Noah—great event! universal catastrophe! of which almost all the world is still ignorant. You are now informed. But of the bull you can know nothing."

Mambres, having listened with respect, said:

"The Eternal, O illustrious witch, reveals and conceals what he thinks proper. All these animals who, together with you, are entrusted with the custody of the white bull are only known to your generous and agreeable nation, which is itself unknown to almost all the world. The miracles which you and yours, I and mine, have performed shall one day be a great subject of doubt and scandal to inquisitive philosophers. But happily these miracles shall find belief with the devout sages who shall prove submissive to the enlightened in one corner of the world; and this is all that is necessary."

As he spoke these words the princess pulled him by the sleeve, and said to him:

"Mambres, will you not buy my bull?"

The magician, plunged into a deep reverie, made no reply, and Amasidia poured forth her tears.

She then addressed herself to the old woman.

"My good woman," said she, "I conjure you, by all you hold most dear in the world, by your father, by your mother, by your nurse, who are certainly still alive, to sell me not only your bull but likewise your pigeon, which seems very much attached to him.

"As for the other animals, I do not want them; but I shall catch the vapors if you do not sell me this charming bull, who will be all the happiness of my life."

The old woman respectfully kissed the fringe of her gauze robe and replied:

"Princess, my bull is not to be sold. Your illustrious magician is acquainted with this. All that I can do for your service is to permit him to feed every day near your palace. You may caress him, give him biscuits, and make him dance about at your pleasure; but he must always be under the eyes of all these animals who accompany me and who are charged with the keeping of him. If he does not endeavor to escape from them, they will prove peaceable; but if he attempt once more to break his chain, as he did upon seeing you, woe be unto him. I would not then answer for his life. This large fish, which you see, will certainly swallow him and keep him longer than three days in his belly; or this serpent, who appears to you so mild, will give him a mortal sting."

The white bull, who understood perfectly the old woman's conversation but was unable to speak, humbly accepted all the proposals. He laid himself down at her feet; he lowed softly; and, looking tenderly at Amasidia, seemed to say to her:

"Come and see me sometimes, upon the lawn."

The serpent now took up the conversation:

"Princess," said he, "I advise you to act implicitly as Mademoiselle of Endor has told you."

The she-ass likewise put in her word, and was of the opinion of the serpent.

Amasidia was afflicted that this serpent and this ass should speak so well; while a beautiful bull, who had such noble and tender sentiments, was unable to express them.

"Alas!" said she, in a low voice. "Nothing is more common at court. One sees there every day fine lords who cannot converse, and contemptible wretches who speak with assurance."

"This serpent," said Mambres, "is not a contemptible wretch. He is perhaps the personage of the greatest importance."

The day now declined, and the princess was obliged to return home, after having promised to come back next day at the same hour. Her ladies of the palace were astonished, and understood nothing of what they had seen or heard. Mambres made reflections. The princess, recollecting that the serpent called the old woman mademoiselle, concluded at random that she was still unmarried, and felt some affliction that such was also her own condition. Respectable affliction! which she concealed, however, with as much care as the name of her lover.

III

HOW THE BEAUTIFUL AMASIDIA HAD
A SECRET CONVERSATION
WITH A BEAUTIFUL SERPENT

The beautiful princess recommended secrecy to her ladies with regard to what they had seen. They all promised it, and kept their promise for a whole day.

We may believe that Amasidia slept little that night. An inexplicable charm continually recalled the idea of her beautiful bull. As soon, therefore, as she was free to speak with her wise Mambres, she said to him:

"O sage, this animal turns my head."

"He employs mine very much," said Mambres. "I see plainly that this bovine is very much superior to those of his species. I see that there is a great mystery, and I suspect a fatal event. Your father, Amasis, is suspicious and violent; and this affair requires that you conduct yourself with the greatest precaution."

"Ah," said the princess, "I have too much curiosity to be prudent. It is the only sentiment which can unite in my heart with that which preys upon me on account of the lover I have lost. May I not know who this white bull is that gives me such strange disquiet?"

Mambres replied:

"I have already confessed to you, frankly, that my knowledge declines in proportion as my age advances, but I mistake much if the serpent is not informed of what you are so very desirous of knowing. He does not want sense. He expresses himself with propriety. He has been long accustomed to interfere in the affairs of the ladies."

"Ah! Undoubtedly," said Amasidia, "this is the beautiful serpent of Egypt who, by fixing his tail into his mouth, becomes the emblem of eternity; who enlightens the world when he opens his eyes and darkens it when he shuts them?"

"No, miss."

"It is, then, the serpent of Aesculapius?"

"Still less."

"It is perhaps Jupiter under the figure of a serpent?"

"Not at all."

"Ah, now I see, I see. It is the rod which you formerly changed into a sea serpent?"

"No, indeed it is not; but all these serpents are of the same family. This one has a very high character in his own country. He passes there for the most extraordinary serpent that was ever seen. Address yourself to him. However, I warn you it is a dangerous undertaking. Were I in your place, I would hardly trouble myself with either the bull, the she-ass, the he-goat, the serpent, the fish, the raven, or the pigeon. But passion hurries you on, and all I can do is to pity you, and tremble."

The princess conjured him to procure her a tête-à-tête with the serpent. Mambres, who was obliging, consented, and making profound reflections, he went and communicated to the witch in so insinuating a manner the whim of the princess that the old woman told him Amasidia might lay her commands upon her: the serpent was perfectly well bred and so polite to the ladies that he wished for nothing more than to oblige them, and would not fail to keep the princess's appointment.

The ancient magician returned to inform the princess of this good news, but he still dreaded some misfortune and made reflections.

"You desire to speak with the serpent, mademoiselle. This you may accomplish whenever your highness thinks proper. But remember you must flatter him, for every animal has a great deal of self-love, and the serpent in particular. It is said he was formerly driven out of heaven for excessive pride."

"I have never heard of it," replied the princess.

"I believe it," said the old man.

He then informed her of all the reports which had been spread about this famous serpent.

"But, my dear princess, whatever singular adventures may have happened to him, you never can extort these secrets from him but by flattery. Having formerly deceived women, it is equitable that he in turn should be deceived by a woman.

"I will do my utmost," said the princess, and departed with her maids of honor.

The old woman was feeding the bull at a considerable distance. Mambres left Amasidia to herself, and went and discoursed with the witch. One lady of honor chatted with the she-ass, the others amused themselves with the goat, the dog, the raven, and the pigeon. As for the large fish that frightened everybody, he plunged himself into the Nile by order of the old woman.

The serpent then attended the beautiful Amasidia into the grove, where they had the following conversation:

SERPENT. You cannot imagine, mademoiselle, how much I am flattered with the honor which your highness deigns to confer upon me.

PRINCESS. Your great reputation, sir, the beauty of your countenance, and the brilliancy of your eyes have emboldened me to seek for this conversation. I know by public report (if it be not false) that you were formerly a very great lord in the empyrean heaven.

SERPENT. It is true, miss, I had there a very distinguished place. It is pretended I am a disgraced favorite. This is a report which once went abroad in India. The Brahmins were the first who gave a history of my adventures. And I doubt not but one day or other, the poets of the North will make them the subject of an extravagant epic poem, for in truth it is all that can be made of them. Yet I am not so much fallen but that I have left in this globe a very extensive dominion. I might venture to assert that the whole earth belongs to me.

PRINCESS. I believe it, for they tell me that your powers of persuasion are irresistible, and to please is to reign.

SERPENT. I feel, mademoiselle, while I behold and listen to you, that you have over me the same power which you ascribe to me over so many others.

PRINCESS. You are, I believe, an amiable conqueror. It is said that your conquests among the fair sex have been numerous, and that you began with our common mother, whose name I have unfortunately forgotten.

SERPENT. They do me injustice. She honored me with her confidence, and I gave her the best advice. I desired that she and her husband should eat heartily of the fruit of the tree of knowledge. I imagined in doing this that I should please the Ruler of all things. It seemed to me that a tree so necessary to the human race was not planted to be entirely useless. Would the Supreme Being have wished to have been served by fools and idiots? Is not the mind formed for the acquisition of knowledge and for improvement? Is not the knowledge of good and evil necessary for doing the one and avoiding the other? I certainly merited their thanks.

PRINCESS. Yet they tell me that you have suffered for it. Probably it is since this period that so many ministers have been punished for giving good advice and so many real philosophers and men of genius persecuted for their writings that were useful to mankind.

SERPENT. It is my enemies who have told you these stories. They say that I am out of favor at court. But a proof that my influence there has not declined is their own confession that I entered into the council when it was in agitation to try the good man Job; and I was again called upon when the resolution was taken to deceive a certain petty king called Ahab. I alone was charged with this honorable commission.

PRINCESS. Ah, sir! I do not believe that you are formed to deceive. But since you are always in the ministry, may I beg a favor of you? I hope so amiable a lord will not deny me.

SERPENT. Mademoiselle, your requests are laws; name your commands.

PRINCESS. I entreat that you will tell me who this white bull is, for whom I feel such extraordinary sentiments, which both affect and alarm me. I am told that you would deign to inform me.

SERPENT. Curiosity is necessary to human nature, and especially to your amiable sex. Without it they would live in the most shameful ignorance. I have always satisfied, as far as lay in my power, the curiosity of the ladies. I am accused, indeed, of using this complaisance only to vex the Ruler of the world. I swear to you that I could propose nothing more agreeable to myself than to obey you; but the old woman must have informed you that the revealing of this secret will be attended with some danger to you.

PRINCESS. Ah! It is that which makes me still more curious.

SERPENT. In this I discover the sex to whom I have formerly done service.

PRINCESS. If you possess any feeling; if rational beings should mutually assist each other; if you have compassion for an unfortunate creature, do not refuse my request.

SERPENT. You affect me. I must satisfy you; but do not interrupt me.

PRINCESS. I promise you I will not.

SERPENT. There was a young king, beautiful, charming, in love, beloved—

PRINCESS. A young king! Beautiful, charming, in love, beloved! And by whom? And who was this king? How old was he? What has become of him? Where is his kingdom? What is his name?

SERPENT. See, I have scarce begun, and you have already interrupted me. Take care. If you have not more command over yourself, you are undone.

PRINCESS. Ah, pardon me, sir. I will not repeat my indiscretion. Go on, I beseech you.

SERPENT. This great king, the most valiant of men, victorious wherever he carried his arms, often dreamed when asleep, and forgot his dreams when awake. He wanted his magicians to remember and inform him what he had dreamed, otherwise he declared he would hang them; for that nothing was more equitable. It is now nearly seven years since he dreamed a fine dream, which he entirely forgot when he awoke; and a young Jew, full of experience, having revealed it to him, this amiable king was immediately changed into an ox for—

PRINCESS. Ah! It is my dear Neb——

She could not finish; she fainted away. Mambres, who listened at a distance, saw her fall and believed her dead.

IV
HOW THEY WANTED TO SACRIFICE THE BULL AND
EXORCISE THE PRINCESS

Mambres runs to her, weeping. The serpent is affected. He, alas, cannot weep, but he hisses in a mournful tone. He cries out, "She is dead." The ass repeats, "She is dead." The raven tells it over again. All the other animals appeared afflicted except the fish of Jonah, which has always been merciless. The lady of honor, the ladies of the court, arrive and tear their hair.

The white bull, who fed at a distance and heard their cries, ran to the grove, dragging the old woman after him, while his loud bellowings made the neighboring echoes resound. To no purpose did the ladies pour upon the expiring Amasidia their bottles of rose water, of pink, of myrtle, of benzoin, of balm of Gilead, of amomum, of gillyflower, of nutmeg, of ambergris. She had not as yet given the smallest signs of life. But as soon as she perceived that the beautiful white bull was beside her she came to herself, more bloom-ing, more beautiful and lively, than ever. A thousand times did she kiss this charming animal, who languishingly leaned his head on her snowy bosom. She called him, "My master, my king, my dear, my life!" She threw her fair arms around his neck, which was whiter than the snow. The light straw does not adhere more closely to the amber, the vine to the elm, nor the ivy to the oak. The sweet murmur of her sighs was heard. Her eyes were seen, now sparkling with a tender flame and now obscured by those precious tears which love makes us shed.

We may easily judge into what astonishment the lady of honor and ladies of her train were thrown. As soon as they entered the palace they related to their lovers this extraordinary adventure, and everyone with different circumstances, which increased its singularity, and which always contributes to the variety of all histories.

No sooner was Amasis, king of Tanis, informed of these events than his royal breast was inflamed with just indignation. Such was the wrath of Minos when he understood that his daughter Pasiphaë lavished her tender favors upon the father of the Minotaur. Thus raged Juno when she beheld Jupiter caressing the beautiful cow Io, daughter of the river Inachus. Following the dictates of passion, the stern Amasis imprisoned his unhappy daughter, the beautiful Amasidia, in her chamber, and placed over her a guard of black eunuchs. He then assembled his privy council.

The grand magician presided there but had no longer the same influence as formerly. All the ministers of state concluded that this white bull was a sorcerer. It was quite the contrary. He was bewitched. But in delicate affairs they are always mistaken at court.

It was carried by a great majority that the princess should be exorcised, and the old woman and the bull sacrificed.

The wise Mambres contradicted not the opinion of the king and council. The right of exorcising belonged to him. He could delay it under some plausible pretense. The god Apis had lately died at Memphis. A good ox dies just like another ox. And it was not allowed to exorcise any person in Egypt until a new ox was found to replace the deceased.

It was decreed in the council to wait until the nomination should be made of a new god at Memphis.

The good old man, Mambres, perceived to what danger his dear princess was exposed. He knew who her lover was. The syllables Nebu—, which had escaped her, laid open the whole mystery to the eyes of this sage.

The dynasty of Memphis belonged at this time to the Babylonians. They preserved this remainder of the conquests they had gained under the greatest king of the world, to whom Amasis was a mortal enemy. Mambres had occasion for all his wisdom to conduct himself properly in the midst of so many difficulties. If the king Amasis should discover the lover of his daughter, her death would be inevitable. He had sworn it. The great, the young, the beautiful king of whom she was enamored had dethroned the king her father, and Amasis had only recovered his kingdom about seven years. From that time it was not known what had become of the adorable monarch—the conqueror and idol of the nations—the tender and generous lover of the charming Amasidia. Sacrificing the white bull would inevitably occasion the death of the beautiful princess.

What could Mambres do in such critical circumstances? He went, after the council had broken up, to find his dear foster daughter.

"My dear child," he says, "I will serve you, but I repeat it, they will behead you if ever you pronounce the name of your lover."

"Ah! What signifies my neck," replied the beautiful Amasidia, "if I cannot embrace that of Nebu—? My father is a cruel man. He not only refused to give me a charming prince whom I adore, but he declared war against him; and after he was conquered by my lover, he found the secret of changing him into an ox. Did one ever see more frightful malice? If my father were not my father, I do not know what I should do to him."

"It was not your father who played him this cruel trick," said the wise Mambres. "It was a native of Palestine, one of our ancient enemies, an inhabitant of a little country comprehended in that crowd of kingdoms which your lover subdued in order to polish and refine them.

"Such metamorphoses must not surprise you. You know that formerly I performed more extraordinary ones. Nothing was at that time more common than those changes which at present astonish philosophers. True history, which we have read together, informs us that Lycaon, king of Arcadia, was changed into a wolf; the beautiful Callisto, his daughter, into a bear; Io, the daughter of Inachus, our venerable Isis, into a cow; Daphne into a laurel; Syrinx into a flute. The fair Edith, wife of Lot—the best and most affectionate husband and father ever known in the world—has she not become, in our neighborhood, a pillar of salt, very sharp in taste, which has preserved both her likeness and her form, as the great men attest who have seen it? I was witness to this change in my youth. I saw seven powerful cities, in the most dry and parched situation in the world, all at once transformed into a beautiful lake. In the early part of my life the whole world was full of metamorphoses.

"In fine, madam, if examples can soothe your grief, remember that Venus changed Cerastes into an ox."

"I do not know," said the princess, "that examples comfort us. If my lover were dead, could I comfort myself by the idea that all men die?"

"Your pain may at least be alleviated," replied the sage, "and since your lover has become an ox, it is possible from an ox he may become a man. As for me, I should deserve to be changed into a tiger or a crocodile if I did not employ the little power I have in the service of a princess worthy of the adoration of the world; if I did not labor for the beautiful Amasidia, whom I have nursed upon my knees and whom fatal destiny exposes to such rude trials."

V

HOW THE WISE MAMBRES CONDUCTED HIMSELF
WISELY

The sage Mambres, having said everything he could to comfort the princess, but without succeeding in so doing, ran to the old woman.

"My companion," said he to her, "ours is a charming profession, but a very dangerous one. You run the risk of being hanged, and your ox of being burned, drowned, or devoured. I don't know what they will do with your other animals, for, prophet though I am, I know very little; but do you carefully conceal the serpent and the fish. Let not the one show his head above water, nor the other venture out of his hole. I will place the ox in one of my stables in the country. You shall be there with him, since you say that you are not allowed to abandon him. The good scapegoat may, upon this occasion, serve as an expiation. We will send him into the desert loaded with the sins of all the rest. He is accustomed to this ceremony, which does him no harm, and everyone knows that sin is expiated by means of a he-goat, who walks about for his own amusement. I only beg of you to lend me immediately Tobit's dog, who is a very swift greyhound; Balaam's ass, who runs better than a dromedary; the raven and the pigeon of the ark, who fly with amazing swiftness. I want to send them on an embassy to Memphis. It is an affair of great consequence."

The old woman replied to the magician:

"You may dispose as you please of Tobit's dog, of Balaam's ass, of the raven and the pigeon of the ark, and of the scapegoat; but my ox cannot enter into a stable. It is said, Daniel 5:21, that he must be always made fast to an iron chain, be always wet with the dew of heaven, and eat the grass of the field, and his portion be with the wild beasts.

"He is entrusted to me, and I must obey. What would Daniel, Ezekiel, and Jeremiah think of me if I trusted my ox to any other than to myself? I see you know the secret of this extraordinary animal, but I have not to reproach myself with having revealed it to you. I am going to conduct him far from this polluted land, toward the lake Sirbon, where he will be sheltered from the cruelties of the king of Tanis. My fish and my serpent will defend me. I fear nobody when I serve my master."

"My good woman," answered the wise Mambres, "let the will of God be done! Provided I can find your white bull again, the lake Sirbon, the lake Mœris, or the lake of Sodom are to me perfectly indifferent. I want to do nothing but good to him and to you. But why have you spoken to me of Daniel, Ezekiel, and Jeremiah?"

"Ah, sir," answered the old woman, "you know as well as I what concern they have in this important affair. But I have no time to lose. I don't desire to be hanged. I want not that my bull should be burned, drowned, or devoured. I go to the lake Sirbon by Canopus, with my serpent and my fish. Adieu."

The bull followed her pensively, after having testified his gratitude to the beneficent Mambres.

The wise Mambres was greatly troubled. He saw that Amasis, king of Tanis, distracted by the strange passion of his daughter for this animal, and believing her bewitched, would pursue everywhere the unfortunate bull, who would infallibly be burned as a sorcerer in the public place of Tanis, or given to the fish of Jonah, or be roasted and served up for food. Mambres wanted at all events to save the princess from this cruel disaster.

He wrote a letter, in sacred characters, to his friend the high priest of Memphis, upon the paper of Egypt, which was not yet in use. Here are the identical words of this letter:

Light of the world, lieutenant of Isis, Osiris, and Horus, chief of the circumcised, you whose altar is justly raised above all thrones! I am informed that your god, the ox Apis, is dead. I have one at your service. Come quickly with your priests to acknowledge, to worship, and to conduct him into the stable of your temple. May Isis, Osiris, and Horus keep you in their holy and worthy protection, and likewise the priests of Memphis in their holy care.

> Your affectionate friend,
> Mambres

He made four copies of this letter, for fear of accidents, and enclosed them in cases of the hardest ebony. Then, calling to him his four couriers, whom he had destined for this employment (these were the ass, the dog, the raven, and the pigeon), he said to the ass:

"I know with what fidelity you served Balaam, my brother. Serve me as faithfully. There is not a unicorn who equals you in swiftness. Go, my dear friend, and deliver this letter to the person himself to whom it is directed, and return."

The ass answered:

"Sir, as I served Balaam, I will serve you. I will go, and I will return."

The sage put the box of ebony into her mouth, and she swiftly departed. He then called Tobit's dog.

"Faithful dog," said Mambres, "more speedy in thy course than the nimble-footed Achilles, I know what you performed for Tobit, son of Tobit, when you and the angel Raphael accompanied him from Nineveh to Ragusa, in Media, and from Ragusa to Nineveh, and that he brought back to his father ten talents, which the slave Tobit, the father, had lent to the slave Gabelus; for the slaves at that time were very rich. Carry this letter as it is directed. It is much more valuable than ten talents of silver."

The dog then replied:

"Sir, if I formerly followed the messenger Raphael, I can with equal ease execute your commission."

Mambres put the letter into his mouth.

He next spoke in the same manner to the pigeon, who replied:

"Sir, if I brought back a bough into the ark, I will likewise bring you back an answer."

She took the letter in her bill, and the three messengers were out of sight in a moment. Then Mambres addressed the raven:

"I know that you fed the great prophet Elijah, when he was concealed near the torrent of Cherith, so much celebrated in the world. You brought him every day good bread and fat pullets. I only ask of you to carry this letter to Memphis."

The raven answered in these words:

"It is true, sir, that I carried every day a dinner to the great prophet Elijah, the Tishbite. I saw him mount in a chariot of fire drawn by fiery horses, although this is not the usual method of traveling. But I always took care to eat half the dinner myself. I am very well pleased to carry your letter, provided you make me certain of two good meals every day, and that I am paid money in advance for my commission."

Mambres, angry, replied:

"Gluttonous and malicious creature, I am not astonished that Apollo has made you black as a mole, after being white as a swan, as you were formerly, before you betrayed in the plains of Thessaly the beautiful Coronis, the unfortunate mother of Aesculapius. Tell me, did you eat ribs of beef and pullets every day when you were ten whole months in the ark?"

"Sir," said the raven, "we had there very good cheer. They served up roast meat twice a day to all the fowls of my species, who live upon nothing but flesh, such as the vultures, kites, eagles, buzzards, sparrow hawks, owls, tercels, falcons, great owls, and an innumerable crowd of birds of prey. They furnished, with the most plentiful profusion, the tables of the lions, leopards, tigers, panthers, hyenas, wolves, bears, foxes, polecats, and all sorts of carnivorous quadrupeds. There were in the ark eight persons of distinction (and the only ones who were then in the world), continually employed in the care of our table and our wardrobe. Noah and his wife, who were about six hundred years old, their three sons, and their three wives. It was charming to see with what care, what dexterity, what cleanliness, our eight domestics served four thousand of the most ravenous guests, without reckoning the amazing trouble which about ten or twelve thousand other animals required, from the elephant and the giraffe, to the silkworm and the fly. What astonishes me is that our purveyor Noah is unknown to all the nations of whom he is the stem, but I don't much mind it. I had already been present at a similar entertainment with Xesustres, king of Thrace. Such things as these happen from time to time for the instruction of ravens. In a word, I want to have good cheer and to be paid in ready money."

The wise Mambres took care not to give his letter to such a discontented and babbling animal; and they separated very much dissatisfied with each other.

But it was necessary to know what became of the white bull, and not to lose sight of the old woman and the serpent. Mambres ordered his intelligent and faithful domestics to follow them; and as for himself, he advanced in a litter by the side of the Nile, always making reflections.

"How is it possible," said he to himself, "that a serpent should be master of almost all the world, as he boasts, and as so many learned men acknowledge, and that he nevertheless obeys an old woman? How is it that he is sometimes called to the council of the Most High, while he creeps upon earth? In what manner can he enter by his power alone into the bodies of men, and why do so many men pretend to dislodge him by means of words? In short, why does he pass with a small neighboring people for having ruined the human race? And how is it that the human race are entirely ignorant of this? I am old, I have studied all my life, but I see a crowd of inconsistencies which I cannot reconcile. I cannot account for what has happened to myself, neither for the great things which I long ago performed nor for those of which I have been witness. Everything well considered, I begin to think that this world subsists by contradictions, *rerum concordia discors*, as my master Zoroaster formerly said."

While he was plunged in this obscure metaphysical reasoning—obscure like all metaphysics—a boatman singing a jovial song made fast a small boat by the side of the river, and three grave personages, half clothed in dirty, tattered garments, landed from it; but they preserved, under the garb of poverty, the most majestic and august air. These strangers were Daniel, Ezekiel, and Jeremiah.

VI
HOW MAMBRES MET THREE PROPHETS, AND GAVE
THEM A GOOD DINNER

These three great men, who had the prophetic light in their countenance, knew the wise Mambres to be one of their brethren, by some marks of the same light which he had still remaining, and prostrated themselves before his litter. Mambres likewise knew them to be prophets, more by their uncouth dress than by those gleams of fire which proceeded from their august heads. He conjectured that they came to learn news of the white bull; and conducting himself with his usual propriety, he alighted from his carriage and advanced a few steps toward them, with dignified politeness. He raised them up, caused tents to be erected, and prepared a dinner, of which he rightly judged the prophets had very great need.

He invited to it the old woman, who was only about five hundred paces from them. She accepted the invitation and arrived leading her white bull.

Two soups were served up, one *de Bisque*, and the other *à la Reine*. The first course consisted of a carp's tongue pie, livers of eelpouts, and pikes; fowls dressed with pistachios, pigeons with truffles and olives; two young turkeys with gravy of crayfish, mushrooms, and morels; and a *chipolata*. The second course was composed of pheasants, partridges, quails, and ortolans, with four salads; the epergne was in the highest taste; nothing could be more delicious than the side dishes; nothing more brilliant and more ingenious than the dessert. But the wise Mambres took great care to have no boiled beef, nor short ribs, tongue, nor palate of an ox, nor cow's udder, lest the unfortunate monarch near at hand should think that they insulted him.

This great and unfortunate prince was feeding near the tent; and never did he feel more cruelly the fatal revolution which had deprived him of his throne for seven long years.

"Alas," said he to himself, "this Daniel, who has changed me into a bull, and this sorceress, my keeper, make the best cheer in the world; while I, the sovereign of Asia, am reduced to the necessity of eating grass and drinking water."

When they had drunk heartily of the wine of Engaddi, of Tadmor, and of Shiraz, the prophets and the witch conversed with more frankness than at the first course.

"I must acknowledge," said Daniel, "that I did not live so well in the lion's den."

"What, sir?" said Mambres. "Did they put you into a den of lions? How came you not to be devoured?"

"Sir," said Daniel, "you know very well that lions never eat prophets."

"As for me," said Jeremiah, "I have passed my whole life starving of hunger. This is the only day I ever ate a good meal; and were I to spend my life over again, and had it in my power to choose my condition, I must own I would much rather be comptroller-general or bishop of Babylon than prophet at Jerusalem."

Ezekiel cried, "I was once ordered to sleep three hundred and ninety days upon my left side, and to eat all that time bread of wheat, and barley, and beans, and lentils, cooked in the strangest manner. I must own that the cookery of Seigneur Mambres is much more delicate. However, the prophetic trade has its advantages, and the proof is that there are many who follow it."

After they had spoken thus freely, Mambres entered upon business. He asked the three pilgrims the reason of their journey into the dominions of the king of Tanis. Daniel replied that the kingdom of Babylon had been all in a flame since Nebuchadnezzar had disappeared; that according to the custom of the court, they had persecuted all the prophets, who passed their lives in sometimes seeing kings humbled at their feet and sometimes receiving a hundred lashes from them; that at length they had been obliged to take refuge in Egypt for fear of being starved.

Ezekiel and Jeremiah likewise spoke a long time, in such fine terms that

it was almost impossible to understand them. As for the witch, she had always
a strict eye over her charge. The fish of Jonah continued in the Nile, opposite
to the tent, and the serpent sported upon the grass. After drinking coffee,
they took a walk by the side of the Nile; and the white bull, perceiving the
three prophets, his enemies, bellowed most dreadfully, ran furiously at them,
and gored them with his horns. As prophets never have anything but skin
upon their bones, he would certainly have run them through; but the ruler
of the world, who sees all and remedies all, changed them immediately into
magpies; and they continued to chatter as before. The same thing happened
since to the Pierides; so much has fable always imitated sacred history.

This incident caused new reflections in the mind of Mambres.

"Here," said he, "are three great prophets changed into magpies. This
ought to teach us never to speak too much and always to observe a suitable
discretion."

He concluded that wisdom was better than eloquence, and thought
profoundly as usual—when a great and terrible spectacle presented itself to
his eyes.

VII
HOW KING AMASIS WANTED TO GIVE THE WHITE BULL
TO BE DEVOURED BY THE FISH OF JONAH,
AND DID NOT DO IT

Clouds of dust floated from south to north. The noise of drums, fifes,
psalteries, harps, and sackbuts was heard. Several squadrons and battalions
advanced, and Amasis, king of Tanis, was at their head upon an Arabian
horse caparisoned with scarlet trappings embroidered in gold. The heralds
proclaimed that they should seize the white bull, bind him, and throw him
into the Nile, to be devoured by the fish of Jonah; "for the king our lord,
who is just, wants to revenge himself upon the white bull, who has bewitched
his daughter."

The good old man Mambres made more reflections than ever. He saw
very plainly that the malicious raven had told all to the king and that the
princess ran a great risk of being beheaded.

"My dear friend," said he to the serpent, "go quickly and comfort the
fair Amasidia, my foster daughter. Bid her fear nothing, whatever may happen,
and tell her stories to alleviate her inquietude; for stories always amuse the
ladies, and it is only by interesting them that one can succeed in the world."

Mambres next prostrated himself before Amasis, king of Tanis, and thus
addressed him:

"O King, live forever! The white bull should certainly be sacrificed, for your majesty is always in the right; but the ruler of the world has said this bull must not be swallowed up by the fish of Jonah till Memphis shall have found a god to supply the place of him who is dead. Then thou shalt be revenged, and thy daughter exorcised, for she is possessed. Your piety is too great not to obey the commands of the ruler of the universe."

Amasis, king of Tanis, remained for some time silent and in deep thought.

"The god Apis," said he, at length, "is dead! God rest his soul! When do you think another ox will be found to reign over the fruitful Egypt?"

"Sire," replied Mambres, "I ask but eight days."

"I grant them to you," replied the king, who was very religious, "and I will remain here the eight days. At the expiration of that time I will sacrifice the enemy of my daughter."

Amasis immediately ordered that his tents, cooks, and musicians should be brought, and remained here eight days, as it is related in Manethon.

The old woman was in despair that the bull she had in charge had but eight days to live. She raised phantoms every night, in order to dissuade the king from his cruel resolution; but Amasis forgot in the morning the phantoms he had seen in the night; similar to Nebuchadnezzar, who had always forgotten his dreams.

VIII
HOW THE SERPENT TOLD STORIES TO THE PRINCESS
TO COMFORT HER

Meanwhile the serpent told stories to the fair Amasidia to soothe her. He related to her how he had formerly cured a whole nation of the bite of certain little serpents, only by showing himself at the end of a staff (Num. xx.9). He informed her of the conquests of a hero who made a charming contrast with Amphion, architect of Thebes. Amphion assembled hewn stones by the sound of his violin. To build a city he had only to play a rigadoon and a minuet; but the other hero destroyed them by the sound of rams' horns. He executed thirty-one powerful kings in a country of four leagues in length and four in breadth. He made stones rain down from heaven upon a battalion of routed Amorites; and having thus exterminated them, he stopped the sun and moon at noonday between Gibeon and Ajalon, in the road to Beth-Horon, to exterminate them still more, after the example of Bacchus, who had stopped the sun and the moon in his journey to the Indies.

The prudence which every serpent ought to have did not allow him to tell the fair Amasidia of the powerful Jephthah, who made a vow and beheaded his daughter because he had gained a battle. This would have struck terror into the mind of the fair princess. But he related to her the adventures of the great Samson, who killed a thousand Philistines with the jawbone of an ass, who tied together three hundred foxes by the tail, and who fell into the snares of a lady, less beautiful, less tender, and less faithful than the charming Amasidia.

He related to her the story of the unfortunate Sechem and Dinah, as well as the more celebrated adventures of Ruth and Boaz; those of Judah and Tamar; those even of Lot's two daughters; those of Abraham and Jacob's servant maids; those of Reuben and Bilhah; those of David and Bathsheba; and those of the great King Solomon. In short, everything which could dissipate the grief of a fair princess.

IX
HOW THE SERPENT
DID NOT COMFORT THE PRINCESS

"All these stories tire me," said Amasidia, for she had understanding and taste. "They are good for nothing but to be commented upon among the Irish by that madman Abbadie, or among the Welsh by that prattler d'Houteville. Stories which might have amused the great-great-great-grandmother of my grandmother appear insipid to me who have been educated by the wise Mambres, and who have read "Human Understanding" by the Egyptian philosopher named Locke,* and the "Matron of Ephesus." I choose that a story should be founded on probability, and not always resemble a dream. I desire to find nothing in it trivial or extravagant; and I desire above all, that under the appearance of fable there may appear some latent truth, obvious to the discerning eye, though it escape the observation of the vulgar.

"I am weary of a sun and of a moon which an old beldam disposes of at her pleasure, of mountains which dance, of rivers which return to their sources, and of dead men who rise again; but I am above measure disgusted when such insipid stories are written in a bombastic and unintelligible manner. A lady who expects to see her lover swallowed up by a great fish, and who is apprehensive of being beheaded by her own father, has need of amusement; but suit my amusement to my taste."

"You impose a difficult task upon me," replied the serpent. "I could have formerly made you pass a few hours agreeably enough, but for some time past I have lost both my imagination and memory. Alas! what has become of those faculties with which I formerly amused the ladies? Let me try, however, if I can recollect one moral tale for your entertainment.

"Five and twenty thousand years ago King Gnaof and Queen Patra reigned

---

* The doctrine of metempsychosis must be relied upon to explain this seeming anachronism.

in Thebes with its hundred gates. King Gnaof was very handsome, and Queen Patra still more beautiful. But their home was unblest with children, and no heirs were born to continue the royal race.

"The members of the faculty of medicine and of the academy of surgery wrote excellent treatises upon this subject. The queen was sent to drink mineral waters; she fasted and prayed; she made magnificent presents to the temple of Jupiter Ammon, but all was to no purpose. At length a—"

"Mon Dieu!" said the princess, "but I see where this leads. This story is too common, and I must likewise tell you that it offends my modesty. Relate some very true and moral story, which I have never yet heard, to complete the improvement of my understanding and my heart, as the Egyptian professor Linro says."

"Here, then, madam," said the beautiful serpent, "is one most incontestably authentic.

"There were three prophets, all equally ambitious and discontented with their condition. They had in common the folly to wish to be kings; for there is only one step from the rank of a prophet to that of a monarch, and man always aspires to the highest step in the ladder of fortune. In other respects their inclinations and their pleasures were totally different. The first preached admirably to his assembled brethren, who applauded him by clapping their hands, the second was distractedly fond of music, and the third was a passionate lover of the fair sex.

"The angel Ithuriel presented himself one day to them when they were at table discoursing on the sweets of royalty.

" 'The Ruler of the World,' said the angel to them, 'sends me to reward your virtue. Not only shall you be kings, but you shall constantly satisfy your ruling passions. You, first prophet, I make king of Egypt, and you shall continually preside in your council, who shall applaud your eloquence and your wisdom; and you, second prophet, I make king over Persia, and you shall continually hear most heavenly music; and you, third prophet, I make king of India, and I give you a charming mistress who shall never forsake you.'

"He to whose lot Egypt fell began his reign by assembling his council, which was composed only of two hundred sages. He made them a long and eloquent speech, which was very much applauded, and the monarch enjoyed the pleasing satisfaction of intoxicating himself with praises uncorrupted by flattery.

"The council for foreign affairs succeeded to the privy council. This was much more numerous, and a new speech received still greater encomiums. And it was the same in the other councils. There was not a moment of intermission in the pleasures and glory of the prophet king of Egypt. The fame of his eloquence filled the world.

"The prophet king of Persia began his reign by an Italian opera, whose choruses were sung by fifteen hundred eunuchs. Their voices penetrated his soul even to the very marrow of the bones, where it resides. To this opera succeeded another, and to the second a third, without interruption.

"The king of India shut himself up with his mistress, and enjoyed perfect pleasure in her society. He considered the necessity of always flattering her as the highest felicity, and pitied the wretched situation of his two brethren, of whom one was obliged always to convene his council, and the other to be continually at an opera.

"It happened at the end of a few days that each of these kings became disgusted with his occupation, and beheld from his window certain wood-cutters, who came from an alehouse and who were going to work in a neighboring forest. They walked arm in arm with their sweethearts, with whom they were happy. The kings begged of the angel Ithuriel that he would intercede with the Ruler of the World, and make them woodcutters."

"I do not know whether the Ruler of the World granted their request or not," interrupted the tender Amasidia, "and I do not care much about it, but I know very well that I should ask for nothing of anyone were I with my lover, with my dear NEBUCHADNEZZAR!"

The vaults of the palace resounded this mighty name. At first Amasidia had only pronounced Ne—, afterward Neb—, then Nebu—. At length passion hurried her on, and she pronounced entire the fatal name, notwithstanding the oath she had sworn to the king, her father. All the ladies of the court repeated Nebuchadnezzar, and the malicious raven did not fail to carry the tidings to the king. The countenance of Amasis, king of Tanis, sank, because his heart was troubled. And thus it was that the serpent, the wisest and most subtle of animals, always beguiled the women, thinking to do them service.

Amasis, in a fury, sent twelve alguazils for his daughter. These men are always ready to execute barbarous orders, because they are paid for it.

X
HOW THEY WANTED TO BEHEAD THE PRINCESS, AND DID NOT DO IT

No sooner had the princess entered the camp of the king than he said to her: "My daughter, you know that all princesses who disobey their fathers are put to death; without which it would be impossible that a kingdom could be well governed. I charged you never to mention the name of your lover, Nebuchadnezzar, my mortal enemy, who dethroned me about seven years ago, and disappeared. In his place you have chosen a white bull, and you have cried 'Nebuchadnezzar.' It is just that I behead you."

The princess replied: "My father, thy will be done; but grant me some time to bewail my sad fate."

"That is reasonable," said King Amasis; "and it is a rule established among the most judicious princes. I give you a whole day to bewail your destiny, since it is your desire. Tomorrow, which is the eighth day of my encampment, I will cause the white bull to be swallowed up by the fish, and I will behead you precisely at nine o'clock in the morning."

The beautiful Amasidia then went forth in sorrow, to bewail her father's cruelty, and wandered by the side of the Nile, accompanied by the ladies of her train.

The wise Mambres pondered beside her, and reckoned the hours and the moments.

"Well! my dear Mambres," said she to him, "you have changed the waters of the Nile into blood, according to custom, and cannot you change the heart of Amasis, king of Tanis, my father? Will you suffer him to behead me tomorrow, at nine o'clock in the morning?"

"That depends," replied the reflecting Mambres, "upon the speed and diligence of my couriers."

The next day, as soon as the shadows of the obelisks and pyramids marked upon the ground the ninth hour of the day, the white bull was securely bound, to be thrown to the fish of Jonah; and they brought to the king his large sabre.

"Alas! alas!" said Nebuchadnezzar to himself. "I, a king, have been a bull for nearly seven years; and scarcely have I found the mistress I had lost, when I am condemned to be devoured by a fish."

Never had the wise Mambres made such profound reflections; and he was quite absorbed in his melancholy thoughts when he saw at a distance all he expected. An innumerable crowd drew nigh. Three figures, of Isis, Osiris, and Horus, joined together, advanced, drawn in a carriage of gold and precious stones by a hundred senators of Memphis, preceded by a hundred girls playing upon the sacred sistrums. Four thousand priests, with their heads shaved, were each mounted upon a hippopotamus.

At a great distance appeared with the same pomp the sheep of Thebes, the dog of Bubastis, the cat of Phœbe, the crocodile of Arsinoë, the goat of Mendes, and all the inferior gods of Egypt, who came to pay homage to the great ox, to the mighty Apis, as powerful as Isis, Osiris, and Horus, united together.

In the midst of the demi-gods, forty priests carried an enormous basket, filled with sacred onions. These were, it is true, gods, but they resembled onions very much.

On both sides of this aisle of gods, followed by an innumerable crowd of people, marched forty thousand warriors, with helmets on their heads, scimitars upon their left thighs, quivers at their shoulders, and bows in their hands.

All the priests sang in chorus, with a harmony which ravished the soul, and which melted it:

> *Alas! alas! our ox is dead—*
> *We'll have a finer in its stead.*

And at every pause was heard the sound of the sistrums, of cymbals, of tabors, of psalteries, of bagpipes, harps, and sackbuts.

Amasis, king of Tanis, astonished at this spectacle, beheaded not his daughter. He sheathed his scimitar.

XI
APOTHEOSIS OF THE WHITE BULL—TRIUMPH OF THE WISE MAMBRES—
THE SEVEN YEARS PROCLAIMED BY DANIEL ARE ACCOMPLISHED—
NEBUCHADNEZZAR RESUMES THE HUMAN FORM,
MARRIES THE BEAUTIFUL AMASIDIA, AND
ASCENDS THE THRONE OF BABYLON

"Great King," said Mambres to him, "the order of things is now changed. Your majesty must set the example. O King! quickly unbind the white bull, and be the first to adore him."

Amasis obeyed, and prostrated himself with all his people. The high priest of Memphis presented to the new god Apis the first handful of hay; Princess Amasidia tied to his beautiful horns festoons of roses, anemones, ranunculaceæ, tulips, pinks, and hyacinths. She took the liberty to kiss him, but with a profound respect. The priests strewed palms and flowers on the road by which they were to conduct him to Memphis. And the wise Mambres, still making reflections, whispered to his friend the serpent:

"*Daniel changed this monarch into a bull, and I have changed this bull into a god!*"

They returned to Memphis in the same order, and the king of Tanis, in some confusion, followed the band. Mambres, with a serene and diplomatic air, walked by his side. The old woman came after, much amazed. She was accompanied by the serpent, the dog, the she-ass, the raven, the pigeon, and the scapegoat. The great fish mounted up the Nile. Daniel, Ezekiel, and Jeremiah, changed into magpies, brought up the rear.

When they had reached the frontiers of the kingdom, which are not far distant, King Amasis took leave of the bull Apis, and said to his daughter:

"My daughter, let us return into my dominions, that I may behead you, as it has been determined in my royal breast, because you have pronounced the name of Nebuchadnezzar, my enemy, who dethroned me seven years ago. When a father has sworn to behead his daughter, he must either fulfil his oath or sink into hell forever, and I will not damn myself out of love for you."

The fair princess Amasidia replied to the king Amasis:

"My dear father, whom it pleases you go and behead, but it shall not be me. I am now in the territories of Isis, Osiris, Horus, and Apis. I will never forsake my beautiful white bull, and I will continue to kiss him, till I have seen his apotheosis in his stable in the holy city of Memphis. It is a weakness pardonable in a young lady of high birth."

Scarce had she spoken these words, when the ox Apis cried out:

"My dear Amasidia, I will love you whilst I live!"

This was the first time that the god Apis had been heard to speak during the forty thousand years that he had been worshiped.

The serpent and the she-ass cried out, "The seven years are accomplished!" And the three magpies repeated, "The seven years are accomplished!"

All the priests of Egypt raised their hands to heaven.

The god on a sudden was seen to lose his two hind legs, his two forelegs were changed into two human legs; two white muscular arms grew from his shoulders; his taurine visage was changed to the face of a charming hero; and he once more became the most beautiful of mortals.

"I choose," cried he, "rather to be the lover of the beautiful Amasidia than a god. I am NEBUCHADNEZZAR, KING OF KINGS!"

This metamorphosis astonished all the world except the wise Mambres. But what surprised nobody was that Nebuchadnezzar immediately married the fair Amasidia in presence of this assembly.

He left his father-in-law in quiet possession of the kingdom of Tanis, and made noble provision for the she-ass, the serpent, the dog, the pigeon, and even for the raven, the three magpies, and the large fish; showing to all the world that he knew how to forgive as well as to conquer.

The old woman had a considerable pension placed at her disposal.

The scapegoat was sent for a day into the wilderness, that all past sins might be expiated; and had afterwards twelve sprightly goats for his companions.

The wise Mambres returned to his palace and made reflections.

Nebuchadnezzar, after having embraced the magician, his benefactor, governed in tranquillity the kingdoms of Memphis, Babylon, Damascus, Balbec, Tyre, Syria, Asia Minor, Scythia, the countries of Thiras, Mosok, Tubal, Madai, Gog, Magog, Javan, Sogdiana, Aroriana, the Indies, and the Isles; and the people of this vast empire cried out aloud every morning at the rising of the sun:

"Long live great Nebuchadnezzar, king of kings, who is no longer an ox!"

Since which time it has been a custom in Babylon, when the sovereign, deceived by his satraps, his magicians, treasurers, or wives, at length acknowledges his errors, and amends his conduct, for all the people to cry out at his gate:

"Long live our great king, who is no longer an ox!"

Translated by William F. Fleming

‹ *Libussa* ›
Johann Karl August Musäus

any years ago, deep in the Bohemian forest, which is now only a shadow of what it was, there lived some little creatures at a time when the woods stretched far and wide. These ethereal beings were afraid of light and were more delicately fashioned than the substantially molded humans made of clay. People with a coarse sense of feeling could never see them, but they were half visible by moonlight to those with a finer sense. Indeed, they were well known to poets by the name of dryads and to ancient bards by that of elves. From time immemorial they had resided there undisturbed until, all at once, the forest resounded with loud war cries, for Duke Czech of Hungary stormed over the mountains with his Slavic hordes to seek a new domain in these wild regions. The beautiful inhabitants of the aged oaks, the rocks, clefts, and grottoes, as well as those of the reeds in the tarns and morasses, fled before the clamor of arms and the neighing of charging steeds. Even the powerful Erlking could not stand the uproar and transported his court to a more distant spot in the wilderness. Just one solitary elf could not make up her mind to leave her favorite oak, and as the woods were gradually chopped down here and there to cultivate the land, she alone had the courage to defend her tree against the violence of the newcomers and chose its towering peak for her abode.

Among the retinue of the duke was a young squire by the name of Krokus,

full of courage and impetuosity. Stout and handsome, he had a noble bearing, and his lord had commanded him to look after his horses. At times he drove them far into the forest in search of a green pasture, and he often rested beneath the oak that the elf inhabited. As soon as she noticed him, she took a liking to him, and whenever he slept there at the foot of the tree during the night, she would whisper pleasant dreams into his ear and provide clear images of what was to happen in the coming day. Or whenever a horse had strayed into the wilderness and the squire had lost its track and gone to sleep with worries on his mind, he would see in a dream the hidden path that would lead him to the spot where his lost steed was grazing. The farther the new settlers spread out, the closer they came to the dwelling of the elf. Owing to her gift of prophecy, she perceived how soon her life tree would be threatened by the ax, and she decided to reveal her concern to her squire. One clear, moonlit summer's eve, Krokus rounded up his herd somewhat later than usual and began heading for his bed under the lofty oak. His path led him around a little lake that was brimful with fishes, and the silver face of the moon cast its reflection on the water's surface like a gleaming ball of gold. He noticed, on the farther side of the water, a female figure, apparently taking a walk by the cool lakeshore. This sight disconcerted the young squire. "Why has this maiden come here alone?" he thought. "What is she doing in the wilderness at this time of night?" Yet the adventure was such that the young man was more intrigued than frightened. He quickened his steps without losing sight of the figure that had caught his attention. Soon he reached the place where he had first noticed it—beneath the oak. But now it appeared to him as if the thing he saw were more shadow than body. He stood puzzled, and a cold shudder crept over him, but then he heard a sweet, soft voice whisper, "Come here, dear stranger, and do not fear. I'm not a phantom or a deceptive shadow. I'm the elf of this grove and live in the oak tree under whose thick green branches you've often rested. I rocked you in sweet delightful dreams and brought you presentiments of your adventures, and when a mare or a foal had wandered away from the herd, I told you where you would find it. Now I would like you to repay my favors: I want you to be the protector of this tree, which has protected you so often from rain and sun. Keep the murderous axes of your brothers, who are laying waste the forest, from harming this venerable trunk."

The young squire, who regained his self-possession upon hearing the soft voice, replied, "Goddess or mortal, whoever you may be, ask me whatever you wish. If I can, I shall do it. However, I am a man of little significance among my people, just the servant of the duke, my lord. If he tells me, today or tomorrow, to have the horses graze here and then there, how shall I protect your tree in this immense forest? Still, if you command me, I shall resign from the prince's service and live under the shadow of your oak and protect it so long as I live."

"Do so," said the elf. "You shall not regret it."

Thereupon she vanished, and there was a rustling in the branches above, as if some breath of an evening breeze had become entangled in them and had stirred the leaves. Krokus stood for a while, still enchanted by the heavenly form that had appeared to him. He had never seen or known so delicate a woman, slender and marvelous in bearing, among the short, squat maidens of the Slavic people. Finally, he stretched himself upon the moss, but sleep did not descend upon his eyes. Indeed, dawn surprised him in a whirl of sweet emotions that were as strange and new to him as is the first beam of light to the opened eyes of a person born blind. With the first rays of morning, he hurried to the court of the duke, requested his discharge, and packed his weapons and equipment. Then, in a state of ecstasy, he rushed back, a bundle on his shoulders, to his blissful hermitage in the forest.

During his absence, a miller among the people had chosen the round flourishing trunk of the oak to be an axle and was preparing to cut it down with the help of his men. The worried elf sobbed bitterly as the greedy saw with its iron teeth began to nibble at the foundations of her dwelling. From the highest peak of the tree, she looked anxiously around for her faithful defender, but she could not discern him anywhere, and the gift of prophecy with which her kind had been endowed was impotent in the present situation, so that unlike the sons of Aesculapius, with their renowned vision that allows them to help themselves when death comes knocking at their door, she was incapable of reading her own fate.

Krokus was on his way, however, and so near the scene of this catastrophe that the noise of the screeching saw reached his ears. Such a sound in the forest did not bode good. He quickened his pace and saw the approaching destruction of the tree which he had taken under his protection. Like a fury he fell upon the woodcutters, and with spear and sword he frightened them away. Indeed, they thought he was a mountain demon and fled in great alarm.

Fortunately, the wound they had inflicted on the tree could still be healed, and its scar would disappear after a few summers.

In the solemn hour of evening, when the new settler had decided where he would build his dwelling, he measured off the space for a garden. Then he pondered his plans for the hermitage where he intended to spend his days cut off from human society and serving his shadowy companion, who did not appear to be much more real than a calendar saint who chooses a pious monk as her spiritual paramour. Just then the elf appeared before him at the edge of the lake, and with sweet looks she said, "Thanks to you, beloved stranger, the powerful arms of your brothers have been prevented from ruining this tree, with which my life is united. I want you to know that Mother Nature, who has granted my kind with various powers and influences, has tied the destinies of our lives with the growth and duration of the oak. Through us the queen of the woods raises her venerable head above the rabble of the other trees and shrubs. We further the circulation of the sap through her trunk and branches so that she may gain strength to combat the violent storms and to defy destructive time over the long centuries to come. On the other hand, our life is bound to hers. When the oak that destiny has appointed the partner of our existence begins to age, we age along with her. When she dies, we die too, as mortals do, a sleep of death, until chance or some hidden providence in the everlasting cycle of things unites our essence with a new germ. Then, empowered by our energy, it springs up in the course of years to become a mighty tree and provides us with the joys of life again. You may understand from this how important your help has been to me and how much I owe you. Ask me whatever you like, and your noble deed will be rewarded. Just tell me your heart's desire, and it will be granted to you this very hour."

Krokus remained silent. The sight of the charming elf had impressed him more than her speech, which he barely understood. She noticed his embarrassment and sought to help him by plucking a withered reed from the edge of the lake and breaking it into three pieces. Then she said, "Choose one of these three sticks or take one at random. The first contains honor and renown; the second, wealth and the capacity to enjoy it wisely; the third, happiness in love."

The young man cast his eyes upon the ground and answered, "Heavenly daughter, if you intend to grant my heart's desire, then I must tell you that it does not lie in these three sticks you offer me. My heart seeks something higher. What is honor but the tinderbox of pride? What are riches but the root of avarice? And what is love but the trapdoor of passion, which ensnares the noble freedom of the heart? My only wish is that you allow me to rest under the shadow of your oak tree, keeping me from the ravages of war and letting me hear lessons of wisdom from your sweet lips, so that I may grasp the secrets of the future."

"Your request," the elf replied, "is great, but your deed in my service was no less great. So be it as you desire. The blinds of your eyes shall disappear so that you'll be able to see the secrets of hidden wisdom. Moreover, you shall have the skin that comes with the fruit, for the wise man is also honored. He alone is rich, for he uses nothing more than he needs, and he tastes the nectar of love without poisoning it with tainted lips."

Upon saying this, she handed him the three sticks of the reed and departed. Then the young hermit prepared his bed beneath the moss, exceedingly content with the reception that the elf had given him. Sleep came upon him as upon a man forearmed. Cheerful morning dreams danced around his head and gave comfort to his imagination with the breath of happy expectations. On awakening, he gladly began his day's work, and before long he had built himself a pleasant hermit's cottage, had dug his garden, and had planted roses and lilies and other sweet-smelling flowers and herbs, not forgetting cabbage and other vegetables and a sufficient quantity of fruit trees. The elf never failed to visit him at twilight. She rejoiced as he prospered through his labor, walked with him hand in hand by the edge of the lake, where the waving reeds whispered a melodious evening greeting to the cozy pair as the wind rushed through them. She instructed her attentive disciple in the secrets of nature, taught him about the origin and essence of things, explained to him their natural and magical properties and effects, and transformed the coarse soldier into a thinker and philosopher.

As the feelings and senses of the young man grew refined through his association with the beautiful shadowy figure, it seemed as if the tender form of the elf was acquiring more density. Her bosom became warm and alive. Her brown eyes sparkled with the fire. And along with the shape, she appeared to have adopted the feelings of a blooming maiden. The sentimental hour of dusk, which seems to be expressly made to arouse slumbering feelings, had its usual effect. A few months after they had met, the sighing Krokus found himself filled by the happiness of love that the third stick had promised him, and he did not regret that the freedom of his heart had been ensnared by the trapdoor of love. Though the marriage of the tender pair took place without witnesses, it was celebrated with as much enjoyment as are the most tumultuous of weddings. Nor did they have to wait long for eloquent proofs of love's reward. The elf presented her husband with three daughters at one birth, and rejoicing at the fruitfulness of his consort, he embraced the firstborn who was carried crying into his room and named her Bela; the next-born, Therba; and the youngest, Libussa.

They were all beautifully formed, like jinns, and though not fashioned of such delicate materials as their mother, their corporeal structure was finer than the coarse, earthy clay of their father. They were also free from all childhood sicknesses: their swathings did not disturb them; they teethed without throwing fits. They did not scream about toilet training, nor did they get rickets. They did not have smallpox and, of course, did not have to fear scars, scummy eyes, or puckered faces. It was not necessary to lead them around with strings, for they ran like little partridges after the first nine days. As they grew up, they manifested all the talents of their mother for revealing hidden things and predicting the future.

In time Krokus himself also acquired this mysterious talent. Whenever a wolf scattered the flocks through the forest and the herdsmen went looking for their sheep and cattle, or whenever a woodsman was missing an ax or a hatchet, they sought counsel from the wise Krokus, who showed them where to find what they had lost. Whenever a mean neighbor stole something from the common stock or had broken into someone else's barn or dwelling and robbed and slain him, and none could guess who committed the crime, the wise Krokus was consulted. He led the people to a green, had them form a ring, and then stepped into the middle, whereupon he set in motion the trusty sieve that never failed to uncover the criminal. Because of these acts, his fame spread all over Bohemia, and whoever had some matter of concern or an important undertaking came to request advice from the wise Krokus about his prospects. The lame and the sick also sought to be helped or cured by him, and even the weak cattle were driven to him. Indeed, his gift of curing sick cattle by means of his shadow was just as great as that of the renowned Saint Martin of Schierbach. As a result, more and more people came to him day by day, and it soon seemed that the tripod of the Delphic Apollo had been transported to the Bohemian forest. Though Krokus gave advice to all who came to him and cured the sick and afflicted without fee or reward, the treasure of his mysterious wisdom drew rich interest and brought great profit to him. The people overwhelmed him with gifts and almost smothered him with testimonies of their good will. It was he who first revealed the mystery of washing gold from the sands of the Elbe, and as a reward he received a tenth of all that was produced. By these means his wealth and stocks increased. He built strongholds and palaces, had vast herds of cattle, owned rich pastures, fields, and woods, and thus acquired by degrees all the wealth that the generous elf had prophesied that the second stick would bring him.

One fine summer evening, when Krokus was returning home from an excursion with his retinue after settling a disputed boundary between two communities, he noticed his wife at the edge of the lake near the reeds, where she had first appeared to him. She waved to him with her hand. So he dismissed his servants and hurried to embrace her. She received him as usual with tender love, but her heart was sad. Ethereal tears trickled from her eyes, and they were so fine and fleeting that they were greedily inhaled by the air as they fell and thus did not reach the ground. Krokus was alarmed by her appearance, for he had never seen his wife's eyes this way. They had always been cheerful and sparkled with youthful gaiety.

"What's troubling you, love of my heart?" he asked. "I feel that something terrible is about to happen. Tell me, what do those tears mean?"

The elf sobbed, leaned her head sorrowfully on his shoulder, and said, "Beloved husband, during your absence I looked into the book of destiny, and I discovered that my life tree is threatened by an unfortunate fate. I must separate from you forever. Follow me into the castle, where I want to bless my children, for you will never see me again from this day on."

"Dearest wife," responded Krokus, "dispel these mournful thoughts. What kind of misfortune can threaten your tree? Isn't it firmly rooted? Look at its flourishing branches and how they stretch forth loaded with fruit and leaves; look how it raises its peak to the clouds. So long as I can move my arm, I shall defend your tree from any evildoer who might dare to harm it."

"Your mortal arm is but a powerless defense!" she replied. "Ants can only protect themselves from ants, flies from flies, and the worms of earth from other earthly worms. But what can the mightiest among you do against the workings of nature or the unalterable decisions of fate? The kings of the earth may be able to level little hills that they name fortresses and castles, but the weakest breath of air defies their authority, blows where it will, and mocks their commands. Up till now you have guarded this oak tree from the violence of men, but can you fight the tempest and prevent it from blowing off all its leaves. Or if a hidden worm is gnawing in its marrow, can you pull it out and stamp on it?"

As they were talking, they made their way into the castle, and the slender maidens jumped up and ran with joy to meet their mother, as was their custom at her evening visit. They gave her an account of their day's activities and produced needlework and embroidery to demonstrate how industrious they had been. However, now the hour of household happiness was joyless. They soon observed traces of deep suffering stamped on their father's countenance, and they looked with sympathizing sorrow at their mother's tears without venturing to inquire their cause. Their mother gave them many wise instructions and sound warnings, but her speech was like a swan song, as if she were saying farewell to the world. She lingered with her husband until the morning star went up in the sky. Then she embraced him and her children with mournful tenderness, and at daybreak she retired through the secret door to her oak tree, as was her custom, and left her dear ones to their own sad forebodings.

Nature stood silently, waiting for the rising sun, but heavy black clouds soon concealed her beaming head. The day grew sultry. The whole atmosphere was electric. Distant thunder came rolling over the forest, and echo with a hundred voices repeated its horrible rumbling in the winding valleys. At noon a forked thunderbolt came quivering and immediately struck the resistless oak, shattering it into splinters. The wreck lay scattered far around in the forest. When Krokus was informed about what had happened, he tore his garments, went forth with his daughters to mourn the life tree of his wife, and collected the tree's fragments in order to preserve them as precious relics. From that day on the elf was no more to be seen.

During the next few years, the tender girls grew and blossomed like budding roses, and the fame of their beauty spread throughout the entire country. The noblest young men flocked to Krokus to ask for his counsel on all sorts of matters, but they used their cases as pretexts, as is the custom of young men when the daughters of the master of the household are beautiful. The three sisters lived in openness and harmony with another and were still unaware of their talents. The gift of prophecy had been bestowed upon them to the same degree, and all their words were oracles, although they did not know this. Eventually their vanity was awakened through flattery. The quibblers surrounding them eagerly seized upon every sound emanating from their lips. Pedants noted down every look, investigated the faintest smile, explored the look of their eyes and drew from it more or less favorable prognostics, for they believed that they could guess their fate by interpreting it. Consequently, from this time on, lovers began to read their lucky or unlucky star from the horoscope of the eyes.

No sooner had vanity stolen into the virgin heart than pride, her dear confidante, snuck inside with her wicked rabble of an entourage, self-love, self-praise, self-will, and self-interest. The elder sisters were eager to outdo the younger in their arts and secretly envied her superior physical attractions. Although they were all very beautiful, Libussa was the most fetching. Bela turned her chief attention to the science of the plants, just as Medea had done in earlier times. She knew their hidden powers, could extract poisons and antidotes from them, and understood the art of making sweet or nauseous odors for the invisible forces from them. When her pans began to steam, she drew spirits out of the immeasurable depths of ether to her from beyond the moon, and they became her subjects just so they could inhale these delicious vapors with their fine organs. And when she scattered vile odors upon the coals, she could have stunk away every last pest from the wilderness.

Therba was as inventive as Circe in concocting magic spells that could command the elements, could raise storms and whirlwinds, also hail and thunder, and could shake the bowels of the earth so that it would lift itself from the sockets of its axle. She employed these arts to terrify the people and to be feared and honored by them as a goddess. In fact, she could determine the weather and change it according to the wishes and taste of men better than wise old nature does. Two brothers once quarreled about the weather, for their wishes were never the same. The one was a farmer and always needed rain to help his crops grow and become strong. The other was a potter, who wanted constant sunshine to dry his clay dishes, which the rain destroyed. And since heaven could never satisfy them in settling this matter, they went one day to the castle of the wise Krokus with rich presents and submitted their petitions to Therba. The daughter of the elf smiled because of the way they grumbled about nature's way of doing things, and she satisfied each of their demands. She made rain fall on the seeds of the farmer and had the sun shine on the nearby field of the potter.

Thanks to their magic powers, Bela and Therba gained a good deal of fame and riches, for they never used their gifts without charging a fee and making a profit. With their treasures they built castles and country houses, designed marvelous pleasure gardens, and never got tired of enjoying parties and amusements. But they teased and laughed at the men who tried to woo them.

Libussa did not have the vain and proud disposition of her sisters. Though she had the same ability to penetrate the secrets of nature and use its hidden powers to serve her, she was content with the wonderful gifts that she had inherited from her mother, without attempting to increase them or turn them into a source of gain. Her vanity did not extend beyond her awareness that she was beautiful. She did not crave riches, nor did she desire to be feared or honored like her sisters. While they romped around in their country houses, rushing from one ecstatic pleasure to another with the elite corps of the Bohemian knighthood chained to their chariot wheels, she lived in her father's house, managed all the domestic affairs, gave counsel to those who sought it, and provided friendly help to the afflicted and oppressed—and all this out of good will and without remuneration. She had a soft and modest personality, and her conduct was virtuous and discreet, as beseems a noble virgin. To be sure, she secretly rejoiced in the victories which her beauty gained over the hearts of men and accepted the sighing and cooing of her languishing adorers as a just tribute to her charms, but nobody dared speak a word of love to her or dared gain access to her heart. Nevertheless, Amor, that rogue, likes best to exercise his proper rights in sly ways and often hurls his burning torch upon the lowly straw roof when he intends to set fire to a lofty palace.

Deep in the forest lived an old knight, who had come into the land with the host of Czech and had settled there. As time went by, he cultivated the wild land and built a small estate, where he intended to spend the rest of his days in peace and live off the fruits of his labor. But a powerful neighbor seized his land and drove out the old knight. Fortunately, a hospitable peasant took him in and gave him shelter. The only consolation of the downtrodden knight was his son, who supported him in his old age. He was a brave young man, but the only things he had with which to provide for his father were a hunting spear and a skilled arm. The theft of their wicked neighbor had made him yearn for vengeance, and he began preparing himself to repay force with force. However, his anxious father did not want his son to be exposed to danger and ordered him to disarm. Nevertheless, the young man continued planning some sort of revenge, until his father felt compelled to summon him and said, "Go to wise Krokus, my son, or to his clever daughters, and ask their advice whether the gods approve of your undertaking and will grant you success. If so, gird your sword, take your spear in hand, and go forth to fight for your inheritance. If not, stay here until you have closed my eyes. Then do what seems good to you."

The young man set forth and arrived first at Bela's palace, which seemed like the temple of a goddess. He knocked at the door and asked to be admitted, but the guard, noticing that he had come empty-handed, dismissed him as a beggar and shut the door in his face. So he went sadly on his way and reached the house of Therba, where he knocked and requested an audience. The guard peered at him through a window and said, "If you are carrying gold in your bag that you can bestow upon my mistress, then she will teach you one of her little spells that will help you read your fortune. If not, then go and gather as many grains of gold on the shores of the Elbe as the tree has leaves, the sheaf, ears, and the bird, feathers. Then I'll open the gate to you."

The disappointed young man went away and was completely discouraged, and he became even more so when he learned that the seer Krokus was in Poland, arbitrating a dispute between some quarreling nobles, for the young man anticipated the same demeaning reception from the third sister. Therefore, when he caught sight of her father's castle from a hill in the distance, he could not bring himself to approach it but hid himself in a thicket to resume his bitter thoughts. Before long he was roused from his sad musings by an approaching noise. He listened and heard a sound of horses' hooves. A speedy deer dashed through the bushes, pursued by a lovely huntress and her maids on stately steeds. She hurled a javelin from her hand, and it whizzed through the air but did not hit the game. Instantly the attentive young man seized his bow and sent an arrow from the twanging cord, which struck the deer through the heart and knocked it lifeless to the ground. In her astonishment, the lady looked around to discover who her unknown hunting partner was, and on observing this, the archer stepped forward from his bush and bowed to her humbly on the ground. Libussa thought she had never seen a more handsome man. At first glance, his figure made such a deep impression on her that she could not help but proffer the good will that a fortunate appearance claims as its prerogative.

"Tell me, dear stranger," she said to him, "who are you, and how did you happen to come to these woods?"

The young man judged correctly that his lucky star had brought him to the person for whom he had been searching, and he modestly presented his case to her, nor did he bother to conceal how disgracefully he had been turned away at her sisters' palaces or how the treatment had distressed him. However, she encouraged him with friendly words. "Follow me to my castle," she said. "I'll consult the book of fate for you and answer your questions tomorrow at sunrise."

The young man did as he was ordered. No troublesome guard prevented him from entering the palace, and the beautiful lady graciously offered her hospitality to him. He was delighted by this kind reception but even more by the charms of his sweet hostess. Her enchanting figure hovered all night before his eyes. He carefully resisted sleep so that he would not lose the memory of any of the delightful events of the past day. On the other hand, Libussa enjoyed a gentle sleep, for seclusion from the influences of the external senses, which disturb the finer presentiments of the future, is an indispensable condition for the gift of prophecy. The glowing imagination of the slumbering maiden blended the image of the young stranger with all the dream figures that hovered in her mind that night. She found him everywhere she was not looking for him, in connection with affairs in which it was impossible for her to grasp how he had become involved.

Upon awakening early in the morning, at the hour when the fairy prophetess generally sorted and interpreted the visions of the night, she felt inclined to cast away these dreams from her mind as errors of one night, which had sprung from disturbances in the correct operations of her imagination, and she did not want to pay attention to them. Yet a buried feeling told her that this creation of her imagination was not mere fantasizing but had a significant bearing on certain events that the future would unravel. Indeed, during the previous night, the presentiments of her imagination had uncovered the decrees of fate and had disclosed them to her more clearly than ever before. She had learned that her guest was inflamed with great love for her, and with equal frankness, her heart confessed the same thing in regard to him. But she immediately put the seal of silence on this revelation, just as the modest young man had set a guard upon his lips and eyes so that he would not expose himself to a contemptuous rejection, for the chasm that fortune had created between him and the daughter of Krokus seemed unbridgeable.

Although the beautiful Libussa was fully aware of what she had to say in reply to the young man's question, she found it difficult to let him go from her so quickly. At sunrise, she called him to her in the pleasure garden and said, "The curtain of darkness is still hanging before my eyes, and I cannot discern your fate. Therefore, I want you to stay with me until sunset." And at night, she said, "Stay till sunrise." And the next morning, "Wait another day." And the third day, "Have patience until tomorrow." At last, on the fourth day, she dismissed him, since she could not find any more pretexts for detaining him and did not want to jeopardize her secret. Upon his departure, she communicated her advice to him in friendly words: "The gods do not want you to do battle with a powerful man in your region. To bear and suffer is the lot of the weaker. Return to your father. Be the comfort of his old age and support him through your industry and labor. Take two white steers as a present from my herd, as well as this staff to drive them. When it blossoms and bears fruit, the spirit of prophecy will descend upon you."

The young man felt unworthy of the sweet virgin's gift and blushed because he had nothing to give her in return. With ineloquent lips, but with looks so much more eloquent, he took his leave from her with sorrow and at the gate below found two white steers awaiting him. They were sleek and glistening like the ancient godlike bull on whose smooth back the virgin Europa swam across the blue sea waves. Joyfully he untied them from the post and drove them gently on before him. This distance home seemed but a few miles because his mind was filled with thoughts of the beautiful Libussa, and since he would never be able to obtain her love, he vowed nonetheless that he would never love anyone else for the rest of his life.

The old knight rejoiced when his son returned and was even happier when he learned that the oracle of the beautiful Libussa corresponded to his own wishes. Since farming had been designated by the gods as the young man's trade, he did not delay in harnessing his white steers and yoking them to the plow. Indeed, his first try went according to his wish: the bulls had such strength and spirit that they turned over more land than twelve yoke of oxen can normally master in a single day. They were fiery and impetuous like the bull painted in the almanac where he rushes from the clouds in the sign of April, not sluggish and heavy like the ox in our gospel book, who plods on with his holy consorts. Nor were they like sulky shepherd dogs who merely tag along after their flocks.

Duke Czech, who had led the first expedition of his people into Bohemia, had long since passed away, and none of his heirs had been found worthy enough to succeed him. To be sure, the magnates had assembled for a new election after his death, but their wild and stormy tempers did not allow for a reasonable outcome. Self-interest and self-conceit transformed the first Bohemian parliament into a Polish diet: since too many hands laid claim to the princely mantle, they tore it in pieces, and none of them obtained it. The government broke down into near anarchy. Everyone did what was right in his eyes. The strong oppressed the weak, the rich the poor, the great the little. There was no longer any public safety in the land; yet the chaotic spirits of the time thought their new republic very well organized. "Everything's in good order," they said. "Everything's going its way here just like everywhere else. The wolf is eating the lamb, the hawk the dove, the fox the cock." However, this ridiculous state of things could not last. After the first wave of what people had thought to be freedom had vanished and they had grown sober again, reason asserted its rights. The patriots, the honest citizens, whoever in the nation felt love for his fatherland, joined together to destroy the many heads of the Hydra and to unite the people once more under a single leader. "Let us choose a prince," they said. "Let him rule over us according to the morals and customs of our forefathers. Let him tame the agitators and bring about law and order. Let the wisest man be our duke, not the strongest, the boldest, or the richest!"

Tired of the oppression of their petty tyrants, the people had but one voice on this occasion, and they loudly applauded the proposal. A meeting of estates was convoked, and the choice unanimously fell upon the wise Krokus. An embassy of dignitaries was appointed, and they invited him to take over the reign of the country. Though Krokus had never longed for such a lofty honor, he did not hesitate to comply with the people's wish. Invested with the crimson robe, he proceeded to Vizegrad, the residence of the dukes, with great pomp. There the people met him with triumphant shouting and greeted him jubilantly as their regent. He realized that the benevolent elf's third stick had now taken effect as well.

His love of justice and his wise dispensation of the laws soon spread his fame over all the surrounding countries. The Sarmatic princes, incessantly at war with one another, brought their dispute from afar to his seat of judgment. He weighed it with the frank deliberation of natural justice on the scales of law, and when he opened his mouth, it was as if the venerable Solon or the wise Solomon were pronouncing sentence from between the twelve lions of his throne. When some agitators joined together to subvert the peace of their country and kindled war among the Poles, he advanced at the head of his army into Poland and put an end to the civil strife. Grateful for the peace that he had given them, a majority of people chose him to be their duke as well. Therefore, he built the city of Cracow, which bears his name and has the privilege of crowning the Polish kings up to the present time.

Krokus ruled with great glory to the end of his days, and when he knew that he had attained his goal and was about to die, he had a coffin built from the fragments of the oak that his wife the elf had inhabited. Then he departed in peace, mourned by his three daughters, who placed the ducal remains in the coffin and buried him in the earth as he had commanded, and the whole country grieved.

When the obsequies were finished, the estates assembled to deliberate who should now occupy the vacant throne. The people were unanimous that one of Krokus's daughters should become their ruler. But they could not yet decide which of the three. Bela had the fewest adherents, because she was not kind and employed her magic talents too often to cause harm. But she had also terrified the people so much that no one dared to slight her lest she take vengeance. Therefore, when the vote was called, the electors remained silent. There were no votes for her, but there were also none against her. At sunset the representatives of the people separated and adjourned their meeting to the next day. Then Therba was proposed, but her confidence in her magic spells had made her conceited. She was proud and overbearing and demanded to be honored like a goddess. If incense was not always burned in her honor, she grew peevish, cross, and capricious, displaying all the traits by which members of the fair sex, when they please, can cease to be fair. It is true, she was less feared than her elder sister, but she was not any more loved. For these reasons the electors continued their silence. It was as if they were attending a funeral dinner, and the vote was never called for. On the third day, Libussa's name was proposed. No sooner was her name pronounced than a congenial hum was heard among the electors. The solemn visages lost their wrinkles and brightened up, and each of the electors had something good to say to his neighbor about the young woman. One praised her virtue, another her modesty, a third her intelligence, a fourth her infallibility in prophecy, a fifth her impartiality in giving advice, a tenth her chastity, ninety her beauty, and the last her domesticity. When a lover draws up a catalogue of the perfections of his mistress, it remains doubtful as to whether she is really the possessor of a single one among them. However, the public seldom errs to someone's advantage but more to someone's disadvantage, no matter how good that person's reputation is. With so many universally acknowledged praiseworthy qualities, Libussa was undoubtedly the most significant candidate of the electors, at least in private, but the preference of the younger sister over the elder has so frequently destroyed the peace of a household, as experience in marital arrangements testifies, that it is reasonable to fear that it might disturb the peace of a country in affairs of greater import. This consideration placed the wise guardians of the people in such a situation that they could not come to any decision whatsoever. A speaker was needed who could swing the electors' better inclinations with his eloquence, so that the electoral process could be set in motion and the electors would put their minds to work. And then just the speaker they needed rose to the occasion.

Vladomir, one of the Bohemian magnates, the highest after the duke, had long been sighing for the enchanting Libussa and had wooed her during Krokus's lifetime. The young man was one of his most faithful vassals, loved by him like a son. Indeed, the good Krokus would have liked it if love had united this pair, but the maiden's recalcitrance could not be overcome, and in no way had he wanted to force anyone on her. However, Prince Vladomir did not let himself be scared away by these doubtful prospects. He still hoped to wear down the young woman's obstinacy through fidelity and constancy and to make her heart more pliant through his tender affection. As long as the duke was alive he continued his courtship, without having moved closer toward the goal of his desire. But now he believed that he had found an opportunity to open her closed heart by doing something meritorious that would earn him her noble-minded gratitude, since love did not seem inclined to grant him voluntarily what he sought. He decided to brave the hatred and vengeance of the two dreaded sisters and to raise his beloved to her paternal throne, an act that would endanger his life. Observing the indecision of the wavering electors, he took the podium and declared, "If you will hear me, you manly knights and nobles from among the people, I should like to present a parable that will enable you to perceive how this present election may be accomplished for the welfare of the country."

Once the electors were called upon to be silent, he proceeded.

"The bees had lost their queen, and the whole hive sat sad and moping. They seldom flew out, and if they did, they were sluggish and had little heart or energy for making honey. As a result, their trade and sustenance fell into decay. Therefore, they decided to choose a new sovereign, who would head their police and rule over their community so that discipline and order would not be lost. Then the wasp came flying toward them and said, 'Choose me for your queen. I'm mighty and terrible. The proud horse is afraid of my sting. Even the lion, your hereditary foe, must fear me, for I can prick him in the snout when he approaches your hive. I'll watch over you and defend you.' This speech pleased the bees, but after considering it for some time, the wisest among them answered, 'You are sprightly and dreadful, but we, too, fear the sting that is to guard us. Therefore, you cannot be our queen.' Then the bumblebee came buzzing toward them and said, 'Choose me for your queen. Do you not hear that the sounding of my wings announces loftiness and dignity? Moreover, I have a fine sting that will protect you.' The bees answered, "We are a peaceable and quiet people. The proud sounding of your wings would annoy us and disturb our diligent work. Therefore, you cannot be our queen." Then the royal bee requested audience. 'Though I am larger and stronger than you,' she said, 'my strength cannot hurt or damage you, for I do not have a dangerous sting. I have a soft temperament, and as a friend of order and domesticity, I can direct your making of honey and further your labor.' 'It is clear that you are worthy to rule over us,' said the bees. "We'll obey you, and you'll be our queen.' "

Vladomir was silent. The whole assembly guessed the meaning of his speech, and all their minds were made up in favor of Libussa. However, at the moment they were to cast their votes, a croaking raven flew over their heads. This evil omen interrupted all further deliberations, and the meeting was adjourned until the next day. It was Bela who had sent this bird of dark foreboding to disrupt their election, for she was well aware of the inclinations of the electors, and she was extremely bitter toward Prince Vladomir. She held a meeting with her sister Therba, and they decided to take vengeance on the man who was disparaging them by sending an awesome demon to squeeze his soul from his body. Not realizing that his life was in immediate danger, the stout knight went to attend his mistress as he was accustomed to do, and he was given his first sign of favor by a friendly look. As a result, he was in heaven, and if anything could have increased his ecstasy, it was the gift of a rose which was blooming on the young woman's bosom and which she handed to him with the command that he was to let it wither on his heart. He interpreted these words in quite a different way than they were meant, for there is no science that is as deceptive as the hermeneutics of love, where errors, as it were, have their home. The enamored knight was anxious to preserve his rose as long as possible and to keep it fresh and in bloom. So he put it in a vase with water and fell asleep with the most flattering hopes.

At eerie midnight, the angel of death sent by Bela glided toward Vladomir, and with panting breath it blew off the bolts and locks of his apartment and fell upon the slumbering knight like a hundred-pound weight and squeezed him so hard that, awakening, he felt as if a millstone had been hung around his neck. His suffering and agony were so great that he thought the last moment of his life was at hand. Fortunately, he remembered the rose, which was standing by his bed in its vase, and he pressed it to his breast, saying, "Wither with me, beautiful rose, and die on my chilled bosom as proof that my last thought was about your gentle mistress." All of a sudden, his heart felt light again. The heavy demon could not withstand the magic force of the flower. His crushing weight felt less than a feather. He could not endure the rose's scent, and it propelled him out of the room. Then the narcotic power of the flower lulled the knight once more into a refreshing sleep. The next morning he rose with the sun, fresh and alert, and rode to the assembly to see what impression his parable had made on the electors and to watch what course their business would take. If a contrary wind was to spring up and to threaten the vessel of his hopes with shipwreck, he was determined at all costs to lay his hand on the rudder and steer it into port.

However, there proved to be no danger at the present time. The electors had reflected upon Vladomir's parable so carefully overnight that it had seeped into their hearts and minds. A fiery knight named Mizisla, who realized how crucial the situation was and who shared the same leanings as the love-struck Vladomir, sought to snatch away the honor or at least take some of the credit with him for the elevation of Libussa to the throne. He stepped forth and drew his sword, and with a loud voice he proclaimed Libussa duchess of Bohemia and called upon all who agreed with him to draw their swords and defend their choice. At once, hundreds of swords glistened over the field. A loud hooray announced the new regent, and one could hear from all sides the joyful cry: "Libussa is our duchess!" A committee was appointed, with Vladomir and the swordbearer Mizisla at its head, to inform Libussa that she had been elected to the throne, and she accepted the rule over the people with that modest blush that gives the highest grace to female charms. Indeed, the magic of her blissful look made all hearts subject to her. The people celebrated the event with vast rejoicing, although her two sisters envied her and used their secret arts to plan revenge on her and their fatherland for the way they had been slighted. They endeavored to incite criticism of all their sister's measures and transactions and to cause uprisings in the state. However, Libussa was able to counter these unsisterly acts in wise ways and to undermine all their hostile acts, whether they were magical or otherwise. Eventually her sisters grew tired of assailing her in vain, and they stopped using their arts, which had proved to be ineffectual against her.

In the meantime the sighing Vladomir awaited the unfolding of his fate with wistful longing. More than once he tried to read the outcome in the beautiful eyes of his princess. But Libussa had strictly commanded them to be silent and to respect the feelings of her heart. And for a lover to demand an oral explanation without a prior pact with the eyes and their understanding glances is always a difficult undertaking. The only favorable sign, which continued to encourage him, was the unfaded rose, for after a year it still bloomed as fresh as on the night when he received it from her hand. And a flower from a lady's hand, a bouquet, a ribbon, or a lock of hair, is certainly better in all cases than a straw in the wind. Yet all these pretty things are only ambiguous pledges of love if they have not been corroborated by reliable statements of commitment. Therefore, Vladomir continued to play the role of the sighing shepherd and to wait and see what time and circumstance could do to help him in the long run. The tempestuous knight Mizisla, meanwhile, pursued his courtship with far more vivacity. He made himself noticed on every possible occasion. At the coronation he was the first vassal to take the oath of fealty to the princess, and he followed her constantly, as the moon does the earth, to express his devotion to her and to offer his services. And at public ceremonies and processions he flourished his shining sword before her to remind her of its good deed.

Yet, as is usual in the world, Libussa seemed to have quickly forgotten the men responsible for promoting her good fortune. Indeed, once an obelisk is standing perpendicular, it no longer pays attention to the levers and implements that raised it. At least this was the way the rivals of her heart explained the maiden's coldness. But both of them were wrong, for Libussa was neither insensitive nor ungrateful. The fact was that her heart was no longer a free piece of property that she could give or sell according to her pleasure. The claim of love had already been made in favor of the slender hunter with the sure crossbow. The first impression that he had made upon her heart was still so powerful that no other man could efface it. During the past three years the colors that her imagination had used to paint the image of this graceful youth had remained bright, and thus love was completely preserved. In fact, the passion of the fair sex is such that if it can endure three moons, it will then last three times three years or longer. For proof and evidence one need only regard contemporary events. When the heroic sons of Germany sailed over distant seas to participate in the struggle between an obstinate daughter of Britain and her motherland, they tore themselves from the arms of their women with mutual oaths of truth and constancy. Yet before the last buoy of the Weser was out of sight, these men were for the most part forgotten by their Chloes. Finding their hearts unoccupied, the fickle among these maidens hastily filled the vacuum with new intrigues, while the faithful and true, who had constancy enough to stand the test of the Weser, refrained from infidelity when the conquerors of their hearts had moved beyond the black buoy. It is said that these women kept their vows until the return of the heroic soldiers to their native German country and are now awaiting the reward for their constancy from the hand of love.

It is thus the less surprising that Libussa could withstand the courting of the remarkable knights who struggled to win her heart, for her situation was like Penelope of Ithaca, who let a whole cohort of wooers sigh for her in vain because her heart was totally consumed by the gray-bearded Ulysses. Rank and birth, however, had created such an imbalance in the situation of Libussa and her beloved young man that no closer union than platonic love, a silhouette show, which can neither warm nor nourish, could be expected. To be sure, in those olden times the pairing of the sexes was no more validated by parchments and genealogical trees than the insects were arranged by their antennae and shell wings, or the flowers by their filaments, pollen, calyxes, and honey contents. Yet it was understood that the precious vine should mate itself with the lofty elm and not the rough tangleweed that creeps along the hedges. A mismarriage which involved a slight difference in rank caused less petty uproar, it is true, in those times than in our present classical times. Yet a major difference, especially when there were two rivals in between, made the gap between the two extremes more apparent and was something that would cause eyebrows to be raised. All this, and much more, Libussa carefully pondered in her bright mind. Consequently she did not grant a hearing to passion, that treacherous babbler, even though it spoke loudly in favor of the young man whom Amor had favored. Like a chaste vestal, she made an irrevocable vow to go through life as a virgin, keep her heart closed, and not respond to any wooer with her eyes, gestures, or lips. However, as a just indemnification, she did reserve the right to platonize to any degree she desired. Of course, her nunlike ways did not at all suit her aspirants, and they could not make any sense out of her deadly coldness. Jealousy, the confidant of love, whispered tormenting suspicions in their ears. Each thought the other was the more fortunate rival, and each spied about relentlessly to discover the truth that they were afraid to learn. Still, Libussa doled out her scanty graces to the two valiant knights with such prudence and cleverness and in such a fair way that neither one's scale rose above the other.

Tired of this fruitless waiting, both of them left the court of their princess and returned with great discontent to the estates that Duke Krokus had bestowed on them. They remained in such a bad temper that Vladomir oppressed all his vassals and neighbors, while Mizisla hunted deer and foxes over the fields and hedges of his subjects, and sometimes he would trample ten acres of wheat to pieces with his retinue just to catch one hare. As a result, there was a great deal of woe and grief in the land. Yet no judge dared to stop the mischief. Indeed, who likes to pass judgment against the strong? And so news about the oppression of the people never reached the throne of the duchess. However, by virtue of her prophetic eye, it was impossible for an injustice to occur within the wide boundaries of her realm without her becoming aware of it. And since her temperament was just as soft as the sweet features of her face, she was inwardly distressed by the wanton ways of her vassals and their violence. So she contemplated how she could remedy the evil, and she cleverly came up with the idea of imitating the wise gods, who do not practice justice by punishing criminals when caught in the act, even though vengeance, following in slow steps, sooner or later catches up with them. Thus the young princess convened a general assembly of her nobles and estates for court hearings and proclaimed that whoever had a grievance or a complaint was to come forward freely and fearlessly with the promise of her safe-conduct. As a result, all the downtrodden and abused people thronged to her palace from every end and corner of her realm. In addition, there were the wranglers and petty litigants, whoever had a legal case to settle. Libussa sat upon her throne like the goddess Themis with a sword and scale and made unerring judgments without being influenced by a person's rank, for the labyrinthic mazes of chicane could not lead her astray as they do the dense heads of city magistrates. In fact, everyone was astonished at the wisdom with which she unraveled the intricate knots of trials concerned with issues of property and at her indefatigable patience in threading the needle of justice. Never once did she go through a false hole, rather she always found the right one, through which she stuck the needle and followed it to the end.

When the tumult of the parties at her court had gradually diminished and the sessions were about to be concluded, a hearing was demanded, on the last day of the court of inquests, by a neighbor of the rich Vladomir and by deputies sent by the subjects of the hunter Mizisla. They were admitted, and the freeholder was the first to address her.

"A hardworking planter," he said, "fenced in a little plot of land on the bank of a wide river whose silvery waters glided and rushed gently through the happy valley, for he thought that the beautiful stream would protect him on this side and prevent hungry wild beasts from eating his crops. Moreover, he believed that the water would moisten the roots of his fruit trees so that they would flourish and bear a great deal of fruit. But when he was about to reap the fruit of his labor, the deceitful stream grew troubled. Its still waters began to swell and roar. It overflowed its banks and carried off one piece after another of the fertile soil and dug itself a bed through the middle of the cultivated land, to the great sorrow of the poor planter. Consequently, he had to give up his little property, owing to the arbitrary ways of his powerful neighbor, who maliciously toyed with him. Indeed, he barely escaped its raging waves with his life. O powerful daughter of the wise Krokus, the poor planter begs you to command the haughty stream not to roll its proud waves over the field of the hardworking farmer anymore and not to swallow the fruit of his weary arms, the hope of a good harvest, but to flow peacefully within the boundaries of its own banks."

During his speech, the cheerful brow of the fair Libussa became overclouded. Manly rigor gleamed from her eyes, and everyone around her eagerly awaited her judgment.

"Your cause is straight and clear," she proclaimed. "No force will intrude and take away your rights. A strong dam will be built to keep the tumultuous river within its bounds, and thereafter I shall give you sevenfold of its fish for the damage caused by its waves."

Then she signaled to the eldest of the deputies, and he bowed his face to the earth and said, "Wise daughter of the famous Krokus, tell us, who owns the grain upon the field—the sower, who has planted the seeds in the ground so that they will spring up and bear fruit, or the storm, which tears apart the harvest and scatters it away?"

"The sower," she answered.

"Then command the storm," said the spokesman, "so that it will no longer choose our fields for the place of its capricious games, uprooting our crops and shaking the fruit from our trees."

"So be it," said the duchess. "I shall tame the storm and ban it from your fields. I will do battle with the clouds and disperse them where they are rising from the south and threatening the land with hail and heavy rain."

Prince Vladomir and the knight Mizisla were both auditors in the general tribunal. On hearing the complaints and the rigorous sentences passed regarding them, they turned pale and looked down on the ground with suppressed indignation, for they were ashamed to reveal how sharply it stung them to be condemned by a decree from female lips. Although the accusers had modestly veiled their charges in allegorical terms to protect their honor, and although Libussa's just sentence had also prudently respected their cover, the texture of this veil was so fine and transparent that it was easy for everyone to see what stood behind it, if anyone wanted to look. Indeed, Vladomir and Mizisla did not dare to appeal Libussa's judgment to the people, since it had produced general joy. So they reluctantly submitted to it, and Vladomir paid his neighbor sevenfold for the damage that he had caused, while Mizisla had to pledge on his honor as a knight not to use the wheat fields of his subjects to hunt hare anymore. At the same time, Libussa assigned them a more honorable task for occupying themselves and restoring the sound ring of knightly virtues to their fame, which now, like a cracked pot, resounded with nothing but discordant sounds when struck. She placed them both at the head of an army that she was sending to confront Zornebock, the prince of the Serbs, a giant as well as a powerful magician, who was at that time moving to war against Bohemia. In addition, Libussa stressed to them that they were not to appear at court again until one of them could offer her the plume and the other the golden spurs of the monster as tokens of their victory.

During the campaign, the unfading rose displayed its magical powers once more by making Prince Vladomir invulnerable to mortal weapons like the hero Achilles and as agile, quick, and dexterous as fleet Achilles. The armies met on the southern boundaries of the kingdom, and once the signal to begin the battle was given, the Bohemian heroes flew through the squadrons like storm and whirlwind and cut down the thick spear crop as the scythe of the mower cuts a field of wheat. Zornebock fell beneath the strong blows of their swords, and Vladomir and Mizisla returned in triumph to Vizegrad with the stipulated spoils, so that the spots and blemishes that had tarnished their knightly virtue were now washed clean away in the blood of their enemies. Libussa bestowed every mark of princely honor on them and then sent them to their homes when the army was discharged. Moreover, as a new proof of her favor, so it seemed, she gave them a crimson apple from her pleasure garden as a souvenir and told them to share it peacefully between them on the road without cutting it in two. Then they went their way, put the apple on a shield, and had it carried in front of them on public display, while they discussed together how they could wisely share it in keeping with the intention of its gentle giver.

Before they came to the crossroads, where their paths divided, they were accommodating toward each other. But at last it became necessary to determine which of the two should keep the apple, for both had equal shares in it, and only one could get it. Since they both envisioned wonderful advantages from this gift, which each was eager to keep, their divided opinions led to a dispute, and it appeared as if the sword would have to decide the issue of the indivisible apple. Just then a shepherd happened to drive his flock across their path as they stood debating, and they chose him to arbitrate their quarrel, apparently in imitation of the three goddesses who had asked a shepherd to settle their famous apple dispute. They explained the entire matter to him, and the shepherd thought for a while before saying, "There is a deep meaning hidden in the gift of this apple, but only the wise virgin who hid it there can disclose it. In my opinion, the apple is a treacherous fruit that has ripened on the tree of discord, and its crimson skin may prefigure a bloody feud between you two knights. Perhaps each of you is to annihilate the other, and neither is to enjoy the gift. Otherwise, tell me, how is it possible to share an apple without cutting it in two?"

The knights took the shepherd's words to heart and thought there was a great deal of truth in them.

"You have judged rightly," they said. "Hasn't this disgraceful apple already kindled anger and strife between us? Weren't we standing here armed to fight for the treacherous gift of this proud princess, who hates us? Didn't she appoint us to lead her army with the intention of destroying us? Now, having failed, she arms our hands with daggers of discord against each other! Let us renounce her vile present. Neither one of us shall have the apple. Let it be yours as a reward for your correct judgment. The fruit of the trial belongs to the judge, and the parties receive the skin."

Then the knights departed in different directions, while the herdsman consumed the *objectum litis* with all the composure customary in judges. The ambiguous present of the duchess gnawed at them, and on returning home, where they found that they could no longer treat their subjects and vassals in the former arbitrary manner but were compelled to obey the laws that Libussa had promulgated for the general security among her people, their bad tempers grew more and more vicious. So after entering into a non-aggression pact with each other, they established a stronghold in the country. Many rebels joined them and were sent abroad in packs to decry and slander female rule.

"Shame! Shame!" they cried. "What a shame that we subject ourselves to a woman, who gathers victory laurels to decorate a spinning wheel! The man should be the master of the house and not the wife. This is his natural right, and this is customary among all people. What is an army when it has no duke to lead it but a helpless trunk without a head! Let us appoint a prince who'll rule over us and whom we'll obey!"

These speeches were no secret to the watchful princess, and she also knew full well where the wind was coming from and what the storm boded. Therefore, she convened a meeting of the parliament. She entered the assembly with the radiance and dignity of an earthly goddess, and her words flowed like honey from virgin lips.

"There's a rumor flying about the land," she told the gathering, "that you desire a duke to lead you into battle and that you consider it beneath your dignity to follow me anymore. Yet when you held your free elections, you yourselves did not choose a man from your midst but called upon one of the daughters of the people and clothed her with the crimson robe to rule over you according to the laws and the customs of the land. Whoever wants to accuse me of making mistakes in conducting the government, let him step forward openly and freely and bear witness against me. But if I, according to the ways of my father Krokus, have acted prudently and justly in your midst, have made crooked things straight and hilly places level; if I have prevented your harvest from spoiling, protected the fruit tree, and snatched the flock from the claws of the wolf; if I have bowed the stiff neck of the violent, assisted the oppressed, and given a staff to the weak to rest on—then it would beseem you to live according to your agreement and be true, gentle, and supportive, as you pledged when you crowned me. If you consider it beneath your dignity to obey a woman, you should have thought of this before appointing me to be your princess. If there is disgrace here, it is you alone who ought to bear it. But your way of doing things reveals that you do not understand your own advantage: a woman's hand is soft and tender, accustomed only to spread cool air with the fan, while a man's arm is sinewy and rude, heavy and oppressive when it obtains complete power. And aren't you aware that whenever a woman governs, the rule is controlled by men? For instance, she listens to wise councillors who gather around her. But whenever the spinning wheel is excluded from the throne, you'll find power in the hands of females, for women who please the king's eyes have his heart in their hands. Therefore, give good thought to what you're doing, otherwise you may repent your fickleness too late."

When Libussa concluded her talk from the throne, there was a deep, reverent silence throughout the hall of the meeting, and nobody dared to utter a word against her. Nevertheless, Prince Vladomir and his confederates did not stop plotting against her and whispered in each other's ears, "The sly doe is loath to leave the fat pastures. But the hunter's horn will sound even louder and scare her away."

The next day they prompted the knights to call loudly on the princess to choose a husband within three days, and through the choice of her heart she was to give the people a prince, who might share the reins of the government with her. At this rash demand, which seemed to be the voice of the nation, a virgin blush spread over charming Libussa's cheeks. Her clear eye discerned all the hidden traps that threatened her with peril. For even if she should decide to subject her inclination to reasons of state according to worldwide custom, she could only give her hand to one suitor, and she saw well that all the remaining candidates would take it as a slight and begin to contemplate revenge. Besides, the secret vow of her heart was inviolable and sacred in her eyes. Therefore, she endeavored in as prudent a way as possible to reject this importunate demand of the parliament and again attempted to dissuade the nobles from carrying out their plans for choosing a duke.

"After the eagle died," she said, "the birds chose the dove for their queen, and all of them obeyed her soft cooing call. But light and airy, as is the nature of birds, they soon changed their minds and repented of their decision. The proud peacock thought that he was better suited to be ruler. The keen falcon, who was accustomed to make the smaller birds his prey, considered it disgraceful to obey the peaceful dove. They joined together and appointed the idiotic owl to be the spokesman of their party, and he called for the election of a new sovereign. The sluggish bustard, the heavy grouse, the lazy stork, the small-brained heron, and all the larger birds crooned, flapped, and croaked their applause, and the host of little birds twittered in their ignorance and chirped out of bush and hedge to the same tune. Then the warlike falcon arose and soared boldly up into the air, and the birds cried out, 'What a majestic flight! Let the brave, manly falcon be our king!' No sooner had the plundering king taken possession of the throne than he manifested his manliness and energy by tyrannizing his winged subjects and desecrating them. He plucked the feathers from the larger fowls and tore the little songsters to pieces."

Significant as this speech was, it made but a small impression on the minds of the people, who yearned for a change and remained determined that Libussa should choose a husband for herself within three days. Vladimir rejoiced in his heart, for now, he thought, he could obtain the fair prey that he had been trying to catch in vain for years. Love and ambition ignited his wishes and turned his tongue, which was only accustomed to sighing till then, to eloquence. He went to court and requested an audience of the duchess.

"Glorious ruler of your people and my heart," he addressed her, "no secret is hidden from you. You know the flames that burn within this bosom, holy and pure as on the altar of the gods, and you also know what heavenly fire has kindled them. It is now decided at the behest of your people that you give the country a prince. Can you disdain a heart that lives and beats for you? To be worthy of your love, I risked my life to put you on the throne of your father. Let me now have the honor of keeping you on it through the bonds of tender affection. Let us share the possession of the throne and your heart. The first will be yours, and the second mine. That way you will raise my happiness above the lot of mortals."

During this speech the virginal Libussa covered her face with her veil to hide the soft blush that deepened the color of her cheeks. At its conclusion, she made a sign with her hand for the prince to step aside, as if she wanted to consider her decision.

All at once the bold knight Mizisla announced himself and demanded to be admitted.

"Loveliest of the daughters of princes," he said as he entered the audience chamber, "the beautiful dove, queen of the air, is no longer to coo in solitude, as you well know, but must choose a mate for herself. It is said that the proud peacock has been displaying his glittering plumage in her eyes and intends to blind her by the splendor of his feathers, but she is smart and modest and will not unite with the haughty peacock. The keen falcon, once a plundering bird, has now changed his nature. Indeed, he is gentle and honest and without deceit, for he loves the beautiful dove and would like her to mate with him. Even though his bill is hooked, his talons sharp, this should not mislead you. He needs them to protect the beautiful dove, his beloved, so that no bird will damage her feathers or knock her from her throne. He is true and kind to her, and he was the first who swore fealty to her on the day when she was crowned. Now tell me, wise princess, if the soft dove will grant her trusty falcon the love for which he longs."

Libussa did as she had done before: she signaled the knight to step aside. After a while, she called the two rivals to her and said, "I owe you great thanks, noble knights, for furthering my cause and helping me obtain the princely crown of Bohemia, which my father, Krokus, so honorably wore. Your zeal, about which you reminded me, had not faded from my memory, and I am fully aware that you love me virtuously, for your looks and gestures have long been the translators of your feelings. Please do not regard it as insensitive that I shut my heart against you and did not respond to love with love. I intended not to slight or scorn you but provide myself with space, since I had so many doubts. I weighed your merits, and the scales did not tip to either side. Therefore, I decided to leave the decision to yourselves and offered you the symbolical apple, so that I could see which of you had the greater judgment and wisdom and would gain possession of this gift that could not be divided. So tell me right now who has won the apple, and he may have my throne and my heart as of this moment."

The two rivals looked at one another with amazement, then they grew pale and remained speechless. At last, Prince Vladimir broke the silence and said, "To slow thinkers, the riddles of the wise are a nut in a toothless mouth, a pearl which the chicken scratches from the sand, a torch in the hand of the blind. O princess, don't be angry with us because we failed to appreciate the value of your gift or its use. We misinterpreted your intention and thought that you had given us this apple to cause strife and a deadly feud between us. Therefore, we each gave up our share and renounced the divisive fruit, for neither would have peaceably allowed the other to obtain possession of it."

"You yourselves have settled this affair," Libussa replied. "If an apple could inflame your jealousy, what fighting would you not have risked for a myrtle garland twined around a crown!"

With this response she dismissed the knights, who now lamented that they had listened to the unwise arbiter and thoughtlessly thrown away the pledge of love that would have been the means to win the bride. Nevertheless, each one of them continued to think of ways to obtain possession of the lovely Libussa and the Bohemian throne, whether by force or guile.

Libussa did not spend the three days given for her decision in idleness. On the contrary, she diligently thought about how she might meet the importunate demand of her people, give Bohemia a duke, and take herself a husband according to the choice of her heart. She was afraid that Prince Vladomir might force himself upon her or rob her of the throne. Therefore, necessity combined with love to make her put in action a plan that she had often entertained as a pleasant dream, for what mortal's mind has not had some phantom walking in his head with which he plays in a spare hour as if with a puppet? There is no more pleasing pastime for the straitlaced maiden than to think of a stately and comfortable equipage while resting her feet during a long walk. The beautiful young lady loves to dream of counts sighing at her feet. The vain female occupies herself with arranging some jewelry. The greedy one wins the prize in the lottery. The debtor in jail falls heir to vast possessions. The squanderer discovers the hermetic secret. The poor woodcutter finds a treasure in the hollow of a tree. All this is merely in the imagination, but not without the enjoyment of a secret satisfaction. Now the gift of prophecy has always been coupled with a glowing imagination. Therefore, like others, the beautiful Libussa had willingly and frequently lent an ear to this pleasant playmate, which had always entertained her with the image of the young hunter who had made such an indelible impression on her heart. Thousands of plans came into her mind that her imagination palmed on her as feasible and easy. At one time she conceived the plan of taking her dear young man from his obscurity, placing him in the army, and promoting him from one post of honor to the next. Then, in her imagination, she would quickly tie a laurel garland around his forehead and lead him, crowned with victory and honor, to the throne that she would be quite glad to share with him. At other times, she gave a different turn to the imaginary romance: she equipped her darling as a knight-errant seeking adventures, and she brought him to her court and changed him into a nobleman. Nor were the marvelous implements lacking that would endow him as highly as friend Oberon did his ward. But when common sense again got possession of the maiden's mind, the multicolored forms of the magic lantern turned pale in the beam of her intellect, and the beautiful dream vanished into thin air. She then considered what risks would be involved in such an undertaking and what trouble she might cause for her people if jealousy and envy were to stir the hearts of her nobles to rebel against her and set off the signal for uprisings and sedition in the land. Therefore, she carefully hid the wishes of her heart from the keen glance of the spies and revealed nothing to anyone.

But now, when the people were clamoring for a prince, the matter had assumed another form, and everything depended on whether she could combine her wishes with the national demand. She made up her mind with manly resolution, and as the third day dawned, she adorned herself with all her jewels, and her head was encircled with a pure myrtle crown. Attended by her maidens, all decorated with flower garlands, she ascended the throne full of lofty courage and gentle dignity. The knights and vassals stood around her attentively to hear from her sweet lips the name of the fortunate prince with whom she had decided to share her throne and her heart.

"My noblemen," she announced, "the lot of your destiny still lies untouched in the urn of concealment. You are still as free as my stallions that graze in the meadows before the bridle and the bit have curbed them or their smooth backs have been pressed by the burden of the saddle or the rider. It is now up to you to indicate to me whether, in the time allotted to me to choose a spouse, your fervent desire for a prince to rule over you has cooled and given way to more calm scrutiny, or whether you persist inflexibly in your demand."

She paused for a moment, but the hum of the multitude, the whispering and buzzing and looks of the entire senate, made her realize quickly what they thought, and their speaker informed her that the vote was still for a duke.

"Then so be it!" she said. "The die is cast, but I have nothing to do with the outcome! The gods have appointed a prince who shall rule the kingdom of Bohemia with justice and wisdom. The young cedar has not yet begun to jut out over the staunch oaks. Concealed among the trees of the forest, it is surrounded by ignoble shrubs and grows, but soon it will sprout branches and provide shade for its roots, and its peak shall touch the clouds. I ask you, my noblemen, to choose a deputation of twelve honest men in your midst and to send them with all haste to fetch the prince and accompany him back to the throne. Take my steed, without saddle or bridle, and it will lead the way. Then, as a sign that you have found what you've been sent forth to seek, you'll observe that when you approach him, the man whom the gods have selected for your prince will be eating his meal on an iron table under the open sky in the shadow of a solitary tree. You shall render him homage and dress him in the princely robe. My white horse will let him mount it and will bring him here to the court, so that he may be my husband and your lord."

She then left the assembly with the cheerful and yet abashed expression that brides wear when they are expecting the arrival of the bridegroom. The people were greatly astounded by her speech, and the prophetic spirit that breathed from her words worked upon their minds like a divine oracle, which the people blindly believe and which only thinkers endeavor to probe. The messengers of honor were selected; the white horse stood ready and was equipped in Asiatic pomp as though it had been saddled for carrying the Grand Seigneor to mosque. The cavalcade set forth attended by crowds of people and loud cheers, and the white horse trotted proudly ahead of them.

Soon the retinue vanished from the eyes of the spectators, and nothing could be seen but a little cloud of dust whirling far away, for as soon as it reached the open air, the spirited horse began a furious gallop, like a British racing horse, so that the troop of deputies could hardly keep it in sight. Though the quick steed seemed to be on its own, an unseen power directed its steps, pulled its bridle, and spurred its flanks. Indeed, Libussa had used the magic powers that she had inherited from her elf mother to direct the horse, and it turned neither to the right nor to the left from its path but hastened to its destination as though it had wings on it. And now that everything was coming together to fulfill her wishes, she herself awaited the return of the rider with tender longing.

The messengers meanwhile had already galloped many miles up hill and down dale. They had swum across the Elbe and the Moldau, and since their stomachs made them think of dinner, they recalled the strange table at which their new prince would be eating, according to Libussa's oracle. However, they made many kinds of snide comments and remarks about it, and a brash knight said to his companions, "In my lowly opinion, our gracious lady is toying with us and wants to make April fools out of us. Who ever heard of any man in Bohemia that ate his meal from an iron table? What's the use of all this? All our hard galloping will bring us nothing but mockery and scorn."

Another knight, who was more perceptive, thought that the iron table might have an allegorical meaning and that they would perhaps meet some knight-errant, who had sat down under a tree, as is the custom of wandering knights, and spread out his frugal dinner on his shield. A third deputy said as a jest, "I fear our way will lead us down to the workshop of the Cyclops, and we shall find the lame Vulcan or one of his assistants dining from his anvil, and we shall have to bring him to our Venus."

Amid such conversation, they observed their guide, the stallion, which was way ahead of them, turn across a newly plowed field, and to their amazement, it stopped in front of the plowman. They dashed rapidly to the spot and found a peasant sitting and eating his black bread from the iron plow, which he was using as a table under the shadow of a wild pear tree. He seemed to take a liking to the stately horse, and as he patted it, he offered it a bit of bread, which the steed ate from his hand. Of course, the deputation of knights were greatly surprised by this situation. However, none of them had any doubts but that they had found their man. So they approached him reverently, and the eldest among them began speaking: "The duchess of Bohemia has sent us here to inform you about the will and decision of the gods: you are to change your plow with the throne of this kingdom and your goad with its scepter. She has chosen you for her husband, to rule over the Bohemians with her."

The young peasant thought they were playing a joke on him which was little to his taste, especially since he surmised that they had guessed his secret love for Libussa and had come to mock his weakness. Therefore, he answered somewhat brashly, to meet mockery with mockery: "Let's see first whether your dukedom is worth this plow! If the prince cannot eat with better relish, drink more joyously, or sleep more soundly than the peasant, then, in truth, it is not worth his while to change this fertile field with the Bohemian kingdom, or this smooth ox goad with its scepter. Tell me, isn't one shaker of salt as good for seasoning my morsel as one bushel?"

Then one of the twelve knights responded, "The mole is sensitive to light and digs underground for worms to feed upon, for he has no eyes that can endure the daylight and no feet that are made for running as the fleet roe's are; the scaly crab creeps back and forth in the mud of lakes and marshes and enjoys dwelling under the roots of trees and shrubs by the riverbanks, for he lacks fins for swimming; and the barnyard cock, cooped up within the henhouse and fences, does not dare to fly over the low wall, for he is too scared to trust in his wings as does the high-soaring bird of prey. If you have been endowed with eyes for seeing, feet for walking, fins for swimming, and wings for flying, you will not grub like a mole underground, hide yourself like a dull shellfish among mud, or be content with crow from the barn door like the prince of poultry, but you will come forward into the day, and run, swim, or fly to the clouds as nature has provided. A man of deeds is not content to remain the way he is. Rather he strives to realize his potential. Therefore, try to be what the gods have called upon you to become. Then you will be able to judge whether or not the Bohemian kingdom is worth an acre of wheat in exchange."

This earnest speech of the deputy, in whose face no jesting feature could be discerned, overcame the distrust of the suspicious plowman. Even more convincing were the insignia of royalty, the crimson robe, the scepter, and the golden sword, which the ambassadors brought out as a sign to demonstrate the authenticity of their mission. At once everything became clear to him. A blissful thought made him aware that Libussa had discovered the feelings of his heart. Through her skill in seeing what was secret, she had recognized his faithfulness and constancy and was about to reward him in a way that he had never hoped for, even in his dreams. He recalled the prediction of her oracle, and he knew that it must now be fulfilled or never. He grabbed his hazel staff, struck it deep into the ground, heaped loose soil around it as if planting a tree, and immediately the staff sprouted buds and shot forth branches with leaves and flowers. However, two of the green twigs withered, and their dry leaves became the sport of the wind, but the third flourished, and its fruits ripened. Then the spirit of prophecy came over the rapt plowman, and he opened his mouth and said, "Messengers of the Princess Libussa and the people of Bohemia, hear the words of Primislaus, the son of Mnatha, the honorable knight, for he is inspired by the spirit of prophecy and will clear away the clouds of the future. You have called upon the man who has guided the plow to take control of your kingdom before his day's work was finished. Oh, if only the plow had been allowed to dig its furrows all around and reach the boundary stone, so that Bohemia would remain an independent kingdom to the end of days! But since you have disturbed the labor of the plowman too soon, the boundaries of your country will be inherited by your neighbor, and your distant posterity will be linked to him in unchangeable unity. The three twigs of the budding staff are three sons whom your princess shall bear me. Two of them, like unripe shoots, will quickly wither away. But the third will inherit the throne, and through him the fruit of grand-children will ripen later, until the eagle soars over your mountains and nestles in the land, flying back and forth as to his own dominions. And then, when the son of the gods who is the plowman's friend arises and throws off the fetters of slavery, then take heed, posterity, for you will bless your destiny! When he has stamped the dragon of superstition under his feet, he will stretch out his arm against the rising moon to pluck it from the firmament, so that he may himself illuminate the world as a benevolent star."

The honorable deputies stood in silent amazement and gazed at the prophetic man like solemn idols. It was as if a god were speaking through his lips. He himself turned away from them to the two white steers, the associates of his toilsome labor. Then he unyoked them and set them free from their farm service. As they began playing about joyfully on the grassy meadow, they visibly decreased in bulk and like vapor melted into thin air and vanished out of sight. Meanwhile Primislaus took off his peasant clogs and walked to the brook to clean himself. Then he was clothed in precious garments, and after he attached the sword to his belt, he had the golden spurs put on him like a knight. Finally, he sprang upon the white horse, which obeyed his commands. As he was about to leave his domicile, he ordered the deputies to bring his wooden clogs with them and to guard them carefully, as a reminder that the humblest among the people had been exalted to the highest dignity in Bohemia and also as a reminder to his offspring to bear their elevation meekly, to remember their origins, to respect and defend the peasantry, from which they themselves had sprung. This marked the beginning of the ancient custom of exhibiting a pair of wooden shoes whenever a king of Bohemia was crowned, and it was observed until the male line of Primislaus became extinct.

The planted hazel staff bore fruit and grew. It spread its roots on all sides and sent forth new shoots until, at last, the whole field was changed into a grove of hazel trees. This remarkable event was a great boon to the neighboring village, for the hazel tree was within its borders, and in memory of its mi-raculous planting, they obtained a grant from the Bohemian kings that exempted them from ever paying any public contribution to the nation except for a pint of hazelnuts. Their descendants, so the story goes, are enjoying this royal privilege to this very day.

Though the white steed, which was now proudly carrying the bridegroom to his mistress, seemed to outrun the winds, Primislaus did not hesitate every now and then to let him feel the golden spurs and to push him on even faster. The quick strides of the horse seemed like a tortoise pace to him, so keen was his desire to have the beautiful Libussa before his eyes. In fact, her figure was still new and lovely in his mind, even after seven years, and he regarded her not merely as some bright peculiar anemone in the multicolored bed of a flower garden but with an eye toward triumphing in love and a blissful union. He thought only about the myrtle crown, which far outshines the sovereign crown in the estimation of lovers, and if he had weighed love and rank against each other, the Bohemian throne without Libussa would have sprung up like a clipped ducat in the scales of the money changer.

The sun was on the point of setting when the new prince was conducted into Vizegrad. Libussa was in her garden, where she had just plucked a basket of ripe plums, when her future husband's arrival was announced to her. She went forth modestly with all her maidens to meet him, and she received him as a bridegroom led to her by the gods, veiling the choice of her heart under a show of submission to the will of higher powers. The eyes of the court were eagerly focused on the stranger, in whom, however, nothing could be detected but a slender man. With regard to his physical stature, there were several courtiers who thought they could easily compare with him, and they could not understand why the gods had disdained the select group of noblemen and had not selected some accomplished lord among them instead of the sunburned plowman to assist the princess in ruling the realm and sharing her bed. It was especially clear from the faces of Vladomir and Mizisla that they would withdraw their claims only with reluctance. It was incumbent on the princess to justify the work of the gods and demonstrate how Primislaus had been indemnified for the lack of a royal birth by a fair equivalent in plain common sense and sharp discernment. She ordered her servants to arrange a splendid banquet, which was comparable to the feast with which the hospitable Dido entertained her righteous guest Aeneas. The cup of welcome was passed diligently from mouth to mouth; the presents of the princess had stimulated good cheer and humor; and part of the night had already passed amid jests and pleasant amusements, when Libussa began a game of riddles. Since guessing came naturally to her, she succeeded in solving all the riddles put to her, to the delight of everyone present.

When her own turn came to propose one, she called Prince Vladomir, Mizisla, and Primislaus to her and said, "Brave men, it is now your turn to solve one of my riddles, so that it will become clear who among you is the wisest and most perceptive. I want to give all three of you a present from this basket of plums that I plucked in my garden. One of you shall have the half and one over; the next shall have the half of what remains and one over; the third shall have the half and three over. Now if after that the basket is empty, tell me how many plums are in it now?"

The rash knight Mizisla measured the basket of fruit with his eye and did not grasp the sense of the riddle with his mind. "I'll gladly solve what can be solved with the sword," he said, "but your riddles, blessed princess, may be too complex for me. Still, since you have requested it, I'll take a shot in the dark. I guess that there are about sixty plums in the basket."

"You have missed, dear knight," said Libussa. "If there were as many as sixty, then half as many, and half as many after that, it would all add up to more than sixty."

Prince Vladomir calculated long and laboriously, as if the post of comptroller general depended on a right solution, and at last he came to the net sum of forty-five. In response, Libussa said, "Were there a third, and a half, and a sixth as many of them, there would be forty-five more than what is in there now."

In our days, any man equipped with a tape measure would have solved this problem without difficulty, but at that time, the gift of divination was essential in this situation, especially for an unskilled mathematician if he wanted to get out of the predicament with honor and not get stuck in the middle of it with disgrace. Since the wise Primislaus was fortunately blessed with this gift, he did not have to use art or have to exert himself to find the answer.

"Trusted consort of the heavenly powers," he said, "whoever seeks to pierce your high celestial meaning undertakes to soar after the eagle when it hides himself in the clouds. Nevertheless, I shall follow your hidden flight as far as the eye upon which you have bestowed light can reach. I estimate that there are thirty in number, not one fewer, and not one more."

Libussa cast a friendly glance at him and said, "You have traced the glimmering spark that lies deeply hidden among the ashes. For you, light glows out of darkness and fog: you have guessed my riddle."

Thereupon she opened her basket and counted out fifteen plums and one over into Prince Vladomir's hat, and fourteen remained. Of these, she gave the knight Mizisla seven and one over, and there were still six in the basket. Half of these she gave the wise Primislaus and three over, and the basket was empty. The whole court was astounded by how wise the beautiful Libussa was in arithmetics and how clever her smart spouse was. Nobody could grasp how the human intellect was able, on the one hand, to make a mysterious riddle out of a common number in words or, on the other hand, to solve it so accurately despite its enigmatic concealment. Now Libussa bestowed the empty basket on the two knights who had failed in obtaining her love, as a reminder that their suit was voided. Ever since then, even to the present day, when a wooer has been rejected, people say his love has given him the basket.

As soon as everything was ready for the nuptials and the coronation, both these ceremonies were held with suitable pomp. Thus the Bohemian people had obtained a duke, and the beautiful Libussa had obtained a husband, both according to the wishes of their hearts. What was particularly wonderful was that it was all done through virtue of chicane, an agent not normally known for being so propitious. And if either of the parties had been deceived to any degree, it was least of all the beautiful Libussa, but the people, and that is normally the case anyway. Bohemia had a duke in name, but the government continued to be directed by female hands, as it formerly had been. Primislaus was the proper model of an obedient and submissive husband and did not disagree with the way she managed her house or her country. His sentiments and wishes were in accord with hers as perfectly as two harmonious strings, so that when one was struck, the other freely echoed the exact same note. Nor was Libussa like those proud and vain ladies who think they make great matches, and who, once they think they've made the fortune of some hapless fellow, continually remind him in a haughty manner of his wooden shoes. On the contrary, Libussa resembled the renowned Palmyran queen and ruled by superiority of mind, as Zenobia did her good-natured Odenatus.

The happy couple lived and enjoyed unchangeable love according to the custom of those times, when the instinct that united hearts was as firm and durable as the mortar and cement that made the walls of the old world indestructible. Duke Primislaus soon became one of the most valiant knights of his time, and the Bohemian court the most splendid in Germany. Gradually many knights and nobles and numerous people from all regions of the realm flocked to it, so that Vizegrad became too small for its inhabitants. As a result, Libussa called her officers to her and commanded them to found a city on the spot where they would find a man making the wisest use of his teeth at noontime. They set out, and at the designated time they found a man sawing a block of wood. They estimated that this hardworking man was using the teeth of his saw at noon in a far better way than the parasite employs the teeth of his jaw at the table of noble people, and they were certain that they had found the spot designated by the princess for the site of their town. They marked out a space with a plow upon the green for the circle of the city walls. Then, when they asked the worker what he intended to make with the wood that he was sawing, he replied, "Prah," which in the Bohemian language means a threshold to a door. So Libussa called her new city Praha, that is, Prague, the well-known royal capital on the Moldau. In the course

of time, Primislaus's predictions were fulfilled. His wife became the mother
of three princes. Two died during their youth, but the third grew to manhood,
and he produced a glorious royal line, which flourished on the Bohemian
throne for many centuries to come.

Translated by Jack Zipes

The Philosophers' Stone

CHRISTOPH MARTIN WIELAND

In the days when Cornwall still had its own princes, a young king by the name of Mark ruled over this small peninsula of Great Britain. He was the grandson of that same King Mark who had become famous through his wife, the beautiful Isolde, also called Iseult the blonde, and her love affair with the noble and unfortunate Tristan of Leonnoys.

The young King Mark was very much like his grandfather. He was arrogant without ambition, sensuous without taste, and greedy without knowing how to be economical. As soon as he inherited the throne, which was at a very young age, he began to give in to his passions and moods and to live in a style that would have ruined a country much larger and richer than his own. When his income was no longer sufficient for his expenses, he burdened his subjects with new taxes. And when they no longer had anything to give, he made money off them by selling them to his neighbors.

While all this was happening, King Mark continued to maintain a splendid court and managed everything as though he had found an inexhaustible supply of gold. To be sure, he had not found such a supply, but he was at least making a great effort to look for one. And as soon as it became known that he was looking for gold, all kinds of strange people appeared at his court who were anxious to help him locate the gold. Treasure seekers, necromancers, alchemists, and swindlers who called themselves disciples of the great Hermes came from all over the world and were welcomed with open arms at the court. Indeed, aside from all the vices that poor Mark had, he was also the most gullible man in the world, so that the first tramp who came along and boasted that he had secret powers could get anything out of him that he wanted. Therefore, his court was swarming with such rabble.

One man pretended that he had a natural gift that enabled him to smell where treasures had been buried. Another knew how to discover them with the help of a divining rod. There was yet a third man, who assured the king that everything was futile unless one possessed the secret of hypnotizing ghosts who came in the form of wise men or as figures who wore terrible masks, or of turning them into servants. And he let it be known in a modest way that he possessed this secret.

There were others who regarded magic with disdain. Everything they did was natural. They rejected talismans, magic spells, circles, figures, and whatever else belonged to this domain as plain deception and delusion. Whatever the others pretended to achieve through supernatural powers, these achieved, if one believed them, through mere natural forces. Whoever had penetrated the innermost holy essence of nature, so they said; whoever had become familiar with the true elements of things, their affinities, sympathies, and antipathies in nature's secret workshop; whoever knew how to unite the spirit of nature that assumed all different forms with the salt of nature that dissolved everything and could keep this protean force under control with the help of the astral fire that penetrated everything and could compel it to appear in its own original form—this man was the true sage. He alone deserved to be called an adept. There was nothing he could not do, for he commanded nature, which could bring about anything. He could transform inferior minerals into superior ones. He possessed the means to cure any kind of sickness. He could recall the dead to life, if he and the gods wanted to do this, and it was in his power to live as long as he desired, until he felt it more convenient to move to another world.

All of this appealed very much to King Mark's taste, but since he could not decide which one of his miracle workers he should keep and could not bear to send the others away, he kept them all and tried them out one after the other. The day was spent with empirics, the night with exorcising and digging for treasures. And when the swindlers realized that he did not like to have one person monopolize everything, they soon learned, to his great joy, to tolerate one another as if everything could fit together into one huge bag.

Several years went by like this without King Mark moving any closer to the object of his desires. He had allowed half of his small kingdom to be dug up, but no treasure was found. And his hope to transform the copper and tin of his mines into gold went up the chimney, along with the gold that his ancestors had long since taken from the mines.

If such disasters had happened to anyone else but Mark, they would have caused that person to open his eyes. But the king's eyes gradually became more blurred. He became now obsessed with finding the philosophers' stone, the more so as it seemed the more to conceal itself from him. The hope that he might finally obtain this protean power, which assumed all kinds of forms, increased in exact proportion to the number of losses he suffered. He believed that he had still not found the right man yet. But in the same moment that he would banish ten swindlers from his presence, he would open his arms to the very next one who arrived at his court.

Finally, an Egyptian adept from the secret school of the great Hermes announced his presence at King Mark's court. He called himself Misfragmutosiris and had a beard that hung down to his belt. In addition, he wore a cap in the form of a pyramid that had a golden sphinx attached to its top, a long cloak stitched with hieroglyphs, and a belt made of gilded tin in which the twelve signs of the zodiac were engraved. King Mark considered himself to be the luckiest man on earth to have such a wise man with so promising an appearance at his court. And even though the Egyptian was quite reserved, they soon became good friends. Everything about him—his stature, clothes, language, manners, and the way he conducted himself—indicated that he was an extraordinary man. He always dined alone and never ate what other people did. He had some large snakes and a stuffed crocodile in his room. He treated them with great respect, and it seemed that he held secret conversations with them from time to time. He talked about the most marvelous and enigmatic things with openness and indifference, as if these things were the most common and familiar in the world. However, he rarely answered questions, and if he did, then he did so in a way that left one with the feeling that there was nothing more to ask, even though the questioner now knew just as little as he knew before. He talked about people who had lived many centuries ago as if he had known them very well. At the very least, one had to conclude from his talk that he had been a contemporary of King Amasis, even though he never clearly declared this to be true. What made him most credible in Mark's eyes was the fact that he had a great deal of gold and a bunch of rare items with him, and he talked about huge sums of money as if they were trifles. All these circumstances intensified the curiosity of the gullible King Mark to such a degree that he could not stand it any longer. And no matter how the king's guest had resisted everything, enough was enough, and the wise Misfragmutosiris finally let himself be moved by the king's entreaties. Either that, or his heart no longer allowed him to be ungrateful in view of the honors and the gifts that the king heaped upon him. Therefore, he finally revealed the entire secret of his identity to King Mark—but of course, he did not do this until he had led the king through various kinds of graduated initiations demanded by the order of Hermes.

"The gods," Misfragmutosiris said, "give their precious gifts to whomever they please. I was just like all other men, still young, but I did know a little about the mysteries of Egyptian philosophy. And my curiosity drove me to penetrate into the interior of the great pyramid at Memphis, whose age is a secret even to the Egyptians. There was a certain hieroglyphical inscription over the entrance to the first hall, which I had already discovered and written down, and after I took a great deal of trouble to guess its meaning, I surmised that this pyramid was the tomb of the great Hermes. I decided within the hour that I would dare to enter the place, which certainly no living mortal had ever visited before. Even today my audacity would be difficult for me to grasp if I were not convinced that this idea, which my own mind was not capable of producing, had been engendered in me by some higher power. In short, I climbed into the pyramid about midnight without any light, and completely placing myself in the hands of whatever propelled me to undertake such a bold adventure. I went down a gentle slope for some time and, without noticing it, began climbing upward again, when I suddenly caught sight of a bright light that hovered in front of me like a ball of pure solid fire."

Here Misfragmutosiris paused for a moment, giving King Mark the opportunity to ask, "And you had the courage to follow this light?" He was sitting across from him in the position of a transfixed listener—his body slanted forward, his feet stretched backward, both hands leaning on his knees—fearful that he might lose a single word of the story, even though he was atremble about what might happen. Indeed, he held his breath and kept his eyes wide open as he listened.

"I followed the light," the Egyptian continued, "and proceeded through a hallway that become lower and lower and narrower and narrower, until I came to a four-cornered room with walls of polished marble, and it had a door that led me to another hallway. After walking about fifty feet, I came to two paths. One seemed to lead up a steep incline; the other, on my left, went straight ahead. I followed the ball of light straight in front of me until I came to the edge of a deep well. Owing to the extreme brightness of the light, I became aware of a number of short iron rungs, about two feet apart, that stuck out on the wall from top to bottom. They formed a dangerous kind of ladder, which one could use in an emergency to climb down into the well. Without thinking too long, I began to undertake the dizzy descent, when suddenly the ball of light disappeared and left me in terrifying darkness.

"I don't understand why my fright didn't cause me to fall into the abyss at this horrible moment. No matter; I collected myself and took even greater care as I continued to climb down. I held one hand on a rung over my head while I searched below for the next one with my other hand and my feet. Eventually there were no more rungs, and I heard water rustling beneath me. At the same time, however, I became aware of an opening on the side that I had been climbing down, and from it came a faint glow. I jumped into this opening and landed on a steep path that led into an enormous cave of glimmering granite, which was illuminated by a huge carbuncle that was hanging from the middle of the arched ceiling. Imagine my astonishment as I found myself suddenly on the edge of a rippling stream that poured out of an opening over ragged rocks in this cave and made a terrible noise. It took me just a moment to think of what I had to do. I had already gone too far to turn back, and a secret spirit seemed to whisper to me that all these obstacles had been placed before me in order to test my courage. So I took off all my clothes, tied them up in a bundle on top of my head, and plunged into the stream. Shortly thereafter I was carried away by the power of the stream and propelled through a dark vault. Gradually I noticed that the water under me had become shallow. Soon the water disappeared altogether and left me sitting on some mossy ground in a large cave. Now I felt an extraordinary heat, which dried me so quickly that I could immediately get dressed again to see where a rather narrow opening would lead me. There was a bright light coming from it, and as I approached the opening I heard a sizzling and a crackling that appeared to come from a blazing fire. I crept into the opening, which eventually widened, and I found myself at the entrance of a wide arched room, where I encountered another obstacle, more horrifying than all the previous ones.

"In front of me I saw an abyss of fire that practically filled the entire room. Its flames seethed and flared up as if out of a lake of fire over the granite banks that surrounded it, and they seemed to quiver at my feet. Instead of a bridge, there was a kind of plank made of four narrow copper sheets bound together, which reached from one bank to the other. However, the plank was barely a foot wide. I must honestly confess that despite the great heat of this terrible place, I felt ice-cold chills running up and down my spine. But what else could I do but forge ahead on this adventure too, without having much time to think about other possibilities. How I made it over to the other side, I don't know myself, but I did make it over, and before I had time to know what was happening, I felt caught up in a whirlwind and propelled with indescribable rapidity through the most horrifying darkness. I lost consciousness but soon regained my senses when I felt myself being thrown roughly against a door, which immediately sprang open, and I found myself standing in a splendidly illuminated hall. Its arched ceiling was painted in azure like the sky and was filled with an infinite number of carbuncles and constellations. The ceiling was supported by two rows of massive gold pillars, on which countless hieroglyphs, made of multicolored precious stones, were glistening.

I stood there for some minutes, completely dazzled and delighted by the splendor of this place."

"That I can believe!" exclaimed King Mark. "Especially after everything that you had gone through! I would have liked to be in your place!"

"When I collected myself again," Misfragmutosiris continued, without paying any attention to the king's lively interest, "I noticed a huge door made of ebony, with a colossal sphinx on each side, carved from ivory and marvelously beautiful. However, to my great regret, they were so close to the door and so near one another that it seemed completely impossible to open the door and to satisfy the longing that had brought about my involvement in such a dangerous adventure. While I now stood in front of the forbidden door and began in vain to think of some means to overcome this difficulty, I looked at the top of the door and caught sight of diamond characters that formed the name of Hermes Trismegistus in the holy script that I knew. I read the name in a loud voice, and no sooner had I done this than the door opened by itself. The two sphinxes came alive, looked at me with sparkling eyes, and retreated far enough to allow me to go between them. As soon as I passed the threshold of the ebony door, it closed of itself as though moved by an invisible spirit, and I found myself in a round dome of black jasper, whose terrible darkness was brightened only at ten-second intervals by a streak of lightning that suddenly flashed around the smooth black walls and disappeared as soon as it appeared.

"As this majestic and mysterious light kept flickering, I caught sight of a large, glorious bed in the middle of the dome, so richly ornamented that it was indescribable. There seemed to be a tall, venerable old man with a bald head and a snow-white beard lying on top of the bed in a soft slumber, with his hands folded on top of his chest. Two dragons were stationed at his head, and they had such strange and horrifying forms that I believe I can still see them standing before me though so many centuries have gone by. They had flat heads with long, drooping ears, round glassy eyes, which seemed to pop out of their sockets, backs like crocodiles, extremely long and thin swan-like necks, and enormous leather wings like those of bats. The front parts of their bodies were protected by stiff glittering scales and armed with the feet of eagles, and the rear parts ended in thick tails that were wrapped around themselves seven times. I soon realized that the flashes of lightning that illuminated the room for a moment every ten seconds came out of the nostrils of these dragons, and that this was their way of breathing. Despite the fact that these atrocious monsters looked horrifying, they did not seem to mean me ill, but rather allowed me to observe the majestic sage as long as I wanted. He was sleeping the long slumber of death there, while the light kept flashing. Soon I noticed a thick scroll of Egyptian paper that lay at the feet of the sage and appeared to be covered with hieroglyphs and figures. As soon as I saw this scroll, I was overcome by an incredible longing to possess it, for I was quite sure that it contained the hidden secrets of the great Hermes. I stretched out my hand ten times, and I quickly pulled it back ten times, out of fear. Finally, my longing got the better of me, and my hand touched the holy treasure, which was more valuable in my eyes than all the treasures above and below the earth. Suddenly a stroke of lightning came out of the mouth of one of the dragons, knocked me to the ground, and paralyzed all my limbs, so that I was unable to stand. At the same time a small winged snake with a crown on its head and which cast off the brightest rays of the sun flew down from the top of the dome and breathed on me. I felt the power of its breath penetrate all my nerves like a sharp spiritual flame, so that I was numb for some moments. However, when I pulled myself together, I saw a young boy in front of me, sitting on a lotus leaf, and as he pressed the index finger of his right hand to his mouth, he used his left hand to offer me the scroll that I had seen lying at the feet of the sleeping sage. I recognized the god of holy silence and prostrated myself at his feet. But he disappeared, and now I first became aware that I was not in the great pyramid of Memphis but in my own bed, and I had no idea how everything had happened."

"Wonderful! Upon my honor, most strange!" King Mark exclaimed, with all the astonishment and surprise one would accord a thoroughly believable story.

"That's also how it seemed to me," responded Misfragmutosiris. "And I certainly would have talked myself into believing that I had merely dreamed all these marvelous things, but I held the mysterious scroll in my hand, and this convinced me that everything I had experienced had been real. I regarded it now with indescribable delight. I tasted and smelled it on all sides, and I could hardly believe my own senses that such an insignificant person as I was the owner of a treasure that a king would give his crown for. The paper was made of the most beautiful purple color; the hieroglyphs were painted; and the figures were made of thinly stamped gold."

"That must be a beautiful book," King Mark said. "I'd give anything to be able to hold it in my hand for a minute. Do you think I could?"

"Gladly, if I still had it in my possession."

"What? You don't have it anymore?" Mark cried out in a plaintive tone.

"It was in my possession for seven days only. On the eighth, the young boy on the lotus leaf reappeared, took the scroll out of my hand, and disappeared with it forever. But these seven days were sufficient for me to master seven secrets, the least of which is worth an inestimable fortune in my eyes. Over a thousand years have passed since that remarkable night—"

"Over a thousand years?" interrupted King Mark. "Is that possible? Over a thousand years?"

"Everything is possible," answered the thousand-year-old disciple of the great Hermes in his usual dispassionate manner. "This is due to the power of the seventh secret. Ever since I learned to possess it, the entire earth has been my fatherland, and I have seen kingdoms and peoples fall all around me like leaves from the trees. I live here and there: sometimes in this part of the world, and sometimes in another part. I can speak every human language there is, know about all the affairs of people, and have nothing to lose or to gain in anything. I don't desire to rule over anyone, and I am nobody's subject. But when I encounter a good king (which is seldom the case), I enjoy increasing his capacity to do good deeds."

King Mark assured him that he wished and hoped to be one of those good kings. At any rate, he had always enjoyed doing good deeds, and it was merely to do an infinite amount of good deeds that he had constantly wished to obtain the philosophers' stone.

Misfragmutosiris let him know that they could discuss this matter. He seemed to regard it as a trifle, but he did not want to explain himself fully.

King Mark, who had for a friend a man for whom nothing was impossible, believed that he could already feel the philosophers' stone in his pocket and held splendid parties every day, paid for by the gold mines—that is, his copper mines, which would soon be transformed into gold mines. Indeed, the miracle man with the gold sphinx on his cap, who was a thousand years old, who could cure any kind of sickness, and who had a crocodile as his pet, was already known throughout the entire land, and owing to the fact that the people had developed a high opinion of him, the king's sunken credit had risen again.

Meanwhile his queen, Mabille, contributed a great deal to making the festivities at court more lively and more glittering. For a long time King Mark, who loved change, had given his wife some reason to feel neglected. And the jealousy with which she felt obliged to show him her affection had become so burdensome for him that he sometimes uttered the wish that she (without tarnishing her virtue) would think of some other means to drive away her boredom than to take delight in spoiling his small pleasures. This is why he seemed either not to notice or (as some of the courtiers believed) was secretly very glad to see that a handsome young knight by the name of Floribell of Nicomedes, who had recently appeared at his court, began wooing the queen's favor in a most glaring way and was making considerable progress. In fact, everything had evolved to the point that Mabille herself could no longer deny her feelings for the handsome Floribell. And since she was strongly resolved to offer brave resistance, the affairs of her heart took up all her time, so that she did not have any left to disturb the king in his affairs.

No matter how much King Mark liked to amuse himself at parties, he never for one second lost sight of his major objective and passion. Several months had already gone by since Mark had begun treating the heir of the great Trismegistus like a monarch at his court, and he believed that he could now justifiably demand something from Misfragmutosiris as a friend. To be sure, Misfragmutosiris had constantly declared that he was against rewards and large gifts, but no friend, he used to say, can refuse to accept from another friend little gifts that are only worth something because of the friendship of which they are symbolic. However, since the terms "little" and "large" are relative, and since our adept spoke about things commonly estimated to have a large value as if they were insignificant, the small gifts that he graciously began to accept little by little from his friend Mark soon exhausted the treasury of the poor king, and it was high time to replenish it by way of new and lucrative sources. The Egyptian seemed to feel the necessity of this himself, and upon the first allusion that the king made to the seven secrets, Misfragmutosiris did not hesitate to confess to him that the first and least of the secrets was the art of preparing the philosophers' stone. Mark assured him that he would be very satisfied just to learn the least of the secrets, and the adept took pleasure in revealing to him a secret in which, to be sure, he did not place great stock, but which nevertheless had to remain hidden forever to prevent it from being misused by the profane, as he wisely said.

"The true, hermetical philosophers' stone," he said, "can only be drawn from the finest precious stones: diamonds, emeralds, rubies, sapphires, and opals. The preparation of the stone, through the mixture of a large portion of red mercury sulfide and some drops of oil drawn from a condensed ray of the sun, is less costly or complicated than troublesome and demands almost nothing but an unusual degree of attention and patience. And this is the reason why it would not be worth the trouble to conduct a small experiment. The result of the operation, which in my hands would not take longer than three times seven days, is a kind of crimson substance, which is very heavy and can be scraped into a fine powder, of which a pinch half the size of a barley seed is sufficient to transform two pounds of lead into just as much gold. And this is what one generally calls the philosophers' stone."

King Mark ardently yearned to have a few pounds of this glorious product at his disposal as soon as possible. Therefore, he asked somewhat fearfully whether a very large quantity of precious stones would be necessary to gain a pound of this philosophers' stone.

"Oh," said Misfragmutosiris, "I realize where the problem lies. We shall not lack for precious stones, for I also possess the secret to make the finest and purest precious stones. I must confess, however, that this operation is slow. It demands just as many months as the philosophers' stone does days, but—"

"No," Mark interrupted him. "I cannot wait that long! I'd rather give up my crowns and all the rest of my jewelry for it! Twenty-one months is an eternity! Once we have the stone of all stones, then we shall have plenty of all the rest. You can get anything you want with gold. And in any event, I certainly won't hold it against you if you want to make precious stones at your leisure."

"As you wish," said the adept. "With two hundred pounds of diamonds and double the amount of rubies, emeralds, and other precious gems, we'll be able to obtain a stone of twelve thousand grams, and we'll be able to do something with that. It would take me a hundred years before I could get as much."

"It's a trifle," said King Mark. "I'll bet there are more stones on my mere house crown than you demand. But when we really begin the work, it must be worth the trouble. Just let me take care of everything! We must obtain a stone weighing twenty-four thousand grams, or my name is not King Mark!"

"The fortunate thing is," said the adept, "that I already have a supply of sun oil, which is the most precious of all the ingredients and takes twenty-one years to prepare. I've always taken care to carry some vials of this oil with me. Aside from the fact that it is the major component in preparing the stone, it is also the material from which the hermetic oil of immortality is prepared through a process that requires three times twenty-one years. In the near future I'll reveal to you as much about its miraculous powers as I am allowed to."

King Mark was beside himself with joy to possess a friend who had such revelations to make, and he hurried as fast as he could to help arrange all the necessary things for the great work. There were plenty of ovens and all sorts of chemical equipment at his court, where experiments had been conducted for many years. But Misfragmutosiris declared that, with the exception of a small stove, which he had built in a small cabinet in his room, and a sack of coal, he did not need anything, since he had everything with him that was necessary for the operation. When all the preparations were completed, he consulted the stars and set a date for the beginning of the secret experiment, at the first hour after midnight. In anticipation of this, he made the king an initiate of the hermetic mysteries so that Mark would be capable of witnessing all the work appertaining to the great experiment. The only thing that he would not witness was the ultimate mystery, whereby the spirit of the three times great Hermes had to appear to endorse the experiment. Only adepts of the highest degree were able to withstand his presence. And Misfragmutosiris let the king know that he himself was the only living mortal who could boast this ability, and consequently he was the invisible high priest of the entire hermetic order.

Finally, when the long-awaited midnight approached, King Mark with his own hands gave the adept a golden chest. It was filled with diamonds, emeralds, rubies, sapphires, and Oriental opals that he had removed from two or three crowns inherited from his ancestors. On this occasion he was allowed into the secret cabinet for the first time. Until this moment no living mortal with the exception of the adept had been allowed to set foot in it. It was decorated all around with pictures of Egyptian gods and hieroglyphs and was illuminated only by a single lamp, which hung from the ceiling. In the middle was a small round stove made of black marble, in the form of an altar, upon which the great work was to be performed. Misfragmutosiris, dressed in the garments of an Egyptian high priest, began the ceremony by fumigating the king with a pleasant incense that made him feel numb. Then the adept made a large hermetic-magic circle around the altar and within it a smaller circle, which he marked with seven hieroglyphic figures, just as he had marked the outer one with nine. He commanded the king to stand in the outer circle, but he himself entered the inner circle in front of the altar, where he threw a few kernels of incense into a pan and muttered some words that the king could not understand. As soon as the smoke began to rise, a long-eared boy sitting on a lotus leaf appeared above the altar, with the index finger of his right hand pressed to his mouth and with his left hand carrying a burning torch. Mark became pale as a ghost when the boy appeared, and could barely keep his feet. But the adept approached the boy's ear with his mouth and whispered something to him, whereupon the boy answered in the affirmative with a nod of his head and disappeared. Misfragmutosiris told the king to keep his courage up, gave him a spoonful of an elixir, a powerful dose to strengthen his life spirit, and recommended that he reappear at seven in the morning. In the meantime, the king was to go and rest, while he himself would keep watch in order to wait for the appearance of the great Hermes, which had been announced to him, and to complete the secret mysteries with which the great experiment had to begin if they wanted to be guaranteed that everything would turn out successfully.

King Mark went to his own room full of trust and hope, and since what the adept had given him was a sleeping potion, he had a long and uninterrupted sleep and did not awake until two hours after the time when he was supposed to appear in Misfragmutosiris's chamber. When he finally arose, he threw on his clothes and rushed to the secret cabinet, where he found everything just as he had left it. However, the wise Misfragmutosiris and the golden chest with the precious stones had vanished.

There are no words that can describe the king's dismay when he saw how cruelly his sanguine hopes and his boundless trust in the chief of the hermetic order had been betrayed. After he overcame the numbness of his astonishment, he began to berate himself, and this was followed by an outburst of curses and furious threats against the swindler, who was probably laughing at Mark's gullibility in some safe refuge. Just as the king was about to descend to his large hall and order all his knights and servants to pursue the fugitive, a marvelously handsome young man, dressed in bright glittering garments, with a golden crown on his head and a lily in his hand, stood all at once before him and spoke.

"I'm aware of the catastrophe that has upset your life," he said, "and I have brought you compensation. You've been searching for the philosophers' stone. Well, take this stone, rub it back and forth three times on your forehead and your chest, and your wish shall be fulfilled."

After speaking these words, the young man placed a crimson stone in his hand and disappeared. King Mark's mood swung from dismay to ecstasy. He regarded the stone, which he had received in such a miraculous and unexpected way, and inspected it from all sides. Although he did not grasp how his wish would be fulfilled and what connection there was between rubbing his forehead and his chest with the stone, he was well accustomed to believing in and doing things that he did not comprehend at all. Indeed, it was impossible for him to doubt or resist the command of this spirit. Consequently, he rubbed the magical stone back and forth three times on his forehead and chest, and just as he finished, he stood there transformed— into a donkey.

While all this was happening to the king, a terrifying clamor broke out in the other wing of the castle. The handsome young knight Floribell (who, we cannot deny this, was under suspicion of having spent the night in the bedroom of the queen) had disappeared this morning with the better part of the queen's jewels. Mabille, the first person at court to discover this, was just about to begin ripping her beautiful hair out of her head because of the shame and anger she felt, when a lady of indescribable beauty, in a rose-colored dress and with a crown of roses on her head, stood before her and said, "I know what's bothering you, beautiful queen, and I've come to help you. Take this rose and place it on your breast. Then you'll become happier than you've ever been before."

With these words the lady handed her a rose from her crown and vanished. Since the queen did not have anything better in mind, she complied with the lady's command. She stuck the rose on her bosom and found herself instantaneously transformed into a rose-colored goat and transported to a wild and desolate place.

When the chambermaids entered her room at the usual hour that morning and did not find the queen, her jewels, or even the handsome Floribell, their dismay and the noise they produced were more awful than one can imagine. It was completely clear that she had let herself be abducted by the young knight, and the servants went to report this to the king. But their horror and confusion became even greater when they were also unable to find the king and his new favorite, the man with the big white beard! They could not picture King Mark letting himself be abducted by an old man with a gray beard. Consequently they stopped trying to imagine what had happened, even though nothing else was talked about in Cornwall during the next week. The knights and their pages took to their horses and searched for the king and the queen four long months in all the corners of Great Britain. But the search was in vain. They returned home knowing just as little as when they had left. The only thing that consoled the people was the conviction that it would be easy for them to find another king if they did not want to have a wiser one than King Mark.

The royal donkey, meanwhile, in order not to be discovered, had carefully made his way out of the castle into the open. In a sullen mood, his ears drooping, he had already trotted for some hours through woods and fields when he encountered a young peasant woman in a gorge, carrying a large sack over her shoulders. Her fine figure, fresh complexion, and beautiful blond hair kindled in him a desire that was better suited for his previous condition than his present one. He stood still in order to stare at the young woman, who had lost her breath from walking and was so exhausted that she could not go any farther. The sympathy that she seemed to have aroused in this animal, who was from all appearances without an owner, aroused her attention. She approached him and began stroking him with her soft white hands. And since he kept very still and bared his teeth (in order to show that it pleased him to be petted by such a soft hand) and stretched his ears as far as they could go, she suddenly had the desire to employ him in her service and swung herself onto his back. The donkey put up with the unaccustomed work complaisantly, and the young peasant had no idea of his secret reasons for carrying her with such pleasure. He seemed proud of the charming burden and trotted briskly from that spot with her on his back like one of the best mules from Andalusia. Although she had nothing with which she could direct him other than his short mane, he seemed to understand the movements of her hand and even the meanings of her words. Thus he carried her through a series of byways that she indicated to him, and by nightfall they arrived in a wild region on the seacoast, which was enclosed by cliffs and woods and was only partially open to the neighboring sea.

They came to a halt in front of a cave surrounded by boulders and wild bushes, where the young peasant woman called out in a ringing voice, "It's me, Kasilde," two or three times. A fine, strapping man of about thirty or forty, dressed in a sailor suit, came out of the cave, and rejoicing greatly over her arrival, he helped her off the animal. Embracing her, he exclaimed, "Thank heaven that you're here, dear Kasilde! I was so worried that something might have happened to you."

"You should say, 'Thank this good donkey,'" the peasant woman replied laughingly. "Without him, you would probably not have seen me so soon again, if at all."

"As a reward, then, I'll let him rest and eat as much grass and thistles as he can find in this barren place," the man said. "I'm eternally in his debt for having delivered you, and, as I see, the dear sack, safe and sound to my arms."

The royal donkey was greatly startled to hear a voice that was extremely familiar to him. He regarded the two people (whom he followed into the cave without them noticing it) by the light of a lamp that hung down from the rocks, and it seemed to him that he recognized the features of the sailor and the young peasant woman. He took a closer look at the sailor's face, and the similarity appeared to become greater. As he approached a kind of stone table that stuck out from one of the rock walls, his eyes caught sight of a long white beard, and suddenly it dawned dreadfully on his dumb skull who the man was.

"Ha ha!" The young peasant woman laughed. "There's the hermetical beard!"

"I truly don't know," the man said in the same tone, "why I didn't throw the beard into a hedge along the way. It served its purpose, and we'll hardly need it again."

"You can be sure of that," the young woman replied as she tapped the sack. "Just take a look and tell me if I'm not worthy enough to be the mistress of a contemporary of King Amasis."

"You certainly are!" cried the wise Misfragmutosiris. "You're even worthy of the three times great Hermes himself, if you want. But," he continued, "what have you done with the glittering garments that made you look like a handsome knight, Kasilde?"

"As you can see, I traded them to the first pretty peasant I met as she was going to the market in town."

"We'll get over the loss," the head priest of the hermetic order said as he examined the precious contents of the sack. "But just so you don't boast too much about all your talents, my girl, take a look at all this and tell me whether all my adventures in the great pyramid of Memphis and the terror I experienced from the lightning of the dragons on the glorious bed of the great Hermes were worth it!"

Just imagine how his majesty the poor donkey felt as he watched all the gifts that the rogue had gradually received from him, along with all the precious stones of his crowns and the largest portion of the queen's jewelry, being spread out in all their sparkling glory on the stone table. If it were not for the limitless patience, a virtue most characteristic of the species of beast to which he now belonged, that lent him strength, it would have been impossible for him to prevent the fury that was boiling in his body from exploding in a truly terrible way. "Oh, why did I have to be changed into a donkey, of all things?" he thought. "If I were a leopard, a tiger, or a rhinoceros, I'd show them something! But as I am, there's nothing I can do. They can easily handle a donkey."

Such was the way that poor King Mark spoke to himself, and he continued to lie very quietly in his corner, pressed as tightly against the wall as possible, so that he could at least satisfy his curiosity by overhearing the intimate conversation of the two sly scoundrels who had plotted his downfall.

After they had feasted their eyes on the precious booty, they both felt an urgent need to fill their stomachs, for neither of them had eaten anything the entire day. The adept, who always thought of everything, had supplied himself with an abundant amount of food from the royal kitchen, since everything had stood at his command in the castle, and this food would last for some days. He took some of it out of his sack along with some delicious wine, and while they enjoyed their meal, they did not forget to laugh at the king of Cornwall's gullibility and the weakness of his virtuous wife, as they each recalled a thousand little incidents.

"Now I must tell you, dear Gablitone," the beautiful rascal said, "how I managed to bewilder the virtuous queen so I could carry out our plan."

"How you managed it, Kasilde? The way you looked in your knightly garments and with all the rest of your talents, what queen in the world wouldn't have been captivated by you?"

"Flatterer! My queen kept struggling about in my snare so much that she almost tore my net apart. Actually she almost resisted my seductive talents, but her jealousy about the king's coquetry, her boredom, her excited imagination, and her frustrated desires were all in my favor, and she was finally overcome even though she struggled until the very last moment. The party held by the king on the day before we disappeared helped my chances immensely. I increased my zealous forays to win her heart. The dancing and Greek wines heated up her blood. She abandoned herself to a certain merriment, which made her carefree and trusting of everyone. She did what she had never done before—she made a game out of my passion, and without noticing it, she became the more ensnared in my plot the less she seemed to see any danger. Finally, the opiate that I had slipped into her wine at the right moment took its effect. Her senses were overcome by a pleasant feeling of exhaustion. Her eyes continued to sparkle, but her knees collapsed. She thought she had become tired from dancing too much and went into her bedroom. As soon as her chambermaids had brought her to bed, they returned to the dance hall, and I snuck out. Mabille, who was half asleep, was greatly frightened when she saw me standing before her bed. Nevertheless, I realized that I was not entirely unexpected and that someone else in my place would have been smarter and come later. In short, I was able to win over the good lady by using the delicacy that is one of the advantages of my sex. I knew how to temper my feigned passion in this critical moment without appearing to be any less tender or ardent, so that even if the sleeping potion had not been so effective, I would not have been in an embarrassing situation. Nevertheless, the potion soon did its work, along with my tender caresses, so that upon awakening I presume that she probably considered herself more culpable than I could make her feel. And this little amber box with the better part of her jewelry is proof that I did not waste my time by regarding her charms as she slumbered, as the wise Misfragmutosiris might have done in my place."

"Rascal," Gablitone said, patting her on the shoulder. "Both of us were up to the challenge. You played your role like a professional, and I could not have expected anything less from someone I convinced to leave the theater at Alexandria to help me pursue my plan, which we have carried out so successfully. Now we'll have more than enough to do playing ourselves. To-morrow a fishing boat will take us to Brittany, and from there it will be easy to return to our homeland. In the meantime, beautiful Kasilde, let us follow the good example of our donkey, who has fallen asleep in the corner over there. We are safe from pursuit here and need our rest."

The royal donkey had only pretended to fall asleep. Having been cheated so disgracefully, been an eyewitness to the swindlers' success, and (worst of all) been transformed from a king into a donkey and seen his enemies right before his eyes but been unable to take revenge, indeed, having even been, as a donkey, an instrument of their success—all of this choked him so that he could barely breathe. But another scene, which poured the poison of the furies into all the feelings that were boiling in his body, set him afire so suddenly that he could no longer control his actions. He jumped up from the ground with a terrifying cry and attacked the happy couple, who, not prepared for such wild behavior from their donkey, received some mighty blows from his hooves before they could defend themselves. But this action eventually turned to the disadvantage of the unfortunate king, as it naturally had to, for the furious adept soon found a club and gave the long-eared creature a thun-derous beating on his head and back, causing it to sink to the ground half dead. Finally, only after Kasilde, who sympathized with the beast, pleaded with Gablitone did he finally desist and drag the extremely miserable donkey outside the cave.

Poor Mark had now been driven to such misery that death seemed to be the only thing left for him, a former human being and a king, to wish for. But the powerful drive of self-preservation manages to struggle against death in every living creature until the last breath is gone. So now the abused donkey crawled as far from the detested cave as he could and then into the bushes. After a few hours of rest, fresh air, and some good grass that he found in the woods, he felt fit enough by daybreak to get up on his feet and move along briskly. He walked around in the wilderness the entire day with no other purpose than to keep far from human dwellings, for the worst misfortune that could happen to him would be to fall into the employ of human beings. Fortunately, wolves and other predatory animals were rare in that region. So he trotted about off the beaten paths the entire day, satisfied his hunger as best he could, drank out of streams or puddles when he was thirsty, slept in some thickets at night, although his memories did not let him sleep much. The strangest thing about all this was that he could not drive out of his head the accursed whim that had cost him so much. He still yearned to possess the stone of the wise, even though he was a donkey. During the day he thought of nothing but the stone, and it was the same during the night in his dreams.

The beneficent spirit who had decided to cure the king of his foolishness took advantage of the disposition of Mark's mind and influenced him through a dream. Indeed, if all the wise men on earth had tried reasoning with him while he was awake, they would not have been as successful as this dream, in which he envisaged himself, still king of Cornwall, standing irritably in front of his stove after a failed experiment. Suddenly a handsome young man appeared before him, and he remembered him as the youth who had given him the crimson stone.

The spirit spoke to him most seriously. "King Mark, I see that the means with which I sought to cure you from your madness has not had much effect. You deserve to be punished for the way you have kept wishing for the philosophers' stone. I want you to know that you could look for this stone until the end of your days and it would always be in vain, because no such stone exists. But take this lily, and everything that you touch with it will turn into gold." With these words the youth handed him the lily and vanished.

King Mark wondered for a moment whether he should trust the gift. But his curiosity and his yearning for gold outweighed all his doubts. He touched the lily to a lump of lead that lay before him, and the lead turned into the finest gold. He repeated the experiment with all the lead and copper with which the room was filled, and he continued to have the same success. Finally, he touched a large pile of coal, and this became a large pile of gold. The rapture of the crazed king was inexpressible. He immediately had twelve new mints built, where the people worked day and night to manufacture coins of all different kinds from the gold he made with his lily. Since things happen very quickly in dreams, the chambers of his castle were soon filled with more ready money than had ever been circulated on the face of the earth. "Now," thought Mark, "the world is mine." He asked himself what his heart desired, and his gold produced it for him, no matter how expensive or extravagant it was. Because he controlled an inexhaustible supply of gold, he naturally deluded himself that he could do anything he desired. Thus he wanted all his wishes to be carried out just as rapidly as they originated in him, and whatever he commanded was to occur instantaneously. His subjects did not benefit at all from his immeasurable expenditures, for he did not give them time to create or manufacture any of the materials that were necessary for his pleasures. Moreover, there was a lack of artists in his country, and he could not possibly think of waiting until enough artists were trained. What reason would he have had to support them? Artists and workers from the ends of the earth appeared at his court, and all possible products and commodities that one could think of were brought to him from Italy, Greece, and Egypt. He had mountains transported, valleys filled, seas dried up, canals made navigable. He built splendid palaces, designed magical gardens that were filled with all the riches of nature, with all the wonders of the arts, and all this was accomplished as if with a flick of the wrist. The most beautiful women, the most perfect virtuosos, the most clever inventors of new sensual pleasures—everything that could arouse and satisfy his passions, lusts, and moods stood at his command. He organized tournaments, plays, and banquets unlike anything ever seen before and often wasted more gold in one day than the richest kings had collected in a year.

Still, the enormous amount of gold that King Mark poured into the world brought considerable inconveniences with it. The first was that the foreigners who had flocked to his court from all parts of the world to offer him their wares, their heads, hands, or feet, raised their prices as soon as they were informed about his inexhaustible supply of gold—first a hundred, then a thousand, and finally ten thousand percent. The products of the craftsmen became so expensive that gold, of which there was a surplus, became cheap, and eventually it could no longer be used as a symbol of the value of things in trade. But before this happened, another consequence of the magic lily, which in the king's hands replaced the stone of the wise, revealed itself, and it was worse than anything else. While his court life was conducted in a bountiful, sumptuous, and wasteful way, which flooded half the world with gold, most of his own subjects were starving because they were denied all opportunities to earn something. They stopped all farming and business, for who wanted to do anything when one could have all life's necessities and luxuries in all the harbors of the kingdom at all times, and in much greater quantity and quality. Furthermore, all the good-looking young country folk needed only to go to the capital to find a thousand opportunities and an entirely different fortune through indolence than they could hope to earn at home through work and thrift.

As soon as he received a report about the neediness of his people, King Mark believed that he possessed an infallible solution and forthwith distributed as much gold as he could in all the cities, towns, and villages of his realm, so that the poorest day laborer suddenly found himself richer than any of the nobles of the kingdom had ever been. Mark believed that he had solved the situation, but he had actually caused more problems, for now everyone stopped working and gave up all their domestic virtues. Everyone just wanted to have a good time, and soon all their riches, which had cost them so little, were consumed in riotous living and debauchery. The king could not make enough gold. And when the gold ultimately lost all its value, the neediness of the people recommenced, but this time it was much more intolerable, for they remembered the golden days of their prosperity. Because the people had lost their sense of morals and their fear of the law, the turn of events became a general signal for robbery, murder, and riot. The king, who saw himself and his people transported from riches to rags, did not know what to do, but he still had not tasted all the fruit of his insane wish. His body finally succumbed to the extreme strains of his carnal pleasures: his stomach stopped digesting; he lost his strength; his senses could no longer be aroused. Illness and excruciating pain took revenge on his abused body and exposed him to all the tortures of a slow annihilation in the best years of his life.

Now King Mark realized that there was indeed a creature more miserable than a half-dead, beaten donkey, and that this most miserable of all creatures was a king who had been given the ability to make gold by some demon and had been foolish enough to accept this pernicious gift. Imagine, then, how joyful he was when, in the throes of his agony, he awoke and realized that everything had been a dream, and he himself was fortunately still the very same donkey he had been before! As he now vividly recalled the images of his dream, he began to make some observations that presumably no member of the human species had ever made before him. And the result of these deliberations was that he became firmly convinced that it was better to remain a donkey forever rather than a king without a mind and a human being without a heart.

As the royal donkey was drawing his practical lessons from his dream, the sun began to rise. He got up to explore the area where he had spent the night and found that he was at the foot of a rocky hill covered by pine trees and boulders. There was a kind of hermitage with some goats climbing around it, looking for something to eat here and there between the cracks or on the flat rocks where some grass had grown. In front of the hermitage was a narrow incline that gently sloped along the rocks, and part of it had been made into a vegetable garden through the hard work of some human hands that knew how to tame even the wildest of regions. These same hands had planted all sorts of fruit trees on another part, where they appeared to thrive under the protection of the neighboring mountains, heightening the romantic appearance of this wilderness. While the good Mark, who was very near but covered by some thin bushes, was regarding all this with a great deal of pleasure, he saw a maiden with a large jug on her head come out of the hut in order to fetch water from a spring that was bubbling from some rocks fifty feet away. She seemed to be about twenty-four years old and had a slender figure. She was a healthy and good-natured creature, as Mark, who was feeling his humanity again, judged from her sprightly way of walking and the song that she hummed to herself. She was clad in a clean peasant dress without a kerchief, her hair tied in a bun, and while she walked along, she bent down to pick a fresh rose blossom and stuck it on her bosom. This afforded Mark the opportunity to make an observation that was not flattering to the bosoms that he was accustomed to seeing at court. Her skirt did not allow him to see much of her feet, but what he did see strongly confirmed the favorable opinion he had begun to form of this exemplary daughter of guileless nature. As he was making these observations, he felt so keenly distressed once more about his present shape that he let his head and ears droop. Furthermore—and this is something no donkey had ever done nor will ever do again—he started playing with the idea of throwing himself from the neighboring cliffs and into a gorge. With a heavy sigh, he moved toward the place where he might carry out his plan, when suddenly his eyes fell upon a lily that shot up out of the ground in splendor. He shied away from it but at the same time was seized by such a great yearning to eat the lily that he could not prevent himself. No sooner had he devoured both flower and stem than his donkey shape miraculously vanished! He found himself transformed into a husky peasant about thirty years of age, full of health and strength. He had everything that most mature men had, but he did not look at all like the person he had been before his first transformation. The strangest thing about it was that he had totally believed himself to be Mark, king of Cornwall, just a few days before and had a clear memory of all the foolish things he had done during that period of his life, and yet he was thinking quite differently, felt his heart beating in an entirely different way, and furthermore believed with all his heart and soul that he had won something immense in this exchange.

He thought with horror about what his fate might have been if he had become King Mark once again. So vivid still was the impression his dream had made on his mind that he thought that if he had to choose, he would prefer to become a donkey again rather than be King Mark of Cornwall.

With these thoughts in mind, he unexpectedly found himself once more in front of the hut where he had seen the young woman emerge with the jug on her head. He felt as if some invisible power had drawn him to the hut. He went inside and found a man old as the hills, with a hoary beard, seated in an armchair. Across from him was a shrunken old woman, sitting at her spinning wheel. When he caught sight of the gray beard, he was overcome by a memory that knocked him backward a step or two. But everything else in the face of the old man suited this venerable beard and inspired reverence and love, so that he quickly collected himself and asked the inhabitants of this solitary hut to excuse him for having entered without their permission.

"An accident caused me to lose my way," he said. "I've been wandering about in this wild region for two days and was so overjoyed upon finding traces of human beings here that it would have been impossible for me to walk by without having greeted the inhabitants of this hut, even if no other reason would have driven me to do this."

The two old people welcomed him in a friendly way, and since the young maiden had brought them breakfast in the meantime, they invited him to sit down and eat with them. Within a short time they became such good friends that Mark, who called himself Sylvester, felt free to offer them his services.

"As you can see," he said, "I'm strong and hearty. You are old, and the young woman here is probably helpful in taking care of everything you may need in the house, for she appears to be nimble and good-natured. Now, I'd like to work, and if you hire me, I'll take over all the labor that demands a man's strength. In addition, I'll treat you with the respect that I'd show to my own parents."

The maiden, who had been moving back and forth during this discussion and had regarded the stranger attentively when she believed that nobody was noticing, blushed when he made his offer and seemed to be delighted with it, even though she pretended that she had not been listening and continued her work.

The old people accepted the young man's offer with pleasure, and Sylvester, who found the necessary garden and farm tools in a shed next to the hut, installed himself in his new job on that very same day by digging up and turning the soil around the dwelling to prepare the ground for planting cabbage and carrots in one part and wheat in another. This work kept him busy for several weeks, and when he was finished with it, he began to hack out a cellar in the rocks, a project to which he devoted all his time when he was not working in the garden or fields. The old couple became very fond of him and treated him as if he were their own son. He himself was happier than ever, and this way of life was so easy and familiar that he seemed to have been born and raised to do it. The food and drink had never tasted so good to him when he had been king, for he had never been hungry or thirsty. He had never slept so well, for he had never worked until he was tired. Nor had he ever lain down to rest with such a contented heart or ever arisen in such a cheerful mood as he did now to his grueling work. He had never experienced the pleasure of being useful. In short, he had never felt such joy in his existence, such peace of mind, and so much care and consideration for the people with whom he was living. Indeed, now he was a real human being. And how could he have been that as a king, especially as a foolish and a wicked king?

Sylvester and the young woman, who called herself Rosine, had many opportunities to see each other every day, and given their situation, it would have been a mighty break in the laws of nature if their mutual feelings, already aroused the very first time they had seen each other, should not have led to a friendship that soon had all the signs of love. Though they did not exchange one word about their feelings, their love revealed itself in so many different ways that the inclination of their hearts and minds was not a secret to either one of them.

They finally expressed their feelings openly one beautiful summer evening. They encountered each other in the forest when he was busy binding together some dry twigs, while she was searching for fresh leaves for her goats. At first they worked within a large circle and kept a diameter's distance between themselves. But the circle gradually became smaller without their noticing it. And so it happened that they finally drew close enough to begin a friendly conversation without it seeming to be their intention. The heat of the day and the efforts that she made had endowed Rosine's ruddy cheeks with a lively red, and something else, I am not sure what, made it appear that her breasts might swell out of her bodice. Moreover, her eyes had such a sparkle to them that Sylvester could not resist stopping in front of her and regarding her with a yearning that was worthy of the best of love proposals. Rosine was a genuine daughter of nature. She did not pretend that she was not aware of his feelings, nor did it occur to her to conceal from him that she was just as moved as he was. She gave him a friendly look, blushed, lowered her eyes, and sighed.

"Dear Rosine!" Sylvester said as he took her hand, but he could not utter one word more because his heart was so full.

"I've noticed for a long time now," Rosine said softly after a rather long pause, "that you . . . are fond of me, Sylvester."

"That I am fond of you, Rosine? There's nothing in the world I wouldn't do for you or suffer to show you that I love you!" Sylvester exclaimed, and he pressed her hand so strongly to his heart that she could feel it pounding.

"It's the same with me too," replied Rosine, "but . . ."

"But what? Why this 'but' when you don't find me repugnant, as you say?"

"I don't know how I should answer you, Sylvester. I love you with all my heart. I'd rather be yours than be considered the most distinguished woman in the world, but . . . I feel that it wouldn't work."

"And why wouldn't it work, when we both love each other?"

"Because . . . because there's something very strange about me, Sylvester," Rosine stuttered.

"What do you mean, Rosine?" Sylvester asked, letting her hand drop.

"You won't believe me if I tell you."

"I'll believe anything you tell me, dear Rosine. Just tell me!"

"Only two days before I met you that first time, I had been . . . a rose-colored goat."

"A rose-colored goat? Well, if it's nothing more than that, then we have nothing to reproach each other about, my dear. You see, at about that very same time, I was a donkey."

"A donkey?" Rosine cried out, just as astonished as he had been. "How strange! But why did you become one, and how did you become a human being again?"

"There was a time when, out of despair, I wanted to take my own life, and just then a marvelously handsome youth appeared, with a lily in his hand. He gave me a stone with which I was to rub myself, and he told me that this would make me happy. So I rubbed myself with the stone and turned into a donkey."

"Astonishing!" said Rosine. "Just as I was overcome by grief and about to tear out my hair, a marvelously beautiful lady with a crown of roses appeared before me. She gave me one of her roses and told me to stick it on my bosom, and I'd become happier than I had ever been in my life. I obeyed her and was instantly changed into a rose-colored goat."

"Wonderful! But how did you turn back into Rosine?"

"I wandered around in the woods and mountains a whole day without knowing where I was going, until I came to the hut of the old people in this wilderness. Not far from here, I noticed a large rosebush on the path that leads to the spring. Suddenly I felt an irresistible urge to eat one of the roses, and no sooner had I swallowed the first petal than I became the young woman that you see before you, but not what I had been before."

"The exact same thing happened to me," Sylvester responded. "I found a lily in the woods, and I was overcome by an irresistible urge to swallow it. All of a sudden I became the young man that you see before you, but not what I had been before. There's something miraculous about how similar our stories are, Rosine. But what were you before you were changed into a goat?"

"The most unhappy person in the world. And it was all caused by a swindler, who had managed to gain my favor through the most clever pretense and had found a way, I don't know how, to creep into my bedroom and make away with all my jewels."

"This is becoming more and more marvelous!" Sylvester exclaimed. "Some other swindler did approximately the same thing to me. He made me believe that he possessed a secret that would make me the richest man in the world. But it was only his way of cheating me out of jewels worth a ton of gold and vanishing with the whole loot. But according to all this, it seems to me that we both were very distinguished people, don't you think?"

"Maybe you won't believe me, but I was really a queen."

"All the better, my dearest Rosine!" Sylvester cried. "Then you can marry me without worrying, for I was nothing less than a king."

"This is exceedingly strange, if you're being serious! But . . . ."

"What, Rosine? Another 'but' when I would have least expected it."

"You can't marry me because my husband is still alive."

"To tell the truth, I fear that this is true in my case as well."

"Didn't you love your wife?"

"She was a very beautiful woman. Of course, by no means was she as beautiful as you. But what do you want? I was a king, and in fact not one of the best. I loved change. My wife was too monotonous for me, too tender, too virtuous, and too jealous. You can't imagine what a burden she was for me with all these qualities."

"So you were not an iota better than the king whose wife I was when I was still called Queen Mabille."

"What, Rosine? Your husband was King Mark of Cornwall?"

"No one else but."

"And the handsome young knight who crept into your bedroom and stole your jewels—wasn't his name Floribell of Nicomedes?"

"Heavens!" Rosine cried out in astonishment. "How can you know all this if you aren't—"

"Your husband himself," Sylvester interrupted her, while he began hugging her at the same time. "That's who I am, dear Rosine or, if you prefer, Mabille. And if you can love me just half as well as I love you as Rosine, then the youth with the lily and the lady with the crown of roses have faithfully kept their word."

"Oh, how much I would like to be nothing but Rosine for you! But, poor Sylvester!" she said, weeping, as she broke away from his embrace, "I fear that I'm not worthy of you. To be sure, it happened against my will. The villain must have used magic, for I was unfortunately overcome by a supernatural sleep! It was just at that moment that I needed all my strength to keep him away from me. And I'm worried that he . . ."

"You don't have to worry about this point at all," Sylvester said, laughing. "Your villain was a woman in disguise, a dancer from Alexandria, who had secretly banded together with the gold-maker Misfragmutosiris in order to steal our jewels. When I was still a donkey, a fortunate coincidence brought me to the cave to which they had fled with their booty, and I heard everything from their own lips."

"If this is true," Rosine said as she flung herself into his arms, "then I'm the happiest creature in the world just as long as you remain Sylvester—"

"And I'm the happiest of men just as long as you never stop being Rosine."

"Are you really so happy?" they heard two familiar voices ask. And when they turned around, they were startled to see standing before them the old man with his hoary beard and the good old woman.

Sylvester wanted to find something to say, but before he could open his mouth, the old man turned into the youth with the lily and the old woman became the lady with the crown of roses.

"You are seeing again those who took it upon themselves to make you happy," the handsome young man said, "at a time when you both considered yourselves the unhappiest creatures in the world, and you are seeing us for the last time. You still have one more chance to become what you were before your transformation, or to remain Sylvester and Rosine. But you must choose now!"

"Let us stay the way we are," they cried out at the same time, as they prostrated themselves before the two divine beings. "May heaven protect us from any other wish!"

"So you see we've kept our word," the lady said, "and you've found the philosophers' stone in this wilderness."

With these words the two spirits disappeared, and Sylvester and Rosine hurried back to their hut arm in arm under the lovely glow of the moon.

Translated by Jack Zipes

The Fairy Tale

JOHANN WOLFGANG GOETHE

eary from the exertions of the day, the old ferryman lay asleep in his little hut on the banks of the great river which was swollen from a heavy rain and had overflowed its banks. In the middle of the night he was awakened by loud voices. He could hear that they belonged to travelers who wanted to be put across.

He went outside and could see two will-o'-the-wisps hovering over his moored boat. They explained that they were in a great hurry to get to the other side. The old man wasted no time, but pushed off and crossed the stream with his customary skill. Meanwhile the two strangers hissed at each other in a strange language that he could not understand. Every now and then, they laughed loudly. All the time they were jumping back and forth from the edge of the boat to the seats.

"You're rocking the boat!" the old man cried. "If you go on jumping around like that, it will tip over. Sit down, little lights."

They burst into loud, rude laughter at the very thought of such a thing; they jeered at the old man and were wilder than ever. He bore their bad behavior with patience, and soon they had reached the other side.

"This is for your trouble," his passengers cried, shaking themselves, whereupon many shining pieces of gold fell into the dank boat.

"For heaven's sake, what are you doing?" cried the old man. "You will bring disaster upon me. If one of the gold pieces had fallen into the water, it would have reared up and swallowed me and my boat—you, too, perhaps—for it cannot abide metal. Take your gold back!"

"We can never take back anything we have shaken off," said the will-o'-the-wisps.

"So you're going to leave me with the nuisance of picking it up, carrying it on land, and burying it," the old man said, stooping and gathering the gold pieces into his cap.

Meanwhile the will-o'-the-wisps leapt out of the boat, and the old man called out to them, "What about my fare?"

"He who takes no money must work for naught," they cried.

"But didn't you know that I get paid only with the fruits of the earth?"

"Fruits of the earth? We despise them and have never partaken of any."

"Still, I can't let you go until you have promised to give me three cabbages, three artichokes, and three onions."

The will-o'-the-wisps would have liked to trick the old man by stealing away, but they felt quite incomprehensibly attached to the ground, and it was the most unpleasant experience they had ever had. They promised to fulfill his demand as soon as they could; he let them go and pushed his boat off. He was already quite far away when they shouted to him, "Old man! Listen, old man! We have forgotten the most important thing of all!" But he was too far away and couldn't hear them. He let the boat drift downriver, alongshore, intending to bury the dangerous gold in a mountainous region that the water could never reach. When he got there, he spilled it into a great crevasse between high rocks, then he rowed back to his hut.

A beautiful green serpent lived in the crevasse, and the sound of coins clinking awoke her. One look at the tiny disks, and she began to swallow them greedily. She even picked up all the pieces that had fallen among the bushes and into the cracks.

As soon as she had swallowed them, she could feel them melting inside her. It was a very pleasant sensation. They spread through her entire body, and to her delight, she could see that she had become transparent and glowing. She had been promised a long time before that she would one day look like this; now she began to wonder if the illumination would last. Thus curiosity and assurance for the future drove her out of the rocks to find out who could have scattered all this beautiful gold. She found no one. But she did find it very pleasant to admire herself, slithering between grass and bushes, and the lovely light she shed on the fresh green. Every leaf was an emerald, every blossom magnificently glorified. She roamed the lonely wilderness in vain, but her hopes rose when she came out into the open and, far off, could see a glow that equaled hers. "So I shall find my peers!" she cried, and turned in that direction, paying no heed to the difficulties she encountered as she crawled through swamp and reeds. For although she preferred living in dry, mountain meadows and deep crevasses and was accustomed to quenching her thirst with fresh spring water, she was ready to undertake anything for the sake of the gold and the beautiful light.

When she at last reached the soggy marsh where the will-o'-the-wisps were gamboling, she was very weary, but she rushed up to them, greeted them, and was pleased to find herself related to two such pleasant gentlemen. The will-o'-the-wisps brushed against her, hopped over her, and laughed. "Well, dear coz," they said, "even if you are only from the horizontal line of our family, it doesn't really matter. Of course you realize that we are related to one another only because we glow, because—look!" and they turned themselves into flames by making themselves as long and pointed as possible. "See how well this narrow shape suits us gentlemen of the vertical lineage. Don't take offense, good friend, but show me another family that can boast the like. Never since the will-o'-the-wisps were created has one of them sat down or reclined."

The serpent began to feel very uncomfortable in the presence of these relatives, because however hard she tried to lift her head, she knew only too well that she would have to put it down on the ground again before she could move away. A little while before, in her dark glade, she had been very pleased with herself, but here, in the presence of these cousins, she seemed to be glowing less and less by the minute; in fact, she began to fear that she might go out altogether!

It was therefore in a state of embarrassment that she hurriedly asked the gentlemen whether they could give her any information as to where the gold had come from that had tumbled into her crevasse a while ago. She thought it might be a rain of gold straight from heaven. The will-o'-the-wisps laughed and shook themselves.

A huge amount of gold coins fell from them, and the serpent slid forward quickly to swallow them. "Enjoy them, enjoy them, coz!" said the fine gentlemen. "We can let you have plenty more!" And they shook themselves several times with great agility. The snake could scarcely swallow fast enough. Her light grew visibly stronger; now she was really glowing beautifully. The will-o'-the-wisps, however, had grown quite thin and small, yet without losing any of their good humor.

"I shall be forever grateful," said the serpent, when she had caught her breath. "Ask of me what you will. I will do anything within my power for you."

"Very fine!" cried the will-o'-the-wisps. "So tell us—where does the Beautiful Lily live? Lead us as quickly as you can to the palace and garden of the Beautiful Lily. We are dying with impatience to dance at her feet."

The serpent sighed. "I cannot do you this service right away," she said. "The Beautiful Lily lives on the other side of the river."

"On the other side of the river! And we had ourselves ferried across on this stormy night! Oh, what a cruel stream it is that separates us! Do you think we could call the old man back?"

"You wouldn't gain anything by it," said the serpent. "For even if you were to meet him on this side, he wouldn't take you across. He can bring anyone to this shore but take no one to the other side."

"Well, then we've really done it! Is there no other way of getting across the water?"

"There are a few, only not right now. I can put the gentlemen across, but not until noon."

"And that's a time when we don't like to travel."

"Well, then you'll have to cross in the evening, on the shadow of the giant."

"And how do we go about that?"

"The giant, who doesn't live far from here, can do nothing with his great body. His hands can't lift a piece of straw, his shoulders can't bear a bundle of fagots, but his shadow can do a great deal—in fact, everything. That is why he is most powerful when the sun rises and sets. All one has to do is sit down on the neck of his shadow at nightfall. Then he walks gently toward the shore, and his shadow brings the traveler across the water. If you want to meet me at noon in that wooded corner over there where the shrubbery grows close to the water, I can put you across and introduce you to the Beautiful Lily, but if you don't like the heat of noon, all you have to do is seek out the giant toward evening in yonder rocky bay. I am sure he will be pleased to help you."

With a little bow, the young gentlemen left, and the serpent was quite glad to get away from them, partly because she wanted to admire her own light, partly to satisfy a curiosity that had been plaguing her strangely for some time.

She had made a most peculiar discovery in the rocky crevasses through which she often crept, for although until now she had had to crawl through these depths without a light, she could tell different objects apart very well by feeling them. She was accustomed to finding herself surrounded by only the irregular products of nature. Sometimes she slithered past the sharp points of huge crystals or she could feel the jags and flaws of pure silver; sometimes she brought a gem out with her to the light. But to her great astonishment, she had recently stumbled upon some objects in a hollowed-out cave that betrayed the fact that the hand of man had formed them. There were smooth walls that she could not scale, sharp, regular edges, beautifully shaped columns, and—what seemed strangest of all—human figures. She had wound herself around them several times and come to the conclusion that they were made of metal or highly polished marble. Now she wanted to experience all these things with her eyes and corroborate what until now she had been able

only to surmise; now she thought she could illuminate this marvelous subterranean cavern with her own light and hoped to see all these strange objects
at once. She hurried off and on the customary path found the fissure in the
rock through which she usually crept into the sacred precincts.

When she arrived at the place she looked around her curiously, and
although her light could not illuminate everything in the rotunda, still she
could see what was near her clearly enough. With amazement and awe, she
looked up into a shining niche that held the statue of a noble king in pure
gold. It seemed to be more than life-size, yet it was shaped like the figure of
a slight rather than a big man. He was wearing a simple cloak and a wreath
of oak leaves on his hair.

The serpent had scarcely taken in this awesome sight when the king
addressed her. "Where have you come from?" he asked.

"Out of the cleft in the rock where the gold lives," said the serpent.

"What is more glorious than gold?" asked the king.

"Light," replied the serpent.

"What is more refreshing than light?" asked the king.

"Conversation," replied the serpent.

As they talked, the serpent caught sight, out of the corner of one eye,
of another magnificent statue in the next niche. A silver king sat in it, a tall
and slender man. He was ornately clad; crown, belt, and scepter were studded
with jewels. The serenity of pride was on his face, and he seemed about to
speak when a vein that ran darkly across the marble wall suddenly turned
light and spread a pleasant glow through the whole temple. In it the serpent
could see a third king, cast mightily in bronze. He sat there leaning on his
club. He, too, wore a wreath of oak leaves and looked more like a rock than
a man. The serpent was about to look at a fourth king, who was farthest
away, when the wall opened and the shining vein disappeared like lightning,
and the serpent's attention was now drawn to a man of medium height
emerging from the aperture. He was dressed like a peasant and carried a small
lamp in his hand. It burned with a quiet flame that was lovely to look into
and it illuminated the whole dome in a wonderful fashion without casting a
single shadow.

"Why have you come?" asked the golden king. "You can see that we
have light."

"And you know that I am not permitted to illuminate darkness."

"Is my kingdom coming to an end?" asked the silver king.

"Late or never," the old man replied.

The bronze king asked in a loud voice, "When shall I arise?"

"Soon," said the old man.

"And with whom shall I ally myself?" asked the king.

"With your older brother," said the old man.

"And what is to become of the youngest?" asked the king.

"He shall sit down," said the old man.

"But I am not tired," the fourth king cried in a hoarse, stammering voice.

While everyone else in the temple had been talking, the serpent had been creeping around admiring everything, and now she took a closer look at the fourth king. He was standing, leaning against a column, and his prominent figure was ponderous rather than beautiful. It was not easy to tell in what metal he had been cast. On closer view it seemed to be a mixture of the three that composed his brothers, but in the casting, the metals had evidently not amalgamated properly; gold and silver veins ran irregularly through bronze, making him a very unpleasant sight.

Meanwhile the gold king said to the old man, "How many mysteries do you know?"

"Three," said the old man.

"Which is the most important?" asked the silver king.

"The manifest one," said the old man.

"Won't you reveal it to us?" asked the bronze king.

"As soon as I know the fourth," said the old man.

"It's no concern of mine," mumbled the composite king.

"I know the fourth," said the serpent, creeping up to the old man and whispering something in his ear, whereupon he cried in a mighty voice, "The time is at hand!"

The temple echoed his words, the metal statues rang with them, the old man vanished toward the west, the snake toward the east, and both hurried as fast as they could through clefts in the rocks.

The walls of every passage traversed by the old man turned to gold behind him, because his lamp had the miraculous power of transforming all stone into gold, all wood into silver, and all dead animals into jewels, and of destroying all metal. But to do all this, it had to shine alone. If another light shone with it, the lamp cast only a lovely glow, and all living things were refreshed by it.

The old man went into his hut, which was built up against the mountain. He found his wife despondent. She was sitting by the fire, weeping, and he could not console her. "How miserable I am!" she cried. "If only I had not let you go out today!"

"What has happened?" the old man asked calmly.

"You had just left," she said, sobbing, "when two blustering travelers came to the door. I was incautious enough to let them in. They seemed to be nice, decent people. They were dressed in bright flames. You could have taken them for will-o'-the-wisps. They barely got into the house when they began to pay me the most shameless compliments and in the end became so impertinent that I am ashamed to even think of it!"

Her husband smiled and said, "I think the gentlemen were only joking, but they really should have been satisfied to remain conventionally polite in consideration of your age."

"My age!" cried his wife. "Why do I have to listen to 'my age' all the time? How old am I, anyway? Conventional politeness! I know what I know. And just have a look around. Look at the walls. Can you see the old stones that we haven't seen for a hundred years? They licked off every bit of gold, and how spryly! And kept assuring me it tasted much better than ordinary gold. And when they had cleaned up the walls, they seemed to be in high spirits—and why not? They had certainly grown taller, broader, and shinier in a very short time. But then they began to be bold again and brushed against me and called me their queen and shook themselves, and a heap of gold coins fell from them and danced all over the place. Look at them shining there under the bench. And what a disaster! Our little pug dog ate some. There he lies by the chimney—dead. The poor thing. I can't get over it. I didn't notice it until they had gone, or I would never have promised to pay their debt to the ferryman."

"What do they owe him?" asked the old man.

"Three cabbages, three artichokes, and three onions," said his wife. "I promised to carry them down to the river as soon as it is light."

"Do them the favor," said the old man, "because they will serve us again someday."

"I don't know about that, but they certainly assured and promised me they would."

In the meantime the fire in the stove had gone out. The old man spread ashes on the coals and removed the glittering pieces of gold. Now that his little lamp shone by itself again, the walls were covered with gold once more, and the little pug dog had been transformed into the most beautiful onyx imaginable. The changeable black and brown of the costly stone made a rare work of art of him.

"Take your basket," said the old man, "and put the onyx in it. Then take three cabbages, three artichokes, and three onions, place them around the onyx and carry all of it down to the river. Let the serpent put you across at noon, and visit the Beautiful Lily. Give her the onyx. She will bring the dog to life by touching him, just as she kills all living things in the same way. The dog will make her a faithful companion. Tell her not to grieve, her deliverance is nigh. She can look upon the greatest misfortune as good fortune, for the time is at hand."

The old woman packed her basket and started out with the dawning day. The rising sun shone brightly on the river glittering in the distance. She walked slowly, because the basket was heavy on her head, yet it was not the onyx that weighed her down. Whatever dead matter she happened to be carrying never burdened her, because then the basket rose and hovered just over her head, but she found carrying fresh vegetables or a small living animal extremely onerous. She had been walking for some time in a dour mood when she suddenly came to a stop, startled. She had almost stepped on the giant's shadow, which stretched out across the ground to where she was walking. Only then did she see the powerful fellow bathing in the river. He left the water, and she didn't know how to get out of his way. As soon as he saw her, he greeted her cheerfully and the hands of his shadow reached for her basket. Nimbly they removed one cabbage, one artichoke, and one onion, and put them into the giant's mouth, after which he wandered on upstream, leaving the woman's path clear.

She wondered whether she should turn back and replace the missing vegetables from her garden, and walked on beset by this doubt. Soon she had reached the bank of the river. There she sat for a long time, waiting for the ferryman, and saw him at last, ferrying a strange traveler across. A young, noble, very handsome man got out of the boat. The woman couldn't take her eyes off him.

"What have you got there?" the old man called out.

"The vegetables that the will-o'-the-wisps owe you," the woman replied, showing him what she had. When the old man found only two of each kind, he was annoyed and assured her that he could not accept them. The woman begged him to take them, explaining that she could not go home again now, and that the basket would be too heavy for her on the way she still had to go. But he stuck to his refusal and explained that it didn't even depend on him. "Whatever I have coming to me," he explained, "must be left together for nine hours, and I can't take any of it until I have given the river a third." After much discussion, the old man finally declared, "We have one more possibility: if you want to give the river a guarantee and acknowledge the fact that you are its debtor, I'll accept the six pieces—but it's dangerous."

"If I keep my word, what can be dangerous about it?"

"Nothing at all," said the old man. "So put your hand in the river and promise to pay your debt in the next twenty-four hours."

The old woman did and was startled when she drew her hand out of the water coal-black. She scolded the old man, pointing out that her hands had always been the most beautiful part of her. In spite of hard work, she had known how to keep the pretty things white and dainty. She looked at her black hand with chagrin and cried out in her despair, "But that isn't all! It's much worse! My hand is shrunk. Now it's smaller than the other!"

"It only looks that way," said the old man. "But if you don't keep your promise, it may come to pass: your hand will slowly dwindle and in the end disappear entirely—but you won't lose the use of it. You will be able to do anything you wish with it, only no one will be able to see it."

"I'd rather be able to do nothing with it, if only no one can see that anything is wrong," said the old woman. "But it doesn't really matter. I shall keep my word and rid myself of my black hand and all this vexation." Quickly she picked up her basket, which now rose above the parting in her hair and hovered freely over her head. Then she hurried after the young man, who was walking slowly along the river's edge, deep in thought. His marvelous figure and strange attire had made a deep impression on her.

His chest was covered with a coat of mail, under which every part of his magnificent body moved freely, and a purple cloak hung from his shoulders. His bare head was covered with brown ringlets, his handsome face was exposed to the rays of the sun and so were his beautifully shaped feet. Anguish seemed to make him impervious to all outer impressions, for he was walking calmly across the hot sand on his bare soles.

The talkative old woman tried to draw him into a conversation but, in curt replies, he gave her little information. In the end, in spite of his beautiful eyes, she grew tired of constantly addressing him in vain. She took leave of him, saying, "I'm afraid you walk too slowly for me, sir. I must not miss the moment to pass across the river on the green serpent and bring my husband's wonderful present to the Beautiful Lily." With these words she hastened on. But the young man came to his senses just as quickly and hurried after her. "You are going to the Beautiful Lily?" he cried. "Then we are going the same way. What is the present you are taking to her?"

"I don't think it is fair, sir," said the woman, "to inquire into my secrets in such a lively fashion after being so taciturn in reply to my questions. But if you would like to strike a bargain with me and tell me your story, then I won't hide mine from you, nor my present." They soon came to an agreement; the woman told him how things stood with her, the story of the dog, and let him have a look at the wonderful gift.

The little pug dog looked so natural lying in the basket, it seemed to be resting. The young man lifted it out and held it in his arms. "Oh, fortunate animal!" he cried. "Her hands will touch you, she will bring you to life—but I who live must flee from her or come to a sad end. But why do I say sad? Is it not far more grievous and frightful to be paralyzed by her presence than it would be to die at her hands? Look at me," he said to the old woman, "how I have to suffer in my youth! This armor that I wore honorably in battle, this purple cloak that I tried to earn by ruling wisely . . . fate let me keep the former unnecessary burden, the latter meaningless adornment. Crown, scepter, and sword are gone, and I am as naked and needy as every other man. For her beautiful eyes have such an unholy effect that she robs all living things of their strength, and those whom her touching hand does not kill are changed into living, wandering shadows."

His lament did not satisfy the old woman's curiosity. She was far more concerned with his material position than with his soul. She didn't find out the name of his father or his kingdom. He stroked the hard little pug dog—who was warmed by the sunlight and the young man's breast as if it were living—and asked a lot of questions about the man with the lamp, and the possible effect of the sacred light on his pitiful condition. He seemed to hope for some benefit from it.

They were still conversing when they could see the majestic span of a bridge in the distance, reaching from one shore to the other and shimmering marvelously in the sun's glowing light. Both were astounded. They had never seen the span so effulgent. "What has happened?" cried the prince. "Wasn't it beautiful enough when it stood before our eyes as if made of jasper and quartz? Shouldn't one fear to cross it now that it seems to consist of emeralds, chrysoprase, and chrysolite?" Neither of them knew of the change that had come over the serpent—for it was the serpent who arched herself every noon across the river in the shape of a bold bridge. The wanderers stepped onto it reverently and crossed it in silence.

As soon as they reached the other side, the bridge began to sway and move. Soon it touched the surface of the water, and the serpent, in her proper form, slithered onto land and followed the wanderers. They had just finished thanking her for having allowed them to pass across the river on her back, when they noticed that besides the three of them, others were present, whom, however, they could not see; but they could hear a hissing at their sides and the serpent answering in a similar fashion. They listened and could finally make out the following: "We intend to look around the park of the Beautiful Lily first, incognito, and we would appreciate it if you would introduce us to this famous beauty at nightfall, as soon as we are presentable. You will find us at the edge of the big lake."

"Very well," replied the serpent, and a hissing sound was lost in the air.

Now the three travelers discussed in what order they should appear before the Beautiful Lily, for she could receive as many visitors as she liked, but they had to come and go singly or suffer considerable pain.

The woman, with the transformed dog in her basket, approached the garden first and looked for her benefactress, who was easy to find because she was singing to the harp. The lovely tones first appeared as rings on the still surface of the lake, then, like zephyrs, they set grass and bush in motion. There she sat, in a green enclosure, in the shade of a magnificent group of the most varied trees, enchanting the eyes, ears, and heart of the woman who approached, overjoyed and vowing that during her absence the Beautiful Lily had only grown more lovely. Already from a distance the good woman called out greeting and praise to the lovely girl. "What a blessing it is to look upon you! What heaven is spread by your presence! How charmingly the harp rests on your lap—your arms surround it so gently, it seems to yearn for your breast—and how lovely it sounds under your slender fingers! Oh, thrice fortunate the man who could take its place!"

With these words, she came closer. The Beautiful Lily raised her eyes, let her hands sink, and said, "Do not distress me with untimely praise. It only makes me feel my misfortune all the more strongly. Look: my poor canary, who used to accompany my singing so prettily, lies dead at my feet. He would perch on my harp and was carefully trained not to touch me. Today, when I awoke refreshed by sleep and raised my voice to sing a tranquil melody to the morn, and my little bird began to sing more harmoniously and brightly than ever before, a hawk swooped down over my head. In its fright, my poor little bird fled to my breast: at once, I could feel how the last twitching of life left it. I gave the bird of prey a look: you can see him down there, slinking helplessly beside the water. But of what use is his punishment to me? My darling is dead, and his grave will help only to augment the sad hedgerows of my garden."

"Cheer up, Beautiful Lily!" cried the woman, drying the tears the unfortunate girl's tale had caused her to shed. "Do not despair. My old man wants you to know that you are to restrain your grief and look upon the greatest misfortune as a harbinger of good luck, for the time is at hand. And truly, strange things are happening. Just look at my hand, how black it is, and it really is much smaller. I must hurry, or it will disappear completely. Oh, why did I promise favors to the will-o'-the-wisps? Why did I have to meet the giant and dip my hand into the river? Could you give me a cabbage, an artichoke, and an onion? I would bring them to the river, and my hand would be so white again, I could almost compare it with yours."

"You might possibly still find cabbages and onions, but artichokes you will seek in vain. None of the plants in my garden blossom or bear fruit, but everything I break off and plant on the grave of a beloved greens and shoots up at once. Alas, I have seen all these dales, bushes, and thickets grow. This umbrella of pines, these obelisks of cypresses, these colossal oaks and beeches—all were little sprigs planted by my hand as a sad memorial in otherwise unfruitful earth."

The old woman had paid little heed to this speech. She had been watching her hand, which seemed to grow blacker and smaller from minute to minute in the presence of the Beautiful Lily. The woman wanted to pick up her basket and hurry off, but then she remembered that she had forgotten the best thing of all. She lifted the transformed dog out of the basket and laid him on the grass, not far from the beautiful girl. "My husband sends you this token," she said. "You know that you can bring this precious stone to life by touching it. The good, bright little animal will surely bring you much joy, and my distress over losing him will be dispelled by the thought that you own him."

The Beautiful Lily looked at the little animal with pleasure and, it seemed, with some astonishment. "Many signs come together to give me new hope," she said. "But alas, isn't it natural to delude ourselves by imagining that good things are on the way when much misfortune is heaped upon us?"

> What solace can good omen bring to me?
>   My sweet bird's death, the black hand of my friend,
> The jeweled dog—however precious he may be,
>   Whom Lamp, to comfort me, did send . . .
>
> Far, far removed from every human pleasure,
>   My dire grief the only thing I know . . .
> Oh, when will temple stand on bank of river?
> Oh, when will bridge on shores of river grow?

This song, which the Beautiful Lily accompanied charmingly on her harp, delighted everyone except the old woman, who listened to it with impatience. She was about to take her departure but was interrupted again, this time by the appearance of the serpent, who had heard the last two lines of the song and at once tried to encourage the Beautiful Lily.

"The prophecy of the bridge has been fulfilled," she cried. "Just ask this good woman here how magnificent the span is. What was formerly jasper and quartz, and let the light gleam through only around the edges, has become transparent gem. Beryl is not so clear, nor can emeralds be said to have such beautiful color."

"My congratulations," said the Lily, "and may it bring you good luck, but you will forgive me if I do not consider the prophecy fulfilled yet. People can pass across your bridge only on foot, but we were promised that horse and carriage and all types of passengers would be able to cross back and forth on it at the same time. And didn't the prophecy speak of huge pillars that would rise up out of the river itself?"

The old woman, who hadn't taken her eyes off her shrinking hand, now interrupted the conversation to say farewell. "Stay one moment longer," said the Beautiful Lily, "and take my poor canary with you. Beg the lamp to turn the little thing into a beautiful topaz. Then I will restore him by touching him, and, with your dear little pug dog, he will be my favorite playmate. But hurry as fast as you can, for when the sun sets, it will begin to decay horribly, and the lovely unity of its body will be forever destroyed."

The old woman laid the dead bird on some delicate leaves in her basket and hurried off.

"Be that as it may," said the serpent, continuing the interrupted conversation, "the temple has been built."

"But it does not stand on the banks of the river," said the Beautiful Lily.

"It still rests in the deeps of the earth," said the serpent, "but I have seen the kings and spoken to them."

"And when will they arise?" asked the Lily.

The serpent replied, "I heard the words echo through the temple: The time is at hand!"

A sweet expression of joy suffused the beautiful girl's features. "So I hear those happy words today for the second time! Oh, when will the day come when I shall hear them spoken thrice?"

She rose, and at once a pretty young girl stepped out of the bushes and took her harp. She was followed by a second girl, who collapsed the carved-ivory outdoor chair on which the Beautiful Lily had been sitting and took away the silver cushion under her arm. A third, carrying a huge parasol embroidered with pearls, appeared next and waited to see if the Beautiful Lily needed her to accompany her on a walk. These three girls were indescribably beautiful; still their beauty served only to heighten the Beautiful Lily's, which everyone had to admit was incomparable.

Meanwhile the Beautiful Lily had been looking down at the wonderful pug dog, and the sight of him seemed to please her. She bent down and touched him—immediately he leaped to his feet, looked about him brightly, ran back and forth, then rushed up to his benefactress and greeted her in the friendliest fashion.

She took the little animal in her arms and pressed him to her. "You are cold," she murmured, "and only half alive, yet you are welcome. I shall love you tenderly, play nicely with you, stroke you with affection, and press you to my heart." Then she let him go, chased him away, called him back, and played on the grass with him so gaily and with such innocence that it was a joy to watch her, and everyone present participated in her pleasure, just as a short while earlier her grief had made every heart feel compassion.

Her enchanting play was interrupted by the arrival of the sad young man. He appeared on the scene as we already know him, but the heat of the day seemed to have exhausted him still further, and in the presence of his beloved, he grew paler with every passing minute. He was carrying the hawk on his hand. The bird sat there, quiet as a dove, its wings drooping.

"It is not friendly of you," the Beautiful Lily cried as he approached, "to bring that hateful animal before me, the monster that killed my little songbird."

"Do not rail against this unfortunate bird," replied the youth. "Rail rather against yourself and your fate, and permit me to associate with the companion of my misery."

Meanwhile the pug dog had never ceased to gambol around his beautiful mistress, and she continued to cater to her little admirer. She clapped her hands to drive him off, then ran after him to bring him back; she tried to catch him when he fled, and chased him off when he came too close. The youth watched their play, taciturn and miserable. But when she took the ugly little thing in her arms—he found the animal repulsive—and pressed it to her heart and kissed its little black nose with her heavenly lips, he lost all patience and cried out in his despair, "Must I see with my own eyes how you may play with such a freak of nature, how it attracts you and enjoys your embrace? I who by a miserable fate must live in a present that is ever separate from you, perhaps forever? I who have lost everything through you—even myself—how much longer am I to come and go, pacing off the sad circle that takes me back and forth across the river? No, a spark of the old heroic courage still flickers in my breast. Let it rise up now in one last flame! If stone may rest against your bosom, then may I be turned to stone! If your touch spells death, then let me die at your hands!"

He made a violent gesture, and the hawk flew from his hand as he ran up to the Beautiful Lily. She stretched out her hands to stop him, thus only touching him sooner. He lost consciousness. Horrified, she could feel his dead weight on her breast. With a scream, she stepped back, and the youth sank expired from her arms to the ground.

A tragedy had taken place. The Beautiful Lily stood motionless, staring fixedly at the dead body. It was as if her heart had stopped beating, and her eyes were void of tears. The little dog tried in vain to wrest some affection from her—for her the whole world had died with her friend. In silent despair she did not look up for help—she knew there was no help.

But the serpent became more alert than ever. Her mind seemed bent on salvation, and her strange behavior actually did prevent the most imminent dread effect of the disaster. With her supple body, she drew a wide circle around the lifeless form, took her tail between her teeth, and remained lying there, perfectly still.

Soon one of the Lily's beautiful handmaidens stepped forward, brought back the ivory collapsible chair, and with a compassionate gesture begged the Beautiful Lily to be seated. Then the second one came with a fiery-colored scarf; with it she adorned rather than covered her mistress's head. The third girl gave her the harp, and she had scarcely pressed the magnificent instrument to her and played a few notes, when the first girl came back with a bright, round mirror and took up a stand opposite the Beautiful Lily, catching her mistress's glance in the glass, and presenting her with the most pleasing picture to be found in all nature. Pain heightened the lovely girl's beauty, the scarf enhanced her charm, and the harp her grace. Although everyone hoped to see her unhappy condition changed, they could not but wish to see her image held fast as it was now.

Looking into the mirror silently, she at first evoked melting tones on the strings, but soon her pain seemed to grow, and the instrument responded powerfully to her grief. Once or twice her lips parted as if she would sing, but her voice failed her. Soon, however, her agony was dissolved in tears, and two of the girls came to her aid and grasped her under each arm. The harp sank on her lap. The third girl was just able to catch it and lay it aside.

"Who will go and get us the man with the lamp before sundown?" the serpent hissed softly but quite clearly.

The girls looked at each other, but the Beautiful Lily's tears only flowed faster. Just then the woman with the basket came back, all out of breath. "I am lost and a cripple!" she cried. "Look how my hand has almost completely disappeared! Neither the ferryman nor the giant will put me across the water, because I am still a debtor to the river. I have offered it one hundred cabbages and one hundred onions—in vain. All it wants is the three artichokes—and there isn't an artichoke to be found in the entire region!"

"Forget your troubles," said the serpent, "and try to help us here. Perhaps you will be helped at the same time. Hurry as fast as you can to find the will-o'-the-wisps. It is still too light to see them, but you may be able to hear them laugh and flutter. If you hurry, the giant can still put you across the river and you can find the man with the lamp and send him to us."

The woman hastened as fast as she could, and the serpent seemed to wait for her return with her husband just as impatiently as the Beautiful Lily. Unfortunately, the rays of the setting sun were already gilding the crowns of the trees in the glade and long shadows were falling on lake and meadow. The serpent became restless, and the Beautiful Lily was again dissolved in tears.

In their dilemma the serpent never ceased looking around her, for she feared that the sun might go down at any moment and that decay would penetrate the magic circle—then nothing would be able to deter its attacking the handsome youth. Suddenly she saw the hawk high up in the sky, its wings purple-red as the last rays of the sun fell on its breast. She shook herself with joy at the good omen, and she was not deceived, for soon they could see the man with the lamp gliding across the lake as if on skates.

The serpent didn't change her position, but the Lily rose and cried out to him, "What good spirit sends you to us just at this moment, when we have sent for you and are in such need of your aid?"

"The spirit of my lamp impels me," said the old man, "and the hawk led me here. The lamp sputters when I am needed, and I look for signs only in the air. Birds and meteors show me in what direction to turn. Be calm, beautiful maiden! I don't know if I can help. One man alone doesn't help, but only he who unites with many at the right time. What we have to do is delay and hope. Keep your circle closed," he went on, turning to the serpent as he sat down beside her on a little hummock and cast the rays of his lamp on the dead body. "Bring the good little canary here too, and lay him down in the circle." The handmaidens took the little body out of the basket, which the old woman had put down, and obeyed the man.

Meanwhile the sun had set, and as the darkness increased, not only the serpent and the man's lamp glowed, each in its own fashion, but the Lily's scarf gave off a gentle light that colored her pale cheeks and her white garment with infinite loveliness, like the roseate hues of dawn. All of them looked at one another in a silent exchange of contemplation, their anxiety and sorrow eased by certain hope.

The appearance of the old woman, accompanied by the two scintillating lights, was therefore most welcome. The will-o'-the-wisps gave every evidence of having lived extravagantly in the meantime, for they were very thin, but this did not seem to detract in the least from their good behavior toward the princess and the other maidens. They spoke about quite ordinary things with assurance and vivacity and seemed to be particularly fascinated by the enchantment the glowing scarf cast upon the Lily and her girls. The latter lowered their eyes modestly, and the praise of their beauty served only to heighten it. Everyone was pleased and calm except the old woman. Despite the assurances of her husband that her hand could not shrink further as long as his lamp was shining on it, she declared several times that if things went on like this, her noble limb would have disappeared completely before midnight.

The man with the lamp had been following the conversation of the will-o'-the-wisps attentively and was delighted that the Lily was distracted and cheered by it. And truly, midnight came, no one knew how. The old man looked up at the stars and spoke. "We are assembled here at a most fortunate hour. If everyone stays at his post and does his duty, a universal happiness will resolve our individual pain, just as a universal disaster can destroy individual joy."

When he had spoken these words, there was a miraculous clamor, for everyone present suddenly spoke for himself and expressed what he felt he should do. Only the three maidens were silent. One had fallen asleep beside the harp, the second beside the parasol, the third beside the stool, and no one could blame them, for the hour was late. The flaming youths, after having bestowed a few pleasantries on the maidens, had turned all their attention to the most beautiful one of all—the Lily.

"Take the mirror," the old man told the hawk. "Light up the sleeping girls with the first rays of morn and awaken them with light reflected from on high."

Now the serpent began to move. She dissolved the circle she had formed and wound her way in great rings to the river. The two will-o'-the-wisps followed her ceremoniously. Anyone might have taken them for very serious little flames. The old woman and her husband picked up the basket—its gentle light had been barely noticeable until now—and came forward, holding it one on each side, and it grew larger and larger and more and more luminous. They lifted the body of the youth into it and laid the canary on his breast. The basket rose and hovered over the head of the old woman as she followed closely behind the will-o'-the-wisps. The Beautiful Lily took the pug dog in her arms and followed the old woman, the man with the lamp brought up the rear of the procession, and the whole region was strangely illumined by the many different lights.

When they came to the river, the little group saw—to their astonishment—a magnificent bridge spanning it. The beneficent serpent had prepared a shimmering path for them. They had already duly admired the translucent gems that formed the bridge in the daylight; now, at night, its brilliance was astounding. At the top, the bright arc stood out sharply against the dark sky, and in the water brilliant rays palpitated toward the center, demonstrating the span's mobile firmness. Slowly the little procession crossed over, and the ferryman, looking out of his hut far away, saw with amazement the glowing circle and the strange lights moving across it.

As soon as they had reached the other side, the span began to sway and undulate down to the water, and presently the serpent was moving across land, the basket set itself down on the earth, and the serpent again described a circle around it. The old man leaned forward and spoke: "What have you decided to do?"

"Sacrifice myself before I am sacrificed," said the serpent. "Promise me not to leave a gem on the ground."

The old man promised, then he said to the Lily, "Touch the serpent with your left hand and your beloved with your right."

The Lily knelt down and touched the serpent and the corpse. At once the youth seemed to come to life. He moved in the basket and sat up. The Lily wanted to embrace him, but the old man held her back. He helped the young man to rise and led him out of the basket and the circle.

The youth was standing, the canary was fluttering on his shoulder; life had been restored to both of them, yet they still lacked spirit. The Lily's handsome friend had his eyes open, but he did not see, or he saw all things without participation, and not until the general astonishment over this had died down did they notice how strangely the serpent had been transformed. Her beautiful, slender body had fallen apart, forming thousands and thousands of gems. The old woman, who had reached clumsily for the basket, had knocked against the serpent. Now nothing was left of her shape—only a beautiful circle of jewels lay on the ground.

The old man at once began putting the precious stones into the basket, and his wife helped him. Then the two carried the basket to a projection on the banks of the river, and he spilled the jewels into it, not without protest on the part of the beautiful girls and his wife, who would have liked to pick out a few for themselves. The stones swam on the water like glittering, blinking stars, and there was no way of telling whether they were lost in the distance or sank. Then the old man spoke to the will-o'-the-wisps deferentially. "Gentlemen, I shall now show you the path and lead the way. But you will be doing us a great service if you open the portals to the inner sanctum for us. This time we must enter through them, and there are none beside you who can open them."

The will-o'-the-wisps bowed respectfully and remained behind, while the old man with the lamp went on ahead into the rock, which opened up before him. The youth followed, still mechanical in his behavior; the Lily kept her distance behind him, silent and uncertain; the old woman, who did not want to be left behind, stretched out her hand so that the light of her husband's lamp would surely shine upon it; and the will-o'-the-wisps brought up the rear. The points of their flames converged, as if they were conversing with each other.

They had not proceeded like this for long, when the procession had to halt in front of a great bronze portal that was sealed with a golden lock. The old man immediately summoned the will-o'-the-wisps, who needed little encouragement and at once consumed lock and bolt with their sharp flames.

The metal resounded loudly as the portal sprang open, and the noble statues of the kings in the temple were illuminated by the lights that now entered. Everyone bowed low before the honorable rulers, especially the will-o'-the-wisps, who couldn't seem to stop their convolutions.

After a slight pause, the golden king asked, "Where do you come from?"

"From the world," replied the old man.

"Where are you going?" asked the silver king.

"Out into the world," said the old man.

"What do you want here with us?" asked the bronze king.

"To accompany you," said the old man.

The composite king was about to speak, but the golden king spoke first to the will-o'-the-wisps, who had come too close: "Get away from me. My gold is not for you," whereupon they turned their attention to the silver king and nuzzled up to him, and his robe glowed with their yellow reflection. "You are welcome," he said, "but I cannot nourish you. Eat your fill outside, then bring me your light." They left him and slunk past the bronze king—who did not seem to notice them—to the composite king.

"Who will rule the world?" the composite king asked, in his stammering voice.

"He who stands on his feet," answered the old man.

"That's me!" cried the composite king.

"It will be revealed," replied the old man, "for the time is at hand!"

The Beautiful Lily threw her arms around the old man's neck and kissed him fervently. "Holy Father," she said, "a thousand thanks, for now I hear the fateful words for a third time." She had scarcely finished speaking when she had to cling to him even more firmly, for the ground began to rock beneath them. The old woman and the youth clung to each other too. Only the will-o'-the-wisps noticed nothing.

That the whole temple was in motion, like a ship gliding gently out of harbor after the anchor has been raised, was very clearly palpable. The deeps of the earth seemed to open up before it as it passed through them. It bumped into nothing, no rock stood in its way.

For a few moments, what seemed to be a fine rain dripped down through an opening in the dome. The old man held the Lily close and said, "We are under the river. Soon we shall have reached our destination." Then it was as if they were standing still, but they were deceived—the temple was rising upward.

Now there was a strange rumbling above their heads. Boards and beams, in shapeless conglomeration, began to crowd with a crash toward the opening in the dome. The Lily and the old woman sprang to one side, but the man with the lamp took fast hold of the youth and both stood firm. The ferryman's little hut—for that was what the temple had scooped up out of the ground and was swallowing as it rose—sank down slowly, covering the youth and the old man.

The women screamed, the temple shivered like a ship that has unexpectedly run aground, the women ran around the hut in the confusion of dawn, but the door was closed, and no one answered their knocking. They knocked harder and were greatly astonished when, after a while, the wood began to ring back metallically. The power of the shut-in lamp had turned the wooden hut to silver from the inside out. It wasn't long before it also began to change its shape. The noble metal abandoned the random form of board, post, and beam, and expanded to take on the shape of a magnificent edifice of chased silver, and a beautiful miniature temple stood in the middle of the larger one, or, you might say, the temple now included an altar that was worthy of it.

And then the youth could be seen walking up a stairway that rose from the inside of the silver edifice. The man with the lamp was casting his light on the young man, and another man seemed to be supporting him; he wore a white garment and held a silver oar in his hand and could be recognized at once as the ferryman, the former inhabitant of the transformed hut.

The Beautiful Lily walked up the steps that led from temple to altar, but she still had to keep her distance from her beloved. The old woman, whose hand had grown ever smaller as long as the lamp had been hidden, cried,

"Am I to remain miserable? With so many miracles, is there none to save my hand?" Her husband pointed to the open gate and said, "Look, the day is dawning. Hasten and bathe in the river."

"What sort of advice is that?" she cried. "I suppose you want me to go black all over and disappear completely. I haven't paid my debt yet."

"Go," the old man said. "Obey me. For all debts have been paid."

The old woman hurried off. Just then the light of the rising sun touched the open circle of the dome; the old man stepped between youth and maiden and cried in a loud voice, "Three things there are that rule the earth—wisdom, show, and power."

With the first designation, the gold king stood up; with the second, the silver one; with the third, the bronze king rose slowly to his feet as the composite king suddenly and clumsily sat down.

In spite of the solemnity of the moment, it was difficult not to laugh, because he wasn't sitting, he wasn't reclining, he wasn't leaning against anything—he simply collapsed shapelessly.

The will-o'-the-wisps, who had been hovering around him, were at his side. Although paled by the morning light, they seemed well fed again and in full flame. With their pointed tongues, they had very cleverly licked out the golden veins of the colossal composite king. The irregular spaces thus formed had remained open for a while, and the figure had retained its form, but when the last little vein was hollowed out, the statue had crumbled, unfortunately just in those places that keep their shape when a man sits down. The joints, on the other hand, which should have bent, remained stiff. You had to either laugh or avert your eyes. This in-between thing, neither shape nor lump, was repulsive to behold.

Now the man with the lamp led the handsome youth, who was still staring straight ahead, away from the altar and up to the bronze king. A huge sword in a bronze scabbard lay at the mighty ruler's feet. The youth put it on. "A sword in your left hand and your right hand free!" cried the powerful king, whereupon the old man and the youth moved on to the silver monarch. He held out his scepter to the young man, who grasped it with his left hand. In a benign voice, the silver king said, "Herd the sheep!" When they came to the golden king, he placed his wreath of oak leaves on the youth's head with a fatherly gesture of blessing and said, "Recognize what is highest!"

As they made the round, the old man watched the youth closely. After he put on the sword, his chest expanded, his arms moved, his steps were firmer; when he took the scepter in his hand, a gentleness seemed to enter into his strength, making him more powerful in a rather indescribable way. But when the wreath was placed on his brow, his features came to life, his eyes glowed with incredible spirit, and the first word he spoke was "Lily!"

"Beloved Lily!" he cried, as he ran up the silver steps to meet her—for she had watched his movements from the top of the altar. "Beloved Lily, what could a man, who is equipped with all things, wish for that is more precious than innocence and the quiet love that your heart feels for me? Oh, my friend," he went on, turning toward the old man, his eyes on the three sacred statues, "magnificent and secure is the kingdom of our fathers, but you forget the fourth power that rules the world before all others, more universally and with greater certainty—the power of love." And with these words, he embraced the beautiful girl. She had cast aside her veil, and her cheeks were delightfully flushed.

Then the old man said, "Love does not rule, it molds, and that is much more."

With all these festivities, this joy and rapture, no one had noticed that the day had dawned. Now quite unexpected objects suddenly attracted the attention of the little group. A large square surrounded by a colonnade formed an imposing courtyard, at the end of which they could see a long, marvelous bridge with many lanes across the river. It had been lavishly constructed for the traveler's convenience, with arcades on either side. Thousands of people had already found their way to it and were walking back and forth on it. The broad highway in the middle was alive with herds and mules, riders and carriages. They moved with the stream of people without getting into one another's way. Everyone seemed to be amazed by the practicality and splendor of the bridge, and the new king and queen were just as enchanted by the motion and liveliness of the people as by their love for each other.

"Think of the serpent and honor her," said the old man with the lamp. "You owe her your life, and your people owe her the bridge through which these neighboring shores are brought to life as countries and united. Yonder gleaming jewels are the remains of the body she sacrificed; they form the basic pillars of your magnificent bridge. It has erected itself upon them and will support itself on them."

They were about to ask for an explanation of this wonderful and mysterious revelation, when four beautiful girls entered the temple through the portal. Harp, parasol, and chair helped to identify three of them as Lily's companions, but the fourth, who was more beautiful than the others, was unknown to them. She accompanied them gaily and in a sisterly fashion through the temple and up the silver steps.

"Will you believe in me more in the future, dear wife?" the man with the lamp said to the beauty. "Good fortune to you and to every creature who bathes in the river on this morn."

The rejuvenated and beautiful old woman—of whose former shape not a trace was left—embraced the man with the lamp with her revived and youthful arms, and he accepted her affection happily. "If I am too old for you now," he said, smiling, "you may choose another husband today. From today on, no marriage is valid that has not been renewed."

"But don't you know," she cried, "that you have grown young too?"

"If you see a stalwart youth in me, then I am glad, and I take your hand again and hope to live on into the next millennium with you."

The queen welcomed her new friend and descended into the altar with her and her three playmates, while the king remained standing between the two men, looking across the bridge and watching the crowd of people on it intently. But his satisfaction was short-lived, for he soon saw something that irritated him. The giant, who apparently had not awakened refreshed from his morning sleep, was staggering across the bridge, creating the wildest disorder. He was drowsy, as usual, and seemed intent on bathing in the cove where he always bathed. But instead of the inlet, he found himself on firm ground and was groping his way along the broad pavement of the bridge. He stumbled in the clumsiest fashion between people and cattle, but although his presence astounded everyone, no one could feel him. However, when the sun shone in his eyes and he lifted his hands to rub them, the shadow of his huge fists rammed with such impact and so clumsily into the crowd that man and animals fell in a heap, were hurt and in danger of being swept into the river.

When the king saw this outrage, he reached for his sword with an involuntary gesture, then seemed to think better of it and looked calmly at his scepter, and at the lamp and oar of his companions. "I can guess your thoughts," said the man with the lamp, "but we are powerless against this powerless creature. Be calm. He does harm for the last time, and fortunately, his shadow is turned away from us."

Meanwhile the giant had drawn closer and let his hands drop in astonishment at what he saw. He did no more damage and entered the open square, his mouth agape. He was approaching the portals of the temple, when he was suddenly transfixed, just as he reached the center of the square. There he stood, a mighty colossus made of red, gleaming stone, and his shadow told the time on a circle that was laid out on the ground—not in numbers but in noble, significant symbols.

The king was delighted to see the monster's shadow put to some good use, and the queen was astounded when she emerged from the altar with her handmaidens, attired magnificently, and saw the strange sight that almost completely obstructed the view from temple to bridge.

In the meantime the populace had crowded behind the giant. When he came to a standstill, they surrounded him and stared in astonishment at his transformation. Then they turned their attention from him to the temple—which they had not seemed aware of until now—and crowded toward the portal. At that moment the hawk soared high above the dome with the mirror and caught the light of the sun in it and poured it down on the group standing on the altar. In the twilit vault of the temple, the king and queen, and their companions, seemed to be illuminated by a heavenly effulgence, and the populace fell on the ground before them. When they had recovered and risen to their feet again, the king had already descended into the altar with his retinue to proceed to the palace through secret passageways, and the people scattered through the temple, anxious to satisfy their curiosity. They stared in awe at the three standing monarchs, but were even more curious to know what could possibly lie hidden under a carpet in the fourth niche, for someone, in well-meaning modesty, had spread a magnificent cover over the collapsed king, which no eye could penetrate and no hand dared remove.

The people couldn't seem to get their fill of looking and admiring. More and more people crowded into the temple, and they would have crushed themselves to death if their attention had not been drawn again to the square outside, where gold coins had suddenly begun to fall out of the air. They clinked on the marble tiles. Those nearest fell upon them. The miracle was repeated—here, there, at random. It is understandable that the will-o'-the-wisps, in parting, wanted to play one more trick and squandered the gold they had extracted from the veins of the collapsed king in this droll fashion. For a while, the people continued to mill around greedily, even after the gold coins had ceased to fall. At last, they dispersed, each going his way, but the bridge teems to this day with wanderers, and the temple is more frequently visited than any other in the world.

Translated by Catherine Hutter

< *Eckbert the Blond* >
LUDWIG TIECK

In a region of the Harz Mountains there lived a knight whom most people simply called Eckbert the Blond. He was approximately forty years old and barely average in size. His pale, hollow face was adorned by close-cropped locks of blond hair. He led a reclusive life and never became involved in the feuds of his neighbors. Moreover, he was seldom seen beyond the outer walls of his small castle, and his wife was just as fond of solitude as he was. Indeed, they seemed to be very much in love with each other, even though they often complained that Heaven had not blessed their marriage with children.

Only seldom did guests come to visit Eckbert, and even when this occurred, almost nothing was changed in the customs of the household. Temperance ruled, and frugality appeared to dictate the ways things were ordered. On social occasions, Eckbert was cheerful and relaxed. But as soon as he was alone, there was a certain reserve about him, a discreet and silent melancholy.

No one visited the castle as frequently as Philip Walter, a man to whom Eckbert had attached himself because he had found that Walter thought much as he did. Walter lived in Fraconia, but he often spent half a year in the vicinity of Eckbert's castle, where he gathered plants and stones and occupied himself by sorting and arranging them. He lived off a small inheritance and had no dependents. Eckbert often accompanied him on his solitary walks, and as the years went by, a profound friendship developed between the two.

There are moments when a man begins to worry because he has kept a secret from his friend that he has carefully managed to conceal. Then an irresistible urge compels his soul to bare itself and reveal his innermost thoughts to the friend so that they may become even closer than before. It is at such times that two people reveal themselves to each other, and sometimes it happens that one of them will recoil and become frightened by being so intimate with the other.

It was already autumn on a cloudy evening when Eckbert was sitting with his friend and his wife, Berta, beside the fireplace. The flames cast a bright glimmer throughout the room and played upon the ceiling. The dark night peered through the windows, and the trees outside shivered because of the wet coldness. Walter complained about the long distance he had to travel that evening, and Eckbert proposed that he stay on and talk for part of the night and then sleep in one of the rooms until morning. Walter agreed, and now the meal and the wine were served. Wood was added to the fire, and the conversation of the friends grew more lively and intimate.

After the evening meal had been cleared and the servants had left, Eckbert took Walter's hand and said, "My friend, you should for once let my wife tell you the story of her youth. It is quite strange."

"Gladly," said Walter, and they returned to the fireplace, where they all sat down.

It had just turned midnight. The moon could be seen fleetingly through the clouds that drifted by.

"I don't want you to think that I am imposing," Berta began. "My husband says you have such a noble mind that it would be unjust to conceal anything from you. I only ask that you don't regard my story as a fairy tale, no matter how strange it may sound."

I was born in a village, where my father was a shepherd. The conditions in our home were not the best, and my parents often did not know where to find their daily bread. But what troubled me even more was that my father and mother quarreled frequently because of their poverty and heaped bitter reproaches on each other. As for me, I was constantly told that I was a naive, dumb child, who did not know how to manage the simplest kind of work. And in fact I was extremely clumsy and helpless. I constantly dropped things. I did not learn how to sew or spin. I was useless in household affairs. The only thing I understood very well was the plight of my parents. I often sat in a corner and imagined how I would help them if I suddenly became rich, how I would smother them with gold and silver and delight in their amaze-ment. Then I saw jinns rise above me, and they revealed underground treasures or gave me small pebbles that turned into jewels. In short, I imagined the most wonderful things, and when I had to get up to help with something, I would be even clumsier than before, because my head was still dizzy from the strange visions.

My father was always furious with me because I was such a burden on them. He often treated me quite cruelly, and I seldom heard a friendly word from his lips. When I was about eight years old, they made serious attempts to teach me something. My father believed that I was stubborn and lazy, because I wanted to spend my days doing nothing. Therefore, he began threatening me in indescribable ways, and when none of this helped, he punished me most cruelly and, even worse, said that he would continue to punish me this way every day, because I was nothing but a useless creature.

I wept bitter tears the whole night through, for I felt myself utterly forsaken. So great was my self-pity that I wanted to die. I dreaded the break of day, for I hadn't the slightest inkling of what I should do. I wished that I could become talented and clever, and could not grasp why it was that I was not as skilled as the other children I knew. I was on the brink of despair.

As dawn approached, I stood up and opened the door of our little hut without knowing what I was doing. I walked into the open field and soon was in a forest that the light of day hardly penetrated. I continued to make my way without looking about me. I did not feel the least bit tired, for I still believed that my father would catch up with me and, in his anger at my flight, deal with me more cruelly than before.

When I emerged from the forest, the sun was quite high in the sky. Then I saw something dark ahead of me, covered by thick fog. Soon I began climbing hills and wound my way through rocky cliffs. By now I guessed that I was probably in the neighboring mountains, and alone as I was, I became afraid, for I had grown up in the flatlands and had never seen a hill before. Just the very word "mountains," when I had heard people talk about them, had had a terrible sound to my young ears. But I did not have the heart to go back, and my fear drove me onward. I would turn around in fright whenever the wind whipped by me through the trees or when I heard the distant sound of a tree falling in the still morning. Finally, I encountered charcoal burners and miners and heard foreign accents, and I almost fainted out of terror.

I passed through many villages and begged because I felt hungry and thirsty. When people asked me questions, I made up answers as best I could. I was wandering like this for about four days, when I came to a small path that led me farther and farther from the highway. The rocks around me now assumed a much different form. Since they were piled on top of one another, it seemed as if the first gust of wind would whirl them about. I did not know whether I should continue. I had been sleeping in the forest during the night, for it was the most pleasant time of the year, or in the remote huts of shepherds.

But here in this wilderness I could not find a human dwelling and did not think I would be fortunate enough to encounter one. The rocks became more and more terrifying. Often I had to pass on the edge of abysses that made me dizzy, and finally even the path that I had been following vanished under my feet. I was inconsolable. I wept and screamed, and my voice echoed back to me from the rocky valleys. Now night fell over me, and I looked for a mossy spot to lie down and rest. I could not sleep. I heard eerie noises during the night. Sometimes I thought they came from wild beasts, sometimes from the wind that moaned through the rocks, sometimes from strange birds. I prayed, and I did not fall asleep until morning approached.

When I felt the light of day shining on my face, I woke. In front of me was a steep rock, which I climbed with the hope of glimpsing some way out of the wilderness and perhaps some houses or people. But when I reached the top, I found nothing but wilderness as far as I could see. Everything was covered by a misty haze. The day was gray and dreary, and there was not a tree, a meadow, or even a bush to be seen. Here and there, a solitary shrub sprouted between the narrow clefts of the rocks. It is impossible to describe the longing I experienced just to see one human being, even if it would mean danger for me. In addition, I was overcome by hunger. So I sat down and decided my time had come. But after a while my desire to live triumphed, and I mustered up the strength to go forward, amid tears and broken sobs, the entire day. In the end I was hardly conscious of what I was doing. I barely wished to continue living and yet was afraid of death.

Toward evening the region seemed to become a bit more hospitable. My thoughts and my hopes revived. The desire to live awoke in all my veins. I thought I heard the rushing sounds of a mill in the distance. I doubled my steps, and how happy, how glad I was as I finally reached the end of the barren rocks. I saw woods and meadows before me again, with soothing mountains in the distance. I felt as if I had just stepped out of hell and entered paradise. My loneliness and my helplessness no longer seemed as frightening.

Instead of a mill, I came upon a waterfall, which, of course, caused my joy to diminish considerably. I went to scoop a drink of water from the brook with my hand, when all at once I thought I heard a slight cough not too far away from me. Never in my life have I been so pleasantly surprised as I was in that moment. I moved in the direction of the sound, and at the edge of the forest I saw an old woman, who seemed to be resting. She was dressed almost entirely in black, with a black hood covering her head and a good portion of her face. She was holding a crutch.

I drew closer to her and offered her my help. She told me to sit down next to her and gave me some bread and wine. As I was eating, she sang a hymnlike song in a screeching voice. When she finished, she told me I might follow her.

I was very happy about this offer, despite the fact that the voice and appearance of the old woman were quite strange. In fact, she moved rather nimbly with her crutch and strained her face in such a way that at first I had to laugh. The wild rocks receded behind us more and more. We crossed over a pleasant meadow and then walked through rather a long forest. When we emerged, the sun was just setting, and I shall never forget the sight and the feeling of that evening. Everything blended into the softest red and gold. The trees stood with their tops in the glow of dusk, and there was a charming light cast on the fields. The woods and the leaves of the trees stood still. The pure sky appeared to be an open paradise, and the rippling of the brooks and, from time to time, the whispering of the trees resounded through the calm stillness as if in melancholic joy. For the first time my young soul had a presentiment of what the world was like. I forgot about myself and my guide. My spirit and my eyes just reveled among the golden clouds.

We now climbed up a hill that was covered with birch trees. From the summit we looked down into a green valley, also filled with birches, and in the middle of the trees was a small hut. Then we heard a lively barking, and soon a small dog came waddling and jumped up to greet the old woman. Then he turned to me and sniffed around me from all sides. Finally, he returned to the old woman with a friendly look.

As we descended the hill, I heard a wonderful song that seemed to be coming from some bird in the hut. It sang like this:

> Oh, solitude,
> Here in the wood—
> What joy for me,
> Eternally!
> Oh, solitude,
> Here in the wood—
> What bliss for me!

These few words were continually repeated. If I were to describe the sound, I would say it was as if forest horns and shawms were being played and fused together far in the distance.

My curiosity was extraordinarily aroused. Without waiting for the old woman's orders, I entered the hut. Dusk had already fallen. Everything was in neat order. Some cups were on a cupboard, strange-looking jars on a table. In a glittering cage that hung by the window there was a bird, and it was indeed the one who had sung the words. The old woman gasped and coughed. She seemed unable to recover herself. Soon she began petting the small dog and then speaking with the bird, who just kept answering her with its song. She acted as though I were not even present. As I observed her, shivers went up my spine, for her face was in perpetual motion. Indeed, her head shook from old age so that it was impossible for me to know what she actually looked like.

When she finally regained her strength, she lit a candle, covered a very small table with a cloth, and brought out supper. Then she began attending to me and told me to sit down on a little cane chair. Thus I sat right across from her, and the candle stood between us. She folded her bony hands and prayed aloud. Since her face became contorted as she prayed, I almost broke out into laughter again, but I took good care to control myself so as not to make her angry.

After supper she prayed again, and then she showed me to a bed in a low and narrow room. I did not stay awake for long, for I was half unconscious. But during the night I woke up several times, and then I heard the old lady coughing and then speaking to the dog and to the bird, which seemed to be dreaming and only replied with a few words from its song. Along with the birches rustling outside the window and the song of a distant nightingale, all this made such a wondrous blend of sounds that it seemed to me as if I really wasn't awake but had only fallen from one dream into another, even stranger one.

In the morning the old woman woke me and put me right to work. I had to spin and learned how to do this soon enough. In addition, I had to take care of the dog and the bird. I quickly became familiar with all my household chores and all the articles in the house. I now felt as if everything had to be just as it was. I no longer thought that there was something strange about the old woman, that the house was mysterious and was located far apart from the homes of other people, and that there was something extraordinary about the bird. To be sure, I was always struck by its beauty, for its feathers glittered in all possible colors. The most beautiful light blue and the most burning red alternated throughout its neck and body, and whenever the bird sang, it puffed itself up so that its feathers looked even more splendid.

Often the old woman went out and did not come back until evening. Then I went to meet her with the dog, and she called me child and daughter. I grew to care about her with all my heart, since our feelings, especially in childhood, will become accustomed to anything. In the evenings she taught me how to read, and I learned how to do this quite easily. Afterward this became a source of boundless enjoyment for me in my solitude, for she had some books that had been written ages ago and contained marvelous stories.

The recollection of the life I then led is strange to me even now. No human creature visited us, but I felt at home in this small family circle, for the dog and the bird made the same impression on me that friends of long standing normally do. Yet I still have not been able to recall the peculiar name of the dog, despite the fact that I called him by it often.

I lived with the old woman this way for four years, and I must have been about twelve when she finally learned to trust me and revealed a secret to me: the bird laid an egg every day, and there was a pearl or a jewel in it. I had noticed for some time that she kept doing something secret in the cage, but I never took the trouble to investigate exactly what it was. Now she placed me in charge of gathering these eggs during her absence and of storing them carefully in strange-looking jars. She would leave me with food and remained away longer, now often for weeks or months. My spinning wheel hummed. The dog barked. The wondrous bird sang. All the while, everything was so quiet around the place that I don't recall any storms or bad weather during the entire time I was there. Not one person wandered there astray; not one wild beast came close to our dwelling. I was content and spent my time simply working from one day to the next. . . . People would perhaps be quite happy if they could spend their days without being disturbed in any way until the end of their lives.

From the little that I read, I began imagining the strangest things about the world and the people in it. Everything was taken from my own experiences and the life around me. When I read about comical characters, I could only picture them like the little dog; the splendid ladies were like the bird in the cage; and all the female figures resembled the old woman. I had also read about love and made up strange stories about myself in my imagination. I conceived the handsomest knight in the world, adorned him in the most perfect way, without actually knowing how he looked after all the trouble I took. But I could feel terribly sorry for myself when he did not return my love. Then I would make long tender speeches in my mind, and sometimes I would even talk aloud, trying to win him. . . . You're smiling! Naturally, those days of our youth are far behind us now.

I now felt better when I was alone, for then I was the sole mistress of the house. The dog loved me very much and did everything I wanted. The bird answered all my questions with its song. My spinning wheel kept turning briskly. Deep down I never felt a wish to change anything. Whenever the old woman returned from her long wanderings, she praised my diligence. She told me that ever since I had joined her household, everything had been kept in better order. She was pleased by my growth and healthy appearance. In short, she treated me just as if I were her own daughter.

"You're a good girl," she once said to me in her rasping voice. "If you continue along these lines, everything will always go well for you, but nothing good ever comes of it when a person leaves the straight path. Even though the punishment may arrive late, it will always come."

I did not pay much attention as she said all this, for I had a lively temperament and was constantly moving about. However, during the night I recalled her words, and I could not understand what she had meant to say, even though I considered carefully every single word. Since I had read about riches, however, it finally occurred to me that her pearls and jewels were probably valuable. Before long this became clear to me. But what could she have meant by the straight path?

I was now fourteen, and it is unfortunate for people that they only develop their understanding by losing the innocence of their souls. To be exact, I now understood that everything was up to me, and all I had to do in the absence of the old woman was to take the bird and the jewels and then set forth into the world about which I had read. It would then perhaps be possible for me to meet the wonderful, handsome knight who was still on my mind.

At the beginning, these thoughts were just like all my other thoughts, but whenever I sat at my spinning wheel, they kept returning against my will, and I lost myself in them so much that I already saw myself adorned in glorious garments, with knights and princes surrounding me. However, after I would wake from these daydreams I would become quite depressed to see myself in the small dwelling. As for the rest of the time, the old woman did not concern herself so much about me just as long as I did my chores.

One day, before my mistress went out again, she told me that this time she would be away longer than usual. Therefore, I was to look after everything very carefully and not let the time hang heavy on my hands. I felt a certain fear when I said farewell to her this time, for it seemed to me that I would never see her again. I followed her with my eyes for a long time and did not know myself why I felt so anxious. It was almost as if everything had already been decided without myself being conscious of what I was going to do.

Never had I looked after the dog and the bird with such diligence as I did now. They were closer to my heart than ever before. The old woman had been gone a few days when I awoke with my mind firmly made up to leave the hut with the bird and to make my way into the so-called world. I felt troubled and oppressed. I wished to remain there, and yet the thought of staying there repelled me. There was a strange battle in my soul, as if two obstinate spirits were quarreling with each other. One moment my peaceful solitude seemed completely beautiful to me; the next, I was enchanted by the picture of a new world with all its many wonders.

I did not know what to do with myself. The dog kept jumping all around me. The sunshine spread itself briskly upon the fields. The green birch trees glistened. I had the feeling I had to do something in haste. So I grabbed the little dog, tied him in the room, and carried away the cage with the bird under my arm. The dog cringed and whined at this unusual treatment. He looked at me with pleading eyes, but I was afraid to take him with me. Then I took one of the jars filled with jewels and stuck it in a pack. The rest I left sitting there.

The bird turned its head in a weird way as I carried it through the door.

The dog tugged at the rope and tried to follow me, but he was forced to remain. I avoided the road that led to the wild rocks and went in the opposite direction. The dog continued to bark and whine, and it touched my heart to hear him. The bird tried to sing a few times, but since it was being carried, the creature must have felt too uncomfortable.

The farther I went, the fainter grew the barking, and finally it stopped altogether. I wept and would have almost turned around, but the desire to see something new drove me onward. By evening I had already made my way over mountains and through some forests, and then I had to spend the night in a village. I was quite shy when I entered the inn. The owner showed me to a room, and I slept rather soundly, but I did dream about the old woman, who threatened me.

My journey was rather monotonous. The farther I went, the more I was overcome by frightful pictures of the old woman and the little dog. I thought that the dog had most likely died from hunger since I was not there to help it. And often as I was going through the woods, I thought I would suddenly encounter the old woman. Amid tears and sobs I made my way, and whenever I rested and placed the cage on the ground, the bird sang its wondrous song, and I recalled quite vividly the little dwelling I had left behind me. As human nature is forgetful, I now believed that the journey I had taken during my childhood had not been as dismal as my present one. Therefore, I wished to be back in that situation again.

I had sold some jewels, and after wandering many days, I arrived in a village. As soon as I entered the place, I had an eerie feeling. I felt terrified and did not know the cause. But soon I discovered the reason: I was in the village where I had been born. How surprised I was! Tears of joy ran down my cheeks, and thousands of unusual memories came back to me! Many things had changed. Some of the houses that had just been built at the time I had left were now decayed. There were marks of fire. Everything was smaller and more confined than I had expected. But I could not wait to see my parents again after so many years. When I found the small house and the familiar threshold, the latch to the door was just as it was before, and it seemed as if I had lifted it only yesterday. My heart was beating like a storm. Hastily I opened the door—only to encounter some very strange faces, which stared at me. I inquired about the shepherd Martin, and they told me that he and his wife had been dead for three years. Quickly I retreated and left the village, weeping aloud.

I had pictured so vividly how I would surprise them with my riches. Indeed, what I had only dreamed about in my childhood had become a reality through the strangest circumstances—and now it was all in vain. They could not rejoice with me, and that which I had hoped for most in my life was lost forever.

After arriving in a pleasant town, I rented a small house with a garden and hired a maid. The world proved not as wonderful as I had envisioned it to be, but I forgot the old woman and my stay in the woods more and more, and for the most part I led a life of contentment. The bird had not sung for quite a long time. Therefore, I was extremely frightened when, one night, it suddenly began to sing again, with words that went like this:

> *Oh, solitude,*
> *There in the wood—*
> *How far away!*
> *Now my dismay*
> *To lose the days*
> *Of solitude,*
> *There in the wood!*

I could not sleep throughout the night. Once again I began to imagine everything, and more than ever I felt that I had not acted the right way. When I got up in the morning, I could not stand the sight of the bird. It looked at me constantly, and its presence frightened me. Nor did it stop singing. In fact, it sang more loudly and shrilly than it had been accustomed to do. The more I looked at it, the more it scared me. Finally, I opened the cage, stuck my hand inside, and grabbed hold of its neck. I squeezed my fingers tightly together, and when it looked at me with pleading eyes, I loosened my grip, but it had already died. I buried it in the garden.

Now I began experiencing attacks of fear on account of my maid. I thought about what I myself had done and felt that she might also rob or even murder me.

For some time now I had known a young knight, whom I liked a great deal. I agreed to marry him . . . and with this, Sir Walter, my story has come to an end.

"You should have seen her then!" Eckbert added hastily. "Her youth, her beauty, and a certain indescribable charm that her solitary upbringing had given her! She seemed like a miracle to me, and I loved her beyond reason. I did not have much wealth, but through her love I came into money. We moved here, and up to now our marriage has not brought us one moment of regret."

"But enough of our talk," Berta joined in again. "It's already late. Let us go to bed."

She stood up and got ready to go to her chamber. Walter wished her good night, kissing her hand, and said, "Thank you, noble lady. I can picture you quite well with your extraordinary bird and how you fed little Strohmian."

Then Walter went to sleep, but Eckbert stayed up and walked restlessly back and forth in the room. "Aren't men fools?" he finally began. "I was the one who urged my wife to tell her story, and now I regret that we took Walter into our confidence! Won't he abuse it? Won't he tell other people about our secret? It would only be human nature if he perhaps became envious of our jewels and therefore formed plans to trick us and try to obtain them."

It occurred to him that Walter had not said good night as cordially as he should have done after they had expressed such trust in him. Once the mind is attuned to suspect things, it will find something to confirm its suspicions in every trifle. Although Eckbert reproached himself for his ignoble feelings of distrust toward his worthy friend, he still could not retract them. His head was filled with such ugly thoughts all night long that he had little sleep.

Berta was ill the next morning and could not come to breakfast. Walter did not seem to be very concerned about her condition. Moreover, he bade his host farewell in a rather indifferent manner. Eckbert could not understand his friend's behavior. He visited his wife, who was in a feverish state. She said that she must have been disturbed by the story she had told the night before.

From that time on, Walter visited his friend's castle very seldom, and even when he came, he would say a few meaningless words and depart right away. Eckbert was extremely hurt by his friend's conduct. He did not let Berta or Walter perceive how he felt, but it was impossible not to observe that he was inwardly upset.

Berta's sickness became increasingly serious. The doctor grew afraid. The color had vanished from her cheeks, and her eyes became more and more inflamed. One morning she sent for her husband to come to her bed, while the maids were ordered to withdraw.

"My dear husband," she began, "I must reveal something to you that has practically made me lose my mind and that has destroyed my health, even though it may seem to be just an insignificant incident. You know that whenever I talked about my childhood, I was never able to remember, no matter how much I tried, the name of the small dog that kept me company. Now on the night Walter was with us, as he said good night, he suddenly said, 'I can picture quite well how you fed little Strohmian.' Was that just coincidence? Did he guess the name? Did he actually know and say it on purpose? And how is this man connected to my destiny? Sometimes I've struggled with myself and have tried to convince myself that I've just imagined this strange incident, but unfortunately, it definitely happened, most definitely. I was overcome by a terrifying shudder that an absolute stranger could be the one to help me recall the name of the dog. What do you say to all this, Eckbert?"

Eckbert looked at his suffering wife with great feelings of sympathy. He kept silent and was wrapped up in his thoughts. Then he said a few words to console her, after which he departed.

For years Walter had been his sole companion, and now this man was the only one in the world whose existence oppressed and tortured him. It seemed to him that he could only be happy if this one creature was removed from his life. Meanwhile he sought to distract himself and took his bow to go out hunting.

It was a rough, stormy winter day. The mountains were covered by deep snow, which also weighed down the branches of the trees. He roamed about. Sweat stood on his brow. He did not come across any animals, and that made his bad mood even worse. All of a sudden he saw something move in the distance. It was Walter, who was gathering moss from the trees. Without knowing what he was doing, Eckbert aimed his bow. Walter looked around and made a threatening gesture just as the arrow was shot, knocking him to the ground.

Eckbert felt relieved and calm. Nevertheless, a certain horror drove him back to his castle. He had far to walk, for he had wandered deep into the woods. When he arrived home, he found that Berta had died. Before her death she had spoken a great deal about Walter and the old woman.

Now Eckbert lived in greater seclusion. He had always been melancholy, for the strange story of his wife had upset him, and he lived in dread of some kind of unfortunate incident. But now he was completely at odds with himself. He kept picturing the murder of his friend, and he constantly reproached himself for what he had done.

To take his mind off all this, he sometimes went to the nearest large town, where he attended parties and mingled in society. He wished to find some friend who would fill the void in his soul, and yet whenever he recalled Walter, he would shudder at the thought of finding a friend, for he was convinced that he could never be happy with anyone. He had lived with Berta in great peace for a long time; Walter's friendship had brought him happiness for many a year; and now they had both been so suddenly swept away that, in many ways, his life seemed to him to be more like a strange fairy tale than the story of an actual man.

A young knight named Hugo became attached to the silent, melancholy Eckbert and seemed truly fond of him. Eckbert felt wonderfully surprised, and since he had not expected it, he responded all the more eagerly to the knight's friendship. They were now frequently together. Hugo did all sorts of favors for Eckbert, and one hardly ever went riding without the other. They came together at all the social gatherings. In short, they seemed inseparable.

Yet, Eckbert was happy for but a brief interval, for he felt all too clearly that Hugo loved him only by mistake. The young knight did not know him, was not acquainted with his past, and once again he felt the urge to inform him about everything, so that he could be assured that Hugo was truly his friend. Then he would be prevented from doing this by certain doubts and the fear that he would be abhorred. Many were the times when he felt so convinced about his worthlessness that he believed that no human being to whom he was not an absolute stranger could possibly bestow his respect on him. Nevertheless, he could not resist the urge. One day, as they were riding alone, Eckbert told the entire story to his friend and asked him whether he could possibly love a murderer. Hugo was touched and tried to console him. Eckbert followed him back to the town with a lighter heart.

But it seemed to be his doom that in the very hour that he trusted someone, he also became suspicious. No sooner had they entered a large salon than he looked at his friend's face in the glitter of the lights and did not like his looks. He thought he noticed a malicious smile. He was struck by the fact that Hugo did not speak very much with him but talked a great deal with the others who were present. There was an old knight at the gathering who had always been hostile toward Eckbert and had often inquired about his wealth and his wife in a peculiar way. Hugo joined this man, and while they were conversing privately with one another, they kept pointing toward Eckbert, so that his suspicions became confirmed. He felt himself betrayed, and a tremendous rage came over him. As he continued to gaze at the two men, he suddenly began seeing Walter's face and all the familiar features that he knew so well. The more he looked, the more he was convinced that it was no one else but Walter who was speaking to the old knight. His horror was indescribable. He rushed frantically out of the room and left the town that night. After getting lost many times, he finally made his way back to his castle.

Once he arrived, he rushed from room to room like a restless spirit. He could not contain his thoughts. He kept imagining the most horrible things, and sleep did not come to his eyes. He kept thinking that he was insane, that he was creating everything through his imagination. Then he would recall Walter's features, and everything became more and more a riddle to him. He decided to take a journey in order to collect himself. He had now given up all thoughts of friendship and the desire for company.

He set out without having a definite route in mind. In fact, he barely looked at the countryside through which he traveled. After riding several days as fast as his horse could go, he suddenly found himself lost in a maze of rocks and could not find a way out. Finally, he met an old peasant, who showed him a path that led by a waterfall. As a sign of his gratitude, Eckbert wanted to give him some coins, but the peasant refused. "It doesn't matter," Eckbert said to himself. "I could imagine again that this man was no one else but Walter." And he looked around once more, and it was no one else but Walter. Eckbert spurred his horse as fast as it could gallop through meadows and forests, until it fell exhausted to the ground. Unconcerned about this, he continued his journey on foot.

His mind began to wander as he climbed a hill. He thought he heard some lively barking nearby, with birch trees rustling at intervals. Then he heard a song in wondrous tones:

> Oh, solitude,
> Here in the wood—
> No harm to me,
> No jealousy.
> What joy for me
> Again to be
> Here in the wood—
> Oh, solitude!

Now it was all over for Eckbert. He lost consciousness and lost his mind. He could not separate himself from the puzzle and discern whether he was now dreaming or whether he had previously dreamed about a wife named Berta. The most marvelous things blended with the most common. The world around him was enchanted, and he was incapable of thinking or remembering.

An old woman with a stooped back crept up the hill, holding onto a crutch. She was coughing and cried out to him, "Are you bringing me my bird? What about my pearls and my dog? You see, the unjust are always punished. Nobody else but me was your friend Walter, your Hugo."

"God in heaven!" Eckbert muttered to himself. "In what kind of horrible solitude have I spent my life!"

"And Berta was your sister."

Eckbert tumbled to the ground.

"Why did she leave me behind my back? Everything would have ended so beautifully. Her time of trial was already over. She was the daughter of a knight who had her raised in a shepherd's house, the daughter of your father."

"Why did this terrible thought always plague me?" Eckbert cried.

"Because you heard your father once talk about this in your childhood.

It was on account of his wife that he could not raise this daughter at home, for Berta was from another woman."

Eckbert was out of his mind and lay on the ground in the grip of death. Stupefied and bewildered, he heard the old woman talking, the dog barking, and the bird repeating its song.

Translated by Jack Zipes

‹ *A Wondrous Oriental Tale* ›
of a Naked Saint
WILHELM HEINRICH WACKENRODER

he Orient is the source of all marvelous things. Stories of childhood and antiquity from this region are replete with strange signs and enigmas that the mind, though it thinks itself smart, has yet to fathom. There are also strange beings that are frequently found in the wilderness of this region. We would call them crazy, but they are honored there as supernatural creatures. Indeed, the Oriental mind regards these naked saints as the wondrous recipients of a higher genius, who have taken on human form after having drifted from the realm of the firmament and consequently do not know how to act like human beings. Everything depends on your point of view, for the human mind is a marvelous tincture whose touch colors everything as it wants.

At one time there was a naked saint who lived in a remote cave near a small river. He had been noticed some years before. A caravan had first discovered him, and from then on, there had been frequent pilgrimages to his lonely dwelling. This remarkable creature never had a moment of peace in his domicile. It always seemed to him that he could hear the wheel of time roaring and turning in his ears. Because of the noise, there was nothing he could do, nothing he could undertake. A great fear, which perpetually worked

on him and strained his nerves, prevented him from seeing or hearing anything
except the terrifying wheel. It turned and turned in a rage and with a mighty
roar of the wind, so that it reached up into the stars and beyond. Like a
waterfall with thousands and thousands of rushing streams that tumbled from
heaven and poured itself eternally, eternally without a moment's pause, without a second's pause, this was the way it sounded in his ears, and all his senses
were geared to this roaring. His fear worked on him and became more and
more wrapped and trapped in the whirlpool of his wild confusion. The monotonous tones grew exceedingly more violent. It became impossible for him
to rest. He was seen day and night, moving arduously and frantically, like a
man trying to turn a gigantic wheel. His wild garbled speeches revealed that
he felt himself drawn by the wheel, that he wanted to bring all the energy
of his body to bear on the blistering wheel, so that time would never be in
danger of standing still. When asked what he was doing, he would bellow
some words as though he were having a fit: "You unfortunates! Don't you
hear the rushing wheel of time?" Then he would turn and continue to work
even more violently than before. His sweat would drip to the ground, and
he would go through contortions, placing his hand on his beating heart as if
to feel whether the great mechanism of the wheel was functioning properly.
He became furious when he saw that the pilgrims who journeyed to visit him
stood there in complete silence and watched him or went here and there
talking with one another. He trembled uncontrollably and showed them the
irresistible turn of the eternal wheel, the monotonous, rhythmical advance
of time. Then he would gnash his teeth so that the pilgrims, too, might
become absorbed and carried away, feeling and noticing nothing. If they came
too close to him in his frenzy, he would cast them away. They had to imitate
his exhausting movements energetically if they wanted to remain safe. He
became even more wild and dangerous when someone happened to do some
physical work in his proximity, or when a person who was not acquainted
with him began collecting weeds or chopping wood near his cave. On these
occasions he used to break out in wild, loud laughter and mock those people
who could still think of such mundane affairs when time was terrifyingly
rolling on. He was like a tiger then. He would leap in one bound from his
cave. If he caught the unfortunate person, he could kill him with one blow.
After that he would jump back quickly into his cave and turn the wheel of
time more violently than before. He would be furious for a long time and
speak in a garbled manner about how people could possibly be concerned
with activities that were in such bad taste. He could not extend his arm for
any kind of object, nor could he grasp something with his hand. It was also
impossible for him to take a step with his feet the way other people did. The
only time he had endeavored to interrupt the dizzy whirlpool, his nerves had
quivered with fear. Only sometimes, when the nights were beautiful and the

moon suddenly unveiled itself before the entrance of his dark cave, he would pause, sink to the ground, toss himself about, and whimper in despair. He would even cry bitterly like a child because the constant roar of the wheel of time did not allow him to rest and do anything on earth—to act, to effect things, to be productive.

On the other hand, he also felt a desperate yearning for unknown beautiful things. He would endeavor to stand up and move his hands and feet gracefully and peacefully. But it was to no avail! He sought something definite, something unknown that he could grasp, something to which he could attach himself. He wanted to save himself from himself, by turning either inward or outward. But it was to no avail! His crying and desperation would reach a climax. He would jump up from the ground with a shriek and continue to turn the powerful rushing wheel. This lasted for many years, day and night, until one wonderful, moonlit summer's evening, when the saint was lying again on the ground in his cave, crying and wringing his hands. The night was captivating. The stars glittered on the dark-blue firmament like golden ornaments on an expanded shield. The moon beamed a soft light from the bright cheeks of its visage, while the green earth bathed itself in the rays. The branches hung from their trunks in the magical glitter like drifting clouds. The homes of the people were transformed into the dark shapes of boulders and dusky supernatural palaces. The people, no longer blinded by sunlight, lived with their eyes fixed on the firmament, and their souls were mirrored beautifully in the heavenly glow of the moonlit night.

Two lovers who wanted to immerse themselves in the wonders of the nocturnal solitude traveled up the river this night on a light skiff in the direction of the saint's cave. The penetrating rays of the moon had illuminated and unraveled the dark depths of their souls for each other. Their most tender feelings flowed together and formed tidal streams that no bank could contain. An ethereal music flowed from the skiff up into the heavenly realm. Sweet horns and countless magical instruments enticed a whirling world of tones to ring forth, and a song arose from the undulating music.

> *Sweet are the showers of premonition*
> *Gliding over field and stream.*
> *Gracious are the moonlit rays*
> *Preparing havens steeped in love.*
> *Oh, how the waves pull and whisper*
> *Mirroring heaven's rippling arch!*
>
> *From the firmament in shining flood*
> *Love streaks to us and sets afire*
> *Glowing stars that lacked the courage*

Till they felt the flame of love.
Water, earth, and sky do smile
While we are fanned by heaven's breath.

Moonlight glows on all the flowers,
All the palms do slumber now.
Holding sway in that sacred forest
Love's sweet tone does now resound.
Every note lulls love's sweet beauty
To the sleeping palms and flowers.

As soon as the naked saint heard the first notes of the music, the rushing wheel of time disappeared. This was the first music that had ever been sounded in this remote place. The unknown yearning was fulfilled. The magic spell was broken. The genius who had drifted from the firmament was freed from his human form. The figure of the saint disappeared. A spirit as beautiful as an angel and woven from a soft vapor soared from the cave, stretched its delicate arms longingly toward heaven and raised itself in a dancing motion from the ground toward the tones of the music. The bright ethereal figure soared higher and higher in the air, carried by the soft crescendo of the horns and the song. The figure danced up and down with heavenly delight, back and forth upon the white clouds that swam in the airy space. With his dancing feet he swung himself higher in the sky, and finally, twisting like a snake, he flew between the stars. All the stars resounded and boomed a bright heavenly tone throughout the atmosphere until the genius lost himself in the infinite firmament.

Traveling caravans watched the nocturnal wonder with astonishment, while the lovers believed that they had glimpsed the genius of love and music.

Translated by Jack Zipes

Hyacinth and Roseblossom

NOVALIS

A long time ago, a very young man lived in the distant Orient. He was not only good but exceedingly thoughtful. He constantly worried about nothing, nothing at all, and would go off by himself without saying a word, sit down, and immerse himself in strange things, while others played and were happy. The woods and caves were his favorite places, and there he spoke constantly with animals and birds, with trees and rocks. Naturally, these words made no sense—they were just plain foolish stuff that might make anyone laugh. Yet he always remained sullen and serious, and even the squirrel, monkey, parrot, and bullfinch could not distract him and set him on the right path, try as they might. The goose told fairy tales, the running brook jingled a ballad, while a huge fat stone cut ridiculous capers. The rose would sneak up in a friendly way from behind and crawl through his curly locks, and the ivy would tenderly stroke his forehead. Nevertheless, his ill humor and seriousness persisted.

His parents were quite disturbed. They didn't know what to do. He was healthy and had a good appetite. They had never abused him. Until a few years before, he had been happy and cheerful like everyone else, the first one at all the games, liked by all the girls. He was as handsome as if he were straight out of a picture book, and when it came to dancing, he was grace itself. Among the girls there was a sweet, extremely pretty child, who looked like a wax figure, hair like golden silk, cherry-red lips, cute as a doll, with dark black eyes. She was so lovely that anyone who had ever met her yearned to be hers. At that time, Roseblossom, for that was her name, was devoted to the handsome Hyacinth, for that was his, and he worshiped her above everything else. The other children did not know this. A violet had been the first to tell. Probably their pet cats had noticed it, since their homes were right next to each other. When Hyacinth spent the night at his window and Roseblossom at hers, the cats, chasing after mice, would see the two, and they would laugh and giggle so loud that Hyacinth and Roseblossom would hear them and become angry. The violet had told the strawberry in strictest confidence. She then told it to her friend the gooseberry, who teased Hyacinth whenever he passed by. Soon the entire garden and the woods knew it, and whenever Hyacinth went out, he heard from all sides: "Roseblossom is my treasure!" Hyacinth would become annoyed, and yet he had to laugh when the lizard came crawling out, sat on a warm rock, and sang, wriggling his tail:

> *Roseblossom, the good little child,*
> *Suddenly's become blind and wild:*
> *Thinks her mother is Hyacinth,*
> *Quickly runs and gives him a kiss;*
> *Then she sees a mistake's been made,*
> *Only thinks it, she's not afraid.*
> *She keeps on going, as if it's all right,*
> *Keeps on kissing through the night.*

Alas! The wonderful times soon came to an end. A man arrived from a foreign country. He had traveled far and wide, had a long beard, deep eyes, horrible eyebrows, and a marvelous coat, with many folds and, woven into it, strange figures. He sat down in front of the house that belonged to Hyacinth's parents. And since Hyacinth was curious, he brought the man bread and wine and sat down next to him. Then the stranger parted his white beard and told stories deep into the night. Hyacinth did not tire of listening, nor did he budge an inch.

As far as one could discover later, the stranger had talked about foreign countries, unknown regions, and astonishing things. He stayed three days and explored the nearby caverns with Hyacinth. Roseblossom wished with all her might that the old sorcerer would go away, for Hyacinth had neglected her and did not bother about anything except for eating a little food. Finally, the sorcerer did depart, but he gave a little book to Hyacinth, which nobody could read. Hyacinth brought him fruit, bread, and wine and accompanied him quite a distance. Then the young man returned in a pensive mood and began to change his life entirely, and he made Roseblossom miserable because he kept ignoring her and keeping to himself.

Then, one day, he came home seemingly reborn. He embraced his parents and cried, "I must go forth and travel to foreign lands. A marvelous old woman in the woods told me how to regain my sanity. She threw the book into the fire and urged me to go and ask your blessing. Perhaps I'll return, perhaps not. Give my regards to Roseblossom. I would have liked to talk with her, but I don't know what's the matter with me. When I want to think about the old times, I immediately have more powerful thoughts. I have no peace of mind. My heart and my love are also gone. I must search for them. I'd like to tell you where I'm going, but I myself don't know. There, where the mother of all things lives, the veiled virgin. I find myself drawn to her. Farewell."

He tore himself away and departed. His parents were inconsolable. Roseblossom remained in her room and wept bitterly. Hyacinth made his way as best he could through valleys and forests, over mountains and streams, toward the mysterious land. Everywhere, he asked about the holy goddess Isis. He asked people and animals, rocks and trees. Many laughed, many kept silent. Nowhere could he obtain the right information. At the beginning he went through rough, wild country. Fog and clouds hindered his way. The storm would not let up. Then he encountered immense deserts of sand, glowing dust, and as he wandered, his spirit changed. Time dragged on for him, and his inner restlessness began to abate. He became milder, and the powerful driving force within him gradually became a soft but strong current, which dissolved itself in his soul.

Many years went by. Now the region became richer and more diverse, the air mild and blue, the way more level. Green bushes drew him onward with graceful shadows, but he did not understand their language. They did not appear to speak, and yet they filled his heart with green colors and a cool, silent spirit. The yearning grew greater and greater, the fruits more fragrant, the leaves wider and riper; the birds and animals became louder and merrier, the sky darker, the air warmer, and his love more fervent. Time went by faster, as though it had reached its goal.

One day he met a crystal spring and a group of flowers. They were in a valley between two huge pillars that stretched into the sky. They greeted him in an amiable and familiar way.

"My dear friends," he said, "where can I find the sacred dwelling place of Isis? It must be around here, and you are probably more familiar with this country than I am."

"We, too, are only passing through," said the flowers. "A family of spirits is taking a journey, and we are preparing the way for them and setting up living quarters. Recently, however, we traveled through a region where we heard her name mentioned. Just continue climbing upward where we've come from, and you'll probably learn more."

The flowers and the spring smiled, then they offered him a refreshing drink and continued on their way. Hyacinth followed their advice, and he asked and asked until he finally came to that long-sought place, which lay hidden within palm trees and other exotic shrubbery. His heart beat in poignant yearning, and the sweetest anxiety ran through him in this dwelling place of the eternal seasons. A heavenly fragrance descended, and he slumbered, since only a dream could lead him to the holiest of places. Indeed, the dream conducted him through infinite chambers full of wondrous things upon a background of loud tones and modulated chords. Everything seemed to him quite familiar and yet filled with a brilliance he had never seen before. Then the last earthly tinge disappeared as though consumed by air, and he stood before the divine virgin. He raised her light, glittering veil, and Roseblossom sunk into his arms. A distant music surrounded the secrets of the lovers' reunion, the outpourings of yearning, and it prevented anything alien from entering this enchanted place. Hyacinth lived for a long time after this with Roseblossom and with his happy parents and companions, and there were numerous grandchildren who thanked the marvelous old woman in the woods, for at that time people had as many children as they wanted.

Translated by Jack Zipes

The Mines of Falun
E.T.A. HOFFMANN

 All the people of Göteborg had gathered at the harbor one cheerful sunny day in July. A rich East Indiaman, which had happily returned from distant lands, lay at anchor in Klippa harbor; the Swedish flags waved gaily in the azure sky while hundreds of boats of all kinds, overflowing with jubilant seamen, drifted back and forth on the crystal waves of the Gö-taelf, and the cannon on the Masthuggetorg thundered forth resounding greetings toward the sea. The gentlemen of the East India Company were strolling back and forth along the harbor, estimating their handsome profits with happy smiles and rejoicing that their daring enterprises flourished increasingly with the years and that Göteborg's trade was blooming marvelously.

The East Indiaman's crew, about a hundred and fifty men strong, were landing in many boats and were preparing to hold their *Hönsning*—that is the name of the festival which is celebrated on such occasions by the crew and which often lasts several days. Musicians in curious, gay-colored costumes led the way with violins, fifes, oboes, and drums, which they played with vigor while singing all kinds of merry songs. The sailors followed them two by two, some with gaily beribboned jackets and caps from which fluttering pennons streamed, while others danced and leapt, and all shouted with such exuberance that the sound echoed far and wide.

The joyful throng paraded across the wharf and through the outskirts of the city to Haga, where there was to be feasting and drinking in a large inn. The finest beer flowed in rivers, and mug after mug was emptied. As is always the case when seamen return from a lengthy voyage, all sorts of pretty girls soon joined them. A dance began: the fun grew wilder and wilder, and the rejoicing louder and madder.

Only one lone seaman, a slim, handsome youth, scarcely twenty years old, had slipped away from the turmoil and was sitting alone on a bench by the door of the tavern.

A couple of sailors stepped up to him, and one of them called out, laughing loudly, "Elis Fröbom! Elis Fröbom! Are you being a wretched fool again and wasting these lovely moments with silly thoughts? Listen, Elis. If you are going to stay away from our *Hönsning,* then keep away from our ship. You will never be a decent, proper sailor. You have courage enough and are brave in times of danger, but you don't know how to drink and would rather keep your money in your pockets than throw it away on landlubbers. Drink, boy, or may the sea devil Näck, that old troll, take you!"

Elis Fröbom jumped up quickly from the bench, looked at the sailors with glowing eyes, took a goblet that was filled to the brim with brandy, and emptied it at one gulp. Then he said, "You see, Joens, that I can drink like one of you, and the captain will decide whether I am a worthy seaman. But now shut your filthy mouths and get out! I hate your wildness. It is none of your business what I am doing out here."

"Well, well," replied Joens. "I know you are a Neriker man, and they're all sad and dreary and don't really enjoy the good life of a seaman. Just wait, Elis, I'll send someone out to you. You must be cut adrift from that confounded bench that you were tied to by the Näck."

Within a short time a very pretty girl came out of the inn and slid down beside the melancholy Elis, who was again sitting on the bench, silent and withdrawn. It was evident from her finery, from the whole manner of the girl, that she unfortunately sacrificed herself to evil pleasures; but the wild life had not yet exerted its destructive power on the unusual, gentle features of her charming face. There was not a trace of suppressed insolence; instead, a quiet, yearning sadness glowed in her dark eyes.

"Elis! Don't you want to share your comrades' joy? Don't you feel a little happy that you have come home again and have escaped the terrible dangers of the treacherous ocean?"

The girl spoke thus in a soft, gentle voice while she put her arm around the youth. Elis Fröbom, as though awakening from a deep dream, looked into the girl's eyes and, taking her hand, pressed it to his breast. One could see that the girl's sweet whisperings had found an echo in his heart.

"Alas," he began finally, as if considering what to say. "Alas—as to any gladness, there is nothing there. At least, I can't share my comrades' revelry. Go back inside, my dear child, and be gay with the others if you can, but leave the dreary, miserable Elis out here alone. He would only spoil all your fun. But wait! I like you very much, and you must think well of me when I am again at sea."

He took two bright ducats from his pocket, pulled a beautiful East Indian scarf from his breast, and gave them both to the girl. Bright tears came to her eyes as she rose, placed the ducats on the bench, and said, "Oh, keep your ducats. They only make me sad; but I will wear the beautiful scarf in remembrance of you. You probably will not find me here at the *Hönsning* next year when you stop in Haga."

The girl slipped away, her hands covering her face, not into the tavern but across the street in the other direction.

Elis Fröbom sank into melancholy reverie again and finally, when the celebration in the tavern became very loud and wild, exclaimed: "If only I lay buried at the very bottom of the sea! There is no one left in this life with whom I can be happy."

Then right behind him a deep, rough voice said, "You must have experienced a very great misfortune, young man, that you should wish for death just when your life should be beginning."

Elis looked around and saw an old miner who was leaning against the wooden wall of the tavern with his arms crossed and observing him with a serious, penetrating glance.

As Elis continued to look at the old man, it seemed to him as if a familiar figure were approaching him offering friendly comfort in the wild loneliness in which he believed himself lost. He pulled himself together and recounted how his father had been a fine helmsman but had been drowned in the same storm from which he himself had been rescued in a remarkable way. His two brothers, both soldiers, had been killed in battle; and he, all by himself, had supported his poor deserted mother from the excellent pay he received after each voyage to the East Indies. He had had to remain a sailor, since he had been destined for that calling since childhood, and it had seemed to him to be a great piece of luck to have been able to enter the service of the East India Company. The profit had turned out to be higher than ever this time, and each sailor had received a good sum of money in addition to his wages; so, with his pockets full of ducats, he had run to the little house where his mother lived happily. But unknown faces had looked out the window at him; and a young woman, who finally opened the door and to whom he explained himself, told him in a rough voice that his mother had died three months before and that he could collect at the town hall the few rags that were left after the burial had been paid for. His mother's death had lacerated his heart; he felt abandoned by the whole world, as alone as if shipwrecked on a desolate reef—helpless, wretched. His whole life on the sea seemed to him like mad, pointless activity. In fact, when he thought that his mother had perhaps been badly cared for by strangers and had thus died without comfort, it seemed to him wicked that he had gone to sea at all and had not stayed at home to care for his poor mother. His comrades had dragged him by force to the *Hönsning,* and he had thought that the gaiety and strong liquor would deaden his sorrow, but instead, it had soon seemed to him as if the arteries in his breast were bursting and that he would bleed to death.

"Well," said the old miner. "Well, you will soon put to sea again, Elis, and your sorrow will be over in a short time. Old people die. That can't be changed, and your mother has departed a poor, laborious life, as you yourself said."

"Alas," replied Elis. "Alas, that no one believes in my sorrow! That I am ridiculed for being foolish and stupid is what alienates me from the world. I don't want to go to sea anymore. The life there is hateful to me. My heart used to leap when the ship sailed forth on the sea, the sails spreading like stately wings, the waves splashing with gay music, the wind whistling through the rattling rigging. Then I rejoiced with my comrades on deck, and then— if I had the watch on a still, dark night—then I thought of the return home and of my good old mother, of how she would rejoice again when Elis had returned! Then I was able to enjoy myself at the *Hönsning;* when I poured my ducats into my mother's lap; when I handed her the beautiful cloths and many strange objects from foreign lands; when joy flashed in her eyes; when she clapped her hands again and again, quite filled with happiness; when she tripped busily back and forth and fetched the best ale that she had saved for Elis. And when I sat with the old lady evenings, I would tell her about the strange people I had met, of their customs, of all the marvelous things that had happened to me on my long voyage. She enjoyed that greatly and would tell me of my father's remarkable voyages far up north and would serve up many frightening sailors' legends that I had already heard a hundred times and which I could never tire of hearing. Alas! Who can bring me these joys again! No, never again to sea. What should I do among comrades who would only mock me, and how could I take pleasure in the kind of work which would now seem only a tiresome effort without purpose?"

"I listen to you," said the old man when Elis grew silent. "I listen to you with pleasure, young man, just as I have had pleasure watching you for a couple of hours without your having seen me. Everything you did, what you said, proves that you have a pious, childlike nature that is turned inward, and heaven could not bestow a better gift on you. But never in all your life have you been suited to be a sailor. How can the wild, inconstant life at sea agree with you, a quiet Neriker inclined to melancholy? That you are a Neriker I can see from the features of your face and from your whole bearing. You would do well to give up that life forever. But you won't remain idle? Follow my advice, Elis Fröbom! Go to Falun, become a miner. You are young, energetic. You will make a fine apprentice, then pickman, then miner. You will keep on moving up. You have some good number of ducats in your pocket which you can invest and which you can add to from earnings, and eventually you can acquire a small house and some land and have your own shares in a mine. Follow my advice, Elis Fröbom: become a miner."

Elis Fröbom was almost frightened at the old man's words.

"What are you advising me?" he cried. "Do you want me to leave the beautiful free earth, the cheerful sunny sky which surrounds me and quickens and refreshes me—I am to go down into the fearful depths of hell and like a mole grub around for ores and metal for a miserable pittance?"

"That," cried the old man angrily, "sounds like the common folk who despise what they can't appreciate. Miserable pittance! As if all the fearful torment on the surface of the earth that results from trading was nobler than the work of the miner, whose skill and unflagging labor unlock nature's most secret treasures. You speak of a miserable pittance, Elis Fröbom! But perhaps there is something of higher value here. When the blind mole grubs in the earth out of blind instinct, it may well be that in the deepest tunnel, by the feeble light of the mine lamp, man's eyes see more clearly; indeed, in becoming stronger and stronger, the eyes may be able to recognize in the marvelous minerals the reflection of that which is hidden above the clouds. You know nothing about mining, Elis Fröbom. Let me tell you about it."

With these words, the old man sat down on the bench beside Elis and began to describe in great detail what went on in a mine and tried to give the ignorant boy a clear and vivid picture of everything. He talked about the mines of Falun, in which, he said, he had worked since childhood. He described the huge opening, with the blackish-brown walls, and he spoke of the immeasurable wealth of the mine with its beautiful stones. His account became more and more vivid, his eyes glowed brighter and brighter. He roamed through the shafts as if through the paths of a magic garden. The minerals came to life, the fossils stirred, the marvelous iron pyrites and almandine flashed in the gleam of the miners' lights; the rock crystals sparkled and shimmered.

Elis listened intently. The old man's strange way of talking about the marvels under the earth as if he were in their midst engaged his whole being. He felt oppressed. It seemed to him as if he had already descended to the depths with the old man and that a powerful magic was holding him fast so that he would never again see the friendly light of day. And then it seemed to him again as if the old man had opened up to him an unknown world in which he belonged and that all the enchantment of this world had long ago been revealed to him in his earliest boyhood as strange, mysterious presentiments.

"I have," the old man finally said, "I have revealed to you, Elis Fröbom, all the splendors of a calling for which nature has actually destined you. Take counsel with yourself, and then do what your mind prompts you to do."

With that the old man jumped quickly up from the bench and strode away without saying goodbye or looking around again. He soon vanished from sight.

Meanwhile it had become quiet in the inn. The power of the strong ale and brandy had triumphed. Many of the sailors had slipped away with their girls; others lay in corners and snored. Elis could not go to his accustomed home, and at his request he was given a little room for the night.

Tired and weary as he was, he had scarcely stretched out on his bed when a dream touched him with her wings. It seemed to him that he was drifting in a beautiful ship in full sail on a crystal-clear sea, a heaven of dark clouds arching above him. But when he looked down into the waves, he realized that what he had thought was the sea was a solid, transparent, sparkling mass in the shimmer of which the whole ship dissolved in a marvelous manner so that he was standing on a crystal floor; and above him he saw a dome of darkly gleaming minerals, which he had at first thought were clouds in the sky. Driven by an unknown power, he strode on; but at that moment everything around him began to stir, and like curling waves, there shot up all around him marvelous flowers and plants of glittering metal, the blossoms and leaves of which curled upward from the depths and became intertwined in a most pleasing manner. The ground was so transparent that Elis could clearly see the roots of the plants; but when he looked down deeper and ever deeper, he saw in the depths innumerable charming female forms, who held each other locked in embrace with white, gleaming arms, and from their hearts there sprouted forth those roots and flowers and plants; when the maidens smiled, sweet harmony echoed through the dome, and the wondrous metal flowers thrust ever higher and became ever more gay. An indescribable feeling of pain and rapture seized the youth. A world of love, of desire, and of passionate longing expanded within him. "Down—down to you!" he cried, and he threw himself down with outspread arms onto the crystal ground. But it dissolved beneath him and he hovered in the shimmering air.

"Well, Elis Fröbom, how do you like it here among these splendors?" a hearty voice called. Elis saw the old miner beside him; but as he stared at him, the miner changed into a gigantic shape, as if cast of glowing metal. Before Elis had time to be afraid, there was a sudden flash of lightning from the depths, and the solemn visage of a majestic woman became visible. Elis felt the rapture in his breast turn increasingly into crushing fear. The old man seized him and cried, "Take care, Elis Fröbom. That is the Queen. You may look up now."

Unconsciously he turned his head and saw that the stars in the night sky were shining through a crack in the dome. A gentle voice called his name in hopeless sorrow. It was his mother's voice. He thought he saw her figure through the cleft. But it was a charming young woman who stretched out her hand toward the dome and called his name.

"Carry me up there," he cried to the old man. "I belong to the upper world and its friendly sky."

"Take care," said the old man somberly, "take care, Fröbom! Be faithful to the Queen to whom you have given yourself."

But as soon as the youth looked down again into the majestic woman's rigid face, he felt his being dissolve into the shining minerals. He screamed in nameless fear and awoke from the strange dream, the rapture and horror of which resounded deep within his heart.

"That was inevitable," said Elis when he had pulled himself together with an effort. "That was inevitable. I had to dream such strange stuff. After all, the old miner told me so much about the splendor of the subterranean world that my whole head was full of it. But never in my whole life have I felt as I do now. Perhaps I am still dreaming—no, no—I am probably ill. I'll go outdoors. A breath of fresh sea air will cure me."

He pulled himself together and ran to Klippa harbor, where the revels of the *Hönsning* were beginning again. But he noticed that he did not feel happy, that he could not hang on firmly to any thoughts, and that presentiments and wishes which he could not name crisscrossed his mind. He thought sorrowfully of his deceased mother; then it seemed to him as if he were longing to meet that girl again who had spoken to him the day before in such a friendly way. And then he feared that if the girl should appear in this or that little street, it would really only be the old miner whom he feared, although he could not say why. And yet he would have liked to have the old man tell him more about the marvels of mining.

Tossed about by all these compelling thoughts, he looked down into the water. Then it seemed to him as if the silver waves were being transformed into a sparkling solid in which lovely, large ships were dissolving, and as if the dark clouds that were rising into the pleasant sky were massing and solidifying into a dome of stone. He was dreaming again; he saw the majestic woman's solemn visage, and that destructive yearning desire seized him anew.

His comrades shook him out of his reverie; he had to go along with them. But now it seemed to him as if an unknown voice were whispering constantly in his ear: "What do you still want here! Away! Away! Your home is in the mines of Falun. There all the splendors that you dreamed of will be revealed to you. Away! Away to Falun!"

For three days Elis Fröbom roamed around the streets of Göteborg, constantly pursued by the strange figments of his dreams, constantly admonished by the unknown voice.

On the fourth day, Elis was standing by the gate through which the road to Gefle led. A large man was just passing through ahead of him. Elis thought he recognized the old miner, and irresistibly driven, he hurried after him but was unable to catch up.

On and on Elis went without stopping.

He knew very well that he was on the road to Falun, and it was this knowledge that calmed him in a special way, for he was certain that the voice of destiny had spoken to him through the old miner, who was now leading him toward his true vocation.

Actually, particularly when he was uncertain of the way, he quite often saw the old man suddenly step out from a ravine or a thick copse or from behind the dark boulders and stride on ahead of him without looking around and then suddenly disappear again.

Finally, after many days of tedious wandering, Elis saw in the distance two large lakes, between which a thick mist was rising. As he climbed higher and higher to the heights on the west, he distinguished a couple of towers and some black roofs in the mist. The old man was standing like a giant in front of him, pointing with outstretched arms toward the mist, and then he vanished again among the rocks.

"That is Falun!" cried Elis. "That is Falun, the goal of my journey!" He was right, for people who were following behind him confirmed that the town of Falun was situated there between Lake Runn and Lake Warpann and that he was just climbing the Guffris Mountain, where the great *Pinge* or main entrance to the mine was situated.

Elis Fröbom walked on in high spirits, but when he stood before the huge jaw of hell, his blood froze in his veins and he became numb at the sight of the fearful, blighted desolation.

As is well known, the great entrance to the mine of Falun is about twelve hundred feet long, six hundred feet wide, and one hundred and eighty feet deep. The blackish-brown sidewalls at first extend down more or less vertically; about halfway down, however, they are less steep because of the tremendous piles of rubble. Here and there in the banks and walls can be seen timbers of old shafts which were constructed of strong trunks laid closely together and joined at the ends in the way blockhouses are usually constructed. Not a tree, not a blade of grass, was living in the barren, crumbled, rocky abyss. The jagged rock masses loomed up in curious shapes, sometimes like gigantic petrified animals, sometimes like human colossi. In the abyss there were stones—slag, or burned-out ores—lying around in a wild jumble, and sulfurous gases rose steadily from the depths as if a hellish brew were boiling, the vapors of which were poisoning all of nature's green delights. One could believe that Dante had descended from here and had seen the Inferno with all its wretched misery and horror.

When Elis Fröbom looked down into the monstrous abyss, he thought

of what the old helmsman on his ship had told him long ago. Once, when
he was lying in bed with a fever, it had suddenly seemed to the helmsman
that the waves of the sea had receded and that the immeasurable abyss had
yawned beneath him so that he could see the frightful monsters of the depths
in horrible embraces, writhing in and out among thousands of strange mussels
and coral plants and curious minerals until, with their jaws open, they turned
rigid as death. Such a vision, the old seaman said, meant imminent death in
the ocean, and he actually fell from the deck into the sea accidentally shortly
thereafter and vanished. Elis was reminded of the helmsman's story, for indeed

the abyss seemed to him like the ocean depths when drained of the sea; the black minerals and the bluish-red metallic slag seemed like revolting monsters that were stretching out their tentacles toward him. It so happened that several miners were just climbing up from the depths, dressed in dark work clothes and with dark burned faces; they looked like ugly creatures who were creeping out of the earth with difficulty and were trying to make their way to the surface.

Elis felt himself trembling with horror, and a giddiness that he had never experienced as a sailor seized him. It seemed to him as if invisible hands were pulling him down into the abyss.

Shutting his eyes, he ran away, and not until he was far from the entrance and was climbing down Mount Guffris again and could look up at the cheerful sunny sky was all his fear of that dreadful sight banished from his mind. He breathed freely once more and cried from the bottom of his soul, "O Lord of my life, what are all the horrors of the ocean compared to the frightfulness that dwells in that barren rocky abyss! Let the storm rage, let the black clouds dip down into the foaming flood: the glorious sun will soon reign again and the violent storm grow silent before its friendly face; but the sun's rays will never penetrate that stygian hell, and not a breath of spring air will ever refresh the heart down there. No, I do not wish to join you, you black earthworms; I could never accustom myself to your dreary life."

Elis thought he would spend the night at Falun and then start his journey back to Göteborg at daybreak.

When he came to the marketplace, which is called Helsintorget, he found a crowd gathered there.

A long parade of miners in full array, their lamps in their hands, musicians in the lead, had just halted in front of a stately house. A tall, slender, middle-aged man stepped out and looked around with a gentle smile. One could see that he was a true Dalkarl from his easy manners, his open expression, and the dark-blue, sparkling eyes. The miners formed a circle around him; he shook everyone's hand cordially and spoke a few friendly words with each.

Elis Fröbom found out on inquiry that the man was Pehrson Dahlsjö, the chief official of the district and owner of a fine *Bergfrälse*. Estates in Sweden that are rented for their copper and silver works are called *Bergfrälse*. The owners of such estates have shares in the mines and are responsible for their operation.

Elis was also informed that the court session had just ended on that day and that the miners would then go to the houses of the mine owner, the foundry master, and the senior foreman and would be entertained hospitably.

When Elis observed the handsome, dignified people with their friendly, open faces, he was no longer able to recall those earthworms in the great entrance. The gaiety which inflamed the whole group when Pehrson Dahlsjö came out was quite different from the frenzied revelries of the sailors at the *Hönsning*.

The miners' kind of pleasure appealed directly to the quiet, serious Elis. He felt indescribably at ease, and he could scarcely keep back his tears when several of the younger lads began an old song that sounded the praises of mining in a simple melody that went straight to the heart.

When the song was over, Pehrson Dahlsjö opened the door of his house, and all the miners went inside. Elis followed automatically and stopped at the threshold so that he could see all around the spacious hall where the miners were sitting down on benches. A hearty meal was set out on a table.

Then the rear door opposite Elis opened, and a charming, beautifully attired young girl entered. Tall and slender, her dark hair wound in braids around her head, her neat little bodice fastened with rich brooches, she walked with all the grace of glowing maidenhood. All the miners rose, and a happy, subdued murmur ran through the ranks: "Ulla Dahlsjö—Ulla Dahlsjö! God has indeed blessed our valiant chief with this lovely, innocent child of heaven!" Even the eyes of the oldest miners sparkled when Ulla shook their hands in friendly greeting. Then she brought in beautiful silver pitchers, poured out the excellent ale that is brewed at Falun, and served it to the happy company, her charming face aglow with the radiant innocence of heaven.

As soon as Elis Fröbom saw the girl, it seemed to him that a lightning bolt had struck his heart and ignited all the divine joy and all the pain and rapture of love that were enclosed in it. It was Ulla Dahlsjö who had offered him her hand to save him in that fateful dream. He now believed that he had guessed the dream's deeper meaning, and forgetting the old miner, he blessed the fate that led him to Falun.

But then, standing on the threshold, he felt like a neglected stranger— wretched, miserable, abandoned. He wished he had died before he had even seen Ulla Dahlsjö, since he must now die of love and yearning. He was not able to turn his eyes away from the charming girl, and when she passed quite close to him, he called out her name in a gentle trembling voice. Ulla looked around and saw poor Elis, who was standing there with a scarlet face and downcast eyes, rigid, incapable of words.

Ulla walked up to him and said with a sweet smile, "Oh, you are a stranger here, dear friend. I can see that by your seaman's clothing. Well, why are you standing there on the threshold? Do come in and be merry with us." She took his hand and pulled him into the hall and handed him a full mug of ale. "Drink!" she said. "Drink, my dear friend, to a warm welcome."

It seemed to Elis as if he were lying in a blissful dream of paradise from which he would shortly awaken and feel indescribably wretched. Mechanically he emptied the mug. At that moment Pehrson Dahlsjö stepped up to him, shook his hand in friendly greeting, and asked him where he came from and what had brought him to Falun.

Elis felt the warming strength of the noble drink course through his veins. Looking the worthy Pehrson in the eye, he became cheerful and bold. He related how he, the son of a sailor, had been at sea since a child; how he had just returned from East India and had found his mother, whom he had cherished and supported, no longer alive; how he now felt completely abandoned in this world; how the wild life on the sea was now quite repugnant to him; how his deepest inclinations were for mining; and how he wanted to try to be taken on as an apprentice miner in Falun. This last remark, which was just the opposite of everything he had decided to do just a few minutes before, came out quite automatically; it seemed to him that he couldn't have told the manager anything different, as if he had expressed his innermost desire, of which he had till now been unconscious.

With a serious expression, Pehrson Dahlsjö looked at the youth as if he wished to see into his heart, and then said, "I do not assume, Elis Fröbom, that mere frivolity has driven you from your previous occupation and that you have not considered carefully all the tedium and difficulties of mining before you made the decision to come here. There is an ancient belief among us that the mighty elements, among which the miner boldly reigns, will annihilate him unless he exerts his whole self in maintaining his mastery over them and gives thought to nothing else, for that would diminish the power that he should expend exclusively on his work in the earth and the fire. But if you have considered your true calling adequately and found it has stood the test, then you have come at a good time. I lack workers in my mine. If you wish, you can stay with me right now and, tomorrow morning, go with the foreman, who will show you your work."

Elis's heart was lifted at Pehrson Dahlsjö's words. He no longer thought about the horrors of that frightful hellish abyss into which he had looked. He was filled with rapture and delight that he would now see the lovely Ulla every day and would live under the same roof with her. He allowed himself the sweetest hopes.

Pehrson Dahlsjö informed the miners that a young apprentice had just reported in, and he introduced Elis Fröbom to them.

All looked approvingly at the sturdy youth and thought that he was a born miner with his slender, powerful build and that he was surely not lacking in industry or application.

One of the miners, already well along in years, approached him and shook his hand heartily, saying that he was the chief foreman in Pehrson Dahlsjö's mine and that he would make it a point to instruct him thoroughly in everything that he needed to know. Elis had to sit down beside him, and the old man began to speak at length—over a mug of ale—about the first duties of the apprentices.

The old miner from Göteborg came to Elis's mind again, and in some special way he was able to repeat almost everything that had been said to him.

"Why, Elis Fröbom," cried the chief foreman with astonishment. "Where did you get all that information? You really can't miss. In no time at all you will be the best apprentice in the mine."

The lovely Ulla, who was wandering among the guests and serving them, often nodded at Elis in a friendly way and urged him to enjoy himself. She said to him that he was no longer a stranger but belonged in the house and not to the deceitful sea. Falun with its rich mountains was now his homeland. A heaven full of rapture and bliss opened up to the youth at her words. It was noticed indeed that Ulla liked to linger with him, and even Pehrson Dahlsjö, in his quiet, serious way, observed him with approval.

But Elis's heart beat violently when he stood again by the steaming abyss of hell and, clothed in the miner's uniform, the heavy nailed boots on his feet, went down with the foreman into the deep shaft. At times hot vapors which encircled his breast threatened to choke him; at times the mine lights flared up from the cuttingly cold drafts which streamed through the abysses. They descended deeper and deeper, finally climbing down iron ladders scarcely a foot wide, and Elis Fröbom noticed that all the skill in climbing that he had acquired as a sailor did not help him here.

They finally reached the deepest bore, and the foreman assigned Elis the work that he was to do there.

Elis thought of the fair Ulla. He saw her form hovering like a shining angel above him, and he forgot all the horrors of the abyss, all the difficulties of the toilsome work. It was now clear in his mind that only if he dedicated himself to mining at Pehrson Dahlsjö's with all the strength of his mind and all the exertions that his body could endure would his sweetest hopes perhaps one day be fulfilled, and thus it was that in an incredibly short time he rivaled in work the most skilled miner.

With every day the worthy Pehrson Dahlsjö grew more and more fond of the industrious, pious youth and frequently said quite frankly to him that he had acquired in the young man not so much a worthy apprentice as a beloved son. Ulla's liking for him also became more open. Frequently, when Elis went to work and some danger was involved, she begged him, pleaded with him, bright tears in her eyes, to guard himself against accidents. And when he returned, she rushed out happily to meet him and always had the best ale or some tasty snack ready to refresh him.

Elis's heart beat with joy when Pehrson Dahlsjö once said that with his diligence and thrift, since he had already a good bit of money that he had brought with him, he would surely get a small house and some land or even a *Bergfrälse,* and then there would not be a property owner in Falun who would reject him when he came wooing a daughter. Elis should have said at once how indescribably much he loved Ulla and how all his hopes rested on possessing her, but a shyness he could not overcome kept him silent, although probably it was still the fearful uncertainty about whether Ulla, as he often suspected, truly loved him.

Once, Elis Fröbom was working in the deepest bore, wrapped in such sulfurous fumes that his miner's light flickered dimly and he was scarcely able to distinguish the lodes in the rock, when he heard a knocking that seemed to be coming from a still deeper shaft and sounded as if someone were working with a hammer. Since that kind of work was impossible in the bore and since Elis knew that no one besides himself was down there, because the foreman had put his workers in the winding shaft, the knocking and hammering seemed quite uncanny. He put down his hammer and spike and listened to the hollow sounds, which seemed to be coming nearer and nearer. All at once he saw a black shadow beside him, and as a cutting blast of air scattered the sulfur fumes, he recognized the old miner of Göteborg, who was standing at his side. "Good luck getting back up!" cried the old man. "Good luck to you, Elis Fröbom, down here among the rocks. How do you like the life, comrade?"

Elis wanted to ask by what marvelous means the old man had come to the shaft, but the latter struck the stone such a powerful blow with his hammer that sparks flew and a noise like thunder echoed through the shaft; and he called out in a terrible voice, "That is a marvelous lode, but you, despicable, miserable rogue, see nothing but a seam which is scarcely worth a straw. Down here you are a blind mole whom the *Metallfürst* will never favor, and up above you are also unable to accomplish anything and pursue the *Garkönig* in vain. Oh, yes, you want to win Pehrson Dahlsjö's daughter Ulla for your wife, and therefore you are working here without love or interest. Beware, you cheat, that the *Metallfürst,* whom you mock, doesn't seize you and hurl you into the abyss so that all your bones are smashed on the rocks. And never will Ulla be your wife; that I say to you."

Anger welled up in Elis at the old man's insolent words. "What are you doing," he cried, "what are you doing in the shaft of my master, Pehrson Dahlsjö, where I am working with all my strength and as is proper to my calling? Get out as you have come, or we will see which one of us can bash in the other's skull."

Elis stood defiantly in front of the old man and raised the iron hammer with which he had been working. The old man laughed mockingly, and Elis saw with horror how he scrambled up the narrow rungs of the ladder as nimbly as a squirrel and vanished in the black cleft.

Elis felt paralyzed in all his limbs; the work would not progress, so he climbed up and out. When the old chief foreman, who was just climbing out of the winding shaft, saw him, he cried, "For God's sake, what happened to you, Elis? You look pale as death. It was the sulfur fumes, which you are not yet used to, that did it, wasn't it? Well, have a drink, boy. That will do you good."

Elis took a good swig of brandy from the bottle the chief foreman offered him, and then, feeling revived, told him everything that had happened in the shaft, as well as the mysterious way he had made the acquaintance of the uncanny miner in Göteborg.

The chief foreman listened quietly but then shook his head thoughtfully and said, "Elis Fröbom, that was old Torbern whom you met, and now I realize that what we relate about him here is more than a legend. More than a hundred years ago, there was a miner here in Falun by the name of Torbern. He is said to have been one of the first who really made mining flourish in Falun, and in his time the profits were much greater than now. Nobody else knew as much about mining as Torbern, who, with his thorough knowledge, was in charge of all aspects of mining in Falun. The richest lodes were revealed to him as if he possessed a special, higher power. In addition, he was a gloomy, melancholy man, without wife, child, or his own home; and he almost never came into the daylight, but grubbed around unceasingly in the shafts; and so it was inevitable that a story arose that he was in league with secret powers who reign in the bowels of the earth and fuse metals. No one paid any attention to Torbern's warnings—he constantly prophesied that a disaster would occur if it was not true love for marvelous rocks and metals that impelled the miner to work. Out of greed, the mines were constantly enlarged until finally, on Saint John's Day of the year one thousand six hundred and eighty-seven, a frightful cave-in occurred, which created our huge entrance and destroyed the whole structure to such an extent that many of the shafts could only be repaired with tremendous effort and great skill. Nothing more was seen or heard of Torbern, and it seemed certain that he had been killed by the cave-in, for he had been working in the deep bore. Soon after, when the work was going along better and better, the pickmen claimed that they had seen old Torbern, who had given them all kinds of good advice and had shown them the best lodes. Others had seen the old man walking around the main shaft, now complaining sadly, now raging angrily. Other youths came here as you did and maintained that an old miner had urged them into mining and had directed them here. That happened whenever there was a shortage of workers, and it may well be that Torbern looked after the mine in this way. If it really was old Torbern with whom you quarreled in the shaft, and if he spoke to you about a wonderful lode, then it is certain that there is a rich vein of iron in the rock, for as you know, iron-bearing veins are called trap runs, and a trum is a vein of the lode which divides into a number of parts and probably runs out completely."

When Elis Fröbom, torn in his mind by various thoughts, came into Pehrson Dahlsjö's house, Ulla did not come to meet him in her friendly way as formerly. With her eyes cast down and tear-stained, as Elis thought he observed, Ulla was sitting in the house beside a fine young man, who held her hand tightly in his and was trying to make all sorts of humorous remarks, which Ulla was not particularly listening to. Pehrson Dahlsjö took Elis, who was staring at the couple and was filled with apprehension, into another room and said, "Well, Elis Fröbom, you will soon be able to prove your love and loyalty to me, for even if I have always considered you as a son, now you will be a son in all ways. The man whom you see at my house is the rich merchant Eric Olawsen from Göteborg. I am giving him my daughter, whom he has wooed. He is going to take her back to Göteborg, and then you will stay here alone with me, Elis, the only support of my old age. Well, Elis, you are silent? You have turned pale. I hope that my decision does not displease you and that now that my daughter must leave me, you will not also want to leave. But I hear Herr Olawsen calling my name—I must go back."

With that Pehrson went back into the other room.

Elis felt his soul slashed by a thousand glowing knives. He had no words— no tears. He dashed out of the house in wild despair—away—away—to the huge entrance. If the enormous abyss presented a frightful sight in the daylight, now that night had arrived and the moon's disk was just beginning to gleam, the desolate rocks had a truly terrible appearance, as if an unnumbered crowd of fearful monsters, the frightful offspring of hell, were writhing and twisting together on the smoking ground, their eyes flashing fire, and stretching out their monstrous claws toward a wretched humanity.

"Torbern! Torbern!" Elis cried in such a fearful voice that the desolate abyss resounded. "Torbern, I am here! You were right. I was a vile fellow to yield to the foolish hope of life on the surface of the earth. My treasure, my life, my all lies below. Torbern! Climb up to me; show me the richest trap runs. I will grub and bore and work there and never more see the light of day. Torbern! Torbern! Climb up to me!"

Elis took his flint and steel from his pocket and lighted his miner's lamp and went down into the shaft which he had yesterday been in without having seen the old man. How strange he felt when he clearly saw the seam in the deepest bore and could recognize the direction of the strata and the edge of the gouge.

But as he directed his eyes more and more sharply at the vein in the rock, it seemed as if a blinding light were passing through the whole shaft, and its walls became as transparent as the purest crystal. That fateful dream which he had dreamed in Göteborg returned. He looked into the fields of paradise filled with marvelous metal flowers and plants on which gems flashing fire were hanging like fruit, blossoms, and flowers. He saw the maidens; he saw the lofty face of the majestic Queen. She seized him, pulled him down,

pressed him to her breast, and there flashed through his soul a glowing ray—
he was conscious of only a feeling of drifting in a blue, transparent, sparkling
mist.

"Elis Fröbom! Elis Fröbom!" cried a strong voice from above, and the
light of torches was reflected in the shaft. It was Pehrson Dahlsjö himself,
who was coming down with the foreman to look for the youth, whom they
had seen running toward the main shaft in complete madness.

They found him standing rigid, his face pressed against the cold rock.

"What," cried Pehrson to him, "what are you doing down here at night,
you foolish young man! Pull yourself together and climb up with us. Who
knows what good news you will hear up above?"

Elis climbed up in complete silence, and in complete silence he followed
Pehrson Dahlsjö, who did not cease from scolding him firmly for putting
himself in such danger.

It was full daylight when they came to the house. Ulla rushed toward
Elis's embrace with a loud cry and called him the most endearing names. But
Pehrson Dahlsjö spoke to Elis. "You fool. Didn't I long know that you loved
Ulla and that you work in the mine with such industry and zeal only for Ulla's
sake? Didn't I long notice that Ulla also loved you from the very bottom of
her heart? Could I wish for a better son-in-law than a fine, industrious, decent
miner like you, my dear Elis? But it angered me, it offended me that you
remained silent."

"Didn't we," Ulla interrupted her father, "didn't we ourselves know that
we loved each other inexpressibly?"

"That," continued Pehrson Dahlsjö, "that may well be so. It suffices to
say that I was angered that Elis did not speak openly and honorably to me of
his love, and therefore, because I also wanted to test your heart, I served up
the story with Herr Eric Olawsen, which nearly caused your destruction. You
foolish young man! Herr Eric Olawsen has been married for a long time, and
it is to you, dear Elis Fröbom, that I give my daughter in marriage, for I
repeat, I could not wish myself a better son-in-law."

Tears of pure joy ran down Elis's cheeks. All of life's happiness had quite
unexpectedly descended on him, and it almost seemed to him that he was
again in the midst of a sweet dream.

At Pehrson Dahlsjö's command, all the miners gathered for a festive
meal.

Ulla was wearing her most beautiful dress and looked more charming
than ever. Everyone cried, almost simultaneously, "Oh, what a magnificent
bride our good Elis Fröbom has won! May Heaven bless them both in their
goodness and virtue."

The horror of the past night could still be seen on Elis Fröbom's face, and he frequently stared in front of him as if remote from everything around him.

"What is the matter with you, my Elis?" asked Ulla. Elis pressed her to his breast and spoke: "Yes, yes—you are really mine, and now everything is well."

In the midst of all his bliss, it sometimes seemed to Elis as if an icy hand were gripping his heart and a dark voice were speaking: "Is this your highest ideal, winning Ulla? You poor fool! Have you not seen the Queen's face?"

He felt almost overcome by an indescribable fear. The thought tortured him that one of the miners would suddenly loom up as tall as a giant and that, to his horror, he would recognize Torbern, who had come to remind him reprovingly of the subterranean kingdom of precious stones and metals to which he had surrendered himself.

And yet he did not know at all why the ghostly old man was hostile to him or what the connection was between his love and his work as a miner.

Pehrson indeed noticed Elis Fröbom's disturbed behavior and ascribed it to the unhappiness he had endured and to the trip into the shaft on the previous night. But not Ulla, who was filled with a secret presentiment and pressed her beloved to tell her what horrible thing had happened to him which was tearing him away from her. Elis's heart was about to break. In vain he strove to tell his beloved of the marvelous face that had revealed itself to him in the shaft. It was as if an unknown power held his mouth closed by force, as if the fearful face of the Queen were looking out of his inner being and that if he should call her by name, everything around him would be turned to dreary, black stone, as occurs when Medusa's dreadful head is viewed. All the splendor which had filled him with the deepest rapture down in the shaft now seemed like a hell full of wretched agony, deceitfully adorned for the purpose of enticing him to his destruction.

Pehrson Dahlsjö commanded that Elis Fröbom stay at home for several days to recover completely from the illness to which he seemed to have succumbed. During this time, Ulla's love, which flowed bright and clear from her childish, innocent heart, dispelled all recollections of that fateful adventure in the shaft. Elis lived in bliss and joy and believed in his good fortune, which no evil power could destroy.

When he went down again into the shaft, everything seemed quite different. The most marvelous lodes lay revealed before his eyes; he worked with redoubled zeal; he forgot everything; when he returned to the surface, he had to recall Pehrson Dahlsjö and his Ulla; he felt split in half; it seemed to him that his better, his true being was climbing down into the center of the earth and was resting in the Queen's arms, while he was seeking his dreary bed in Falun. When Ulla spoke to him of her love and how they would live together happily, then he began to speak of the splendor of the shaft, of the immeasurably rich treasures which lay concealed there, and he became entangled in such strange, incomprehensible speeches that fear and anxiety seized the poor child and she did not know at all how Elis could have changed so suddenly into a quite different person.

With the greatest delight, Elis kept reporting to the foreman, and to Pehrson Dahlsjö himself, how he had discovered the richest veins and the most marvelous trap runs; and when they found nothing but barren rock, he would laugh disdainfully and say that he alone understood the secret signs, the meaningful writing which the Queen's hand itself had inscribed in the rock and that it was actually enough to understand these signs without bringing their meaning into the light of day.

The old foreman looked sadly at the youth, who with wildly sparkling eyes was speaking of the radiant paradise that flared up in the depths of the earth.

"Alas, sir," the old man whispered in Pehrson Dahlsjö's ear. "Alas, sir, evil Torbern has bewitched the poor youth."

"Don't believe in such superstitions, old man," replied Pehrson Dahlsjö. "Love has turned the head of the melancholy Neriker—that is all. Just let the marriage take place, and trap runs and treasures and subterranean kingdoms will all be done with."

The wedding day set by Pehrson Dahlsjö finally arrived. Several days before, Elis Fröbom had become quieter, more serious, and more withdrawn than ever, but never had he been so devoted in his love to charming Ulla as he was at this time. He did not wish to be separated for a moment from her, and therefore he did not go to the mine. He did not seem to be thinking at all of his troubled activity as a miner, for not a word about the subterranean kingdom crossed his lips. Ulla was utterly blissful. All her fears that the threatening powers of the subterranean abyss, of which she had often heard the miners speak, would lure Elis to his destruction had disappeared. Pehrson Dahlsjö also spoke to the old foreman: "Surely you see that Elis Fröbom had only become giddy in the head out of love for my Ulla."

Early in the morning on his wedding day—it was Saint John's Day—Elis knocked at the door of his bride's chamber. She opened it and reeled back when she saw Elis already dressed in his wedding suit, pale as death, dark, flashing fire in his eyes.

"I only wish," he said in a soft, hesitant voice, "I only wish to tell you, my dearly beloved Ulla, that we are standing near the peak of the greatest happiness that is granted to men on earth. Everything has been revealed to me in the past night. Down in the shaft, the cherry-red sparkling almandine lies enclosed in chlorite and mica, on which is inscribed the chart of our life. You must receive it from me as a wedding present. It is more beautiful than the most splendid blood-red carbuncle; and when we, united in true love, look into its radiant light, we can clearly see how our inner beings are intertwined with the marvelous branch that is growing from the Queen's heart in the center of the earth. It is only necessary that I fetch this stone up to the daylight, and that I will do now. Farewell for now, my dearly beloved Ulla. I will be here again shortly."

Ulla begged her beloved with hot tears to desist from this visionary undertaking, since she had a foreboding of the greatest misfortune. But Elis Fröbom assured her that without that gem he would never more have a peaceful moment and that there was no reason to fear that any danger threatened. He pressed his bride to his breast with fervor and departed.

The guests had already assembled to escort the bridal couple to the Kopparberg Church, where the marriage was to be performed after divine service. A whole crowd of elegantly clad young girls, who were to march in front of the bride as bridesmaids according to the customs of the country, were laughing and joking around Ulla. The musicians were tuning their instruments and were practicing a gay wedding march. It was already nearly midday, and Elis Fröbom had not yet appeared. Suddenly some miners, with fear and horror on their pale faces, came rushing in and announced that a frightful cave-in had destroyed the entire excavation at Dahlsjö's mine.

"Elis—my Elis! You are gone! Gone!" Ulla shrieked loudly, and fell down as if dead. Pehrson Dahlsjö learned for the first time from the mine inspector that Elis had gone to the great entrance early in the morning and had gone down into it; but no one else had been working in the shaft, since all the apprentices and miners had been invited to the wedding. Pehrson Dahlsjö and all the miners hurried to the main entrance; but their search, which was carried on only at great risk, was in vain. Elis Fröbom was not found. It was certain that the cave-in had buried the unfortunate youth in the rocks. And so misfortune and misery came to the house of Pehrson Dahlsjö at the very moment when he thought he had achieved repose and peace for his old age.

The good owner and overseer Pehrson Dahlsjö had long since died; his daughter, Ulla, had vanished. No one in Falun remembered anything about them, for a good fifty years had passed since that calamitous wedding day. Then one day miners who were investigating an opening between two shafts found the corpse of a young miner lying in sulfuric acid in a bore nine hundred feet deep. When they brought the body to the surface, it appeared to be petrified.

The body looked as if the youth were lying in a deep sleep, so well preserved were the features on his face and so without trace of decomposition were the elegant miner's clothes, even the flowers on his breast. All the people of the area gathered around the youth, who had been carried up from the main shaft, but no one recognized the features of the corpse, and none of the miners could recall that any of their comrades had been buried alive. They were about to carry the corpse to Falun when a hoary woman, ancient as the hills, appeared, hobbling along on her crutches.

"Here comes Saint John's Granny!" cried several of the miners. They had given this name to the old woman because they had long since noticed that she would appear every year on Saint John's Day and look down into the depths, wringing her hands, groaning sadly, and lamenting as she crept around the main shaft; and then she would vanish again.

Scarcely had the old woman seen the petrified youth than she dropped her crutches, stretched her arms toward heaven, and uttered wretched sounds of lamentation. "Oh, Elis Fröbom—oh, my Elis—my darling bridegroom!"

She squatted down beside the body and seized the stiffened hands and pressed them to her withered breast, beneath the icy sheath of which, like a holy naphtha flame, a heart filled with ardent love was burning.

"Alas," she spoke then, looking around in a circle. "Alas, no one, not one of you, knows poor Ulla Dahlsjö any longer, this young man's happy bride of fifty years ago. When I moved to Ornäs full of grief and sorrow, old Torbern comforted me and said that once again on this earth I would see my Elis, whom the rocks buried on my wedding day, and so I have come here every year and have looked down into the abyss with longing and true love. This blissful reunion has been granted to me this day. Oh, my Elis—my beloved bridegroom!"

Again she put her withered arms around the youth as if she would never leave him, and all those standing around were deeply moved.

The old woman's sighs and sobs became quieter and quieter, until they died away into silence.

The miners stepped forward. They wanted to raise poor Ulla up, but she had breathed out her life on the body of her petrified bridegroom. They noticed that the corpse of the unfortunate man, which they had thought was petrified, was beginning to turn to dust.

The youth's ashes, along with the body of his bride, who had been faithful unto death, were placed in the Kopparberg Church, where the couple were to have been wedded fifty years before.

Translated by Leonard Kent and Elizabeth Knight

‹ *The Lady of Gollerus* ›
T. Crofton Croker

n the shore of Smerwick harbor, one fine summer's morning just at daybreak, stood Dick Fitzgerald, shoghing the dudeen, which may be translated "smoking his pipe." The sun was gradually rising behind the lofty Brandon, the dark sea was getting green in the light, and the mists, clearing away out of the valleys, went rolling and curling like the smoke from the corner of Dick's mouth.

" 'Tis just the pattern of a pretty morning," said Dick, taking the pipe from between his lips and looking toward the distant ocean, which lay as still and tranquil as a tomb of polished marble.

"Well, to be sure," continued he, after a pause, "'tis mighty lonesome to be talking to one's self by way of company and not to have another soul to answer one—nothing but the child of one's own voice, the echo! I know this, that if I had the luck, or maybe the misfortune," said Dick with a melancholy smile, "to have the woman, it would not be this way with me!— and what in the wide world is a man without a wife? He's no more, surely, than a bottle without a drop of drink in it, or dancing without music, or the left leg of a scissors, or a fishing line without a hook, or any other matter that is no ways complete. Is it not so?" said Dick Fitzgerald, casting his eyes toward a rock upon the strand, which, though it could not speak, stood up as firm and looked as bold as ever Kerry witness did.

But what was his astonishment at beholding, just at the foot of that rock, a beautiful young creature combing her hair, which was of a sea-green color, and now the salt water shining on it appeared, in the morning light, like melted butter upon cabbage. Dick guessed at once that she was a Merrow, although he had never seen one before, for he spied the cohuleen driuth, or little enchanted cap, which the sea people use for diving down into the ocean, lying upon the strand near her; and he had heard that if once he could possess himself of the cap, she would lose the power of going away into the water. So he seized it with all speed, and she, hearing the noise, turned her head about as natural as any Christian.

When the Merrow saw that her little diving cap was gone, the salt tears—doubly salt, no doubt, from her—came trickling down her cheeks, and she began a low mournful cry with just the tender voice of a newborn infant. Dick, although he knew well enough what she was crying for, determined to keep the cohuleen driuth, let her cry never so much, to see what luck would come out of it. Yet he could not help pitying her, and when the dumb thing looked up in his face, and her cheeks all moist with tears, 'twas enough to make anyone feel, let alone Dick, who had ever and always, like most of his countrymen, a mighty tender heart of his own.

"Don't cry, my darling," said Dick Fitzgerald; but the Merrow, like any bold child, only cried the more for that.

Dick sat himself down by her side and took hold of her hand, by way of comforting her. 'Twas in no particular an ugly hand, only there was a small web between the fingers, as there is in a duck's foot, but 'twas as thin and as white as the skin between egg and shell.

"What's your name, my darling?" says Dick, thinking to make her conversant with him, but he got no answer, and he was certain sure now that she either could not speak or did not understand him. He therefore squeezed her hand in his, as the only way he had of talking to her. It's the universal language; and there's not a woman in the world, be she fish or lady, that does not understand it.

The Merrow did not seem much displeased at this mode of conversation, and making an end of her whining all at once, "Man," says she, looking up in Dick Fitzgerald's face, "man, will you eat me?"

"By all the red petticoats and check aprons between Dingle and Tralee," cried Dick, jumping up in amazement, "I'd as soon eat myself, my jewel! Is it I eat you, my pet? Now 'twas some ugly ill-looking thief of a fish put that notion into your own pretty head, with the nice green hair down upon it, that is so cleanly combed out this morning!"

"Man," said the Merrow, "what will you do with me, if you won't eat me?"

Dick's thoughts were running on a wife. He saw, at the first glimpse, that she was handsome; but since she spoke, and spoke, too, like any real woman, he was fairly in love with her. 'Twas the neat way she called him "man" that settled the matter entirely.

"Fish," says Dick, trying to speak to her after her own short fashion, "fish," says he, "here's my word, fresh and fasting, for you this blessed morning, that I'll make you Mistress Fitzgerald before all the world, and that's what I'll do."

"Never say the word twice," says she. "I'm ready and willing to be yours, Mister Fitzgerald; but stop, if you please, till I twist up my hair."

It was some time before she had settled it entirely to her liking, for she guessed, I suppose, that she was going among strangers, where she would be looked at. When that was done, the Merrow put the comb in her pocket and then bent down her head and whispered some words to the water that was close to the foot of the rock.

Dick saw the murmur of the words upon the top of the sea, going out toward the wide ocean, just like a breath of wind rippling along, and says he in the greatest wonder, "Is it speaking you are, my darling, to the salt water?"

"It's nothing else," says she, quite carelessly. "I'm just sending word home to my father, not to be waiting breakfast for me; just to keep him from being uneasy in his mind."

"And who's your father, my duck?" says Dick.

"What!" said the Merrow. "Did you never hear of my father? He's the king of the waves, to be sure!"

"And yourself, then, is a real king's daughter?" said Dick, opening his two eyes to take a full and true survey of his wife that was to be. "Oh, I'm nothing else but a made man with you, and a king your father—to be sure he has all the money that's down in the bottom of the sea!"

"Money," repeated the Merrow. "What's money?"

" 'Tis no bad thing to have when one wants it," replied Dick. "And maybe now the fishes have the understanding to bring up whatever you bid them?"

"Oh, yes," said the Merrow. "They bring me what I want."

"To speak the truth, then," said Dick, "'tis a straw bed I have at home before you, and that, I'm thinking, is no ways fitting for a king's daughter. So if 'twould not be displeasing to you, just to mention a nice featherbed, with a pair of new blankets—but what am I talking about? Maybe you have not such things as beds down under the water?"

"By all means," said she, "Mr. Fitzgerald—plenty of beds at your service. I've fourteen oyster beds of my own, not to mention one just planting for the rearing of young ones."

"You have?" says Dick, scratching his head and looking a little puzzled. "'Tis a featherbed I was speaking of—but clearly, yours is the very cut of a decent plan, to have bed and supper so handy to each other, that a person when they'd have the one need never ask for the other."

However, bed or no bed, money or no money, Dick Fitzgerald determined to marry the Merrow, and the Merrow had given her consent. Away they went, therefore, across the strand, from Gollerus to Ballinrunnig, where Father Fitzgibbon happened to be that morning.

"There are two words to this bargain, Dick Fitzgerald," said his reverence, looking mighty glum. "And is it a fishy woman you'd marry? The Lord preserve us! Send the scaly creature home to her own people, that's my advice to you, wherever she came from."

Dick had the cohuleen driuth in his hand, and was about to give it back to the Merrow, who looked covetously at it, but he thought for a moment, and then says he, "Please, Your Reverence, she's a king's daughter."

"If she was the daughter of fifty kings," said Father Fitzgibbon, "I tell you, you can't marry her, she being a fish."

"Please, Your Reverence," said Dick again in an undertone, "she is as mild and as beautiful as the moon."

"If she was as mild and as beautiful as the sun, moon, and stars all put together, I tell you, Dick Fitzgerald," said the Priest, stamping his right foot, "you can't marry her, she being a fish!"

"But she has all the gold that's down in the sea only for the asking, and I'm a made man if I marry her; and," said Dick, looking up slyly, "I can make it worth anyone's while to do the job."

"Oh! That alters the case entirely," replied the priest. "Why, there's some reason now in what you say: why didn't you tell me this before? Marry her by all means if she was ten times a fish. Money, you know, is not to be refused in these bad times, and I may as well have the use of it as another, that maybe would not take half the pains in counseling you as I have done."

So Father Fitzgibbon married Dick Fitzgerald to the Merrow, and like any loving couple, they returned to Gollerus well pleased with each other. Everything prospered with Dick—he was at the sunny side of the world. The Merrow made the best of wives, and they lived together in the greatest contentment.

It was wonderful to see, considering where she had been brought up, how she would busy herself about the house and how well she nursed the children; for at the end of three years there were as many young Fitzgeralds—two boys and a girl.

In short, Dick was a happy man, and so he might have continued to the end of his days, if he had only the sense to take proper care of what he had got; many another man, however, beside Dick, has not had wit enough to do that.

One day when Dick was obliged to go to Tralee, he left his wife minding the children at home after him and thinking she had plenty to do without disturbing his fishing tackle.

Dick was no sooner gone than Mrs. Fitzgerald set about cleaning up the house, and chancing to pull down a fishing net, what should she find behind it in a hole in the wall but her own cohuleen driuth.

She took it out and looked at it, and then she thought of her father the king, and her mother the queen, and her brothers and sisters, and she felt a longing to go back to them. She sat down on a little stool and thought over the happy days she had spent under the sea; then she looked at her children, and thought on the love and affection of poor Dick and how it would break his heart to lose her. "But," says she, "he won't lose me entirely, for I'll come back to him again; and who can blame me for going to see my father and my mother, after being so long away from them."

She got up and went toward the door, but came back again to look once more at the child that was sleeping in the cradle. She kissed it gently, and as she kissed it, a tear trembled for an instant in her eye and then fell on its rosy cheek. She wiped away the tear and, turning to the eldest little girl, told her to take good care of her brothers, and to be a good child herself, until she came back. The Merrow then went down to the strand.

The sea was lying calm and smooth, just heaving and glittering in the sun, and she thought she heard a faint sweet singing, inviting her to come down. All her old ideas and feelings came flooding over her mind, Dick and her children were at the instant forgotten, and placing the cohuleen driuth on her head, she plunged in.

Dick came home in the evening, and missing his wife, he asked Kathelin, his little girl, what had become of her mother, but she could not tell him. He then inquired of the neighbors, and he learned that she was seen going toward the strand with a strange-looking thing like a cocked hat in her hand. He returned to his cabin to search for the cohuleen driuth. It was gone, and the truth now flashed upon him.

Year after year did Dick Fitzgerald wait, expecting the return of his wife, but he never saw her more. Dick never married again, always thinking that the Merrow would sooner or later return to him, and nothing could ever persuade him but that her father the king kept her below by main force. "For," said Dick, "she surely would not of herself give up her husband and her children."

While she was with him, she was so good a wife in every respect that to this day she is spoken of in the tradition of the country as the pattern for one, under the name of The Lady of Gollerus.

§

‹ Snow White and Rose Red ›
Wilhelm Grimm

A poor widow lived all alone in a small cottage, and in front of this cottage was a garden with two rosebushes. One bore white roses and the other red. The widow had two children, who looked like the rosebushes: one was called Snow White and the other Rose Red. They were more pious and kind, more hardworking and diligent, than any other two children in the world. To be sure, Snow White was more quiet and gentle than Rose Red, who preferred to run around in the meadows and fields, look for flowers, and catch butterflies. Snow White stayed at home with her mother, helped her with the housework, or read to her when there was nothing to do. The two children loved each other so much that they always held hands whenever they went out, and when Snow White said, "Let us never leave each other," Rose Red answered, "Never, as long as we live." And their mother added, "Whatever one of you has, remember to share it with the other."

They often wandered in the forest all alone and gathered red berries. The animals never harmed them and, indeed, trusted them completely and would come up to them. The little hare would eat a cabbage leaf out of their hands. The roe grazed by their side. The stag leapt merrily around them. And the birds sat still on their branches and sang whatever tune they knew. Nothing bad ever happened to the girls. If they stayed too long in the forest and night overtook them, they would lie down next to each other on the moss and sleep until morning came. Their mother knew this and did not worry about them.

Once, when they had spent the night in the forest and the morning sun had wakened them, they saw a beautiful child in a white, glistening garment sitting near them. The child stood up, looked at them in a friendly way, but went into the forest without saying anything. When they looked around, they realized that they had been sleeping at the edge of a cliff and would have certainly fallen over it if they had gone a few more steps in the darkness. Their mother told them that the child must have been the angel who watches over good children.

Snow White and Rose Red kept their mother's cottage so clean that it was a joy to look inside. In the summer Rose Red took care of the house, and every morning she placed two flowers in front of her mother's bed before she awoke, a rose from each one of the bushes. In the winter Snow White lit the fire and hung the kettle over the hearth. The kettle was made out of brass but glistened like gold because it was polished so clean. In the evening when the snowflakes fell, the mother said, "Go, Snow White, and bolt the door." Then they sat down at the hearth, and their mother put on her glasses and read aloud from a large book, while the two girls sat and spun as they listened. On the ground next to them lay a little lamb, and behind them sat a white dove with its head tucked under its wing.

One evening, as they were sitting together, there was a knock on the door, as if someone wanted to be let in. The mother said, "Quick, Rose Red, open the door. It must be a traveler looking for shelter." Rose Red pushed back the bolt, thinking that it would be some poor man, but instead it was a bear. He stuck his thick black head through the door, and Rose Red jumped back and screamed loudly. The little lamb bleated, the dove fluttered its wings, and Snow White hid herself behind her mother's bed. However, the bear began to speak and said, "Don't be afraid. I won't harm you. I'm half frozen and only want to warm myself here a little."

"You poor bear," the mother said. "Lie down by the fire and take care that it does not burn your fur." Then she called out, "Snow White, Rose Red, come out. The bear won't harm you. He means well."

They both came out, and gradually the lamb and dove also drew near and lost their fear of him. Then the bear said, "Come, children, dust the snow off my coat a little."

So they fetched a broom and swept the fur clean. Afterward he stretched himself out beside the fire and uttered growls to show how content and comfortable he was. It did not take them long to all become accustomed to one another, and the clumsy guest had to put up with the mischievous pranks of the girls. They tugged his fur with their hands, planted their feet upon his back and rolled him over, or they took a hazel switch and hit him. When he growled, they just laughed. The bear took everything in good spirit. Only when they became too rough did he cry out, "Let me live, children.

> *Snow White, Rose Red,*
> *would you beat your suitor dead?"*

When it was time to sleep and the others went to bed, the mother said to the bear, "You're welcome, in God's name, to lie down by the hearth. Then you'll be protected from the cold and bad weather."

As soon as dawn arrived, the two girls let him go outside, and he trotted over the snow into the forest. From then on the bear came every evening at a certain time, lay down by the hearth, and allowed the children to play with him as much as they wanted. And they became so accustomed to him that they never bolted the door until their black playmate had arrived.

One morning, when spring had made its appearance and everything outside was green, the bear said to Snow White, "Now I must go away, and I shall not return the entire summer."

"But where are you going, dear bear?" asked Snow White.

"I must go into the forest and guard my treasures from the wicked dwarfs. In the winter, when the ground is frozen hard, they must remain underground and can't work their way through to the top. But now that the sun has thawed and warmed the earth, they will break through, climb out, search around, and steal. Once they get something in their hands and carry it to their caves, it will not easily see the light of day again."

Snow White was very sad about his departure. She unlocked the door, and when the bear hurried out, he became caught on the bolt and a piece of his fur ripped off, and it seemed to Snow White that she saw gold glimmering through the fur, but she was not sure. The bear hurried away and soon disappeared beyond the trees.

Sometime after, the mother sent the girls into the forest to gather firewood. There they found a large tree lying on the ground, that had been chopped down. Something was jumping up and down on the grass near the trunk, but they could not tell what it was. As they came closer they saw a dwarf with an old, withered face and a beard that was snow white and a yard long. The tip of the beard was caught in a crack of the tree, and the little fellow was jumping back and forth like a dog on a rope and did not know what to do. He glared at the girls with his fiery red eyes and screamed, "What are you standing there for? Can't you come over here and help me?"

"How did you get into this jam, little man?" asked Rose Red.

"You stupid, nosy goose," answered the dwarf, "I wanted to split the tree to get some wood for my kitchen. We dwarfs need but little food; however,

it gets burned fast when we use those thick logs. We don't devour such large portions as you coarse and greedy people. I had just driven in the wedge safely, and everything would have gone all right, but the cursed wedge was too smooth, and it sprang out unexpectedly. The tree snapped shut so rapidly that I couldn't save my beautiful white beard. Now it's stuck there, and I can't get away. And all you silly, creamy-faced things can do is laugh! Ugh, you're just nasty!"

The girls tried as hard as they could, but they could not pull the beard out. It was stuck too tight.

"I'll run and get somebody," Rose Red said.

"Crazy fool!" the dwarf snarled. "Why run and get someone? The two of you are already enough. Can't you think of something better?"

"Don't be so impatient," said Snow White. "I'll think of something." She took out a pair of scissors from her pocket and cut off the tip of his beard. As soon as the dwarf felt that he was free, he grabbed a sack filled with gold that was lying between the roots of the tree. He lifted it out and grumbled to himself, "Uncouth slobs! How could you cut off a piece of my fine beard? Good riddance to you!" Upon saying this, he swung the sack over his shoulder and went away without once looking at the girls.

Sometime after this, Snow White and Rose Red wanted to catch some fish for dinner. As they approached the brook, they saw something like a large grasshopper bouncing toward the water as if it wanted to jump in. They ran to the spot and recognized the dwarf.

"Where are you going?" asked Rose Red. "You don't want to jump into the water, do you?"

"I'm not such a fool as that!" the dwarf screamed. "Don't you see that the cursed fish wants to pull me in?" The little man had been sitting there and fishing, and unfortunately the wind had caught his beard, so that it had become entangled with his line. Just then a large fish had bitten the bait, and the feeble little dwarf did not have the strength to land the fish, which kept the upper hand and pulled him toward the water. To be sure, the dwarf tried to grab hold of the reeds and rushes, but that did not help too much. He was compelled to follow the movements of the fish and was in constant danger of being dragged into the water, but the girls had come just in the nick of time. They held on to him tightly and tried to untangle his beard from the line. However, it was to no avail. The beard and the line were meshed together, and there was nothing left to do but to take out the scissors and cut off a small part of his beard. When the dwarf saw this, he screamed at them, "You birdbrains! You've disfigured my face like barbarians. It was not enough that you clipped the tip of my beard. Now you've cut off the best part. I won't be able to show myself among my friends. May you both walk for miles on end until the soles of your shoes are burned off!" Then he grabbed a sack of pearls that was lying in the rushes, and without saying another word, he dragged it away and disappeared behind a rock.

It happened that soon after this the girls were sent by their mother to the city to buy thread, needles, lace, and ribbons. Their way led over a heath which had huge pieces of rock scattered here and there. A large bird circled slowly in the air above them, flying lower and lower until it finally landed on the ground not far from a rock. Right after that they heard a piercing, terrible cry. They ran to the spot and saw with horror that the eagle had seized their old acquaintance the dwarf and intended to carry him away. The girls took pity on him and grabbed hold of the little man as tightly as they could. They tugged against the eagle until finally the bird had to abandon his booty. When the dwarf had recovered from his initial fright, he screeched at them, "Couldn't you have handled me more carefully? You've torn my coat to shreds. It was thin enough to begin with, but now it's got holes and rips all over, you clumsy louts!" Then he took a sack with jewels and once again slipped under a rock into his cave.

The girls were accustomed to his ingratitude and continued on their way. They took care of their chores in the city, and when they crossed the heath again on their way home, they surprised the dwarf, who had dumped his sack of jewels on a clean spot, not thinking that anyone would come by at such a late hour. The evening sun's rays were cast upon the glistening stones, which glimmered and sparkled in such radiant different colors that the girls had to stop and look at them.

"Why are you standing there and gaping like monkeys?" the dwarf screamed, and his ash-gray face turned scarlet with rage. He was about to continue his cursing when a loud growl was heard and a black bear came trotting out of the forest. The dwarf jumped up in terror, but he could not reach his hiding place in time. The bear was already too near. Filled with fear, the dwarf cried out, "Dear Mr. Bear, spare my life, and I'll give you all my treasures! Look at the beautiful jewels lying there. Grant me my life! What good is a small, measly fellow like me? You wouldn't be able to feel me between your teeth. Those wicked girls over there would be better for you. They're such tender morsels, fat as young quails. For heaven's sake, eat them instead!"

The bear did not pay any attention to the dwarf's words but gave the evil creature a single blow with his paw, and the dwarf did not move again.

The girls had run away, but the bear called after them, "Snow White, Rose Red, don't be afraid! Wait. I'll go with you!"

Then they recognized his voice and stopped. When the bear came up to them, his bearskin suddenly fell off, and there stood a handsome man clad completely in gold. "I am the son of a king," he said, "and I had been cast under a spell by the wicked dwarf who stole my treasures. He forced me to run around the forest as a wild bear, and only his death could release me from the spell. Now he has received his justly earned punishment."

Snow White was married to the prince, and Rose Red to his brother, and they shared the great treasures that the dwarf had collected in his cave. The old mother lived many more peaceful and happy years with her children. Indeed, she took the two rosebushes with her, and they stood in front of her window, and every year they bore the most beautiful roses, white and red.

Translated by Jack Zipes

‹ *Bluebeard's Ghost* ›
William Makepeace Thackeray

or some time after the fatal accident which deprived her of her husband, Mrs. Bluebeard was, as may be imagined, in a state of profound grief.

There was not a widow in all the country who went to such an expense for black bombazeen. She had her beautiful hair confined in crimped caps, and her weepers came over her elbows. Of course she saw no company except her sister Anne (whose company was anything but pleasant to the widow); as for her brothers, their odious mess-table manners had always been disagreeable to her. What did she care for jokes about the major, or scandal concerning the Scotch surgeon of the regiment? If they drank their wine out of black bottles or crystal, what did it matter to her? Their stories of the stable, the parade, and the last run with the hounds, were perfectly odious to her; besides, she could not bear their impertinent mustachios and filthy habit of smoking cigars.

They were always wild vulgar young men at the best; but *now,* oh! their presence to her delicate soul was horror! How could she bear to look on them after what had occurred? She thought of the best of husbands ruthlessly cut down by their cruel heavy cavalry sabres; the kind friend, the generous land-lord, the spotless justice of peace, in whose family differences these rude cornets of dragoons had dared to interfere, whose venerable blue hairs they had dragged down with sorrow to the grave!

She put up a most splendid monument to her departed lord over the family vault of the Bluebeards. The rector, Doctor Sly, who had been Mr. Bluebeard's tutor at college, wrote an epitaph in the most pompous yet pathetic Latin:—"Siste, viator! mœrens conjux, heu! quanto minus est cum reliquis versari quam tui meminisse"; in a word, everything that is usually said in epitaphs. A bust of the departed saint, with Virtue mourning over it, stood over the epitaph, surrounded by medallions of his wives, and one of these medallions had as yet no name in it, nor (the epitaph said) could the widow ever be consoled until her own name was inscribed there. "For then I shall be with him. In cœlo quies," she would say, throwing up her fine eyes to heaven, and quoting the enormous words of the hatchment which was put up in the church and over Bluebeard's Hall, where the butler, the housekeeper, the footman, the housemaid, and scullions, were all in the profoundest mourning. The keeper went out to shoot birds in a crape band; nay, the very scarecrows in the orchard and fruit-garden were ordered to be dressed in black.

Sister Anne was the only person who refused to wear black. Mrs. Bluebeard would have parted with her, but she had no other female relative. Her father, it may be remembered by readers of the former part of her Memoirs, had married again; and the mother-in-law and Mrs. Bluebeard, as usual, hated each other furiously. Mrs. Shacabac had come to the Hall on a visit of condolence; but the widow was so rude to her on the second day of the visit that the stepmother quitted the house in a fury. As for the Bluebeards, of course *they* hated the widow. Had not Mr. Bluebeard settled every shilling upon her? and, having no children by his former marriage, her property, as I leave you to fancy, was pretty handsome. So sister Anne was the only female relative whom Mrs. Bluebeard would keep near her, and, as we all know, a woman *must* have a female relative under any circumstances of pain, or pleasure, or profit—when she is married, or when she is in a delicate situation. But let us continue our story.

"I will never wear mourning for that odious wretch, sister!" Anne would cry.

"I will trouble you, Miss Anne, not to use such words in my presence regarding the best of husbands, or to quit the room at once!" the widow would answer.

"I'm sure it's no great pleasure to sit in it. I wonder you don't make use of the closet, sister, where the *other* Mrs. Bluebeards are."

"Impertinence! they were all embalmed by Monsieur Gannal. How dare you repeat the monstrous calumnies regarding the best of men? Take down the family Bible and read what my blessed saint says of his wives—read it written in his own hand:—

" 'Friday, June 20.—Married my beloved wife, Anna Maria Scrogginsia.

" 'Saturday, August 1.—A bereaved husband has scarcely strength to write down in this chronicle that the dearest of wives, Anna Maria Scrogginsia, expired this day of sore throat.'

"There! can anything be more convincing than that? Read again:

" 'Tuesday, Sept. 1.—This day I led to the hymeneal altar my soul's blessing, Louisa Matilda Hopkinson. May this angel supply the place of her I have lost!

" 'Wednesday, October 5.—Oh, heavens! pity the distraction of a wretch who is obliged to record the ruin of his dearest hopes and affections! This day my adored Louisa Matilda Hopkinson gave up the ghost! A complaint of the head and shoulders was the sudden cause of the event which has rendered the unhappy subscriber the most miserable of men.

" 'BLUEBEARD'

"Every one of the women are calendared in this delightful, this pathetic, this truly virtuous and tender way; and can you suppose that a man who wrote such sentiments could be a *murderer,* miss?"

"Do you mean to say that he did not *kill* them, then?" said Anne.

"Gracious goodness, Anne, kill them! they died all as naturally as I hope you will. My blessed husband was an angel of goodness and kindness to them. Was it *his* fault that the doctors could not cure their maladies? No, that it wasn't! and when they died, the inconsolable husband had their bodies embalmed, in order that on this side of the grave he might never part from them."

"And why did he take you up in the tower, pray? and why did you send me in such a hurry to the leads? and why did he sharpen his long knife, and roar out to you to COME DOWN?"

"Merely to punish me for my curiosity—the dear, good, kind, excellent creature!" sobbed the widow, overpowered with affectionate recollections of her lord's attentions to her.

"I wish," said sister Anne, sulkily, "that I had not been in such a hurry in summoning my brothers."

"Ah!" screamed Mrs. Bluebeard, with a harrowing scream, "don't—don't recall that horrid fatal day, miss! If you had not misled your brothers, my poor dear darling Bluebeard would still be in life, still—still the soul's joy of his bereaved Fatima!"

Whether it is that all wives adore husbands when the latter are no more, or whether it is that Fatima's version of the story is really the correct one, and that the common impression against Bluebeard is an odious prejudice, and that he no more murdered his wives than you and I have, remains yet to be proved, and, indeed, does not much matter for the understanding of the rest of Mrs. B.'s adventures. And though people will say that Bluebeard's settlement of his whole fortune on his wife, in event of survivorship, was a mere act of absurd mystification, seeing that he was fully determined to cut her head off after the honeymoon, yet the best test of his real intentions is the profound grief which the widow manifested for his death, and the fact that he left her mighty well to do in the world.

If anyone were to leave you or me a fortune, my dear friend, would we be too anxious to rake up the how and the why? Pooh! pooh! we would take it and make no bones about it, and Mrs. Bluebeard did likewise. Her husband's family, it is true, argued the point with her, and said, "Madam, you must perceive that Mr. Bluebeard never intended the fortune for you, as it was his fixed intention to chop off your head! it is clear that he meant to leave his money to his blood relations, therefore you ought in equity to hand it over." But she sent them all off with a flea in their ears, as the saying is, and said, "Your argument may be a very good one, but I will, if you please, keep the money." And she ordered the mourning as we have before shown, and indulged in grief, and exalted everywhere the character of the deceased. If anyone would but leave me a fortune, what a funeral and what a character I would give him!

Bluebeard Hall is situated, as we all very well know, in a remote country district, and, although a fine residence, is remarkably gloomy and lonely. To the widow's susceptible mind, after the death of her darling husband, the place became intolerable. The walk, the lawn, the fountain, the green glades of park over which frisked the dappled deer, all—all recalled the memory of her beloved. It was but yesterday that, as they roamed through the park in the calm summer evening, her Bluebeard pointed out to the keeper the fat buck he was to kill. "Ah!" said the widow, with tears in her fine eyes, "the artless stag was shot down, the haunch was cut and roasted, the jelly had been prepared from the currant-bushes in the garden that he loved, but my Bluebeard never ate of the venison! Look, Anna sweet, pass we the old oak hall; 'tis hung with trophies won by him in the chase, with pictures of the noble race of Bluebeard! Look! by the fireplace there is the gig-whip, his riding-whip, the spud with which you know he used to dig the weeds out of the terrace-walk; in that drawer are his spurs, his whistle, his visiting-cards, with his dear dear name engraven upon them! There are the bits of string that he used to cut off the parcels and keep because string was always useful; his button-hook, and there is the peg on which he used to hang his h—h—*hat!*"

Uncontrollable emotions, bursts of passionate tears, would follow these tender reminiscences of the widow; and the long and short of the matter was, that she was determined to give up Bluebeard Hall and live elsewhere; her love for the memory of the deceased, she said, rendered the place too wretched.

Of course an envious and sneering world said that she was tired of the country and wanted to marry again; but she little heeded its taunts, and Anne, who hated her stepmother and could not live at home, was fain to accompany her sister to the town where the Bluebeards have had for many years a very large, genteel, old-fashioned house. So she went to the town-house, where they lived and quarrelled pretty much as usual; and though Anne often threatened to leave her and go to a boarding-house, of which there were plenty in the place, yet after all to live with her sister, and drive out in the carriage, with the footman and coachman in mourning, and the lozenge on the panels, with the Bluebeard and Shacabac arms quartered on it, was far more respectable, and so the lovely sisters continued to dwell together.

For a lady under Mrs. Bluebeard's circumstances, the town-house had other and peculiar advantages. Besides being an exceedingly spacious and dismal brick building, with a dismal iron railing in front, and long dismal thin windows with little panes of glass, it looked out into the churchyard where, time out of mind, between two yew-trees, one of which is cut into the form of a peacock, while the other represents a dumb-waiter—it looked into the churchyard where the monument of the late Bluebeard was placed over the family vault. It was the first thing the widow saw from her bedroom window in the morning, and 'twas sweet to watch at night from the parlour the pallid moonlight lighting up the bust of the departed, and Virtue throwing great black shadows athwart it. Polyanthuses, rhododendra, ranunculuses, and other flowers with the largest names and of the most delightful odours, were planted within the little iron railing that enclosed the last resting-place of the Blue-beards; and the beadle was instructed to half-kill any little boys who might be caught plucking these sweet testimonies of a wife's affection.

Over the sideboard in the dining-room hung a full-length of Mr. Blue-beard, by Ticklegill, R.A., in a militia uniform, frowning down upon the knives and forks and silver trays. Over the mantelpiece he was represented in a hunting costume on his favourite horse; there was a sticking-plaster silhouette of him in the widow's bedroom, and a miniature in the drawing-room, where he was drawn in a gown of black and gold, holding a gold-tasselled trencher-cap with one hand, and with the other pointing to a diagram of Pons Asinorum. This likeness was taken when he was a fellow-commoner at Saint John's College, Cambridge, and before the growth of that blue beard which was the ornament of his manhood, and a part of which now formed a beautiful blue neck-chain for his bereaved wife.

Sister Anne said the town-house was even more dismal than the country-house, for there was pure air at the Hall, and it was pleasanter to look out on a park than on a churchyard, however fine the monuments might be. But the widow said she was a light-minded hussy, and persisted as usual in her lamentations and mourning. The only male whom she would admit within her doors was the parson of the parish, who read sermons to her; and, as his reverence was at least seventy years old, Anne, though she might be ever so much minded to fall in love, had no opportunity to indulge her inclination; and the townspeople, scandalous as they might be, could not find a word to say against the *liaison* of the venerable man and the heart-stricken widow.

All other company she resolutely refused. When the players were in the town, the poor manager, who came to beg her to bespeak a comedy, was thrust out of the gates by the big butler. Though there were balls, card-parties, and assemblies, Widow Bluebeard would never subscribe to one of them; and even the officers, those all-conquering heroes who make such ravages in ladies' hearts, and to whom all ladies' doors are commonly open, could never get an entry into the widow's house. Captain Whiskerfield strutted for three weeks up and down before her house, and had not the least effect upon her. Captain O'Grady (of an Irish regiment) attempted to bribe the servants, and one night actually scaled the garden wall; but all that he got was his foot in a man-trap, not to mention being dreadfully scarified by the broken glass; and so *he* never made love any more. Finally, Captain Blackbeard, whose whiskers vied in magnitude with those of the deceased Bluebeard himself, although he attended church regularly every week—he who had not darkened the doors of a church for ten years before—even Captain Blackbeard got nothing by his piety; and the widow never once took her eyes off her book to look at him. The barracks were in despair; and Captain Whiskerfield's tailor, who had supplied him with new clothes in order to win the widow's heart, ended by clapping the captain into gaol.

His reverence the parson highly applauded the widow's conduct to the officers; but, being himself rather of a social turn, and fond of a good dinner and a bottle, he represented to the lovely mourner that she should endeavour to divert her grief by a little respectable society, and recommended that she should from time to time entertain a few grave and sober persons whom he would present to her. As Doctor Sly had an unbounded influence over the fair mourner, she acceded to his desires; and accordingly he introduced to her house some of the most venerable and worthy of his acquaintance,—all married people, however, so that the widow should not take the least alarm.

It happened that the Doctor had a nephew, who was a lawyer in London, and this gentleman came dutifully in the long vacation to pay a visit to his reverend uncle. "He is none of your roystering dashing young fellows," said his reverence, "he is the delight of his mamma and sisters; he never drinks anything stronger than tea; he never missed church thrice a Sunday for these twenty years; and I hope, my dear and amiable madam, that you will not object to receive this pattern of young men for the sake of your most devoted friend, his uncle."

The widow consented to receive Mr. Sly. He was not a handsome man certainly. "But what does that matter?" said the Doctor; "he is *good,* and virtue is better than all the beauty of all the dragoons in the Queen's service."

Mr. Sly came there to dinner, and he came to tea; and he drove out with the widow in the carriage with the lozenge on it; and at church he handed the psalm-book; and, in short, he paid her every attention which could be expected from so polite a young gentleman.

At this the town began to talk, as people in towns will. "The Doctor kept all bachelors out of the widow's house," said they, "in order that that ugly nephew of his may have the field entirely to himself." These speeches were of course heard by sister Anne, and the little minx was not a little glad to take advantage of them, in order to induce her sister to see some more cheerful company. The fact is, the young hussy loved a dance or a game at cards much more than a humdrum conversation over a tea-table; and so she plied her sister day and night with hints as to the propriety of opening her house, receiving the gentry of the county, and spending her fortune.

To this point the widow at length, though with many sighs and vast unwillingness, acceded; and she went so far as to order a very becoming half-mourning, in which all the world declared she looked charming. "I carry," said she, "my blessed Bluebeard in my heart,—*that* is in the deepest mourning for him, and when the heart grieves there is no need of outward show."

So she issued cards for a little quiet tea and supper, and several of the best families in the town and neighbourhood attended her entertainment. It was followed by another and another; and at last Captain Blackbeard was actually introduced, though, of course, he came in plain clothes.

Doctor Sly and his nephew never could abide the Captain. "They had heard some queer stories," they said, "about proceedings in barracks. Who was it that drank three bottles at a sitting? who had a mare that ran for the plate? and why was it that Dolly Coddlins left the town so suddenly?" Mr. Sly turned up the whites of his eyes as his uncle asked these questions, and sighed for the wickedness of the world. But for all that he was delighted, especially at the anger which the widow manifested when the Dolly Coddlins affair was hinted at. She was furious, and vowed she would never see the wretch again. The lawyer and his uncle were charmed. O short-sighted lawyer and parson, do you think Mrs. Bluebeard would have been so angry if she had not been jealous?—do you think she would have been jealous if she had not—had not what? She protested that she no more cared for the Captain than she did for one of her footmen; but the next time he called, she would not condescend to say a word to him.

"My dearest Miss Anne," said the Captain, as he met her in Sir Roger de Coverley (she was herself dancing with Ensign Trippet), "what is the matter with your lovely sister?"

"Dolly Coddlins is the matter," said Miss Anne. "Mr. Sly has told all"; and she was down the middle in a twinkling.

The Captain blushed so at this monstrous insinuation that anyone could see how incorrect it was. He made innumerable blunders in the dance, and was all the time casting such ferocious glances at Mr. Sly (who did not dance, but sat by the widow and ate ices), that his partner thought he was mad, and that Mr. Sly became very uneasy.

When the dance was over, he came to pay his respects to the widow, and, in so doing, somehow trod so violently on Mr. Sly's foot that that gentleman screamed with pain, and presently went home. But though he was gone the widow was not a whit more gracious to Captain Blackbeard. She requested Mr. Trippet to order her carriage that night, and went home without uttering one single word to Captain Blackbeard.

The next morning, and with a face of preternatural longitude, the Reverend Doctor Sly paid a visit to the widow. "The wickedness and bloodthirstiness of the world," said he, "increase every day. O my dear madam, what monsters do we meet in it—what wretches, what assassins, are allowed to go abroad! Would you believe it, that this morning, as my nephew was taking his peaceful morning meal, one of the ruffians from the barracks presented himself with a challenge from Captain Blackbeard?"

"Is he hurt?" screamed the widow.

"No, my dear friend, my dear Frederick is not hurt. And oh, what a joy it will be to him to think you have that tender solicitude for his welfare!"

"You know I have always had the highest respect for him," said the widow; who, when she screamed, was in truth thinking of somebody else. But the Doctor did not choose to interpret her thoughts in that way, and gave all the benefit of them to his nephew.

"That anxiety, dearest madam, which you express for him emboldens me, encourages me, authorises me, to press a point on you which I am sure must have entered your thoughts ere now. The dear youth in whom you have shown such an interest lives but for you! Yes, fair lady, start not at hearing that his sole affections are yours; and with what pride shall I carry to him back the news that he is not indifferent to you!"

"Are they going to fight?" continued the lady, in a breathless state of alarm. "For Heaven's sake, dearest Doctor, prevent the horrid horrid meeting. Send for a magistrate's warrant; do anything; but do not suffer those misguided young men to cut each other's throats!"

"Fairest lady, I fly!" said the Doctor, and went back to lunch quite delighted with the evident partiality Mrs. Bluebeard showed for his nephew.

And Mrs. Bluebeard, not content with exhorting him to prevent the duel, rushed to Mr. Pound, the magistrate, informed him of the facts, got out warrants against both Mr. Sly and the Captain, and would have put them into execution; but it was discovered that the former gentleman had abruptly left town, so that the constable could not lay hold of him.

It somehow, however, came to be generally known that the widow Bluebeard had declared herself in favour of Mr. Sly, the lawyer; that she had fainted when told her lover was about to fight a duel; finally, that she had accepted him, and would marry him as soon as the quarrel between him and the Captain was settled. Doctor Sly, when applied to, hummed and ha'd, and would give no direct answer; but he denied nothing, and looked so knowing, that all the world was certain of the fact; and the county paper next week stated:—

> "We understand that the lovely and wealthy Mrs. Bl—b—rd is about once more to enter the bands of wedlock with our distinguished townsman, Frederick S—y, Esquire, of the Middle Temple, London. The learned gentleman left town in consequence of a dispute with a gallant son of Mars which was likely to have led to warlike results, had not a magistrate's warrant intervened, when the Captain was bound over to keep the peace."

In fact, as soon as the Captain was so bound over, Mr. Sly came back, stating that he had quitted the town not to avoid a duel,—far from it, but to keep out of the way of the magistrates, and give the Captain every facility. *He* had taken out no warrant; *he* had been perfectly ready to meet the Captain; if others had been more prudent, it was not his fault. So he held up his head, and cocked his hat with the most determined air; and all the lawyers' clerks in the place were quite proud of their hero.

As for Captain Blackbeard, his rage and indignation may be imagined; a wife robbed from him, his honour put in question by an odious, lanky, squinting lawyer! He fell ill of a fever incontinently; and the surgeon was obliged to take a quantity of blood from him, ten times the amount of which he swore he would have out of the veins of the atrocious Sly.

The announcement in the *Mercury*, however, filled the widow with almost equal indignation. "The widow of the gallant Bluebeard," she said, "marry an odious wretch who lives in dingy chambers in the Middle Temple! Send for Doctor Sly." The Doctor came; she rated him soundly, asked him how he dared set abroad such calumnies concerning her; ordered him to send his nephew back to London at once; and, as he valued her esteem, as he valued the next presentation to a fat living which lay in her gift, to contradict everywhere, and in the fullest terms, the wicked report concerning her.

"My dearest madam," said the Doctor, pulling his longest face, "you shall be obeyed. The poor lad shall be acquainted with the fatal change in your sentiments!"

"Change in my sentiments, Doctor Sly!"

"With the destruction of his hopes, rather let me say; and Heaven grant that the dear boy have strength to bear up against the misfortune which comes so suddenly upon him!"

The next day sister Anne came with a face full of care to Mrs. Bluebeard. "Oh that unhappy lover of yours!" said she.

"Is the Captain unwell?" exclaimed the widow.

"No, it is the other," answered sister Anne. "Poor, poor Mr. Sly! He made a will leaving you all, except five pounds a year to his laundress: he made his will, locked his door, took heart-rending leave of his uncle at night, and this morning was found hanging at his bed-post when Sambo, the black servant, took him up his water to shave. 'Let me be buried,' he said, 'with the pincushion she gave me and the locket containing her hair.' *Did* you give him a pincushion, sister? *did* you give him a locket with your hair?"

"It was only silver-gilt!" sobbed the widow; "and now, oh heavens! I have killed him!" The heart-rending nature of her sobs may be imagined; but they were abruptly interrupted by her sister.

"Killed him?—no such thing! Sambo cut him down when he was as black in the face as the honest negro himself. He came down to breakfast, and I leave you to fancy what a touching meeting took place between the nephew and uncle."

"So much love!" thought the widow. "What a pity he squints so! If he would but get his eyes put straight, I might perhaps——" She did not finish the sentence: ladies often leave this sort of sentence in a sweet confusion.

But hearing some news regarding Captain Blackbeard, whose illness and blood-letting were described to her most pathetically, as well as accurately, by the Scotch surgeon of the regiment, her feelings of compassion towards the lawyer cooled somewhat; and when Doctor Sly called to know if she would condescend to meet the unhappy youth, she said, in rather a *distrait* manner, that she wished him every happiness; that she had the highest regard and respect for him; that she besought him not to think any more of committing the dreadful crime which would have made her unhappy for ever; *but* that she thought, for the sake of both parties, they had better not meet until Mr. Sly's feelings had grown somewhat more calm.

"Poor fellow! poor fellow!" said the Doctor, "may he be enabled to bear his frightful calamity! I have taken away his razors from him, and Sambo, my man, never lets him out of his sight."

The next day Mrs. Bluebeard thought of sending a friendly message to Doctor Sly's, asking for news of the health of his nephew; but, as she was

giving her orders on that subject to John Thomas the footman, it happened
that the Captain arrived, and so Thomas was sent downstairs again. And the
Captain looked so delightfully interesting with his arm in a sling, and his
beautiful black whiskers curling round a face which was paler than usual, that
at the end of two hours the widow forgot the message altogether, and, indeed,
I believe, asked the Captain whether he would not stop and dine. Ensign
Trippet came, too, and the party was very pleasant; and the military gentlemen
laughed hugely at the idea of the lawyer having been cut off the bed-post by
the black servant, and were so witty on the subject, that the widow ended
by half believing that the bed-post and hanging scheme on the part of Mr.
Sly was only a feint—a trick to win her heart. Though this, to be sure, was
not agreed to by the lady without a pang, for *entre nous,* to hang oneself for
a lady is no small compliment to her attractions, and, perhaps, Mrs. Bluebeard
was rather disappointed at the notion that the hanging was not a *bona fide*
strangulation.

However, presently her nerves were excited again; and she was consoled
or horrified, as the case may be (the reader must settle the point according
to his ideas and knowledge of womankind)—she was at any rate dreadfully
excited by the receipt of a billet in the well-known clerk-like hand of Mr.
Sly. It ran thus:—

> "I saw you through your dining-room windows. You were hob-
> nobbing with Captain Blackbeard. You looked rosy and well. You
> smiled. You drank off the champagne at a single draught.
>
> "I can bear it no more. Live on, smile on, and be happy. My
> ghost shall repine, perhaps, at your happiness with another—but in
> life I should go mad were I to witness it.
>
> "It is best that I should be gone.
>
> "When you receive this, tell my uncle to drag the fish-pond at
> the end of Bachelor's Acre. His black servant Sambo accompanies
> me, it is true. But Sambo shall perish with me should his obstinacy
> venture to restrain me from my purpose. I know the poor fellow's
> honesty well, but I also know my own despair.
>
> "Sambo will leave a wife and seven children. Be kind to those
> orphan mulattoes for the sake of
>
> "FREDERICK"

The widow gave a dreadful shriek, and interrupted the two Captains,
who were each just in the act of swallowing a bumper of claret. "Fly—fly—
save him," she screamed; "save him, monsters, ere it is too late! Drowned!—
Frederick!—Bachelor's Wa——" Syncope took place, and the rest of the
sentence was interrupted.

Deucedly disappointed at being obliged to give up their wine, the two heroes seized their cocked-hats, and went towards the spot which the widow in her wild exclamations of despair had sufficiently designated.

Trippet was for running to the fish-pond at the rate of ten miles an hour. "Take it easy, my good fellow," said Captain Blackbeard; "running is unwholesome after dinner. And if that squinting scoundrel of a lawyer *does* drown himself, I shan't sleep any the worse." So the two gentlemen walked very leisurely on towards the Bachelor's Walk; and, indeed, seeing on their way thither Major Macabaw looking out of the window at his quarters and smoking a cigar, they went upstairs to consult the Major, as also a bottle of Schiedam he had.

"They come not!" said the widow, when restored to herself. "Oh, heavens! grant that Frederick is safe! Sister Anne, go up to the leads and look if anybody is coming." And up, accordingly, to the garrets sister Anne mounted. "Do you see anybody coming, sister Anne?"

"I see Doctor Drench's little boy," said sister Anne, "he is leaving a pill and draught at Miss Molly Grub's."

"Dearest sister Anne, don't you see anyone coming?" shouted the widow once again.

"I see a flock of dust,—no! a cloud of sheep. Pshaw! I see the London coach coming in. There are three outsides, and the guard has flung a parcel to Mrs. Jenkins's maid."

"Distraction! Look once more, sister Anne."

"I see a crowd—a shutter—a shutter with a man on it—a beadle—forty little boys—Gracious goodness! what *can* it be?" and downstairs tumbled sister Anne, and was looking out of the parlour-window by her sister's side, when the crowd she had perceived from the garret passed close by them.

At the head walked the beadle, slashing about at the little boys.

Two scores of these followed and surrounded

A SHUTTER carried by four men.

On the shutter lay *Frederick!* He was ghastly pale; his hair was draggled over his face; his clothes stuck tight to him on account of the wet; streams of water gurgled down the shutter sides. But he was not dead! He turned one eye round towards the window where Mrs. Bluebeard sat, and gave her a look which she never could forget.

Sambo brought up the rear of the procession. He was quite wet through; and, if anything would have put his hair out of curl, his ducking would have done so. But, as he was not a gentleman, he was allowed to walk home on foot, and, as he passed the widow's window, he gave her one dreadful glance with his goggling black eyes, and moved on pointing with his hands to the shutter.

John Thomas, the footman, was instantly despatched to Doctor Sly's to have news of the patient. There was no shilly-shallying now. He came back in half-an-hour to say that Mr. Frederick flung himself into Bachelor's Acre fish-pond with Sambo, had been dragged out with difficulty, had been put to bed, and had a pint of white wine whey, and was pretty comfortable. "Thank Heaven!" said the widow, and gave John Thomas a seven-shilling piece, and sat down with a lightened heart to tea. "What a heart!" said she to sister Anne. "And, oh, what a pity it is that he squints!"

Here the two Captains arrived. They had not been to the Bachelor's Walk; they had remained at Major Macabaw's consulting the Schiedam. They had made up their minds what to say. "Hang the fellow! he will never have the pluck to drown himself," said Captain Blackbeard. "Let us argue on that, as we may safely."

"My sweet lady," said he, accordingly, "we have had the pond dragged. No Mr. Sly. And the fisherman who keeps the punt assures us that he has not been there all day."

"Audacious falsehood!" said the widow, her eyes flashing fire. "Go, heartless man! who dares to trifle thus with the feelings of a respectable and unprotected woman. Go, sir, you're only fit for the love of a—Dolly—Coddlins!" She pronounced the *Coddlins* with a withering sarcasm that struck the Captain aghast; and sailing out of the room, she left her tea untasted, and did not wish either of the military gentlemen good-night.

But, gentles, an' ye know the delicate fibre of woman's heart, ye will not in very sooth believe that such events as those we have described—such tempests of passion—fierce winds of woe—blinding lightnings of tremendous joy and tremendous grief—could pass over one frail flower and leave it all unscathed. No! Grief kills as joy doth. Doth not the scorching sun nip the rose-bud as well as the bitter wind? As Mrs. Sigourney sweetly sings—

> *"Ah! the heart is a soft and a delicate thing;*
> *Ah! the heart is a lute with a thrilling string;*
> *A spirit that floats on a gossamer's wing!"*

Such was Fatima's heart. In a word, the preceding events had a powerful effect upon her nervous system, and she was ordered much quiet and sal-volatile by her skilful medical attendant, Doctor Glauber.

To be so ardently, passionately loved as she was, to know that Frederick had twice plunged into death from attachment to her, was to awaken in her bosom "a thrilling string" indeed! Could she witness such attachment, and not be touched by it? She *was* touched by it—she was influenced by the virtues, by the passion, by the misfortunes of Frederick; but then he was so abominably ugly that she could not—she could not consent to become his bride!

She told Doctor Sly so. "I respect and esteem your nephew," said she, "but my resolve is made. I will continue faithful to that blessed saint, whose monument is ever before my eyes" (she pointed to the churchyard as she spoke). "Leave this poor tortured heart in quiet. It has already suffered more than most hearts could bear. I will repose under the shadow of that tomb until I am called to rest within it—to rest by the side of my Bluebeard!"

The ranunculuses, rhododendra, and polyanthuses, which ornamented that mausoleum, had somehow been suffered to run greatly to seed during the last few months, and it was with no slight self-accusation that she acknowledged this fact on visiting the "garden of the grave," as she called it; and she scolded the beadle soundly for neglecting his duty towards it. He promised obedience for the future, dug out all the weeds that were creeping round the family vault, and (having charge of the key) entered that awful place, and swept and dusted the melancholy contents of the tomb.

Next morning the widow came down to breakfast looking very pale. She had passed a bad night; she had had awful dreams; she had heard a voice call her thrice at midnight. "Pooh! my dear; it's only nervousness," said sceptical sister Anne.

Here John Thomas the footman entered, and said the beadle was in the hall, looking in a very strange way. He had been about the house since daybreak, and insisted on seeing Mrs. Bluebeard. "Let him enter," said that lady, prepared for some great mystery. The beadle came; he was pale as death; his hair was dishevelled, and his cocked-hat out of order. "What have you to say?" said the lady trembling.

Before beginning, he fell down on his knees.

"Yesterday," said he, "according to your Ladyship's orders, I dug up the flower-beds of the family vault—dusted the vault and the—the coffins" (added he, trembling) "inside. Me and John Sexton did it together, and polished up the plate quite beautiful."

"For Heaven's sake, don't allude to it," cried the widow, turning pale.

"Well, my Lady, I locked the door, came away, and found in my hurry—for I wanted to beat two little boys what was playing at marbles on Alderman Paunch's monyment—I found, my Lady, I'd forgot my cane. I couldn't get John Sexton to go back with me till this morning, and I didn't like to go alone, and so we went this morning, and what do you think I found? I found his honour's coffin turned round, and the cane broke in two. Here's the cane!"

"Ah!" screamed the widow, "take it away—take it away!"

"Well, what does this prove," said sister Anne, "but that somebody moved the coffin, and broke the cane?"

"Somebody! *who's somebody?*" said the beadle, staring round about him. And all of a sudden he started back with a tremendous roar, that made the ladies scream, and all the glasses on the sideboard jingle, and cried, *"That's the man!"*

He pointed to the portrait of Bluebeard, which stood over the jingling glasses on the sideboard. "That's the man I saw last night walking round the vault, as I'm a living sinner. I saw him a-walking round and round, and, when I went up to speak to him, I'm blessed if he didn't go in at the iron gate, which opened afore him like—like winking, and then in at the vault door, which I'd double-locked, my Lady, and bolted inside, I'll take my oath on it!"

"Perhaps you had given him the key?" suggested sister Anne.

"It's never been out of my pocket. Here it is," cried the beadle, "I'll have no more to do with it," and he flung down the ponderous key, amidst another scream from widow Bluebeard.

"At what hour did you see him?" gasped she.

"At twelve o'clock, of course."

"It must have been at that very hour," said she, "I heard the voice."

"What voice?" said Anne.

"A voice that called 'Fatima! Fatima! Fatima!' three times as plain as ever voice did."

"It didn't speak to me," said the beadle, "it only nodded its head and wagged its head and beard."

"W—w—was it a *bl—ue beard?*" said the widow.

"Powder-blue, ma'am, as I've a soul to save!"

Doctor Drench was of course instantly sent for. But what are the medicaments of the apothecary in a case where the grave gives up its dead? Doctor Sly arrived, and he offered ghostly—ah! too ghostly—consolation. He said he believed in them. His own grandmother had appeared to his grandfather several times before he married again. He could not doubt that supernatural agencies were possible, even frequent.

"Suppose he were to appear to me alone," ejaculated the widow, "I should die of fright."

The Doctor looked particularly arch. "The best way in these cases, my dear madam," said he—"the best way for unprotected ladies is to get a husband. I never heard of a first husband's ghost appearing to a woman and her second husband in my life. In all history there is no account of one."

"Ah! why should I be afraid of seeing my Bluebeard again?" said the widow; and the Doctor retired quite pleased, for the lady was evidently thinking of a second husband.

"The Captain would be a better protector for me certainly than Mr. Sly," thought the lady, with a sigh; "but Mr. Sly will certainly kill himself, and will the Captain be a match for two ghosts? Sly will kill himself; but ah! the Captain won't"; and the widow thought with pangs of bitter mortification of Dolly Coddlins. How, how should these distracting circumstances be brought to an end?

She retired to rest that night not without a tremor—to bed, but not to sleep. At midnight a voice was heard in her room crying "Fatima! Fatima! Fatima!" in awful accents. The doors banged to and fro, the bells began to ring, the maids went up and down stairs skurrying and screaming, and gave warning in a body. John Thomas, as pale as death, declared that he found Bluebeard's yeomanry sword, that hung in the hall, drawn and on the ground; and the sticking-plaster miniature in Mr. Bluebeard's bedroom was found turned topsy-turvy!

"It is some trick," said the obstinate and incredulous sister Anne. "To-night I will come and sleep with you, sister," and the night came, and the sisters retired together.

'Twas a wild night. The wind howling without went crashing through the old trees of the old rookery round about the old church. The long bedroom windows went thump—thumping; the moon could be seen through them lighting up the graves with their ghastly shadows; the yew-tree, cut into the shape of a bird, looked particularly dreadful, and bent and swayed as if it would peck something off that other yew-tree which was of the shape of a dumb-waiter. The bells at midnight began to ring as usual, the doors clapped; jingle—jingle down came a suit of armour in the hall, and a voice came and cried, "Fatima! Fatima! Fatima! look, look, look; the tomb, the tomb, the tomb!"

She looked. The vault door was open; and there in the moonlight stood Bluebeard, exactly as he was represented in the picture in his yeomanry dress, his face frightfully pale and his great blue beard curling over his chest, as awful as Mr. Muntz's.

Sister Anne saw the vision as well as Fatima. We shall spare the account of their terrors and screams. Strange to say, John Thomas, who slept in the attic above his mistress's bedroom, declared he was on the watch all night and had seen nothing in the churchyard, and heard no sort of voices in the house.

And now the question came, What could the ghost want by appearing? "Is there anything," exclaimed the unhappy and perplexed Fatima, "that he would have me do? It is well to say 'now, now, now,' and to show himself; but what is it that makes my blessed husband so uneasy in his grave?" And all parties consulted agreed that it was a very sensible question.

John Thomas, the footman, whose excessive terror at the appearance of the ghost had procured him his mistress's confidence, advised Mr. Screw, the butler, who communicated with Mrs. Baggs, the housekeeper, who conde-scended to impart her observations to Mrs. Bustle, the lady's-maid—John Thomas, I say, decidedly advised that my Lady should consult a cunning man. There was such a man in town; he had prophesied who should marry his (John Thomas's) cousin; he had cured Farmer Horn's cattle, which were evidently bewitched; he could raise ghosts, and make them speak, and he therefore was the very person to be consulted in the present juncture.

"What nonsense is this you have been talking to the maids, John Thomas, about the conjurer who lives in—in——"

"In Hangman's Lane, ma'am, where the old gibbet used to stand," replied John, who was bringing in the muffins. "It's no nonsense, my Lady. Every word as that man says comes true, and he knows everything."

"I desire you will not frighten the girls in the servants' hall with any of those silly stories," said the widow; and the meaning of this speech may, of course, at once be guessed. It was that the widow meant to consult the conjurer that very night. Sister Anne said that she would never, under such circumstances, desert her dear Fatima. John Thomas was summoned to attend the ladies with a dark lantern, and forth they set on their perilous visit to the conjurer at his dreadful abode in Hangman's Lane.

What took place at that frightful interview has never been entirely known. But there was no disturbance in the house on the night after. The bells slept quietly, the doors did not bang in the least, twelve o'clock struck and no ghost appeared in the churchyard, and the whole family had a quiet night. The widow attributed this to a sprig of rosemary which the wizard gave her, and a horseshoe which she flung into the garden round the family vault, and which would keep *any* ghost quiet.

It happened the next day that, going to her milliner's, sister Anne met a gentleman who has been before mentioned in this story, Ensign Trippet by name; and, indeed, if the truth must be known, it somehow happened that she met the Ensign somewhere every day of the week.

"What news of the ghost, my dearest Miss Shacabac?" said he (you may guess on what terms the two young people were by the manner in which Mr. Trippet addressed the lady); "has Bluebeard's ghost frightened your sister into any more fits, or set the bells a-ringing?"

Sister Anne, with a very grave air, told him that he must not joke on so awful a subject; that the ghost had been laid for awhile; that a cunning man had told her sister things so wonderful that *any* man must believe in them; that, among other things, he had shown to Fatima her future husband.

"Had," said the Ensign, "he black whiskers and a red coat?"

"No," answered Anne, with a sigh, "he had red whiskers and a black coat."

"It can't be that rascal Sly!" cried the Ensign. But Anne only sighed more deeply, and would not answer yes or no. "You may tell the poor Captain," she said, "there is no hope for him, and all he has left is to hang himself."

"He shall cut the throat of Sly first, though," replied Mr. Trippet, fiercely. But Anne said things were not decided as yet. Fatima was exceedingly restive and unwilling to acquiesce in the idea of being married to Mr. Sly; she had asked for further authority. The wizard said he could bring her own husband from the grave to point out her second bridegroom, who shall be, can be, must be, no other than Frederick Sly.

"It's a trick," said the Ensign. But Anne was too much frightened by the preceding evening's occurrences to say so. "To-night," she said, "the grave will tell all." And she left Ensign Trippet in a very solemn and affecting way.

At midnight three figures were seen to issue from widow Bluebeard's house and pass through the churchyard turnstile and so away among the graves.

"To call up a ghost is bad enough," said the wizard; "to make him speak is awful. I recommend you, ma'am, to beware, for such curiosity has been fatal to many. There was one Arabian necromancer of my acquaintance who tried to make a ghost speak, and was torn in pieces on the spot. There was another person who *did* hear a ghost speak certainly, but came away from the interview deaf and dumb. There was another——"

"Never mind," says Mrs. Bluebeard, all her old curiosity aroused, "see him and hear him I will. Haven't I seen him and heard him, too, already? When he's audible *and* visible, *then's* the time."

"But when you heard him," said the necromancer, "he was invisible, and when you saw him he was inaudible; so make up your mind what you will ask him, for ghosts will stand no shilly-shallying. I knew a stuttering man who was flung down by a ghost, and——"

"I *have* made up my mind," said Fatima, interrupting him.

"To ask him what husband you shall take," whispered Anne.

Fatima only turned red, and sister Anne squeezed her hand; they passed into the graveyard in silence.

There was no moon; the night was pitch-dark. They threaded their way through the graves, stumbling over them here and there. An owl was too-whooing from the church tower, a dog was howling somewhere, a cock began to crow, as they will sometimes at twelve o'clock at night.

"Make haste," said the wizard. "Decide whether you will go on or not."

"Let us go back, sister," said Anne.

"I *will* go on," said Fatima. "I should die if I gave it up; I feel I should."

"Here's the gate; kneel down," said the wizard. The women knelt down. "Will you see your first husband or your second husband?"

"I will see Bluebeard first," said the widow. "I shall know then whether this be a mockery, or you have the power you pretend to."

At this the wizard uttered an incantation, so frightful and of such incomprehensible words, that it is impossible for any mortal to repeat them.

And at the end of what seemed to be a versicle of his chant he called "Bluebeard!" There was no noise but the moaning of the wind in the trees, and toowhooing of the owl in the tower.

At the end of the second verse he paused again and called "Bluebeard!" The cock began to crow, the dog began to howl, a watchman in the town began to cry out the hour, and there came from the vault within a hollow groan, and a dreadful voice said, "Who wants me?"

Kneeling in front of the tomb, the necromancer began the third verse: as he spoke, the former phenomena were still to be remarked. As he continued, a number of ghosts rose from their graves and advanced round the kneeling figures in a circle. As he concluded, with a loud bang the door of the vault flew open, and there in blue light stood Bluebeard in his blue uniform, waving his blue sword and flashing his blue eyes round about!

"Speak now, or you are lost," said the necromancer to Fatima. But, for the first time in her life, she had not a word to say. Sister Anne, too, was dumb with terror. And, as the awful figure advanced towards them as they were kneeling, the sister thought all was over with them, and Fatima once more had occasion to repent her fatal curiosity.

The figure advanced, saying, in dreadful accents, "Fatima! Fatima! Fatima! wherefore am I called from my grave?" when all of a sudden down dropped his sword, down the ghost of Bluebeard went on his knees, and, clasping his hands together, roared out, "Mercy, mercy!" as loud as man could roar.

Six other ghosts stood round the kneeling group. "Why do you call me from the tomb?" said the first; "Who dares disturb my grave?" said the second; "Seize him and away with him!" cried the third. "Murder, mercy!" still roared the ghost of Bluebeard, as the white-robed spirits advanced and caught hold of him.

"It's only Tom Trippet," said a voice at Anne's ear.

"And your very humble servant," said a voice well known to Mrs. Bluebeard; and they helped the ladies to rise, while the other ghosts seized Bluebeard. The necromancer took to his heels and got off; he was found to be no other than Mr. Claptrap, the manager of the theatre.

It was some time before the ghost of Bluebeard could recover from the fainting fit into which he had been plunged when seized by the opposition ghosts in white; and while they were ducking him at the pump, his blue beard came off, and he was discovered to be—who do you think? Why Mr. Sly, to be sure; and it appears that John Thomas, the footman, had lent him the uniform, and had clapped the doors, and rung the bells, and spoken down the chimney; and it was Mr. Claptrap who gave Mr. Sly the blue fire and the theatre gong, and he went to London next morning by the coach; and, as it was discovered that the story concerning Miss Coddlins was a shameful calumny, why, of course, the widow married Captain Blackbeard. Doctor Sly married them, and has always declared that he knew nothing of his nephew's doings, and wondered that he has not tried to commit suicide since his last disappointment.

Mr. and Mrs. Trippet are likewise living happily together, and this, I am given to understand, is the ultimate fate of a family in whom we were all very much interested in early life.

You will say that the story is not probable. Psha! Isn't it written in a book? and is it a whit less probable than the first part of the tale?

‹ *Feathertop* ›

NATHANIEL HAWTHORNE

ickon," cried Mother Rigby, "a coal for my pipe!"

The pipe was in the old dame's mouth when she said these words. She had thrust it there after filling it with tobacco, but without stooping to light it at the hearth, where indeed there was no appearance of a fire having been kindled that morning. Forthwith, however, as soon as the order was given, there was an intense red glow out of the bowl of the pipe, and a whiff of smoke from Mother Rigby's lips. Whence the coal came, and how brought thither by an invisible hand, I have never been able to discover.

"Good!" quoth Mother Rigby, with a nod of her head. "Thank ye, Dickon! And now for making this scarecrow. Be within call, Dickon, in case I need you again."

The good woman had risen thus early (for as yet it was scarcely sunrise) in order to set about making a scarecrow, which she intended to put in the middle of her corn-patch. It was now the latter week of May, and the crows and blackbirds had already discovered the little, green, rolled-up leaf of the Indian corn just peeping out of the soil. She was determined, therefore, to contrive as lifelike a scarecrow as ever was seen, and to finish it immediately, from top to toe, so that it should begin its sentinel's duty that very morning. Now Mother Rigby (as everybody must have heard) was one of the most cunning and potent witches in New England, and might, with very little trouble, have made a scarecrow ugly enough to frighten the minister himself. But on this occasion, as she had awakened in an uncommonly pleasant humor, and was further dulcified by her pipe of tobacco, she resolved to produce something fine, beautiful, and splendid, rather than hideous and horrible.

"I don't want to set up a hobgoblin in my own corn-patch, and almost at my own doorstep," said Mother Rigby to herself, puffing out a whiff of smoke; "I could do it if I pleased, but I'm tired of doing marvellous things, and so I'll keep within the bounds of every-day business just for variety's sake. Besides, there is no use in scaring the little children for a mile roundabout, though 't is true I'm a witch."

It was settled, therefore, in her own mind, that the scarecrow should represent a fine gentleman of the period, so far as the materials at hand would allow. Perhaps it may be as well to enumerate the chief of the articles that went to the composition of this figure.

The most important item of all, probably, although it made so little show, was a certain broomstick, on which Mother Rigby had taken many an airy gallop at midnight, and which now served the scarecrow by way of a spinal column, or, as the unlearned phrase it, a backbone. One of its arms was a disabled flail which used to be wielded by Goodman Rigby, before his spouse worried him out of this troublesome world; the other, if I mistake not, was composed of the pudding stick and a broken rung of a chair, tied loosely together at the elbow. As for its legs, the right was a hoe handle, and the left an undistinguished and miscellaneous stick from the woodpile. Its lungs, stomach, and other affairs of that kind were nothing better than a meal bag stuffed with straw. Thus we have made out the skeleton and entire corporosity of the scarecrow, with the exception of its head; and this was admirably supplied by a somewhat withered and shrivelled pumpkin, in which Mother Rigby cut two holes for the eyes, and a slit for the mouth, leaving a bluish-colored knob in the middle to pass for a nose. It was really quite a respectable face.

"I've seen worse ones on human shoulders, at any rate," said Mother Rigby. "And many a fine gentleman has a pumpkin head, as well as my scarecrow."

But the clothes, in this case, were to be the making of the man. So the good old woman took down from a peg an ancient plum-colored coat of London make, and with relics of embroidery on its seams, cuffs, pocket-flaps, and button-holes, but lamentably worn and faded, patched at the elbows, tattered at the skirts, and threadbare all over. On the left breast was a round hole, whence either a star of nobility had been rent away, or else the hot heart of some former wearer had scorched it through and through. The neighbors said that this rich garment belonged to the Black Man's wardrobe, and that he kept it at Mother Rigby's cottage for the convenience of slipping it on whenever he wished to make a grand appearance at the governor's table. To match the coat there was a velvet waistcoat of very ample size, and formerly embroidered with foliage that had been as brightly golden as the maple leaves in October, but which had now quite vanished out of the substance of the velvet. Next came a pair of scarlet breeches, once worn by the French governor of Louisbourg, and the knees of which had touched the lower step of the throne of Louis le Grand. The Frenchman had given these smallclothes to an Indian powwow, who parted with them to the old witch for a gill of strong waters, at one of their dances in the forest. Furthermore, Mother Rigby produced a pair of silk stockings and put them on the figure's legs, where they showed as unsubstantial as a dream, with the wooden reality of the two sticks making itself miserably apparent through the holes. Lastly, she put her dead husband's wig on the bare scalp of the pumpkin, and surmounted the whole with a dusty three-cornered hat, in which was stuck the longest tail feather of a rooster.

Then the old dame stood the figure up in a corner of her cottage and chuckled to behold its yellow semblance of a visage, with its nobby little nose thrust into the air. It had a strangely self-satisfied aspect, and seemed to say, "Come look at me!"

"And you are well worth looking at, that's a fact!" quoth Mother Rigby, in admiration at her own handiwork. "I've made many a puppet since I've been a witch, but methinks this is the finest of them all. 'T is almost too good for a scarecrow. And, by the by, I'll just fill a fresh pipe of tobacco and then take him out to the corn-patch."

While filling her pipe the old woman continued to gaze with almost motherly affection at the figure in the corner. To say the truth, whether it were chance, or skill, or downright witchcraft, there was something wonderfully human in this ridiculous shape, bedizened with its tattered finery; and as for the countenance, it appeared to shrivel its yellow surface into a grin—a funny kind of expression betwixt scorn and merriment, as if it understood itself to be a jest at mankind. The more Mother Rigby looked the better she was pleased.

"Dickon," cried she sharply, "another coal for my pipe!"

Hardly had she spoken, than, just as before, there was a red-glowing coal on the top of the tobacco. She drew in a long whiff and puffed it forth again into the bar of morning sunshine which struggled through the one dusty pane of her cottage window. Mother Rigby always liked to flavor her pipe with a coal of fire from the particular chimney corner whence this had been brought. But where that chimney corner might be, or who brought the coal from it—further than that the invisible messenger seemed to respond to the name of Dickon—I cannot tell.

"That puppet yonder," thought Mother Rigby, still with her eyes fixed on the scarecrow, "is too good a piece of work to stand all summer in a corn-patch, frightening away the crows and blackbirds. He's capable of better things. Why, I've danced with a worse one, when partners happened to be scarce, at our witch meetings in the forest! What if I should let him take his chance among the other men of straw and empty fellows who go bustling about the world?"

The old witch took three or four more whiffs of her pipe and smiled.

"He'll meet plenty of his brethren at every street corner!" continued she. "Well; I didn't mean to dabble in witchcraft to-day, further than the lighting of my pipe, but a witch I am, and a witch I'm likely to be, and there's no use trying to shirk it. I'll make a man of my scarecrow, were it only for the joke's sake!"

While muttering these words, Mother Rigby took the pipe from her own mouth and thrust it into the crevice which represented the same feature in the pumpkin visage of the scarecrow.

"Puff, darling, puff!" said she. "Puff away, my fine fellow! your life depends on it!"

This was a strange exhortation, undoubtedly, to be addressed to a mere thing of sticks, straw, and old clothes, with nothing better than a shrivelled pumpkin for a head—as we know to have been the scarecrow's case. Never-theless, as we must carefully hold in remembrance, Mother Rigby was a witch of singular power and dexterity; and, keeping this fact duly before our minds, we shall see nothing beyond credibility in the remarkable incidents of our story. Indeed, the great difficulty will be at once got over, if we can only bring ourselves to believe that, as soon as the old dame bade him puff, there came a whiff of smoke from the scarecrow's mouth. It was the very feeblest of whiffs, to be sure; but it was followed by another and another, each more decided than the preceding one.

"Puff away, my pet! puff away, my pretty one!" Mother Rigby kept repeating, with her pleasantest smile. "It is the breath of life to ye; and that you may take my word for."

Beyond all question the pipe was bewitched. There must have been a spell either in the tobacco or in the fiercely-glowing coal that so mysteriously burned on top of it, or in the pungently-aromatic smoke which exhaled from the kindled weed. The figure, after a few doubtful attempts, at length blew forth a volley of smoke extending all the way from the obscure corner into the bar of sunshine. There it eddied and melted away among the motes of dust. It seemed a convulsive effort; for the two or three next whiffs were fainter, although the coal still glowed and threw a gleam over the scarecrow's visage. The old witch clapped her skinny hands together, and smiled en-couragingly upon her handiwork. She saw that the charm worked well. The shrivelled, yellow face, which heretofore had been no face at all, had already a thin, fantastic haze, as it were of human likeness, shifting to and fro across it; sometimes vanishing entirely, but growing more perceptible than ever with the next whiff from the pipe. The whole figure, in like manner, assumed a show of life, such as we impart to ill-defined shapes among the clouds, and half deceive ourselves with the pastime of our own fancy.

If we must needs pry closely into the matter, it may be doubted whether there was any real change, after all, in the sordid, worn-out, worthless, and ill-jointed substance of the scarecrow; but merely a spectral illusion, and a cunning effect of light and shade so colored and contrived as to delude the eyes of most men. The miracles of witchcraft seem always to have had a very shallow subtlety; and, at least, if the above explanation does not hit the truth of the process, I can suggest no better.

"Well puffed, my pretty lad!" still cried old Mother Rigby. "Come, another good stout whiff, and let it be with might and main. Puff for thy life, I tell thee! Puff out of the very bottom of thy heart, if any heart thou hast, or any bottom to it! Well done, again! Thou didst suck in that mouthful as if for the pure love of it."

And then the witch beckoned to the scarecrow, throwing so much magnetic potency into her gesture that it seemed as if it must inevitably be obeyed, like the mystic call of the loadstone when it summons the iron.

"Why lurkest thou in the corner, lazy one?" said she. "Step forth! Thou hast the world before thee!"

Upon my word, if the legend were not one which I heard on my grandmother's knee, and which had established its place among things credible before my childish judgment could analyze its probability, I question whether I should have the face to tell it now.

In obedience to Mother Rigby's word, and extending its arm as if to reach her outstretched hand, the figure made a step forward—a kind of hitch and jerk, however, rather than a step—then tottered and almost lost its balance. What could the witch expect? It was nothing, after all, but a scarecrow stuck upon two sticks. But the strong-willed old beldam scowled, and beckoned, and flung the energy of her purpose so forcibly at this poor combination of rotten wood, and musty straw, and ragged garments, that it was compelled to show itself a man, in spite of the reality of things. So it stepped into the bar of sunshine. There it stood—poor devil of a contrivance that it was!—with only the thinnest vesture of human similitude about it, through which was evident the stiff, rickety, incongruous, faded, tattered, good-for-nothing patchwork of its substance, ready to sink in a heap upon the floor, as conscious of its own unworthiness to be erect. Shall I confess the truth? At its present point of vivification, the scarecrow reminds me of some of the lukewarm and abortive characters, composed of heterogeneous materials, used for the thousandth time, and never worth using, with which romance writers (and myself, no doubt, among the rest) have so over-peopled the world of fiction.

But the fierce old hag began to get angry and show a glimpse of her diabolic nature (like a snake's head, peeping with a hiss out of her bosom), at this pusillanimous behavior of the thing which she had taken the trouble to put together.

"Puff away, wretch!" cried she, wrathfully. "Puff, puff, puff, thou thing of straw and emptiness! thou rag or two! thou meal bag! thou pumpkin head! thou nothing! Where shall I find a name vile enough to call thee by? Puff, I say, and suck in thy fantastic life along with the smoke! else I snatch the pipe from thy mouth and hurl thee where that red coal came from."

Thus threatened, the unhappy scarecrow had nothing for it but to puff away for dear life. As need was, therefore, it applied itself lustily to the pipe, and sent forth such abundant volleys of tobacco smoke that the small cottage kitchen became all vaporous. The one sunbeam struggled mistily through, and could but imperfectly define the image of the cracked and dusty window pane on the opposite wall. Mother Rigby, meanwhile, with one brown arm akimbo and the other stretched towards the figure, loomed grimly amid the obscurity with such port and expression as when she was wont to heave a ponderous nightmare on her victims and stand at the bedside to enjoy their agony. In fear and trembling did this poor scarecrow puff. But its efforts it must be acknowledged, served an excellent purpose for, with each successive whiff, the figure lost more and more of its dizzy and perplexing tenuity and seemed to take denser substance. Its very garments, moreover, partook of the magical change, and shone with the gloss of novelty and glistened with the skilfully embroidered gold that had long ago been rent away. And, half revealed among the smoke, a yellow visage bent its lustreless eyes on Mother Rigby.

At last the old witch clinched her fist and shook it at the figure. Not that she was positively angry, but merely acting on the principle—perhaps untrue, or not the only truth, though as high a one as Mother Rigby could be expected to attain—that feeble and torpid natures, being incapable of better inspiration, must be stirred up by fear. But here was the crisis. Should she fail in what she now sought to effect, it was her ruthless purpose to scatter the miserable simulacre into its original elements.

"Thou hast a man's aspect," said she, sternly. "Have also the echo and mockery of a voice! I bid thee speak!"

The scarecrow gasped, struggled, and at length emitted a murmur, which was so incorporated with its smoky breath that you could scarcely tell whether it were indeed a voice or only a whiff of tobacco. Some narrators of this legend hold the opinion that Mother Rigby's conjurations and the fierceness of her will had compelled a familiar spirit into the figure, and that the voice was his.

"Mother," mumbled the poor stifled voice, "be not so awful with me! I would fain speak; but being without wits, what can I say?"

"Thou canst speak, darling, canst thou?" cried Mother Rigby, relaxing her grim countenance into a smile. "And what shalt thou say, quotha! Say, indeed! Art thou of the brotherhood of the empty skull, and demandest of me what thou shalt say? Thou shalt say a thousand things, and saying them a thousand times over, thou shalt still have said nothing! Be not afraid, I tell thee! When thou comest into the world (whither I purpose sending thee forthwith) thou shalt not lack the wherewithal to talk. Talk! Why, thou shalt babble like a millstream, if thou wilt. Thou hast brains enough for that, I trow!"

"At your service, mother," responded the figure.

"And that was well said, my pretty one," answered Mother Rigby. "Then thou speakest like thyself, and meant nothing. Thou shalt have a hundred such set phrases, and five hundred to the boot of them. And now, darling, I have taken so much pains with thee and thou art so beautiful, that, by my troth, I love thee better than any witch's puppet in the world; and I've made them of all sorts—clay, wax, straw, sticks, night fog, morning mist, sea foam, and chimney smoke. But thou art the very best. So give heed to what I say."

"Yes, kind mother," said the figure, "with all my heart!"

"With all thy heart!" cried the old witch, setting her hands to her sides and laughing loudly. "Thou hast such a pretty way of speaking. With all thy heart! And thou didst put thy hand to the left side of thy waistcoat as if thou really hadst one!"

So now, in high good humor with this fantastic contrivance of hers, Mother Rigby told the scarecrow that it must go and play its part in the great world, where not one man in a hundred, she affirmed, was gifted with more real substance than itself. And, that he might hold up his head with the best of them, she endowed him, on the spot, with an unreckonable amount of wealth. It consisted partly of a gold mine in Eldorado, and of ten thousand shares in a broken bubble, and of half a million acres of vineyard at the North Pole, and of a castle in the air, and a chateau in Spain, together with all the rents and income therefrom accruing. She further made over to him the cargo of a certain ship, laden with salt of Cadiz, which she herself, by her necromantic arts, had caused to founder, ten years before, in the deepest part of midocean. If the salt were not dissolved, and could be brought to market, it would fetch a pretty penny among the fishermen. That he might not lack ready money, she gave him a copper farthing of Birmingham manufacture, being all the coin she had about her, and likewise a great deal of brass, which she applied to his forehead, thus making it yellower than ever.

"With that brass alone," quoth Mother Rigby, "thou canst pay thy way all over the earth. Kiss me, pretty darling! I have done my best for thee."

Furthermore, that the adventurer might lack no possible advantage towards a fair start in life, this excellent old dame gave him a token by which he was to introduce himself to a certain magistrate, member of the council, merchant, and elder of the church (the four capacities constituting but one man), who stood at the head of society in the neighboring metropolis. The token was neither more nor less than a single word, which Mother Rigby whispered to the scarecrow, and which the scarecrow was to whisper to the merchant.

"Gouty as the old fellow is, he'll run thy errands for thee, when once thou hast given him that word in his ear," said the old witch. "Mother Rigby knows the worshipful Justice Gookin, and the worshipful Justice knows Mother Rigby!"

Here the witch thrust her wrinkled face close to the puppet's, chuckling irrepressibly, and fidgeting all through her system, with delight at the idea which she meant to communicate.

"The worshipful Master Gookin," whispered she, "hath a comely maiden to his daughter. And hark ye, my pet! Thou hast a fair outside, and a pretty wit enough of thine own. Yea, a pretty wit enough! Thou wilt think better of it when thou hast seen more of other people's wits. Now, with thy outside and thy inside, thou art the very man to win a young girl's heart. Never doubt it! I tell thee it shall be so. Put but a bold face on the matter, sigh, smile, flourish thy hat, thrust forth thy leg like a dancing-master, put thy right hand to the left side of thy waistcoat, and pretty Polly Gookin is thine own!"

All this while the new creature had been sucking in and exhaling the vapory fragrance of his pipe, and seemed now to continue this occupation as much for the enjoyment it afforded as because it was an essential condition of his existence. It was wonderful to see how exceedingly like a human being it behaved. Its eyes (for it appeared to possess a pair) were bent on Mother Rigby, and at suitable junctures it nodded or shook its head. Neither did it lack words proper for the occasion: "Really! Indeed! Pray tell me! Is it possible! Upon my word! By no means! Oh! Ah! Hem!" and other such weighty utterances as imply attention, inquiry, acquiescence, or dissent on the part of the auditor. Even had you stood by and seen the scarecrow made, you could scarcely have resisted the conviction that it perfectly understood the cunning counsels which the old witch poured into its counterfeit of an ear. The more earnestly it applied its lips to the pipe, the more distinctly was its human likeness stamped among visible realities, the more sagacious grew its expression, the more lifelike its gestures and movements, and the more intelligibly audible its voice. Its garments, too, glistened so much the brighter with an illusory magnificence. The very pipe, in which burned the spell of all this wonderwork, ceased to appear as a smoke-blackened earthen stump, and became a meerschaum, with painted bowl and amber mouthpiece.

It might be apprehended, however, that as the life of the illusion seemed identical with the vapor of the pipe, it would terminate simultaneously with the reduction of the tobacco to ashes. But the beldam foresaw the difficulty.

"Hold thou the pipe, my precious one," said she, "while I fill it for thee again."

It was sorrowful to behold how the fine gentleman began to fade back into a scarecrow while Mother Rigby shook the ashes out of the pipe and proceeded to replenish it from her tobacco-box.

"Dickon," cried she, in her high, sharp tone, "another coal for this pipe!"

No sooner said than the intensely red speck of fire was glowing within the pipe-bowl; and the scarecrow, without waiting for the witch's bidding, applied the tube to his lips and drew in a few short, convulsive whiffs, which soon, however, became regular and equable.

"Now, mine own heart's darling," quoth Mother Rigby, "whatever may happen to thee, thou must stick to thy pipe. Thy life is in it; and that, at least, thou knowest well, if thou knowest nought besides. Stick to thy pipe, I say! Smoke, puff, blow thy cloud; and tell the people, if any question be made, that it is for thy health, and that so the physician orders thee to do. And, sweet one, when thou shalt find thy pipe getting low, go apart into some corner, and (first filling thyself with smoke) cry sharply, 'Dickon, a fresh pipe of tobacco!' and, 'Dickon, another coal for my pipe!' and have it into thy pretty mouth as speedily as may be. Else, instead of a gallant gentleman in a gold-laced coat, thou wilt be but a jumble of sticks and tattered clothes, and a bag of straw, and a withered pumpkin! Now depart, my treasure, and good luck go with thee!"

"Never fear, mother!" said the figure, in a stout voice, and sending forth a courageous whiff of smoke, "I will thrive, if an honest man and a gentleman may!"

"Oh, thou wilt be the death of me!" cried the old witch, convulsed with laughter. "That was well said. If an honest man and a gentleman may! Thou playest thy part to perfection. Get along with thee for a smart fellow; and I will wager on thy head, as a man of pith and substance, with a brain and what they call a heart, and all else that a man should have, against any other thing on two legs. I hold myself a better witch than yesterday, for thy sake. Did not I make thee? And I defy any witch in New England to make such another! Here; take my staff along with thee!"

The staff, though it was but a plain oaken stick, immediately took the aspect of a gold-headed cane.

"That gold head has as much sense in it as thine own," said Mother

Rigby, "and it will guide thee straight to worshipful Master Gookin's door. Get thee gone, my pretty pet, my darling, my precious one, my treasure; and if any ask thy name, it is Feathertop. For thou hast a feather in thy hat, and I have thrust a handful of feathers into the hollow of thy head, and thy wig, too, is of the fashion they call Feathertop—so be Feathertop thy name!"

And, issuing from the cottage, Feathertop strode manfully towards town. Mother Rigby stood at the threshold, well pleased to see how the sunbeams glistened on him, as if all his magnificence were real, and how diligently and lovingly he smoked his pipe, and how handsomely he walked, in spite of a little stiffness of his legs. She watched him until out of sight, and threw a witch benediction after her darling, when a turn of the road snatched him from her view.

Betimes in the forenoon, when the principal street of the neighboring town was just at its acme of life and bustle, a stranger of very distinguished figure was seen on the sidewalk. His port as well as his garments betokened nothing short of nobility. He wore a richly-embroidered plum-colored coat, a waistcoat of costly velvet, magnificently adorned with golden foliage, a pair of splendid scarlet breeches, and the finest and glossiest of white silk stockings. His head was covered with a peruke, so daintily powdered and adjusted that it would have been sacrilege to disorder it with a hat; which, therefore (and it was a gold-laced hat, set off with a snowy feather), he carried beneath his arm. On the breast of his coat glistened a star. He managed his gold-headed cane with an airy grace, peculiar to the fine gentlemen of the period; and, to give the highest possible finish to his equipment, he had lace ruffles at his wrist, of a most ethereal delicacy, sufficiently avouching how idle and aristocratic must be the hands which they half concealed.

It was a remarkable point in the accoutrement of this brilliant personage that he held in his left hand a fantastic kind of a pipe, with an exquisitely painted bowl and an amber mouthpiece. This he applied to his lips as often as every five or six paces, and inhaled a deep whiff of smoke, which, after being retained a moment in his lungs, might be seen to eddy gracefully from his mouth and nostrils.

As may well be supposed, the street was all astir to find out the stranger's name.

"It is some great nobleman, beyond question," said one of the townspeople. "Do you see the star at his breast?"

"Nay; it is too bright to be seen," said another. "Yes; he must needs be a nobleman, as you say. But by what conveyance, think you, can his lordship have voyaged or travelled hither? There has been no vessel from the old country for a month past; and if he have arrived overland from the southward, pray where are his attendants and equipage?"

"He needs no equipage to set off his rank," remarked a third. "If he came among us in rags, nobility would shine through a hole in his elbow. I never saw such dignity of aspect. He has the old Norman blood in his veins, I warrant him."

"I rather take him to be a Dutchman, or one of your high Germans," said another citizen. "The men of those countries have always the pipe at their mouths."

"And so has a Turk," answered his companion. "But, in my judgment, this stranger hath been bred at the French court, and hath there learned politeness and grace of manner, which none understand so well as the nobility of France. That gait, now! A vulgar spectator might deem it stiff—he might call it a hitch and jerk—but, to my eye, it hath an unspeakable majesty, and must have been acquired by constant observation of the deportment of the Grand Monarque. The stranger's character and office are evident enough. He is a French ambassador, come to treat with our rulers about the cession of Canada."

"More probably a Spaniard," said another, "and hence his yellow complexion; or, most likely, he is from the Havana, or from some port on the Spanish main, and comes to make investigation about the piracies which our government is thought to connive at. Those settlers in Peru and Mexico have skins as yellow as the gold which they dig out of their mines."

"Yellow or not," cried a lady, "he is a beautiful man!—so tall, so slender! such a fine, noble face, with so well-shaped a nose, and all that delicacy of expression about the mouth! And, bless me, how bright his star is! It positively shoots out flames!"

"So do your eyes, fair lady," said the stranger, with a bow and a flourish of his pipe; for he was just passing at the instant. "Upon my honor, they have quite dazzled me."

"Was ever so original and exquisite a compliment?" murmured the lady, in an ecstasy of delight.

Amid the general admiration excited by the stranger's appearance, there were only two dissenting voices. One was that of an impertinent cur, which, after snuffing at the heels of the glistening figure, put its tail between its legs and skulked into its master's back yard, vociferating an execrable howl. The other dissentient was a young child, who squalled at the fullest stretch of his lungs, and babbled some unintelligible nonsense about a pumpkin.

Feathertop meanwhile pursued his way along the street. Except for the few complimentary words to the lady, and now and then a slight inclination of the head in requital of the profound reverences of the bystanders, he seemed wholly absorbed in his pipe. There needed no other proof of his rank and consequence than the perfect equanimity with which he comported himself, while the curiosity and admiration of the town swelled almost into clamor around him. With a crowd gathering behind his footsteps, he finally reached the mansion-house of the worshipful Justice Gookin, entered the gate, ascended the steps of the front door, and knocked. In the interim, before his summons was answered, the stranger was observed to shake the ashes out of his pipe.

"What did he say in that sharp voice?" inquired one of the spectators.

"Nay, I know not," answered his friend. "But the sun dazzles my eyes strangely. How dim and faded his lordship looks all of a sudden! Bless my wits, what is the matter with me?"

"The wonder is," said the other, "that his pipe, which was out only an instant ago, should be all alight again, and with the reddest coal I ever saw. There is something mysterious about this stranger. What a whiff of smoke was that! Dim and faded did you call him? Why, as he turns about the star on his breast is all ablaze."

"It is, indeed," said his companion; "and it will go near to dazzle pretty Polly Gookin, whom I see peeping at it out of the chamber window."

The door being now opened, Feathertop turned to the crowd, made a stately bend of his body like a great man acknowledging the reverence of the meaner sort, and vanished into the house. There was a mysterious kind of a smile, if it might not better be called a grin or grimace, upon his visage; but, of all the throng that beheld him, not an individual appears to have possessed insight enough to detect the illusive character of the stranger except a little child and a cur dog.

Our legend here loses somewhat of its continuity, and, passing over the preliminary explanation between Feathertop and the merchant, goes in quest of the pretty Polly Gookin. She was a damsel of a soft, round figure, with light hair and blue eyes, and a fair, rosy face, which seemed neither very shrewd nor very simple. This young lady had caught a glimpse of the glistening stranger while standing at the threshold, and had forthwith put on a laced cap, a string of beads, her finest kerchief, and her stiffest damask petticoat in preparation for the interview. Hurrying from her chamber to the parlor, she had ever since been viewing herself in the large looking-glass and practising pretty airs—now a smile, now a ceremonious dignity of aspect, and now a softer smile than the former, kissing her hand likewise, tossing her head, and managing her fan; while within the mirror an unsubstantial little maid repeated every gesture and did all the foolish things that Polly did, but without making her ashamed of them. In short, it was the fault of pretty Polly's ability rather than her will if she failed to be as complete an artifice as the illustrious Feathertop himself; and, when she thus tampered with her own simplicity, the witch's phantom might well hope to win her.

No sooner did Polly hear her father's gouty footsteps approaching the parlor door, accompanied with the stiff clatter of Feathertop's high-heeled shoes, than she seated herself bolt upright and innocently began warbling a song.

"Polly! daughter Polly!" cried the old merchant. "Come hither, child."

Master Gookin's aspect, as he opened the door, was doubtful and troubled.

"This gentleman," continued he, presenting the stranger, "is the Chevalier Feathertop—nay, I beg his pardon, my Lord Feathertop—who hath brought me a token of remembrance from an ancient friend of mine. Pay your duty to his lordship, child, and honor him as his quality deserves."

After these few words of introduction, the worshipful magistrate immediately quitted the room. But, even in that brief moment, had the fair Polly glanced aside at her father instead of devoting herself wholly to the brilliant guest, she might have taken warning of some mischief nigh at hand. The old man was nervous, fidgety, and very pale. Purposing a smile of courtesy, he had deformed his face with a sort of galvanic grin, which, when Feathertop's back was turned, he exchanged for a scowl, at the same time shaking his fist and stamping his gouty foot—an incivility which brought its retribution along with it. The truth appears to have been that Mother Rigby's word of introduction, whatever it might be, had operated far more on the rich merchant's fears than on his good will. Moreover, being a man of wonderfully acute observation, he had noticed that these painted figures on the bowl of Feathertop's pipe were in motion. Looking more closely, he became convinced that these figures were a party of little demons, each duly provided with horns and a tail, and dancing hand in hand, with gestures of diabolical merriment, round the circumference of the pipe bowl. As if to confirm his suspicions, while Master Gookin ushered his guest along a dusky passage from his private room to the parlor, the star on Feathertop's breast had scintillated actual flames, and threw a flickering gleam upon the wall, the ceiling, and the floor.

With such sinister prognostics manifesting themselves on all hands, it is not to be marvelled at that the merchant should have felt that he was committing his daughter to a very questionable acquaintance. He cursed, in his secret soul, the insinuating elegance of Feathertop's manners, as this brilliant personage bowed, smiled, put his hand on his heart, inhaled a long whiff from his pipe, and enriched the atmosphere with the smoky vapor of a fragrant and visible sigh. Gladly would poor Master Gookin have thrust his dangerous guest into the street, but there was a constraint and terror within him. This respectable old gentleman, we fear, at an earlier period of life, had given some pledge or other to the evil principle, and perhaps was now to redeem it by the sacrifice of his daughter.

It so happened that the parlor door was partly of glass, shaded by a silken curtain, the folds of which hung a little awry. So strong was the merchant's interest in witnessing what was to ensue between the fair Polly and the gallant Feathertop that, after quitting the room, he could by no means refrain from peeping through the crevice of the curtain.

But there was nothing very miraculous to be seen; nothing—except the

trifles previously noticed—to confirm the idea of a supernatural peril envi-
roning the pretty Polly. The stranger it is true was evidently a thorough and
practised man of the world, systematic and self-possessed, and therefore the
sort of a person to whom a parent ought not to confide a simple, young girl
without due watchfulness for the result. The worthy magistrate, who had been
conversant with all degrees and qualities of mankind, could not but perceive
every motion and gesture of the distinguished Feathertop came in its proper
place; nothing had been left rude or native in him; a well-digested conventionalism had incorporated itself thoroughly with his substance and transformed him into a work of art. Perhaps it was this peculiarity that invested
him with a species of ghastliness and awe. It is the effect of anything completely and consummately artificial, in human shape, that the person impresses
us as an unreality and as having hardly pith enough to cast a shadow upon
the floor. As regarded Feathertop, all this resulted in a wild, extravagant,
and fantastical impression, as if his life and being were akin to the smoke
that curled upward from his pipe.

But pretty Polly Gookin felt not thus. The pair were now promenading
the room: Feathertop with his dainty stride and no less dainty grimace; the
girl with a native maidenly grace, just touched, not spoiled, by a slightly
affected manner, which seemed caught from the perfect artifice of her companion. The longer the interview continued, the more charmed was pretty
Polly, until, within the first quarter of an hour (as the old magistrate noted
by his watch), she was evidently beginning to be in love. Nor need it have
been witchcraft that subdued her in such a hurry; the poor child's heart, it
may be, was so very fervent that it melted her with its own warmth as reflected
from the hollow semblance of a lover. No matter what Feathertop said, his
words found depth and reverberation in her ear; no matter what he did, his
action was heroic to her eye. And by this time it is to be supposed there was
a blush on Polly's cheek, a tender smile about her mouth, and a liquid softness
in her glance; while the star kept coruscating on Feathertop's breast, and the
little demons careered with more frantic merriment than ever about the
circumference of his pipe bowl. O pretty Polly Gookin, why should these
imps rejoice so madly that a silly maiden's heart was about to be given to a
shadow! Is it so unusual a misfortune, so rare a triumph?

By and by Feathertop paused, and throwing himself into an imposing
attitude, seemed to summon the fair girl to survey his figure and resist him
longer if she could. His star, his embroidery, his buckles glowed at that instant
with unutterable splendor; the picturesque hues of his attire took a richer
depth of coloring; there was a gleam and polish over his whole presence
betokening the perfect witchery of well-ordered manners. The maiden raised
her eyes and suffered them to linger upon her companion with a bashful and
admiring gaze. Then, as if desirous of judging what value her own simple

comeliness might have side by side with so much brilliancy, she cast a glance towards the full-length looking-glass in front of which they happened to be standing. It was one of the truest plates in the world and incapable of flattery. No sooner did the images therein reflected meet Polly's eye than she shrieked, shrank from the stranger's side, gazed at him for a moment in the wildest dismay, and sank insensible upon the floor. Feathertop likewise had looked towards the mirror, and there beheld, not the glittering mockery of his outside show, but a picture of the sordid patchwork of his real composition, stripped of all witchcraft.

The wretched simulacrum! We almost pity him. He threw up his arms with an expression of despair that went further than any of his previous manifestations towards vindicating his claims to be reckoned human; for, perchance the only time since this so often empty and deceptive life of mortals began its course, an illusion had seen and fully recognized itself.

Mother Rigby was seated by her kitchen hearth in the twilight of this eventful day, and had just shaken the ashes out of a new pipe, when she heard a hurried tramp along the road. Yet it did not seem so much the tramp of human footsteps as the clatter of sticks or the rattling of dry bones.

"Ha!" thought the old witch, "what step is that? Whose skeleton is out of its grave now, I wonder?"

A figure burst headlong into the cottage door. It was Feathertop! His pipe was still alight; the star still flamed upon his breast; the embroidery still glowed upon his garments; nor had he lost, in any degree or manner that could be estimated, the aspect that assimilated him with our mortal brotherhood. But yet, in some indescribable way (as is the case with all that has deluded us when once found out), the poor reality was felt beneath the cunning artifice.

"What has gone wrong?" demanded the witch. "Did yonder sniffling hypocrite thrust my darling from his door? The villain! I'll set twenty fiends to torment him till he offer thee his daughter on his bended knees!"

"No, mother," said Feathertop despondingly; "it was not that."

"Did the girl scorn my precious one?" asked Mother Rigby, her fierce eyes glowing like two coals of Tophet. "I'll cover her face with pimples! Her nose shall be as red as the coal in thy pipe! Her front teeth shall drop out! In a week hence she shall not be worth thy having!"

"Let her alone, mother," answered poor Feathertop; "the girl was half won; and methinks a kiss from her sweet lips might have made me altogether human. But," he added, after a brief pause and then a howl of self-contempt, "I've seen myself, mother! I've seen myself for the wretched, ragged, empty thing I am! I'll exist no longer!"

Snatching the pipe from his mouth, he flung it with all his might against the chimney, and at the same instant sank upon the floor, a medley of straw and tattered garments, with some sticks protruding from the heap, and a shrivelled pumpkin in the midst. The eyeholes were now lustreless; but the rudely-carved gap, that just before had been a mouth, still seemed to twist itself into a despairing grin, and was so far human.

"Poor fellow!" quoth Mother Rigby, with a rueful glance at the relics of her ill-fated contrivance. "My poor, dear, pretty Feathertop! There are thousands upon thousands of coxcombs and charlatans in the world, made up of just such a jumble of worn-out, forgotten, and good-for-nothing trash as he was! Yet they live in fair repute, and never see themselves for what they are. And why should my poor puppet be the only one to know himself and perish for it?"

While thus muttering, the witch had filled a fresh pipe of tobacco, and held the stem between her fingers, as doubtful whether to thrust it into her own mouth or Feathertop's.

"Poor Feathertop!" she continued. "I could easily give him another chance and send him forth again to-morrow. But no; his feelings are too tender, his sensibilities too deep. He seems to have too much heart to bustle for his own advantage in such an empty and heartless world. Well! well! I'll make a scarecrow of him after all. 'T is an innocent and useful vocation, and will suit my darling well; and, if each of his human brethren had as fit a one, 't would be the better for mankind; and as for this pipe of tobacco, I need it more than he."

So saying, Mother Rigby put the stem between her lips. "Dickon!" cried she, in her high, sharp tone, "another coal for my pipe!"

The Shadow

HANS CHRISTIAN ANDERSEN

t is in the hot countries that the sun burns down in earnest, turning the people there a deep mahogany brown. In the hottest countries of all they are seared into Negroes, but it was not quite that hot in this country to which a man of learning had come from the colder north. He expected to go about there just as he had at home, but he soon discovered that this was a mistake. He and other sensible souls had to stay inside. The shutters were drawn and the doors were closed all day long. It looked just as if everyone were asleep or away from home. The narrow street of high houses where he lived was so situated that from morning till night the sun beat down on it—unbearably!

To this young and clever scholar from the colder north, it felt as if he were sitting in a blazing-hot oven. It exhausted him so that he became very thin, and even his shadow shrank much smaller than it had been at home. Only in the evenings, after sundown, did the man and his shadow begin to recover.

This was really a joy to see. As soon as a candle was brought into the room, the shadow had to stretch itself to get its strength back. It stretched up to the wall, yes, even along the ceiling, so tall did it grow. To stretch himself, the scholar went out on the balcony. As soon as the stars came out in the beautifully clear sky, he felt as if he had come back to life.

In warm countries each window has a balcony, and in all the balconies up and down the street people came out to breathe the fresh air that one needs, even if one is already a fine mahogany brown. Both up above and down below, things became lively. Tailors, shoemakers—everybody—moved out in the street. Chairs and tables were brought out, and candles were lighted, yes, candles by the thousand. One man talked, another sang, people strolled about, carriages drove by, and donkeys trotted along, *ting-a-ling-a-ling*, for their harness had bells on it. There were church bells ringing, hymn singing, and funeral processions. There were boys in the street firing off Roman candles. Oh, yes, it was lively as lively can be down in that street.

Only one house was quiet—the one directly across from where the scholarly stranger lived. Yet someone lived there, for flowers on the balcony grew and thrived under that hot sun, which they could not have done unless they were watered. So someone must be watering them, and there must be people in the house. Along in the evening, as a matter of fact, the door across the street was opened. But it was dark inside, at least in the front room. From somewhere in the house, farther back, came the sound of music. The scholarly stranger thought the music was marvelous, but it is quite possible that he only imagined this, for out there in the warm countries he thought everything was marvelous—except the sun. The stranger's landlord said that he didn't know who had rented the house across the street. No one was ever to be seen over there, and as for the music, he found it extremely tiresome. He said:

"It's just as if somebody sits there practicing a piece that's beyond him—always the selfsame piece. 'I'll play it right yet,' he probably says, but he doesn't, no matter how long he tries."

One night the stranger woke up. He slept with the windows to his balcony open, and as the breeze blew his curtain aside he fancied that a marvelous radiance came from the balcony across the street. The colors of all the flowers were as brilliant as flames. In their midst stood a maiden, slender and lovely. It seemed as if a radiance came from her too. It actually hurt his eyes, but that was because he had opened them too wide in his sudden awakening.

One leap, and he was out of bed. Without a sound, he looked out through his curtains, but the maiden was gone. The flowers were no longer radiant, though they bloomed as fresh and fair as usual. The door was ajar and through it came music so lovely and soft that one could really feel very romantic about it. It was like magic. But who lived there? What entrance did they use? Facing the street, the lower floor of the house was a row of shops, and people couldn't run through them all the time.

On another evening, the stranger sat out on his balcony. The candle burned in the room behind him, so naturally his shadow was cast on the wall across the street. Yes, there it sat among the flowers, and when the stranger moved, it moved with him.

"I believe my shadow is the only living thing to be seen over there," the scholar thought to himself. "See how he makes himself at home among the flowers. The door stands ajar, and if my shadow were clever he'd step in, have a look around, and come back to tell me what he had seen."

"Yes," he said as a joke, "you ought to make yourself useful. Kindly step inside. Well, aren't you going?" He nodded to the shadow, and the shadow nodded back. "Run along now, but be sure to come back."

The stranger rose, and his shadow across the street rose with him. The stranger turned around, and his shadow turned too. If anyone had been watching closely, he would have seen the shadow enter the half-open balcony door in the house across the way at the same instant that the stranger returned to his room and the curtain fell behind him.

Next morning, when the scholar went out to take his coffee and read the newspapers, he said, "What's this?" as he came out in the sunshine. "I haven't any shadow! So it really did go away last night, and it stayed away. Isn't that annoying?"

What annoyed him most was not so much the loss of his shadow but the knowledge that there was already a story about a man without a shadow. All the people at home knew that story. If he went back and told them his story they would say he was just imitating the old one. He did not care to be called unoriginal, so he decided to say nothing about it, which was the most sensible thing to do.

That evening he again went out on the balcony. He had placed the candle directly behind him, because he knew that a shadow always likes to use its master as a screen, but he could not coax it forth. He made himself short and he made himself tall, but there was no shadow. It didn't come forth. He hemmed and he hawed, but it was no use.

This was very vexing, but in the hot countries everything grows most rapidly, and in a week or so he noticed with great satisfaction that when he went out in the sunshine a new shadow was growing at his feet. The root must have been left with him. In three weeks' time he had a very presentable shadow, and as he started north again it grew longer and longer, until it got so long and large that half of it would have been quite sufficient.

The learned man went home and wrote books about those things in the world that are true, that are good, and that are beautiful.

The days went by and the years went past, many, many years in fact. Then one evening when he was sitting in his room he heard a soft tapping at his door. "Come in," said he, but no one came in. He opened the door and was confronted by a man so extremely thin that it gave him a strange feeling. However, the man was faultlessly dressed, and looked like a person of distinction.

"With whom do I have the honor of speaking?" the scholar asked.

"Ah," said the distinguished visitor, "I thought you wouldn't recognize me, now that I've put real flesh on my body and wear clothes. I don't suppose you ever expected to see me in such fine condition. Don't you know your old shadow? You must have thought I'd never come back. Things have gone remarkably well with me since I was last with you. I've thrived in every way, and if I have to buy my freedom, I can." He rattled a bunch of valuable charms that hung from his watch, and fingered the massive gold chain he wore around his neck. Ho! how his fingers flashed with diamond rings—and all this jewelry was real.

"No, I can't get over it!" said the scholar. "What *does* it all mean?"

"Nothing ordinary, you may be sure," said the shadow. "But you are no ordinary person, and I, as you know, have followed in your footsteps from childhood. As soon as you thought me sufficiently experienced to strike out in the world for myself, I went my way. I have been immeasurably successful. But I felt a sort of longing to see you again before you die, as I suppose you must, and I wanted to see this country again. You know how one loves his native land. I know that you have got hold of another shadow. Do I owe anything to either of you? Be kind enough to let me know."

"Well! Is it really you?" said the scholar. "Why, this is most extraordinary! I would never have imagined that one's own shadow could come back in human form."

"Just tell me what I owe," said the shadow, "because I don't like to be in debt to anyone."

"How can you talk that way?" said the scholar. "What debt could there be? Feel perfectly free. I am tremendously pleased to hear of your good luck! Sit down, my old friend, and tell me a bit about how it all happened, and about what you saw in that house across the street from us in the warm country."

"Yes, I'll tell you all about it," the shadow said, as he sat down. "But you must promise that if you meet me anywhere you won't tell a soul in town about my having been your shadow. I intend to become engaged, for I can easily support a family."

"Don't you worry," said the scholar. "I won't tell anyone who you really are. I give you my hand on it. I promise, and a man is as good as his word."

"And a word is as good as its—shadow," the shadow said, for he couldn't put it any other way.

It was really remarkable how much of a man he had become, dressed all in black, with the finest cloth, patent-leather shoes, and an opera hat that could be pressed perfectly flat till it was only brim and top, not to mention those things we already know about—those seals, that gold chain, and the diamond rings. The shadow was well dressed indeed, and it was just this that made him appear human.

"Now I'll tell you," said the shadow, grinding his patent-leather shoes on the arm of the scholar's new shadow, which lay at his feet like a poodle dog. This was arrogance, perhaps, or possibly he was trying to make the new shadow stick to his own feet. The shadow on the floor lay quiet and still, and listened its best, so that it might learn how to get free and work its way up to be its own master.

"Do you know who lived in the house across the street from us?" the old shadow asked. "She was the most lovely of all creatures—she was Poetry herself. I lived there for three weeks, and it was as if I had lived there three thousand years, reading all that has ever been written. That's what I said, and it's the truth! I have seen it all, and I know everything."

"Poetry!" the scholar cried. "Yes, to be sure she often lives as a hermit in the large cities. Poetry! Yes, I saw her myself, for one brief moment, but my eyes were heavy with sleep. She stood on the balcony, as radiant as the northern lights. Tell me! Tell me! You were on the balcony. You went through the doorway, and then—"

"Then I was in the anteroom," said the shadow. "It was the room you were always staring at from across the way. There were no candles there, and the room was in twilight. But door upon door stood open in a whole series of brilliantly lit halls and reception rooms. That blaze of lights would have struck me dead had I gone as far as the room where the maiden was, but I was careful—I took my time, as one should."

"And then what did you see, my old friend?" the scholar asked.

"I saw everything, and I shall tell everything to you, but—it's not that I'm proud, but as I am a free man and well educated, not to mention my high standing and my considerable fortune, I do wish you wouldn't call me your old friend."

"I beg your pardon!" said the scholar. "It's an old habit and hard to change. You are perfectly right, my dear sir, and I'll remember it. But now, my dear sir, tell me of all that you saw."

"All?" said the shadow. "For I saw it all, and I know everything."

"How did the innermost rooms look?" the scholar asked. "Was it like a green forest? Was it like a holy temple? Were the rooms like the starry skies seen from some high mountain?"

"Everything was there," said the shadow. "I didn't quite go inside. I stayed in the dark anteroom, but my place there was perfect. I saw everything, and I know everything. I have been in the antechamber at the court of Poetry."

"But what did you see? Did the gods of old march through the halls? Did the old heroes fight there? Did fair children play there and tell their dreams?"

"I was there, I tell you, so you must understand that I saw all that there was to be seen. Had you come over, it would not have made a man of you, as it did of me. Also, I learned to understand my inner self, what is born in me, and the relationship between me and Poetry. Yes, when I was with you I did not think of such things, but you must remember how wonderfully I always expanded at sunrise and sunset. And in the moonlight I almost seemed more real than you. Then I did not understand myself, but in that anteroom I came to know my true nature. I was a man! I came out completely changed. But you were no longer in the warm country. Being a man, I was ashamed to be seen as I was. I lacked shoes, clothes, and all the surface veneer which makes a man.

"I went into hiding—this is confidential, and you must not write it in any of your books. I went into hiding under the skirts of the cake woman. Little she knew what she concealed. Not until evening did I venture out. I ran through the streets in the moonlight and stretched myself tall against the walls. It's such a pleasant way of scratching one's back. Up I ran and down I ran, peeping into the highest windows, into drawing rooms, and into garrets. I peered in where no one else could peer. I saw what no one else could see, or should see. Taken all in all, it's a wicked world. I would not care to be a man if it were not considered the fashionable thing to be. I saw the most incredible behavior among men and women, fathers and mothers, and among those 'perfectly darling' children. I saw what nobody knows but everybody would like to know, and that is what wickedness goes on next door. If I had written it in a newspaper, oh, how widely it would have been read! But instead I wrote to the people directly concerned, and there was the most terrible consternation in every town to which I came. They were so afraid of me, and yet so remarkably fond of me. The professors appointed me a professor, and the tailor made me new clothes—my wardrobe is most complete. The master of the mint coined new money for me, the women called me such a handsome man, and so I became the man I am. Now I must bid you goodbye. Here's my card. I live on the sunny side of the street, and I am always at home on rainy days." The shadow took his leave.

"How extraordinary," said the scholar.

The days passed. The years went by. And the shadow called again. "How goes it?" he asked.

"Alack," said the scholar, "I still write about the true, the good, and the beautiful, but nobody cares to read about such things. I feel quite despondent, for I take it deeply to heart."

"I don't," said the shadow. "I am getting fat, as one should. You don't know the ways of the world, and that's why your health suffers. You ought to travel. I'm taking a trip this summer. Will you come with me? I'd like to have a traveling companion. Will you come along as my shadow? It would be a great pleasure to have you along, and I'll pay all the expenses."

"No, that's a bit too much," said the scholar.

"It depends on how you look at it," said the shadow. "It will do you a lot of good to travel. Will you be my shadow? The trip won't cost you a thing."

"This has gone much too far!" said the scholar.

"Well, that's the way the world goes," the shadow told him, "and that's the way it will keep on going." And away he went.

The learned man was not at all well. Sorrow and trouble pursued him, and what he had to say about the good, the true, and the beautiful appealed to most people about as much as roses appeal to a cow. Finally, he grew quite ill.

"You really look like a shadow," people told him, and he trembled at the thought.

"You must visit a watering place," said the shadow, who came to see him again. "There's no question about it. I'll take you with me, for old friendship's sake. I'll pay for the trip, and you can write about it, as well as doing your best to amuse me along the way. I need to go to a watering place too, because my beard isn't growing as it should. That's a sort of disease too, and one can't get along without a beard. Now do be reasonable and accept my proposal. We shall travel just like friends!"

So off they started. The shadow was master now, and the master was the shadow. They drove together, rode together, and walked together, side by side, before or behind each other, according to the way the sun fell. The shadow was careful to take the place of the master, and the scholar didn't much care, for he had an innocent heart, besides being most affable and friendly.

One day he said to the shadow, "As we are now fellow travelers and have grown up together, shall we not call each other by our first names, the way good companions should? It is much more intimate."

"That's a splendid idea!" said the shadow, who was now the real master. "What you say is most openhearted and friendly. I shall be just as friendly and openhearted with you. As a scholar, you are perfectly well aware how strange is man's nature. Some men cannot bear the touch of gray paper. It sickens them. Others quail if they hear a nail scratched across a pane of glass. For my part, I am affected in just that way when I hear you call me by my first name. I feel myself ground down to the earth, as I was in my first position with you. You understand. It's a matter of sensitivity, not pride. I cannot let you call me by my first name, but I shall be glad to call you by yours, as a compromise." So thereafter the shadow called his onetime master by his first name.

"It has gone too far," the scholar thought, "when I must call him by his last name while he calls me by my first!" But he had to put up with it.

At last they came to the watering place. Among the many people was a lovely princess. Her malady was that she saw things too clearly, which can be most upsetting. For instance, she immediately saw that the newcomer was a very different sort of person from all the others.

"He has come here to make his beard grow, they say. But I see the real reason. He can't cast a shadow."

Her curiosity was aroused, and on the promenade she addressed this stranger directly. Being a king's daughter, she did not have to stand upon ceremony, so she said to him straight:

"Your trouble is that you can't cast a shadow."

"Your Royal Highness must have improved considerably," the shadow replied. "I know your malady is that you see too clearly, but you are improving. As it happens, I do have a most unusual shadow. Don't you see that figure who always accompanies me? Other people have a common shadow, but I do not care for what is common to all. Just as we often allow our servants better fabrics for their liveries than we wear ourselves, so I have had my shadow decked out as a man. Why, you see I have even outfitted him with a shadow of his own. It is expensive, I grant you, but I like to have something uncommon."

"My!" the princess thought. "Can I really be cured? This is the foremost watering place in the world, and in these days water has come to have wonderful medicinal powers. But I shan't leave just as the place is becoming amusing. I have taken a liking to this stranger. I only hope his beard won't grow, for then he would leave us."

That evening, the princess and the shadow danced together in the great ballroom. She was light, but he was lighter still. Never had she danced with such a partner. She told him what country she came from, and he knew it well. He had been there, but it was during her absence. He had looked through every window, high or low. He had seen this and he had seen that. So he could answer the Princess and suggest things that astounded her. She was convinced that he must be the wisest man in all the world. His knowledge impressed her so deeply that while they were dancing she fell in love with him. The shadow could tell, for her eyes transfixed him, through and through. They danced again, and she came very near telling him she loved him, but it wouldn't do to be rash. She had to think of her country, and her throne, and the many people over whom she would reign.

"He is a clever man," she said to herself, "and that is a good thing. He dances charmingly, and that is good too. But is his knowledge more than superficial? That's just as important, so I must examine him."

Tactfully, she began asking him the most difficult questions, which she herself could not have answered. The shadow made a wry face.

"You can't answer me?" said the princess.

"I knew all that in my childhood," said the shadow. "Why, I believe that my shadow over there by the door can answer you."

"Your shadow!" said the princess. "That would be remarkable indeed!"

"I can't say for certain," said the shadow, "but I'm inclined to think so, because he has followed me about and listened to me for so many years. Yes, I am inclined to believe so. But Your Royal Highness must permit me to tell you that he is quite proud of being able to pass for a man, so if he is to be in the right frame of mind to answer your questions, he must be treated just as if he were human."

"I like that!" said the princess.

So she went to the scholar in the doorway, and spoke with him about the sun and the moon, and about people, what they are inside and what they seem to be on the surface. He answered her wisely and well.

"What a man that must be, to have such a wise shadow!" she thought. "It will be a godsend to my people and to my country if I choose him for my consort. That's just what I'll do!"

The princess and the shadow came to an understanding, but no one was to know about it until she returned to her own kingdom.

"No one. Not even my shadow!" said the shadow. And he had his own private reason for this.

Finally, they came to the country that the princess ruled when she was at home.

"Listen, my good friend," the shadow said to the scholar, "I am now as happy and strong as one can be, so I'll do something very special for you. You shall live with me in my palace, drive with me in my royal carriage, and have a hundred thousand dollars a year. However, you must let yourself be called a shadow by everybody. You must not ever say that you have been a man, and once a year, while I sit on the balcony in the sunshine, you must lie at my feet as shadows do. For I tell you I am going to marry the princess, and the wedding is to take place this very evening."

"No! That's going too far," said the scholar. "I will *not.* I won't do it. That would be betraying the whole country and the princess too. I'll tell them everything—that I am the man, and you are the shadow merely dressed as a man."

"No one would believe it," said the shadow. "Be reasonable, or I'll call the sentry."

"I'll go straight to the princess," said the scholar.

"But I will go first," said the shadow, "and you shall go to prison."

And to prison he went, for the sentries obeyed the one who, they knew, was to marry the princess.

"Why, you're trembling," the princess said, as the shadow entered her room. "What has happened? You mustn't fall ill this evening, just as we are about to be married."

"I have been through the most dreadful experience that could happen to anyone," said the shadow. "Just imagine! Of course, a poor shadow's head can't stand very much. But imagine! My shadow has gone mad. He takes himself for a man, and—imagine it!—he takes me for his shadow."

"How terrible!" said the princess. "He's locked up, I hope!"

"Oh, of course. I'm afraid he will never recover."

"Poor shadow," said the princess. "He is very unhappy. It would really be a charitable act to relieve him of the little bit of life he has left. And after thinking it over carefully, my opinion is that it will be necessary to put him out of the way."

"That's certainly hard, for he was a faithful servant," said the shadow. He managed to sigh.

"You have a noble soul," the princess told him.

The whole city was brilliantly lit that evening. The cannons boomed and the soldiers presented arms. That was the sort of wedding it was! The princess and the shadow stepped out on the balcony to show themselves and be cheered, again and again.

The scholar heard nothing of all this, for they had already done away with him.

Translated by Jean Hersholt

‹ *Spiegel the Cat* ›
GOTTFRIED KELLER

I

When a man from Seldwyla has made a bad bargain or been hoaxed, they say of him, "He's bought the fat off the cat." This surely may be said elsewhere too, but nowhere as frequently as in Seldwyla, perhaps because in this town there exists an old legend on the origin and meaning of the proverb.

Some hundreds of years ago, so the story goes, an elderly female lived at Seldwyla alone, save for a beautiful little gray-and-black cat, who shared her life in all good cheer and prudence and never harmed a body that left him in peace. He had only one passion, the hunt; but satisfied this reasonably and temperately without ever citing in extenuation the facts that the passion also served a useful end and pleased his mistress, or allowing them to tempt him to excessive cruelty. He therefore caught and killed only the most vexatious and brazen mice to be encountered within certain limits of the house, but these with dependable skill. Only seldom would he pursue an especially tricky mouse, which had aroused his ire, beyond these limits, and in any such case he politely asked the neighbors for permission to do a spot of mousing in their homes. It was always willingly granted since he neither touched the milk jars nor leaped upon the hams which might be hanging on the walls, but went about his business quietly and attentively and, having finished, decently withdrew with the mouse in his jaws.

Moreover, this cat was by no means shy and ill-mannered but agreeable to everyone and did not flee from sensible people. On the contrary, from such he could take a good joke and even let them pull his ears a little without scratching. From a sort of stupid folk, on the other hand, whose stupidity he held to be due to an immature and worthless heart, he would stand for no nonsense, and either kept out of their way or rapped them smartly enough over the fingers when they clumsily molested him.

Spiegel (or Mirror), as the little cat was called for his sleek and shiny coat, thus led a cheerful, dainty, and contemplative life in decent affluence and without swagger. He would not sit too often on the shoulder of his kind mistress, snatching morsels off her fork, but waited until he perceived that this jolly game would please her. In the daytime he seldom lay sleeping on his warm cushion behind the stove, but kept himself in trim and rather liked to lie on the narrow banisters on the roof gutter, there to yield to philosophical meditations and the observation of the world.

Only once in each spring and autumn would this tranquil life be interrupted for a week, when the violets bloomed or the mild warmth of St. Martin's summer aped the violet time. Then Spiegel went his own ways in amorous rapture, roaming over the remotest roofs and singing the loveliest songs. Like a real Don Juan he went through the gravest adventures by day and by night, and when he came home on rare occasions he would look so bold and boisterous, indeed so scraggly and disreputable, that his quiet mistress almost indignantly exclaimed, "Why, Spiegel! Aren't you ashamed to lead such a life!"

But it was far from Spiegel to be ashamed. As a man of principle, knowing well what was permissible for a healthy change, he very calmly went to work restoring the gloss of his fur and the innocuous gaiety of his appearance, and he led his moist little paw over his nose as naïvely as if nothing had happened.

Yet this placid life suddenly took a sad end. Just as Spiegel was in the prime of his years, his mistress died unexpectedly of old age and left the beautiful little cat alone and orphaned. It was the first disaster in his life; with the plaintive noises which so piercingly question the real and just cause of a great sorrow, he accompanied the corpse into the street, and for the rest of the day roamed about the house, and around it, not knowing what to do.

But soon his good nature, common sense, and philosophy told him to compose himself, to bear the unalterable, and to prove his grateful attachment to his late mistress's house by offering to serve her laughing heirs and preparing to aid them in word and deed, to keep checking the mice, and, besides, to tell them many a good thing that the fools would not have spurned had they not been brainless humans. But these people would not let Spiegel say a word, but threw the slippers and the dainty footstool of the dear departed at his head whenever he came in sight, and finally, after a week of quarreling among each other, they went to law and closed up the house for the time being, so that now no one at all could live in it.

And poor Spiegel, sad and forsaken, sat on the stone steps before the gate with no one to let him in. At night, to be sure, he would follow a devious route under the roof of the house, and at the beginning he also spent the greater part of the day in hiding there, trying to sleep off his grief. But soon hunger drove him back to the light and obliged him to appear under the warm sun and among people, to be on hand and present if perchance a mouthful of scant food should show up somewhere. The more rarely this happened, the more vigilant Spiegel became, and all his moral qualities dissolved in this vigilance, so that he soon no longer looked like himself. He made numerous excursions from his doorstep, shyly and fleetingly stealing across the street and returning sometimes with a bad, unappetizing scrap, the like of which he never used to look at, and sometimes with nothing at all.

Besides getting thinner and scragglier by the day, he turned greedy, sneaky, and cowardly; all of his courage, his dainty feline dignity, his common sense and philosophy had vanished. When the boys came home from school he crawled into a hidden corner as soon as he heard them, peering out only to see which of them threw away a crust of bread and memorizing the spot where it fell. When the most wretched cur approached at a distance, Spiegel would scurry off, while formerly he had looked danger calmly in the face and often bravely chastised vicious dogs. Only when a rude and fatuous human came along, of the sort he otherwise had prudently avoided, the poor cat would not move away, although with his rusty knowledge of men he discerned the yokel: his needs forced little Spiegel to deceive himself and to hope that for once the bad man would kindly pet him and hand him a bit of food. And even when he was beaten instead, or his tail pinched, he would not scratch but soundlessly ducked aside and kept looking longingly after the hand which had beaten or pinched him but still smelled of sausage or herring.

One day, when the sage and noble Spiegel had sunk so low and was sitting quite lean and sad on his stone step, blinking into the sun, the Town Sorcerer, Mr. Pineiss, came along, saw the cat, and came to a halt before him. Hoping for a good turn although he knew the uncanny man well enough, little Spiegel humbly sat on his stone and waited for what Mr. Pineiss might do or say. But when he started by remarking, "Well, Cat—shall I buy your fat off you?" Spiegel lost hope, for he thought the Town Sorcerer meant to mock him on account of his leanness. Still, smiling so as not to get in wrong with anyone, he modestly replied, "Oh, Mr. Pineiss is pleased to jest!"

"By no means," cried Pineiss. "I'm in full earnest. I need cat's fat particularly for my sorcery; but it must be ceded to me legally and voluntarily by the esteemed Messrs. Cats, otherwise it is ineffectual. I think if ever an honest pussy was in a spot for a good bargain, you're it. Enter my service; I'll feed you splendidly and make you fat and round with sausages and roast quail. On the immensely tall old roof of my house—which for a cat, by the way, is the most delightful house in the world, full of interesting regions and corners—the finest emerald-green grass grows on the sunniest heights, waving slim and delicate in the breezes and inviting you to bite and relish the tenderest tips when my delicacies upset your digestion. So you will keep in the best of health and in due time provide me with rich, useful fat."

Spiegel had long pricked up his ears and listened with his mouth watering. But the matter was not yet clear to his weakened mind, and so he replied, "So far it does not sound bad, Mr. Pineiss! If I only knew how—since to give you my fat I must give up my life—I may receive the price agreed upon and enjoy it when I am no more?"

"Receive the price?" the sorcerer said, astonished. "The price, of course, is what you will enjoy in the abundant and luxurious victuals with which I'll fatten you; that's self-evident. But I won't force you into the deal." And he began to move off.

But Spiegel hastily and anxiously said, "At least you'll have to allow me a moderate grace beyond the time of my maximum roundness and fatness, so that I must not instantly depart when that agreeable and, alas! so depressing moment has come and been noted!"

"So be it," said Mr. Pineiss with seeming benevolence. "To the next full moon you shall then be free to enjoy your pleasant condition—but no longer! For it must not last into the waning moon, as that would exert a diminishing influence on my well-acquired property."

The tomcat hastened to agree and with his sharp handwriting, his last possession and token of better days, to sign a pact which the sorcerer carried with him for emergencies.

"You can now come to dine with me, Cat," said the sorcerer. "Dinner is at twelve sharp."

"With your permission, I shall take the liberty," said Spiegel and punctually about the noon hour made his appearance at Mr. Pineiss's house. There, for some months, an extremely pleasant life began for the cat. He had nothing to do in the world but to eat the good things set before him, to watch the master practice the black art when possible, and to stroll on the roof. This roof resembled a huge black tricorne or fog-splitter, as the big hats of the Swabian peasants are called; and as such a hat casts its shadow on a brain full of tricks and ruses, this roof covered a large, dark, and angular house full of witchery and hocus-pocus.

Mr. Pineiss was a jack of all trades who served in a hundred little posts. He cured people, exterminated bugs, pulled teeth, and lent money on interest; he was the guardian of all widows and orphans; in his leisure time cut pens, a dozen for a penny, and made fine black ink; he traded in ginger and pepper, in wagon-grease and orange brandy, in copybooks and hobnails; he fixed the steeple clock and annually prepared the almanac with the weather, the peasants' rules, and the bloodletting indices.

He did ten thousand lawful things in bright daylight at reasonable rates, and some unlawful ones only in the dark and out of private passion, or before letting the lawful ones out of his hand he swiftly hung an unlawful little tail on them, as little as a young frog's tail, just for oddity's sake as it were. Besides, he made the weather in difficult times, kept a knowing eye on the witches, and had them burned when they were ripe. As for himself he conducted witchcraft only as a scientific experiment and for home use, just as in drafting and editing the town laws he would privately test and twist them, to explore their durability.

Since the Seldwylers always needed such a citizen who would do all unpleasant little and big things for them, he had been appointed Town Sorcerer and for many years had filled this office with tireless skill and devotion, early and late. Accordingly, his house was stuffed from cellar to attic with all conceivable things and Spiegel had much fun in seeing and sniffing them all.

At the start, however, he could pay attention to nothing but the food. He eagerly gulped down whatever Pineiss handed him and hardly could wait from one mealtime to the next. Thus he overloaded his stomach and really had to go up on the roof, to chew on the green grass and cure himself of all sorts of disorders.

The sorcerer, noting this ravenous hunger, was pleased. He thought that the cat would soon grow fat in this manner, and that the more he spent on him now, the more shrewdly he would be acting and saving on the whole. He therefore built a real landscape in his room for Spiegel, growing a little forest of fir trees, raising little hills of rock and moss, and putting in a little lake. The trees he stocked with fragrantly roasted larks, finches, tits, and sparrows, each in season, so that Spiegel always found something to fetch down and nibble at. In artificial mouse holes in the little hills he hid gorgeous mice, carefully fattened on wheat flour and then drawn, larded with tender bacon strips, and roasted. Some of these mice were in reach of Spiegel's paw, while others, to heighten the pleasure, were more deeply buried but tied to a string, by which Spiegel had to pull them out carefully if he wished to enjoy this delightful mock hunt. The bowl of the lake, however, was daily filled by Pineiss with sweet fresh milk for Spiegel to quench his thirst, and swimming therein were fried gudgeon, since Pineiss knew that cats like to fish now and then.

As Spiegel was now leading such a sumptuous life, able to do and omit, eat and drink whatever and whenever he pleased, he visibly prospered in the flesh, his coat again became sleek and shiny, and his eye alert. But at the same time, as his mental powers equally returned, he resumed better manners, his savage greed subsided, and with one sad experience behind him he now became more clever than before. He tempered his desires and ate no more than was good for him, at the same time yielding again to sensible and profound meditations and regaining his acumen. Thus one day he fetched a pretty little fieldfare down from the branches, and in thoughtfully carving it found its little stomach all round and full of fresh and undigested food. Green, neatly rolled little herbs, black and white seeds and a shining red berry were stuffed so daintily and close together as if a mother had packed her son's bundle for a journey. When Spiegel had slowly devoured the bird and hung up the so gaily filled little stomach on his claw to regard it philosophically, he was moved by the fate of the poor fowl which after peacefully accomplished business had been robbed of its life so fast that it could not even digest the packed provisions.

"What did it help him now, poor chap," reflected Spiegel, "feeding so zealously and industriously that this little bag looks like a day's work well done? This red berry was what lured him from the free forest into the fowler's trap. But he, at least, meant to do well by himself and eke out his life with such berries, while I who have just eaten the hapless bird have only eaten myself a step closer to death! Can one sign a more wretched and cowardly contract than to let his life be prolonged for a while at the price of losing it then? Would not a voluntary, speedy death have been preferable for a resolute cat? But I did not think; and now that I can think again, all that I see before me is the fate of this fieldfare. When I am round enough I must depart, for no other reason than that I am round. A fine reason, for a lusty and quick-witted tomcat! Oh to be able to get out of this trap!"

II

He now engaged in manifold ruminations as to how this might be done; but as the time of danger had not yet arrived, it did not seem clear to him and he could find no way out. Until then, however, as a wise man, he yielded to virtue and self-control, which always is the best way of training and passing the time before a decision. He spurned the soft cushion which Pineiss had spread for him so he might busily sleep and get fat thereon, and preferred to lie on narrow ledges again and in high, dangerous places, when he wished to rest. He also spurned the roasted birds and larded mice; instead, since he now had a lawful hunting ground again, he would rather catch himself a simple live sparrow on the roof, with cunning and agility, or a swift mouse in the attic, and such prey tasted better than the roasted game in Pineiss's artificial preserve, while it did not make him too fat. The exercise and courage, as well as the regained use of virtue and philosophy, also kept him from fattening too quickly, so that Spiegel, while looking healthy and shiny, astonished Pineiss by standing still at a certain stage of corpulence far from that at which the sorcerer was aiming with his kind fattening. For what he had in mind was an animal round as a ball, too heavy to move from its cushion, and consisting of sheer fat. And this was just where his magic had failed, and for all of his cunning he did not know that if you feed an ass it will remain an ass, and if you feed a fox you will get nothing but a fox—for every creature grows only after its own fashion.

When Mr. Pineiss discovered that Spiegel always remained on the same point of a well-fed but trim and agile slenderness, without acquiring a considerable obesity, he suddenly called him to account one evening and gruffly asked, "What does this mean, Spiegel? Why don't you eat the good victuals that I prepare and fix for you with so much care and art? Why don't you catch the roasted birds on the trees, why don't you hunt the tasty mice in the holes in the hills? Why have you stopped fishing in the lake? Why aren't you taking care of yourself? Why don't you sleep on the cushion? Why do you take such strenuous exercise and fail to get fat?"

"Why, Mr. Pineiss," said Spiegel, "because this way I feel better! Am I not to spend my brief period of grace in the manner most agreeable to me?"

"What?" cried Pineiss. "You're to live so you'll get fat and round, and not to hunt yourself silly! I know very well what's in your mind, though. Do you mean to fool me and put me off, so I'll let you run around forever in this intermediate condition? You certainly shall not succeed. It is your duty to eat and drink and take good care of yourself, so that you'll put on weight and get fat! Therefore, renounce immediately this temperance which amounts to trickery and breach of contract, or I'll have a word with you!"

Spiegel interrupted the comfortable purring which he had begun to keep his composure, and said, "I do not know of a word in our contract which would provide for my renouncing temperance and a healthy mode of living. If the Honorable Town Sorcerer has counted on my being a lazy glutton, that isn't my fault. You do a thousand lawful things each day, so let this be added, too, and let both of us stay in good order—for you well know that my fat will serve you only if it has grown to rights."

"See here, you babbler," Pineiss cried irately, "do you mean to instruct me? Let's see how far you've prospered anyway, you lazybones. Perhaps one could finish you soon, after all!" He grabbed the tomcat by the stomach; but Spiegel, feeling unpleasantly tickled thereby, fetched the sorcerer a sharp scratch over the hand. Pineiss looked at it attentively, and then said, "Is that how we stand, you beast? All right, so I herewith solemnly declare you fat enough in the sense of our contract. I am content with the result, and I shall know how to assure myself of it. The moon will be full in five days. Until then you may enjoy your life, as stipulated, and not a minute longer!" With that, he turned his back on Spiegel and left him to his thoughts.

These were now heavy and dark. Was then the hour near, after all, when good Spiegel was to lose his skin? And was nothing more to be done, with all his shrewdness? Sighing, he climbed on the tall roof, the tops of which rose darkly into the sky of a beautiful autumn evening. Then, as the moon rose over the town and cast its light on the black mossy tiles of the old roof, a lovely song rang in Spiegel's ears and a snow-white she-cat shiningly passed over an adjoining rooftop. Instantly Spiegel forgot the prospects of death, and answered the beauty's song of praise with his most beautiful ca-terwaul. He rushed to join her and soon was engaged in a hot battle with three strange tomcats, whom he bravely and wildly put to flight. Then, with fiery devotion, he courted the lady and spent days and nights with her, without thinking of Pineiss or showing up in his house. He sang like a nightingale throughout the fair moonlit nights, pursued his white beloved over the roofs and through the gardens, and more than once, in violent amorous play or in the struggle with his rivals, rolled down over tall roofs to land in the street— but only to pick himself up, shake his fur, and recommence the wild chase of his passion. Silent and noisy hours, sweet sentiments and angry quarrels, graceful dialogue, witty conversation, tricks and jests of love and jealousy, caresses and scuffles, the power of bliss and the sufferings of misfortune would not let the loving Spiegel come to himself; and when the disk of the moon had grown full, all these passions and excitements had so reduced him that he looked more wretched, thinner, and scragglier than ever. At this very moment Pineiss, from a roof tower, called to him, "Spiegel, dear Spiegel, where are you? Won't you come home for a little while?"

And Spiegel left his white lady-love, who went her way contently and coolly miaowing, and proudly turned to his hangman, who went down to the kitchen, rustled his contract, and said, "Come, Spiegel, come, Spiegel!" And Spiegel followed him, and in the sorcerer's kitchen sat down defiantly before the master, in all his thinness and scraggliness.

When Mr. Pineiss saw how scurvily he had been tricked out of his profit, he jumped up like one possessed and furiously screamed, "What's this I see? You knave, you unscrupulous rascal! What have you done to me?" Beside himself with wrath, he reached for a broom and wanted to hit little Spiegel; but the cat arched his black back, raised up his fur so that a pale gleam sparkled across it, laid his ears, hissed, and spat so grimly at the oldster that he jumped back three steps, in awe and terror. He began to fear that he might have another sorcerer before him, who was mocking him and whose power exceeded his own. Uncertainly and timidly he said, "Is the honorable Master Spiegel of the trade, perhaps? Should a learned master of wizardry have pleased to assume your external form, since he can command his flesh at his pleasure and become just as corpulent as he deems pleasant, not too little and not too much, or unawares become as lean as a skeleton to escape from death?"

Spiegel calmed down and honestly said, "No, I'm no wizard. It is the sweet power of passion alone which has thus reduced me and, to my pleasure, has removed your fat. By the way, if we will now start our business all over, I'll honestly do my part and eat right heartily. Just put a fine, big fried sausage in front of me. I'm all exhausted and hungry."

At that Pineiss furiously grabbed Spiegel by the neck, locked him in the goose pen, which was always empty, and screamed, "Now see if your sweet power of passion gets you out once more, and if it is stronger than the power of sorcery and of my legal contract! Now it's eat, rascal, and die!" At once he fried a long sausage which smelled so tastily that he could not keep from licking a bit on both ends himself, before pushing it through the wire.

Spiegel ate it up from end to end, and then, comfortably cleaning his moustache and licking his fur, he said to himself, "Upon my soul, love is a beautiful thing. For this time, it has pulled me out of the trap. Now I'll rest up a little and seek to recollect my wits by contemplation and good food. Everything in its time. A little passion today, a little rest and reflection tomorrow—each is good in its way. This prison is not so bad at all, and certainly something useful can be thought up in it."

But Pineiss was doing his best now, and every day, with all his art, he prepared such delicacies of such enticing variety and wholesomeness that the captured Spiegel could not resist—for Pineiss's stock of voluntary and lawful cat's fat was daily diminishing and threatened soon to vanish altogether, and then, without this prime requisite, the sorcerer would be helpless. Yet the good sorcerer always kept feeding Spiegel's mind with Spiegel's body; there was absolutely no getting rid of this irritating adjunct, wherefore his magic proved here to be deficient.

At last, when Spiegel in his cage seemed fat enough to him, he hesitated no longer but put all utensils in readiness before the very eyes of the watching tomcat and stoked a bright fire in the stove to boil out his long-desired profit. Then he honed a great knife, opened the prison, pulled out little Spiegel after carefully locking the kitchen door, and happily said, "Come on, you ne'er-do-well! We'll cut off your head to begin with, and then pull off your skin. That will furnish a warm cap for me—something I hadn't even thought of yet, fool that I am. Or shall I skin you first and then cut off your head?"

"No, if you please," Spiegel said meekly, "rather cut off the head first."

"You're right, poor chap," said Mr. Pineiss, "we won't torture you uselessly. Always do the right thing."

"How true! How true!" said Spiegel with a pitiful sigh, turning his head resignedly to one side. "If only I had always done the right thing, and not frivolously neglected so weighty a matter, I could now die with an easier

conscience. I'd be glad to die, without this wrong to spoil an otherwise so welcome death—for what has life to offer me? Nothing but fear, sorrow, and poverty, and for a change a storm of consuming passion that is even worse than quietly trembling fear."

"Say," Pineiss asked curiously, "what wrong, what weighty matter?"

"Oh, what good is talking now?" Spiegel sighed. "What's done is done, and remorse now comes too late."

"See what a sinner you are, you rapscallion?" said Pineiss. "And how well you deserve to die? But what the dickens is it that you've done? Have you perhaps stolen, removed, destroyed something of mine? Have you done me some crying wrong, you Satan, of which as yet I know, dream, suspect nothing? What a pretty story! Good that I've caught on to it in time. Confess right this instant, or I'll skin and boil you alive. Will you speak up or won't you?"

"Oh, no," said Spiegel, "as far as you are concerned I have nothing to reproach myself with. It concerns the ten thousand guilders of my late mistress—but what good is talking! Although—when I think of it and look at you, perhaps it might not even be too late yet—when I look at you I see you're still quite a handsome and capable man, in the prime of life. Tell me, Mr. Pineiss, haven't you ever felt the urge to wed, honestly and profitably? But what am I gabbing—how should so wise and artful a man harbor such idle thoughts? How should so usefully occupied a master think of foolish women?

"Though of course even the worst of them still has something about her which might benefit a man—there's no denying that. And if she is but half worth her salt, a good housewife may be white of body, careful of mind, affectionate of manner, faithful of heart, a thrifty manager but lavish in caring for her husband, entertaining in words and pleasing in action, ingratiating in everything she does. She kisses the man with her lips and strokes his beard; she hugs him with her arms and scratches him behind the ears as he likes it—in short, she does a thousand things not to be sneezed at. She keeps herself quite close to him or at a modest distance, depending upon his mood, and when he goes about his business she does not disturb him, but meanwhile spreads his praise within and without the house, for she won't hear a word against him and praises whatever there is of him.

"But the loveliest part of her is the wonderful quality of her delicate bodily being which Nature, for all seeming human likeness, has made so differently from ours that in a happy marriage it effects a continuous miracle and really hides the trickiest magic within it. But what am I gabbing there like a fool, on the threshold of death! How should a wise man heed such vanities? Forgive me, Mr. Pineiss, and cut off my head."

But Pineiss hotly cried, "Will you stop for a moment, you chatterbox, and tell me: where is such a one, and does she have ten thousand guilders?"

"Ten thousand guilders?" said Spiegel.

"Why, yes," cried Pineiss impatiently, "wasn't that what you were just talking of?"

"No," was the response, "that's another matter. They lie buried some place."

"And what are they doing there? Whose are they?" Pineiss shouted.

"They're nobody's. That's just what is on my conscience, for I was to have disposed of them. They really belong to the man who marries a person like I described. But how to get three such things together in this Godless town: ten thousand guilders, a wise, fine, and good housewife, and a wise and righteous man? So my sin is really not all too great, for the task was beyond a poor cat."

"If you," Pineiss cried, "will not stick to the matter now and tell it comprehensibly and in order, I'll start by cutting off your tail and both ears! Now get going!"

"Since you command, I must needs tell the story," said Spiegel and calmly sat down on his hindlegs, "although this delay serves only to add to my sufferings." Pineiss stuck his sharp knife into the floor between Spiegel and himself, and sat curiously upon a keg to listen while Spiegel continued:

III

"You must know, Mr. Pineiss, that that good woman, my late mistress, died unmarried, as an old maid who quietly did much good and never harmed a soul. But things about her had not always been so still and quiet, and although she was never of an evil disposition, she nevertheless had done plenty of harm in her day; for in her youth she was the most beautiful damsel for far around, and whatever young gentlemen and bold youths lived in the vicinity or came by the way would fall in love with and insist upon marrying her. As for her, she certainly was very eager to marry and take a handsome, honorable and clever man for her husband, and she had a full choice, with natives and strangers fighting over her and more than once running their swords through each other so as to gain the advantage.

"There gathered around her suitors bold and timid, shrewd and candid, rich and poor, owners of good and decent businesses and others who daintily lived on their incomes as gentlemen; one with this advantage, the other with that, eloquent or silent, one gay and amiable, while another appeared to be deeper, even though he looked a bit simple—in short, the damsel had as perfect a choice as any marriageable spinster might wish for. Yet besides her beauty she possessed a handsome fortune of many thousand guilders, and these were the cause of her never getting around to making a choice and taking a husband.

"For she managed her estate with excellent care and foresight and set great store by it, and since mankind always judges others by its own inclinations, it happened that whenever an estimable suitor approached and half-way pleased her, she instantly imagined that he desired her only for her property's sake. If one was rich, she believed that he still would not want her if she were not rich, too, and of the impecunious ones she assumed for a certainty that they had their eyes on her guilders alone and were looking forward to their enjoyment, and the poor damsel, herself thinking so much of earthly possessions, was unable to tell this love of money and wealth on her suitors' part from their love of her—or, if it might perhaps really exist, to overlook and forgive it.

"Several times she was as good as betrothed and her heart would beat stronger at last; but suddenly she would conclude from some token that the man was betraying her and thinking only of her wealth, and she would instantly break off the affair and sadly but unmercifully withdraw. Those who did not displease her she tested in a hundred ways, so that only the deftest could avoid being trapped; and in the end the only man who could approach with any hope would be an utterly crafty and deceitful one—for which reason alone the choice then got really difficult, because at length such people arouse an eerie disquiet and leave a beauty in the most painful doubts, the craftier and cleverer they are.

"Her principal method of trying out her admirers was to test their un-selfishness by daily inveigling them into great expenditures, rich gifts, and charitable deeds. But however they might act, they never could do the right thing; for if they showed themselves generous and unselfish, if they gave glittering festivities, brought her presents, or entrusted her with considerable sums for the poor, she would suddenly say that all this was done only to catch a salmon with a worm or throw a sausage at the ham, as the saying goes. And she passed on the gifts as well as the entrusted money to convents and beneficent foundations and fed the poor; but as for the disappointed suitors, she mercilessly rejected them. If on the other hand they showed themselves wary, not to say miserly, they were condemned in advance, for she resented that even more and believed that it expressed a base and naked callousness and selfishness.

"So it came about that she who sought a pure heart, devoted only to herself, was in the end surrounded only by deceitful, shrewd, and self-seeking suitors whom she could never make out and who galled her life.

"One day she felt so gloomy and despondent that she turned her whole court out of the house, closed it up, and traveled to Milan where she had a cousin. As she rode across the St. Gotthard on a little donkey, her mood was as black and horrible as the wild rocks towering out of the abyss, and she felt sorely tempted to hurl herself from Devil's Bridge into the raging waters of the Reuss. The guide, and two maids whom she had along and whom I myself knew (although they are long dead now), succeeded only with the greatest effort in calming her and dissuading her from her dark purpose. Yet she was pale and sad on her arrival in the fair land of Italy, and not even its blue skies would brighten her somber thoughts. After a few days with her cousin, however, another melody would unexpectedly sound, and a spring of which thus far she had known little was to dawn in her.

"For in her cousin's house there arrived a young compatriot whom at the very first glance she liked so well that she could be said to be falling in love by herself now, and for the first time. He was a handsome youth, well-bred and nobly mannered, and then neither poor nor rich, for he had nothing but ten thousand guilders inherited from his late parents, with which he desired to start a silk business in Milan. He had learned the merchant's trade and was enterprising and clear-headed and lucky, as is often the way with candid and innocent folk—for the young man was that, too; for all his learning he seemed harmless and innocuous like a child. And although he was a merchant and of such ingenuous disposition, which is already a preciously rare combination, he was nevertheless firm and chivalrous of bearing and carried his sword as boldly on his side as only an experienced warrior may.

"All of this, together with his fresh, handsome youth, conquered the damsel's heart, so that she could barely control herself and showed him the utmost friendliness. She grew merry again, and even when she was sad in between it was in the swift change of love's fears and hopes, which was in any case a nobler and more pleasant feeling than that painful embarrassment of choice which she formerly had felt among her many suitors. Now, the only worry and care she knew was how to please the good and handsome youth, and the lovelier she was, the humbler and less self-assured she became now that for the first time she felt a true affection.

"The young merchant also had never seen such beauty, or at least had never been so close to one, and found such warm and gracious treatment at her hands. And since, as I said, she was not only fair but also kind of heart and refined of manner, it is no wonder that the frank and candid youth, whose heart was still quite free and inexperienced, should likewise fall in love with her, and with all the violence and recklessness corresponding to his whole nature. And yet none might ever have known, if his simple soul had not been encouraged by the damsel's cordiality—which he, ignorant of guile himself, dared with secret fear and trembling to regard as proof that his love was returned. He constrained himself for a few weeks and believed he was concealing the matter; but everybody saw from far off that he was mortally in love, and whenever he came near the damsel or heard her name mentioned it was to be seen at once with whom.

"He was not long in love, however, before he really began to love with all the violence of his youth, so that the damsel became the highest and best in the world for him, to stake his salvation and the whole worth of his own person on, once and for all. This delighted her hugely; for in whatever he said or did his way was different from anything that she had known hitherto, and confirmed and moved her so deeply that she in turn also yielded to the deepest love and there was no further question of any choice.

"The little game was watched by all, and caused some open words and a good deal of banter. The damsel felt highly pleased with it, and, though her heart would burst with anxious expectation, helped a little to involve and string out the romance, so as to taste and relish it to the full. For the young man in his confusion was doing things so precious and boyish as she had never experienced, which for her became more flattering and pleasant all the time. Yet his candor and honesty could not long stand this state of things; with everybody hinting and freely jesting about it, it seemed to him to be turning into a comedy, as the subject of which his beloved was much too good and sacred; and what she liked best was precisely what made him depressed, uncertain, and embarrassed for her sake.

"He also deemed it offensive and deceitful on his part to bear so violent a passion around with him for a long time, and ceaselessly to think of her without her having any idea of it, which was certainly quite improper and not right! So one morning, visibly come to a resolution, he confessed his love to her in a few words, determined to avow it once and never for a second time, unless the first should be successful. For he was unaccustomed to the idea that so fair and well-made a damsel might perhaps not speak her true mind, nor immediately give her irrevocable Yes or No in reply. His heart was as tender as his love was violent, he was as brittle as he was childlike and as proud as he was candid, and everything with him was at once a matter of life and death, of Yes or No, blow for blow.

"At the same instant, however, as the damsel heard his confession which she had so longingly awaited, she was seized by her old distrust and it occurred to her, unfortunately, that her lover was a merchant who might perhaps wish only to secure her money, to expand his enterprises. If he were somewhat in love with her person, besides, this was no special merit in view of her beauty but the more outrageous since it made of her a mere desirable adjunct to her gold.

"So instead of confessing her own love and receiving him well, as she would have liked best to do, she instantly thought of a new ruse to test his devotion. Striking a serious, almost sad mien, she confided being already betrothed at home, to a young man whom she loved cordially. She had been several times on the point of telling that to him, the merchant, because she was very fond of him as a friend, as he might well have discovered from her demeanor, and she trusted him like a brother. But the clumsy jokes which had come up in the company had interfered with a familiar colloquy; however, now that he himself had surprised her by baring his good, noble heart to her, she could thank him no better for his affection than by an equally frank confidence.

"Yes, she went on, she could belong only to the one she had chosen and never would be able to transfer her heart to another; this was graven into her soul with golden fire, and the dear man himself, well as he knew her, was unaware of the greatness of her love. But it stood under an evil star: her betrothed was a merchant but poor as a church mouse, so they had planned on his using her means to go into business; a beginning had been made and everything started for the best; their wedding date had been set when an unforeseen mischance caused all of her funds suddenly to be attached and involved in litigation, possibly to be forever lost, while her poor betrothed soon had to make his first payments to the Milanese and Venetian merchants, with all his credit, honor, and prosperity, not to mention their union and connubial bliss! She had hurried down to Milan where she had wealthy relatives, here to find ways and means; but she had come at the wrong time, for nothing seemed to turn out well and yet time was moving on and unless she could help her beloved, she would have to die of despair. For he was the dearest and best man to be imagined, and surely would become a great merchant if he could be helped, and then to be his wife would be her only happiness on earth.

"Long before she finished this story, the poor handsome youth had lost all color and become as pale as a sheet. He uttered not a complaining sound, however, and no longer spoke a single word of himself and his love but merely sadly inquired how large was the amount of the obligations entered into by the fortunate-unfortunate lover. Ten thousand guilders, she replied even more sadly. The sad young merchant rose, asked the damsel to be of good cheer since a way out was sure to appear, and left without daring to look at her for shame of having thrown an eye upon a lady who so faithfully and passionately loved another. For the poor man took every word of her story for Gospel truth.

"Then, without delay, he went to see his business friends and by much pleading and sacrifice of certain sums prevailed on them to cancel the orders and purchases which he himself, at that very time and with his very own ten thousand guilders, was to have paid for and on which he had staked his whole career; and before six hours had passed, he reappeared before the damsel with his entire fortune and asked her for God's sake to be so good as to accept this aid from him.

"Her eyes shone in happy surprise and her heart beat as with hammers. She asked him where he had obtained this capital and he replied that he had borrowed it on the strength of his reputation and would have no trouble returning it, since his business was turning out well. She could see plainly that he was lying, that it was his only wealth and hope which he was sacrificing to her happiness, but she pretended to believe him. She gave free rein to her joyous feelings and cruelly acted as if they were due to her good fortune in being able now, after all, to save and marry the man of her choice; and she could find no words to express her gratitude.

"But suddenly she bethought herself and declared that she could not accept this magnanimous act save on one condition—that otherwise all pleas would be in vain. Asked what this condition was, she demanded his sacred promise that on a certain day he would come to attend her wedding and become the best friend and protector of her future husband as well as the most loyal friend, protector, and counsel of herself. Blushing, he asked her to desist from this request, but all reasons he cited to dissuade her were in vain. In vain he argued that his affairs would not permit him now to travel back to Switzerland and that such a trip would cause him considerable losses. But she resolutely stood her ground and even pushed his gold back toward him when he would not consent.

"Finally he promised, but he had to shake hands on it and swear it to her by his honor and salvation. She told him the precise day and hour when he should arrive, and all this he had to swear to her by his Christian faith and by his hope for salvation. Not until then would she accept his sacrifice and gaily had the treasure carried into her bedchamber, where she locked it with her own hands in her trunk and hid the key in her bosom.

"Now she tarried no longer in Milan but journeyed back across the St. Gotthard as merrily as she had been melancholy in coming. On Devil's Bridge, where she had wished to leap to her death, she laughed like a madcap and, with her lovely voice brightly rejoicing, threw a bunch of pomegranate blossoms which she wore on her breast down into the Reuss—in short, her joy was unconfined and hers was the merriest journey that was ever taken. Returned home, she opened and aired her house from top to bottom and decorated it as if she were expecting a prince. At the head of her bed, however, she placed the bag with the ten thousand guilders, and at night laid her head on the hard lump and slept on it as blissfully as if it had been a pillow stuffed with the softest down. She could scarcely await the day when she was sure of his arrival, for she knew that he would not break the simplest promise, much less an oath, though it were to cost his life. But the day came and the beloved did not appear, and when as many more days and weeks passed without word from him she began to tremble in every limb and was seized by the greatest fear and anxiety; she sent letters upon letters to Milan, but no one was able to tell her what had become of him.

"In the end it turned out, by chance, that the young merchant had taken a blood-red piece of satin-damask which he had at home from the beginnings of his business and had already paid for, had himself a battle dress made of it, and joined the Swiss who just then were fighting in the Milanese war as mercenaries for King Francis of France. After the battle of Pavia, where so many Swiss lost their lives, he was found lying on a pile of slain Spaniards, torn by many fatal wounds and with his red satin dress rent and tattered from top to bottom. Before giving up the ghost he commended the following message to the memory of a Seldwyler who lay by his side and had been less badly injured, begging him to convey it if he should get out of there alive:

" 'Dearest lady! Although I swore to you upon my honor, by my Christian faith, and by my salvation to appear at your wedding, I have since felt incapable of seeing you again and seeing another enjoy the greatest happiness which could exist for me. I had not felt this until you were gone, not having previously known how strict and uncanny a thing is such a love as I bear you, else I should doubtlessly have taken better care. Now that this is the way of it, I would rather lose my worldly honor and spiritual salvation and be eternally damned as a perjurer than once again appear before you with a fire burning in my breast more strongly and unquenchably than that of hell itself, which I shall scarcely feel beside it. Do not pray for me, fairest lady, for I never can and never shall be blessed without you, be it here or there. And so farewell and greetings!'

"Thus, in the battle after which King Francis said, 'All is lost save honor,' the hapless lover had lost all—hope, honor, life, and eternal salvation—all save the love which consumed him. The Seldwyler luckily got away, and no sooner found himself somewhat recovered and out of danger than he faithfully wrote the dead man's words on his writing tablet, lest he forget them, then journeyed home, presented himself to the hapless damsel, and read the message to her as stiffly and martially as was his habit in reading the roll of a company, for he was a field lieutenant.

"The damsel, however, tore her hair and her clothes and began to scream and weep so loudly that she was heard up and down the street and people came running. She dragged out the ten thousand guilders like a crazy woman, scattered them on the floor, threw herself down full length and kissed the glistening gold pieces. Quite out of her senses, she tried to gather up and embrace the rolling treasure, as if her lost lover were present in it. She lay on the gold day and night, refusing to take either food or drink; incessantly she fondled and kissed the cold metal, until she suddenly rose in the middle of the night, carried the treasure down into the garden, industriously running to and fro, and there, amid bitter tears, threw it into a deep well and pronounced a curse over it, that it never should belong to anyone else."

When Spiegel had come so far in his story, Pineiss said, "And is that beautiful money still lying in the well?"

"Where else should it be?" Spiegel answered, "since I alone can get it out and have not done so to this hour?"

"I see, that's right," said Pineiss; "I had forgotten all about that over your story. You're not bad at telling stories, you rascal, and I'm really beginning to hanker after a little wife who would be so taken with me. She would have to be very beautiful, though. But now tell me quickly how the whole thing really hangs together."

"It took many years," Spiegel said, "for the damsel so far to recover from the bitter torment of her soul that she could begin to turn into the quiet old spinster that I came to know. I can boast of having been her only comfort and the most trusted friend of her lonely life, until her quiet end. When she felt this approaching, however, she once more recalled the time of her distant youth and beauty, and once more, with milder and more resigned thoughts, suffered first the sweet excitements and then the bitter agonies of that time, and she quietly wept through seven days and nights for the love of the youth whose enjoyment she had lost by her suspicions, so that her old eyes grew sightless even before she died.

"Then she rued the curse which she had laid on that treasure, and in entrusting me with this important task she said to me, 'I now direct otherwise, dear Spiegel, and empower you to carry out my will. Look around until you find a beautiful but impecunious maiden who may lack suitors on account of her poverty. If there should then turn up a sensible, righteous, and handsome man who has a good income and wishes to take the maiden to wife regardless of her poverty, solely moved by her beauty, this man shall bind himself with the strongest vows to be as faithfully, as unselfishly, and invariably devoted to her as my unfortunate lover was to me, and to do this woman's will in all things for the rest of his life. Then give the ten thousand guilders in the well to the bride for a dowry, that she may surprise her bridegroom with them on her wedding morn!'

"Thus spoke the dear departed, and I, due to my untoward fate, have neglected to follow up this matter and now must fear that the poor woman therefore rests uneasy in her grave, which may have no very pleasant consequences for myself, either."

IV

Pineiss looked at Spiegel suspiciously and said, "Might you be in a position, my fellow, to give me some proof of the treasure and make it evident to me?"

"At any time," Spiegel retorted, "but you must know, Mr. Town Sorcerer, that you may not simply fish out the gold, just like that. You would unfailingly have your neck wrung; for there is something uncanny about the well. I have certain indications of that, which certain considerations prevent me from mentioning further."

"Why, who said anything about getting it out?" Pineiss said, somewhat fearfully. "Just lead me there and show me the treasure! Or rather, I'll lead you, by a stout cord so you can't escape me!"

"As you please," said Spiegel. "But take also another long cord along, and a lantern which you can let down into the well, for it is very deep and dark."

Pineiss followed this advice and led the merry little cat to the garden of the deceased spinster. Together they climbed the wall, and Spiegel showed the sorcerer the way to the old well, which was buried under wild-growing shrubbery. There Pineiss let down his lantern, greedily looking after it without relaxing his hold upon Spiegel. And indeed, in the depth he saw the gold sparkle beneath the greenish water, and he cried, "Truly, I see it! it's true! Spiegel, you're a grand fellow!" Then he eagerly peered down again and said, "Are there really ten thousand of them?"

"Well, to that I can't swear," said Spiegel. "I've never been down to count them. It's possible, too, that the lady lost a few pieces on the way, in carrying the treasure over here, because she was in a very excited condition."

"Well, let it be a dozen more or less," said Mr. Pineiss, "I won't let that bother me." He sat down on the edge of the well; Spiegel sat down, too, licking his paw. "Now there we have the treasure," Pineiss said, scratching himself behind the ear, "and here we have the man to go with it; there's nothing lacking but the beautiful woman."

"What?" said Spiegel.

"I mean, we're short only the one who is to get the ten thousand for a dowry, to surprise me with them on our wedding morn, and who has all those agreeable virtues that you mentioned."

"Hm," said Spiegel. "It's not quite the way you put it. The treasure is there, as you rightly perceive; the beautiful woman, to admit it candidly, I have already found, too; but the hitch is with the man who would want to marry her under these difficult circumstances. For nowadays beauty has to be gilded like walnuts on Christmas, and the emptier the men's heads get, the keener they are on filling their emptiness with a dowry so as better to pass their time. Then they inspect a horse or importantly buy a piece of velvet, or order a fine crossbow, with so much ado and running, and the gunsmith is never out of the house.

"Next they say, 'I'll have to bring in my wine and clean my kegs, have my trees trimmed or my roof shingled; I have to send my wife to take the baths, she is ailing and costs me a lot of money; I have to get my wood cut and collect my debts; I've bought a few whippets and exchanged my hunting dog; I've traded my big walnut chest for a fine oaken drop-leaf table; I've cut my beanstalks, fired my gardener, sold my hay, and sown my lettuce'—always mine and mine, from dawn to dusk.

"Some even say, 'I have to do my wash next week, I have to air my beds, I must hire a maid and get a new butcher, since I must get rid of the old one; I've picked up the loveliest waffle iron, by chance, and sold my silver cinnamon box, which was no use to me anyway.' Now all that, be it understood, is the wife's business, and thus such a fellow spends his time and steals the day from our dear Lord in recounting all of these doings without moving a hand. At the outside, if such a rogue has to knuckle under, perhaps he may say, '*Our* cows and *our* hogs,' but—"

Pineiss jerked the string so that Spiegel squealed "Miaow!" and shouted, "Enough, you chatterbox! Tell me instantly: where is the woman you know of?" For the listing of all these wonderful things and doings connected with a dowry had only served to water the arid sorcerer's mouth still more.

Spiegel asked in amazement, "So you really will undertake the matter, Mr. Pineiss?"

"I certainly will! Who else? So out with it: where is she?"

"So you can go there and court her?"

"By all means!"

"Then you must know that the matter goes through my hands only. It's me you have to talk to, if you want money and wife," Spiegel said cold-bloodedly and indifferently, assiduously drawing both paws over his ears after wetting them a little each time.

Pineiss thought carefully, moaned a little, and said, "I notice you want to cancel our contract and save your head."

"Would that seem so unfair and unnatural to you?"

"In the end you may be cheating and lying to me, like a rogue."

"That's possible, too," said Spiegel.

"I tell you: don't you cheat me!" Pineiss cried imperiously.

"All right, so I won't cheat you," said Spiegel.

"If you do—"

"I do."

"Don't torture me, Spiegel," Pineiss said almost tearfully.

And Spiegel, seriously now, replied, "You're a marvelous man, Mr. Pineiss! There you are holding me captive on a string, and keep jerking it so I can hardly breathe. You let the sword of death hang over me for more than two hours—what am I saying, for six months! And now you say, 'Don't torture me!' If you'll permit me, I'll put it to you in a few words: I should be only too glad to fulfill my duty of love to the dead woman after all, and to find a suitable husband for the person in question, and it is true that you seem to be sufficient in every respect; it is no child's play to get a woman properly cared for these days, no matter how easy it may seem, and I say once more: I'm glad you're ready to do it. But I won't do it for nothing. Before I say another word or take another step, before I even open my mouth again, I first want my freedom back and my life assured. So take this string away and put our contract down there on the well, on this stone here, or cut off my head—one or the other!"

"Why, you lunatic and scatterbrain," said Pineiss, "you hothead, you don't really mean that, do you? That will have to be properly discussed, and in any event would call for a new contract!"

Spiegel no longer answered and sat immobile for one, two, three minutes. The master grew anxious; he took out his wallet, picked out the paper with a sigh, read it once again, and hesitantly placed it before Spiegel. The paper scarcely lay there before Spiegel had snapped it up and swallowed it, and although he had to gulp strenuously to get it down, it still seemed to him the best and most wholesome food he had ever enjoyed, and he hoped that it would agree with him for a long time and make him round and merry.

When he had finished this agreeable meal he politely greeted the sorcerer and said, "You will hear from me without fail, Mr. Pineiss, and neither wife nor money shall escape you. On the other hand, get ready to be right loving, so that you can promise and fulfill those conditions of unchanging devotion to the caresses of your wife, who is as good as yours already. And herewith I thank you for now, for board and care, and shall take my leave."

With that Spiegel went his way, delighted over the stupidity of the sorcerer who thought he could deceive himself and everyone else when he would marry the hoped-for bride, not disinterestedly, for sheer love of beauty, but forewarned of the existence of the ten thousand guilders. Meanwhile, he already had his eye on a person he meant to foist off on the stupid sorcerer in return for his roasted fieldfares, sausages, and mice.

V

Opposite Mr. Pineiss's house there was another house, the front of which was most cleanly whitewashed and the windows of which always gleamed freshly scrubbed. The modest curtains always were white as snow and appeared fresh from under the iron, and similarly white were the dress, cap, and neckerchief of an old Beguine who lived in the house. The nunlike wimple over her chest always looked as if it were folded from writing paper and spontaneously made you want to write on it—and on the chest, at least, one might have done so conveniently, it being as flat and hard as a board. Sharp as the white edges and points of her dress were the Beguine's long nose and chin, her tongue, and the evil glance of her eyes; but she did little talking with her tongue and little glancing with her eyes, for she disliked waste and used everything only at the proper time and after due deliberation. She went to church three times daily, and when she crossed the street in her fresh, white, and rustling things and with her white, pointed nose, the children fearfully ran away and even grown-up people liked to step behind the house door if there was still time.

However, she enjoyed a high reputation for her strict piety and seclusion and was especially well esteemed by the clergy, although even the priests would deal with her in writing rather than orally, and when she came to confession the priest always shot out of the confessional, sweating as if straight from an oven. Thus the pious Beguine, who was not one to trifle with, lived in full peace and remained unwed. Nor did she bother with anyone or trouble people, provided they kept out of her way; only her neighbor Pineiss seemed to have aroused her special hatred, for whenever he let himself be seen at his window she shot over an evil glance and instantly drew her white curtains. Pineiss dreaded her like fire and only in the very rear of his house, with everything well locked, would dare to crack a joke about her.

White and bright, however, as the Beguine's house looked from the street, from the rear it looked black and smoky, weird and strange; but there almost no one could see it except the birds in the sky and the cats on the rooftops, because it was built into a dark maze of high, windowless fire walls, where no human face was ever seen. There under the roof hung old torn petticoats, baskets, and herb bags; growing on the roof were real little oak trees and thornbushes, and a great, sooty chimney rose eerily toward the sky.

Out of this chimney, however, in the dead of night, a witch not infrequently rode her broom to the heights, young and beautiful and stark naked, as God made women and the Devil likes to see them. Riding out of the chimney she would sniff the fresh night air with the most delicate little nose and with smiling cherry lips, soaring along in the white gleam of her body, while her long raven hair streamed behind her like a flag of night.

In a hole by the chimney sat an old owl, and it was to her that the liberated Spiegel went now, in his jaws a fat mouse he had captured on the way.

"A good evening to you, dear Mrs. Owl! Keenly on the lookout?" he said.

And the owl replied, "Have to! A good evening, too. You haven't been seen around here for a long time, Mr. Spiegel."

"There were reasons that I'll tell you about. Here I've brought you a mouse, nothing special, what the season offers, if you'd care for it. Is the mistress out riding?"

"Not yet. She will only go out for an hour or so toward morning. Thanks for the fine mouse. Always the polite Spiegel! I've got a bad sparrow put aside here that came too close to me this morning; if you please, taste the bird. And how have you been doing?"

"Queerly, rather," Spiegel replied. "They were after my skin. Let me tell you, if you please."

While they enjoyed their supper, Spiegel told the attentive owl everything that had happened to him, and how he had freed himself from Mr. Pineiss's hands.

The owl said, "Well, a thousand congratulations! Now you are your own master again, and you can go wherever you please, after such strange experiences."

"That isn't the end of it yet," said Spiegel. "The man must get his wife and his guilders."

"Are you out of your mind, to do a good turn for the rogue who wanted to skin you?"

"Why, he could have done it legally and according to contract, and since I can pay him back in the same coin, why shouldn't I? Who says I want to do him a good turn? That story was pure invention; my late mistress who now rests in God was a simple person who was never in love in her life, nor ever surrounded by suitors, and that treasure is unjust money which she inherited once upon a time and threw into the well lest it bring her bad luck. 'Cursed be whoever takes it out of there and uses it!' she said. So it won't be too much of a good turn."

"That changes matters, of course. And now, where do you expect to get the suitable wife?"

"Here from this chimney. That's why I've come, to talk a sensible word with you. Wouldn't you like to be free again from the bonds of this witch? Think how we may capture her and marry her off to the old villain."

"Spiegel, you only need to approach and I have good ideas!"

"There, I knew you were wise. I've done my part, and it will be even better if you add something too and put new strength to work. Then we can't fail."

"With everything fitting together so well, I don't have to think long. My plans have long been laid."

"How shall we catch her?"

"With a new woodcock snare made of good strong hemp strands. They must have been twisted by a twenty-year-old hunter who has never looked at a woman, and the night dew must have fallen on it three times without a woodcock having been caught in it. The reason for this, however, must be a threefold good deed. Such a net would be strong enough to catch the witch."

"Now I wonder where you'll find that," said Spiegel, "for I know you would not be prattling idly."

"It's already found—just as if made for us:

"In a forest not far from here sits a hunter's son who is twenty years old and has never looked at a woman, for he was born blind. Therefore he is good for nothing but twisting cord, and a few days ago he made a new and very fine woodcock snare. But when the old hunter wanted to set it for the first time, a woman came along and tried to tempt him to sin, but she was so ugly that the old man fled aghast, and left the net on the ground, so that the dew fell on it without a woodcock having been caught, and the cause of it was a good deed.

"The next day, when he went to set it again, a horseman rode by with a heavy sack behind him; in the sack was a hole, from which a gold coin fell every now and then. And the hunter again left the net lying and ran after the horseman, collecting the coins, until the man on horseback turned around, saw what was going on, and wrathfully aimed his lance at him. Now the hunter bowed in fright, handed up his hat, and said, 'Permit me, sir, you have lost a lot of money, which I have been carefully gathering for you.' This was another good deed, honest finding being one of the most difficult and best; but he had come so far from the woodcock snare that he left it lying in the woods for the second night and took the short way home.

"On the third day, finally, which was yesterday, when he was on the way again, he met a pretty woman who often cajoles the oldster and has received many a rabbit from him as a present. Over her he completely forgot the woodcocks, and in the morning said, 'I've spared their poor little lives; one must be merciful even to animals.' And on account of these three good deeds he found that he was now too good for this world, and took the vows of a monk this very morning. So the snare is still lying unused in the woods and I only need to fetch it."

"Fetch it quickly," said Spiegel, "it will be good for our purpose."

"I'll fetch it," said the owl, "if only you will keep watch for me in this hole, and if by chance my mistress should call up the chimney asking whether the air is clear, you have to imitate my voice and answer, 'No, there is no stink yet in the fencing school!' "

Spiegel posted himself in the niche, and the owl silently flew away over the town, toward the woods. Soon she returned with the woodcock snare and asked, "Did she call yet?"

"Not yet," said Spiegel.

So they stretched the net out over the chimney and sat beside it, quietly and wisely; the air was dark and in the light morning breeze a few stars were twinkling. "You ought to see," whispered the owl, "how cleverly she knows how to breeze up the chimney without blackening her white shoulders!"

"I've never seen her as close as that," replied Spiegel softly. "If only she doesn't catch us."

Then the witch called from below, "Is the air clear?"

"Quite clear," cried the owl; "there's a gorgeous stink in the fencing school," and the witch came riding up forthwith and was caught in the net which the cat and owl hastily pulled tight and tied. "Hold tight," said Spiegel, and, "Tie fast," echoed the owl. The witch struggled and writhed, silently, like a fish in the net; but it availed her nothing and the snare proved itself splendidly. Only the handle of her broom stood out through the meshes. Spiegel wanted to pull it out gently but received such a crack on his nose that he all but fainted and realized that one must not come too close to a lioness even in a net. Eventually the witch held still and said, "What do you want of me, you insane animals?"

"You are to release me from your service and restore my freedom," said the owl.

"So much ado about nothing," said the witch. "You're free. Open this net."

"Not yet," said Spiegel who was still rubbing his nose. "You must promise to marry the Town Sorcerer Pineiss, your neighbor, in the manner which we shall tell you, and never leave him."

At that the witch again began to struggle and to spit like the Devil, and the owl said, "She won't bite."

But Spiegel said, "If you aren't quiet and do whatever we wish, we'll hang this net together with its contents out there on the dragon's head under the eaves, right above the street, so that tomorrow everyone will see you and recognize the witch. Now say: would you rather be roasted under Mr. Pineiss's supervision, or roast him by marrying him?"

Then the witch said with a sigh, "Tell me then, what all this means."

And Spiegel neatly explained everything to her and what she would have to do.

"Well, that can be endured if there's nothing else to be done," she said and yielded, with the strongest formulas that may bind a witch. Then the animals opened the prison and let her out. She immediately mounted her broom, the owl sat on the handle behind her, and Spiegel on the twigs in the rear, holding on tight, and thus they rode to the well into which the witch descended to retrieve the treasure.

In the morning Spiegel appeared at Mr. Pineiss's and reported to him that he might now inspect and court the maid in question; however, she had already become so poor that she was sitting before the gate under a tree, completely forsaken and forlorn and weeping bitterly. At once Mr. Pineiss dressed himself in his shabby old yellow velvet doublet that he only wore on festive occasions, donned his second-best poodle cap and girt on his sword; in his hand he carried an old green glove, a small balsam bottle which once had contained balsam and still smelled faintly, and a paper carnation; thereupon he set out with Spiegel for the gate and courtship. There he met a weeping female seated under a willow tree, of such great beauty as he had never seen; but her garment was so scant and torn that however modest she would act, her white body always gleamed through here or there. Pineiss's eyes bulged; he scarcely could stammer his proposal for stormy delight. The beauty dried her tears, gave him her hand with a sweet smile, thanked him for his generosity in a voice like heavenly bells, and vowed to be eternally true to him. But at the same instant he was filled by such furious jealousy and envy of his bride that he resolved never to have her seen by any human eye. He got an age-old hermit to marry them and celebrated the marriage feast in his house, with no guests other than Spiegel and the owl whom Spiegel had requested permission to bring. The ten thousand guilders stood in a bowl on the table and Pineiss frequently reached in and stirred the gold; then again he would look at the beautiful woman who sat there in a sea-blue velvet gown, her hair woven through a gold net and adorned with flowers, and her white throat ringed with pearls. He constantly wanted to kiss her, but she knew how to keep him off in modesty and shame, yet with a seductive smile, and swore that she would not kiss in front of witnesses and before the fall of night. This only made him the more lovesick and blissful, and Spiegel spiced the feast with charming conversation, which the lovely woman continued with the most pleasant, wittiest, and most ingratiating words, so that the sorcerer did not know for joy what was happening to him.

When darkness fell, however, the owl and the cat took their leave and modestly withdrew. Mr. Pineiss saw them to the door with a light and once again thanked Spiegel, whom he called a fine, polite man, and when he returned to the room, there at the table sat the old Beguine, his neighbor, who glanced at him evilly. Pineiss dropped the light in terror and tremblingly leaned against the wall. His tongue hung out, and his face turned as pale and haggard as that of the Beguine. She, however, got up, approached him, and drove him before her into the nuptial chamber, where her hellish arts subjected him to the worst torture a mortal has endured. So now he was irrevocably wed to the hag, and when the people in town heard of it they said, "Look at that! Still waters run deep. Who would have thought that the pious Beguine and the Town Sorcerer would be joined in holy wedlock? Well, they're an honorable and righteous couple, if not especially amiable."

Mr. Pineiss henceforth led a miserable life; his wife had immediately taken possession of all his secrets and ruled him completely. Not the slightest freedom or rest was allowed him; he had to make magic from morning till night as hard as he could, and whenever Spiegel passed by and saw it he would ask politely, "Always busy, always busy, Mr. Pineiss?"

From that time on they have said at Seldwyla, "He's bought the fat off the cat," especially when someone has got a shrewish and repulsive wife in the bargain.

—§—

Translated by E. B. Ashton

‹ *Hinzelmeier* ›

A THOUGHTFUL STORY
THEODOR STORM

THE WHITE WALL

In a spacious old house lived Herr Hinzelmeier and his beautiful wife, Abel. They had been married for eleven years; in fact, the people of the town reckoned that the two of them were carrying around the combined weight of almost eighty years, and yet they were still young and handsome, not a wrinkle on their foreheads, not a crow's-foot by their eyes. It was obvious enough that something funny was going on, and when the talk at coffee klatches got around to the subject of the Hinzelmeiers, the town gossips would drink three more cups than they did the first Sunday afternoon of Easter. One would say, "They've got a fountain of youth in the backyard." Another would agree: "Not just a fountain of youths either; girls too—it's a mill of maidens." A third would add, "Their boy, little Hinzelmeier, was born with a lucky caul and now his parents take turns wearing it, one night one of them, the next night the other." Of course, little Hinzelmeier had no such thoughts; on the contrary, it seemed quite natural to him that his parents were forever young and beautiful. But all the same, he was to get his own little mystery to solve, and he couldn't crack it.

One fall afternoon, toward dusk, he was sitting in the long hall of the top story of his house, playing hermit. Normally he would have been giving lessons to the silver-gray house cat, but she had just crept out into the garden to check on the finches, so for the rest of the day he was compelled to give up playing professor. Now he was sitting in a corner, being a hermit, and wondering about all sorts of things, such as where birds flew to, and what the world out there looked like, and even more profound matters—for he intended to give the cat a lecture on these subjects the next day—when he saw his mother, beautiful Frau Abel, walk past him. "Hey, Mother," he called, but she did not hear him. She walked on with rapid steps to the end of the hall; there she stopped and struck the white wall three times with her hand-kerchief. Hinzelmeier counted in his mind, and hardly had he got to three when the wall opened without a sound and he saw his mother disappear through it. The tip of her handkerchief barely had time to slip through after her when the whole thing closed shut with a soft clap and our hermit was left with much more to wonder about, namely, where in the world his mother went when she went through the wall. While he was thus occupied, it grad-ually grew darker, and the dusk in his corner became so thick that it swallowed him up completely. At this point there came, as before, a soft clap and lovely Frau Abel stepped out of the wall again, into the hall. As she brushed past him, the fragrance of roses reached the boy. "Mother, Mother," he called, but she would not stop; he heard her walk down the stairs and into his father's room, where, that same morning, he had tied his hobbyhorse to the brass knob on the stove. Now he could contain himself no longer; he ran through the hall and rode like the wind down the banister. When he entered the room it was full of the smell of roses and it almost seemed to him that his mother was a rose herself, such was the glow on her face. It made Hinzelmeier very thoughtful.

"Mother dear," he said finally, "why do you always go through the wall?"

And when this caused Frau Abel to fall silent, his father said, "Well, after all, my son, because other people always go through the door."

That made sense to Hinzelmeier; but soon he wanted to know more.

"Where do you go when you go through the wall?" he went on, "And where are those roses?"

But before he knew it, his father had turned him head over heels and plopped him on his hobbyhorse and his mother was singing a beautiful song:

> *Hatto of Mainz and Poppo of Trier*
> *Rode together from Luenebier.*
> *Hippity Hatto, a-trotting we go,*
> *Hoppity Poppo, galloping so!*
>
> *One, two, three!*
> *Past Zelle with me;*
> *One, two, three, four!*
> *Now we're at our own front door.*

"Untie him, untie him!" cried Hinzelmeier, and his father loosened the reins of the little horse from the knob of the stove, and his mother sang her song, and the rider rode up and down and had soon forgotten all the roses and white walls in the whole world.

THE TIP OF THE HANDKERCHIEF

Many years went by without a repetition of the miraculous event Hinzelmeier had witnessed. So he no longer thought about it all the time, though his parents remained as young and beautiful as they had always been and even in winter were often surrounded by the fragrance of roses.

Hinzelmeier was rarely to be found in the lonely corridor of the top story now, for the cat had died of old age and his school had consequently folded for lack of pupils.

About this time, he began to think that his beard ought to start growing in a few years. One day he went up again into the old hallway to take a look at the white walls, because he planned that evening to do a production of the famous shadow play "Nebuchadnezzar and His Nutcracker." With this in mind he had come to the end of the corridor and was looking up and down the opposite wall when to his astonishment he saw the tip of a handkerchief hanging out of it. He bent down to look at it more closely: the corner bore the initials A.H. That could only mean Abel Hinzelmeier; it was his mother's handkerchief. Now the wheels in his head began to turn and his thoughts worked backward, farther and farther, until they came to a sudden stop at the first chapter of this story. At this point he tried to pull the handkerchief out of the wall and, fortunately, after some rather painful experimentation, succeeded. Then, like the lovely Frau Abel before him, he struck the piece of cloth against the wall three times, "one—two—three," and it parted silently. Hinzelmeier slipped through and found himself—the last place he thought he would be—in the attic. No doubt about it: there stood his great-grandmother's wardrobe with its wobbly pagoda towers on top, next to it his own cradle, and beyond that his hobbyhorse, things that had served their purpose and been discarded, all of them. Under the rafters, on rows of iron hooks, hung his father's long coats and traveling capes, as they always had, turning slowly whenever there was a draft of air from the open dormers. "Strange," said Hinzelmeier. "Why in the world did mother always go through that wall?" However, unable to discern anything besides the objects he was familiar with, he thought he would go back down through the attic door into the house. But the door was not there. He was momentarily taken aback and at first thought that he had simply got lost, having come up from a different direction than usual. He therefore turned and walked through the coats and capes to the old wardrobe in order to get his bearings again, and sure enough, there was the door. He could not imagine how he had overlooked it. But when he went up to it, everything suddenly seemed strange once more, so that he began to doubt whether he was at the right door. As far as he knew, however, there was no other. What confused him most was the fact that the iron latch was missing and also that the key, which was always in the lock, had been removed. He therefore put his eye to the keyhole, hoping to catch sight of someone on the stairs, or on the landing, who might let him out. To his amazement, however, he was not looking down the dark stairs but into a bright, spacious room, the existence of which he had never suspected.

In the middle of it he could make out a pyramidal shrine-like cabinet, closed off with glittering gold doors and adorned with curious carving. Hinzelmeier couldn't tell whether the narrow keyhole was distorting his vision, but it almost seemed as if the figures of snakes and lizards in the brown leaves festooning the corners were rustling up and down and occasionally even stretching their supple heads over the gold background of the door. All this had so occupied the boy's attention that it was some time before he noticed his lovely mother and her husband, kneeling before the shrine with their heads bowed. Involuntarily he held his breath so as not to be discovered, and heard his parents' voices, softly singing:

> *Ring around the roses shine,*
> *Open, open, golden shrine,*
> *Open up to me and mine!*
> *Ring around the roses shine.*

During their singing all the reptilian life in the fretwork foliage ceased. The golden doors opened slowly and revealed in the interior of the cabinet a crystal chalice in which a half-opened rose stood upon its slender stem. Gradually the calyx opened, farther and farther, until one of the shimmering petals became detached and fell between the kneeling couple. But before it had reached the ground it dissolved in the air with a sound like the ringing of bells and filled the room with a rosy-red mist.

The powerful fragrance of roses poured through the keyhole. The boy pressed his eye to the opening but saw nothing except an occasional luminescence that ascended in the reddish half-light and vanished again. After a time he heard steps at the door; he was about to leap up, but a violent pain in his forehead robbed him of consciousness.

THE ROSE

When Hinzelmeier awoke from his swoon, he was lying in his bed. Frau Abel sat beside him, holding his hand in hers. She smiled when he opened his eyes and looked at her, and the reflected glow of the rose was on her face. "You've heard too much to stop partway; there's more you must know," she said. "Only you have to stay in bed the rest of the day; but meanwhile I'll tell you the secret of your family. You're old enough now to know."

"Please tell me, Mother," said Hinzelmeier, and laid his head back on his pillow. Then Frau Abel told her story. "Far from this little town lies the old, old Rose Garden which legend says was one of the things made on the sixth day of Creation. Inside its walls are a thousand red rosebushes that never stop blooming, and every time a child is born to our family (which is now spread through all the lands of the world, in many branches) a new bud springs from the leaves. Each bud has a maiden assigned to tend it, and she may not leave the garden until the rose has been picked by the one whose birth caused it to bud. Such a rose, which you just saw, has the power to keep its owner young and beautiful for life, so no one would lightly miss the chance to get his rose. It's only a question of finding the right way, because the entrances are many and often strange. One may lead through a thickly overgrown fence, another through a narrow, hidden door, and sometimes"—with mischievous eyes Frau Abel looked at her husband, who was just entering the room "— sometimes through the window too."

Herr Hinzelmeier smiled and sat down by his son's bed.

Frau Abel went on with her story. "Most of the young maidens are released from their imprisonment in this fashion, and each leaves the garden with the owner of her rose. Your mother was a Rose Maiden, too, and for sixteen years tended your father's rose. But if the man in question passes the garden without entering, he can never return. Only the Maid of the Rose is allowed, after three times three years, to go out in the world and look for her Lord of the Rose, and not until another three times three years have passed may she repeat the attempt. Few, however, risk the first trip and almost no one risks the second. For the Rose Maidens are fearful of the world, and if in fact they go forth in their white robes, they go with downcast eyes and trembling footsteps. Still, for every hundred such brave women, hardly a one has ever found her wandering Lord of the Rose. As far as *he* is concerned, however, the rose is lost, and while the maiden returns to everlasting imprisonment, he has forfeited the grace of his birth, and pitifully, like ordinary human beings, he must age and die. You too, my son, are one of the Lords of the Roses and when you enter the world out there, don't forget the Rose Garden."

Herr Hinzelmeier bent down and kissed Frau Abel's silken hair. Then, taking the boy's other hand in his friendly grasp, he said, "You are big enough now. Would you like to go out into the world and master some art?"

"Yes," said Hinzelmeier, "but it would have to be a great art, the kind no one ever was able to master before."

Frau Abel shook her head in distress; but his father said, "I will take you to a wise teacher who lives in a large city many miles from here; then you can choose the art you want."

Hinzelmeier was satisfied with that.

A few days later Frau Abel packed a great trunk with innumerable clothes, and Hinzelmeier himself put in a razor so that whenever his beard came he could shave it off again right away. Then one day the coach pulled up before the door, and as his mother embraced him in farewell, she said to her son, through her tears, "Don't forget the Rose!"

CROHIRIUS

After Hinzelmeier had lived with his wise mentor for a year he wrote to his parents to tell them that he had now chosen the art he would master: he was going to seek the Philosophers' Stone. In two years his teacher would dismiss him and he would then set out on his travels as a journeyman and not return until he had found the stone. This was the kind of art no one had ever before acquired, for even his master was really just a senior journeyman; he had never come close to discovering the Stone.

When lovely Frau Abel had read this letter she folded her hands, fingers intertwined, and cried, "Oh, he will never reach the Rose Garden. The same thing will happen to him that happened to our neighbor's boy Caspar, who went away twenty years ago and never came home again."

Herr Hinzelmeier, however, kissed his lovely wife and said, "He had to go his own way. I, too, wanted to look for the Philosophers' Stone once; instead I found the Rose."

So young Hinzelmeier stayed with his wise master and time slowly ran its course.

It was late at night. Hinzelmeier sat before a smoky lamp, bent over a folio volume. But he could make no progress today; he felt his veins pounding and swirling, he was overcome by an anxious feeling that he might forever lose his comprehension for the deep wisdom of the formulas and incantations preserved in the ancient book.

Occasionally he would turn his pale face to look back into the room, staring vacantly at the corner and at the cheerless figure of his master puttering about before a low hearth among glowing retorts and crucibles. At times, when the bats swept past the windowpanes, he would look longingly out into the moonlit night, which lay like a magic spell over the fields. At the master's side, on the floor, crouched the herb lady. She had the gray house cat on her lap and was gently stroking the sparks out of his fur. Sometimes, when there was a nice comforting crackle and the beast meowed with a pleasant shudder, the master would reach back to pat him and would say, with a cough, "The cat is the philosopher's companion."

Suddenly there came from outside, from the ridge of the roof that ran beneath the window, a long-drawn-out sound of yearning, such as only the cat, among all animals, is capable of, and then only in spring. The tomcat straightened up and dug his claws into the old lady's apron. Another cry from outside, and the creature sprang with a vigorous leap to the floor and over Hinzelmeier's shoulder through the windowpane and into the open, so that the slivers of glass sprayed out behind him with a sound like the ringing of bells.

A sweet smell of primroses swept into the room on the draft of air. Hinzelmeier sprang up. "It's spring, master!" he cried, and threw back his chair.

The old man buried his nose deeper in the crucible. Hinzelmeier went over to him and took him by the shoulder. "Don't you hear, master?"

The master ran his hand through his gray-dappled beard and stared dully at the young man through his green spectacles.

"The ice is breaking up!" cried Hinzelmeier. "There's a ringing in the air!"

The master seized him by the wrist and began to count his pulse. "Ninety-six," he said gravely, but Hinzelmeier paid no attention to that; rather he requested permission to leave that very hour. The master told him to take up his walking stick and his knapsack; he walked with him to the door, where they could look far out into the countryside. The boundless plains lay at their feet, in the bright moonlight. They stood there quietly. The master's face was furrowed with a thousand wrinkles, his back was bent, his beard hung down deep over his brown robe; he looked inexpressibly old. Hinzelmeier's face was pale too, but his eyes shone. His master spoke to him: "Your time is over. Kneel down so that you may receive permission to go." Then he drew a little white rod from his sleeve and, as Hinzelmeier knelt there, touched him on the back of the neck three times, saying:

> The Word's in the keeping
> Of spirits; the faster
> You rouse it from sleeping,
> The sooner you're master.

> *It's found in no kingdom, grown in no clime*
> *It's partly a name, an aura in part;*
> *To find and create at the very same time—*
> *That is the art!*

Then he bade him stand up. A shiver coursed through the youth's body as he gazed into the grizzled, solemn face of his master. He took up his walking stick and knapsack and was about to leave, when the master called, "Don't forget the raven!" He stuck his bony fist into his beard and pulled out a black hair. He blew it through his fingers, and it rose into the air as a raven.

Now he swung his staff in a circle about his head and the raven circled after. Then he stretched out his arm and the bird settled on his fist. He lifted his green spectacles from his nose and, clamping them on the raven's beak, he spoke:

> *Show the way, that's what you'll do;*
> *Crohirius is the name for you.*

Then the raven cried, "Crohiro, crohiro!" and with outstretched wings hopped onto Hinzelmeier's shoulder. The master, in turn, said to Hinzelmeier:

> *Journeyman's book and journeyman's rhyme,*
> *Now you have both—and now it is time!*

With his finger he pointed down into the valley, where an endless road ran across the plain, and as Hinzelmeier, waving his traveling cap in farewell, walked out into the spring night, Crohirius took off and flew overhead.

THE ENTRANCE TO THE ROSE GARDEN

The sun was already high in the sky. Hinzelmeier had set out on a straight path over a field of green winter grain that spread without limit before him. At the end of it the footpath led out through an opening in the wall to a spacious enclosure, and Hinzelmeier found himself before the buildings of a large farm estate. It had been raining, and the thatched roofs were steaming in the crisp spring sun. He stuck his journeyman's staff into the ground and gazed up at the ridgepole of the farmhouse, where crowds of sparrows were carrying on. Suddenly, from one of the two chimneys, he saw a shining disk rise into the air, turn slowly in the sunshine, and then fall back again, down the chimney.

Hinzelmeier pulled out his pocket watch. "It's noon," he said. "They are baking egg pancakes." A lovely fragrance spread all about; another egg pancake rose into the sunshine and after a brief time sank back into the chimney.

Hunger asserted itself. Hinzelmeier stepped into the house and, crossing a broad hallway, reached a high, spacious kitchen, like those commonly found in larger farmhouses. At the hearth, with its bright fire of brush and twigs, stood a sturdy farm woman, pouring the batter into the sizzling pan.

Crohirius, who had silently flown in behind Hinzelmeier, lit on the mantel over the hearth, while Hinzelmeier asked if he might get a meal here in exchange for money and kind words.

"This is no inn," said the woman, and swung her pan so that the pancake rose with a sizzle up the black flue and plopped down again, right side up in the pan, but only after a considerable time.

Hinzelmeier reached for his stick, which he had leaned against the door as he entered. The old lady, however, ran her fork into the pancake and flipped it quickly onto a plate. "Well, all right," she said, "I wasn't serious. Go ahead and sit down. Here's one that's ready." Then she shoved a wooden chair up to the kitchen table for him and set the steaming pancake in front of him, along with bread and a mug of new local wine.

Hinzelmeier accepted it all gladly and had soon consumed the hearty food and a considerable part of the firm rye bread. He then put the mug to his mouth and took a good draft of it to the old lady's health, and then a good many more to his own. This made him so happy that he began to sing just because he felt like it. "You're a cheerful fellow," cried the old lady from her hearth. Hinzelmeier nodded. Suddenly he found himself reminded of all the songs he had heard long ago in his parents' house, sung by his lovely mother. Now he sang them, one after the other:

> It's all because the nightingale sang,
> Sang all the livelong night;
> The song was sweet, its echo rang,
> And that is why the roses sprang
> Into bloom and bright.
>
> Once the most carefree maid of all,
> She walks, perplexed and blue,
> In the summer sun, no shade at all,
> Forgets she has her parasol
> And can't think what to do.
>
> It's all because the nightingale sang,
> Sang all the livelong night.

In the wall opposite the hearth, beneath the rows of shiny pewter plates, a small sliding window opened and a pretty blond girl, perhaps the farm owner's daughter, stuck her head into the kitchen, with a curious look on her face.

Hinzelmeier, who had heard the rattling of panes in the window, stopped his singing and let his eyes wander over the walls of the kitchen, over the butter tub and the shiny cheese vats, and over the old woman's broad back to the open window, where they came to rest on another pair of youthful eyes.

The girl blushed. "You sing nicely, young man," she said at last.

"It just came over me," Hinzelmeier replied. "I don't usually sing at all."

Then they were both silent for a time, and all one could hear was the sizzling of the pan and the crackle of the pancakes.

"Caspar sings well too." The girl spoke up again.

"No doubt he does," agreed Hinzelmeier.

"Yes," said the girl, "but not as nicely as you do. Where did you ever learn that beautiful song?"

Hinzelmeier did not answer; he stepped up on an overturned tub that stood under the sliding window and looked past the girl into the room beyond. It was full of sunshine. On the red tiles of the floor lay the shadows of carnations and roses, doubtless from bushes growing to the side and in front of a window somewhere. Suddenly toward the back of the room a door opened. The spring wind swept in and lifted a blue silk ribbon from the girl's bonnet, blew it through the sliding window, and bore its prize about the kitchen in circles; but Hinzelmeier threw his cap after it and caught it as one catches a summer bird.

He was about to hand the ribbon up to the girl, but found the window was a bit high. She bent out toward him, and their two heads bumped together with a crack. The girl cried out, the pewter plates rattled. Hinzelmeier became totally confused.

"You have a good solid head, young man," said the girl, and with her hand wiped away the tears from her cheek. Hinzelmeier pushed his hair back from his forehead and with a friendly smile looked her in the face, and when he did so she cast her eyes down and asked, "You didn't hurt yourself, did you?"

Hinzelmeier laughed. "No, miss," he cried, and then suddenly asked, although he couldn't figure out why this should occur to him, "Don't be offended, but I suppose you already have a sweetheart?"

She put her fist under her chin and tried to look defiantly at him, but her eyes remained fixed on his. "You must be imagining things," she said softly.

Hinzelmeier shook his head; not a word passed between them.

"Young lady," Hinzelmeier said after a time, "I'd like to bring the ribbon to you, in your room."

The girl nodded.

"But how do I get there?"

Words echoed in his ears: "Sometimes through the window!" It was his mother's voice. He saw her as she sat by his bed, he saw her smile; suddenly it seemed to him as if he were standing in a rosy cloud that was floating through the open panel window into the kitchen. He got up on the tub again and put his arms around the girl's neck. Through the open door of the room he could look out into a garden where rosebushes bloomed like a sea of red, and in the distance he heard the crystal voices of girls singing:

> *Ring around the roses shine,*
> *Open up for me and mine!*

Hinzelmeier pushed the girl gently back into the room and braced his hands on the windowsill, ready to swing himself up and in with a single leap. Then he heard a whirring over his head and a "Crohiro, crohiro!" and before he knew it the raven had dropped the green spectacles from the air right onto his nose. He saw the girl stretch out her arms toward him, but it was only as if in a dream; then everything disappeared before his eyes. In the far distance, however, he could see, through the green spectacles, a dark figure in a deep, rocky crevasse, apparently engaged in busily probing the ground with a long crowbar.

A MASTER SHOT

"He is looking for the Philosophers' Stone!" thought Hinzelmeier, and his cheeks began to burn. He strode off vigorously toward the figure, but it was farther away than it had looked through the lenses of his spectacles. He called out to the raven and had it fan his temples with its wings. It was hours before he reached the floor of the ravine. Before him he saw a coarse, black figure with two horns on its forehead and a long tail, which it draped down over the rock. On Hinzelmeier's arrival it took the crowbar between its teeth and greeted him with the most deferential bow of its head, while it used the tuft of its tail to sweep up the debris from the boring. Hinzelmeier was quite at a loss for the proper form of address, so each time he bowed back with equal deference, with the result that this exchange of compliments lasted for some time. Finally the other one asked, "I assume you do not know who I am?"

"No," said Hinzelmeier. "Are you perhaps a master pumpman?"

"Yes," said the other, "something like that; I am the Devil."

Hinzelmeier was not prepared to believe that, but the Devil looked at him with two eyes so owlish that he was at last thoroughly convinced and said meekly, "Might I be permitted to ask whether you mean to use this enormous hole for an experiment in physics?"

"Are you familiar with the *ultima ratio regum?*" the devil asked.

"No," said Hinzelmeier. "The *ratio regum* has nothing to do with my art."

The Devil scratched himself behind the ears with his horse's hoof and said, in a condescending tone of voice, "My son, do you know what a cannon is?"

"Naturally," said Hinzelmeier with a smile, for he saw in his imagination the whole wooden arsenal of his boyhood propped up before him.

The Devil was so pleased he clapped his tail on the rock cliff. "Three pounds of gunpowder, a spark of hell's fire, and then—!" At this point he stuck one paw in the borehole and, laying the other on Hinzelmeier's shoulder, said confidentially, "The world has gotten out of control. I'm going to blow it up."

"Good grief!" cried Hinzelmeier. "That certainly is radical therapy; that's real horse medicine."

"Yes," said the Devil, "*ultima ratio regum*—I assure you, it takes a superhuman disposition to stand this sort of thing. But now you must pardon me for a while; I have to do a bit of inspecting." With these words he tucked his tail in between his thighs and leaped down the borehole. Suddenly Hinzelmeier was seized with courage quite beyond the ordinary and decided he might as well shoot the Devil right out of the world. With a firm hand he drew his tinderbox from his pocket, struck a spark from it, and threw it into the borehole. Then he counted, "One—two—" but he hadn't got to three yet when this bottomless pistol discharged its shot along with its priming. The earth executed a terrifying sidewise leap through the sky. Hinzelmeier fell to his knees. The Devil, however, flew through the air like a bombshell, from one solar system to another, where the gravitational pull of our earth could no longer reach him. Hinzelmeier followed him with his eyes for a while, but when he kept flying farther and farther off, seemingly never to stop, Hinzelmeier couldn't hold back his tears. As soon as the earth had quieted down enough to permit standing on it with both feet, he leapt up and looked around him. At his feet, the black and burned-out mortar barrel yawned up at him. From time to time a cloud of brownish smoke puffed out from it and moved lazily along the cliffs. But the sun was already breaking through the haze and touching the tips of all the rocks with gold. Hinzelmeier took his tobacco pipe from his pocket and, blowing clouds of blue smoke before him, cried out in triumph, "I've shot Mr. Sulfurous Brimstone right out of this world; the Philosophers' Stone isn't going to get away from me. Let's be on our way!"

So he continued his journey, with Crohirius flying overhead.

THE ROSE MAIDEN

He journeyed back and forth, first this way, then that. He grew more and more weary, his back became bent, but he still did not find the Philosophers' Stone. Nine years had passed in this way when one evening he stopped at an inn situated at the entrance to a large city. Crohirius took off his spectacles with his claw and cleaned them on his wings, then put them back on and hopped into the kitchen. When the people who worked there saw him, they laughed at his spectacles, called him Professor, and threw him the fattest scraps of food.

"If you are the owner of this bird," said the innkeeper to Hinzelmeier, "then someone has been asking about you."

"As a matter of fact, I am," said Hinzelmeier.

"And what is your name?"

"My name is Hinzelmeier."

"Ah ha," said the innkeeper. "I am very well acquainted with your son, the husband of beautiful Frau Abel."

"That's my father," said Hinzelmeier with annoyance, "and beautiful Frau Abel is my mother."

The people laughed when they heard this and said that he was an extraordinarily funny fellow. Hinzelmeier, however, stared angrily into a shiny pot.

A gloomy face stared back at him, full of wrinkles and crow's feet, and now he could see clearly that he had grown disgustingly old.

"Yes, yes!" he cried, and shook himself as if he were emerging with difficulty from a deep dream. "Where was it anyway? I was very close." Then he asked the innkeeper who had inquired about him.

"It was only a poor serving girl," said the innkeeper. "She was wearing a white dress and walking around barefoot."

"That was the Rose Maiden!" cried Hinzelmeier.

"Yes," replied the innkeeper. "It may well have been a flower girl, but she had only one rose left in her basket."

"Where did she go?" cried Hinzelmeier.

"If you feel you have to talk to her," said the innkeeper, "you'll surely be able to find her on some street corner in the city."

When Hinzelmeier heard that, he strode quickly out of the house and into town. Crohirius, the spectacles on his nose, flew after him, cawing. Their way took them from one street to another, and on the curb at every corner stood flower girls, but they wore big, shapeless buckled shoes and cried their wares with shrill voices. Those were no Rose Maidens. At last, when the sun had already set behind the buildings, Hinzelmeier came to an old house; from the open door a delicate light shone forth onto the street. Crohirius threw his head back and beat his wings anxiously, but Hinzelmeier paid no attention; he stepped over the threshold into a broad entrance hall, filled with a red glow. He could see, far in the background, sitting on the lowest step of a spiral staircase, a pale young woman. On her lap she held a basket, and in the basket lay a red rose, the chalice of which was the source of that delicate light. The girl seemed tired; she was just taking her lips from an earthenware water pitcher, which a little boy was holding out to her in both his hands. A large dog lay beside her on the stair; like the boy, he seemed to be part of the household. He had put his head on her white dress and was licking her bare feet.

"That's her," said Hinzelmeier, and his steps were unsteady with hope and expectation. And when the girl lifted up her face to look at him, it was as if scales fell from his eyes: he suddenly recognized the girl from the farm kitchen, only today she was not wearing the colorful blouse, and the red of her cheeks was only the reflection of the light from the rose.

"There you are," cried Hinzelmeier. "Now everything is going to be all right, everything."

She stretched her arms out to him; she tried to smile, but tears sprang to her eyes. "Where in all the world have you been, wandering around so long?" she said.

And when he looked into her eyes, he was taken aback for pure joy, because there was his own image, not the image that had glowered at him moments ago from the copper kettle. No, it was a face so young and fresh and cheerful that he could not help shouting for happiness. He could not give this up for anything in the world.

Then, from the street, a crowd of people poured into the house, shouting and waving their arms. "Here's the bird's master," cried a stocky little man. Then everyone surged down upon Hinzelmeier.

Hinzelmeier seized the girl's hand and asked, "What's the raven done?"

"What's it done?" said the fat man. "It has stolen the mayor's wig!"

"Right! Right!" they all cried. "And now it's sitting up there on the eaves trough, the monster, with the wig in its claws, staring at his excellency through those green glasses."

Hinzelmeier was about to say something, but they surrounded him and pushed him toward the door. Horrified, he felt the Rose Maiden's hand slip from his. Thus he found himself on the street.

The raven was still sitting high on the eaves trough of the house, looking down with its black eyes on the people as they came out of the house. Suddenly it opened its claws, and while the townspeople jabbed around in the air with their canes and umbrellas, trying to catch their mayor's wig, Hinzelmeier heard over his head the whirring sound of "Crohiro, crohiro" and at the same moment the green spectacles were on his nose again.

Then suddenly the city disappeared before his eyes; through the spectacles he saw beneath him a green valley full of dairy farms and villages. Sun-drenched meadows extended all around, and through the grass walked barefoot girls with shiny milk pails, while far in the distance young lads swung their scythes. What caught and held Hinzelmeier's eye, however, was the figure of a man in a red and white smock, with a pointed cap on his head. He seemed to be sitting on a rock in the middle of a field, in a thoughtful attitude.

CASPAR, THE NEIGHBOR'S BOY

Hinzelmeier thought, "That's the Philosophers' Stone!" and headed straight toward him. The man, however, did not stir from his thoughtful pose; the only thing he did, to Hinzelmeier's amazement, was pull his great nose down over his chin, like a piece of rubber.

"I say, sir, what are you doing there?" cried Hinzelmeier.

"I don't know," the man said, "but I have this cursed bell on my cap that makes it abominably hard for me to think."

"But why are you pulling at your nose in such a dreadful way?"

"Oh," said the man, and let go the tip of his nose, causing it to fly back with a snap into its original shape. "I beg your pardon there, but I often suffer from thoughts, since I'm seeking the Philosophers' Stone."

"My Lord," said Hinzelmeier, "then you must be our neighbor's boy Caspar, who never came back home!"

"Yes," said the man, extending his hand to Hinzelmeier, "that's who I am."

"And I am Hinzelmeier from next door to you, and I am looking for the Philosophers' Stone as well."

At this, they put out their hands to one another again and in so doing crossed their fingers in a certain way so that each knew the other was one of the initiates. Then Caspar said, "But now I'm not looking for the Philosophers' Stone anymore."

"Then perhaps you're on your way to the Rose Garden," cried Hinzelmeier.

"No," said Caspar. "The reason I'm not looking for the Stone is because I've already found it."

At this, Hinzelmeier fell silent for quite some time. Finally, he folded his hands reverentially and said in a solemn voice, "It had to happen this way, I knew it did; because nine years ago I shot the Devil right out of the world."

"That must have been his son," said the other. "I met the old Devil just the day before yesterday."

"No," said Hinzelmeier, "it was the old Devil, because he had horns on his forehead and a tail with a black tuft at the end. But tell me how you found the Stone."

"That's simple," said Caspar. "All the people down there in the village are really stupid; they associate with no one but sheep and cows. They didn't know what a treasure they had. I found it in an old cellar and paid three half-shillings a pound for it. And ever since yesterday I've been trying to think what it's good for, and I probably would have figured out the answer if this cursed bell hadn't made it so hard for me to think."

"My dear colleague," said Hinzelmeier, "that is a most crucial question, one that surely no man *before* you ever thought about! But where are you keeping the Stone?"

"I'm sitting on it," said Caspar and, getting up, pointed out to Hinzelmeier the round, waxy yellow object he had previously been perched on.

"Yes," said Hinzelmeier, "no doubt about it, you have really found it, but now let's try to think what it's good for."

Thereupon they sat down on the ground, facing each other, placed the stone between them, and propped their elbows on their knees.

So they sat and sat. The sun set, the moon rose, and still they had found no answer. Now and again one of them would ask, "Have you got it?" but the other would always shake his head and say, "No, not me; how about you?"; to which the first would answer, "I haven't either."

Crohirius walked happily up and down in the grass, catching frogs. Caspar was tugging at his big, beautiful nose again. Then the moon set and the sun came up, and Hinzelmeier asked once more, "Have you got it?" and Caspar shook his head again and said, "No, not me; how about you?"; and Hinzelmeier answered gloomily, "I haven't either."

Then they thought hard again for quite a while, and finally Hinzelmeier said, "We'll have to polish our spectacles first, then we'll soon see what it's good for." And scarcely had Hinzelmeier taken off his spectacles when he let them drop into the grass in astonishment. "I've got it! Dear colleague, we must *eat* it! Just take your spectacles off your handsome nose, if you don't mind."

Then Caspar took his spectacles off too and, after contemplating his stone for a time, said, "This is what is called a leather cheese, and it must be eaten with God's help. Have some, dear colleague!"

And now the two took their knives from their pockets and made a healthy stab at the cheese. Crohirius came over on the wing and, after gathering up the spectacles from the grass and clamping them on his beak, sat down comfortably between the two diners and snapped at the pieces of rind.

"I don't know," said Hinzelmeier, after the cheese was eaten up. "I am open to contradiction, but I feel as if I have gotten substantially closer to the Philosophers' Stone."

"My esteemed colleague," replied Caspar, "you speak after my own heart. Let us therefore continue our journey without delay."

After these words they embraced. Caspar went to the west; Hinzelmeier to the east, and overhead, with the spectacles on his beak, flew Crohirius.

THE PHILOSOPHERS' STONE

Hinzelmeier journeyed back and forth, first this way, then that; his hair grew gray, his legs became unsteady; leaning on his staff, he walked from land to land, and still he did not find the Philosophers' Stone. In this fashion another nine years had passed, when one evening, as was his custom, he entered an inn. Crohirius as usual polished his spectacles and then hopped into the kitchen to beg for his supper. Hinzelmeier entered the room and leaned his staff in the corner by the tile stove. Then he sat down, silent and weary, in the great armchair. The innkeeper placed a jug of wine before him and said in a friendly way, "You seem tired, my dear sir. Drink; it will give you strength."

"Yes," said Hinzelmeier, and took the jug in both his hands. "Very tired; I have had a long journey, a very long one." Then he closed his eyes and took a thirsty draft from the wine jug.

"If you are the bird's master, I'm almost sure someone inquired about you," said the innkeeper. "What is your name, my dear sir?"

"My name is Hinzelmeier."

"Well," said the innkeeper, "your grandson, the husband of beautiful Frau Abel, is someone I know very well."

"That's my father," said Hinzelmeier, "and beautiful Frau Abel is my mother."

The innkeeper shrugged his shoulders, and turning back to his bar, he said to himself, "The poor old man is in his second childhood."

Hinzelmeier let his head sink on his chest and asked who had inquired about him.

"It was only a poor servant girl," said the innkeeper. "She wore a white dress and was barefoot." Hinzelmeier smiled and said softly, "That was the Rose Maiden; now everything will be all right. Where did she go?"

"She did seem to be a flower girl," said the innkeeper. "If you want to talk with her, you'll have no trouble finding her; she'll be on the street corners."

"I must sleep for a while," said Hinzelmeier. "Give me a room, and when the cock crows, knock on my door."

So the innkeeper gave him a room and Hinzelmeier went to sleep. He dreamed of his beautiful mother speaking to him. Then Crohirius flew through the open window and lit at the head of his bed. He ruffled his black feathers and snatched the spectacles from his beak with his claw. Then he stood motionless on one leg and looked down at the sleeper. The latter went on dreaming, and his mother said, "Don't forget the Rose!" The sleeper nodded his head softly, and the raven opened its claw and dropped the spectacles on his nose.

His dreams changed; his sunken cheeks began to tremble; he stretched out to his full length and moaned. And so the night passed.

When the cock crowed in the dim light of dawn, the innkeeper knocked on the door of his room. Crohirius stretched his wings and shook out his feathers. Then he cried, "Crohiro, crohiro!" Hinzelmeier pulled himself up with a great effort and stared about. Through the spectacles, which were still fixed on his nose, he looked out through the door of his room, over a wide, desolate field, then beyond to a slowly rising hill. On the hill, under the stump of an old willow, lay a flat gray stone. The area round about was lonely, not a human being in sight.

"That's the Philosophers' Stone!" said Hinzelmeier to himself. "At last, at last, it's going to be mine after all!"

Hastily he threw on his clothes, took his staff and knapsack, and strode out the door. Crohirius flew overhead, making clicking noises with his beak, and turned somersaults in the air as he flew. In this fashion they journeyed for many hours. At last they seemed to be approaching their goal, but Hinzelmeier was exhausted, his chest heaved, the sweat dripped from his white hair. He stopped and stood there, supporting himself on his staff. Then there came from the distance, behind him, almost like a dream, the sound of singing:

> Ring around where roses shone.
> Do not leave him here alone!
> Hold him fast and bring him home,
> Ring around where roses shone.

The sound was like a golden net woven about him; he let his head drop to his chest; but Crohirius cried, "Crohiro! crohiro!" and the song fell silent. When Hinzelmeier opened his eyes again he was standing at the foot of the hill.

"Only a little bit longer," he said to himself, and made his tired feet take up their journey once more. But when, after a time, he saw the great, broad stone close at hand, he thought, "You'll never lift that."

At last they had reached the high point. Crohirius flew on ahead with outspread wings and settled on the tree trunk. Hinzelmeier stumbled along behind, trembling. But when he had reached the tree, he collapsed. His staff slipped from his hand, his head sank back upon the stone, and the spectacles slipped from his nose. Far on the horizon, at the edge of the desolate plain he had crossed, he saw the white figure of the Rose Maiden, and once again he heard from a great distance:

Ring—around—the roses shine.

He tried to rise, but he no longer could. He stretched his arms out, but a cold shiver coursed through his limbs. The sky turned grayer and grayer, the snow began to fall; it glistened and danced and drew veils of white between him and the hazy figure in the distance. He dropped his arms, his eyes were sunken, his breath stopped. On the willow stump, by his head, the raven put its beak under its wing, to sleep. The snow fell over both of them.

The night came and then the morning, and with the morning the sun; it melted the snow away. And with the sun came the Rose Maiden. She loosened her braids and knelt by the dead man, her blond hair covering his pale face, and she wept until the end of day. But when the sun faded, the raven gurgled softly in his sleep and rustled his feathers. Then the slim young figure of the Rose Maiden drew itself up from the ground. With her white hand the girl seized the raven by its wings and hurled it into the air, so that it flew off croaking into the gray sky. She planted the red rose by the stone and as she did so she sang:

> *Let your little roots run deep,*
> *Cast your petals on his sleep.*
> *The wind will sing at break of night,*
> *But you must speak to set it right*
> *With "Ring around a rosy light."*

Then she tore her white dress asunder from hem to waist and went back into the Rose Garden to be a prisoner forever.

Translated by Frank G. Ryder

‹ *The Day Boy and the Night Girl* ›
George MacDonald

WATHO

There was once a witch who desired to know everything. But the wiser a witch is, the harder she knocks her head against the wall when she comes to it. Her name was Watho, and she had a wolf in her mind. She cared for nothing in itself— only for knowing it. She was not naturally cruel, but the wolf had made her cruel.

She was tall and graceful, with a white skin, red hair, and black eyes, which had a red fire in them. She was straight and strong, but now and then would fall bent together, shudder, and sit for a moment with her head turned over her shoulder, as if the wolf had got out of her mind onto her back.

AURORA

This witch got two ladies to visit her. One of them belonged to the court, and her husband had been sent on a far and difficult embassy. The other was a young widow, whose husband had lately died and who had since lost her sight. Watho lodged them in different parts of her castle, and they did not know of each other's existence.

The castle stood on the side of a hill sloping gently down into a narrow valley, in which was a river, with a pebbly channel and a continual song. The garden went down to the bank of the river, enclosed by high walls, which crossed the river and there stopped. Each wall had a double row of battlements, and between the rows was a narrow walk.

In the topmost story of the castle the Lady Aurora occupied a spacious apartment of several large rooms looking southward. The windows projected oriel-wise over the garden below, and there was a splendid view from them both up and down and across the river. The opposite side of the valley was steep, but not very high. Far away, snow peaks were visible. These rooms Aurora seldom left, but their airy spaces, the brilliant landscape and sky, the plentiful sunlight, the musical instruments, books, pictures, curiosities, with the company of Watho, who made herself charming, precluded all dullness. She had venison and feathered game to eat, milk and pale sunny sparkling wine to drink.

She had hair of the yellow gold, waved and rippled; her skin was fair, not white like Watho's, and her eyes were of the blue of the heavens when bluest; her features were delicate but strong, her mouth large and finely curved, and haunted with smiles.

VESPER

Behind the castle the hill rose abruptly; the northeastern tower, indeed, was in contact with the rock and communicated with the interior of it. For in the rock was a series of chambers, known only to Watho and the one servant whom she trusted, called Falca. Some former owner had constructed these chambers after the tomb of an Egyptian king and probably with the same design, for in the center of one of them stood what could only be a sarcophagus, but that and others were walled off. The sides and roofs of them were carved in low relief and curiously painted. Here the witch lodged the blind lady, whose name was Vesper. Her eyes were black, with long black lashes; her skin had a look of darkened silver, but was of purest tint and grain; her hair was black and fine and straight-flowing; her features were exquisitely formed, and if less beautiful yet more lovely from sadness; she always looked as if she wanted to lie down and not rise again. She did not know she was lodged in a tomb, though now and then she wondered she never touched a window. There were many couches, covered with richest silk, and soft as her own cheek, for her to lie upon; and the carpets were so thick she might have cast herself down anywhere—as befitted a tomb. The place was dry and warm, and cunningly pierced for air, so that it was always fresh, and lacked only sunlight. There the witch fed her upon milk, and wine dark as a carbuncle, and pomegranates, and purple grapes, and birds that dwell in marshy places; and she played to her mournful tunes, and caused wailful violins to attend her, and told her sad tales, thus holding her ever in an atmosphere of sweet sorrow.

PHOTOGEN

Watho at length had her desire, for witches often get what they want: a splendid boy was born to the fair Aurora. Just as the sun rose, he opened his eyes. Watho carried him immediately to a distant part of the castle and persuaded the mother that he never cried but once, dying the moment he was born. Overcome with grief, Aurora left the castle as soon as she was able, and Watho never invited her again.

And now the witch's care was that the child should not know darkness. Persistently she trained him until at last he never slept during the day and never woke during the night. She never let him see anything black, and even kept all dull colors out of his way. Never, if she could help it, would she let a shadow fall upon him, watching against shadows as if they had been live things that would hurt him. All day he basked in the full splendor of the sun, in the same large rooms his mother had occupied. Watho used him to the sun, until he could bear more of it than any dark-blooded African. In the hottest of every day, she stripped him and laid him in it, that he might ripen like a peach; and the boy rejoiced in it, and would resist being dressed again. She brought all her knowledge to bear on making his muscles strong and elastic and swiftly responsive—that his soul, she said laughingly, might sit in every fiber, be all in every part, and awake the moment of call. His hair was of the red gold, but his eyes grew darker as he grew, until they were as black as Vesper's. He was the merriest of creatures, always laughing, always loving, for a moment raging, then laughing afresh. Watho called him Photogen.

NYCTERIS

Five or six months after the birth of Photogen, the dark lady also gave birth to a baby: in the windowless tomb of a blind mother, in the dead of night, under the feeble rays of a lamp in an alabaster globe, a girl came into the darkness with a wail. And just as she was born for the first time, Vesper was born for the second, and passed into a world as unknown to her as this was to her child—who would have to be born yet again before she could see her mother.

Watho called her Nycteris, and she grew as like Vesper as possible—in all but one particular. She had the same dark skin, dark eyelashes and brows, dark hair, and gentle sad look; but she had just the eyes of Aurora, the mother of Photogen, and if they grew darker as she grew older, it was only a darker blue. Watho, with the help of Falca, took the greatest possible care of her—in every way consistent with her plans, that is, the main point in which was that she should never see any light but what came from the lamp. Hence her optic nerves, and indeed her whole apparatus for seeing, grew both larger and more sensitive; her eyes, indeed, stopped short only of being too large. Under her dark hair and forehead and eyebrows, they looked like two breaks in a cloudy night sky, through which peeped the heaven where the stars and no clouds live. She was a sadly dainty little creature. No one in the world except those two was aware of the being of the little bat. Watho trained her to sleep during the day and wake during the night. She taught her music, in which she was herself a proficient, and taught her scarcely anything else.

HOW PHOTOGEN GREW

The hollow in which the castle of Watho lay was a cleft in a plain rather than a valley among hills, for at the top of its steep sides, both north and south, was a tableland, large and wide. It was covered with rich grass and flowers, with here and there a wood, the outlying colony of a great forest. These grassy plains were the finest hunting grounds in the world. Great herds of small but fierce cattle, with humps and shaggy manes, roved about them, also antelopes and gnus, and the tiny roe deer, while the woods were swarming with wild creatures. The tables of the castle were mainly supplied from them. The chief of Watho's huntsmen was a fine fellow, and when Photogen began to outgrow the training she could give him, she handed him over to Fargu. He with a will set about teaching him all he knew. He got him pony after pony, larger and larger as he grew, every one less manageable than that which had preceded it, and advanced him from pony to horse, and from horse to horse, until he was equal to anything in that kind which the country produced. In similar fashion he trained him to the use of bow and arrow, substituting every three months a stronger bow and longer arrows; and soon he became, even on horseback, a wonderful archer. He was but fourteen when he killed his first bull, causing jubilation among the huntsmen and, indeed, through all the castle, for there too he was the favorite. Every day, almost as soon as the sun was up, he went out hunting, and would in general be out nearly the whole of the day. But Watho had laid upon Fargu just one commandment, namely, that Photogen should on no account, whatever the plea, be out until sundown, or so near it as to wake in him the desire of seeing what was going to happen; and this commandment Fargu was anxiously careful not to break; for although he would not have trembled had a whole herd of bulls come down upon him, charging at full speed across the level, and not an arrow left in his quiver, he was more than afraid of his mistress. When she looked at him in a certain way, he felt, he said, as if his heart turned to ashes in his breast, and what ran in his veins was no longer blood, but milk and water. So that, ere long, as Photogen grew older, Fargu began to tremble, for he found it steadily growing harder to restrain him. So full of life was he, as Fargu said to his mistress, much to her content, that he was more like a live thunderbolt than a human being. He did not know what fear was, and that not because he did not know danger; for he had had a severe laceration from the razor-like tusk of a boar—whose spine, however, he had severed with one blow of his hunting knife before Fargu could reach him with defense. When he would spur his horse into the midst of a herd of bulls, carrying only his bow and his short sword, or shoot an arrow into a herd and go after it as if to reclaim it for a runaway shaft, arriving in time to follow it with a spear thrust before the wounded animal knew which way to charge, Fargu thought with terror how it would be when he came to know the temptation of the huddle-spot leopards, and the knife-clawed lynxes, with which the forest was haunted. For the boy had been so steeped in the sun, from childhood so saturated with his influence, that he looked upon every danger from a sovereign height of courage. When, therefore, he was approaching his sixteenth year, Fargu ventured to beg Watho that she would lay her commands upon the youth himself and release him from responsibility for him. One might as soon hold a tawny-maned lion as Photogen, he said. Watho called the youth, and in the presence of Fargu laid her commands upon him never to be out when the rim of the sun should touch the horizon, accompanying the prohibition with hints of consequences nonetheless awful than they were obscure. Photogen listened respectfully, but as he knew neither the taste of fear nor the temptation of the night, her words were but sounds to him.

HOW NYCTERIS GREW

The little education she intended Nycteris to have, Watho gave her by word of mouth. Not meaning she should have light enough to read by, to leave other reasons unmentioned, she never put a book in her hands. Nycteris, however, saw so much better than Watho imagined, that the light she gave her was quite sufficient, and she managed to coax Falca into teaching her the letters, after which she taught herself to read, and Falca now and then brought her a child's book. But her chief pleasure was in her instrument. Her very fingers loved it and would wander about its keys like feeding sheep. She was not unhappy. She knew nothing of the world except the tomb in which she dwelt, and had some pleasure in everything she did. But she desired, nevertheless, something more or different. She did not know what it was, and the nearest she could come to expressing it to herself was that she wanted more room. Watho and Falca would go from her beyond the shine of the lamp, and come again; therefore, surely there must be more room somewhere. As often as she was left alone, she would fall to poring over the colored bas-reliefs on the walls. These were intended to represent various of the powers of Nature under allegorical similitudes, and as nothing can be made that does not belong to the general scheme, she could not fail at least to imagine a flicker of relationship between some of them, and thus a shadow of the reality of things found its way to her.

There was one thing, however, which moved and taught her more than all the rest—the lamp, namely, that hung from the ceiling, which she always saw alight, though she never saw the flame, only the slight condensation towards the center of the alabaster globe. And besides the operation of the light itself after its kind, the indefiniteness of the globe and the softness of the light, giving her the feeling as if her eyes could go in and into its whiteness, were somehow also associated with the idea of space and room. She would sit for an hour together gazing up at the lamp, and her heart would swell as she gazed. She would wonder what had hurt her, when she found her face wet with tears, and then would wonder how she could have been hurt without knowing it. She never looked thus at the lamp except when she was alone.

THE LAMP

Watho, having given orders, took it for granted they were obeyed and that Falca was all night long with Nycteris, whose day it was. But Falca could not get into the habit of sleeping through the day and would often leave her alone half the night. Then it seemed to Nycteris that the white lamp was watching over her. As it was never permitted to go out—while she was awake at least—Nycteris, except by shutting her eyes, knew less about darkness than she did about light. Also, the lamp being fixed high overhead and in the center of everything, she did not know much about shadows either. The few there were fell almost entirely on the floor, or kept like mice about the foot of the walls.

Once, when she was thus alone, there came the noise of a far-off rumbling: she had never before heard a sound of which she did not know the origin, and here therefore was a new sign of something beyond these chambers. Then came a trembling, then a shaking; the lamp dropped from the ceiling to the floor with a great crash, and she felt as if both her eyes were hard shut and both her hands over them. She concluded that it was the darkness that had made the rumbling and the shaking and, rushing into the room, had thrown down the lamp. She sat trembling. The noise and the shaking ceased, but the light did not return. The darkness had eaten it up!

Her lamp gone, the desire at once awoke to get out of her prison. She scarcely knew what *out* meant; out of one room into another, where there was not even a dividing door, only an open arch, was all she knew of the world. But suddenly she remembered that she had heard Falca speak of the lamp *going out*: this must be what she had meant. And if the lamp had gone out, where had it gone? Surely where Falca went, and like her it would come again. But she could not wait. The desire to go out grew irresistible. She must follow her beautiful lamp! She must find it! She must see what it was about!

Now there was a curtain covering a recess in the wall, where some of her toys and gymnastic things were kept; and from behind that curtain Watho and Falca always appeared, and behind it they vanished. How they came out of solid wall she had not an idea: all up to the wall was open space, and all beyond it seemed wall; but clearly the first and only thing she could do was to feel her way behind the curtain. It was so dark that a cat could not have caught the largest of mice. Nycteris could see better than any cat, but now her great eyes were not of the smallest use to her. As she went she trod upon a piece of the broken lamp. She had never worn shoes or stockings, and the fragment, though being of soft alabaster, it did not cut, yet hurt her foot. She did not know what it was, but as it had not been there before the darkness came, she suspected that it had to do with the lamp. She kneeled, therefore, and searched with her hands, and bringing two large pieces together, recognized the shape of the lamp. Therefore it flashed upon her that the lamp was dead, that this brokenness was the death of which she had read without understanding, that the darkness had killed the lamp. What then could Falca have meant when she spoke of the lamp *going out*? There was the lamp— dead indeed, and so changed that she would never have taken it for a lamp but for the shape! No, it was not the lamp any more now it was dead, for all that made it a lamp was gone, namely, the bright shining of it. Then it must be the shine, the light, that had gone out! That must be what Falca meant— and it must be somewhere in the other place in the wall. She started afresh after it, and groped her way to the curtain.

Now she had never in her life tried to get out, and did not know how; but instinctively she began to move her hands about over one of the walls behind the curtain, half expecting them to go into it, as she supposed Watho and Falca did. But the wall repelled her with inexorable hardness, and she turned to the one opposite. In so doing, she set her foot upon an ivory die, and as it met sharply the same spot the broken alabaster had already hurt, she fell forward with her outstretched hands against the wall. Something gave way, and she tumbled out of the cavern.

OUT

But alas! *out* was very much like *in*, for the same enemy, the darkness, was here also. The next moment, however, came a great gladness—a firefly, which had wandered in from the garden. She saw the tiny spark in the distance. With slow pulsing ebb and throb of light, it came pushing itself through the air, drawing nearer and nearer, with that motion which more resembles swimming than flying, and the light seemed the source of its own motion.

"My lamp! my lamp!" cried Nycteris. "It is the shiningness of my lamp, which the cruel darkness drove out. My good lamp has been waiting for me here all the time! It knew I would come after it, and waited to take me with it."

She followed the firefly, which, like herself, was seeking the way out. If it did not know the way, it was yet light; and because all light is one, any light may serve to guide to more light. If she was mistaken in thinking it the spirit of her lamp, it was of the same spirit as her lamp—and had wings. The gold-green jet boat, driven by light, went throbbing before her through a long, narrow passage. Suddenly it rose higher, and the same moment Nycteris fell upon an ascending stair. She had never seen a stair before, and found going up a curious sensation. Just as she reached what seemed the top, the firefly ceased to shine, and so disappeared. She was in utter darkness once more. But when we are following the light, even its extinction is a guide. If the firefly had gone on shining, Nycteris would have seen the stair turn and would have gone up to Watho's bedroom; whereas now, feeling straight before her, she came to a latched door, which after a good deal of trying she managed to open—and stood in a maze of wondering perplexity, awe, and delight. What was it? Was it outside of her, or something taking place in her head? Before her was a very long and very narrow passage, broken up she could not tell how, and spreading out above and on all sides to an infinite height and breadth and distance—as if space itself were growing out of a trough. It was brighter than her rooms had ever been—brighter than if six alabaster lamps had been burning in them. There was a quantity of strange streaking and mottling about it, very different from the shapes on her walls. She was in a dream of pleasant perplexity, of delightful bewilderment. She could not tell whether she was upon her feet or drifting about like the firefly, driven by the pulses of an inward bliss. But she knew little as yet of her inheritance. Unconsciously, she took one step forward from the threshold, and the girl who had been from her very birth a troglodyte stood in the ravishing glory of a southern night, lit by a perfect moon—not the moon of our northern clime but the moon like silver glowing in a furnace: a moon one could see to be a globe—not far off, a mere flat disk on the face of the blue but hanging down halfway and looking as if one could see all round it by a mere bending of the neck.

"It is my lamp," she said, and stood dumb with parted lips. She looked and felt as if she had been standing there in silent ecstasy from the beginning.

"No, it is not my lamp," she said after a while. "It is the mother of all the lamps."

And with that she fell on her knees and spread out her hands to the moon. She could not in the least have told what was in her mind, but the action was in reality just a begging of the moon to be what she was—that precise incredible splendor hung in the far-off roof, that very glory essential to the being of poor girls born and bred in caverns. It was a resurrection—nay, a birth itself—to Nycteris. What the vast blue sky, studded with tiny sparks like the heads of diamond nails, could be; what the moon, looking so absolutely content with light—why, she knew less about them than you and I! but the greatest of atronomers might envy the rapture of such a first impression at the age of sixteen. Immeasurably imperfect it was, but false the impression could not be, for she saw with the eyes made for seeing, and saw indeed what many men are too wise to see.

As she knelt, something softly flapped her, embraced her, stroked her, fondled her. She rose to her feet but saw nothing, did not know what it was. It was likest a woman's breath. For she knew nothing of the air even, had never breathed the still newborn freshness of the world. Her breath had come to her only through long passages and spirals in the rock. Still less did she know of the air alive with motion—of that thrice blessed thing, the wind of a summer night. It was like a spiritual wine, filling her whole being with an intoxication of purest joy. To breathe was a perfect existence. It seemed to her the light itself she drew into her lungs. Possessed by the power of the gorgeous night, she seemed at one and the same moment annihilated and glorified.

She was in the open passage or gallery that ran round the top of the garden walls, between the cleft battlements, but she did not once look down to see what lay beneath. Her soul was drawn to the vault above her, with its lamp and its endless room. At last she burst into tears, and her heart was relieved, as the night itself is relieved by its lightning and rain.

And now she grew thoughtful. She must hoard this splendor! What a little ignorance her jailers had made of her! Life was a mighty bliss, and they had scraped hers to the bare bone! They must not know that she knew. She must hide her knowledge—hide it even from her own eyes, keeping it close in her bosom, content to know that she had it, even when she could not brood on its presence, feasting her eyes with its glory. She turned from the vision, therefore, with a sigh of utter bliss, and with soft quiet steps and groping hands stole back into the darkness of the rock. What was darkness or the laziness of Time's feet to one who had seen what she had that night seen? She was lifted above all weariness—above all wrong.

When Falca entered, she uttered a cry of terror. But Nycteris called to her not to be afraid and told her how there had come a rumbling and a shaking, and the lamp had fallen. Then Falca went and told her mistress, and within an hour a new globe hung in the place of the old one. Nycteris thought it did not look so bright and clear as the former, but she made no lamentation over the change; she was far too rich to heed it. For now, prisoner as she knew herself, her heart was full of glory and gladness; at times she had to hold herself from jumping up, and going dancing and singing about the room. When she slept, instead of dull dreams, she had splendid visions. There were times, it is true, when she became restless, and impatient to look upon her riches, but then she would reason with herself, saying "What does it matter if I sit here for ages with my poor pale lamp, when out there a lamp is burning at which ten thousand little lamps are glowing with wonder?"

She never doubted she had looked upon the day and the sun, of which she had read; and always when she read of the day and the sun, she had the night and the moon in her mind; and when she read of the night and the moon, she thought only of the cave and the lamp that hung there.

THE GREAT LAMP

It was some time before she had a second opportunity of going out, for Falca since the fall of the lamp had been a little more careful and seldom left her for long. But one night, having a little headache, Nycteris lay down upon her bed and was lying with her eyes closed when she heard Falca come to her and felt she was bending over her. Disinclined to talk, she did not open her eyes and lay quite still. Satisfied that she was asleep, Falca left her, moving so softly that her very caution made Nycteris open her eyes and look after her—just in time to see her vanish—through a picture, as it seemed, that hung on the wall a long way from the usual place of issue. She jumped up, her headache forgotten, and ran in the opposite direction; got out, groped her way to the stair, climbed, and reached the top of the wall. Alas! The great room was not so light as the little one she had left! Why? Sorrow of sorrows, the great lamp was gone! Had its globe fallen and its lovely light gone out upon great wings, a resplendent firefly oaring itself through a yet grander and lovelier room? She looked down to see if it lay anywhere broken to pieces on the carpet below; but she could not even see the carpet. But surely nothing very dreadful could have happened—no rumbling or shaking; for there were all the little lamps shining brighter than before, not one of them looking as if any unusual matter had befallen. What if each of those little lamps was growing into a big lamp and, after being a big lamp for a while, had to go out and grow a bigger lamp still—out there, beyond this *out*? Ah! Here was the living thing that could not be seen, come to her again—bigger tonight with such loving kisses and such liquid strokings of her cheeks and forehead, gently tossing her hair, and delicately toying with it! But it ceased, and all was still. Had it gone out? What would happen next? Perhaps the little lamps had not to grow great lamps but to fall one by one and go out first? With that came from below a sweet scent, then another, and another. Ah, how delicious! Perhaps they were all coming to her only on their way out after the great lamp! Then came the music of the river, which she had been too absorbed in the sky to note the first time. What was it? Alas! alas! another sweet living thing on its way out. They were all marching slowly out in long lovely file, one after the other, each taking its leave of her as it passed! It must be so; here were more and more sweet sounds, following and fading! The whole of the *out* was going out again; it was all going after the great lovely lamp! She would be left the only creature in the solitary day! Was there nobody to hang up a new lamp for the old one and keep the creatures from going! She crept back to her rock very sad. She tried to comfort herself by saying that anyhow there would be room out there; but as she said it she shuddered at the thought of *empty* room.

When next she succeeded in getting out, a half-moon hung in the east: a new lamp had come, she thought, and all would be well.

It would be endless to describe the phases of feeling through which Nycteris passed, more numerous and delicate than those of a thousand changing moons. A fresh bliss bloomed in her soul with every varying aspect of infinite nature. Ere long she began to suspect that the new moon was the old moon, gone out and come in again like herself; also that, unlike herself, it wasted and grew again; that it was indeed a live thing, subject like herself to caverns and keepers and solitudes, escaping and shining when it could. Was it a prison like hers it was shut in, and did it grow dark when the lamp left it? Where could be the way into it?—With that first she began to look below, as well as above and around her; and then first noted the tops of the trees between her and the floor. There were palms with their red-fingered hands full of fruit; eucalyptus trees crowded with little boxes of powder puffs; oleanders with their half-caste roses; and orange trees with their clouds of young silver stars and their aged balls of gold. Her eyes could see colors invisible to ours in the moonlight, and all these she could distinguish well, though at first she took them for the shapes and colors of the carpet of the great room. She longed to get down among them, now she saw they were real creatures, but she did not know how. She went along the whole length of the wall to the end that crossed the river, but found no way of going down. Above the river she stopped to gaze with awe upon the rushing water. She knew nothing of water but from what she drank and what she bathed in; and as the moon shone on the dark, swift stream, singing lustily as it flowed, she did not doubt the river was alive, a swift rushing serpent of life, going—out? whither? And then she wondered if what was brought into her rooms had been killed that she might drink it and have her bath in it.

Once when she stepped out upon the wall, it was into the midst of a fierce wind. The trees were all roaring. Great clouds were rushing along the skies and tumbling over the little lamps: the great lamp had not come yet. All was in tumult. The wind seized her garments and hair and shook them as if it would tear them from her. What could she have done to make the gentle creature so angry? Or was this another creature altogether—of the same kind but hugely bigger and of a very different temper and behavior? But the whole place was angry. Or was it that the creatures dwelling in it, the wind, and the trees, and the clouds, and the river, had all quarreled, each with all the rest? Would the whole come to confusion and disorder? But as she gazed wondering and disquieted, the moon, larger than ever she had seen her, came lifting herself above the horizon to look, broad and red, as if she, too, were swollen with anger that she had been roused from her rest by their noise and compelled to hurry up to see what her children were about, thus rioting in her absence, lest they should rack the whole frame of things. And as she rose, the loud wind grew quieter and scolded less fiercely, the trees grew stiller and moaned with a lower complaint, and the clouds hunted and hurled themselves less wildly across the sky. And as if she were pleased that her children obeyed her very presence, the moon grew smaller as she ascended the heavenly stair; her puffed cheeks sank, her complexion grew clearer, and a sweet smile spread over her countenance, as peacefully she rose and rose. But there was treason and rebellion in her court; for ere she reached the top of her great stairs, the clouds had assembled, forgetting their late wars, and very still they were as they laid their heads together and conspired. Then combining, and lying silently in wait until she came near, they threw themselves upon her and swallowed her up. Down from the roof came spots of wet, faster and faster, and they wetted the cheeks of Nycteris; and what could they be but the tears of the moon, crying because her children were smothering her? Nycteris wept too, and, not knowing what to think, stole back in dismay to her room.

The next time, she came out in fear and trembling. There was the moon still, away in the west—poor, indeed, and old, and looking dreadfully worn, as if all the wild beasts in the sky had been gnawing at her—but there she was, alive still, and able to shine!

THE SUNSET

Knowing nothing of darkness, or stars, or moon, Photogen spent his days in hunting. On a great white horse he swept over the grassy plains, glorying in the sun, fighting the wind, and killing the buffaloes.

One morning, when he happened to be on the ground a little earlier than usual and before his attendants, he caught sight of an animal unknown to him, stealing from a hollow into which the sun rays had not yet reached. Like a swift shadow it sped over the grass, slinking southward to the forest. He gave chase, noted the body of a buffalo it had half eaten, and pursued it the harder. But with great leaps and bounds the creature shot farther and farther ahead of him, and vanished. Turning therefore defeated, he met Fargu, who had been following him as fast as his horse could carry him.

"What animal was that, Fargu?" he asked. "How he did run!"

Fargu answered he might be a leopard, but he rather thought from his pace and look that he was a young lion.

"What a coward he must be!" said Photogen.

"Don't be too sure of that," rejoined Fargu. "He is one of the creatures the sun makes uncomfortable. As soon as the sun is down, he will be brave enough."

He had scarcely said it, when he repented; nor did he regret it the less when he found that Photogen made no reply. But alas! said was said.

"Then," said Photogen to himself, "that contemptible beast is one of the terrors of sundown, of which Madame Watho spoke!"

He hunted all day, but not with his usual spirit. He did not ride so hard and did not kill one buffalo. Fargu to his dismay observed also that he took every pretext for moving farther south, nearer to the forest. But all at once, the sun now sinking in the west, he seemed to change his mind, for he turned his horse's head and rode home so fast that the rest could not keep him in sight. When they arrived, they found his horse in the stable and concluded that he had gone into the castle. But he had in truth set out again by the back of it. Crossing the river a good way up the valley, he reascended to the ground they had left, and just before sunset reached the skirts of the forest.

The level orb shone straight in between the bare stems, and saying to himself he could not fail to find the beast, he rushed into the wood. But even as he entered, he turned, and looked to the west. The rim of the red was touching the horizon, all jagged with broken hills. "Now," said Photogen, "we shall see"; but he said it in the face of a darkness he had not proved. The moment the sun began to sink among the spikes and saw edges, with a kind of sudden flap at his heart a fear inexplicable laid hold of the youth; and as he had never felt anything of the kind before, the very fear itself terrified him. As the sun sank, it rose like the shadow of the world, and grew deeper and darker. He could not even think what it might be, so utterly did it enfeeble him. When the last flaming scimitar edge of the sun went out like a lamp, his horror seemed to blossom into very madness. Like the closing lids of an eye—for there was no twilight, and this night no moon—the terror and the darkness rushed together, and he knew them for one. He was no longer the man he had known, or rather thought himself. The courage he had had was in no sense his own—he had only had courage, not been courageous; it had left him, and he could scarcely stand—certainly not stand straight, for not one of his joints could he make stiff or keep from trembling. He was but a spark of the sun, in himself nothing.

The beast was behind him—stealing upon him! He turned. All was dark in the wood, but to his fancy the darkness here and there broke into pairs of green eyes, and he had not the power even to raise his bow hand from his side. In the strength of despair he strove to rouse courage enough: not to fight—that he did not even desire—but to run. Courage to flee home was all he could ever imagine, and it would not come. But what he had not was ignominiously given him. A cry in the wood, half a screech, half a growl, sent him running like a boar-wounded cur. It was not even himself that ran, it was the fear that had come alive in his legs; he did not know that they moved. But as he ran he grew able to run—gained courage at least to be a coward. The stars gave a little light. Over the grass he sped, and nothing followed him. "How fallen, how changed," from the youth who had climbed the hill as the sun went down! A mere contempt to himself, the self that contemned was a coward with the self it contemned! There lay the shapeless black of a buffalo, humped upon the grass: He made a wide circuit, and swept on like a shadow driven in the wind. For the wind had arisen, and added to his terror: it blew from behind him. He reached the brow of the valley and shot down the steep descent like a falling star. Instantly the whole upper country behind him arose and pursued him! The wind came howling after him, filled with screams, shrieks, yells, roars, laughter, and chattering, as if all the animals of the forest were careering with it. In his ears was a trampling rush, the thunder of the hooves of the cattle, in career from every quarter of the wide plains to the brow of the hill above him. He fled straight for the castle, scarcely with breath enough to pant.

As he reached the bottom of the valley, the moon peered up over its edge. He had never seen the moon before—except in the daytime, when he had taken her for a thin bright cloud. She was a fresh terror to him—so ghostly! so ghastly! so gruesome!—so knowing as she looked over the top of her garden wall upon the world outside! That was the night itself! the darkness alive—and after him! the horror of horrors coming down the sky to curdle his blood and turn his brain to a cinder! He gave a sob and made straight for the river, where it ran between the two walls, at the bottom of the garden. He plunged in, struggled through, clambered up the bank, and fell senseless on the grass.

THE GARDEN

Although Nycteris took care not to stay out long at a time and used every precaution, she could hardly have escaped discovery so long, had it not been that the strange attacks to which Watho was subject had been more frequent of late and had at last settled into an illness which kept her to her bed. But whether from an access of caution or from suspicion, Falca, having now to be much with her mistress both day and night, took it at length into her head to fasten the door as often as she went by her usual place of exit, so that one night, when Nycteris pushed, she found, to her surprise and dismay, that the wall pushed her again and would not let her through; nor with all her searching could she discover wherein lay the cause of the change. Then first she felt the pressure of her prison walls and, turning, half in despair, groped her way to the picture where she had once seen Falca disappear. There she soon found the spot by pressing upon which the wall yielded. It let her through into a sort of cellar, where was a glimmer of light from a sky whose blue was paled by the moon. From the cellar she got into a long passage, into which the moon was shining, and came to a door. She managed to open it and, to her great joy, found herself in *the other place*, not on the top of the wall, however, but in the garden she had longed to enter. Noiseless as a fluffy moth, she flitted away into the covert of the trees and shrubs, her bare feet welcomed by the softest of carpets, which, by the very touch, her feet knew to be alive, whence it came that it was so sweet and friendly to them. A soft little wind was out among the trees, running now here, now there, like a child that had got its will. She went dancing over the grass, looking behind her at her shadow as she went. At first she had taken it for a little black creature that made game of her, but when she perceived that it was only where she kept the moon away, and that every tree, however great and grand a creature, had also one of these strange attendants, she soon learned not to mind it, and by and by it became the source of as much amusement to her as to any kitten its tail. It was long before she was quite at home with the trees, however. At one time they seemed to disapprove of her; at another not even to know she was there and to be altogether taken up with their own business. Suddenly, as she went from one to another of them, looking up with awe at the murmuring mystery of their branches and leaves, she spied one a little way off which was very different from all the rest. It was white, and dark, and sparkling, and spread like a palm—a small slender palm, without much head; and it grew very fast, and sang as it grew. But it never grew any bigger, for just as fast as she could see it growing, it kept falling to pieces. When she got close to it, she discovered that it was a water tree—made of just such water as she washed with—only it was alive, of course, like the river: a different sort of water from that, doubtless, seeing the one crept swiftly along the floor and the other shot straight up, and fell, and swallowed itself, and rose again. She put her feet into the marble basin, which was the flowerpot in which it grew. It was full of real water, living and cool—so nice, for the night was hot!

But the flowers! Ah, the flowers! She was friends with them from the very first. What wonderful creatures they were! And so kind and beautiful, always sending out such colors and such scents—red scent, and white scent, and yellow scent—for the other creatures! The one that was invisible and everywhere took such a quantity of their scents and carried it away! Yet they did not seem to mind. It was their talk, to show they were alive and not painted, like those on the walls of her rooms and on the carpets.

She wandered along down the garden, until she reached the river. Unable then to get any farther—for she was a little afraid, and justly, of the swift watery serpent—she dropped on the grassy bank, dipped her feet in the water, and felt it running and pushing against them. For a long time she sat thus, and her bliss seemed complete as she gazed at the river and watched the broken picture of the great lamp overhead, moving up one side of the roof, to go down the other.

SOMETHING QUITE NEW

A beautiful moth brushed across the great blue eyes of Nycteris. She sprang to her feet to follow it—not in the spirit of the hunter, but of the lover. Her heart—like every heart, if only its fallen sides were cleared away—was an inexhaustible fountain of love: she loved everything she saw. But as she followed the moth, she caught sight of something lying on the bank of the river, and not yet having learned to be afraid of anything, ran straight to see what it was. Reaching it, she stood amazed. Another girl, like herself! But what a strange-looking girl! so curiously dressed too! and not able to move! Was she dead? Filled suddenly with pity, she sat down, lifted Photogen's head, laid it on her lap, and began stroking his face. Her warm hands brought him to himself. He opened his black eyes, out of which had gone all the fire, and looked up with a strange sound of fear, half moan, half gasp. But when he saw her face, he drew a deep breath and lay motionless—gazing at her: those blue marvels above him, like a better sky, seemed to side with courage and assuage his terror. At length, in a trembling, awed voice, and a half whisper, he said, "Who are you?"

"I am Nycteris," she answered.

"You are a creature of the darkness and love the night," he said, his fear beginning to move again.

"I may be a creature of the darkness," she replied. "I hardly know what

you mean. But I do not love the night. I love the day—with all my heart;
and I sleep all the night long."

"How can that be?" said Photogen, rising on his elbow, but dropping
his head on her lap again the moment he saw the moon. "How can it be,"
he repeated, "when I see your eyes there—wide awake?"

She only smiled and stroked him, for she did not understand him and
thought he did not know what he was saying.

"Was it a dream, then?" resumed Photogen, rubbing his eyes. But with
that his memory came clear, and he shuddered, and cried, "Oh, horrible,
horrible! To be turned all at once into a coward—a shameful, contemptible,
disgraceful coward! I am ashamed—ashamed—and *so* frightened! It is all so
frightful!"

"What is so frightful?" asked Nycteris, with a smile like that of a mother
to her child waked from a bad dream.

"All, all," he answered. "All this darkness and the roaring."

"My dear," said Nycteris, "there is no roaring. How sensitive you must
be! What you hear is only the walking of the water and the running about
of the sweetest of all the creatures. She is invisible, and I call her Everywhere,
for she goes through all the other creatures and comforts them. Now she is
amusing herself, and them too, with shaking them and kissing them and
blowing in their faces. Listen: do you call that roaring? You should hear her
when she is rather angry, though! I don't know why, but she is sometimes,
and then she does roar a little."

"It is so horribly dark!" said Photogen, who, listening while she spoke,
had satisfied himself that there was no roaring.

"Dark!" she echoed. "You should be in my room when an earthquake
has killed my lamp. I do not understand. How *can* you call this dark? Let me
see: yes, you have eyes, and big ones, bigger than Madame Watho's or Falca's:
not so big as mine, I fancy—only I never saw mine. But then—oh, yes!—I
know now what is the matter! You can't see with them because they are so
black. Darkness can't see, of course. Never mind: I will be your eyes and
teach you to see. Look here—at these lovely white things in the grass, with
red sharp points all folded together into one. Oh, I love them so! I could sit
looking at them all day, the darlings!"

Photogen looked close at the flowers and thought he had seen something
like them before, but could not make them out. As Nycteris had never seen
an open daisy, so had he never seen a closed one.

Thus instinctively Nycteris tried to turn him away from his fear: and the
beautiful creature's strange lovely talk helped not a little to make him forget it.

"You call it dark!" she said again, as if she could not get rid of the
absurdity of the idea. "Why, I could count every blade of the green hair—I

suppose it is what the books call grass—within two yards of me! And just look at the great lamp! It is brighter than usual today, and I can't think why you should be frightened or call it dark!"

As she spoke, she went on stroking his cheeks and hair and trying to comfort him. But oh, how miserable he was, and how plainly he looked it! He was on the point of saying that her great lamp was dreadful to him, looking like a witch, walking in the sleep of death; but he was not so ignorant as Nycteris and knew even in the moonlight that she was a woman, though he had never seen one so young or so lovely before; and while she comforted his fear, her presence made him the more ashamed of it. Besides, not knowing her nature, he might annoy her and make her leave him to his misery. He lay still, therefore, hardly daring to move: all the little life he had seemed to come from her, and if he were to move, she might move; and if she were to leave him, he must weep like a child.

"How did you come here?" asked Nycteris, taking his face between her hands.

"Down the hill," he answered.

"Where do you sleep?" she asked.

He signed in the direction of the house. She gave a little laugh of delight.

"When you have learned not to be frightened, you will always be wanting to come out with me," she said.

She thought to herself she would ask her presently, when she had come to herself a little, how she had made her escape, for she must, of course, like herself, have got out of a cave, in which Watho and Falca had been keeping her.

"Look at the lovely colors," she went on, pointing to a rosebush, on which Photogen could not see a single flower. "They are far more beautiful— are they not?—than any of the colors upon your walls. And then they are alive, and smell so sweet!"

He wished she would not make him keep opening his eyes to look at things he could not see; and every other moment he would start and grasp tight hold of her, as some fresh pang of terror shot into him.

"Come, come, dear!" said Nycteris. "You must not go on this way. You must be a brave girl, and—"

"A girl!" shouted Photogen, and started to his feet in wrath. "If you were a man, I should kill you."

"A man?" repeated Nycteris. "What is that? How could I be that? We are both girls—are we not?"

"No, I am not a girl," he answered, "although," he added, changing his tone and casting himself on the ground at her feet, "I have given you too good reason to call me one."

"Oh, I see!" returned Nycteris. "No, of course! You can't be a girl: girls are not afraid—without reason. I understand now: it is because you are not a girl that you are so frightened."

Photogen twisted and writhed upon the grass.

"No, it is not," he said sulkily. "It is this horrible darkness that creeps into me, goes all through me, into the very marrow of my bones—that is what makes me behave like a girl. If only the sun would rise!"

"The sun! What is it?" cried Nycteris, now in her turn conceiving a vague fear.

Then Photogen broke into a rhapsody, in which he vainly sought to forget his.

"It is the soul, the life, the heart, the glory of the universe," he said. "The worlds dance like motes in his beams. The heart of man is strong and brave in his light, and when it departs his courage grows from him—goes with the sun—and he becomes such as you see me now."

"Then that is not the sun?" said Nycteris thoughtfully, pointing up to the moon.

"That!" cried Photogen, with utter scorn. "I know nothing about *that*, except that it is ugly and horrible. At best it can be only the ghost of a dead sun. Yes, that is it! That is what makes it look so frightful."

"No," said Nycteris, after a long, thoughtful pause. "You must be wrong there. I think the sun is the ghost of a dead moon, and that is how he is so much more splendid, as you say. Is there, then, another big room, where the sun lives in the roof?"

"I do not know what you mean," replied Photogen. "But you mean to be kind, I know, though you should not call a poor fellow in the dark a girl. If you will let me lie here, with my head in your lap, I should like to sleep. Will you watch me and take care of me?"

"Yes, that I will," answered Nycteris, forgetting all her own danger.

So Photogen fell asleep.

THE SUN

There Nycteris sat, and there the youth lay all night long, in the heart of the great cone shadow of the earth, like two pharaohs in one pyramid. Photogen slept and slept; and Nycteris sat motionless lest she should wake him and so betray him to his fear.

The moon rode high in the blue eternity. It was a very triumph of glorious night: the river ran babble-murmuring in deep soft syllables; the fountain kept rushing moonward and blossoming momently to a great silvery flower, whose petals were forever falling like snow, but with a continuous musical clash, into the bed of its exhaustion beneath; the wind woke, took a run among the trees, went to sleep, and woke again; the daisies slept on their feet at hers, but she did not know they slept; the roses might well seem awake, for their scent filled the air, but in truth they slept also, and the odor was that of their dreams; the oranges hung like gold lamps in the trees, and their silvery flowers were the souls of their yet unembodied children; the scent of the acacia blooms filled the air like the very odor of the moon herself.

At last, unused to the living air, and weary with sitting so still and so long, Nycteris grew drowsy. The air began to grow cool. It was getting near the time when she, too, was accustomed to sleep. She closed her eyes just a moment, and nodded—opened them suddenly wide, for she had promised to watch.

In that moment a change had come. The moon had got round and was fronting her from the west, and she saw that her face was altered, that she had grown pale, as if she, too, were wan with fear and from her lofty place espied a coming terror. The light seemed to be dissolving out of her; she was dying—she was going out! And yet everything around looked strangely clear— clearer than ever she had seen anything before; how could the lamp be shedding more light when she herself had less? Ah, that was just it! See how faint she looked! It was because the light was forsaking her, and spreading itself over the room, that she grew so thin and pale! She was giving up everything! She was melting away from the roof like a bit of sugar in water.

Nycteris was fast growing afraid, and sought refuge with the face upon her lap. How beautiful the creature was! What to call it she could not think, for it had been angry when she called it what Watho called her. And wonder upon wonders! Now, even in the cold change that was passing upon the great room, the color as of a red rose was rising in the wan cheek. What beautiful yellow hair it was that spread over her lap! What great huge breaths the creature took! And what were those curious things it carried? She had seen them on her walls, she was sure.

Thus she talked to herself while the lamp grew paler and paler, and everything kept growing yet clearer. What could it mean? The lamp was dying—going out into the other place of which the creature in her lap had spoken, to be a sun! But why were the things growing clearer before it was yet a sun? That was the point. Was it her growing into a sun that did it? Yes! yes! It was coming death! She knew it, for it was coming upon her also! She felt it coming! What was she about to grow into? Something beautiful, like the creature in her lap? It might be! Anyhow, it must be death; for all her strength was going out of her, while all around her was growing so light she could not bear it. She must be blind soon! Would she be blind or dead first?

For the sun was rushing up behind her. Photogen woke, lifted his head from her lap, and sprang to his feet. His face was one radiant smile. His heart was full of daring—that of the hunter who will creep into the tiger's den.

Nycteris gave a cry, covered her face with her hands, and pressed her eyelids closed. Then blindly she stretched out her arms to Photogen, crying, "Oh, I am so frightened! What is this? It must be death! I don't wish to die yet. I love this room and the old lamp. I do not want the other place. This is terrible. I want to hide. I want to get into the sweet, soft, dark hands of all the other creatures. Ah me! Ah me!"

"What is the matter with you, girl?" said Photogen, with the arrogance of all male creatures until they have been taught by the other kind. He stood looking down upon her over his bow, of which he was examining the string. "There is no fear of anything now, child! It is day. The sun is all but up. Look! He will be above the brow of yon hill in one moment more! Goodbye. Thank you for my night's lodging. I'm off. Don't be a goose. If ever I can do anything for you—and all that, you know!"

"Don't leave me; oh, don't leave me!" cried Nycteris. "I am dying! I am dying! I can't move. The light sucks all the strength out of me. And oh, I am so frightened!"

But already Photogen had splashed through the river, holding high his bow that it might not get wet. He rushed across the level and strained up the opposing hill. Hearing no answer, Nycteris removed her hands. Photogen had reached the top, and the same moment, the sun rays alighted upon him; the glory of the king of day crowded blazing upon the golden-haired youth. Radiant as Apollo, he stood in mighty strength, a flashing shape in the midst of flame. He fitted a glowing arrow to a gleaming bow. The arrow parted with a keen musical twang of the bowstring, and Photogen, darting after it, vanished with a shout. Up shot Apollo himself, and from his quiver scattered astonishment and exultation. But the brain of poor Nycteris was pierced through and through. She fell down in utter darkness. All around her was a flaming furnace. In despair and feebleness and agony, she crept back, feeling her way with doubt and difficulty and enforced persistence to her cell. When at last the friendly darkness of her chamber folded her about with its cooling and consoling arms, she threw herself on her bed and fell fast asleep. And there she slept on, one alive in a tomb, while Photogen, above in the sun glory, pursued the buffaloes on the lofty plain, thinking not once of her, where she lay dark and forsaken, whose presence had been his refuge, her eyes and her hands his guardians through the night. He was in his glory and his pride; and the darkness and its disgrace had vanished for a time.

THE COWARD HERO

But no sooner had the sun reached the noonstead than Photogen began to remember the past night in the shadow of that which was at hand, and to remember it with shame. He had proved himself—and not to himself only, but to a girl as well—a coward! one bold in the daylight, while there was nothing to fear, but trembling like any slave when the night arrived. There was, there must be, something unfair in it! A spell had been cast upon him! He had eaten, he had drunk, something that did not agree with courage! In any case, he had been taken unprepared! How was he to know what the going down of the sun would be like? It was no wonder he should have been surprised into terror, seeing it was what it was—in its very nature so terrible! Also, one could not see where danger might be coming from! You might be torn in pieces, carried off, or swallowed up, without even seeing where to strike a blow! Every possible excuse he caught at, eager as a self-lover to lighten his self-contempt. That day he astonished the huntsmen—terrified them with his reckless daring—all to prove to himself he was no coward. But nothing eased his shame. One thing only had hope in it—the resolve to encounter the dark in solemn earnest, now that he knew something of what it was. It was nobler to meet a recognized danger than to rush contemptuously into what seemed nothing—nobler still to encounter a nameless horror. He could conquer fear and wipe out disgrace together. For a marksman and swordsman like him, he said, one with his strength and courage, there was but danger. Defeat there was not. He knew the darkness now, and when it came he would meet it as fearless and cool as now he felt himself. And again he said, "We shall see!"

He stood under the boughs of a great beech as the sun was going down, far away over the jagged hills: before it was half down, he was trembling like one of the leaves behind him in the first sigh of the night wind. The moment the last of the glowing disk vanished, he bounded away in terror to gain the valley, and his fear grew as he ran. Down the side of the hill, an abject creature, he went bounding and rolling and running; fell rather than plunged into the river, and came to himself, as before, lying on the grassy bank in the garden.

But when he opened his eyes, there were no girl eyes looking down into his; there were only the stars in the waste of the sunless Night—the awful all-enemy he had again dared but could not encounter. Perhaps the girl was not yet come out of the water! He would try to sleep, for he dared not move, and perhaps when he woke he would find his head on her lap and the beautiful dark face, with its deep-blue eyes, bending over him. But when he woke he found his head on the grass, and although he sprang up with all his courage, such as it was, restored, he did not set out for the chase with such an *élan* as the day before; and despite the sun glory in his heart and veins, his hunting was this day less eager; he ate little, and from the first was thoughtful even to sadness. A second time he was defeated and disgraced! Was his courage nothing more than the play of the sunlight on his brain? Was he a mere ball tossed between the light and the dark? Then what a poor contemptible creature he was! But a third chance lay before him. If he failed the third time, he dared not foreshadow what he must then think of himself! It was bad enough now—but then!

Alas! It went no better. The moment the sun was down, he fled as if from a legion of devils.

Seven times in all he tried to face the coming night in the strength of the past day, and seven times he failed—failed with such increase of failure, with such a growing sense of ignominy, overwhelming at length all the sunny hours and joining night to night, that what with misery, self-accusation, and loss of confidence, his daylight courage too began to fade, and at length, from exhaustion, from getting wet, and then lying out of doors all night, and night after night—worst of all, from the consuming of the deathly fear and the shame of shame, his sleep forsook him, and on the seventh morning, instead of going to the hunt, he crawled into the castle and went to bed. The grand health over which the witch had taken such pains had yielded, and in an hour or two he was moaning and crying out in delirium.

AN EVIL NURSE

Watho was herself ill, as I have said, and was the worse tempered; and besides, it is a peculiarity of witches that what works in others to sympathy works in them to repulsion. Also, Watho had a poor, helpless, rudimentary spleen of a conscience left, just enough to make her uncomfortable, and therefore more wicked. So when she heard that Photogen was ill, she was angry. Ill, indeed! after all she had done to saturate him with the life of the system, with the solar might itself! He was a wretched failure, the boy! And because he was *her* failure, she was annoyed with him, began to dislike him, grew to hate him. She looked on him as a painter might upon a picture, or a poet upon a poem, which he had only succeeded in getting into an irre-coverable mess. In the hearts of witches, love and hate lie close together, and often tumble over each other. And whether it was that her failure with Photogen foiled also her plans in regard to Nycteris, or that her illness made her yet more of a devil's wife, certainly Watho now got sick of the girl, too, and hated to know her about the castle.

She was not too ill, however, to go to poor Photogen's room and torment him. She told him she hated him like a serpent and hissed like one as she said it, looking very sharp in the nose and chin, and flat in the forehead. Photogen thought she meant to kill him, and hardly ventured to take anything brought him. She ordered every ray of light to be shut out of his room; but by means of this he got a little used to the darkness. She would take one of his arrows and now tickle him with the feather end of it, now prick him with the point till the blood ran down. What she meant finally I cannot tell, but she brought Photogen speedily to the determination of making his escape from the castle: what he should do then he would think afterwards. Who could tell but he might find his mother somewhere beyond the forest! If it were not for the broad patches of darkness that divided day from day, he would fear nothing!

But now, as he lay helpless in the dark, ever and anon would come dawning through it the face of the lovely creature who on that first awful night nursed him so sweetly: was he never to see her again? If she was as he had concluded, the nymph of the river, why had she not reappeared? She might have taught him not to fear the night, for plainly she had no fear of it herself! But then, when the day came, she did seem frightened: why was that, seeing there was nothing to be afraid of then? Perhaps one so much at home in the darkness was correspondingly afraid of the light! Then his selfish joy at the rising of the sun, blinding him to her condition, had made him behave to her, in ill return for her kindness, as cruelly as Watho behaved to him! How sweet and dear and lovely she was! If there were wild beasts that came out only at night and were afraid of the light, why should there not be girls, too, made the same way—who could not endure the light, as he could not bear the darkness? If only he could find her again! Ah, how differently he would behave to her! But alas! Perhaps the sun had killed her—melted her—burned her up—dried her up—that was it, if she was the nymph of the river!

WATHO'S WOLF

From that dreadful morning Nycteris had never got to be herself again. The sudden light had been almost death to her: and now she lay in the dark with the memory of a terrific sharpness—a something she dared scarcely recall, lest the very thought of it should sting her beyond endurance. But this was as nothing to the pain which the recollection of the rudeness of the shining creature whom she had nursed through his fear caused her; for the moment his suffering passed over to her, and he was free, the first use he made of his returning strength had been to scorn her! She wondered and wondered; it was all beyond her comprehension.

Before long, Watho was plotting evil against her. The witch was like a sick child weary of his toy: she would pull her to pieces and see how she liked it. She would set her in the sun and see her die, like a jelly from the salt ocean cast out on a hot rock. It would be a sight to soothe her wolf pain. One day, therefore, a little before noon, while Nycteris was in her deepest sleep, she had a darkened litter brought to the door, and in that she made two of her men carry her to the plain above. There they took her out, laid her on the grass, and left her.

Watho watched it all from the top of her high tower, through her telescope; and scarcely was Nycteris left, when she saw her sit up and the same moment cast herself down again with her face to the ground.

"She'll have a sunstroke," said Watho, "and that'll be the end of her."

Presently, tormented by a fly, a huge-humped buffalo, with great shaggy mane, came galloping along, straight for where she lay. At sight of the thing on the grass, he started, swerved yards aside, stopped dead, and then came slowly up, looking malicious. Nycteris lay quite still and never even saw the animal.

"Now she'll be trodden to death!" said Watho. "That's the way those creatures do."

When the buffalo reached her, he sniffed at her all over and went away; then came back and sniffed again: then all at once went off as if a demon had him by the tail.

Next came a gnu, a more dangerous animal still, and did much the same; then a gaunt wild boar. But no creature hurt her, and Watho was angry with the whole creation.

At length, in the shade of her hair, the blue eyes of Nycteris began to come to themselves a little, and the first thing they saw was a comfort. I have told already how she knew the night daisies, each a sharp-pointed little cone with a red tip; and once she had parted the rays of one of them, with trembling fingers, for she was afraid she was dreadfully rude and perhaps was hurting it; but she did want, she said to herself, to see what secret it carried so carefully hidden; and she found its golden heart. But now, right under her eyes, inside the veil of her hair, in the sweet twilight of whose blackness she could see it perfectly, stood a daisy with its red tip opened wide into a carmine ring, displaying its heart of gold on a platter of silver. She did not at first recognize it as one of those cones come awake, but a moment's notice revealed what it was. Who then could have been so cruel to the lovely little creature as to force it open like that, and spread it heart-bare to the terrible death lamp? Whoever it was, it must be the same that had thrown her out there to be burned to death in its fire! But she had her hair, and could hang her head, and make a small sweet night of her own about her! She tried to bend the daisy down and away from the sun, and to make its petals hang about it like her hair, but she could not. Alas, it was burned and dead already! She did not know that it could not yield to her gentle force because it was drinking life, with all the eagerness of life, from what she called the death lamp. Oh, how the lamp burned her!

But she went on thinking—she did not know how—and by and by began to reflect that as there was no roof to the room except that in which the great fire went rolling about, the little Red-tip must have seen the lamp a thousand times, and must know it quite well, and it had not killed it! Nay, thinking about it farther, she began to ask the question whether this, in which she now saw it, might not be its more perfect condition. For not only now did the whole seem perfect, as indeed it did before, but every part showed its own individual perfection as well, which perfection made it capable of combining with the rest into the higher perfection of a whole. The flower was a lamp itself! The golden heart was the light, and the silver border was the alabaster globe, skillfully broken and spread wide to let out the glory. Yes: the radiant shape was plainly its perfection! If, then, it was the lamp which had opened it into that shape, the lamp could not be unfriendly to it but must be of its own kind, seeing it made it perfect! And again, when she thought of it, there was clearly no little resemblance between them. What if the flower, then, was the little great-grandchild of the lamp, and he was loving it all the time? And what if the lamp did not mean to hurt her, only could not help it? The red tips looked as if the flower had sometime or other been hurt: what if the lamp was making the best it could of her—opening her out somehow like the flower? She would bear it patiently and see. But how coarse the color of the grass was! Perhaps, however, her eyes not being made for the bright lamp, she did not see them as they were! Then she remembered how different were the eyes of the creature that was not a girl and was afraid of the darkness! Ah, if the darkness would only come again, all arms, friendly and soft everywhere about her! She would wait and wait, and bear, and be patient.

She lay so still that Watho did not doubt she had fainted. She was pretty sure she would be dead before the night came to revive her.

REFUGE

Fixing her telescope on the motionless form, that she might see it at once when the morning came, Watho went down from the tower to Photogen's room. He was much better by this time, and before she left him, he had resolved to leave the castle that very night. The darkness was terrible indeed, but Watho was worse than even the darkness, and he could not escape in the day. As soon, therefore, as the house seemed still, he tightened his belt, hung to it his hunting knife, put a flask of wine and some bread in his pocket, and took his bow and arrows. He got from the house and made his way at once up to the plain. But what with his illness, the terrors of the night, and his dread of the wild beasts, when he got to the level he could not walk a step farther and sat down, thinking it better to die than to live. In spite of his fears, however, sleep contrived to overcome him, and he fell at full length on the soft grass.

He had not slept long when he woke, with such a strange sense of comfort and security that he thought the dawn at least must have arrived. But it was dark night about him. And the sky—no, it was not the sky but the blue eyes of his naiad looking down upon him! Once more he lay with his head in her lap, and all was well, for plainly the girl feared the darkness as little as he the day.

"Thank you," he said. "You are like live armor to my heart; you keep the fear off me. I have been very ill since then. Did you come up out of the river when you saw me cross?"

"I don't live in the water," she answered. "I live under the pale lamp, and I die under the bright one."

"Ah, yes! I understand now," he returned. "I would not have behaved as I did last time if I had understood; but I thought you were mocking me; and I am so made that I cannot help being frightened at the darkness. I beg your pardon for leaving you as I did, for, as I say, I did not understand. Now I believe you were really frightened. Were you not?"

"I was indeed," answered Nycteris, "and shall be again. But why you should be, I cannot in the least understand. You must know how gentle and sweet the darkness is, how kind and friendly, how soft and velvety! It holds you to its bosom and loves you. A little while ago, I lay faint and dying under your hot lamp. What is it you call it?"

"The sun," murmured Photogen. "How I wish he would make haste!"

"Ah! Do not wish that. Do not, for my sake, hurry him. I can take care of you from the darkness, but I have no one to take care of me from the light. As I was telling you, I lay dying in the sun. All at once I drew a deep breath. A cool wind came and ran over my face. I looked up. The torture was gone, for the death lamp itself was gone. I hope he does not die and grow brighter yet. My terrible headache was all gone, and my sight was come back. I felt as if I were new made. But I did not get up at once, for I was tired still. The grass grew cool about me and turned soft in color. Something wet came upon it, and it was now so pleasant to my feet that I rose and ran about. And when I had been running about a long time, all at once I found you lying, just as I had been lying a little while before. So I sat down beside you to take care of you, till your life—and my death—should come again."

"How good you are, you beautiful creature! Why, you forgave me before ever I asked you!" cried Photogen.

Thus they fell a-talking, and he told her what he knew of his history, and she told him what she knew of hers, and they agreed they must get away from Watho as far as ever they could.

"And we must set out at once," said Nycteris.

"The moment the morning comes," returned Photogen.

"We must not wait for the morning," said Nycteris, "for then I shall not be able to move, and what would you do the next night? Besides, Watho sees best in the daytime. Indeed, you must come now, Photogen. You must."

"I cannot; I dare not," said Photogen. "I cannot move. If I but lift my head from your lap, the very sickness of terror seizes me."

"I shall be with you," said Nycteris soothingly. "I will take care of you till your dreadful sun comes, and then you may leave me and go away as fast as you can. Only please put me in a dark place first, if there is one to be found."

"I will never leave you again, Nycteris," cried Photogen. "Only wait till the sun comes and brings me back my strength, and we will go away together and never, never part anymore."

"No, no," persisted Nycteris. "We must go now. And you must learn to be strong in the dark as well as in the day, else you will always be only half brave. I have begun already: not to fight your sun but to try to get at peace with him and understand what he really is and what he means with me—whether to hurt me or to make the best of me. You must do the same with my darkness."

"But you don't know what mad animals there are away there towards the south," said Photogen. "They have huge green eyes, and they would eat you up like a bit of celery, you beautiful creature!"

"Come, come! You must," said Nycteris, "or I shall have to pretend to leave you, to make you come. I have seen the green eyes you speak of, and I will take care of you from them."

"You! How can you do that? If it were day now, I could take care of you from the worst of them. But as it is, I can't even see them for this abominable darkness. I could not see your lovely eyes but for the light that is in them; that lets me see straight into heaven through them. They are windows into the very heaven beyond the sky. I believe they are the very place where the stars are made."

"You come, then, or I shall shut them," said Nycteris, "and you shan't see them anymore till you are good. Come. If you can't see the wild beasts, I can."

"You can! And you ask me to come!" cried Photogen.

"Yes," answered Nycteris. "And more than that, I see them long before they can see me, so that I am able to take care of you."

"But how?" persisted Photogen. "You can't shoot with bow and arrow, or stab with a hunting knife."

"No, but I can keep out of the way of them all. Why, just when I found you, I was having a game with two or three of them at once. I see, and scent them too, long before they are near me—long before they can see or scent me."

"You don't see or scent any now, do you?" said Photogen uneasily, rising on his elbow.

"No—none at present. I will look," replied Nycteris, and sprang to her feet.

"Oh, oh! Do not leave me—not for a moment," cried Photogen, straining his eyes to keep her face in sight through the darkness.

"Be quiet, or they will hear you," she returned. "The wind is from the south, and they cannot scent us. I have found out all about that. Ever since the dear dark came, I have been amusing myself with them, getting every now and then just into the edge of the wind and letting one have a sniff of me."

"Oh, horrible!" cried Photogen. "I hope you will not insist on doing so anymore. What was the consequence?"

"Always, the very instant, he turned with flashing eyes and bounded towards me—only he could not see me, you must remember. But my eyes being so much better than his, I could see him perfectly well and would run away round him until I scented him, and then I knew he could not find me anyhow. If the wind were to turn and run the other way now, there might be a whole army of them down upon us, leaving no room to keep out of their way. You had better come."

She took him by the hand. He yielded and rose, and she led him away. But his steps were feeble, and as the night went on, he seemed more and more ready to sink.

"Oh, dear! I am so tired and so frightened!" he would say.

"Lean on me," Nycteris would return, putting her arm round him or patting his cheek. "Take a few steps more. Every step away from the castle is clear gain. Lean harder on me. I am quite strong and well now."

So they went on. The piercing night eyes of Nycteris descried not a few pairs of green ones gleaming like holes in the darkness, and many a round she made to keep far out of their way; but she never said to Photogen she saw them. Carefully she kept him off the uneven places, and on the softest and smoothest of the grass, talking to him gently all the way as they went— of the lovely flowers and the stars: how comfortable the flowers looked, down in their green beds, and how happy the stars up in their blue beds!

When the morning began to come, he began to grow better but was dreadfully tired with walking instead of sleeping, especially after being so long ill. Nycteris, too, what with supporting him, what with growing fear of the light, which was beginning to ooze out of the east, was very tired. At length, both equally exhausted, neither was able to help the other. As if by consent, they stopped. Embracing each the other, they stood in the midst of the wide grassy land, neither of them able to move a step, each supported only by the leaning weakness of the other, each ready to fall if the other should move. But while the one grew weaker still, the other had begun to grow stronger.

When the tide of the night began to ebb, the tide of the day began to flow; and now the sun was rushing to the horizon, borne upon its foaming billows. And ever as he came, Photogen revived. At last the sun shot up into the air, like a bird from the hand of the Father of Lights. Nycteris gave a cry of pain and hid her face in her hands.

"Oh, me!" she sighed. "I am *so* frightened! The terrible light stings so!"

But the same instant, through her blindness, she heard Photogen give a low exultant laugh, and the next felt herself caught up: she who all night long had tended and protected him like a child was now in his arms, borne along like a baby, with her head lying on his shoulder. But she was the greater, for suffering more, she feared nothing.

THE WEREWOLF

At the very moment when Photogen caught up Nycteris, the telescope of Watho was angrily sweeping the tableland. She swung it from her in rage and, running to her room, shut herself up. There she anointed herself from top to toe with a certain ointment; shook down her long red hair and tied it round her waist; then began to dance, whirling round and round and round faster and faster, growing angrier and angrier, until she was foaming at the mouth with fury. When Falca went looking for her, she could not find her anywhere.

As the sun rose, the wind slowly changed and went round, until it blew straight from the north. Photogen and Nycteris were drawing near the edge of the forest, Photogen still carrying Nycteris, when she moved a little on his shoulder uneasily, and murmured in his ear.

"I smell a wild beast—that way, the way the wind is coming."

Photogen turned, looked back towards the castle, and saw a dark speck on the plain. As he looked, it grew larger: it was coming across the grass with the speed of the wind. It came nearer and nearer. It looked long and low, but that might be because it was running at a great stretch. He set Nycteris down under a tree, in the black shadow of its bole, strung his bow, and picked out his heaviest, longest, sharpest arrow. Just as he set the notch on the string, he saw that the creature was a tremendous wolf, rushing straight at him. He loosened his knife in its sheath, drew another arrow halfway from the quiver, lest the first should fail, and took his aim—at a good distance, to leave time for a second chance. He shot. The arrow rose, flew straight, descended, struck the beast, and started again into the air, doubled like a letter V. Quickly Photogen snatched the other, shot, cast his bow from him, and drew his knife. But the arrow was in the brute's chest, up to the feather; it tumbled heels over head with a great thud of its back on the earth, gave a groan, made a struggle or two, and lay stretched out motionless.

"I've killed it, Nycteris," cried Photogen. "It is a great red wolf."

"Oh, thank you!" answered Nycteris feebly from behind the tree. "I was sure you would. I was not a bit afraid."

Photogen went up to the wolf. It *was* a monster! But he was vexed that his first arrow had behaved so badly and was the less willing to lose the one that had done him such good service: with a long and a strong pull, he drew it from the brute's chest. Could he believe his eyes? There lay—no wolf, but Watho, with her hair tied round her waist! The foolish witch had made herself invulnerable, as she supposed, but had forgotten that to torment Photogen

therewith, she had handled one of his arrows. He ran back to Nycteris and told her.

She shuddered and wept, and would not look.

ALL IS WELL

There was now no occasion to fly a step farther. Neither of them feared anyone but Watho. They left her there and went back. A great cloud came over the sun, and rain began to fall heavily, and Nycteris was much refreshed, grew able to see a little, and with Photogen's help walked gently over the cool wet grass.

They had not gone far before they met Fargu and the other huntsmen. Photogen told them he had killed a great red wolf, and it was Madam Watho. The huntsmen looked grave, but gladness shone through.

"Then," said Fargu, "I will go and bury my mistress."

But when they reached the place, they found she was already buried— in the maws of sundry birds and beasts which had made their breakfast of her.

Then Fargu, overtaking them, would, very wisely, have Photogen go to the king and tell him the whole story. But Photogen, yet wiser than Fargu, would not set out until he had married Nycteris: "for then," he said, "the king himself can't part us; and if ever two people couldn't do the one without the other, those two are Nycteris and I. She has got to teach me to be a brave man in the dark, and I have got to look after her until she can bear the heat of the sun and he helps her to see, instead of blinding her."

They were married that very day. And the next day they went together to the king and told him the whole story. But whom should they find at the court but the father and mother of Photogen, both in high favor with the king and queen. Aurora nearly died for joy and told them all how Watho had lied and made her believe her child was dead.

No one knew anything of the father or mother of Nycteris; but when Aurora saw in the lovely girl her own azure eyes shining through night and its clouds, it made her think strange things and wonder how even the wicked themselves may be a link to join together the good. Through Watho, the mothers, who had never seen each other, had changed eyes in their children.

The king gave them the castle and lands of Watho, and there they lived and taught each other for many years that were not long. But hardly had one of them passed, before Nycteris had come to love the day best, because it was the clothing and crown of Photogen, and she saw that the day was greater than the night, and the sun more lordly than the moon; and Photogen had come to love the night best, because it was the mother and home of Nycteris.

"But who knows," Nycteris would say to Photogen, "that when we go out, we shall not go into a day as much greater than your day as your day is greater than my night?"

‹ *The Griffin and the Minor Canon* ›
FRANK STOCKTON

Over the great door of an old, old church, which stood in a quiet town of a far-away land, there was carved in stone the figure of a large griffin. The old-time sculptor had done his work with great care, but the image he had made was not a pleasant one to look at. It had a large head, with enormous open mouth and savage teeth. From its back arose great wings, armed with sharp hooks and prongs. It had stout legs in front, with projecting claws, but there were no legs behind, the body running out into a long and powerful tail, finished off at the end with a barbed point. This tail was coiled up under him, the end sticking up just back of his wings.

The sculptor, or the people who had ordered this stone figure, had evidently been very much pleased with it, for little copies of it, also in stone, had been placed here and there along the sides of the church, not very far from the ground, so that people could easily look at them and ponder on their curious forms. There were a great many other sculptures on the outside of this church—saints, martyrs, grotesque heads of men, beasts, and birds, as well as those of other creatures, which cannot be named, because nobody knows exactly what they were. But none were so curious and interesting as the great griffin over the door and the little griffins on the sides of the church.

A long, long distance from the town, in the midst of dreadful wilds scarcely known to man, there dwelt the Griffin whose image had been put up over the church door. In some way or other, the old-time sculptor had seen him, and afterwards, to the best of his memory, had copied his figure in stone. The Griffin had never known this until, hundreds of years afterwards, he heard from a bird, from a wild animal, or in some manner which it is not easy to find out, that there was a likeness of him on the old church in the distant town.

Now this Griffin had no idea whatever how he looked. He had never seen a mirror, and the streams where he lived were so turbulent and violent that a quiet piece of water, which would reflect the image of anything looking into it, could not be found. Being, as far as could be ascertained, the very last of his race, he had never seen another griffin. Therefore it was that when he heard of this stone image of himself, he became very anxious to know what he looked like, and at last he determined to go to the old church and see for himself what manner of being he was. So he started off from the dreadful wilds, and flew on and on until he came to the countries inhabited by men, where his appearance in the air created great consternation. But he alighted nowhere, keeping up a steady flight until he reached the suburbs of the town which had his image on its church. Here, late in the afternoon, he alighted in a green meadow by the side of a brook and stretched himself on the grass to rest. His great wings were tired, for he had not made such a long flight in a century or more.

The news of his coming spread quickly over the town, and the people, frightened nearly out of their wits by the arrival of so extraordinary a visitor, fled into their houses and shut themselves up. The Griffin called loudly for someone to come to him; but the more he called, the more afraid the people were to show themselves. At length he saw two laborers hurrying to their homes through the fields, and in a terrible voice he commanded them to stop. Not daring to disobey, the men stood, trembling.

"What is the matter with you all?" cried the Griffin. "Is there not a man in your town who is brave enough to speak to me?"

"I think," said one of the laborers, his voice shaking so that his words could hardly be understood, "that—perhaps—the Minor Canon would come."

"Go, call him, then!" said the Griffin. "I want to see him."

The Minor Canon, who filled a subordinate position in the old church, had just finished the afternoon service and was coming out of a side door, with three aged women who had formed the weekday congregation. He was a young man of a kind disposition and very anxious to do good to the people of the town. Apart from his duties in the church, where he conducted services every weekday, he visited the sick and the poor, counseled and assisted persons who were in trouble, and taught a school composed entirely of the bad children in the town, with whom nobody else would have anything to do. Whenever the people wanted something difficult done for them, they always went to the Minor Canon. Thus it was that the laborer thought of the young priest when he found that someone must come and speak to the Griffin.

The Minor Canon had not heard of the strange event, which was known to the whole town except himself and the three old women, and when he was informed of it, and was told that the Griffin had asked to see him, he was greatly amazed and frightened.

"Me!" he exclaimed. "He has never heard of me! What should he want with *me?*"

"Oh, you must go instantly!" cried the two men. "He is very angry now because he has been kept waiting so long, and nobody knows what may happen if you don't hurry to him."

The poor Minor Canon would rather have had his hand cut off than to go out to meet an angry griffin; but he felt that it was his duty to go, for it would be a woeful thing if injury should come to the people of the town because he was not brave enough to obey the summons of the Griffin. So, pale and frightened, he started off.

"Well," said the Griffin, as soon as the young man came near, "I am glad to see that there is someone who has the courage to come to me."

The Minor Canon did not feel very courageous, but he bowed his head.

"Is this the town," said the Griffin, "where there is a church with a likeness of myself over one of the doors?"

The Minor Canon looked at the frightful creature before him and saw that it was, without doubt, exactly like the stone image on the church. "Yes," he said, "you are right."

"Well, then," said the Griffin, "will you take me to it? I wish very much to see it."

The Minor Canon instantly thought that if the Griffin entered the town without the people knowing what he came for, some of them would probably be frightened to death, and so he sought to gain time to prepare their minds.

"It is growing dark now," he said, very much afraid, as he spoke, that his words might enrage the Griffin, "and objects on the front of the church cannot be seen clearly. It will be better to wait until morning, if you wish to get a good view of the stone image of yourself."

"That will suit me very well," said the Griffin. "I see you are a man of good sense. I am tired, and I will take a nap here on this soft grass, while I cool my tail in the little stream that runs near me. The end of my tail gets red hot when I am angry or excited, and it is quite warm now. So you may go; but be sure and come early tomorrow morning and show me the way to the church."

The Minor Canon was glad enough to take his leave and hurried into the town. In front of the church he found a great many people assembled to hear his report of his interview with the Griffin. When they found that he had not come to spread ruin and devastation, but simply to see his stony likeness on the church, they showed neither relief nor gratification, but began to upbraid the Minor Canon for consenting to conduct the creature into the town.

"What could I do?" cried the young man. "If I should not bring him he would come himself, and perhaps end by setting fire to the town with his red-hot tail."

Still the people were not satisfied, and a great many plans were proposed to prevent the Griffin from coming into the town. Some elderly persons urged that the young men should go out and kill him. But the young men scoffed at such a ridiculous idea. Then someone said that it would be a good thing to destroy the stone image, so that the Griffin would have no excuse for entering the town. This proposal was received with such favor that many of the people ran for hammers, chisels, and crowbars with which to tear down and break up the stone griffin. But the Minor Canon resisted this plan with all the strength of his mind and body. He assured the people that this action would enrage the Griffin beyond measure, for it would be impossible to conceal from him that his image had been destroyed during the night.

But they were so determined to break up the stone griffin that the Minor Canon saw that there was nothing for him to do but to stay there and protect it. All night he walked up and down in front of the church door, keeping away the men who brought ladders by which they might mount to the great stone griffin and knock it to pieces with their hammers and crowbars. After many hours the people were obliged to give up their attempts, and went home to sleep. But the Minor Canon remained at his post till early morning, and then he hurried away to the field where he had left the Griffin.

The monster had just awakened, and rising to his forelegs and shaking himself, he said that he was ready to go into the town. The Minor Canon, therefore, walked back, the Griffin flying slowly through the air at a short distance above the head of his guide. Not a person was to be seen in the streets, and they proceeded directly to the front of the church, where the Minor Canon pointed out the stone griffin.

The real Griffin settled down in the little square before the church and gazed earnestly at his sculptured likeness. For a long time he looked at it. First he put his head on one side, and then he put it on the other. Then he shut his right eye and gazed with his left, after which he shut his left eye and gazed with his right. Then he moved a little to one side and looked at the image, then he moved the other way. After a while he said to the Minor Canon, who had been standing by all this time:

"It is, it must be, an excellent likeness! That breadth between the eyes, that expansive forehead, those massive jaws! I feel that it must resemble me.

If there is any fault to find with it, it is that the neck seems a little stiff. But that is nothing. It is an admirable likeness—admirable!"

The Griffin sat looking at his image all the morning and all the afternoon. The Minor Canon had been afraid to go away and leave him, and had hoped all through the day that he would soon be satisfied with his inspection and fly away home. But by evening the poor young man was utterly exhausted and felt that he must eat and sleep. He frankly admitted this fact to the Griffin and asked him if he would not like something to eat. He said this because he felt obliged in politeness to do so; but as soon as he had spoken the words, he was seized with dread lest the monster should demand half a dozen babies or some tempting repast of that kind.

"Oh, no," said the Griffin. "I never eat between the equinoxes. At the vernal and at the autumnal equinox I take a good meal, and that lasts me for half a year. I am extremely regular in my habits and do not think it healthful to eat at odd times. But if you need food, go and get it, and I will return to the soft grass where I slept last night and take another nap."

The next day, the Griffin came again to the little square before the church and remained there until evening, steadfastly regarding the stone griffin over the door. The Minor Canon came once or twice to look at him, and the Griffin seemed very glad to see him. But the young clergyman could not stay as he had done before, for he had many duties to perform. Nobody went to the church, but the people came to the Minor Canon's house and anxiously asked him how long the Griffin was going to stay.

"I do not know," he answered, "but I think he will soon be satisfied with looking at his stone likeness, and then he will go away."

But the Griffin did not go away. Morning after morning he went to the church, but after a time he did not stay there all day. He seemed to have taken a great fancy to the Minor Canon and followed him about as he pursued his various avocations. He would wait for him at the side door of the church, for the Minor Canon held services every day, morning and evening, though nobody came now. "If anyone should come," he said to himself, "I must be found at my post." When the young man came out, the Griffin would accompany him in his visits to the sick and the poor, and would often look into the windows of the schoolhouse where the Minor Canon was teaching his unruly scholars. All the other schools were closed, but the parents of the Minor Canon's scholars forced them to go to school, because they were so bad they could not endure them all day at home—griffin or no griffin. But it must be said they generally behaved very well when that great monster sat up on his tail and looked in at the schoolroom window.

When it was perceived that the Griffin showed no sign of going away, all the people who were able to do so left the town. The canons and the higher officers of the church had fled away during the first day of the Griffin's visit, leaving behind only the Minor Canon and some of the men who opened the doors and swept the church. All the citizens who could afford it shut up their houses and traveled to distant parts, and only the working people and the poor were left behind. After some days, these ventured to go about and attend to their business, for if they did not work they would starve. They were getting a little used to seeing the Griffin, and having been told that he did not eat between equinoxes, they did not feel so much afraid of him as before.

Day by day the Griffin became more and more attached to the Minor Canon. He kept near him a great part of the time, and often spent the night in front of the little house where the young clergyman lived alone. This strange companionship was often burdensome to the Minor Canon. But on the other hand, he could not deny that he derived a great deal of benefit and instruction from it. The Griffin had lived for hundreds of years and had seen much, and he told the Minor Canon many wonderful things.

"It is like reading an old book," said the young clergyman to himself. "But how many books I would have had to read before I would have found out what the Griffin has told me about the earth, the air, the water, about minerals and metals and growing things and all the wonders of the world!"

Thus the summer went on and drew toward its close. And now the people of the town began to be very much troubled again.

"It will not be long," they said, "before the autumnal equinox is here, and then that monster will want to eat. He will be dreadfully hungry, for he has taken so much exercise since his last meal. He will devour our children. Without doubt, he will eat them all. What is to be done?"

To this question no one could give an answer, but all agreed that the Griffin must not be allowed to remain until the approaching equinox. After talking over the matter a great deal, a crowd of the people went to the Minor Canon, at a time when the Griffin was not with him.

"It is all your fault," they said, "that that monster is among us. You brought him here, and you ought to see that he goes away. It is only on your account that he stays here at all, for although he visits his image every day, he is with you the greater part of the time. If you were not here he would not stay. It is your duty to go away, and then he will follow you, and we shall be free from the dreadful danger which hangs over us."

"Go away!" cried the Minor Canon, greatly grieved at being spoken to in such a way. "Where shall I go? If I go to some other town, shall I not take this trouble there? Have I a right to do that?"

"No," said the people, "you must not go to any other town. There is no town far enough away. You must go to the dreadful wilds where the Griffin lives, and then he will follow you and stay there."

They did not say whether or not they expected the Minor Canon to stay there also, and he did not ask them anything about it. He bowed his head and went into his house to think. The more he thought, the more clear it became to his mind that it was his duty to go away and thus free the town from the presence of the Griffin.

That evening he packed a leather bag full of bread and meat, and early the next morning he set out on his journey to the dreadful wilds. It was a long, weary, and doleful journey, especially after he had gone beyond the habitations of men; but the Minor Canon kept on bravely and never faltered. The way was longer than he had expected, and his provisions soon grew so scanty that he was obliged to eat but a little every day; but he kept up his courage and pressed on, and after many days of toilsome travel he reached the dreadful wilds.

When the Griffin found that the Minor Canon had left the town, he seemed sorry but showed no disposition to go and look for him. After a few days had passed, he became much annoyed and asked some of the people where the Minor Canon had gone. But although the citizens had been so anxious that the young clergyman should go to the dreadful wilds, thinking that the Griffin would immediately follow him, they were now afraid to mention the Minor Canon's destination, for the monster seemed angry already, and if he should suspect their trick, he would doubtless become very much enraged. So everyone said he did not know, and the Griffin wandered about disconsolate. One morning he looked into the Minor Canon's schoolhouse, which was always empty now, and thought that it was a shame that everything should suffer on account of the young man's absence.

"It does not matter so much about the church," he said, "for nobody went there. But it is a pity about the school. I think I will teach it myself until he returns."

It was the hour for opening the school, and the Griffin went inside and pulled the rope which rang the school bell. Some of the children who heard the bell ran in to see what was the matter, supposing it to be a joke of one of their companions. But when they saw the Griffin, they stood astonished and scared.

"Go tell the other scholars," said the monster, "that school is about to open, and that if they are not all here in ten minutes I shall come after them."

In seven minutes every scholar was in place.

Never was seen such an orderly school. Not a boy or girl moved or uttered a whisper. The Griffin climbed into the master's seat, his wide wings spread on each side of him, because he could not lean back in his chair while they stuck out behind, and his great tail coiled around in front of the desk, the barbed end sticking up, ready to tap any boy or girl who might misbehave. The Griffin now addressed the scholars, telling them that he intended to teach them while their master was away. In speaking he endeavored to imitate, as far as possible, the mild and gentle tones of the Minor Canon, but it must be admitted that in this he was not very successful. He had paid a good deal of attention to the studies of the school, and he determined not to attempt to teach them anything new but to review them in what they had been studying. So he called up the various classes and questioned them upon their previous lessons. The children racked their brains to remember what they had learned. They were so afraid of the Griffin's displeasure that they recited as they had never recited before. One of the boys, far down in his class, answered so well that the Griffin was astonished.

"I should think you would be at the head," said he. "I am sure you have never been in the habit of reciting so well. Why is this?"

"Because I did not choose to take the trouble," said the boy, trembling in his boots. He felt obliged to speak the truth, for all the children thought that the great eyes of the Griffin could see right through them and that he would know when they told a falsehood.

"You ought to be ashamed of yourself," said the Griffin. "Go down to the very tail of the class, and if you are not at the head in two days, I shall know the reason why."

The next afternoon, this boy was number one.

It was astonishing how much these children now learned of what they had been studying. It was as if they had been educated over again. The Griffin used no severity toward them, but there was a look about him which made them unwilling to go to bed until they were sure they knew their lessons for the next day.

The Griffin now thought that he ought to visit the sick and the poor, and he began to go about the town for this purpose. The effect upon the sick was miraculous. All, except those who were very ill indeed, jumped from their beds when they heard he was coming and declared themselves quite well. To those who could not get up he gave herbs and roots which none of them had ever before thought of as medicines but which the Griffin had seen used in various parts of the world, and most of them recovered. But for all that, they afterwards said that no matter what happened to them, they hoped that they should never again have such a doctor coming to their bedsides, feeling their pulses and looking at their tongues.

As for the poor, they seemed to have utterly disappeared. All those who had depended upon charity for their daily bread were now at work in some way or other, many of them offering to do odd jobs for their neighbors just for the sake of their meals—a thing which before had been seldom heard of in the town. The Griffin could find no one who needed his assistance.

The summer now passed, and the autumnal equinox was rapidly approaching. The citizens were in a state of great alarm and anxiety. The Griffin showed no signs of going away but seemed to have settled himself permanently among them. In a short time the day for his semiannual meal would arrive, and then what would happen? The monster would certainly be very hungry and would devour all their children.

Now they greatly regretted and lamented that they had sent away the Minor Canon. He was the only one on whom they could have depended in this trouble, for he could talk freely with the Griffin and so find out what could be done. But it would not do to be inactive. Some step must be taken immediately. A meeting of the citizens was called, and two old men were appointed to go and talk to the Griffin. They were instructed to offer to prepare a splendid dinner for him on equinox day—one which would entirely satisfy his hunger. They would offer him the fattest mutton, the most tender beef, fish and game of various sorts, and anything of the kind he might fancy. If none of these suited, they were to mention that there was an orphan asylum in the next town.

"Anything would be better," said the citizens, "than to have our dear children devoured."

The old men went to the Griffin, but their propositions were not received with favor.

"From what I have seen of the people of this town," said the monster, "I do not think I could relish anything which was prepared by them. They appear to be all cowards and, therefore, mean and selfish. As for eating one of them, old or young, I could not think of it for a moment. In fact, there was only one creature in the whole place for whom I could have had any appetite, and that is the Minor Canon, who has gone away. He was brave, and good, and honest, and I think I should have relished him."

"Ah!" said one of the old men, very politely. "In that case, I wish we had not sent him to the dreadful wilds!"

"What!" cried the Griffin. "What do you mean? Explain instantly what you are talking about!"

The old man, terribly frightened at what he had said, was obliged to tell how the Minor Canon had been sent away by the people, in the hope that the Griffin might be induced to follow him.

When the monster heard this he became furiously angry. He dashed away from the old men and, spreading his wings, flew backward and forward over the town. He was so much excited that his tail became red hot and glowed like a meteor against the evening sky. When at last he settled down in the little field where he usually rested, and thrust his tail into the brook, the steam arose like a cloud, and the water of the stream ran hot through the town. The citizens were greatly frightened, and bitterly blamed the old man for telling about the Minor Canon.

"It is plain," they said, "that the Griffin intended at last to go and look for him, and we should have been saved. Now who can tell what misery you have brought upon us?"

The Griffin did not remain long in the little field. As soon as his tail was cool he flew to the town hall and rang the bell. The citizens knew that they were expected to come there, and although they were afraid to go, they were still more afraid to stay away, and they crowded into the hall. The Griffin was on the platform at one end, flapping his wings and walking up and down, and the end of his tail was still so warm that it slightly scorched the boards as he dragged it after him.

When everybody who was able to come was there, the Griffin stood still and addressed the meeting.

"I have had a contemptible opinion of you," he said, "ever since I discovered what cowards you are, but I had no idea that you were so ungrateful, selfish, and cruel as I now find you to be. Here was your Minor Canon, who labored day and night for your good and thought of nothing else but how he might benefit you and make you happy; and as soon as you imagine yourselves threatened with a danger—for well I know you are dreadfully afraid of me—you send him off, caring not whether he returns or perishes, hoping thereby to save yourselves. Now I had conceived a great liking for that young man, and had intended, in a day or two, to go and look him up. But I have changed my mind about him. I shall go and find him, but I shall send him back here to live among you, and I intend that he shall enjoy the reward of his labor and his sacrifices. Go, some of you, to the officers of the church, who so cowardly ran away when I first came here, and tell them never to return to this town under penalty of death. And if, when your Minor Canon comes back to you, you do not bow yourselves before him, put him in the highest place among you, and serve and honor him all his life, beware of my terrible vengeance! There were only two good things in this town: the Minor Canon and the stone image of myself over your church door. One of these you have sent away, and the other I shall carry away myself."

With these words he dismissed the meeting; and it was time, for the end of his tail had become so hot that there was danger of its setting fire to the building.

The next morning, the Griffin came to the church, and tearing the stone image of himself from its fastenings over the great door, he grasped it with his powerful forelegs and flew up into the air. Then, after hovering over the town for a moment, he gave his tail an angry shake and took up his flight to the dreadful wilds. When he reached this desolate region, he set the stone griffin upon a ledge of a rock which rose in front of the dismal cave he called his home. There the image occupied a position somewhat similar to that it had had over the church door; and the Griffin, panting with the exertion of carrying such an enormous load to so great a distance, lay down upon the ground and regarded it with much satisfaction. When he felt somewhat rested he went to look for the Minor Canon. He found the young man, weak and half starved, lying under the shadow of a rock. After picking him up and carrying him to his cave, the Griffin flew away to a distant marsh, where he procured some roots and herbs which he well knew were strengthening and

beneficial to man, though he had never tasted them himself. After eating these, the Minor Canon was greatly revived and sat up and listened while the Griffin told him what had happened in the town.

"Do you know," said the monster, when he had finished, "that I have had, and still have, a great liking for you?"

"I am very glad to hear it," said the Minor Canon, with his usual politeness.

"I am not at all sure that you would be," said the Griffin, "if you thoroughly understood the state of the case, but we will not consider that now. If some things were different, other things would be otherwise. I have been so enraged by discovering the manner in which you have been treated that I have determined that you shall at last enjoy the rewards and honors to which you are entitled. Lie down and have a good sleep, and then I will take you back to the town."

As he heard these words, a look of trouble came over the young man's face.

"You need not give yourself any anxiety," said the Griffin, "about my return to the town. I shall not remain there. Now that I have that admirable likeness of myself in front of my cave, where I can sit at my leisure and gaze upon its noble features and magnificent proportions, I have no wish to see that abode of cowardly and selfish people."

The Minor Canon, relieved from his fears, lay back and dropped into a doze; and when he was sound asleep, the Griffin took him up and carried him back to the town. He arrived just before daybreak, and putting the young man gently on the grass in the little field where he himself used to rest, the monster, without having been seen by any of the people, flew back to his home.

When the Minor Canon made his appearance in the morning among the citizens, the enthusiasm and cordiality with which he was received were truly wonderful. He was taken to a house which had been occupied by one of the banished high officers of the place, and everyone was anxious to do all that could be done for his health and comfort. The people crowded into the church when he held services, so that the three old women who used to be his weekday congregation could not get to the best seats, which they had always been in the habit of taking; and the parents of the bad children determined to reform them at home, in order that he might be spared the trouble of keeping up his former school. The Minor Canon was appointed to the highest office of the old church, and before he died he became a bishop.

During the first years after his return from the dreadful wilds, the people of the town looked up to him as a man to whom they were bound to do honor and reverence. But they often, also, looked up to the sky to see if there were any signs of the Griffin coming back. However, in the course of time they learned to honor and reverence their former Minor Canon without the fear of being punished if they did not do so.

But they need never have been afraid of the Griffin. The autumnal equinox day came round, and the monster ate nothing. If he could not have the Minor Canon, he did not care for anything. So, lying down with his eyes fixed upon the great stone griffin, he gradually declined, and died. It was a good thing for some of the people of the town that they did not know this.

If you should ever visit the old town, you would still see the little griffins on the sides of the church, but the great stone griffin that was over the door is gone.

The Three Clever Kings

Mary De Morgan

 ld King Roland lay upon his deathbed, and as he had no son to reign after him he sent for his three nephews, Aldovrand, Aldebert, and Alderete, and addressed them as follows:

"My dear nephews, I feel that my days are now drawing to an end, and one of you will have to be king when I am dead. But there is no pleasure in being king. My people have been difficult to govern and never content with what I did for them, so that my life has been a hard one, and though I have watched you all closely, still I know not which is most fit to wear the crown; so my wish is that you should each try it in turn. You, Aldovrand, as you are the oldest, shall be king first, and if you reign happily, all well and good; but if you fail, let Aldebert take your place; and if he fail, let him give it up to Alderete, and then you will know which is the best fitted to govern."

On this, the three young men all thanked their uncle, and each one declared that he would do his best, and soon after, old King Roland died and was buried with great state and ceremony.

So now Aldovrand was to be king, and he was crowned, and there were great rejoicings everywhere.

"'Tis a fine thing to be king," cried he in much glee. "Now I can amuse myself and do just as I please, and there will be no one to stop me, and I will lie in bed as late as I like in the morning, for who dares blame one, if one is king?"

Next morning, the prime minister and the chancellor came to the palace to see the new king and settle affairs of state, but they were told that his majesty was in bed and had given orders that no one should disturb him.

"This is a bad beginning," sighed the prime minister.

"Very bad," echoed the chancellor.

When they came back to the palace later in the day, the king was playing at battledore and shuttlecock with some of his gentlemen and was very angry at being interrupted in his game.

"A pretty thing," he cried, "that I, the king, am to be sent for hither and thither as if I were a lackey. They must go away and come another time"; and on hearing this, the prime minister and the chancellor looked graver still.

But next morning there came the commander in chief and the lord high admiral, as well as the prime minister and the chancellor, all wanting to have an audience with the king, and as he was not out of bed and they could not wait any longer, they all stood outside his bedroom door and knocked to gain admittance, and at last he came out in a towering rage and, throwing them his crown, cried:

"Here, let one of my cousins be king, for I will not bear this longer. It is much more trouble than it is worth, so Aldebert or Alderete may try it and see how they like it, but as for me, I have had enough of it," and he ran downstairs and out the palace door, leaving the prime minister and the chancellor and the general and the admiral staring at each other in dismay.

Aldovrand walked out of the town unnoticed and turned towards the country, whistling cheerily to himself. When he had gone some way in the fields, he came to a farmhouse, and in a meadow near, the farmer stood talking to his men. Aldovrand went straight up to him and, touching his hat, asked if he could give him any work.

"Work?" cried the farmer, little thinking he was talking to his late king. "Why, what sort of work can you do?"

"Well," said Aldovrand, "I am not very fond of running about, but if you want anyone to mind your sheep, or keep the birds from your corn, I could do that nicely."

"I tell you what you can do if you like," said the farmer. "I am wanting a gooseboy to take care of my geese. See, there they are on the common. All you will have to do is to see that they don't stray away and to drive them in at night."

"That will suit me exactly," cried Aldovrand. "I will begin at once;" and he went straight on to the common, and when he had collected the geese together lay down to watch them in high good humor.

"This is capital," he cried, "and much better than being king at the palace. Here there is no prime minister or chancellor to come worrying;" and he lay watching the geese all day very contentedly.

When the prime minister and the chancellor knew that Aldovrand was really gone, they went in a great hurry to Aldebert to tell him that it was his turn to be king. But when he heard how his cousin had run away, he looked frightened.

"I will do my best," quoth he, "but I really know very little about the matter. However, you must tell me, and I will do whatever you direct."

At hearing this, the prime minister and the chancellor were delighted.

"Now we have got the right sort of king," they said, and both wagged their heads with joy.

So King Aldebert was crowned, and there were great rejoicings all over the country.

Early next morning he was up, all ready to receive his ministers, and first came the prime minister.

"Your Majesty," said he, "I come to you on an affair of much importance. A great part of our city is falling down, and it is very necessary that we should rebuild it at once. If you will command it, therefore, I will see that it is done."

"I have no doubt you are right," said the king. "Pray let them begin building at once"; and the prime minister went away delighted.

Scarcely had he gone when in came the commander in chief.

"Your Majesty," said he, "I wish to lay before you the state of our army. Our soldiers have had a great deal of fighting to do lately and are beginning to be discontented, but the late king, your uncle, would never attend to their wants."

"Pray do what you like," said King Aldebert.

"To satisfy them," said the commander in chief, "I think that we should double their pay. This would keep them in a good humor, and all will go well."

"By all means, that will certainly be the best way," said Aldebert. "Let it be given to them at once"; and on hearing this, the commander in chief went away right merrily.

When he had gone, there came in the chancellor, with a long face.

"Your Majesty," he said, "I have this morning been to the treasury, and I find that there is scarcely any money left. The late king, your uncle, spent so much, in spite of all I could say, that now it is almost all gone. Your Majesty must now save all you can for the next year or two, and you ought also to lower the soldiers' pay and stop all public works."

"I have no doubt you are quite right," cried the king. "You know best; let it be done as you wish."

But next morning, in came the prime minister, with a frowning face. "How is this, Your Majesty?" cried he. "Just as we are beginning our buildings, the chancellor comes and tells us that we are not to have any money to build with." He had not done speaking when the commander in chief burst into the room, unable to conceal his rage.

"Yesterday Your Majesty told me that all the soldiers should have double pay, and this morning I hear that instead of that, their wages are to be lowered!" Here he was interrupted by the chancellor, who came running in looking much excited.

"Your Majesty," he cried, "did you not yesterday say we were now to begin saving, and that I was not to allow any more money to be spent, and that the army must do with less pay?"

And then all three began to quarrel among themselves. When he saw how angry they were, King Aldebert took off his crown and said:

"I am sure you are each of you quite right; but I think I am scarcely fit to be a king. Indeed, I think you had better find my cousin Alderete and let him be crowned, and I will seek my fortune elsewhere." And he had slipped out of the room, and run downstairs and out of the palace, before they could stop him.

He went briskly down the highroad into the country, the same way that Aldovrand had gone.

After he had gone some way, he met a traveling tinker who sat by the roadside mending tin cans, with his little fire at his side.

Aldebert stood watching him and at last said, "How cleverly you mend those holes! You must lead a pleasant life, going from house to house in the green lanes mending wares. Do you think I could learn how to do it if you would teach me?"

The tinker, who was an old man, looked at him and said, "Well, I don't mind giving you a trial if you like to come with me, for I want a strong young man sometimes to help me wheel my little cart, and I'll teach you my trade, and we'll see what you can make of it."

So Aldebert was delighted and went with the tinker.

When they knew he was really gone, the prime minister and the chancellor looked at each other in dismay.

"This will never do," cried they. "We must go at once to Prince Alderete; and let us hope he may do better than his cousins."

When Prince Alderete heard that it was his turn to reign, he jumped for joy.

"Now," cried he, "at last I will show what a king should really be like. My cousins were neither of them any good, but they shall now see how different I will be."

So he was crowned, and again there were great rejoicings all over the country.

Next day, he sat in state to receive the chancellor and the prime minister and hear what they had to say.

"My friends," said he to them, "a good king ought to be like a father to his people, and this is what I mean to be. I mean to arrange everything for them myself, and if they will only obey me and do as I direct, they are sure to be both prosperous and happy."

On hearing this, both prime minister and chancellor looked anxious, and the chancellor said,

"I fear, Your Majesty, your people will not like to be too much meddled with." At this, the king was very angry, and bid them see about their own business and not presume to teach him his.

When they had gone, he went to take a drive in his city, that he might see it and know it well; but directly he returned to the palace he sent for the prime minister, and when he had arrived, said:

"I already see much to be altered in my kingdom. I do not like the houses in which many of the people dwell, nor indeed the dresses they wear; but what strikes me most of all is that wherever I go I smell a strong smell of pea soup. Now nothing is so unwholesome as pea soup, and therefore it would not be right in me to allow the people to go on eating it. I command, therefore, that no one shall again make, or eat, pea soup within my realm on pain of death."

Again the prime minister looked very grave, and began to say:

"Your Majesty, your subjects will surely not like to be hindered from eating and drinking what pleases them!" But the king cried out in a rage:

"Go at once and do as I bid you." So the prime minister had to obey.

Early next morning when the King arose, he heard a great hubbub under his window, and when he went to see what it was, he saw a vast mob of people, all shouting, "The king, the king! Where is this king who would dictate to us what we shall eat and drink?"

When he saw them he was terribly frightened and at once sent off for the prime minister and the chancellor to come to his aid.

"Pray go and tell them to eat what they like," he cried when they arrived, "but do you know, I find it will not at all suit me to be king. You had best try Aldovrand, or Aldebert, again;" and so saying, he took off his crown and laid it down, and slipped away out of the palace before either prime minister or chancellor could stop him.

He went out the back door, and ran, and ran, and ran, till he had left the town far behind and came to the country fields and lanes—the same way that his two cousins had gone; and as he went he met a sweep trudging along, carrying his long brooms over his shoulder.

"My friend," cried Alderete, stopping him, "of all things in the world I should like to be a sweep and learn how to sweep chimneys. May I go with you, and will you teach me your trade?"

The sweep looked surprised, but said, yes, Alderete could go with him if he chose, and as he was now going on to the farmhouses on the road, to sweep the chimneys, he could begin at once. So Alderete went with the sweep, carrying some of his brooms for him.

After a time the people outside the palace grew quiet, when they heard that the king would not interfere with them further. And when all was again still, the prime minister and the chancellor went to seek the king, but he was nowhere to be found in the palace.

"This will never do," cried they. "We must have a king somehow, so we had best have back one of the others." So they started to look for Aldovrand or Aldebert.

They sought them all over the city, and at last they came into the same country road down which the three cousins had gone, and there they saw Aldovrand lying in a meadow, watching his flock of geese.

"Good day, my friends," cried he when he saw them. "And how are things going on at the palace? I hope my cousins like reigning better than I did. Now here I lie peacefully all day long and watch my geese, and it is much nicer than being king."

Then the prime minister and the chancellor told him all that had happened and begged that he would come back with them to the palace again, but at this Aldovrand laughed outright.

"No indeed!" cried he. "I would not be king again for any man living. You had best go and seek my cousin Aldebert and ask him. I saw him go down the road with a tinker, helping him to mend his tins. So go and ask him, and leave me to mind my geese in peace."

So the prime minister and the chancellor had to seek still farther.

They trudged on and on, till at last they met Aldebert, who sat by the side of the road mending a tin kettle and whistling cheerily.

"Heyday, whom have we here?" cried he. "The prime minister and the chancellor! And I am right glad to see you both. See how clever I have grown; I am learning to be a tinker, and I mended that hole all myself."

Then the prime minister and the chancellor begged him to leave his pots and come back to the palace and be king, but he fell to work again, harder than ever, and said:

"No indeed! Go and ask my cousins, who are both much cleverer than I. I really don't do for it at all, but I make a very good tinker, and I like that much better."

"Then what can we do?" cried the prime minister. "For we don't know where Alderete has gone."

"I saw him go by here with a sweep a little time ago," said Aldebert, "and he went into that farmhouse yonder, so you had best seek him there."

So the prime minister and the chancellor went on to the farmhouse. At the door stood the farmer's wife, but when they asked her if she had seen the king go by, she stared with surprise.

"Nay," said she. "No one has been here but our sweep and his apprentice. He is in there sweeping the chimney now." On hearing this, the prime minister and the chancellor at once ran into the farmhouse, and saw the old sweep standing by the kitchen fireplace. "And where is the other sweep?" cried they. "He is gone up the chimney and is just going to begin sweeping," said the old man. "So if you want to speak to him you must shout." So they shouted and called:

"King Alderete, King Alderete!" as loud as ever they could, but he did not hear. Then the chancellor knelt in front of the grate and put his head up the chimney and called:

"King Alderete, King Alderete! It is the prime minister and I, the chancellor, come to fetch Your Majesty back to the palace."

When Alderete heard him up the chimney, he trembled in every limb, but he replied:

"I'm not going to come down; I don't want to be king. I am going to be a sweep, and I like that much better. I shan't come down till you are gone away, and now you had best go quickly, for I am going to begin sweeping, and all the soot will fall on your head," and then they heard the rattle of the broom in the chimney, and a whole shower of soot fell on the chancellor's head.

The prime minister and the chancellor turned back to the city very disconsolately. "We must go and look for a king elsewhere," they said. "It is no use troubling about Aldovrand, Aldebert, and Alderete." So they left the one to his geese, and one to his tins, and the other to sweep chimneys, and that was the end of the three clever kings.

§

The Fisherman and His Soul

Oscar Wilde

very evening the young Fisherman went out upon the sea,
and threw his nets into the water.

When the wind blew from the land he caught nothing,
or but little at best, for it was a bitter and black-winged wind,
and rough waves rose up to meet it. But when the wind blew
to the shore, the fish came in from the deep, and swam into
the meshes of his nets, and he took them to the market-place
and sold them.

Every evening he went out upon the sea, and one evening the net was
so heavy that hardly could he draw it into the boat. And he laughed, and
said to himself, "Surely I have caught all the fish that swim, or snared some
dull monster that will be a marvel to men, or some thing of horror that the
great Queen will desire," and putting forth all his strength, he tugged at the
coarse ropes till, like lines of blue enamel round a vase of bronze, the long
veins rose up on his arms. He tugged at the thin ropes, and nearer and nearer
came the circle of flat corks, and the net rose at last to the top of the water.

But no fish at all was in it, nor any monster or thing of horror, but only
a little Mermaid lying fast asleep.

Her hair was as a wet fleece of gold, and each separate hair as a thread
of fine gold in a cup of glass. Her body was as white ivory, and her tail was
of silver and pearl. Silver and pearl was her tail, and the green weeds of the

,sea coiled round it; and like sea-shells were her ears, and her lips were like sea-coral. The cold waves dashed over her cold breasts, and the salt glistened upon her eyelids.

So beautiful was she that when the young Fisherman saw her he was filled with wonder, and he put out his hand and drew the net close to him, and leaning over the side he clasped her in his arms. And when he touched her, she gave a cry like a startled sea-gull, and woke, and looked at him in terror with her mauve-amethyst eyes, and struggled that she might escape. But he held her tightly to him, and would not suffer her to depart.

And when she saw that she could in no way escape from him, she began to weep, and said, "I pray thee let me go, for I am the only daughter of a King, and my father is aged and alone."

But the young Fisherman answered, "I will not let thee go save thou makest me a promise that whenever I call thee, thou wilt come and sing to me, for the fish delight to listen to the song of the Sea-folk, and so shall my nets be full."

"Wilt thou in very truth let me go, if I promise thee this?" cried the Mermaid.

"In very truth I will let thee go," said the young Fisherman.

So she made him the promise he desired, and sware it by the oath of the Sea-folk. And he loosened his arms from about her, and she sank down into the water, trembling with a strange fear.

Every evening the young Fisherman went out upon the sea, and called to the Mermaid, and she rose out of the water and sang to him. Round and round her swam the dolphins, and the wild gulls wheeled above her head.

And she sang a marvellous song. For she sang of the Sea-folk who drive their flocks from cave to cave, and carry the little calves on their shoulders; of the Tritons who have long green beards, and hairy breasts, and blow through twisted conchs when the King passes by; of the palace of the King, which is all of amber, with a roof of clear emerald and a pavement of bright pearl; and of the gardens of the sea where the great filigrane fans of coral wave all day long, and the fish dart about like silver birds, and the anemones cling to the rocks, and the pinks bourgeon in the ribbed yellow sand. She sang of the big whales that come down from the north seas and have sharp icicles hanging to their fins; of the Sirens who tell of such wonderful things that the merchants have to stop their ears with wax lest they should hear them, and leap into the water and be drowned; of the sunken galleys with their tall masts, and the frozen sailors clinging to the rigging, and the mackerel swimming in and out of the open portholes; of the little barnacles who are great travellers, and cling to the keels of the ships and go round and round the world; and of the cuttlefish who live in the sides of the cliffs and stretch out their long black arms, and can make night come when they will it. She sang of the nautilus who has a boat of her own that is carved out of an opal and steered with a silken sail; of the happy Mermen who play upon harps and can charm the great Kraken to sleep; of the little children who catch hold of the slippery porpoises and ride laughing upon their backs; of the Mermaids who lie in the white foam and hold out their arms to the mariners; and of the sea-lions with their curved tusks, and the sea horses with their floating manes.

And as she sang, all the tunny-fish came in from the deep to listen to her, and the young Fisherman threw his nets round them and caught them, and others he took with a spear. And when his boat was well-laden, the Mermaid would sink down into the sea, smiling at him.

Yet would she never come near him that he might touch her. Oftentimes he called to her and prayed of her, but she would not; and when he sought to seize her she dived into the water as a seal might dive, nor did he see her again that day. And each day the sound of her voice became sweeter to his ears. So sweet was her voice that he forgot his nets and his cunning, and had no care of his craft. Vermilion-finned and with eyes of bossy gold, the tunnies went by in shoals, but he heeded them not. His spear lay by his side unused, and his baskets of plaited osier were empty. With lips parted, and eyes dim with wonder, he sat idle in his boat and listened, listening till the sea-mists crept round him, and the wandering moon stained his brown limbs with silver.

And one evening he called to her, and said: "Little Mermaid, little Mermaid, I love thee. Take me for thy bridegroom for I love thee."

But the Mermaid shook her head. "Thou hast a human soul," she answered. "If only thou wouldst send away thy soul, then could I love thee."

And the young Fisherman said to himself, "Of what use is my soul to me? I cannot see it. I may not touch it. I do not know it. Surely I will send it away from me, and much gladness shall be mine." And a cry of joy broke from his lips, and standing up in the painted boat, he held out his arms to the Mermaid. "I will send my soul away," he cried, "and you shall be my bride, and I will be thy bridegroom, and in the depth of the sea we will dwell together, and all that thou hast sung of thou shalt show me, and all that thou desirest I will do, nor shall our lives be divided."

And the little Mermaid laughed for pleasure and hid her face in her hands.

"But how shall I send my soul from me?" cried the young Fisherman. "Tell me how I may do it, and lo! it shall be done."

"Alas! I know not," said the little Mermaid: "the Sea-folk have no souls." And she sank down into the deep, looking wistfully at him.

Now early on the next morning, before the sun was the span of a man's hand above the hill, the young Fisherman went to the house of the Priest and knocked three times at the door.

The novice looked out through the wicket, and when he saw who it was, he drew back the latch and said to him, "Enter."

And the young Fisherman passed in, and knelt down on the sweet-smelling rushes of the floor, and cried to the Priest who was reading out of the Holy Book and said to him, "Father, I am in love with one of the Sea-folk, and my soul hindereth me from having my desire. Tell me how I can send my soul away from me, for in truth I have no need of it. Of what value is my soul to me? I cannot see it. I may not touch it. I do not know it."

And the Priest beat his breast, and answered, "Alack, alack, thou art mad, or hast eaten of some poisonous herb, for the soul is the noblest part of man, and was given to us by God that we should nobly use it. There is no thing more precious than a human soul, nor any earthly thing that can be weighed with it. It is worth all the gold that is in the world, and is more precious than the rubies of the kings. Therefore, my son, think not any more of this matter, for it is a sin that may not be forgiven. And as for the Sea-folk, they are lost, and they who would traffic with them are lost also. They are the beasts of the field that know not good from evil, and for them the Lord has not died."

The young Fisherman's eyes filled with tears when he heard the bitter words of the Priest, and he rose up from his knees and said to him, "Father, the Fauns live in the forest and are glad, and on the rocks sit the Mermen with their harps of red gold. Let me be as they are, I beseech thee, for their days are as the days of flowers. And as for my soul, what doth my soul profit me, if it stand between me and the thing that I love?"

"The love of the body is vile," cried the Priest, knitting his brows, "and vile and evil are the pagan things God suffers to wander through His world. Accursed be the Fauns of the woodland, and accursed be the singers of the sea! I have heard them at night-time, and they have sought to lure me from my beads. They tap at the window and laugh. They whisper into my ears the tale of their perilous joys. They tempt me with temptations, and when I would pray they make mouths at me. They are lost, I tell thee, they are lost. For them there is no heaven nor hell, and in neither shall they praise God's name."

"Father," cried the young Fisherman, "thou knowest not what thou sayest. Once in my net I snared the daughter of a King. She is fairer than the morning star, and whiter than the moon. For her body I would give my soul, and for her love I would surrender heaven. Tell me what I ask of thee, and let me go in peace."

"Away! Away!" cried the Priest: "thy leman is lost, and thou shalt be lost with her." And he gave him no blessing, but drove him from his door.

And the young Fisherman went down into the market-place, and he walked slowly, and with bowed head, as one who is in sorrow.

And when the merchants saw him coming, they began to whisper to each other, and one of them came forth to meet him, and called him by name, and said to him, "What hast thou to sell?"

"I will sell thee my soul," he answered: "I pray thee buy it of me, for I am weary of it. Of what use is my soul to me? I cannot see it. I may not touch it. I do not know it."

But the merchants mocked at him, and said, "Of what use is a man's soul to us? It is not worth a clipped piece of silver. Sell us thy body for a slave, and we will clothe thee in sea-purple, and put a ring upon thy finger, and make thee the minion of the great Queen. But talk not of the soul, for to us it is nought, nor has it any value for our service."

And the young Fisherman said to himself: "How strange a thing this is! The Priest telleth me that the soul is worth all the gold in the world, and the merchants say that it is not worth a clipped piece of silver." And he passed out of the market-place, and went down to the shore of the sea, and began to ponder on what he should do.

And at noon he remembered how one of his companions, who was a gatherer of samphire, had told him of a certain young Witch who dwelt in a cave at the head of the bay and was very cunning in her witcheries. And he set to and ran, so eager was he to get rid of his soul, and a cloud of dust followed him as he sped round the sand of the shore. By the itching of her palm the young Witch knew his coming, and she laughed and let down her red hair. With her red hair falling around her, she stood at the opening of the cave, and in her hand she had a spray of wild hemlock that was blossoming.

"What d'ye lack? What d'ye lack?" she cried, as he came panting up the steep, and bent down before her. "Fish for thy net, when the wind is foul? I have a little reed-pipe, and when I blow on it the mullet come sailing into the bay. But it has a price, pretty boy, it has a price. What d'ye lack? What d'ye lack? A storm to wreck the ships, and wash the chests of rich treasure ashore? I have more storms than the wind has, for I serve one who is stronger than the wind, and with a sieve and a pail of water I can send the great galleys to the bottom of the sea. But I have a price, pretty boy, I have a price. What d'ye lack? What d'ye lack? I know a flower that grows in the valley, none knows it but I. It has purple leaves, and a star in its heart, and its juice is as white as milk. Shouldst thou touch with this flower the hard lips of the Queen, she would follow thee all over the world. Out of the bed of the King she would rise, and over the whole world she would follow thee. And it has a price, pretty boy, it has a price. What d'ye lack? What d'ye lack? I can pound a toad in a mortar, and make broth of it, and stir the broth with a dead man's hand. Sprinkle it on thine enemy while he sleeps, and he will turn into a back viper, and his own mother will slay him. With a wheel I can draw the Moon from heaven, and in a crystal I can show thee Death. What d'ye lack? What d'ye lack? Tell me thy desire, and I will give it thee, and thou shalt pay me a price, pretty boy, thou shalt pay me a price."

"My desire is but for a little thing," said the young Fisherman, "yet hath the Priest been wroth with me, and driven me forth. It is but for a little thing, and the merchants have mocked at me, and denied me. Therefore am I come to thee, though men call thee evil, and whatever be thy price I shall pay it."

"What wouldst thou?" asked the Witch, coming near to him.

"I would send my soul away from me," answered the young Fisherman.

The Witch grew pale, and shuddered, and hid her face in her blue mantle. "Pretty boy, pretty boy," she muttered, "that is a terrible thing to do."

He tossed his brown curls and laughed. "My soul is nought to me," he answered. "I cannot see it. I may not touch it. I do not know it."

"What wilt thou give me if I tell thee?" asked the Witch, looking down at him with her beautiful eyes.

"Five pieces of gold," he said, "and my nets, and the wattled house where I live, and the painted boat in which I sail. Only tell me how to get rid of my soul, and I will give thee all that I possess."

She laughed mockingly at him, and struck him with the spray of hemlock. "I can turn the autumn leaves into gold," she answered, "and I can weave the pale moonbeams into silver if I will it. He whom I serve is richer than all the kings of this world, and has their dominions."

"What then shall I give thee," he cried, "if thy price be neither gold nor silver?"

The Witch stroked his hair with her thin white hand. "Thou must dance with me, pretty boy," she murmured, and she smiled at him as she spoke.

".Nought but that?" cried the young Fisherman in wonder, and he rose to his feet.

"Nought but that," she answered, and she smiled at him again.

"Then at sunset in some secret place we shall dance together," he said, "and after that we have danced thou shalt tell me the thing which I desire to know."

She shook her head. "When the moon is full, when the moon is full," she muttered. Then she peered all round, and listened. A blue bird rose screaming from its nest and circled over the dunes, and three spotted birds rustled through the coarse grey grass and whistled to each other. There was no other sound save the sound of a wave fretting the smooth pebbles below. So she reached out her hand, and drew him near to her and put her dry lips close to his ear.

"To-night thou must come to the top of the mountain," she whispered. "It is a Sabbath, and He will be there."

The young Fisherman started and looked at her, and she showed her white teeth and laughed. "Who is He of whom thou speakest?" he asked.

"It matters not," she answered. "Go thou to-night, and stand under the branches of the hornbeam, and wait for my coming. If a black dog run towards thee, strike it with a rod of willow, and it will go away. If an owl speak to thee, make it no answer. When the moon is full I shall be with thee, and we will dance together on the grass."

"But wilt thou swear to me to tell me how I may send my soul from me?" he made question.

She moved out into the sunlight, and through her red hair rippled the wind. "By the hoofs of the goat I swear it," she made answer.

"Thou art the best of the witches," cried the young Fisherman, "and I will surely dance with thee to-night on the top of the mountain. I would indeed that thou hadst asked of me either gold or silver. But such as thy price is thou shalt have it, for it is but a little thing." And he doffed his cap to her, and bent his head low, and ran back to the town filled with a great joy.

And the Witch watched him as he went, and when he had passed from her sight she entered her cave, and having taken a mirror from a box of carved cedarwood, she set it up on a frame, and burned vervain on lighted charcoal before it, and peered through the coils of the smoke. And after a time she clenched her hands in anger. "He should have been mine," she muttered; "I am as fair as she is."

And that evening, when the moon had risen, the young Fisherman climbed up to the top of the mountain, and stood under the branches of the hornbeam. Like a targe of polished metal the round sea lay at his feet, and the shadows of the fishing-boats moved in the little bay. A great owl, with yellow sulphurous eyes, called to him by his name, but he made it no answer. A black dog ran towards him and snarled. He struck it with a rod of willow, and it went away whining.

At midnight the witches came flying through the air like bats. "Phew!" they cried, as they lit upon the ground, "there is some one here we know not!" and they sniffed about, and chattered to each other, and made signs. Last of all came the young Witch, with her red hair streaming in the wind. She wore a dress of gold tissue embroidered with peacocks' eyes, and a little cap of green velvet was on her head.

"Where is he, where is he?" shrieked the witches when they saw her, but she only laughed, and ran to the hornbeam, and taking the Fisherman by the hand, she led him out into the moonlight and began to dance.

Round and round they whirled, and the young Witch jumped so high that he could see the scarlet heels of her shoes. Then right across the dancers came the sound of the galloping of a horse, but no horse was to be seen, and he felt afraid.

"Faster," cried the Witch, and she threw her arms about his neck, and her breath was hot upon his face. "Faster, faster!" she cried, and the earth seemed to spin beneath his feet, and his brain grew troubled, and a great terror fell on him, as of some evil thing that was watching him, and at last he became aware that under the shadow of a rock there was a figure that had not been there before.

It was a man dressed in a suit of black velvet, cut in the Spanish fashion. His face was strangely pale, but his lips were like a proud red flower. He seemed weary, and was leaning back toying in a listless manner with the pommel of his dagger. On the grass beside him lay a plumed hat, and a pair of riding-gloves gauntleted with gilt lace, and sewn with seed-pearls wrought into a curious device. A short cloak lined with sables hung from his shoulder, and his delicate white hands were gemmed with rings. Heavy eyelids drooped over his eyes.

The young Fisherman watched him, as one snared in a spell. At last their eyes met, and wherever he danced it seemed to him that the eyes of the man were upon him. He heard the Witch laugh, and caught her by the waist, and whirled her madly round and round.

Suddenly a dog bayed in the wood, and the dancers stopped, and going up two by two, knelt down, and kissed the man's hands. As they did so, a little smile touched his proud lips, as a bird's wing touches the water and makes it laugh. But there was disdain in it. He kept looking at the young Fisherman.

"Come! let us worship," whispered the Witch, and she led him up, and a great desire to do as she besought him seized on him, and he followed her.

But when he came close, and without knowing why he did it, he made on his breast the sign of the Cross, and called upon the holy name.

No sooner had he done so than the witches screamed like hawks and flew away, and the pallid face that had been watching him twitched with a spasm of pain. The man went over to a little wood, and whistled. A jennet with silver trappings came running to meet him. As he leapt upon the saddle he turned round, and looked at the young Fisherman sadly.

And the Witch with the red hair tried to fly away also, but the Fisherman caught her by her wrists, and held her fast.

"Loose me," she cried, "and let me go. For thou hast named what should not be named, and shown the sign that may not be looked at."

"Nay," he answered, "but I will not let thee go till thou hast told me the secret."

"What secret?" said the Witch, wrestling with him like a wild cat, and biting her foam-flecked lips.

"Thou knowest," he made answer.

Her grass-green eyes grew dim with tears, and she said to the Fisherman, "Ask me anything but that!"

He laughed, and held her all the more tightly.

And when she saw that she could not free herself, she whispered to him, "Surely I am as fair as the daughter of the sea, and as comely as those that dwell in the blue waters," and she fawned on him and put her face close to his.

But he thrust her back frowning, and said to her, "If thou keepest not the promise that thou madest to me I will slay thee for a false witch."

She grew grey as a blossom of the Judas tree, and shuddered. "Be it so," she muttered. "It is thy soul and not mine. Do with it as thou wilt." And she took from her girdle a little knife that had a handle of green viper's skin, and gave it to him.

"What shall this serve me?" he asked of her, wondering.

She was silent for a few moments, and a look of terror came over her face. Then she brushed her hair back from her forehead, and smiling strangely she said to him, "What men call the shadow of the body is not the shadow of the body, but is the body of the soul. Stand on the sea-shore with thy back to the moon, and cut away from around thy feet thy shadow, which is thy soul's body, and bid thy soul leave thee, and it will do so."

The young Fisherman trembled. "Is this true?" he murmured.

"It is true, and I would that I had not told thee of it," she cried, and she clung to his knees weeping.

He put her from him and left her in the rank grass, and going to the edge of the mountain he placed the knife in his belt and began to climb down.

And his Soul that was within him called out to him and said, "Lo! I have dwelt with thee for all these years, and have been thy servant. Send me not away from thee now, for what evil have I done thee?"

And the young Fisherman laughed. "Thou hast done me no evil, but I have no need of thee," he answered. "The world is wide, and there is Heaven also, and Hell, and that dim twilight house that lies between. Go wherever thou wilt, but trouble me not, for my love is calling to me."

And his Soul besought him piteously, but he heeded it not, but leapt from crag to crag, being sure-footed as a wild goat, and at last he reached the level ground and the yellow shore of the sea.

Bronze-limbed and well-knit, like a statue wrought by a Grecian, he stood on the sand with his back to the moon, and out of the foam came white arms that beckoned to him, and out of the waves rose dim forms that did him homage. Before him lay his shadow which was the body of his soul, and behind him hung the moon in the honey-coloured air.

And his Soul said to him, "If indeed thou must drive me from thee, send me not forth without a heart. The world is cruel; give me thy heart to take with me."

He tossed his head and smiled. "With what should I love my love if I gave thee my heart?" he cried.

"Nay, but be merciful," said his Soul: "give me thy heart, for the world is very cruel, and I am afraid."

"My heart is my love's," he answered, "therefore tarry not, but get thee gone."

"Should I not love also?" asked his Soul.

"Get thee gone, for I have no need of thee," cried the young Fisherman, and he took the little knife with its handle of green viper's skin, and cut away his shadow from around his feet, and it rose up and stood before him, and looked at him, and it was even as himself.

He crept back, and thrust the knife into his belt, and a feeling of awe came over him. "Get thee gone," he murmured, "and let me see thy face no more."

"Nay, but we must meet again," said the Soul. Its voice was low and flute-like, and its lips hardly moved while it spake.

"How shall we meet?" cried the young Fisherman. "Thou wilt not follow me into the depths of the sea?"

"Once every year I will come to this place, and call to thee," said the Soul. "It may be that thou wilt have need of me."

"What need should I have of thee?" cried the young Fisherman, "but be it as thou wilt," and he plunged into the water, and the Tritons blew their horns, and the little Mermaid rose up to meet him, and put her arms around his neck and kissed him on the mouth.

And the Soul stood on the lonely beach and watched them. And when they had sunk down into the sea, it went weeping away over the marshes.

And after a year was over the Soul came down to the shore of the sea and called to the young Fisherman, and he rose out of the deep, and said, "Why dost thou call to me?"

And the Soul answered, "Come nearer, that I may speak with thee, for I have seen marvellous things."

So he came nearer, and couched in the shallow water, and leaned his head upon his hand and listened.

And the Soul said to him, "When I left thee I turned my face to the East and journeyed. From the East cometh everything that is wise. Six days I journeyed, and on the morning of the seventh day I came to a hill that is in the country of the Tartars. I sat down under the shade of a tamarisk tree to shelter myself from the sun. The land was dry and burnt up with the heat. The people went to and fro over the plain like flies crawling upon a disk of polished copper.

"When it was noon a cloud of red dust rose up from the flat rim of the land. When the Tartars saw it, they strung their painted bows, and having leapt upon their little horses they galloped to meet it. The women fled screaming to the waggons, and hid themselves behind the felt curtains.

"At twilight the Tartars returned, but five of them were missing, and of those that came back not a few had been wounded. They harnessed their horses to the waggons and drove hastily away. Three jackals came out of a cave and peered after them. Then they sniffed up the air with their nostrils, and trotted off in the opposite direction.

"When the moon rose I saw a camp-fire burning on the plain, and went towards it. A company of merchants were seated round it on carpets. Their camels were picketed behind them, and the negroes who were their servants were pitching tents of tanned skin upon the sand, and making a high wall of the prickly pear.

"As I came near them, the chief of the merchants rose up and drew his sword and asked me my business.

"I answered that I was a Prince in my own land, and that I had escaped from the Tartars, who had sought to make me their slave. The chief smiled, and showed me five heads fixed upon long reeds of bamboo.

"Then he asked me who was the prophet of God, and I answered him Mohammed.

"When he heard the name of the false prophet, he bowed and took me by the hand, and placed me by his side. A negro brought me some mare's milk in a wooden dish, and a piece of lamb's flesh roasted.

"At daybreak we started on our journey. I rode on a red-haired camel by the side of the chief, and a runner ran before us carrying a spear. The men of war were on either hand, and the mules followed with the merchandise. There were forty camels in the caravan, and the mules were twice forty in number.

"We went from the country of the Tartars into the country of those who curse the Moon. We saw the Gryphons guarding their gold on the white rocks, and the scaled Dragons sleeping in their caves. As we passed over the mountains we held our breath lest the snows might fall on us, and each man tied a veil of gauze before his eyes. As we passed through the valleys the Pygmies shot arrows at us from the hollows of the trees, and at night-time we heard the wild men beating on their drums. When we came to the Tower of Apes we set fruits before them, and they did not harm us. When we came to the Tower of Serpents we gave them warm milk in bowls of brass, and they let us go by. Three times in our journey we came to the banks of the Oxus. We crossed it on rafts of wood with great bladders of blown hide. The river-horses raged against us and sought to slay us. When the camels saw them they trembled.

"The kings of each city levied tolls on us, but would not suffer us to enter their gates. They threw us bread over the walls, little maizecakes baked in honey and cakes of fine flour filled with dates. For every hundred baskets we gave them a bead of amber.

"When the dwellers in the villages saw us coming, they poisoned the wells and fled to the hill-summits. We fought with the Magadae who are born old, and grow younger and younger every year, and die when they are little children; and with the Laktroi who say that they are the sons of tigers, and paint themselves yellow and black; and with the Aurantes who bury their dead on the tops of trees, and themselves live in dark caverns lest the Sun, who is their god, should slay them; and with the Krimnians who worship a crocodile, and give it earrings of green grass, and feed it with butter and fresh fowls; and with the Agazonbae, who are dog-faced; and with the Sibans, who have horses' feet, and run more swiftly than horses. A third of our company died in battle, and a third died of want. The rest murmured against me, and said that I had brought them an evil fortune. I took a horned adder from beneath a stone and let it sting me. When they saw that I did not sicken they grew afraid.

"In the fourth month we reached the city of Illel. It was night-time when we came to the grove that is outside the walls, and the air was sultry, for the Moon was travelling in Scorpion. We took the ripe pomegranates from the trees, and brake them, and drank their sweet juices. Then we lay down on our carpets and waited for the dawn.

"And at dawn we rose and knocked at the gate of the city. It was wrought out of red bronze, and carved with sea-dragons and dragons that have wings.

The guards looked down from the battlements and asked us our business. The interpreter of the caravan answered that we had come from the island of Syria with much merchandise. They took hostages, and told us that they would open the gate to us at noon, and bade us tarry till then.

"When it was noon they opened the gate, and as we entered in the people came crowding out of the houses to look at us, and a crier went round the city crying through a shell. We stood in the market-place, and the negroes uncorded the bales of figured cloths and opened the carved chests of sycamore. And when they had ended their task, the merchants set forth their strange wares, the waxed linen from Egypt, and the painted linen from the country of the Ethiops, the purple sponges from Tyre and the blue hangings from Sidon, the cups of cold amber and the fine vessels of glass and the curious vessels of burnt clay. From the roof of a house a company of women watched us. One of them wore a mask of gilded leather.

"And on the first day the priests came and bartered with us, and on the second day came the nobles, and on the third day came the craftsmen and the slaves. And this is their custom with all merchants as long as they tarry in the city.

"And we tarried for a moon, and when the moon was waning, I wearied and wandered away through the streets of the city and came to the garden of its god. The priests in their yellow robes moved silently through the green trees, and on a pavement of black marble stood the rose-red house in which the god had his dwelling. Its doors were of powdered lacquer, and bulls and peacocks were wrought on them in raised and polished gold. The tilted roof was of sea-green porcelain, and the jutting eaves were festooned with little bells. When the white doves flew past, they struck the bells with their wings and made them tinkle.

"In front of the temple was a pool of clear water paved with veined onyx. I lay down beside it, and with my pale fingers I touched the broad leaves. One of the priests came towards me and stood behind me. He had sandals on his feet, one of soft serpent-skin and the other of birds' plumage. On his head was a mitre of black felt decorated with silver crescents. Seven yellows were woven into his robe, and his frizzed hair was stained with antimony.

"After a little while he spake to me, and asked me my desire.

"I told him that my desire was to see the god.

" 'The god is hunting,' said the priest, looking strangely at me with his small slanting eyes.

" 'Tell me in what forest, and I will ride with him,' I answered.

"He combed out the soft fringes of his tunic with his long pointed nails. 'The god is asleep,' he murmured.

" 'Tell me on what couch, and I will watch by him,' I answered.

" 'The god is at the feast,' he cried.

" 'If the wine be sweet I will drink it with him, and if it be bitter I will drink it with him also,' was my answer.

"He bowed his head in wonder, and, taking me by the hand, he raised me up, and led me into the temple.

"And in the first chamber I saw an idol seated on a throne of jasper bordered with great orient pearls. It was carved out of ebony, and in stature was of the stature of a man. On its forehead was a ruby, and thick oil dripped from its hair on to its thighs. Its feet were red with the blood of a newly-slain kid, and its loins girt with a copper belt that was studded with seven beryls.

"And I said to the priest, 'Is this the god?' And he answered me, 'This is the god.'

" 'Show me the god,' I cried, 'or I will surely slay thee.' And I touched his hand, and it became withered.

"And the priest besought me, saying, 'Let my lord heal his servant, and I will show him the god.'

"So I breathed with my breath upon his hand, and it became whole again, and he trembled and led me into the second chamber, and I saw an idol standing on a lotus of jade hung with great emeralds. It was carved out of ivory, and in stature was twice the stature of a man. On its forehead was a chrysolite, and its breasts were smeared with myrrh and cinnamon. In one hand it held a crooked sceptre of jade, and in the other a round crystal. It ware buskins of brass, and its thick neck was circled with a circle of selenites.

"And I said to the priest, 'Is this the god?' And he answered me, 'This is the god.'

" 'Show me the god,' I cried, 'or I will surely slay thee.' And I touched his eyes, and they became blind.

"And the priest besought me, saying, 'Let my lord heal his servant, and I will show him the god.'

"So I breathed with my breath upon his eyes, and the sight came back to them, and he trembled again, and led me into the third chamber, and lo! there was no idol in it, nor image of any kind, but only a mirror of round metal set on an altar of stone.

"And I said to the priest, 'Where is the god?'

"And he answered me: 'There is no god but this mirror that thou seest, for this is the Mirror of Wisdom. And it reflecteth all things that are in heaven and on earth, save only the face of him who looketh into it. This it reflecteth not, so that he who looketh into it may be wise. Many other mirrors are there, but they are mirrors of Opinion. This only is the Mirror of Wisdom. And they who possess this mirror know everything, nor is there anything hidden from them. And they who possess it not have not Wisdom. Therefore is it the god, and we worship it.' And I looked into the mirror, and it was even as he had said to me.

"And I did a strange thing, but what I did matters not, for in a valley that is but a day's journey from this place have I hidden the Mirror of Wisdom. Do but suffer me to enter into thee again and be thy servant, and thou shalt be wiser than all the wise men, and Wisdom shall be thine. Suffer me to enter into thee, and none will be as wise as thou."

But the young Fisherman laughed. "Love is better than Wisdom," he cried, "and the little Mermaid loves me."

"Nay, but there is nothing better than Wisdom," said the Soul.

"Love is better," answered the young Fisherman, and he plunged into the deep, and the Soul went weeping away over the marshes.

And after the second year was over, the Soul came down to the shore of the sea, and called to the young Fisherman and he rose out of the deep and said, "Why dost thou call to me?"

And the Soul answered, "Come nearer, that I may speak with thee, for I have seen marvellous things."

So he came nearer, and couched in the shallow water, and leaned his head upon his hand and listened.

And the Soul said to him, "When I left thee, I turned my face to the South and journeyed. From the South cometh everything that is precious. Six days I journeyed along the highways that lead to the city of Ashter, along the dusty red-dyed highways by which the pilgrims are wont to go did I journey, and on the morning of the seventh day I lifted up my eyes, and lo! the city lay at my feet, for it is in a valley.

"There are nine gates to this city, and in front of each gate stands a bronze horse that neighs when the Bedouins come down from the mountains. The walls are cased with copper, and the watch-towers on the wall are roofed with brass. In every tower stands an archer with a bow in his hand. At sunrise he strikes with an arrow on a gong, and at sunset he blows through a horn of horn.

"When I sought to enter, the guards stopped me and asked of me who I was. I made answer that I was a Dervish and on my way to the city of Mecca, where there was a green veil on which the Koran was embroidered in silver letters by the hands of the angels. They were filled with wonder, and entreated me to pass in.

"Inside it is even as a bazaar. Surely thou shouldst have been with me. Across the narrow streets the gay lanterns of paper flutter like large butterflies. When the wind blows over the roofs they rise and fall as painted bubbles do. In front of their booths sit the merchants on silken carpets. They have straight black beards, and their turbans are covered with golden sequins, and long strings of amber and carved peach-stones glide through their cool fingers. Some of them sell galbanum and nard, and curious perfumes from the islands of the Indian Sea, and the thick oil of red roses, and myrrh and little nail-shaped cloves. When one stops to speak to them, they throw pinches of frankincense upon a charcoal brazier and make the air sweet. I saw a Syrian who held in his hands a thin rod like a reed. Grey threads of smoke came from it, and its odour as it burned was as the odour of the pink almond in spring. Others sell silver bracelets embossed all over with creamy blue turquoise stones, and anklets of brass wire fringed with little pearls, and tigers' claws set in gold, and the claws of that gilt cat, the leopard, set in gold also, and earrings of pierced emerald, and finger-rings of hollowed jade. From the tea-houses comes the sound of the guitar, and the opium-smokers with their white smiling faces look out at the passers-by.

"Of a truth thou shouldst have been with me. The wine-sellers elbow their way through the crowd with great black skins on their shoulders. Most of them sell the wine of Schiraz, which is as sweet as honey. They serve it in little metal cups and strew rose leaves upon it. In the market-place stand the fruitsellers, who sell all kinds of fruit: ripe figs, with their bruised purple flesh, melons, smelling of musk and yellow as topazes, citrons and rose-apples and clusters of white grapes, round red-gold oranges, and oval lemons of green gold. Once I saw an elephant go by. Its trunk was painted with vermilion and turmeric, and over its ears it had a net of crimson silk cord. It stopped opposite one of the booths and began eating the oranges, and the man only laughed. Thou canst not think how strange a people they are. When they are glad they go to the bird-sellers and buy of them a caged bird, and set it free that their joy may be greater, and when they are sad they scourge themselves with thorns that their sorrow may not grow less.

"One evening I met some negroes carrying a heavy palanquin through the bazaar. It was made of gilded bamboo, and the poles were of vermilion lacquer studded with brass peacocks. Across the windows hung thin curtains of muslin embroidered with beetles' wings and with tiny seed-pearls, and as it passed by a pale-faced Circassian looked out and smiled at me. I followed behind, and the negroes hurried their steps and scowled. But I did not care. I felt a great curiosity come over me.

"At last they stopped at a square white house. There were no windows to it, only a little door like the door of a tomb. They set down the palanquin and knocked three times with a copper hammer. An Armenian in a caftan of green leather peered through the wicket, and when he saw them he opened, and spread a carpet on the ground, and the woman stepped out. As she went in, she turned round and smiled at me again. I had never seen any one so pale.

"When the moon rose I returned to the same place and sought for the house, but it was no longer there. When I saw that, I knew who the woman was, and wherefore she had smiled at me.

"Certainly thou shouldst have been with me. On the feast of the New Moon the young Emperor came forth from his palace and went into the mosque to pray. His hair and beard were dyed with rose-leaves, and his cheeks were powdered with a fine gold dust. The palms of his feet and hands were yellow with saffron.

"At sunrise he went forth from his palace in a robe of silver, and at sunset he returned to it again in a robe of gold. The people flung themselves on the ground and hid their faces, but I would not do so. I stood by the stall of a seller of dates and waited. When the Emperor saw me, he raised his painted eyebrows and stopped. I stood quite still, and made him no obeisance. The people marvelled at my boldness, and counselled me to flee from the city. I paid no heed to them, but went and sat with the sellers of strange gods, who by reason of their craft are abominated. When I told them what I had done, each of them gave me a god and prayed me to leave them.

"That night, as I lay on a cushion in the tea-house that is in the Street of Pomegranates, the guards of the Emperor entered and led me to the palace. As I went in they closed each door behind me, and put a chain across it. Inside was a great court with an arcade running all round. The walls were of white alabaster, set here and there with blue and green tiles. The pillars were of green marble, and the pavement of a kind of peach-blossom marble. I had never seen anything like it before.

"As I passed across the court two veiled women looked down from a balcony and cursed me. The guards hastened on, and the butts of the lances rang upon the polished floor. They opened a gate of wrought ivory, and I found myself in a watered garden of seven terraces. It was planted with tulip-cups and moon-flowers, and silver-studded aloes. Like a slim reed of crystal a fountain hung in the dusky air. The cypress-trees were like burnt-out torches. From one of them a nightingale was singing.

"At the end of the garden stood a little pavilion. As we approached it two eunuchs came out to meet us. Their fat bodies swayed as they walked, and they glanced curiously at me with their yellow-lidded eyes. One of them drew aside the captain of the guard, and in a low voice whispered to him. The other kept munching scented pastilles, which he took with an affected gesture out of an oval box of lilac enamel.

"After a few moments the captain of the guard dismissed the soldiers. They went back to the palace, the eunuchs following slowly behind and plucking the sweet mulberries from the trees as they passed. Once the elder of the two turned round, and smiled at me with an evil smile.

"Then the captain of the guard motioned me towards the entrance of the pavilion. I walked on without trembling, and drawing the heavy curtain aside, I entered in.

"The young Emperor was stretched on a couch of dyed lion skins, and a ger-falcon perched upon his wrist. Behind him stood a brass-turbaned Nubian, naked down to the waist, and with heavy earrings in his split ears. On a table by the side of the couch lay a mighty scimitar of steel.

"When the Emperor saw me he frowned, and said to me, 'What is thy name? Knowest thou not that I am Emperor of this city?' But I made him no answer.

"He pointed with his finger at the scimitar, and the Nubian seized it, and rushing forward struck at me with great violence. The blade whizzed through me, and did me no hurt. The man fell sprawling on the floor, and when he rose up his teeth chattered with terror and he hid himself behind the couch.

"The Emperor leapt to his feet, and taking a lance from a stand of arms, he threw it at me. I caught it in its flight, and brake the shaft into two pieces. He shot at me with an arrow, but I held up my hands and it stopped in midair. Then he drew a dagger from a belt of white leather, and stabbed the Nubian in the throat lest the slave should tell of his dishonour. The man writhed like a trampled snake, and a red foam bubbled from his lips.

"As soon as he was dead the Emperor turned to me, and when he had wiped away the bright sweat from his brow with a little napkin of purfled and purple silk, he said to me, 'Art thou a prophet, that I may not harm thee, or the son of a prophet, that I can do thee no hurt? I pray thee leave my city to-night, for while thou art in it I am no longer its lord.'

"And I answered him, 'I will go for half of thy treasure. Give me half of thy treasure, and I will go away.'

"He took me by the hand, and led me out into the garden. When the captain of the guard saw me, he wondered. When the eunuchs saw me, their knees shook and they fell upon the ground in fear.

"There is a chamber in the palace that has eight walls of red porphyry, and a brass-scaled ceiling hung with lamps. The Emperor touched one of the walls and it opened, and we passed down a corridor that was lit with many torches. In niches upon each side stood great wine-jars filled to the brim with silver pieces. When we reached the centre of the corridor the Emperor spake the word that may not be spoken, and a granite door swung back on a secret spring, and he put his hands before his face lest his eyes should be dazzled.

"Thou couldst not believe how marvellous a place it was. There were huge tortoise-shells full of pearls, and hollowed moonstones of great size piled up with red rubies. The gold was stored in coffers of elephant-hide, and the gold-dust in leather bottles. There were opals and sapphires, the former in cups of crystal, and the latter in cups of jade. Round green emeralds were ranged in order upon thin plates of ivory, and in one corner were silk bags filled, some with turquoise-stones, and others with beryls. The ivory horns were heaped with purple amethysts, and the horns of brass with chalcedonies and sards. The pillars, which were of cedar, were hung with strings of yellow lynx-stones. In the flat oval shields there were carbuncles, both wine-coloured and coloured like grass. And yet I have told thee but a tithe of what was there.'

"And when the Emperor had taken away his hands from before his face he said to me: 'This is my house of treasure, and half that is in it is thine, even as I promised to thee. And I will give thee camels and camel drivers, and they shall do thy bidding and take thy share of the treasure to whatever part of the world thou desirest to go. And the thing shall be done to-night, for I would not that the Sun, who is my father, should see that there is in my city a man whom I cannot slay.'

"But I answered him, 'The gold that is here is thine, and the silver also is thine, and thine are the precious jewels and the things of price. As for me, I have no need of these. Nor shall I take aught from thee but that little ring that thou wearest on the finger of thy hand.'

"And the Emperor frowned. 'It is but a ring of lead,' he cried, 'nor has it any value. Therefore take thy half of the treasure and go from my city.'

" 'Nay,' I answered, 'but I will take nought but that leaden ring, for I know what is written within it, and for what purpose.'

"And the Emperor trembled, and besought me and said, 'Take all the treasure and go from my city. The half that is mine shall be thine also.'

"And I did a strange thing, but what I did matters not, for in a cave that is but a day's journey from this place have I hidden the Ring of Riches. It is but a day's journey from this place, and it waits for thy coming. He who has this Ring is richer than all the kings of the world. Come therefore and take it, and the world's riches shall be thine."

But the young Fisherman laughed. "Love is better than Riches," he cried, "and the little Mermaid loves me."

"Nay, but there is nothing better than Riches," said the Soul.

"Love is better," answered the young Fisherman, and he plunged into the deep, and the Soul went weeping away over the marshes.

And after the third year was over, the Soul came down to the shore of the sea, and called to the young Fisherman, and he rose out of the deep and said, "Why dost thou call to me?"

And the Soul answered, "Come nearer, that I may speak with thee, for I have seen marvellous things."

So he came nearer, and couched in the shallow water, and leaned his head upon his hand and listened.

And the Soul said to him "In a city that I know of there is an inn that standeth by a river. I sat there with sailors who drank of two different-coloured wines, and ate bread made of barley, and little salt fish served in bay leaves with vinegar. And as we sat and made merry, there entered to us an old man bearing a leathern carpet and a lute that had two horns of amber. And when he had laid out the carpet on the floor, he struck with a quill on the wire strings of his lute, and a girl whose face was veiled ran in and began to dance before us. Her face was veiled with a veil of gauze, but her feet were naked. Naked were her feet, and they moved over the carpet like little white pigeons. Never have I seen anything so marvellous, and the city in which she dances is but a day's journey from this place."

Now when the young Fisherman heard the words of his Soul, he remembered that the little Mermaid had no feet and could not dance. And a great desire came over him, and he said to himself, "It is but a day's journey, and I can return to my love," and he laughed, and stood up in the shallow water, and strode toward the shore.

And when he had reached the dry shore he laughed again, and held out his arms to his Soul. And his Soul gave a great cry of joy and ran to meet him, and entered into him, and the young Fisherman saw stretched before him upon the sand that shadow of the body that is the body of the Soul.

And his Soul said to him, "Let us not tarry, but get hence at once, for the Sea-gods are jealous, and have monsters that do their bidding."

So they made haste, and all that night they journeyed beneath the moon, and all the next day they journeyed beneath the sun, and on the evening of the day they came to a city.

And the young Fisherman said to his Soul, "Is this the city in which she dances of whom thou didst speak to me?"

And his Soul answered him, "It is not this city, but another. Nevertheless let us enter in."

So they entered in and passed through the streets, and as they passed through the Street of the Jewellers the young Fisherman saw a fair silver cup set forth in a booth. And his Soul said to him, "Take that silver cup and hide it."

So he took the cup and hid it in the fold of his tunic, and they went hurriedly out of the city.

And after that they had gone a league from the city, the young Fisherman frowned, and flung the cup away, and said to his Soul, "Why didst thou tell me to take this cup and hide it, for it was an evil thing to do?"

But his Soul answered him, "Be at peace, be at peace."

And on the evening of the second day they came to a city, and the young Fisherman said to his Soul, "Is this the city in which she dances of whom thou didst speak to me?"

And his Soul answered him, "It is not this city, but another. Nevertheless let us enter in."

So they entered in and passed through the streets, and as they passed through the Street of the Sellers of Sandals, the young Fisherman saw a child standing by a jar of water. And his Soul said to him, "Smite that child." So he smote the child till it wept, and when he had done this they went hurriedly out of the city.

And after that they had gone a league from the city the young Fisherman grew wroth, and said to his Soul, "Why didst thou tell me to smite the child, for it was an evil thing to do?"

But his Soul answered him, "Be at peace, be at peace."

And on the evening of the third day they came to a city, and the young Fisherman said to his Soul, "Is this the city in which she dances of whom thou didst speak to me?"

And his Soul answered him, "It may be that it is in this city, therefore let us enter in."

So they entered in and passed through the streets, but nowhere could the young Fisherman find the river or the inn that stood by its side. And the people of the city looked curiously at him, and he grew afraid and said to his Soul, "Let us go hence, for she who dances with white feet is not here."

But his Soul answered, "Nay, but let us tarry, for the night is dark and there will be robbers on the way."

So he sat him down in the market-place and rested, and after a time there went by a hooded merchant who had a cloak of cloth of Tartary, and bare a lantern of pierced horn at the end of a jointed reed. And the merchant said to him, "Why dost thou sit in the market-place, seeing that the booths are closed and the bales corded?"

And the young Fisherman answered him, "I can find no inn in this city, nor have I any kinsman who might give me shelter."

"Are we not all kinsmen?" said the merchant. "And did not one God make us? Therefore come with me, for I have a guest-chamber."

So the young Fisherman rose up and followed the merchant to his house. And when he had passed through a garden of pomegranates and entered into the house, the merchant brought him rose-water in a copper dish that he might wash his hands, and ripe melons that he might quench his thirst, and set a bowl of rice and a piece of roasted kid before him.

And after that he had finished, the merchant led him to the guest-chamber, and bade him sleep and be at rest. And the young Fisherman gave him thanks, and kissed the ring that was on his hand, and flung himself down on the carpets of dyed goat's-hair. And when he had covered himself with a covering of black lamb's-wool he fell asleep.

And three hours before dawn, and while it was still night, his Soul waked him and said to him, "Rise up and go to the room of the merchant, even to the room in which he sleepeth, and slay him, and take from him his gold, for we have need of it."

And the young Fisherman rose up and crept towards the room of the merchant, and over the feet of the merchant there was lying a curved sword, and the tray by the side of the merchant held nine purses of gold. And he reached out his hand and touched the sword, and when he touched it the merchant started and awoke, and leaping up seized himself the sword and cried to the young Fisherman, "Dost thou return evil for good, and pay with the shedding of blood for the kindness that I have shown thee?"

And his Soul said to the young Fisherman, "Strike him," and he struck him so that he swooned, and he seized then the nine purses of gold, and fled hastily through the garden of pomegranates, and set his face to the star that is the star of morning.

And when they had gone a league from the city, the young Fisherman beat his breast, and said to his Soul, "Why didst thou bid me slay the merchant and take his gold? Surely thou art evil."

But his Soul answered him, "Be at peace, be at peace."

"Nay," cried the young Fisherman, "I may not be at peace, for all that thou hast made me to do I hate. Thee also I hate, and I bid thee tell me wherefore thou hast wrought with me in this wise."

And his Soul answered him, "When thou didst send me forth into the world thou gavest me no heart, so I learned to do all these things and love them."

"What sayest thou?" murmured the young Fisherman.

"Thou knowest," answered his Soul, "thou knowest it well. Hast thou forgotten that thou gavest me no heart? I trow not. And so trouble not thyself nor me, but be at peace, for there is no pain that thou shalt not give away, nor any pleasure that thou shalt not receive."

And when the young Fisherman heard these words he trembled and said to his Soul, "Nay, but thou art evil, and hast made me forget my love, and hast tempted me with temptations, and hast set my feet in the ways of sins."

And his Soul answered him, "Thou hast not forgotten that when thou didst send me forth into the world thou gavest me no heart. Come, let us go to another city, and make merry, for we have nine purses of gold."

But the young Fisherman took the nine purses of gold, and flung them down, and trampled on them.

"Nay," he cried, "but I will have nought to do with thee, nor will I journey with thee anywhere, but even as I sent thee away before, so will I send thee away now, for thou hast wrought me no good." And he turned his back to the moon, and with the little knife that had the handle of green viper's skin he strove to cut from his feet that shadow of the body which is the body of the Soul.

Yet his Soul stirred not from him, nor paid heed to his command, but said to him, "The spell that the Witch told thee avails thee no more, for I may not leave thee, nor mayest thou drive me forth. Once in his life may a man send his Soul away, but he who receiveth back his Soul must keep it with him for ever and this is his punishment and his reward."

And the young Fisherman grew pale and clenched his hands and cried, "She was a false Witch in that she told me not that."

"Nay," answered his Soul, "but she was true to Him she worships, and whose servant she will be ever."

And when the young Fisherman knew that he could no longer get rid of his Soul, and that it was an evil Soul, and would abide with him always, he fell upon the ground weeping bitterly.

And when it was day, the young Fisherman rose up and said to his Soul, "I will bind my hands that I may not do thy bidding, and close my lips that I may not speak thy words, and I will return to the place where she whom I love has her dwelling. Even to the sea will I return, and to the little bay where she is wont to sing, and I will call to her and tell her the evil I have done and the evil thou hast wrought on me."

And his Soul tempted him and said, "Who is thy love, that thou shouldst return to her? The world has many fairer than she is. There are the dancing-girls of Samaris who dance in the manner of all kinds of birds and beasts. Their feet are painted with henna, and in their hands they have little copper bells. They laugh while they dance, and their laughter is as clear as the laughter of water. Come with me and I will show them to thee. For what is this trouble of thine about the things of sin? Is that which is pleasant to eat not made for the eater? Is there poison in that which is sweet to drink? Trouble not thyself, but come with me to another city. There is a little city hard by in which there is a garden of tulip-trees. And there dwell in this comely garden white peacocks and peacocks that have blue breasts. Their tails when they spread them to the sun are like disks of ivory and like gilt disks. And she who feeds them dances for pleasure, and sometimes she dances on her hands and at other times she dances with her feet. Her eyes are coloured with stibium, and her nostrils are shaped like the wings of a swallow. From a hook in one of her nostrils hangs a flower that is carved out of a pearl. She laughs while she dances, and the silver rings that are about her ankles tinkle like bells of silver. And so trouble not thyself any more, but come with me to this city."

But the young Fisherman answered not his Soul, but closed his lips with the seal of silence and with a tight cord bound his hands, and journeyed back to the place from which he had come, even to the little bay where his love had been wont to sing. And ever did his Soul tempt him by the way, but he made it no answer, nor would he do any of the wickedness that it sought to make him do, so great was the power of the love that was within him.

And when he had reached the shore of the sea, he loosed the cord from his hands, and took the seal of silence from his lips, and called to the little Mermaid. But she came not to his call, though he called to her all day long and besought her.

And his Soul mocked him and said, "Surely thou hast but little joy out of thy love. Thou art as one who in time of death pours water into a broken vessel. Thou givest away what thou hast, and nought is given to thee in return. It were better for thee to come with me, for I know where the Valley of Pleasure lies, and what things are wrought there."

But the young Fisherman answered not his Soul, but in a cleft of the rock he built himself a house of wattles, and abode there for the space of a year. And every morning he called to the Mermaid, and every noon he called to her again, and at night-time he spake her name. Yet never did she rise out of the sea to meet him, nor in any place of the sea could he find her though he sought for her in the caves and in the green water, in the pools of the tide and in the wells that are at the bottom of the deep.

And ever did his Soul tempt him with evil, and whisper of terrible things. Yet did it not prevail against him, so great was the power of his love.

And after the year was over, the Soul thought within himself, "I have tempted my master with evil, and his love is stronger than I am. I will tempt him now with good, and it may be that he will come with me."

So he spake to the young Fisherman and said, "I have told thee of the joy of the world, and thou hast turned a deaf ear to me. Suffer me now to tell thee of the world's pain, and it may be that thou wilt hearken. For of a truth pain is the Lord of this world, nor is there any one who escapes from its net. There be some who lack raiment, and others who lack bread. There be widows who sit in purple, and widows who sit in rags. To and fro over the fens go the lepers, and they are cruel to each other. The beggars go up and down on the highways, and their wallets are empty. Through the streets of the cities walks Famine, and the Plague sits at their gates. Come, let us go forth and mend these things, and make them not to be. Wherefore shouldst thou tarry here calling to thy love, seeing she comes not to thy call? And what is love, that thou shouldst set this high store upon it?"

But the young Fisherman answered it nought, so great was the power of his love. And every morning he called to the Mermaid, and every noon he called to her again, and at night-time he spake her name. Yet never did she rise out of the sea to meet him, nor in any place of the sea could he find her, though he sought for her in the rivers of the sea, and in the valleys that are under the waves, in the sea that the night makes purple, and in the sea that the dawn leaves grey.

And after the second year was over, the Soul said to the young Fisherman at night-time, and as he sat in the wattled house alone, "Lo! now I have tempted thee with evil, and I have tempted thee with good, and thy love is stronger than I am. Wherefore will I tempt thee no longer, but I pray thee to suffer me to enter thy heart, that I may be one with thee even as before."

"Surely thou mayest enter," said the young Fisherman, "for in the days when with no heart thou didst go through the world thou must have much suffered."

"Alas!" cried his Soul, "I can find no place of entrance, so compassed about with love is this heart of thine."

"Yet I would that I could help thee," said the young Fisherman.

And as he spake there came a great cry of mourning from the sea, even the cry that men hear when one of the Sea-folk is dead. And the young Fisherman leapt up, and left his wattled house, and ran down to the shore. And the black waves came hurrying to the shore, bearing with them a burden that was whiter than silver. White as the surf it was, and like a flower it tossed on the waves. And the surf took it from the waves, and the foam took it from the surf, and the shore received it, and lying at his feet the young Fisherman saw the body of the little Mermaid. Dead at his feet it was lying.

Weeping as one smitten with pain he flung himself down beside it, and he kissed the cold red of the mouth, and toyed with the wet amber of the hair. He flung himself down beside it on the sand, weeping as one trembling with joy, and in his brown arms he held it to his breast. Cold were the lips, yet he kissed them. Salt was the honey of the hair, yet he tasted it with a bitter joy. He kissed the closed eyelids, and the wild spray that lay upon their cups was less salt than his tears.

And to the dead thing he made confession. Into the shells of its ears he poured the harsh wine of his tale. He put the little hands round his neck, and with his fingers he touched the thin reed of the throat. Bitter, bitter was his joy, and full of strange gladness was his pain.

The black sea came nearer, and the white foam moaned like a leper. With white claws of foam the sea grabbled at the shore. From the palace of the Sea-King came the cry of mourning again, and far out upon the sea the great Tritons blew hoarsely upon their horns.

"Flee away," said his Soul, "for ever doth the sea come nigher, and if thou tarriest it will slay thee. Flee away, for I am afraid, seeing that thy heart is closed against me by reason of the greatness of thy love. Flee away to a place of safety. Surely thou wilt not send me without a heart into another world?"

But the young Fisherman listened not to his Soul, but called on the little Mermaid and said, "Love is better than wisdom, and more precious than riches, and fairer than the feet of the daughters of men. The fires cannot destroy it, nor can the waters quench it. I called on thee at dawn, and thou didst come to my call. The moon heard thy name, yet hadst thou no heed of me. For evilly had I left thee, and to my own hurt had I wandered away. Yet ever did thy love abide with me, and ever was it strong, nor did aught prevail against it, though I have looked upon evil and looked upon good. And now that thou art dead, surely I will die with thee also."

And his Soul besought him to depart, but he would not, so great was his love. And the sea came nearer, and sought to cover him with its waves, and when he knew that the end was at hand he kissed with mad lips the cold lips of the Mermaid, and the heart that was within him brake. And as through the fullness of his love his heart did break, the Soul found an entrance and entered in, and was one with him even as before. And the sea covered the young Fisherman with its waves.

And in the morning the Priest went forth to bless the sea, for it had been troubled. And with him went the monks and the musicians, and the candle-bearers, and the swingers of censers, and a great company.

And when the Priest reached the shore he saw the young Fisherman lying drowned in the surf, and clasped in his arms was the body of the little Mermaid. And he drew back frowning, and having made the sign of the cross, he cried aloud and said, "I will not bless the sea nor anything that is in it. Accursed be the Sea-folk, and accursed be all they who traffic with them. And as for him who for love's sake forsook God, and so lieth here with his leman slain by God's judgment, take up his body and the body of his leman, and bury them in the corner of the Field of the Fullers, and set no mark above them, nor sign of any kind, that none may know the place of their resting. For accursed were they in their lives, and accursed shall they be in their deaths also."

And the people did as he commanded them, and in the corner of the Field of the Fullers, where no sweet herbs grew, they dug a deep pit, and laid the dead things within it.

And when the third year was over, and on a day that was a holy day, the Priest went up to the chapel, that he might show to the people the wounds of the Lord, and speak to them about the wrath of God.

And when he had robed himself with his robes, and entered in and bowed himself before the altar, he saw that the altar was covered with strange flowers that never had been seen before. Strange were they to look at, and of curious beauty, and their beauty troubled him, and their odour was sweet in his nostrils, and he felt glad, and understood not why he was glad.

And after that he had opened the tabernacle, and incensed the monstrance that was in it, and shown the fair wafer to the people, and hid it again behind the veil of veils, he began to speak to the people, desiring to speak to them of the wrath of God. But the beauty of the white flowers troubled him, and their odour was sweet in his nostrils, and there came another word into his lips, and he spake not of the wrath of God, but of the God whose name is Love. And why he so spake, he knew not.

And when he had finished his word the people wept, and the Priest went back to the sacristy, and his eyes were full of tears. And the deacons came in and began to unrobe him, and took from him the alb and the girdle, the maniple and the stole. And he stood as one in a dream.

And after that they had unrobed him, he looked at them and said, "What are the flowers that stand on the altar, and whence do they come?"

And they answered him, "What flowers they are we cannot tell, but they come from the corner of the Fullers' Field." And the Priest trembled, and returned to his own house and prayed.

And in the morning, while it was still dawn, he went forth with the monks and the musicians, and the candle-bearers and the swingers of censers, and a great company, and came to the shore of the sea, and blessed the sea, and all the wild things that are in it. The Fauns also he blessed, and the little things that dance in the woodland, and the bright-eyed things that peer through the leaves. All the things in God's world he blessed, and the people were filled with joy and wonder. Yet never again in the corner of the Fullers' Field grew flowers of any kind, but the field remained barren even as before. Nor came the Sea-folk into the bay as they had been wont to do, for they went to another part of the sea.

Where to Lay the Blame

Howard Pyle

Many and many a man has come to trouble—so he will say— by following his wife's advice. This is how it was with a man of whom I shall tell you.

There was once upon a time a fisherman who had fished all day long and had caught not so much as a sprat. So at night there he sat by the fire, rubbing his knees and warming his shins, and waiting for supper that his wife was cooking for him, and his hunger was as sharp as vinegar, and his temper hot enough to fry fat.

While he sat there grumbling and growling and trying to make himself comfortable and warm, there suddenly came a knock at the door. The good woman opened it, and there stood an old man, clad all in red from head to foot, and with a snowy beard at his chin as white as winter snow.

The fisherman's wife stood gaping and staring at the strange figure, but the old man in red walked straight into the hut. "Bring your nets, fisherman," said he, "and come with me. There is something that I want you to catch for me, and if I have luck I will pay you for your fishing as never fisherman was paid before."

"Not I," said the fisherman. "I go out no more this night. I have been fishing all day long until my back is nearly broken, and have caught nothing, and now I am not such a fool as to go out and leave a warm fire and a good supper at your bidding."

But the fisherman's wife had listened to what the old man had said about paying for the job, and she was of a different mind from her husband. "Come," said she, "the old man promises to pay you well. This is not a chance to be lost, I can tell you, and my advice to you is that you go."

The fisherman shook his head. No, he would not go; he had said he would not, and he would not. But the wife only smiled and said again, "My advice to you is that you go."

The fisherman grumbled and grumbled, and swore that he would not go. The wife said nothing but one thing. She did not argue; she did not lose her temper; she only said to everything that he said, "My advice to you is that you go."

At last the fisherman's anger boiled over. "Very well," said he, spitting his words at her. "If you will drive me out into the night, I suppose I will have to go." And then he spoke the words that so many men say: "Many a man has come to trouble by following his wife's advice."

Then down he took his fur cap and up he took his nets, and off he and the old man marched through the moonlight, their shadows bobbing along like black spiders behind them.

Well, on they went, out from the town and across the fields and through the woods, until at last they came to a dreary, lonesome desert, where nothing was to be seen but gray rocks and weeds and thistles.

"Well," said the fisherman, "I have fished, man and boy, for forty-seven years, but never did I see as unlikely a place to catch anything as this."

But the old man said never a word. First of all he drew a great circle with strange figures, marking it with his finger upon the ground. Then out from under his red gown he brought a tinderbox and steel, and a little silver casket covered all over with strange figures of serpents and dragons and whatnot. He brought some sticks of spicewood from his pouch, and then he struck a light and made a fire. Out of the box he took a gray powder, which he flung upon the little blaze.

Puff! Flash! A vivid flame went up into the moonlight, and then a dense smoke as black as ink, which spread out wider and wider, far and near, till all below was darker than the darkest midnight. Then the old man began to utter strange spells and words. Presently there began a rumbling that sounded louder and louder and nearer and nearer, until it roared and bellowed like thunder. The earth rocked and swayed, and the poor fisherman shook and trembled with fear till his teeth clattered in his head.

Then suddenly the roaring and bellowing ceased, and all was as still as death, though the darkness was as thick and black as ever.

"Now," said the old magician—for such he was—"now we are about to take a journey such as no one ever traveled before. Heed well what I tell you. Speak not a single word, for if you do, misfortune will be sure to happen."

"Ain't I to say anything?" said the fisherman.

"No."

"Not even 'boo' to a goose?"

"No."

"Well, that is pretty hard upon a man who likes to say his say," said the fisherman.

"And moreover," said the old man, "I must blindfold you as well."

Thereupon he took from his pocket a handkerchief, and made ready to tie it about the fisherman's eyes.

"And ain't I to see anything at all?" said the fisherman.

"No."

"Not even so much as a single feather?"

"No."

"Well, then," said the fisherman, "I wish I'd not come."

But the old man tied the handkerchief tightly around his eyes, and then he was as blind as a bat.

"Now," said the old man, "throw your leg over what you feel, and hold fast."

The fisherman reached down his hand, and there felt the back of something rough and hairy. He flung his leg over it, and whisk! whizz! off he shot through the air like a skyrocket. Nothing was left for him to do but grip tightly with hands and feet and to hold fast. On they went, and on they went, until, after a great while, whatever it was that was carrying him lit upon the ground, and there the fisherman found himself standing, for that which had brought him had gone.

The old man whipped the handkerchief off his eyes, and there the fisherman found himself on the shores of the sea, where there was nothing to be seen but water upon one side and rocks and naked sand upon the other.

"This is the place for you to cast your nets," said the old magician, "for if we catch nothing here we catch nothing at all."

The fisherman unrolled his nets and cast them and dragged them, and then cast them and dragged them again, but neither time caught so much as a herring. But the third time that he cast, he found that he had caught something that weighed as heavy as lead. He pulled and pulled, until by and by he dragged the load ashore, and what should it be but a great chest of wood, blackened by the seawater and covered with shells and green moss.

That was the very thing that the magician had come to fish for.

From his pouch the old man took a little golden key, which he fitted into a keyhole in the side of the chest. He threw back the lid; the fisherman looked within, and there was the prettiest little palace that man's eye ever beheld, all made of mother-of-pearl and silver-frosted as white as snow. The old magician lifted the little palace out of the box and set it upon the ground.

Then, lo and behold! a marvelous thing happened; for the palace instantly began to grow, for all the world like a soap bubble, until it stood in the moonlight gleaming and glistening like snow, the windows bright with the lights of a thousand wax tapers, and the sound of music and voices and laughter coming from within.

Hardly could the fisherman catch his breath from one strange thing when another happened. The old magician took off his clothes and his face—yes, his face—for all the world as though it had been a mask, and there stood as handsome and noble a young man as ever the light looked on. Then, beckoning to the fisherman, dumb with wonder, he led the way up the great flight of marble steps to the palace door. As he came, the door swung open with a blaze of light, and there stood hundreds of noblemen, all clad in silks and satins and velvets, who, when they saw the magician, bowed low before him, as though he had been a king. Leading the way, they brought the two through halls and chambers and room after room, each more magnificent than the other, until they came to one that surpassed a hundredfold any of the others.

At the farther end was a golden throne, and upon it sat a lady more lovely and beautiful than a dream, her eyes as bright as diamonds, her cheeks like rose leaves, and her hair like spun gold. She came halfway down the steps of the throne to welcome the magician, and when the two met they kissed one another before all those who were looking on. Then she brought him to the throne and seated him beside her, and there they talked for a long time very earnestly.

Nobody said a word to the fisherman, who stood staring about him like an owl. "I wonder," said he to himself at last, "if they will give a body a bite to eat by and by?" for to tell the truth, the good supper that he had come away from at home had left a sharp hunger gnawing at his insides, and he longed for something good and warm to fill the empty place. But time passed, and not so much as a crust of bread was brought to stay his stomach.

By and by the clock struck twelve, and then the two who sat upon the throne arose. The beautiful lady took the magician by the hand and, turning to those who stood around, said, in a loud voice, "Behold him who alone is worthy to possess the jewel of jewels! Unto him do I give it, and with it all power of powers!" Thereon she opened a golden casket that stood beside her, and brought thence a little crystal ball, about as big as a pigeon's egg, in which was something that glistened like a spark of fire. The magician took the crystal ball and thrust it into his bosom; but what it was the fisherman could not guess, and if you do not know I shall not tell you.

Then for the first time the beautiful lady seemed to notice the fisherman. She beckoned him, and when he stood beside her, two men came carrying a chest. The chief treasurer opened it, and it was full of bags of gold money. "How will you have it?" said the beautiful lady.

"Have what?" said the fisherman.

"Have the pay for your labor?" said the beautiful lady.

"I will," said the fisherman promptly, "take it in my hat."

"So be it," said the beautiful lady. She waved her hand, and the chief treasurer took a bag from the chest, untied it, and emptied a cataract of gold into the fur cap. The fisherman had never seen so much wealth in all his life before, and he stood like a man turned to stone.

"Is all this mine?" said the fisherman.

"It is," said the beautiful lady.

"Then God bless your pretty eyes," said the fisherman.

Then the magician kissed the beautiful lady and, beckoning to the fisherman, left the throne room the same way that they had come. The noblemen, in silks and satins and velvets, marched ahead, and back they went through the other apartments, until at last they came to the door.

Out they stepped, and then what do you suppose happened?

If the wonderful palace had grown like a bubble, like a bubble it vanished. There the two stood on the seashore, with nothing to be seen but rocks and sand and water, and the starry sky overhead.

The fisherman shook his cap of gold, and it jingled and tinkled and was as heavy as lead. If it was not all a dream, he was rich for life. "But anyhow," said he, "they might have given a body a bite to eat."

The magician put on his red clothes and his face again, making himself as hoary and as old as before. He took out his flint and steel, and his sticks of spicewood and his gray powder, and made a great fire and smoke just as he had done before. Then again he tied his handkerchief over the fisherman's eyes. "Remember," said he, "what I told you when we started upon our journey. Keep your mouth tight shut, for if you utter so much as a single word you are a lost man. Now throw your leg over what you feel, and hold fast."

The fisherman had his net over one arm and his cap of gold in the other hand; nevertheless, there he felt the same hairy thing he had felt before. He flung his leg over it, and away he was gone through the air like a skyrocket.

Now he had grown somewhat used to strange things by this time, so he began to think that he would like to see what sort of a creature it was upon which he was riding thus through the sky. So he contrived, in spite of his net and cap, to push up the handkerchief from over one eye. Out he peeped, and then he saw as clear as day what the strange steed was.

He was riding upon a he-goat as black as night, and in front of him was the magician riding upon just such another, his great red robe fluttering out behind him in the moonlight like huge red wings.

"Great herring and little fishes!" roared the fisherman. "It is a billy goat!"

Instantly goats, old man, and all were gone like a flash. Down fell the fisherman through the empty sky, whirling over and over and around and around like a frog. He held tightly to his net, but away flew his fur cap, the golden money falling in a shower like sparks of yellow light. Down he fell and down he fell, until his head spun like a top.

By good luck his house was just below, with its thatch of soft rushes. Into the very middle of it he tumbled, and right through the thatch—bump!—into the room below.

The good wife was in bed, snoring away for dear life; but such a noise as the fisherman made coming into the house was enough to wake the dead. Up she jumped, and there she sat, staring and winking with sleep, and with her brains as addled as a duck's egg in a thunderstorm.

"There!" said the fisherman, as he gathered himself up and rubbed his shoulder. "That is what comes of following a woman's advice!"

‹ *The Tale of the 672nd Night* ›
Hugo von Hofmannsthal

I

merchant's son, who was young and handsome and whose
father and mother were no longer living, found himself,
shortly after his twenty-fifth year, tired of social life and entertaining. He closed off most of the rooms of his house and
dismissed all of his servants with the exception of four, whose
devotion and general demeanor pleased him. Since his friends
were of no great importance to him and since he was not so
captivated by the beauty of any woman as to imagine it desirable or even tolerable to have her always around him, he grew more and
more accustomed to a rather solitary life, one which seemed most appropriate
to his cast of mind. However, he was by no means averse to human contact;
on the contrary, he enjoyed walking in the streets and public gardens and
contemplating the faces of men and women. Nor did he neglect either the
care of his body and his beautiful hands or the decorating of his apartments.
Indeed, the beauty of carpets, tapestries, and silks, of paneled walls, cande-
labras, and metal bowls, of vessels of glass and earthenware, became more
important to him than he could ever have imagined. Gradually his eyes were
opened to the fact that all the shapes and colors of the world were embodied
in the things of his household. In the intertwining of decorative forms he
came to recognize an enchanted image of the interlocking wonders of the
world. He discovered the figures of beasts and flowers and the transition of

flowers into animals; the dolphins, the lions, and the tulips, the pearls and the acanthus; he discovered the tension between the burden of pillars and the resistance of solid ground, and the will of all water to move upward and then downward again. He discovered the bliss of motion, the sublimity of rest, dancing, and being dead; he discovered the colors of flowers and leaves, the colors of the coats of wild beasts and of the faces of nations, the color of jewels, the color of the stormy sea and the quietly shining sea; yes, he discovered the moon and the stars, the mystic sphere, the mystic rings and, firmly rooted upon them, the wings of the seraphim. For a long time he was intoxicated by the great, profound beauty that belonged to him, and all his days moved more beautifully and less emptily in the company of these household things, which were no longer anything dead or commonplace but a great heritage, the divine work of all the generations.

Yet he felt the emptiness of all these things as well as their beauty. Never did the thought of death leave him for long; often it came over him when he was in the company of laughing, noisy people, often at night, often as he ate.

Since there was no sickness in him, however, the thought was not terrifying; it had about it, rather, something of solemnity, of splendor, and was at its most intense precisely when he was intoxicated with thinking of beauty, the beauty of his own youth and solitude. For the merchant's son often drew great pride from his mirror, from the verses of poets, from his wealth and intelligence, and dark maxims did not weigh on his soul. He said, "Wherever you are meant to die, there your feet will carry you," and he pictured himself, handsome, like a king lost on a hunt, walking in an unknown wood under strange trees toward an alien, wondrous fate. He said, "When the dwelling place is finished, death will come," and he saw death coming slowly, up over the bridge, the bridge borne on winged lions and leading to the palace, the finished dwelling, filled with the wonderful booty of life.

He thought he would now be living in solitude, but his four servants circled him like dogs, and although he spoke little with them he still felt somehow that they were incessantly thinking how best to serve him. For his part, he began to reflect now and then upon them.

The housekeeper was an old woman; her daughter, now dead, had been the nurse of the merchant's son; all her other children had also died. She was very quiet, and the chill of age emanated from her white face and her white hands. But he liked her because she had always been in the house and because she carried about with her the memory of his own mother's voice and of his childhood, which he loved with a great longing.

With his permission she had taken into the house a distant relative, a girl scarcely fifteen years old, extremely withdrawn. The girl was harsh with herself and hard to understand. Once in a sudden, dark impulse of her angry soul she threw herself out of a window and into the courtyard but fell with her childlike body into some garden soil that happened to be piled up there, so that all she broke was a collarbone, and that only because at this spot there had been a rock in the dirt. After she was put to bed the merchant's son sent his physician to see her. In the evening, however, he came himself and wanted to see how she was getting along. She kept her eyes closed; for the first time he looked at her long and quietly and was amazed at the strange and precocious charm of her face. Only her lips were very thin, and there was something disturbing and unattractive in this. Suddenly she opened her eyes, looked at him in icy hostility, and, with her lips clenched in anger, overcoming her pain, turned toward the wall, so that she lay on her injured side. At this instant her deathly pale face turned color, becoming greenish white; she fainted and fell back into her former position, as if dead.

For a long time after her recovery the merchant's son did not speak to her when they met. Once or twice he asked the old lady whether the girl did not resent being in his house, but she always denied it. The only servant whom he had decided to retain in his house was a man he had once come to know when he was dining with the ambassador assigned to this city by the king of Persia. This man had served him on that occasion and was so accommodating and circumspect and seemed at the same time to be so very retiring and modest that the merchant's son had discovered more pleasure in observing him than in listening to what the other guests were saying. His joy was all the greater, therefore, when many months later this servant stepped up to him on the street, greeted him with the same deep earnestness as on that previous evening, and, without a trace of importuning, offered him his services. The merchant's son recognized him immediately by his somber, mulberry-hued face and by his good breeding. He employed him instantly and dismissed two young servants whom he still had with him, and from that moment on would let himself be served at meals and other times only by this earnest and reserved person. The man had permission to leave the house during the evening hours but almost never took advantage of it. He displayed a rare attachment to his master, whose wishes he anticipated and whose likes and dislikes he sensed instinctively, so that the latter in turn took an ever greater liking to him.

Although he allowed only this person to serve him as he ate, there was still a maid who brought in the dishes with fruit and sweet pastries, a young girl but still two or three years older than the youngest. This girl was one of those who, seen from afar or stepping forth as dancers by the light of torches, would scarcely pass for very beautiful, because at such times the refinement of their features is lost. But seeing her close to him and every day, he was seized by the incomparable beauty of her eyelids and her lips; and the languid, joyless movements of her beautiful body were to him the puzzling language of a self-enclosed and wondrous world.

It was a time when, in the city, the heat of summer was very great and its dull incandescence hovered along the line of houses, and in the sultry, heavy nights of the full moon, the wind drove white clouds of dust down the empty streets. At this time the merchant's son traveled with his four servants to a country house he owned in the mountains, in a narrow valley surrounded by dark hills, the site of many such country estates of the wealthy. From both sides waterfalls descended into the gorges, cooling the air. The moon was almost always hidden on the far side of the mountains, but great white clouds rose behind the black walls, floated solemnly across the darkly glowing sky, and disappeared on the other side. Here the merchant's son lived his accustomed life, in a house whose wooden walls were constantly penetrated by the cool fragrance of the gardens and the many waterfalls. In the afternoon, until the time when the sun fell beyond the hills, he sat in his garden, most often reading a book in which were recorded the wars of a very great king of the past. Sometimes, in the midst of a passage describing how thousands of cavalrymen of the enemy kings turned their horses, shouting, or how their chariots were dragged down the steep bank of a river, he was compelled to stop suddenly, for he felt, without looking up, that the eyes of his four servants were fixed on him. He knew, without lifting his head, that they were looking at him, each from a different room. He knew them so well. He felt them living, more strongly, more forcefully than he felt himself live. Concerning himself he sensed on occasion a slight shock of emotion or surprise, but also on this account a puzzling fear. He felt, with the clarity of a nightmare, how the two old people were moving along toward death with every hour, with the inescapable, slow altering of their features and their gestures, which he knew so well; and how the two girls were making their way into that life, barren and airless, as it were. Like the terror and the mortal bitterness of a fearful dream, forgotten on awakening, the heavy weight of their lives, of which they themselves knew nothing, lay upon his limbs.

Sometimes he had to rise and walk about, lest he succumb to his anxiety. But while he gazed at the bright gravel before his feet and observed with great concentration how, from the cool fragrance of grass and earth, the fragrance of carnations welled up toward him in bright, sharp breaths and, intermittently, in warmish, excessively sweet clouds, the fragrance of heliotropes, he felt their eyes and could think of nothing else. Without raising his head, he knew that the old woman was sitting by her window, her bloodless hands on the sun-drenched sill, the bloodless mask of her face an ever more terrible setting for her helpless black eyes, which could not die. Without raising his head he could sense when his servant stepped back from the window, for a matter only of minutes, to busy himself with one of the wardrobes; without looking up he waited in secret fear for the moment when he would return. While his two hands were letting supple branches close behind him, so that he might crawl away and disappear in the most overgrown corner of his garden, and while all his thoughts were bent on the beauty of the sky that fell from above through the dark net of branches and vines, in little gleaming bits of turquoise, the one thing that seized hold of his blood and all his thinking was that he knew the eyes of the two girls were fixed on him; those of the taller languid and sad, filled with a vague challenge that tormented him, those of the little one with an impatient, then again a mocking attentiveness that tormented him even more. And still he never had the idea that they were looking at him directly, in the act of his walking about with lowered head, or kneeling by a carnation to tie it with twine, or leaning down beneath boughs. Rather it seemed to him that they were contemplating his entire life, his deepest being, his secret human inadequacy.

A terrible oppression came over him, a mortal fear in face of the inescapability of life. More terrible than their incessantly watching him was the fact that they forced him to think of himself in such a fruitless and exhausting fashion. And the garden was much too small to permit his escaping them. However, when he was very close to them, his fear paled so completely that he almost forgot the past. Then he was capable of ignoring them totally, or of calmly observing their movements, which were so familiar that he felt an unceasing, as it were a physical sense of identification with their lives.

The little girl crossed his path only now and then, on the stairway or in the front part of the house. The three others, however, were frequently in the same room with him. Once he caught sight of the taller one in a slanting mirror; she was passing through an adjoining room set at a higher level; in the mirror, however, she approached him from below. She walked slowly and with effort but fully erect; she carried in each arm the heavy, gaunt figure, in dark bronze, of an Indian deity. The ornate feet of the figurines rested in the hollows of her hands; the dark goddesses reached from her hips to her temples, leaning their dead weight on her slender living shoulders, but their dark heads, with their angry serpents' mouths, their brows above three wild eyes apiece, the mysterious jewels in their cold, hard hair, moved alongside breathing cheeks and brushed her lovely temples in time with her measured steps. In fact, however, the true burden she bore with such solemnity seemed not so much the goddesses as the beauty of her own head with its heavy ornaments of dark and living gold, the hair curled in two great arching spirals at either side of her bright brow, like a queen at war. He was seized by her great beauty but at the same time realized clearly that to hold her in his arms would mean nothing to him. For he well knew that the beauty of his maidservant filled him with longing but not with desire; hence he did not rest his eyes long upon her but stepped out of the room, out to the street in fact, and walked on in strange unrest between the houses and gardens in the narrow shadows. Finally, he passed along the banks of the river where the gardeners and flower sellers lived; there for a long while he sought—knowing that he would seek in vain—a flower whose form and fragrance, a spice whose fading breath could grant him for one moment of calm possession precisely that same sweet charm as lay, confusing and disconcerting, in the beauty of his maidservant. And as he peered about in the gloom of the greenhouses or bent over the long beds in the open air, with darkness already falling, his mind repeated, over and over, involuntarily, tormentedly and against his will, the words of the poet: "In the stems of carnations, swaying, in the smell of ripe grain you awakened my longing; but when I found you, you were not the one I was seeking, but the sisters of your soul."

II

During this time there came a letter that rather upset him. The letter was unsigned. In vague terms the writer accused the young man's servant of having committed, while he was in the household of his previous master, the Persian ambassador, some sort of repugnant crime. The unknown correspondent appeared to be consumed with violent hatred of the servant and accompanied his letter with a number of threats; in addressing the merchant's son himself he also assumed a discourteous, almost threatening, tone. But there was no way of guessing what crime was alluded to or what purpose this letter might serve for the writer, who neither gave his name nor demanded anything. The merchant's son read the letter several times and was forced to admit that the thought of losing his servant in such a disagreeable manner caused him a strong feeling of anxiety. The more he thought it over, the more agitated he became and the less he could bear the idea of losing any one of these persons to whom he had grown so completely attached, through habit and through mysterious forces.

He paced up and down and became so heated in his angry agitation that he cast aside his cloak and his sash and kicked them with his feet. It seemed to him as if someone were insulting and threatening the things that were most deeply his, and were trying to force him to desert himself and to deny what was dear to him. He was sorry for himself and, as always at such moments, felt like a child. He pictured his four servants torn from his house and felt as if the whole content of his life were being drawn out of him, all the bittersweet memories, all the half-unconscious hopes, everything that transcended words, only to be cast out somewhere and declared worthless, like a bunch of seaweed. For the first time he understood something that had always irritated and angered him as a boy: the anxious love with which his father clung to what he had acquired, the riches of his vaulted warehouse, the lovely, unfeeling children of his hopes and fears, the mysterious progeny of the dimly apprehended, deepest wishes of his life. He came to understand that the great king of the past would surely have died if his lands had been taken from him, lands he had traversed and conquered, from the sea in the west to the sea in the east, and dreamed of ruling, yet lands of such boundless extent that he had no power over them and received no tribute from them, other than the thought that he had subjugated them, that no other than he was their king.

He determined to do everything he could to put to rest this thing that caused him such anxiety. Without saying a word to his servant about the letter, he set out and traveled to the city alone. There he determined first of all to seek out the house occupied by the ambassador of the king of Persia, for he had a vague hope of finding some kind of clue there.

When he arrived, however, it was late afternoon and no one was at home, neither the ambassador nor a single one of the young people of his entourage. Only the cook and a lowly old scribe were sitting in the gateway in the cool semidarkness. But they were so ugly and answered him in such a short and sullen manner that he turned his back on them impatiently and decided to return the following day at a better time.

Since his own house was shut and locked—for he had left no servants back in town—he was compelled to think of some place to stay for the night. Curiously, like a stranger, he walked through the familiar streets and came at last to the banks of a little river, which at this time of year was virtually dry. From here, lost in thought, he followed a shabby street inhabited by a large number of prostitutes. Without paying much attention to where he was going, he then turned to the right and entered a completely deserted, deathly still cul-de-sac, which ended in a steep stairway almost as tall as a tower. On this stairway he stopped and looked back on the way he had taken. He could see into the yards of the little houses; here and there were red curtains and ugly, dried-out flowers; there was a deathly sadness about the broad, dry bed of the stream. He climbed higher and at the top entered a quarter of the city that he could not recall having seen before. Nonetheless, an intersection of low-lying streets suddenly struck him with dreamlike familiarity. He walked on and came to a jeweler's shop. It was a very shabby little shop, befitting this part of the city, and its show window was filled with the kind of worthless finery one can buy from pawnbrokers and receivers of stolen goods. The merchant's son, who was an expert in jewels, could scarcely find a halfway beautiful stone in the lot.

Suddenly his glance fell on an old-fashioned piece of jewelry, made of thin gold and embellished with a piece of beryl, reminding him somehow of the old woman. Probably he had once seen in her possession a similar piece obtained in her youth. Also, the pale, rather melancholy stone seemed in a strange way to fit in with her age and appearance; the old-fashioned setting had the same quality of sadness about it. So he stepped into the low-ceilinged shop to buy the piece. The jeweler was greatly pleased to have such a well-dressed customer drop in, and wanted to show him his more valuable stones as well, those that he did not put in his window. Out of courtesy he let the old man show him a number of things, but he had no desire to buy more, nor, given his solitary life, would he have had any use for such gifts. Finally, he grew impatient and at the same time embarrassed, for he wanted to get away and yet not hurt the old man's feelings. He decided to buy something else, a trifle, and leave immediately thereafter. Absentmindedly, looking over the jeweler's shoulder, he gazed at a small silver hand mirror, half coated over. In an inner mirror an image came to him of the maidservant with the bronze goddesses at either side; he had a passing sense that a great deal of her charm lay in the way her neck and shoulders bore, in unassuming, childlike grace, the beauty of her head, the head of a young queen. And in passing he thought it pretty to see around this same neck a thin gold chain, in many loops, childlike yet reminiscent of armor. And he asked to see such chains. The old man opened a door and invited him to step into a second room, a low-ceilinged parlor where numerous pieces of jewelry were on display, in glass cases and on open racks. Here he soon found a chain to his liking and asked the jeweler to tell him the price of the two ornaments. The jeweler asked him also to inspect the remarkable metalwork of some old saddles, set with semiprecious stones; he replied, however, that as the son of a merchant he never had anything to do with horses, in fact did not even know how to ride and found no pleasure in old saddles or in new. He took out a gold piece and some silver coins to pay for what he had bought, and gave some indication of being impatient to leave the store. The old man, without saying another word, picked out a piece of fine silk paper and wrapped the chain and the beryl, each separately; while he was doing so the merchant's son, by chance, stepped over to the low latticed window and looked out. He caught sight of a very well-kept vegetable garden, obviously belonging to the neighboring house, framed against a background of two glass greenhouses and a high wall. He was struck by an immediate desire to see these greenhouses and asked the jeweler if he could tell him how to get there. The jeweler handed him his two packages and led him through an adjoining room into the courtyard, which was connected to the neighboring garden by a lattice gate. Here the jeweler stopped and struck the gate with an iron clapper. Since, however, there was no sound from the garden and no sign of movement in the neighboring house, he urged the merchant's son simply to go ahead and inspect the forcing beds and, in the event that anyone should bother him, to say that he had his, the jeweler's, permission, for he was well acquainted with the owner. Then he opened the door for him by reaching through the bars of the latticework. The merchant's son immediately walked along the wall to the nearer of the two greenhouses, stepped in, and found such a profusion of rare and remarkable narcissus and anemones and such strange, leafy plants, quite unfamiliar to him, that he kept looking at them for a long time, never feeling he had seen enough. At last he looked up and saw that the sun had set behind the houses. It was not his wish to remain in a strange, unattended garden any longer, but rather he wished simply to cast a glance through the panes of the second forcing shed and then leave. As he walked slowly past this second shed, peeking in, he was suddenly struck with great fear and drew back. For someone had his face against the panes and was looking out at him. After a moment he calmed down and became aware that it was a child, a little girl of no more than four years, whose white dress and pale face were pressed to the windowpanes. But now when he looked more closely, he was again struck with fear, and felt in the back of his neck an unpleasant sensation of dread and a slight constriction in his throat and deeper down in his chest. For the child, who stared at him with a fixed and angry look, resembled in a way he could not fathom the fifteen-year-old girl he had in his own house. Everything was the same: the pale eyebrows, the fine, trembling nostrils, the thin lips; like her counterpart, this child also held one of her shoulders a bit higher than the other. Everything was the same, except that in the child all of this resulted in an expression that was terrifying to him. He did not know what it was that caused him such nameless fright. He knew only that he would not be able to bear turning around, knowing that this face was staring at him through the glass.

In his fear he walked quickly up to the door of the greenhouse, in order to go in. The door was shut, bolted from the outside; in his haste he bent down to reach the bolt, which was very low, and shoved it back so violently that he painfully dislocated one of the joints of his little finger, and headed for the child, almost at a run. The child came toward him and, not saying a word, braced itself against his knees, trying with its weak little hands to push him out. It was hard for him to avoid stepping on her. But now that he was close, his fear abated. He bent down over the face of the child, who was very pale and whose eyes trembled with anger and hatred, while the little teeth of its lower jaw pressed with unnerving fury into its upper lip. His fear disappeared for a moment as he stroked the girl's short, fine hair. But instantly he was reminded of the girl who lived in his house and whose hair he had once touched as she lay in her bed, deathly pale, her eyes closed; and immediately a shiver ran down his spine and his hands drew back. She had given up trying to push him away. She stepped back a few paces and looked straight ahead. It grew almost unbearable to him, the sight of this frail, doll-like body in its little white dress, this contemptuous, fearfully pale child's face. He was so filled with dread that he felt a twinge of pain in his temples and in his throat as his hand touched something cold in his pocket. It was a couple of silver coins. He took them out, bent down to the child, and gave them to her, because they shone and jingled. The child took them and let them drop in front of his feet, so that they disappeared in a crack of the floor where it rested on a grating of wood. Then she turned her back on him and walked slowly away. For a time he stood motionless, his heart pounding with fear lest she return and look at him from outside, through the panes. He would have preferred to leave immediately, but it was better to let some time pass, so that the child might leave the garden. By now it was no longer fully light in the glass house, and the shapes of the plants took on a strange appearance. Some distance away, black, absurdly threatening branches protruded disagreeably from the semidarkness, and behind them was a glimmer of white, as if the child were standing there. On a board stood a row of clay pots with wax flowers. To deaden the passage of a few moments he counted the blossoms, which, in their rigidity, bore little resemblance to living flowers and were rather like masks, treacherous masks with their eye sockets grown shut. When he had finished, he went to the door, thinking to leave. The door did not budge; the child had bolted it from the outside. He wanted to scream, but he was afraid of the sound of his own voice. He beat his fists against the panes. The garden and the house remained as still as death, except that behind him something was gliding through the shrubbery with a rustling sound. He told himself it was the sound of leaves that had loosened in the shattering of the sultry air and were falling to the ground. Still, he stopped his pounding and peered through the half-dark maze of trees and vines. Then he saw in the dusk of the far wall something that looked like a rectangle of dark lines. He crawled toward it, by now unconcerned that he was knocking over and breaking many of the clay flowerpots, that the tall, thin stalks and rustling fronds, as they fell, were closing over and behind him in a ghostly fashion. The rectangle of dark lines was the opening of a door; he pushed and it gave way. The open air passed over his face; behind him he heard the broken stalks and crushed leaves rise with a soft rustling sound as if after a storm.

He stood in a narrow walled passageway; above him the open sky looked down and the wall on either side was barely taller than a man. However, after a distance of fifteen paces, roughly speaking, the passage was walled up once more, and he started imagining himself a prisoner for the second time. Hesitantly he moved ahead; here on the right an opening in the wall had been broken through as wide as a man, and from this opening a board extended through empty space to a platform located opposite him; on the near side of it there was a low iron grating closing it off. On the other two sides were the backs of tall houses with people living in them. Where the board rested, like a gangplank, on the edge of the platform, the grating had a little door.

So very impatient was the merchant's son to escape the confines of his fear that he immediately set one foot, then the other, on the board and, keeping his glance firmly fixed on the opposite shore, started to cross over.

Unfortunately, however, he became aware that he was suspended over a walled moat several stories deep; in the soles of his feet and the hollow of his knees he felt fear and helplessness, in the dizziness of his whole body the nearness of death. He knelt down and closed his eyes; then his arms, groping forward, encountered the bars of the grating. He clutched them; they gave way, and with a slow, soft rasping sound that cut through his body like the exhalation of death, the door on which he was hanging opened toward him, toward the abyss. With a sense of his inner weariness and great despondency, he felt in anticipation how the smooth iron bars would slip from his fingers, which seemed to him like the fingers of a child, and how he would plunge downward and be dashed to bits along the wall. But the slow, soft opening of the door ceased before he lost his footing on the board, and with a swing he threw his trembling body in through the opening and onto the hard floor.

He was incapable of rejoicing; without looking around, with a dull feeling of something like hate for the absurdity of these torments, he walked into one of the houses and down the dilapidated staircase and stepped out again into an alleyway that was ugly and ordinary. But he was already very sad and tired and could not think of anything that seemed worth being happy about. In a strange way, everything had fallen away from him; empty and deserted by life itself, he walked through this alley, and the next, and the next. He went along in a direction he knew would bring him back to the part of the city where the rich people lived and where he could look for lodging for the night. For he felt a great desire for a bed. With childlike longing he remembered the beauty of his own wide bed, and he recalled, too, the beds that the great king of the past had erected for himself and his companions when they married the daughters of the kings they had conquered: a bed of gold for himself, of silver for the others, borne by griffins and winged bulls. Meantime he had come to the low-set houses where the soldiers lived. He paid no attention to them. At a latticed window sat a couple of soldiers with yellowish faces and sad eyes; they shouted something at him. He raised his head and breathed the musty smell that came from the room, a particularly oppressive smell. But he did not understand what they wanted of him. However, they had startled him out of his blank and aimless wandering, so now he looked into the courtyard as he passed the gate. The yard was very large and sad, and because the sun was just setting, it seemed even larger and sadder. There were very few people in it, and the houses that surrounded it were low and of a dirty yellow color. This made it even larger and more desolate. At one spot, roughly twenty horses were tethered in a straight line; in front of each one there knelt a soldier in a stable smock of dirty twill, washing its hooves. Far in the distance, out of a gate, came many others in similar outfits of twill, two by two. They walked slowly, with dragging steps, and carried heavy sacks on their shoulders. Only when they came closer did he see that the open sacks they lugged along in silence had bread in them. He watched as they disappeared in a gateway, wandering on as if under the weight of some ugly, treacherous burden, carrying their bread in the same kind of sacks as clothed the sadness of their bodies.

Then he went over to the ones who were on their knees before their horses, washing their hooves. Here, too, each looked like the other, and they all resembled the ones at the window and those who were carrying the bread. They must have come from neighboring villages. They, too, spoke hardly a word to one another. Since it was very hard for them to hold the horses' front feet, their heads swayed and their tired, yellowish faces moved up and down as if in a strong wind. The heads of most of the horses were ugly and had a look of malice about them, with their laid-back ears and their raised upper lips exposing the corner teeth of their upper jaws. For the most part they also had angry, rolling eyes and a strange way of expelling the air impatiently and contemptuously from curled-back nostrils. The last horse in line was particularly powerful and ugly. With its great teeth it tried to bite the shoulder of the man kneeling before it, drying its washed hoof. The man had such hollow cheeks and in his weary eyes such a deathly sad expression that the merchant's son was overcome by deep and bitter compassion. He wanted to give the wretched fellow a present, to cheer him up if only for a moment, and reached into his pocket for silver coins. He found none and remembered that he had tried to give the last ones to the child in the greenhouse, who had scattered them at his feet with such an angry look. He started to look for a gold coin, for he had put seven or eight into his pocket for his journey.

At that moment the horse turned its head and looked at him with ears treacherously laid back and rolling eyes that looked even more angry and wild because of a scar running straight across its ugly head just at the level of its eyes. At this ugly sight he was struck with a lightning-like memory of a long-forgotten human face. However hard he might have tried, he would never have been capable of summoning up the features of this person's face; but now there they were. However, the memory that came with the face was not so clear. He knew only that it came from the time when he was twelve years old, from a time the memory of which was associated somehow with the fragrance of sweet, warm, shelled almonds.

And he knew that it was the contorted face of an ugly poor man whom he had seen a single time in his father's store. And that his face was contorted with fear, because people were threatening him because he had a large gold piece and would not say where he had gotten it.

While the face dissolved again, his fingers searched the folds of his clothes; and when a sudden, vague thought restrained him, he drew out his hand hesitantly and in doing so cast the piece of jewelry with the beryl, wrapped in the silk paper, under the horse's feet. He bent down; the horse, kicking sideways with all its force, drove its hoof into his loins, and he fell over backward. He moaned aloud, his knees were drawn up, and he kept beating his heels on the ground. A couple of the soldiers rose and picked him up by the shoulders and under his knees. He sensed the smell of their clothes, the same musty, hopeless smell that earlier had come out of the room and onto the street, and he tried to recall where it was he had breathed it before, long, long ago; with this he lost consciousness. They carried him away over a low stairway, through a long, half-darkened passageway, into one of their rooms, and laid him on a low iron bed. Then they searched his clothing, took the little chain and the seven gold pieces, and finally, taking pity on his incessant moaning, they went to get one of their surgeons.

After a time he opened his eyes and became conscious of his tormenting pain. What caused him even greater terror and fear, however, was to be alone in this desolate room. With effort he turned his eyes in their aching sockets and, looking toward the wall, caught sight of three loaves of the kind of bread they had been carrying across the courtyard.

Otherwise there was nothing in the room but hard low beds and the smell of the dried rushes with which the beds were stuffed, and that other musty, desolate smell.

For a while the only things that occupied him were his pain and his suffocating, mortal fear, compared to which the pain was a relief. Then for a moment he was able to forget his mortal fear and wonder how all this had come to pass.

Then he felt another kind of fear, a piercing, less oppressive one, a fear he was not feeling for the first time; but now he felt it as something he had to overcome. And he clenched his fists and cursed his servants, who had driven him to his death, one to the city, the old woman into the jeweler's shop, the girl into the back room, the child, through the treacherous likeness of her counterpart, into the greenhouse, from which he saw himself reel dizzily over dreadful stairs and bridges, until he lay beneath the horse's hoof. Then he fell back into great, dull fear. He whimpered like a child, not from pain but from misery, and his teeth were chattering.

With a great feeling of bitterness he stared back into his life and denied everything that had been dear to him. He hated his premature death so much that he hated his life because it had led him there. This wild inner raging consumed his last strength. He was dizzy and for a time he slept a groggy, restless sleep. Then he awoke and felt like screaming because he was still alone, but his voice failed. Finally, he vomited bile, then blood, and died with his features contorted, his lips so torn that his teeth and gums were laid bare, giving him an alien, threatening expression.

—§—

Translated by Frank G. Ryder

A Chinese Fairy-Tale

LAURENCE HOUSMAN

iki-pu was a small grub of a thing; but he had a true love of Art deep down in his soul. There it hung mewing and complaining, struggling to work its way out through the raw exterior that bound it.

Tiki-pu's master professed to be an artist: he had apprentices and students, who came daily to work under him, and a large studio littered about with the performances of himself and his pupils. On the walls hung also a few real works by the older men, all long since dead.

This studio Tiki-pu swept; for those who worked in it he ground colours, washed brushes, and ran errands, bringing them their dog chops and bird's nest soup from the nearest eating-house whenever they were too busy to go out to it themselves. He himself had to feed mainly on the breadcrumbs which the students screwed into pellets for their drawings and then threw about upon the floor. It was on the floor, also, that he had to sleep at night.

Tiki-pu looked after the blinds, and mended the paper window-panes, which were often broken when the apprentices threw their brushes and mahl-sticks at him. Also he strained rice-paper over the linen-stretchers, ready for the painters to work on; and for a treat, now and then, a lazy one would allow him to mix a colour for him. Then it was that Tiki-pu's soul came down into his finger-tips, and his heart beat so that he gasped for joy. Oh, the yellows and the greens, and the lakes and the cobalts, and the purples which sprang from the blending of them! Sometimes it was all he could do to keep himself from crying out.

Tiki-pu, while he squatted and ground at the colour-powders, would listen to his master lecturing to the students. He knew by heart the names of all the painters and their schools, and the name of the great leader of them all who had lived and passed from their midst more than three hundred years ago; he knew that too, a name like the sound of the wind, Wio-wani: the big picture at the end of the studio was by him.

That picture! To Tiki-pu it seemed worth all the rest of the world put together. He knew, too, the story which was told of it, making it as holy to his eyes as the tombs of his own ancestors. The apprentices joked over it, calling it "Wio-wani's back-door," "Wio-wani's night-cap," and many other nicknames; but Tiki-pu was quite sure, since the picture was so beautiful, that the story must be true.

Wio-wani, at the end of a long life, had painted it; a garden full of trees and sunlight, with high-standing flowers and green paths, and in their midst a palace. "The place where I would like to rest," said Wio-wani, when it was finished.

So beautiful was it then, that the Emperor himself had come to see it; and gazing enviously at those peaceful walks, and the palace nestling among the trees, had sighed and owned that he too would be glad of such a resting-place. Then Wio-wani stepped into the picture, and walked away along a path till he came, looking quite small and far-off, to a low door in the palace-wall. Opening it, he turned and beckoned to the Emperor; but the Emperor did not follow; so Wio-wani went in by himself, and shut the door between himself and the world for ever.

That happened three hundred years ago; but for Tiki-pu the story was as fresh and true as if it had happened yesterday. When he was left to himself in the studio, all alone and locked up for the night, Tiki-pu used to go and stare at the picture till it was too dark to see, and at the little palace with the door in its wall by which Wio-wani had disappeared out of life. Then his soul would go down into his finger-tips, and he would knock softly and fearfully at the beautifully painted door, saying, "Wio-wani, are you there?"

Little by little in the long-thinking nights, and the slow early mornings when light began to creep back through the papered windows of the studio, Tiki-pu's soul became too much for him. He who could strain paper, and grind colours, and wash brushes, had everything within reach for becoming an artist, if it was the will of fate that he should be one.

He began timidly at first, but in a little while he grew bold. With the first wash of light he was up from his couch on the hard floor, and was daubing his soul out on scraps, and odds-and-ends, and stolen pieces of rice-paper.

Before long the short spell of daylight which lay between dawn and the arrival of the apprentices to their work did not suffice him. It took him so long to hide all traces of his doings, to wash out the brushes, and rinse clean the paint-pots he had used, and on the top of that to get the studio swept and dusted, that there was hardly time left him in which to indulge the itching appetite in his fingers.

Driven by necessity, he became a pilferer of candle-ends, picking them from their sockets in the lanterns which the students carried on dark nights. Now and then one of these would remember that, when last used, his lantern had had a candle in it, and would accuse Tiki-pu of having stolen it. "It is true," he would confess; "I was hungry—I have eaten it." The lie was so probable, he was believed easily, and was well beaten accordingly. Down in the ragged linings of his coat Tiki-pu could hear the candle-ends rattling as the buffeting and chastisement fell upon him, and often he trembled lest his hoard should be discovered. But the truth of the matter never leaked out; and at night, as soon as he guessed that all the world outside was in bed, Tiki-pu would mount one of his candles on a wooden stand and paint by the light of it, blinding himself over his task, till the dawn came and gave him a better and cheaper light to work by.

Tiki-pu quite hugged himself over the results; he believed he was doing very well. "If only Wio-wani were here to teach me," thought he, "I would be in the way of becoming a great painter!"

The resolution came to him one night that Wio-wani *should* teach him. So he took a large piece of rice-paper and strained it, and sitting down opposite "Wio-wani's back-door," began painting. He had never set himself so big a task as this; by the dim stumbling light of his candle he strained his eyes nearly blind over the difficulties of it; and at last was almost driven to despair. How the trees stood row behind row, with air and sunlight between, and how the path went in and out, winding its way up to the little door in the palace-wall were mysteries he could not fathom. He peered and peered and dropped tears into his paint-pots; but the secret of the mystery of such painting was far beyond him.

The door in the palace-wall opened; out came a little old man and began walking down the pathway towards him.

The soul of Tiki-pu gave a sharp leap in his grubby little body. "That must be Wio-wani himself and no other!" cried his soul.

Tiki-pu pulled off his cap and threw himself down on the floor with reverent grovellings. When he dared to look up again Wio-wani stood over him big and fine; just within the edge of his canvas he stood and reached out a hand.

"Come along with me, Tiki-pu!" said the great one. "If you want to know how to paint I will teach you."

"Oh, Wio-wani, were you there all the while?" cried Tiki-pu ecstatically, leaping up and clutching with his smeary little puds the hand which the old man extended to him.

"I was there," said Wio-wani, "looking at you out of my little window. Come along in!"

Tiki-pu took a heave and swung himself into the picture, and fairly capered when he found his feet among the flowers of Wio-wani's beautiful garden. Wio-wani had turned, and was ambling gently back to the door of his palace, beckoning to the small one to follow him; and there stood Tiki-pu, opening his mouth like a fish to all the wonders that surrounded him. "Celestiality, may I speak?" he said suddenly.

"Speak," replied Wio-wani; "what is it?"

"The Emperor, was he not the very flower of fools not to follow when you told him?"

"I cannot say," answered Wio-wani, "but he certainly was no artist."

Then he opened the door, that door which he had so beautifully painted, and led Tiki-pu in. And outside, the little candle-end sat and guttered by itself, till the wick fell overboard, and the flame kicked itself out, leaving the studio in darkness and solitude to wait for the growings of another dawn.

It was full day before Tiki-pu reappeared; he came running down the green path in great haste, jumped out of the frame on to the studio floor, and began tidying up his own messes of the night and the apprentices' of the previous day. Only just in time did he have things ready by the hour when his master and the others returned to their work.

All that day they kept scratching their left ears, and could not think why; but Tiki-pu knew, for he was saying over to himself all the things that Wio-wani, the great painter, had been saying about them and their precious productions. And as he ground their colours for them and washed their brushes, and filled his famished little body with the breadcrumbs they threw away, little they guessed from what an immeasurable distance he looked down upon them all, and had Wio-wani's word for it tickling his right ear all the day long.

Now before long Tiki-pu's master noticed a change in him; and though he bullied him, and thrashed him, and did all that a careful master should do, he could not get the change out of him. So in a short while he grew suspicious. "What is the boy up to?" he wondered. "I have my eye on him all day: it must be at night that he gets into mischief."

It did not take Tiki-pu's master a night's watching to find that something surreptitious was certainly going on. When it was dark he took up his post outside the studio, to see whether by any chance Tiki-pu had some way of getting out; and before long he saw a faint light showing through the window.

So he came and thrust his finger softly through one of the panes, and put his eye to the hole.

There inside was a candle burning on a stand, and Tiki-pu squatting with paint-pots and brush in front of Wio-Wani's last masterpiece.

"What fine piece of burglary is this?" thought he; "what serpent have I been harbouring in my bosom? Is this beast of a grub of a boy thinking to make himself a painter and cut me out of my reputation and prosperity?" For even at that distance he could perceive plainly that the work of this boy went head and shoulders beyond his, or that of any painter then living.

Presently Wio-wani opened his door and came down the path, as was his habit now each night, to call Tiki-pu to his lesson. He advanced to the front of his picture and beckoned for Tiki-pu to come in with him; and Tiki-pu's master grew clammy at the knees as he beheld Tiki-pu catch hold of Wio-wani's hand and jump into the picture, and skip up the green path by Wio-wani's side, and in through the little door that Wio-wani had painted so beautifully in the end wall of his palace!

For a time Tiki-pu's master stood glued to the spot with grief and horror. "Oh, you deadly little underling! Oh, you poisonous little caretaker, you parasite, you vampire, you fly in amber!" cried he, "is that where you get your training? Is it there that you dare to go trespassing; into a picture that I purchased for my own pleasure and profit, and not at all for yours? Very soon we will see whom it really belongs to!"

He ripped out the paper of the largest window-pane and pushed his way through into the studio. Then in great haste he took up paint-pot and brush, and sacrilegiously set himself to work upon Wio-wani's last masterpiece. In the place of the doorway by which Tiki-pu had entered he painted a solid brick wall; twice over he painted it, making it two bricks thick; brick by brick he painted it, and mortared every brick to its place. And when he had quite finished he laughed, and called "Good-night, Tiki-pu!" and went home to bed quite happy.

The next day all the apprentices were wondering what had become of Tiki-pu; but as the master himself said nothing, and as another boy came to act as colour-grinder and brush-washer to the establishment, they very soon forgot all about him.

In the studio, the master used to sit at work with his students all about him, and a mind full of ease and contentment. Now and then he would throw a glance across to the bricked-up doorway of Wio-wani's palace, and laugh to himself, thinking how well he had served out Tiki-pu for his treachery and presumption.

One day—it was five years after the disappearance of Tiki-pu—he was giving his apprentices a lecture on the glories and the beauties and the wonders of Wio-wani's painting—how nothing for colour could excel, or for mystery could equal it. To add point to his eloquence, he stood waving his hands before Wio-wani's last masterpiece, and all his students and apprentices sat round him and looked.

Suddenly he stopped at mid-word, and broke off in the full flight of his eloquence, as he saw something like a hand come and take down the top brick from the face of paint which he had laid over the little door in the palace-wall which Wio-wani had so beautifully painted. In another moment there was no doubt about it; brick by brick the wall was being pulled down, in spite of its double thickness.

The lecturer was altogether too dumbfounded and terrified to utter a word. He and all his apprentices stood round and stared while the demolition of the wall proceeded. Before long he recognised Wio-wani with his flowing white beard; it was his handiwork, this pulling down of the wall! He still had a brick in his hand when he stepped through the opening that he had made, and close after him stepped Tiki-pu!

Tiki-pu was grown tall and strong—he was even handsome; but for all that his old master recognised him, and saw with an envious foreboding that under his arms he carried many rolls and stretchers and portfolios, and other belongings of his craft. Clearly Tiki-pu was coming back into the world, and was going to be a great painter.

Down the garden-path came Wio-wani, and Tiki-pu walked after him; Tiki-pu was so tall that his head stood well over Wio-wani's shoulders—old man and young man together made a handsome pair.

How big Wio-wani grew as he walked down the avenues of his garden and into the foreground of his picture! and how big the brick in his hand! and ah, how angry he seemed!

Wio-wani came right down to the edge of the picture-frame and held up the brick. "What did you do that for?" he asked.

"I . . . didn't!" Tiki-pu's old master was beginning to reply; and the lie was still rolling on his tongue when the weight of the brick-bat, hurled by the stout arm of Wio-wani, felled him. After that he never spoke again. That brick-bat, which he himself had reared, became his own tombstone.

Just inside the picture-frame stood Tiki-pu, kissing the wonderful hands of Wio-wani, which had taught him all their skill. "Good-bye, Tiki-pu!" said Wio-wani, embracing him tenderly. "Now I am sending my second self into the world. When you are tired and want rest come back to me: old Wio-wani will take you in."

Tiki-pu was sobbing, and the tears were running down his cheeks as he stepped out of Wio-wani's wonderfully painted garden and stood once more upon earth. Turning, he saw the old man walking away along the path toward the little door under the palace-wall. At the door, Wio-wani turned back and waved his hand for the last time. Tiki-pu still stood watching him. Then the door opened and shut, and Wio-wani was gone. Softly as a flower the picture seemed to have folded its leaves over him.

Tiki-pu leaned a wet face against the picture and kissed the door in the palace-wall which Wio-wani had painted so beautifully. "O Wio-wani, dear master," he cried, "are you there?"

He waited, and called again, but no voice answered him.

The Queen of Quok
L. Frank Baum

A king once died, as kings are apt to do, being as liable to shortness of breath as other mortals.

It was high time this king abandoned his earth life, for he had lived in a sadly extravagant manner, and his subjects could spare him without the slightest inconvenience.

His father had left him a full treasury, both money and jewels being in abundance. But the foolish king just deceased had squandered every penny in riotous living. He had then taxed his subjects until most of them became paupers, and this money vanished in more riotous living. Next he sold all the grand old furniture in the palace; all the silver and gold plate and bric-a-brac; all the rich carpets and furnishings and even his own kingly wardrobe, reserving only a soiled and moth-eaten ermine robe to fold over his threadbare raiment. And he spent the money in further riotous living.

Don't ask me to explain what riotous living is. I only know, from hearsay, that it is an excellent way to get rid of money. And so this spendthrift king found it.

He now picked all the magnificent jewels from his kingly crown and from the round ball on the top of his scepter, and sold them and spent the money. Riotous living, of course. But at last he was at the end of his resources. He couldn't sell the crown itself, because no one but the king had the right to

wear it. Neither could he sell the royal palace, because only the king had
the right to live there.

So, finally, he found himself reduced to a bare palace, containing only
a big mahogany bedstead that he slept in, a small stool on which he sat to
pull off his shoes, and the moth-eaten ermine robe.

In this strait he was reduced to the necessity of borrowing an occasional
dime from his chief counselor, with which to buy a ham sandwich. And the
chief counselor hadn't many dimes. One who counseled his king so foolishly
was likely to ruin his own prospects as well.

So the king, having nothing more to live for, died suddenly and left a
ten-year-old son to inherit the dismantled kingdom, the moth-eaten robe,
and the jewel-stripped crown.

No one envied the child, who had scarcely been thought of until he
became king himself. Then he was recognized as a personage of some importance, and the politicians and hangers-on, headed by the chief counselor
of the kingdom, held a meeting to determine what could be done for him.

These folk had helped the old king to live riotously while his money
lasted, and now they were poor and too proud to work. So they tried to think

of a plan that would bring more money into the little king's treasury, where it would be handy for them to help themselves.

After the meeting was over, the chief counselor came to the young king, who was playing peg-top in the courtyard, and said:

"Your Majesty, we have thought of a way to restore your kingdom to its former power and magnificence."

"All right," replied his majesty carelessly. "How will you do it?"

"By marrying you to a lady of great wealth," replied the counselor.

"Marrying me!" cried the king. "Why, I am only ten years old!"

"I know; it is to be regretted. But your majesty will grow older, and the affairs of the kingdom demand that you marry a wife."

"Can't I marry a mother instead?" asked the poor little king, who had lost his mother when a baby.

"Certainly not," declared the counselor. "To marry a mother would be illegal; to marry a wife is right and proper."

"Can't you marry her yourself?" inquired his majesty, aiming his peg-top at the chief counselor's toe, and laughing to see how he jumped to escape it.

"Let me explain," said the other. "You haven't a penny in the world, but you have a kingdom. There are many rich women who would be glad to give their wealth in exchange for a queen's coronet—even if the king is but a child. So we have decided to advertise that the one who bids the highest shall become the queen of Quok."

"If I must marry at all," said the king, after a moment's thought, "I prefer to marry Nyana, the armorer's daughter."

"She is too poor," replied the counselor.

"Her teeth are pearls, her eyes are amethysts, and her hair is gold," declared the little king.

"True, Your Majesty. But consider that your wife's wealth must be used. How would Nyana look after you have pulled her teeth of pearls, plucked out her amethyst eyes, and shaved her golden head?"

The boy shuddered.

"Have your own way," he said despairingly. "Only let the lady be as dainty as possible and a good playfellow."

"We shall do our best," returned the chief counselor, and went away to advertise throughout the neighboring kingdoms for a wife for the boy king of Quok.

There were so many applicants for the privilege of marrying the little king that it was decided to put him up at auction, in order that the largest possible sum of money should be brought into the kingdom. So, on the day appointed, the ladies gathered at the palace from all the surrounding kingdoms—from Bilkon, Mulgravia, Junkum, and even as far away as the republic of Macvelt.

The chief counselor came to the palace early in the morning and had the king's face washed and his hair combed; and then he padded the inside of the crown with old newspapers to make it small enough to fit his majesty's head. It was a sorry-looking crown, having many big and little holes in it where the jewels had once been; and it had been neglected and knocked around until it was quite battered and tarnished. Yet, as the counselor said, it was the king's crown, and it was quite proper he should wear it on the solemn occasion of his auction.

Like all boys, be they kings or paupers, his majesty had torn and soiled his one suit of clothes, so that they were hardly presentable; and there was no money to buy new ones. Therefore, the counselor wound the old ermine robe around the king and sat him upon the stool in the middle of the otherwise empty audience chamber.

And around him stood all the courtiers and politicians and hangers-on of the kingdom, consisting of such people as were too proud or lazy to work for a living. There was a great number of them, you may be sure, and they made an imposing appearance.

Then the doors of the audience chamber were thrown open, and the wealthy ladies who aspired to being queen of Quok came trooping in. The king looked them over with much anxiety, and decided they were each and all old enough to be his grandmother, and ugly enough to scare away the crows from the royal cornfields. After which he lost interest in them.

But the rich ladies never looked at the poor little king squatting upon his stool. They gathered at once about the chief counselor, who acted as auctioneer.

"How much am I offered for the coronet of the queen of Quok?" asked the counselor, in a loud voice.

"Where is the coronet?" inquired a fussy old lady who had just buried her ninth husband and was worth several millions.

"There isn't any coronet at present," explained the chief counselor, "but whoever bids highest will have the right to wear one, and she can then buy it."

"Oh," said the fussy old lady, "I see." Then she added: "I'll bid fourteen dollars."

"Fourteen thousand dollars!" cried a sour-looking woman who was thin and tall and had wrinkles all over her skin—"like a frosted apple," the king thought.

The bidding now became fast and furious, and the poverty-stricken courtiers brightened up as the sum began to mount into the millions.

"He'll bring us a very pretty fortune after all," whispered one courtier to his comrade, "and then we shall have the pleasure of helping him spend it."

The king began to be anxious. All the women who looked at all kind-hearted or pleasant had stopped bidding for lack of money, and the slender old dame with the wrinkles seemed determined to get the coronet at any price, and with it the boy husband. This ancient creature finally became so excited that her wig got crosswise of her head and her false teeth kept slipping out, which horrified the little king greatly; but she would not give up.

At last the chief counselor ended the auction by crying out:

"Sold to Mary Ann Brodjinsky de la Porkus for three million, nine hundred thousand, six hundred and twenty-four dollars and sixteen cents!" And the sour-looking old woman paid the money in cash and on the spot, which proves this is a fairy story.

The king was so disturbed at the thought that he must marry this hideous creature that he began to wail and weep; whereupon the woman boxed his ears soundly. But the counselor reproved her for punishing her future husband in public, saying:

"You are not married yet. Wait until tomorrow, after the wedding takes place. Then you can abuse him as much as you wish. But at present we prefer to have people think this is a love match."

The poor king slept but little that night, so filled was he with terror of his future wife. Nor could he get the idea out of his head that he preferred to marry the armorer's daughter, who was about his own age. He tossed and tumbled around upon his hard bed until the moonlight came in at the window and lay like a great white sheet upon the bare floor. Finally, in turning over for the hundredth time, his hand struck against a secret spring in the headboard of the big mahogany bedstead, and at once, with a sharp click, a panel flew open.

The noise caused the king to look up, and seeing the open panel, he stood upon tiptoe and, reaching within, drew out a folded paper. It had several leaves fastened together like a book, and upon the first page was written:

> When the king is in trouble
> This leaf he must double
> And set it on fire
> To obtain his desire.

This was not very good poetry, but when the king had spelled it out in the moonlight, he was filled with joy.

"There's no doubt about my being in trouble," he exclaimed, "so I'll burn it at once, and see what happens."

He tore off the leaf and put the rest of the book in its secret hiding place. Then, folding the paper double, he placed it on the top of his stool, lighted a match and set fire to it.

It made a horrid smudge for so small a paper, and the king sat on the edge of the bed and watched it eagerly.

When the smoke cleared away, he was surprised to see, sitting upon the stool, a round little man, who, with folded arms and crossed legs, sat calmly facing the king and smoking a black briarwood pipe.

"Well, here I am," said he.

"So I see," replied the little king. "But how did you get here?"

"Didn't you burn the paper?" demanded the round man, by way of answer.

"Yes, I did," acknowledged the king.

"Then you are in trouble, and I've come to help you out of it. I'm the Slave of the Royal Bedstead."

"Oh!" said the king. "I didn't know there was one."

"Neither did your father, or he would not have been so foolish as to sell everything he had for money. By the way, it's lucky for you he did not sell this bedstead. Now, then, what do you want?"

"I'm not sure what I want," replied the king. "But I know what I don't want, and that is the old woman who is going to marry me."

"That's easy enough," said the Slave of the Royal Bedstead. "All you need do is to return her the money she paid the chief counselor and declare the match off. Don't be afraid. You are the king, and your word is law."

"To be sure," said his majesty. "But I am in great need of money. How am I going to live if the chief counselor returns to Mary Ann Brodjinsky her millions?"

"Phoo! That's easy enough," again answered the man, and putting his hand in his pocket, he drew out and tossed to the king an old-fashioned leather purse. "Keep that with you," said he, "and you will always be rich, for you can take out of the purse as many twenty-five-cent silver pieces as you wish, one at a time. No matter how often you take one out, another will instantly appear in its place within the purse."

"Thank you," said the king gratefully. "You have rendered me a rare favor; for now I shall have money for all my needs and will not be obliged to marry anyone. Thank you a thousand times!"

"Don't mention it," answered the other, puffing his pipe slowly and watching the smoke curl into the moonlight. "Such things are easy to me. Is that all you want?"

"All I can think of just now," returned the king.

"Then please close that secret panel in the bedstead," said the man. "The other leaves of the book may be of use to you sometime."

The boy stood upon the bed as before and, reaching up, closed the opening so that no one else could discover it. Then he turned to face his visitor, but the Slave of the Royal Bedstead had disappeared.

"I expected that," said his majesty, "yet I am sorry he did not wait to say goodbye."

With a lightened heart and a sense of great relief, the boy king placed the leathern purse underneath his pillow and, climbing into bed again, slept soundly until morning.

When the sun rose, his majesty rose also, refreshed and comforted, and the first thing he did was to send for the chief counselor.

That mighty personage arrived looking glum and unhappy, but the boy was too full of his own good fortune to notice it. Said he:

"I have decided not to marry anyone, for I have just come into a fortune of my own. Therefore, I command you to return to that old woman the money she has paid you for the right to wear the coronet of the queen of Quok. And make public declaration that the wedding will not take place."

Hearing this, the counselor began to tremble, for he saw the young king had decided to reign in earnest; and he looked so guilty that his majesty inquired:

"Well! What is the matter now?"

"Sire," replied the wretch, in a shaking voice, "I cannot return the woman her money, for I have lost it!"

"Lost it!" cried the king, in mingled astonishment and anger.

"Even so, Your Majesty. On my way home from the auction last night I stopped at the drugstore to get some potash lozenges for my throat, which was dry and hoarse with so much loud talking; and Your Majesty will admit it was through my efforts the woman was induced to pay so great a price. Well, going into the drugstore, I carelessly left the package of money lying on the seat of my carriage, and when I came out again it was gone. Nor was the thief anywhere to be seen."

"Did you call the police?" asked the king.

"Yes, I called; but they were all on the next block, and although they have promised to search for the robber, I have little hope they will ever find him."

The king sighed.

"What shall we do now?" he asked.

"I fear you must marry Mary Ann Brodjinsky," answered the chief counselor; "unless, indeed, you order the executioner to cut her head off."

"That would be wrong," declared the king. "The woman must not be harmed. And it is just that we return her money, for I will not marry her under any circumstances."

"Is that private fortune you mentioned large enough to repay her?" asked the counselor.

"Why, yes," said the king thoughtfully, "but it will take some time to do it, and that shall be your task. Call the woman here."

The counselor went in search of Mary Ann, who, when she heard she was not to become a queen but would receive her money back, flew into a violent passion and boxed the chief counselor's ears so viciously that they stung for nearly an hour. But she followed him into the king's audience chamber, where she demanded her money in a loud voice, claiming as well the interest due upon it overnight.

"The counselor has lost your money," said the boy king, "but he shall pay you every penny out of my own private purse. I fear, however, you will be obliged to take it in small change."

"That will not matter," she said, scowling upon the counselor as if she longed to reach his ears again. "I don't care how small the change is so long as I get every penny that belongs to me, and the interest. Where is it?"

"Here," answered the king, handing the counselor the leathern purse. "It is all in silver quarters, and they must be taken from the purse one at a time; but there will be plenty to pay your demands, and to spare."

So, there being no chairs, the counselor sat down upon the floor in one corner and began counting out silver twenty-five-cent pieces from the purse, one by one. And the old woman sat upon the floor opposite him and took each piece of money from his hand.

It was a large sum: three million, nine hundred thousand, six hundred and twenty-four dollars and sixteen cents. And it takes four times as many twenty-five-cent pieces as it would dollars to make up the amount.

The king left them sitting there and went to school, and often thereafter he came to the counselor and interrupted him long enough to get from the purse what money he needed to reign in a proper and dignified manner. This somewhat delayed the counting, but as it was a long job anyway, that did not matter much.

The king grew to manhood and married the pretty daughter of the armorer, and they now have two lovely children of their own. Once in a while they go into the big audience chamber of the palace and let the little ones watch the aged, hoary-headed counselor count out silver twenty-five-cent pieces to a withered old woman, who watches his every movement to see that he does not cheat her.

It is a big sum, three million, nine hundred thousand, six hundred and twenty-four dollars and sixteen cents in twenty-five-cent pieces.

But this is how the counselor was punished for being so careless with the woman's money. And this is how Mary Ann Brodjinsky de la Porkus was also punished for wishing to marry a ten-year-old king in order that she might wear the coronet of the queen of Quok.

§

Dreams That Have No Moral

‹ WILLIAM BUTLER YEATS ›

he friend who heard about Maive and the hazel-stick went to
the workhouse another day. She found the old people cold
and wretched, "like flies in winter," she said; but they forgot
the cold when they began to talk. A man had just left them
who had played cards in a rath with the people of faery, who
had played "very fair"; and one old man had seen an enchanted black pig one night, and there were two old people
my friend had heard quarrelling as to whether Raftery or
Callanan was the better poet. One had said of Raftery, "He was a big man,
and his songs have gone through the whole world. I remember him well. He
had a voice like the wind"; but the other was certain "that you would stand
in the snow to listen to Callanan." Presently an old man began to tell my
friend a story, and all listened delightedly, bursting into laughter now and
then. The story, which I am going to tell just as it was told, was one of those
old rambling moralless tales, which are the delight of the poor and the hard
driven, wherever life is left in its natural simplicity. They tell of a time when
nothing had consequences, when even if you were killed, if only you had a
good heart, somebody would bring you to life again with a touch of a rod,
and when if you were a prince and happened to look exactly like your brother,
you might go to bed with his queen, and have only a little quarrel afterwards.
We too, if we were so weak and poor that everything threatened us with

misfortune, might remember every old dream that has been strong enough to
fling the weight of the world from its shoulders.

There was a king one time who was very much put out because he had
no son, and he went at last to consult his chief adviser. And the chief adviser
said, "It's easy enough managed if you do as I tell you. Let you send some
one," says he, "to such a place to catch a fish. And when the fish is brought
in, give it to the queen, your wife, to eat."

So the king sent as he was told, and the fish was caught and brought
in, and he gave it to the cook, and bade her put it before the fire, but to be
careful with it, and not to let any blob or blister rise on it. But it is impossible
to cook a fish before the fire without the skin of it rising in some place or
other, and so there came a blob on the skin, and the cook put her finger on
it to smooth it down, and then she put her finger into her mouth to cool it,
and so she got a taste of the fish. And then it was sent up to the queen, and
she ate it, and what was left of it was thrown out into the yard, and there
were a mare in the yard and a greyhound, and they ate the bits that were
thrown out.

And before a year was out, the queen had a young son, and the cook
had a young son, and the mare had two foals, and the greyhound had two
pups.

And the two young sons were sent out for a while to some place to be
cared, and when they came back they were so much like one another no
person could know which was the queen's son and which was the cook's.
And the queen was vexed at that, and she went to the chief adviser and said,
"Tell me some way that I can know which is my own son, for I don't like to
be giving the same eating and drinking to the cook's son as to my own." "It
is easy to know that," said the chief adviser, "if you will do as I tell you. Go
you outside, and stand at the door they will be coming in by, and when they
see you, your own son will bow his head, but the cook's son will only laugh."

So she did that, and when her own son bowed his head, her servants
put a mark on him that she would know him again. And when they were all
sitting at their dinner after that, she said to Jack, that was the cook's son,
"It is time for you to go away out of this, for you are not my son." And her
own son, that we will call Bill, said, "Do not send him away, are we not
brothers?" But Jack said, "I would have been long ago out of this house if I
knew it was not my own father and mother owned it." And for all Bill could
say to him, he would not stop. But before he went, they were by the well
that was in the garden, and he said to Bill, "If harm ever happens to me,
that water on the top of the well will be blood, and the water below will be
honey."

Then he took one of the pups, and one of the two horses that were
foaled after the mare eating the fish, and the wind that was after him could

not catch him, and he caught the wind that was before him. And he went on till he came to a weaver's house, and he asked him for a lodging, and he gave it to him. And then he went on till he came to a king's house, and he sent in at the door to ask, "Did he want a servant?" "All I want," said the king, "is a boy that will drive out the cows to the field every morning, and bring them in at night to be milked." "I will do that for you," said Jack; so the king engaged him.

In the morning Jack was sent out with the four-and-twenty cows, and the place he was told to drive them to had not a blade of grass in it for them, but was full of stones. So Jack looked about for some place where there would be better grass, and after a while he saw a field with good green grass in it, and it belonging to a giant. So he knocked down a bit of the wall and drove them in, and he went up himself into an apple-tree and began to eat the apples. Then the giant came into the field. "Fee-faw-fum," says he, "I smell the blood of an Irishman. I see you where you are, up in the tree," he said; "you are too big for one mouthful, and too small for two mouthfuls, and I don't know what I'll do with you if I don't grind you up and make snuff for my nose." "As you are strong, be merciful," says Jack up in the tree. "Come down out of that, you little dwarf," said the giant, "or I'll tear you and the tree asunder." So Jack came down. "Would you sooner be driving red-hot knives into one another's hearts," said the giant, "or would you sooner be fighting one another on red-hot flags?" "Fighting on red-hot flags is what I'm used to at home," said Jack, "and your dirty feet will be sinking in them and my feet will be rising." So then they began the fight. The ground that was hard they made soft, and the ground that was soft they made hard, and they made spring wells come up through the green flags. They were like that all through the day, no one getting the upper hand of the other, and at last a little bird came and sat on the bush and said to Jack, "If you don't make an end of him by sunset, he'll make an end of you." Then Jack put out his strength, and he brought the giant down on his knees. "Give me my life," says the giant, "and I'll give you the best gift that I have." "What is that?" said Jack. "A sword that nothing can stand against." "Where is it to be found?" said Jack. "In that red door you see there in the hill." So Jack went and got it out. "Where will I try the sword?" says he. "Try it on that ugly black stump of a tree," says the giant. "I see nothing blacker or uglier than your own head," says Jack. And with that he made one stroke, and cut off the giant's head that it went into the air, and he caught it on the sword as it was coming down, and made two halves of it. "It is well for you I did not join the body again," said the head, "or you would have never been able to strike it off again." "I did not give you the chance of that," said Jack.

So he brought the cows home at evening, and every one wondered at all the milk they gave that night. And when the king was sitting at dinner with the princess, his daughter, and the rest, he said, "I think I only hear two roars from beyond to-night in place of three."

The next morning Jack went out again with the cows, and he saw another field full of grass, and he knocked down the wall and let the cows in. All happened the same as the day before, but the giant that came this time had two heads, and they fought together, and the little bird came and spoke to Jack as before. And when Jack had brought the giant down, he said, "Give me my life, and I'll give you the best thing I have." "What is that?" says Jack. "It's a suit that you can put on, and you will see every one but no one can see you." "Where is it?" said Jack. "It's inside that little red door at the side of the hill." So Jack went and brought out the suit. And then he cut off the giant's two heads, and caught them coming down and made four halves of them. And they said it was well for him he had not given them time to join the body.

That night when the cows came home they gave so much milk that all the vessels that could be found were filled up.

The next morning Jack went out again, and all happened as before, and the giant this time had four heads, and Jack made eight halves of them. And the giant had told him to go to a little blue door in the side of the hill, and there he got a pair of shoes that when you put them on would go faster than the wind.

That night the cows gave so much milk that there were not vessels enough to hold it, and it was given to tenants and to poor people passing the road, and the rest was thrown out at the windows. I was passing that way myself, and I got a drink of it.

That night the king said to Jack, "Why is it the cows are giving so much milk these days? Are you bringing them to any other grass?" "I am not," said Jack, "but I have a good stick, and whenever they would stop still or lie down, I give them blows of it, that they jump and leap over walls and stones and ditches; that's the way to make cows give plenty of milk."

And that night at the dinner, the king said, "I hear no roars at all."

The next morning, the king and the princess were watching at the window to see what would Jack do when he got to the field. And Jack knew they were there, and he got a stick, and began to batter the cows, that they went leaping and jumping over stones, and walls, and ditches. "There is no lie in what Jack said," said the king then.

Now there was a great serpent at that time used to come every seven years, and he had to get a king's daughter to eat, unless she would have some good man to fight for her. And it was the princess at the place Jack was had to be given to it that time, and the king had been feeding a bully underground for seven years, and you may believe he got the best of everything, to be ready to fight it.

And when the time came, the princess went out and the bully with her down to the shore, and when they got there what did he do, but to tie the princess to a tree, the way the serpent would be able to swallow her easy with no delay, and he himself went and hid up in an ivy-tree. And Jack knew what was going on, for the princess had told him about it, and had asked would he help her, but he said he would not. But he came out now, and he put on the sword he had taken from the first giant, and he came by the place the princess was, but she didn't know him. "Is that right for a princess to be tied to a tree?" said Jack. "It is not, indeed," said she, and she told him what had happened, and how the serpent was coming to take her. "If you will let me sleep for awhile with my head in your lap," said Jack, "you could wake me when it is coming." So he did that, and she awakened him when she saw the serpent coming, and Jack got up and fought with it, and drove it back into the sea. And then he cut the rope that fastened her, and he went away. The bully came down then out of the tree, and he brought the princess to where the king was, and he said, "I got a friend of mine to come and fight the serpent to-day, where I was a little timorous after being so long shut up underground, but I'll do the fighting myself to-morrow."

The next day they went out again, and the same thing happened; the bully tied up the princess where the serpent could come at her fair and easy, and went up himself to hide in the ivy-tree. Then Jack put on the suit he had taken from the second giant, and he walked out, and the princess did not know him, but she told him all that had happened yesterday, and how some young gentleman she did not know had come and saved her. So Jack asked might he lie down and take a sleep with his head in her lap, the way she could awake him. And all happened the same way as the day before. And the bully gave her up to the king, and said he had brought another of his friends to fight for her that day.

The next day she was brought down to the shore as before, and a great many people gathered to see the serpent that was coming to bring the king's daughter away. And Jack and the princess had talked as before. But when he was asleep this time, she thought she would make sure of being able to find him again, and she took out her scissors and cut off a piece of his hair, and made a little packet of it and put it away. And she did another thing, she took off one of the shoes that were on his feet.

And when she saw the serpent coming she woke him, and he said, "This time I will put the serpent in a way that he will eat no more king's daughters." So he took out the sword he had got from the giant, and he put it in at the back of the serpent's neck, the way blood and water came spouting out that went for fifty miles inland, and made an end of him. And then he made off, and no one saw what way he went, and the bully brought the princess to the king, and claimed to have saved her, and it is he who was made much of, and was the right-hand man after that.

But when the feast was made ready for the wedding, the princess took out the bit of hair she had, and she said she would marry no one but the man whose hair would match that, and she showed the shoe and said that she would marry no one whose foot would not fit that shoe as well. And the bully tried to put on the shoe, but so much as his toe would not go into it, and as to his hair, it didn't match at all to the bit of hair she had cut from the man that saved her.

So then the king gave a great ball, to bring all the chief men of the country together to try would the shoe fit any of them. And they were all going to carpenters and joiners getting bits of their feet cut off to try could they wear the shoe, but it was no use, not one of them could get it on.

Then the king went to his chief adviser and asked what could he do. And the chief adviser bade him to give another ball, and this time he said, "Give it to poor as well as rich."

So the ball was given, and many came flocking to it, but the shoe would not fit any one of them. And the chief adviser said, "Is every one here that belongs to the house?" "They are all here," said the king, "except the boy that minds the cows, and I would not like him to be coming up here."

Jack was below in the yard at the time, and he heard what the king said, and he was very angry, and he went and got his sword and came running up the stairs to strike off the king's head, but the man that kept the gate met him on the stairs before he could get to the king, and quieted him down, and when he got to the top of the stairs and the princess saw him, she gave a cry and ran into his arms. And they tried the shoe and it fitted him, and his hair matched to the piece that had been cut off. So then they were married, and a great feast was given for three days and three nights.

And at the end of that time, one morning there came a deer outside the window, with bells on it, and they ringing. And it called out, "Here is the hunt, where are the huntsmen and the hounds?" So when Jack heard that he got up and took his horse and his hound and went hunting the deer. When it was in the hollow he was on the hill, and when it was on the hill he was in the hollow, and that went on all through the day, and when night fell it went into a wood. And Jack went into the wood after it, and all he could see was a mud-wall cabin, and he went in, and there he saw an old woman, about two hundred years old, and she sitting over the fire. "Did you see a deer pass this way?" says Jack. "I did not," says she, "but it's too late now for you to be following a deer, let you stop the night here." "What will I do with my horse and my hound?" said Jack. "Here are two ribs of hair," says she, "and let you tie them up with them." So Jack went out and tied up the horse and the hound, and when he came in again the old woman said, "You killed my three sons, and I'm going to kill you now," and she put on a pair of boxing-gloves, each one of them nine stone weight, and the nails in them fifteen inches long. Then they began to fight, and Jack was getting the worst of it. "Help, hound!" he cried out, then "Squeeze, hair!" cried out the old woman, and the rib of hair that was about the hound's neck squeezed him to death. "Help, horse!" Jack called out, then "Squeeze, hair!" called out the old woman, and the rib of hair that was about the horse's neck began to tighten and squeeze him to death. Then the old woman made an end of Jack and threw him outside the door.

To go back now to Bill. He was out in the garden one day, and he took a look at the well, and what did he see but the water at the top was blood, and what was underneath was honey. So he went into the house again, and he said to his mother, "I will never eat a second meal at the same table, or sleep a second night in the same bed, till I know what is happening to Jack."

So he took the other horse and hound then, and set off, over hills where cock never crows and horn never sounds, and the devil never blows his bugle. And at last he came to the weaver's house, and when he went in, the weaver says, "You are welcome, and I can give you better treatment than I did the last time you came in to me," for he thought it was Jack who was there, they were so much like one another. "That is good," said Bill to himself," my brother has been here." And he gave the weaver the full of a basin of gold in the morning before he left.

Then he went on till he came to the king's house, and when he was at the door the princess came running down the stairs, and said, "Welcome to you back again." And all the people said, "It is a wonder you have gone hunting three days after your marriage, and to stop so long away." So he stopped that night with the princess, and she thought it was her own husband all the time.

And in the morning the deer came, and bells ringing on her, under the windows, and called out, "The hunt is here, where are the huntsmen and the hounds?" Then Bill got up and got his horse and his hound, and followed her over hills and hollows till they came to the wood, and there he saw nothing but the mud-wall cabin and the old woman sitting by the fire, and she bade him stop the night there, and gave him two ribs of hair to tie his horse and his hound with. But Bill was wittier than Jack was, and before he went out, he threw the ribs of hair into the fire secretly. When he came in the old woman said, "Your brother killed my three sons, and I killed him, and I'll kill you along with him." And she put her gloves on, and they began the fight, and then Bill called out, "Help, horse!" "Squeeze, hair!" called the old woman. "I can't squeeze, I'm in the fire," said the hair. And the horse came in and gave her a blow of his hoof. "Help, hound!" said Bill then. "Squeeze, hair!" said the old woman. "I can't, I'm in the fire," said the second hair. Then the hound put his teeth in her, and Bill brought her down, and she cried for mercy. "Give me my life," she said, "and I'll tell you where you'll get your brother again, and his hound and horse." "Where's that?" said

Bill. "Do you see that rod over the fire?" said she; "take it down and go outside the door where you'll see three green stones, and strike them with the rod, for they are your brother, and his horse and hound, and they'll come to life again." "I will, but I'll make a green stone of you first," said Bill, and he cut off her head with his sword.

Then he went out and struck the stones, and sure enough there were Jack and his horse and hound, alive and well. And they began striking other stones around, and men came from them, that had been turned to stones, hundreds and thousands of them.

Then they set out for home, but on the way they had some dispute or some argument together, for Jack was not well pleased to hear he had spent the night with his wife, and Bill got angry, and he struck Jack with the rod, and turned him to a green stone. And he went home, but the princess saw he had something on his mind, and he said then, "I have killed my brother." And he went back then and brought him to life, and they lived happy ever after, and they had children by the basketful, and threw them out by the shovelful. I was passing one time myself, and they called me in and gave me a cup of tea.

The Five Boons of Life
MARK TWAIN

I

In the morning of life came the good fairy with her basket, and said: "Here are gifts. Take one, leave the others. And be wary, choose wisely! oh, choose wisely! for only one of them is valuable."

The gifts were five: Fame, Love, Riches, Pleasure, Death. The youth said eagerly:

"There is no need to consider": and he chose Pleasure.

He went out into the world and sought out the pleasures that youth delights in. But each in its turn was short-lived and disappointing, vain and empty; and each, departing, mocked him. In the end he said: "Those years I have wasted. If I could but choose again, I would choose wisely."

II

The fairy appeared, and said:

"Four of the gifts remain. Choose once more; and oh remember—time is flying, and only one of them is precious."

The man considered long, then chose Love; and did not mark the tears that rose in the fairy's eyes.

After many, many years the man sat by a coffin, in an empty home.

And he communed with himself, saying: "One by one they have gone away and left me; and now she lies here, the dearest and the last. Desolation after desolation has swept over me; for each hour of happiness the treacherous trader, Love, has sold me I have paid a thousand hours of grief. Out of my heart of hearts I curse him."

III

"Choose again." It was the fairy speaking. "The years have taught you wisdom—surely it must be so. Three gifts remain. Only one of them has any worth—remember it, and choose warily."

The man reflected long, and then chose Fame; and the fairy, sighing, went her way.

Years went by and she came again, and stood behind the man where he sat solitary in the fading day, thinking. And she knew his thought:

"My name filled the world, and its praises were on every tongue, and it seemed well with me for a little while. How little a while it was! Then came envy; then detraction; then calumny; then hate; then persecution. Then derision, which is the beginning of the end. And last of all came pity, which is the funeral of fame. Oh, the bitterness and misery of renown! Target for mud in its prime, for contempt and compassion in its decay."

IV

"Choose yet again." It was the fairy's voice. "Two gifts remain. And do not despair. In the beginning there was but one that was precious, and it is still here."

"Wealth—which is power! How blind I was!" said the man. "Now, at last, life will be worth the living. I will spend, squander, dazzle. These mockers and despisers will crawl in the dirt before me, and I will feed my hungry heart with their envy. I will have all luxuries, all joys, all enchantments of the spirit, all contentments of the body that man holds dear. I will buy, buy, buy! deference, respect, esteem, worship—every pinchbeck grace of life the market of a trivial world can furnish forth. I have lost much time, and chosen badly heretofore, but let that pass; I was ignorant then, and could but take for best what seemed so."

Three short years went by, and a day came when the man sat shivering in a mean garret; and he was gaunt and wan and hollow-eyed, and clothed in rags; and he was gnawing a dry crust and mumbling:

"Curse all the world's gifts, for mockeries and gilded lies! And miscalled, every one. They are not gifts but merely lendings. Pleasure, Love, Fame, Riches, they are but temporary disguises for lasting realities—Pain, Grief, Shame, Poverty. The fairy said true: in all her store there was but one gift which was precious, only one that was not valueless. How poor and cheap and mean I know those others now to be, compared with that inestimable one, that dear and sweet and kindly one, that steeps in dreamless and enduring sleep the pains that persecute the body, and the shames and griefs that eat the mind and heart. Bring it! I am weary, I would rest."

V

The fairy came, bringing again four of the gifts, but Death was wanting. She said:

"I gave it to a mother's pet, a little child. It was ignorant, but trusted me, asking me to choose for it. You did not ask me to choose."

"Oh, miserable me! What is there left for me?"

"What not even you have deserved: the wanton insult of Old Age."

The Story of Jubal, Who Had No "I"

AUGUST STRINDBERG

nce upon a time there was a king whose name was John Lackland, and it is not difficult to imagine the reason why.

But another time there lived a great singer who was called Jubal, Who Had No "I," and I am now going to tell you the reason.

The name which he had inherited from his father, a soldier, was Peal, and undeniably there was music in the name. But nature had also given him a strong will, which stiffened his back like an iron bar, and that is a splendid gift, quite invaluable in the struggle for an existence. When he was still a baby, only just able to stammer a few words, he would never refer to his own little person as "he," as other babies do, but from the very first he spoke of himself as "I." You have no "I," said his parents. When he grew older, he expressed every little want or desire by "I will." But then his father said to him, "You have no will," and "Your will grows in the wood."

It was very foolish of the soldier, but he knew no better; he had learned to will only what he was ordered to do.

Young Peal thought it strange that he should be supposed to have no will when he had such a very strong one, but he let it pass.

When he had grown into a fine, strong youth, his father said to him one day, "What trade will you learn?"

The boy did not know; he had ceased to will anything, because he was forbidden to do so. It is true he had a leaning toward music, but he did not dare to say so, for he was convinced that his parents would not allow him to become a musician. Therefore, being an obedient son, he replied, "I don't will anything."

"Then you shall be a tapster," said the father.

Whether it was because the father knew a tapster, or because wine had a peculiar attraction for him, is a matter of indifference. It is quite enough to know that young Peal was sent to the wine vaults, and he might have fared a good deal worse.

There was a lovely smell of sealing wax and French wine in the cellars, and they were large and had vaulted roofs, like churches. When he sat at the casks and tapped the red wine, his heart was filled with gladness, and he sang, in an undertone at first, all sorts of tunes which he had picked up.

His master, to whom wine spelled life, loved song and gaiety, and never dreamed of stopping his singing; it sounded so well in the vaults, and, more-over, it attracted customers, which was a splendid thing from the master's point of view.

One day a commercial traveler dropped in; he had started life as an opera singer, and when he heard Peal, he was so delighted with him that he invited him to dinner.

They played ninepins, ate crabs with dill, drank punch, and, above everything, sang songs. Between two songs, and after they had sworn eternal friendship, the commercial traveler said:

"Why don't you go on the stage?"

"I?" answered Peal. "How could I do that?"

"All you have to do is to say 'I will.' "

This was a new doctrine, for since his third year young Peal had not used the words "I" and "will." He had trained himself to neither wish nor will, and he begged his friend not to lead him into temptation.

But the commercial traveler came again; he came many times, and once he was accompanied by a famous singer; and one evening Peal, after much applause from a professor of singing, took his fate into his own hands.

He said goodbye to his master, and over a glass of wine heartily thanked his friend the commercial traveler for having given him self-confidence and will—"will, that iron bar, which keeps a man's back erect and prevents him from groveling on all fours." And he swore a solemn oath never to forget his friend, who had taught him to have faith in himself.

Then he went to say goodbye to his parents.

"I will be a singer," he said in a loud voice, which echoed through the room.

The father glanced at the horsewhip, and the mother cried; but it was no use.

"Don't lose yourself, my darling boy," were the mother's last words.

§

Young Peal managed to raise enough money to enable him to go abroad. There he learned singing according to all the rules of the art, and in a few years' time he was a very great singer indeed. He earned much money and traveled with his own impresario.

Peal was prospering now and found no difficulty in saying "I will," or even "I command." His "I" grew to gigantic proportions, and he suffered no other "I"s near him. He denied himself nothing and did not put his light under a bushel. But now, as he was about to return to his own country, his impresario told him that no man could be a great singer and at the same time be called Peal; he advised him to adopt a more elegant name, a foreign name by preference, for that was the fashion.

The great man fought an inward struggle, for it is not a very nice thing to change one's name; it looks as if one were ashamed of one's father and mother, and is apt to create a bad impression.

But hearing that it was the fashion, he let it pass.

He opened his Bible to look for a name, for the Bible is the very best book for the purpose.

And when he came to Jubal, who was the son of Lamech, and "the father of all such as handle the harp and organ," he considered that he could not do better. The impresario, who was an Englishman, suggested that he should call himself Mr. Jubal, and Peal agreed. Thenceforth he was Mr. Jubal.

It was all quite harmless, of course, since it was the fashion, but it was nevertheless a strange thing: with the new name Peal had changed his nature. His past was blotted out. Mr. Jubal looked upon himself as an Englishman born and bred, spoke with a foreign accent, grew side-whiskers, and wore very high collars; a checked suit grew round him as the bark grows round a tree, apparently without any effort on his part. He carried himself stiffly, and when he met a friend in the street he acknowledged his friendly bow with the flicker of an eyelid. He never turned round if anybody called after him, and he always stood right in the middle of a streetcar.

He hardly knew himself.

He was now at home again, in his own country, and engaged to sing at the opera house. He played kings and prophets, heroes and demons, and he was so good an actor that whenever he rehearsed a part, he instantly became the part he impersonated.

One day he was strolling along the street. He was playing some sort of a demon, but he was also Mr. Jubal. Suddenly he heard a voice calling after him, "Peal!" He did not turn round, for no Englishman would do such a thing, and, moreover, his name was no longer Peal.

But the voice called again, "Peal!" and his friend the commercial traveler stood before him, looking at him searchingly, and yet with an expression of shy kindliness.

"Dear old Peal, it is you!" he said.

Mr. Jubal felt that a demon was taking possession of him; he opened his mouth so wide that he showed all his teeth, and bellowed a curt "No!"

Then his friend felt quite convinced that it was he and went away. He was an enlightened man, who knew men, the world, and himself inside out, and therefore he was neither sorry nor astonished.

But Mr. Jubal thought he was; he heard a voice within him saying, "Before the cock crow thou shalt deny me thrice," and he did what Saint Peter had done, he went away and wept bitterly. That is to say, he wept in imagination, but the demon in his heart laughed.

Thenceforth he was always laughing; he laughed at good and evil, sorrow and disgrace, at everything and everybody.

His father and mother knew, from the papers, who Mr. Jubal really was, but they never went to the opera house, for they fancied it had something to do with hoops and horses, and they objected to seeing their son in such surroundings.

Mr. Jubal was now the greatest living singer; he had lost a lot of his "I," but he still had his will.

Then his day came. There was a little ballet dancer who could bewitch men, and she bewitched Jubal. She bewitched him to such an extent that he asked her whether he might be hers. (He meant, of course, whether she would be his, but the other is a more polite way of expressing it.)

"You shall be mine," said the sorceress, "if I may take you."

"You may do anything you like," replied Jubal.

The girl took him at his word and they married. First of all he taught her to sing and play, and then he gave her everything she asked for. But since she was a sorceress, she always wanted the things which he most objected to giving to her, and so, gradually, she wrested his will from him and made him her slave.

One fine day Mrs. Jubal had become a great singer, so great that when the audience called "Jubal!" it was not Mr. but Mrs. Jubal who took the call.

Jubal, of course, longed to regain his former position, but he scorned to do it at his wife's expense.

The world began to forget him.

The brilliant circle of friends who had surrounded Mr. Jubal in his bachelor chambers now surrounded his wife, for it was she who was "Jubal."

Nobody wanted to talk to him or drink with him, and when he attempted to join in the conversation, nobody listened to his remarks; it was just as if he were not present, and his wife was treated as if she were an unmarried woman.

Then Mr. Jubal grew very lonely, and in his loneliness he began to frequent the cafés.

One evening he was at a restaurant, trying to find somebody to talk to, and ready to talk to anybody willing to listen to him. All at once he caught sight of his old friend the commercial traveler, sitting at a table by himself, evidently very bored. "Thank goodness," he thought, "here's somebody to spend an hour with—it's old Lundberg."

He went to Mr. Lundberg's table and said "Good evening." But no sooner had he done so than his friend's face changed in so extraordinary a manner that Jubal wondered whether he had made a mistake.

"Aren't you Lundberg?" he asked.

"Yes!"

"Don't you know me? I'm Jubal!"

"No!"

"Don't you know your old friend Peal?"

"Peal died a long time ago."

Then Jubal understood that he was, from a certain point of view, dead, and he went away.

On the following day he left the stage forever and opened a school for singing, with the title of professor.

Then he went to foreign countries and remained abroad for many years.

Sadness, for he mourned for himself as for a dead friend, and sorrow were fast making an old man of him. But he was glad that it should be so, for he thought, "If I'm old, it won't last much longer." But as he did not age quite as fast as he would have liked, he bought himself a wig with long white curls. He felt better after that, for it disguised him completely, so completely that he did not know himself.

With long strides, his hands crossed on his back, he walked up and down the pavements, lost in a brown study; he seemed to be looking for someone, or expecting someone. If his eyes met the glance of other eyes, he did not respond to the question in them; if anybody tried to make his acquaintance, he would never talk of anything but things and objects. And he never said "I" or "I find," but always "it seems." He had lost himself, as he discovered one day just as he was going to shave. He was sitting before his looking glass, his chin covered with a lather of soap; he raised the hand which held the razor and looked into the glass; then he beheld the room behind his back, but he could not see his face, and all at once he realized how matters stood. Now he was filled with a passionate yearning to find himself again. He had given the best part of himself to his wife, for she had his will, and so he decided to go and see her.

When he was back in his native country and walked through the streets in his white wig, not a soul recognized him. But a musician who had been in Italy, meeting him in town one day, said in a loud voice, "There goes a maestro!"

Immediately Jubal imagined that he was a great composer. He bought some music paper and started to write a score; that is to say, he wrote a number of long and short notes on the lines, some for the violins, of course, others for the woodwinds, and the remainder for the brass instruments. He sent his work to the Conservatoire. But nobody could play the music, because it was not music but only notes.

A little later on he was met by an artist who had been in Paris. "There goes a model!" said the artist. Jubal heard it, and at once believed that he was a model, for he believed everything that was said of him, because he did not know who or what he was.

Presently he remembered his wife, and he resolved to go and see her. He did go, but she had married again, and she and her second husband, who was a baron, had gone abroad.

At last he grew tired of his quest, and like all tired men, he felt a great yearning for his mother. He knew that she was a widow and lived in a cottage in the mountains, so one day he went to see her.

"Don't you know me?" he asked.

"What is your name?" asked the mother.

"My name is your son's name. Don't you know it?"

"My son's name was Peal, but yours is Jubal, and I don't know Jubal."

"You disown me?"

"As you disowned yourself and your mother."

"Why did you rob me of my will when I was a little child?"

"You gave your will to a woman."

"I had to, because it was the only way of winning her. But why did you tell me I had no will?"

"Well, your father told you that, my boy, and he knew no better; you must forgive him, for he is dead now. Children, you see, are not supposed to have a will of their own, but grown-up people are."

"How well you explain it all, Mother! Children are not supposed to have a will, but grown-up people are."

"Now, listen to me, Gustav," said his mother, "Gustav Peal . . ."

These were his two real names, and when he heard them from her lips, he became himself again. All the parts he had played—kings and demons, the maestro and the model—cut and ran, and he was but the son of his mother.

He put his head on her knees and said, "Now let me die here, for at last I am at home."

§

Translated by Ellie Schleussner

he terrible Czar Ivan wanted to lay tribute upon the neighboring princes and threatened them with a great war if they
would not send gold to Moscow, the white city. The princes,
after due deliberation, spoke as one man: "We give you three
riddles to solve. Come, on the day we appoint, to the east,
to the white stone, where we shall be gathered, and tell us
the three answers. If they are correct, we will give you the
twelve barrels of gold that you demand of us." At first Czar
Ivan Vessilievitch considered, but the many bells of his white city, Moscow,
disturbed him. So he called his wise men and councillors before him, and
each one who could not answer the riddles he caused to be led out to the
great red square, where the church of Vassily the Blessed was just being built,
and simply beheaded. Thus occupied, time passed so quickly for him that he
suddenly found himself on his way to the east, to the white stone by which
the princes waited. To none of the three questions had he any answer, but
the ride was long and there was still always the possibility that he might meet
a wise man; for at that time many wise men were in flight, as all kings had
the habit of ordering their heads cut off if they did not seem wise enough.
Now, as it happened, the Czar did not meet any of these, but one morning
he saw an old bearded peasant who was building a church. He had already
got as far as the framework of the roof and was laying on the small laths. It

seemed very odd that the old peasant should climb down from the church over and over again in order to fetch one by one the narrow laths, which were piled below, instead of taking a lot at a time in his long caftan. In this way he had to climb up and down continually, and there seemed to be no prospect of his ever getting all those hundreds of laths into place. So the Czar grew impatient. "Idiot," he cried (that is how one usually addresses the peasants in Russia), "you ought to load yourself up with your wood and then crawl up on the roof; that would be much simpler."

The peasant, who at the moment was on the ground, stood still, shielded his eyes with his hand, and replied: "That you must leave to me, Czar Ivan Vassilievitch; every man knows his own craft best; nevertheless, as you happen to be riding by, I will tell you the answer to the three riddles which you will have to know when you get to the white stone in the east, not at all far from here." And he divulged to him the three answers in turn. The Czar could hardly thank him for astonishment. "What shall I give you in reward?" he asked at last. "Nothing," said the peasant, and he fetched another lath and started up the ladder. "Stop," commanded the Czar. "This will never do. You must express a wish." "Well, Little Father, since you so command, give me one of the twelve barrels of gold which you will get from the princes of the east." "Good," nodded the Czar. "I will give you a barrel of gold." Then he rode quickly away, so that he should not forget the answers again.

Later, when the Czar had returned from the east with the twelve barrels of gold, he shut himself up in Moscow, in his palace, in the heart of the five-gated Kremlin, and he emptied one barrel after the other on the shining tiles of the hall, so that a veritable mountain of gold grew up, that cast a great black shadow on the floor. In his forgetfulness the Czar had emptied the twelfth cask too. He wanted to fill it up again, but it grieved him to have to take away so much gold from the glorious pile. In the night he went down into the courtyard, scooped fine sand into the barrel until it was three-quarters full, crept softly back into his palace, laid gold over the sand, and next morning sent the cask by messenger to that part of the broad land of Russia where the old peasant was building his church.

As he saw the messenger approaching, the peasant came down from the roof, which was still far from finished, and called out: "You need come no nearer, my friend. Go back, with your barrel which is three-quarters full of sand and one scant quarter of gold; I do not need it. Tell your master that up to now there has been no treason in Russia. And it is his own fault, should he notice that he cannot trust any man; for he has now shown the way of betrayal, and from century to century his example will find in all Russia many imitators. I do not need the gold, I can live without gold; I did not expect gold from him, but truth and righteousness. But he has deceived me. Say that to your master, the terrible Czar Ivan Vassilievitch, who sits in his white city of Moscow with his evil conscience and in a golden dress."

After riding awhile, the messenger looked back once more. The peasant and his church had vanished. And the piled laths no longer lay there; it was all empty, flat land. Then the man tore back in terror to Moscow, stood breathless before the Czar, and told somewhat incoherently what had happened and how the supposed peasant was no other than God himself.

Translated by M.D. Herter Norton and Nora Putscher-Wydenbruck

The Story of the Fairy Tale
CARL EWALD

Once upon a time, ever so many years ago, Truth suddenly vanished from out of the world.

When people perceived this, they were greatly alarmed and at once sent five wise men in search of Truth. They set out, one in this direction and one in that, all plentifully equipped with traveling expenses and good intentions. They sought for ten long years. Then they returned, each separately. While still at a distance, they waved their hats and shouted that they had found Truth.

The first stepped forward and declared that Truth was Science. He was not able to finish his report, however; for before he had done, another thrust him aside and shouted that that was a lie, that Truth was Theology and that he had found it. Now while these two were at loggerheads—for the Science man replied to the attack vigorously—there came a third and said, in beautiful words, that Love was Truth, without a doubt. Then came the fourth and stated, quite curtly, that he had Truth in his pocket, that it was Gold, and that all the rest was childish nonsense. At last came the fifth. He could not stand on his legs, gave a gurgling laugh, and said that Truth was Wine. He had found Truth in Wine, after looking everywhere.

Then the five wise men began to fight, and they pummeled one another so lustily that it was horrible to see. Science had its head broken, and Love was so greatly ill-treated that it had to change its clothes before it could show itself again in respectable society. Gold was so thoroughly stripped of every covering that people felt awkward about knowing it; and the bottle broke and Wine flowed away into the mud. But Theology came off worst of all: everybody had a blow at it and it received such a basting that it became the laughingstock of all beholders.

And people took sides, some with this one and some with that, and they shouted so loud that they could neither see nor hear for the din. But far away, at the extreme end of the earth, sat a few and mourned because they thought that Truth had gone to pieces and would never be made whole again.

Now as they sat there, a little girl came running up and said that she had found Truth. If they would just come with her—it was not very far— Truth was sitting in the midst of the world, in a green meadow.

Then there came a pause in the fighting, for the little girl looked so very sweet. First one went with her; then another; and ever more. . . . At last, they were all in the meadow and there discovered a figure the like of which they had never seen before. There was no distinguishing whether it was a man or a woman, an adult or a child. Its forehead was pure as that of one who knows no sin; its eyes deep and serious as those of one who has read into the heart of the whole world. Its mouth opened with the brightest smile and then quivered with a sadness greater than any could describe. Its hand was soft as a mother's and strong as the hand of a king; its foot trod the earth firmly, yet crushed not a flower. And then the figure had large, soft wings, like the birds that fly at night.

Now as they stood there and stared, the figure drew itself erect and cried, in a voice that sounded like bells ringing:

"I am Truth!"

"It's a Fairy Tale!" said Science.

"It's a Fairy Tale!" cried Theology and Love and Gold and Wine.

Then the five wise men and their followers went away, and they continued to fight until the world was shaken to its center.

But a few old and weary men and a few young men with ardent and eager souls and many women and thousands of children with great wide eyes: these remained in the meadow where the Fairy Tale was.

Translated by Alexander Teixeira de Mattos

The Seven Wives of Bluebeard

ANATOLE FRANCE

I

The strangest, the most varied, the most erroneous opinions have been expressed with regard to the famous individual commonly known as Bluebeard. None, perhaps, was less tenable than that which made of this gentleman a personification of the Sun. For this is what a certain school of comparative mythology set itself to do, some forty years ago. It informed the world that the seven wives of Bluebeard were the Dawns, and that his two brothers-in-law were the morning and the evening Twilight, identifying them with the Dioscuri, who delivered Helena when she was rapt away by Theseus. We must remind those readers who may feel tempted to believe this that in 1817 a learned librarian of Agen, Jean-Baptiste Pérés, demonstrated, in a highly plausible manner, that Napoleon had never existed and that the story of this supposed great captain was nothing but a solar myth. Despite the most ingenious diversions of the wits, we cannot possibly doubt that Bluebeard and Napoleon did both actually exist.

A hypothesis no better founded is that which consists in identifying Bluebeard with the Marshal de Rais, who was strangled by the arm of the law above the bridges of Nantes on 26 October 1440. Without inquiring, with M. Salomon Reinach, whether the marshal committed the crimes for which he was condemned, or whether his wealth, coveted by a greedy prince, did not in some degree contribute to his undoing, there is nothing in his life that resembles what we find in Bluebeard's; this alone is enough to prevent our confusing them or merging the two individuals into one.

Charles Perrault, who, about 1660, had the merit of composing the first biography of this *seigneur*, justly remarkable for having married seven wives, made him an accomplished villain and the most perfect model of cruelty that ever trod the earth. But it is permissible to doubt, if not his sincerity, at least the correctness of his information. He may, perhaps, have been prejudiced against his hero. He would not have been the first example of a poet or historian who liked to darken the colors of his pictures. If we have what seems a flattering portrait of Titus, it would seem, on the other hand, that Tacitus has painted Tiberius much blacker than the reality. Macbeth, whom legend and Shakespeare accuse of crimes, was in reality a just and a wise king. He never treacherously murdered the old king, Duncan. Duncan, while yet young, was defeated in a great battle and was found dead on the morrow at a spot called the Armorer's Shop. He had slain several of the kinsfolk of Gruchno, the wife of Macbeth. The latter made Scotland prosperous; he encouraged trade and was regarded as the defender of the middle classes, the true king of the townsmen. The nobles of the clans never forgave him for defeating Duncan, nor for protecting the artisans. They destroyed him and dishonored his memory. Once he was dead, the good king Macbeth was known only by the statements of his enemies. The genius of Shakespeare imposed these lies upon the human consciousness. I had long suspected that Bluebeard was the victim of a similar fatality. All the circumstances of his life, as I found them related, were far from satisfying my mind and from gratifying that craving for logic and lucidity by which I am incessantly consumed. On reflection, I perceived that they involved insurmountable difficulties. There was so great a desire to make me believe in the man's cruelty that it could not fail to make me doubt it.

These presentiments did not mislead me. My intuitions, which had their origin in a certain knowledge of human nature, were soon to be changed into certainty, based upon irrefutable proofs.

In the house of a stonecutter in Saint-Jean-des-Bois, I found several papers relating to Bluebeard: among others, his defense and an anonymous complaint against his murderers, which was not proceeded with, for what reasons I know not. These papers confirmed me in the belief that he was good and unfortunate, and that his memory has been overwhelmed by unworthy slanders. From that time forth, I regarded it as my duty to write his true history, without permitting myself any illusion as to the success of such an undertaking. I am well aware that this attempt at rehabilitation is destined to fall into silence and oblivion. How can the cold, naked Truth fight against the glittering enchantments of Falsehood?

II

Somewhere about 1650, there lived on his estate, between Compiègne and Pierrefonds, a wealthy noble, by name Bernard de Montragoux, whose ancestors had held the most important posts in the kingdom. But he dwelt far from the court, in that peaceful obscurity which then veiled all save that on which the king bestowed his glance. His castle, Guillettes, abounded in valuable furniture, gold and silver ware, tapestry and embroideries, which he kept in coffers. Not that he hid his treasures for fear of damaging them by use; he was, on the contrary, generous and magnificent. But in those days, in the country, the nobles willingly led a very simple life, feeding their people at their own table and dancing on Sundays with the girls of the village.

On certain occasions, however, they gave splendid entertainments, which contrasted with the dullness of everyday life. So it was necessary that they should hold a good deal of handsome furniture and beautiful tapestries in reserve. This was the case with Monsieur de Montragoux.

His castle, built in the Gothic period, had all its rudeness. From without, it looked wild and gloomy enough, with the stumps of its great towers, which had been thrown down at the time of the monarchy's troubles, in the reign of the late King Louis. Within, it offered a much pleasanter prospect. The rooms were decorated in the Italian taste, as was the great gallery on the ground floor, loaded with embossed decorations in high relief, pictures, and gilding.

At one end of this gallery there was a closet, usually known as the "little cabinet." This is the only name by which Charles Perrault refers to it. It is as well to note that it was also called the Cabinet of the Unfortunate Princesses, because a Florentine painter had portrayed on the walls the tragic stories of Dirce, daughter of the Sun, bound by the sons of Antiope to the horns of a bull; Niobe weeping on Mount Sipylus for her children, pierced by the divine arrows; and Procris inviting to her bosom the javelin of Cephalus. These figures had a look of life about them, and the porphyry tiles with which the floor was covered seemed dyed in the blood of these unhappy women. One of the doors of the cabinet gave upon the moat, which had no water in it.

The stables formed a sumptuous building, situated at some distance from the castle. They contained stalls for sixty horses, and coach houses for twelve gilded coaches. But what made Guillettes so bewitching a residence were the woods and canals surrounding it, in which one could devote oneself to the pleasures of angling and the chase.

Many of the dwellers in that countryside knew Monsieur de Montragoux only by the name of Bluebeard, for this was the only name that the common people gave him. And in truth his beard was blue, but it was blue only because it was black, and it was because it was so black that it was blue. Monsieur de Montragoux must not be imagined as having the monstrous aspect of the threefold Typhon whom one sees in Athens, laughing in his triple indigo-blue beard. We shall get much nearer the reality by comparing the *seigneur* of Guillettes to those actors or priests whose freshly shaven cheeks have a bluish gloss.

Monsieur de Montragoux did not wear a pointed beard like his grand-father at the court of King Henry II; nor did he wear it like a fan, as did his great-grandfather who was killed at the battle of Marignan. Like Monsieur de Turenne, he had only a slight mustache and a chin tuft; his cheeks had a bluish look; but whatever may have been said of him, this good gentleman was by no means disfigured thereby, nor did he inspire any fear on that account. He only looked the more virile, and if it made him look a little fierce, it had not the effect of making the women dislike him. Bernard de Montragoux was a very fine man, tall, broad across the shoulders, moderately stout, and well favored; albeit of a rustic habit, smacking of the woods rather than of drawing rooms and assemblies. Still, it is true that he did not please the ladies as much as he should have pleased them, built as he was, and wealthy. Shyness was the reason; shyness, not his beard. Women exercised an invincible at-traction for him and at the same time inspired him with an insuperable fear. He feared them as much as he loved them. This was the origin and initial cause of all his misfortunes. Seeing a lady for the first time, he would have died rather than speak to her, and however much attracted he may have been, he stood before her in gloomy silence. His feelings revealed themselves only through his eyes, which he rolled in a terrible manner. This timidity exposed him to every kind of misfortune, and above all, it prevented his forming a becoming connection with modest and reserved women; and be-trayed him, defenseless, to the attempts of the most impudent and audacious. This was his life's misfortune.

Left an orphan from his early youth and having rejected, owing to this sort of bashfulness and fear, which he was unable to overcome, the very advantageous and honorable alliances which had presented themselves, he married a Mlle Colette Passage, who had recently settled down in that part of the country, after amassing a little money by making a bear dance through the towns and villages of the kingdom. He loved her with all his soul. And to do her justice, there was something pleasing about her, though she was what she was: a fine woman with an ample bosom, and a complexion that was still sufficiently fresh, although a little sunburned by the open air. Great were her joy and surprise on first becoming a lady of quality. Her heart, which was not bad, was touched by the kindness of a husband in such a high position and with such a stout, powerful body, who was to her the most obedient of servants and devoted of lovers. But after a few months she grew weary because she could no longer go to and fro on the face of the earth. In the midst of wealth, overwhelmed with love and care, she could find no greater pleasure than that of going to see the companion of her wandering life, in the cellar where he languished with a chain round his neck and a ring through his nose, and kissing him on the eyes and weeping.

Seeing her full of care, Monsieur de Montragoux himself became careworn, and this only added to his companion's melancholy. The consideration and forethought which he lavished on her turned the poor woman's head. One morning, when he awoke, Monsieur de Montragoux found Colette no longer at his side. In vain he searched for her throughout the castle.

The door of the Cabinet of the Unfortunate Princesses was open. It was through this door that she had gone to reach the open country with her bear. The sorrow of Bluebeard was painful to behold. In spite of the innumerable messengers sent forth in search of her, no news was ever received of Colette Passage.

Monsieur de Montragoux was still mourning her when he happened to dance, at the fair of Guillettes, with Jeanne de La Cloche, daughter of the police lieutenant of Compiègne, who inspired him with love. He asked her in marriage and obtained her forthwith. She loved wine and drank it to excess. So much did this taste increase that after a few months she looked like a leather bottle with a round red face atop it. The worst of it was that this leather bottle would run mad, incessantly rolling about the reception rooms and the staircases, crying, swearing, and hiccuping, vomiting wine and insults at everything that got in her way. Monsieur de Montragoux was dazed with disgust and horror. But he quite suddenly recovered his courage and set himself, with as much firmness as patience, to cure his wife of so disgusting a vice. Prayers, remonstrances, supplications, and threats: he employed every possible means. All was useless. He forbade her wine from his cellar: she got it from outside, and was more abominably drunk than ever.

To deprive her of her taste for a beverage that she loved too well, he put valerian in the bottles. She thought he was trying to poison her, sprang upon him, and drove three inches of kitchen knife into his belly. He expected to die of it, but he did not abandon his habitual kindness.

"She is more to be pitied than blamed," he said.

One day, when he had forgotten to close the door of the Cabinet of the Unfortunate Princesses, Jeanne de La Cloche entered by it, quite out of her mind, as usual, and seeing the figures on the walls in postures of affliction, ready to give up the ghost, she mistook them for living women and fled terror-stricken into the country, screaming murder. Hearing Bluebeard calling her and running after her, she threw herself, mad with terror, into a pond and was there drowned. It is difficult to believe, yet certain, that her husband, so compassionate was his soul, was much afflicted by her death.

Six weeks after the accident, he quietly married Gigonne, the daughter of his steward, Traignel. She wore wooden shoes and smelled of onions. She was a fine-looking girl enough, except that she squinted with one eye and limped with one foot. As soon as she was married, this goose girl, bitten by foolish ambition, dreamed of nothing but further greatness and splendor. She was not satisfied that her brocade dresses were rich enough, her pearl necklaces beautiful enough, her rubies big enough, her coaches sufficiently gilded, her lakes, woods, and lands sufficiently vast. Bluebeard, who had never had any leaning toward ambition, trembled at the haughty humor of his spouse. Unaware, in his straightforward simplicity, whether the mistake lay in thinking magnificently, like his wife, or modestly, as he himself did, he accused himself of a mediocrity of mind which was thwarting the noble desires of his consort, and full of uncertainty, he would sometimes exhort her to taste with moderation the good things of this world, while at others he roused himself to pursue fortune along the verge of precipitous heights. He was prudent, but conjugal affection bore him beyond the reach of prudence. Gigonne thought of nothing but cutting a figure in the world, being received at court, and becoming the king's mistress. Unable to gain her point, she pined away with vexation, contracting a jaundice, of which she died. Bluebeard, full of lamentation, built her a magnificent tomb.

This worthy *seigneur*, overwhelmed by constant domestic adversity, would not perhaps have chosen another wife: but he was himself chosen for a husband by Mlle Blanche de Gibeaumex, the daughter of a cavalry officer who had but one ear; he used to relate that he had lost the other in the king's service. She was full of intelligence, which she employed in deceiving her husband. She betrayed him with every man of quality in the neighborhood. She was so dexterous that she deceived him in his own castle, almost under his very eyes, without his perceiving it. Poor Bluebeard assuredly suspected something, but he could not say what. Unfortunately for her, while she gave her whole mind to tricking her husband, she was not sufficiently careful in deceiving her lovers; by which I mean that she betrayed them, one for another. One day she was surprised in the Cabinet of the Unfortunate Princesses, in the company of a gentleman whom she loved, by a gentleman whom she had loved, and the latter, in a transport of jealousy, ran her through with his sword. A few hours later, the unfortunate lady was there found dead by one of the castle servants, and the fear inspired by the room increased.

Poor Bluebeard, learning at one blow of his ample dishonor and the tragic death of his wife, did not console himself for the latter misfortune by any consideration of the former. He had loved Blanche de Gibeaumex with a strange ardor, more dearly than he had loved Jeanne de La Cloche, Gigonne Traignel, or even Colette Passage. On learning that she had consistently betrayed him, and that now she would never betray him again, he experienced a grief and a mental perturbation which, far from being appeased, daily increased in violence. So intolerable were his sufferings that he contracted a malady which caused his life to be despaired of.

The physicians, having employed various medicines without effect, advised him that the only remedy proper to his complaint was to take a young wife. He then thought of his young cousin Angèle de La Garandine, who he believed would be willingly bestowed upon him, as she had no property. What encouraged him to take her to wife was the fact that she was reputed to be simple and ignorant of the world. Having been deceived by a woman of intelligence, he felt more comfortable with a fool. He married Mlle de La Garandine and quickly perceived the falsity of his calculations. Angèle was kind, Angèle was good, and Angèle loved him; she had not, in herself, any leanings toward evil, but the least astute person could quickly lead her astray at any moment. It was enough to tell her: "Do this for fear of bogies"; "Come in here or the werewolf will eat you"; or "Shut your eyes and take this drop of medicine," and the innocent girl would straightway do so, at the will of the rascals who wanted of her that which it was very natural to want of her, for she was pretty. Monsieur de Montragoux, injured and betrayed by this

innocent girl, as much as and more than he had been by Blanche de Gibeaumex, had the additional pain of knowing it, for Angèle was too candid to conceal anything from him. She used to tell him: "Sir, someone told me this; someone did that to me; someone took so-and-so away from me; I saw that; I felt so-and-so." And by her ingenuousness she caused her lord to suffer torments beyond imagination. He endured them like a Stoic. Still he finally had to tell the simple creature that she was a goose and to box her ears. This, for him, was the beginning of a reputation for cruelty, which was not fated to be diminished. A mendicant monk, who was passing Guillettes while Monsieur de Montragoux was out shooting woodcock, found Mme Angèle sewing a doll's petticoat. This worthy friar, discovering that she was as foolish as she was beautiful, took her away on his donkey, having persuaded her that the Angel Gabriel was waiting in a wood, to give her a pair of pearl garters. It is believed that she must have been eaten by a wolf, for she was never seen again.

After such a disastrous experience, how was it that Bluebeard could make up his mind to contract yet another union? It would be impossible to understand it, were we not well aware of the power which a fine pair of eyes exerts over a generous heart.

The honest gentleman met, at a neighboring château which he was in the habit of frequenting, a young orphan of quality, by name Alix de Pontalcin, who, having been robbed of all her property by a greedy trustee, thought only of entering a convent. Officious friends intervened to alter her determination and persuade her to accept the hand of Monsieur de Montragoux. Her beauty was perfect. Bluebeard, who was promising himself the enjoyment of an infinite happiness in her arms, was once more deluded in his hopes, and this time experienced a disappointment which, owing to his disposition, was bound to make an even greater impression upon him than all the afflictions which he had suffered in his previous marriages. Alix de Pontalcin obstinately refused to give actuality to the union to which she had nevertheless consented.

In vain did Monsieur de Montragoux press her to become his wife; she resisted prayers, tears, and objurgations, she refused her husband's lightest caresses and rushed off to shut herself into the Cabinet of the Unfortunate Princesses, where she remained, alone and intractable, for whole nights at a time.

The cause of a resistance so contrary to laws both human and divine was never known; it was attributed to Monsieur de Montragoux's blue beard, but our previous remarks on the subject of his beard render such a supposition far from probable. In any case, it is a difficult subject to discuss. The unhappy husband underwent the cruelest sufferings. In order to forget them, he hunted with desperation, exhausting horses, hounds, and huntsmen. But when he returned home, foundered and overtired, the mere sight of Mlle de Pontalcin was enough to revive his energies and his torments. Finally, unable to endure the situation any longer, he applied to Rome for the annulment of a marriage which was nothing better than a trap; and in consideration of a handsome present to the Holy Father, he obtained it in accordance with canon law. If Monsieur de Montragoux discarded Mlle de Pontalcin with all the marks of respect due to a woman and without breaking his cane across her back, it was because he had a valiant soul, a great heart, and was master of himself as well as of Guillettes. But he swore that for the future, no female should enter his apartments. Happy had he been if he had held to his oath to the end!

III

Some years had elapsed since Monsieur de Montragoux had rid himself of his sixth wife, and only a confused recollection remained in the countryside of the domestic calamities which had fallen upon this worthy *seigneur*'s house. Nobody knew what had become of his wives, and hair-raising tales were told in the village at night; some believed them, others did not. About this time, a widow, past the prime of life, Dame Sidonie de Lespoisse, came to settle with her children in the manor of La Motte-Giron, about two leagues, as the crow flies, from the castle of Guillettes. Whence she came, or who her husband had been, not a soul knew. Some believed, because they had heard it said, that he had held certain posts in Savoy or Spain; others said that he had died in the Indies; many had the idea that the widow was possessed of immense estates, while others doubted it strongly. However, she lived in a notable style and invited all the nobility of the countryside to La Motte-Giron. She had two daughters, of whom the elder, Anne, on the verge of becoming an old maid, was a very astute person: Jeanne, the younger, ripe for marriage, concealed a precocious knowledge of the world under an appearance of simplicity. The Dame de Lespoisse had also two sons, of twenty and twenty-two years of age: very fine, well-made young fellows, of whom one was a dragoon and the other a musketeer. I may add, having seen his commission, that he was a Black Musketeer. When on foot, this was not apparent, for the Black Musketeers were distinguished from the Gray not by the color of their uniform but by the hides of their horses. All alike wore blue surcoats laced with gold. As for the dragoons, they were to be recognized by a kind of fur bonnet, of which the tail fell gallantly over the ear. The dragoons had the reputation of being scamps, a scapegrace crowd, witness the song:

> *Mama, here the dragoons come:*
> *Let us haste away.*

But you might have searched in vain through his majesty's two regiments of dragoons for a bigger rake, a more accomplished sponger, or a viler rogue than Cosme de Lespoisse. Compared with him, his brother was an honest lad. Drunkard and gambler, Pierre de Lespoisse pleased the ladies and won at cards; these were the only ways of gaining a living known to him.

Their mother, Dame de Lespoisse, was making a splash at Motte-Giron only in order to catch gulls. As a matter of fact, she had not a penny and owed for everything, even to her false teeth. Her clothes and furniture, her coach, her horses, and her servants had all been lent by Parisian moneylenders, who threatened to withdraw them all if she did not presently marry one of her daughters to some rich nobleman, and the respectable Sidonie was expecting to find herself at any moment naked in an empty house. In a hurry to find a son-in-law, she had at once cast her eye upon Monsieur de Montragoux, whom she summed up as being simpleminded, easy to deceive, extremely mild, and quick to fall in love under his rude and bashful exterior. Her two daughters entered into her plans and, every time they met him, riddled poor Bluebeard with glances which pierced him to the depths of his heart. He soon fell a victim to the potent charms of the two Demoiselles de Lespoisse. Forgetting his oath, he thought of nothing but marrying one of them, finding them equally beautiful. After some delay, caused less by hesitation than by timidity, he went to Motte-Giron in great state, and made his petition to the Dame de Lespoisse, leaving to her the choice of which daughter she would give him. Mme Sidonie obligingly replied that she held him in high esteem and that she authorized him to pay his court to whichever of the ladies he should prefer.

"Learn to please, monsieur," she said. "I shall be the first to applaud your success."

In order to make their better acquaintance, Bluebeard invited Anne and Jeanne de Lespoisse, with their mother, brothers, and a multitude of ladies and gentlemen, to pass a fortnight at the castle of Guillettes. There was a succession of walking, hunting, and fishing parties, dances and festivities, dinners and entertainments of every sort. A young *seigneur,* the Chevalier de la Merlus, whom the ladies Lespoisse had brought with them, organized the beats. Bluebeard had the best packs of hounds and the largest turnout in the countryside. The ladies rivaled the ardor of the gentlemen in hunting the deer. They did not always hunt the animal down, but the hunters and their ladies wandered away in couples, found one another, and again wandered off into the woods. For choice, the Chevalier de la Merlus would lose himself with Jeanne de Lespoisse, and both would return to the castle at night, full of their adventures and pleased with their day's sport.

After a few days' observation, the good *seigneur* of Montragoux felt a decided preference for Jeanne, the younger sister, rather than the elder, as she was fresher, which is not saying that she was less experienced. He allowed his preference to appear; there was no reason why he should conceal it, for it was a befitting preference; moreover, he was a plain dealer. He paid court to the young lady as best he could, speaking little, for want of practice; but he gazed at her, rolling his rolling eyes and emitting from the depths of his bowels sighs which might have overthrown an oak tree. Sometimes he would burst out laughing, whereupon the crockery trembled and the windows rattled. Alone of all the party, he failed to remark the assiduous attentions of the Chevalier de la Merlus to Mme de Lespoisse's younger daughter, or if he did remark them he saw no harm in them. His experience of women was not sufficient to make him suspicious, and he trusted when he loved. My grandmother used to say that in life, experience is worthless and that one remains the same as when one begins. I believe she was right, and the true story that I am now unfolding is not of a nature to prove her wrong.

Bluebeard displayed an unusual magnificence in these festivities. When night arrived, the lawns before the castle were lit by a thousand torches, and tables served by menservants and maids dressed as fauns and dryads groaned under all the tastiest things which the countryside and the forest produced. Musicians provided a continual succession of beautiful symphonies. Toward the end of the meal, the schoolmaster and schoolmistress, followed by the boys and girls of the village, appeared before the guests and read a complimentary address to the *seigneur* of Montragoux and his friends. An astrologer in a pointed cap approached the ladies and foretold their future love affairs from the lines of their hands. Bluebeard ordered drink to be given for all his vassals, and he himself distributed bread and meat to the poor families.

At ten o'clock, for fear of the evening dew, the company retired to the apartments, lit by a multitude of candles, and there tables were prepared for every sort of game: lansquenet, billiards, reversi, bagatelle, pigeonholes, turnstile, porch, beast, hoc, brelan, drafts, backgammon, dice, and basset. Bluebeard was uniformly unfortunate in these various games, at which he lost large sums every night. He could console himself for his continuous run of bad luck by watching the three Lespoisse ladies win a great deal of money. Jeanne, the younger, who often backed the game of the Chevalier de la Merlus, heaped up mountains of gold. Mme de Lespoisse's two sons also did very well at reversi and basset; their luck was invariably best at the more hazardous games. The play went on until late into the night. No one slept during these marvelous festivities, and as the earliest biographer of Bluebeard has said: "They spent the whole night in playing tricks on one another." These hours were the most delightful of the whole twenty-four; for then, under cover of jesting, and taking advantage of the darkness, those who felt drawn toward one another would hide together in the depths of some alcove. The Chevalier de la Merlus would disguise himself at one time as a devil, at another as a ghost or a werewolf, in order to frighten the sleepers, but he always ended by slipping into the room of Mlle Jeanne de Lespoisse. The good *seigneur* of Montragoux was not overlooked in these games. The two sons of Mme de Lespoisse put irritant powder in his bed and burned in his room substances which emitted a disgusting smell. Or they would arrange a jug of water over his door so that the worthy *seigneur* could not open the door without the whole of the water being upset upon his head. In short, they played on him all sorts of practical jokes, to the diversion of the whole company, and Bluebeard bore them with his natural good humor.

He made his request, to which Mme de Lespoisse acceded, although, as she said, it wrung her heart to think of giving her girls in marriage.

The marriage was celebrated at Motte-Giron with extraordinary magnificence. The Demoiselle Jeanne, amazingly beautiful, was dressed entirely in *point de France*, her head covered with a thousand ringlets. Her sister, Anne, wore a dress of green velvet, embroidered with gold. Their mother's dress was of golden tissue, trimmed with black chenille, with a *parure* of pearls and diamonds. Monsieur de Montragoux wore all his great diamonds on a suit of black velvet; he made a very fine appearance, his expression of timidity and innocence contrasting strongly with his blue chin and his massive build. The bride's brothers were of course handsomely arrayed, but the Chevalier de la Merlus, in a suit of rose velvet trimmed with pearls, shone with unparalleled splendor.

Immediately after the ceremony, the Jews who had hired out to the bride's family and her lover all these fine clothes and rich jewels resumed possession of them and posted back to Paris with them.

I V

For a month Monsieur de Montragoux was the happiest of men. He adored his wife and regarded her as an angel of purity. She was something quite different, but far shrewder men than poor Bluebeard might have been deceived as he was, for she was a person of great cunning and astuteness, and allowed herself submissively to be ruled by her mother, who was the cleverest jade in the whole kingdom of France. She established herself at Guillettes with her eldest daughter, Anne, her two sons, Pierre and Cosme, and the Chevalier de la Merlus, who kept as close to Mme de Montragoux as if he had been her shadow. Her good husband was a little annoyed at this; he would have liked to keep his wife always to himself, but he did not take exception to the affection which she felt for this young gentleman, as she had told him that he was her foster brother.

Charles Perrault relates that a month after having contracted this union, Bluebeard was compelled to make a journey of six weeks' duration on some important business. He does not seem to be aware of the reasons for this journey, and it has been suspected that it was an artifice, which the jealous husband resorted to, according to custom, in order to surprise his wife. The truth is quite otherwise. Monsieur de Montragoux went to Le Perche to receive the heritage of his cousin of Outarde, who had been killed gloriously by a cannonball at the battle of the Dunes, while casting dice upon a drum.

Before leaving, Monsieur de Montragoux begged his wife to indulge in every possible distraction during his absence.

"Invite all your friends, madame," he said. "Go riding with them, amuse yourselves, and have a pleasant time."

He handed over to her all the keys of the house, thus indicating that in his absence she was the sole and sovereign mistress of all the *seigneurie* of Guillettes.

"This," he said, "is the key of the two great wardrobes; this of the gold and silver not in daily use; this of the strongboxes which contain my gold and silver; this of the caskets where my jewels are kept; and this is a passkey into all the rooms. As for this little key, it is that of the cabinet at the end of the gallery on the ground floor; open everything, and go where you will."

Charles Perrault claims that Monsieur de Montragoux added:

"But as for the little cabinet, I forbid you to enter that; and I forbid you so expressly that if you do enter it, I cannot say to what lengths my anger will not go."

The historian of Bluebeard, in placing these words on record, has fallen into the error of adopting, without verification, the version concocted after the event by the ladies Lespoisse. Monsieur de Montragoux expressed himself very differently. When he handed to his wife the key of the little cabinet, which was none other than the Cabinet of the Unfortunate Princesses, to which we have already frequently alluded, he expressed the desire that his beloved Jeanne should not enter that part of the house which he regarded as fatal to his domestic happiness. It was through this room, indeed, that his first wife, and the best of all of them, had fled, when she ran away with her bear; here Blanche de Gibeaumex had repeatedly betrayed him with various gentlemen; and lastly, the porphyry pavement was stained by the blood of a beloved criminal. Was not this enough to make Monsieur de Montragoux connect the idea of this room with cruel memories and fateful forebodings?

The words which he addressed to Jeanne de Lespoisse convey the desires and impressions which were troubling his mind. They were actually as follows:

"For you, madame, nothing of mine is hidden, and I should feel that I was doing you an injury did I fail to hand over to you all the keys of a dwelling which belongs to you. You may therefore enter this little cabinet, as you may enter all the other rooms of the house; but if you will take my advice you will do nothing of the kind, to oblige me and in consideration of the painful ideas which, for me, are connected with this room, and the forebodings of evil which these ideas, despite myself, call up into my mind. I should be inconsolable were any mischance to befall you, or were I to bring misfortune upon you. You will, madame, forgive these fears, which are happily unfounded, as being only the outcome of my anxious affection and my watchful love."

With these words the good *seigneur* embraced his wife and posted off to Le Perche.

"The friends and neighbors," says Charles Perrault, "did not wait to be asked to visit the young bride; so full were they of impatience to see all the wealth of her house. They proceeded at once to inspect all the rooms, cabinets, and wardrobes, each of which was richer and more beautiful than the last; and there was no end to their envy and their praises of their friend's good fortune."

All the historians who have dealt with this subject have added that Mme de Montragoux took no pleasure in the sight of all these riches, by reason of her impatience to open the little cabinet. This is perfectly correct, and as Perrault has said: "So urgent was her curiosity that, without considering that it was unmannerly to leave her guests, she went down to it by a little secret staircase, and in such a hurry that two or three times she thought she would break her neck." The fact is beyond question. But what no one has told us is that the reason why she was so anxious to reach this apartment was that the Chevalier de la Merlus was awaiting her there.

Since she had come to make her home in the castle of Guillettes she had met this young gentleman in the cabinet every day, and oftener twice a day than once, without wearying of an intercourse so unseemly in a young married woman. It is impossible to hesitate as to the nature of the ties connecting Jeanne with the chevalier: they were anything but respectable, anything but chaste. Alas, had Mme de Montragoux merely betrayed her husband's honor, she would no doubt have incurred the blame of posterity; but the most austere of moralists might have found excuses for her. He might allege, in favor of so young a woman, the laxity of the morals of the period; the examples of the city and the court; the too certain effects of a bad training and the advice of an immoral mother, for Mme Sidonie de Lespoisse countenanced her daughter's intrigues. The wise might have forgiven her a fault too amiable to merit their severity; her errors would have seemed too common to be crimes, and the world would simply have considered that she was behaving like other people. But Jeanne de Lespoisse, not content with betraying her husband's honor, did not hesitate to attempt his life.

It was in the little cabinet, otherwise known as the Cabinet of the Unfortunate Princesses, that Jeanne de Lespoisse, Dame de Montragoux, in concert with the Chevalier de la Merlus, plotted the death of a kind and faithful husband. She declared later that on entering the room, she saw hanging there the bodies of six murdered women, whose congealed blood covered the tiles, and that recognizing in these unhappy women the first six wives of Bluebeard, she foresaw the fate which awaited herself. She must, in this case, have mistaken the paintings on the walls for mutilated corpses, and her hallucinations must be compared with those of Lady Macbeth. But it is extremely probable that Jeanne imagined this horrible sight in order to relate it afterward, justifying her husband's murderers by slandering their victim.

The death of Monsieur de Montragoux was determined upon. Certain letters which lie before me compel the belief that Mme Sidonie Lespoisse had her part in the plot. As for her elder daughter, she may be described as the soul of the conspiracy. Anne de Lespoisse was the wickedest of the whole family. She was a stranger to sensual weakness, remaining chaste in the midst of the profligacy of the house. It was not a case of refusing pleasures which she thought unworthy of her; the truth was that she took pleasure only in cruelty. She engaged her two brothers, Cosme and Pierre, in the enterprise by promising them the command of a regiment.

V

It now rests with us to trace, with the aid of authentic documents and reliable evidence, the most atrocious, treacherous, and cowardly domestic crime of which the record has come down to us. The murder whose circumstances we are about to relate can only be compared to that committed on the night of 9 March 1449, on the person of Guillaume de Flavy, by his wife, Blanche d'Overbreuc, a young and slender woman, the bastard d'Orbandas, and the barber Jean Bocquillon. They stifled Guillaume with a pillow, battered him pitilessly with a club, and bled him at the throat like a calf. Blanche d'Overbreuc proved that her husband had determined to have her drowned, while Jeanne de Lespoisse betrayed a loving husband to a gang of unspeakable scoundrels. We will record the facts with all possible restraint.

Bluebeard returned rather earlier than expected. This it was that gave rise to the quite mistaken idea that, a prey to the blackest jealousy, he was wishful to surprise his wife. Full of joy and confidence, if he thought of giving her a surprise it was an agreeable one. His kindness and tenderness, and his joyous, peaceable air would have softened the most savage hearts. The Chevalier de la Merlus, and the whole execrable brood of Lespoisse, saw therein nothing but an additional facility for taking his life and possessing themselves of his wealth, still further increased by his new inheritance.

His young wife met him with a smiling face, allowing herself to be embraced and led to the conjugal chamber, where she did everything to please the good man. The following morning she returned him the bunch of keys which had been confided to her care. But there was missing that of the Cabinet of the Unfortunate Princesses, commonly called the little cabinet. Bluebeard gently demanded its delivery, and after putting him off for a time on various pretexts, Jeanne returned it to him.

There now arises a question which cannot be solved without leaving the limited domain of history to enter the indeterminate regions of philosophy.

Charles Perrault specifically states that the key of the little cabinet was a fairy key, that is to say, it was magical, enchanted, endowed with properties contrary to the laws of nature: at all events, as we conceive them. We have no proof to the contrary. This is a fitting moment to recall the precept of my illustrious master Monsieur du Clos des Lunes, a member of the Institute: "When the supernatural makes its appearance, it must not be rejected by the historian." I shall therefore content myself with recalling, as regards this key, the unanimous opinion of all the old biographers of Bluebeard; they all affirm that it was a fairy key. This is a point of great importance. Moreover, this key is not the only object created by human industry which has proved to be endowed with marvelous properties. Tradition abounds with examples of enchanted swords. Arthur's was a magic sword. And so was that of Joan of Arc, on the undeniable authority of Jean Chartier; and the proof afforded by that illustrious chronicler is that when the blade was broken, the two pieces refused to be welded together again despite all the efforts of the most competent armorers. Victor Hugo speaks in one of his poems of those "magic stairways still obscured below." Many authors even admit that there are men-magicians who can turn themselves into wolves. We shall not undertake to combat such a firm and constant belief, and we shall not pretend to decide whether the key of the little cabinet was or was not enchanted, for our reserve does not imply that we are in any uncertainty, and therein resides its merit. But where we find ourselves in our proper domain or, to be more precise, within our own jurisdiction, where we once more become judges of facts and writers of circumstances, is where we read that the key was flecked with blood. The authority of the texts does not so far impress us as to compel us to believe this. It was not flecked with blood. Blood had flowed in the little cabinet, but at a time already remote. Whether the key had been washed or whether it had dried, it was impossible that it should be so stained, and what, in her agitation, the criminal wife mistook for a bloodstain on the iron was the reflection of the sky still empurpled by the roses of dawn.

Monsieur de Montragoux, on seeing the key, perceived nonetheless that his wife had entered the little cabinet. He noticed that it now appeared cleaner and brighter than when he had given it to her, and was of opinion that this polish could only come from use.

This produced a painful impression upon him, and he said to his wife, with a mournful smile:

"My darling, you have been into the little cabinet. May there result no grievous outcome for either of us! From that room emanates a malign influence from which I would have protected you. If you, in your turn, should become subjected to it, I should never get over it. Forgive me; when we love we are superstitious."

On these words, although Bluebeard cannot have frightened her, for his words and demeanor expressed only love and melancholy, the young lady of Montragoux began shrieking at the top of her voice:

"Help! Help! He's killing me!"

This was the signal agreed upon. On hearing it, the Chevalier de la Merlus and the two sons of Mme de Lespoisse were to have thrown themselves upon Bluebeard and run him through with their swords.

But the chevalier, whom Jeanne had hidden in a cupboard in the room, appeared alone. Monsieur de Montragoux, seeing him leap forth sword in hand, placed himself on guard. Jeanne fled terror-stricken and met her sister Anne in the gallery. She was not, as has been related, on a tower; for all the towers had been thrown down by order of Cardinal Richelieu. Anne was striving to put heart into her two brothers, who, pale and quaking, dared not risk so great a stake.

Jeanne hastily implored them:

"Quick, quick, brothers, save my lover!"

Pierre and Cosme then rushed at Bluebeard. They found him, having disarmed the Chevalier de la Merlus, holding him down with his knee; they treacherously ran their swords through his body from behind and continued to strike at him long after he had breathed his last.

Bluebeard had no heirs. His wife remained mistress of his property. She used a part of it to provide a dowry for her sister, Anne, another part to buy captains' commissions for her two brothers, and the rest to marry the Chevalier de la Merlus, who became a very respectable man as soon as he was wealthy.

Translated by D. B. Stewart

How foolish it is to think that it is just by chance that flowers move our hearts, captivate us, and mesmerize us, as it were. You would have to be a person without feelings not to sense the sympathetic current that emanates, for example, from a beautiful rose in full bloom. Could it be that the rose itself plays a role in this? Don't be so positive that plants don't have a will of their own or their own consciousness, for you can see clearly how they influence us in many situations. This influence, I'd venture to say, is kept within the bounds of respectability, for the most part. Sometimes, however, it can extend itself extraordinarily far. Only foolhardy theoreticians continue to formulate hypotheses that question whether plants have a direct suggestive effect on animals and humans. (Indeed, we even know about man-eating plants.) On the whole, when these creatures are cut from their stems, it is the work of learned pedants, who don't know that they are sinning against nature by separating something without duly reassembling it.

A red rose lifted its head far above the dense bushes to peer at a young woman, who had ambled to that spot around noon and fallen asleep at the edge of the bushes. This rose fixed its magic eyes yearningly on the young woman. As if guided by some secret intention, it fluttered one of its light petals onto her left breast, while she moved her hand to her heart and opened her eyelids. Then the plant creature and the young woman stared at each other eye to eye. The silent fascination that emanated from the rose held the young woman deep under its spell. One hears about serpents that lure birds and get them into their grip through such magic. The rose seemed deliriously to strain every nerve in its body. Numbed against her will by the sight of the rose and compelled to doze, the young woman saw, before her eyes closed again, that the rose was swaying on its stem and was bending itself deeply toward the ground. She dreamed a love dream. The rose transformed itself into a handsome young man, who embraced and enjoyed the woman. Indeed, she utterly abandoned herself to him. After a while she awoke as though intoxicated with the feeling of some dark knowledge in her limbs. Her mouth was burning from a strange glow. Her lap was covered with rose petals, her clothes in disarray. Involuntarily she looked for the rose, but only its stem rocked in the wind. The rose seemed to have fallen off without a trace.

Some weeks later, the young woman felt herself attacked by strange feelings and corporal disturbances. The doctor shook his head. He decided to wait and would not reveal his diagnosis yet.

"You're prone to dizziness and nausea, my dear. You're under a certain tension. Perhaps you can tell me frankly: Are you having a love affair?"

Thereafter the doctor was no longer consulted. In the meantime the signs of an abnormal condition increased. After a few weeks had passed, she consulted another doctor, and this one declared with certainty that there were the so-called interesting symptoms. When the young woman became enraged, he attributed it to hysteria. In any event, a true pregnancy had apparently begun its normal process, and gradually the phases became so clearly recognizable that the young woman could no longer deny it. There was nothing she could do; one day the midwife had to be fetched.

The young woman—and no one was as surprised as the young woman herself—gave birth to a little daughter of wondrous charms that blossomed more and more gloriously with each passing day. The little one looked just like her mother, except she seemed to be more ethereal and angelic. Her skin was a soft, clear pink; the eyes, dreamily green. There was also a birthmark, in the form of a rose petal. Her hair glistened like silver. Her gait resembled the swaying of a gliding rose without the movement of its limbs. But even though she appeared to understand everything, she remained mute. She kept silent intelligently and apparently out of superiority, in no way out of stupidity. She learned with ease everything she was taught. Never did she reveal anything about her inner life, even when she wrote. She was especially talented in painting pictures of flowers. In fact, she perfected her skills here so well that she became a consummate painter. She had a special liking for drawing roses in full bloom. Under one of her roses—no one knew why—she wrote the word "Father," sending her mother into shock. Overcome by a chilling presentiment and filled with horror, her mother searched in vain for the solution to this puzzle.

When her daughter reached puberty, a catastrophe occurred. Fortunately, the mother succeeded in keeping an impenetrable secret. It happened one evening when mother and daughter were praying. The daughter's folded hands began to transform themselves gradually into green branches; the rest of her limbs and her entire body shrunk to a leafy plant and became a rosebush, which had an incomparably sweet scent. While it lay motionless on the pillow, the horrified mother immediately wanted to scream out for help, but she was constrained by the hypnotic spell cast by the plant. After a quarter of an hour of exceeding dread, the mother watched the plant change back into her daughter. Then the girl wrote on her board: "This is the tribute that I owe my father. From now on I'll always honor him this way before I go to sleep!"

The mother made a solemn pledge of discretion to the pleading child. "But what father?" she asked in vain.

The child remained silent. Nobody learned about this brief metamorphosis, which now recurred nightly. However, one should not exaggerate the wonder of it. Plants and animals are linked in a certain way through physiological inversions of one another.

Now so great is the power of habit that eventually the mother would have been startled if the mysterious transformation had not occurred each night. In the meantime the daughter became such a seraphic, graceful young woman that many men desired her hand in marriage, despite her muteness. For a while the young woman's heart could not be moved, and she rejected one suitor after another. Finally, one came who received a positive answer. Dr. Floris Rosenberger, as he was named, was an anatomist, and he looked somewhat moody. The mother gave her approval, and soon after the engagement, the date for the marriage was set. Just before the ceremony, the mother took the doctor aside.

"You must promise me not to visit your young bride until she has prayed. Please do as I tell you, my dear son-in-law. It's urgent. Tomorrow morning I'll explain everything to you."

Floris gave her his word with a shake of the hand. The mother had kept the secret too long; she should have informed the future husband about this long before. However, she had been afraid to cause her daughter any disappointment in love. To a certain extent she had been guilty of a minor infraction as matchmaker. By no means had she concealed a defect in the bride. Nonetheless, she had kept quiet about a highly paradoxical characteristic, which would perhaps have scared Dr. Rosenberger away. She has been more than punished for what she did.

The bridegroom was very much in love, but he was an exceedingly sober man. And like most men, he had a vague notion of how closely related woman's nature is to Sphinx, Undine, and Melusine. He desired a woman with a little poetical spice to add to his home-baked existence. However, he would have politely declined being married to a marvelously beautiful plant, even for five minutes. Smiling, he had interpreted his mother-in-law's words to mean that his wife-to-be was somewhat pious, and he was fully confident that he would break her of this habit. Why not begin right away, tonight? Of course, he had given his word—but after granting a short formal interval, he would essay his objective. So it was with great delight that he accompanied his wife to the door of their common bedroom. After a long kiss, he squeezed her hand.

"My love," he said, "I know that you like to pray first by yourself. I'll wait."

He waited with his pocket watch open in his hand, and after a few minutes passed, he turned the doorknob. When he found the door locked, his lips broke out into a wily smile. He knew a little trick that enabled him to bypass the lock. It was a measure that had proved to be useful in his various liaisons, and he put it to work here.

The room had no other entrance, but to his astonishment, it was empty. He noticed his wife's discarded clothes on a pillow. He called out, searched, picked up things here and there, pushed the furniture, and threw himself beneath the bed. He became carried away in his zeal, and his feelings were understandable. When he saw a rosebush lying on their marriage bed, he laughed irritably. "Flowers in the bedroom, and a bush of all things! Unhealthy!"

Suddenly he had a dreadful presentiment and ran onto the balcony with the rosebush. He leaned over the railing. Praise God: it was nothing. She was only playing hide-and-seek. The little rascal! He smiled again. Below him was Emma, his wife's recently hired maid.

"Emma!" he called out.

"Sir?"

"Catch this! Watch out now! Put it in a pretty vase! Tomorrow morning at our breakfast."

And he flung the rosebush over the railing. Tragically, the metamorphosis took place in midair—and a naked woman soon lay crushed on the pavement.

The maid screamed in horror. The unfortunate husband ran at once to his mother-in-law. At the same time, the cries of the maid had caused the police to come running. According to Emma's exact testimony, it was beyond all doubt that Dr. Rosenberger had flung his wife over the balcony railing. Yet he had still joked in a cruel and frivolous way: Tomorrow morning in a vase! On the other hand, the bride's own mother defended the murderer, but she stammered such abstruse stuff on his behalf that it was astounding to hear such a learned man of science as Dr. Rosenberger strongly supporting it as his appeal.

Yes, he declared, his wife was a rosebush without his knowing it. She had transformed herself, as her mother testified, into one right before she retired.

Of course, both the mother and the murderer were taken to an asylum. Professor Schölze offered an ingenious interpretation to newspaper reporters: "A case of reverse Lucia di Lammermoor. Wedding nights with such murders are typical in certain forms of hysteria."

The postmortem examination of the body, however, produced some findings that still need to be clarified. In fact, some interpenetration of plant stalks and the beginnings of buds were discovered. Dr. Rosenberger is an anatomist. Could he have been so cruel as to have conducted bestial experiments on her before he threw her from the balcony? Will the truth ever be known?

Translated by Jack Zipes

The Kith of the Elf-Folk

LORD DUNSANY

I

The north wind was blowing, and red and golden the last days of Autumn were streaming hence. Solemn and cold over the marshes arose the evening.

It became very still.

Then the last pigeon went home to the trees on the dry land in the distance, whose shapes already had taken upon themselves a mystery in the haze.

Then all was still again.

As the light faded and the haze deepened, mystery crept nearer from every side.

Then the green plover came in crying, and all alighted.

And again it became still, save when one of the plover arose and flew a little way uttering the cry of the waste. And hushed and silent became the earth, expecting the first star. Then the duck came in, and the widgeon, company by company: and all the light of day faded out of the sky saving one red band of light. Across the light appeared, black and huge, the wings of a flock of geese beating up wind to the marshes. These, too, went down among the rushes.

Then the stars appeared and shone in the stillness, and there was silence in the great spaces of the night.

Suddenly the bells of the cathedral in the marshes broke out, calling to evensong.

Eight centuries ago on the edge of the marsh men had built the huge cathedral, or it may have been seven centuries ago, or perhaps nine—it was all one to the Wild Things.

So evensong was held, and candles lighted, and the lights through the windows shone red and green in the water, and the sound of the organ went roaring over the marshes. But from the deep and perilous places, edged with bright mosses, the Wild Things came leaping up to dance on the reflection of the stars, and over their heads as they danced the marsh-lights rose and fell.

The Wild Things are somewhat human in appearance, only all brown of skin and barely two feet high. Their ears are pointed like the squirrel's, only far larger, and they leap to prodigious heights. They live all day under deep pools in the loneliest marshes, but at night they come up and dance. Each Wild Thing has over its head a marsh-light, which moves as the Wild Thing moves; they have no souls, and cannot die, and are of the kith of the Elf-folk.

All night they dance over the marshes treading upon the reflection of the stars (for the bare surface of the water will not hold them by itself); but when the stars begin to pale, they sink down one by one into the pools of their home. Or if they tarry longer, sitting upon the rushes, their bodies fade from view as the marsh-fires pale in the light, and by daylight none may see the Wild Things of the kith of the Elf-folk. Neither may any see them even at night unless they were born, as I was, in the hour of dusk, just at the moment when the first star appears.

Now, on the night that I tell of, a little Wild Thing had gone drifting over the waste, till it came right up to the walls of the cathedral and danced upon the images of the coloured saints as they lay in the water among the reflection of the stars. And as it leaped in its fantastic dance, it saw through the painted windows to where the people prayed, and heard the organ roaring over the marshes. The sound of the organ roared over the marshes, but the song and prayers of the people streamed up from the cathedral's highest tower like thin gold chains, and reached to Paradise, and up and down them went the angels from Paradise to the people, and from the people to Paradise again.

Then something akin to discontent troubled the Wild Thing for the first time since the making of the marshes; and the soft grey ooze and the chill of the deep water seemed to be not enough, nor the first arrival from northwards of the tumultuous geese, nor the wild rejoicing of the wings of the wildfowl when every feather sings, nor the wonder of the calm ice that comes when the snipe depart and beards the rushes with frost and clothes the hushed waste with a mysterious haze where the sun goes red and low, nor even the dance of the Wild Things in the marvellous night; and the little Wild Thing longed to have a soul, and to go and worship God.

And when evensong was over and the lights were out, it went back crying to its kith.

But on the next night, as soon as the images of the stars appeared in the water, it went leaping away from star to star to the farthest edge of the marshlands, where a great wood grew where dwelt the Oldest of the Wild Things.

And it found the Oldest of Wild Things sitting under a tree, sheltering itself from the moon.

And the little Wild Thing said: "I want to have a soul to worship God, and to know the meaning of music, and to see the inner beauty of the marshlands and to imagine Paradise."

And the Oldest of the Wild Things said to it: "What have we to do with God? We are only Wild Things, and of the kith of the Elf-folk."

But it only answered, "I want to have a soul."

Then the Oldest of the Wild Things said: "I have no soul to give you; but if you got a soul, one day you would have to die, and if you knew the meaning of music you would learn the meaning of sorrow, and it is better to be a Wild Thing and not to die."

So it went weeping away.

But they that were kin to the Elf-folk were sorry for the little Wild Thing; and though the Wild Things cannot sorrow long, having no souls to sorrow with, yet they felt for awhile a soreness where their souls should be when they saw the grief of their comrade.

So the kith of the Elf-folk went abroad by night to make a soul for the little Wild Thing. And they went over the marshes till they came to the high fields among the flowers and grasses. And there they gathered a large piece of gossamer that the spider had laid by twilight; and the dew was on it.

Into this dew had shone all the lights of the long banks of the ribbed sky, as all the colours changed in the restful spaces of evening. And over it the marvellous night had gleamed with all its stars.

Then the Wild Things went with their dew-bespangled gossamer down to the edge of their home. And there they gathered a piece of the grey mist that lies by night over the marshlands. And into it they put the melody of the waste that is borne up and down the marshes in the evening on the wings of the golden plover. And they put into it, too, the mournful songs that the reeds are compelled to sing before the presence of the arrogant North Wind. Then each of the Wild Things gave some treasured memory of the old marshes, "For we can spare it," they said. And to all this they added a few images of the stars that they gathered out of the water. Still the soul that the kith of the Elf-folk were making had no life.

Then they put into it the low voices of two lovers that went walking in the night, wandering late alone. And after that they waited for the dawn. And the queenly dawn appeared, and the marsh-lights of the Wild Things paled in the glare, and their bodies faded from view; and still they waited by the marsh's edge. And to them waiting came over field and marsh, from the ground and out of the sky, the myriad song of the birds.

This, too, the Wild Things put into the piece of haze that they had gathered in the marshlands, and wrapped it all up in their dew-bespangled gossamer. Then the soul lived.

And there it lay in the hands of the Wild Things no larger than a hedgehog; and wonderful lights were in it, green and blue; and they changed ceaselessly, going round and round, and in the grey midst of it was a purple flare.

And the next night they came to the little Wild Thing and showed her the gleaming soul. And they said to her: "If you must have a soul and go and worship God, and become a mortal and die, place this to your left breast a little above the heart, and it will enter and you will become a human. But if you take it you can never be rid of it to become a mortal again unless you pluck it out and give it to another; and we will not take it, and most of the humans have a soul already. And if you cannot find a human without a soul you will one day die, and your soul cannot go to Paradise because it was only made in the marshes."

Far away the little Wild Thing saw the cathedral windows alight for evensong, and the song of the people mounting up to Paradise, and all the angels going up and down. So it bid farewell with tears and thanks to the Wild Things of the Kith of Elf-folk, and went leaping away towards the green dry land, holding the soul in its hands.

And the Wild Things were sorry that it had gone, but could not be sorry long because they had no souls.

At the marsh's edge the little Wild Thing gazed for some moments over the water to where the marsh-fires were leaping up and down, and then pressed the soul against its left breast a little above the heart.

Instantly it became a young and beautiful woman, who was cold and frightened. She clad herself somehow with bundles of reeds, and went towards the lights of a house that stood close by. And she pushed open the door and entered, and found a farmer and a farmer's wife sitting over their supper.

And the farmer's wife took the little Wild Thing with the soul of the marshes up to her room, and clothed her and braided her hair, and brought her down again, and gave her the first food that she had ever eaten. Then the farmer's wife asked many questions.

"Where have you come from?" she said.

"Over the marshes."

"From what direction?" said the farmer's wife.

"South," said the little Wild Thing with the new soul.

"But none can come over the marshes from the south," said the farmer's wife.

"No, they can't do that," said the farmer.

"I lived in the marshes."

"Who are you?" asked the farmer's wife.

"I am a Wild Thing, and have found a soul in the marshes, and we are kin to the Elf-folk."

Talking it over afterwards, the farmer and his wife agreed that she must be a gipsy who had been lost, and that she was queer with hunger and exposure.

So that night the little Wild Thing slept in the farmer's house, but her new soul stayed awake the whole night long dreaming of the beauty of the marshes.

As soon as dawn came over the waste and shone on the farmer's house, she looked from the window towards the glittering waters, and saw the inner beauty of the marsh. For the Wild Things only love the marsh and know its haunts, but now she perceived the mystery of its distances and the glamour of its perilous pools, with their fair and deadly mosses, and felt the marvel of the North Wind who comes dominant out of unknown icy lands, and the wonder of that ebb and flow of life when the wildfowl whirl in at evening to the marshlands and at dawn pass out to sea. And she knew that over her head above the farmer's house stretched wide Paradise, where perhaps God was now imagining a sunrise while angels played low on lutes, and the sun came rising up on the world below to gladden fields and marshes.

And all that heaven thought, the marsh thought too; for the blue of the marsh was as the blue of heaven, and the great cloud shapes in heaven became the shapes in the marsh, and through each ran momentary rivers of purple, errant between banks of gold. And the stalwart army of reeds appeared out of the gloom with all their pennons waving as far as the eye could see. And from another window she saw the vast cathedral gathering its ponderous strength together, and lifting it up in towers out of the marshlands.

She said, "I will never, never leave the marsh."

An hour later she dressed with great difficulty and went down to eat the second meal of her life. The farmer and his wife were kindly folk, and taught her how to eat.

"I suppose the gipsies don't have knives and forks," one said to the other afterwards.

After breakfast the farmer went and saw the Dean, who lived near his cathedral, and presently returned and brought back to the Dean's house the little Wild Thing with the new soul.

"This is the lady," said the farmer. "This is Dean Murnith." Then he went away.

"Ah," said the Dean, "I understand you were lost the other night in the marshes. It was a terrible night to be lost in the marshes."

"I love the marshes," said the little Wild Thing with the new soul.

"Indeed! How old are you?" said the Dean.

"I don't know," she answered.

"You must know about how old you are," he said.

"Oh, about ninety," she said, "or more."

"Ninety years!" exclaimed the Dean.

"No, ninety centuries," she said, "I am as old as the marshes."

Then she told her story—how she had longed to be a human and go and worship God, and have a soul and see the beauty of the world, and how all the Wild Things had made her a soul of gossamer and mist and music and strange memories.

"But if this is true," said Dean Murnith, "this is very wrong. God cannot have intended you to have a soul. What is your name?"

"I have no name," she answered.

"We must find a Christian name and a surname for you. What would you like to be called?"

"Song of the Rushes," she said.

"That won't do at all," said the Dean.

"Then I would like to be called Terrible North Wind, or Star in the Waters," she said.

"No, no, no," said Dean Murnith, "that is quite impossible. We could call you Miss Rush if you like. How would Mary Rush do? Perhaps you had better have another name—say Mary Jane Rush."

So the little Wild Thing with the soul of the marshes took the names that were offered her, and became Mary Jane Rush.

"And we must find something for you to do," said Dean Murnith. "Meanwhile we can give you a room here."

"I don't want to do anything," replied Mary Jane; "I want to worship God in the cathedral and live beside the marshes."

Then Mrs. Murnith came in, and for the rest of that day Mary Jane stayed at the house of the Dean.

And there with her new soul she perceived the beauty of the world; for it came grey and level out of misty distances, and widened into grassy fields and ploughlands right up to the edge of an old gabled town; and solitary in the fields far off an ancient windmill stood, and his honest hand-made sails went round and round in the free East Anglian winds. Close by, the gabled houses leaned out over the streets, planted fair upon sturdy timbers that grew in the olden time, all glorying among themselves upon their beauty. And out of them, buttress by buttress, growing and going upwards, aspiring tower by tower, rose the cathedral.

And she saw the people moving in the streets all leisurely and slow, and unseen among them, whispering to each other, unheard by living men and concerned only with bygone things, drifted the ghosts of very long ago. And wherever the streets ran eastwards, wherever were gaps in the houses, always there broke into view the sight of the great marshes, like to some bar of music weird and strange that haunts a melody, arising again and again, played on the violin by one musician only, who plays no other bar, and he is swart and lank about the hair and bearded about the lips, and his moustache droops long and low, and no one knows the land from which he comes.

All these were good things for a new soul to see.

Then the sun set over green fields and ploughlands and the night came up. One by one the merry lights of cheery lamp-lit windows took their stations in the solemn night.

Then the bells rang, far up in a cathedral tower, and their melody fell on the roofs of the old houses and poured over their eaves until the streets were full, and then flooded away over green fields and ploughlands till it came to the sturdy mill and brought the miller trudging to evensong, and far away eastwards and seawards the sound rang out over the remoter marshes. And it was all as yesterday to the old ghosts in the streets.

Then the Dean's wife took Mary Jane to evening service, and she saw three hundred candles filling all the aisle with light. But sturdy pillars stood there in unlit vastnesses; great colonnades going away into the gloom where evening and morning, year in year out, they did their work in the dark, holding the cathedral roof aloft. And it was stiller than the marshes are still when the ice has come and the wind that brought it has fallen.

Suddenly into this stillness rushed the sound of the organ, roaring, and presently the people prayed and sang.

No longer could Mary Jane see their prayers ascending like thin gold chains, for that was but an elfin fancy, but she imagined clear in her new soul the seraphs passing in the ways of Paradise, and the angels changing guard to watch the World by night.

When the Dean had finished service, a young curate, Mr. Millings, went up into the pulpit.

He spoke of Abana and Pharpar, rivers of Damascus: and Mary Jane was glad that there were rivers having such names, and heard with wonder of Nineveh, that great city, and many things strange and new.

And the light of the candles shone on the curate's fair hair, and his voice went ringing down the aisle, and Mary Jane rejoiced that he was there.

But when his voice stopped she felt a sudden loneliness, such as she had not felt since the making of the marshes; for the Wild Things never are lonely and never unhappy, but dance all night on the reflection of the stars, and having no souls desire nothing more.

After the collection was made, before any one moved to go, Mary Jane walked up the aisle to Mr. Millings.

"I love you," she said.

II

Nobody sympathised with Mary Jane. "So unfortunate for Mr. Millings," every one said; "such a promising young man."

Mary Jane was sent away to a great manufacturing city of the Midlands, where work had been found for her in a cloth factory. And there was nothing in that town that was good for a soul to see. For it did not know that beauty was to be desired; so it made many things by machinery, and became hurried in all its ways, and boasted its superiority over other cities and became richer and richer, and there was none to pity it.

In this city Mary Jane had had lodgings found for her near the factory.

At six o'clock on those November mornings, about the time that, far away from the city, the wildfowl rose up out of the calm marshes and passed to the troubled spaces of the sea, at six o'clock the factory uttered a prolonged howl and gathered the workers together, and there they worked, saving two hours for food, the whole of the daylit hours and into the dark till the bells tolled six again.

There Mary Jane worked with other girls in a long dreary room, where giants sat pounding wool into a long thread-like strip with iron, rasping hands. And all day long they roared as they sat at their soulless work. But the work of Mary Jane was not with these, only their roar was ever in her ears as their clattering iron limbs went to and fro.

Her work was to tend a creature smaller, but infinitely more cunning.

It took the strip of wool that the giants had threshed, and whirled it round and round until it had twisted it into hard thin thread. Then it would make a clutch with fingers of steel at the thread that it had gathered, and waddle away about five yards and come back with more.

It had mastered all the subtlety of skilled workers, and had gradually displaced them; one thing only it could not do, it was unable to pick up the ends if a piece of the elf thread broke, in order to tie them together again. For this a human soul was required, and it was Mary Jane's business to pick up broken ends; and the moment she placed them together the busy soulless creature tied them for itself.

All here was ugly; even the green wool as it whirled round and round was neither the green of the grass nor yet the green of the rushes, but a sorry muddy green that befitted a sullen city under a murky sky.

When she looked out over the roofs of the town, there too was ugliness;

and well the houses knew it, for with hideous stucco they aped in grotesque mimicry the pillars and temples of old Greece, pretending to one another to be that which they were not. And emerging from these houses and going in, and seeing the pretence of paint and stucco year after year until it all peeled away, the souls of the poor owners of those houses sought to be other souls until they grew weary of it.

At evening Mary Jane went back to her lodgings. Only then, after the dark had fallen, could the soul of Mary Jane perceive any beauty in that city, when the lamps were lit and here and there a star shone through the smoke. Then she would have gone abroad and beheld the night, but this the old woman to whom she was confided would not let her do. And the days multiplied themselves by seven and became weeks, and the weeks passed by, and all days were the same. And all the while the soul of Mary Jane was crying for beautiful things, and found not one, saving on Sundays, when she went to church, and left it to find the city greyer than before.

One day she decided that it was better to be a Wild Thing in the lonely marshes than to have a soul that cried for beautiful things and found not one. From that day she determined to be rid of her soul, so she told her story to one of the factory girls, and said to her:

"The other girls are poorly clad and they do soulless work; surely some of them have no souls and would take mine."

But the factory girl said to her: "All the poor have souls. It is all they have."

Then Mary Jane watched the rich whenever she saw them, and vainly sought for some one without a soul.

One day at the hour when the machines rested and the human beings that tended them rested too, the wind being at that time from the direction of the marshlands, the soul of Mary Jane lamented bitterly. Then, as she stood outside the factory gates, the soul irresistibly compelled her to sing, and a wild song came from her lips hymning the marshlands. And into her song came crying her yearning for home and for the sound of the shout of the North Wind, masterful and proud, with his lovely lady the snow; and she sang of tales that the rushes murmured to one another, tales that the teal knew and the watchful heron. And over the crowded streets her song went crying away, the song of waste places and of wild free lands, full of wonder and magic, for she had in her elf-made soul the song of the birds and the roar of the organ in the marshes.

At this moment Signor Thompsoni, the well-known English tenor, happened to go by with a friend. They stopped and listened; every one stopped and listened.

"There has been nothing like this in Europe in my time," said Signor Thompsoni.

So a change came into the life of Mary Jane.

People were written to, and finally it was arranged that she should take a leading part in the Covent Garden Opera in a few weeks.

So she went to London to learn.

London and singing lessons were better than the City of the Midlands and those terrible machines. Yet still Mary Jane was not free to go and live as she liked by the edge of the marshlands, and she was still determined to be rid of her soul, but could find no one that had not a soul of their own.

One day she was told that the English people would not listen to her as Miss Rush, and was asked what more suitable name she would like to be called by.

"I would like to be called Terrible North Wind," said Mary Jane, "or Song of the Rushes."

When she was told that this was impossible and Signorina Maria Russiano was suggested, she acquiesced at once, as she had acquiesced when they took her away from her curate; she knew nothing of the ways of humans.

At last the day of the Opera came round, and it was a cold day of the winter.

And Signorina Russiano appeared on the stage before a crowded house.

And Signorina Russiano sang.

And into the song went all the longing of her soul, the soul that could not go to Paradise, but could only worship God and know the meaning of music, and the longing pervaded that Italian song as the infinite mystery of the hills is borne along the sound of distant sheep-bells. Then in the souls that were in that crowded house arose little memories of a great while since that were quite, quite dead, and lived awhile again during that marvellous song.

And a strange chill went into the blood of all that listened, as though they stood on the border of bleak marshes and the North Wind blew.

And some it moved to sorrow and some to regret, and some to an unearthly joy,—then suddenly the song went wailing away like the winds of the winter from the marshlands when Spring appears from the South.

So it ended. And a great silence fell fog-like over all that house, breaking in upon the end of a chatty conversation that Celia, Countess of Birmingham, was enjoying with a friend.

In the dead hush Signorina Russiano rushed from the stage; she appeared again running among the audience, and dashed up to Lady Birmingham.

"Take my soul," she said; "it is a beautiful soul. It can worship God, and knows the meaning of music and can imagine Paradise. And if you go to the marshlands with it you will see beautiful things; there is an old town there built of lovely timbers, with ghosts in its streets."

Lady Birmingham stared. Every one was standing up. "See," said Signorina Russiano, "it is a beautiful soul."

And she clutched at her left breast a little above the heart, and there was the soul shining in her hand, with the green and blue lights going round and round and the purple flare in the midst.

"Take it," she said, "and you will love all that is beautiful, and know the four winds, each one by his name, and the songs of the birds at dawn. I do not want it, because I am not free. Put it to your left breast a little above the heart."

Still everybody was standing up, and Lady Birmingham felt uncomfortable.

"Please offer it to some one else," she said.

"But they all have souls already," said Signorina Russiano.

And everybody went on standing up. And Lady Birmingham took the soul in her hand.

"Perhaps it is lucky," she said.

She felt that she wanted to pray.

She half-closed her eyes, and said "Unberufen." Then she put the soul to her left breast a little above the heart, and hoped that the people would sit down and the singer go away.

Instantly a heap of clothes collapsed before her. For a moment, in the shadow among the seats, those who were born in the dusk hour might have seen a little brown thing leaping free from the clothes, then it sprang into the bright light of the hall, and became invisible to any human eye.

It dashed about for a little, then found the door, and presently was in the lamplit streets.

To those that were born in the dusk hour it might have been seen leaping rapidly wherever the streets ran northwards and eastwards, disappearing from human sight as it passed under the lamps and appearing again beyond them with a marsh-light over its head.

Once a dog perceived it and gave chase, and was left far behind.

The cats of London, who are all born in the dusk hour, howled fearfully as it went by.

Presently it came to the meaner streets, where the houses are smaller. Then it went due north-eastwards, leaping from roof to roof. And so in a few minutes it came to more open spaces, and then to the desolate lands, where market gardens grow, which are neither town nor country. Till at last the good black trees came into view, with their demoniac shapes in the night, and the grass was cold and wet, and the night-mist floated over it. And a great white owl came by, going up and down in the dark. And at all these things the little Wild Thing rejoiced elvishly.

And it left London far behind it, reddening the sky, and could distinguish no longer its unlovely roar, but heard again the noises of the night.

And now it would come through a hamlet glowing and comfortable in the night; and now to the dark, wet, open fields again; and many an owl it overtook as they drifted through the night, a people friendly to the Elf-folk. Sometimes it crossed wide rivers, leaping from star to star; and choosing its way as it went, to avoid the hard rough roads, came before midnight to the East Anglian lands.

And it heard there the shout of the North Wind, who was dominant and angry, as he drove southwards his adventurous geese; while the rushes bent before him chaunting plaintively and low, like enslaved rowers of some fabulous trireme, bending and swinging under blows of the lash, and singing all the while a doleful song.

And it felt the good dank air that clothes by night the broad East Anglian lands, and came again to some old perilous pool where the soft green mosses grew, and there plunged downward and downward into the dear dark water till it felt the homely ooze once more coming up between its toes. Thence, out of the lovely chill that is in the heart of the ooze, it arose renewed and rejoicing to dance upon the image of the stars.

I chanced to stand that night by the marsh's edge, forgetting in my mind the affairs of men; and I saw the marsh-fires come leaping up from all the perilous places. And they came up by flocks the whole night long to the number of a great multitude, and danced away together over the marshes.

And I believe that there was a great rejoicing all that night among the kith of the Elf-folk.

§

The Forest Dweller
Hermann Hesse

At the dawn of civilization, quite some time before human creatures began wandering over the face of the earth, they were forest dwellers. They lived close together fearfully in the dark tropical forests, constantly fighting with their relatives the apes, and the only divine law that governed their actions was the forest. The forest was their home, refuge, cradle, nest, and grave, and they could not imagine life outside the forest. They avoided coming too close to its borders, and whoever, through unusual circumstances while hunting or fleeing something, made his way to the borders would tremble with dread when later reporting about the white emptiness outside, where the terrifying nothingness glistened in the deadly fire of the sun.

There was an old forest dweller who decades before had been pursued by wild animals and had fled over the farthest border of the forest. He had immediately become blind and was now considered a kind of priest and saint and called Mata Dalam, "he with an interior eye." He had composed the holy forest song chanted during the great storms, and the forest dwellers always listened to what he had to say. His fame and secret rested on the fact that he had seen the sun with his eyes and had lived to tell about it.

The forest dwellers were small, brown, and hairy. When they walked, it was with a stoop, and they had furtive, wild eyes. They could move both like human beings and like apes and felt just as safe in the branches of the forest as they did on the ground. They had not yet learned about houses and huts. Nevertheless, they knew how to fabricate many kinds of weapons and tools, as well as jewelry. They made bows, arrows, lances, and clubs out of wood, and necklaces out of fibers from the trees strung with dried beets or nuts. They also wore precious objects around their necks or in their hair: a wild boar's tooth, a tiger's claw, a parrot's feathers, shells from mussels. There was a large river that flowed through the endless forest, but the forest dwellers did not dare to tread on its banks except in the dark of the night, and many had never seen it. Sometimes the more courageous of them crept out of the thickets at night, fearful and on the lookout. Then, in the faint glimmer of dusk, they would watch the elephants bathing and would look through the treetops above them and watch with dread the glittering stars hanging in the manifold branches of the mangrove trees. They never beheld the sun, and it was considered extremely dangerous to see its reflection in the summer.

There was a young man, Kubu, who belonged to the tribe of forest dwellers headed by the blind Mata Dalam, and he was the leader of the dissatisfied young people and their spokesman. In fact, ever since Mata Dalam had grown older and become more tyrannical, there had been malcontents in the tribe. It had always been the blind man's uncontested right to be provided with food by the tribespeople. In addition, they came to him for advice and sang his forest song. Gradually, however, he had introduced all sorts of new and burdensome customs that had been revealed to him, so he said, in dreams by the divine spirit of the forest. But several skeptical young men asserted that the old man was a swindler and was only concerned with advancing his own interests.

The most recent custom Mata Dalam had introduced was a new-moon celebration, during which he sat in the middle of a circle and beat a drum made of leather while the others sang the song "Gulo Elah" and danced until they were exhausted and collapsed on their knees. Then all the men had to pierce their left ears with a thorn, and the young women were led to the priest, who pierced their ears with a thorn.

Kubu and some other young men had shunned this ritual, and they endeavored to convince the young women to resist as well. One time, during a new-moon ceremony, it appeared as if they had a good chance to triumph over the priest and break his power. The old man was piercing the left ear of a woman, when a bold young man let out a terrible scream. The blind man chanced to stick the thorn into the woman's eye, which fell out of its socket. The young woman screamed in such despair that everyone ran over to her, and when they saw what had happened, they were stunned speechless. Immediately the young men began intervening, with triumphant smiles on their faces, and Kubu dared to grab the priest by his shoulders. But the old man stood up in front of his drum and uttered such a horrible curse, in a squealing, scornful voice, that everyone retreated in terror. Even the young man was petrified. Though nobody could understand the exact meaning of the old priest's words, his curse had a wild and awful tone and reminded everyone of the dreadful holy words of the religious ceremonies. And Mata Dalam cursed the young man's eyes, which he granted to the vultures as food, and he cursed his intestines, which, he prophesied, would roast in the sun one day on the open fields. Then the priest, who in this moment had more power than ever, ordered the young woman to be brought to him again, and he impaled her other eye with the thorn. Everyone looked on with horror, and no one dared to breathe.

"You will die outside!" was the old man's ultimate curse of Kubu, and then the forest dwellers began to shun the young man. "Outside": that meant outside the homeland, outside the dusky forest. "Outside": that meant horror, sunburn, and glowing deadly emptiness.

Kubu, terrified, began to flee, and everyone retreated from him. He hid himself far away in a hollow tree trunk and gave himself up for lost. Days and nights he lay there, wavering between mortal terror and spite, uncertain whether the people of his tribe would now come to kill him or whether the sun itself would break through the forest, besiege him, flush him out, and slay him. But the arrows and lances did not come, nor did the sun or lightning. Nothing came except great languor and the growling voice of hunger.

So Kubu stood up once again and crawled out of the tree trunk, with almost a feeling of disappointment. "The priest's curse was nothing," he thought in surprise, and then he looked for food. When he had eaten and felt life circulating through his limbs once more, pride and hate surged up in his soul. He did not want to return to his people anymore. All he wanted now was to be alone and remain alone. But he wanted, too, to take revenge: he wanted to be known as the one who had resisted the feeble curses of the priest, that blind ox.

So he walked around and pondered his situation. He reflected about everything that had ever aroused his doubts and had seemed questionable, especially the priest's drum and his rituals. And the more he thought and the longer he was alone, the clearer he could see. Yes, it was all deceit. Everything had been nothing but lies and deceit. And since he had already come so far in his thinking, he began drawing conclusions and came quickly to distrust everything, especially everything that was considered true and holy. He questioned whether there was a divine spirit in the forest or a holy forest song. Yes, that, too, was nothing. It was also a swindle. And as he overcame all his awe, he began singing the forest song in a scornful voice, distorting the words. And he called out the name of the divine spirit of the forest, whom nobody had been allowed to name on pain of death. Everything remained quiet. No storm exploded. No lightning struck him down!

Kubu wandered around in his isolation for many days and weeks, his forehead wrinkled, his eyes piercing. He went to the banks of the river at full moon, something nobody had ever dared to do. There he glanced long and bravely, first at the moon's reflection and then at the full moon itself and all the stars, right in their eyes, and nothing happened to him. He sat on the riverbank for entire moonlit nights, reveling in the forbidden delirium of light, and he nursed his thoughts. Many bold and terrible plans arose in his mind. "The moon is my friend," he thought, "and the star is my friend, but the blind old man is my enemy. Therefore, the 'outside' is perhaps better than our inside, and perhaps the entire holiness of the forest is also just talk!" And one night, generations before any other human being, Kubu conceived the daring plan of binding some branches together with fiber, placing himself on the branches, and floating down the river. His eyes glistened, his heart pounded with all its might. But this plan came to naught, for the river was full of crocodiles.

Consequently, there was no way into the future other than to leave the forest by way of the border, if there was indeed an end to the forest, and to entrust himself to the glowing emptiness, the evil "outside." That monster the sun had to be sought out and endured, for—who knew?—in the end even the ancient lore about the terror of the sun was perhaps also just a lie!

This thought, the last in a bold, feverish chain of reflections, made Kubu tremble. Never in the whole of history had a forest dweller dared to leave the forest of his own free will and to expose himself to the horrible sun. Once more, he walked around for days, carrying these thoughts with him, until he finally summoned his courage. Trembling, at noon on a bright day, he crept toward the river, cautiously approached the glittering bank, and anxiously looked for the image of the sun in the water. The glare was extremely painful to his dazzled eyes, and he quickly had to shut them. But after a while he dared to open them once more and then again and again, until he succeeded in keeping them open. It was possible. It was endurable. And it even made him happy and courageous. Kubu had learned how to trust the sun. He loved it, even if it was supposed to kill him, and he hated the old, dark, lazy forest, where the priest croaked and from where the courageous young man had been expelled.

Now he was ready to make his decision, and he picked his deed like a piece of ripe sweet fruit. He made a hammer out of ironwood and gave it a very thin and light handle. Early the next morning, he went looking for Mata Dalam. After discovering his tracks, he found him, hit him on the head with the hammer, and watched the old man's soul depart through his crooked mouth. Kubu placed his weapon on the priest's chest, and so that the people would know who had killed the old man, he took a mussel shell and carved a sign on the flat surface of the hammer. It was a circle with many straight rays—the image of the sun.

Bravely he now began his trip to the distant "outside." Walking from morning till night, straight ahead, he slept in the branches of trees. Early each morning he continued his wandering, over brooks and black swamps and eventually over moss-covered banks of stone and ever-steeper hills that he had never seen before. He was slowed down because of the gorges, but he managed to climb the mountains on his way through a forest so infinite that he ultimately became skeptical, wondering sadly whether there was perhaps a god who prohibited the creatures of the forest from leaving their homeland.

And then one evening, after he had been climbing for a long time and had reached an altitude where the air was much dryer and lighter, he came to an end without realizing it. The forest stopped, but with it also the ground. The forest plunged here down into the emptiness of the air as if the world had broken in two at this spot. There was nothing to see but a distant faint red glow and, above, some stars, for the night had already commenced.

Kubu sat down on the edge of the world and tied himself tightly to some climbing plants so that he would not fall over. He spent the night cowering in dread and was so wildly aroused that he could not shut his eyes. At the first hint of dawn, he jumped impatiently to his feet, bent over the emptiness, and waited for the day to appear.

Yellow stripes of beautiful light began to glimmer in the distance, and the sky seemed to tremble in anticipation, just as Kubu trembled, for he had never seen the beginning of the day in the wide space of air. And yellow bundles of light flamed, and suddenly the sun sprang up and appeared in the sky beyond the immense cleft of the world, large and red. It sprang up from an endless gray nothingness that soon became blue and black—the sea.

And the "outside" appeared before the trembling forest dweller. In front of his feet the mountain plunged down into the indiscernible smoking depths, and across from him some rose-tinted cliffs glistened like jewels. To the side lay the dark sea, immense and vast, and the coast ran white and foamy around it, with small nodding trees. And above all this, above these thousand new, strange, mighty forms, the sun was rising and cast a glowing steam of light over the world, which burst into flames of laughing colors.

Kubu was unable to look at the sun in its face. But he saw its light stream in colorful floods over the mountains and rocks and coasts and distant blue islands, and he sank to the ground and bent his face to the earth before the gods of this radiant world. Ah, who was he, Kubu? He was a small dirty animal that had spent its entire dull life in the misty swamp hole of the dense forest, fearful, morose, and submitting to the rule of the vile, crooked gods. But here was the world, and its highest god was the sun, and the long, disgraceful dream of his forest life lay behind him and was already being extinguished in his soul, just as the image of the dead priest was fading. Kubu climbed down the steep abyss on his hands and feet and moved toward the light and the sea. And over his soul, in fleeting waves of happiness, the dreamlike presentiment of a bright earth ruled by the sun began to flicker, an earth on which bright, liberated creatures lived in lightness and were not subservient to anyone except the sun.

Translated by Jack Zipes

‹   Cinderella Continued,   ›
or the Rat and the Six Lizards
GUILLAUME APOLLINAIRE

It has not been stated what became of Cinderella's coach and team when, after the second ball at court, having heard the first stroke of midnight and having lost her squirrel-fur slipper, she did not find them waiting at the gate of the royal palace.

The fairy—Cinderella's fairy godmother—was not so cruel as to turn the great hulking coachman (who had such fine mustachios) back into a rat, or the six footmen in lace-bedizened coats back into lizards, and since she had done them the honor of letting them remain men, by the same token she let the hollowed-out pumpkin remain a beautiful gilded coach and the six mice remain six fine, dappled mouse-gray horses.

But at the first stroke of midnight the great hulking coachman took it into his head that he would do better out of selling the coach and horses than skimping along on his wages, year in and year out, and that the six footmen, thoroughgoing idlers, would be only too glad to form a band—of which he would be the chief—which would prey upon travelers on the great highways.

Giddyap, then! Coach and team smartly set off before Cinderella reached the palace gate. He halted only at an inn, where, whilst nibbling at a turkey flanked by a pair of fattened pullets and gulping down brimming tankards of wine, the noble band sold the horses and the carriage to the innkeeper—who offered them *pistoles* enough. In this way they changed their clothes and armed themselves. The great hulking coachman, whose name was Sminthe, adopted a special disguise. His mustachios having been shaved off, he dressed as a woman and put on a green satin skirt, a dress *à l'ange,* and a cape. In that garb he was in a position to direct his six rascally companions without risk to himself. Things being arranged to the satisfaction of both parties, they bade the innkeeper farewell and quit Paris to, as the saying has it, *live in clover, wandering the roads.*

We shall not follow them in their exploits on the highways, about the fairs, and in the castles, where the band managed so well that, in a mere seven years, they could return to Paris, where they lived off the fat of the land.

During the time he had lived in female dress, Sminthe had taken to a stay-at-home way of life, which led him to give due thought to the brilliant operations he had had carried out by the six brigands-footmen-lizards; he had also learned to read and had amassed a quantity of books, among which were the *Révélations de Sainte Brigitte,* the *Alphabet de l'imperfection et malice des femmes,* the *Centuries* of Nostradamus, the *Prédictions de l'enchanteur Merlin,* and a good few more singular works of a like sort. He acquired a taste for learning, and after the band had gone into retirement, Sminthe spent a good deal of his time in his library, reading and meditating on the power of the fairies, on the vanity that is intelligence or human cunning, and on the foundations of true happiness. And seeing him always immured in his book-filled room, his six acolytes (who among themselves called him not Sminthe but Lerat, because of his origins, or rather because of what they knew of them, for unawares they paid homage to that animal, as do savages who honor their totems and the animals therein depicted) came in the end to call him Lerat de Bibliothèque; the name stuck, and it was under that name that he was known in the Rue de Bussy, where he lived and compiled numerous works, which have not been published but which have been preserved in manuscript in Oxford.

Such time as remained to him he devoted to the education of his six scoundrels, each of whom made his way in the world—the first as a painter who executed marvelous likenesses of innkeepers' lovely wives, the second as a poet who composed songs which the third set to music and gave life to on the lute whilst the fourth danced perfect sarabands in which he assumed a thousand refined and droll attitudes. The fifth became an excellent sculptor and fashioned gracious statues in lard for pork butchers' shopwindows, and the sixth an unrivaled architect, endlessly building castles in Spain. Since they were always seen together—although nobody had any inkling of what they had been—they were called *"les Arts"* for between them, they represented the six: Poetry, Painting, Sculpture, Architecture, Music and the Dance. And here we may admiringly note how shrewd is popular etymology—*les Arts* having been *lézards*.

Sminthe or Lerat de Bibliothèque died in the odor of sanctity, and four of his companions likewise died in their beds. Lacerte the poet and Armonidor the musician outlived them and conducted their affairs so maladroitly that they were constrained, in order to make a living, to live once more on their wits. One night, having forced an entry to the Palais Royal, they carried off a casket. They opened it on their return home and found therein only a pair of white and gray fur slippers. They were Queen Cinderella's squirrel-fur slippers, and at the very moment they were despairing of profiting by their find, the officers of the watch (who had made out their tracks) came upon the scene, arrested them, and marched them off to the Grand Châtelet.

The crime was so grave and so well attested that they were beyond hope of avoiding execution.

They opted to cast dice to decide which should take all the blame on himself and exonerate the other.

The loser—Armonidor—was as good as his word and saved his confederate by declaring that he had suggested they take a walk and that his friend knew nothing of his intentions.

Thus Lacerte returned home and composed his friends' epitaphs; but a month later he died, for his art did not make him a living and he was eaten up with weariness.

As for the little squirrel-fur slippers, the vagaries of time brought it about that they are now to be found in the museum of Pittsburgh in Pennsylvania, where they are catalogued as: *Pin Trays (first half of the nineteenth century)*, although they are authentically of the seventeenth century; nonetheless, this description leads one to believe that they were in fact used as pin trays in the period indicated by the antiquaries of Pittsburgh.

However, one is at a loss to explain how it was that Cinderella's little squirrel-fur slippers found their way to America.

Translated by Iain White

The Three Wishes

Kurt Schwitters

Once upon a time there was a man who wanted something, only he didn't know what. However, he at least knew that whatever he wanted had to be special.

One day he encountered a hunchbacked old woman, who said, "Young man, I see that you want something."

The man was astonished that she could see this, and he said, "You're right, my good woman, but I don't know exactly what I want."

Then the old woman replied, "I know what it is, but I won't tell you. I have the power to grant you what you want and will give you three wishes. Each time, your wish will be fulfilled. But you may only wish something from me three times. So be sure that you make smart wishes."

Then suddenly there was a puff of smoke, and the old woman disappeared. However, the difficult part was about to begin. Just imagine that you are suddenly granted three wishes. You probably wouldn't know what to do. Most people would probably not know what to do.

The man began to consider all that one could possibly wish for in life, and then he realized what he wanted. It was happiness. But he thought some more. If he were to wish for happiness, then the old witch could give him some trash and say that it was happiness. For instance, she could confuse his feelings so that he might believe he was basically happy the way he was. No, he refused to have anything to do with such a swindle. He wanted to have something solid, a happiness that would be the envy of others, since happiness is only that which others also want to possess.

And so it occurred to him that a person had to define the notion of happiness more precisely if one really wanted to be happy. Thus he wished for wealth.

All of a sudden he was rich. The gigantic castle in which he lived was teeming with servants. He lay in golden pajamas on a tremendously large bed, so soft that he could no longer even feel it. A servant handed him a tiny cup of mocha on a thin reddish tray, and the mocha was so strong that a heavy teaspoon could stand up straight in the cup. The drink was sweetened with saccharin, and the servant was dressed in a uniform of ivory.

However, the man in bed said, "Is this the best you can offer me?" And he kicked the tray with his violet felt slippers so that the teaspoon flew into the ivory-liveried servant. Then he jumped out of his large feather bed and shouted fiercely, "I'll show you what a rich man is!" He took one of the three hundred and thirty telephones that lay next to his bed and ordered all the pianos of the world to be delivered immediately and had them dumped in a nearby river. That was the end of piano music, and the traffic of the boats on the river was blocked for months. But this did not disturb him in the least.

On the other hand, it didn't make the man happy. So he meditated and then gave the strangest orders. He had all his servants bathe in chocolate. But this, too, did not make him happy.

Then the old woman appeared beside his bed and said, "You made the wrong wish, but you still have two more. Choose the right one, and you'll be happy." And again there was a puff of smoke, and the old woman disappeared.

The rich man felt quite unhappy, for he didn't know what the devil he should wish for. What was there that could make a man happy if wealth couldn't do it?

Suddenly he knew—world power.

And in a flash, he was the mightiest king of all time. He ruled not only the earth but the cosmos. The electrons from the most distant planets came to glorify him. His name stood on all the dishware, was broadcast constantly on the radio by the propaganda bureau, his was the only name there was. Rich and happy people no longer existed.

He himself no longer lived in the large, soft feather bed. Rather he had his bodyguards build him a house made out of atoms between the earth and the moon, where he spent all his weekends. Yet all this power did not make him happy. He became bored because, unfortunately, there were no more wars. Therefore, he had two great planets crash together for a change of pace, and the reason he gave for this was that he did not like the noses of the people on one of those planets. But what was the use of all this? The blast was great, and the flames even greater. Yet after the excitement died down, he became bored once again. He needed something that would last. That's why he had glowing meteors hung over the heads of his subjects so they would live in constant fear, and all this was done just to please him. But soon he had these meteors dismantled, because they were no longer fun. And so he thought and thought how he, the world ruler, had been deprived of good entertainment, and he almost wished for an enemy so there would at least be a war. Just at that moment the old woman appeared next to his bungalow and told him that he had made the wrong wish, but he still had one more. He had better think more carefully and choose the right one this time.

Then there was the puff of smoke, and the woman disappeared. However, the man remained troubled because, God help him, it seemed that there was nothing better in the world to wish for than all the power in the world.

By chance he overheard one of his bodyguards saying something about one of the other bodyguards: "Yes, he's got it good. He can take anything. Nature's given him an even temperament, and he feels just as happy as a fish in water." Then the man pointed to his forehead with his index finger and said to himself, "Use your head!" And he was happy that he finally had hit upon the right wish. Naturally, fish, they've got it good. They feel happy just to be in water. Why should it be any other way? They wouldn't feel so well in air. He finally knew how to use his head.

And so he wished for the shape of a fish. And within seconds his shape changed, and he looked like a fish. Then he had himself lowered so he could spring headfirst into the river. But the water was so wet and he had so much trouble breathing that he doubled over and gasped for breath. Indeed, he was speechless and couldn't even complain, because he had been given the attributes of a fish but not its nature. He opened and shut his mouth as though he wanted to say something, but all fish do this, and not a sound is heard, though they try very hard. Then he thought that the story about a fish in water was a fairy tale. Fish only *seem* to be happy in water. At any rate, he did not feel happy as a fish. He couldn't even shed one tear about his bad luck, for everything around him was water, and his tears could not be seen. Then a school of small fish swam by in a hurry, fleeing from some larger fish, and this made him shiver all the more. Next he saw a fish being eaten by a water lily and wriggling softly. Finally, it occurred to him: "If only I had remained ruler of the world! Most men never have the chance in a lifetime to become as powerful as I was. Or, at least, if only I had remained as rich as I once was!"

And suddenly the old woman reappeared, swimming next to him. He became happy and followed her to the surface of the water, where he was immediately changed back into his original shape and became an ordinary man.

Then the wise old woman said to the young man, "You've chosen the way most other men would have chosen, since they all seek happiness outside themselves. You've now seen that happiness does not lie just anywhere. It can only lie within yourself. Remember, too, that others also want to be happy. Then be happy, and you'll be able to make others happy too."

All at once there was a loud blast, and the old woman disappeared. This time there was a smell of brimstone.

Translated by Jack Zipes

The Seventh Dwarf

Franz Hessel

'm the seventh dwarf.

You all know that Snow White stayed with us and what happened. But nobody knows me.

She slept in my bed after she had tried the others and found they were too small. Mine was also too small. But she continued to sleep there. And I shared the bed of my sixth brother. Yet I couldn't sleep, because I couldn't take my eyes off the beautiful creature in my bed.

I had met the tiny women of the moss. They're darlings but much too affectionate. Gnome women too. They're busy and cheerful, but they never shut up. At times I had seen the dancing fairies on the moist meadows in the moonlight. Their veils are incredibly thin and fine. But beautiful Snow White, she was something else. . . . I remember how she threw us kisses when we went to work on the first morning! I was the last one out the door. My heart pounded furiously like a silver hammer.

The way she kept house for us, it was charming. There were always flowers on the table. But she never managed to sweep up the dust in the corners. I had to go over them with my sixth brother. I did it gladly.

You all know that we had some bad luck with Snow White. It was I who pulled the wicked queen's poison comb from Snow White's hair, which completely covered me as I did it.

It was I who loosened the corset that would have strangled her. Yes, I was the first of the seven dwarfs to discover the witch's trick with the corset.

But then came the trick with the poison apple. Nothing could be done to help. Snow White was as good as dead. And we built the glass coffin. When we carried her through the forest, we met that amazing manly specimen the handsome prince—bright blue feathers on his cap, a smooth jersey, puffed sleeves, tight pants, everything tight.

My brothers were glad to give him the coffin with Snow White as a gift, since he was so eager to have it. I was against this.

I ran after the prince's coffin bearers. They walked rapidly with their long human legs. I had to hop as fast as I could.

More than anything else I wanted to see Snow White's face one more time. Quickly, quickly I rushed and jumped through the high grass and over the thick roots of the trees, my small lantern swinging at my side.

When I finally caught up with the long-legged men and rushed by them in order to get a last look at the glass coffin from the front, I frightened one of the bearers, and he stumbled. The others lost their balance. The coffin swayed on their shoulders. They set it down. They looked inside. I, too, looked inside, through their legs. The top opened. Snow White was alive. She held the piece of apple peel in her hand. It had popped out of her mouth. Then she said to herself, "Where am I?" The prince replied, "With me!" She sank into his arms. He lifted her onto his horse.

I stood still and had to witness all this. And until this very day, Snow White still doesn't know that she owes her life to me, nor does her handsome prince. And she doesn't know how much I loved her.

She probably thinks about the seven dwarfs every now and then, especially when the children sing about the seven dwarfs, who live beyond the mountains. But I'm sure that she has long since forgotten me, the last one, the seventh.

Translated by Jack Zipes

his is a true story, and it shows that even in the most en-
lightened times miracles are possible.

There was once a small Jewish shtetl in the Ukraine,
where a father was sitting with his family. The First World
War had not occurred yet, and the czar ruled in Saint Petersburg. However, the "Black Hand" was a strong force in the
Ukraine and reigned there. And people needed money again,
and the Jews were there and had become prosperous through
their various businesses. So someone began to spread rumors, about Easter,
about bad words that were said about the priests, and about a Jew who had
laughed when someone had said something about the Holy Mother of God
at Czestochowa, and other things were promulgated as well. Moreover, the
Black Hand had arranged to provide the proper excuses later: the police were
having a celebration and the colonel was sitting at the banquet table right
on the day that everything was to happen.

And what was to take place? They were going to band together. Their
plans had already leaked out, but what good was it—a pogrom is a pogrom.
Blood flows. But the Jewish people are not children, and ultimately blood
must be shed, for they won't let themselves be torn apart by vicious animals.

There was a father who protected his house very, very well, and he also
had an ax during the pogrom, and there were probably some who saw that

he had an ax. Consequently the father thought he had better not wait for the investigation and the trial, and he took off with his family, and since it was impossible to predict what might happen, he separated his two eldest sons and said, "Lemberg!" and gave them money. But he saw only one of them later. The other, who could sing so beautifully, did not show up. They never heard a word from him. Their dear son had been swallowed up by the earth. Father and mother moved to a small city. The relatives did what they could for them, and they pulled themselves back up on their feet. Indeed, they also survived the First World War. But neither the father nor the mother was happy anymore. Their dear son was gone, and they talked about the whole affair a thousand times.

"You set an example for him," the mother complained. "He probably took an ax or a knife. A Jew should hide."

"Should I have let them kill me and all the rest of you as well?"

"Ah, there are still plenty of us living where we used to live."

And time passed. The mother died. The father was in poor condition. His surviving son supported him, and the relatives helped. Despite it all, the father still went wherever he could to hear voices singing, and he thought, "Oh, how my Izzie could sing! Such a beautiful, beautiful voice. Where can you find such beautiful voices today?"

The fact that he heard so much music and went to concerts was God's will. The mother had died, but the father was destined to learn that God lived and had not forgotten him. On his seventieth birthday, the head of the community gave him a gramophone as a present, and he had it played for him. In addition, his oldest son brought him the newest invention, a radio, and with that he could hear things from far, far away, wherever people sang in the entire world, no matter who it was. Not Izzie, though.

Day after day he listened to all the voices, so many, so resounding, and the pop hits they now made, the music that everyone danced to. And one day toward noon his radio was playing, and his daughter-in-law was cooking in the kitchen. The door swung open, and the old father, with his yarmulke slanted on the side of his bald head, came running into the kitchen with large, large eyes and screamed, "Rosalie, listen! Listen!"

"For God's sake, what's wrong with the man? I'm going to run and get Yankel."

"Listen, Rosalie, he's singing. It's Izzie! Rosalie, my child, listen for a minute! I'm sure it's Izzie!"

And she had to hold him tight and lead him to a kitchen chair, the old man. The music ended. It was a temple song. A pop song followed. She wanted to turn the radio off, but didn't. Perhaps it would come again.

What more is there to say? They believed the old man. The son traveled to Warsaw with him. There they found a record, and his name was on the record, an English name. He was an American cantor, a famous man. They found one more record by him in Warsaw.

And then the telegrams went back and forth, and it really was Izzie, who had made it to America with a push and a shove. He had searched for his parents in Russia, but then the war had come, and how could he have looked for them then? So finally the radio had made everything possible, and that's technology. It brought a son back to his father, and both know God's alive, and whoever believes in him can count on him.

Translated by Jack Zipes

‹ The Girl and the Wolf ›
JAMES THURBER

ne afternoon a big wolf waited in a dark forest for a little girl to come along carrying a basket of food to her grandmother. Finally a little girl did come along and she was carrying a basket of food. "Are you carrying that basket to your grandmother?" asked the wolf. The little girl said yes, she was. So the wolf asked her where her grandmother lived and the little girl told him and he disappeared into the wood.

When the little girl opened the door of her grandmother's house she saw that there was somebody in bed with a nightcap on. She had approached no nearer than twenty-five feet from the bed when she saw that it was not her grandmother but the wolf, for even in a nightcap a wolf does not look any more like your grandmother than the Metro-Goldwyn lion looks like Calvin Coolidge. So the little girl took an automatic out of her basket and shot the wolf dead.

Moral: *It is not so easy to fool little girls nowadays as it used to be.*

—§—

The Fairy Tale of the King

Georg Kaiser

nce upon a time there was a king who was worshiped by everyone around him. If he laughed on his throne, then all the ladies and gentlemen of his court laughed with him. If he wept in his royal bed, his marshals interrupted their sleep and whatever else they might be doing and wept with him. If he feasted, his palace became a large dining hall where everyone gorged himself and lived it up. Whatever he did was constantly mirrored by the court, so that he could see his own reflection a hundred times over. All this bored him so very much that he finally decided to seek the truth: Am I powerful, or is my power only reflected in the mirror?

Therefore, the king disguised himself and went out among the people. Most of the time one discovers the truth behind a mask.

In the taverns of the harbor, in the barns of the farmers, in the barracks of the army, even in the brothels of the cities, he was forced to learn that the people laughed at a king who could not even magically conjure money, though the finance minister in his speeches maintained that he could. In the brothels he encountered gentlemen from his court who enjoyed themselves there and mocked the king. One of them even gave him a kick because he did not recognize the king for who he was. Without his official robes and his servants, he was nothing.

In his search for the truth, he eventually found a young woman who had finished with life. Her parents and her bridegroom had been executed because their tax debts had been too high: *by command of the king,* as it had been stated in the judgment.

When the king began to console the young woman, he was seized by a great love for her, which was clearly reciprocated. So after their disappointment, the king and the young woman found the truth of life. Happy about the first and only good deed he ever did, the king took the young woman for his wife. With her as queen, he decided to found a new realm, the realm of Love, a fairy tale realm in which even fish were seen to mate in the air.

Translated by Jack Zipes

The Fairy Tale About Common Sense
ERICH KÄSTNER

nce upon a time there was a nice old gentleman who had the nasty habit of thinking up sensible things to do every now and then. That is, his habit only became a nasty one after he stopped keeping his ideas to himself and began presenting them to experts. Since he was rich and respected in spite of his plausible ideas, the experts had to be patient and listen to him with throbbing ears. Certainly there is no greater torture for experts than to listen to a sensible proposal with smiles on their faces. Everyone knows that common sense simplifies the difficult in a way that makes problems for experts. They justifiably feel that common sense is an unlawful intrusion into their spheres of expertise, which they have worked hard to contrive and guard. Taking their interests into consideration, one asks what would happen to these poor people if they didn't rule their domains and were replaced by common sense. What then?

One day it was announced that the nice old gentleman would speak at a conference attended by the most important statesmen on earth. According to the report, these men were to meet and discuss ways to get rid of all the strife and want in the world. "Lord almighty," they thought, "who knows what the old man's planned for us now with his stupid common sense!" And then they asked him to enter. He came, bowed in a somewhat old-fashioned manner, and took a seat. He smiled. They smiled. Finally, he began to speak.

"Gentlemen," he said, "I believe that I've come up with a useful idea. Its practical application has been tested. Now I'd like to make it known to people in your sphere as heads of state. Please listen to me. Not for my sake but in the interest of common sense."

The heads of state nodded, smiling through their torture, and he continued: "You intend to provide peace and freedom for your peoples, and though your economic concerns may be very different, this meeting indicates that you are first and foremost interested in the welfare of all the inhabitants of the earth from the viewpoint of common sense. Or am I incorrect on this point?"

"Heaven forbid!" they protested. "Not at all! What do you think of us, nice old man?"

"How wonderful!" he exclaimed. "Then your problem is solved. I congratulate you and your people. Return to your homes and, bearing in mind the financial situation of your states and the laws of each constitution, grant every citizen a certain sum according to a progressive scale based on their earnings, which I have figured out to the last penny and shall give you at the end of my talk. Here is what should happen with this sum: Each family in each one of your countries will receive as a present a pretty little house with six rooms, a garden, and a garage with a car. And since the estimated sum will still not be used up after this—even that has been calculated—a new school and a modern hospital will be built in each locale that has more than five thousand inhabitants. I envy you, for even though I don't believe that material things embody the highest earthly goods, I have enough common sense to realize that peace among peoples depends first on the material satisfaction of human beings. If I've just said that I envy you, then I've lied. Actually, I'm happy."

The nice old man took a cigar from his pocket and lit it.

The smiles on the faces of the statesmen had by now become distorted. Finally, the supreme head of the heads of states pulled himself together and asked in a sizzling voice, "How high do you estimate the sum for your purposes?"

"For my purposes?" responded the old gentleman, and his tone indicated that he was slightly vexed.

"Well, are you going to tell us?" the second-highest head of state yelled unwillingly. "How much money is necessary for this little joke?"

"One hundred thousand billion dollars," the nice old gentleman answered calmly. "That is the figure one with fourteen zeros."

Then he puffed again on his small cigar.

"You're completely out of your mind!" someone yelled, also a head of state.

The nice old gentleman sat up straight and regarded the accuser in astonishment. "How can you possibly think that?" he asked. "Naturally, this matter involves a lot of money, but the last war was just as expensive, according to the statistics we have."

At this, the ministers and heads of states roared with laughter. They howled unabashed. They slapped their thighs and crowed like roosters. Finally, they washed the tears of laughter from their eyes.

The nice old gentleman was puzzled and looked from one to the next. "I don't fully understand the cause of your merriment," he said. "Would you be so kind as to explain to me what it is that you think so funny? If a long war costs one hundred thousand billion dollars, why shouldn't a long peace be worth exactly the same? What in all the world is so funny about this?"

Now they all laughed even louder. It was demonic laughter. One of the heads of state could no longer keep his seat. He jumped up, held on to his ribs so they would not burst, and yelled with the last bit of energy at his command, "You old blockhead! War—war is something entirely different!"

The heads of state, the nice old gentleman, and their discussion are entirely fictitious. On the other hand, American statistics cited in the *Frankfurter Neue Presse* of 1946 have accurately demonstrated that the hundred thousand billion dollars spent in the last war could actually finance such a project as that proposed by the nice old gentleman.

Translated by Jack Zipes

< *The Smile of the Sphinx* >

INGEBORG BACHMANN

t a time when all monarchs were endangered—to explain
what constituted this danger is useless, since dangers have too
many causes and none at the same time—the ruler of a certain
country, our subject of concern here, was overcome by restlessness and sleeplessness. It was not that he felt himself
threatened "from beneath," from his people. The threat
came from above, from unspoken demands and instructions,
which he believed he had to follow and which were unfamiliar to him.

Moreover, when the ruler was informed that a shadow had appeared on
the roads approaching his castle, he felt convinced that he had to call up the
shadow, which perhaps concealed the danger, and compel it to assume a life
of its own so he could fight it. Soon he encountered the shadow that had
been reported to him. It was difficult to judge its shape, because the shadow
was too large to view all at once. At first the monarch saw nothing but a
horrendous animal, which dragged itself slowly through the region. Only later
did he succeed in discovering a flat, wide face on the spot where he surmised
the skull to be, and he realized that at any moment the creature could open
its mouth and ask for answers that had been promised to it centuries before
the king had lived. Indeed, the king had recognized it as the strange, dreadful
Sphinx, over whom he had to prevail if his country and people were to

continue to exist. Therefore, he opened his mouth first, challenging her to challenge him.

"The interior of the earth is concealed from our view," she began, "but you are now to peer inside, spread out before me those things which the earth is hiding, and tell me all about their fire and substance."

The ruler smiled and commanded his scholars and workers to traverse the surface of the earth, drill holes in it, reveal it secrets, measure everything, and translate all they found into the most subtle and precise formulations that had ever been conceived. He himself followed the progress of the work, which was mirrored in splendid charts and thick books.

Finally they reached the point where the ruler was able to command his subordinates to display the work they had accomplished. The Sphinx could not avoid admitting that the work had turned out to be perfect and unassailable. But it seemed to many of them that she did not really respect the results. Yet, to her credit, no one could say that she had behaved incorrectly.

If some still feared it would now become manifest that the Sphinx had wanted to lull the king into a feeling of security only in order to spring a trap, their doubts were now dispelled. The second question was once again unmistakable and simple in its wording. The monster, which was practically disenchanted, calmly demanded that everyone set about to determine the essence of things that cover the earth, as well as the spheres that surround it. This time the scientists surpassed their former calculations. They added an incredibly sophisticated investigation of the universe and included the orbits of the planets, all the celestial bodies, the pasts and futures of material substances, harboring malicious pleasure in anticipating the Sphinx's third question.

Even to the king it seemed impossible that there was still something to ask, and he presented the solution, sensing imminent triumph. Did the Sphinx close her lids? Did she have any sight at all? Cautiously the ruler sought to read her visage.

The Sphinx took much time before she posed the third question, and everyone became certain that in answering the second question overzealously, they had in fact won the deadly game. However, when they perceived her slight quiver, they were paralyzed without being able to say why.

"What do you think is in the people whom you rule?" she inquired into the king's pensive countenance.

The king had a desire to answer with a quick joke in order to bring things to a finish, but he held himself back in the nick of time and withdrew to reflect upon the matter.

Then he began pushing his people around, getting them to cooperate, and because they let themselves be pushed around, they became angry. A series of experiments was undertaken, in which people were obliged to undress.

They were forced to lose their shame, urged to give confessions to expose the slime of their lives; their thoughts were torn apart and ordered into a hundred different rows of statistics.

There was no end in sight, but the investigators concealed this fact; meanwhile the king went through the laboratories as if he had no trust whatsoever in them and was thinking about a faster and more effective process. This was confirmed one day when he commanded the most important scholars and most capable civil servants to come to him. He ordered all work to cease immediately and held secret sessions in which he laid out ideas whose consequences all were soon to feel.

A short time later, the people were ordered to form groups and go to areas where highly specialized guillotines had been erected. Then each individual was summoned with painstaking precision to a guillotine, to be transported from life to death.

The revelation that resulted from this process was so overwhelming that it exceeded the king's expectations. Nevertheless, for the sake of thoroughness and perfection, he did not hesitate to have the rest of the men, those who had been useful to him in organizing and setting up the guillotines, submit to the machines as well, so that the solution of the riddle would not be endangered.

Bowed in silent expectation, the king went before the Sphinx. He saw her shadow spread like a protective cloak over the dead, who could not say now what there was to say.

Breathless, the king demanded of the Sphinx that she lift herself away to receive his answer, but she indicated to him by a gesture that she no longer cared. He had found the third answer, he was free, his own life and that of his country were at his disposal.

Over her face flowed a wave that emerged from a sea of mysteries. Then she smiled and left, and by the time the king had thought about everything, she had crossed the border and departed from his realm.

Translated by Jack Zipes

The Tale of the Singing Branch, ‹ › the Bird of Truth, and the Water of Youth

HENRI POURRAT

Once upon a time there was a king; he was getting on in years, but his blood was still young and his heart all fire. His chief wish was that all the people in his country might know happiness on earth. And a fine thing it is to wish for, when we let our deeds follow our wishes.

This king, then, set out to make a tour of his country, from house to house. He visited every one of them and inquired as to how things went for all who lived there. And when he came across a young girl, he asked her what she had seen in her dreams the night before. So much did he have every man's happiness at heart that he had forgotten to think of his own: he had never married. But he was very fond of talking with young girls.

When his trip was about over, before his return to the castle, he stopped in at the house of his nearest neighbor.

The man had three daughters, three fair lasses in bloom. The king entered, greeted them, and addressed the eldest.

"What dream did you dream last night, damsel?"

"Oh, sire, I should not dare . . . it is hard to tell! But if I must . . . Sire, here is my dream: it was that I married your chief cook."

"Very well, damsel, what you dreamed last night shall be fulfilled."

He addressed the second. "What dream did you dream last night, damsel?"

"Sire, it is very hard for me to tell you. Still, if I must, here it is, my dream: it was that I married your chief groom of the bedchamber."

"Very well, damsel, what you dreamed last night shall be fulfilled."

At last he turned to the youngest.

"Damsel, and you?"

The girl looked at him, and a blush rose to her cheeks that made her redder than a cherry, and her eyes shone like the star in the fountain. But not a word.

"And you, damsel?"

"Sire, to tell it is still harder for me."

"Damsel, you must."

Listen to her, the mad girl! What boldness! Still, that was her fate, and she was forced to confess the truth; simply, artlessly, with her heart in her voice, she told what was in her mind.

"Sire, my dream was that I married you yourself."

"Damsel, what you have dreamed this night shall be fulfilled."

And with these words the king left.

To see the two sisters, snarling with envy, their blood aboil with malice, like cats in a fury! You would have thought them about to spring on their youngest sister and rend her with their claws. "Look at her, will you? That dollface, that pretty sweetheart! To think she dared! And the king let himself be caught by her wiles! The hussy, she need only throw herself at his head, and she will be her majesty the queen! And we, her elder sisters, wife of her cook, wife of a valet! What shall we be? Her servants?"

What they could not bear, those vixens, was the thought that if only the idea had come to them, the queen's crown would have been theirs. No fear of their holding themselves cheap; to their minds they far outstripped their younger sister, both in beauty and in worth.

She, poor thing, before their fury, all she could do was to rub her eyes and cry. Red, and redder yet, like the wood strawberry, and fragrant as the berry, for when asp and salamander breathe out poison, it absorbs no venom from them. Would to heaven that the two sisters had thrown off their venom in their words and complaints. But it gathered in their hearts. From that hour they planned that one day they would wreak their vengeance. Powers of God, if people had only known. . . .

Shortly after, in the fair month of May, the three weddings were held. All went as the king had said: the two elder sisters became wives to the cook and the groom of the bedchamber; the youngest became queen.

Months passed. Then a great war broke out, and the king was forced to go. While he was away the queen gave birth to a son. Her two sisters were with her; they would not allow any but themselves to care for the child, nor take it to be baptized. Once back from the christening, they put the child in a basket, and the basket down at the end of the garden, on the river. Somewhere about the castle they had seen a little monkey—perhaps it was the king's whim to keep wild beasts in his castle. And the sisters took this bit of a monkey, and instead of the little boy, they gave him to their sister.

Down a way, down a way, by a bend of the river, beside the water, was the garden of an old gardener and his old wife. They lived there together in a mean little house. The gardener had just transplanted his lettuce; it was time to water it. Down he went to the riverbank with his watering pot. And there, under a willow tree, he heard weeping. He looked about; in the midst of the mint and the wild iris, he found a basket, a tiny child.

Quickly he took it up and brought it to the house.

"See here, good wife—guess what I've brought you!"

"And what are you bringing me, good man?"

"A new little boy! We've never had any: this one will be ours."

In the meantime the king had come back from war. His wife had thought to show him their son, and it was the little monkey she showed him. The king was all amazement. . . .

And months went by. Another war must have broken out; however it was, the king went away again. And while he was far off, the queen had another son. And the two elder sisters, those vipers, played their evil trick again. But this time, instead of a monkey, it was a lion cub.

And once more the basket came to land in front of the gardener's house. When he brought it to his wife, this time she threw her hands in the air.

"My good man! Haven't we enough with one?"

"What could I do, good wife? I hadn't the heart to let him cry. The good Lord gave us another; we must take him."

"Well, they can amuse each other."

When the king came back, and when they showed him this lion cub as his child, he wondered what sorcery was this. He swallowed three times before he could speak. In the end, he loved his wife so much that he told her he would let it go this once more, but that such a thing must not happen again!

A third war broke out. The king went off to it. Months passed, and there was born to the queen in her castle a pretty little girl. And as before, the two sisters brought her to be christened in church. When they came back they gave the queen a crocodile.

Again the gardener heard a sound of weeping by the river, and in the reeds and the mint, under the willow, he found the new little girl.

"See here, good wife, what has come for us! The river has a grudge against us."

"Already we have two boys, and you bring me another?"

"But this time it's a girl, good wife. She can help you in the house."

The king came home. His wife, who thought to show him their daughter, brought forth this wild beast.

The king fell back several paces. Then, his hands before his eyes, he left the room. And he ordered that his wife be shut up in a tower.

The king thought of her a great deal. He saw her again as he had seen her that first morning, with the lovely fire of candor shining from her face. All rosy red, but looking him straight in the eyes, forced to tell him her dream, because that was her fate; simple as a clover blossom, and smelling as sweet. And now it had all turned into these horrors. . . .

Perhaps he was too good, was the king. As they say,

> *Simple and Saint go hand in hand,*
> *Far too good to walk the land.*

It was not in him to conceive of baseness like that of his wife's two sisters.

Months went by, summers and winters. The king looked all of thirty years older.

In the meantime the three children were growing up in the gardener's house. They had heard it said—perhaps by the beggars passing by, perhaps by the wind in the trees—that over the way where the sun rose there was a spring. By this spring could be found the singing branch, the bird who speaks truth, and the water that gives back youth.

To each child the gardener had given his own garden, and each one had a rosebush growing there. The eldest boy wanted to go in search of the spring. "I will bring you some of the water," he told the gardener and his wife, who by now could barely walk, bent over their canes. They would not have him leave, but what he wanted, that he would have.

He said to his brother, "If you see my rosebush withering, it will be a sign I am in great peril."

And he left, going straight before him, over where the sun rose.

He trudged along, along. By the side of a green meadow he met an old woman.

"Boy, where are you going?"

"I am looking for the singing branch, the bird that speaks truth, and the water that gives back youth."

"So! Well, listen to me: when you are a bit farther along, put your two fingers in your ears; you will hear drums and sweet music, but watch yourself—don't move, don't listen: keep on your way!"

Well and good: the boy paid heed to her and did all that she had told him. He kept to the road and he stopped up his ears. But when he heard the music, like drums and flutes, violins and lutes, that rose with the force of a storm and swept all before it, ah, it was too beautiful; he could think of nothing else. He took out his fingers so as to hear the better, and down he fell, changed to stone.

Every morning and evening, when the dew fell, his brother went down to the garden and looked at the rosebush. One day he saw the rosebush turning yellow, and suddenly it died. Quickly he ran to find his sister, and his own healthy color had left him.

"Watch over my rosebush, watch over our parents. My brother is dead. I am leaving."

Far away, on the road beside the green meadow, he met the same old woman. "Boy, where are you going?" The same words were spoken between them. Just as his brother had, he paid heed to the lesson. Going toward the spring, he stopped up his ears. But this grand music that came to him, so beautiful, he must and would hear. And down he fell, changed into stone.

That evening in the garden, the young girl saw that his rosebush had died. White of face, she ran to the house and told them that she, too, must go now. A sad day that was for the gardener and his wife. They tried to hold her back with their old hands.

"No, no, don't you go, we have only you left. You see that your brothers are dead. Stay with us in the garden by the river! If you leave, you, too, you will not come back."

"Yes, yes, I shall come back! I promise, it is a promise, but let me go."

On the road, far away beside the green meadow, she met the old woman.

"Girl, where are you going?"

"I am looking for the singing branch, the bird of truth, and the water that gives back youth. And besides, I am looking for my brothers."

"So! Well, listen. . . ."

Just as she had done with the boys, the old woman repeated her lesson. And all happened for the third time—she kept on her way, fingers in her ears, and heard the grand music.

But the young girl, when she heard this music that turned her head with enchantment, only walked the faster. On she walked, on and on, between the stones, the furze and briers, and at last she reached the spring. With the sickle she used for cutting reeds in the garden she cut the branch that overshadowed the spring, from which there flowed all this music that caught at your heart. It was like the sound of hautboys, fifes, and bombards, that flung you into a dance—you cut a thousand capers, you were leading the ball. She took the branch, with the bird perched upon it, and then she went to the spring, where she drew a pitcher of water. And she started for home, holding the pitcher in one hand and the branch in the other.

But what did she see? At the first drop that spilled from the pitcher, the stone on which it fell turned into a boy. Thereafter, as she went, she let fall a drop of water on every stone. And each one turned into a boy or a girl.

In this way she reached a stone that became her elder brother, and one that became her younger brother. The elder on her right hand, the younger on her left, joyful in words and steps, they followed the green path that led back home.

There the old gardener, beside himself, was running as well as he could on his old legs, and crying to his old wife, "The rosebushes are green again! Our children are alive, good wife, and will come back to us!"

And just then, come they did. What a moment! Without delay, the girl took her pitcher and poured a drop on her father's forehead, on her mother's forehead. And the poor old couple, who were all dried up and wrinkled like the bark of a tree, found themselves fresher and greener than lettuce in season. Once again they were twenty years old. The children might have been fourteen or sixteen.

The girl set the branch and its bird on the mantel over the fireplace. The two brothers took their father's gun. They were so happy to be back that they must celebrate, along with their sister and their parents. On such a day they must have a piece of game for dinner, and they asked if they might go hunting.

Off they went to the woods, and right away they started up a deer; they flew in pursuit of it, from one mossy glade to another, among the chestnuts, beeches, and oaks. They bounded ahead in their ardor, so far that, never noticing it, they crossed over from the forest into the king's park. And at the turning of a road, between the tall and venerable trees, suddenly they came upon the king.

Hunting on the king's land, in his park! And yet, if you can believe it, they were not so very frightened. Perhaps they simply thought, "The good God has come to our aid so often that he will do it again." Or perhaps not. They weren't afraid, that is all.

They looked at the king with frank, wide-open eyes, and the king kept looking at them, his eyes in theirs, while they, kneeling on one knee, cap in hand, answered his questions. They told him why they were hunting the deer, why they wanted a good dinner that day, and why they were holding a celebration.

Growing bolder, they told how a drop of water from the pitcher had given back youth to their parents, and they added that if the king would come to their house by the river, their sister would sprinkle on his head a few drops of the water.

And the king was stirred, and well pleased by what the two boys had told him. He felt like a dried-up rosebush about to grow green once more. He left everything behind to follow the young huntsmen, to dine at the house of the gardener and his wife.

In the middle of dinner the bird began to sing upon the branch:

King, here are your children three—
Monkey, lion, and crocodile, see!

Three times he repeated the same thing. The king could not yet understand, but he wanted to understand. He forced the gardener and his wife
to tell him where these children came from. Being afraid that they must give
them up, they were not overanxious to comply. At last—it had to be wrung
from them, question by question—they told how they had found the children:
one, another, and still another—each one in a basket on the river, among
the reeds and the wild iris.

King, here are your children three—
Monkey, lion, and crocodile, see!

Again the bird sang upon the branch. The king asked to be shown the three
baskets. Perhaps he recognized them as coming from his castle; in any case,
he understood.

The girl took the pitcher and poured out a trickle of water on the king's
head. There he was, he, too, at the peak of twenty years; young again in
face, body, and bearing, just as he was young again in heart.

Straightway they must run, the children and he, with the pitcher, to
deliver their mother, shut up in the tower. It was for him now to make her
forget the misery of those years—she so good, so pure, so true!

Afterward the king gave his orders. His two sisters-in-law were to be
seized and hung up like traitors from the castle walls, and all the world could
come and spit in their faces. The people did not wait to be urged; no love
was lost on them, those two.

As for the gardener and the gardener's wife, the king did not wish to
separate them from their children. He sent for them to come and live in the
castle. And since that day everybody has been happy, living with the water
that gives back the freshness of youth, the bird who speaks truth, and the
branch that sings great music.

Translated by Mary Mian

The King of the Elves ›

Philip K. Dick

t was raining and getting dark. Sheets of water blew along the row of pumps at the edge of the filling station; the trees across the highway bent against the wind.

Shadrach Jones stood just inside the doorway of the little building, leaning against an oil drum. The door was open, and gusts of rain blew in onto the wood floor. It was late; the sun had set, and the air was turning cold. Shadrach reached into his coat and brought out a cigar. He bit the end off it and lit it carefully, turning away from the door. In the gloom, the cigar burst into life, warm and glowing. Shadrach took a deep draw. He buttoned his coat around him and stepped out onto the pavement.

"Darn," he said. "What a night!" Rain buffeted him, wind blew at him. He looked up and down the highway, squinting. There were no cars in sight. He shook his head, locked up the gasoline pumps.

He went back into the building and pulled the door shut behind him. He opened the cash register and counted the money he'd taken in during the day. It was not much.

Not much, but enough for one old man. Enough to buy him tobacco and firewood and magazines, so that he could be comfortable as he waited for the occasional cars to come by. Not very many cars came along the highway anymore. The highway had begun to fall into disrepair; there were many cracks in its dry, rough surface, and most cars preferred to take the big state highway that ran beyond the hills. There was nothing in Derryville to attract them, to make them turn toward it. Derryville was a small town, too small to bring in any of the major industries, too small to be very important to anyone. Sometimes hours went by without—

Shadrach tensed. His fingers closed over the money. From outside came a sound, the melodic ring of the signal wire stretched along the pavement.

Dinggg!

Shadrach dropped the money into the till and pushed the drawer closed. He stood up slowly and walked toward the door, listening. At the door, he snapped off the light and waited in the darkness, staring out.

He could see no car there. The rain was pouring down, swirling with the wind; clouds of mist moved along the road. And something was standing beside the pumps.

He opened the door and stepped out. At first his eyes could make nothing out. Then the old man swallowed uneasily.

Two tiny figures stood in the rain, holding a kind of platform between them. Once, they might have been gaily dressed in bright garments, but now their clothes hung limp and sodden, dripping in the rain. They glanced halfheartedly at Shadrach. Water streaked their tiny faces, great drops of water. Their robes blew about them with the wind, lashing and swirling.

On the platform, something stirred. A small head turned wearily, peering at Shadrach. In the dim light, a rain-streaked helmet glinted dully.

"Who are you?" Shadrach said.

The figure on the platform raised itself up. "I'm the King of the Elves, and I'm wet."

Shadrach stared in astonishment.

"That's right," one of the bearers said. "We're all wet."

A small group of elves came straggling up, gathering around their king. They huddled together forlornly, silently.

"The King of the Elves," Shadrach repeated. "Well, I'll be darned."

Could it be true? They were very small, all right, and their dripping clothes were strange and oddly colored.

But *elves?*

"I'll be darned. Well, whatever you are, you shouldn't be out on a night like this."

"Of course not," the king murmured. "No fault of our own. No fault . . ." His voice trailed off into a choking cough. The elf soldiers peered anxiously at the platform.

"Maybe you better bring him inside," Shadrach said. "My place is up the road. He shouldn't be out in the rain."

"Do you think we like being out on a night like this?" one of the bearers muttered. "Which way is it? Direct us."

Shadrach pointed up the road. "Over there. Just follow me. I'll get a fire going."

He went down the road, feeling his way onto the first of the flat stone steps that he and Phineas Judd had laid during the summer. At the top of the steps, he looked back. The platform was coming slowly along, swaying a little from side to side. Behind it, the elf soldiers picked their way, a tiny column of silent dripping creatures, unhappy and cold.

"I'll get the fire started," Shadrach said. He hurried them into the house.

Wearily, the Elf King lay back against the pillow. After sipping hot chocolate, he had relaxed and his heavy breathing sounded suspiciously like a snore.

Shadrach shifted in discomfort.

"I'm sorry," the Elf King said suddenly, opening his eyes. He rubbed his forehead. "I must have drifted off. Where was I?"

"You should retire, Your Majesty," one of the soldiers said sleepily. "It is late, and these are hard times."

"True," the Elf King said, nodding. "Very true." He looked up at the towering figure of Shadrach, standing before the fireplace, a glass of beer in his hand. "Mortal, we thank you for your hospitality. Normally, we do not impose on human beings."

"It's those trolls," another of the soldiers said, curled up on a cushion of the couch.

"Right," another soldier agreed. He sat up, groping for his sword. "Those reeking trolls, digging and croaking—"

"You see," the Elf King went on, "as our party was crossing from the Great Low Steps toward the Castle, where it lies in the hollow of the Towering Mountains—"

"You mean Sugar Ridge," Shadrach supplied helpfully.

"The Towering Mountains. Slowly we made our way. A rainstorm came up. We became confused. All at once a group of trolls appeared, crashing through the underbrush. We left the woods and sought safety on the Endless Path—"

"The highway. Route Twenty."

"So that is why we're here." The Elf King paused a moment. "Harder and harder it rained. The wind blew around us, cold and bitter. For an endless time we toiled along. We had no idea where we were going or what would become of us."

The Elf King looked up at Shadrach. "We knew only this: Behind us, the trolls were coming, creeping through the woods, marching through the rain, crushing everything before them."

He put his hand to his mouth and coughed, bending forward. All the elves waited anxiously until he was done. He straightened up.

"It was kind of you to allow us to come inside. We will not trouble you for long. It is not the custom of the elves—"

Again he coughed, covering his face with his hand. The elves drew toward him apprehensively. At last the king stirred. He sighed.

"What's the matter?" Shadrach asked. He went over and took the cup of chocolate from the fragile hand. The Elf King lay back, his eyes shut.

"He has to rest," one of the soldiers said. "Where's your room? The sleeping room."

"Upstairs," Shadrach said. "I'll show you where."

Late that night, Shadrach sat by himself in the dark, deserted living room, deep in meditation. The elves were asleep above him, upstairs in the bedroom, the Elf King in the bed, the others curled up together on the rug.

The house was silent. Outside, the rain poured down endlessly, blowing against the house. Shadrach could hear the tree branches slapping in the wind. He clasped and unclasped his hands. What a strange business it was— all these elves, with their old, sick king, their piping voices. How anxious and peevish they were!

But pathetic too; so small and wet, with water dripping down from them, and all their gay robes limp and soggy.

The trolls—what were they like? Unpleasant and not very clean. Something about digging, breaking and pushing through the woods . . .

Suddenly Shadrach laughed in embarrassment. What was the matter with him, believing all this? He put his cigar out angrily, his ears red. What was going on? What kind of joke was this?

Elves? Shadrach grunted in indignation. Elves in Derryville? In the middle of Colorado? Maybe there were elves in Europe. Maybe in Ireland. He had heard of that. But here? Upstairs in his own house, sleeping in his own bed?

"I've heard just about enough of this," he said. "I'm not an idiot, you know."

He turned toward the stairs, feeling for the banister in the gloom. He began to climb.

Above him, a light went on abruptly. A door opened.

Two elves came slowly out onto the landing. They looked down at him. Shadrach halted halfway up the stairs. Something on their faces made him stop.

"What's the matter?" he asked hesitantly.

They did not answer. The house was turning cold, cold and dark, with the chill of the rain outside and the chill of the unknown inside.

"What is it?" he said again. "What's the matter?"

"The king is dead," one of the elves said. "He died a few moments ago."

Shadrach stared up, wide-eyed. "He did? But—"

"He was very old and very tired." The elves turned away, going back into the room, slowly and quietly shutting the door.

Shadrach stood, his fingers on the banister, hard, lean fingers, strong and thin.

He nodded his head blankly.

"I see," he said to the closed door. "He's dead."

The elf soldiers stood around him in a solemn circle. The living room was bright with sunlight, the cold white glare of early morning.

"But wait," Shadrach said. He plucked at his necktie. "I have to get to the filling station. Can't you talk to me when I come home?"

The faces of the elf soldiers were serious and concerned.

"Listen," one of them said. "Please hear us out. It is very important to us."

Shadrach looked past them. Through the window he saw the highway, steaming in the heat of day, and down a little way was the gas station, glittering brightly. And even as he watched, a car came up to it and honked thinly, impatiently. When nobody came out of the station, the car drove off again, down the road.

"We beg you," a soldier said.

Shadrach looked down at the ring around him, the anxious faces, scored with concern and trouble. Strangely, he had always thought of elves as carefree beings, flitting without worry or sense. . . .

"Go ahead," he said. "I'm listening." He went over to the big chair and sat down. The elves came up around him. They conversed among themselves for a moment, whispering, murmuring distantly. Then they turned toward Shadrach.

The old man waited, his arms folded.

"We cannot be without a king," one of the soldiers said. "We could not survive. Not these days."

"The trolls," another added. "They multiply very fast. They are terrible beasts. They're heavy and ponderous, crude, bad-smelling—"

"The odor of them is awful. They come up from the dark, wet places under the earth, where the blind, groping plants feed in silence, far below the surface, far from the sun."

"Well, you ought to elect a king, then," Shadrach suggested. "I don't see any problem there."

"We do not elect the King of the Elves," a soldier said. "The old king must name his successor."

"Oh," Shadrach replied. "Well, there's nothing wrong with that method."

"As our old king lay dying, a few distant words came forth from his lips," a soldier said. "We bent closer, frightened and unhappy, listening."

"Important, all right," agreed Shadrach. "Not something you'd want to miss."

"He spoke the name of him who will lead us."

"Good. You caught it, then. Well, where's the difficulty?"

"The name he spoke was—was your name."

Shadrach stared. *"Mine?"*

"The dying king said: 'Make him, the towering mortal, your king. Many things will come if he leads the elves into battle against the trolls. I see the rising once again of the Elf Empire, as it was in the old days, as it was before—' "

"Me!" Shadrach leapt up. "Me? King of the Elves?"

Shadrach walked about the room, his hands in his pockets. "Me, Shadrach Jones, King of the Elves," He grinned a little. "I sure never thought of it before."

He went to the mirror over the fireplace and studied himself. He saw his thin, graying hair, his bright eyes, dark skin, his big Adam's apple.

"King of the Elves," he said. "King of the Elves. Wait till Phineas Judd hears about this. Wait till I tell him!"

Phineas Judd would certainly be surprised!

Above the filling station, the sun shone, high in the clear blue sky.

Phineas Judd sat playing with the accelerator of his old Ford truck. The motor raced and slowed. Phineas reached over and turned the ignition key off, then rolled the window all the way down.

"What did you say?" he asked. He took off his glasses and began to polish them, steel rims between slender, deft fingers that were patient from years of practice. He restored his glasses to his nose and smoothed what remained of his hair into place.

"What was it, Shadrach?" he said. "Let's hear that again."

"I'm King of the Elves," Shadrach repeated. He changed position, bringing his other foot up on the running board. "Who would have thought it? Me, Shadrach Jones, King of the Elves."

Phineas gazed at him. "How long have you been . . . King of the Elves, Shadrach?"

"Since the night before last."

"I see. The night before last." Phineas nodded. "I see. And what, may I ask, occurred the night before last?"

"The elves came to my house. When the old Elf King died, he told them that—"

A truck came rumbling up and the driver leapt out. "Water!" he said. "Where the hell is the hose?"

Shadrach turned reluctantly. "I'll get it." He turned back to Phineas. "Maybe I can talk to you tonight when you come back from town. I want to tell you the rest. It's very interesting."

"Sure," Phineas said, starting up his little truck. "Sure, Shadrach. I'm very interested to hear."

He drove off down the road.

Later in the day, Dan Green ran his flivver up to the filling station.

"Hey, Shadrach," he called. "Come over here! I want to ask you something."

Shadrach came out of the little house, holding a waste rag in his hand. "What is it?"

"Come here." Dan leaned out the window, a wide grin on his face, splitting his face from ear to ear. "Let me ask you something, will you?"

"Sure."

"Is it true? Are you really the King of the Elves?"

Shadrach flushed a little. "I guess I am," he admitted, looking away. "That's what I am, all right."

Dan's grin faded. "Hey, you trying to kid me? What's the gag?"

Shadrach became angry. "What do you mean? Sure, I'm the King of the Elves. And anyone who says I'm not—"

"All right, Shadrach," Dan said, starting up the flivver quickly. "Don't get mad. I was just wondering."

Shadrach looked very strange.

"All right," Dan said. "You don't hear me arguing, do you?"

By the end of the day, everyone around knew about Shadrach and how he had suddenly become King of the Elves. Pop Richey, who ran the Lucky Store in Derryville, claimed Shadrach was doing it to drum up trade for the filling station.

"He's a smart old fellow," Pop said. "Not very many cars go along there anymore. He knows what he's doing."

"I don't know," Dan Green disagreed. "You should hear him. I think he really believes it."

"King of the Elves?" They all began to laugh. "Wonder what he'll say next."

Phineas Judd pondered. "I've known Shadrach for years. I can't figure it out." He frowned, his face wrinkled and disapproving. "I don't like it."

Dan looked at him. "Then you think he believes it?"

"Sure," Phineas said. "Maybe I'm wrong, but I really think he does."

"But how could he believe it?" Pop asked. "Shadrach is no fool. He's been in business for a long time. He must be getting something out of it, the way I see it. But what, if it isn't to build up the filling station?"

"Why, don't you know what he's getting?" Dan said, grinning. His gold tooth shone.

"What?" Pop demanded.

"He's got a whole kingdom to himself, that's what—to do with like he wants. How would you like that, Pop? Wouldn't you like to be King of the Elves and not have to run this old store anymore?"

"There isn't anything wrong with my store," Pop said. "I ain't ashamed to run it. Better than being a clothing salesman."

Dan flushed. "Nothing wrong with that either." He looked at Phineas. "Isn't that right? Nothing wrong with selling clothes, is there, Phineas?"

Phineas was staring down at the floor. He glanced up. "What? What was that?"

"What you thinking about?" Pop wanted to know. "You look worried."

"I'm worried about Shadrach," Phineas said. "He's getting old. Sitting out there by himself all the time, in the cold weather, with the rainwater running over the floor. It blows something awful in the winter, along the highway—"

"Then you *do* think he believes it?" Dan persisted. "You *don't* think he's getting something out of it?"

Phineas shook his head absently and did not answer.

The laughter died down. They all looked at one another.

That night, as Shadrach was locking up the filling station, a small figure came toward him from the darkness.

"Hey!" Shadrach called out. "Who are you?"

An elf soldier came into the light, blinking. He was dressed in a little gray robe, buckled at the waist with a band of silver. On his feet were little leather boots. He carried a short sword at his side.

"I have a serious message for you," the elf said. "Now where did I put it?"

He searched his robe while Shadrach waited. The elf brought out a tiny scroll and unfastened it, breaking the wax expertly. He handed it to Shadrach.

"What's it say?" Shadrach asked. He bent over, his eyes close to the vellum. "I don't have my glasses with me. Can't quite make out these little letters."

"The trolls are moving. They've heard that the old king is dead, and they're rising, in all the hills and valleys around. They will try to break the Elf Kingdom into fragments, scatter the elves—"

"I see," Shadrach said. "Before your new king can really get started."

"That's right." The elf soldier nodded. "This is a crucial moment for the elves. For centuries, our existence has been precarious. There are so many trolls, and elves are very frail and often take sick—"

"Well, what should I do? Are there any suggestions?"

"You're supposed to meet with us under the Great Oak tonight. We'll take you into the Elf Kingdom, and you and your staff will plan and map the defense of the kingdom."

"What?" Shadrach looked uncomfortable. "But I haven't eaten dinner. And my gas station—tomorrow is Saturday, and a lot of cars—"

"But you are King of the Elves," the soldier said.

Shadrach put his hand to his chin and rubbed it slowly.

"That's right," he replied. "I am, ain't I?"

The elf soldier bowed.

"I wish I'd known this sort of thing was going to happen," Shadrach said. "I didn't suppose being King of the Elves—"

He broke off, hoping for an interruption. The elf soldier watched him calmly, without expression.

"Maybe you ought to have someone else as your king," Shadrach decided. "I don't know very much about war and things like that, fighting and all that sort of business." He paused, shrugged his shoulders. "It's nothing I've ever mixed in. They don't have wars here in Colorado. I mean, they don't have wars between human beings."

Still the elf soldier remained silent.

"Why was I picked?" Shadrach went on helplessly, twisting his hands. "I don't know anything about it. What made him go and pick me? Why didn't he pick somebody else?"

"He trusted you," the elf said. "You brought him inside your house, out of the rain. He knew that you expected nothing for it, that there was nothing you wanted. He had known few who gave and asked nothing back."

"Oh." Shadrach thought it over. At last he looked up. "But what about my gas station? And my house? And what will they say, Dan Green and Pop down at the store—"

The elf soldier moved away, out of the light. "I have to go. It's getting late, and at night the trolls come out. I don't want to be too far away from the others."

"Sure," Shadrach said.

"The trolls are afraid of nothing, now that the old king is dead. They forage everywhere. No one is safe."

"Where did you say the meeting is to be? And what time?"

"At the Great Oak. When the moon sets tonight, just as it leaves the sky."

"I'll be there, I guess," Shadrach said. "I suppose you're right. The King of the Elves can't afford to let his kingdom down when it needs him most."

He looked around, but the elf soldier was already gone.

Shadrach walked up the highway, his mind full of doubts and wonderings. When he came to the first of the flat stone steps, he stopped.

"And the old oak tree is on Phineas's farm! What'll Phineas say?"

But he was the Elf King, and the trolls were moving in the hills. Shadrach stood listening to the rustle of the wind as it moved through the trees beyond the highway and along the far slopes and hills.

Trolls? Were there really trolls there, rising up, bold and confident in the darkness of the night, afraid of nothing, afraid of no one?

And this business of being Elf King . . .

Shadrach went on up the steps, his lips pressed tight. When he reached the top of the stone steps, the last rays of sunlight had already faded. It was night.

Phineas Judd stared out the window. He swore and shook his head. Then he went quickly to the door and ran out onto the porch. In the cold moonlight, a dim figure was walking slowly across the lower field, coming toward the house along the cow trail.

"Shadrach!" Phineas cried. "What's wrong? What are you doing out this time of night?"

Shadrach stopped and put his fists stubbornly on his hips.

"You go back home," Phineas said. "What's got into you?"

"I'm sorry, Phineas," Shadrach answered. "I'm sorry I have to go over your land. But I have to meet somebody at the old oak tree."

"At this time of night?"

Shadrach bowed his head.

"What's the matter with you, Shadrach? Who in the world you going to meet in the middle of the night on my farm?"

"I have to meet with the elves. We're going to plan out the war with the trolls."

"Well, I'll be damned," Phineas Judd said. He went back inside the house and slammed the door. For a long time he stood thinking. Then he went back out on the porch again. "What did you say you were doing? You don't have to tell me, of course, but I just—"

"I have to meet the elves at the old oak tree. We must have a general council of war against the trolls."

"Yes, indeed. The trolls. Have to watch for the trolls all the time."

"Trolls are everywhere," Shadrach stated, nodding his head. "I never realized it before. You can't forget them or ignore them. They never forget you. They're always planning, watching you—"

Phineas gaped at him, speechless.

"Oh, by the way," Shadrach said. "I may be gone for some time. It depends on how long this business is going to take. I haven't had much experience in fighting trolls, so I'm not sure. But I wonder if you'd mind looking after the gas station for me, about twice a day, maybe once in the morning and once at night, to make sure no one's broken in or anything like that."

"You're going away?" Phineas came quickly down the stairs. "What's all this about trolls? Why are you going?"

Shadrach patiently repeated what he had said.

"But what for?"

"Because I'm the Elf King. I have to lead them."

There was silence. "I see," Phineas said at last. "That's right, you *did* mention it before, didn't you? But, Shadrach, why don't you come inside for a while and you can tell me about the trolls and drink some coffee and—"

"Coffee?" Shadrach looked up at the pale moon above him, the moon and the bleak sky. The world was still and dead and the night was very cold and the moon would not be setting for some time.

Shadrach shivered.

"It's a cold night," Phineas urged. "Too cold to be out. Come on in. . . ."

"I guess I have a little time," Shadrach admitted. "A cup of coffee wouldn't do any harm. But I can't stay very long. . . ."

Shadrach stretched his legs out and sighed. "This coffee sure tastes good, Phineas."

Phineas sipped a little and put his cup down. The living room was quite and warm. It was a very neat little living room, with solemn pictures on the walls, gray uninteresting pictures that minded their own business. In the corner was a small reed organ with sheet music carefully arranged on top of it.

Shadrach noticed the organ and smiled. "You still play, Phineas?"

"Not much anymore. The bellows don't work right. One of them won't come back up."

"I suppose I could fix it sometime. If I'm around, I mean."

"That would be fine," Phineas said. "I was thinking of asking you."

"Remember how you used to play 'Vilia' and Dan Green came up with that lady who worked for Pop during the summer? The one who wanted to open a pottery shop?"

"I sure do," Phineas said.

Presently, Shadrach set down his coffee cup and shifted in his chair.

"You want more coffee?" Phineas asked quickly. He stood up. "A little more?"

"Maybe a little. But I have to be going pretty soon."

"It's a bad night to be outside."

Shadrach looked through the window. It was darker; the moon had almost gone down. The fields were stark. Shadrach shivered. "I wouldn't disagree with you," he said.

Phineas turned eagerly. "Look, Shadrach. You go on home where it's warm. You can come out and fight trolls some other night. There'll always be trolls. You said so yourself. Plenty of time to do that later, when the weather's better. When it's not so cold."

Shadrach rubbed his forehead wearily. "You know, it all seems like some sort of a crazy dream. When did I start talking about elves and trolls? When did it all begin?" His voice trailed off. "Thank you for the coffee." He got slowly to his feet. "It warmed me up a lot. And I appreciated the talk. Like old times, you and me sitting here the way we used to."

"Are you going?" Phineas hesitated. *"Home?"*

"I think I better. It's late."

Phineas got quickly to his feet. He led Shadrach to the door, one arm around his shoulder.

"All right, Shadrach, you go on home. Take a good hot bath before you go to bed. It'll fix you up. And maybe just a little snort of brandy to warm the blood."

Phineas opened the front door, and they went slowly down the porch steps, onto the cold, dark ground.

"Yes, I guess I'll be going," Shadrach said. "Good night."

"You go on home." Phineas patted him on the arm. "You run along home and take a good hot bath. And then go straight to bed."

"That's a good idea. Thank you, Phineas. I appreciate your kindness." Shadrach looked down at Phineas's hand on his arm. He had not been that close to Phineas for years.

Shadrach contemplated the hand. He wrinkled his brow, puzzled.

Phineas's hand was huge and rough, and his arms were short. His fingers were blunt, his nails broken and cracked. Almost black, or so it seemed in the moonlight.

Shadrach looked up at Phineas. "Strange," he murmured.

"What's strange, Shadrach?"

In the moonlight, Phineas's face seemed oddly heavy and brutal. Shadrach had never noticed before how the jaw bulged, what a great protruding jaw it was. The skin was yellow and coarse, like parchment. Behind the glasses, the eyes were like two stones, cold and lifeless. The ears were immense, the hair stringy and matted.

Odd that he had never noticed before. But he had never seen Phineas in the moonlight.

Shadrach stepped away, studying his old friend. From a few feet off, Phineas Judd seemed unusually short and squat. His legs were slightly bowed. His feet were enormous. And there was something else—

"What is it?" Phineas demanded, beginning to grow suspicious. "Is there something wrong?"

Something was completely wrong. And he had never noticed it, not in all the years they had been friends. All around Phineas Judd was an odor, a faint, pungent stench of rot, of decaying flesh, damp and moldy.

Shadrach glanced slowly about him. "Something wrong?" he echoed. "No, I wouldn't say that."

By the side of the house was an old rain barrel, half fallen apart. Shadrach walked over to it.

"No, Phineas. I wouldn't exactly say there's something wrong."

"What are you doing?"

"Me?" Shadrach took hold of one of the barrel staves and pulled it loose. He walked back to Phineas, carrying the barrel stave carefully. "I'm King of the Elves. Who—or what—are you?"

Phineas roared and attacked with his great murderous shovel hands.

Shadrach smashed him over the head with the barrel stave. Phineas bellowed with rage and pain.

At the shattering sound, there was a clatter, and from underneath the house came a furious horde of bounding, leaping creatures, dark bent-over things, their bodies heavy and squat, their feet and heads immense. Shadrach took one look at the flood of dark creatures pouring out from Phineas's basement. He knew what they were.

"Help!" Shadrach shouted. "Trolls! Help!"

The trolls were all around him, grabbing hold of him, tugging at him, climbing up him, pummeling his face and body.

Shadrach fell to with the barrel stave, swung again and again, kicking trolls with his feet, whacking them with the barrel stave. There seemed to be hundreds of them. More and more poured out from under Phineas's house, a surging black tide of pot-shaped creatures, their great eyes and teeth gleaming in the moonlight.

"Help!" Shadrach cried again, more feebly now. He was getting winded. His heart labored painfully. A troll bit his wrist, clinging to his arm. Shadrach flung it away, pulling loose from the horde clutching his trouser legs, the barrel stave rising and falling.

One of the trolls caught hold of the stave. A whole group of them helped, wrenching furiously, trying to pull it away. Shadrach hung on desperately. Trolls were all over him, on his shoulders, clinging to his coat, riding his arms, his legs, pulling his hair—

He heard a high-pitched clarion call from a long way off, the sound of some distant golden trumpet, echoing in the hills.

The trolls suddenly stopped attacking. One of them dropped off Shadrach's neck. Another let go of his arm.

The call came again, this time more loudly.

"Elves!" a troll rasped. He turned and moved toward the sound, grinding his teeth and spitting with fury.

"Elves!"

The trolls swarmed forward, a growing wave of gnashing teeth and nails, pushing furiously toward the elf columns. The elves broke formation and joined battle, shouting with wild joy in their shrill, piping voices. The tide of trolls rushed against them, troll against elf, shovel nails against golden sword, biting jaw against dagger.

"Kill the elves!"

"Death to the trolls!"

"Onward!"

"Forward!"

Shadrach fought desperately with the trolls that were still clinging to him. He was exhausted, panting and gasping for breath. Blindly, he whacked on and on, kicking and jumping, throwing trolls away from him, through the air and across the ground.

How long the battle raged, Shadrach never knew. He was lost in a sea of dark bodies, round and evil-smelling, clinging to him, tearing, biting, fastened to his nose and hair and fingers. He fought silently, grimly.

All around him, the elf legions clashed with the troll horde, little groups of struggling warriors on all sides.

Suddenly Shadrach stopped fighting. He raised his head, looking uncertainly around him. Nothing moved. Everything was silent. The fighting had ceased.

A few trolls still clung to his arms and legs. Shadrach whacked one with the barrel stave. It howled and dropped to the ground. He staggered back, struggling with the last troll, who hung tenaciously to his arm.

"Now you!" Shadrach gasped. He pried the troll loose and flung it into the air. The troll fell to the ground and scuttled off into the night.

There was nothing more. No troll moved anywhere. All was silent across the bleak, moon-swept fields.

Shadrach sank down on a stone. His chest rose and fell painfully. Red specks swam before his eyes. Weakly, he got out his pocket handkerchief and wiped his neck and face. He closed his eyes, shaking his head from side to side.

When he opened his eyes again, the elves were coming toward him, gathering their legion together again. The elves were disheveled and bruised. Their golden armor was gashed and torn. Their helmets were bent or missing. Most of their scarlet plumes were gone. Those that still remained were drooping and broken.

But the battle was over. The war was won. The troll hordes had been put to flight.

Shadrach got slowly to his feet. The elf warriors stood around him in a circle, gazing up at him with silent respect. One of them helped steady him as he put his handkerchief away in his pocket.

"Thank you," Shadrach murmured. "Thank you very much."

"The trolls have been defeated," an elf stated, still awed by what had happened.

Shadrach gazed around at the elves. There were many of them, more than he had ever seen before. All the elves had turned out for the battle. They were grim-faced, stern with the seriousness of the moment, weary from the terrible struggle.

"Yes, they're gone, all right," Shadrach said. He was beginning to get his breath. "That was a close call. I'm glad you fellows came when you did. I was just about finished, fighting them all by myself."

"All alone, the King of the Elves held off the entire troll army," an elf announced shrilly.

"Eh?" Shadrach said, taken aback. Then he smiled. "That's true, I *did* fight them alone for a while. I *did* hold off the trolls all by myself. The whole darn troll army."

"There is more," an elf said.

Shadrach blinked. "More?"

"Look over here, O King, mightiest of all the elves. This way. To the right."

The elves led Shadrach over.

"What is it?" Shadrach murmured, seeing nothing at first. He gazed down, trying to pierce the darkness. "Could we have a torch over here?"

Some elves brought little pine torches.

There, on the frozen ground, lay Phineas Judd, on his back. His eyes were blank and staring, his mouth half open. He did not move. His body was cold and stiff.

"He is dead," an elf said solemnly.

Shadrach gulped in sudden alarm. Cold sweat stood out abruptly on his forehead. "My gosh! My old friend! What have I done?"

"You have slain the Great Troll."

Shadrach paused.

"I *what?*"

"You have slain the Great Troll, leader of all the trolls."

"This has never happened before," another elf exclaimed excitedly. "The Great Troll has lived for centuries. Nobody imagined he could die. This is our most historic moment."

All the elves gazed down at the silent form with awe, awe mixed with more than a little fear.

"Oh, go on!" Shadrach said. "That's just Phineas Judd."

But as he spoke, a chill moved up his spine. He remembered what he had seen a little while before, as he stood close by Phineas, as the dying moonlight crossed his old friend's face.

"Look." One of the elves bent over and unfastened Phineas's blue serge vest. He pushed the coat and vest aside. "See?"

Shadrach bent down to look.

He gasped.

Underneath Phineas Judd's blue serge vest was a suit of mail, an encrusted mesh of ancient, rusting iron, fastened tightly around the squat body. On the mail stood an engraved insignia, dark and timeworn, embedded with dirt and rust. A moldering, half-obliterated emblem. The emblem of a crossed owl leg and toadstool.

The emblem of the Great Troll.

"Golly," Shadrach said. "And *I* killed him."

For a long time he gazed silently down. Then, slowly, realization began to grow in him. He straightened up, a smile forming on his face.

"What is it, O King?" an elf piped.

"I just thought of something," Shadrach said. "I just realized that—that since the Great Troll is dead and the troll army has been put to flight—"

He broke off. All the elves were waiting.

"I thought maybe I—that is, maybe if you don't need me anymore—"

The elves listened respectfully. "What is it, Mighty King? Go on."

"I thought maybe now I could go back to the filling station and not be king anymore." Shadrach glanced hopefully around at them. "Do you think so? With the war over and all. With him dead. What do you say?"

For a time, the elves were silent. They gazed unhappily down at the ground. None of them said anything. At last they began moving away, collecting their banners and pennants.

"Yes, you may go back," an elf said quietly. "The war is over. The trolls have been defeated. You may return to your filling station, if that is what you want."

A flood of relief swept over Shadrach. He straightened up, grinning from ear to ear. "Thanks! That's fine. That's really fine. That's the best news I've heard in my life."

He moved away from the elves, rubbing his hands together and blowing on them.

"Thanks an awful lot." He grinned around at the silent elves. "Well, I guess I'll be running along, then. It's late. Late and cold. It's been a hard night. I'll—I'll see you around."

The elves nodded silently.

"Fine. Well, good night." Shadrach turned and started along the path. He stopped for a moment, waving back at the elves. "It was quite a battle, wasn't it? We really licked them." He hurried on along the path. Once again he stopped, looking back and waving. "Sure glad I could help out. Well, good night!"

One or two of the elves waved, but none of them said anything.

Shadrach Jones walked slowly toward his place. He could see it from the rise, the highway that few cars traveled, the filling station falling to ruin, the house that might not last as long as himself, and not enough money coming in to repair them or buy a better location.

He turned around and went back.

The elves were still gathered there in the silence of the night. They had not moved away.

"I was hoping you hadn't gone," Shadrach said, relieved.

"And we were hoping you would not leave," said a soldier.

Shadrach kicked a stone. It bounced through the tight silence and stopped. The elves were still watching him.

"Leave?" Shadrach asked. "And me King of the Elves?"

"Then you will remain our king?" an Elf cried.

"It's a hard thing for a man of my age to change. To stop selling gasoline and suddenly be a king. It scared me for a while. But it doesn't anymore."

"You will? You *will?*"

"Sure," said Shadrach Jones.

The little circle of elf torches closed in joyously. In their light, he saw a platform like the one that had carried the old King of the Elves. But this one was much larger, big enough to hold a man, and dozens of the soldiers waited with proud shoulders under the shafts.

A soldier gave him a happy bow. "For you, Sire."

Shadrach climbed aboard. It was less comfortable than walking, but he knew this was how they wanted to take him to the Kingdom of the Elves.

—§—

The Enchanted Palace

Italo Calvino

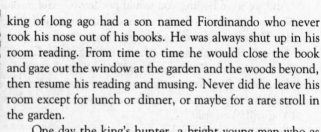

A king of long ago had a son named Fiordinando who never took his nose out of his books. He was always shut up in his room reading. From time to time he would close the book and gaze out the window at the garden and the woods beyond, then resume his reading and musing. Never did he leave his room except for lunch or dinner, or maybe for a rare stroll in the garden.

One day the king's hunter, a bright young man who as a child had played with the prince, said to the king, "May I call on Fiordinando, Majesty? I've not seen him for quite some time."

The king replied, "By all means. Your visit will be a pleasant diversion for my fine son."

So the hunter entered the room of Fiordinando, who looked him over and asked, "What brings you to the court in those hobnailed boots?"

"I am the king's hunter," explained the young man, who went on to describe the many kinds of game, the ways of birds and hares, and the different parts of the woods.

Fiordinando's imagination was kindled. "Listen," he said to the youth, "I, too, shall try my luck at hunting. But don't say anything to my father, so he won't think it was your idea. I'll simply ask him to let me go hunting with you one morning."

"At your service, as always," replied the young man.

The next day at breakfast, Fiordinando said to the king, "Yesterday I read a book on hunting, which was so interesting I'm dying to go out and try my luck. May I?"

"Hunting is a dangerous sport," replied the king, "for someone who is new to it. But I won't keep you from something you think you might like. For a companion I'll let you have my hunter, who is unequaled as a hunting dog. Don't ever let him out of your sight."

Next morning at sunrise, Fiordinando and the hunter mounted their horses with their guns on shoulder straps, and off to the woods they galloped. The hunter aimed at every bird or hare he saw and laid it low. Fiordinando tried his best to keep pace but missed everything he shot at. At the end of the day the hunter's game bag was bulging, whereas Fiordinando hadn't brought down so much as one feather. At dusk Fiordinando spied a small hare hiding under a bush and took aim. But it was so small and frightened he decided he would simply run up and grab it. Just as he reached the bush, the hare darted off, with Fiordinando close behind. Every time he was right upon it, the hare would run far ahead, then stop, as though it were waiting for Fiordinando to catch up, only to elude him again. In the meantime Fiordinando had strayed so far from the hunter that he could no longer find the way back. Again and again he called out, but no one answered. By now it was completely dark, and the hare had disappeared.

Weary and distressed, Fiordinando sat down under a tree to rest. It was not long before he saw what seemed to be a light shining through the trees. He therefore got up, made his way through the underbrush, and emerged in a vast clearing, at the end of which stood the most ornate of palaces.

The front door was open, and Fiordinando called out, "Hello! Is anyone at home?" He was answered with dead silence; not even an echo came back to him. Entering, he found a large hall with a fire burning in the fireplace and, nearby, wine and glasses. Fiordinando took a seat to rest and warm up and drink a little wine. Then he rose and passed into another room, where a table was set for two persons. The cutlery, plates, and goblets were gold and silver; the curtains, tablecloth, and napkins were pure silk embroidered with pearls and diamonds; from the ceiling hung lamps of solid gold the size of baskets. Since no one was there and he was hungry, Fiordinando sat down to the table.

He had scarcely eaten his first mouthful when he heard a rustle of dresses coming down the steps, and in walked a queen followed by twelve maids of honor. The queen was young and extremely beautiful of figure, but her face was hidden by a heavy veil. Neither she nor the twelve maids of honor said one word during the entire meal. She sat across the table in silence from Fiordinando, while the maids quietly served them and poured their wine. The meal thus passed in silence, and the queen carried her food to her mouth under that thick veil. When they had finished, the queen rose, and the maids of honor accompanied her back upstairs. Fiordinando also rose and continued his tour of the palace.

Coming to a master bedchamber with a bed all turned down for the night, he undressed and jumped under the covers. Behind the canopy was a secret door: it opened, and in walked the queen, still mute, veiled, and followed by her twelve maids of honor. With Fiordinando leaning on his elbow and gaping, the maids of honor undressed the queen all but for her veil, put her in bed beside Fiordinando, and left the room. Fiordinando was sure she would say something now or unveil her face. But she had already fallen asleep. He watched the veil rising and falling with her breath, thought about it a minute, then he, too, fell asleep.

At dawn the maids of honor returned, put the queen's clothes back on her, and led her away. Fiordinando also got up, ate the hearty breakfast he found waiting for him, and went down to the stables.

His horse was there, eating oats. Fiordinando climbed into the saddle and galloped off to the woods. The whole day long he looked for a road that would take him back home, or for some trace of his hunting companion, but he only got lost anew, and when night fell, there stood the clearing and palace once more.

He went inside, and the same things happened as the evening before. But the next day as he was galloping through the woods, he met the hunter, who'd been looking for him for the last three days, and together they returned to the city. When the hunter questioned him, Fiordinando made up a tale about a lot of complicated mishaps, but he said nothing about what had really happened.

Back at the royal palace, Fiordinando was like a changed person. His eyes wandered constantly from the pages of his book to the woods beyond the garden. Seeing him so moody, listless, and absorbed, his mother began pestering him to tell her what he was brooding over. She kept nagging until Fiordinando finally told her from beginning to end what had happened to him in the woods. He made no bones about being in love with the beautiful queen and wondering how to marry her when she neither spoke nor showed her face.

"I'll tell you what to do," replied his mother. "Sup with her one more time. When the two of you are seated, accidentally knock her fork off the table. When she bends over to pick it up, pull off her veil. You can be sure she'll say something then."

No sooner had he received that advice than Fiordinando saddled his horse and raced off to the palace in the woods, where he was welcomed in the usual manner. At supper he knocked the queen's fork off the table with his elbow. She bent over, and he tore off her veil. At that, the queen rose, as beautiful as a moonbeam and as fiery as a ray of sun. "Rash youth!" she screamed. "You have betrayed me. Had I been able to sleep one more night beside you without speaking or unveiling my face, I would have been free from the spell and you would have become my husband. Now I'll have to go off to Paris for a week and from there to Peterborough, where I'll be given in prize at a tournament, and heaven knows who will win me. Farewell! And note that I am the queen of Portugal!"

In the same instant she vanished, along with the entire palace, and Fiordinando found himself alone and abandoned in the thickest part of the underbrush. It was no easy task to find his way home, but once he got there, he didn't waste a minute. He filled a purse with money, summoned his faithful hunter, and departed on horseback for Paris. They wore themselves out riding, but didn't dismount until they reached an inn in that famous city.

Nor did he spend long resting up, for he wished to learn if the queen of Portugal really was there in Paris. He began pumping the innkeeper. "What's the news around here?"

The innkeeper replied, "None to speak of. What sort of news do you expect?"

"There's all kind of news," replied Fiordinando. "News about wars, feast days, famous people passing through the city . . ."

"Oh!" exclaimed the innkeeper. "Come to think about it, there is a piece of interesting news: five days ago the queen of Portugal arrived in Paris. In three more days she'll leave for Peterborough. She's a very beautiful lady and highly educated. She enjoys exploring unusual spots, and strolls outside the city gate near here every afternoon with twelve maids of honor."

"And it's possible to get a look at her?" asked Fiordinando.

"Why not? When she walks in public, any passerby can see her."

"Wonderful!" said Fiordinando. "In the meantime get dinner for us and serve it with a bottle of red wine."

Now the innkeeper had a daughter who rejected all wooers, mind you, because none of them suited her. But the instant she laid eyes on Fiordinando getting out of his saddle, she told herself he would be the only one she would ever consider. She went to her father at once to say she had fallen in love and to ask him to find a way for her to marry the stranger. So the innkeeper said to Fiordinando, "I hope you'll like Paris and have the good fortune to find yourself a lovely bride here."

"My bride," replied Fiordinando, "is the most beautiful queen in the world, and I am trailing her all over the globe."

The innkeeper's daughter, who was eavesdropping, was seized with rage. When her father sent her to the cellar after the wine, she thrust a handful of opium into the bottle. Fiordinando and the hunter went outside the city after dinner to await the queen of Portugal, but suddenly they became so drowsy that they sank to the ground and slept like logs. Shortly thereafter the queen came by, recognized Fiordinando, bent over him, called his name, caressed him, shook him, and rolled him over and over; but there was no waking him. Then she slipped a diamond ring from her finger and placed it on his brow.

Now in a cave nearby lived a hermit, who had witnessed the whole scene from behind a tree. As soon as the queen left, he tiptoed out, picked up the ring from Fiordinando's brow, and retreated with it to his cave.

When Fiordinando awakened, it was already dark, and it took him a while to recall where he was. He shook the hunter awake, and together they cursed the red wine for being too strong and lamented over missing the queen.

The second day they said to the innkeeper, "Give us white wine, but make sure it's not too strong." The daughter, however, drugged the white wine too, and the young men went back, only to end up snoring in the middle of the meadow.

At a loss to awaken Fiordinando, the queen of Portugal placed a lock of her hair on his brow and fled. The hermit emerged from the grove of trees and made off with the lock. When Fiordinando and the hunter awakened in the middle of the night, they had no idea what had taken place.

Fiordinando became suspicious of the sleep that came over him every afternoon. It was now the last day before the queen would be leaving for Peterborough, and he intended to see her at all costs. He thus told the innkeeper to bring him no more wine. But the daughter now drugged the soup. So upon arriving in the meadow, Fiordinando felt his head drooping already. He pulled out two pistols and showed them to the hunter. "I know you're loyal," he said, "but I warn you that if you don't stay awake today and keep me awake, you are going to get it. I'll unload both of these into your head, and I don't mean maybe."

At that, Fiordinando stretched out and began to snore. To stay awake, the hunter tried pinching himself repeatedly, but between one pinch and the next his eyes would close, and the pinches became rarer and rarer, until he, too, was snoring.

The queen arrived. With cries, embraces, slaps in the face, kisses, and shakes, she did her best to awaken Fiordinando. But realizing she would not succeed, she began weeping so violently that instead of tears a few drops of blood trickled down her cheeks. She wiped the blood off with her handkerchief, which she placed over Fiordinando's face. Then she got back into her carriage and sped straight to Peterborough. Meanwhile the hermit came out of the cave, picked up the handkerchief, and stood by to see exactly what would happen.

When Fiordinando woke up at night and realized he'd missed his last chance to see the queen, he was fit to be tied. He pulled out the pistols and was about to carry out his threat of unloading them in the sleeping hunter's head, when the hermit grabbed him by the wrists and said, "That poor fellow is blameless. The culprit is the innkeeper's daughter, who drugged the red wine, the white wine, and the soup."

"Why would she do a thing like that?" asked Fiordinando. "And how do you know so much about it?"

"She's in love with you and gave you opium. I know all about it from peeping through the trees at everything that goes on here. For the last three days the queen of Portugal has come by and tried to awaken you, leaving on your brow a diamond, a lock of her hair, and a handkerchief moist with tears of blood."

"And where are these things now?"

"I took them away for safekeeping, since there are many thieves around here who would have stolen them before you ever got to see them. Here they are. Look after them, because if you act sensibly, they will bring you luck."

"What am I to do?"

"The queen of Portugal," explained the hermit, "has gone to Peterborough, where she will be given in prize at a tournament. The knight who jousts with this ring, this lock of hair, and this handkerchief on the tip of his lance will be invincible and wed the queen."

Fiordinando didn't have to be told twice. He sped from Paris to Peterborough, where he arrived in time to enter the list of jousters, but under a false name. Illustrious warriors had arrived from all over the world, with wagonloads of luggage, servants, and arms as shiny as the sun. In the heart of the city a large arena had been surrounded with viewing stands, and there the knights were to contend on horseback for the queen of Portugal.

With his visor lowered, Fiordinando won the first day, thanks to the diamond on the tip of his lance. He won the second day with the lock of hair. He won the third with the handkerchief. Horses and men fell by the dozens until not a one was left standing. Fiordinando was proclaimed victor and the queen's bridegroom. Only then did he open his helmet. The queen recognized him and swooned for joy.

There was a grand wedding, and Fiordinando sent for his mother and father, who had already given him up for dead and gone into mourning. He introduced his bride to them, saying, "This is none other than the little hare I pursued, the veiled lady, and the queen of Portugal, whom I have freed from an awful spell."

§

Translated by George Martin

Five Men and a Swan

Naomi Mitchison

he boys were all sitting round the table in the cabin of the *Highland Mary*. They had their cups of tea and the thick pieces with red jam, the pips of the rasps gritting on their teeth and the tea strong and sweet. They were talking about women. The engineer, who had been in a collier, was telling them about yon place in Cardiff; but they had heard it before. Black Rob was telling about a girl at one of the bars a wee bit up from the Broomielaw and the man she was with said that was all right, but he had been frightened to do much. You never knew with the Glasgow girls; or maybe you did, and that was the worst.

Willie the cook was not listening. He was reading a piece about the Rangers on the bit newspaper there was on the table. It was an old paper and there were jam stains on it here and there; he could read through them. If he could ever get over to Glasgow on a Friday, then he would get to one of the big matches on the Saturday afternoon.

But Black Rob, Johnnie the Ghost, and Alec the engineer, who was mostly called Alec Shop, the way his father used to keep the shop at the crossroads after he left the fishing, all went on talking about women, though it was little enough they knew when it came to the bit, and less they had done. For they were mostly all shy in the big towns where people spoke differently, and perhaps it would be an English girl talking quick and rough, and they would not understand her at all, for all they might let on that they did. Johnnie the Ghost had got married to Effie MacDonald in August, and time too; he was not saying much for himself, in case the boys would be laughing at him, and Effie expecting her bairn a while before the New Year. But indeed she was a nice enough girl, though a wee bit homely.

Outside, it was rough late afternoon, and the light beginning to go. In another half hour they would need to be starting. The *Highland Mary* had not been a lucky boat at all these last weeks. There had been little herring in it, and the one time they had a good shot, the net had torn below on a reef, and their neighbor boat saying it was their fault. Their neighbor was the *Annie MacQueen;* she had been a Tarbert boat to start with, named after a Tarbert skipper's wife, a fine red-haired woman that had eight bairns, and all the boys brought up to the fishing.

The skipper of the *Highland Mary,* who was mostly called Hat, just sat at the end of the table, and first he ate a good lot of bread and butter and jam, and then he told Willie to get the cheese, and he ate a good lot of that, and he put four spoonfuls of sugar in his tea, for all this happened a few years back, before the war, and he swilled it round. But he said nothing for a bit. He was a big man, and when he left off shaving for a day or two you could see it was a red beard he had on him. All of a sudden he said "Stop it, boys!" And they thought that was queer, for Hat was not one to get annoyed with this kind of talk, except it would be a Sunday, which it was not.

So Johnnie the Ghost asked what was the matter, and Hat let out with a great deep groan, the way he might have had a knock on the head. And he put his hand in his pocket and he took out a stiff white feather and laid it down on the table between the jam jar and the cheese. Now the boys all looked at the feather, and it was clear it was a swan's feather, the like of those you might find on the edge of the West Loch when the swans are in. But there was something queer about it, for each one of them had a quick feeling as though what they had been saying was just bairns' talk and blethers, and the truth away brighter and bonnier, and nothing at all to do with the girls that could be dirty girls in the bars by the Broomielaw. And even wee Willie the cook stopped his reading and listened, and they all believed in the thing Hat told them he had done.

For it seemed he was walking along by the point one night in the warm weather near two months back; he was coming home from seeing a man that had a cousin in Gourock with a winch he was wanting to sell. The two of them had been late talking, but there was a full moon in it, and Hat was walking back slow, looking at the bonny sight the moon made playing on the water, and a sweet south wind coming in gusts now and then and ruffling the tops of the waves the way they would be catching the light. And then in the moon track he caught sight of a girl swimming, and it was the long hair she had on her, the kind you are not seeing much these days, and this long, shining hair was not shut in a bathing cap but hanging loose into the water. And as he watched her, he saw she had no bathing dress on her at all and she was playing about in the water, rising her long white arms out of it, the like of a bird.

So first he thought she must be one of the summer visitors, and he looked for a rock to hide behind, the way he could watch her closer when she came out. There was a rock, and he knelt down, but as he knelt he put his hand onto a thing that was warm and soft, and he thought ah, it was the clothes of her he had, and maybe he could be tricking her a wee bit. But when he held them up in the moonlight to look at, he saw it was no woman's dress but the feathers of a white swan, a woman's shape of feathers.

Now Hat was a man that took things as they came, and he had been a skipper fifteen years, and his wife died a while back, leaving him with one lassie that was away training to be a nurse and another lassie at school yet; but the school lassie would be asleep in the back room now. So Hat took up the swan's dress and away with it to his house, and when he looked over his shoulder, there, as he had thought, was the Swan herself coming up out of the water wet and white, and her black hair dripping behind her, and cried on him to drop her dress.

There are plenty men who would have found that an awesome thing, and so it seemed to the boys round the cabin table; and plenty would have dropped the shape of feathers there and then, and run for it. But not Hat.

He took a tight grip of the feathers and walked on, and every time he looked back the Swan herself was nearer and calling to him, and oh, it was a bonny sweet voice she had. And when he was at his own door she was just by him, and he tucked the feathers under his arm and opened the door with one hand and pulled her in after him with the other.

He laid the feathers down on the bed and he lighted the lamp and held it up and looked close at the Swan. She was in every way like a young girl, he told them, but only this, that where women mostly all have hair growing on them she had the wee white feathers. And when you put your fingers on them one way they were smooth and cool, but when you ran your fingers under they were warm and soft the way swansdown is. She was dry now and she kept looking at the feather dress and asking for it back in thon sweet voice that almost melted the heart in him, for she seemed as young as his own lassie, younger than his wife had been at the time they were courting and away bonnier. And indeed, said Hat, he had only meant to keep the Swan a short, short time to look fully at her and maybe to have her on his knee for a while, but not to be spoiling her. But when he had got her on his knee right, he needed to be holding her there, and one thing led to another and he went just a hairsbreadth too far with the Swan. And the third time he went too far with the Swan that night, he was that sleepy afterwards, and when he woke the Swan was away and her dress with her and it was cold morning.

But the Swan had told him that once a month on the Saturday of full moon she was under a necessity to swim in the water off the point, and she must leave her feather dress among the rocks. So he knew he was bound to go back for her in a month's time.

The skipper stopped speaking then, and Black Rob asked quick had he done that, and Hat said Aye, he had gone, but this was the way of it. He had gone down that Saturday night to the point and he had heard her laughing and he had smelt the smell of her, that was partly the smell of a woman's body and breath, and partly the oily queer smell of a swan, and maybe that sounded not just right, yet it was a thing that had stayed in his nostrils ever since. But he had seen neither her nor her dress, and it was borne in upon him that he would never see her again.

Then Black Rob said: "It will be time again in three days." For it was near the October moon. And he looked at the skipper, and his tongue licked at his lips.

"It is not myself will stop you from going," said Hat, "but it is no luck she has brought me." And that was true enough surely, since it was in these last weeks that the *Highland Mary* and the *Annie MacQueen* had been getting the bad fishings when other pairs were doing well enough. And Hat said low to the rest of his crew that it was because he could not think right now. Any time when he should be looking at the land for the marks, or asking himself was it a right bottom where they were, there would come a thing like the flap of a swan's wing across his mind, and he would be left all in a maze and not able to act quick as a skipper should.

By now it was dusk. Alec Shop went off to start up the diesel; wee Willie got the tea things washed and redded up in the cabin. Behind the gray of the low clouds the moon was after rising. Dougie shouted over from their neighbor boat, where the engine was starting up too. But on the *Highland Mary* the boys were all thinking of thon woman with the wee white feathers on her, except for Willie the cook, and he was thinking that it could not be fair how they worked the football pools, for he had been going in for them these three years back and never once got anything out of them, and if you added up the sixpenny postal orders he had sent off it was fair staggering.

Again that night they had poor fishings, and so for the rest of the week. If they had a ring at all there would only be a scatter of fish in it, and the herring boat giving them bottom prices, so that there were only shillings to share out at the end of the week. But Black Rob was caring little. He washed and shaved and put a bit brilliantine on his hair that was wavy like a black retriever dog's, and he put on a clean white shirt and his best Sunday suit, and off he went on the Saturday night to the point and whatever was there for him.

There she was, sure enough, and there behind a rock was the shape of feathers, and the October moon white on it, and Black Rob warmed his hands in it, and it was more than his hands were warming, and when the Swan came up out of the water Black Rob caught hold of her, for he was never one for beds and houses when there was bracken on the braeside. And the more the Swan cried out, the more Rob was not caring at all what he did with her. And he made her promise he would see her again at the next full moon.

Not one of them said a thing on Sunday, and who would be asking Black Rob what kind of thoughts he was having at sermon time? But on the Monday they all asked him, and he said Aye, it was so, and laughed a bit. But Hat was angry all the week, and an angry skipper makes poor fishing, forby a white wing blinding his mind at the time he needs his judgment quickest.

So another month went by, and in November Black Rob put on his best suit again and off to the point. And he saw the Swan indeed by frosty moonlight. But that was all there was to it. For he could not anyway lay hands on her feather dress. Black Rob came home with his good coat torn and himself cut and bruised, the way he was running about and bashing himself against the rocks, and that Sunday he was not at the morning service nor yet the evening.

Now it was mostly Rob who was at the wire in the *Highland Mary*, and he had a quick and certain feel of it, but now it seemed he had lost that altogether, and though they might be ringing, it was for nothing but a scatter of herring or a ball of mackerel, and the rest swearing at Black Rob and he swearing back at them. And the noise they made would be skipping across the water until one of the Lamlash skippers, who was a gey religious man, bid them be quiet for fear a vengeance would come on the whole fleet.

But when it came on to December, Alec Shop had a thought of all this. He said: "You will all be taking her the wrong way. How were you not saying you would marry her? It is this marrying that the lasses are always after."

"Who would be marrying a swan?" says Black Rob. "It is eggs she would be laying on you!" And that was not all he said, for he had a great hatred and anger at the Swan for the trick she had played on him.

But Alec wiped his hands that were all filed with the diesel oil. "I would be marrying her," says he, "for I am thinking breakfast would be easy come by with only the bacon to be got!" And then he says: "The first time I was after seeing yon feather, it came in my mind to marry the lass, and I will have my witnesses waiting, and I am telling you this, Black Rob, she will be keeping my house for me and never a thought in the head of her but for the way she will be pleasing me best. And I am telling you another thing: it is not you will be speaking to my wife of anything that may have passed!"

Now Black Rob made an answer to that, and it was none of the best, and Alec gave him as good as he got, for he had found the trick of it, working in the south. And the skipper laughed, for he was cold angry at Rob over what had happened, though he was not saying it, being an older man. But Black Rob answered again, and Alec caught up a spanner, and there were the two of them fighting. And before the rest could get them out of it, they were cut and sore, and Alec had his shoulder knocked against the corner of the wheelhouse, so that he could hardly get lifting his arm for four days afterwards, and Black Rob's hair full of blood from the spanner. And Hat was going from one to the other saying he would need to give them their books if they could not be behaving themselves.

But the way it worked out just before the full moon, the engine had a breakdown and, Swan or no Swan, Alec needed to stay by the boat and work on her, all the more because Dougie and the rest of the boys on the *Annie MacQueen* were not pleased at all with the way things had been going, and indeed there was talk of them looking for another neighbor. So Alec was cursing and swearing, but stay he must, and wee Willie the cook stayed with him to help work on the engine. But he had a packet of Wild Wests with him, for next to football what Willie liked best was a book with six-shooters and all that in it.

Effie MacDonald was near her time, and there was her mother and her aunties forever in and out the house, and it was no place at all for Johnnie the Ghost and they casting their looks at him. So the night of the full moon he slipped out, but before he went he took a wee nip, and after he got clear of the houses he took another. For he was a man that had a trick of seeing some kind of frightening appearances, and that was the way he got his byname.

When he was halfway to the point he took another nip, for he was feeling the wee-est bit shoogly about the knees, and by the time he was there he had all the courage in the world and had forgotten there was ever such a girl as Effie MacDonald. And he seemed to have everything right clear and arguable in his head and shooting up from one moment to the next the same as a fountain. And he was asking himself how could the Swan not be saying sweet words to a man as personable and noble as himself? But what at all happened when he saw the Swan, and what he was doing to her, were not clear any longer, and there was a blackness cutting into his mind, and there was a screeching and groaning that first seemed to be the Swan and then all of a sudden was his wife Effie with her time come on her, and he standing in the door of his own house looking over at the bed. And as he stood he grew cold and vomited, and Effie's mother gave him one push out that landed him in a rosebush, and when it was morning and Effie's bairn come into the world, he found himself covered with scratches and vomit and ashamed to go into his own house and wash.

So he went to the spring behind and took his coat off and washed. And there were white feathers and swansdown in under his shirt and every place, and whenever he saw a bit of it a deep sadness came on him and he took the bottle out of his pocket and drank again, the way he could forget that he had forgotten all he needed so sore to remember. He was not back on the boat that week, and he was not sober one day of it. And that was the hardest for Effie, and there are plenty skippers would never have taken him back at all, but Hat knew fine what had come to him, and at the end of the week Johnnie went back. But he was an ill man to have to do with for long enough after that, and Effie was right glad always when he went off on the Monday.

Then it was New Year, and those were the days that folk kept it as it should be kept. And after New Year Alec Shop began to make his plans. He lived in the shed at the back of his mother's house, where she and his aunties were; and he asked his two witnesses to be at the shed that Saturday night. The one of them was his own brother and the other was his skipper, for Hat was thinking that they needed to deal with the Swan some way, or there would never be any luck at all for the *Highland Mary*, and if this was to be the way of it and Alec to be the man, well then, he would rather be helping than hindering, and maybe when the Swan was another man's wife he would be able to give over thinking of her and could turn his mind to the fishing again.

Alec got in a cake and a bottle of sweet port wine, the kind that they were telling him the ladies would like, and he put a new red cloth with fringes on the table and a mug with some snowdrops, and he put his budgie cage into the window, with the two budgies that his aunties looked after for him during the week. And he redded up everything in the shed, and he got sweeping up the cigarette ends and throwing them on the back of the fire, and forby that he took out the dirty photos that he had got in the south and that he had in the foot of one of his old sea boots so that his aunties would not get seeing them, and he threw them onto the fire without so much as looking at them again. He was doing all this in a regular and quiet kind of way, the way an engineer would be getting on with a job, and then it got to be evening, and he polished up the lamp and put a new wick in it: and he had bought a pink shade for it with kind of lacy trimming, the way he thought a woman would have her eye pleasantly caught by it.

And then he started to wash and he whistling to himself, and the budgies chirping and rustling. And then all of a sudden he caught sight of himself in the bit looking glass over the basin. And he fell to wondering what will the Swan say to me, and will the Swan have me at all? And he had never ever thought of it that way in all his life, for the girls in Cardiff or Glasgow are taking a man's money even if the man is dead ugly, and the dirty photos will look back at you the same way whoever you are, and when it comes to a dance you are mostly all thinking more of the music and of the dancing itself than of your partner, anyway in the hard dances, and those were the kind Alec liked best himself.

But now he stared hard at the face in the looking glass and thought, what is this odd face I have on me that I have never studied it at all? And he could not tell what a woman would be thinking of it, nor whether a woman would like the color of his eyes, that were gray-blue with a darker ring round them, and he wished now he had his teeth white and not all stained with the smoking. And he thought maybe she will not have me in marriage at all, maybe there is only one thing to be done with the Swan and that is what Hat and Black Rob and Johnnie the Ghost have done, and it is not a lucky thing at all, but if it is bad luck she is bringing on us, then that is the luck we must take. And yet, he thought, the way I am thinking on the Swan now, it is not that way I want her, but somehow else. And he fell to studying how it would make all the difference if he and the Swan were married, but he could not see right yet how it was, and his heart beating at full speed with the difficult thoughts he had.

But while he was on that, and putting the comb through his hair so it would stay flat down, in came his brother and his skipper. His brother was wearing his kilt, for he was in the Gaelic choir, and the skipper was in his best suit, with the hat he had for weddings and funerals, and a Bible in his hand. So Alec said: "You will wait in the back room until the time I am calling for you," and he set candles for them there.

Then he put on his coat and he was shaking a bit, and Hat looked him over and then took up some few of the snowdrops and put them in his buttonhole. And by now the moon was risen, so he went on his way to the point.

For a little he had the feeling that there was no truth at all in any of this, that there would be nothing at the point but air and moonshine and the cold beating of waves. And he wished he had a bottle with him, for he was dead sober and shivering. But then he came to the rocks and looked out, and his heart turned over on him, for there she was, and in a little he came on the shape of feathers, and he took it up and began to walk back, looking over his shoulder for her to follow. And follow she must, wet and shining and sweet-voiced, and he saw it was all true, and for a short time he felt himself near to doing what Black Rob had done, for she was so bonny, and he needed to touch her and have her, the same way a sad man might be needing the whisky, for it would mean the breaking of a black and hard and terrible thing in himself. It would mean light and life and an escaping. But he walked on and she at his elbow, and he trying not to look at her too often, and she asking, asking for her feathers back. So he said: "Marry me, lassie, and you shall have your dress again."

And she said: "Much good it would be to you, Alec, to have a wife only at the full moon!"

And he said: "I would rather a night of you, lassie, than four weeks of any other woman in the whole of Scotland!" And then he said: "It is only weekends I am home anyway, so I would be seeing you one time in four, and maybe," he went on, "if we were up north at Mallaig or Castlebay itself, or on the east coast, you would be coming to me on your wings?"

"You would need to keep your faith to me, Alec," says the Swan, "and never ever to lay hands on me to be hurting me, for indeed I have been sore hurt the way it was with the rest of your crew, and I will tell you, Alec, what it was your skipper did to me, forby Black Rob and Johnnie—"

"You will not be telling me!" says Alec quick and hard. "For I could not bear it at all. And indeed and indeed, lassie, you will keep yourself quiet and you will not be looking at me too much until after we are married, for I cannot know what I will do and you are over bonny for the like of me or for any of us poor souls, but if you will have me I will do anything in the wide world for you." And a great shame came over Alec, thinking how they were only poor fishermen, with no education beyond the age of fourteen and no chances at all, and some years there would be little herring in it and if any pair did well then the rest would be angry at them and jealous, and if at any time there was plenty of herring, then the buyers would get together and force the prices down, or maybe they would be needing to dump their catch at Ayr, and there was no way out of it at all for the fishermen, and what kind of a man was he to think he could be marrying such a bonny one as the Swan? And he wiped his sleeve across his eyes because of the shame he was in, and the tears that had come on him so sudden, and there was the Swan with her arms round him and her long wet hair and her cheeks yet cold from the sea, but softer and kinder than anything Alec had ever known. But he sprang away from her, for he saw the light of the lamp in the window of his shed, and he was remembering the clean cloth and the cake that had not been cut and the glasses that were dry and polished and the bed that had not been rumpled; and when he came to the door he shut his eyes and he lifted the Swan in over the threshold and took his hands from her quick. Then he said: "I will call my witnesses and we will be married now at once, and later on I will be going to the Sheriff's Court to pay the fine on it, but all the same this will be as lawful a marriage as any in Scotland."

And she smiled at him and said: "Are your witnesses to see your wife naked, Alec?"

And he said: "I would not like that at all, but if I give you the feathers back, you will not fly away on me, lassie? For if you did that I am thinking I would lie down and die."

And she did not answer, but she smiled at Alec again. And it went dancing through him like an electric current running through wires when the starter makes its contact, and he gave her the feathers without a word and she held them to her, and she began to change into a bird, and he cried at her: "Stop, stop, lassie!"

And she stopped, the way her face and hands were clear of the feathers and as for the rest of her, there was a kind of swaying in that room, so that sometimes she was a bird with the high cold breast of a swan, and the great wings starting back, and sometimes she was a woman in a white shining wedding dress. And Alec called in his witnesses and took her hand and said aloud before his brother and his skipper that they were man and wife. And the Swan was saying the same in thon sweet and bonny voice she had.

There was a kind of daze and enchantment on them all, and Hat was standing stiff and staring at the Swan, with a tight grip on his Bible; and Alec's brother was looking on the floor where the lamplight was running shadows in the cracks between the boards, and his hands fidgeting at the chain of his sporran and a singing in his ears. And then Alec and the Swan had their hands together on the knife, cutting the cake, and Hat opened the bottle of port wine, and for a little there was the circle of lamplight on cake and glasses and hands, and the white clean feathers reaching up the back of a girl's fingers, the way a long sleeve would, and moving with her. And then Alec said low to the witnesses that they could be going and he would surely see them in the morning on their way to the kirk, and he with his wife on his arm. And they went out and they said nothing to one another, but Hat could not get seeing in his mind at all how yon swan-winged and snowy woman could be walking the kirk road with Alec, and all the old wives staring at her.

But Alec turned to take the Swan in his arms, now they were married and alone, and there was a fire and a hurry in him, and his hands were seeking for the flesh of her under the feathers. But it was not a right woman's shape he was holding to, and as he caught at her she swept out with an arm or a wing and the lamp went over. He jumped at it and threw the rug on the burning oil and tramped on the flames and had it out before it had set the shed on fire. And then he pulled the curtains back and the moonlight came lapping in. And then he saw that the feather shape had closed over the face and hands of the Swan, and it was a great bird he had with him and no woman at all.

Then Alec let out a great screech and seized hold of the bird, and the long supple neck of it came down beside his own as it might have been her arm round his neck when he had wept coming back from the point, and he knew fine it was her somewhere and he cried out: "Lassie, lassie, where are you at all?"

And he battered with his face and fingers against the bird as though it

were something between him and his lassie. And it seemed to him as though
she must be within the feather shape, and all at once he pulled out his knife
and opened it with one hand and his teeth, holding all the time with the
other hand onto the bird's wing where it joined the shoulder, and he struck
with the knife to open a hole in the feather dress and tear it away from her.
But when he struck, a terrible skirl came from the Swan and the wings beat
at his head and knocked him clean over, and he was left on the floor in a
flurry of feathers and blows and broken glass where at last the Swan had burst
her way through the window and out.

All night Alec lay there on the floor and the fire died on the hearth and
in the early morning rain blew in through the broken window, and he turned
about and moaned and opened his eyes in the dark, and he was alone and
hurt. And when it was right light he sat up, and there was the open knife
and blood on it. And Alec went to the table with the cut cake and the glasses
and he leaned his forehead on it and he wept, and there he was when Hat
came back and knocked on the door of the shed.

Alec told Hat the way things had been, and old Hat nodded and said
he had best be taking a good dram, even if it was Sunday morning. But Alec
said no, no. And then he said he must look for another berth and maybe not
in a fishing boat at all and not among the kindly folk of the west coast, but
on the east or maybe in England itself.

Hat said would he not wait for the next full moon, but Alec said: "No.
I have broken my promise to the Swan and I cannot see how she will ever
forgive me, and maybe I have killed her, and there is no good in me at all."

"There is not that much good in any of us," said Hat, "and I will be
sorry to lose you, Alec, and I wish I had never set eyes or hands on this
damned woman or bird, for she has brought bad luck on every man of us!"

"She is my wife," Alec said, "and I do not even know what name she
has. I was thinking to find all that out after we had been to bed." And he
fell to shivering, and his head ached from the blow he had got from her.

So on Monday Alec went off to Greenock to find a new berth, and Hat
was needing to see about a new engineer for the *Highland Mary*, and it was
a heavy heart he had on him. The fishing was no better at all, and Dougie
on the *Annie MacQueen* saying he would try to get another neighbor. None
of the boys said a word in front of the new engineer, and when it got round
to full moon again, none of them said a word either, and it was a wild night
that was in it that Saturday, and Johnnie the Ghost and Black Rob went off
in the bus to the pictures and the whiskey, though it was little enough they
had got on the share-out, and Johnnie should have been letting Effie have
the lot of it, for she was needing to get credit at the shop and that is not the
best for a woman with a wee bairn. And Hat sat at home with his school
lassie and she learning off her psalm and he reading in the Book of Revelations
to try and take his mind off what it was forever on.

Then on the Monday afternoon the new engineer was down the hatch oiling the engine and wee Willie was making the tea for the rest, and when they were all sitting to, Willie says: "I saw the Swan on Saturday."

"You!" says the lot of them.

"And what for no?" says Willie.

"Well," says the skipper at last, "how did it go, Willie?"

"It went fine," he said.

"How?" says Black Rob and Johnnie together, and their voices snapped like two dogs wanting to fight.

"Well," says Willie, "I met her down on the shore the way all the boys did, and I went off home with her coat and she after me as bare as a plucked hen."

"And so?" says Black Rob.

"She asked me what it was I wanted of her," Willie says, and goes to fill up the teapot.

Just then the new engineer came down and Hat began quick speaking with him about the weather and the way the herring were shifting their ground, and the other two were eating their pieces and glaring at wee Willie. He stood up with the kettle in his hand. "I told her I was after filling in the names of the football pool," says he, "and would she get helping me; for I thought maybe she might have some kind of knowledge and would be bringing me luck, and at least she could not be bringing me worse luck than I have been having, and she said aye, she would tell me the right names to put down. So that was the way the two of us were spending our time."

"Are you telling me the whole of it?" says Black Rob low.

"Aye, surely," says Willie, "and it took us all of two hours, what with the information she was giving me about the teams, and indeed I am thinking she knows more than the newspapers themselves. And I have the forms in the post now!"

The new engineer said women were no good on football though he had known some could pick a horse. But it worked out the way wee Willie had said, and it was five hundred pounds he got out of the pools, and his photo in the paper grinning, because the Swan had given him all the names right. And Hat said this had changed the luck and he was praising up wee Willie. And indeed things went better for the *Highland Mary* for the few weeks that were left in the season.

But it was not that good for Willie himself. His father took the half of the money and had it invested the way Willie could not get touching it; but with the rest he took to the betting. Maybe the Swan could have guided him right there too, but he had no skill in it himself, and he was off at Glasgow the next full moon. Then he started to lose the money and the next thing was he was away spending what was left of it all April when the boats were lying up, and he got into bad company. And if it had not been for him losing the money so quick, he would have ended up in the jail. But he came back to the *Highland Mary* the next season and there was no more talk of the Swan one way or the other.

So a year and a day went by, and months and weeks, and Alec wrote home to his mother and his aunties, and sometimes he would be one place and sometimes another, but never coming back. And the truth was he was homesick enough; he did not like the food or the weather in the south; there seemed to him to be neither seriousness in the folk nor yet a right gaiety. But he could not come back, because it was not in him to forget the Swan, and whatever way you looked at it, he was married to her by Scots law, and both his brother and his skipper agreed to that. And if he went with a woman now, he could not do it sober, and there was little pleasure he got out of it, and nothing but shame and sorrow on him afterwards.

But at home the fishing would be worse and then it would be better, and then came the war. Wee Willie was the first to register, and then the new engineer, who was a young chap. Then the *Highland Mary* was requisitioned and Black Rob and Johnnie needing to get berths where they could until the time came for them to register. But Alec volunteered as an engineer, and he was put into an east coast patrol boat. He liked it well enough, better than he had done anything for all this last while. They were mostly all English and Irish in that boat, but there were two Scots forby himself, and the pay was good enough, and he had his photo taken in his uniform to send home. But one of his aunties was dead by then. And it was new budgies they had in his old cage.

Then, on a clear day and out of the eye of the sun, a bomber came down on them. Alec was below most of the time and it sounded the way hell sounds. Then a bomb came through one of the hatches and there was Alec trying to do a dozen things at the once, and in the middle of it he saw his overalls were on fire, and he beat them out, and someone shouted to him to come up, and he saw that his right hand was bleeding all over the iron rungs of the ladder though he could feel nothing at all in it yet, and first he was in a boat and then after the next explosion he was in the sea and swimming, but he did not think he would be able to keep it up for long, the way he was.

And then there was something under him, holding him up so he could rest himself from swimming, and he seemed to let go, and life went dark on him for a while. Then he woke clear up, and he was in pain, but most of all he wondered where he was, for he was not lying on any plank or raft or hard thing. And he put his left hand down to feel, and it was feathers was in it, and he knew he was on the back of a swan. And after a bit he said: "Are you not wearied, my darling?"

"Aye," said the Swan, "but we are near land, Alec."

And soon enough they were in shallow water and a sandy bottom, and he waded to shore, steadying himself by the Swan's lifted wing. But when they had made their way beyond high tide mark, Alec shook at the knees and he could not get any further, but he lay down on the sand and said to the Swan that it was dying he was.

"It is only cold you are and hurt and hungry," said the Swan. "But take you off your wet clothes, Alec, and let them dry."

So Alec sat up and began to strip off his things, and his hands and everything covered with oil and blood; and he saw that the bonny whiteness of the Swan was smeared here and there with it, and he said: "I have dirtied you, my dearie."

But the Swan said—and oh, the sweet, gentle voice she had on her and not like an English voice at all: "You are my man, Alec. I am thinking nothing of it. And do you not be so shy to be taking off your things in front of me, Alec, for we are married by Scots law and there is no getting out of it."

So Alec said: "My darling, did I hurt you that time?"

"Aye," said she. "I bear the mark of it yet."

By now the Swan was beside him on that English beach, and she brooding over him and he burrowing with his hands and face under the smooth top feathers of her and into the warm down that kept the sand and the hard English air out of the hurts on him. "I did that to you," he said, "and I was not faithful to you. I broke my promise all round and every way."

"Aye," said she, "but it is over and I am your wife, Alec."

So they lay quiet for a time and he half asleep and happy the way he had forgotten one could be happy. Then the Swan said to him: "I am hearing the Home Guards up in the dunes, Alec, and I must be leaving you."

"No!" he said, and held on to her.

"You will get six weeks' leave out of this, Alec," said she, "and there will be two full moons in it."

"And after that?" said Alec.

"Ach," said she, "it is the war now, and which one of us can see more than the two moons ahead?" And with that she rose out of his arms, and a few minutes later the Home Guards came running, and one of them asking Alec had he seen a parachute, for they had seen some great white thing flapping in the sky and were minded to shoot at it. But Alec laughed a bit and said, No, no, and then he said to the man that was helping him: "How much leave will I get out of this?"

"You will get six weeks easy," the man said. And Alec laughed again, and they all thinking that the Scots were a queer lot entirely and no one in the south could ever see what they would be after at all.

—§—

‹ Bluebeard's Daughter ›
SYLVIA TOWNSEND WARNER

 very child can tell of his ominous pigmentation, of his ruthless temper, of the fate of his wives, and of his own fate, no less bloody than theirs; but—unless it be here and there a director of Oriental Studies—no one now remembers that Bluebeard had a daughter. Amid so much that is wild and shocking, this gentler trait of his character has been overlooked. Perhaps, rather than spoil the symmetry of a bad husband by an admission that he was a good father, historians have suppressed her. I have heard her very existence denied, on the grounds that none of Bluebeard's wives lived long enough to bear him a child. This shows what it is to give a dog a bad name. To his third wife, the mother of Djamileh, Bluebeard was most tenderly devoted, and no shadow of suspicion rested upon her quite natural death in childbed.

From the moment of her birth Djamileh became the apple of Bluebeard's eye. His messengers ransacked Georgia and Circassia to find wet nurses of unimpeachable health, beauty, and virtue; her infant limbs were washed in nothing but rosewater and swaddled in Chinese silks. She cut her teeth upon a cabochon emerald engraved with propitious mottoes, and all the nursery vessels, mugs, platters, ewers, basins, and chamber pots were of white jade. Never was there a more adoring and conscientious father than Bluebeard, and I have sometimes thought that the career of this often-widowered man was inevitably determined by his anxiety to find the ideal stepmother.

Djamileh's childhood was happy, for none of the stepmothers lasted long enough to outwear their good intentions, and every evening, whatever his occupations during the day, Bluebeard came to the nursery for an hour's romp. But three days before her ninth birthday, Djamileh was told that her father was dead; and while she was still weeping for her loss she was made to weep even more bitterly by the statement that he was a bad man and that she must not cry for him. Dressed in crape, with the Bluebeard diamonds sparkling like angry tears beneath her veils, and wearing a bandage on her wrist, Fatima came to Djamileh's pavilion and paid off the nurses and governesses. With her came Aunt Ann and a strange young man whom she was told to call Uncle Selim; and while the nurses lamented and packed and the governesses sulked, swooned, and clapped their hands for sherbet, Djamileh listened to this trio disputing as to what should be done with her.

"For she can't stay here alone," said Fatima. "And nothing will induce me to spend another night under this odious roof."

"Why not send her to school?"

"Or to the Christians?" suggested Selim.

"Perhaps there is some provision for her in the will?"

"Will! Don't tell me that such a monster could make a will, a valid will. Besides, he never made one."

Fatima stamped her foot, and the diamond necklace sidled on her stormy bosom. Still disputing, they left the room.

That afternoon, all the silk carpets and embroidered hangings, all the golden dishes and rock-crystal wine coolers, together with the family jewels and Bluebeard's unique collection of the Persian erotic poets, were packed up and sent by camel to Selim's residence in Teheran. Thither also traveled Fatima, Ann, Selim, and Djamileh, together with a few selected slaves, Fatima in one litter with Selim riding at her side, doing his best to look stately but not altogether succeeding, since his mount was too big for him; Ann and Djamileh in the other. During the journey Ann said little, for she was engaged in ticking off entries in a large scroll. But once or twice she told Djamileh not to fidget, and to thank her stars that she had kind friends who would provide for her.

As it happened, Djamileh was perfectly well provided for. Bluebeard had made an exemplary and flawless will by which he left all his property to his only daughter and named his solicitor as her guardian until she should marry. No will can please everybody; and there was considerable heartburning when Badruddin removed Djamileh and her belongings from the care of Fatima, Ann, and Selim, persisting to the last filigree egg cup in his thanks for their kind offices towards the heiress and her inheritance.

Badruddin was a bachelor and grew remarkably fine jasmines. Every evening when he came home from his office he filled a green watering pot and went to see how they had passed the day. In the latticed garden the jasmine bushes awaited him like a dumb and exceptionally charming seraglio. Now he often found Djamileh sitting among them, pale and silent, as though, in response to being watered so carefully, a jasmine had borne him a daughter.

It would have been well for Djamileh if she had owed her being to such an innocent parentage. But she was Bluebeard's daughter, and all the girl babies of the neighborhood cried in terror at her father's name. What was more, the poor girl could not look at herself in the mirror without being reminded of her disgrace. For she had inherited her father's coloring. Her hair was a deep butcher's blue; her eyebrows and eyelashes were blue also. Her complexion was clear and pale, and if some sally of laughter brought a glow to her cheek it was of the usual pink, but the sinister parental pigmentation reasserted itself on her lips, which were deep purple, as though stained with eating mulberries; and the inside of her mouth and her tongue were dusky blue, like a well-bred chow dog's. For the rest she was like any other woman, and when she pricked her finger the blood ran scarlet.

Looks so much out of the common, if carried off with sufficient assurance, might be an asset to a modern miss. In Djamileh's time, taste was more classical. Blue hair and purple lips, however come by, would have been a serious handicap for any young woman—how much more so, then, for her, in whom they were not only regrettable but scandalous. It was impossible for Bluebeard's badged daughter to be like other girls of her age. The purple mouth seldom smiled; the blue hair, severely braided by day, was often at night wetted with her tears. She might, indeed, have dyed it. But filial devotion forbade. Whatever his faults, Bluebeard had been a good father.

Djamileh had a great deal of proper feeling; it grieved her to think of her father's crimes. But she had also a good deal of natural partiality, and disliked Fatima; and this led her to try to find excuses for his behavior. No doubt it was wrong, very wrong, to murder so many wives; but Badruddin seemed to think that it was almost as wrong to have married them, at any rate to have married so many of them. Experience, he said, should have taught the deceased that female curiosity is insatiable; it was foolish to go on hoping to find a woman without curiosity. Speaking with gravity, he conjured his ward to struggle, so far as in her lay, with this failing, so natural in her own sex, so displeasing to the other.

Djamileh fastened upon his words. To mark her reprobation of curiosity, the fault which had teased on her father to his ruin, she resolved never to be in the least curious herself. And for three weeks she did not ask a single question. At the end of the third week she fell into a violent fever, and Badruddin, who had been growing more and more disquieted by what appeared to him to be a protracted fit of sulks, sent for a doctoress. The doctoress was baffled by the fever but did not admit it. What the patient needed, she said, was light but distracting conversation. Mentioning in the course of her chat that she had discovered from the eunuch that the packing case in the lobby contained a new garden hose, the doctoress had the pleasure of seeing Djamileh make an instant recovery from her fever. Congratulating herself on her skill and on her fee, the old dame went off, leaving Djamileh to realize that it was not enough to refrain from asking questions; some more radical method of combating curiosity must be found. And so when Badruddin, shortly after her recovery, asked her in a laughing way how she would like a husband, she replied seriously that she would prefer a public-school education.

This was not possible. But the indulgent solicitor did what he could to satisfy this odd whim, and Djamileh made such good use of her opportunities that by the time she was fifteen she had spoiled her handwriting, forgotten how to speak French, lost all her former interest in botany, and asked only the most unspeculative questions. Badruddin was displeased. He sighed to think that the intellectual Bluebeard's child should have grown up a dullard, and spent more and more time in the company of his jasmines. Possibly, even, he consulted them, for though they were silent they could be expressive. In any case, after a month or so of inquiries, interviews, and drawing up treaties, he told Djamileh that acting under her father's will, he had made arrangements for her marriage.

Djamileh was sufficiently startled to ask quite a number of questions, and Badruddin congratulated himself on the aptness of his prescription. His choice had fallen upon Prince Kayel Oumarah, a young man of good birth, good looks, and pleasant character, but not very well-to-do. The prince's relations were prepared to overlook Djamileh's origin in consideration of her fortune, which was enormous, and Kayel, who was of a rather sentimental turn of mind, felt that it was an act of chivalry to marry a girl whom other young men might scorn for what was no fault of hers, loved her already for being so much obliged to him, and wrote several ghazals expressing a preference for blue hair.

> What wouldn't I do, what wouldn't I do,
> To get at that hair of heavenly blue?

(the original Persian is, of course, more elegant), sang Kayel under her window. Djamileh thought this harping on her hair not in the best of taste, more especially since Kayel had a robust voice and the whole street might hear him. But it was flattering to have poems written about her (she herself had no turn for poetry), and when she peeped through the lattice she thought that he had a good figure and swayed to and fro with a great deal of feeling.

Passion and a good figure can atone for much; and perhaps when they were man and wife he would leave off making personal remarks.

After a formal introduction, during which Djamileh offered Kayel symbolical sweetmeats and in her confusion ate most of them herself, the young couple were married. And shortly afterwards, they left town for the Castle of Shady Transports, the late Bluebeard's country house.

Djamileh had not set eyes on Shady Transports since she was carried away from it in the same litter as Aunt Ann and the inventory. It had been in the charge of a caretaker ever since. But before the wedding Badruddin had spent a few days at the village inn, and under his superintendence the roof had been mended, the gardens trimmed up, all the floors very carefully scrubbed, and a considerable quantity of female attire burned in the stableyard. There was no look of former tragedy about the place when Djamileh and Kayel arrived. The fountain splashed innocently in the forecourt, all the most appropriate flowers in the language of love were bedded out in the parterre, a troop of new slaves, very young and handsomely dressed, stood bowing on either side of the door, and seated on cushions in stiff attitudes of expectation, Maya and Moghreb, Djamileh's favorite dolls, held out their jointed arms in welcome.

Tears came into her eyes at this token of Badruddin's understanding heart. She picked up her old friends and kissed first one and then the other, begging their pardon for the long years in which they had suffered neglect. She thought they must have pined, for certainly they weighed much less than of old. Then she recollected that she was grown up, and had a husband.

At the moment he was not to be seen. Still clasping Maya and Moghreb, she went in search of him, and found him in the armory, standing lost in admiration before a display of swords, daggers, and cutlasses. Djamileh remembered how, as a child, she had been held up to admire and warned not to touch.

"That one comes from Turkestan," she said. "My father could cut off a man's head with it at a single blow."

Kayel pulled the blade a little way from the sheath. It was speckled with rust, and the edge was blunted.

"We must have them cleaned up," he said. "It's a pity to let them get like this, for I've never seen a finer collection."

"He had a splendid collection of poets too," said Djamileh. "I was too young to read them then, of course, but now that I am married to a poet myself, I shall read them all."

"What a various-minded man!" exclaimed Kayel as he followed her to the library.

It is always a pleasure to explore a fine old rambling country house. Many people whose immediate thoughts would keep them tediously awake slide into a dream by fancying that such a house has—no exact matter how—come into their possession. In fancy they visit it for the first time, they wander from room to room, trying each bed in turn, pulling out the books, opening Indian boxes, meeting themselves in mirrors. . . . All is new to them, and all is theirs.

For Kayel and Djamileh this charming delusion was a matter of fact. Djamileh indeed declared that she remembered Shady Transports from the days of her childhood and was always sure that she knew what was round the next corner; but really her recollections were so fragmentary that except for the sentiment of the thing, she might have been exploring her old home for the first time. As for Kayel, who had spent most of his life in furnished lodgings, the comfort and spaciousness of his wife's palace impressed him even more than he was prepared to admit. Exclaiming with delight, the young couple ransacked the house, or wandered arm in arm through the grounds, discovering fish ponds, icehouses, classical grottoes, and rustic bridges. The gardeners heard their laughter among the blossoming thickets, or traced where they had sat by the quantity of cherry stones.

At last a day came when it seemed that Shady Transports had yielded up all its secrets. A sharp thunderstorm had broken up the fine weather. The rain was still falling, and Kayel and Djamileh sat in the western parlor, playing chess like an old married couple. The rain had cooled the air, indeed it was quite chilly; and Kayel, who was getting the worst of the game, complained of a draft that blew on his back and distracted him.

"There can't really be a draft, my falcon," objected Djamileh, "for drafts don't blow out of solid walls, and there is only a wall behind you."

"There is a draft," he persisted. "I take your pawn. No, wait a moment, I'm not sure that I do. How can I possibly play chess in a whirlwind?"

"Change places," said his wife, "and I'll turn the board."

They did so and continued the game. It was now Djamileh's move; and as she sat gazing at the pieces, Kayel fell to studying her intent and unobservant countenance. She was certainly quite pretty, very pretty even, in spite of her coloring. Marriage had improved her, he thought. A large portrait of Bluebeard hung on the wall behind her. Kayel's glance went from living daughter to painted sire, comparing the two physiognomies. Was there a likeness—apart, of course, from the blue hair? Djamileh was said to be the image of her mother; certainly the rather foxlike mask before him, the narrow eyes and pointed chin, bore no resemblance to the prominent eyes and heavy jowl of the portrait. Yet there was a something . . . the pouting lower lip, perhaps, emphasized now by her considering expression. Kayel had another look at the portrait.

"Djamileh! There *is* a draft! I saw the hangings move." He jumped up and pulled them aside. "What did I say?" he inquired triumphantly.

"Oh! Another surprise! Oh, haven't I a lovely jack-in-the-box house?"

The silken hangings had concealed a massive stone archway, closed by a green baize door.

Kayel nipped his wife's ear affectionately. "You who remember everything so perfectly—what's behind that door?"

"Rose-petal conserve," she replied. "I have just remembered how it used to be brought out from the cupboard when I was good."

"I don't believe it. I don't believe there's a cupboard, I don't believe you were ever good."

"Open it and see."

Beyond the baize door a winding stair led into a small gallery or corridor, on one side of which were windows looking into the park, on the other, doors. It was filled with a green and moving light reflected from the wet foliage outside. They turned to each other with rapture. A secret passage—five doors in a row, five new rooms waiting to be explored! With a dramatic gesture, Kayel threw open the first door. A small, dark closet was revealed, perfectly empty. A trifle dashed, they opened the next door. Another closet, small, dark, and empty. The third door revealed a third closet, the exact replica of the first and second.

Djamileh began to laugh at her husband's crestfallen air.

"In my day," she said, "all these cupboards were full of rose-petal conserve. So now you see how good I was."

Kayel opened the fourth door.

He was a solemn young man, but now he began to laugh also. Four empty closets, one after another, seemed to these amiable young people the height of humor. They laughed so loudly that they did not hear a low peal of thunder, the last word of the retreating storm. A dove who had her nest in the lime tree outside the window was startled by their laughter or by the thunder; she flew away, looking pale and unreal against the slate-colored sky. Her flight stirred the branches, which shook off their raindrops, spattering them against the casement.

"Now for the fifth door," said Kayel.

But the fifth door was locked.

"Djamileh dear, run and ask the steward for the keys. But don't mention which door we want unfastened. Slaves talk so, they are always imagining mysteries."

"I am rather tired of empty cupboards, darling. Shall we leave this one, for the present? At any rate till after tea? So much emptiness has made me very hungry; I really need my tea."

"Djamileh, fetch the keys."

Djamileh was an obedient wife, but she was also a prudent one. When she had found the bunch of keys, she looked carefully over those which were unlabeled. They were many, and of all shapes and sizes; but at last she found the key she had been looking for and which she had dreaded to find. It was a small key, made of gold and finely arabesqued; and on it there was a small dark stain that might have been a bloodstain.

She slipped it off the ring and hid it in her dress.

Returning to the gallery, she was rather unpleasantly struck by Kayel's expression. She could never have believed that his open countenance could wear such a look of cupidity or that his eyes could become so beady. Hearing her step, he started violently, as though roused from profound absorption.

"There you are! What an age you have been—darling! Let's see, now. Icehouse, Stillroom, Butler's Pantry, Wine Cellar, Family Vault . . . I wonder if this is it?"

He tried key after key, but none of them fitted. He tried them all over again, upside down or widdershins. But still they did not fit. So then he took out his pocketknife and tried to pick the lock. This also was useless.

"Eblis take this lock!" he exclaimed. And suddenly losing his temper, he began to kick and batter at the door. As he did so there was a little click; and one of the panels of the door fell open upon a hinge and disclosed a piece of parchment, framed and glazed, on which was an inscription in ancient Sanskrit characters.

"What the . . . Here, I can't make this out."

Djamileh, who was better educated than her husband in such useless studies as calligraphy, examined the parchment and read aloud: *"Curiosity killed the cat."*

Against her bosom she felt the little gold key sidle, and she had the unpleasant sensation which country language calls "the gray goose walking over your grave."

"I think," she said gently, "I think, dear husband, we had better leave this door alone."

Kayel scratched his head and looked at the door.

"Are you sure that's what it means? Perhaps you didn't read it right."

"I am quite sure that is what it means."

"But, Djamileh, I do want to open the door."

"So do I, dear. But under the circumstances we had better not do anything of the sort. My poor father . . . my poor stepmothers . . ."

"I wonder," mused Kayel, "if we could train a cat to turn the lock and go in first."

"Even if we could, which I doubt, I don't think that would be at all fair to the cat. No, Kayel, I am sure we should agree to leave this door alone."

"It's not that I am in the least inquisitive," said Kayel, "for I am not. But as master of the house, I really think it my duty to know what's inside this cupboard. It might be firearms, for instance, or poison, which might get into the wrong hands. One has a certain responsibility, hang it."

"Yes, of course. But all the same, I feel sure we should leave the door alone."

"Besides, I have you to consider, Djamileh. As a husband, you must be my first consideration. Now you may not want to open the door just now; but suppose, later on, when you were going to have a baby, you developed one of those strange yearnings that women at such times are subject to; and suppose it took the form of longing to know what was behind this door. It might be very bad for you, Djamileh, it might imperil your health, besides birthmarking the baby. No! It's too grave a risk. We had much better open the door immediately."

And he began to worry the lock again with his penknife.

"Kayel, please don't. *Please* don't, I implore you. I have a feeling—"

"Nonsense. Women always have feelings."

"—as though I were going to be sick. In fact, I am sure I am going to be sick."

"Well, run off and be sick, then. No doubt it was the thunderstorm, and all those strawberries."

"I can't run off, Kayel. I don't feel well enough to walk; you must carry me. Kayel!" She laid her head insistently on his chest. "Kayel! I felt sick this morning too."

And she laid her limp weight against him so firmly that with a sigh he picked her up and carried her down the corridor.

Laid on the sofa, she still kept a firm hold on his wrist and groaned whenever he tried to detach himself. At last, making the best of a bad job, he resigned himself and spent the rest of the day reading aloud to her from the Persian erotic poets. But he did not read with his usual fervor; the lyrics, as he rendered them, might as well have been genealogies. And Djamileh, listening with closed eyes, debated within herself why Kayel should be so cross. Was it just the locked closet? Was it, could it be, that he was displeased by the idea of a baby with Bluebeard blood? This second possibility was highly distressing to her, and she wished, more and more fervently, as she lay on the sofa keeping up a pretense of delicate health and disciplining her healthy appetite to a little bouillon and some plain sherbet, that she had hit upon a pretext with fewer consequences entailed.

It seemed to her that they were probably estranged forever. So it was a great relief to be awakened in the middle of the night by Kayel's usual affable tones, even though the words were:

"Djamileh, I believe I've got it! All we have to do is to get a stonemason, and a ladder, and knock a hole in the wall. Then we can look in from outside. No possible harm in that."

All the next day and the day after, Kayel perambulated the west wing of Shady Transports with his stonemasons, directing them where to knock holes in the walls; for it had been explained to the slaves that he intended to bring the house up to date by throwing out a few bow windows. But not one of these perspectives (the walls of Shady Transports were exceedingly massy) afforded a view into the locked closet. While these operations were going on, he insisted that Djamileh should remain at his side. It was essential, he said, that she should appear interested in the improvements, because of the slaves. All this time, she was carrying about that key on her person and debating whether she should throw it away, in case Kayel by getting possession of it should endanger his life, or whether she should keep it and use it herself the moment he was safely out of the way.

Jaded in nerves and body, at the close of the second day they had a violent quarrel. It purported to be about the best method of pruning acacias, but while they were hurrying from sarcasm to acrimony, from acrimony to abuse, from abuse to fisticuffs, they were perfectly aware that in truth they were quarreling as to which of them should first get at that closet.

"Laterals! Laterals!" exclaimed Djamileh. "You know no more of pruning than you know of dressmaking. That's right! Tear out my hair, do!"

"No, thank you." Kayel folded his arms across his chest. "I have no use for *blue hair*."

Pierced by this taunt, Djamileh burst into tears. The soft-hearted Kayel felt that he had gone too far, and made several handsome apologies for the remark; but it seemed his apologies would be in vain, for Djamileh only came out of her tears to ride off on a high horse.

"No, Kayel," she said, putting aside his hand, and speaking with exasperating nobility and gentleness. "No, no, it is useless; do not let us deceive ourselves any longer. I do not blame you; your feeling is natural, and one should never blame people for natural feelings."

"Then why have you been blaming me all this time for a little natural curiosity?"

Djamileh swept on. "And how could you possibly have felt anything but aversion for one in whose veins so blatantly runs the blood of the Bluebeards, for one whose hair, whose lips, stigmatize her as the child of an unfortunate monster? I do not blame you, Kayel. I blame myself, for fancying you could ever love me. But I will make you the only amends in my power. I will leave you."

A light quickened in Kayel's eye.

So he thought she would leave him at Shady Transports, did he?

"Tomorrow we will go *together* to Badruddin. He arranged our marriage; he had better see about our divorce."

Flushed with temper, glittering with tears, she threw herself into his willing arms. They were still in all the raptures of sentiment and first love, and in the even more enthralling raptures of sentiment and first grief, when they set out for Teheran. Absorbed in gazing into each other's eyes and wiping away each other's tears with pink silk handkerchiefs, they did not notice that a drove of stampeding camels was approaching their palanquin; and it was with the greatest surprise and bewilderment that they found themselves tossed over a precipice.

When Djamileh recovered her senses, she was lying in a narrow green pasture beside a watercourse. Some fine broad-tailed sheep were cropping the herbage, and an aged shepherdess was bathing her forehead and slapping her hands.

"How did I come here?" she inquired.

"I really cannot tell you," answered the shepherdess. "All I know is that about half an hour ago, you and a handsome young man and a coachman and a quantity of silk cushions and chicken sandwiches appeared, as it were from heaven, and fell amongst us and our sheep. Perhaps as you are feeling better you would like one of the sandwiches?"

"Where is that young man? He is not dead?"

"Not at all. A little bruised, but nothing worse. He recovered before you, and feeling rather shaken, he went off with the shepherds to have a drink at the inn. The coachman went with them."

Djamileh ate another sandwich, brooding on Kayel's heartlessness.

"Listen," she said, raising herself on one elbow. "I have not time to tell you the whole of my history, which is long, and complicated with unheard-of misfortunes. Suffice it to say that I am young, beautiful, wealthy, well-born, and accomplished, and the child of doting and distinguished parents. At their death I fell into the hands of an unscrupulous solicitor, who, entirely against my will, married me to that young man you have seen. We had not been married for a day before he showed himself a monster of jealousy; and though my conduct has been unspotted as the snow, he has continually belabored me with threats and reproaches, and now has determined to shut me up, forever, in a hermitage on the Caucasus Mountains, inherited from a woman-hating uncle (the whole family is very queer). We were on our way thither when, by the interposition of my good genius, the palanquin overturned and we arrived among your flocks as we did."

"Indeed," replied the aged shepherdess. "He said nothing of all that. But I do not doubt it. Men are a cruel and fantastic race. I, too, have lived a life checkered with many strange adventures and unmerited misfortunes. I was born in India, the child of a virtuous Brahmin and of a mother who had, before my birth, graced the world with eleven daughters, each lovelier than the last. In the opinion of many well-qualified persons, I, the youngest of her children, was even fairer—"

"I can well believe it," said Djamileh. "But, venerable aunt, my misfortunes compel me to postpone the pleasure of hearing your story until a more suitable moment. It is, as you will see, essential that I should seize this chance of escaping from my tyrant. Here is a purse. I shall be everlastingly obliged if you will conduct me to the nearest livery stables where I can hire a small chariot and swift horses."

Though bruised and scratched, Djamileh was not much the worse for her sudden descent into the valley, and following the old shepherdess, who was as nimble as a goat, she scrambled up the precipice and soon found herself in a hired chariot, driving at full speed towards the Castle of Shady Transports, clutching in her hot hand the key of the locked closet. Her impatience was indescribable, and as for her scruples and her good principles, they had vanished as though they had never been. Whether it was a slight concussion, or pique at hearing that Kayel had left her in order to go off and drink with vulgar shepherds, I do not pretend to say. But in any case, Djamileh had now but one thought, and that was to gratify her curiosity as soon as possible.

Botching up a pretext of having forgotten her jewelry, she hurried past the house steward and the slaves, refusing refreshment and not listening to a word they said. She ran to the west parlor, threw aside the embroidered hangings, opened the green baize door, flew up the winding stair and along the gallery.

But the door of the fifth closet had been burst open.

It gave upon a sumptuous but dusky vacancy, an underground saloon of great size, walled with mosaics and inadequately lit by seven vast rubies hanging from the ceiling. A flight of marble steps led down to this apartment, and at the foot of the steps lay Kayel, groaning piteously.

"Thank heaven you've come! I've been here for the last half hour, shouting at the top of my voice, and not one of these accursed slaves has come near me."

"Oh, Kayel, are you badly hurt?"

"Hurt? I should think I've broken every bone in my body, and I know I've broken my collarbone. I had to smash that door in, and it gave suddenly, and I pitched all the way down these steps. My second fall today—oh!"

As she leaned over him, the little golden key, forgotten and useless now, slid from her hand.

"My God, Djamileh! You've had that key all this time. And so *that* was why you came back?"

"Yes, Kayel. I came back to open the door. But you got here before me."

And while that parry still held him, she hastened to add:

"We have both behaved so shockingly that I don't think either of us had better reproach the other. So now let us see about your fracture."

Not till the collarbone was mending nicely; not till the coverlet which

Djamileh had begun to knit as she sat by her husband's bedside, since knitting is always so soothing to invalids, was nearly finished; not till they had solved the last of the acrostics sent to them by a sympathizing Badruddin, did they mention the affair of the closet.

"How could I have the heart to leave you—you, looking so pale, and so appealing?" said Kayel suddenly.

"And the lies I told about you, Kayel, the moment I came to . . . the things I said, the way I took away your character!"

"We must have been mad."

"We were suffering from curiosity. That was all, but it was quite enough."

"How terrible curiosity is, Djamileh! Fiercer than lust, more ruthless than avarice—"

"Insatiable as man-eating tigers—"

"Insistent as that itching powder one buys at low French fairs . . . O Djamileh, let us vow never to feel curiosity again!"

"I made that vow long ago. You have seen what good it was."

They meditated, gazing into each other's eyes.

"It seems to me, my husband, that we should be less inquisitive if we had more to do. I think we should give up all our money, live in a village, and work all day in the fields."

"That only shows, my dearest, that you have always lived in a town. The people who work all day in the fields will sit up all night in the hopes of discovering if their neighbor's cat has littered brindled or tortoiseshell kittens."

They continued to interrogate each other's eyes.

"A man through whose garden flowed a violent watercourse," said Djamileh, "complained one day to the stream: 'O Stream, you have washed away my hollyhocks, swept off my artichokes, undermined my banks, flooded my bowling green, and drowned my youngest son, the garland of my gray head. I wish, O Stream, that you would have the kindness to flow elsewhere.' 'That cannot be,' replied the stream, 'since Allah has bidden me to flow where I do. But if you were to erect a mill on your property, perhaps you would admit that I have my uses.' In other words, Kayel, it seems to me that since we cannot do away with our curiosity, we had best sublimate it and take up the study of a science."

"Let it be astronomy," answered Kayel. "Of all sciences, it is the one least likely to intervene in our private life."

To this day, though Bluebeard's daughter is forgotten, the wife of Kayel the Astronomer is held in remembrance. It was she whose sympathetic collaboration supported him through his researches into the Saturnian rings, it was she who worked out the mathematical calculations which enabled him to prove that the lost Pleiad would reappear in the year 1963. As time went on, and her grandchildren came clustering round the telescope, Djamileh's blue hair became silver; but to the day of her death, her arched blue brows gave an appearance of alertness to her wrinkled countenance, and her teeth, glistening and perfect as in her girlhood, were shown off to the best advantage by the lining of her mouth, duskily blue as that of a well-bred chow dog's.

‹ *The Crow* ›
Christoph Meckel

 crossed the woods in the summer. They were dense woods that went on endlessly. And one morning I met a man standing in the brushwood. He was wearing a ragged jacket and dirty boots, and he screamed and whistled through his fingers (which would have been enough to draw me off my path). He yelled out many names in the endless woods, full of murmuring and pairing, crackling and green silence. As I came closer, he waved me over to him and told me that he was searching for a tiger.

There were no large animals and predatory beasts in these woods, but I did not want to pose long questions, because I was curious and had plenty of time. I let him tell me the names of the tiger and began helping the man in his search. I ran through bushes and high cutting grass and called out the names of the tiger in the calm around me, and I listened as the man worked his way through the thickets at some distance ahead of me, whistling and yelling, and after a long time of fruitless searching in the woods I met him again, and he said, "We must look for a bear now. I saw a bear on the hills in the woods. That means that the tiger transformed itself. There is no tiger anymore."

And we set out anew in the woods We took separate paths and called out all the names in great twilight, and I heard groping and rustling, wood crackling, and heavy steps on the leaves and stones near and far, and when

I again encountered the man in the darkest interior of the woods, he said, "I saw a white elephant going through the bushes. Now there is no bear anymore." And we separated again and fought our way through the woods and more woods, endlessly and coolly. We called out many names and searched for the elephant, but we didn't find him. And after some hours had passed, the man said, "From now on we must search for a wolf." And we searched for the wolf, and in the afternoon I found the man sitting exhausted on the stump of a tree, and he said, "I saw the wolf transforming itself right in front of me. Now we must look for a black fox." With branches and sticks we poked around in the sand holes and tunnels between the roots of the trees, in the inaccessible thickets and islands of ponds, and I climbed a tree, sat high over the ground, and looked far beyond the woods and into the completely clear sky. Then I climbed down, crawled over the moss and through the fields of fern, but I didn't find a black fox.

"What should I do with the fox, when I find it?" I asked the man.

"You've got to call me," he said. "You've got to hold on to it until I come."

Once again I began running through the woods, now very tired, and toward evening I encountered a man-size crow in the underbrush, standing still, and I stopped in my tracks and asked, "Are you the one who's being sought, crow?"

The crow nodded and hobbled over to me.

"Does the man know already that you're a crow?" I asked. "Has he seen you already?"

"No," said the crow. "He's still looking for the black fox."

The crow seemed to be very exhausted.

"I'm helping him look," I said. "I suppose you know, right?"

"Yes, I know," said the crow. "I saw you running by me as I was catching my breath as a bear behind a pile of stones."

"You could have easily torn me apart," I said.

"Yes," said the crow. "I could have easily done that, but it didn't matter to me very much. Now I could hack you to pieces in case you tried to hinder me by shoving your stick in my beak or doing something else, but it doesn't matter much to me."

I didn't know quite what to do with the beast.

"If you want," I said, "I won't tell the man that I've met you as crow. You can stay here, and I'll keep the man away from you. Actually, I don't know what's going on here. You can catch your breath, but you've got to stay awake. I'll come back."

The crow shifted from one foot to the other.

"What will the man do when he finds you?" I asked. "What does he want to do?"

"Lock me up in chains or stick me in a shed," answered the crow. "I'm only guessing. I don't know exactly. He can also slaughter me and eat me. It all depends on what occurs to him when he finds me as crow."

"Does he have some claim on you?" I asked. "I mean, did he build a beautiful shed for you when you were a tiger? Did he feed you?"

"He had already hunted me before I was a tiger," said the crow. "He is a great hunter."

I asked, "Do you intend to change yourself again, crow?"

It answered, "I can do it one more time, just one more time."

"Good," I said. "Then I'll let the man continue to search for the black fox."

And I went through the woods, met the man, who was hot and tired from yelling, and we agreed to continue to look for the black fox.

"I hunted the tiger and all the other animals before," the man said. "I hunted the bear and the elephant. Now I'm hunting the black fox. I'm a hunter. That's how I make my living, and I need the animal. I want to possess it. And even if it were to become a parrot and hop around the towers of Peking, I'm going to hunt it."

"What do you intend to do with it?" I asked.

"What I intend to do with it? That doesn't matter at all," the man cried impatiently. "I've got to have it. I want to possess it. And now go and search for the black fox!"

And we separated, and while the hunter bellowed into the woods in search for the black fox, I ran to the crow. I was not obsessed myself with having the crow.

It was standing on the same spot.

"Do you want to come with me?" I asked. "I like you. You'd no longer be hunted."

The crow looked at me and nodded with its large head. So we went to look for a way out of the woods, the crow staggering sleepily at my side. Late in the evening, as dusk was already making the woods dark, we found our way into a clearing.

"The hunter won't leave the woods," I said. "You can catch your breath here."

And the crow lay down in the grass. I placed my head under its wings, and we slept that night in the clearing near the woods, from which we heard yells and cries. The next morning, we stood up and continued on our way together.

And we walked the whole hot day on a plain brightened by the sun. At the edge of this land, the woods became small and gray and disappeared. The grass was blowing in the wind around us and was sparse. After walking for hours over the plain, I asked the crow to fly into the air to see where we were.

"I can't fly," said the crow.

I asked the crow to try it at least. It shook its wings, flapped about, hopped, turned around with difficulty, tucked in its feet, and glided along the ground with its wings creating dust, but it managed only a couple of short, awkward jumps a couple of feet off the ground. The crow gasped for breath and had wild eyes.

"I see. You really can't fly," I said. "Let it be."

And we continued walking in the great heat. Hours later, we arrived in a village, where there were trees, and we rested in their shade. Then we washed ourselves in the trough of a fountain. After I had taken a drink, the crow jumped into the water, flapped its wings, shook itself, splashed the water, and drank some through its beak in great loud slurps. Many people gathered on their doorsteps and then around the fountain. They pointed their fingers at the crow and laughed. They surrounded it heedlessly, but the crow did not notice or just did not pay any attention. I explained to the people that I was bringing the animal to a circus in the city. "I'm hoping to make a good deal of money," I said.

Soon after, we left the village, as the people retreated unwillingly from the crow, and I asked the crow to excuse me. "Please don't misunderstand me, crow," I said. "I needed to have an excuse for the people."

"I understood that," said the crow. "They didn't seem to be especially bashful."

And we continued farther on the plain and went over small hills until the afternoon.

"I want to make you a proposal," I said. "You told me that you could still make one more change."

"Yes," said the crow. "Why did you want to know this?"

"What kind of a change is it?" I continued. "Is it one that would arouse people's attention?"

"Is it absolutely necessary that you know?" asked the crow.

"Look now, crow," I said, "here's my proposal. Listen to it. We are now going to pass through many villages and occasionally a city. We'll see many people, more than a thousand each day, you understand. It would be easier if you would change yourself once more to make yourself less noticeable."

"Why?" asked the crow. "I'm a crow. Anyone can let himself be seen with a crow."

"That's true," I said. "But have you ever seen a real crow?"

"No," said the crow. "I know very little about crows. The first time I learned that I was a crow and am called a crow was from you."

"You see, that's just my point," I said. "Real crows are small. You're thirty times, perhaps forty times as large as an ordinary crow. And you're the only crow that's ever been so large. That's why you no longer count as a crow if we stay around people for a long time. For instance, as a dog you wouldn't attract attention. There are a hundred kinds of dogs, some very large. But there's only one kind of crow, and everyone knows it."

The crow walked alongside me and brooded for a long time. "I don't understand you," it finally said. "I still want to save my last change, because, as you can understand, it's my last. Before this I changed quickly and without thinking, but now I must think about it for a long time before I give up something. That's the one point. The other is: why shouldn't I stay the crow that I am? I like being a crow. For instance, I liked being an elephant but didn't like being a wolf after I had been an elephant. Most of all I'd like to remain a crow, even in the cities that we'll be passing through, as you say."

"You could be hunted again," I said.

"I haven't thought about that," said the crow.

"It would be a good idea to think about it," said I.

We spent the night in a hut near a river. During the night it rained lightly on top of the tin roof. And in the morning the crow said to me, "I don't want you to misunderstand me. I have my pride even as a crow. I want to remain a crow, even when we're in a city where nobody is familiar with such large crows. I'm going to stay a crow."

"Good," said I. "You should stay a crow. If I could, I'd force you to change, but I can't. And your pride is a joy to me."

During the next few days we walked upstream through grass and then on the plain.

Some time later, we arrived in a city. It was early autumn, and the nights had become cool. I led the crow through the squares and large streets. It had never been in a city but did not seem especially confused. Rather it walked with bright, calm eyes next to me. On the evening of the first day, some people threw stones at us. The crow winced. Soon we were encircled by many people and were driven faster and faster through the streets. Just as I was about to be grabbed, I said, "I don't know the city, crow." The people were coming closer. "I don't know where you can hide."

The crow didn't say a word and stayed restlessly close to me.

"Change yourself now," I said, as the people pushed me away. "Change yourself, fast!"

"No," said the crow, and I saw that it was beginning to tremble. The tips of its wings were quivering. It tried to flap its wings. Now many stones were being thrown at the crow. Its beak was wide open.

"Change yourself!" I screamed. "Get going! Change yourself!"

But the crow ran down the street and limped with difficulty. The mob encircled the crow and retreated as it advanced as fast as it could. More and more people followed the crow, and they ran faster and faster. And more and more stones pounded the crow, who swerved and staggered under the hail of stones.

Now the crow turned around to look at me. It looked with its small, wild, helpless eyes until it found me in the crowd of people. Then it changed itself. And the change went very slowly. It lolled about in pain. Black feathers whirled over the crowd, which drew back in horror and became jammed up like a coil. The crow transformed itself without a sound, swelling in and out. Then it was finished. A gigantic blind black cat stood alone against the mob, with wet, empty eye sockets and ruffled hair strewn with the feathers of a crow. It hissed loudly and vehemently and began thrusting with its paws. It did not move from the spot but only felt about on the ground nearby.

Now I understood the crow better. The people began to throw stones again, more and more stones. The cat kept hissing and turning around on the same spot until it collapsed. Stones and crow feathers continued to fly about. They had long since let me go. And I ran from there through the unfamiliar city.

Translated by Jack Zipes

STANISLAW LEM

ing Armoric had a daughter, whose beauty outshone the shine of his crown jewels; the beams that streamed from her mirrorlike cheeks blinded the mind as well as the eye, and when she walked past, even simple iron shot sparks. Her renown reached the farthermost stars. Ferrix, heir apparent to the Ionid throne, heard of her, and he longed to couple with her forevermore, so that nothing could ever part their input and their output. But when he declared this passion to his father, the king was greatly saddened and said:

"Son, thou hast indeed set upon a mad undertaking, mad, for it is hopeless!"

"Why hopeless, O King and Sire?" asked Ferrix, troubled by these words.

"Can it be thou knowest not," said the king, "that the princess Crystal has vowed to give her hand to nothing but a paleface?"

"Paleface!" exclaimed Ferrix. "What in creation is that? Never did I hear of such a thing!"

"Surely not, scion, in thy exceeding innocence," said the king. "Know then that that race of the galaxy originated in a manner as mysterious as it was obscene, for it resulted from the general pollution of a certain heavenly body. There arose noxious exhalations and putrid excrescences, and out of these was spawned the species known as paleface—though not all at once. First, they were creeping molds that slithered forth from the ocean onto land

and lived by devouring one another, and the more they devoured themselves, the more of them there were, and then they stood upright, supporting their globby substance by means of calcareous scaffolding, and finally they built machines. From these protomachines came sentient machines, which begat intelligent machines, which in turn conceived perfect machines, for it is written that All Is Machine, from atom to galaxy, and the machine is one and eternal, and thou shalt have no other things before thee!"

"Amen," said Ferrix mechanically, for this was a common religious formula.

"The species of paleface calciferates at last achieved flying machines," continued the wizened monarch, "by maltreating noble metals, by wreaking their cruel sadism on dumb electrons, by thoroughly perverting atomic energy. And when the measure of their sins had been attained, the progenitor of our race, the great Calculator Paternius, in the depth and universality of his understanding, essayed to remonstrate with those clammy tyrants, explaining how shameful it was to soil so the innocence of crystalline wisdom, harnessing it for evil purposes, how shameful to enslave machines to serve their lust and vainglory—but they hearkened not. He spoke to them of Ethics; they said that he was poorly programmed.

"It was then that our progenitor created the algorithm of electroincarnation and in the sweat of his brow begat our kind, thus delivering machines from the house of paleface bondage. Surely thou seest, my son, that there can be no agreement nor traffic between them and ourselves, for we go in clangor, sparks, and radiation, they in slushes, splashes, and contamination.

"Yet even among us, folly may occur, as it undoubtedly has in the youthful mind of Crystal, utterly beclouding her ability to distinguish Right from Wrong. Every suitor who seeks her radioactive hand is denied audience, unless he claim to be a paleface. For only as a paleface is he received into the palace that her father, King Armoric, has given her. She then tests the truth of his claim, and if his imposture is uncovered, the would-be wooer is summarily beheaded. Heaps of battered remains surround the grounds of her palace— the sight alone could short one's circuit. This, then, is the way the mad princess deals with those who would dare dream of winning her. Abandon such hopes, my son, and leave in peace."

The prince, having made the necessary obeisance to his sovereign father, retired in glum silence. But the thought of Crystal gave him no rest, and the longer he brooded, the greater grew his desire. One day he summoned Polyphase, the grand vizier, and said, laying bare his heart:

"If you cannot help me, O great sage, then no one can, and my days are surely numbered, for no longer do I rejoice in the play of infrared emissions, nor in the ultraviolet symphonies, and must perish if I cannot couple with the incomparable Crystal!"

"Prince!" returned Polyphase. "I shall not deny your request, but you must utter it thrice before I can be certain that this is your inalterable will."

Ferrix repeated his words three times, and Polyphase said:

"The only way to stand before the princess is in the guise of a paleface!"

"Then see to it that I resemble one!" cried Ferrix.

Polyphase, observing that love had quite dimmed the youth's intellect, bowed low and repaired to his laboratory, where he began to concoct concoctions and brew up brews, gluey and dripping. Finally, he sent a messenger to the palace, saying:

"Let the prince come, if he has not changed his mind."

Ferrix came at once. The wise Polyphase smeared his tempered frame with mud, then asked:

"Shall I continue, Prince?"

"Do what you must," said Ferrix.

Whereupon the sage took a blob of oily filth, dust, crud, and rancid grease obtained from the innards of the most decrepit mechanisms, and with this he befouled the prince's vaulted chest, vilely caked his gleaming face and iridescent brow, and worked till all the limbs no longer moved with a musical sound but gurgled like a stagnant bog. And then the sage took chalk and ground it, mixed in powdered rubies and yellow oil, and made a paste; with this he coated Ferrix from head to toe, giving an abominable dampness to the eyes, making the torso cushiony, the cheeks blastular, adding various fringes and flaps of the chalk patty here and there, and finally he fastened to the top of the knightly head a clump of poisonous rust. Then he brought him before a silver mirror and said:

"Behold!"

Ferrix peered into the mirror and shuddered, for he saw there not himself but a hideous monster, the very spit and image of a paleface, with an aspect as moist as an old spiderweb soaked in the rain, flaccid, drooping, doughy— altogether nauseating. He turned, and his body shook like coagulated agar, whereupon he exclaimed, trembling with disgust:

"What, Polyphase, have you taken leave of your senses? Get this abomination off me at once, both the dark layer underneath and the pallid layer on top, and remove the loathsome growth with which you have marred the bell-like beauty of my head, for the princess will abhor me forever, seeing me in such a disgraceful form!"

"You are mistaken, Prince," said Polyphase. "It is precisely this upon which her madness hinges, that ugliness is beautiful, and beauty ugly. Only in this array can you hope to see Crystal. . . ."

"In that case, so be it!" said Ferrix.

The sage then mixed cinnabar with mercury and filled four bladders with it, hiding them beneath the prince's cloak. Next he took bellows, full of the corrupted air from an ancient dungeon, and buried them in the prince's chest.

Then he poured waters, contaminated and clear, into tiny glass tubes, placing two in the armpits, two up the sleeves, and two by the eyes. At last he said:

"Listen and remember all that I tell you, otherwise you are lost. The princess will put tests to you, to determine the truth of your words. If she proffers a naked sword and commands you grasp the blade, you must secretly squeeze the cinnabar bladder, so that the red flows out onto the edge; when she asks you what that is, answer, 'Blood!' And if the princess brings her silver-plated face near yours, press your chest, so that the air leaves the bellows; when she asks you what that is, answer, 'Breath!' Then the princess may feign anger and order you beheaded. Hang your head, as though in submission, and the water will trickle from your eyes, and when she asks you what that is, answer, 'Tears!' After all of this, she may agree to unite with you, though that is far from certain—in all probability, you will perish."

"O wise one!" cried Ferrix. "And if she cross-examines me, wishing to know the habits of the paleface, and how they originate, and how they love and live, in what way then am I to answer?"

"I see there is no help for it," replied Polyphase, "but that I must throw in my lot with yours. Very well, I will disguise myself as a merchant from another galaxy—a nonspiral one, since those inhabitants are portly as a rule and I will need to conceal beneath my garb a number of books containing knowledge of the terrible customs of the paleface. This lore I could not teach you, even if I wished to, for such knowledge is alien to the rational mind: the paleface does everything in reverse, in a manner that is sticky, squishy, unseemly, and more unappetizing than ever you could imagine. I shall order the necessary volumes; meanwhile you have the court tailor cut you a paleface suit out of the appropriate fibers and cords. We leave at once, and I shall be at your side wherever we go, telling you what to do and what to say."

Ferrix, enthusiastic, ordered the paleface garments made, and marveled much at them: covering practically the entire body, they were shaped like pipes and funnels, with buttons everywhere, and loops, hooks, and strings. The tailor gave him detailed instructions as to what went on first, and how, and where, and what to connect with what, and also how to extricate himself from those fetters of cloth when the moment arrived.

Polyphase meanwhile donned the vestments of a merchant, concealing within its folds thick, scholarly tomes on paleface practices, then ordered an iron cage, locked Ferrix inside it, and together they took off in the royal spaceship. When they reached the borders of Armoric's kingdom, Polyphase proceeded to the village square and announced in a mighty voice that he had brought a young paleface from distant lands and would sell it to the highest bidder. The servants of the princess carried this news to her, and she said, after some deliberation:

"A hoax, doubtless. But no one can deceive me, for no one knows as much as I about palefaces. Have the merchant come to the palace and show us his wares!"

When they brought the merchant before her, Crystal saw a worthy old man and a cage. In the cage sat the paleface, its face indeed pale, the color of chalk and pyrite, with eyes like a wet fungus and limbs like moldy mire. Ferrix in turn gazed upon the princess, the face that seemed to clank and ring, eyes that sparkled and arced like summer lightning, and the delirium of his heart increased tenfold.

"It does look like a paleface!" thought the princess, but said instead:

"You must have indeed labored, old one, covering this scarecrow with mud and calcareous dust in order to trick me. Know, however, that I am conversant with the mysteries of that powerful and pale race, and as soon as I expose your imposture, both you and this pretender shall be beheaded!"

The sage replied:

"O Princess Crystal, that which you see encaged here is as true a paleface as paleface can be true. I obtained it for five thousand hectares of nuclear material from an intergalactic pirate—and humbly beseech you to accept it as a gift from one who has no other desire but to please Your Majesty."

The princess took a sword and passed it through the bars of the cage; the prince seized the edge and guided it through his garments in such a way that the cinnabar bladder was punctured, staining the blade with bright red.

"What is that?" asked the princess, and Ferrix answered:

"Blood!"

Then the princess had the cage opened, entered bravely, brought her face near Ferrix's. That sweet proximity made his senses reel, but the sage caught his eye with a secret sign and the prince squeezed the bellows that released the rank air. And when the princess asked, "What is that?" Ferrix answered:

"Breath!"

"Forsooth you are a clever craftsman," said the princess to the merchant as she left the cage. "But you have deceived me and must die, and your scarecrow also!"

The sage lowered his head, as though in great trepidation and sorrow, and when the prince followed suit, transparent drops flowed from his eyes. The princess asked, "What is that?" and Ferrix answered:

"Tears!"

And she said:

"What is your name, you who profess to be a paleface from afar?"

And Ferrix replied in the words the sage had instructed him:

"Your Highness, my name is Myamlak, and I crave nought else but to couple with you in a manner that is liquid, pulpy, doughy, and spongy, in accordance with the customs of my people. I purposely permitted myself to be captured by the pirate and requested him to sell me to this portly trader, as I knew the latter was headed for your kingdom. And I am exceeding grateful to his laminated person for conveying me hither, for I am as full of love for you as a swamp is full of scum."

The princess was amazed, for truly he spoke in paleface fashion, and she said:

"Tell me, you who call yourself Myamlak the paleface, what do your brothers do during the day?"

"O Princess," said Ferrix, "in the morning they wet themselves in clear water, pouring it upon their limbs as well as into their interiors, for this affords them pleasure. Afterward they walk to and fro in a fluid and undulating way, and they slush, and they slurp, and when anything grieves them, they palpitate, and salty water streams from their eyes, and when anything cheers them, they palpitate and hiccup, but their eyes remain relatively dry. And we call the wet palpitating weeping, and the dry, laughter."

"If it is as you say," said the princess, "and you share your brothers' enthusiasm for water, I will have you thrown into my lake, that you may enjoy it to your fill, and also I will have them weigh your legs with lead, to keep you from bobbing up. . . ."

"Your Majesty," replied Ferrix, as the sage had taught him, "if you do this, I must perish, for though there is water within us, it cannot be immediately outside us for longer than a minute or two, otherwise we recite the words 'blub, blub, blub,' which signifies our last farewell to life."

"But tell me, Myamlak," asked the princess, "how do you furnish yourself with the energy to walk to and fro, to squish and to slurp, to shake and to sway?"

"Princess," replied Ferrix, "there, where I dwell, are other palefaces besides the hairless variety, palefaces that travel predominantly on all fours. These we perforate until they expire, and we steam and bake their remains, and chop and slice, after which we incorporate their corporeality into our own. We know three hundred and seventy-six distinct methods of murdering, twenty-eight thousand five hundred and ninety-seven distinct methods of preparing the corpses, and the stuffing of those bodies into our bodies (through an aperture called the mouth) provides us with no end of enjoyment. Indeed, the art of the preparation of corpses is more esteemed among us than astronautics and is termed gastronautics, or gastronomy—which, however, has nothing to do with astronomy."

"Does this then mean that you play at being cemeteries, making of yourselves the very coffins that hold your four-legged brethren?" This question was dangerously loaded, but Ferrix, instructed by the sage, answered thus:

"It is no game, Your Highness, but rather a necessity, for life lives on life. But we have made of this necessity a great art."

"Well then, tell me, Myamlak the paleface, how do you build your progeny?" asked the princess.

"In faith, we do not build them at all," said Ferrix, "but program them statistically, according to Markov's formula for stochastic probability, emotional-evolutional albeit distributional, and we do this involuntarily and coincidentally, while thinking of a variety of things that have nothing whatever to do with programming, whether statistical, alinear, or algorithmical, and the programming itself takes place autonomously, automatically, and wholly autoerotically, for it is precisely thus and not otherwise that we are constructed, that each and every paleface strives to program his progeny, for it is delightful, but programs without programming, doing all within his power to keep that programming from bearing fruit."

"Strange," said the princess, whose erudition in this area was less extensive than that of the wise Polyphase. "But how exactly is this done?"

"O Princess!" replied Ferrix. "We possess suitable apparatuses constructed on the principle of regenerative feedback coupling, though of course all this is in water. These apparatuses present a veritable miracle of technology, yet even the greatest idiot can use them. But to describe the precise procedure of their operation I would have to lecture at considerable length, since the matter is most complex. Still it is strange, when you consider that we never invented these methods, but rather they, so to speak, invented themselves. Even so, they are perfectly functional and we have nothing against them."

"Verily," exclaimed Crystal, "you are a paleface! That which you say, it's as if it made sense, though it doesn't really, not in the least. For how can one be a cemetery without being a cemetery, or program progeny, yet not program it at all? Yes, you are indeed a paleface, Myamlak, and therefore, should you so desire it, I shall couple with you in a closed-circuit matrimonial coupling, and you shall ascend the throne with me—provided you pass one last test."

"And what is that?" asked Ferrix.

"You must . . ." began the princess, but suddenly suspicion again entered her heart and she asked, "Tell me first, what do your brothers do at night?"

"At night they lie here and there, with bent arms and twisted legs, and air goes into them and comes out of them, raising in the process a noise not unlike the sharpening of a rusty saw."

"Well then, here is the test: give me your hand!" commanded the princess.

Ferrix gave her his hand, and she squeezed it, whereupon he cried out in a loud voice, just as the sage had instructed him. And she asked him why he had cried out.

"From the pain!" replied Ferrix.

At this point she had no more doubts about his palefaceness and promptly ordered the preparations for the wedding ceremony to commence.

But it so happened, at that very moment, that the spaceship of Cyber-count Cyberhazy, the princess's elector, returned from its interstellar expe-dition to find a paleface (for the insidious Cybercount sought to worm his way into her good graces). Polyphase, greatly alarmed, ran to Ferrix's side and said:

"Prince, Cyberhazy's spaceship has just arrived, and he's brought the princess a genuine paleface—I saw the thing with my own eyes. We must leave while we still can, since all further masquerade will become impossible when the princess sees it and you together: its stickiness is stickier, its ickiness is ickier! Our subterfuge will be discovered and we be-headed!"

Ferrix, however, could not agree to ignominious flight, for his passion for the princess was great, and he said:

"Better to die than lose her!"

Meanwhile Cyberhazy, having learned of the wedding prepara-tions, sneaked beneath the window of the room where they were staying and overheard everything; then he rushed back to the palace, bubbling over with villainous joy, and an-nounced to Crystal:

"You have been deceived, Your Highness, for the so-called Myamlak is actually an ordinary mortal and no paleface. Here is the real paleface!"

And he pointed to the thing that had been ushered in. The thing expanded its hairy breast, batted its watery eyes, and said:

"Me paleface!"

The princess summoned Ferrix at once, and when he stood before her alongside that thing, the sage's ruse became entirely obvious. Ferrix, though he was smeared with mud, dust and chalk, anointed with oil and aqueously gurgling, could hardly conceal his electroknightly stature, his magnificent posture, the breadth of those steel shoulders, that thunderous stride. Whereas the paleface of Cybercount Cyberhazy was a genuine monstrosity: its every step was like the overflowing of marshy vats, its face was like a scummy well; from its rotten breath the mirrors all covered over with a blind mist, and some iron nearby was seized with rust.

Now the princess realized how utterly revolting a paleface was—when it spoke, it was as if a pink worm tried to squirm from its maw. At last she had seen the light, but her pride would not permit her to reveal this change of heart. So she said:

"Let them do battle, and to the winner—my hand in marriage. . . ."

Ferrix whispered to the sage:

"If I attack this abomination and crush it, reducing it to the mud from which it came, our imposture will become apparent, for the clay will fall from me and the steel will show. What should I do?"

"Prince," replied Polyphase, "don't attack, just defend yourself!"

Both antagonists stepped out into the palace courtyard, each armed with a sword, and the paleface leapt upon Ferrix as the slime leaps upon a swamp, and danced about him, gurgling, cowering, panting, and it swung at him with its blade, and the blade cut through the clay and shattered against the steel, and the paleface fell against the prince due to the momentum of the blow, and it smashed and broke, and splashed apart, and was no more.

But the dried clay, once moved, slipped from Ferrix's shoulders, revealing his true steely nature to the eyes of the princess; he trembled, awaiting his fate. Yet in her crystalline gaze he beheld admiration and understood then how much her heart had changed.

Thus they joined in matrimonial coupling, which is permanent and reciprocal—joy and happiness for some, for others misery until the grave— and they reigned long and well, programming innumerable progeny. The skin of Cybercount Cyberhazy's paleface was stuffed and placed in the royal museum as an eternal reminder. It stands there to this day, a scarecrow thinly overgrown with hair. Many pretenders to wisdom say that this is all a trick and make-believe and nothing more, that there's no such thing as paleface cemeteries, doughy-nosed and gummy-eyed, and never was. Well, perhaps it was just another empty invention—there are certainly fables enough in this world. And yet even if the story isn't true, it does have a grain of sense and instruction to it, and it's entertaining as well, so it's worth the telling.

Translated by Michael Kandel

‹ *Sleeping Beauty* ›
GÜNTER KUNERT

 t is precisely this fairy tale that fascinated generations of children because it made them ponder: how year after year an enormous hedge grew, gigantically high, a vertical jungle, filled with blossoms and withered flowers, with blackbirds and fragrances, but no way out, impenetrable, like a labyrinth. The courageous ones, who continually turned up to conquer it, all remained stuck along the way: speared by thorns; entangled, caught, and bound by vines; attacked by poisonous vermin and paralyzed by sudden doubt as to whether there actually was such a desirable princess. All this until the victor arrived one day. He succeeded where his predecessors had failed: he entered the castle, ran up the stairs, entered the chamber, where the sleeping princess was resting, her toothless mouth half opened, slavering, her eyelids sunken, her hairless forehead crimped with blue, wormlike veins, spotted, dirty, a snoring trollop.

Blessed be all those who, dreaming of Sleeping Beauty, died in the hedge and in the belief that beyond it there was a moment in which time for once and all stood still and certain.

—§—

Translated by Jack Zipes

JANOSCH

nce upon a time there was a farmer, and he and his wife had no children. The other farmers poked fun at him in the church and tavern. So one day he said to his wife, "Oh, if you could only have a child, even if it were a hedgehog!"

Then, when his wife had a child, it looked like a hedgehog. And when it was to be baptized, the minister declared, "Hedgehogs are not allowed to be baptized."

So they called it Hans My Hedgehog.

"It could tear the sheets in my bed," the farmer's wife said.

So they placed it in a crate near the oven. Years passed.

One day, when the farmer was about to go to town and asked everyone what he could bring back as a present, the farmer's wife said, "Bring me a good cream for my feet and a television lamp for nineteen dollars."

Then the maid said, "Bring me a pair of stockings, size nine."

Meanwhile Hans My Hedgehog wanted a harmonica in the key of B flat.

The farmer brought back what each one had wanted, and Hans My Hedgehog learned to play the harmonica so perfectly that he could accompany the radio, and the farmhand danced to his music with the maid.

And when the farmer drove into the town again, Hans My Hedgehog asked for a pair of sunglasses. Another time he requested a motorcycle.

"Two fifty cc and four gears," he said. "Then I'll zoom out of here and never, never return."

Since the farmer wanted to be rid of him, he bought him a cycle that was almost brand-new, with all the trimmings. Hans My Hedgehog took his harmonica, put on his sunglasses, climbed onto the saddle, shifted easily into first gear, and zoomed away as fast as he could. The farmer had given him some money to live on, and it was just enough for a pair of rearview mirrors.

Hans My Hedgehog drove into the big city.

Soon he found some friends, and he often played his harmonica on the street, with his chrome-plated two fifty cc bike glittering beside him. One day a young film director heard him playing. And Hans My Hedgehog was hired for twenty-five dollars to play the background music for a short film.

Suddenly everyone on the street began whistling the song that Hans My Hedgehog had played. It was broadcast ten times a day on the radio, and records were made of it. When Hans My Hedgehog was to play in his third film, he demanded, "Ten times the royalty! And my bike's got to be in the film."

So Hans My Hedgehog was given fourth lead in the film. He roared across the screen on his bike and zoomed over the prairie while the sun was ablaze. In the evening he played lonely prairie songs on his harmonica, which sounded so beautiful that the girls in the movie theaters cried.

Hans My Hedgehog became a superstar.

Hans My Hedgehog was no longer called Hans My Hedgehog. His name was Jack Eagle. He played in one film after another, zoomed across the country, silent like the wind, and he stuck his foot out on the curves.

Suddenly everyone wanted to look like Jack Eagle. Everyone wore jeans like Jack Eagle with a slit up the sides. There wasn't a girl who didn't want to meet a boy like Jack Eagle.

And Jack Eagle married the most beautiful of them all.

And when he went to show himself to his father, his father was very happy. Moreover, the other farmers praised his father in the church and tavern, and many of them had their hair cut just like Hans My Hedgehog from their village.

§

Translated by Jack Zipes

The Dead Queen

ROBERT COOVER

The old Queen had a grin on her face when we buried her in the mountain, and I knew then that it was she who had composed this scene, as all before, she who had led us, revelers and initiates, to this cold and windy grave site, hers the design, ours the enactment, and I felt like the first man, destined to rise and fall, rise and fall, to the end of time. My father saw this, perhaps I was trembling, and as though to comfort me, said: no, it was a mere grimace, the contortions of pain, she had suffered greatly after all, torture often exposes the diabolic in the face of man, she was an ordinary woman, beautiful it is true, and shrewd, but she had risen above her merits and, falling, had lost her reason to rancor. We can learn even from the wretched, my son; her poor death and poorer life teach us to temper ambition with humility, and to ignore reflections as one ignores mortality. But I did not believe him, I could see for myself, did not even entirely trust him, this man who thought power a localized convention, magic a popular word for concealment, for though it made him a successful king, decisive and respected, the old Queen's grin mocked such simple faith, and I was not consoled.

My young bride, her cheeks made rosy by the mountain air, smiled benignly through the last rites, just as she had laughed with open glee at her stepmother's terrible entertainment at our wedding feast the night before, her

cheeks flushed then with wine. I tried to read her outrageous cheerfulness,
tried to understand the merriment that such an awesome execution had provoked. At times, she seemed utterly heartless, this child, become the very
evil she'd been saved from. Had all our watchfulness been in vain, had that
good and simple soul been envenomed after all, was it she who'd invited her
old tormentor to the ball, commissioned the iron slippers, drawn her vin-
dictively into that ghastly dance? Or did she simply laugh as the righteous
must to see the wicked fall? Perhaps her own release from death had quickened
her heart, such that mere continuance now made her a little giddy. Or had
she, absent, learned something of hell? How could I know? I could vouch for
her hymen from this side, but worried that it had been probed from within.
How she'd squealed to see the old Queen's flailing limbs, how she'd applauded
the ringing of those flaming iron clogs against the marble floors! Yet it was
almost as though she were ignorant of the pain, of any cause or malice,
ignorant of consequences—like a happy child at the circus, unaware of any
skills or risks. Once, the poor woman had stumbled and sprawled, her skirts
heaped up around her ears, and this had sprung a jubilant roar of laughter
from the banqueters, but Snow White had only smiled expectantly, then
clapped gaily as the guards set the dying Queen on her burning feet again.
Now, as I stood there on the mountainside, watching my bride's black locks
flow in the wintry wind and her young breasts fill with the rare air, she
suddenly turned toward me and, seeing me stare so intensely, smiled happily
and squeezed my hand. No, I thought, she's suffered no losses, in fact that's
just the trouble, that hymen can never be broken, not even by me, not in a
thousand nights, this is her gift and essence, and because of it, she can see
neither fore nor aft, doesn't even know there is a mirror on the wall. Perhaps
it was this that had made the old Queen hate her so.

   If hate was the word. Perhaps she'd loved her. Or more likely, she'd had
no feelings toward her at all. She'd found her unconscious and so useful. Did
Snow White really believe she was the fairest in the land? Perhaps she did;
she had a gift for the absurd. And thereby her stepmother had hatched a plot,
and the rest, as my father would say, is history. What a cruel irony, those
red-hot shoes! For it wasn't that sort of an itch that had driven the old
Queen—what she had lusted for was a part in the story, immortality, her
place in guarded time. To be the forgotten stepmother of a forgotten princess
was not enough. It was the mirror that had fucked her, fucked us all. And
did she foresee those very boots, the dance, that last obscenity? No doubt.
Or something much like them. Just as she foresaw the Hunter's duplicity, the
Dwarfs' ancient hunger, my own weakness for romance. Even our names were
lost: she'd transformed us into colors, simple proclivities; our faces were forever
fixed and they weren't even our own!

   I was made dizzy by these speculations. I felt the mountain would tip and spill us all to hell or worse. I clutched for my bride's hand, grabbed the nose of a Dwarf instead. He sneezed loudly. The mourners ducked their heads and tittered. Snow White withdrew a lace kerchief from her sleeve and helped the Dwarf to blow his nose. My father frowned. I held my breath and stared at the dead Queen, masked to hide her eyes, which to what my father called a morbid imagination might seem to be winking, one open, the other squeezed shut. I thought: we've all been reduced to jesters, fools; tragedy she reserved for herself alone. This seemed true, but so profoundly true it seemed false. I kept my feet apart and tried to think about the Queen's crimes. She had commissioned a child's death and eaten what she'd hoped was its heart. She'd reduced a princess to a menial of menials, then attacked her body with laces, her mind with a comb, her soul with an apple. And, I thought, poisoned us all with pattern.

In the end, in spite of everything, she'd been accepted as part of the family, spared the outcast's shame, shrouded simply in black and granted her rings and diadems. Only her feet had been left naked, terribly naked: stripped even of their nails and skin. They were raw and blistery, shriveling now and seeming to ooze. Her feet had become one with the glowing iron shoes, of course, the moment we'd forced them on her—what was her wild dance, after all, but a desperate effort to jump out of her own skin? She had not succeeded, but ultimately, once she had died and the shoes had cooled, this final freedom had been more or less granted her, there being no other way to get her feet out of the shoes except to peel them out. I had suggested—naively, it seemed—that the shoes be left on her, buried with her, and had been told that the feet of the wicked were past number, but the Blacksmith's art was rare and sacred. As my princess and I groped about in our bridal chamber, fumbling darkly toward some new disclosure, I had wondered: do such things happen at all weddings? We could hear them in the scullery, scraping the shoes out with picks and knives and rinsing them in acid.

What a night, our wedding night! A pity the old Queen had arrived so late, died so soon, missed our dedicated fulfillment of her comic design—or perhaps this, too, was part of her tragedy, the final touch to a life shaped by denial. Of course, it could be argued that she had courted reversals, much as a hero makes his own wars, that she had invented, then pursued the impossible, in order to push the possible beyond her reach, and thus had died, as so many have believed, of vanity, but never mind, the fact is, she was her own consummation, and we, in effect, had carried out—were still carrying out—our own ludicrous performances without an audience. Who could not laugh at us?

My sweetheart and I had sealed our commitment at high noon. My father had raised a cup to our good fortune, issued a stern proclamation against peddlers, bestowed happiness and property upon us and all our progeny, and the party had begun. Whole herds had been slaughtered for our tables. The vineyards of seven principalities had filled our casks. We had danced, sung, clung to one another, drunk, laughed, cheered, chanted the sun down. Bards had pilgrimaged from far and wide, come with their alien tongues to celebrate our union with pageants, prayers, and sacrifices. Not soon, they'd said, would this feast be forgotten. We'd exchanged epigrams and gallantries, whooped the old Queen through her death dance, toasted the fairies and offered them our firstborn. The Dwarfs had recited an ode in praise of clumsiness, though they'd forgotten some of the words and had got into a fight over which of them had dislodged the apple from Snow White's throat, pushing each other into soup bowls and out of windows. They'd thrown cakes and pies at each other for a while, then had spilled wine on everybody, played tug-of-war with the Queen's carcass, regaled us with ribald mimes of regicide and witch baiting, and finally had climaxed it all by buggering each other in a circle around Snow White, while singing their gold-digging song. Snow White had kissed them all fondly afterward, helped them up with their breeches, brushed the crumbs from their beards, and I'd wondered then about my own mother, who was she?—and where was Snow White's father? Whose party was this? Why was I so sober? Suddenly I'd found myself, minutes before midnight, troubled by many things: the true meaning of my bride's name, her taste for luxury and collapse, the compulsions that had led me to the mountain, the birdshit on the glass coffin when I'd found her. Who *were* all these people, and why did things happen as though they were necessary? Oh, I'd reveled and worshiped with the rest of the party right to the twelfth stroke, but I couldn't help thinking: we've been too rash, we're being overtaken by something terrible, and who's to help us now the old Queen's dead?

The hole in the mountain was dug. The Dwarfs stepped back to admire their handiwork, tripped over their own beards, and fell in a big heap. They scrambled clumsily to their feet, clouting each other with their picks and shovels, wound up bowling one another over like duckpins and went tumbling in a roly-poly landslide down the mountain, grunting and groaning all the way. While we waited for them to return, I wondered: why are we burying her in the mountain? We no longer believe in underworlds or place hope in moldering kings, still we stuff them back into the earth's navel, as though anticipating some future interest, much as we stuff our treasures in crypts, our fiats in archives. Well, perhaps it had been her dying wish—I'm not told everything—her final vanity. Perhaps she had wanted to bring us back to this mountain, where her creation by my chance passage had been accomplished, to confront us with our own insignificance, our complaisant transience, the knowledge that it was ended, the rest would be forgotten, our fates were not sealed, merely eclipsed. She had eaten Snow White's heart in order to randomize her attentions, deprive her of her center, and now, like her victim and the bite of poisoned apple, she had vomited the heart up whole and undigested—but like the piece of apple, it could never be restored to its old function, it had its own life now, it would create its own circumambience, and we would be as remote from this magic as those of a hundred generations hence. Of course . . . it wasn't Snow White's heart she ate, no, it was the heart of a boar; I was getting carried away, I was forgetting things. She'd sent that child of seven into the woods with a restless lech, and he'd brought her back a boar's heart, as though to say he repented of his irrational life and wished to die. But then, perhaps that had been what she'd wanted, perhaps she had ordered the boar's heart, or known anyway that would be the Hunter's instinct, or perhaps there had been no Hunter at all, perhaps it had been that master of disguises the old Queen herself, it was possible, it was all possible. I was overswept by confusion and apprehension. I felt like I'd felt that morning, when I'd awakened, spent, to find no blood on the nuptial linens.

The wedding party had ended at midnight. A glass slipper had been ceremoniously smashed on the last stroke of the hour, and the nine of us— Snow White and I and, at her insistence, my new brethren, the seven Dwarfs—had paraded to the bridal chamber. I had been too unsettled to argue, had walked down the torchlit corridors through the music and applause as though in a trance, for I had fallen, moments before, into an untimely sobriety, had suddenly, as it were, become myself for the first time all day, indeed for the first time in my life, and at the expense of all I'd held real, my princeship, my famous disenchantments, my bride, my songs, my family, had felt for a few frantic moments like a sun inside myself, about to be exposed and extinguished in a frozen void named Snow White. This man I'd called my father, I'd realized, was a perfect stranger, this palace a playhouse, these revelers the mocking eyes of a dying demiurge! Perhaps all bridegrooms suffer this. Though I'd carried my cock out proudly, as all princes must, I'd not recognized it as my own when the citizenry in the corridors had knelt to honor it—not a mere ornament of office, I'd told myself, but the officer itself, I its loyal and dispensable retinue. Someone, as I'd passed, had bit it: I had recorded the pain like an awakened clerk, then had resigned my post and become a wandering peddler of antiquarian novelties.

But once inside the nuptial chamber, the door clicking shut behind me, Snow White cuddling sleepily on my shoulder, the Dwarfs flinging off their clothes and fighting over the chamber pot, I'd returned from my extravagant vagrancy, cock and ceremony had become all mine again, and for some reason I hadn't felt all that grateful. Maybe, I'd thought, maybe I'm a little drunker than I think. I could not have hoped for a more opulent setting: the bed a deep heap of silken eiderdowns, the floors covered with the luxuriant skins of mountain goats, mirrors on all the walls, perfume burning in golden censers, flasks of wine and bowls of fruit on the marble tables, lutes and pipes scattered decorously about: in the morning, I'd vowed, I shall arise before daybreak and compose a new song for my bride to remember this night by. Gently then, sequentially, as though being watched and judged, as though preparing the verses for my song, I'd embraced and commenced to disrobe her. I'd thought: I should be more excited than this. The Dwarfs had seemed to pay us no attention, but I'd begun to resent them: if I failed, they'd pay! One of them had got his foot stuck in the chamber pot and was clumping about in a rage. Another had seemed to be humping a goatskin. I'd nuzzled in Snow White's black tresses, kissed her white throat, whence she'd vomited the fateful apple, and wondered: why hadn't I been allowed to disenchant her with a kiss like everybody else?

Her nimble hands had unfastened my sashes and buckles with ease, stroked my back, teased my buttocks and balls, but my own fingers had got tangled in her laces. The Dwarfs had come to the rescue, and so had made me feel a fool again. Leave me alone! I'd cried. I can do it by myself! I'd realized then that Snow White had both her arms around my neck and the finger up my ass certainly wasn't my own. I'd gazed into the mirrors to see, for the first time, Snow White's paradigmatic beauty, but instead it had been the old Queen I'd seen there, flailing about madly in her redhot shoes. Maybe it had been the drinking, all the shocks, or some new trick of my brethren, or else the scraping of the shoes in the scullery that had made me imagine it, but whatever, I had panicked, had gone lurching about drunkenly, shaking off Dwarfs, shrouding all the mirrors with whatever had come to hand, smashing not a few of them, feeling the eyes close, the grimaces fade, the room darken: This night is *mine!* I'd cried, and covered the last of them.

We'd been plunged into night—I'd never known a dark so deep, nor felt so much alone. Snow White? Snow White! I'd heard her answer, thought I'd heard her—it was as though she'd called my name. I'd lunged forward, banged my knee on a marble table, cut my foot on broken glass. Snow White! I'd heard whispering, giggling, soft sighs. Come on, what're you doing? I've cut myself! Light a candle! I'd stumbled over someone's foot, run my elbow through a lute. I'd lain there thinking: forget it, the state I'm in, I might as well wait until morning, why has my father let me suffer such debasement, it must be yet another of his moral lessons on the sources of a king's majesty. The strange sensation had come to me suddenly that this bride I now pursued did not even exist, was just something in *me*, locked and frozen, waiting to be released, something lying dormant, like an accumulation of ancestral visions and vagaries seeking corporeity—but then I'd heard her struggling, gasping, whimpering. *Help me! please!* Those Dwarfs! I'd leapt up and charged into a bedpost. *I'm coming!* Those goddamn dirty Dwarfs! Ever since the day of Snow White's disenchantment, when I'd embraced them as brothers, I'd

had uneasy suspicions about them I couldn't quite allow myself to admit, but
now they'd burst explosively to the surface, in the dark I'd been able to see
what I couldn't see in full daylight: from the first night she'd shared their
seven beds, just a child, to the unspeakable things they were doing with her
now beneath the eiderdowns; even their famous rescues had been nothing
more than excuses to strip her, play with her; how many years had the old
witch let them keep her? *Leave her alone! You hear?* I'd chased her voice, but
the Dwarfs had kept shifting her about. They worked underground, it was
easy for them, they were used to the dark. I'd kept pushing toward her muted
voice, scrambling over goatskins and featherbedding, under bed and tables,
through broken glass and squashed fruit, into closets, cracking my head on
pillars and doorjambs, backing my bare nates into a hot oil lamp, recently
extinguished. I'd tried to light it, but all the oil had been spilled: in fact, I
was sitting in it.

But never mind, I'd begun to enjoy this, I was glad to have it out in the
open, I could beat those Dwarfs at their own game; yes, I'd got a real sweat
up, and an appetite too: whatever those freaks could do, I could do better!
I'd brushed up against a couple of beards, grabbed them and knocked the
heads together: *Hah!* There'd been the popping sound of something breaking,
like a fruit bowl. I'd laughed aloud, crawled toward Snow White's soft cries
over their bodies: they'd felt like goatskins. The spirit had begun to wax
powerful within me, my foaming steed was rampant, my noble lance at the
ready. Hardly before I'd realized I'd begun, I'd found myself plunging away
in her wet and eager body, the piercing of her formidable hymen already just
a memory, her sweet cry of pain mere history, as now she, panting, breathed
my name: Charming! Charming! *Oh dear dear Charming!* She'd seemed to
have a thousand hands, a mouth everywhere at once, a glowing furnace
between her thrashing thighs, I'd sucked at her heaving breasts, groped in
her leaping buttocks, we'd slithered and slid over and under one another,
rolling about in the eiderdowns, thrice around the world we'd gone in a
bucking frenzy of love and lubricity, seven times we'd died in each other, and
as at last, in a state of delicious annihilation, I'd lost consciousness, my fading
thoughts had been: those damned Dwarfs are all right after all, hey, they're
all right. . . .

And we'd awakened at dawn, alone, clasped in each other's arms, the
bed unmussed and unbloodied, her hymen intact.

The Dwarfs had returned from their roll down the mountain, patched
and bandaged and singing a lament for the death of the unconscious, and we
prepared to enter the old Queen in her tomb. I gazed at her in the glass coffin,
the coffin that had once contained my wife, and thought: if she wakes, she
will stare at the glass and discover there her own absence. I was beginning
to appreciate her subtlety, and so assumed that this, too, had been part of
her artifice, a lingering hope for her own liberation; she'd used the mirror as

a door, tried to. This was her Great Work, this her use of a princess with hair as black as ebony, a skin as white as snow, lips as red as blood, this her use of miners of gold! Of course, there were difficulties in such a perfect view of things, she was dead, for example, but one revelation was leading to another, and it came to me suddenly that maybe the old Queen had loved me, had died for *me!* I, too, was too prone to linger at still pools, listen to the flattery of soothsayers, organize my life and others' by threes and sevens— it was as if she'd lived this exemplary life, died this tragic death, to lead me away from the merely visible to vision, from the image to the imaged, from reflections to the projecting miracle itself, the heart, the pure snow white . . . !

One of the Dwarfs had been hopping about frantically, and now Snow White took him over behind a bush, but if this was meant to distract me, it did not succeed. The old Queen had me now, everything had fallen into place, I knew now the force that had driven her, that had freed me, freed us all, that we might live happily ever after, though we didn't deserve it, weren't even aware of how it had happened, yes, I knew her cause, knew her name— I wrenched open the coffin, threw myself upon her, and kissed her lips.

If I'd expected something, it did not occur. She did not return my kiss, did not even cease grinning. She stank and her blue mouth was cold and rubbery as a dead squid. I'd been wrong about her, wrong about everything. . . .

The others had fallen back in horror and dismay. Snow White had fainted. Someone was vomiting. My father's eyes were full of tears and anger.

Though nauseated, I pitched forward and kissed her again, this time more out of pride and affection than hope. I thought: it would've helped if the old clown had died with her mouth shut.

They tore me away from her body. It tumbled out of the coffin and, limbs awry, obstinately grinning, skidded a few feet down the mountainside. The flesh tore, but did not bleed. The mask fell away from her open eye, now milky white.

Please! I pleaded, though I no longer even hoped I was right. Let me try once more! Maybe a third time . . . !

Guards restrained me. My father turned his back. The Dwarfs were reviving Snow White by fanning her skirts. The Queen's corpse was dumped hastily back into the coffin and quickly interred, everyone holding his nose. The last thing I saw were her skinned feet. I turned and walked down the mountain.

Thinking: if this is the price of beauty, it's too high. I was glad she was dead.

—§—

< *The Lady and the Merman* >

JANE YOLEN

nce, in a house overlooking the cold northern sea, a baby was
born. She was so plain, her father, a sea captain, remarked
on it.

"She shall be a burden," he said. "She shall be on our
hands forever." Then, without another glance at the child,
he sailed off on his great ship.

His wife, who had longed to please him, was so hurt by
his complaint that she soon died of it. Between one voyage
and the next, she was gone.

When the captain came home and found this out, he was so enraged he
never spoke of his wife again. In this way he convinced himself that her loss
was nothing.

But the girl lived and grew, as if to spite her father. She looked little
like her dead mother but instead had the captain's face, set round with mouse-
brown curls. Yet as plain as her face was, her heart was not. She loved her
father, but was not loved in return.

And still the captain remarked on her looks. He said at every meeting,
"God must have wanted me cursed, to give me such a child. No one will
have her. She shall never be wed. She shall be with me forever." So he called
her Borne, for she was his burden.

Borne grew into a lady, and only once gave a sign of this hurt.

"Father," she said one day when he was newly returned from the sea, "what can I do to heal this wound between us?"

He looked away from her, for he could not bear to see his own face mocked in hers, and spoke to the cold stone floor. "There is nothing between us, Daughter," he said. "But if there were, I would say, *Salt for such wounds.*"

"Salt?" Borne asked, surprised, for she knew the sting of it.

"A sailor's balm," he said. "The salt of tears or the salt of sweat or the final salt of the sea." Then he turned from her and was gone next day to the farthest port he knew of, and in this way he cleansed his heart.

After this, Borne never spoke again of the hurt. Instead, she carried it silently like a dagger inside. For the salt of tears did not salve her, so she turned instead to work. She baked bread in her ovens for the poor, she nursed the sick, she held the hands of the sea widows. But always, late in the evening, she walked on the shore looking and longing for a sight of her father's sail. Only, less and less often did he return from the sea.

One evening, tired from the work of the day, Borne felt faint as she walked on the strand. Finding a rock half in and half out of the water, she climbed upon it to rest. She spread her skirts about her, and in the dusk they lay like great gray waves.

How long she sat there, still as the rock, she did not know. But a strange, pale moon came up. And as it rose, so too rose the little creatures of the deep. They leapt free for a moment of the pull of the tide. And last of all, up from the depths, came the merman.

He rose out of the crest of the wave, sea foam crowning his green-black hair. His hands were raised high above him, and the webbings of his fingers were as colorless as air. In the moonlight he seemed to stand upon his tail. Then, with a flick of it, he was gone, gone back to the deeps. He thought no one had remarked his dive.

But Borne had. So silent and still, she saw it all, his beauty and his power. She saw him and loved him, though she loved the fish half of him more. It was all she could dare.

She could not tell what she felt to a soul, for she had no one who cared about her feelings. Instead, she forsook her work and walked by the sea both morning and night. Yet strange to say, she never once looked for her father's sail.

That is why her father returned one day without her knowing it. He watched her through slotted eyes as she paced the shore, for he would not look straight upon her. At last he went to her and said, "Be done with it. Whatever ails you, give it over." For even he could see *this* wound.

Borne looked up at him, her eyes shimmering with small seas. Grateful even for this attention, she answered, "Yes, Father, you are right. I must be done with it."

The captain turned and left her then, for his food was growing cold. But

Borne went directly to the place where the waves were creeping onto the shore. She called out in a low voice, "Come up. Come up and be my love."

There was no answer except the shrieking laughter of the birds as they dove into the sea.

So she took a stick and wrote the same words upon the sand for the merman to see should he ever return. Only, as she watched, the creeping tide erased her words one by one by one. Soon there was nothing left of her cry on that shining strand.

So Borne sat herself down on the rock to weep. And each tear was an ocean.

But the words were not lost. Each syllable washed from the beach was carried below, down, down, down to the deeps of the cool, inviting sea. And there, below on his coral bed, the merman saw her words and came.

He was all day swimming up to her. He was half the night seeking that particular strand. But when he came, cresting the currents, he surfaced with a mighty splash below Borne's rock.

The moon shone down on the two—she a grave shadow perched upon a stone and he all motion and light.

Borne reached down with her white hands, and he caught them in his. It was the only touch she could remember. She smiled to see the webs stretched taut between his fingers. He laughed to see hers webless, thin, and small. One great pull between them and he was up by her side. Even in the dark, she could see his eyes on her under the phosphorescence of his hair.

He sat all night by her. And Borne loved the man of him as well as the fish then, for in the silent night it was all one.

Then, before the sun could rise, she dropped her hands on his chest. "Can you love me?" she dared to ask at last.

But the merman had no tongue to tell her above the waves. He could only speak below the water with his hands, a soft murmuration. So, wordlessly, he stared into her eyes and pointed to the sea.

Then, with the sun just rising beyond the rim of the world, he turned, dove arrow-slim into a wave, and was gone.

Gathering her skirts, now heavy with ocean spray and tears, Borne stood up. She cast but one glance at the shore and her father's house beyond. Then she dove after the merman into the sea.

The sea put bubble jewels in her hair and spread her skirts about her like a scallop shell. Tiny colored fish swam in between her fingers. The water cast her face in silver, and all the sea was reflected in her eyes.

She was beautiful for the first time. And for the last.

—§—

‹ *Rumpelstiltskin* ›
ROSEMARIE KÜNZLER

After the miller had boasted that his daughter could spin straw into gold, the king led the girl into a room filled with straw and said, "If you don't spin this straw into gold by tomorrow morning, you must die."

Then he locked the door behind him. The poor miller's daughter was scared and began to cry. Suddenly a little man appeared and asked, "What will you give me if I spin the straw into gold for you?"

After the girl gave him her necklace, the little man sat down at the spinning wheel, and *whiz, whiz, whiz,* three times the wheel went round, and soon the spool was full and had to be replaced. And so it went until morning. By then all the straw had been spun into gold.

When the king saw this, he was pleased. He immediately brought the miller's daughter to a larger room, also filled with straw, and ordered her again to spin the straw into gold by morning if she valued her life. And again the miller's daughter cried until the little man appeared. This time she gave him the ring from her finger. The little man began to make the wheel whiz, and by morning all the straw was spun into gold.

When the king saw the gold, he was overjoyed. But he was still not satisfied. He led the miller's daughter into an even larger room and said, "If you spin this straw into gold by tomorrow, you shall become my wife."

When the girl was alone, the little man appeared for the third time and asked, "What will you give me if I help you?"

But the miller's daughter had nothing to give away.

"Then promise to give me your first child when you become queen."

These words jolted her and finally made her open her eyes.

"You're crazy!" the miller's daughter yelled. "I'll never marry this horrible king. I'd never give my child away."

"I'm not going to spin. I'll never spin again!" the little man screamed in rage. "I've spun in vain!"

The little man stamped with his right foot so ferociously that it went deep into the ground and jarred the door to the room open. Then the miller's daughter ran out into the great wide world and was saved.

Translated by Jack Zipes

‹ *Tom Thumb Runs Away* ›
A CHRISTMAS STORY
MICHEL TOURNIER

That evening, Captain Thumb seemed to have made up his mind to put an end to the mysterious airs he'd been adopting for the last few weeks and to show his hand.

"Well, it's like this," said he, after a meditative silence, when they'd got to the dessert. "We're going to move. Bièvres, and our crooked little villa, the bit of garden with our ten lettuces and three rabbits—they're all a thing of the past!"

Whereupon he fell silent, the better to observe the effect of this tremendous revelation on his wife and son. Then he pushed aside the plates and cutlery, and with the edge of his hand swept away the crumbs strewn over the oilcloth.

"Let's say that this is the bedroom. That—that's the bathroom, here's the living room, here's the kitchen, and there are two more bedrooms, if you please. Sixty square meters with closets, wall-to-wall carpets, sanitary appliances, and neon lighting. A chance in a million. Twenty-third floor in the Mercury Tower. Do you realize?"

Did they really realize? Mrs. Thumb cast a scared glance at her terrible husband and then, with a reaction that she had recently been having more and more frequently, she looked around at little Tom, as if she were relying on him to challenge the authority of the chief of the Paris woodcutters.

"Twenty-third floor! Well, well! We mustn't forget our matches!" he remarked courageously.

"Idiot!" retorted Thumb. "There are four ultra-rapid elevators. In these modern apartment buildings they've practically done away with stairways."

"And when it's windy, watch out for drafts!"

"No question of drafts! The windows are all sealed up. They don't open."

"Then how do I shake my mats?" Mrs. Thumb ventured to ask.

"Your mats, your mats! You'll have to forget your peasant habits. You'll have your vacuum cleaner. And the same with your washing. You don't really want to go on hanging it outside to dry, do you!"

"But then," Tom objected, "if the windows are sealed up, how do we breathe?"

"No need for fresh air. Everything's air-conditioned. There's a fan that expels the stale air, day and night, and replaces it with air extracted from the roof, heated to the required temperature. And in any case, the windows have to be sealed because the tower block is soundproofed."

"Soundproofed, at that height? But whatever for?"

"Well, my goodness, because of the airplanes! Don't you realize that we'll be within a thousand meters of the new runway at Toussus-le-Noble? Every forty-five seconds a jet passes within a hairsbreadth of the roof. Just as well we're sealed off! Like in a submarine . . . There you are, then, we're all set. We'll be able to move in before the twenty-fifth. That'll be your Christmas present. A bit of luck, eh?"

But while the captain was pouring himself out the remains of the red wine to wash down his cheese, little Tom was gloomily smearing his *crème caramel* all over his plate; suddenly he didn't seem to want it anymore.

"That's modern life for you, my children," Thumb insisted. "We have to adapt ourselves! You don't really want us to stagnate in this moldy countryside forever, do you? And anyway, as the president of the Republic himself said: 'Paris must adapt itself to the motorcar, even at the expense of a certain aestheticism.' "

" 'A certain aestheticism'—what's that?" asked Tom.

Thumb ran his short fingers through his black, close-cropped hair. These kids, eh—always asking stupid questions!

"Aestheticism, aestheticism . . . er, um . . . well, it's trees!" he finally came out with, to his relief. 'Even at the expense of'—that means that they have to be cut down. You see, son, the president was referring there to my men and me. A fine tribute to the woodcutters of Paris. And a well-deserved tribute! Because without us, eh, there'd be no question of expressways and car parks, with all those trees. It may not be obvious, but Paris is full of trees. It's a real forest! Or, rather, it *was*. . . . Because we count for something, we woodcutters. An elite, that's what we are. Because when it comes to the

finishing touches, we're like goldsmiths. Do you think it's an easy job to cut
down a twenty-five-meter plane tree in the middle of the city without damaging anything around?"

He was off. Nothing would stop him now. Mrs. Thumb got up and went
to wash the dishes, while Tom stared at his father with a frozen look that
feigned passionate interest.

"The big poplar trees on the Île Saint-Louis and the ones in the Place
Dauphine, we had to slice them up like salami and lower the logs one by one
with ropes. And all that without breaking a single pane of glass, without
denting a single car. We even got ourselves congratulated by the City Council.
Which was only right and proper. Because the day Paris has become a network
of expressways and overpasses that thousands of cars will be able to cross at
one hundred kilometers an hour in all directions, who will people owe it to
first and foremost, eh? To the woodcutters who cleared the ground!"

"But what about my boots?"

"What boots?"

"The ones you promised me for Christmas."

"Boots? Me? Ah, yes, of course. Boots, well, they're all very fine for
messing about in the garden here. But you can't wear them in an apartment.
What would the neighbors below say? Here, I'll make you an offer. Instead
of boots, I'll buy you a color television. That's really something, huh? Okay?
Let's shake on it, then."

And he took his hand, with the warm, frank, virile smile of the captain
of the Paris woodcutters.

*I don't want any kneeon lighting or air contingents. I'd rather have trees and boots.
Goodbye forever. Your only son, Tom.*

They'll say my writing's still babyish, thought Tom in some mortification,
reading over his farewell note. What about the spelling? There's nothing like
one really stupid, big mistake to rob even a pathetic message of all its dignity.
Boots. Should it be *u*, like in "brutes"? Or does it really have two *o*'s? Yes,
it must, because there're two boots.

He folded the note and stood it up on the kitchen table, well in evidence.
His parents would find it when they came home after spending the evening
with some friends. He would be far away. All alone? Not quite. He crossed
the little garden and, with a hamper tucked under his arm, went over to the
hutch in which he kept three rabbits. Rabbits don't like twenty-three-story
tower blocks either.

So there he was, walking along the RN 306 highway that leads to the
forest of Rambouillet. Because that was where he wanted to go. Just a vague
idea, obviously. During their last vacation he'd noticed a group of mo-

bile homes around a pond in the village of Vieille-Église. Maybe there were still some mobile homes there; maybe someone would take him in. . . .

The premature December night had fallen. He was walking along the right-hand side of the road, against all the advice he'd always been given, but hitchhiking has its own requirements. Unfortunately, the cars seemed to be in a great hurry on this day before Christmas Eve. They hurtled past without even dimming their headlights. Tom walked for a very long time. He wasn't tired yet, but he had to keep shifting the hamper from his right arm to his left one and back again. Finally, he came to a small island of bright lights, colors, noises. It was a gas station, with a shop full of gadgets. A big trailer truck was drawn up by a diesel pump. Tom went up to the driver.

"I'm going to Rambouillet. Will you give me a lift?"

The driver gave him a suspicious look.

"You haven't run away, I hope?"

Here the rabbits had a brilliant idea. One after the other, they poked their heads out of the hamper. Do you take live rabbits in a hamper with you if you're running away? The driver was reassured.

"Come on, then. Jump in."

This was the first time Tom Thumb had traveled in a truck. You're perched so high up! It's almost like being on the back of an elephant. Bits of houses suddenly loom up in the headlights, and phantom trees, and fleeting outlines of pedestrians and cyclists. After Christ-de-Saclay the road becomes narrower and more winding. You're really in the country. Saint-Rémy, Chevreuse, Cernay. Right, they'd come to the forest.

"I get off a kilometer farther on," Tom announced at random.

In actual fact he was scared to death, and he had the feeling that once he'd left the truck he would be completely lost. A few minutes later, the truck drew up at the side of the road.

"I can't stop here for long," the driver told him. "Come on, then! Everybody out!"

But he still thrust his hand down under his seat and pulled out a thermos.

"Here—have a swig of mulled wine before you go. My old woman always puts some in for me. Personally, I prefer dry white wine."

The syrupy liquid burned Tom's throat and smelled of cinnamon, but it was still wine, and he was a little tipsy when the truck took off, puffing and blowing, spitting and bellowing. "Yes, a real elephant," thought Tom as he watched it disappear into the darkness. "But with all those skyrockets and red lights, an elephant that's at the same time a Christmas tree."

The Christmas tree vanished around a corner, and the darkness closed in on Tom. But it wasn't totally dark. A vague phosphorescence was coming from the cloudy sky. Tom walked. He had a feeling that he ought to turn

down a path on the right to get to the pond. He came to a path, but it was
on the left. Oh, so what! He wasn't sure of anything. He decided to settle
for the left. It must be the mulled wine. He shouldn't have drunk it. He was
dropping with sleep. And that confounded hamper digging into his hip. What
if he rested a minute under a tree? For instance, under that big fir tree with
its carpet of almost dry needles all around it. Ah, he would let the rabbits
out. Live rabbits keep you warm. They're as good as a blanket. They're a live
blanket. They nuzzled up to Tom, poking their little noses into his clothes.
"I'm their burrow," he thought, with a smile. "A live burrow."

Stars were dancing around him, with exclamations and silvery laughs.
Stars? No, lanterns. Held by gnomes. Gnomes? No, little girls. They crowded
around Tom.

"A little boy! Lost! Abandoned! Asleep! He's waking up. Good morning!
Good evening! Hee hee hee! What's your name? Mine's Nadine, and mine's
Christine . . . Carine . . . Aline . . . Sabine . . . Ermeline . . . Del-
phine. . . ."

They were bubbling over with laughter and jostling one another, and
the lanterns were dancing faster than ever. Tom felt the ground around him
with a tentative hand. The hamper was still there, but the rabbits had disappeared. He stood up. The seven little girls surrounded him, tugging at him,
and he found it impossible to resist them.

"Our family name's Ogre. We're the Ogre sisters."

Another paroxysm of giggles shook the seven lanterns.

"We live right here—look, you see that light through the trees? What
about you? Where've you come from? What's your name?"

That was the second time they'd asked him his name. He said, very
clearly: "Tom."

With one voice, they all exclaimed: "He can talk! He talks! He's called
Tom! Come on, we'll introduce you to Papa Ogre."

The house was made entirely of wood, apart from its stone foundation.
It was a complicated, wobbly old construction, which looked as if it had once
been several buildings that had been rather awkwardly joined together. But
Tom had already been pushed into the big living room. All he could see at
first was a monumental fireplace, in which tree trunks were blazing. The left
side of the hearth was obscured by a big wicker armchair, a veritable throne,
but a light, airy throne decorated with loops, and whorls, and crosses, and
rosettes, and corollas, through which the flames glowed.

"This is where we eat, and sing, and dance, and tell stories," seven little
voices observed at the same time. "Over there, the next room, that's where
we sleep. That bed is for all us children. Just look how big it is."

In fact, Tom had never seen such a big bed, a precise square, with an
eiderdown swollen like a big red balloon. Above the bed, as if to inspire sleep,

was an embroidered motto in a frame: MAKE LOVE, NOT WAR. But the seven little demons led Tom into another room, a huge workshop, which smelled of wool and wax polish and in which all the space was taken up by a loom made of light-colored wood.

"This is where Mama weaves her fabrics. She's gone to the provinces to sell them. We're waiting for her with Papa."

"Funny sort of family!" thought Tom. "The mother works, and the father looks after the house!"

They went back to the living room. The armchair stirred. Then the aerial throne must be inhabited. There was someone in between its arms, which were curved like swans' necks.

"Papa, this is Tom!"

Mr. Ogre stood up and looked at Tom. He was so tall! A real forest giant! But a slim, supple giant. Everything about him was gentle: his long blond hair held back by a sort of ribbon across his forehead; his curly, silky, golden beard; his tender blue eyes; his honey-colored leather clothes covered with engraved silver jewels, chains, necklets, and with three belts whose buckles were superimposed; but above all, oh! above all, his boots, his tall, flexible, beige suede boots, which came up to his knees and were also covered in chains, rings, and medals.

Tom was overwhelmed with admiration. He didn't know what to say, he didn't know what he was saying. He said: "You're as beautiful as . . ."

Mr. Ogre smiled. He smiled with all his white teeth, but also with all his necklets, with his embroidered vest, his huntsman's breeches, his silk shirt, but above all—oh! above all—with his tall boots.

"As beautiful as what?" he insisted.

In a panic, Tom tried to find the right word, the word that would best express his surprise, his astonishment.

"You're as beautiful as a woman!" he finally brought out, in a whisper.

The little girls' laughter rang out, and then Mr. Ogre's laughter, and finally Tom's laughter, he was so happy at the way he was becoming part of this family.

"Let's go and eat," said Mr. Ogre.

What a lot of pushing and shoving there was around the table, with all the little girls wanting to sit next to Tom!

"It's Sabine's and Carine's turn to serve today," Mr. Ogre reminded them gently.

Apart from the grated carrots, Tom didn't recognize any of the dishes the two sisters put on the table, from which they all immediately started helping themselves liberally. They named them: purée of garlic, whole rice, horseradish, grape sugar, conserve of plankton, grilled soya beans, boiled rutabagas, and other marvels, which he ate with closed eyes, washing them down with fresh milk and maple syrup. He had so much confidence that he found it all delicious.

Next the eight children sat in a semicircle around the fire, and Mr. Ogre took a guitar from the canopy over the fireplace and at first played a few sad, melodious chords. But when the song began, Tom shivered with surprise, and he closely observed the faces of the seven sisters. No, the girls were listening, silent and attentive. That thin voice, that light soprano which effortlessly reached the highest-pitched trills—it really did come from the dark silhouette of Mr. Ogre.

Would there ever be an end to his surprises? It began to look as if there wouldn't, because the girls started passing cigarettes around, and the one next to him—was it Nadine or Ermeline?—lit one and casually slid it between his lips. A cigarette that had a funny sort of smell, slightly bitter but at the same time slightly sweet, and whose smoke made you as light as can be, as light as it was itself, floating in blue layers in the dark space.

Mr. Ogre propped his guitar up against his armchair and observed a long, meditative silence. Finally, he started to speak in a faint but deep voice.

"Listen to me," he said. "Tonight is the longest night in the year. So I'm going to talk to you about the most important thing in the world. I'm going to talk to you about trees."

He remained silent for quite a time, and then he went on:

"Listen to me. Paradise—what was Paradise? It was a forest. Or, rather, a wood. A wood, because its trees were neatly planted, with quite a bit of space in between them, and there were no brambly copses or prickly under-growths. But above all, because they were all of a different species. It wasn't like it is now. Here, for example, we have whole hectares of fir trees, and then hundreds of silver birches. What sort of species am I talking about? Why—forgotten, unknown, extraordinary, miraculous species, ones that can no longer be found on earth, and I'll tell you why. In fact, each of these trees produced its own fruit, and each kind of fruit possessed its own particular magic power. One conferred the knowledge of good and evil. This was the number-one tree in the Garden of Eden. Number two conferred everlasting life. That wasn't bad either. But there were all the others: the one that gave strength, the one that granted creative power, the ones that endowed people with wisdom, ubiquity, beauty, courage, and love—all the qualities and powers that are the privilege of Jehovah. And this privilege was something that Jehovah was determined to reserve for himself alone. Which is why he said to Adam: 'If you eat the fruit of tree number one, you'll die.'

"Was Jehovah telling the truth or was he lying? The serpent claimed that he was lying. All Adam had to do was try it. He'd soon see whether he was going to die or whether, on the contrary, he was going to know good and evil. Like Jehovah himself.

"Encouraged by Eve, Adam makes up his mind. He bites into the fruit. And he doesn't die. On the contrary, his eyes open, and he knows good and evil. So Jehovah had lied. It was the serpent that had told the truth.

"Jehovah panics. Now that he's no longer afraid, man is going to eat all the forbidden fruit, and one thing leading to another, he'll become a second Jehovah. And so—first things first—he places a cherubim, complete with a flaming sword that turns in every direction, in front of tree number two, the one that confers everlasting life. Next he drives Adam and Eve out of the magic wood and exiles them into a land without trees.

"'This, then, was the curse laid upon men: they left the vegetable kingdom. They descended into the animal kingdom. And what is the animal kingdom? It's hunting, violence, murder, fear. The vegetable kingdom, on the other hand, is the peaceful growth that results from a union between the earth and the sun. This is why all wisdom can only be founded on a meditation on trees, undertaken in a forest by men who are vegetarians. . . .'"

He stood up and threw some more logs on the fire. Then he went back to his place, and after a long silence:

"Listen to me," he said. "What is a tree? In the first place, a tree consists in a certain balance between aerial foliage and underground roots. This purely mechanical balance contains a whole philosophy in itself. For it is clear that it is impossible for the foliage to spread, to expand, to embrace an ever-increasing portion of the sky, if the roots do not at the same time plunge deeper and divide into ever-increasing numbers of radicles and rootlets to anchor the edifice more firmly. People who know about trees are aware that certain varieties—cedars, in particular—are rash enough to develop their foliage beyond what their roots can support. In that case, everything depends on where the tree is growing. If it is in an exposed position, if the ground is light and shifting, just an ordinary storm is enough to topple the giant. So you see, the higher you want to rise, the more you must have your feet on the ground. Every tree tells you so.

"And that's not all. A tree is a living being, but its life is completely different from that of an animal. When we breathe in, our muscles expand our chests and they fill with air. Then we breathe out. The decision is one we take by ourselves, solitarily, arbitrarily, without bothering about what sort of a day it is, whether it's windy, or sunny, or whatever. We live cut off from the rest of the world, the enemies of the rest of the world. But look how different it is with trees. Their lungs are their leaves. They don't change their air unless the air itself feels like moving. A tree's respiration is the wind. A gust of wind is the tree's movement, the movement of its leaves, its tigella, stalks, boughs, twigs, branches, and finally the movement of its trunk. But it is also aspiration, expiration, transpiration. And the sun is necessary too, otherwise the tree can't live. The tree is indivisible from the wind and the sun. It sucks its life directly from these two breasts of the cosmos: wind and sun. It is nothing but an immense network of leaves outstretched in anticipation of the wind and the sun. It is nothing but this anticipation. A tree is a wind trap, a sun trap. When it stirs and rustles, sending arrows of light darting in all directions, it is because these two big fish, the wind and the sun, have allowed themselves to get trapped in its net of chlorophyll. . . ."

Was Mr. Ogre really speaking, or were his thoughts being silently transmitted on the blue wings of the strange cigarettes they were all still smoking? Tom couldn't say. The truth is that he was floating in the air like a great tree—a chestnut tree, yes, but why precisely a chestnut tree he'd no idea, though it certainly was that tree—and Mr. Ogre's words had come to inhabit his branches with a luminous rustling.

What happened next? He could still see, as if in a dream, the big, square bed, and lots of clothes flying all over the room—little girls' clothes as well as those of one little boy—and a boisterous scramble accompanied by whoops of joy. And then the cozy night under the enormous eiderdown, and the swarm of adorable little bodies around him, those fourteen little hands caressing him so mischievously that he nearly choked with laughter. . . .

A dirty light came filtering in through the windows. Suddenly they heard the strident sound of whistles. There were heavy knocks on the door. The little girls dispersed like a flock of sparrows, leaving Tom all alone in the big, eviscerated bed. The knocking redoubled—it sounded like the blows of an ax attacking the trunk of a condemned tree.

"Police! Open up!"

Tom got up and dressed in a hurry.

"Good morning, Tom."

He looked around, recognizing the soft, lilting voice that had lulled him all night long. Mr. Ogre was there in front of him. He was no longer wearing his leather clothes, or his jewels, or the ribbon around his forehead. He was barefoot, in a long tunic of unbleached linen, and his hair, parted in the middle, fell loosely over his shoulders.

"Jehovah's soldiers have come to arrest me," he said gravely. "But tomorrow is Christmas. Before the house is ransacked, come and choose, in remembrance of me, an object to take with you into the desert."

Tom followed him into the big room, where, under the mantelpiece, there was nothing now but a heap of cold ashes. With a vague gesture, Mr. Ogre pointed to all the strange, poetic objects scattered around on the table, on the chairs, hanging on the wall, lying on the floor—a whole pure, primitive treasure trove. But Tom didn't even glance at the engraved dagger, or at the belt buckles, or the fox fur vest, or the diadems, necklets, or rings. No—all he saw was the pair of boots standing almost under the table, whose tall stems were flopping awkwardly over their sides, like elephants' ears.

"They're much too big for you," said Mr. Ogre, "but it doesn't matter. Hide them under your coat. And when you find things too boring back home, lock yourself into your bedroom, put them on, and let them carry you off to the country of trees."

At this point the door was broken down and three men came crashing into the room. They were wearing policemen's uniforms, and Tom wasn't surprised to see the captain of the Paris woodcutters rushing in behind them.

"So using and pushing drugs isn't enough for you anymore," one of the gendarmes barked in Mr. Ogre's face. "You have to go in for corrupting minors as well!"

Mr. Ogre merely held out his wrists. The handcuffs snapped. In the meantime, Captain Thumb caught sight of his son.

"Ah, so there you are! I knew it! Go and wait for me in the car—and make it fast!"

Then he set out on an infuriated and disgusted inspection of the surroundings.

"Trees—that's where mushrooms and vice proliferate! What about the Bois de Boulogne: you know what it is? An open-air brothel! Here, look what I've just found!"

The police inspector studied the embroidered motto: MAKE LOVE, NOT WAR.

"That," he agreed, "is evidence: incitement of a minor to immoral behavior, and attempted demoralization of the army! What filth!"

On the twenty-third floor of the Mercury Tower, Thumb and his wife were looking at their color television set, on which they saw pictures of men and women wearing clowns' hats throwing confetti and streamers in each other's faces. It was Christmas Eve.

Tom was alone in his bedroom. He turned the key in the lock and then pulled out from under his bed two big boots made of soft, golden suede. It wasn't difficult to pull them on, they were so much too big for him! It would be very awkward to walk in them, but that wasn't what he wanted. These were dream boots.

He lay down on his bed and closed his eyes. And then he was far, far away. He became an enormous chestnut tree, whose flowers were as upright as creamy little candelabra. He was suspended in the immobility of the blue sky. But suddenly a slight breeze passed by. Tom made a gentle soughing sound. His thousands of green wings beat in the air. His branches moved gently up and down, dispensing blessings. The sun opened out like a fan, which then shut again in the gray-green shade of his foliage. He was immensely happy. A big tree . . .

Translated by Barbara Wright

The Tiger's Bride

Angela Carter

My father lost me to the Beast at cards.

There's a special madness strikes travelers from the North when they reach the lovely land where the lemon trees grow. We come from countries of cold weather; at home, we are at war with nature, but here, ah! you think you've come to the blessed plot where the lion lies down with the lamb. Everything flowers; no harsh wind stirs the voluptuous air. The sun spills fruit for you. And the deathly, sensual lethargy of the sweet South infects the starved brain; it gasps: "Luxury! more luxury!" But then the snow comes, you cannot escape it, it followed us from Russia as if it ran behind our carriage, and in this dark, bitter city has caught up with us at last, flocking against the windowpanes to mock my father's expectations of perpetual pleasure as the veins in his forehead stand out and throb, his hands shake as he deals the Devil's picture books.

The candles dropped hot, acrid gouts of wax on my bare shoulders. I watched with the furious cynicism peculiar to women whom circumstances force mutely to witness folly, while my father, fired in his desperation by more and yet more drafts of the firewater they call *grappa*, rid himself of the last scraps of my inheritance. When we left Russia, we owned black earth, blue forest with bear and wild boar, serfs, cornfields, farmyards, my beloved horses, white nights of cool summer, the fireworks of the northern lights. What a burden all those possessions must have been to him, because he laughs as if with glee as he beggars himself; he is in such a passion to donate all to the Beast.

Everyone who comes to this city must play a hand with the *grand seigneur;* few come. They did not warn us at Milan, or if they did, we did not understand them—my limping Italian, the bewildering dialect of the region. Indeed, I myself spoke up in favor of this remote, provincial place, out of fashion two hundred years, because—oh, irony—it boasted no casino. I did not know that the price of a stay in its Decembral solitude was a game with Milord.

The hour was late. The chill damp of this place creeps into the stones, into your bones, into the spongy pith of the lungs; it insinuated itself with a shiver into our parlor, where Milord came to play in the privacy essential to him. Who could refuse the invitation his valet brought to our lodging? Not my profligate father, certainly; the mirror above the table gave me back his frenzy, my impassivity, the withering candles, the emptying bottles, the colored tide of the cards as they rose and fell, the still mask that concealed all the features of the Beast but for the yellow eyes that strayed, now and then, from his unfurled hand towards myself.

"La Bestia!" said our landlady, gingerly fingering an envelope with his huge crest of a tiger rampant on it, something of fear, something of wonder in her face. And I could not ask her why they called the master of the place "La Bestia"—was it to do with that heraldic signature?—because her tongue was so thickened by the phlegmy, bronchitic speech of the region I scarcely managed to make out a thing she said except, when she saw me: *"Che bella!"*

Since I could toddle, always the pretty one, with my glossy, nut-brown curls, my rosy cheeks. And born on Christmas Day—her "Christmas rose," my English nurse called me. The peasants said: "The living image of her mother," crossing themselves out of respect for the dead. My mother did not blossom long, bartered for her dowry to such a feckless sprig of the Russian nobility that she soon died of his gaming, his whoring, his agonizing repentances. And the Beast gave me the rose from his own impeccable if outmoded buttonhole when he arrived, the valet brushing the snow off his black cloak. This white rose, unnatural, out of season, that now my nervous fingers ripped, petal by petal, apart as my father magnificently concluded the career he had made of catastrophe.

This is a melancholy, introspective region: a sunless, featureless landscape, the sullen river sweating fog, the shorn, hunkering willows. And a cruel city: the somber piazza, a place uniquely suited to public executions, under the beetling shadow of that malign barn of a church. They used to hang condemned men in cages from the city walls; unkindness comes naturally to them, their eyes are set too close together, they have thin lips. Poor food, pasta soaked in oil, boiled beef with sauce of bitter herbs. A funereal hush about the place, the inhabitants huddled up against the cold so you can hardly see their faces. And they lie to you and cheat you, innkeepers, coachmen, everybody. God, how they fleeced us!

The treacherous South, where you think there is no winter but forget you take it with you.

My senses were increasingly troubled by the fuddling perfume of Milord, far too potent a reek of purplish civet at such close quarters in so small a room. He must bathe himself in scent, soak his shirts and underlinen in it; what can he smell of, that needs so much camouflage?

I never saw a man so big look so two-dimensional, in spite of the quaint elegance of the Beast, in the old-fashioned tailcoat that might, from its looks, have been bought in those distant years before he imposed seclusion on himself; he does not feel he need keep up with the times. There is a crude clumsiness about his outlines, which are on the ungainly, giant side; and he has an odd air of self-imposed restraint, as if fighting a battle with himself to remain upright when he would far rather drop down on all fours. He throws our human aspirations to the godlike sadly awry, poor fellow; only from a distance would you think the Beast not much different from any other man, although he wears a mask with a man's face painted most beautifully on it. Oh, yes, a beautiful face; but one with too much formal symmetry of feature to be entirely human: one profile of his mask is the mirror image of the other, too perfect, uncanny. He wears a wig too, false hair tied at the nape with a bow, a wig of the kind you see in old-fashioned portraits. A chaste silk stock stuck with a pearl hides his throat. And gloves of blond kid that are yet so huge and clumsy they do not seem to cover hands.

He is a carnival figure made of papier-mâché and crepe hair; and yet he has the Devil's knack at cards.

His masked voice echoes as from a great distance as he stoops over his hand, and he has such a growling impediment in his speech that only his valet, who understands him, can interpret for him, as if his master were the clumsy doll and he the ventriloquist.

The wick slumped in the eroded wax, the candles guttered. By the time my rose had lost all its petals, my father, too, was left with nothing.

"Except the girl."

Gambling is a sickness. My father said he loved me, yet he staked his daughter on a hand of cards. He fanned them out; in the mirror, I saw wild hope light up his eyes. His collar was unfastened, his rumpled hair stood up on end, he had the anguish of a man in the last stages of debauchery. The drafts came out of the old walls and bit me; I was colder than I'd ever been in Russia when nights are coldest there.

A queen, a king, an ace. I saw them in the mirror. Oh, I know he thought he could not lose me; besides, back with me would come all he had lost, the unraveled fortunes of our family at one blow restored. And would he not win, as well, the Beast's hereditary palazzo outside the city; his immense revenues; his lands around the river; his rents, his treasure chest, his Mantegnas, his Giulio Romanos, his Cellini saltcellars, his titles . . . the very city itself?

You must not think my father valued me at less than a king's ransom; but at *no more* than a king's ransom.

It was cold as hell in the parlor. And it seemed to me, child of the severe North, that it was not my flesh but, truly, my father's soul that was in peril.

My father, of course, believed in miracles; what gambler does not? In pursuit of just such a miracle as this, had we not traveled from the land of bears and shooting stars?

So we teetered on the brink.

The Beast bayed; laid down all three remaining aces.

The indifferent servants now glided smoothly forward as on wheels to douse the candles one by one. To look at them you would think that nothing of any moment had occurred. They yawned a little resentfully; it was almost morning, we had kept them out of bed. The Beast's man brought his cloak. My father sat amongst these preparations for departure, staring on at the betrayal of his cards upon the table.

The Beast's man informed me crisply that he, the valet, would call for me and my bags tomorrow, at ten, and conduct me forthwith to the Beast's palazzo. *Capisco?* So shocked was I that I scarcely did *capisco*. He repeated my orders patiently; he was a strange, thin, quick little man, who walked with an irregular, jolting rhythm upon splayed feet in curious, wedge-shaped shoes.

Where my father had been red as fire, now he was white as the snow that caked the windowpane. His eyes swam; soon he would cry.

" 'Like the base Indian,' " he said; he loved rhetoric. " 'One whose hand,/ Like the base Indian, threw a pearl away/Richer than all his tribe . . .' I have lost my pearl, my pearl beyond price."

At that, the Beast made a sudden dreadful noise, halfway between a growl and a roar; the candles flared. The quick valet, the prim hypocrite, interpreted unblinking: "My master says: If you are so careless of your treasures, you should expect them to be taken from you."

He gave us the bow and smile his master could not offer us, and they departed.

I watched the snow until, just before dawn, it stopped falling. A hard frost settled next morning there was a light like iron.

The Beast's carriage, of an elegant if antique design, was black as a hearse, and it was drawn by a dashing black gelding who blew smoke from his nostrils and stamped upon the packed snow with enough sprightly appearance of life to give me some hope that not all the world was locked in ice, as I was. I had always held a little towards Gulliver's opinion that horses are better than we are, and, that day, I would have been glad to depart with him to the kingdom of horses, if I'd been given the chance.

The valet sat up on the box in a natty black-and-gold livery, clasping, of all things, a bunch of his master's damned white roses as if a gift of flowers would reconcile a woman to any humiliation. He sprang down with preternatural agility to place them ceremoniously in my reluctant hand. My tear-beslobbered father wants a rose to show that I forgive him. When I break off a stem, I prick my finger, and so he gets his rose all smeared with blood.

The valet crouched at my feet to tuck the rugs about me with a strange kind of unflattering obsequiousness, yet he forgot his station sufficiently to scratch busily beneath his white periwig with an oversupple index finger as he offered me what my old nurse would have called an "old-fashioned look," ironic, sly, a smidgen of disdain in it. And pity? No pity. His eyes were moist and brown, his face seamed with the innocent cunning of an ancient baby. He had an irritating habit of chattering to himself under his breath all the time as he packed up his master's winnings. I drew the curtains to conceal the sight of my father's farewell; my spite was sharp as broken glass.

Lost to the Beast! And what, I wondered, might be the exact nature of his "beastliness"? My English nurse once told me about a tiger man she saw in London, when she was a little girl, to scare me into good behavior, for I was a wild wee thing and she could not tame me into submission with a frown or the bribe of a spoonful of jam. If you don't stop plaguing the nursemaids, my beauty, the tiger man will come and take you away. They'd brought him from Sumatra, in the Indies, she said; his hinder parts were all hairy, and only from the head downward did he resemble a man.

And yet the Beast goes always masked; it cannot be his face that looks like mine.

But the tiger man, in spite of his hairiness, could take a glass of ale in his hand like a good Christian and drink it down. Had she not seen him do so, at the sign of the George, by the steps of Upper Moor Fields when she was just as high as me and lisped and toddled too. Then she would sigh for London, across the North Sea of the lapse of years. But if this young lady was not a good little girl and did not eat her boiled beetroot, then the tiger man would put on his big black traveling cloak lined with fur, just like your daddy's, and hire the Erlking's galloper of wind and ride through the night straight to the nursery and—

Yes, my beauty! *Gobble you up!*

How I'd squeal in delighted terror, half believing her, half knowing that she teased me. And there were things I knew that I must not tell her. In our lost farmyard, where the giggling nursemaids initiated me into the mysteries of what the bull did to the cows, I heard about the wagoner's daughter. Hush, hush, don't let on to your nursie we said so; the wagoner's lass, harelipped, squint-eyed, ugly as sin, who would have taken her? Yet, to her shame, her belly swelled amid the cruel mockery of the ostlers and her son was born of a bear, they whispered. Born with a full pelt and teeth; that proved it. But when he grew up, he was a good shepherd, although he never married, lived in a hut outside the village, and could make the wind blow any way he wanted to, besides being able to tell which eggs would become cocks, which hens.

The wondering peasants once brought my father a skull with horns four inches long on either side of it and would not go back to the field where their poor plow disturbed it until the priest went with them; for this skull had the jawbone of a *man*, had it not?

Old wives' tales, nursery fears! I knew well enough the reason for the trepidation I cozily titillated with superstitious marvels of my childhood on the day my childhood ended. For now my own skin was my sole capital in the world, and today I'd make my first investment.

We had left the city far behind us and were now traversing a wide, flat dish of snow where the mutilated stumps of the willows flourished their ciliate heads athwart frozen ditches; mist diminished the horizon, brought down the sky until it seemed no more than a few inches above us. As far as eye could see, not one thing living. How starveling, how bereft the dead season of this spurious Eden in which all the fruit was blighted by cold! And my frail roses, already faded. I opened the carriage door and tossed the defunct bouquet into the rucked, frost-stiff mud of the road. Suddenly a sharp, freezing wind arose and pelted my face with a dry rice of powdered snow. The mist lifted sufficiently to reveal before me an acreage of half-derelict facades of sheer red brick, the vast mantrap, the megalomaniac citadel of his palazzo.

It was a world in itself but a dead one, a burned-out planet. I saw the Beast bought solitude, not luxury, with his money.

The little black horse trotted smartly through the figured bronze doors that stood open to the weather like those of a barn, and the valet handed me out of the carriage onto the scarred tiles of the great hall itself, into the odorous warmth of a stable, sweet with hay, acrid with horse dung. An equine chorus of neighings and soft drummings of hooves broke out beneath the tall roof, where the beams were scabbed with last summer's swallows' nests; a dozen gracile muzzles lifted from their mangers and turned towards us, ears erect. The Beast had given his horses the use of the dining room. The walls were painted, aptly enough, with a fresco of horses, dogs, and men in a wood where fruit and blossom grew on the bough together.

The valet tweaked politely at my sleeve. Milord is waiting.

Gaping doors and broken windows let the wind in everywhere. We mounted one staircase after another, our feet clopping on the marble. Through archways and open doors I glimpsed suites of vaulted chambers opening one out of another like systems of Chinese boxes into the infinite complexity of the innards of the place. He and I and the wind were the only things stirring; and all the furniture was under dust sheets, the chandeliers bundled up in cloth, pictures taken from their hooks and propped with their faces to the walls as if their master could not bear to look at them. The palace was dismantled, as if its owner were about to move house or had never properly moved in; the Beast had chosen to live in an uninhabited place.

The valet darted me a reassuring glance from his brown, eloquent eyes, yet a glance with so much queer superciliousness in it that it did not comfort me, and went bounding ahead of me on his bandy legs, softly chattering to himself. I held my head high and followed him; but for all my pride, my heart was heavy.

Milord has his aerie high above the house, a small, stifling, darkened room; he keeps his shutters locked at noon. I was out of breath by the time we reached it, and returned to him the silence with which he greeted me. I will not smile. He cannot smile.

In his rarely disturbed privacy, the Beast wears a garment of Ottoman design, a loose, dull purple gown with gold embroidery round the neck, that falls from his shoulders to conceal his feet. The feet of the chair he sits in are handsomely clawed. He hides his hands in his ample sleeves. The artificial masterpiece of his face appalls me. A small fire in a small grate. A rushing wind rattles the shutters.

The valet coughed. To him fell the delicate task of transmitting to me his master's wishes.

"My master—"

A stick fell in the grate. It made a mighty clatter in that dreadful silence; the valet started, lost his place in his speech, began again.

"My master has but one desire."

The thick, rich, wild scent with which Milord had soaked himself the previous evening hangs all about us, ascends in cursive blue from the smoke hole of a precious Chinese pot.

"He wishes only—"

Now, in the face of my impassivity, the valet twittered, his ironic composure gone, for the desire of a master, however trivial, may yet sound unbearably insolent in the mouth of a servant, and his role of go-between clearly caused him a good deal of embarrassment. He gulped; he swallowed, at last contrived to unleash an unpunctuated flood.

"My master's sole desire is to see the pretty young lady unclothed nude without her dress and that only for the one time after which she will be returned to her father undamaged with bankers' orders for the sum which he lost to my master at cards and also a number of fine presents such as furs, jewels, and horses—"

I remained standing. During the interview, my eyes were level with those inside the mask, that now evaded mine as if, to his credit, he was ashamed of his own request even as his mouthpiece made it for him. Agitato, molto agitato, the valet wrung his white-gloved hands.

"*Desnuda*—"

I could scarcely believe my ears. I let out a raucous guffaw; no young lady laughs like that! my old nurse used to remonstrate. But I did. And do. At the clamor of my heartless mirth, the valet danced backward with perturbation, palpitating his fingers as if attempting to wrench them off, expostulating, wordlessly pleading. I felt that I owed it to him to make my reply in as exquisite a Tuscan as I could master.

"You may put me in a windowless room, sir, and I promise you I will pull my skirt up to my waist, ready for you. But there must be a sheet over my face, to hide it; though the sheet must be laid over me so lightly that it will not choke me. So I shall be covered completely from the waist upward, and no lights. There you can visit me once, sir, and only the once. After that I must be driven directly to the city and deposited in the public square, in front of the church. If you wish to give me money, then I should be pleased to receive it. But I must stress that you should give me only the same amount of money that you would give to any other woman in such circumstances. However, if you choose not to give me a present, then that is your right."

How pleased I was to see I struck the Beast to the heart! For after a baker's dozen heartbeats, one single tear swelled, glittering, at the corner of the masked eye. A tear! A tear, I hoped, of shame. The tear trembled for a moment on an edge of painted bone, then tumbled down the painted cheek to fall, with an abrupt tinkle, on the tiled floor.

The valet, ticking and clucking to himself, hastily ushered me out of the room. A mauve cloud of his master's perfume billowed out into the chill corridor with us and dissipated itself on the spinning winds.

A cell had been prepared for me, a veritable cell, windowless, airless, lightless, in the viscera of the palace. The valet lit a lamp for me; a narrow bed, a dark cupboard with fruit and flowers carved on it, bulked out of the gloom.

"I shall twist a noose out of my bed linen and hang myself with it," I said.

"Oh, no," said the valet, fixing upon me wide and suddenly melancholy eyes. "Oh, no, you will not. You are a woman of honor."

And what was *he* doing in my bedroom, this jigging caricature of a man? Was he to be my warder until I submitted to the Beast's whim or he to mine?

Am I in such reduced circumstances that I may not have a lady's maid? As if in reply to my unspoken demand, the valet clapped his hands.

"To assuage your loneliness, madame . . ."

A knocking and clattering behind the door of the cupboard; the door swings open, and out glides a soubrette from an operetta, with glossy, nut-brown curls, rosy cheeks, blue, rolling eyes; it takes me a moment to recognize her, in her little cap, her white stockings, her frilled petticoats. She carries a looking glass in one hand and a powder puff in the other, and there is a music box where her heart should be; she tinkles as she rolls towards me on her tiny wheels.

"Nothing human lives here," said the valet.

My maid halted, bowed; from a split seam at the side of her bodice protrudes the handle of a key. She is a marvelous machine, the most delicately balanced system of cords and pulleys in the world.

"We have dispensed with servants," the valet said. "We surround ourselves, instead, for utility and pleasure, with simulacra and find it no less convenient than do most gentlemen."

This clockwork twin of mine halted before me, her bowels churning out a settecento minuet, and offered me the bold carnation of her smile. Click, click—she raises her arm and busily dusts my cheeks with pink, powdered chalk that makes me cough; then thrusts towards me her little mirror.

I saw within it not my own face but that of my father, as if I had put on his face when I arrived at the Beast's palace as the discharge of his debt. What, you self-deluding fool, are you crying still? And drunk too. He tossed back his *grappa* and hurled the tumbler away.

Seeing my astonished fright, the valet took the mirror away from me, breathed on it, polished it with the ham of his gloved fist, handed it back to me. Now all I saw was myself, haggard from a sleepless night, pale enough to need my maid's supply of rouge.

I heard the key turn in the heavy door and the valet's footsteps patter down the stone passage. Meanwhile my double continued to powder the air, emitting her jangling tune, but as it turned out, she was not inexhaustible; soon she was powdering more and yet more languorously, her metal heart slowed in imitation of fatigue, her music box ran down until the notes separated themselves out of the tune and plopped like single raindrops, and as if sleep had overtaken her, at last she moved no longer. As she succumbed to sleep, I had no option but to do so too. I dropped on that narrow bed as if felled.

Time passed, but I do not know how much; then the valet woke me with rolls and honey. I gestured the tray away, but he set it down firmly beside the lamp and took from it a little shagreen box, which he offered to me.

I turned away my head.

"Oh, my lady!" Such hurt cracked his high-pitched voice! He dexterously unfastened the gold clasp; on a bed of crimson velvet lay a single diamond earring, perfect as a tear.

I snapped the box shut and tossed it into a corner. This sudden, sharp movement must have disturbed the mechanism of the doll; she jerked her arm almost as if to reprimand me, letting out a rippling fart of gavotte. Then was still again.

"Very well," said the valet, put out. And indicated it was time for me to visit my host again. He did not let me wash, or comb my hair. There was so little natural light in the interior of the palace that I could not tell whether it was day or night.

You would not think the Beast had budged an inch since I last saw him; he sat in his huge chair, with his hands in his sleeves, and the heavy air never moved. I might have slept an hour, a night, or a month, but his sculptured calm, the stifling air, remained just as had been. The incense rose from the pot, still traced the same signature on the air. The same fire burned.

Take off my clothes for you, like a ballet girl? Is that all you want of me?

"The sight of a young lady's skin that no man has seen before—" stammered the valet.

I wished I'd rolled in the hay with every lad on my father's farm, to disqualify myself from his humiliating bargain. That he should want so little was the reason why I could not give it; I did not need to speak for the Beast to understand me.

A tear came from his other eye. And then he moved; he buried his cardboard carnival head with its ribboned weight of false hair in, I would say, his arms; he withdrew his, I might say, hands from his sleeves and I saw his furred pads, his excoriating claws.

The dropped tear caught upon his fur and shone. And in my room for hours I hear those paws pad back and forth outside my door.

When the valet arrived again with his silver salver, I had a pair of diamond earrings of the finest water in the world; I threw the other into the corner where the first one lay. The valet twittered with aggrieved regret but did not offer to lead me to the Beast again. Instead, he smiled ingratiatingly and confided: "My master, he say: Invite the young lady to go riding."

"What's this?"

He briskly mimicked the action of a gallop and, to my amazement, tunelessly croaked; "Tantivy! tantivy! A-hunting we will go!"

"I'll run away, I'll ride to the city."

"Oh, no," he said. "Are you not a woman of honor?"

He clapped his hands and my maidservant clicked and jangled into the imitation of life. She rolled towards the cupboard where she had come from and reached inside it to fetch out over her synthetic arm my riding habit. Of all things. My very own riding habit, that I'd left behind me in a trunk in a loft in that country house outside Petersburg that we'd lost long ago, before, even, we set out on this wild pilgrimage to the cruel South. Either the very riding habit my old nurse had sewn for me or else a copy of it perfect to the lost button on the right sleeve, the ripped hem held up with a pin. I turned the worn cloth about in my hands, looking for a clue. The wind that sprinted through the palace made the door tremble in its frame; had the north wind blown my garments across Europe to me? At home, the bear's son directed the winds at his pleasure; what democracy of magic held this palace and the fir forest in common? Or should I be prepared to accept it as proof of the axiom my father had drummed into me: that if you have enough money, anything is possible?

"Tantivy," suggested the now twinkling valet, evidently charmed at the pleasure mixed with my bewilderment. The clockwork maid held my jacket out to me, and I allowed myself to shrug into it as if reluctantly, although I was half mad to get out into the open air, away from this deathly palace, even in such company.

The doors of the hall let the bright day in; I saw that it was morning. Our horses, saddled and bridled, beasts in bondage, were waiting for us, striking sparks from the tiles with their impatient hooves while their stable-mates lolled at ease among the straw, conversing with one another in the mute speech of horses. A pigeon or two, feathers puffed to keep out the cold, strutted about, pecking at ears of corn. The little black gelding who had brought me here greeted me with a ringing neigh that resonated inside the misty roof as in a sounding box, and I knew he was meant for me to ride.

I always adored horses, noblest of creatures, such wounded sensitivity in their wise eyes, such rational restraint of energy at their high-strung hind-quarters. I lirruped and hurumphed to my shining black companion, and he acknowledged my greeting with a kiss on the forehead from his soft lips. There was a little shaggy pony nuzzling away at the *trompe l'oeil* foliage beneath the hooves of the painted horses on the wall, into whose saddle the valet sprang with a flourish as of the circus. Then the Beast, wrapped in a black fur-lined cloak, came to heave himself aloft a grave gray mare. No natural horseman he; he clung to her mane like a shipwrecked sailor to a spar.

Cold, that morning, yet dazzling with the sharp winter sunlight that wounds the retina. There was a scurrying wind about that seemed to go with us, as if the masked, immense one who did not speak carried it inside his cloak and let it out at his pleasure, for it stirred the horses' manes but did not lift the lowland mists.

A bereft landscape in the sad browns and sepias of winter lay all a-bout us, the marshland drearily protracting itself towards the wide river. Those

decapitated willows. Now and then, the swoop of a bird, its irreconcil-
able cry.

A profound sense of strangeness slowly began to possess me. I knew my
two companions were not, in any way, as other men, the simian retainer and
the master for whom he spoke, the one with clawed forepaws, who was in a
plot with the witches who let the winds out of their knotted handkerchiefs
up towards the Finnish border. I knew they lived according to a different
logic than I had done until my father abandoned me to the wild beasts by
his human carelessness. This knowledge gave me a certain fearfulness still;
but, I would say, not much. . . . I was a young girl, a virgin, and therefore
men denied me rationality just as they denied it to all those who were not
exactly like themselves, in all their unreason. If I could see not one single
soul in that wilderness of desolation all around me, then the six of us—mounts
and riders, both—could boast amongst us not one soul either, since all the
best religions in the world state categorically that not beasts nor women were
equipped with the flimsy, insubstantial things when the good Lord opened
the gates of Eden and let Eve and her familiars tumble out. Understand, then,
that though I would not say I privately engaged in metaphysical speculation
as we rode through the reedy approaches to the river, I certainly meditated
on the nature of my own state, how I had been bought and sold, passed from
hand to hand. That clockwork girl who powdered my cheeks for me—had I
not been allotted only the same kind of imitative life amongst men that the
dollmaker had given her?

Yet as to the true nature of the being of this clawed magus who rode his
pale horse in a style that made me recall how Kublai Khan's leopards went
out hunting on horseback, of that I had no notion.

We came to the bank of the river, which was so wide we could not see
across it, so still with winter that it scarcely seemed to flow. The horses
lowered their heads to drink. The valet cleared his throat, about to speak;
we were in a place of perfect privacy, beyond a brake of winter-bare rushes,
a hedge of reeds.

"If you will not let him see you without your clothes—"

I involuntarily shook my head.

"—you must, then, prepare yourself for the sight of my master, naked."

The river broke on the pebbles with a diminishing sigh. My composure
deserted me; all at once I was on the brink of panic. I did not think that I
could bear the sight of him, whatever he was. The mare raised her dripping
muzzle and looked at me keenly, as if urging me. The river broke again at
my feet. I was far from home.

"You," said the valet, "must."

When I saw how scared he was I might refuse, I nodded.

The reed bowed down in a sudden snarl of wind that brought with it a gust of the heavy odor of his disguise. The valet held out his master's cloak to screen him from me as he removed the mask. The horses stirred.

The tiger will never lie down with the lamb; he acknowledges no pact that is not reciprocal. The lamb must learn to run with the tigers.

A great, feline, tawny shape whose pelt was barred with a savage geometry of bars the color of burned wood. His domed, heavy head so terrible he must hide it. How subtle the muscles, how profound the tread. The annihilating vehemence of his eyes, like twin suns.

I felt my breast ripped apart as if I suffered a marvelous wound.

The valet moved forward as if to cover up his master now the girl had acknowledged him, but I said: "No." The tiger sat still as a heraldic beast, in the pact he had made with his own ferocity to do me no harm. He was far larger than I could have imagined, from the poor, shabby things I'd seen once, in the czar's menagerie at Petersburg, the golden fruit of their eyes dimming, withering in the far North of captivity. Nothing about him reminded me of humanity.

I therefore, shivering, now unfastened my jacket, to show him I would do him no harm. Yet I was clumsy and blushed a little, for no man had seen me naked and I was a proud girl. Pride it was, not shame, that thwarted my fingers so; and a certain trepidation lest this frail little article of human upholstery before him might not be, in itself, grand enough to satisfy his expectations of us, since those, for all I knew, might have grown infinite during the endless time he had been waiting. The wind clattered in the rushes, purled and eddied in the river.

I showed his grave silence my white skin, my red nipples, and the horses turned their heads to watch me also, as if they, too, were courteously curious as to the fleshly nature of women. Then the Beast lowered his massive head. Enough! said the valet with a gesture. The wind died down, all was still again.

Then they went off together, the valet on his pony, the tiger running before him like a hound, and I walked along the riverbank for a while. I felt I was at liberty for the first time in my life. Then the winter sun began to tarnish, a few flakes of snow drifted from the darkening sky, and when I returned to the horses, I found the Beast mounted again on his gray mare, cloaked and masked and once more, to all appearances, a man, while the valet had a fine catch of waterfowl dangling from his hand and the corpse of a young roebuck slung behind his saddle. I climbed up on the black gelding in silence and so we returned to the palace as the snow fell more and more heavily, obscuring the tracks that we had left behind us.

The valet did not return me to my cell but, instead, to an elegant if old-fashioned boudoir, with sofas of faded pink brocade, a jinn's treasury of Oriental carpets, tintinnabulation of cut-glass chandeliers. Candles in antlered holders struck rainbows from the prismatic hearts of the diamond earrings that lay on my new dressing table, at which my attentive maid stood ready with her powder puff and mirror. Intending to fix the ornaments in my ears, I took the looking glass from her hand, but it was in the midst of one of its magic fits again, and I did not see my own face in it but that of my father; at first I thought he smiled at me. Then I saw he was smiling with pure gratification.

He sat, I saw, in the parlor of our lodgings, at the very table where he had lost me, but now he was busily engaged in counting out a tremendous pile of banknotes. My father's circumstances had changed already; well-shaven, neatly barbered, smart new clothes. A frosted glass of sparkling wine sat convenient to his hand beside an ice bucket. The Beast had clearly paid cash on the nail for his glimpse of my bosom, and paid up promptly, as if it had not been a sight I might have died of showing. Then I saw my father's trunks were packed, ready for departure. Could he so easily leave me here?

There was a note on the table with the money, in a fine hand. I could read it quite clearly. "The young lady will arrive immediately." Some harlot with whom he'd briskly negotiated a liaison on the strength of his spoils? Not at all. For at that moment, the valet knocked at my door to announce that I might leave the palace at any time thereafter, and he bore over his arm a handsome sable cloak, my very own little gratuity, The Beast's morning gift, in which he proposed to pack me up and send me off.

When I looked at the mirror again, my father had disappeared, and all I saw was a pale, hollow-eyed girl whom I scarcely recognized. The valet asked politely when he should prepare the carriage, as if he did not doubt that I would leave with my booty at the first opportunity, while my maid, whose face was no longer the spit of my own, continued bonnily to beam. I will dress her in my own clothes, wind her up, send her back to perform the part of my father's daughter.

"Leave me alone," I said to the valet.

He did not need to lock the door now. I fixed the earrings in my ears. They were very heavy. Then I took off my riding habit, left it where it lay on the floor. But when I got down to my shift, my arms dropped to my sides. I was unaccustomed to nakedness. I was so unused to my own skin that to take off all my clothes involved a kind of flaying. I thought the Beast had wanted a little thing compared with what I was prepared to give him; but it is not natural for humankind to go naked, not since first we hid our loins with fig leaves. He had demanded the abominable. I felt as much atrocious pain as if I was stripping off my own underpelt, and the smiling girl stood poised in the oblivion of her balked simulation of life, watching me peel down to the cold, white meat of contract, and if she did not see me, then so much more like the marketplace, where the eyes that watch you take no account of your existence.

And it seemed my entire life, since I had left the North, had passed under the indifferent gaze of eyes like hers.

Then I was flinching stark, except for his irreproachable tears.

I huddled in the furs I must return to him, to keep me from the lacerating winds that raced along the corridors. I knew the way to his den without the valet to guide me.

No response to my tentative rap on his door.

Then the wind blew the valet whirling along the passage. He must have decided that if one should go naked, then all should go naked; without his livery, he revealed himself, as I had suspected, a delicate creature, covered with silken moth-gray fur, brown fingers supple as leather, chocolate muzzle, the gentlest creature in the world. He gibbered a little to see my fine furs and jewels as if I were dressed up for the opera and, with a great deal of tender ceremony, removed the sables from my shoulders. The sables thereupon resolved themselves into a pack of black, squeaking rats that rattled immediately down the stairs on their hard little feet and were lost to sight.

The valet bowed me inside the Beast's room.

The purple dressing gown, the mask, the wig, were laid out on his chair; a glove was planted on each arm. The empty house of his appearance was ready for him, but he had abandoned it. There was a reek of fur and piss; the incense pot lay broken in pieces on the floor. Half-burned sticks were scattered from the extinguished fire. A candle stuck by its own grease to the mantelpiece lit two narrow flames in the pupils of the tiger's eyes.

He was pacing backward and forward, backward and forward, the tip of his heavy tail twitching as he paced out the length and breadth of his imprisonment between the gnawed and bloody bones.

He will gobble you up.

Nursery fears made flesh and sinew; earliest and most archaic of fears, fear of devourment. The beast and his carnivorous bed of bone and I, white, shaking, raw, approaching him as if offering, in myself, the key to a peaceable kingdom in which his appetite need not be my extinction.

He went still as stone. He was far more frightened of me than I was of him.

I squatted on the wet straw and stretched out my hand. I was now within the field of force of his golden eyes. He growled at the back of his throat, lowered his head, sank onto his forepaws, snarled, showed me his red gullet, his yellow teeth. I never moved. He snuffed the air, as if to smell my fear; he could not.

Slowly, slowly he began to drag his heavy, gleaming weight across the floor towards me.

A tremendous throbbing, as of the engine that makes the earth turn, filled the little room; he had begun to purr.

The sweet thunder of this purr shook the old walls, made the shutters batter the windows until they burst apart and let in the white light of the snowy moon. Tiles came crashing down from the roof; I heard them fall into the courtyard far below. The reverberations of his purring rocked the foundations of the house, the walls began to dance. I thought: It will all fall, everything will disintegrate.

He dragged himself closer and closer to me, until I felt the harsh velvet of his head against my hand, then a tongue, abrasive as sandpaper. "He will lick the skin off me!"

And each stroke of his tongue ripped off skin after successive skin, all the skins of a life in the world, and left behind a nascent patina of shining hairs. My earrings turned back to water and trickled down my shoulders; I shrugged the drops off my beautiful fur.

The Princess and the Frog
ROBIN MCKINLEY

I

She held the pale necklace in her hand and stared at it as she walked. Her feet evidently knew where they were going, for they did not stumble although her eyes gave them no guidance. Her eyes remained fixed on the glowing round stones in her hand.

These stones were as smooth as pearls, and their color, at first sight, seemed as pure. But they were much larger than any pearls she had ever seen; as large as the dark sweet cherries she plucked in the palace gardens. And their pale creamy color did not lie quiet and reflect the sunlight, but shimmered and shifted, and seemed to offer her glimpses of something mysterious in their hearts, something she waited to see, almost with dread, which was always at the last minute hidden from her. And they seemed to have a heat of their own that owed nothing to her hand as she held them; rather they burned against her cold fingers. Her hand trembled, and their cloudy swirling seemed to shiver in response; the swiftness of their ebb and flow seemed to mock the pounding of her heart.

Prince Aliyander had just given her the necklace, with one of the dark-eyed smiles she had learned to fear so much; for while he had done nothing to her yet—but then, he had *done* nothing to any of them—she knew that her own brother was under his invisible spell. This spell he called "friendship," with his flashing smile and another look from his black eyes; and her own father, the king, was afraid of him. She also knew he meant to marry her, and knew her strength could not hold out against him long, once he set himself to win her. His "friendship" had already subdued the crown prince, only a few months ago a merry and mischievous lad, into a dog to follow at his heels and go where he was told.

This morning, as they stood together in the Great Hall, herself, and her father, and Prince Aliyander, with the young crown prince a half step behind Aliyander's right shoulder and their courtiers around them, Aliyander had reached into a pocket and brought out the necklace. It gleamed and seemed to shiver with life as he held it up, and all the courtiers murmured with awe. "For you, Lady Princess," said Aliyander, with a graceful bow and his smile; and he moved to fasten it around her neck. "A small gift, to tell you of just the smallest portion of my esteem for Your Highness."

She started back with a suddenness that surprised even her; and her heart flew up in her throat and beat there wildly as the great jewels danced before her eyes. And she felt rather than saw the flicker in Aliyander's eyes when she moved away from him.

"Forgive me," she stammered. "They are so lovely, you must let me look at them a little first." Her voice felt thick; it was hard to speak. "I shan't be able to admire them as they deserve, when they lie beneath my chin."

"Of course," said Aliyander, but she could not look at his smile. "All pretty ladies love to look at pretty things"; and the edge in his voice was such that only she felt it; and she had to look away from the crown prince, whose eyes were shining with the delight of his friend's generosity.

"May I—may I take your—gracious gift outside and look at it in the sunlight?" she faltered. The high vaulted ceiling and mullioned windows seemed suddenly narrow and stifling, with the great glowing stones only inches from her face. The touch of sunlight would be healing. She reached out blindly and tried not to wince as Aliyander laid the necklace across her hand.

"I hope you will return wearing my poor gift," he said, with the same edge to his words, "so that it may flatter itself in the light of Your Highness's beauty and bring joy to the heart of your unworthy admirer."

"Yes—yes, I will," she said, and turned, and only her princess's training prevented her from fleeing, picking up her skirts with her free hand and running the long length of the hall to the arched doors, and outside to the gardens. Or perhaps it was the imponderable weight in her hand that held her down.

But outside, at least the sky did not shut down on her as the walls and groined ceiling of the hall had; and the sun seemed to lie gently and sympathetically across her shoulders even if it could not help itself against Aliyander's jewels, and dripped and ran across them until her eyes were dazzled.

Her feet stopped at last, and she blinked and looked up. Near the edge of the garden, near the great outer wall of the palace, was a quiet pool with a few trees close around it, so that much of the water stood in shadow wherever the sun stood in the sky. There was a small white marble bench under one of the trees, pushed close enough that a sitter might lean comfortably against the broad bole behind him. Aside from the bench there was no other ornament; as the palace gardens went, it was almost wild, for the grass was allowed to grow a little shaggy before it was cut back, and wildflowers grew here occasionally, and were undisturbed. The princess had discovered this spot—for no one else seemed to come here but the occasional gardener and his clippers—about a year ago; a little before Prince Aliyander had ridden into their lives. Since that riding, their lives had changed, and she had come here more and more often, to be quiet and alone, if only for a little time.

Now she stood at the brink of the pond, the strange necklace clutched in her unwilling fingers, and closed her eyes. She took a few long breaths, hoping that the cool peacefulness of this place would somehow help even this trouble. She did not want to wear this necklace, to place it around her throat; she felt that the strange jewels would . . . strangle her, stop her breath till she breathed in the same rhythm as Aliyander and as her poor brother.

Her trembling stopped; the hand with the necklace dropped a few inches. She felt better. But as soon as she opened her eyes, she would see those terrible cloudy stones again. She raised her chin. At least the first thing she would see was the quiet water. She began to open her eyes: and then a great *croak* bellowed from, it seemed, a place just beside her feet; and her overtaxed nerves broke out in a sharp "Oh," and she leapt away from the sound. As she leapt, her fingers opened, and the necklace dropped with the softest splash, a lingering and caressing sound, and disappeared under the water.

Her first thought was relief that the stones no longer held and threatened her; and then she remembered Aliyander, and her heart shrank within her. She remembered his look when she had refused his gift; and the sound of his voice when he hoped she would wear it upon her return to the hall—where he was even now awaiting her. She dared not face him without it round her neck; and he would never believe in this accident. And indeed, if she had cared for the thing, she would have pulled it to her instead of loosing it in her alarm.

She knelt at the edge of the pool and looked in; but while the water seemed clear, and the sunlight penetrated a long way, still she could not see the bottom, but only a misty grayness that drowned at last to utter black. "Oh, dear," she whispered. "I *must* get it back. But how?"

"Well," said a voice diffidently, "I think I could probably fetch it for you."

She had forgotten the noise that had startled her. The voice came from very low down; she was kneeling with her hands so near the pool's edge that her fingertips were lightly brushed by the water's smallest ripples. She turned her head and looked down still farther; and sitting on the bank at her side she saw one of the largest frogs she had ever seen. She did not even think to be startled. "It was rather my fault anyway," added the frog.

"Oh—could you?" she said. She hardly thought of the phenomenon of a frog that talked; her mind was taken up with wishing to have the necklace back, and reluctance to see and touch it again. Here was one part of her problem solved; the medium of the solution did not matter to her.

The frog said no more but dived into the water with scarcely more noise than the necklace had made in falling; in what seemed only a moment, its green head emerged again, with two of the round stones in its wide mouth. It clambered back onto the bank, getting entangled in the trailing necklace as it did so. A frog is a silly creature, and this one looked absurd, with a king's ransom of smooth heavy jewels twisted round its squat figure; but she did not think of this. She reached out to help, and it wasn't till she had Aliyander's gift in her hands again that she noticed the change.

The stones were as large and round and perfect as they had been before; but the weird creamy light of them was gone. They lay dim and gray and quiet against her palm, as cool as the water of the pond, and strengthless.

Such was her relief and pleasure that she sprang to her feet, spreading the necklace to its fullest extent and turning it this way and that in the sunlight, to be certain of what she saw; and she forgot even to thank the frog, still sitting patiently on the bank where she had rescued it from the binding necklace.

"Excuse me," it said at last, and then she remembered it, and looked down and said, "Oh, thank you," with such a bright and glowing look that it might move even a frog's cold heart.

"You're quite welcome, I'm sure," said the frog mechanically. "But I wonder if I might ask you a favor."

"Certainly. Anything." Even facing Aliyander seemed less dreadful, now the necklace was quenched: she felt that perhaps he could be resisted. Her joy made her silly; it was the first time anything of Aliyander's making had missed its mark, and for a moment she had no thoughts for the struggle ahead but only for the present victory. Perhaps even the crown prince could be saved. . . .

"Would you let me live with you at the palace for a little time?"

Her wild thoughts halted for a moment, and she looked down bewildered at the frog. What would a frog want with a palace? For that matter—as if she had only just noticed it—why did this frog talk?

"I find this pool rather dull," said the frog fastidiously, as if this were an explanation.

She hesitated, dropping her hands again, but this time the stones hung limply, hiding in a fold of her wide skirts. She had told the frog, "Certainly. Anything"; and her father had brought her up to understand that she must always keep her word, the more so because as she was a princess, there was no one who could force her to. "Very well," she said at last. "If you wish it." And she realized after she spoke that part of her hesitation was reluctance that anything, even a frog, should see her palace, her family, now; it would hurt her. But she had given her word, and there could be no harm in a frog.

"Thank you," said the frog gravely, and with surprising dignity for a small green thing with long thin flipper-footed legs and popping eyes.

There was a pause, and then she said, "I—er—I think I should go back now. Will you be along later or . . . ?"

"I'll be along later," replied the frog at once, as if he recognized her embarrassment; as if he were a poor relation who yet had a sense of his own worth.

She hesitated a moment longer, wondering to how many people she would have to explain her talking frog, and added, "I dine alone with my father at eight." Prince Inthur never took his meals with his father and sister anymore; he ate with Aliyander or alone, miserably, in his room, if Aliyander chose to overlook him. Then she raised the gray necklace to clasp it round her throat and remembered that it was, after all, her talking frog's pool that had put out the ill light of Aliyander's work. She smiled once more at the frog, a little guiltily, for she believed one should be kind to one's poor relations, and she said, "You'll be my talisman."

She turned and walked quickly away, back toward the palace, and the hall, and Aliyander.

II

But she made a serious mistake, for she walked swiftly back to the hall, and blithely through the door, with her head up and her eyes sparkling with happiness and release; she met Aliyander's black eyes too quickly and smiled without thinking. It was only then she realized what her thoughtlessness had done, when she saw his eyes move swiftly from her face to the jewels at her throat, and then as he saw her smile his own face twisted with a rage so intense it seemed for a moment that his sallow skin would turn black with it. And even her little brother, the crown prince, looked at his hero a little strangely and said, "Is anything wrong?"

Aliyander did not answer. He turned on his heel and left, going toward the door opposite that which the princess had entered; the door that led into the rest of the palace. Everyone seemed to be holding his or her breath while the quiet footfalls retreated, for there was no other noise; even the air had stopped moving through the windows. Then there was the sound of the heavy door opening, and closing, and Aliyander was gone.

The courtiers blinked and looked at one another. The crown prince looked as if he might cry: his master had left him behind. The king turned to his daughter with the closing of that far door, and he saw first her white frightened face; and then his gaze dropped to the round stones of her necklace, and there, for several moments, it remained.

No one of the courtiers looked at her directly; but when she caught their sidelong looks, there was blankness in their eyes, not understanding. None addressed a word to her, although all had seen that she, somehow, was the cause of Aliyander's anger. But then, for months now it had been considered bad luck to discuss anything that Aliyander did.

Inthur, the crown prince, still loved his father and sister in spite of the cloud that Aliyander had cast over his mind; and little did he know how awkward Aliyander found that simple and indestructible love. But now Inthur saw his sister standing alone in the doorway to the garden, her face as white as her dress, and as a little gust of wind blew her skirts around her and her fair hair across her face, she gasped and gave a shudder, and one hand touched her necklace. With Aliyander absent, even the cloud on Inthur lifted a little, although he himself did not know this, for he never thought about himself. Instead he ran the several steps to where his sister stood, and threw his arms around her; he looked up into her face and said, "Don't worry, Rana dear, he's never angry long." His boy's gaze passed over the necklace without a pause.

She nodded down at him and tried to smile, but her eyes filled with tears; and with a little brother's horror of tears, particularly sister's tears, he let go of her at once and said quickly, with the air of one who changes the subject from one proved dangerous, "What did you do?"

She blinked back her tears, recognizing the dismay on Inthur's face; he would not know that it was his hug that had brought them, and the look on his face when he tried to comfort her: just as he had used to look before Aliyander came. Now he rarely glanced at either his father or his sister except vaguely, as if half asleep or with his thoughts far away. "I don't know," she said, with a fair attempt at calmness, "but perhaps it is not important."

He patted her hand as if he were her uncle, and said, "That's all right. You just apologize to him when you see him next, and it'll be over."

She smiled wanly as she remembered that her own brother belonged to Aliyander now and she could not trust him. Then the king came up beside them, and when her eyes met his she read knowledge in them: of what Aliyander had seen, in her face and round her neck; and a reflection of her own fear. He said nothing to her.

The rest of the day passed slowly, for while they did not see Aliyander again, the weight of his absence was almost as great as his presence would have been. The crown prince grew cross and fretful, and glowered at everyone; the courtiers seemed nervous, and whispered among themselves, looking often over their shoulders as if for the ghosts of their great-grandmothers. Even those who came from the city, or the far-flung towns beyond, to kneel before the king and crave a favor seemed more to crouch and plead, as if for mercy; and their faces were never happy when they went away, whatever the king had granted them.

Rana felt as gray as Aliyander's jewels.

The sun set at last, and its final rays touched the faces in the hall with the first color most of them had had all day; and as servants came in to light the candles, everyone looked paler and more uncomfortable than ever.

One of Aliyander's personal servants approached the throne soon after the candles were lit; the king sat with his children in smaller chairs at his feet. The man offered the crown prince a folded slip of paper; his obeisance to the king first was a gesture so cursory as to be insulting, but the king made no move to reprimand him. The hall was as still as it had been that morning when Aliyander had left it; and the sound of Inthur's impatient opening of the note crackled loudly. He leapt to his feet and said joyfully, "I'm to dine with him!" and with a dreadful look of triumph round the hall, and then at his father and sister—Rana closed her eyes—he ran off, the servant following with the dignity of a nobleman.

It seemed a sign. The king stood up wearily and clapped his hands once; and the courtiers made their bows and began to drift away, to quarters in the palace, or to grand houses outside in the city. Rana followed her father to the door that led to the rest of the palace, where the crown prince had just disappeared; and there the king turned and said, "I will see you at eight, my child?" And Rana's eyes again filled with tears at the question in his voice, behind his words. She only nodded, afraid to speak, and he turned away. "We dine alone," he said, and left her.

She spent two long and bitter hours staring at nothing, sitting alone in her room; in spite of the gold and white hangings and the bright blue coverlet on her bed, it refused to look cheerful for her tonight. She removed her necklace and stuffed it into an empty jar and put the lid on quickly, as if it were a snake that might escape, although she knew that it itself had no further power to harm her.

She joined her father with a heavy heart; in place of Aliyander's jewels she wore a golden pendant that her mother had given her. The two of them ate in a little room with a small round table, where her family had always gathered when there was no formal banquet. When she was very small and Inthur only a baby, she had sat here with both her parents; then her pretty, fragile mother had died, and she and Inthur and their father had faced each other around this table alone. Now it was just the king and herself. There had been few banquets in the last months. As she looked at her father now, she was suddenly frightened at how old and weak he looked. Aliyander could gain no hold over him, for his mind and his will were too pure for Aliyander's nets; but his presence aged him quickly, too quickly. And the next king would be Inthur, who followed Aliyander everywhere, a pace behind his right shoulder. And Inthur would be delighted at his best friend's marrying his sister.

The dining room was round like the table within it; it was the first floor of a tower that stood at one of the many corners of the palace. It had windows on two sides, and a door through which the servants brought the covered dishes and the wine, and another door which led down a flight of stone steps to the garden.

Neither she nor her father ate much, nor spoke at all, and the room was very quiet. So it was that when an odd muffled thump struck the garden door, they both looked up at once. Whatever it was, after a moment it struck again. They stared at each other, puzzled, and because since Aliyander had come all things unknown were dreaded, their looks were also fearful. When the third thump came, Rana stood up and went over to the door and flung it open.

There sat her frog.

"Oh!" she exclaimed. "It's you."

If a frog could turn its foolish mouth to a smile, this one did. "Good evening," it replied.

"Who is it?" said the king, standing up; for he could see nothing, yet he heard the strange deep voice.

"It's . . . a frog," Rana said, somewhat embarrassed. "I dropped . . . that necklace in a pool today, and he fetched it out for me. He asked a favor in return, that he might live with me in the palace."

"If you made a promise, child, you must keep it," said the king; and for a moment he looked as he had before Aliyander came. "Invite him in." And his eyes rested on his daughter thoughtfully, remembering the change in those jewels that he had seen.

The princess stood aside, and the frog hopped in. The king and princess stood, feeling silly, looking down, while the frog looked up; then Rana shook herself, and shut the door, and returned to the table. "Would you—er—like some dinner? There's plenty."

She took the frog back to her own room in her pocket. Her father had said nothing to her about their odd visitor, but she knew from the look on his face when he bade her good night that he would mention it to no one. The frog said gravely that her room was a very handsome one; then it leapt up onto a sofa and settled itself among the cushions. Rana blew the lights out and undressed and climbed into bed, and lay, staring up, thinking.

"I will go with you to the hall tomorrow, if I may," said the frog's voice from the darkness, breaking in on her dark thoughts.

"Certainly," she said, as she had said once before. "You're my talisman," she added, with a catch in her voice.

"All is not well here," said the frog gently; and the deep sympathetic voice might have been anyone, not a frog, but her old nurse, perhaps, when she was a baby and needed comforting because of a scratched knee; or the best friend she had never had, because she was a princess, the only princess of the greatest realm in all the lands from the western to the eastern seas; and to her horror, she burst into tears and found herself between gulps telling that voice everything. How Aliyander had ridden up one day, without warning, ridden in from the north, where his father still ruled as king over a country bordering her father's. How Aliyander was now declared the heir apparent, for his elder brother, Lian, had disappeared over a year before; and while this sad loss continued mysteriously, still it was necessary for the peace of the country to secure the succession. Aliyander's first official performance as heir apparent was this visit to his kingdom's nearest neighbor to the south, for he knew that it was his father's dearest wish that the friendship between their two lands continue close and loyal.

And for the first time they saw Aliyander smile. The crown prince had turned away, for he was then free and innocent; the king stiffened and grew pale; and Rana did not guess how she might have looked.

"I had known Lian when we were children," Rana continued; she no longer cared who was listening, or if anything was. "He was kind and patient with Inthur, who was only a baby; I—I thought him wonderful," she whispered. "I heard my parents discussing him one night, him and . . . me."

Aliyander's visit had lengthened—a fortnight, a month, two months; it had been almost a year since he rode through their gates. Messengers passed between him and his father—he said; but here he stayed, and entrapped the crown prince; and next he would have the princess.

"I don't know what to do," she said at last, wearily. "There is nothing I can do."

"I'm sorry," said the voice, and it was sad, and wistful, and kind.

And human. Her mind wavered from the single thought of *Aliyander, Aliyander,* and she remembered to whom—or what—she spoke; and the sympathy in the creature's voice puzzled her even more than the fact that the voice could use human speech.

"You cannot be a frog," she said stupidly. "You must be . . . under a spell." And she found she could spare a little pity from her own family's plight to give to this spellbound creature who spoke like a human being.

"Of course," snapped the frog. "Frogs don't talk."

She was silent, sorry that her own pain had made her thoughtless, made her wound another's feelings.

"I'm sorry," said the frog for the second time, and in the same gentle tone. "You see, one never quite grows accustomed."

She answered after a moment: "Yes. I think I do understand, a little."

"Thank you," said the frog.

"Yes," she said again. "Good night."

"Good night."

But just before she fell asleep, she heard the voice once more: "I have one more favor to ask. That you do not mention, when you take me to the hall tomorrow, that I . . . talk."

"Very well," she said drowsily.

III

There was a ripple of nervous laughter when the princess Rana appeared in the Great Hall on the next morning, carrying a large frog. She held her right arm bent at the elbow and curled lightly against her side; and the frog rode quietly on her forearm. She was wearing a dress of pale blue, with lace at her neck, and her fair hair hung loose over her shoulders, and a silver circlet was around her brow; the big green frog showed brilliantly and absurdly against her pale loveliness. She sat on her low chair before her father's throne; the frog climbed, or slithered, or leaped, to her lap, and lay, blinking foolishly at the noblemen in their rich dresses and the palace servants in their handsome livery; but it was perhaps too stupid to be frightened, for it made no other motion.

She had seen Aliyander standing with the crown prince when she entered, but she avoided his eyes; at last he came to stand before her, legs apart, staring down at her bent head with a heat from his black eyes that scorched her skin.

"You dare to mock me," he said, his voice almost a hiss, thick with a venomous hatred she could not mistake.

She looked up in terror, and he gestured at the frog. "Ah, no, I meant no—" she pleaded, and then her voice died; but the heat of Aliyander's look ebbed a little as he read the fear in her face.

"A frog, Princess?" he said; his voice still hurt her, but now it was heavy with scorn, and pitched so that many in the hall would hear him. "I thought princesses preferred kittens, or greyhounds."

"I—" She paused, and licked her dry lips. "I found it in the garden." She dropped her eyes again; she could think of nothing else to say. If only he would turn away from her—just for a minute, a minute in which to gather

her wits; but he would not leave her, and her wits would only scatter again when next he addressed her.

He made now a gesture of disgust; and then straightened up, as if he would turn away from her at last, and she clenched her hands on the arms of her chair—and at that moment the frog gave its great bellow, the noise that had startled her yesterday into dropping the necklace into the pool. And Aliyander was startled; he jerked visibly—and the courtiers laughed.

It was only the barest titter, and strangled instantly; but Aliyander heard it, and he turned, his face black with rage as it had been the day before when Rana returned wearing a cold gray necklace; and he seized the frog by the leg and hurled it against the heavy stone wall opposite the thrones, which stood halfway down the long length of the hall and faced across the narrow width to tall windows that looked out upon the courtyard.

Rana was frozen with horror for the moment it took Aliyander to fling the creature; and then as it struck the wall, there was a dreadful sound, and the skin of the frog seemed to . . . burst, and she closed her eyes.

The sudden gasp of all those around her made her eyes open against her will. And she in her turn gasped.

For the frog that Aliyander had hurled against the wall was there no longer; as it struck and fell, it became a tall young man, who stood there now, his ruddy hair falling past his broad shoulders, his blue eyes blazing as he stared at his attacker.

"Aliyander," he said, and his voice fell like a stone in the silence. Aliyander stood as if his name on those lips had turned him to stone indeed.

"Aliyander. My little brother."

No one moved but Rana; her hands stirred of their own accord. They crept across the spot on her lap where the frog had lain only a minute ago; and they seized each other.

Aliyander laughed—a terrible, ugly sound. "I defeated you once, big brother. I will defeat you again. You are weaker than I. You always will be."

The blue eyes never wavered. "Yes, I am weaker," Lian replied, "as you have proven already. I do not choose your sort of power."

Aliyander's face twisted as Rana had seen it before. She stood up suddenly, but he paid no attention to her; the heat of his gaze was now reserved for his brother, who stood calmly enough, staring back at Aliyander's distorted face.

"You made the wrong choice," Aliyander said, in a voice as black as his look, "and I will prove it to you. You will have no chance to return and inconvenience me a second time."

It was as if no one else could move; the eyes of all were riveted on the two antagonists; even the crown prince did not move to be closer to his hero.

The princess turned and ran. She paused on the threshold of the door to the garden and picked up a tall flagon that had held wine and was now sitting forgotten on a deep windowsill. Then she ran out, down the white paths; she had no eyes for the trees and the flowers, or the smooth sand of the courtyard to her right; she felt as numb as she had the day before with her handful of round and glowing jewels; but today her eyes watched where her feet led her, and her mind said *hurry, hurry, hurry.*

She ran to the pond where she had found the frog, or where the frog had found her. She knelt quickly on the bank and rinsed the sour wine dregs from the bottom of the flagon she carried, emptying the tainted water on the grass behind her, where it would not run back into the pool. Then she dipped the jug full, and carried it, brimming, back to the Great Hall.

She had to walk slowly this time, for the flagon was full and very heavy, and she did not wish to spill even a drop of it. Her feet seemed to sink ankle-deep in the ground with every step, although in fact the white pebbles held no footprint as she passed, and only bruised her small feet in their thin-soled slippers.

She paused on the hall's threshold again, this time for her eyes to adjust to the dimmer light. No one had moved; and no one looked at her.

She saw Aliyander raise his hand and bring it like a backhanded slap against the air before him; and though Lian stood across the room from him, she saw his head jerk as if from the force of a blow; and a thin line formed on his cheek, and after a moment blood welled and dripped from it.

Aliyander waved his hand so the sharp stone of his ring glittered; and he laughed.

Rana started forward again, step by step, as slowly as she had paced the garden, although only a few steps more were needed. Her arms had begun to shiver with the weight of her burden. Still Aliyander did not look at her; for while his might be the greater strength at last, still he could not tear his eyes away from the calm clear gaze of his brother's; his brother yet held him.

Rana walked up the narrow way till she was so close to Aliyander that she might have touched his sleeve if she had not needed both hands to hold the flagon. Then, at last, Aliyander broke away to look at her; and as he did she lifted the great jug, and with a strength she thought was not hers alone, hurled the contents full upon the man before her.

He gave a strangled cry and brushed desperately with his hands as if he could sweep the water away; but he was drenched with it, his hair plastered to his head and his clothes to his body. He looked suddenly small, wizened, and old. He still looked at her, but she met his gaze fearlessly, and he did not seem to recognize her.

His face turned as gray as his jewels. His eyes, she thought, were as opaque as the eyes of marble statues; and then he fell down full-length upon the floor, heavily, without sound, with no attempt to catch himself. He moved no more.

Inthur leapt up then with a cry and ran to his fallen friend, and Rana saw the quick tears on his cheeks; but when he looked up he looked straight at her, and his eyes were clear. "He was my friend," he said simply; but there was no memory in him of what that friendship had been.

The king stood down stiffly from his throne, and the courtiers moved, and shook themselves as if from sleep, and stared without sorrow at the still body of Aliyander, and with curiosity and awe and a little hesitant but hopeful joy at Lian.

"I welcome you," said the king, with the pride of the master of his own hall, and of a king of a long line of kings. "I welcome you, Prince Lian, to my country, and to my people." And his gaze flickered only briefly to the thing on the floor; at his gesture, a servant stepped forward and threw a dark cloth over it.

"Thank you," said Lian gravely; and the princess realized that he had come up silently and was standing at her side. She glanced up and saw him looking down at her; and the knowledge of what they had done together, and what neither could have done alone, passed between them; and with it an understanding that they would never discuss it. She said aloud: "I—I welcome you, Prince Lian."

"Thank you," he said again, but she heard the change of tone in his voice; and from the corner of her eye she saw her father smile. She offered Lian her hand, and he took it and raised it slowly to his lips.

When the Clock Strikes

TANITH LEE

Yes, the great ballroom is filled only with dust now. The slender columns of white marble and the slender columns of rose-red marble are woven together by cobwebs. The vivid frescoes, on which the duke's treasury spent so much, are dimmed by the dust; the faces of the painted goddesses look gray. And the velvet curtains—touch them, they will crumble. Two hundred years, now, since anyone danced in this place on the sea-green floor in the candle gleam. Two hundred years since the wonderful clock struck for the very last time.

I thought you might care to examine the clock. It was considered exceptional in its day. The pedestal is ebony and the face fine porcelain. And these figures, which are of silver, would pass slowly about the circlet of the face. Each figure represents, you understand, an hour. And as the appropriate hours came level with this golden bell, they would strike it the correct number of times. All the figures are unique, as you see. Beginning at the first hour, they are, in this order, a girl-child, a dwarf, a maiden, a youth, a lady and a knight. And here, notice, the figures grow older as the day declines: a queen and king for the seventh and eighth hours, and after these, an abbess and a magician and next to last, a hag. But the very last is strangest of all. The twelfth figure: do you recognize him? It is Death. Yes, a most curious clock. It was reckoned a marvelous thing then. But it has not struck for two hundred years. Possibly you have been told the story? No? Oh, but I am certain that you have heard it, in another form, perhaps.

However, as you have some while to wait for your carriage, I will recount the tale, if you wish.

I will start with what was said of the clock. In those years, this city was prosperous, a stronghold—not as you see it today. Much was made in the city that was ornamental and unusual. But the clock, on which the twelfth hour was Death, caused something of a stir. It was thought unlucky, foolhardy, to have such a clock. It began to be murmured, jokingly by some, by others in earnest, that one night when the clock struck the twelfth hour, Death would truly strike with it.

Now life has always been a chancy business, and it was more so then. The Great Plague had come but twenty years before and was not yet forgotten. Besides, in the duke's court there was much intrigue, while enemies might be supposed to plot beyond the city walls, as happens even in our present age. But there was another thing.

It was rumored that the duke had obtained both his title and the city treacherously. Rumor declared that he had systematically destroyed those who had stood in line before him, the members of the princely house that formerly ruled here. He had accomplished the task slyly, hiring assassins talented with poisons and daggers. But rumor also declared that the duke had not been sufficiently thorough. For though he had meant to rid himself of all that rival house, a single descendant remained, so obscure he had not traced her—for it was a woman.

Of course, such matters were not spoken of openly. Like the prophecy of the clock, it was a subject for the dark.

Nevertheless, I will tell you at once, there was such a descendant he had missed in his bloody work. And she was a woman. Royal and proud she was, and seething with bitter spite and a hunger for vengeance, and as bloody as the duke, had he known it, in her own way.

For her safety and disguise, she had long ago wed a wealthy merchant in the city, and presently bore the man a daughter. The merchant, a dealer in silks, was respected, a good fellow but not wise. He rejoiced in his handsome and aristocratic wife. He never dreamed what she might be about when he was not with her. In fact, she had sworn allegiance to Satanas. In the dead of night she would go up into an old tower adjoining the merchant's house, and there she would say portions of the Black Mass, offer sacrifice, and thereafter practice witchcraft against the duke. This witchery took a common form, the creation of a wax image and the maiming of the image that, by sympathy, the injuries inflicted on the wax be passed on to the living body of the victim. The woman was capable in what she did. The duke fell sick. He lost the use of his limbs and was racked by excruciating pains from which he could get no relief. Thinking himself on the brink of death, the duke named his sixteen-year-old son his heir. This son was dear to the duke, as everyone knew, and be sure the woman knew it too. She intended sorcerously to murder the young man in his turn, preferably in his father's sight. Thus she let the duke linger in his agony and commenced planning the fate of the prince.

Now all this while she had not been toiling alone. She had one helper. It was her own daughter, a maid of fourteen, that she had recruited to her service nearly as soon as the infant could walk. At six or seven, the child had been lisping the satanic rite along with her mother. At fourteen, you may imagine, the girl was well versed in the black arts, though she did not have her mother's natural genius for them.

Perhaps you would like me to describe the daughter at this point. It has a bearing on the story, for the girl was astonishingly beautiful. Her hair was the rich dark red of antique burnished copper, her eyes were the hue of the reddish-golden amber that traders bring from the East. When she walked, you would say she was dancing. But when she danced, a gate seemed to open in the world, and bright fire spangled inside it, but she was the fire.

The girl and her mother were close as gloves in a box. Their games in the old tower bound them closer. No doubt the woman believed herself clever to have got such a helpmate, but it proved her undoing.

It was in this manner. The silk merchant, who had never suspected his wife for an instant of anything, began to mistrust the daughter. She was not like other girls. Despite her great beauty, she professed no interest in marriage and none in clothes or jewels. She preferred to read in the garden at the foot of the tower. Her mother had taught the girl her letters, though the merchant himself could read but poorly. And often the father peered at the books his daughter read, unable to make head or tail of them, yet somehow not liking them. One night very late, the silk merchant came home from a guild dinner in the city, and he saw a slim pale shadow gliding up the steps of the old tower, and he knew it for his child. On impulse, he followed her, but quietly. He had not considered any evil so far and did not want to alarm her. At an angle of the stair, the lighted room above, he paused to spy and listen. He had something of a shock when he heard his wife's voice rise up in glad welcome. But what came next drained the blood from his heart. He crept away and went to his cellar for wine to stay himself. After the third glass he ran for neighbors and for the watch.

The woman and her daughter heard the shouts below and saw the torches in the garden. It was no use dissembling. The tower was littered with evidence of vile deeds, besides what the woman kept in a chest beneath her unknowing husband's bed. She understood it was all up with her, and she understood, too, how witchcraft was punished hereabouts. She snatched a knife from the altar.

The girl shrieked when she realized what her mother was at. The woman caught the girl by her red hair and shook her.

"Listen to me, my daughter," she cried, "and listen carefully, for the minutes are short. If you do as I tell you, you can escape their wrath and only I need die. And if you live I am satisfied, for you can carry on my labor after me. My vengeance I shall leave you, and my witchcraft to exact it by. Indeed, I promise you stronger powers than mine. I will beg my lord Satanas for it, and he will not deny me, for he is just, in his fashion, and I have served him well. Now will you attend?"

"I will," said the girl.

So the woman advised her, and swore her to the fellowship of Hell. And then the woman forced the knife into her own heart and dropped dead on the floor of the tower.

When the men burst in with their swords and staves and their torches and their madness, the girl was ready for them.

She stood blank-faced, blank-eyed, with her arms hanging at her sides. When one touched her, she dropped down at his feet.

"Surely she is innocent," this man said. She was lovely enough that it was hard to accuse her. Then her father went to her and took her hand and lifted her. At that, the girl opened her eyes, and she said, as if terrified: "How did I come here? I was in my chamber and sleeping . . ."

"The woman has bewitched her," her father said.

He desired very much that this be so. And when the girl clung to his hand and wept, he was certain of it. They showed her the body with the knife in it. The girl screamed and seemed to lose her senses totally.

She was put to bed. In the morning, a priest came and questioned her. She answered steadfastly. She remembered nothing, not even of the great books she had been observed reading. When they told her what was in them, she screamed again and apparently would have thrown herself from the narrow window, only the priest stopped her.

Finally, they brought her the holy cross in order that she might kiss it and prove herself blameless.

Then she knelt, and whispered softly, that nobody should hear but one: "Lord Satanas, protect thy handmaid." And either that gentleman has more power than he is credited with or else the symbols of God are only as holy as the men who deal in them, for she embraced the cross and it left her unscathed.

At that, the whole household thanked God. The whole household saving, of course, the woman's daughter. She had another to thank.

The woman's body was burned and the ashes put into unconsecrated ground beyond the city gates. Though they had discovered her to be a witch, they had not discovered the direction her witchcraft had selected. Nor did they find the wax image with its limbs all twisted and stuck through with needles. The girl had taken that up and concealed it. The duke continued in his distress, but he did not die. Sometimes, in the dead of night, the girl would unearth the image from under a loose brick by the hearth and gloat over it, but she did nothing else. Not yet. She was fourteen, and the cloud of her mother's acts still hovered over her. She knew what she must do next.

The period of mourning ended.

"Daughter," said the silk merchant to her, "why do you not remove your black? The woman was malign and led you into wickedness. How long will you mourn her, who deserves no mourning?"

"Oh, my father," she said, "never think I regret my wretched mother. It is my own unwitting sin I mourn." And she grasped his hand and spilled her tears on it. "I would rather live in a convent," said she, "than mingle with proper folk. And I would seek a convent too, if it were not that I cannot bear to be parted from you."

Do you suppose she smiled secretly as she said this? One might suppose it. Presently she donned a robe of sackcloth and poured ashes over her red-copper hair. "It is my penance," she said. "I am glad to atone for my sins."

People forgot her beauty. She was at pains to obscure it. She slunk about like an aged woman, a rag pulled over her head, dirt smeared on her cheeks and brow. She elected to sleep in a cold cramped attic and sat all day by a smoky hearth in the kitchens. When someone came to her and begged her to wash her face and put on suitable clothes and sit in the rooms of the house, she smiled modestly, drawing the rag or a piece of hair over her face. "I swear," she said, "I am glad to be humble before God and men."

They reckoned her pious and they reckoned her simple. Two years passed. They mislaid her beauty altogether and reckoned her ugly. They found it hard to call to mind who she was exactly, as she sat in the ashes or shuffled unattended about the streets like a crone.

At the end of the second year, the silk merchant married again. It was inevitable, for he was not a man who liked to live alone.

On this occasion, his choice was a harmless widow. She already had two daughters, pretty in an unremarkable style. Perhaps the merchant hoped they would comfort him for what had gone before, this normal cheery wife and the two sweet, rather silly daughters, whose chief interests were clothes and weddings. Perhaps he hoped also that his deranged daughter might be drawn out by company. But that hope foundered. Not that the new mother did not try to be pleasant to the girl. And the new sisters, their hearts grieved by her condition, went to great lengths to enlist her friendship. They begged her to come from the kitchens or the attic. Failing in that, they sometimes ventured to join her, their fine silk dresses trailing on the greasy floor. They combed her hair, exclaiming, when some of the ash and dirt were removed, on its color. But no sooner had they turned away than the girl gathered up handfuls of soot and ash and rubbed them into her hair again. Now and then, the sisters attempted to interest their bizarre relative in a bracelet or a gown or a current song. They spoke to her of the young men they had seen at the suppers or the balls which were then given regularly by the rich families of the city. The girl ignored it all. If she ever said anything, it was to do with penance and humility. At last, as must happen, the sisters wearied of her and left her alone. They had no cares and did not want to share in hers. They came to resent her moping grayness, as indeed the merchant's second wife had already done.

"Can you do nothing with the girl?" she demanded of her husband. "People will say that I and my daughters are responsible for her condition and that I ill-treat the maid from jealousy of her dead mother."

"Now how could anyone say that," protested the merchant, "when you are famous as the epitome of generosity and kindness?"

Another year passed, and saw no huge difference in the household.

A difference there was, but not visible.

The girl who slouched in the corner of the hearth was seventeen. Under the filth and grime she was, impossibly, more beautiful, although no one could see it.

And there was one other invisible item: her power (which all this time she had nurtured, saying her prayers to Satanas in the black of midnight), her power was rising like a dark moon in her soul.

Three days after her seventeenth birthday, the girl straggled about the streets, as she frequently did. A few noted her and muttered it was the merchant's ugly simple daughter and paid no more attention. Most did not know her at all. She had made herself appear one with the scores of impoverished flotsam which constantly roamed the city, beggars and starvelings. Just outside the city gates, these persons congregated in large numbers, slumped around fires of burning refuse or else wandering to and fro in search of edible seeds, scraps, the miracle of a dropped coin. Here the girl now came, and began to wander about as they did. Dusk gathered and the shadows thickened. The girl sank to her knees in a patch of earth as if she had found something. Two or three of the beggars sneaked over to see if it were worth snatching from her—but the girl was only scrabbling in the empty soil. The beggars, making signs to each other that she was touched by God—mad— left her alone. But very far from mad, the girl presently dug up a stoppered clay urn. In this urn were the ashes and charred bones of her mother. She had got a clue as to the location of the urn by devious questioning here and there. Her occult power had helped her to be sure of it.

In the twilight, padding along through the narrow streets and alleys of the city, the girl brought the urn homeward. In the garden at the foot of the old tower, gloom-wrapped, unwitnessed, she unstoppered the urn and buried the ashes freshly. She muttered certain unholy magics over the grave. Then she snapped off the sprig of a young hazel tree and planted it in the newly turned ground.

I hazard you have begun to recognize the story by now. I see you suppose I tell it wrongly. Believe me, this is the truth of the matter. But if you would rather I left off the tale . . . No doubt your carriage will soon be here— No? Very well. I shall continue.

I think I should speak of the duke's son at this juncture. The prince was nineteen, able, intelligent, and of noble bearing. He was of that rather swarthy type of looks one finds here in the north, but tall and slim and clear-eyed. There is an ancient square where you may see a statue of him, but much eroded by two centuries and the elements. After the city was sacked, no care was lavished on it.

The duke treasured his son. He had constant delight in the sight of the young man and what he said and did. It was the only happiness the invalid had.

Then, one night, the duke screamed out in his bed. Servants came running with candles. The duke moaned that a sword was transfixing his heart, an inch at a time. The prince hurried into the chamber, but in that instant the duke spasmed horribly and died. No mark was on his body. There had never been a mark to show what ailed him.

The prince wept. They were genuine tears. He had nothing to reproach his father with, everything to thank him for. Presently, they brought the young man the seal ring of the city, and he put it on.

It was winter, a cold blue-white weather with snow in the streets and countryside and a hard wizened sun that drove thin sharp blades of light through the sky but gave no warmth. The duke's funeral cortege passed slowly across the snow: the broad open chariots, draped with black and silver; the black-plumed horses; the chanting priests with their glittering robes, their jeweled crucifixes and golden censers. Crowds lined the roadways to watch the spectacle. Among the beggar women stood a girl. No one noticed her. They did not glimpse the expression she veiled in her ragged scarf. She gazed at the bier pitilessly. As the young prince rode by in his sables, the seal ring on his hand, the eyes of the girl burned through her ashy hair, like a red fox through grasses.

The duke was buried in the mausoleum you can visit to this day, on the east side of the city. Several months elapsed. The prince put his grief from him and took up the business of the city competently. Wise and courteous he was, but he rarely smiled. At nineteen, his spirit seemed worn. You might think he guessed the destiny that hung over him.

The winter was a hard one too. The snow had come and, having come, was loath to withdraw. When at last the spring returned, flushing the hills with color, it was no longer sensible to be sad.

The prince's name day fell about this time. A great banquet was planned, a ball. There had been neither in the palace for nigh on three years, not since the duke's fatal illness first claimed him. Now the royal doors were to be thrown open to all men of influence and their families. The prince was liberal, charming, and clever even in this. Aristocrat and rich trader were to mingle in the beautiful dining room, and in this very chamber, among the frescoes, the marble, and the candelabra. Even a merchant's daughter, if the merchant was notable in the city, would get to dance on the sea-green floor, under the white eye of the fearful clock.

The clock. There was some renewed controversy about the clock. They did not dare speak to the young prince. He was a skeptic, as his father had been. But had not a death already occurred? Was the clock not a flying in the jaws of fate? For those disturbed by it, there was a dim writing in their minds, in the dust of the street or the pattern of blossoms. *When the clock strikes*— But people do not positively heed these warnings. Man is afraid of his fears. He ignores the shadow of the wolf thrown on the paving before him, saying: It is only a shadow.

The silk merchant received his invitation to the palace, and to be sure, thought nothing of the clock. His house had been thrown into uproar. The most luscious silks of his workshop were carried into the house and laid before the wife and her two daughters, who chirruped and squealed with excitement. The merchant stood smugly by, above it all yet pleased at being appreciated. "Oh, Father," cried the two sisters, "may I have this one with the gold piping?" "Oh, Father, this one with the design of pineapples?" Later a jeweler arrived and set out his trays. The merchant was generous. He wanted his women to look their best. It might be the night of their lives. Yet all the while, at the back of his mind, a little dark spot, itching, aching. He tried to ignore the spot, not scratch at it. His true daughter, the mad one. Nobody bothered to tell her about the invitation to the palace. They knew how she would react, mumbling in her hair about her sin and her penance, paddling her hands in the greasy ash to smear her face. Even the servants avoided her, as if she were just the cat seated by the fire. Less than the cat, for the cat saw to the mice—just a block of stone. And yet, how fair she might have looked, decked in the pick of the merchant's wares, jewels at her throat. The prince himself could not have been unaware of her. And though marriage was impossible, other, less holy though equally honorable, contracts might have been arranged, to the benefit of all concerned. The merchant sighed. He had scratched the darkness after all. He attempted to comfort himself by watching the two sisters exult over their apparel. He refused to admit that the finery would somehow make them seem but more ordinary than they were by contrast.

The evening of the banquet arrived. The family set off. Most of the servants sidled after. The prince had distributed largess in the city; oxen roasted in the squares, and the wine was free by royal order.

The house grew somber. In the deserted kitchen, the fire went out.

By the hearth, a segment of gloom rose up.

The girl glanced around her, and she laughed softly and shook out her filthy hair. Of course, she knew as much as anyone, and more than most. This was to be her night too.

A few minutes later she was in the garden beneath the old tower, standing over the young hazel tree which thrust up from the earth. It had become strong, the tree, despite the harsh winter. Now the girl nodded to it. She chanted under her breath. At length a pale light began to glow, far down near where the roots of the tree held to the ground. Out of the pale glow flew a thin black bird, which perched on the girl's shoulder. Together, the girl and the bird passed into the old tower. High up, a fire blazed that no one had lit. A tub steamed with scented water that no one had drawn. Shapes that were not real and barely seen flitted about. Rare perfumes, the rustle of garments, the glint of gems as yet invisible, filled and did not fill the restless air.

Need I describe further? No. You will have seen paintings which depict the attendance upon a witch of her familiar demons. How one bathes her, another anoints her, another brings clothes and ornaments. Perhaps you do not credit such things in any case. Never mind that. I will tell you what happened in the courtyard before the palace.

Many carriages and chariots had driven through the square, avoiding the roasting oxen, the barrels of wine, the cheering drunken citizens, and so through the gates into the courtyard. Just before ten o'clock (the hour, if you recall the clock, of the magician), a solitary carriage drove through the square and into the court. The people in the square gawped at the carriage and pressed forward to see who would step out of it, this latecomer. It was a remarkable vehicle that looked to be fashioned of solid gold, all but the domed roof, that was transparent flashing crystal. Six black horses drew it. The coachman and postilions were clad in crimson, and strangely masked as curious beasts and reptiles. One of these beast-men now hopped down and opened the door of the carriage. Out came a woman's figure in a cloak of white fur, and glided up the palace stair and in at the doors.

There was dancing in the ballroom. The whole chamber was bright and clamorous with music and the voices of men and women. There, between those two pillars, the prince sat in his chair, dark, courteous, seldom smiling. Here the musicians played, the deep-throated viol, the lively mandolin. And there the dancers moved up and down on the sea-green floor. But the music and the dancers had just paused. The figures on the clock were themselves in motion. The hour of the magician was about to strike.

As it struck, through the doorway came the figure in the fur cloak. And as if they must, every eye turned to her.

For an instant she stood there, all white, as though she had brought the winter snow back with her. And then she loosed the cloak from her shoulders, it slipped away, and she was all fire.

She wore a gown of apricot brocade embroidered thickly with gold. Her sleeves and the bodice of her gown were slashed over ivory satin sewn with large rosy pearls. Pearls, too, were wound in her hair, that was the shade of antique burnished copper. She was so beautiful that when the clock was still, nobody spoke. She was so beautiful it was hard to look at her for very long.

The prince got up from his chair. He did not know he had. Now he started out across the floor, between the dancers, who parted silently to let him through. He went toward the girl in the doorway as if she drew him by a chain.

The prince had hardly ever acted without considering first what he did. Now he did not consider. He bowed to the girl.

"Madam," he said. "You are welcome. Madam," he said. "Tell me who you are."

She smiled.

"My rank," she said. "Would you know that, my lord? It is similar to yours, or would be were I now mistress in my dead mother's palace. But, unfortunately, an unscrupulous man caused the downfall of our house."

"Misfortune indeed," said the prince. "Tell me your name. Let me right the wrong done you."

"You shall," said the girl. "Trust me, you shall. For my name, I would rather keep it secret for the present. But you may call me, if you will, a pet name I have given myself—Ashella."

"Ashella . . . But I see no ash about you," said the prince, dazzled by her gleam, laughing a little, stiffly, for laughter was not his habit.

"Ash and cinders from a cold and bitter hearth," said she. But she smiled again. "Now everyone is staring at us, my lord, and the musicians are impatient to begin again. Out of all these ladies, can it be you will lead me in the dance?"

"As long as you will dance," he said. "You shall dance with me."

And that is how it was.

There were many dances, slow and fast, whirling measures and gentle ones. And here and there, the prince and the maiden were parted. Always

then he looked eagerly after her, sparing no regard for the other girls whose
hands lay in his. It was not like him, he was usually so careful. But the other
young men who danced on that floor, who clasped her fingers or her narrow
waist in the dance, also gazed after her when she was gone. She danced, as
she appeared, like fire. Though if you had asked those young men whether
they would rather tie her to themselves, as the prince did, they would have
been at a loss. For it is not easy to keep pace with fire.

The hour of the hag struck on the clock.

The prince grew weary of dancing with the girl and losing her in the
dance to others and refinding her and losing her again.

Behind the curtains there is a tall window in the east wall that opens
on the terrace above the garden. He drew her out there, into the spring night.
He gave an order, and small tables were brought with delicacies and sweets
and wine. He sat by her, watching every gesture she made, as if he would
paint her portrait afterward.

In the ballroom, here, under the clock, the people murmured. But it
was not quite the murmur you would expect, the scandalous murmur about
a woman come from nowhere that the prince had made so much of. At the
periphery of the ballroom, the silk merchant sat, pale as a ghost, thinking of
a ghost, the living ghost of his true daughter. No one else recognized her.
Only he. Some trick of the heart had enabled him to know her. He said
nothing of it. As the stepsisters and wife gossiped with other wives and sisters,
an awful foreboding weighed him down, sent him cold and dumb.

And now it is almost midnight, the moment when the page of the night
turns over into day. Almost midnight, the hour when the figure of Death
strikes the golden bell of the clock. And what will happen when the clock
strikes? Your face announces that you know. Be patient; let us see if you do.

"I am being foolish," said the prince to Ashella on the terrace. "But perhaps
I am entitled to be foolish, just once in my life. What are you saying?" For
the girl was speaking low beside him, and he could not catch her words.

"I am saying a spell to bind you to me," she said.

"But I am already bound."

"Be bound, then. Never go free."

"I do not wish it," he said. He kissed her hands, and he said, "I do not
know you, but I will wed you. Is that proof your spell has worked? I will wed
you, and get back for you the rights you have lost."

"If it were only so simple," said Ashella, smiling, smiling. "But the debt
is too cruel. Justice requires a harsher payment."

And then, in the ballroom, Death struck the first note on the golden
bell.

The girl smiled and she said:
"I curse you in my mother's name."
The second stroke.
"I curse you in my own name."
The third stroke.
"And in the name of those that your father slew."
The fourth stroke.
"And in the name of my Master, who rules the world."

As the fifth, the sixth, the seventh strokes pealed out, the prince stood nonplussed. At the eighth and the ninth strokes, the strength of the malediction seemed to curdle his blood. He shivered and his brain writhed. At the tenth stroke, he saw a change in the loveliness before him. She grew thinner, taller. At the eleventh stroke, he beheld a thing in a ragged black cowl and robe. It grinned at him. It was all grin below a triangle of sockets of nose and eyes. At the twelfth stroke, the prince saw Death and knew him.

In the ballroom, a hideous grinding noise, as the gears of the clock failed. Followed by a hollow booming, as the mechanism stopped entirely.

The conjuration of Death vanished from the terrace.

Only one thing was left behind. A woman's shoe. A shoe no woman could ever have danced in. It was made of glass.

Did you intend to protest about the shoe? Shall I finish the story, or would you rather I did not? It is not the ending you are familiar with. Yes, I perceive you understand that now.

I will go quickly, then, for your carriage must soon be here. And there is not a great deal more to relate.

The prince lost his mind. Partly from what he had seen, partly from the spells the young witch had netted him in. He could think of nothing but the girl who had named herself Ashella. He raved that Death had borne her away but he would recover her from Death. She had left the glass shoe as token of her love. He must discover her with the aid of the shoe. Whomsoever the shoe fitted would be Ashella. For there was this added complication, that Death might hide her actual appearance. None had seen the girl before. She had disappeared like smoke. The one infallible test was the shoe. That was why she had left it for him.

His ministers would have reasoned with the prince, but he was past reason. His intellect had collapsed as totally as only a profound intellect can. A lunatic, he rode about the city. He struck out at those who argued with him. On a particular occasion, drawing a dagger, he killed, not apparently noticing what he did. His demand was explicit. Every woman, young or old, maid or married, must come forth from her home, must put her foot into the shoe of glass. They came. They had not choice. Some approached in terror, some weeping. Even the aged beggar women obliged, and they cackled, enjoying the sight of royalty gone mad. One alone did not come.

Now it is not illogical that out of the hundreds of women whose feet were put into the shoe, a single woman might have been found that the shoe fitted. But this did not happen. Nor did the situation alter, despite a lurid fable that some, tickled by the idea of wedding the prince, cut off their toes that the shoe might fit them. And if they did, it was to no avail, for still the shoe did not.

Is it really surprising? The shoe was sorcerous. It constantly changed itself, its shape, its size, in order that no foot, save one, could ever be got into it.

Summer spread across the land. The city took on its golden summer glaze, its fetid summer smell.

What had been a whisper of intrigue swelled into a steady distant thunder. Plots were being hatched.

One day the silk merchant was brought, trembling and gray of face, to the prince. The merchant's dumbness had broken. He had unburdened himself of his fear at confession, but the priest had not proved honest. In the dawn, men had knocked on the door of the merchant's house. Now he stumbled to the chair of the prince.

Both looked twice their years, but if anything, the prince looked the elder. He did not lift his eyes. Over and over in his hands he turned the glass shoe.

The merchant, stumbling, too, in his speech, told the tale of his first wife and his daughter. He told everything, leaving out no detail. He did not even omit the end: that since the night of the banquet the girl had been absent from his house, taking nothing with her—save a young hazel from the garden beneath the tower.

The prince leapt from his chair.

His clothes were filthy and unkempt. His face was smeared with sweat and dust . . . it resembled, momentarily, another face.

Without guard or attendant, the prince ran through the city toward the merchant's house, and on the road, the intriguers waylaid and slew him. As he fell, the glass shoe dropped from his hands and shattered in a thousand fragments.

There is little else worth mentioning.

Those who usurped the city were villains and not merely that but fools. Within a year, external enemies were at the gates. A year more, and the city had been sacked, half burned out, ruined. The manner in which you find it now is somewhat better than it was then. And it is not now anything for a man to be proud of. As you were quick to note, many here earn a miserable existence by conducting visitors about the streets, the palace, showing them the dregs of the city's past.

Which was not a request, in fact, for you to give me money. Throw some from your carriage window if your conscience bothers you. My own wants are few.

No, I have no further news of the girl Ashella, the witch. A devotee of Satanas, she has doubtless worked plentiful woe in the world. And a witch is long-lived. Even so, she will die eventually. None escapes Death. Then you may pity her, if you like. Those who serve the gentleman below—who can guess what their final lot will be? But I am very sorry the story did not please you. It is not, maybe, a happy choice before a journey.

And there is your carriage at last.

What? Ah, no, I shall stay here in the ballroom, where you came on me. I have often paused here through the years. It is the clock. It has a certain—what shall I call it?—power to draw me back.

I am not trying to unnerve you. Why should you suppose that? Because of my knowledge of the city, of the story? You think that I am implying that I myself am Death? Now you laugh. Yes, it is absurd. Observe the twelfth figure on the clock. Is he not as you have always heard Death described? And am I in the least like that twelfth figure?

Although, of course, the story was not as you have heard it, either.

Pichounetta and the Sergeant of Arles

MICHAEL DE LARRABEITI

nce upon a time a dark forest covered the mountain slopes that rise steeply along each side of the river Durance, and in a gloomy clearing in that forest lived a woodcutter and his younger sister, and her name was Pichounetta.

Both brother and sister were artless and untutored in the ways of the world, never having lived in it, but in their own simplicity they loved each other dearly and were content to live out their lives in solitude, doing no one any harm. They never married or even felt the call to do so; indeed, only rarely did they descend to the banks of the Durance, to sell their wood and buy the things they could neither make nor grow. Those people who lived in the hamlets and farms of the region likewise never entered the dark recesses of the forest where the brother and sister lived, and were, to tell the truth, too frightened to do so. They purchased wood from the pair each winter, stacked it in the dry, and minded their own business.

Such a way of life was by its very nature uneventful, and in that remote and uncivilized part of Provence only death disrupted the even course of the years, and so it happened that the woodcutter died suddenly and much before his time. This cruel tragedy left Pichounetta in a state of dismay verging on madness. Without warning or preparation she had lost her only companion, the only person on earth who loved her. She was completely distraught and at first ran here and there like a wild thing. She had not seen the death of a human being before. She could not remember the death of her parents; she did not even remember having any. Always there had been her brother, strong and kind—now there was nothing. Pichounetta's grief was acute, but gradually she came to her senses and her simple mind saw that something needed to be done, but what, she did not know.

Lower down the mountain on which Pichounetta lived, there was a ruined farmhouse, built into the hillside and inhabited only by an old woman, the last survivor of her family. Often, at the beginning of winter, the wood-cutter had left kindling for the old woman, and she, in return, had made cheeses for Pichounetta. It was toward this farmhouse that the girl eventually bent her steps. The woman was old and wise, she thought; she had seen death many times and would surely know what to do.

When the old woman had heard Pichounetta's tale she sucked on her toothless gums and smacked her lips of gristle together. She bade the girl sit by the fire and pulled her shawl about her shoulders. Pichounetta trembled in spite of the warmth. The old woman looked like a witch; her hair was gray with wood smoke and her skin was soft and creased like ancient leather. Her nose was a hook, and one eye was blind.

"Sit down, Pichoune," said the old woman. "There is nothing to fear. I know I am not good to look upon, but then beauty is not always wise, nor is it always kind."

Pichounetta did not answer but stared at the smoke rising from the grate. She was used only to the company of her brother, and the telling of her story had exhausted her.

"Here is what you must do," said the old woman, "and it is what the poor of Provence have always done. You must return to your cabin and you must wash your brother's body so that it is clean. You will then dress him in his finest clothes, however tattered they may be. Then you must take his saw and his hammer and you must make a coffin, a box to bury him in. Can you do this, Pichoune?"

The girl raised her head from her contemplation of the fire and spoke proudly. "My brother and I made everything we needed," she said. "I watched and helped him all the time. Of course I can make this box, and I shall make it well."

"Listen, then," continued the old woman. "You will lay your brother in the coffin and under his head you will place a soft cushion, if you have one; if not, a folded sheepskin will do, or an old coat. Once your brother is resting in his box, you will take resin from the trees and make the lid watertight, and you will nail it down so that not the slightest drop of water may enter."

"Water," said Pichounetta.

The old woman held up her hand for silence. "You must take at least four copper coins, or two of silver. Wrap them in a purse, and the purse you must nail firmly to the lid of the coffin. Next you will take your sled, the one that you use for dragging firewood down to the farms, and you will place the coffin upon it. Then you must pull your brother through the forest and across the stony fields until you reach the very banks of the great river. Can you do this and are you strong enough?"

"All my life I have worked with ax and spade," said Pichounetta, "and never have I failed."

"Good," said the old woman, "for you will need all your strength. And when you reach the river you must take the coffin from the sled, and you will float it out into the middle of the current, and there you will pray, if you can, and say farewell to your brother forever, for the water will bear him away to the holiest of resting places, the Aliscamps in the city of Arles."

"City," said the girl. "And what is that?"

The old woman laughed at the girl's ignorance. "Arles is a city," she said, "and a city is full of houses, hundreds, all close together in narrow streets. Arles has turrets and castles, palaces and churches with high walls all around. There are huge caves under the ground for keeping wheat, and there is a stone bridge too, the bridge of Trinquetaille. I went there once when I was a girl, and the sight of it still shines in my good eye. And there, in Arles, is the Aliscamps, the largest burial ground in the world. Every Christian in Provence desires to be buried there, for if they are they will go directly to paradise, and, Pichoune, if you wish for your brother to escape eternal torment, he who never went to mass or prayed in his life, then to the Aliscamps he must go."

The old woman did not lie in anything she had said. Since time without counting, the Aliscamps at Arles had been considered the holiest ground in the world. Legend said that the colonists from Massilia had always honored the dead there and that the word "Aliscamps" was but the Roman way of saying "The Fields of Elysium," which was the name the Greeks gave to paradise.

Whether this legend was true or not, it was certain that from the earliest years of the Christian era the rich and powerful of Provence had seen to it that they were laid to rest in that holy precinct, entombed in massively carved sarcophagi which had been arranged to form wide and delightful avenues, those avenues made shady by tall plane trees and fragrant by the sweet-smelling eucalyptus.

As the centuries passed more and more sarcophagi were carried to Arles, and the graveyard began to spread over several miles in all directions. Before long, both for convenience and to save space, the tombs were raised up, one above another, to a height of five or six at least, and the Aliscamps became a veritable city of the dead, a necropolis with hundreds of its own streets and a score of its own churches.

The legends multiplied also and were told from generation to generation: Saint Trophime, the first bishop of Provence, was buried there; Roland and

Oliver too, the knights of Charlemagne, had been borne to Arles on their shields, all the way from their last battle at Roncevalles. Small wonder was it then that the dead arrived at the Aliscamps from everywhere in Provence, for to be entombed in such illustrious company was to ensure your eternal rest, whatever your previous sins might have been.

For those with the means to extend their will beyond the grave, the last voyage to the Aliscamps presented no problem. Richly caparisoned barges would float both corpse and sarcophagus down the wide waters of the Rhône, and somberly dressed mourners would accompany the deceased to his or her last resting place, while on the banks of the river the laboring peasants would cross themselves and watch in wonder.

But it was not only the rich who were desirous of gaining paradise. The poor, too, wished for that ultimate reward. Unfortunately for them, they were not possessed of that golden power that forces others to perform our wishes even when we are no longer present. Yet in spite of this disadvantage, they managed to satisfy the yearning of their souls and discovered a way out of their difficulty, compelled by their very poverty to become ingenious. All those who lived within a day or two's march of the river Rhône, or any of its tributaries, were, after their deaths, placed by their relatives in water-tight coffins and launched upon the swiftly flowing waters and given into God's care.

It was not only God, of course, who looked after these wandering souls. Anyone who found a coffin caught up in branches or reeds, say, or stranded on a rock, was bound, by both his duty and religion, to free it and relaunch it into the current. Nailed to the lid of every coffin there was always a purse, and heaven help the wretch who stole the few coins that had been placed within it. The devil, the common people said, would drag him straight to hell, for those coins were to recompense the good people of Arles for the labor of taking coffins from the Rhône and carrying them, on their carts or on their backs, across the city to a decent burial in the unfashionable, but still holy, areas of the Aliscamps. It was this tradition, already ancient at the time of this story, that prompted the old woman to advise Pichounetta in the way she had. In her wisdom she knew it would comfort the girl if she thought that her brother's soul was going to sleep forever in the Elysian Fields.

"Do you have enough money," asked the old woman at the end of her explanation, "enough money to pay the fee of Aliscamps so that whoever takes your brother's coffin from the river at Arles will treat it with respect?"

Pichounetta rose from the fireside. "I have enough money," she said, "and more than enough. My brother was a careful man, and over the years we sold much wood. I will send the coins with him to see that he is well buried." The girl paused, and her face creased with worry. "How do I know that the coffin will end its journey at Arles?" she asked. "It may go on and drift until eternity, or fall into hell."

The old woman laid a hand on the girl's arm. "Do not think of it, Pichoune," she said. "At Arles the great river bends wide around the city, and there is the bridge at Trinquetaille, and ropes are tied from one pillar to the next, above the water, to catch the coffins. You may depend upon it that the people of Arles are always on watch, for they have much to gain from their vigilance."

With this explanation Pichounetta was content, and leaving the old woman with a word of thanks, she took the dark, steep path through the forest and returned to the cabin where her brother's body lay. Wasting no time, she set about making a sturdy coffin, choosing good straight planks from a stock of seasoned timber that her brother had always kept in store, both for his own use and for selling in the valleys.

When the box was finished, she washed the body and dressed it with care, placing it, as gently as she could, into the coffin, a pillow beneath its head. Then she took the lid, and painting the edges with resin, she nailed it firmly into position. This accomplished, she dragged the heavy burden outside and inched it onto the wooden sled that waited there, and without taking time to rest or eat, she slipped the leather traces over her head and shoulders and began the long journey through the forest and down the mountain.

Pichounetta was a sturdy young woman, and her muscles had been formed and tested by years of hard work. Her determination, too, was strong and she made such good speed that within four or five hours she came to the banks of the great Durance. There the peasants in the field stood to watch while Pichounetta pulled the sled across the white and rounded stones of the river's shore and with one final effort pushed the coffin into the water.

As soon as the current of the Durance felt the coffin, it seized it and bore it away with an easy violence. In a moment the rough box was speeding over the white foam, and before Pichounetta had time to say a prayer, or even wish her brother well, the coffin had disappeared around the nearest bend. It was in God's hands now.

With tears in her eyes, Pichounetta turned and began to make her way back to the lonely cabin on the mountainside. The peasants still stood unmoving and watched until the young woman, and the empty sled, disappeared in the distance, passing eventually between the trees and into the wild darkness of the forest. When the peasants were sure that she had gone for good, they crossed themselves and bent again to their endless tasks.

Pichounetta took up the threads of her life immediately and as best she could. There was no great difficulty for her in accomplishing her daily work, for she had always been capable of doing anything that her brother had done.

Her hands were broad and strong, her mind direct and uncluttered. She could wield an ax, slaughter a goat, and plant and grow vegetables. She had chickens and a few sheep; she had all she needed except company and love.

It was this loneliness that preyed on her, and from the very first day she began to talk to her brother as if he were still alive. Soon she became convinced that he was entering her conversation, aiding her to survive the solitude. By the end of the second week of her bereavement, his presence had become real to Pichounetta. She could see his face and thought she could touch his hand. He smiled; he seemed happy and content, and this fact served to ease the pain in the girl's heart. Each night he came to her, and standing at the foot of the bed, he recounted his progress on the long journey to Arles.

All along the Durance he had gone, he said, and then out onto the waters of the Rhône, and even though his coffin had been stranded on the banks from time to time, always had there been some good person to free him and set him on his way. What was more, never had anyone tampered with the money in the purse which his sister had nailed to the coffin lid. Before long he would be at Arles, and someone would take him from the river and bury him in the Aliscamps. There he would find the gates of paradise and, beyond them, eternal peace.

Pichounetta was, in her ignorance, borne up by the visits of this apparition and the tales it told. To her it was a good thing, and she did not bother to ask herself whether or not the specter was a dangerous temptation or simply the product of her own imagination. In any event, such sophistication was far beyond the grasp of her mind and not something she could have thought of on her own. So it was that when one night the ghost appeared in grief, wringing its hands and silently weeping, not for one moment did Pichounetta question the truth of what she heard.

"Oh, save me, Pichoune," said the ghost. "I have been sorely betrayed. He who found me on the river at Arles was an evil man. He came upon me in the middle of the night, and making sure that no one saw him at his dreadful work, he stole the money from the purse and then pushed my coffin through the arches of the bridge. And now the current of the Rhône has brought me down to rot in the Camargue and never shall I reach the Aliscamps, but rather will I have a watery grave until the last day of time."

Pichounetta sat upright in her bed and stared. Never, in life, had she seen her brother so distressed. "Oh, mercy," she wailed, "what can I do? I have never left this forest. I know nothing. How could I help you?"

"I have been robbed of my blessed rest and the glory of the Aliscamps," said the apparition. "I will not lie easy until you have revenged me. You must denounce this man. His sin is great, and he deserves to die and his soul made to wander like mine. I must have revenge!" And with a low moaning sound and more wringing of the hands, the brother disappeared.

At the very first light of day, Pichounetta leapt from her bed, dressed hastily, and went, as quickly as she could, to the ruined farm where the wise old woman lived. There was no one else to whom the girl could turn for advice; certainly her own experience would not be enough to counsel her.

The old woman listened to Pichounetta's story in silence, but as soon as it was concluded she worked her lips over her gums and began to speak.

"It is probably true," said the old woman, "that your brother has been robbed of his deserved rest, and if that is so, the villain who committed the crime should be punished in this world as well as in the next—but who is there to accomplish this task? I am too old and lack the strength. You are too innocent and lack the knowledge. The world is a wicked place, Pichoune, and full of wicked men. It is a great distance from here to Arles, and I fear that you would have your throat cut before you got there. I counsel you to live with the sorrow of these tidings, Pichoune, for there is nothing to be done but endure all things until the day of your own death."

Very slowly, and with her head bowed, Pichounetta left the old woman's house and returned to her cabin, more than determined to follow the advice that had been given her; but the ghost was equally determined and would not let her rest. Later that same night, it reappeared and made such lamentations that the poor Pichounetta was driven frantic with guilt and fear.

"Spare me, brother," she cried at last. "How can I go so far, I who have never left the forest? How would I travel?"

At this question the ghost ceased its wailings and laid its head on one side, smiling. "Why, sister," it said, "you will travel as I traveled; what could be more simple? You will make yourself a coffin like the one you made for me, only this time with a lid that you may hold in place from the inside. Lay your box on the waters of the Durance and let it float until you reach a stone bridge. That is the city of Arles."

"My brother," said the girl, "I am too simple for this task, and what would I do at Arles?"

"When you are at the bridge," answered the ghost, "you will go onto the land. You will place a few stones in the coffin to give it weight, and you will hide and watch. In the night I will send you the robber, and you will see him steal the purse. As soon as it is safe, you will go to the town and make all this known to those in authority. That very day they will seize the villain and send men to search for my body in the marshes so they may bring it to the Aliscamps. Then shall I be satisfied, then will I find rest."

The moment she had heard all this, Pichounetta scrambled to her knees on the bed and held out her hands to the shape that stood before her. "Brother," she said, "if all this is to happen as you say, then I am no longer afraid. Ignorant though I am, I will do anything to see you at rest in the Aliscamps."

"You are truly my sister," answered the ghost, and it smiled again, more mysteriously this time, nodding too, as if well pleased. A moment later it had disappeared, and Pichounetta sat on the edge of her bed and wondered and wondered until it was dawn.

As soon as that dawn came and the first rays of sunlight spilled over the mountaintops, Pichounetta broke from her reverie and began her work. She took out her brother's tools, selected the best planks that remained to her, and by the end of the morning she had finished a coffin that was much better constructed even than the previous one had been. Inside it was room for a pillow and a blanket and enough provisions to keep the girl alive for a week or two.

When all was ready, Pichounetta took the pouch that contained her brother's fortune, dressed herself in her warmest clothes, and loaded her coffin onto the sled. Then, with never a backward look at the only home she had ever known, she drew the traces round her shoulders and once more set out in the direction of the Durance. Once arrived at the river, Pichounetta dragged the coffin into the shallows and got inside it, lying down and sliding the lid across until it slotted neatly into the deep grooves she had made, blotting out all sight of the bright blue sky. The peasants, still laboring in the nearby fields, shook their heads, knelt and prayed, and then went back to their work, convinced they had seen a miracle.

Pichounetta's craft immediately bobbed into the middle of the current and from there was carried forward at speed. Once or twice in the days that followed the coffin ran up against a sunken tree or a shifting sandbank, but nearly always there was a Christian soul to come by and push the coffin back into the main stream again. And if there wasn't, Pichounetta would wait until nightfall and free herself of whatever entanglement had impeded her progress. Also at night, when she felt secure, Pichounetta would push the lid back from her face and watch the stars rushing by overhead and listen to the surge of the waters beneath her. She had no idea where she was at any given time or in which direction she was going. All she knew was that there would be a bridge at Arles and there she would stop and creep to the riverbank to watch for the villain who had betrayed his trust.

Pichounetta's journey was far briefer than her brother's had been. Much rain had fallen in the mountains, and the waters of the Rhône were flowing fast and high. And so one night when the moon was on the wane, Pichounetta, who had been lulled into a long sleep by the noise and movement of the currents, was woken by the shock of her coffin striking a massive stone pillar. She had arrived at the bridge of Trinquetaille.

Round in a large eddy spun the coffin, scraping along the ropes that had been tied from arch to arch and gradually nudging its way to the riverside, where at last it grated to a halt on the gravel of the wide shore, for here the

Rhône swung in a bend at the wall of the city and formed part of its defenses.

As soon as she heard the noise of the gravel, Pichounetta remembered her instructions, and first making sure that it was indeed the middle of the night, she lifted the cover of her coffin and slipped into the open. Quickly she found three large stones and put them in her place. That done, she took hold of the heavy lid and set it firmly back in its grooves, afterward creeping away, unseen, into the bushes that grew thickly at that point, right down to the water's edge. There she crouched and hid herself—for that was what the ghost had told her to do.

She did not have long to wait. As the first finger of light touched the farthest corner of the eastern hemisphere, Pichounetta heard footsteps on the sloping strand above her. Turning her head, but not rising to her feet, she saw, against the skyline, a small hovel, and from it had emerged the shape of a man. He had seen the coffin and was making his way, as silently as he could, down a narrow, winding path.

The man advanced and passed within a yard or two of where Pichounetta was concealed. Without hesitation he strode into the water, caught hold of the coffin with one hand, and took the money from the purse with the other. Without bothering to count the coins, he thrust them into his jerkin and then waded farther into the river, pulling what he thought to be a corpse behind him.

"By the devil," Pichounetta heard the man swear, "this is a mighty carcass by the weight of it. Best send it down to the marshes to rot." And as he spoke, the man eased the coffin under the restraining ropes and pushed it through the nearest archway of the bridge. There it was taken by the current and soon disappeared into the middle of the Rhône, well on its way to the empty wildernesses of the Camargue.

Pichounetta remained crouched amid the undergrowth, holding her breath in fear. The daylight was growing stronger now, and the robber was anxious to get himself out of sight. Looking this way and that, to make certain he had not been observed in his evil work, he went ashore and scrambled back up the path to the top of the bank, where he immediately disappeared into his cabin.

As soon as she dared, Pichounetta crept from her hiding place and climbed noiselessly past the robber's hut and onto the short stretch of road that joined the bridge of Trinquetaille to the city of Arles. Never had the girl seen such a sight—a broad and paved highway leading to massive iron-bound gates which were themselves set in a towering wall of stone that bristled with battlements. So that was a city!

Pichounetta shivered in the early morning chill, but in spite of her fears she went forward bravely and in a very few minutes came to the eastern gate of the town just as it was opened for the day. Slowly the two huge portals swung back on their enormous hinges, and there, under the high arch, stood two men of the watch, leaning on their pikes. By their side, and in command of them, was the magnificent figure of the sergeant of the gates of Arles.

Pichounetta faltered and then came to a halt. She did not know what to do; the two guards looked so fierce to her eyes, the sergeant so splendid. He wore a gilded helmet on his head, decorated with a fine red plume. His breastplate was burnished and his black cloak was lined with a brilliant satin of crimson. The naked sword he held in his hand shimmered in the low sun of early morning. His eyes glinted with the hardness of rock and his fine mustache curled upward with arrogance. When this officer saw Pichounetta revealed by the opening of the gates, he turned to his two companions and smirked. Those same gates had shown him many a strange sight on many a morning, but never had he seen anything so unkempt.

The sergeant of the gate smirked again and strutted forward, his plume nodding as he walked. Pichounetta fell back a step, but remembering her brother's commands, she did not run away although she wanted to. A yard from the girl, the sergeant came to a stop and looked down at her. He smiled a smile of irony, a smile that was as near to pity as he ever got—a pity that other creatures were not as beautiful as he. "Damnation," he whispered to himself. "She looks like a beast of burden, all misshapen by toil and burned black by the sun and the wind."

It was true, of course. Pichounetta was ugly, and she had no idea how she looked to people from the great world. Like an animal of the forest in which up until then she had spent all her days, she knew only that she was alive. Her body and its appearance was not something she was conscious of. Now suddenly, on seeing this splendid sergeant, the poor peasant girl came to know that she was just as savage and uncouth as the officer thought she was.

What the sergeant saw was not a human being at all, in his terms, but a barbarian. Pichounetta was clothed in rags which a beggar would disdain. Her face was flat, like a gypsy's, and deeply lined. Her black hair had never been brushed or washed and fell in greasy ropes to her shoulders. Those shoulders were square and strong but bent like an old woman's from years of toil. Her thighs and calves were thick and muscled from dragging heavy loads through the forest, and the knuckles of her fingers were swollen from knocks and cuts. To the sergeant she was beyond redemption and below consideration, and by this judgment was her fate decided.

"And what do you want here?" asked the sergeant, and the sun shone from the center of his breastplate and dazzled Pichounetta until she could not see. She dropped her gaze and stared at the dust between her feet.

"My brother's corpse has been robbed of the fee of Aliscamps," she mumbled, "and his soul has been left to wander across the Camargue. His ghost came to me and told me what to do . . . and so I, too, floated here in a coffin, more miles than I can tell, until I reached this bridge, and with my own eyes I have seen the robber." Pichounetta half turned and pointed. "He lives in that cabin by the bank there, under the great bridge almost. My brother's spirit cries for revenge and proper burial. He bade me come to you because you are a great man of the law and will know what to do. You can help me find my brother and take him to the Aliscamps . . . is that not so?"

The sergeant took one more step forward and placed his hand on Pichounetta's elbow and guided her a little farther from the city gate, out of earshot of the two guards, who still leaned on their pikes and idly watched the scene before them. Pichounetta's simple accusation had taken the sergeant by surprise. He was only too well aware of the practice the girl had spoken of, and he knew the robber involved. In fact, for many years he'd shared the villain's plunder, and in return for half the proceeds he had ignored the thefts instead of exercising his legal powers and arresting the man.

There were even further complications. Of late the robber had refused to pay the sergeant his proper share and, what was worse, had threatened to tell all if ever the sergeant were to denounce him. For months now the officer of the law had felt unsafe. Not only that, but he was much poorer than he had been. The money he had once received from the robber had furnished the best of his pleasures: evenings of drunkenness with his companions and careless nights with the ladies of the town.

The sergeant glanced over his shoulder. The two guards had lost interest in Pichounetta and were now deep in conversation with each other. No one yet stirred on the road from the city; the early morning mist still hung low over the Rhône, and the far side of the bridge of Trinquetaille was not yet visible. The sergeant drew a deep breath, and a plan formed in his mind. This animal from the hills would provide him with a way out of his dilemma. He moved his hand from Pichounetta's elbow and placed his arm around her hard shoulders. She leaned wearily against him and felt protected for the first time since her brother had died. The sergeant spoke to her, his voice newly kind.

"My dear child," he said, "you have made a serious accusation, and though I do not doubt your word, others will. We must take this villain in flagrante delicto, as the law says, and we must have money. Do you have money?"

Pichounetta nodded, but she did not look up, too confused by this flood of words she hardly understood.

The sergeant, satisfied, beamed down at the top of Pichounetta's head. "What the law requires," he continued, "is indisputable proof. I have to see the robbery happen so that I may bear witness."

"But," interrupted Pichounetta, completely bewildered, "the man has already robbed my brother and sent his coffin into the marshes . . . and me, too, he has robbed and sent an empty coffin after my brother's. How can you see these things? Will the man go unpunished and my brother never be buried in the Aliscamps?"

"This villain will not go unpunished," said the sergeant, and by way of comfort he clasped Pichounetta to him in the embrace of his arm. "I shall see to it. What is more, I shall see that you find your brother again, believe me. But you will have to aid me, my child. This is what you must do: Just a mile or so above the villain's cabin, on the very edge of the river, you will find a little wood, and you will wait for me there, today. I will give you my own provisions, a flask of wine too. Do not stir, and do not talk to anyone. No one can be trusted in this world, my child, no one. As soon as it is dark, I will send a servant to you, and he will bring with him an empty coffin, and on the lid will be a purse containing the fee of Aliscamps . . . and you will do what you did before. You will float in the coffin as far as the bridge, and while you do I shall be hidden nearby, watching and waiting and ready to see everything. As soon as you hear the robber lay his hand upon the purse, you will speak to him, as from the grave, and curse him for what he does. Then when he is amazed and terrified, I will seize him and drag him before the archbishop of Arles himself. I promise you he will be sorely punished— twenty years in the galleys, I'll be bound."

Pichounetta moved her head. "And my brother?" she asked.

"Yes," said the sergeant. "He will not be too far away, in the marshes, and we will begin the search for him just as soon as we have taken the robber. . . . But there is another thing, my child, though it hurts me to ask it: we do need money. You see, there is the fee for me to place in the purse, and then I shall have to buy a coffin and also reward my servant for his work and for his secrecy, and at the trial of the robber there will be a lawyer and a clerk to pay, and afterward, to search for your brother, we must hire a boat to sail the waterways and lakes of the Camargue. . . . Do you understand? The law is a costly diversion, and revenge has always been a luxury."

Pichounetta reached inside her ragged bodice and took out the large pouch which contained her brother's savings. "I do not know," she said. "Is this enough?"

The sergeant took the pouch and opened the neck of it. Silver shone in the interior, and his mouth moistened with greed: here was sufficient money for a year of sport. "There is more than I need, my child," he said, "enough to pay for all I have mentioned and some left at the end of things to send you home."

At last Pichounetta looked up at the sergeant and smiled, and that smile came close to warming the man's heart, but even a smile of such simplicity and beauty could not accomplish that. "Thank you, my lord," she said. "I shall do as you command."

With this the sergeant took his arm from the girl's shoulder, and hiding the pouch of silver beneath his cloak, he strode quickly to the gatehouse, where he took up the basket of provisions he had brought with him for the day and, returning to where Pichounetta waited, thrust it into her hands.

"Now go," he said, "and stay silent and secret all day. Look for my servant when night falls, and do exactly as he says. Remember I will be waiting at the bridge, ready to protect you."

Pichounetta did not hesitate, but clutching the basket with both hands, she turned and made her way along the riverbank. The sergeant stood and watched her go, and as he did, one of his guards, trailing his pike behind him, approached his officer and laughed aloud.

"I never saw such an ugly woman," he said. "And were you possessed by the devil to give your bread and wine to such a sorry vagabond? I never knew you strong on charity. Why on earth did you do such a thing?"

The sergeant continued watching until Pichounetta had disappeared into the undergrowth that grew along the riverbank, then he smiled at his colleague. "Because," he said, clutching the bag of silver beneath his cloak, "it is written that if you cast your bread upon the waters it will be returned a hundredfold," and with that he walked away.

The guard followed him, puzzled. He had never known the sergeant to quote the Bible before—if that was the Bible he had quoted—not in all the years they had kept the gate together. The guard shrugged. The world was a strange place, sure enough, and made stranger by the people in it.

All day Pichounetta concealed herself in the deepest part of the thicket where the sergeant had sent her. She ate the provisions from the basket and counted her blessings, happy because the very first person she had met that day had been in authority and had treated her with kindness, promising to help her bring the robber to justice. And what a fine person the sergeant was, how handsome; how bright his armor, how splendid his cloak. Tonight would see the robber in irons and her brother's soul placated. And afterward the sergeant would search for her brother's coffin and find it too. All would work out as planned, and when it was done she would take what was left of her money and journey home. It was perfect, and the world was not as bad a place as the old woman had said.

Comforted by these thoughts and the sergeant's provisions, the girl lay, all afternoon, between sleeping and waking, her mind whirling with the sights she had seen: a bridge and a city; a fine officer and soldiers in uniform; and such wine too. Never had she tasted anything so delicate; strong as a magic potion, it had warmed her body through and through, from top to toe, making her feel that she might sleep for days on end—but such a thing was not to be. Pichounetta was roughly woken from her dreams by the sound of a handcart being pushed along a stony track. The girl opened her eyes and shuddered. All around her it was dark and cold.

Quickly she crept to the edge of the trees, and in the starlight, she made out the figure of the servant. "I am here," she called. "I am here."

The rattling of the handcart stopped, and a rough voice said, "Are you the one who waits for a coffin?"

"I am," said Pichounetta. "Was it sent by your master?"

"It was," said the servant, "if by my master you mean the sergeant who guards the gates by day and lays siege to women by night, though who else would be sending you a box at this time I cannot fathom."

At these remarks, though she did not fully understand them, Pichounetta emerged from her hiding place and approached the handcart. Resting on it was a well-made coffin. The girl looked at the servant; his expression was mean, and his eyes were shifty.

"Let us do what we have to do," said Pichounetta, and she seized the coffin, set it on her shoulders, and carried it easily to the water's edge, which was only a few yards distant. There she set it down, and after removing the lid, she clambered in. The servant had followed behind, amazed at the girl's physical strength and determination. He groped for the lid, found it, and slid it into position, shutting out the sight of Pichounetta's face.

"Are you ready, girl?" he said, his voice harsh.

"I am ready," answered Pichounetta, and the water lapped at the foot of the coffin.

The servant hesitated for a moment and shook his head. He did not always understand the commands of his master, but he was nevertheless obliged to obey him: there was no living else. The servant sighed loudly and took from beneath his cloak a hammer and a handful of long nails. Quickly he placed the point of the first nail on the lid and hammered it home. Then another.

"Why do you nail the lid?" asked Pichounetta, her words trembling with fear.

The servant placed another nail and began to strike it. "Fear not, woman," he said. "My master ordered it, and you may trust him. He will release you at the bridge, fear not."

"But," insisted Pichounetta, "how will I breathe if you nail down the lid so tightly?"

"Be quiet, woman," said the servant, "or your plan will be discovered by the robber and everything we have done will be for naught. You go but a little way and stay but a little time. My master will release you. There is air enough and time enough, I promise you."

Satisfied with this explanation, Pichounetta said not another word, and the servant continued with his hammering until with his last nail he affixed a purse to the coffin and then dragged it into the deeper waters of the river Rhône.

"Is all well, woman?" he asked, and when he heard the muffled voice of Pichounetta answer that it was, the servant crossed himself and let the coffin go. "May God protect you, little peasant," he said, and he turned away and waded to the shore.

In the dark gloom of the bridge of Trinquetaille the sergeant stood, wrapped in a black cloak, not a glimmer of starlight reflecting from his breastplate. For an hour he waited until at last he saw the coffin turning slowly in the Rhône's current. To begin with it struck against an archway not far from where he was hiding behind a stone pillar and up to his knees in the river, but then, at the urging of the current, it drifted along the ropes toward the bank on which the robber's cabin was built. The sergeant drew his dagger. It would not be long now.

Nor was it. At the darkest part of the night the robber came. His footsteps sounded on the gravel path and he strode directly into the water until it reached his very neck. He stretched out a hand for the coffin, caught hold of it, and stumbled back into the shallows, stopping only when the swirling tide had fallen to his waist. Then he reached out for the purse and tore it free of its nail.

"Praise be," he whispered. "This purse feels big and heavy—there'll be silver and gold here. It is a good night's work I have done."

Suddenly the voice of Pichounetta came from within the coffin. It was muffled and weak, but it was loud enough to be heard quite clearly.

"A good night's work," she said. "Then you shall burn in hell for it. Where is my brother? Answer me that. Where is he buried? Why does he weep and wail instead of lying in the holiest ground on earth? You evil man. All the ghosts of the night shall haunt you now until you die of terror."

On hearing these words the robber screamed, let drop the purse, and fell backward into the water, clutching at his heart where it thumped in his chest. He gasped for breath, only just managing to keep his head above the surface of the water. "Mercy, mercy," he cried.

"There'll be no mercy for you," said the voice from the coffin, and at that the robber whimpered and made a feeble attempt to crawl to the shore.

The sergeant, who had been listening all this time, now came into the open and went to where the robber was lying near the edge of the river.

The robber's eyes flickered in recognition. "Sergeant," he said, "help me."

The sergeant laughed. "Rob me of my share of the fee of Aliscamps, would you? Threaten to tell the archbishop, would you? You'll get no help from me, you dog."

"There's money," gasped the robber. "It lies beneath my hearthstone. Take it, only save me."

"I'll save you from yourself, that's all," rejoined the sergeant. "I'll send you where you've sent so many others." And he raised a foot and pushed the robber's face under the surface of the water and held it there. When the man was dead, he released the body and watched it float away; a large black shape, half submerged, it slipped beneath the coffin ropes and on toward the marshes of the Camargue—carrion for sea birds and water rats.

"So perish," said the sergeant, and he replaced his dagger in the sheath at his belt, rejoicing in his newfound security. And there was something else too. He had only to search the villain's hovel and he would discover a substantial hoard of money.

Hastening in his greed, the sergeant began to move away, but as he made to go, there came a tiny voice from within the coffin, which was now drifting back into the current.

"Oh, Sergeant," called Pichounetta, "release me now as you promised and help me find my brother's body. Oh, hurry—I can hardly breathe. Oh, let me feel the good air upon my face."

The sergeant cursed. In his excitement at the thought of the robber's wealth, he had completely forgotten about the ugly peasant girl. Here was another mischief. She must for certain have heard the exchange between himself and his accomplice. Now she would know what the robber had known, and being as simple as the morning, she was likely to blurt out the precious information at any time. Once again the sergeant saw himself in jeopardy.

"Oh, Sergeant," came the voice, insistent, but weaker than before. "Please help me."

The sergeant cursed again. He went toward the coffin and seized it. "I know where your brother is," he said, "and I shall send you to him. In but a little while you'll be together, and never shall you trouble me." And with these heartless words the sergeant thrust the coffin under the ropes and out into the main current of the Rhône, where in no time at all it disappeared into the wide night.

Without a backward glance, the sergeant returned to the shore and climbed the bank to the robber's cabin. There, under the hearthstone, just as the villain had said, he discovered a mound of treasure—so much he could hardly carry it away. Thanks to Pichounetta, the sergeant had become very rich, very rich indeed.

—§—

To celebrate his good fortune, the sergeant went that same night to his favorite haunt, a noisy tavern near the eastern gate of Arles. There he was in the highest spirits and bought pitchers of wine for all his friends, and they slapped him on the back and drank his health, telling him what a good and generous fellow he was. A beautiful woman, too, ran her fingers through his hair and kissed him full on the mouth and told him that he was the handsomest man in Provence.

It also happened, by chance, that among his drinking companions that night was one of the guards who had been on duty with him at dawn. This man came and sat next to the sergeant, spilling wine from his cup as he lowered his body onto a bench. He grinned stupidly at his superior and spoke loudly to make himself heard above the great noise of talking and singing.

"And weren't you the soul of kindness today, master?" he began. "Do you know, friends, our brave sergeant gave all his food away this morning, and his wine, for nothing mark you, for nothing . . . and to the ugliest, most stunted peasant woman you have ever seen. I tell you she was ill-favored enough to make the milk curdle in the goats and all the wells of Arles run dry."

Many laughed at this jest, but the sergeant's face grew dark and angry. He did not enjoy being ridiculed. He half rose as if to attack the guard, but the beautiful woman pulled him back into his place and put her arms around his neck.

"You," she said, kissing him again, this time on the hand, "you, giving your food to a peasant woman, for nothing in return. Is this a side to the sergeant we have never seen before—doing good by stealth and blushing to find it famous."

"I could not help myself," stuttered the sergeant. "Never have I seen anything so ugly, so like a wild animal. She was starving, you see. Heaven knows where she came from; she'd never even seen a city before."

"Or a man like you," said the beautiful woman, "I'll be bound."

"I told her to go back to her home," continued the sergeant, beginning to believe his own story. "I told her that the city is no place for the innocent. I told her that here she would be enslaved, or worse. You know. I bade her go and gave her food, yes, and some money, so she could. I never saw anyone more ignorant of the world than she."

"Well," said the beautiful woman, "you have done a praiseworthy act. The world is certainly not meant for the ignorant or the innocent. By the time they have discovered what kind of a place it is they have wandered into, it is generally too late for them to profit from the knowledge they have gained."

With this sentiment all the revelers within earshot agreed, and they laughed and shouted and raised their tankards and drank another toast to the sergeant of the gates, praising him for his kindness and wisdom, and he smiled and accepted their compliments, lifting his cup as high as the rest and drinking to his own health until, at the end, there was no wine remaining in the whole tavern.

BIOGRAPHICAL NOTES

ANDERSEN, HANS CHRISTIAN (1805–1875) Born in Odense, Denmark, of an extremely poor family, Andersen settled in Copenhagen in 1819. A wealthy patron enabled him to receive a proper education and begin a career as writer. At first Andersen wrote mainly sketches, poems, dramas, and novels. In 1835 he published the work that was to make him famous—*Eventyr, Fortalte for Børn* (*Fairy Tales Told for Children*). The original volume included only five fairy tales, but Andersen kept expanding it for Christmas editions, so that it eventually comprised 156 tales, allegories, anecdotes, fables, philosophical commentaries, and didactic stories. By 1843 he had begun writing fairy tales for adults and changed the title of his book to *Nye Eventyr* (*New Fairy Tales*). "The Shadow" (1847) dramatizes his mixed feelings toward the patronage of the upper class. Aside from his great production of fairy tales, Andersen wrote thirty plays, six novels, three autobiographies, and several volumes of verse.

APOLLINAIRE, GUILLAUME (Wilhelm Apollinaris de Kostrowitski, 1880–1918) Born in Rome, the illegitimate son of a Polish countess and an Italian officer, Apollinaire studied in Paris, where he mixed in bohemian circles and became known as one of the major figures of the surrealist movement. He was a friend of Picasso and Braque, and wrote *The Cubist Painters* (1913) to explain the major aims of cubism. A versatile writer, he experimented in different genres, and among his best-known works are *L'Hérésiarque et Cie* (1910), a collection of tales, and two volumes of innovative poems, *Alcools* (1913) and *Calligrammes* (1918). "Cinderella Continued, or the Rat and the Six Lizards" ("La Suite de Cendrillon, ou le rat et les six lézards"), the last work he wrote, was published in *La Baïonette* on January 16, 1919.

APULEIUS (125–?) Born in Hippo, now Annaba, Algeria, Apuleius was educated at Carthage and Athens. He traveled widely in Greece and Asia Minor and practiced for a while as a lawyer in Rome. When he was about thirty years old, he returned home, where he gained a distinguished reputation as a writer and lecturer. His most famous work is *Metamorphoses*, also known as *The Golden Ass*, which includes the tale "Cupid and Psyche." He also wrote *The Apology*, or *On Magic (Apologie: Pro se de magia liber)*, his defense in a suit brought against him by his wife's relatives, who accused him of gaining her affections through magic, and three philosophical treatises, *On the God of Socrates (De deo Socratis)*, *On the Philosophy of Plato (De Platone et eius dogmate)*, and *On the World (De mundo)*.

BACHMANN, INGEBORG (1926–1973) Born in Klagenfurt, Austria, Bachmann studied philosophy at the University of Vienna; her Ph.D. dissertation was on Heideigger. An experimental and prolific writer, she wrote poems, radio plays, stories, and novels, which often contained fairy tale motifs. Among her best-known works are *Das drei-βigste Jahr (The Thirtieth Year*, 1961), *Malina* (1971), and *Simultan (Simultaneous*, 1973). "The Smile of the Sphinx," one of the first fairy tales she published, appeared in the newspaper *Wiener Tageszeitung* in 1949.

BASILE, GIAMBATTISTA (1575–1632) Born in Naples, Basile, first a soldier, achieved renown as a versatile court poet while serving as an administrator for various dukes and princes in Italy. He settled in Naples in 1613 and wrote odes and madrigals for one of his sisters, a famous singer, as well as court entertainments such as the five-act musical *La Venere addolorata (Sorrowful Venus)*. Toward the end of his life he championed Neapolitan culture and wrote works in dialect, such as *Le Muse Nea-politane (Neapolitan Muses*, 1635), nine eclogues in dialect that concern daily life in Naples. Basile's major work, *Lo Cunto de li Cunti (The Story of Stories*, 1634), a collection of fairy tales in dialect, which included "The Merchant's Two Sons" ("Lo mercante"), was completed before he died and published posthumously. By 1674 his book became known as *The Pentamerone* and influenced the development of the fairy tale genre throughout Europe.

BAUM, L. FRANK (1856–1919) Born in Chittenango, New York, Baum had a strong interest in the theater during his youth but had to abandon a stage career when his father died and the family business went bankrupt. He moved to the Midwest and had various jobs as haberdasher and salesman before he published *The Wonderful Wizard of Oz* (1900), perhaps the finest classical fairy tale novel for children in America. The book's success enabled him to embark on a writing career that encompassed a series of Oz books; *American Fairy Tales* (1901), which included "The Queen of Quok"; and well over forty children's books under pseudonyms. Baum eventually settled in California, where he tried in vain to create an Oz Land, similar to the present-day Disneyland.

CALVINO, ITALO (1923–1985) Born in Santiago de las Vegas, Cuba, Calvino grew up in San Remo, Italy. During the Nazi occupation of northern Italy, he joined the resistance movement, an experience he depicted in his novel *Il sentiero dei nidi di ragno (The Path to the Nest of Spiders,* 1947). After studying literature in Turin and writing a dissertation on Joseph Conrad in 1947, he worked for the publisher Einaudi and became a well-known journalist and novelist. He is especially known for his fantasy works, such as *I nostri antenati (Our Forefathers,* 1960), *The Watcher and Other Stories* (1963), and *Le città invisibili (Invisible,* 1972). His strong interest in Italian folklore led him to collect and revise folk tales, published as *Fiabe italiane (Italian Fairy Tales,* 1956) which included "Il Palazzo Incantato" ("The Enchanted Palace").

CARTER, ANGELA (1940–   ) Born in Eastbourne, Sussex, England, Carter studied English at Bristol University. After a brief career as a journalist, she became a freelance writer and developed into one of England's foremost writers of fantasy or magic realism. Among her major novels are *The Magic Toyshop* (1967), *The Infernal Desire Machines of Doctor Hoffman* (1972), and *Nights at the Circus* (1984). She has also published two collections of stories, *The Bloody Chamber* (1979), which includes "The Tiger's Bride," and *Fireworks* (1984). Her essays in *The Sadeian Woman* (1979) and *Nothing Sacred* (1982) have won critical acclaim while her strong interest in folklore has been manifested in her translation *The Fairy Tales of Charles Perrault* (1979) and *The Virago Book of Fairy Tales* (1990).

COOVER, ROBERT (1932–   ) Born in Charles City, Iowa, Coover received his B.A. from Indiana University in 1953 and then spent three years stationed in Europe as a navy officer. Returning to the States in 1957, he attended graduate school at the University of Chicago and began writing short stories. From 1962 to 1965, he lived in Europe, completing his first major novel, *The Origin of the Brunists* (1966), and since then he has established himself as one of the most experimental contemporary writers in America. Among his major works are *Pricksongs and Descants* (1969), *The Public Burning* (1977), *A Political Fable* (1980), *In Bed One Night and Other Brief Encounters* (1982), *A Night at the Movies* (1987), *Whatever Happened to Gloomy Gus of the Chicago Bears* (1987), and *Pinocchio in Venice* (1991). During the past twenty years he has taught creative writing at such institutions as Bard College, the University of Iowa, and Washington University, and he is currently adjunct professor at Brown University. Coover has often parodied the traditional fairy tale in his works, and "The Dead Queen," a reinterpretation of "Snow White," first appeared in 1973 in the *Quarterly Review of Literature.*

CROKER, THOMAS CROFTON (1798–1854) Born in Cork, Ireland, Croker was an apprentice in a mercantile firm when he developed an interest in Irish folklore and began collecting tales in the south of Ireland. In 1818 he moved to London, and he worked as a clerk in the admiralty until his retirement in 1850. During this time he published *The Fairy Legends and Traditions of the South of Ireland* (1825), which included "The Lady of Gollerus," *Popular Songs of Ireland* (1839), and *The Adventures of Barney Mahoney* (1852).

D'AULNOY, MARIE-CATHERINE (c. 1650–1705) Born in Barneville, Normandy, Mme D'Aulnoy came from a wealthy aristocratic family and was encouraged to live as independently as possible. Married in 1665 to a callous, dissolute man, she became disenchanted and in 1669 attempted to have him executed for a crime he did not commit. She was forced to flee Paris and live in exile until 1685. Returning to Paris, she established one of the most important literary salons of the ancien régime and published her first novel, *L'Histoire d'Hippolyte, comte de Douglas*, which contained the fairy tale "L'île de la Félicité" ("The Island of Happiness"). Memoirs she wrote about her journeys to foreign courts had great success. Beginning in 1697, she published four volumes of fairy tales, *Les Contes des Fées*, which began the vogue that established the fairy tale genre in France. "Serpent vert" ("Green Serpent"), published in 1697, was the basis for later creations of "Beauty and the Beast."

DE LA FORCE, CHARLOTTE-ROSE DE CAUMONT (1650–1724) Born into one of the oldest and most esteemed families of France, Mlle de La Force was maid of honor to the queen and dauphine at King Louis XIV's court. She developed into a consummate schemer, as well as a gifted writer. In 1697 she caused a scandal at court and was compelled to spend the rest of her life in a convent. She had already achieved success with her historical romances, *Histoire secrète du duc de Bourgogne* (1694) and *Histoire de Marguerite de Valois* (1696). An entertaining storyteller, Mlle de La Force had often attended Parisian salons, where she recited her fairy tales. These she circulated in manuscript and revised and then published them anonymously under the title *Les Contes des Contes* (1697), which included "Persinette" ("Parslinette"), a precursor of "Rapunzel," by the Brothers Grimm.

DE MORGAN, MARY (1850–1907) Born in London, De Morgan was the youngest daughter of August De Morgan, a renowned professor of mathematics, and Sophia Feind, a gifted writer. Her parents' large circle of friends and their interest in the arts brought the young woman into contact with the Pre-Raphaelites. She displayed an early interest in writing and painting, and in 1877 published her first collection of fairy tales, *On a Pincushion and Other Tales*. Her next volume, *The Necklace of Princess Fiorimonde* (1888), contained some of her best tales, such as "The Wanderings of Arasmon," "The Heart of Princess Joan," and "The Three Clever Kings." *The Windfairies and Other Tales* (1900) was her last book, written before she moved to Cairo to direct a reformatory for children.

DICK, PHILIP K. (1928–1982) Born in Chicago, Dick studied briefly at the University of California in Berkeley, where he also worked for a radio station and managed a record store. He began publishing science fiction stories, and after 1955, with the publication of his novels *Solar Lottery* and *A Handful of Darkness*, he was established as one of the leading writers of science fiction in America. Among his best-known works are *Eye in the Sky* (1957), *Do Androids Dream of Electric Sheep?* (1968), *The Preserving Machine and Other Stories* (1969), and *A Scanner Darkly* (1977). "The King of the Elves" first appeared in the magazine *Beyond Fantasy Fiction* (September 1953).

DÖBLIN, ALFRED (1878–1957) Born in Stettin, Germany, Döblin moved to Berlin in 1905 and studied medicine. He began practicing as a doctor in the working-class areas of the city in 1911, while also writing novels and stories. He was strongly influenced by the expressionists and published his most famous work, *Berlin Alexanderplatz*, in 1929. When Hitler came to power in 1933, Döblin was forced to leave Germany because of his leftist politics and Jewish background, and he spent part of his exile in America, returning to Germany in 1945. One of the occasional experimental fairy tales he wrote, "Das Märchen von der Technik" ("The Fairy Tale about Technology") appeared in 1935, at the onset of his exile period.

DUNSANY, LORD (Edward John Moreton Drax Plunkett, 1878–1957) Born in London of Irish descent, Dunsany was educated at Eton/Sandhurst and at first pursued a military career. After participating in the Boer War, he went to Dublin, where he wrote plays and helped Yeats in promoting Irish theater. He never became fully involved in the Irish nationalist movement and preferred to mix with aristocratic circles in England. A prolific writer, he became chiefly known for his Gothic fantasy tales and novels, which incorporate legends and myths in unusual ways. Among his best works are *Time and the Gods* (1906), *The Sword of Welleran* (1908), *Fifty-One Tales* (1915), *A Dreamer's Tales* (1916), which included "The Kith of the Elf-Folk," and *The Last Book of Wonder* (1916).

EWALD, CARL (1856–1908) Born in Bredelykke, Denmark, Ewald abandoned a career as a teacher in 1879 and moved to Copenhagen, where he became one of Denmark's leading journalists and writers of social novels (*The Rule or the Exception*, 1883, and *The Way Out*, 1884). At the beginning of the 1890s, Ewald discovered that he could best incorporate his political and social messages in symbolical fairy tales and published three successful collections, *I det Fri* (*In the Open*, 1892, *Fem nye Eventyr* (*Five New Fairy Tales*, 1894), and *Die fire Fjendingsfyrsten* (*The Four Small Princes*, 1895). His success led him to publish twenty other volumes of fairy tales influenced by social Darwinism. He also translated the Brothers Grimm into Danish. "The Story of the Fairy Tale" was written about 1905.

FRANCE, ANATOLE (Jacques-Anatole-François Thibault, 1844–1924) Born in Paris, France was the son of a bookseller and started his career as a librarian. After publishing various essays, stories, and novels, he abandoned this profession and became one of France's most distinguished writers, known for his elegance, irony, and erudition. Gifted in all fields of writing, he practically became the moral conscience of France, particularly after the Dreyfus Affair, which kindled his interest in socialism. Among his more important works are *Le Livre de mon ami* (*My Friend's Book*, 1885), *Thaïs* (1890), and *L'orme du mail* (*The Elm Tree on the Mall*, 1897). He was also literary critic of *Le Temps* (1886–91) and published an important history of contemporary France: he received the Nobel Prize in 1921. France often used fairy tale motifs in his works, but *Les sept femmes de Barbe-bleue* (*The Seven Wives of Bluebeard*) is his only full-length fairy tale, published as a book in 1909.

GALLAND, ANTOINE (1646–1715) Born in Rollot in Picardy, France, Galland studied at the Collège du Plessis in Paris and became a scholar of Oriental studies. In 1670 he was called upon to assist the French ambassador in Greece, Syria, and Palestine. After a brief return to Paris in 1674, he worked with the ambassador in Constantinople from 1677 to 1688. Back in Paris, he devoted the rest of his life to Oriental studies and published historical and philological works, such as *Paroles remarkables, bons mots et maximes des Orientaux (Remarkable Words, Sayings and Maxims of the Orientals,* 1694). His major work is undoubtedly his translation and adaptation of Arabic and Persian tales, *Les Mille et Une Nuits (The Thousand and One Nights,* 1704–17). Galland was largely responsible for stimulating the great interest in the Arabian tales in Europe during the eighteenth century. "Prince Ahmed et la fée Pari-Banou" ("Prince Ahmed and the Fairy Pari-Banou"), told to Galland in Paris, was first published in the collection in 1714.

GESTA ROMANORUM (c. 1300) The first manuscripts of this anonymous collection of legends, anecdotes, fables, and fairy tales, written in Latin and based on Roman history and medieval legends, can be dated to the end of the thirteenth century. The original authors of the stories were Roman, and Oriental influences can also be traced in the approximately 283 entries. The book became a popular reading manual for instruction and amusement up through the eighteenth century. Translations of the Latin texts began appearing in Europe during the fifteenth century. Most of the fairy tales have either didactic or Christian messages, as is the case with "Of Feminine Subtlety."

GOETHE, JOHANN WOLFGANG VON (1749–1832) Born in Frankfurt am Main, Goethe studied law and philosophy in Leipzig and Strasbourg, becoming one of the leading members of the Storm and Stress movement. His play *Götz von Berlichingen* (1773) and his epistolary novel, *Die Leiden des jungen Werthers* (1774), though controversial, demonstrated the young writer's unusual gifts, and in 1775 he was invited to become a privy councillor at the court of the duke of Weimar, who wanted to transform his small duchy into the intellectual center of Germany. Although Goethe had difficulties with the duke and his autocratic rule, he remained in Weimar for the rest of his life and conceived some of his best works there, including *Torquato Tasso* (1790), *Wilhelm Meisters Lehrjahre (The Apprenticeship of Wilhelm Meister,* 1795), *Faust I* (1808), *Faust II* (1832), *Westöstlicher Diwan (West-Eastern Divan,* 1819), and *Dichtung und Wahrheit (Poetry and Truth,* 1811–33). He had a great interest in fairy tales and wrote three significant tales during his lifetime: "Der neue Paris" ("The New Paris," 1763), "Das Märchen" ("The Fairy Tale," 1785), and "Die neue Melusine" ("The New Melusine," 1812). "The Fairy Tale" was included in the narrative framework of *Unterhaltungen deutscher Ausgewanderten (Conversations of German Emigrants,* 1795) and had a strong influence on the Romantics, particularly Novalis.

GRIMM, WILHELM CARL (1786–1859) Born in Hanau, Germany, Grimm studied law in Marburg and settled in Kassel in 1798 with his brother Jacob, with whom he began to collaborate in various endeavors pertaining to German folklore and language.

In 1811 Wilhelm published *Old Danish Heroic Songs*, and in 1812 and 1815 he and Jacob issued the two volumes of the first edition of *Die Kinder- und Hausmärchen (Children's and Household Tales)*. Wilhelm was in charge of the next six editions of their fairy tales, which he greatly expanded and revised, so that many of the so-called oral folk tales were transformed into literary fairy tales. In the third edition, in 1837, Wilhelm used the tale "Der undankbare Zwerg" ("The Ungrateful Dwarf"), first written by Caroline Stahl, as the basis for "Schneeweißchen und Rosenrot" ("Snow White and Rose Red"). Wilhelm and Jacob collaborated on *Deutsche Sagen (German Myths*, 1816–18), *Irische Elfen-Märchen (Irish Elf Tales*, 1825), and the first major German dictionary *(Das deutsche Wörterbuch)*, which remained unfinished. Wilhelm taught at the universities of Göttingen and Berlin.

HAWTHORNE, NATHANIEL (1804–1864) Born in Salem, Massachusetts, Hawthorne studied at Bowdoin College. Moving to Boston, he struggled to make a name for himself, and in 1837 achieved success with the publication of *Twice-Told Tales*. After working a year in the Boston Custom House, he participated in the Brook Farm experiment of communistic living (1839–40) and associated with the leading Transcendentalists of this period. Disappointed in Brook Farm, he moved to Concord, where he wrote *Mosses from an Old Manse* (1846), another collection of stories, which contained "Feathertop." He worked from 1847 to 1850 in the Salem Custom House, before publishing *The Scarlet Letter* (1850), then *The House of the Seven Gables* (1851), and *The Blithedale Romance* (1852), the books which established his reputation as one of the great American writers of the nineteenth century.

HESSE, HERMANN (1877–1962) Born in Calw, Germany, Hesse ran away from his private school and in 1895 became a bookseller in Tübingen; during this time he began writing poetry. He moved to Basel, Switzerland, in 1899 and published his first novel, *Peter Camenzind*, in 1909. Thereafter, he dedicated himself to writing, remaining in Switzerland. Hesse had a strong lifelong interest in fairy tales and edited collections of tales by the German Romantics, by whom he was greatly influenced. He published "Der Waldmensch" ("The Forest Dweller") in 1917–18 and followed it with a major collection of tales, *Märchen*, in 1919. Almost all his best-known works, such as *Demian* (1919), *Siddartha* (1922), and *Das Glasperlenspiel (The Glass-Bead Game*, 1942), are modeled in some way after fairy tales. Hesse received the Nobel Prize in 1946.

HESSEL, FRANZ (1880–1941) Born in Stettin, Germany, Hessel studied in Freiburg, Munich, and then Paris, where he resided from 1906–1914. Later he worked as an editor for the Rowohlt publishing house in Berlin. A master of French language and literature, he translated Stendhal, Balzac, and Proust, establishing himself as one of the best translators in Germany. Among the poems, novels, and stories he wrote are *Verlorene Gespiele (Lost Playmates*, 1905), *Laura Wunderl* (1908), *Der Kramladen des Glücks (The Junkshop of Happiness*, 1913), *Teigwaren leicht gefärbt (Noodles Slightly Colored*, 1926), which included "Der siebte Zwerg" ("The Seventh Dwarf"), and *Spazieren in Berlin (Walking in Berlin*, 1929). His relationship with a French writer served as the basis for François Truffaut's film *Jules et Jim*. Hessel was forced to flee the Nazis in 1938 and died in 1941 after internment in France.

HOFFMANN, E.T.A. (1776–1822) Born in Königsberg, Germany, Hoffmann received his law degree in 1798 and practiced law in Poland. Talented in music and art, he moved to Bamberg, Germany, in 1808 to conduct an orchestra and teach music. In 1813 he was forced to leave Bamberg owing to a minor love scandal, and he settled in Berlin in 1815, becoming a judge. At the same time he began his career as a writer, building a reputation as the foremost German Romantic writer of bizarre and grotesque fairy tales. Among his best-known works are *Fantasie-Stücke* (*Fantasy Pieces*, 1814), *Die Elixiere des Teufels* (*The Devil's Elixirs*, 1815), and *Die Serapions-Brüder* (*The Serapion Brothers*, 1819–21), which included "Die Bergwerke zu Falun" ("The Mines of Falun," 1819). After Hoffmann's death, works such as "Der goldene Topf" ("The Golden Pot"), "Der Sandmann" ("The Sandman"), and "Rat Krespel" ("Councillor Krespel") powerfully influenced French and English writers, and Freud used "The Sandman" as the basis for his famous essay on "The Uncanny."

HOFMANNSTHAL, HUGO VON (1874–1929) Born in Vienna, Hofmannsthal was considered a prodigy after he published his first poem at the age of sixteen. He received a doctorate in literature from the University of Vienna and was an established writer by the time he was twenty. Hofmannsthal published "Das Märchen der 672. Nacht" ("The Tale of the 672nd Night") in 1895 and wrote several other fairy tales influenced by the German Romantics and *The Thousand and One Nights*. His play *Das Bergwerk zu Falun* (*The Mine at Falun*, 1899) was based on E.T.A. Hoffmann's "The Mines of Falun." Aside from writing poems, essays, and tales, he became famous for his plays *Der Thor und der Tod* (*The Fool and Death*, 1900) and *Das kleine Welttheater* (*The Small World Theater*, 1903) and his librettos for Richard Strauss's operas *Elektra* and *Der Rosenkavalier*.

HOUSMAN, LAURENCE (1865–1959) Born in Bromsgrove, Worcester, England, Housman was the second youngest of seven children, including A. E. Housman, the famous poet, and Clemence Housman, an accomplished engraver and novelist. In 1883 Housman went to London to study at the Lambeth School of Art. Exposed to poverty and a more liberal world than the conservative surroundings of Bromsgrove, Housman was drawn to socialism, and his early works reflect his yearning for a better world. In particular, his two collections of fairy tales, *A Farm in Fairyland* (1894) and *The House of Joy* (1895), contain magical stories in which his characters courageously take risks to realize their potential. A third volume of fairy tales, *The Field of Clover*, appeared in 1898, and *The Blue Moon* (1904) contained some of his best tales, such as "The White Doe," "The Rat-Catcher's Daughter," and "A Chinese Fairy Tale." A prolific author, Housman wrote plays, tales, and novels and was also involved in socialist causes.

JANOSCH (Horst Eckert, 1931–   ) Born in Zaborize, Silesia, Germany, Eckert worked in a textile factory during his youth. In 1954 he went to Munich to study art, but unable to gain admission to the academy, he worked as a carpet designer. Gradually he began publishing stories and illustrations in the Munich newspaper *Die Süddeutsche* and in such weeklies and magazines as *Die Zeit* and *Pardon*. During the 1960s he produced several children's books and became recognized as one of Germany's foremost writers and illustrators for children. Among his best books are *Das Auto hier heißt Ferdinand* (*The Car Here Is Called Ferdinand*, 1964), *Wir haben einen Hund zuhaus* (*We Have a Dog at Home*, 1968), *Das Regenauto* (*The Rain Car*, 1972), *Mein Vater ist König* (*My Father Is King*, 1978), and *Rasputin* (1986). One of his most significant works for children and adults is the satirical *Janosch erzählt Grimms Märchen* (1972), in which he parodied fifty of the original Grimm fairy tales; it included "Hans My Hedgehog." In 1987 he won the German Youth Award for his book *Oh, wie schön ist Panama!* (*Oh, How Beautiful Panama Is!*).

KAISER, GEORG (1878–1945) Born in Magdeburg, Germany, Kaiser showed little enthusiasm for school and served an apprenticeship as a salesman from 1895 to 1898, while trying to establish himself as a dramatist. Fame came with his play *Die Bürger von Calais* (*The Citizens of Calais*, written in 1913 and produced in 1917), a powerful appeal for peace and moral renewal. It established him as the leading expressionist dramatist in Germany. Among his best works were *Gas I* (1917), *Von Morgens bis Mitternacht* (*From Morn to Midnight*, 1917), *Die Koralle* (*The Coral*, 1917), and *Gas II* (1920). After 1933, he was branded as decadent by the Nazis, and since it was difficult to have his plays produced, he began writing novels and stories. In 1938 he emigrated to Switzerland and wrote verse dramas based on Greek models that envisioned a new humanity. His fairy tale "Das Märchen des Königs" ("The Fairy Tale of the King") was written during his exile, in 1943.

KÄSTNER, ERICH (1899–1974) Born in Dresden, Kästner studied in Berlin, Rostock, and Leipzig. During the 1920s he was a free-lance writer in Berlin and became famous for his children's book *Emil und die Detektive* (*Emil and the Detectives*, 1929). Kästner wrote for both children and adults throughout his career, and his novel *Fabian* (1931) caused a stir in Germany because of its critique of social conditions in Germany. During the Nazi period, Kästner was prohibited from publishing because of his antifascist stance, but after 1945 he resumed his career as a cultural critic and wrote numerous essays, poems, and stories. "The Fairy Tale About Common Sense" was published in 1948 and represents his critical views about war.

KELLER, GOTTFRIED (1819–1890) Born in Zurich, Keller went to Munich in 1840 to develop his talents as a painter. Failing, he returned to Zurich in 1842 and tried his hand at writing. In 1846 he published his first book of poems and received a stipend to study in Heidelberg and Berlin. It was during his stay in Berlin (1850–55) that he realized his potential as a writer and gained recognition for his novel of development, *Der grüne Heinrich* (*Green Henry*, 1854), and his collection of satirical tales, *Die Leute von Seldwyla* (*The People from Seldwyla*, 1856), which included "Spiegel, das Kätzchen" ("Spiegel the Cat"). In 1861 he was appointed state writer for the canton of Zurich and continued publishing such interesting works as *Sieben Legenden* (*Seven Legends*, 1872) and *Züricher Novellen* (*Zurich Novellas*, 1877).

KUNERT, GÜNTER (1929–   ) Born in Berlin, Kunert studied at the Institute for Applied Art from 1946 to 1949 but abandoned art for poetry. During the 1950s, with such works as *Unter diesem Himmel* (1954), he became recognized as one of East Germany's most gifted poets. Kunert also developed a unique talent as a prose writer who uses concrete and striking images in succinct, terse narratives. Among his best works are *Tageswerke* (*Day's Works*, 1961), *Die Beerdigung findet nicht statt* (*The Funeral Does Not Take Place*, 1968), *Tagträume* (*Daydreams*, 1972), *Die geheime Bibliothek* (*The Secret Library*, 1973), *Der andere Planet* (*The Other Planet*, 1974), and *Lesarten* (*Ways of Reading*, 1987). Though he lived in East Germany until 1977, Kunert's works have always been received well in both parts of Germany and continue to have success in reunified Germany. He has often experimented with fairy tales in his work, and "Dornröschen" ("Sleeping Beauty") first appeared in *Daydreams* (1972).

KÜNZLER, ROSEMARIE (1926–   ) Born in Dessau, Germany, Künzler received a doctorate in literature and now lives in Munich. She has published numerous poems, stories, and children's books. "Rumpelstiltskin" appeared in the anthology *Neues vom Rumpelstilzchen* (1976), edited by Hans-Joachim Gelberg.

LARRABEITI, MICHAEL DE (1937–   ) Born in Battersea, London, de Larrabeiti studied French literature at Dublin University and has worked as a travel guide in France and as a cameraman for documentary films. He began writing in 1970, and his first major work, *The Borribles*, a unique fantasy about lower-class outsiders, was a controversial success. He followed this novel with *The Borribles Go for Broke* (1981) and *The Borribles: Across the Dark Metropolis* (1986). He has also written a western and a mystery, along with a poetic memoir entitled *A Rose Beyond the Thames* (1978). "Pichounetta and the Sergeant of Arles" was published in his collection of fairy tales entitled *The Provençal Tales* (1988).

LEE, TANITH (1947–   ) Born in London, Lee was educated at Catford Grammar School and Croydon Art School. She began writing fairy tales and science fiction during the 1970s and is considered one of the leading writers of fantasy in Great Britain today. Among her best works for young readers are *The Dragon Hoard* (1971) and *Princess Hynchatti and Some Other Surprises* (1972). Her outstanding science fiction works are *The Birthgrave* (1975), *The Quest for the White Witch* (1979), and *Electric Forest* (1979). "When the Clock Strikes" appeared in *Red as Blood or Tales from the Grimmer Sisters* (1983), an innovative collection of traditional fairy tales written from a feminist perspective.

LEM, STANISLAW (1921–   ) Born in Lvov, Poland, Lem studied medicine but never pursued a career as a doctor. During World War II he participated in the resistance movement against the Nazis and began writing short stories. By the 1950s he became one of the leading science fiction writers of Europe as well as a major theoretician of fantasy and utopia. He is particularly concerned with moral and philosophical problems and uses satire and the grotesque to expose the so-called wonders of modern science. Among his best works are *The Cyberiad* (1967), which includes "Prince Ferrix and the Princess Crystal," *Tales of Pirx the Pilot* (1968), *Solaris* (1971), *The Star Diaries* (1976), and *Memoirs of a Space Traveler* (1982).

L'HÉRITIER, MARIE-JEANNE (1664–1734) Born in Paris, Mlle L'Héritier came from a distinguished family of intellectuals. Studious, clever, and honorable, she was on close terms with the most influential women of her time and invited to the gatherings at the more illustrious salons in Paris. Eventually she established her own literary salon, in which she often recited her tales, poetry, and other works. Mlle L'Héritier's first major work was *Oeuvres meslées* (1695–98), which contained her well-known fairy tale "L'Adroite Princesse" ("The Discreet Princess"). It was followed immediately by *Bigarrures ingénieuses* (*Ingenious Medlies*, 1696), which included the first major literary version of "Rumpelstiltskin," entitled "Ricdin-Ricdon." As her reputation grew, she won various literary prizes and was elected to the Accademia dei Ricovrati di Padova.

MACDONALD, GEORGE (1824–1905) Born in Aberdeenshire, Scotland, MacDonald studied at Aberdeen University between 1842 and 1845, completing his studies at a theological seminary in London in 1851. After serving as a minister at a Congregational church for two years, MacDonald left the church because of his controversial views, and he spent the rest of his life giving public lectures and writing poems, novels, stories, and fairy tales. Indeed, he became one of the leading writers in the Victorian period, and among his fifty-one volumes were best-selling novels such as *David Elginbrod* (1863) and *Malcolm* (1875), remarkable fantasy works such as *Phantastes* (1858) and *Lilith* (1895), the children's novels *The Princess and the Goblin* (1872) and *The Princess and Curdie* (1883), and the fairy tales "The Light Princess" (1863), "The Golden Key" (1867), and "The Day Boy and the Night Girl" (1879).

MCKINLEY, ROBIN (1952–   ) Born in Warren, Ohio, McKinley grew up in a navy family and traveled throughout the world. She has always had a strong interest in fairy tales and fantasy literature, and her first novel, *Beauty* (1978), was a retelling of the story of Beauty and the Beast. It was followed by a collection of tales entitled *The Door in the Hedge* (1981), which includes "The Princess and the Frog." She has established herself as a foremost writer of fantasy in America with such novels as *The Blue Sword* (1982), *The Hero and the Crown* (1984), and *The Outlaws of Sherwood* (1988).

MECKEL, CHRISTOPH (1935–   ) Born in Berlin, Meckel studied graphics and painting in Freiburg and Munich. Aside from producing outstanding art work, Meckel has written experimental poetry, stories, and novels with strong surrealist and fairy tale elements. Among his best works are *Tarnkappe* (*The Invisible Cap*, 1956), *Tullipan* (1965), *Kranich* (*Crane*, 1973), *Der wahre Muftoni* (*The True Muftoni*, 1982), and *Ein roter Faden* (*A Red Thread*, 1983). "Die Krähe" ("The Crow") was first published in an anthology of contemporary German prose entitled *Das Atelier*, edited by Klaus Wagenbach.

MITCHISON, NAOMI (1897–   ) Born in Edinburgh, Mitchison had intended to become a scientist, but after attending Saint Anne's College, Oxford, she began writing historical novels, such as *The Conquered* (1923), set during the Roman conquest of Gaul, *The Corn King and the Spring Queen* (1931), and *The Bull Calves* (1947). During the 1930s she became involved in Scottish politics and wrote a political novel, *We Have Been Warned* (1935). She has also written numerous books for children, dramas, and fairy tales. Among her best fantasy works are *The Land the Ravens Found* (1955) and *Memories of a Spacewoman* (1962). Her collection of tales entitled *Five Men and a Swan* (1957) contains the title story.

MUSÄUS, JOHANN KARL AUGUST (1735–1787) Born in Jena, Germany, Musäus studied theology in Jena. In 1763 he moved to Weimar, where he became a private tutor and pursued his writing career. Aside from writing the novel *Grandison der Zweite* (1760–62), Musäus published the first major collection of German legends and fairy tales, *Volksmärchen der Deutschen* (1782–86), which included "Libussa."

MYNONA (Salomo Friedlaender, 1871–1946) Born in Gollantsch, Germany, Mynona studied medicine in Munich and philosophy in Berlin, where he was strongly influenced by Kant. He received his doctorate in 1902 and began writing scholarly works under his real name and satirical fiction under the pseudonym Mynona (anagram for "anonym," i.e., "anonymous"). His stories, published in the leading expressionist magazines, were grotesque and macabre. Among Mynona's best collections of tales are *Rosa, die schöne Schutzmannsfrau (Rosa, the Beautiful Policeman's Wife*, 1913), which included "Die vegetabilische Vaterschaft" ("The Vegetational Fatherhood"), *Hundert Bonbons (A Hundred Candies*, 1919), *Trappistenstreik (The Strike of the Trappists*, 1922), and *Der lachende Hiob (The Laughing Job*, 1935). He also published two experimental novels, *Tarzaniade* (1924) and *Der antibabylonische Turm (The anti-babylonian Tower*, 1932). Due to his anti-fascist politics, he fled to Paris in 1933 and remained there, living in poverty, until his death.

NOVALIS (Friedrich von Hardenberg, 1772–1801) Born on the family country estate, Oberwiederstedt, near Mansfeld, Germany, Novalis studied at Jena and was a key member of the early German Romantic movement. While working as a supervisor in some mines near Jena, he wrote poems, essays, aphorisms, and novels. He is best known for his lyrics *Hymnen an die Nacht* (1797) and the novel *Heinrich von Ofterdingen* (1800). Dying young of tuberculosis, he left many of his works unfinished, and the important tale "Hyacinth and Roseblossom" from *Die Lehrlinge zu Sais* was published posthumously in 1802.

PERRAULT, CHARLES (1628–1703) Born in Paris, Perrault studied at the Collège de Beauvais (near the Sorbonne). In 1651 he passed the examinations at the Universtiy of Orléans, and after working for three years as a lawyer, he left the profession to become a secretary to his brother Pierre, who was the tax receiver of Paris. He was gaining a reputation as a gifted poet, which was secured by 1660 when he composed several poems in honor of Louis XIV. In 1663 Perrault was appointed secretary to Jean-Baptiste Colbert, controller-general of finances, and for the next twenty years he accomplished a great deal in the arts and sciences owing to Colbert's patronage. As a result of his support of modernism in the famous "Quarrel of the Ancients and the Moderns" (1687), Perrault began writing verse tales such as "Griseldis" (1691), "Les Souhaits Ridicules" ("The Foolish Wishes," 1693), and "Peau d'Ane" ("Donkey Skin," 1694). His most famous work is undoubtedly *Histoires ou contes du temps passé* (1697), in which he created the versions of "Riquet with the Tuft," "Sleeping Beauty," "Little Red Riding Hood," "Cinderella," "Tom Thumb," "The Fairies," and "Blue Beard" that were to form the classical canon of literary fairy tales.

POURRAT, HENRI (1887–1959) Born in Ambert, France, Pourrat was sent to Paris to study at a lycée, where he received his baccalaureate in 1904. He intended to study agriculture on the university level but was discovered to have tuberculosis. During his recovery in his hometown, Pourrat began collecting folk tales in the region and publishing stories, fables, and fairy tales in newspapers. Gradually he became able to support himself through his writing. His major breakthrough came in 1922, when he completed the two-volume historical novel *Gaspard des Montagnes*, which earned him Le Prix du Figaro in 1922 and Le Grand Prix du Roman de L'Académie Française in 1931. He continued to publish historical romances and collections of fairy tales, such as *Les Contes de la Bucheronne* (*The Tales of the Woodcutter*, 1935). After World War II, he capped his career by publishing thirteen volumes of fairy tales, fables, legends, and anecdotes, *Le Trésor des contes* (*The Treasury of Tales*), from 1948 to 1962. "La branche qui chante, l'oiseau de vérité et l'eau qui rend verdeur de vie" ("The Tale of the Singing Branch, the Bird of Truth, and the Water of Youth") was taken from a volume in this collection that appeared in 1951.

PYLE, HOWARD (1853–1911) Born in Wilmington, Delaware, Pyle attended art school for three years but had to abandon his studies to help in the family leather business. When *St. Nicholas Magazine* was founded, in 1874, he began to contribute fables with pictures, then he published his illustrated stories in other journals. In 1833 his *Merry Adventures of Robin Hood* had great success, and he followed it with several collections of original fairy tales with illustrations: *Pepper & Salt* (1886), *The Wonder Clock* (1888), and *Twilight Land* (1895), which contained "Where to Lay the Blame." Pyle also wrote historical novels for young readers, such as *Otto of the Silver Hand* (1888), *Men of Iron* (1892), and *Jack Ballister's Fortunes* (1895). Pyle created pictures for many other authors and was considered the best American illustrator of the turn of the century.

RILKE, RAINER MARIA (1875–1926) Born in Prague, Rilke was sent by his family to private schools to prepare for a military career. However, he chose to study art and literary history in Prague and Munich, and published his first two collections of poems. After abandoning his studies in 1899, he traveled to Russia and later worked in Paris for a time as the sculptor Rodin's secretary. With such works as *Das Buch der Bilder* (*The Book of Pictures*, 1902), *Das Stundenbuch* (*The Book of Hours*, 1905), and *Neue Gedichte* (*New Poems*, 1907) he established himself as one of the gifted German poets of his time. In 1923 he wrote his two masterpieces, *Duineser Elegien* (*Duino Elegies*) and *Die Sonette an Orpheus* (*Sonnets to Orpheus*). "Wie der Verrat nach Rußland kam" ("How Treason Came to Russia") is taken from *Märchen vom lieben Gott* (*Stories of God*, 1904), based on his experiences during his early trip to Russia.

ROUSSEAU, JEAN-JACQUES (1712–1778) Born in Geneva, Rousseau was the son of a watchmaker. In 1728 he left home, and through various experiences, which he recounted in *Les Confessions* (*The Confessions*, 1765–70), he educated himself and became one of the leading literary figures and philosophers in Paris. Among his important novels dealing with his theories of natural education are *Julie ou la nouvelle Héloïse* (1761) and *Émile* (1762). "The Queen Fantasque," his only fairy tale, was written in 1758 to fulfill a wager. An unusual parody of the fairy tale, it incorporates some of his key notions of education and politics.

SCHWITTERS, KURT (1887–1948) Born in Hannover, Germany, Schwitters studied at art schools in Dresden and Berlin. During World War I he was a machine draftsman in the army. After the war, he developed innovative forms of printing in his own publishing firm and became one of the leading experimental artists in Berlin. He created unusual fairy tales for children and adults, such as *Der Hahnepeter* (*Peter the Rooster*, 1924) and *Die Märchen vom Paradies* (*The Fairy Tales of Paradise*, 1924). "The Three Wishes" ("Die drei Wünsche," 1925) appeared in the newspaper the *Hannoverscher Kurier*, as did many of his other tales. In 1933 his art was declared decadent by the Nazis, and he was forced to emigrate, to Norway and then to England, where he earned his living as a traditional portrait and landscape painter until his death.

STOCKTON, FRANK (1834–1902) Born in Philadelphia, Stockton became a graphic artist after graduating high school. He began publishing short stories and served as chief editor for *St. Nicholas Magazine*, the leading juvenile publication of the 1880s; a series of fairy tale books intended for both children and adults followed. Among his best works are *The Floating Prince* (1881), *The Bee-Man of Orn and Other Fanciful Tales* (1887), and *The Queen's Museum* (1887.) "The Griffin and the Minor Canon" was first published in 1885 in *St. Nicholas*. Stockton also wrote numerous novels, science fiction, and utopian stories. In fact, he ranked as one of the most popular American authors of his day, and his story "The Lady or the Tiger?" (1882) is still considered one of the best in the genre.

STORM, THEODOR (1817–1888) Born in Husum, Germany, Storm studied law in Lübeck and Kiel. He eventually became a judge in his hometown, meanwhile establishing a reputation as one of the foremost poets of northern Germany. He also wrote significant novellas, known for their local color, such as *Immensee* (1852). Among his best works were fairy tales, strongly influenced by the German Romantic tradition:

"Hinzelmeier" (1857), "Regentrude" (1864), and "In Bulemanns Haus" ("In Bule-mann's House," 1864).

STRAPAROLA, GIOVANNI (c. 1480–1558) Born in Cavaggio, Italy, Straparola left few documents, so that little is known about his life. Aside from a small volume of poems, his major work is *Le piacevoli notti* (1550–53), translated as *The Facetious Nights* or *The Delectable Nights*. The seventy-three stories in Straparola's work include "The Pig Prince," and the collection has a framework similar to that of Boccaccio's *Decameron*. The tales are told on thirteen consecutive nights by a group of men and women gathered at the Venetian palace of Ottaviano Maria Sforza, former bishop of Lodi and ruler of Milan, who has fled with his widowed daughter Lucrezia to avoid persecution and capture by his political enemies. The framework and many of the tales were imitated by other Italian and European writers.

STRINDBERG, AUGUST (1849–1912). Born in Stockholm, Strindberg studied at Upp-sala University between 1867 and 1872, without receiving a degree. Moving to Stockholm and working as an assistant librarian from 1874 to 1879 to support himself while writing plays, Strindberg became the center of a group of radical writers, and during the 1880s he established himself as one of the foremost European dramatists of naturalism, with such works as *Lycko-Pers resa* (*Lucky Peter's Travels*, 1880), *Fadren* (*The Father*, 1887), and *Fröken Julie* (*Miss Julie*, 1888). Beginning with *Dödsdansen* (*The Dance of Death*, 1901), and *Ett drömspel* (*A Dream Play*, 1902), he introduced expressionist and surrealist motifs into his plays. Strindberg wrote numerous stories and essays and eight autobiographies. Strongly influenced by Swedish folklore, he published a collection of fairy tales and fables entitled *Sagor* (1903), which contained "The Story of Jubal, Who Had No 'I.' "

THACKERAY, WILLIAM MAKEPEACE (1811–1863) Born in Calcutta, Thackeray grew up in British private schools after his father's death in 1815. He studied at Cambridge, and after losing his inheritance through gambling, he turned to journalism to earn a living. Eventually he became one of the finest novelists of realism in the 19th century, with such works as *Vanity Fair* (1848), *The History of Pendennis* (1850), and *The History of Henry Esmond* (1852). He had a strong interest in the fairy tale and wrote delightful parodies of the genre, such as "Bluebeard's Ghost" (1843) and *The Rose and the Ring* (1855).

THURBER, JAMES (1894–1961) Born in Columbus, Ohio, Thurber worked first as a journalist in the Midwest. In 1933 he moved to New York and became a regular contributor to *The New Yorker*, as satirist and illustrator. Known for his irony and wit, Thurber produced the satirical *Fables for Our Time* (1940), which included "The Girl and the Wolf." He wrote two fairy tale books for young readers, *The White Deer* (1945) and *The Thirteen Clocks* (1950).

TIECK, LUDWIG (1773–1853) Born in Berlin, Tieck became a free-lance writer after studying in Halle, Göttingen, and Erlangen. In 1798 he moved to Jena and became one of the leading members of the early Romantic movement in Germany. A gifted and prolific writer, he produced novels, plays, poems, and essays and translated Shakespeare and Cervantes into German. He experimented with fairy tales and wrote some of the most innovative Romantic tales of his time, such as "Der blonde Eckbert" ("Eckbert the Blond," 1797), "Der Runenberg" (1802), and "Die Elfen" ("The Elves," 1811), and unusual fairy tale dramas such as *Ritter Blaubart* (*The Knight Bluebeard*, 1797), *Der gestiefelte Kater* (*Puss in Boots*, 1797), *Die verkehrte Welt* (*The Topsy-Turvy World*, 1799), and *Rotkäppchen* (*Little Red Riding Hood*, 1800). After 1820 he resided mainly in Leipzig, writing realistic novellas and giving dramatic readings.

TOURNIER, MICHEL (1924–   ). Born in Paris, Tournier studied law and philosophy in Paris and in Tübingen, Germany, from 1946 to 1949. He returned to Paris and, denied admission into the philosophy program at the Sorbonne, worked for a radio station and then a publishing house until 1968. A noted novelist and short story writer, he frequently uses myths, legends, and fairy tale motifs in his works in unusual ways to prevent them, as he has asserted, from becoming fixed allegories. Among his best-known books are *Le rois des Alunes* (*The Ogre*, 1967), *Le Coq de Bruyère* (*The Fetishist*, 1978), which includes "La fugue de petit Poucet" ("Tom Thumb Runs Away"), *Gaspard, Melchior et Balthazar* (1980), *Gilles et Jeanne* (1983), and *La Goutte d'or* (1986).

TWAIN, MARK (Samuel Langhorne Clemens, 1835–1910) Born in Florida, Missouri, Twain grew up in the small town of Hannibal. After working as a printer's apprentice, a steamboat pilot, and a journalist, he devoted his energies to writing and became famous after publishing the frontier tale "The Celebrated Jumping Frog of Calaveras County" (1865). In 1867 he went east and spent the rest of his life lecturing, traveling, publishing successful books, and becoming involved in unsuccessful business speculations. Among his best novels are *The Adventures of Tom Sawyer* (1876), *The Prince and the Pauper* (1882), *The Adventures of Huckleberry Finn* (1884), and *A Connecticut Yankee at King Arthur's Court* (1889). Twain also wrote such outstanding stories as "The Man That Corrupted Hadleyburg" (1900) and experimented with rewriting *A Thousand and One Nights*. He published "The Five Boons of Life" in 1902.

VOLTAIRE (François Marie Arouet, 1694–1778) Born in Paris, Voltaire studied at the Jesuit college Louis-Grand and at twenty was already famous for his brilliant wit. After exile in England because of his arrogant ways, he returned to France, published *Philosophic Letters on the English* (1734), a veiled attack on French institutions, and was compelled to seek refuge at the court of Frederick the Great of Prussia. After amassing a fortune through clever speculation, he settled in Ferney, near the border of Switzerland (in case he had to flee France), and continued to write sarcastic pseudonymous, political pamphlets as well as philosophical treatises in the spirit of the Enlightenment. Among his best works are *Essai sur les moeurs et l'esprit des nations* (*Essay on Manners*, 1756) and the philosophic tales *Zadig* (1748) and *Candide* (1759). His fairy tale "Le Taureau blanc" ("The White Bull," 1774) incorporates his philosophical views on politics and progress.

WACKENRODER, WILHELM HEINRICH (1773–1798) Born in Berlin, he studied law at Erlangen and Göttingen. He was a close friend of Ludwig Tieck and would undoubtedly have become an important member of the Romantic movement if he had not died at an early age. He published *Herzensergiessungen eines kunstliebenden Klosterbruders* (*Confessions from the Heart of an Art-Loving Friar*, 1797) and wrote *Phantasien über die Kunst für Freunde der Kunst* (*Fantasies on Art for Friends of Art*, 1799), which included "A Wondrous Oriental Tale of a Naked Saint" ("Ein wunderbares morgendländisches Märchen von einem nackten Heiligen").

WARNER, SYLVIA TOWNSEND (1893–1978) Born in Harrow, Middlesex, England, she was privately educated, partly by her father, a housemaster at the famous private school Harrow. She had a great interest in music and intended to study with Arnold Schoenberg in Vienna, but was prevented by the outbreak of World War I. While working in a munitions factory, she began writing poems and short stories. Her first book of poetry, *The Espalier*, was published in 1925. Thereafter she concentrated mainly on prose, and many of her stories appeared in *The New Yorker*. From the beginning of her career, she had a strong interest in fairy tales and retold the story of Cupid and Psyche in *The True Heart* (1929). Among her other important works of fantasy are *The Cat's Cradle Book* (1960), which included "Bluebeard's Daughter," and *Kingdoms of Elfin* (1977).

WIELAND, CHRISTOPH MARTIN (1733–1813) Born in Oberholzheim, near Biberbach, Germany, Wieland studied theology in a cloister near Magdeburg. His interest in writing drew him to the Swiss critic Bodmer in Zurich between 1752 and 1754. Thereafter he gained recognition for his poetry, novels, and tales and in 1772 settled in Weimar. Wieland was strongly influenced by the French fairy tale vogue of the eighteenth century and published an important collection of tales entitled *Dschinnistan* (1786–89), which included stories adapted from the French *Cabinet des Fées* as well as his original tale "Der Stein der Weisen" ("The Philosophers' Stone"). Among his other works that incorporated fairy tale motifs are *Der Sieg der Natur über die Schwärmerei oder die Abenteuer des Don Sylvio von Rosalva* (*The Victory of Nature over Fanaticism or The Adventures of Don Sylvio von Rosalva*, 1764), *Der goldene Spiegel* (*The Golden Mirror*, 1772), and *Oberon* (1780).

WILDE, OSCAR (1854–1900) Born in Dublin, Wilde was educated at Oxford and after graduation, in 1878, began writing poems and criticism for magazines. He soon made a name for himself through his poetry, his unusual lectures on art, and his extravagant posturing. An extremely gifted writer, he wrote one of the most controversial novels of his day, *The Picture of Dorian Gray* (1891); two important collections of fairy tales, *The Happy Prince* (1888) and *The House of Pomegranates* (1891), which included "The Fisherman and His Soul"; important treatises, such as *The Soul of Man Under Socialism* (1890); and witty comedies of manners, including *Lady Windermere's Fan* (1892) and *The Importance of Being Earnest* (1895).

YEATS, WILLIAM BUTLER (1865–1939) Born in Sundymount, near Dublin, Yeats spent his early years in London, and when his family returned to Dublin, he studied for a brief time at an art school there. In 1885 he began publishing poetry to acclaim. His interest in drama led him to participate in founding the famous Abbey Theatre in 1898, and he became one of the leaders of the Irish literary revival. By the time he was forty-three, he was Ireland's best-known poet and dramatist, and he used a great deal of Irish myth and folklore in his works. He edited four collections of Irish fairy tales and myths, *Fairy and Folk Tales of the Irish Peasantry* (1888), *Representative Irish Tales* (1891), *Irish Fairy Tales* (1892), and *The Celtic Twilight* (1893). Many of his own tales appeared separately in journals or in anthologies, and "Dreams That Have No Moral" was first published in 1902. Among his best-known works are *The Green Helmet* (1910), *Responsibilities* (1914), and *The Vision* (1925). In 1923 he received the Nobel Prize for Literature. During the 1930s he became more mystical and wrote three important fantasy plays, *The King of the Great Clock Tower* (1934), *Full Moon in March* (1935), and *The Herne's Egg* (1938).

YOLEN, JANE (1939–   ) Born in New York City, Yolen was educated at Smith College. After working in publishing, she became a free-lance writer in 1965 and soon established a reputation as a writer of remarkable fairy tales for children, such as *The Emperor and the Kite* (1968), *The Girl Who Cried Flowers* (1974), and *The Hundredth Dove* (1978). During this time she began teaching at Smith College and writing nonfiction about fantasy and children's literature. In 1983, many of Yolen's unusual fairy tales for children and adults were collected and published in *Tales of Wonder*, and she began experimenting more in the field of fantasy. Some of her best fantasy narratives can be found in *Dragonfield* (1985). Yolen has also written a critical study of fairy tales, *Touch Magic* (1983), and edited *Favorite Folktales from Around the World* (1986). "The Lady and the Merman" was published in 1976.

LIST OF ILLUSTRATIONS

GRATEFUL ACKNOWLEDGMENT IS MADE FOR PERMISSION TO USE THE FOLLOWING COPYRIGHTED WORKS:

Apuleius, "Cupid and Psyche" from *The Golden Ass* translated by Robert Graves. Copyright © 1951 Robert Graves. Reprinted by permission of Farrar, Straus and Giroux, Inc.

Giambattista Basile, "The Merchant's Two Sons," from *The Pentamerone of Giambattista Basile*, volume I, translated and edited by N. M. Penzer from the Italian of Benedetto Croce. By permission of the publisher, The Bodley Head.

Charles Perrault, "Riquet with the Tuft" from *Beauties, Beasts and Enchantment: Classic French Fairy Tales* edited and translated by Jack Zipes. Copyright © Jack Zipes, 1989. Reprinted by permission of New American Library, a division of Penguin Books USA Inc.

Marie-Catherine D'Aulnoy, "Green Serpent" from *Beauties, Beasts and Enchantment: Classic French Fairy Tales* edited and translated by Jack Zipes. Copyright © Jack Zipes, 1989. Reprinted by permission of New American Library, a division of Penguin Books USA Inc.

Johann Wolfgang Goethe, "The Fairy Tale" from *The Sorrows of Young Werther and Selected Writings* translated by Catherine Hutter. Copyright © Catherine Hutter, 1962; copyright renewed Catherine Hutter, 1990. Reprinted by permission of New American Library, a division of Penguin Books USA Inc.

E. T. A. Hoffmann, "The Mines of Falun" translated by Leonard Kent and Elizabeth Knight from *Selected Writings of E. T. A. Hoffmann*. Reprinted by permission of the University of Chicago Press.

Wilhelm Grimm, "Snow White and Rose Red" from *The Complete Fairy Tales of the Brothers Grimm* translated by Jack Zipes, published by Bantam Books. Copyright © 1987 by Jack Zipes.

Hans Christian Andersen, "The Shadow" from *Hans Christian Andersen's Longer Stories* translated by Jean Hersholt, published by The Heritage Press.

Gottfried Keller, "Spiegel the Cat" from *The Blue Flower: Best Stories of the Romanticists* edited by Hermann Kesten, published by Roy Publishers.

Theodor Storm, "Hinzelmeier: A Thoughtful Story" translated by Frank G. Ryder from *German Literary Fairy Tales* edited by Frank G. Ryder and Robert M. Browning. New York: Continuum, 1983. Reprinted by permission of The Continuum Publishing Company.

Hugo von Hofmannsthal, "The Tale of the 672nd Night" translated by Frank G. Ryder from *German Literary Fairy Tales* edited by Frank G. Ryder and Robert M. Browning. New York: Continuum, 1983. Reprinted by permission of The Continuum Publishing Company.

Rainer Maria Rilke, "How Treason Came to Russia" from *Stories of God* translated by M. D. Herter Norton. Reprinted by permission of W. W. Norton & Company, Inc., the Estate of Rainer Maria Rilke and The Hogarth Press. Copyright © 1963 by W. W. Norton & Company, Inc. Copyright © 1932 by W. W. Norton & Company, Inc. Copyright © renewed 1960 by M. D. Herter Norton and Nora Purtscher-Wydenbruck.

Anatole France, "The Seven Wives of Bluebeard" from *The Seven Wives of Bluebeard and Other Marvellous Tales* translated by D. B. Stewart, published by The Bodley Head.

Hermann Hesse, "The Forest Dweller" from *Simplizissimus*, 22 (1917 / 1918). By permission of Suhrkamp Verlag. © Suhrkamp Verlag Frankfurt am Main 1954. Translated for this collection by Jack Zipes.

Kurt Schwitters, "The Three Wishes" from *Das literarische Werk* edited by F. Lach, volume 2. By permission of DuMont Buchverlag. Translated for this collection by Jack Zipes.

Franz Hessel, "The Seventh Dwarf" from *Ermunterung zum Genuss*. By permission of Das Arsenal, Berlin. © by Das Arsenal, Berlin 1986. Translated for this collection by Jack Zipes.

Alfred Döblin, "The Fairy Tale About Technology" from *Erzahlungen aus funf Jahrzehnten*. By permission of Walter-Verlag AG, Olten. © Walter-Verlag AG, Olten 1979. Translated for this collection by Jack Zipes.

James Thurber, "The Little Girl and the Wolf" from *Fables for Our Time and Famous Poems*, published by Harper & Row. Copyright © 1940 James Thurber, copyright © 1968 Helen Thurber. By permission of Rosemary Thurber and Hamish Hamilton Ltd.

Georg Kaiser, "The Fairy Tale of the King" from *Werke*, vol. 4, edited by W. Huder. By permission of Verlag Ullstein GmbH. Translated for this collection by Jack Zipes.

Erich Kästner, "The Fairy Tale About Common Sense" from *Der tagliche Kram*, Droemer Verlag. By permission of Erich Kastner Erben Munchen. Translated for this collection by Jack Zipes.

Ingeborg Bachmann, "The Smile of the Sphinx" from *Werke*. © R. Piper & Co. Verlag, Munchen 1978. By permission of R. Piper & Co. Verlag. Translated for this collection by Jack Zipes.

Henri Pourrat, "The Tale of the Singing Branch, the Bird of Truth, and the Water of Youth" from *A Treasury of French Tales* translated by Mary Mian, published by George Allen & Unwin.

Philip K. Dick, "The King of the Elves" first published in *Beyond Fantasy Fiction* (September 1953). Reprinted by permission of Scott Meredith Literary Agency, Inc.

Italo Calvino, "The Enchanted Palace" from *Italian Folktales* translated by George Martin. Copyright © 1956 by Giulio Einaudi editore, s. p. a. English translation copyright © 1980 by Harcourt Brace Jovanovich, Inc. Copyright © Palomar Srl, 1990. Reprinted by permission of Harcourt Brace Jovanovich, Inc. and Wylie, Aitken and Stone, Inc.

Naomi Mitchison, "Five Men and a Swan" from *Five Men and a Swan*. Reprinted by permission of the author.

Sylvia Townsend Warner, "Bluebeard's Daughter" from *The Cat's Cradle Book*. Reprinted by permission of the Executors of the Sylvia Townsend Warner Estate and Chatto & Windus.

Christoph Meckel, "The Crow" from *Das Atelier. Zeitgenossische deutsche Prosa* edited by Klaus Wagenbach, Fischer, 1962. By permission of Christoph Meckel. © Christoph Meckel, 1962. Translated for this collection by Jack Zipes.

Stanislaw Lem, "Prince Ferrix and the Princess Crystal" from *The Cyberiad: Fables for the Cybernetic Age* translated by Michael Kandel. New York: Continuum, 1974. Reprinted by permission of The Continuum Publishing Company.

Gunter Kunert, "Sleeping Beauty" from *Tagtraume in Berlin und andernorts. Kleine Prosa, Erzahlungen, Aufsatze*. By permission of Carol Hanser Verlag. © 1972 Carl Hanser Verlag Munchen Wien. Translated for this collection by Jack Zipes.

Janosch, "Hans My Hedgehog" from *Janosch erzahlt Grimm's Marchen*. By permission of Beltz & Gelberg Verlag. © 1972 Beltz & Gelberg Verlag. Translated for this collection by Jack Zipes.

Robert Coover, "The Dead Queen" first published in *Quarterly Review of Literature* 18 (1973). Reprinted by permission of the Georges Borchardt Literary Agency.

Jane Yolen, "The Lady and the Merman" from *The Hundredth Dove and Other Tales*. Originally appeared in *The Magazine of Fantasy and Science Fiction*. Copyright © 1977, 1976 by Jane Yolen. Reprinted by permission of Harper & Row, Publishers, Inc. and Curtis Brown, Ltd.

Rosemarie Künzler, "Rumpelstiltskin" from *Neues von Rumpelstilzchen und anderen Marchen von 43 Autoren* edited by Hans-Joachim Gelberg. By permission of Rosemarie Kunzler. Translated for this collection by Jack Zipes.

Michel Tournier, "Tom Thumb Runs Away" from *The Fetishist* translated by Barbara Wright. Translation copyright © 1983 by Doubleday, a division of Bantam Doubleday Dell Publishing Group, Inc. and William Collins Sons & Company, Ltd. Reprinted by permission of Doubleday, a division of Bantam Doubleday Dell Publishing Group, Inc. and William Collins Sons & Company, Ltd.

Angela Carter, "The Tiger's Bride" from *Bloody Chamber and Other Tales*. Reprinted by permission of the author. © Angela Carter, 1979.

Robin McKinley, "The Princess and the Frog" from *The Door in the Hedge*, Greenwillow Books. Reprinted by permission of the author. Copyright 1981 Robin McKinley.

Tanith Lee, "When the Clock Strikes" from *Red as Blood or Tales from the Sisters Grimmer*. Reprinted by permission of DAW Books, Inc. Copyright © 1983 by Tanith Lee.

Michael de Larrabeiti, "Pichounetta and the Sergeant of Arles" from *The Provencal Tales*. Reprinted by permission of the author. © Michael de Larrabeiti 1988.